bitlit

A **bundled** eBook edition is available
with the purchase of this print book.

ℓ **ENGAGE BOOKS**

Mailing address
PO BOX 4608
Main Station Terminal
349 West Georgia Street
Vancouver, BC
Canada, V6B 4A1

John Carter: Barsoom Series
Burroughs, Edgar Rice, 1875–1950
A Princess of Mars
First published by A.C. McClurg & Co in 1917
The Gods of Mars
First published by A.C. McClurg & Co in 1918
The Warlord of Mars
First published by A.C. McClurg & Co in 1919
Thuvia, Maid of Mars
First published by A.C. McClurg & Co in 1920
The Chessmen of Mars
First published by A.C. McClurg & Co in 1922
The Master Mind of Mars
First published by A.C. McClurg & Co in 1928
A Fighting Man of Mars
First published by Metropolitan Books in 1931
This edition published by Engage Books in 2014
Design © 2014 Engage Books

Every reasonable effort has been made to
contact the copyright holders of all material
reproduced in this book.

www.engagebooks.ca

Designed by: A.R. Roumanis

Cover backdrop painted by Atkinson Grimshaw in 1893. Cover illustrations by J. Allen St. John in 1920. Original text illustrations by Frank Schoonover, J. Allan St. John, J. W. Small, P. J. Monahan, Frank R. Paul, J. H. Hartley & Laurence Herndon.

Text set in Minion Pro. Chapter headings set in News Gothic Standard.

ISBN:
paperback: 978-1-926606-84-2
hardcover: 978-1-926606-85-9
limited edition: 978-1-77226-000-7
epub: 978-1-926606-75-0
kindle: 978-1-927970-47-8
pdf: 978-1-927970-48-5

FIRST EDITION / FIRST PRINTING

SEVEN NOVELS IN ONE
A PRINCESS OF MARS; GODS OF MARS; WARLORD OF MARS; THUVIA, MAID OF MARS;
CHESSMEN OF MARS; MASTER MIND OF MARS; A FIGHTING MAN OF MARS
By EDGAR RICE BURROUGHS

JOHN CARTER

BARSOOM SERIES

ENGAGE BOOKS / VANCOUVER

Edgar Rice Burroughs

CONTENTS

A PRINCESS OF MARS

Foreword 11

1 On the Arizona Hills 14

2 The Escape of the Dead 20

3 My Advent on Mars 24

4 A Prisoner 30

5 I Elude My Watch Dog 35

6 A Fight that Won Friends 39

7 Child-Raising on Mars 44

8 A Fair Captive from the Sky 49

9 I Learn the Language 54

10 Champion and Chief 58

11 With Dejah Thoris 66

12 A Prisoner with Power 72

13 Love-Making on Mars 77

14 A Duel to the Death 82

15 Sola Tells Me Her Story 90

16 We Plan Escape 97

17 A Costly Recapture 106

18 Chained in Warhoon 113

19 Battling in the Arena 117

20 In the Atmosphere Factory 121

21 An Air Scout for Zodanga 129

22 I Find Dejah 137

23 Lost in the Sky 145

24 Tars Tarkas Finds a Friend 150

25 The Looting of Zodanga 156

26 Through Carnage to Joy 160

27 From Joy to Death 166

28 At the Arizona Cave 171

THE GODS OF MARS

Foreword 175

1 The Plant Men 178

2 A Forest Battle 187

3 The Chamber of Mystery 197

4 Thuvia 207

5 Corridors of Peril 216

6 The Black Pirates of Barsoom 223

7 A Fair Goddess 230

8 The Depths of Omean 239

9 Issus, Goddess of Life Eternal 249

10 The Prison Isle of Shador 256

11 When Hell Broke Loose 263

12 Doomed to Die 273

13 A Break for Liberty 279

14 The Eyes in the Dark 289

15 Flight and Pursuit 300

16 Under Arrest 307

17 The Death Sentence 315

18 Sola's Story 322

19 Black Despair 328

20 The Air Battle 338

21 Through Flood and Flame 348

22 Victory and Defeat 354

THE WARLORD OF MARS

1 On the River Iss 365

2 Under the Mountains 374

3 The Temple of the Sun 383

4 The Secret Tower 391

5 On the Kaolian Road 400

6 A Hero in Kaol 410

7 New Allies 418

8 Through the Carrion Caves 427

9 With the Yellow Men 436

10 In Durance 444

11 The Pit of Plenty 452

12 "Follow the Rope!" 460

13 The Magnet Switch 468

14 The Tide of Battle 476

15 Rewards 482

16 The New Ruler 490

THUVIA, MAID OF MARS

1 Carthoris and Thuvia 501

2 Slavery 510

3 Treachery 519

4 A Green Man's Captive 524

5 The Fair Race 533

6 The Jeddak of Lothar 544

7 The Phantom Bowmen 552

8 The Hall of Doom 560

9 The Battle in the Plain 569

10 Kar Komak, the Bowman 576

11 Green Men and White Apes 584

12 To Save Dusar 593

13 Turjun, the Panthan 600

14 Kulan Tith's Sacrifice 609

THE CHESSMEN OF MARS

Prelude 623

1 Tara in a Tantrum 626

2 At the Gale's Mercy 634

3 The Headless Humans 642

4 Captured 652

5 The Perfect Brain 662

6 In the Toils of Horror 670

7 A Repellent Sight 681

8 Close Work 690

9 Adrift Over Strange Regions 698

10 Entrapped 708

11 The Choice of Tara 717

12 Ghek Plays Pranks 726

13 A Desperate Deed 735

14 At Ghek's Command 744

15 The Old Man of the Pits 753

16 Another Change of Name 762

17 A Play to the Death 771

18 A Task for Loyalty 780

19 The Menace of the Dead 790

20 The Charge of Cowardice 797

21 A Risk for Love 806

22 At the Moment of Marriage 815

Jetan, or Martian Chess 826

THE MASTER MIND OF MARS

A Letter 831

1 The House of the Dead 834

2 Preferment 843

3 Valla Dia 849

4 The Compact 860

5 Danger 869

6 Suspicions 875

7 Escape 883

8 Hands Up! 890

9 The Palace of Mu Tel 901

10 Phundahl 913

11 Xaxa 921

12 The Great Tur 932

13 Back to Thavas 941

14 John Carter 949

A FIGHTING MAN OF MARS

Foreword 959

1 Sanoma Tora 965

2 Brought Down 976

3 Cornered 985

4 Tavia 996

5 To the Pits 1006

6 Sentenced to Die 1017

7 The Death 1030

8 The Spider of Ghasta 1044

9 Phor Tak of Jhama 1054

10 The Flying Death 1066

11 "Let the Fire be Hot!" 1075

12 The Cloak of Invisibility 1085

13 Tul Axtar's Women 1098

14 The Cannibals of U-Gor 1107

15 The Battle of Jahar 1118

16 Despair 1133

17 I Find a Princess 1145

Glossary 1151

LIST OF ILLUSTRATIONS

A Princess of Mars

1	Frank Schoonover	10
2	Frank Schoonover	41
3	Frank Schoonover	85
4	Frank Schoonover	101
5	Frank Schoonover	124

The Gods of Mars

1	Frank Schoonover	174

The Warlord of Mars

1	J. Allan St. John	364
2	F. W. Small	416

Thuvia, Maid of Mars

1	P. J. Monahan	500
2	J. Allen St. John	503
3	J. Allen St. John	512
4	J. Allen St. John	528
5	J. Allen St. John	540
6	J. Allen St. John	550
7	J. Allen St. John	563
8	J. Allen St. John	583
9	J. Allen St. John	606
10	J. Allen St. John	611
11	J. Allen St. John	618

The Chessmen of Mars

1	J. Allen St. John	622
2	J. Allen St. John	678

3	J. Allen St. John	699
4	J. Allen St. John	713
5	J. Allen St. John	728
6	J. Allen St. John	779
7	J. Allen St. John	813
8	J. Allen St. John	819

The Master Mind of Mars

1	J. Allen St. John	830
2	J. Allen St. John	840
3	J. Allen St. John	858
4	Frank R. Paul	893
5	Frank R. Paul	896
6	J. Allen St. John	899
7	Frank R. Paul	909
8	J. Allen St. John	911
9	Frank R. Paul	925
10	J. Allen St. John	934
11	Frank R. Paul	950

A Fighting Man of Mars

1	J. H. Hartley	958
2	Laurence Herndon	964
3	Laurence Herndon	995
4	Laurence Herndon	1029
5	Laurence Herndon	1065
6	Laurence Herndon	1097
7	Laurence Herndon	1132

A PRINCESS OF MARS

BOOK ONE

FOREWORD

To the Reader of this Work:
In submitting Captain Carter's strange manuscript to you in book form, I believe that a few words relative to this remarkable personality will be of interest.

My first recollection of Captain Carter is of the few months he spent at my father's home in Virginia, just prior to the opening of the civil war. I was then a child of but five years, yet I well remember the tall, dark, smooth-faced, athletic man whom I called Uncle Jack.

He seemed always to be laughing; and he entered into the sports of the children with the same hearty good fellowship he displayed toward those pastimes in which the men and women of his own age indulged; or he would sit for an hour at a time entertaining my old grandmother with stories of his strange, wild life in all parts of the world. We all loved him, and our slaves fairly worshipped the ground he trod.

He was a splendid specimen of manhood, standing a good two inches over six feet, broad of shoulder and narrow of hip, with the carriage of the trained fighting man. His features were regular and clear cut, his hair black and closely cropped, while his eyes were of a steel gray, reflecting a strong and loyal character, filled with fire and initiative. His manners were perfect, and his courtliness was that of a typical southern gentleman of the highest type.

His horsemanship, especially after hounds, was a marvel and delight even in that country of magnificent horsemen. I have often heard my father caution him against his wild recklessness, but he would only laugh, and say that the tumble that killed him would be from the back of a horse yet unfoaled.

When the war broke out he left us, nor did I see him again for some fifteen or sixteen years. When he returned it was without warning, and I was much surprised to note that he had not aged apparently a moment, nor had he changed in any other outward way. He was, when others were with him, the same genial, happy fellow we had known of old, but when he thought himself alone I have seen him sit for hours gazing off into space, his face set in a look of wistful longing and hopeless misery; and at night he would sit thus looking up into the heavens, at what I did not know until I read his manuscript years afterward.

He told us that he had been prospecting and mining in Arizona part of the time since the war; and that he had been very successful was evidenced by the unlimited amount of money with which he was supplied. As to the details of his life during these years he was very reticent, in fact he would not talk of them at all.

He remained with us for about a year and then went to New York, where he purchased a little place on the Hudson, where I visited him once a year on the occasions of my trips to the New York market – my father and I owning and operating a string of general stores throughout Virginia at that time. Captain Carter had a small but beautiful cottage, situated on a bluff overlooking the river, and during one of my last visits, in the winter of 1885, I observed he was much occupied in writing, I presume now, upon this manuscript.

He told me at this time that if anything should happen to him he wished me to take charge of his estate, and he gave me a key to a compartment in the safe which stood in his study, telling me I would find his will there and some personal instructions which he had me pledge myself to carry out with absolute fidelity.

After I had retired for the night I have seen him from my window standing in the moonlight on the brink of the bluff overlooking the Hudson with his arms stretched out to the heavens as though in appeal. I thought at the time that he was praying, although I never understood that he was in the strict sense of the term a religious man.

Several months after I had returned home from my last visit, the first of March, 1886, I think, I received a telegram from him asking me to come to him at once. I had always been his favorite among the younger generation of Carters and so I hastened to comply with his demand.

I arrived at the little station, about a mile from his grounds, on the morning of March 4, 1886, and when I asked the livery man to drive me out to Captain Carter's he replied that if I was a friend of the Captain's he had some very bad news for me; the Captain had been found dead shortly after daylight that very morning by the watchman attached to an adjoining property.

For some reason this news did not surprise me, but I hurried out to his place as quickly as possible, so that I could take charge of the body and of his affairs.

I found the watchman who had discovered him, together with the local police chief and several townspeople, assembled in his little study. The watchman related the few details connected with the finding of the body, which he said had been still warm when he came upon it. It lay, he said, stretched full length in the snow with the arms outstretched above the head toward the edge of the bluff, and when he showed me the spot it flashed upon me that it was the identical one where I had seen him on those other nights, with his arms raised in supplication to the skies.

There were no marks of violence on the body, and with the aid of a local physician the coroner's jury quickly reached a decision of death from heart failure. Left alone in the study, I opened the safe and withdrew the contents of the drawer in which he had told me I would find my instructions. They were in part peculiar indeed, but I have followed them to each last detail as faithfully as I was able.

He directed that I remove his body to Virginia without embalming, and that he be laid in an open coffin within a tomb which he previously had had constructed and which, as I later learned, was well ventilated. The instructions impressed upon me that I must personally see that this was carried out just as he directed, even in secrecy if necessary.

His property was left in such a way that I was to receive the entire income for twenty-five years, when the principal was to become mine. His further instructions related to this manuscript which I was to retain sealed and unread, just as I found it, for eleven years; nor was I to divulge its contents until twenty-one years after his death.

A strange feature about the tomb, where his body still lies, is that the massive door is equipped with a single, huge gold-plated spring lock which can be opened *only from the inside.*

Yours very sincerely,

Edgar Rice Burroughs.

CHAPTER ONE

On the Arizona Hills

I AM A VERY OLD MAN; how old I do not know. Possibly I am a hundred, possibly more; but I cannot tell because I have never aged as other men, nor do I remember any childhood. So far as I can recollect I have always been a man, a man of about thirty. I appear today as I did forty years and more ago, and yet I feel that I cannot go on living forever; that some day I shall die the real death from which there is no resurrection. I do not know why I should fear death, I who have died twice and am still alive; but yet I have the same horror of it as you who have never died, and it is because of this terror of death, I believe, that I am so convinced of my mortality.

And because of this conviction I have determined to write down the story of the interesting periods of my life and of my death. I cannot explain the phenomena; I can only set down here in the words of an ordinary soldier of fortune a chronicle of the strange events that befell me during the ten years that my dead body lay undiscovered in an Arizona cave.

I have never told this story, nor shall mortal man see this manuscript until after I have passed over for eternity. I know that the average human mind will not believe what it cannot grasp, and so I do not purpose being pilloried by the public, the pulpit, and the press, and held up as a colossal liar when I am but telling the simple truths which some day science will substantiate. Possibly the suggestions which I gained upon Mars, and the knowledge which I can set down in this chronicle, will aid in an earlier understanding of the mysteries of our sister planet; mysteries to you, but no longer mysteries to me.

My name is John Carter; I am better known as Captain Jack Carter of Virginia. At the close of the Civil War I found myself possessed of several hundred thousand dollars (Confederate) and a captain's commission in the cavalry arm of an army which no longer existed; the servant of a state which had vanished with the hopes of the South. Masterless, penniless, and with my only means of livelihood, fighting, gone, I determined to work my way to the southwest and attempt to retrieve my fallen fortunes in a search for gold.

I spent nearly a year prospecting in company with another Confederate officer, Captain James K. Powell of Richmond. We were extremely fortunate, for late in the winter of 1865, after many hardships and privations, we located the most remarkable gold-bearing quartz vein that our wildest dreams had ever pictured. Powell, who was a mining engineer by education, stated that we had uncovered over a million dollars worth of ore in a trifle over three months.

As our equipment was crude in the extreme we decided that one of us must return to civilization, purchase the necessary machinery and return with a sufficient force of men properly to work the mine.

As Powell was familiar with the country, as well as with the mechanical requirements of mining we determined that it would be best for him to make the trip. It was agreed that I was to hold down our claim against the remote possibility of its being jumped by some wandering prospector.

On March 3, 1866, Powell and I packed his provisions on two of our burros, and bidding me good-bye he mounted his horse, and started down the mountainside toward the valley, across which led the first stage of his journey.

The morning of Powell's departure was, like nearly all Arizona mornings, clear and beautiful; I could see him and his little pack animals picking their way down the mountainside toward the valley, and all during the morning I would catch occasional glimpses of them as they topped a hog back or came out upon a level plateau. My last sight of Powell was about three in the afternoon as he entered the shadows of the range on the opposite side of the valley.

Some half hour later I happened to glance casually across the valley and was much surprised to note three little dots in about the same place I had last seen my friend and his two pack animals. I am not given to needless worrying, but the more I tried to convince myself that all was well with Powell, and that the dots I had seen on his trail were antelope or wild horses, the less I was able to assure myself.

Since we had entered the territory we had not seen a hostile Indian, and we had, therefore, become careless in the extreme, and were wont to ridicule the stories we had heard of the great numbers of these vicious marauders that were supposed to haunt the trails, taking their toll in lives and torture of every white party which fell into their merciless clutches.

Powell, I knew, was well armed and, further, an experienced Indian fighter; but I too had lived and fought for years among the Sioux in the North, and I knew that his chances were small against a party of cunning trailing Apaches. Finally I could endure the suspense no longer, and, arming myself with my two Colt revolvers and a carbine, I strapped two belts of cartridges about me and catching my saddle horse, started down the trail taken by Powell in the morning.

As soon as I reached comparatively level ground I urged my mount into a canter and continued this, where the going permitted, until, close upon dusk, I discovered the point where other tracks joined those of Powell. They were the tracks of unshod ponies, three of them, and the ponies had been galloping.

I followed rapidly until, darkness shutting down, I was forced to await the rising of the moon, and given an opportunity to speculate on the question of the wisdom of my chase. Possibly I had conjured up impossible dangers, like some nervous old housewife, and when I should catch up with Powell would get a good laugh for my pains. However, I am not prone to sensitiveness, and the following of a sense of duty, wherever it may lead, has always been a kind of fetich with me throughout my life; which may account for the honors bestowed upon me by three republics and the decorations and friendships of an old and powerful emperor and several lesser kings, in whose service my sword has been red many a time.

About nine o'clock the moon was sufficiently bright for me to proceed on my way and I had no difficulty in following the trail at a fast walk, and in some places at a brisk trot until, about midnight, I reached the water hole where Powell had expected to camp. I came upon the spot unexpectedly, finding it entirely deserted, with no signs of having been recently occupied as a camp.

I was interested to note that the tracks of the pursuing horsemen, for such I was now convinced they must be, continued after Powell with only a brief stop at the hole for water; and always at the same rate of speed as his.

I was positive now that the trailers were Apaches and that they wished to capture Powell alive for the fiendish pleasure of the torture, so I urged my horse onward at a most dangerous pace, hoping against hope that I would catch up with the red rascals before they attacked him.

Further speculation was suddenly cut short by the faint report of two shots far ahead of me. I knew that Powell would need me now if ever, and I instantly urged my horse to his topmost speed up the narrow and difficult mountain trail.

I had forged ahead for perhaps a mile or more without hearing further sounds, when the trail suddenly debouched onto a small, open plateau near the summit of the pass. I had passed through a narrow, overhanging gorge just before entering suddenly upon this table land, and the sight which met my eyes filled me with consternation and dismay.

The little stretch of level land was white with Indian tepees, and there were probably half a thousand red warriors clustered around some object near the center of the camp. Their attention was so wholly riveted to this point of interest that they did not notice me, and I easily could have turned back into the dark recesses of the gorge and made my escape with perfect safety. The fact, however, that this thought did not occur to me until the following day removes any possible right to a claim to heroism to which the narration of this episode might possibly otherwise entitle me.

I do not believe that I am made of the stuff which constitutes heroes, because, in all of the hundreds of instances that my voluntary acts have placed me face to face with death, I cannot recall a single one where any alternative step to that I took occurred to me until many hours later. My mind is evidently so constituted that I am subconsciously forced into the path of duty without recourse to tiresome mental processes. However that may be, I have never regretted that cowardice is not optional with me.

In this instance I was, of course, positive that Powell was the center of attraction, but whether I thought or acted first I do not know, but within an instant from the moment the scene broke upon my view I had whipped out my revolvers and was charging down upon the entire army of warriors, shooting rapidly, and whooping at the top of my lungs. Singlehanded, I could not have pursued better tactics, for the red men, convinced by sudden surprise that not less than a regiment of regulars was upon them, turned and fled in every direction for their bows, arrows, and rifles.

The view which their hurried routing disclosed filled me with apprehension and with rage. Under the clear rays of the Arizona moon lay Powell, his body fairly bristling with the hostile arrows of the braves. That he was already dead I could not but be convinced, and yet I would have saved his body from mutilation at the hands of the Apaches as quickly as I would have saved the man himself from death.

Riding close to him I reached down from the saddle, and grasping his cartridge belt drew him up across the withers of my mount. A backward glance convinced me that to return by the way I had come would be more hazardous than to continue across the plateau, so, putting spurs to my poor beast, I made a dash for the opening to the pass which I could distinguish on the far side of the table land.

The Indians had by this time discovered that I was alone and I was pursued with imprecations, arrows, and rifle balls. The fact that it is difficult to aim anything but imprecations accurately by moonlight, that they were upset by the sudden and unexpected manner of my advent, and that I was a rather rapidly moving target saved me from the various deadly projectiles of the enemy and permitted me to reach the shadows of the surrounding peaks before an orderly pursuit could be organized.

My horse was traveling practically unguided as I knew that I had probably less knowledge of the exact location of the trail to the pass than he, and thus it happened that he entered a defile which led to the summit of the range and not to the pass which I had hoped would carry me to the valley and to safety. It is probable, however, that to this fact I owe my life and the remarkable experiences and adventures which befell me during the following ten years.

My first knowledge that I was on the wrong trail came when I heard the yells of the pursuing savages suddenly grow fainter and fainter far off to my left.

I knew then that they had passed to the left of the jagged rock formation at the edge of the plateau, to the right of which my horse had borne me and the body of Powell.

I drew rein on a little level promontory overlooking the trail below and to my left, and saw the party of pursuing savages disappearing around the point of a neighboring peak.

I knew the Indians would soon discover that they were on the wrong trail and that the search for me would be renewed in the right direction as soon as they located my tracks.

I had gone but a short distance further when what seemed to be an excellent trail opened up around the face of a high cliff. The trail was level and quite broad and led upward and in the general direction I wished to go. The cliff arose for several hundred feet on my right, and on my left was an equal and nearly perpendicular drop to the bottom of a rocky ravine.

I had followed this trail for perhaps a hundred yards when a sharp turn to the right brought me to the mouth of a large cave. The opening was about four feet in height and three to four feet wide, and at this opening the trail ended.

It was now morning, and, with the customary lack of dawn which is a startling characteristic of Arizona, it had become daylight almost without warning.

Dismounting, I laid Powell upon the ground, but the most painstaking examination failed to reveal the faintest spark of life. I forced water from my canteen between his dead lips, bathed his face and rubbed his hands, working over him continuously for the better part of an hour in the face of the fact that I knew him to be dead.

I was very fond of Powell; he was thoroughly a man in every respect; a polished southern gentleman; a staunch and true friend; and it was with a feeling of the deepest grief that I finally gave up my crude endeavors at resuscitation.

Leaving Powell's body where it lay on the ledge I crept into the cave to reconnoiter. I found a large chamber, possibly a hundred feet in diameter and thirty or forty feet in height; a smooth and well-worn floor, and many other evidences that the cave had, at some remote period, been inhabited. The back of the cave was so lost in dense shadow that I could not distinguish whether there were openings into other apartments or not.

As I was continuing my examination I commenced to feel a pleasant drowsiness creeping over me which I attributed to the fatigue of my long and strenuous ride, and the reaction from the excitement of the fight and the pursuit. I felt comparatively safe in my present location as I knew that one man could defend the trail to the cave against an army.

I soon became so drowsy that I could scarcely resist the strong desire to throw myself on the floor of the cave for a few moments' rest, but I knew that this would never do, as it would mean certain death at the hands of my red friends, who might be upon me at any moment. With an effort I started toward the opening of the cave only to reel drunkenly against a side wall, and from there slip prone upon the floor.

CHAPTER TWO

The Escape of the Dead

A SENSE OF DELICIOUS DREAMINESS overcame me, my muscles relaxed, and I was on the point of giving way to my desire to sleep when the sound of approaching horses reached my ears. I attempted to spring to my feet but was horrified to discover that my muscles refused to respond to my will. I was now thoroughly awake, but as unable to move a muscle as though turned to stone. It was then, for the first time, that I noticed a slight vapor filling the cave. It was extremely tenuous and only noticeable against the opening which led to daylight. There also came to my nostrils a faintly pungent odor, and I could only assume that I had been overcome by some poisonous gas, but why I should retain my mental faculties and yet be unable to move I could not fathom.

I lay facing the opening of the cave and where I could see the short stretch of trail which lay between the cave and the turn of the cliff around which the trail led. The noise of the approaching horses had ceased, and I judged the Indians were creeping stealthily upon me along the little ledge which led to my living tomb. I remember that I hoped they would make short work of me as I did not particularly relish the thought of the innumerable things they might do to me if the spirit prompted them.

I had not long to wait before a stealthy sound apprised me of their nearness, and then a war-bonneted, paint-streaked face was thrust cautiously around the shoulder of the cliff, and savage eyes looked into mine. That he could see me in the dim light of the cave I was sure for the early morning sun was falling full upon me through the opening.

The fellow, instead of approaching, merely stood and stared; his eyes bulging and his jaw dropped. And then another savage face appeared, and a third and fourth and fifth, craning their necks over the shoulders of their fellows whom they could not pass upon the narrow ledge. Each face was the picture of awe and fear, but for what reason I did not know, nor did I learn until ten years later. That there were still other braves behind those who regarded me was apparent from the fact that the leaders passed back whispered word to those behind them.

Suddenly a low but distinct moaning sound issued from the recesses of the cave behind me, and, as it reached the ears of the Indians, they turned and fled in terror, panic-stricken. So frantic were their efforts to escape from the unseen thing behind me that one of the braves was hurled headlong from the cliff to the rocks below. Their wild cries echoed in the canyon for a short time, and then all was still once more.

The sound which had frightened them was not repeated, but it had been sufficient as it was to start me speculating on the possible horror which lurked in the shadows at my back. Fear is a relative term and so I can only measure my feelings at that time by what I had experienced in previous positions of danger and by those that I have passed through since; but I can say without shame that if the sensations I endured during the next few minutes were fear, then may God help the coward, for cowardice is of a surety its own punishment.

To be held paralyzed, with one's back toward some horrible and unknown danger from the very sound of which the ferocious Apache warriors turn in wild stampede, as a flock of sheep would madly flee from a pack of wolves, seems to me the last word in fearsome predicaments for a man who had ever been used to fighting for his life with all the energy of a powerful physique.

Several times I thought I heard faint sounds behind me as of somebody moving cautiously, but eventually even these ceased, and I was left to the contemplation of my position without interruption. I could but vaguely conjecture the cause of my paralysis, and my only hope lay in that it might pass off as suddenly as it had fallen upon me.

Late in the afternoon my horse, which had been standing with dragging rein before the cave, started slowly down the trail, evidently in search of food and water, and I was left alone with my mysterious unknown companion and the dead body of my friend, which lay just within my range of vision upon the ledge where I had placed it in the early morning.

From then until possibly midnight all was silence, the silence of the dead; then, suddenly, the awful moan of the morning broke upon my startled ears, and there came again from the black shadows the sound of a moving thing, and a faint rustling as of dead leaves. The shock to my already overstrained nervous system was terrible in the extreme, and with a superhuman effort I strove to break my awful bonds. It was an effort of the mind, of the will, of the nerves; not muscular, for I could not move even so much as my little finger, but none the less mighty for all that. And then something gave, there was a momentary feeling of nausea, a sharp click as of the snapping of a steel wire, and I stood with my back against the wall of the cave facing my unknown foe.

And then the moonlight flooded the cave, and there before me lay my own body as it had been lying all these hours, with the eyes staring toward the open ledge and the hands resting limply upon the ground. I looked first at my lifeless clay there upon the floor of the cave and then down at myself in utter bewilderment; for there I lay clothed, and yet here I stood but naked as at the minute of my birth.

The transition had been so sudden and so unexpected that it left me for a moment forgetful of aught else than my strange metamorphosis. My first thought was, is this then death! Have I indeed passed over forever into that other life! But I could not well believe this, as I could feel my heart pounding against my ribs from the exertion of my efforts to release myself from the anaesthesis which had held me. My breath was coming in quick, short gasps, cold sweat stood out from every pore of my body, and the ancient experiment of pinching revealed the fact that I was anything other than a wraith.

Again was I suddenly recalled to my immediate surroundings by a repetition of the weird moan from the depths of the cave. Naked and unarmed as I was, I had no desire to face the unseen thing which menaced me.

My revolvers were strapped to my lifeless body which, for some unfathomable reason, I could not bring myself to touch. My carbine was in its boot, strapped to my saddle, and as my horse had wandered off I was left without means of defense. My only alternative seemed to lie in flight and my decision was crystallized by a recurrence of the rustling sound from the thing which now seemed, in the darkness of the cave and to my distorted imagination, to be creeping stealthily upon me.

Unable longer to resist the temptation to escape this horrible place I leaped quickly through the opening into the starlight of a clear Arizona night. The crisp, fresh mountain air outside the cave acted as an immediate tonic and I felt new life and new courage coursing through me. Pausing upon the brink of the ledge I upbraided myself for what now seemed to me wholly unwarranted apprehension. I reasoned with myself that I had lain helpless for many hours within the cave, yet nothing had molested me, and my better judgment, when permitted the direction of clear and logical reasoning, convinced me that the noises I had heard must have resulted from purely natural and harmless causes; probably the conformation of the cave was such that a slight breeze had caused the sounds I heard.

I decided to investigate, but first I lifted my head to fill my lungs with the pure, invigorating night air of the mountains. As I did so I saw stretching far below me the beautiful vista of rocky gorge, and level, cacti-studded flat, wrought by the moonlight into a miracle of soft splendor and wondrous enchantment.

Few western wonders are more inspiring than the beauties of an Arizona moonlit landscape; the silvered mountains in the distance, the strange lights and shadows upon hog back and arroyo, and the grotesque details of the stiff, yet beautiful cacti form a picture at once enchanting and inspiring; as though one were catching for the first time a glimpse of some dead and forgotten world, so different is it from the aspect of any other spot upon our earth.

As I stood thus meditating, I turned my gaze from the landscape to the heavens where the myriad stars formed a gorgeous and fitting canopy for the wonders of the earthly scene. My attention was quickly riveted by a large red star close to the distant horizon. As I gazed upon it I felt a spell of overpowering fascination – it was Mars, the god of war, and for me, the fighting man, it had always held the power of irresistible enchantment. As I gazed at it on that far-gone night it seemed to call across the unthinkable void, to lure me to it, to draw me as the lodestone attracts a particle of iron.

My longing was beyond the power of opposition; I closed my eyes, stretched out my arms toward the god of my vocation and felt myself drawn with the suddenness of thought through the trackless immensity of space. There was an instant of extreme cold and utter darkness.

CHAPTER THREE

My Advent on Mars

I OPENED MY EYES upon a strange and weird landscape. I knew that I was on Mars; not once did I question either my sanity or my wakefulness. I was not asleep, no need for pinching here; my inner consciousness told me as plainly that I was upon Mars as your conscious mind tells you that you are upon Earth. You do not question the fact; neither did I.

I found myself lying prone upon a bed of yellowish, mosslike vegetation which stretched around me in all directions for interminable miles. I seemed to be lying in a deep, circular basin, along the outer verge of which I could distinguish the irregularities of low hills.

It was midday, the sun was shining full upon me and the heat of it was rather intense upon my naked body, yet no greater than would have been true under similar conditions on an Arizona desert. Here and there were slight outcroppings of quartz-bearing rock which glistened in the sunlight; and a little to my left, perhaps a hundred yards, appeared a low, walled enclosure about four feet in height. No water, and no other vegetation than the moss was in evidence, and as I was somewhat thirsty I determined to do a little exploring.

Springing to my feet I received my first Martian surprise, for the effort, which on Earth would have brought me standing upright, carried me into the Martian air to the height of about three yards. I alighted softly upon the ground, however, without appreciable shock or jar. Now commenced a series of evolutions which even then seemed ludicrous in the extreme. I found that I must learn to walk all over again, as the muscular exertion which carried me easily and safely upon Earth played strange antics with me upon Mars.

Instead of progressing in a sane and dignified manner, my attempts to walk resulted in a variety of hops which took me clear of the ground a couple of feet at each step and landed me sprawling upon my face or back at the end of each second or third hop. My muscles, perfectly attuned and accustomed to the force of gravity on Earth, played the mischief with me in attempting for the first time to cope with the lesser gravitation and lower air pressure on Mars.

I was determined, however, to explore the low structure which was the only evidence of habitation in sight, and so I hit upon the unique plan of reverting to first principles in locomotion, creeping. I did fairly well at this and in a few moments had reached the low, encircling wall of the enclosure.

There appeared to be no doors or windows upon the side nearest me, but as the wall was but about four feet high I cautiously gained my feet and peered over the top upon the strangest sight it had ever been given me to see.

The roof of the enclosure was of solid glass about four or five inches in thickness, and beneath this were several hundred large eggs, perfectly round and snowy white. The eggs were nearly uniform in size being about two and one-half feet in diameter.

Five or six had already hatched and the grotesque caricatures which sat blinking in the sunlight were enough to cause me to doubt my sanity. They seemed mostly head, with little scrawny bodies, long necks and six legs, or, as I afterward learned, two legs and two arms, with an intermediary pair of limbs which could be used at will either as arms or legs. Their eyes were set at the extreme sides of their heads a trifle above the center and protruded in such a manner that they could be directed either forward or back and also independently of each other, thus permitting this queer animal to look in any direction, or in two directions at once, without the necessity of turning the head.

The ears, which were slightly above the eyes and closer together, were small, cup-shaped antennae, protruding not more than an inch on these young specimens. Their noses were but longitudinal slits in the center of their faces, midway between their mouths and ears.

There was no hair on their bodies, which were of a very light yellowish-green color. In the adults, as I was to learn quite soon, this color deepens to an olive green and is darker in the male than in the female. Further, the heads of the adults are not so out of proportion to their bodies as in the case of the young.

The iris of the eyes is blood red, as in Albinos, while the pupil is dark. The eyeball itself is very white, as are the teeth. These latter add a most ferocious appearance to an otherwise fearsome and terrible countenance, as the lower tusks curve upward to sharp points which end about where the eyes of earthly human beings are located. The whiteness of the teeth is not that of ivory, but of the snowiest and most gleaming of china. Against the dark background of their olive skins their tusks stand out in a most striking manner, making these weapons present a singularly formidable appearance.

Most of these details I noted later, for I was given but little time to speculate on the wonders of my new discovery. I had seen that the eggs were in the process of hatching, and as I stood watching the hideous little monsters break from their shells I failed to note the approach of a score of full-grown Martians from behind me.

Coming, as they did, over the soft and soundless moss, which covers practically the entire surface of Mars with the exception of the frozen areas at the poles and the scattered cultivated districts, they might have captured me easily, but their intentions were far more sinister. It was the rattling of the accouterments of the foremost warrior which warned me.

On such a little thing my life hung that I often marvel that I escaped so easily. Had not the rifle of the leader of the party swung from its fastenings beside his saddle in such a way as to strike against the butt of his great metal-shod spear I should have snuffed out without ever knowing that death was near me. But the little sound caused me to turn, and there upon me, not ten feet from my breast, was the point of that huge spear, a spear forty feet long, tipped with gleaming metal, and held low at the side of a mounted replica of the little devils I had been watching.

But how puny and harmless they now looked beside this huge and terrific incarnation of hate, of vengeance and of death. The man himself, for such I may call him, was fully fifteen feet in height and, on Earth, would have weighed some four hundred pounds. He sat his mount as we sit a horse, grasping the animal's barrel with his lower limbs, while the hands of his two right arms held his immense spear low at the side of his mount; his two left arms were outstretched laterally to help preserve his balance, the thing he rode having neither bridle or reins of any description for guidance.

And his mount! How can earthly words describe it! It towered ten feet at the shoulder; had four legs on either side; a broad flat tail, larger at the tip than at the root, and which it held straight out behind while running; a gaping mouth which split its head from its snout to its long, massive neck.

Like its master, it was entirely devoid of hair, but was of a dark slate color and exceeding smooth and glossy. Its belly was white, and its legs shaded from the slate of its shoulders and hips to a vivid yellow at the feet. The feet themselves were heavily padded and nailless, which fact had also contributed to the noiselessness of their approach, and, in common with a multiplicity of legs, is a characteristic feature of the fauna of Mars. The highest type of man and one other animal, the only mammal existing on Mars, alone have well-formed nails, and there are absolutely no hoofed animals in existence there.

Behind this first charging demon trailed nineteen others, similar in all respects, but, as I learned later, bearing individual characteristics peculiar to themselves; precisely as no two of us are identical although we are all cast in a similar mold. This picture, or rather materialized nightmare, which I have described at length, made but one terrible and swift impression on me as I turned to meet it.

Unarmed and naked as I was, the first law of nature manifested itself in the only possible solution of my immediate problem, and that was to get out of the vicinity of the point of the charging spear. Consequently I gave a very earthly and at the same time superhuman leap to reach the top of the Martian incubator, for such I had determined it must be.

My effort was crowned with a success which appalled me no less than it seemed to surprise the Martian warriors, for it carried me fully thirty feet into the air and landed me a hundred feet from my pursuers and on the opposite side of the enclosure.

I alighted upon the soft moss easily and without mishap, and turning saw my enemies lined up along the further wall. Some were surveying me with expressions which I afterward discovered marked extreme astonishment, and the others were evidently satisfying themselves that I had not molested their young.

They were conversing together in low tones, and gesticulating and pointing toward me. Their discovery that I had not harmed the little Martians, and that I was unarmed, must have caused them to look upon me with less ferocity; but, as I was to learn later, the thing which weighed most in my favor was my exhibition of hurdling.

While the Martians are immense, their bones are very large and they are muscled only in proportion to the gravitation which they must overcome. The result is that they are infinitely less agile and less powerful, in proportion to their weight, than an Earth man, and I doubt that were one of them suddenly to be transported to Earth he could lift his own weight from the ground; in fact, I am convinced that he could not do so.

My feat then was as marvelous upon Mars as it would have been upon Earth, and from desiring to annihilate me they suddenly looked upon me as a wonderful discovery to be captured and exhibited among their fellows.

The respite my unexpected agility had given me permitted me to formulate plans for the immediate future and to note more closely the appearance of the warriors, for I could not disassociate these people in my mind from those other warriors who, only the day before, had been pursuing me.

I noted that each was armed with several other weapons in addition to the huge spear which I have described. The weapon which caused me to decide against an attempt at escape by flight was what was evidently a rifle of some description, and which I felt, for some reason, they were peculiarly efficient in handling.

These rifles were of a white metal stocked with wood, which I learned later was a very light and intensely hard growth much prized on Mars, and entirely unknown to us denizens of Earth. The metal of the barrel is an alloy composed principally of aluminum and steel which they have learned to temper to a hardness far exceeding that of the steel with which we are familiar. The weight of these rifles is comparatively little, and with the small caliber, explosive, radium projectiles which they use, and the great length of the barrel, they are deadly in the extreme and at ranges which would be unthinkable on Earth. The theoretic effective radius of this rifle is three hundred miles, but the best they can do in actual service when equipped with their wireless finders and sighters is but a trifle over two hundred miles.

This is quite far enough to imbue me with great respect for the Martian firearm, and some telepathic force must have warned me against an attempt to escape in broad daylight from under the muzzles of twenty of these death-dealing machines.

The Martians, after conversing for a short time, turned and rode away in the direction from which they had come, leaving one of their number alone by the enclosure. When they had covered perhaps two hundred yards they halted, and turning their mounts toward us sat watching the warrior by the enclosure.

He was the one whose spear had so nearly transfixed me, and was evidently the leader of the band, as I had noted that they seemed to have moved to their present position at his direction. When his force had come to a halt he dismounted, threw down his spear and small arms, and came around the end of the incubator toward me, entirely unarmed and as naked as I, except for the ornaments strapped upon his head, limbs, and breast.

When he was within about fifty feet of me he unclasped an enormous metal armlet, and holding it toward me in the open palm of his hand, addressed me in a clear, resonant voice, but in a language, it is needless to say, I could not understand. He then stopped as though waiting for my reply, pricking up his antennae-like ears and cocking his strange-looking eyes still further toward me.

As the silence became painful I concluded to hazard a little conversation on my own part, as I had guessed that he was making overtures of peace. The throwing down of his weapons and the withdrawing of his troop before his advance toward me would have signified a peaceful mission anywhere on Earth, so why not, then, on Mars!

Placing my hand over my heart I bowed low to the Martian and explained to him that while I did not understand his language, his actions spoke for the peace and friendship that at the present moment were most dear to my heart. Of course I might have been a babbling brook for all the intelligence my speech carried to him, but he understood the action with which I immediately followed my words.

Stretching my hand toward him, I advanced and took the armlet from his open palm, clasping it about my arm above the elbow; smiled at him and stood waiting. His wide mouth spread into an answering smile, and locking one of his intermediary arms in mine we turned and walked back toward his mount. At the same time he motioned his followers to advance. They started toward us on a wild run, but were checked by a signal from him. Evidently he feared that were I to be really frightened again I might jump entirely out of the landscape.

He exchanged a few words with his men, motioned to me that I would ride behind one of them, and then mounted his own animal. The fellow designated reached down two or three hands and lifted me up behind him on the glossy back of his mount, where I hung on as best I could by the belts and straps which held the Martian's weapons and ornaments.

The entire cavalcade then turned and galloped away toward the range of hills in the distance.

CHAPTER FOUR
A Prisoner

WE HAD GONE PERHAPS TEN MILES when the ground began to rise very rapidly. We were, as I was later to learn, nearing the edge of one of Mars' long-dead seas, in the bottom of which my encounter with the Martians had taken place.

In a short time we gained the foot of the mountains, and after traversing a narrow gorge came to an open valley, at the far extremity of which was a low table land upon which I beheld an enormous city. Toward this we galloped, entering it by what appeared to be a ruined roadway leading out from the city, but only to the edge of the table land, where it ended abruptly in a flight of broad steps.

Upon closer observation I saw as we passed them that the buildings were deserted, and while not greatly decayed had the appearance of not having been tenanted for years, possibly for ages. Toward the center of the city was a large plaza, and upon this and in the buildings immediately surrounding it were camped some nine or ten hundred creatures of the same breed as my captors, for such I now considered them despite the suave manner in which I had been trapped.

With the exception of their ornaments all were naked. The women varied in appearance but little from the men, except that their tusks were much larger in proportion to their height, in some instances curving nearly to their high-set ears. Their bodies were smaller and lighter in color, and their fingers and toes bore the rudiments of nails, which were entirely lacking among the males. The adult females ranged in height from ten to twelve feet.

The children were light in color, even lighter than the women, and all looked precisely alike to me, except that some were taller than others; older, I presumed.

I saw no signs of extreme age among them, nor is there any appreciable difference in their appearance from the age of maturity, about forty, until, at about the age of one thousand years, they go voluntarily upon their last strange pilgrimage down the river Iss, which leads no living Martian knows whither and from whose bosom no Martian has ever returned, or would be allowed to live did he return after once embarking upon its cold, dark waters.

Only about one Martian in a thousand dies of sickness or disease, and possibly about twenty take the voluntary pilgrimage. The other nine hundred and seventy-nine die violent deaths in duels, in hunting, in aviation and in war; but perhaps by far the greatest death loss comes during the age of childhood, when vast numbers of the little Martians fall victims to the great white apes of Mars.

The average life expectancy of a Martian after the age of maturity is about three hundred years, but would be nearer the one-thousand mark were it not for the various means leading to violent death. Owing to the waning resources of the planet it evidently became necessary to counteract the increasing longevity which their remarkable skill in therapeutics and surgery produced, and so human life has come to be considered but lightly on Mars, as is evidenced by their dangerous sports and the almost continual warfare between the various communities.

There are other and natural causes tending toward a diminution of population, but nothing contributes so greatly to this end as the fact that no male or female Martian is ever voluntarily without a weapon of destruction.

As we neared the plaza and my presence was discovered we were immediately surrounded by hundreds of the creatures who seemed anxious to pluck me from my seat behind my guard. A word from the leader of the party stilled their clamor, and we proceeded at a trot across the plaza to the entrance of as magnificent an edifice as mortal eye has rested upon.

The building was low, but covered an enormous area. It was constructed of gleaming white marble inlaid with gold and brilliant stones which sparkled and scintillated in the sunlight. The main entrance was some hundred feet in width and projected from the building proper to form a huge canopy above the entrance hall. There was no stairway, but a gentle incline to the first floor of the building opened into an enormous chamber encircled by galleries.

On the floor of this chamber, which was dotted with highly carved wooden desks and chairs, were assembled about forty or fifty male Martians around the steps of a rostrum. On the platform proper squatted an enormous warrior heavily loaded with metal ornaments, gay-colored feathers and beautifully wrought leather trappings ingeniously set with precious stones. From his shoulders depended a short cape of white fur lined with brilliant scarlet silk.

What struck me as most remarkable about this assemblage and the hall in which they were congregated was the fact that the creatures were entirely out of proportion to the desks, chairs, and other furnishings; these being of a size adapted to human beings such as I, whereas the great bulks of the Martians could scarcely have squeezed into the chairs, nor was there room beneath the desks for their long legs. Evidently, then, there were other denizens on Mars than the wild and grotesque creatures into whose hands I had fallen, but the evidences of extreme antiquity which showed all around me indicated that these buildings might have belonged to some long-extinct and forgotten race in the dim antiquity of Mars.

Our party had halted at the entrance to the building, and at a sign from the leader I had been lowered to the ground. Again locking his arm in mine, we had proceeded into the audience chamber. There were few formalities observed in approaching the Martian chieftain. My captor merely strode up to the rostrum, the others making way for him as he advanced. The chieftain rose to his feet and uttered the name of my escort who, in turn, halted and repeated the name of the ruler followed by his title.

At the time, this ceremony and the words they uttered meant nothing to me, but later I came to know that this was the customary greeting between green Martians. Had the men been strangers, and therefore unable to exchange names, they would have silently exchanged ornaments, had their missions been peaceful – otherwise they would have exchanged shots, or have fought out their introduction with some other of their various weapons.

My captor, whose name was Tars Tarkas, was virtually the vice-chieftain of the community, and a man of great ability as a statesman and warrior. He evidently explained briefly the incidents connected with his expedition, including my capture, and when he had concluded the chieftain addressed me at some length.

I replied in our good old English tongue merely to convince him that neither of us could understand the other; but I noticed that when I smiled slightly on concluding, he did likewise. This fact, and the similar occurrence during my first talk with Tars Tarkas, convinced me that we had at least something in common; the ability to smile, therefore to laugh; denoting a sense of humor. But I was to learn that the Martian smile is merely perfunctory, and that the Martian laugh is a thing to cause strong men to blanch in horror.

The ideas of humor among the green men of Mars are widely at variance with our conceptions of incitants to merriment. The death agonies of a fellow being are, to these strange creatures provocative of the wildest hilarity, while their chief form of commonest amusement is to inflict death on their prisoners of war in various ingenious and horrible ways.

The assembled warriors and chieftains examined me closely, feeling my muscles and the texture of my skin. The principal chieftain then evidently signified a desire to see me perform, and, motioning me to follow, he started with Tars Tarkas for the open plaza.

Now, I had made no attempt to walk, since my first signal failure, except while tightly grasping Tars Tarkas' arm, and so now I went skipping and flitting about among the desks and chairs like some monstrous grasshopper. After bruising myself severely, much to the amusement of the Martians, I again had recourse to creeping, but this did not suit them and I was roughly jerked to my feet by a towering fellow who had laughed most heartily at my misfortunes.

As he banged me down upon my feet his face was bent close to mine and I did the only thing a gentleman might do under the circumstances of brutality, boorishness, and lack of consideration for a stranger's rights; I swung my fist squarely to his jaw and he went down like a felled ox. As he sunk to the floor I wheeled around with my back toward the nearest desk, expecting to be overwhelmed by the vengeance of his fellows, but determined to give them as good a battle as the unequal odds would permit before I gave up my life.

My fears were groundless, however, as the other Martians, at first struck dumb with wonderment, finally broke into wild peals of laughter and applause. I did not recognize the applause as such, but later, when I had become acquainted with their customs, I learned that I had won what they seldom accord, a manifestation of approbation.

The fellow whom I had struck lay where he had fallen, nor did any of his mates approach him. Tars Tarkas advanced toward me, holding out one of his arms, and we thus proceeded to the plaza without further mishap. I did not, of course, know the reason for which we had come to the open, but I was not long in being enlightened. They first repeated the word "sak" a number of times, and then Tars Tarkas made several jumps, repeating the same word before each leap; then, turning to me, he said, "sak!" I saw what they were after, and gathering myself together I "sakked" with such marvelous success that I cleared a good hundred and fifty feet; nor did I this time, lose my equilibrium, but landed squarely upon my feet without falling. I then returned by easy jumps of twenty-five or thirty feet to the little group of warriors.

My exhibition had been witnessed by several hundred lesser Martians, and they immediately broke into demands for a repetition, which the chieftain then ordered me to make; but I was both hungry and thirsty, and determined on the spot that my only method of salvation was to demand the consideration from these creatures which they evidently would not voluntarily accord. I therefore ignored the repeated commands to "sak," and each time they were made I motioned to my mouth and rubbed my stomach.

Tars Tarkas and the chief exchanged a few words, and the former, calling to a young female among the throng, gave her some instructions and motioned me to accompany her. I grasped her proffered arm and together we crossed the plaza toward a large building on the far side.

My fair companion was about eight feet tall, having just arrived at maturity, but not yet to her full height. She was of a light olive-green color, with a smooth, glossy hide. Her name, as I afterward learned, was Sola, and she belonged to the retinue of Tars Tarkas. She conducted me to a spacious chamber in one of the buildings fronting on the plaza, and which, from the litter of silks and furs upon the floor, I took to be the sleeping quarters of several of the natives.

The room was well lighted by a number of large windows and was beautifully decorated with mural paintings and mosaics, but upon all there seemed to rest that indefinable touch of the finger of antiquity which convinced me that the architects and builders of these wondrous creations had nothing in common with the crude half-brutes which now occupied them.

Sola motioned me to be seated upon a pile of silks near the center of the room, and, turning, made a peculiar hissing sound, as though signaling to someone in an adjoining room. In response to her call I obtained my first sight of a new Martian wonder. It waddled in on its ten short legs, and squatted down before the girl like an obedient puppy. The thing was about the size of a Shetland pony, but its head bore a slight resemblance to that of a frog, except that the jaws were equipped with three rows of long, sharp tusks.

CHAPTER FIVE

I Elude My Watch Dog

SOLA STARED INTO the brute's wicked-looking eyes, muttered a word or
two of command, pointed to me, and left the chamber. I could not but
wonder what this ferocious-looking monstrosity might do when left
alone in such close proximity to such a relatively tender morsel of meat;
but my fears were groundless, as the beast, after surveying me intently
for a moment, crossed the room to the only exit which led to the street,
and lay down full length across the threshold.

This was my first experience with a Martian watch dog, but it was
destined not to be my last, for this fellow guarded me carefully during
the time I remained a captive among these green men; twice saving my
life, and never voluntarily being away from me a moment.

While Sola was away I took occasion to examine more minutely the
room in which I found myself captive. The mural painting depicted
scenes of rare and wonderful beauty; mountains, rivers, lake, ocean,
meadow, trees and flowers, winding roadways, sun-kissed gardens –
scenes which might have portrayed earthly views but for the different
colorings of the vegetation. The work had evidently been wrought by
a master hand, so subtle the atmosphere, so perfect the technique; yet
nowhere was there a representation of a living animal, either human or
brute, by which I could guess at the likeness of these other and perhaps
extinct denizens of Mars.

While I was allowing my fancy to run riot in wild conjecture on the
possible explanation of the strange anomalies which I had so far met
with on Mars, Sola returned bearing both food and drink. These she
placed on the floor beside me, and seating herself a short ways off regarded me intently. The food consisted of about a pound of some solid
substance of the consistency of cheese and almost tasteless, while the

liquid was apparently milk from some animal. It was not unpleasant to the taste, though slightly acid, and I learned in a short time to prize it very highly. It came, as I later discovered, not from an animal, as there is only one mammal on Mars and that one very rare indeed, but from a large plant which grows practically without water, but seems to distill its plentiful supply of milk from the products of the soil, the moisture of the air, and the rays of the sun. A single plant of this species will give eight or ten quarts of milk per day.

After I had eaten I was greatly invigorated, but feeling the need of rest I stretched out upon the silks and was soon asleep. I must have slept several hours, as it was dark when I awoke, and I was very cold. I noticed that someone had thrown a fur over me, but it had become partially dislodged and in the darkness I could not see to replace it. Suddenly a hand reached out and pulled the fur over me, shortly afterwards adding another to my covering.

I presumed that my watchful guardian was Sola, nor was I wrong. This girl alone, among all the green Martians with whom I came in contact, disclosed characteristics of sympathy, kindliness, and affection; her ministrations to my bodily wants were unfailing, and her solicitous care saved me from much suffering and many hardships.

As I was to learn, the Martian nights are extremely cold, and as there is practically no twilight or dawn, the changes in temperature are sudden and most uncomfortable, as are the transitions from brilliant daylight to darkness. The nights are either brilliantly illumined or very dark, for if neither of the two moons of Mars happen to be in the sky almost total darkness results, since the lack of atmosphere, or, rather, the very thin atmosphere, fails to diffuse the starlight to any great extent; on the other hand, if both of the moons are in the heavens at night the surface of the ground is brightly illuminated.

Both of Mars' moons are vastly nearer her than is our moon to Earth; the nearer moon being but about five thousand miles distant, while the further is but little more than fourteen thousand miles away, against the nearly one-quarter million miles which separate us from our moon. The nearer moon of Mars makes a complete revolution around the planet in a little over seven and one-half hours, so that she may be seen hurtling through the sky like some huge meteor two or three times each night, revealing all her phases during each transit of the heavens.

The further moon revolves about Mars in something over thirty and one-quarter hours, and with her sister satellite makes a nocturnal Martian scene one of splendid and weird grandeur. And it is well that nature has so graciously and abundantly lighted the Martian night, for

the green men of Mars, being a nomadic race without high intellectual development, have but crude means for artificial lighting; depending principally upon torches, a kind of candle, and a peculiar oil lamp
which generates a gas and burns without a wick.

This last device produces an intensely brilliant far-reaching white
light, but as the natural oil which it requires can only be obtained by
mining in one of several widely separated and remote localities it is
seldom used by these creatures whose only thought is for today, and
whose hatred for manual labor has kept them in a semi-barbaric state
for countless ages.

After Sola had replenished my coverings I again slept, nor did I
awaken until daylight. The other occupants of the room, five in number, were all females, and they were still sleeping, piled high with a
motley array of silks and furs. Across the threshold lay stretched the
sleepless guardian brute, just as I had last seen him on the preceding
day; apparently he had not moved a muscle; his eyes were fairly glued
upon me, and I fell to wondering just what might befall me should I
endeavor to escape.

I have ever been prone to seek adventure and to investigate and experiment where wiser men would have left well enough alone. It therefore
now occurred to me that the surest way of learning the exact attitude of
this beast toward me would be to attempt to leave the room. I felt fairly
secure in my belief that I could escape him should he pursue me once I
was outside the building, for I had begun to take great pride in my ability
as a jumper. Furthermore, I could see from the shortness of his legs that
the brute himself was no jumper and probably no runner.

Slowly and carefully, therefore, I gained my feet, only to see that my
watcher did the same; cautiously I advanced toward him, finding that by
moving with a shuffling gait I could retain my balance as well as make
reasonably rapid progress. As I neared the brute he backed cautiously
away from me, and when I had reached the open he moved to one side
to let me pass. He then fell in behind me and followed about ten paces in
my rear as I made my way along the deserted street.

Evidently his mission was to protect me only, I thought, but when
we reached the edge of the city he suddenly sprang before me, uttering strange sounds and baring his ugly and ferocious tusks. Thinking
to have some amusement at his expense, I rushed toward him, and
when almost upon him sprang into the air, alighting far beyond him
and away from the city. He wheeled instantly and charged me with the
most appalling speed I had ever beheld. I had thought his short legs
a bar to swiftness, but had he been coursing with greyhounds the lat-

ter would have appeared as though asleep on a door mat. As I was to learn, this is the fleetest animal on Mars, and owing to its intelligence, loyalty, and ferocity is used in hunting, in war, and as the protector of the Martian man.

I quickly saw that I would have difficulty in escaping the fangs of the beast on a straightaway course, and so I met his charge by doubling in my tracks and leaping over him as he was almost upon me. This maneuver gave me a considerable advantage, and I was able to reach the city quite a bit ahead of him, and as he came tearing after me I jumped for a window about thirty feet from the ground in the face of one of the buildings overlooking the valley.

Grasping the sill I pulled myself up to a sitting posture without looking into the building, and gazed down at the baffled animal beneath me. My exultation was short-lived, however, for scarcely had I gained a secure seat upon the sill than a huge hand grasped me by the neck from behind and dragged me violently into the room. Here I was thrown upon my back, and beheld standing over me a colossal ape-like creature, white and hairless except for an enormous shock of bristly hair upon its head.

CHAPTER SIX
A Fight that Won Friends

THE THING, which more nearly resembled our earthly men than it did the Martians I had seen, held me pinioned to the ground with one huge foot, while it jabbered and gesticulated at some answering creature behind me. This other, which was evidently its mate, soon came toward us, bearing a mighty stone cudgel with which it evidently intended to brain me.

The creatures were about ten or fifteen feet tall, standing erect, and had, like the green Martians, an intermediary set of arms or legs, midway between their upper and lower limbs. Their eyes were close together and non-protruding; their ears were high set, but more laterally located than those of the Martians, while their snouts and teeth were strikingly like those of our African gorilla. Altogether they were not unlovely when viewed in comparison with the green Martians.

The cudgel was swinging in the arc which ended upon my upturned face when a bolt of myriad-legged horror hurled itself through the doorway full upon the breast of my executioner. With a shriek of fear the ape which held me leaped through the open window, but its mate closed in a terrific death struggle with my preserver, which was nothing less than my faithful watch-thing; I cannot bring myself to call so hideous a creature a dog.

As quickly as possible I gained my feet and backing against the wall I witnessed such a battle as it is vouchsafed few beings to see. The strength, agility, and blind ferocity of these two creatures is approached by nothing known to earthly man. My beast had an advantage in his first hold, having sunk his mighty fangs far into the breast of his adversary; but the great arms and paws of the ape, backed by muscles far transcending those of the Martian men I had seen, had locked the throat of my guardian and slowly were choking out his life, and bending back his head and neck upon his body, where I momentarily expected the former to fall limp at the end of a broken neck.

In accomplishing this the ape was tearing away the entire front of its breast, which was held in the vise-like grip of the powerful jaws. Back and forth upon the floor they rolled, neither one emitting a sound of fear or pain. Presently I saw the great eyes of my beast bulging completely from their sockets and blood flowing from its nostrils. That he was weakening perceptibly was evident, but so also was the ape, whose struggles were growing momentarily less.

Suddenly I came to myself and, with that strange instinct which seems ever to prompt me to my duty, I seized the cudgel, which had fallen to the floor at the commencement of the battle, and swinging it with all the power of my earthly arms I crashed it full upon the head of the ape, crushing his skull as though it had been an eggshell.

Scarcely had the blow descended when I was confronted with a new danger. The ape's mate, recovered from its first shock of terror, had returned to the scene of the encounter by way of the interior of the building. I glimpsed him just before he reached the doorway and the sight of him, now roaring as he perceived his lifeless fellow stretched upon the floor, and frothing at the mouth, in the extremity of his rage, filled me, I must confess, with dire forebodings.

I am ever willing to stand and fight when the odds are not too overwhelmingly against me, but in this instance I perceived neither glory nor profit in pitting my relatively puny strength against the iron muscles and brutal ferocity of this enraged denizen of an unknown world; in fact, the only outcome of such an encounter, so far as I might be concerned, seemed sudden death.

I was standing near the window and I knew that once in the street I might gain the plaza and safety before the creature could overtake me; at least there was a chance for safety in flight, against almost certain death should I remain and fight however desperately.

It is true I held the cudgel, but what could I do with it against his four great arms? Even should I break one of them with my first blow, for I figured that he would attempt to ward off the cudgel, he could reach out and annihilate me with the others before I could recover for a second attack.

In the instant that these thoughts passed through my mind I had turned to make for the window, but my eyes alighting on the form of my erstwhile guardian threw all thoughts of flight to the four winds. He lay gasping upon the floor of the chamber, his great eyes fastened upon me in what seemed a pitiful appeal for protection. I could not

withstand that look, nor could I, on second thought, have deserted my rescuer without giving as good an account of myself in his behalf as he had in mine.

Without more ado, therefore, I turned to meet the charge of the infuriated bull ape. He was now too close upon me for the cudgel to prove of any effective assistance, so I merely threw it as heavily as I could at his advancing bulk. It struck him just below the knees, eliciting a howl of pain and rage, and so throwing him off his balance that he lunged full upon me with arms wide stretched to ease his fall.

Again, as on the preceding day, I had recourse to earthly tactics, and swinging my right fist full upon the point of his chin I followed it with a smashing left to the pit of his stomach. The effect was marvelous, for, as I lightly sidestepped, after delivering the second blow, he reeled and fell upon the floor doubled up with pain and gasping for wind. Leaping over his prostrate body, I seized the cudgel and finished the monster before he could regain his feet.

As I delivered the blow a low laugh rang out behind me, and, turning, I beheld Tars Tarkas, Sola, and three or four warriors standing in the doorway of the chamber. As my eyes met theirs I was, for the second time, the recipient of their zealously guarded applause.

My absence had been noted by Sola on her awakening, and she had quickly informed Tars Tarkas, who had set out immediately with a handful of warriors to search for me. As they had approached the limits of the city they had witnessed the actions of the bull ape as he bolted into the building, frothing with rage.

They had followed immediately behind him, thinking it barely possible that his actions might prove a clew to my whereabouts and had witnessed my short but decisive battle with him. This encounter, together with my set-to with the Martian warrior on the previous day and my feats of jumping placed me upon a high pinnacle in their regard. Evidently devoid of all the finer sentiments of friendship, love, or affection, these people fairly worship physical prowess and bravery, and nothing is too good for the object of their adoration as long as he maintains his position by repeated examples of his skill, strength, and courage.

Sola, who had accompanied the searching party of her own volition, was the only one of the Martians whose face had not been twisted in laughter as I battled for my life. She, on the contrary, was sober with apparent solicitude and, as soon as I had finished the monster, rushed to me and carefully examined my body for possible wounds or injuries. Satisfying herself that I had come off unscathed she smiled quietly, and, taking my hand, started toward the door of the chamber.

Tars Tarkas and the other warriors had entered and were standing over the now rapidly reviving brute which had saved my life, and whose life I, in turn, had rescued. They seemed to be deep in argument, and finally one of them addressed me, but remembering my ignorance of his language turned back to Tars Tarkas, who, with a word and gesture, gave some command to the fellow and turned to follow us from the room.

There seemed something menacing in their attitude toward my beast, and I hesitated to leave until I had learned the outcome. It was well I did so, for the warrior drew an evil looking pistol from its holster and was on the point of putting an end to the creature when I sprang forward and struck up his arm. The bullet striking the wooden casing of the window exploded, blowing a hole completely through the wood and masonry.

I then knelt down beside the fearsome-looking thing, and raising it to its feet motioned for it to follow me. The looks of surprise which my actions elicited from the Martians were ludicrous; they could not understand, except in a feeble and childish way, such attributes as gratitude and compassion. The warrior whose gun I had struck up looked enquiringly at Tars Tarkas, but the latter signed that I be left to my own devices, and so we returned to the plaza with my great beast following close at heel, and Sola grasping me tightly by the arm.

I had at least two friends on Mars; a young woman who watched over me with motherly solicitude, and a dumb brute which, as I later came to know, held in its poor ugly carcass more love, more loyalty, more gratitude than could have been found in the entire five million green Martians who rove the deserted cities and dead sea bottoms of Mars.

CHAPTER SEVEN

Child-Raising on Mars

AFTER A BREAKFAST, which was an exact replica of the meal of the preceding day and an index of practically every meal which followed while I was with the green men of Mars, Sola escorted me to the plaza, where I found the entire community engaged in watching or helping at the harnessing of huge mastodonian animals to great three-wheeled chariots. There were about two hundred and fifty of these vehicles, each drawn by a single animal, any one of which, from their appearance, might easily have drawn the entire wagon train when fully loaded.

The chariots themselves were large, commodious, and gorgeously decorated. In each was seated a female Martian loaded with ornaments of metal, with jewels and silks and furs, and upon the back of each of the beasts which drew the chariots was perched a young Martian driver. Like the animals upon which the warriors were mounted, the heavier draft animals wore neither bit nor bridle, but were guided entirely by telepathic means.

This power is wonderfully developed in all Martians, and accounts largely for the simplicity of their language and the relatively few spoken words exchanged even in long conversations. It is the universal language of Mars, through the medium of which the higher and lower animals of this world of paradoxes are able to communicate to a greater or less extent, depending upon the intellectual sphere of the species and the development of the individual.

As the cavalcade took up the line of march in single file, Sola dragged me into an empty chariot and we proceeded with the procession toward the point by which I had entered the city the day before. At the head of the caravan rode some two hundred warriors, five abreast, and a like number brought up the rear, while twenty-five or thirty outriders flanked us on either side.

Every one but myself – men, women, and children – were heavily armed, and at the tail of each chariot trotted a Martian hound, my own beast following closely behind ours; in fact, the faithful creature never left me voluntarily during the entire ten years I spent on Mars. Our way led out across the little valley before the city, through the hills, and down into the dead sea bottom which I had traversed on my journey from the incubator to the plaza. The incubator, as it proved, was the terminal point of our journey this day, and, as the entire cavalcade broke into a mad gallop as soon as we reached the level expanse of sea bottom, we were soon within sight of our goal.

On reaching it the chariots were parked with military precision on the four sides of the enclosure, and half a score of warriors, headed by the enormous chieftain, and including Tars Tarkas and several other lesser chiefs, dismounted and advanced toward it. I could see Tars Tarkas explaining something to the principal chieftain, whose name, by the way, was, as nearly as I can translate it into English, Lorquas Ptomel, Jed; jed being his title.

I was soon appraised of the subject of their conversation, as, calling to Sola, Tars Tarkas signed for her to send me to him. I had by this time mastered the intricacies of walking under Martian conditions, and quickly responding to his command I advanced to the side of the incubator where the warriors stood.

As I reached their side a glance showed me that all but a very few eggs had hatched, the incubator being fairly alive with the hideous little devils. They ranged in height from three to four feet, and were moving restlessly about the enclosure as though searching for food.

As I came to a halt before him, Tars Tarkas pointed over the incubator and said, "Sak." I saw that he wanted me to repeat my performance of yesterday for the edification of Lorquas Ptomel, and, as I must confess that my prowess gave me no little satisfaction, I responded quickly, leaping entirely over the parked chariots on the far side of the incubator. As I returned, Lorquas Ptomel grunted something at me, and turning to his warriors gave a few words of command relative to the incubator. They paid no further attention to me and I was thus permitted to remain close and watch their operations, which consisted in breaking an opening in the wall of the incubator large enough to permit of the exit of the young Martians.

On either side of this opening the women and the younger Martians, both male and female, formed two solid walls leading out through the chariots and quite away into the plain beyond. Between these walls the little Martians scampered, wild as deer; being permitted to run the full length of the aisle, where they were captured one at a time by the women and older children; the last in the line capturing the first little one to reach the end of the gauntlet, her opposite in the line capturing the second, and so on until all the little fellows had left the enclosure and been appropriated by some youth or female. As the women caught the young they fell out of line and returned to their respective chariots, while those who fell into the hands of the young men were later turned over to some of the women.

I saw that the ceremony, if it could be dignified by such a name, was over, and seeking out Sola I found her in our chariot with a hideous little creature held tightly in her arms.

The work of rearing young, green Martians consists solely in teaching them to talk, and to use the weapons of warfare with which they are loaded down from the very first year of their lives. Coming from eggs in which they have lain for five years, the period of incubation, they step forth into the world perfectly developed except in size. Entirely unknown to their mothers, who, in turn, would have difficulty in pointing out the fathers with any degree of accuracy, they are the common children of the community, and their education devolves upon the females who chance to capture them as they leave the incubator.

Their foster mothers may not even have had an egg in the incubator, as was the case with Sola, who had not commenced to lay, until less than a year before she became the mother of another woman's offspring. But this counts for little among the green Martians, as parental and filial love is as unknown to them as it is common among us. I believe this horrible system which has been carried on for ages is the direct cause of the loss of all the finer feelings and higher humanitarian instincts among these poor creatures. From birth they know no father or mother love, they know not the meaning of the word home; they are taught that they are only suffered to live until they can demonstrate by their physique and ferocity that they are fit to live. Should they prove deformed or defective in any way they are promptly shot; nor do they see a tear shed for a single one of the many cruel hardships they pass through from earliest infancy.

I do not mean that the adult Martians are unnecessarily or intentionally cruel to the young, but theirs is a hard and pitiless struggle for existence upon a dying planet, the natural resources of which have dwindled to a point where the support of each additional life means an added tax upon the community into which it is thrown.

By careful selection they rear only the hardiest specimens of each species, and with almost supernatural foresight they regulate the birth rate to merely offset the loss by death.

Each adult Martian female brings forth about thirteen eggs each year, and those which meet the size, weight, and specific gravity tests are hidden in the recesses of some subterranean vault where the temperature is too low for incubation. Every year these eggs are carefully examined by a council of twenty chieftains, and all but about one hundred of the most perfect are destroyed out of each yearly supply. At the end of five years about five hundred almost perfect eggs have been chosen from the thousands brought forth. These are then placed in the almost air-tight incubators to be hatched by the sun's rays after a period of another five years. The hatching which we had witnessed today was a fairly representative event of its kind, all but about one per cent of the eggs hatching in two days. If the remaining eggs ever hatched we knew nothing of the fate of the little Martians. They were not wanted, as their offspring might inherit and transmit the tendency to prolonged incubation, and thus upset the system which has maintained for ages and which permits the adult Martians to figure the proper time for return to the incubators, almost to an hour.

The incubators are built in remote fastnesses, where there is little or no likelihood of their being discovered by other tribes. The result of such a catastrophe would mean no children in the community for another five years. I was later to witness the results of the discovery of an alien incubator.

The community of which the green Martians with whom my lot was cast formed a part was composed of some thirty thousand souls. They roamed an enormous tract of arid and semi-arid land between forty and eighty degrees south latitude, and bounded on the east and west by two large fertile tracts. Their headquarters lay in the southwest corner of this district, near the crossing of two of the so-called Martian canals.

As the incubator had been placed far north of their own territory in a supposedly uninhabited and unfrequented area, we had before us a tremendous journey, concerning which I, of course, knew nothing.

After our return to the dead city I passed several days in comparative idleness. On the day following our return all the warriors had ridden forth early in the morning and had not returned until just before darkness fell. As I later learned, they had been to the subterranean vaults in which the eggs were kept and had transported them to the incubator, which they had then walled up for another five years, and which, in all probability, would not be visited again during that period.

The vaults which hid the eggs until they were ready for the incubator were located many miles south of the incubator, and would be visited yearly by the council of twenty chieftains. Why they did not arrange to build their vaults and incubators nearer home has always been a mystery to me, and, like many other Martian mysteries, unsolved and unsolvable by earthly reasoning and customs.

Sola's duties were now doubled, as she was compelled to care for the young Martian as well as for me, but neither one of us required much attention, and as we were both about equally advanced in Martian education, Sola took it upon herself to train us together.

Her prize consisted in a male about four feet tall, very strong and physically perfect; also, he learned quickly, and we had considerable amusement, at least I did, over the keen rivalry we displayed. The Martian language, as I have said, is extremely simple, and in a week I could make all my wants known and understand nearly everything that was said to me. Likewise, under Sola's tutelage, I developed my telepathic powers so that I shortly could sense practically everything that went on around me.

What surprised Sola most in me was that while I could catch telepathic messages easily from others, and often when they were not intended for me, no one could read a jot from my mind under any circumstances. At first this vexed me, but later I was very glad of it, as it gave me an undoubted advantage over the Martians.

CHAPTER EIGHT

A Fair Captive from the Sky

THE THIRD DAY after the incubator ceremony we set forth toward home, but scarcely had the head of the procession debouched into the open ground before the city than orders were given for an immediate and hasty return. As though trained for years in this particular evolution, the green Martians melted like mist into the spacious doorways of the nearby buildings, until, in less than three minutes, the entire cavalcade of chariots, mastodons and mounted warriors was nowhere to be seen.

Sola and I had entered a building upon the front of the city, in fact, the same one in which I had had my encounter with the apes, and, wishing to see what had caused the sudden retreat, I mounted to an upper floor and peered from the window out over the valley and the hills beyond; and there I saw the cause of their sudden scurrying to cover. A huge craft, long, low, and gray-painted, swung slowly over the crest of the nearest hill. Following it came another, and another, and another, until twenty of them, swinging low above the ground, sailed slowly and majestically toward us.

Each carried a strange banner swung from stem to stern above the upper works, and upon the prow of each was painted some odd device that gleamed in the sunlight and showed plainly even at the distance at which we were from the vessels. I could see figures crowding the forward decks and upper works of the air craft. Whether they had discovered us or simply were looking at the deserted city I could not say, but in any event they received a rude reception, for suddenly and without warning the green Martian warriors fired a terrific volley from the windows of the buildings facing the little valley across which the great ships were so peacefully advancing.

Instantly the scene changed as by magic; the foremost vessel swung broadside toward us, and bringing her guns into play returned our fire, at the same time moving parallel to our front for a short distance and then turning back with the evident intention of completing a great circle which would bring her up to position once more opposite our firing line; the other vessels followed in her wake, each one opening upon us as she swung into position. Our own fire never diminished, and I doubt if twenty-five per cent of our shots went wild. It had never been given me to see such deadly accuracy of aim, and it seemed as though a little figure on one of the craft dropped at the explosion of each bullet, while the banners and upper works dissolved in spurts of flame as the irresistible projectiles of our warriors mowed through them.

The fire from the vessels was most ineffectual, owing, as I afterward learned, to the unexpected suddenness of the first volley, which caught the ship's crews entirely unprepared and the sighting apparatus of the guns unprotected from the deadly aim of our warriors.

It seems that each green warrior has certain objective points for his fire under relatively identical circumstances of warfare. For example, a proportion of them, always the best marksmen, direct their fire entirely upon the wireless finding and sighting apparatus of the big guns of an attacking naval force; another detail attends to the smaller guns in the same way; others pick off the gunners; still others the officers; while certain other quotas concentrate their attention upon the other members of the crew, upon the upper works, and upon the steering gear and propellers.

Twenty minutes after the first volley the great fleet swung trailing off in the direction from which it had first appeared. Several of the craft were limping perceptibly, and seemed but barely under the control of their depleted crews. Their fire had ceased entirely and all their energies seemed focused upon escape. Our warriors then rushed up to the roofs of the buildings which we occupied and followed the retreating armada with a continuous fusillade of deadly fire.

One by one, however, the ships managed to dip below the crests of the outlying hills until only one barely moving craft was in sight. This had received the brunt of our fire and seemed to be entirely unmanned, as not a moving figure was visible upon her decks. Slowly she swung from her course, circling back toward us in an erratic and pitiful manner. Instantly the warriors ceased firing, for it was quite apparent that the vessel was entirely helpless, and, far from being in a position to inflict harm upon us, she could not even control herself sufficiently to escape.

As she neared the city the warriors rushed out upon the plain to meet her, but it was evident that she still was too high for them to hope to reach her decks. From my vantage point in the window I could see the bodies of her crew strewn about, although I could not make out what manner of creatures they might be. Not a sign of life was manifest upon her as she drifted slowly with the light breeze in a southeasterly direction.

She was drifting some fifty feet above the ground, followed by all but some hundred of the warriors who had been ordered back to the roofs to cover the possibility of a return of the fleet, or of reinforcements. It soon became evident that she would strike the face of the buildings about a mile south of our position, and as I watched the progress of the chase I saw a number of warriors gallop ahead, dismount and enter the building she seemed destined to touch.

As the craft neared the building, and just before she struck, the Martian warriors swarmed upon her from the windows, and with their great spears eased the shock of the collision, and in a few moments they had thrown out grappling hooks and the big boat was being hauled to ground by their fellows below.

After making her fast, they swarmed the sides and searched the vessel from stem to stern. I could see them examining the dead sailors, evidently for signs of life, and presently a party of them appeared from below dragging a little figure among them. The creature was considerably less than half as tall as the green Martian warriors, and from my balcony I could see that it walked erect upon two legs and surmised that it was some new and strange Martian monstrosity with which I had not as yet become acquainted.

They removed their prisoner to the ground and then commenced a systematic rifling of the vessel. This operation required several hours, during which time a number of the chariots were requisitioned to transport the loot, which consisted in arms, ammunition, silks, furs, jewels, strangely carved stone vessels, and a quantity of solid foods and liquids, including many casks of water, the first I had seen since my advent upon Mars.

After the last load had been removed the warriors made lines fast to the craft and towed her far out into the valley in a southwesterly direction. A few of them then boarded her and were busily engaged in what appeared, from my distant position, as the emptying of the contents of various carboys upon the dead bodies of the sailors and over the decks and works of the vessel.

This operation concluded, they hastily clambered over her sides, sliding down the guy ropes to the ground. The last warrior to leave the deck turned and threw something back upon the vessel, waiting an instant to note the outcome of his act. As a faint spurt of flame rose from the point where the missile struck he swung over the side and was quickly upon the ground. Scarcely had he alighted than the guy ropes were simultaneous released, and the great warship, lightened by the removal of the loot, soared majestically into the air, her decks and upper works a mass of roaring flames.

Slowly she drifted to the southeast, rising higher and higher as the flames ate away her wooden parts and diminished the weight upon her. Ascending to the roof of the building I watched her for hours, until finally she was lost in the dim vistas of the distance. The sight was awe-inspiring in the extreme as one contemplated this mighty floating funeral pyre, drifting unguided and unmanned through the lonely wastes of the Martian heavens; a derelict of death and destruction, typifying the life story of these strange and ferocious creatures into whose unfriendly hands fate had carried it.

Much depressed, and, to me, unaccountably so, I slowly descended to the street. The scene I had witnessed seemed to mark the defeat and annihilation of the forces of a kindred people, rather than the routing by our green warriors of a horde of similar, though unfriendly, creatures. I could not fathom the seeming hallucination, nor could I free myself from it; but somewhere in the innermost recesses of my soul I felt a strange yearning toward these unknown foemen, and a mighty hope surged through me that the fleet would return and demand a reckoning from the green warriors who had so ruthlessly and wantonly attacked it.

Close at my heel, in his now accustomed place, followed Woola, the hound, and as I emerged upon the street Sola rushed up to me as though I had been the object of some search on her part. The cavalcade was returning to the plaza, the homeward march having been given up for that day; nor, in fact, was it recommenced for more than a week, owing to the fear of a return attack by the air craft.

Lorquas Ptomel was too astute an old warrior to be caught upon the open plains with a caravan of chariots and children, and so we remained at the deserted city until the danger seemed passed.

As Sola and I entered the plaza a sight met my eyes which filled my whole being with a great surge of mingled hope, fear, exultation, and depression, and yet most dominant was a subtle sense of relief and happiness; for just as we neared the throng of Martians I caught a glimpse of the prisoner from the battle craft who was being roughly dragged into a nearby building by a couple of green Martian females.

And the sight which met my eyes was that of a slender, girlish figure, similar in every detail to the earthly women of my past life. She did not see me at first, but just as she was disappearing through the portal of the building which was to be her prison she turned, and her eyes met mine. Her face was oval and beautiful in the extreme, her every feature was finely chiseled and exquisite, her eyes large and lustrous and her head surmounted by a mass of coal black, waving hair, caught loosely into a strange yet becoming coiffure. Her skin was of a light reddish copper color, against which the crimson glow of her cheeks and the ruby of her beautifully molded lips shone with a strangely enhancing effect.

She was as destitute of clothes as the green Martians who accompanied her; indeed, save for her highly wrought ornaments she was entirely naked, nor could any apparel have enhanced the beauty of her perfect and symmetrical figure.

As her gaze rested on me her eyes opened wide in astonishment, and she made a little sign with her free hand; a sign which I did not, of course, understand. Just a moment we gazed upon each other, and then the look of hope and renewed courage which had glorified her face as she discovered me, faded into one of utter dejection, mingled with loathing and contempt. I realized I had not answered her signal, and ignorant as I was of Martian customs, I intuitively felt that she had made an appeal for succor and protection which my unfortunate ignorance had prevented me from answering. And then she was dragged out of my sight into the depths of the deserted edifice.

CHAPTER NINE

I Learn the Language

As I CAME BACK TO MYSELF I glanced at Sola, who had witnessed this encounter and I was surprised to note a strange expression upon her usually expressionless countenance. What her thoughts were I did not know, for as yet I had learned but little of the Martian tongue; enough only to suffice for my daily needs.

As I reached the doorway of our building a strange surprise awaited me. A warrior approached bearing the arms, ornaments, and full accouterments of his kind. These he presented to me with a few unintelligible words, and a bearing at once respectful and menacing.

Later, Sola, with the aid of several of the other women, remodeled the trappings to fit my lesser proportions, and after they completed the work I went about garbed in all the panoply of war.

From then on Sola instructed me in the mysteries of the various weapons, and with the Martian young I spent several hours each day practicing upon the plaza. I was not yet proficient with all the weapons, but my great familiarity with similar earthly weapons made me an unusually apt pupil, and I progressed in a very satisfactory manner.

The training of myself and the young Martians was conducted solely by the women, who not only attend to the education of the young in the arts of individual defense and offense, but are also the artisans who produce every manufactured article wrought by the green Martians. They make the powder, the cartridges, the firearms; in fact everything of value is produced by the females. In time of actual warfare they form a part of the reserves, and when the necessity arises fight with even greater intelligence and ferocity than the men.

The men are trained in the higher branches of the art of war; in strategy and the maneuvering of large bodies of troops. They make the laws as they are needed; a new law for each emergency. They are unfettered by precedent in the administration of justice. Customs have been handed down by ages of repetition, but the punishment for ignoring a custom is a matter for individual treatment by a jury of the culprit's peers, and I may say that justice seldom misses fire, but seems rather to rule in inverse ratio to the ascendency of law. In one respect at least the Martians are a happy people; they have no lawyers.

I did not see the prisoner again for several days subsequent to our first encounter, and then only to catch a fleeting glimpse of her as she was being conducted to the great audience chamber where I had had my first meeting with Lorquas Ptomel. I could not but note the unnecessary harshness and brutality with which her guards treated her; so different from the almost maternal kindliness which Sola manifested toward me, and the respectful attitude of the few green Martians who took the trouble to notice me at all.

I had observed on the two occasions when I had seen her that the prisoner exchanged words with her guards, and this convinced me that they spoke, or at least could make themselves understood by a common language. With this added incentive I nearly drove Sola distracted by my importunities to hasten on my education and within a few more days I had mastered the Martian tongue sufficiently well to enable me to carry on a passable conversation and to fully understand practically all that I heard.

At this time our sleeping quarters were occupied by three or four females and a couple of the recently hatched young, beside Sola and her youthful ward, myself, and Woola the hound. After they had retired for the night it was customary for the adults to carry on a desultory conversation for a short time before lapsing into sleep, and now that I could understand their language I was always a keen listener, although I never proffered any remarks myself.

On the night following the prisoner's visit to the audience chamber the conversation finally fell upon this subject, and I was all ears on the instant. I had feared to question Sola relative to the beautiful captive, as I could not but recall the strange expression I had noted upon her face after my first encounter with the prisoner. That it denoted jealousy I could not say, and yet, judging all things by mundane standards as I still did, I felt it safer to affect indifference in the matter until I learned more surely Sola's attitude toward the object of my solicitude.

Sarkoja, one of the older women who shared our domicile, had been present at the audience as one of the captive's guards, and it was toward her the question turned.

"When," asked one of the women, "will we enjoy the death throes of the red one? or does Lorquas Ptomel, Jed, intend holding her for ransom?"

"They have decided to carry her with us back to Thark, and exhibit her last agonies at the great games before Tal Hajus," replied Sarkoja.

"What will be the manner of her going out?" inquired Sola. "She is very small and very beautiful; I had hoped that they would hold her for ransom."

Sarkoja and the other women grunted angrily at this evidence of weakness on the part of Sola.

"It is sad, Sola, that you were not born a million years ago," snapped Sarkoja, "when all the hollows of the land were filled with water, and the peoples were as soft as the stuff they sailed upon. In our day we have progressed to a point where such sentiments mark weakness and atavism. It will not be well for you to permit Tars Tarkas to learn that you hold such degenerate sentiments, as I doubt that he would care to entrust such as you with the grave responsibilities of maternity."

"I see nothing wrong with my expression of interest in this red woman," retorted Sola. "She has never harmed us, nor would she should we have fallen into her hands. It is only the men of her kind who war upon us, and I have ever thought that their attitude toward us is but the reflection of ours toward them. They live at peace with all their fellows, except when duty calls upon them to make war, while we are at peace with none; forever warring among our own kind as well as upon the red men, and even in our own communities the individuals fight amongst themselves. Oh, it is one continual, awful period of bloodshed from the time we break the shell until we gladly embrace the bosom of the river of mystery, the dark and ancient Iss which carries us to an unknown, but at least no more frightful and terrible existence! Fortunate indeed is he who meets his end in an early death. Say what you please to Tars Tarkas, he can mete out no worse fate to me than a continuation of the horrible existence we are forced to lead in this life."

This wild outbreak on the part of Sola so greatly surprised and shocked the other women, that, after a few words of general reprimand, they all lapsed into silence and were soon asleep. One thing the episode had accomplished was to assure me of Sola's friendliness toward the poor girl, and also to convince me that I had been extremely fortunate in falling into her hands rather than those of some of the other females. I knew that she was fond of me, and now that I had discovered that she hated cruelty and barbarity I was confident that I could depend upon her to aid me and the girl captive to escape, provided of course that such a thing was within the range of possibilities.

I did not even know that there were any better conditions to escape to, but I was more than willing to take my chances among people fashioned after my own mold rather than to remain longer among the hideous and bloodthirsty green men of Mars. But where to go, and how, was as much of a puzzle to me as the age-old search for the spring of eternal life has been to earthly men since the beginning of time.

I decided that at the first opportunity I would take Sola into my confidence and openly ask her to aid me, and with this resolution strong upon me I turned among my silks and furs and slept the dreamless and refreshing sleep of Mars.

CHAPTER TEN

Champion and Chief

EARLY THE NEXT MORNING I was astir. Considerable freedom was allowed me, as Sola had informed me that so long as I did not attempt to
leave the city I was free to go and come as I pleased. She had warned
me, however, against venturing forth unarmed, as this city, like all other
deserted metropolises of an ancient Martian civilization, was peopled
by the great white apes of my second day's adventure.

In advising me that I must not leave the boundaries of the city Sola
had explained that Woola would prevent this anyway should I attempt
it, and she warned me most urgently not to arouse his fierce nature
by ignoring his warnings should I venture too close to the forbidden
territory. His nature was such, she said, that he would bring me back
into the city dead or alive should I persist in opposing him; "preferably
dead," she added.

On this morning I had chosen a new street to explore when suddenly
I found myself at the limits of the city. Before me were low hills pierced
by narrow and inviting ravines. I longed to explore the country before
me, and, like the pioneer stock from which I sprang, to view what the
landscape beyond the encircling hills might disclose from the summits
which shut out my view.

It also occurred to me that this would prove an excellent opportunity
to test the qualities of Woola. I was convinced that the brute loved me; I
had seen more evidences of affection in him than in any other Martian
animal, man or beast, and I was sure that gratitude for the acts that had
twice saved his life would more than outweigh his loyalty to the duty
imposed upon him by cruel and loveless masters.

As I approached the boundary line Woola ran anxiously before me,
and thrust his body against my legs. His expression was pleading rather

than ferocious, nor did he bare his great tusks or utter his fearful guttural warnings. Denied the friendship and companionship of my kind, I had developed considerable affection for Woola and Sola, for the normal earthly man must have some outlet for his natural affections, and so I decided upon an appeal to a like instinct in this great brute, sure that I would not be disappointed.

I had never petted nor fondled him, but now I sat upon the ground and putting my arms around his heavy neck I stroked and coaxed him, talking in my newly acquired Martian tongue as I would have to my hound at home, as I would have talked to any other friend among the lower animals. His response to my manifestation of affection was remarkable to a degree; he stretched his great mouth to its full width, baring the entire expanse of his upper rows of tusks and wrinkling his snout until his great eyes were almost hidden by the folds of flesh. If you have ever seen a collie smile you may have some idea of Woola's facial distortion.

He threw himself upon his back and fairly wallowed at my feet; jumped up and sprang upon me, rolling me upon the ground by his great weight; then wriggling and squirming around me like a playful puppy presenting its back for the petting it craves. I could not resist the ludicrousness of the spectacle, and holding my sides I rocked back and forth in the first laughter which had passed my lips in many days; the first, in fact, since the morning Powell had left camp when his horse, long unused, had precipitately and unexpectedly bucked him off headforemost into a pot of frijoles.

My laughter frightened Woola, his antics ceased and he crawled pitifully toward me, poking his ugly head far into my lap; and then I remembered what laughter signified on Mars – torture, suffering, death. Quieting myself, I rubbed the poor old fellow's head and back, talked to him for a few minutes, and then in an authoritative tone commanded him to follow me, and arising started for the hills.

There was no further question of authority between us; Woola was my devoted slave from that moment hence, and I his only and undisputed master. My walk to the hills occupied but a few minutes, and I found nothing of particular interest to reward me. Numerous brilliantly colored and strangely formed wild flowers dotted the ravines and from the summit of the first hill I saw still other hills stretching off toward the north, and rising, one range above another, until lost in mountains of quite respectable dimensions; though I afterward found that only a few peaks on all Mars exceed four thousand feet in height; the suggestion of magnitude was merely relative.

My morning's walk had been large with importance to me for it had resulted in a perfect understanding with Woola, upon whom Tars Tarkas relied for my safe keeping. I now knew that while theoretically a prisoner I was virtually free, and I hastened to regain the city limits before the defection of Woola could be discovered by his erstwhile masters. The adventure decided me never again to leave the limits of my prescribed stamping grounds until I was ready to venture forth for good and all, as it would certainly result in a curtailment of my liberties, as well as the probable death of Woola, were we to be discovered.

On regaining the plaza I had my third glimpse of the captive girl. She was standing with her guards before the entrance to the audience chamber, and as I approached she gave me one haughty glance and turned her back full upon me. The act was so womanly, so earthly womanly, that though it stung my pride it also warmed my heart with a feeling of companionship; it was good to know that someone else on Mars beside myself had human instincts of a civilized order, even though the manifestation of them was so painful and mortifying.

Had a green Martian woman desired to show dislike or contempt she would, in all likelihood, have done it with a sword thrust or a movement of her trigger finger; but as their sentiments are mostly atrophied it would have required a serious injury to have aroused such passions in them. Sola, let me add, was an exception; I never saw her perform a cruel or uncouth act, or fail in uniform kindliness and good nature. She was indeed, as her fellow Martian had said of her, an atavism; a dear and precious reversion to a former type of loved and loving ancestor.

Seeing that the prisoner seemed the center of attraction I halted to view the proceedings. I had not long to wait for presently Lorquas Ptomel and his retinue of chieftains approached the building and, signing the guards to follow with the prisoner entered the audience chamber. Realizing that I was a somewhat favored character, and also convinced that the warriors did not know of my proficiency in their language, as I had pleaded with Sola to keep this a secret on the grounds that I did not wish to be forced to talk with the men until I had perfectly mastered the Martian tongue, I chanced an attempt to enter the audience chamber and listen to the proceedings.

The council squatted upon the steps of the rostrum, while below them stood the prisoner and her two guards. I saw that one of the women was Sarkoja, and thus understood how she had been present at the hearing of the preceding day, the results of which she had reported to the occupants of our dormitory last night. Her attitude toward the captive was most harsh and brutal. When she held her, she sunk her rudimentary nails into the poor girl's flesh, or twisted her arm in a most painful manner. When it was necessary to move from one spot to another she either jerked her roughly, or pushed her headlong before her. She seemed to be venting upon this poor defenseless creature all the hatred, cruelty, ferocity, and spite of her nine hundred years, backed by unguessable ages of fierce and brutal ancestors.

The other woman was less cruel because she was entirely indifferent; if the prisoner had been left to her alone, and fortunately she was at night, she would have received no harsh treatment, nor, by the same token would she have received any attention at all.

As Lorquas Ptomel raised his eyes to address the prisoner they fell on me and he turned to Tars Tarkas with a word, and gesture of impatience. Tars Tarkas made some reply which I could not catch, but which caused Lorquas Ptomel to smile; after which they paid no further attention to me.

"What is your name?" asked Lorquas Ptomel, addressing the prisoner.

"Dejah Thoris, daughter of Mors Kajak of Helium."

"And the nature of your expedition?" he continued.

"It was a purely scientific research party sent out by my father's father, the Jeddak of Helium, to rechart the air currents, and to take atmospheric density tests," replied the fair prisoner, in a low, well-modulated voice.

"We were unprepared for battle," she continued, "as we were on a peaceful mission, as our banners and the colors of our craft denoted. The work we were doing was as much in your interests as in ours, for you know full well that were it not for our labors and the fruits of our scientific operations there would not be enough air or water on Mars to support a single human life. For ages we have maintained the air and water supply at practically the same point without an appreciable loss, and we have done this in the face of the brutal and ignorant interference of your green men.

"Why, oh, why will you not learn to live in amity with your fellows, must you ever go on down the ages to your final extinction but little above the plane of the dumb brutes that serve you! A people without written language, without art, without homes, without love; the victim of eons of the horrible community idea. Owning everything in common, even to your women and children, has resulted in your owning nothing in common. You hate each other as you hate all else except yourselves. Come back to the ways of our common ancestors, come back to the light of kindliness and fellowship. The way is open to you, you will find the hands of the red men stretched out to aid you.

Together we may do still more to regenerate our dying planet. The granddaughter of the greatest and mightiest of the red jeddaks has asked you. Will you come?"

Lorquas Ptomel and the warriors sat looking silently and intently at the young woman for several moments after she had ceased speaking. What was passing in their minds no man may know, but that they were moved I truly believe, and if one man high among them had been strong enough to rise above custom, that moment would have marked a new and mighty era for Mars.

I saw Tars Tarkas rise to speak, and on his face was such an expression as I had never seen upon the countenance of a green Martian warrior. It bespoke an inward and mighty battle with self, with heredity, with age-old custom, and as he opened his mouth to speak, a look almost of benignity, of kindliness, momentarily lighted up his fierce and terrible countenance.

What words of moment were to have fallen from his lips were never spoken, as just then a young warrior, evidently sensing the trend of thought among the older men, leaped down from the steps of the rostrum, and striking the frail captive a powerful blow across the face, which felled her to the floor, placed his foot upon her prostrate form and turning toward the assembled council broke into peals of horrid, mirthless laughter.

For an instant I thought Tars Tarkas would strike him dead, nor did the aspect of Lorquas Ptomel augur any too favorably for the brute, but the mood passed, their old selves reasserted their ascendency, and they smiled. It was portentous however that they did not laugh aloud, for the brute's act constituted a side-splitting witticism according to the ethics which rule green Martian humor.

That I have taken moments to write down a part of what occurred as that blow fell does not signify that I remained inactive for any such length of time. I think I must have sensed something of what was coming, for I realize now that I was crouched as for a spring as I saw the blow aimed at her beautiful, upturned, pleading face, and ere the hand descended I was halfway across the hall.

Scarcely had his hideous laugh rang out but once, when I was upon him. The brute was twelve feet in height and armed to the teeth, but I believe that I could have accounted for the whole roomful in the terrific intensity of my rage. Springing upward, I struck him full in the face as he turned at my warning cry and then as he drew his short-sword I drew mine and sprang up again upon his breast, hooking one leg over the butt of his pistol and grasping one of his huge tusks with my left hand while I delivered blow after blow upon his enormous chest.

He could not use his short-sword to advantage because I was too close to him, nor could he draw his pistol, which he attempted to do in direct opposition to Martian custom which says that you may not fight a fellow warrior in private combat with any other than the weapon with which you are attacked. In fact he could do nothing but make a wild and futile attempt to dislodge me. With all his immense bulk he was little if any stronger than I, and it was but the matter of a moment or two before he sank, bleeding and lifeless, to the floor.

Dejah Thoris had raised herself upon one elbow and was watching the battle with wide, staring eyes. When I had regained my feet I raised her in my arms and bore her to one of the benches at the side of the room.

Again no Martian interfered with me, and tearing a piece of silk from my cape I endeavored to staunch the flow of blood from her nostrils. I was soon successful as her injuries amounted to little more than an ordinary nosebleed, and when she could speak she placed her hand upon my arm and looking up into my eyes, said:

"Why did you do it? You who refused me even friendly recognition in the first hour of my peril! And now you risk your life and kill one of your companions for my sake. I cannot understand. What strange manner of man are you, that you consort with the green men, though your form is that of my race, while your color is little darker than that of the white ape? Tell me, are you human, or are you more than human?"

"It is a strange tale," I replied, "too long to attempt to tell you now, and one which I so much doubt the credibility of myself that I fear to hope that others will believe it. Suffice it, for the present, that I am your friend, and, so far as our captors will permit, your protector and your servant."

"Then you too are a prisoner? But why, then, those arms and the regalia of a Tharkian chieftain? What is your name? Where your country?"

"Yes, Dejah Thoris, I too am a prisoner; my name is John Carter, and I claim Virginia, one of the United States of America, Earth, as my home; but why I am permitted to wear arms I do not know, nor was I aware that my regalia was that of a chieftain."

We were interrupted at this juncture by the approach of one of the warriors, bearing arms, accouterments and ornaments, and in a flash one of her questions was answered and a puzzle cleared up for me. I saw that the body of my dead antagonist had been stripped, and I read in the menacing yet respectful attitude of the warrior who had brought me these trophies of the kill the same demeanor as that evinced by the other who had brought me my original equipment, and now for the first time I realized that my blow, on the occasion of my first battle in the audience chamber had resulted in the death of my adversary.

The reason for the whole attitude displayed toward me was now apparent; I had won my spurs, so to speak, and in the crude justice, which always marks Martian dealings, and which, among other things, has caused me to call her the planet of paradoxes, I was accorded the honors due a conqueror; the trappings and the position of the man I killed. In truth, I was a Martian chieftain, and this I learned later was the cause of my great freedom and my toleration in the audience chamber.

As I had turned to receive the dead warrior's chattels I had noticed that Tars Tarkas and several others had pushed forward toward us, and the eyes of the former rested upon me in a most quizzical manner. Finally he addressed me:

"You speak the tongue of Barsoom quite readily for one who was deaf and dumb to us a few short days ago. Where did you learn it, John Carter?"

"You, yourself, are responsible, Tars Tarkas," I replied, "in that you furnished me with an instructress of remarkable ability; I have to thank Sola for my learning."

"She has done well," he answered, "but your education in other respects needs considerable polish. Do you know what your unprecedented temerity would have cost you had you failed to kill either of the two chieftains whose metal you now wear?"

"I presume that that one whom I had failed to kill, would have killed me," I answered, smiling.

"No, you are wrong. Only in the last extremity of self-defense would a Martian warrior kill a prisoner; we like to save them for other purposes," and his face bespoke possibilities that were not pleasant to dwell upon.

"But one thing can save you now," he continued. "Should you, in recognition of your remarkable valor, ferocity, and prowess, be considered by Tal Hajus as worthy of his service you may be taken into the community and become a full-fledged Tharkian. Until we reach the headquarters of Tal Hajus it is the will of Lorquas Ptomel that you be accorded the respect your acts have earned you. You will be treated by us as a Tharkian chieftain, but you must not forget that every chief who ranks you is responsible for your safe delivery to our mighty and most ferocious ruler. I am done."

"I hear you, Tars Tarkas," I answered. "As you know I am not of Barsoom; your ways are not my ways, and I can only act in the future as I have in the past, in accordance with the dictates of my conscience and guided by the standards of mine own people. If you will leave me alone I will go in peace, but if not, let the individual Barsoomians with whom I must deal either respect my rights as a stranger among you, or take whatever consequences may befall. Of one thing let us be sure, whatever may be your ultimate intentions toward this unfortunate young woman, whoever would offer her injury or insult in the future must figure on making a full accounting to me. I understand that you belittle all sentiments of generosity and kindliness, but I do not, and I can convince your most doughty warrior that these characteristics are not incompatible with an ability to fight."

Ordinarily I am not given to long speeches, nor ever before had I descended to bombast, but I had guessed at the keynote which would strike an answering chord in the breasts of the green Martians, nor was I wrong, for my harangue evidently deeply impressed them, and their attitude toward me thereafter was still further respectful.

Tars Tarkas himself seemed pleased with my reply, but his only comment was more or less enigmatical – "And I think I know Tal Hajus, Jeddak of Thark."

I now turned my attention to Dejah Thoris, and assisting her to her feet I turned with her toward the exit, ignoring her hovering guardian harpies as well as the inquiring glances of the chieftains. Was I not now a chieftain also! Well, then, I would assume the responsibilities of one. They did not molest us, and so Dejah Thoris, Princess of Helium, and John Carter, gentleman of Virginia, followed by the faithful Woola, passed through utter silence from the audience chamber of Lorquas Ptomel, Jed among the Tharks of Barsoom.

CHAPTER ELEVEN

With Dejah Thoris

As WE REACHED THE OPEN the two female guards who had been detailed to watch over Dejah Thoris hurried up and made as though to assume custody of her once more. The poor child shrank against me and I felt her two little hands fold tightly over my arm. Waving the women away, I informed them that Sola would attend the captive hereafter, and I further warned Sarkoja that any more of her cruel attentions bestowed upon Dejah Thoris would result in Sarkoja's sudden and painful demise.

My threat was unfortunate and resulted in more harm than good to Dejah Thoris, for, as I learned later, men do not kill women upon Mars, nor women, men. So Sarkoja merely gave us an ugly look and departed to hatch up deviltries against us.

I soon found Sola and explained to her that I wished her to guard Dejah Thoris as she had guarded me; that I wished her to find other quarters where they would not be molested by Sarkoja, and I finally informed her that I myself would take up my quarters among the men.

Sola glanced at the accouterments which were carried in my hand and slung across my shoulder.

"You are a great chieftain now, John Carter," she said, "and I must do your bidding, though indeed I am glad to do it under any circumstances. The man whose metal you carry was young, but he was a great warrior, and had by his promotions and kills won his way close to the rank of Tars Tarkas, who, as you know, is second to Lorquas Ptomel only. You are eleventh, there are but ten chieftains in this community who rank you in prowess."

"And if I should kill Lorquas Ptomel?" I asked.

"You would be first, John Carter; but you may only win that honor by the will of the entire council that Lorquas Ptomel meet you in combat, or should he attack you, you may kill him in self-defense, and thus win first place."

I laughed, and changed the subject. I had no particular desire to kill Lorquas Ptomel, and less to be a jed among the Tharks.

I accompanied Sola and Dejah Thoris in a search for new quarters, which we found in a building nearer the audience chamber and of far more pretentious architecture than our former habitation. We also found in this building real sleeping apartments with ancient beds of highly wrought metal swinging from enormous gold chains depending from the marble ceilings. The decoration of the walls was most elaborate, and, unlike the frescoes in the other buildings I had examined, portrayed many human figures in the compositions. These were of people like myself, and of a much lighter color than Dejah Thoris. They were clad in graceful, flowing robes, highly ornamented with metal and jewels, and their luxuriant hair was of a beautiful golden and reddish bronze. The men were beardless and only a few wore arms. The scenes depicted for the most part, a fair-skinned, fair-haired people at play.

Dejah Thoris clasped her hands with an exclamation of rapture as she gazed upon these magnificent works of art, wrought by a people long extinct; while Sola, on the other hand, apparently did not see them.

We decided to use this room, on the second floor and overlooking the plaza, for Dejah Thoris and Sola, and another room adjoining and in the rear for the cooking and supplies. I then dispatched Sola to bring the bedding and such food and utensils as she might need, telling her that I would guard Dejah Thoris until her return.

As Sola departed Dejah Thoris turned to me with a faint smile.

"And whereto, then, would your prisoner escape should you leave her, unless it was to follow you and crave your protection, and ask your pardon for the cruel thoughts she has harbored against you these past few days?"

"You are right," I answered, "there is no escape for either of us unless we go together."

"I heard your challenge to the creature you call Tars Tarkas, and I think I understand your position among these people, but what I cannot fathom is your statement that you are not of Barsoom."

"In the name of my first ancestor, then," she continued, "where may you be from? You are like unto my people, and yet so unlike. You speak my language, and yet I heard you tell Tars Tarkas that you had but learned it recently. All Barsoomians speak the same tongue from the ice-clad south to the ice-clad north, though their written languages differ. Only in the valley Dor, where the river Iss empties into the lost sea of Korus, is there supposed to be a different language spoken, and, except in the legends of our ancestors, there is no record of a Barsoomian returning up the river Iss, from the shores of Korus in the valley of Dor. Do not tell me that you have thus returned! They would kill you horribly anywhere upon the surface of Barsoom if that were true; tell me it is not!"

Her eyes were filled with a strange, weird light; her voice was pleading, and her little hands, reached up upon my breast, were pressed against me as though to wring a denial from my very heart.

"I do not know your customs, Dejah Thoris, but in my own Virginia a gentleman does not lie to save himself; I am not of Dor; I have never seen the mysterious Iss; the lost sea of Korus is still lost, so far as I am concerned. Do you believe me?"

And then it struck me suddenly that I was very anxious that she should believe me. It was not that I feared the results which would follow a general belief that I had returned from the Barsoomian heaven or hell, or whatever it was. Why was it, then! Why should I care what she thought? I looked down at her; her beautiful face upturned, and her wonderful eyes opening up the very depth of her soul; and as my eyes met hers I knew why, and – I shuddered.

A similar wave of feeling seemed to stir her; she drew away from me with a sigh, and with her earnest, beautiful face turned up to mine, she whispered: "I believe you, John Carter; I do not know what a 'gentleman' is, nor have I ever heard before of Virginia; but on Barsoom no man lies; if he does not wish to speak the truth he is silent. Where is this Virginia, your country, John Carter?" she asked, and it seemed that this fair name of my fair land had never sounded more beautiful than as it fell from those perfect lips on that far-gone day.

"I am of another world," I answered, "the great planet Earth, which revolves about our common sun and next within the orbit of your Barsoom, which we know as Mars. How I came here I cannot tell you, for I do not know; but here I am, and since my presence has permitted me to serve Dejah Thoris I am glad that I am here."

She gazed at me with troubled eyes, long and questioningly. That it was difficult to believe my statement I well knew, nor could I hope that she would do so however much I craved her confidence and respect. I would much rather not have told her anything of my antecedents, but no man could look into the depth of those eyes and refuse her slightest behest.

Finally she smiled, and, rising, said: "I shall have to believe even though I cannot understand. I can readily perceive that you are not of the Barsoom of today; you are like us, yet different – but why should I trouble my poor head with such a problem, when my heart tells me that I believe because I wish to believe!"

It was good logic, good, earthly, feminine logic, and if it satisfied her I certainly could pick no flaws in it. As a matter of fact it was about the only kind of logic that could be brought to bear upon my problem. We fell into a general conversation then, asking and answering many questions on each side. She was curious to learn of the customs of my people and displayed a remarkable knowledge of events on Earth. When I questioned her closely on this seeming familiarity with earthly things she laughed, and cried out:

"Why, every school boy on Barsoom knows the geography, and much concerning the fauna and flora, as well as the history of your planet fully as well as of his own. Can we not see everything which takes place upon Earth, as you call it; is it not hanging there in the heavens in plain sight?"

This baffled me, I must confess, fully as much as my statements had confounded her; and I told her so. She then explained in general the instruments her people had used and been perfecting for ages, which permit them to throw upon a screen a perfect image of what is transpiring upon any planet and upon many of the stars. These pictures are so perfect in detail that, when photographed and enlarged, objects no greater than a blade of grass may be distinctly recognized. I afterward, in Helium, saw many of these pictures, as well as the instruments which produced them.

"If, then, you are so familiar with earthly things," I asked, "why is it that you do not recognize me as identical with the inhabitants of that planet?"

She smiled again as one might in bored indulgence of a questioning child.

"Because, John Carter," she replied, "nearly every planet and star having atmospheric conditions at all approaching those of Barsoom, shows forms of animal life almost identical with you and me; and, further, Earth men, almost without exception, cover their bodies with strange, unsightly pieces of cloth, and their heads with hideous contraptions the purpose of which we have been unable to conceive; while you, when found by the Tharkian warriors, were entirely undisfigured and unadorned.

"The fact that you wore no ornaments is a strong proof of your un-Barsoomian origin, while the absence of grotesque coverings might cause a doubt as to your earthliness."

I then narrated the details of my departure from the Earth, explaining that my body there lay fully clothed in all the, to her, strange garments of mundane dwellers. At this point Sola returned with our meager belongings and her young Martian protege, who, of course, would have to share the quarters with them.

Sola asked us if we had had a visitor during her absence, and seemed much surprised when we answered in the negative. It seemed that as she had mounted the approach to the upper floors where our quarters were located, she had met Sarkoja descending. We decided that she must have been eavesdropping, but as we could recall nothing of importance that had passed between us we dismissed the matter as of little consequence, merely promising ourselves to be warned to the utmost caution in the future.

Dejah Thoris and I then fell to examining the architecture and decorations of the beautiful chambers of the building we were occupying. She told me that these people had presumably flourished over a hundred thousand years before. They were the early progenitors of her race, but had mixed with the other great race of early Martians, who were very dark, almost black, and also with the reddish yellow race which had flourished at the same time.

These three great divisions of the higher Martians had been forced into a mighty alliance as the drying up of the Martian seas had compelled them to seek the comparatively few and always diminishing fertile areas, and to defend themselves, under new conditions of life, against the wild hordes of green men.

Ages of close relationship and intermarrying had resulted in the race of red men, of which Dejah Thoris was a fair and beautiful daughter. During the ages of hardships and incessant warring between their own various races, as well as with the green men, and before they had fitted themselves to the changed conditions, much of the high civilization and many of the arts of the fair-haired Martians had become lost; but the red race of today has reached a point where it feels that it has made up in new discoveries and in a more practical civilization for all that lies irretrievably buried with the ancient Barsoomians, beneath the countless intervening ages.

These ancient Martians had been a highly cultivated and literary race, but during the vicissitudes of those trying centuries of readjustment to new conditions, not only did their advancement and production cease entirely, but practically all their archives, records, and literature were lost.

Dejah Thoris related many interesting facts and legends concerning this lost race of noble and kindly people. She said that the city in which we were camping was supposed to have been a center of commerce and culture known as Korad. It had been built upon a beautiful, natural harbor, landlocked by magnificent hills. The little valley on the west front of the city, she explained, was all that remained of the harbor, while the pass through the hills to the old sea bottom had been the channel through which the shipping passed up to the city's gates.

The shores of the ancient seas were dotted with just such cities, and lesser ones, in diminishing numbers, were to be found converging toward the center of the oceans, as the people had found it necessary to follow the receding waters until necessity had forced upon them their ultimate salvation, the so-called Martian canals.

We had been so engrossed in exploration of the building and in our conversation that it was late in the afternoon before we realized it. We were brought back to a realization of our present conditions by a messenger bearing a summons from Lorquas Ptomel directing me to appear before him forthwith. Bidding Dejah Thoris and Sola farewell, and commanding Woola to remain on guard, I hastened to the audience chamber, where I found Lorquas Ptomel and Tars Tarkas seated upon the rostrum.

CHAPTER TWELVE

A Prisoner with Power

As I ENTERED AND SALUTED, Lorquas Ptomel signaled me to advance, and, fixing his great, hideous eyes upon me, addressed me thus:

"You have been with us a few days, yet during that time you have by your prowess won a high position among us. Be that as it may, you are not one of us; you owe us no allegiance.

"Your position is a peculiar one," he continued; "you are a prisoner and yet you give commands which must be obeyed; you are an alien and yet you are a Tharkian chieftain; you are a midget and yet you can kill a mighty warrior with one blow of your fist. And now you are reported to have been plotting to escape with another prisoner of another race; a prisoner who, from her own admission, half believes you are returned from the valley of Dor. Either one of these accusations, if proved, would be sufficient grounds for your execution, but we are a just people and you shall have a trial on our return to Thark, if Tal Hajus so commands.

"But," he continued, in his fierce guttural tones, "if you run off with the red girl it is I who shall have to account to Tal Hajus; it is I who shall have to face Tars Tarkas, and either demonstrate my right to command, or the metal from my dead carcass will go to a better man, for such is the custom of the Tharks.

"I have no quarrel with Tars Tarkas; together we rule supreme the greatest of the lesser communities among the green men; we do not wish to fight between ourselves; and so if you were dead, John Carter, I should be glad. Under two conditions only, however, may you be killed by us without orders from Tal Hajus; in personal combat in self-defense, should you attack one of us, or were you apprehended in an attempt to escape.

"As a matter of justice I must warn you that we only await one of these two excuses for ridding ourselves of so great a responsibility. The safe delivery of the red girl to Tal Hajus is of the greatest importance. Not in a thousand years have the Tharks made such a capture; she is the grand-daughter of the greatest of the red jeddaks, who is also our bitterest enemy. I have spoken. The red girl told us that we were without the softer sentiments of humanity, but we are a just and truthful race. You may go."

Turning, I left the audience chamber. So this was the beginning of Sarkoja's persecution! I knew that none other could be responsible for this report which had reached the ears of Lorquas Ptomel so quickly, and now I recalled those portions of our conversation which had touched upon escape and upon my origin.

Sarkoja was at this time Tars Tarkas' oldest and most trusted female. As such she was a mighty power behind the throne, for no warrior had the confidence of Lorquas Ptomel to such an extent as did his ablest lieutenant, Tars Tarkas.

However, instead of putting thoughts of possible escape from my mind, my audience with Lorquas Ptomel only served to center my every faculty on this subject. Now, more than before, the absolute necessity for escape, in so far as Dejah Thoris was concerned, was impressed upon me, for I was convinced that some horrible fate awaited her at the headquarters of Tal Hajus.

As described by Sola, this monster was the exaggerated personification of all the ages of cruelty, ferocity, and brutality from which he had descended. Cold, cunning, calculating; he was, also, in marked contrast to most of his fellows, a slave to that brute passion which the waning demands for procreation upon their dying planet has almost stilled in the Martian breast.

The thought that the divine Dejah Thoris might fall into the clutches of such an abysmal atavism started the cold sweat upon me. Far better that we save friendly bullets for ourselves at the last moment, as did those brave frontier women of my lost land, who took their own lives rather than fall into the hands of the Indian braves.

As I wandered about the plaza lost in my gloomy forebodings Tars Tarkas approached me on his way from the audience chamber. His demeanor toward me was unchanged, and he greeted me as though we had not just parted a few moments before.

"Where are your quarters, John Carter?" he asked.

"I have selected none," I replied. "It seemed best that I quartered either by myself or among the other warriors, and I was awaiting an opportunity to ask your advice. As you know," and I smiled, "I am not yet familiar with all the customs of the Tharks."

"Come with me," he directed, and together we moved off across the plaza to a building which I was glad to see adjoined that occupied by Sola and her charges.

"My quarters are on the first floor of this building," he said, "and the second floor also is fully occupied by warriors, but the third floor and the floors above are vacant; you may take your choice of these.

"I understand," he continued, "that you have given up your woman to the red prisoner. Well, as you have said, your ways are not our ways, but you can fight well enough to do about as you please, and so, if you wish to give your woman to a captive, it is your own affair; but as a chieftain you should have those to serve you, and in accordance with our customs you may select any or all the females from the retinues of the chieftains whose metal you now wear."

I thanked him, but assured him that I could get along very nicely without assistance except in the matter of preparing food, and so he promised to send women to me for this purpose and also for the care of my arms and the manufacture of my ammunition, which he said would be necessary. I suggested that they might also bring some of the sleeping silks and furs which belonged to me as spoils of combat, for the nights were cold and I had none of my own.

He promised to do so, and departed. Left alone, I ascended the winding corridor to the upper floors in search of suitable quarters. The beauties of the other buildings were repeated in this, and, as usual, I was soon lost in a tour of investigation and discovery.

I finally chose a front room on the third floor, because this brought me nearer to Dejah Thoris, whose apartment was on the second floor of the adjoining building, and it flashed upon me that I could rig up some means of communication whereby she might signal me in case she needed either my services or my protection.

Adjoining my sleeping apartment were baths, dressing rooms, and other sleeping and living apartments, in all some ten rooms on this floor. The windows of the back rooms overlooked an enormous court, which formed the center of the square made by the buildings which faced the four contiguous streets, and which was now given over to the quartering of the various animals belonging to the warriors occupying the adjoining buildings.

While the court was entirely overgrown with the yellow, moss-like vegetation which blankets practically the entire surface of Mars, yet numerous fountains, statuary, benches, and pergola-like contraptions bore witness to the beauty which the court must have presented in bygone times, when graced by the fair-haired, laughing people whom stern and unalterable cosmic laws had driven not only from their homes, but from all except the vague legends of their descendants.

One could easily picture the gorgeous foliage of the luxuriant Martian vegetation which once filled this scene with life and color; the graceful figures of the beautiful women, the straight and handsome men; the happy frolicking children – all sunlight, happiness and peace. It was difficult to realize that they had gone; down through ages of darkness, cruelty, and ignorance, until their hereditary instincts of culture and humanitarianism had risen ascendant once more in the final composite race which now is dominant upon Mars.

My thoughts were cut short by the advent of several young females bearing loads of weapons, silks, furs, jewels, cooking utensils, and casks of food and drink, including considerable loot from the air craft. All this, it seemed, had been the property of the two chieftains I had slain, and now, by the customs of the Tharks, it had become mine. At my direction they placed the stuff in one of the back rooms, and then departed, only to return with a second load, which they advised me constituted the balance of my goods. On the second trip they were accompanied by ten or fifteen other women and youths, who, it seemed, formed the retinues of the two chieftains.

They were not their families, nor their wives, nor their servants; the relationship was peculiar, and so unlike anything known to us that it is most difficult to describe. All property among the green Martians is owned in common by the community, except the personal weapons, ornaments and sleeping silks and furs of the individuals. These alone can one claim undisputed right to, nor may he accumulate more of these than are required for his actual needs. The surplus he holds merely as custodian, and it is passed on to the younger members of the community as necessity demands.

The women and children of a man's retinue may be likened to a military unit for which he is responsible in various ways, as in matters of instruction, discipline, sustenance, and the exigencies of their continual roamings and their unending strife with other communities and with the red Martians. His women are in no sense wives. The green Martians use no word corresponding in meaning with this earthly word. Their mating is a matter of community interest solely, and is directed without reference to natural selection. The council of chieftains of each community control the matter as surely as the owner of a Kentucky racing stud directs the scientific breeding of his stock for the improvement of the whole.

In theory it may sound well, as is often the case with theories, but the results of ages of this unnatural practice, coupled with the community interest in the offspring being held paramount to that of the mother, is shown in the cold, cruel creatures, and their gloomy, loveless, mirthless existence.

It is true that the green Martians are absolutely virtuous, both men and women, with the exception of such degenerates as Tal Hajus; but better far a finer balance of human characteristics even at the expense of a slight and occasional loss of chastity.

Finding that I must assume responsibility for these creatures, whether I would or not, I made the best of it and directed them to find quarters on the upper floors, leaving the third floor to me. One of the girls I charged with the duties of my simple cuisine, and directed the others to take up the various activities which had formerly constituted their vocations. Thereafter I saw little of them, nor did I care to.

CHAPTER THIRTEEN

Love-Making on Mars

FOLLOWING THE BATTLE with the air ships, the community remained within the city for several days, abandoning the homeward march until they could feel reasonably assured that the ships would not return; for to be caught on the open plains with a cavalcade of chariots and children was far from the desire of even so warlike a people as the green Martians.

During our period of inactivity, Tars Tarkas had instructed me in many of the customs and arts of war familiar to the Tharks, including lessons in riding and guiding the great beasts which bore the warriors. These creatures, which are known as thoats, are as dangerous and vicious as their masters, but when once subdued are sufficiently tractable for the purposes of the green Martians.

Two of these animals had fallen to me from the warriors whose metal I wore, and in a short time I could handle them quite as well as the native warriors. The method was not at all complicated. If the thoats did not respond with sufficient celerity to the telepathic instructions of their riders they were dealt a terrific blow between the ears with the butt of a pistol, and if they showed fight this treatment was continued until the brutes either were subdued, or had unseated their riders.

In the latter case it became a life and death struggle between the man and the beast. If the former were quick enough with his pistol he might live to ride again, though upon some other beast; if not, his torn and mangled body was gathered up by his women and burned in accordance with Tharkian custom.

My experience with Woola determined me to attempt the experiment of kindness in my treatment of my thoats. First I taught them that they could not unseat me, and even rapped them sharply between the ears to impress upon them my authority and mastery. Then, by degrees, I won their confidence in much the same manner as I had adopted countless times with my many mundane mounts. I was ever a good hand with animals, and by inclination, as well as because it brought more lasting and satisfactory results, I was always kind and humane in my dealings with the lower orders. I could take a human life, if necessary, with far less compunction than that of a poor, unreasoning, irresponsible brute.

In the course of a few days my thoats were the wonder of the entire community. They would follow me like dogs, rubbing their great snouts against my body in awkward evidence of affection, and respond to my every command with an alacrity and docility which caused the Martian warriors to ascribe to me the possession of some earthly power unknown on Mars.

"How have you bewitched them?" asked Tars Tarkas one afternoon, when he had seen me run my arm far between the great jaws of one of my thoats which had wedged a piece of stone between two of his teeth while feeding upon the moss-like vegetation within our court yard.

"By kindness," I replied. "You see, Tars Tarkas, the softer sentiments have their value, even to a warrior. In the height of battle as well as upon the march I know that my thoats will obey my every command, and therefore my fighting efficiency is enhanced, and I am a better warrior for the reason that I am a kind master. Your other warriors would find it to the advantage of themselves as well as of the community to adopt my methods in this respect. Only a few days since you, yourself, told me that these great brutes, by the uncertainty of their tempers, often were the means of turning victory into defeat, since, at a crucial moment, they might elect to unseat and rend their riders."

"Show me how you accomplish these results," was Tars Tarkas' only rejoinder.

And so I explained as carefully as I could the entire method of training I had adopted with my beasts, and later he had me repeat it before Lorquas Ptomel and the assembled warriors. That moment marked the beginning of a new existence for the poor thoats, and before I left the community of Lorquas Ptomel I had the satisfaction of observing a regiment of as tractable and docile mounts as one might care to see. The effect on the precision and celerity of the military movements was so remarkable that Lorquas Ptomel presented me with a massive anklet of gold from his own leg, as a sign of his appreciation of my service to the horde.

On the seventh day following the battle with the air craft we again took up the march toward Thark, all probability of another attack being deemed remote by Lorquas Ptomel.

During the days just preceding our departure I had seen but little of Dejah Thoris, as I had been kept very busy by Tars Tarkas with my lessons in the art of Martian warfare, as well as in the training of my thoats. The few times I had visited her quarters she had been absent, walking upon the streets with Sola, or investigating the buildings in the near vicinity of the plaza. I had warned them against venturing far from the plaza for fear of the great white apes, whose ferocity I was only too well acquainted with. However, since Woola accompanied them on all their excursions, and as Sola was well armed, there was comparatively little cause for fear.

On the evening before our departure I saw them approaching along one of the great avenues which lead into the plaza from the east. I advanced to meet them, and telling Sola that I would take the responsibility for Dejah Thoris' safekeeping, I directed her to return to her quarters on some trivial errand. I liked and trusted Sola, but for some reason I desired to be alone with Dejah Thoris, who represented to me all that I had left behind upon Earth in agreeable and congenial companionship. There seemed bonds of mutual interest between us as powerful as though we had been born under the same roof rather than upon different planets, hurtling through space some forty-eight million miles apart.

That she shared my sentiments in this respect I was positive, for on my approach the look of pitiful hopelessness left her sweet countenance to be replaced by a smile of joyful welcome, as she placed her little right hand upon my left shoulder in true red Martian salute.

"Sarkoja told Sola that you had become a true Thark," she said, "and that I would now see no more of you than of any of the other warriors."

"Sarkoja is a liar of the first magnitude," I replied, "notwithstanding the proud claim of the Tharks to absolute verity."

Dejah Thoris laughed.

"I knew that even though you became a member of the community you would not cease to be my friend; 'A warrior may change his metal, but not his heart,' as the saying is upon Barsoom."

"I think they have been trying to keep us apart," she continued, "for whenever you have been off duty one of the older women of Tars Tarkas' retinue has always arranged to trump up some excuse to get Sola and me out of sight. They have had me down in the pits below the buildings helping them mix their awful radium powder, and make their terrible projectiles. You know that these have to be manufactured by artificial light, as exposure to sunlight always results in an explosion. You have noticed that their bullets explode when they strike an object? Well, the opaque, outer coating is broken by the impact, exposing a glass cylinder, almost solid, in the forward end of which is a minute particle of radium powder. The moment the sunlight, even though diffused, strikes this powder it explodes with a violence which nothing can withstand. If you ever witness a night battle you will note the absence of these explosions, while the morning following the battle will be filled at sunrise with the sharp detonations of exploding missiles fired the preceding night. As a rule, however, non-exploding projectiles are used at night." [I have used the word radium in describing this powder because in the light of recent discoveries on Earth I believe it to be a mixture of which radium is the base. In Captain Carter's manuscript it is mentioned always by the name used in the written language of Helium and is spelled in hieroglyphics which it would be difficult and useless to reproduce.]

While I was much interested in Dejah Thoris' explanation of this wonderful adjunct to Martian warfare, I was more concerned by the immediate problem of their treatment of her. That they were keeping her away from me was not a matter for surprise, but that they should subject her to dangerous and arduous labor filled me with rage.

"Have they ever subjected you to cruelty and ignominy, Dejah Thoris?" I asked, feeling the hot blood of my fighting ancestors leap in my veins as I awaited her reply.

"Only in little ways, John Carter," she answered. "Nothing that can harm me outside my pride. They know that I am the daughter of ten thousand jeddaks, that I trace my ancestry straight back without a break to the builder of the first great waterway, and they, who do not even know their own mothers, are jealous of me. At heart they hate their horrid fates, and so wreak their poor spite on me who stand for everything they have not, and for all they most crave and never can attain. Let us pity them, my chieftain, for even though we die at their hands we can afford them pity, since we are greater than they and they know it."

Had I known the significance of those words "my chieftain," as applied by a red Martian woman to a man, I should have had the surprise of my life, but I did not know at that time, nor for many months thereafter. Yes, I still had much to learn upon Barsoom.

"I presume it is the better part of wisdom that we bow to our fate with as good grace as possible, Dejah Thoris; but I hope, nevertheless, that I may be present the next time that any Martian, green, red, pink, or violet, has the temerity to even so much as frown on you, my princess."

Dejah Thoris caught her breath at my last words, and gazed upon me with dilated eyes and quickening breath, and then, with an odd little laugh, which brought roguish dimples to the corners of her mouth, she shook her head and cried:

"What a child! A great warrior and yet a stumbling little child."

"What have I done now?" I asked, in sore perplexity.

"Some day you shall know, John Carter, if we live; but I may not tell you. And I, the daughter of Mors Kajak, son of Tardos Mors, have listened without anger," she soliloquized in conclusion.

Then she broke out again into one of her gay, happy, laughing moods; joking with me on my prowess as a Thark warrior as contrasted with my soft heart and natural kindliness.

"I presume that should you accidentally wound an enemy you would take him home and nurse him back to health," she laughed.

"That is precisely what we do on Earth," I answered. "At least among civilized men."

This made her laugh again. She could not understand it, for, with all her tenderness and womanly sweetness, she was still a Martian, and to a Martian the only good enemy is a dead enemy; for every dead foeman means so much more to divide between those who live.

I was very curious to know what I had said or done to cause her so much perturbation a moment before and so I continued to importune her to enlighten me.

"No," she exclaimed, "it is enough that you have said it and that I have listened. And when you learn, John Carter, and if I be dead, as likely I shall be ere the further moon has circled Barsoom another twelve times, remember that I listened and that I – smiled."

It was all Greek to me, but the more I begged her to explain the more positive became her denials of my request, and, so, in very hopelessness, I desisted.

Day had now given away to night and as we wandered along the great avenue lighted by the two moons of Barsoom, and with Earth looking down upon us out of her luminous green eye, it seemed that we were alone in the universe, and I, at least, was content that it should be so.

The chill of the Martian night was upon us, and removing my silks I threw them across the shoulders of Dejah Thoris. As my arm rested for an instant upon her I felt a thrill pass through every fiber of my being such as contact with no other mortal had even produced; and it seemed to me that she had leaned slightly toward me, but of that I was not sure. Only I knew that as my arm rested there across her shoulders longer than the act of adjusting the silk required she did not draw away, nor did she speak. And so, in silence, we walked the surface of a dying world, but in the breast of one of us at least had been born that which is ever oldest, yet ever new.

I loved Dejah Thoris. The touch of my arm upon her naked shoulder had spoken to me in words I would not mistake, and I knew that I had loved her since the first moment that my eyes had met hers that first time in the plaza of the dead city of Korad.

CHAPTER FOURTEEN

A Duel to the Death

MY FIRST IMPULSE was to tell her of my love, and then I thought of the helplessness of her position wherein I alone could lighten the burdens of her captivity, and protect her in my poor way against the thousands of hereditary enemies she must face upon our arrival at Thark. I could not chance causing her additional pain or sorrow by declaring a love which, in all probability she did not return. Should I be so indiscreet, her position would be even more unbearable than now, and the thought that she might feel that I was taking advantage of her helplessness, to influence her decision was the final argument which sealed my lips.

"Why are you so quiet, Dejah Thoris?" I asked. "Possibly you would rather return to Sola and your quarters."

"No," she murmured, "I am happy here. I do not know why it is that I should always be happy and contented when you, John Carter, a stranger, are with me; yet at such times it seems that I am safe and that, with you, I shall soon return to my father's court and feel his strong arms about me and my mother's tears and kisses on my cheek."

"Do people kiss, then, upon Barsoom?" I asked, when she had explained the word she used, in answer to my inquiry as to its meaning.

"Parents, brothers, and sisters, yes; and," she added in a low, thoughtful tone, "lovers."

"And you, Dejah Thoris, have parents and brothers and sisters?"

"Yes."

"And a – lover?"

She was silent, nor could I venture to repeat the question.

"The man of Barsoom," she finally ventured, "does not ask personal questions of women, except his mother, and the woman he has fought for and won."

"But I have fought – " I started, and then I wished my tongue had been cut from my mouth; for she turned even as I caught myself and ceased, and drawing my silks from her shoulder she held them out to me, and without a word, and with head held high, she moved with the carriage of the queen she was toward the plaza and the doorway of her quarters.

I did not attempt to follow her, other than to see that she reached the building in safety, but, directing Woola to accompany her, I turned disconsolately and entered my own house. I sat for hours cross-legged, and cross-tempered, upon my silks meditating upon the queer freaks chance plays upon us poor devils of mortals.

So this was love! I had escaped it for all the years I had roamed the five continents and their encircling seas; in spite of beautiful women and urging opportunity; in spite of a half-desire for love and a constant search for my ideal, it had remained for me to fall furiously and hopelessly in love with a creature from another world, of a species similar possibly, yet not identical with mine. A woman who was hatched from an egg, and whose span of life might cover a thousand years; whose people had strange customs and ideas; a woman whose hopes, whose pleasures, whose standards of virtue and of right and wrong might vary as greatly from mine as did those of the green Martians.

Yes, I was a fool, but I was in love, and though I was suffering the greatest misery I had ever known I would not have had it otherwise for all the riches of Barsoom. Such is love, and such are lovers wherever love is known.

To me, Dejah Thoris was all that was perfect; all that was virtuous and beautiful and noble and good. I believed that from the bottom of my heart, from the depth of my soul on that night in Korad as I sat cross-legged upon my silks while the nearer moon of Barsoom raced through the western sky toward the horizon, and lighted up the gold and marble, and jeweled mosaics of my world-old chamber, and I believe it today as I sit at my desk in the little study overlooking the Hudson. Twenty years have intervened; for ten of them I lived and fought for Dejah Thoris and her people, and for ten I have lived upon her memory.

The morning of our departure for Thark dawned clear and hot, as do all Martian mornings except for the six weeks when the snow melts at the poles.

I sought out Dejah Thoris in the throng of departing chariots, but she turned her shoulder to me, and I could see the red blood mount to her cheek. With the foolish inconsistency of love I held my peace when I might have plead ignorance of the nature of my offense, or at least the gravity of it, and so have effected, at worst, a half conciliation.

I sought out Dejah Thoris in the throng of departing chariots.

My duty dictated that I must see that she was comfortable, and so I glanced into her chariot and rearranged her silks and furs. In doing so I noted with horror that she was heavily chained by one ankle to the side of the vehicle.

"What does this mean?" I cried, turning to Sola.

"Sarkoja thought it best," she answered, her face betokening her disapproval of the procedure.

Examining the manacles I saw that they fastened with a massive spring lock.

"Where is the key, Sola? Let me have it."

"Sarkoja wears it, John Carter," she answered.

I turned without further word and sought out Tars Tarkas, to whom I vehemently objected to the unnecessary humiliations and cruelties, as they seemed to my lover's eyes, that were being heaped upon Dejah Thoris.

"John Carter," he answered, "if ever you and Dejah Thoris escape the Tharks it will be upon this journey. We know that you will not go without her. You have shown yourself a mighty fighter, and we do not wish to manacle you, so we hold you both in the easiest way that will yet ensure security. I have spoken."

I saw the strength of his reasoning at a flash, and knew that it were futile to appeal from his decision, but I asked that the key be taken from Sarkoja and that she be directed to leave the prisoner alone in future.

"This much, Tars Tarkas, you may do for me in return for the friendship that, I must confess, I feel for you."

"Friendship?" he replied. "There is no such thing, John Carter; but have your will. I shall direct that Sarkoja cease to annoy the girl, and I myself will take the custody of the key."

"Unless you wish me to assume the responsibility," I said, smiling.

He looked at me long and earnestly before he spoke.

"Were you to give me your word that neither you nor Dejah Thoris would attempt to escape until after we have safely reached the court of Tal Hajus you might have the key and throw the chains into the river Iss."

"It were better that you held the key, Tars Tarkas," I replied

He smiled, and said no more, but that night as we were making camp I saw him unfasten Dejah Thoris' fetters himself.

With all his cruel ferocity and coldness there was an undercurrent of something in Tars Tarkas which he seemed ever battling to subdue. Could it be a vestige of some human instinct come back from an ancient forbear to haunt him with the horror of his people's ways!

As I was approaching Dejah Thoris' chariot I passed Sarkoja, and the black, venomous look she accorded me was the sweetest balm I had felt for many hours. Lord, how she hated me! It bristled from her so palpably that one might almost have cut it with a sword.

A few moments later I saw her deep in conversation with a warrior named Zad; a big, hulking, powerful brute, but one who had never made a kill among his own chieftains, and so was still as an o mad, or man with one name; he could win a second name only with the metal of some chieftain. It was this custom which entitled me to the names of either of the chieftains I had killed; in fact, some of the warriors addressed me as Dotar Sojat, a combination of the surnames of the two warrior chieftains whose metal I had taken, or, in other words, whom I had slain in fair fight.

As Sarkoja talked with Zad he cast occasional glances in my direction, while she seemed to be urging him very strongly to some action. I paid little attention to it at the time, but the next day I had good reason to recall the circumstances, and at the same time gain a slight insight into the depths of Sarkoja's hatred and the lengths to which she was capable of going to wreak her horrid vengeance on me.

Dejah Thoris would have none of me again on this evening, and though I spoke her name she neither replied, nor conceded by so much as the flutter of an eyelid that she realized my existence. In my extremity I did what most other lovers would have done; I sought word from her through an intimate. In this instance it was Sola whom I intercepted in another part of camp.

"What is the matter with Dejah Thoris?" I blurted out at her. "Why will she not speak to me?"

Sola seemed puzzled herself, as though such strange actions on the part of two humans were quite beyond her, as indeed they were, poor child.

"She says you have angered her, and that is all she will say, except that she is the daughter of a jed and the granddaughter of a jeddak and she has been humiliated by a creature who could not polish the teeth of her grandmother's sorak."

I pondered over this report for some time, finally asking, "What might a sorak be, Sola?"

"A little animal about as big as my hand, which the red Martian women keep to play with," explained Sola.

Not fit to polish the teeth of her grandmother's cat! I must rank pretty low in the consideration of Dejah Thoris, I thought; but I could not help laughing at the strange figure of speech, so homely and in this respect so earthly. It made me homesick, for it sounded very much like "not fit to polish her shoes." And then commenced a train of thought quite new to me. I began to wonder what my people at home were doing. I had not seen them for years. There was a family of Carters in Virginia who claimed close relationship with me; I was supposed to be a great uncle, or something of the kind equally foolish. I could pass anywhere for twenty-five to thirty years of age, and to be a great uncle always seemed the height of incongruity, for my thoughts and feelings were those of a boy. There was two little kiddies in the Carter family whom I had loved and who had thought there was no one on Earth like Uncle Jack; I could see them just as plainly, as I stood there under the moonlit skies of Barsoom, and I longed for them as I had never longed for any mortals before. By nature a wanderer, I had never known the true meaning of the word home, but the great hall of the Carters had always stood for all that the word did mean to me, and now my heart turned toward it from the cold and unfriendly peoples I had been thrown amongst. For did not even Dejah Thoris despise me! I was a low creature, so low in fact that I was not even fit to polish the teeth of her grandmother's cat; and then my saving sense of humor came to my rescue, and laughing I turned into my silks and furs and slept upon the moon-haunted ground the sleep of a tired and healthy fighting man.

We broke camp the next day at an early hour and marched with only a single halt until just before dark. Two incidents broke the tediousness of the march. About noon we espied far to our right what was evidently an incubator, and Lorquas Ptomel directed Tars Tarkas to investigate it. The latter took a dozen warriors, including myself, and we raced across the velvety carpeting of moss to the little enclosure.

It was indeed an incubator, but the eggs were very small in comparison with those I had seen hatching in ours at the time of my arrival on Mars.

Tars Tarkas dismounted and examined the enclosure minutely, finally announcing that it belonged to the green men of Warhoon and that the cement was scarcely dry where it had been walled up.

"They cannot be a day's march ahead of us," he exclaimed, the light of battle leaping to his fierce face.

The work at the incubator was short indeed. The warriors tore open the entrance and a couple of them, crawling in, soon demolished all the eggs with their short-swords. Then remounting we dashed back to join the cavalcade. During the ride I took occasion to ask Tars Tarkas if these Warhoons whose eggs we had destroyed were a smaller people than his Tharks.

"I noticed that their eggs were so much smaller than those I saw hatching in your incubator," I added.

He explained that the eggs had just been placed there; but, like all green Martian eggs, they would grow during the five-year period of incubation until they obtained the size of those I had seen hatching on the day of my arrival on Barsoom. This was indeed an interesting piece of information, for it had always seemed remarkable to me that the green Martian women, large as they were, could bring forth such enormous eggs as I had seen the four-foot infants emerging from. As a matter of fact, the new-laid egg is but little larger than an ordinary goose egg, and as it does not commence to grow until subjected to the light of the sun the chieftains have little difficulty in transporting several hundreds of them at one time from the storage vaults to the incubators.

Shortly after the incident of the Warhoon eggs we halted to rest the animals, and it was during this halt that the second of the day's interesting episodes occurred. I was engaged in changing my riding cloths from one of my thoats to the other, for I divided the day's work between them, when Zad approached me, and without a word struck my animal a terrific blow with his long-sword.

I did not need a manual of green Martian etiquette to know what reply to make, for, in fact, I was so wild with anger that I could scarcely refrain from drawing my pistol and shooting him down for the brute he was; but he stood waiting with drawn long-sword, and my only choice was to draw my own and meet him in fair fight with his choice of weapons or a lesser one.

This latter alternative is always permissible, therefore I could have used my short-sword, my dagger, my hatchet, or my fists had I wished, and been entirely within my rights, but I could not use firearms or a spear while he held only his long-sword.

I chose the same weapon he had drawn because I knew he prided himself upon his ability with it, and I wished, if I worsted him at all, to do it with his own weapon. The fight that followed was a long one and delayed the resumption of the march for an hour. The entire community surrounded us, leaving a clear space about one hundred feet in diameter for our battle.

Zad first attempted to rush me down as a bull might a wolf, but I was much too quick for him, and each time I side-stepped his rushes he would go lunging past me, only to receive a nick from my sword upon his arm or back. He was soon streaming blood from a half dozen minor wounds, but I could not obtain an opening to deliver an effective thrust. Then he changed his tactics, and fighting warily and with extreme dexterity, he tried to do by science what he was unable to do by brute strength. I must admit that he was a magnificent swordsman, and had it not been for my greater endurance and the remarkable agility the lesser gravitation of Mars lent me I might not have been able to put up the creditable fight I did against him.

We circled for some time without doing much damage on either side; the long, straight, needle-like swords flashing in the sunlight, and ringing out upon the stillness as they crashed together with each effective parry. Finally Zad, realizing that he was tiring more than I, evidently decided to close in and end the battle in a final blaze of glory for himself; just as he rushed me a blinding flash of light struck full in my eyes, so that I could not see his approach and could only leap blindly to one side in an effort to escape the mighty blade that it seemed I could already feel in my vitals. I was only partially successful, as a sharp pain in my left shoulder attested, but in the sweep of my glance as I sought to again locate my adversary, a sight met my astonished gaze which paid me well for the wound the temporary blindness had caused me. There, upon Dejah Thoris' chariot stood three figures, for the purpose evidently of witnessing the encounter above the heads of the intervening Tharks. There were Dejah Thoris, Sola, and Sarkoja, and as my fleeting glance swept over them a little tableau was presented which will stand graven in my memory to the day of my death.

As I looked, Dejah Thoris turned upon Sarkoja with the fury of a young tigress and struck something from her upraised hand; something which flashed in the sunlight as it spun to the ground. Then I knew what had blinded me at that crucial moment of the fight, and how Sarkoja had found a way to kill me without herself delivering the final thrust. Another thing I saw, too, which almost lost my life for me then and there, for it took my mind for the fraction of an instant entirely from my antagonist; for, as Dejah Thoris struck the tiny mirror from her hand, Sarkoja, her face livid with hatred and baffled rage, whipped out her dagger and aimed a terrific blow at Dejah Thoris; and then Sola, our dear and faithful Sola, sprang between them; the last I saw was the great knife descending upon her shielding breast.

My enemy had recovered from his thrust and was making it extremely interesting for me, so I reluctantly gave my attention to the work in hand, but my mind was not upon the battle.

We rushed each other furiously time after time, 'til suddenly, feeling the sharp point of his sword at my breast in a thrust I could neither parry nor escape, I threw myself upon him with outstretched sword and with all the weight of my body, determined that I would not die alone if I could prevent it. I felt the steel tear into my chest, all went black before me, my head whirled in dizziness, and I felt my knees giving beneath me.

CHAPTER FIFTEEN

Sola Tells Me Her Story

WHEN CONSCIOUSNESS RETURNED, and, as I soon learned, I was down but a moment, I sprang quickly to my feet searching for my sword, and there I found it, buried to the hilt in the green breast of Zad, who lay stone dead upon the ochre moss of the ancient sea bottom. As I regained my full senses I found his weapon piercing my left breast, but only through the flesh and muscles which cover my ribs, entering near the center of my chest and coming out below the shoulder. As I had lunged I had turned so that his sword merely passed beneath the muscles, inflicting a painful but not dangerous wound.

Removing the blade from my body I also regained my own, and turning my back upon his ugly carcass, I moved, sick, sore, and disgusted, toward the chariots which bore my retinue and my belongings. A murmur of Martian applause greeted me, but I cared not for it.

Bleeding and weak I reached my women, who, accustomed to such happenings, dressed my wounds, applying the wonderful healing and remedial agents which make only the most instantaneous of death blows fatal. Give a Martian woman a chance and death must take a back seat. They soon had me patched up so that, except for weakness from loss of blood and a little soreness around the wound, I suffered no great distress from this thrust which, under earthly treatment, undoubtedly would have put me flat on my back for days.

As soon as they were through with me I hastened to the chariot of Dejah Thoris, where I found my poor Sola with her chest swathed in bandages, but apparently little the worse for her encounter with Sarkoja, whose dagger it seemed had struck the edge of one of Sola's metal breast ornaments and, thus deflected, had inflicted but a slight flesh wound.

As I approached I found Dejah Thoris lying prone upon her silks and furs, her lithe form wracked with sobs. She did not notice my presence, nor did she hear me speaking with Sola, who was standing a short distance from the vehicle.

"Is she injured?" I asked of Sola, indicating Dejah Thoris by an inclination of my head.

"No," she answered, "she thinks that you are dead."

"And that her grandmother's cat may now have no one to polish its teeth?" I queried, smiling.

"I think you wrong her, John Carter," said Sola. "I do not understand either her ways or yours, but I am sure the granddaughter of ten thousand jeddaks would never grieve like this over any who held but the highest claim upon her affections. They are a proud race, but they are just, as are all Barsoomians, and you must have hurt or wronged her grievously that she will not admit your existence living, though she mourns you dead.

"Tears are a strange sight upon Barsoom," she continued, "and so it is difficult for me to interpret them. I have seen but two people weep in all my life, other than Dejah Thoris; one wept from sorrow, the other from baffled rage. The first was my mother, years ago before they killed her; the other was Sarkoja, when they dragged her from me today."

"Your mother!" I exclaimed, "but, Sola, you could not have known your mother, child."

"But I did. And my father also," she added. "If you would like to hear the strange and un-Barsoomian story come to the chariot tonight, John Carter, and I will tell you that of which I have never spoken in all my life before. And now the signal has been given to resume the march, you must go."

"I will come tonight, Sola," I promised. "Be sure to tell Dejah Thoris I am alive and well. I shall not force myself upon her, and be sure that you do not let her know I saw her tears. If she would speak with me I but await her command."

Sola mounted the chariot, which was swinging into its place in line, and I hastened to my waiting thoat and galloped to my station beside Tars Tarkas at the rear of the column.

We made a most imposing and awe-inspiring spectacle as we strung out across the yellow landscape; the two hundred and fifty ornate and brightly colored chariots, preceded by an advance guard of some two hundred mounted warriors and chieftains riding five abreast and one hundred yards apart, and followed by a like number in the same formation, with a score or more of flankers on either side; the fifty extra mastodons, or heavy draught animals, known as zitidars, and the five or six hundred extra thoats of the warriors running loose within the hollow square formed by the surrounding warriors. The gleaming metal and jewels of the gorgeous ornaments of the men and women, duplicated in the trappings of the zitidars and thoats, and interspersed with the flashing colors of magnificent silks and furs and feathers, lent a barbaric splendor to the caravan which would have turned an East Indian potentate green with envy.

The enormous broad tires of the chariots and the padded feet of the animals brought forth no sound from the moss-covered sea bottom; and so we moved in utter silence, like some huge phantasmagoria, except when the stillness was broken by the guttural growling of a goaded zitidar, or the squealing of fighting thoats. The green Martians converse but little, and then usually in monosyllables, low and like the faint rumbling of distant thunder.

We traversed a trackless waste of moss which, bending to the pressure of broad tire or padded foot, rose up again behind us, leaving no sign that we had passed. We might indeed have been the wraiths of the departed dead upon the dead sea of that dying planet for all the sound or sign we made in passing. It was the first march of a large body of men and animals I had ever witnessed which raised no dust and left no spoor; for there is no dust upon Mars except in the cultivated districts during the winter months, and even then the absence of high winds renders it almost unnoticeable.

We camped that night at the foot of the hills we had been approaching for two days and which marked the southern boundary of this particular sea. Our animals had been two days without drink, nor had they had water for nearly two months, not since shortly after leaving Thark; but, as Tars Tarkas explained to me, they require but little and can live almost indefinitely upon the moss which covers Barsoom, and which, he told me, holds in its tiny stems sufficient moisture to meet the limited demands of the animals.

After partaking of my evening meal of cheese-like food and vegetable milk I sought out Sola, whom I found working by the light of a torch upon some of Tars Tarkas' trappings. She looked up at my approach, her face lighting with pleasure and with welcome.

"I am glad you came," she said; "Dejah Thoris sleeps and I am lonely. Mine own people do not care for me, John Carter; I am too unlike them. It is a sad fate, since I must live my life amongst them, and I often wish that I were a true green Martian woman, without love and without hope; but I have known love and so I am lost.

"I promised to tell you my story, or rather the story of my parents. From what I have learned of you and the ways of your people I am sure that the tale will not seem strange to you, but among green Martians it has no parallel within the memory of the oldest living Thark, nor do our legends hold many similar tales.

"My mother was rather small, in fact too small to be allowed the responsibilities of maternity, as our chieftains breed principally for size. She was also less cold and cruel than most green Martian women, and caring little for their society, she often roamed the deserted avenues of Thark alone, or went and sat among the wild flowers that deck the nearby hills, thinking thoughts and wishing wishes which I believe I alone among Tharkian women today may understand, for am I not the child of my mother?

"And there among the hills she met a young warrior, whose duty it was to guard the feeding zitidars and thoats and see that they roamed not beyond the hills. They spoke at first only of such things as interest a community of Tharks, but gradually, as they came to meet more often, and, as was now quite evident to both, no longer by chance, they talked about themselves, their likes, their ambitions and their hopes. She trusted him and told him of the awful repugnance she felt for the cruelties of their kind, for the hideous, loveless lives they must ever lead, and then she waited for the storm of denunciation to break from his cold, hard lips; but instead he took her in his arms and kissed her.

"They kept their love a secret for six long years. She, my mother, was of the retinue of the great Tal Hajus, while her lover was a simple warrior, wearing only his own metal. Had their defection from the traditions of the Tharks been discovered both would have paid the penalty in the great arena before Tal Hajus and the assembled hordes.

"The egg from which I came was hidden beneath a great glass vessel upon the highest and most inaccessible of the partially ruined towers of ancient Thark. Once each year my mother visited it for the five long years it lay there in the process of incubation. She dared not come oftener, for in the mighty guilt of her conscience she feared that her every move was watched. During this period my father gained great distinction as a warrior and had taken the metal from several chieftains. His love for my mother had never diminished, and his own ambition in life was to reach a point where he might wrest the metal from Tal Hajus himself, and thus, as ruler of the Tharks, be free to claim her as his own, as well as, by the might of his power, protect the child which otherwise would be quickly dispatched should the truth become known.

"It was a wild dream, that of wresting the metal from Tal Hajus in five short years, but his advance was rapid, and he soon stood high in the councils of Thark. But one day the chance was lost forever, in so far as it could come in time to save his loved ones, for he was ordered away upon a long expedition to the ice-clad south, to make war upon the natives there and despoil them of their furs, for such is the manner of the green Barsoomian; he does not labor for what he can wrest in battle from others.

"He was gone for four years, and when he returned all had been over for three; for about a year after his departure, and shortly before the time for the return of an expedition which had gone forth to fetch the fruits of a community incubator, the egg had hatched. Thereafter my mother continued to keep me in the old tower, visiting me nightly and lavishing upon me the love the community life would have robbed us both of. She hoped, upon the return of the expedition from the incubator, to mix me with the other young assigned to the quarters of Tal Hajus, and thus escape the fate which would surely follow discovery of her sin against the ancient traditions of the green men.

"She taught me rapidly the language and customs of my kind, and one night she told me the story I have told to you up to this point, impressing upon me the necessity for absolute secrecy and the great caution I must exercise after she had placed me with the other young Tharks to permit no one to guess that I was further advanced in education than they, nor by any sign to divulge in the presence of others my affection for her, or my knowledge of my parentage; and then drawing me close to her she whispered in my ear the name of my father.

"And then a light flashed out upon the darkness of the tower chamber, and there stood Sarkoja, her gleaming, baleful eyes fixed in a frenzy of loathing and contempt upon my mother. The torrent of hatred and abuse she poured out upon her turned my young heart cold in terror. That she had heard the entire story was apparent, and that she had suspected something wrong from my mother's long nightly absences from her quarters accounted for her presence there on that fateful night.

"One thing she had not heard, nor did she know, the whispered name of my father. This was apparent from her repeated demands upon my mother to disclose the name of her partner in sin, but no amount of abuse or threats could wring this from her, and to save me from needless torture she lied, for she told Sarkoja that she alone knew nor would she even tell her child.

"With final imprecations, Sarkoja hastened away to Tal Hajus to report her discovery, and while she was gone my mother, wrapping me in the silks and furs of her night coverings, so that I was scarcely noticeable, descended to the streets and ran wildly away toward the outskirts of the city, in the direction which led to the far south, out toward the man whose protection she might not claim, but on whose face she wished to look once more before she died.

"As we neared the city's southern extremity a sound came to us from across the mossy flat, from the direction of the only pass through the hills which led to the gates, the pass by which caravans from either north or south or east or west would enter the city. The sounds we heard were the squealing of thoats and the grumbling of zitidars, with the occasional clank of arms which announced the approach of a body of warriors. The thought uppermost in her mind was that it was my father returned from his expedition, but the cunning of the Thark held her from headlong and precipitate flight to greet him.

"Retreating into the shadows of a doorway she awaited the coming of the cavalcade which shortly entered the avenue, breaking its formation and thronging the thoroughfare from wall to wall. As the head of the procession passed us the lesser moon swung clear of the overhanging roofs and lit up the scene with all the brilliancy of her wondrous light. My mother shrank further back into the friendly shadows, and from her hiding place saw that the expedition was not that of my father, but the returning caravan bearing the young Tharks. Instantly her plan was formed, and as a great chariot swung close to our hiding place she slipped stealthily in upon the trailing tailboard, crouching low in the shadow of the high side, straining me to her bosom in a frenzy of love.

"She knew, what I did not, that never again after that night would she hold me to her breast, nor was it likely we would ever look upon each other's face again. In the confusion of the plaza she mixed me with the other children, whose guardians during the journey were now free to relinquish their responsibility. We were herded together into a great room, fed by women who had not accompanied the expedition, and the next day we were parceled out among the retinues of the chieftains.

"I never saw my mother after that night. She was imprisoned by Tal Hajus, and every effort, including the most horrible and shameful torture, was brought to bear upon her to wring from her lips the name of my father; but she remained steadfast and loyal, dying at last amidst the laughter of Tal Hajus and his chieftains during some awful torture she was undergoing.

"I learned afterwards that she told them that she had killed me to save me from a like fate at their hands, and that she had thrown my body to the white apes. Sarkoja alone disbelieved her, and I feel to this day that she suspects my true origin, but does not dare expose me, at the present, at all events, because she also guesses, I am sure, the identity of my father.

"When he returned from his expedition and learned the story of my mother's fate I was present as Tal Hajus told him; but never by the quiver of a muscle did he betray the slightest emotion; only he did not laugh as Tal Hajus gleefully described her death struggles. From that moment on he was the cruelest of the cruel, and I am awaiting the day when he shall win the goal of his ambition, and feel the carcass of Tal Hajus beneath his foot, for I am as sure that he but waits the opportunity to wreak a terrible vengeance, and that his great love is as strong in his breast as when it first transfigured him nearly forty years ago, as I am that we sit here upon the edge of a world-old ocean while sensible people sleep, John Carter."

"And your father, Sola, is he with us now?" I asked.

"Yes," she replied, "but he does not know me for what I am, nor does he know who betrayed my mother to Tal Hajus. I alone know my father's name, and only I and Tal Hajus and Sarkoja know that it was she who carried the tale that brought death and torture upon her he loved."

We sat silent for a few moments, she wrapped in the gloomy thoughts of her terrible past, and I in pity for the poor creatures whom the heartless, senseless customs of their race had doomed to loveless lives of cruelty and of hate. Presently she spoke.

"John Carter, if ever a real man walked the cold, dead bosom of Barsoom you are one. I know that I can trust you, and because the knowledge may someday help you or him or Dejah Thoris or myself, I am going to tell you the name of my father, nor place any restrictions or conditions upon your tongue. When the time comes, speak the truth if it seems best to you. I trust you because I know that you are not cursed with the terrible trait of absolute and unswerving truthfulness, that you could lie like one of your own Virginia gentlemen if a lie would save others from sorrow or suffering. My father's name is Tars Tarkas."

CHAPTER SIXTEEN

We Plan Escape

THE REMAINDER OF OUR JOURNEY to Thark was uneventful. We were twenty days upon the road, crossing two sea bottoms and passing through or around a number of ruined cities, mostly smaller than Korad. Twice we crossed the famous Martian waterways, or canals, so-called by our earthly astronomers. When we approached these points a warrior would be sent far ahead with a powerful field glass, and if no great body of red Martian troops was in sight we would advance as close as possible without chance of being seen and then camp until dark, when we would slowly approach the cultivated tract, and, locating one of the numerous, broad highways which cross these areas at regular intervals, creep silently and stealthily across to the arid lands upon the other side. It required five hours to make one of these crossings without a single halt, and the other consumed the entire night, so that we were just leaving the confines of the high-walled fields when the sun broke out upon us.

Crossing in the darkness, as we did, I was unable to see but little, except as the nearer moon, in her wild and ceaseless hurtling through the Barsoomian heavens, lit up little patches of the landscape from time to time, disclosing walled fields and low, rambling buildings, presenting much the appearance of earthly farms. There were many trees, methodically arranged, and some of them were of enormous height; there were animals in some of the enclosures, and they announced their presence by terrified squealings and snortings as they scented our queer, wild beasts and wilder human beings.

Only once did I perceive a human being, and that was at the intersection of our crossroad with the wide, white turnpike which cuts each cultivated district longitudinally at its exact center. The fellow must have been sleeping beside the road, for, as I came abreast of him, he raised upon one elbow and after a single glance at the approaching caravan leaped shrieking to his feet and fled madly down the road, scaling a nearby wall with the agility of a scared cat. The Tharks paid him not the slightest attention; they were not out upon the warpath, and the only sign that I had that they had seen him was a quickening of the pace of the caravan as we hastened toward the bordering desert which marked our entrance into the realm of Tal Hajus.

Not once did I have speech with Dejah Thoris, as she sent no word to me that I would be welcome at her chariot, and my foolish pride kept me from making any advances. I verily believe that a man's way with women is in inverse ratio to his prowess among men. The weakling and the saphead have often great ability to charm the fair sex, while the fighting man who can face a thousand real dangers unafraid, sits hiding in the shadows like some frightened child.

Just thirty days after my advent upon Barsoom we entered the ancient city of Thark, from whose long-forgotten people this horde of green men have stolen even their name. The hordes of Thark number some thirty thousand souls, and are divided into twenty-five communities. Each community has its own jed and lesser chieftains, but all are under the rule of Tal Hajus, Jeddak of Thark. Five communities make their headquarters at the city of Thark, and the balance are scattered among other deserted cities of ancient Mars throughout the district claimed by Tal Hajus.

We made our entry into the great central plaza early in the afternoon. There were no enthusiastic friendly greetings for the returned expedition. Those who chanced to be in sight spoke the names of warriors or women with whom they came in direct contact, in the formal greeting of their kind, but when it was discovered that they brought two captives a greater interest was aroused, and Dejah Thoris and I were the centers of inquiring groups.

We were soon assigned to new quarters, and the balance of the day was devoted to settling ourselves to the changed conditions. My home now was upon an avenue leading into the plaza from the south, the main artery down which we had marched from the gates of the city. I was at the far end of the square and had an entire building to myself. The same grandeur of architecture which was so noticeable a characteristic of Korad was in evidence here, only, if that were possible, on a larger and richer scale. My quarters would have been suitable for housing the greatest of earthly emperors, but to these queer creatures nothing about a building appealed to them but its size and the enormity of its chambers; the larger the building, the more desirable; and so Tal Hajus occupied what must have been an enormous public building, the largest in the city, but entirely unfitted for residence purposes; the next largest was reserved for Lorquas Ptomel, the next for the jed of a lesser rank, and so on to the bottom of the list of five jeds. The warriors occupied the buildings with the chieftains to whose retinues they belonged; or, if they preferred, sought shelter among any of the thousands of untenanted buildings in their own quarter of town; each community being assigned a certain section of the city. The selection of building had to be made in accordance with these divisions, except in so far as the jeds were concerned, they all occupying edifices which fronted upon the plaza.

When I had finally put my house in order, or rather seen that it had been done, it was nearing sunset, and I hastened out with the intention of locating Sola and her charges, as I had determined upon having speech with Dejah Thoris and trying to impress on her the necessity of our at least patching up a truce until I could find some way of aiding her to escape. I searched in vain until the upper rim of the great red sun was just disappearing behind the horizon and then I spied the ugly head of Woola peering from a second-story window on the opposite side of the very street where I was quartered, but nearer the plaza.

Without waiting for a further invitation I bolted up the winding runway which led to the second floor, and entering a great chamber at the front of the building was greeted by the frenzied Woola, who threw his great carcass upon me, nearly hurling me to the floor; the poor old fellow was so glad to see me that I thought he would devour me, his head split from ear to ear, showing his three rows of tusks in his hobgoblin smile.

Quieting him with a word of command and a caress, I looked hurriedly through the approaching gloom for a sign of Dejah Thoris, and then, not seeing her, I called her name. There was an answering murmur from the far corner of the apartment, and with a couple of quick strides I was standing beside her where she crouched among the furs and silks upon an ancient carved wooden seat. As I waited she rose to her full height and looking me straight in the eye said:

"What would Dotar Sojat, Thark, of Dejah Thoris his captive?"

"Dejah Thoris, I do not know how I have angered you. It was furtherest from my desire to hurt or offend you, whom I had hoped to protect and comfort. Have none of me if it is your will, but that you must aid me in effecting your escape, if such a thing be possible, is not my request, but my command. When you are safe once more at your father's court you may do with me as you please, but from now on until that day I am your master, and you must obey and aid me."

She looked at me long and earnestly and I thought that she was softening toward me.

"I understand your words, Dotar Sojat," she replied, "but you I do not understand. You are a queer mixture of child and man, of brute and noble. I only wish that I might read your heart."

"Look down at your feet, Dejah Thoris; it lies there now where it has lain since that other night at Korad, and where it will ever lie beating alone for you until death stills it forever."

She took a little step toward me, her beautiful hands outstretched in a strange, groping gesture.

"What do you mean, John Carter?" she whispered. "What are you saying to me?"

"I am saying what I had promised myself that I would not say to you, at least until you were no longer a captive among the green men; what from your attitude toward me for the past twenty days I had thought never to say to you; I am saying, Dejah Thoris, that I am yours, body and soul, to serve you, to fight for you, and to die for you. Only one thing I ask of you in return, and that is that you make no sign, either of condemnation or of approbation of my words until you are safe among your own people, and that whatever sentiments you harbor toward me they be not influenced or colored by gratitude; whatever I may do to serve you will be prompted solely from selfish motives, since it gives me more pleasure to serve you than not."

"I will respect your wishes, John Carter, because I understand the motives which prompt them, and I accept your service no more willingly than I bow to your authority; your word shall be my law. I have twice wronged you in my thoughts and again I ask your forgiveness."

Further conversation of a personal nature was prevented by the entrance of Sola, who was much agitated and wholly unlike her usual calm and possessed self.

"That horrible Sarkoja has been before Tal Hajus," she cried, "and from what I heard upon the plaza there is little hope for either of you."

"What do they say?" inquired Dejah Thoris.

"That you will be thrown to the wild calots [dogs] in the great arena as soon as the hordes have assembled for the yearly games."

"Sola," I said, "you are a Thark, but you hate and loathe the customs of your people as much as we do. Will you not accompany us in one supreme effort to escape? I am sure that Dejah Thoris can offer you a home and protection among her people, and your fate can be no worse among them than it must ever be here."

"Yes," cried Dejah Thoris, "come with us, Sola, you will be better off among the red men of Helium than you are here, and I can promise you not only a home with us, but the love and affection your nature craves and which must always be denied you by the customs of your own race. Come with us, Sola; we might go without you, but your fate would be terrible if they thought you had connived to aid us. I know that even that fear would not tempt you to interfere in our escape, but we want you with us, we want you to come to a land of sunshine and happiness, amongst a people who know the meaning of love, of sympathy, and of gratitude. Say that you will, Sola; tell me that you will."

"The great waterway which leads to Helium is but fifty miles to the south," murmured Sola, half to herself; "a swift thoat might make it in three hours; and then to Helium it is five hundred miles, most of the way through thinly settled districts. They would know and they would follow us. We might hide among the great trees for a time, but the chances are small indeed for escape. They would follow us to the very gates of Helium, and they would take toll of life at every step; you do not know them."

"Is there no other way we might reach Helium?" I asked. "Can you not draw me a rough map of the country we must traverse, Dejah Thoris?"

"Yes," she replied, and taking a great diamond from her hair she drew upon the marble floor the first map of Barsoomian territory I had ever seen. It was crisscrossed in every direction with long straight lines, sometimes running parallel and sometimes converging toward some great circle. The lines, she said, were waterways; the circles, cities; and one far to the northwest of us she pointed out as Helium. There were other cities closer, but she said she feared to enter many of them, as they were not all friendly toward Helium.

Finally, after studying the map carefully in the moonlight which now flooded the room, I pointed out a waterway far to the north of us which also seemed to lead to Helium.

"Does not this pierce your grandfather's territory?" I asked.

"Yes," she answered, "but it is two hundred miles north of us; it is one of the waterways we crossed on the trip to Thark."

"They would never suspect that we would try for that distant waterway," I answered, "and that is why I think that it is the best route for our escape."

Sola agreed with me, and it was decided that we should leave Thark this same night; just as quickly, in fact, as I could find and saddle my thoats. Sola was to ride one and Dejah Thoris and I the other; each of us carrying sufficient food and drink to last us for two days, since the animals could not be urged too rapidly for so long a distance.

I directed Sola to proceed with Dejah Thoris along one of the less frequented avenues to the southern boundary of the city, where I would overtake them with the thoats as quickly as possible; then, leaving them to gather what food, silks, and furs we were to need, I slipped quietly to the rear of the first floor, and entered the courtyard, where our animals were moving restlessly about, as was their habit, before settling down for the night.

In the shadows of the buildings and out beneath the radiance of the Martian moons moved the great herd of thoats and zitidars, the latter grunting their low gutturals and the former occasionally emitting the sharp squeal which denotes the almost habitual state of rage in which these creatures passed their existence. They were quieter now, owing to the absence of man, but as they scented me they became more restless and their hideous noise increased. It was risky business, this entering a paddock of thoats alone and at night; first, because their increasing noisiness might warn the nearby warriors that something was amiss, and also because for the slightest cause, or for no cause at all some great bull thoat might take it upon himself to lead a charge upon me.

Having no desire to awaken their nasty tempers upon such a night as this, where so much depended upon secrecy and dispatch, I hugged the shadows of the buildings, ready at an instant's warning to leap into the safety of a nearby door or window. Thus I moved silently to the great gates which opened upon the street at the back of the court, and as I neared the exit I called softly to my two animals. How I thanked the kind providence which had given me the foresight to win the love and confidence of these wild dumb brutes, for presently from the far side of the court I saw two huge bulks forcing their way toward me through the surging mountains of flesh.

They came quite close to me, rubbing their muzzles against my body and nosing for the bits of food it was always my practice to reward them with. Opening the gates I ordered the two great beasts to pass out, and then slipping quietly after them I closed the portals behind me.

I did not saddle or mount the animals there, but instead walked quietly in the shadows of the buildings toward an unfrequented avenue which led toward the point I had arranged to meet Dejah Thoris and Sola. With the noiselessness of disembodied spirits we moved stealthily along the deserted streets, but not until we were within sight of the plain beyond the city did I commence to breathe freely. I was sure that Sola and Dejah Thoris would find no difficulty in reaching our rendezvous undetected, but with my great thoats I was not so sure for myself, as it was quite unusual for warriors to leave the city after dark; in fact there was no place for them to go within any but a long ride.

I reached the appointed meeting place safely, but as Dejah Thoris and Sola were not there I led my animals into the entrance hall of one of the large buildings. Presuming that one of the other women of the same household may have come in to speak to Sola, and so delayed their departure, I did not feel any undue apprehension until nearly an hour had passed without a sign of them, and by the time another half hour had crawled away I was becoming filled with grave anxiety. Then there broke upon the stillness of the night the sound of an approaching party, which, from the noise, I knew could be no fugitives creeping stealthily toward liberty. Soon the party was near me, and from the black shadows of my entranceway I perceived a score of mounted warriors, who, in passing, dropped a dozen words that fetched my heart clean into the top of my head.

"He would likely have arranged to meet them just without the city, and so – " I heard no more, they had passed on; but it was enough. Our plan had been discovered, and the chances for escape from now on to the fearful end would be small indeed. My one hope now was to return undetected to the quarters of Dejah Thoris and learn what fate had overtaken her, but how to do it with these great monstrous thoats upon my hands, now that the city probably was aroused by the knowledge of my escape was a problem of no mean proportions.

Suddenly an idea occurred to me, and acting on my knowledge of the construction of the buildings of these ancient Martian cities with a hollow court within the center of each square, I groped my way blindly through the dark chambers, calling the great thoats after me. They had difficulty in negotiating some of the doorways, but as the buildings fronting the city's principal exposures were all designed upon a magnificent scale, they were able to wriggle through without sticking fast; and thus we finally made the inner court where I found, as I had expected, the usual carpet of moss-like vegetation which would prove their food and drink until I could return them to their own enclosure. That they would be as quiet and contented here as elsewhere I was confident, nor was there but the remotest possibility that they would be discovered, as the green men had no great desire to enter these outlying buildings, which were frequented by the only thing, I believe, which caused them the sensation of fear – the great white apes of Barsoom.

Removing the saddle trappings, I hid them just within the rear doorway of the building through which we had entered the court, and, turning the beasts loose, quickly made my way across the court to the rear of the buildings upon the further side, and thence to the avenue beyond. Waiting in the doorway of the building until I was assured that no one was approaching, I hurried across to the opposite side and through the first doorway to the court beyond; thus, crossing through court after court with only the slight chance of detection which the necessary crossing of the avenues entailed, I made my way in safety to the courtyard in the rear of Dejah Thoris' quarters.

Here, of course, I found the beasts of the warriors who quartered in the adjacent buildings, and the warriors themselves I might expect to meet within if I entered; but, fortunately for me, I had another and safer method of reaching the upper story where Dejah Thoris should be found, and, after first determining as nearly as possible which of the buildings she occupied, for I had never observed them before from the court side, I took advantage of my relatively great strength and agility and sprang upward until I grasped the sill of a second-story window which I thought to be in the rear of her apartment. Drawing myself inside the room I moved stealthily toward the front of the building, and not until I had quite reached the doorway of her room was I made aware by voices that it was occupied.

I did not rush headlong in, but listened without to assure myself that it was Dejah Thoris and that it was safe to venture within. It was well indeed that I took this precaution, for the conversation I heard was in the low gutturals of men, and the words which finally came to me proved a most timely warning. The speaker was a chieftain and he was giving orders to four of his warriors.

"And when he returns to this chamber," he was saying, "as he surely will when he finds she does not meet him at the city's edge, you four are to spring upon him and disarm him. It will require the combined strength of all of you to do it if the reports they bring back from Korad are correct. When you have him fast bound bear him to the vaults beneath the jeddak's quarters and chain him securely where he may be found when Tal Hajus wishes him. Allow him to speak with none, nor permit any other to enter this apartment before he comes. There will be no danger of the girl returning, for by this time she is safe in the arms of Tal Hajus, and may all her ancestors have pity upon her, for Tal Hajus will have none; the great Sarkoja has done a noble night's work. I go, and if you fail to capture him when he comes, I commend your carcasses to the cold bosom of Iss."

CHAPTER SEVENTEEN

A Costly Recapture

As THE SPEAKER CEASED he turned to leave the apartment by the door where I was standing, but I needed to wait no longer; I had heard enough to fill my soul with dread, and stealing quietly away I returned to the courtyard by the way I had come. My plan of action was formed upon the instant, and crossing the square and the bordering avenue upon the opposite side I soon stood within the courtyard of Tal Hajus.

The brilliantly lighted apartments of the first floor told me where first to seek, and advancing to the windows I peered within. I soon discovered that my approach was not to be the easy thing I had hoped, for the rear rooms bordering the court were filled with warriors and women. I then glanced up at the stories above, discovering that the third was apparently unlighted, and so decided to make my entrance to the building from that point. It was the work of but a moment for me to reach the windows above, and soon I had drawn myself within the sheltering shadows of the unlighted third floor.

Fortunately the room I had selected was untenanted, and creeping noiselessly to the corridor beyond I discovered a light in the apartments ahead of me. Reaching what appeared to be a doorway I discovered that it was but an opening upon an immense inner chamber which towered from the first floor, two stories below me, to the dome-like roof of the building, high above my head. The floor of this great circular hall was thronged with chieftains, warriors and women, and at one end was a great raised platform upon which squatted the most hideous beast I had ever put my eyes upon. He had all the cold, hard, cruel, terrible features of the green warriors, but accentuated and debased by the animal passions to which he had given himself over for many years. There was not a mark of dignity or pride upon his bestial countenance, while his enormous bulk spread itself out upon the platform where he squatted like some huge devil fish, his six limbs accentuating the similarity in a horrible and startling manner.

But the sight that froze me with apprehension was that of Dejah Thoris and Sola standing there before him, and the fiendish leer of him as he let his great protruding eyes gloat upon the lines of her beautiful figure. She was speaking, but I could not hear what she said, nor could I make out the low grumbling of his reply. She stood there erect before him, her head high held, and even at the distance I was from them I could read the scorn and disgust upon her face as she let her haughty glance rest without sign of fear upon him. She was indeed the proud daughter of a thousand jeddaks, every inch of her dear, precious little body; so small, so frail beside the towering warriors around her, but in her majesty dwarfing them into insignificance; she was the mightiest figure among them and I verily believe that they felt it.

Presently Tal Hajus made a sign that the chamber be cleared, and that the prisoners be left alone before him. Slowly the chieftains, the warriors and the women melted away into the shadows of the surrounding chambers, and Dejah Thoris and Sola stood alone before the jeddak of the Tharks.

One chieftain alone had hesitated before departing; I saw him standing in the shadows of a mighty column, his fingers nervously toying with the hilt of his great-sword and his cruel eyes bent in implacable hatred upon Tal Hajus. It was Tars Tarkas, and I could read his thoughts as they were an open book for the undisguised loathing upon his face. He was thinking of that other woman who, forty years ago, had stood before this beast, and could I have spoken a word into his ear at that moment the reign of Tal Hajus would have been over; but finally he also strode from the room, not knowing that he left his own daughter at the mercy of the creature he most loathed.

Tal Hajus arose, and I, half fearing, half anticipating his intentions, hurried to the winding runway which led to the floors below. No one was near to intercept me, and I reached the main floor of the chamber unobserved, taking my station in the shadow of the same column that Tars Tarkas had but just deserted. As I reached the floor Tal Hajus was speaking.

"Princess of Helium, I might wring a mighty ransom from your people would I but return you to them unharmed, but a thousand times rather would I watch that beautiful face writhe in the agony of torture; it shall be long drawn out, that I promise you; ten days of pleasure were all too short to show the love I harbor for your race. The terrors of your death shall haunt the slumbers of the red men through all the ages to come; they will shudder in the shadows of the night as their fathers tell them of the awful vengeance of the green men; of the power and might and hate and cruelty of Tal Hajus. But before the torture you shall be mine for one short hour, and word of that too shall go forth to Tardos Mors, Jeddak of Helium, your grandfather, that he may grovel upon the ground in the agony of his sorrow. Tomorrow the torture will commence; tonight thou art Tal Hajus'; come!"

He sprang down from the platform and grasped her roughly by the arm, but scarcely had he touched her than I leaped between them. My short-sword, sharp and gleaming was in my right hand; I could have plunged it into his putrid heart before he realized that I was upon him; but as I raised my arm to strike I thought of Tars Tarkas, and, with all my rage, with all my hatred, I could not rob him of that sweet moment for which he had lived and hoped all these long, weary years, and so, instead, I swung my good right fist full upon the point of his jaw. Without a sound he slipped to the floor as one dead.

In the same deathly silence I grasped Dejah Thoris by the hand, and motioning Sola to follow we sped noiselessly from the chamber and to the floor above. Unseen we reached a rear window and with the straps and leather of my trappings I lowered, first Sola and then Dejah Thoris to the ground below. Dropping lightly after them I drew them rapidly around the court in the shadows of the buildings, and thus we returned over the same course I had so recently followed from the distant boundary of the city.

We finally came upon my thoats in the courtyard where I had left them, and placing the trappings upon them we hastened through the building to the avenue beyond. Mounting, Sola upon one beast, and Dejah Thoris behind me upon the other, we rode from the city of Thark through the hills to the south.

Instead of circling back around the city to the northwest and toward the nearest waterway which lay so short a distance from us, we turned to the northeast and struck out upon the mossy waste across which, for two hundred dangerous and weary miles, lay another main artery leading to Helium.

No word was spoken until we had left the city far behind, but I could hear the quiet sobbing of Dejah Thoris as she clung to me with her dear head resting against my shoulder.

"If we make it, my chieftain, the debt of Helium will be a mighty one; greater than she can ever pay you; and should we not make it," she continued, "the debt is no less, though Helium will never know, for you have saved the last of our line from worse than death."

I did not answer, but instead reached to my side and pressed the little fingers of her I loved where they clung to me for support, and then, in unbroken silence, we sped over the yellow, moonlit moss; each of us occupied with his own thoughts. For my part I could not be other than joyful had I tried, with Dejah Thoris' warm body pressed close to mine, and with all our unpassed danger my heart was singing as gaily as though we were already entering the gates of Helium.

Our earlier plans had been so sadly upset that we now found ourselves without food or drink, and I alone was armed. We therefore urged our beasts to a speed that must tell on them sorely before we could hope to sight the ending of the first stage of our journey.

We rode all night and all the following day with only a few short rests. On the second night both we and our animals were completely fagged, and so we lay down upon the moss and slept for some five or six hours, taking up the journey once more before daylight. All the following day we rode, and when, late in the afternoon we had sighted no distant trees, the mark of the great waterways throughout all Barsoom, the terrible truth flashed upon us – we were lost.

Evidently we had circled, but which way it was difficult to say, nor did it seem possible with the sun to guide us by day and the moons and stars by night. At any rate no waterway was in sight, and the entire party was almost ready to drop from hunger, thirst and fatigue. Far ahead of us and a trifle to the right we could distinguish the outlines of low mountains. These we decided to attempt to reach in the hope that from some ridge we might discern the missing waterway. Night fell upon us before we reached our goal, and, almost fainting from weariness and weakness, we lay down and slept.

I was awakened early in the morning by some huge body pressing close to mine, and opening my eyes with a start I beheld my blessed old Woola snuggling close to me; the faithful brute had followed us across that trackless waste to share our fate, whatever it might be. Putting my arms about his neck I pressed my cheek close to his, nor am I ashamed that I did it, nor of the tears that came to my eyes as I thought of his love for me. Shortly after this Dejah Thoris and Sola awakened, and it was decided that we push on at once in an effort to gain the hills.

We had gone scarcely a mile when I noticed that my thoat was commencing to stumble and stagger in a most pitiful manner, although we had not attempted to force them out of a walk since about noon of the preceding day. Suddenly he lurched wildly to one side and pitched violently to the ground. Dejah Thoris and I were thrown clear of him and fell upon the soft moss with scarcely a jar; but the poor beast was in a pitiable condition, not even being able to rise, although relieved of our weight. Sola told me that the coolness of the night, when it fell, together with the rest would doubtless revive him, and so I decided not to kill him, as was my first intention, as I had thought it cruel to leave him alone there to die of hunger and thirst. Relieving him of his trappings, which I flung down beside him, we left the poor fellow to his fate, and pushed on with the one thoat as best we could. Sola and I walked, making Dejah Thoris ride, much against her will. In this way we had progressed to within about a mile of the hills we were endeavoring to reach when Dejah Thoris, from her point of vantage upon the thoat, cried out that she saw a great party of mounted men filing down from a pass in the hills several miles away. Sola and I both looked in the direction she indicated, and there, plainly discernible, were several hundred mounted warriors. They seemed to be headed in a southwesterly direction, which would take them away from us.

They doubtless were Thark warriors who had been sent out to capture us, and we breathed a great sigh of relief that they were traveling in the opposite direction. Quickly lifting Dejah Thoris from the thoat, I commanded the animal to lie down and we three did the same, presenting as small an object as possible for fear of attracting the attention of the warriors toward us.

We could see them as they filed out of the pass, just for an instant, before they were lost to view behind a friendly ridge; to us a most providential ridge; since, had they been in view for any great length of time, they scarcely could have failed to discover us. As what proved to be the last warrior came into view from the pass, he halted and, to our consternation, threw his small but powerful fieldglass to his eye and scanned the sea bottom in all directions. Evidently he was a chieftain, for in certain marching formations among the green men a chieftain brings up the extreme rear of the column. As his glass swung toward us our hearts stopped in our breasts, and I could feel the cold sweat start from every pore in my body.

Presently it swung full upon us and – stopped. The tension on our nerves was near the breaking point, and I doubt if any of us breathed for the few moments he held us covered by his glass; and then he lowered it and we could see him shout a command to the warriors who had passed from our sight behind the ridge. He did not wait for them to join him, however, instead he wheeled his thoat and came tearing madly in our direction.

There was but one slight chance and that we must take quickly. Raising my strange Martian rifle to my shoulder I sighted and touched the button which controlled the trigger; there was a sharp explosion as the missile reached its goal, and the charging chieftain pitched backward from his flying mount.

Springing to my feet I urged the thoat to rise, and directed Sola to take Dejah Thoris with her upon him and make a mighty effort to reach the hills before the green warriors were upon us. I knew that in the ravines and gullies they might find a temporary hiding place, and even though they died there of hunger and thirst it would be better so than that they fell into the hands of the Tharks. Forcing my two revolvers upon them as a slight means of protection, and, as a last resort, as an escape for themselves from the horrid death which recapture would surely mean, I lifted Dejah Thoris in my arms and placed her upon the thoat behind Sola, who had already mounted at my command.

"Good-bye, my princess," I whispered, "we may meet in Helium yet. I have escaped from worse plights than this," and I tried to smile as I lied.

"What," she cried, "are you not coming with us?"

"How may I, Dejah Thoris? Someone must hold these fellows off for a while, and I can better escape them alone than could the three of us together."

She sprang quickly from the thoat and, throwing her dear arms about my neck, turned to Sola, saying with quiet dignity: "Fly, Sola! Dejah Thoris remains to die with the man she loves."

Those words are engraved upon my heart. Ah, gladly would I give up my life a thousand times could I only hear them once again; but I could not then give even a second to the rapture of her sweet embrace, and pressing my lips to hers for the first time, I picked her up bodily and tossed her to her seat behind Sola again, commanding the latter in peremptory tones to hold her there by force, and then, slapping the thoat upon the flank, I saw them borne away; Dejah Thoris struggling to the last to free herself from Sola's grasp.

Turning, I beheld the green warriors mounting the ridge and looking for their chieftain. In a moment they saw him, and then me; but scarcely had they discovered me than I commenced firing, lying flat upon my belly in the moss. I had an even hundred rounds in the magazine of my rifle, and another hundred in the belt at my back, and I kept up a continuous stream of fire until I saw all of the warriors who had been first to return from behind the ridge either dead or scurrying to cover.

My respite was short-lived however, for soon the entire party, numbering some thousand men, came charging into view, racing madly toward me. I fired until my rifle was empty and they were almost upon me, and then a glance showing me that Dejah Thoris and Sola had disappeared among the hills, I sprang up, throwing down my useless gun, and started away in the direction opposite to that taken by Sola and her charge.

If ever Martians had an exhibition of jumping, it was granted those astonished warriors on that day long years ago, but while it led them away from Dejah Thoris it did not distract their attention from endeavoring to capture me.

They raced wildly after me until, finally, my foot struck a projecting piece of quartz, and down I went sprawling upon the moss. As I looked up they were upon me, and although I drew my long-sword in an attempt to sell my life as dearly as possible, it was soon over. I reeled beneath their blows which fell upon me in perfect torrents; my head swam; all was black, and I went down beneath them to oblivion.

CHAPTER EIGHTEEN

Chained in Warhoon

IT MUST HAVE BEEN several hours before I regained consciousness and I well remember the feeling of surprise which swept over me as I realized that I was not dead.

I was lying among a pile of sleeping silks and furs in the corner of a small room in which were several green warriors, and bending over me was an ancient and ugly female.

As I opened my eyes she turned to one of the warriors, saying, "He will live, O Jed."

"'Tis well," replied the one so addressed, rising and approaching my couch, "he should render rare sport for the great games."

And now as my eyes fell upon him, I saw that he was no Thark, for his ornaments and metal were not of that horde. He was a huge fellow, terribly scarred about the face and chest, and with one broken tusk and a missing ear. Strapped on either breast were human skulls and depending from these a number of dried human hands.

His reference to the great games of which I had heard so much while among the Tharks convinced me that I had but jumped from purgatory into gehenna.

After a few more words with the female, during which she assured him that I was now fully fit to travel, the jed ordered that we mount and ride after the main column.

I was strapped securely to as wild and unmanageable a thoat as I had ever seen, and, with a mounted warrior on either side to prevent the beast from bolting, we rode forth at a furious pace in pursuit of the column. My wounds gave me but little pain, so wonderfully and rapidly had the applications and injections of the female exercised their therapeutic powers, and so deftly had she bound and plastered the injuries.

Just before dark we reached the main body of troops shortly after they had made camp for the night. I was immediately taken before the leader, who proved to be the jeddak of the hordes of Warhoon.

Like the jed who had brought me, he was frightfully scarred, and also decorated with the breastplate of human skulls and dried dead hands which seemed to mark all the greater warriors among the Warhoons, as well as to indicate their awful ferocity, which greatly transcends even that of the Tharks.

The jeddak, Bar Comas, who was comparatively young, was the object of the fierce and jealous hatred of his old lieutenant, Dak Kova, the jed who had captured me, and I could not but note the almost studied efforts which the latter made to affront his superior.

He entirely omitted the usual formal salutation as we entered the presence of the jeddak, and as he pushed me roughly before the ruler he exclaimed in a loud and menacing voice.

"I have brought a strange creature wearing the metal of a Thark whom it is my pleasure to have battle with a wild thoat at the great games."

"He will die as Bar Comas, your jeddak, sees fit, if at all," replied the young ruler, with emphasis and dignity.

"If at all?" roared Dak Kova. "By the dead hands at my throat but he shall die, Bar Comas. No maudlin weakness on your part shall save him. O, would that Warhoon were ruled by a real jeddak rather than by a water-hearted weakling from whom even old Dak Kova could tear the metal with his bare hands!"

Bar Comas eyed the defiant and insubordinate chieftain for an instant, his expression one of haughty, fearless contempt and hate, and then without drawing a weapon and without uttering a word he hurled himself at the throat of his defamer.

I never before had seen two green Martian warriors battle with nature's weapons and the exhibition of animal ferocity which ensued was as fearful a thing as the most disordered imagination could picture. They tore at each others' eyes and ears with their hands and with their gleaming tusks repeatedly slashed and gored until both were cut fairly to ribbons from head to foot.

Bar Comas had much the better of the battle as he was stronger, quicker and more intelligent. It soon seemed that the encounter was done saving only the final death thrust when Bar Comas slipped in breaking away from a clinch. It was the one little opening that Dak Kova needed, and hurling himself at the body of his adversary he buried his single mighty tusk in Bar Comas' groin and with a last powerful effort ripped the young jeddak wide open the full length of his body, the great tusk finally wedging in the bones of Bar Comas' jaw. Victor and vanquished rolled limp and lifeless upon the moss, a huge mass of torn and bloody flesh.

Bar Comas was stone dead, and only the most herculean efforts on the part of Dak Kova's females saved him from the fate he deserved. Three days later he walked without assistance to the body of Bar Comas which, by custom, had not been moved from where it fell, and placing his foot upon the neck of his erstwhile ruler he assumed the title of Jeddak of Warhoon.

The dead jeddak's hands and head were removed to be added to the ornaments of his conqueror, and then his women cremated what remained, amid wild and terrible laughter.

The injuries to Dak Kova had delayed the march so greatly that it was decided to give up the expedition, which was a raid upon a small Thark community in retaliation for the destruction of the incubator, until after the great games, and the entire body of warriors, ten thousand in number, turned back toward Warhoon.

My introduction to these cruel and bloodthirsty people was but an index to the scenes I witnessed almost daily while with them. They are a smaller horde than the Tharks but much more ferocious. Not a day passed but that some members of the various Warhoon communities met in deadly combat. I have seen as high as eight mortal duels within a single day.

We reached the city of Warhoon after some three days march and I was immediately cast into a dungeon and heavily chained to the floor and walls. Food was brought me at intervals but owing to the utter darkness of the place I do not know whether I lay there days, or weeks, or months. It was the most horrible experience of all my life and that my mind did not give way to the terrors of that inky blackness has been a wonder to me ever since. The place was filled with creeping, crawling things; cold, sinuous bodies passed over me when I lay down, and in the darkness I occasionally caught glimpses of gleaming, fiery eyes, fixed in horrible intentness upon me. No sound reached me from the world above and no word would my jailer vouchsafe when my food was brought to me, although I at first bombarded him with questions.

Finally all the hatred and maniacal loathing for these awful creatures who had placed me in this horrible place was centered by my tottering reason upon this single emissary who represented to me the entire horde of Warhoons.

I had noticed that he always advanced with his dim torch to where he could place the food within my reach and as he stooped to place it upon the floor his head was about on a level with my breast. So, with the cunning of a madman, I backed into the far corner of my cell when next I heard him approaching and gathering a little slack of the great chain which held me in my hand I waited his coming, crouching like some beast of prey. As he stooped to place my food upon the ground I swung the chain above my head and crashed the links with all my strength upon his skull. Without a sound he slipped to the floor, stone dead.

Laughing and chattering like the idiot I was fast becoming I fell upon his prostrate form my fingers feeling for his dead throat. Presently they came in contact with a small chain at the end of which dangled a number of keys. The touch of my fingers on these keys brought back my reason with the suddenness of thought. No longer was I a jibbering idiot, but a sane, reasoning man with the means of escape within my very hands.

As I was groping to remove the chain from about my victim's neck I glanced up into the darkness to see six pairs of gleaming eyes fixed, unwinking, upon me. Slowly they approached and slowly I shrank back from the awful horror of them. Back into my corner I crouched holding my hands palms out, before me, and stealthily on came the awful eyes until they reached the dead body at my feet. Then slowly they retreated but this time with a strange grating sound and finally they disappeared in some black and distant recess of my dungeon.

CHAPTER NINETEEN

Battling in the Arena

Slowly I regained my composure and finally essayed again to attempt to remove the keys from the dead body of my former jailer. But as I reached out into the darkness to locate it I found to my horror that it was gone. Then the truth flashed on me; the owners of those gleaming eyes had dragged my prize away from me to be devoured in their neighboring lair; as they had been waiting for days, for weeks, for months, through all this awful eternity of my imprisonment to drag my dead carcass to their feast.

For two days no food was brought me, but then a new messenger appeared and my incarceration went on as before, but not again did I allow my reason to be submerged by the horror of my position.

Shortly after this episode another prisoner was brought in and chained near me. By the dim torch light I saw that he was a red Martian and I could scarcely await the departure of his guards to address him. As their retreating footsteps died away in the distance, I called out softly the Martian word of greeting, kaor.

"Who are you who speaks out of the darkness?" he answered

"John Carter, a friend of the red men of Helium."

"I am of Helium," he said, "but I do not recall your name."

And then I told him my story as I have written it here, omitting only any reference to my love for Dejah Thoris. He was much excited by the news of Helium's princess and seemed quite positive that she and Sola could easily have reached a point of safety from where they left me. He said that he knew the place well because the defile through which the Warhoon warriors had passed when they discovered us was the only one ever used by them when marching to the south.

"Dejah Thoris and Sola entered the hills not five miles from a great waterway and are now probably quite safe," he assured me.

My fellow prisoner was Kantos Kan, a padwar (lieutenant) in the navy of Helium. He had been a member of the ill-fated expedition which had fallen into the hands of the Tharks at the time of Dejah Thoris' capture, and he briefly related the events which followed the defeat of the battleships.

Badly injured and only partially manned they had limped slowly toward Helium, but while passing near the city of Zodanga, the capital of Helium's hereditary enemies among the red men of Barsoom, they had been attacked by a great body of war vessels and all but the craft to which Kantos Kan belonged were either destroyed or captured. His vessel was chased for days by three of the Zodangan war ships but finally escaped during the darkness of a moonless night.

Thirty days after the capture of Dejah Thoris, or about the time of our coming to Thark, his vessel had reached Helium with about ten survivors of the original crew of seven hundred officers and men. Immediately seven great fleets, each of one hundred mighty war ships, had been dispatched to search for Dejah Thoris, and from these vessels two thousand smaller craft had been kept out continuously in futile search for the missing princess.

Two green Martian communities had been wiped off the face of Barsoom by the avenging fleets, but no trace of Dejah Thoris had been found. They had been searching among the northern hordes, and only within the past few days had they extended their quest to the south.

Kantos Kan had been detailed to one of the small one-man fliers and had had the misfortune to be discovered by the Warhoons while exploring their city. The bravery and daring of the man won my greatest respect and admiration. Alone he had landed at the city's boundary and on foot had penetrated to the buildings surrounding the plaza. For two days and nights he had explored their quarters and their dungeons in search of his beloved princess only to fall into the hands of a party of Warhoons as he was about to leave, after assuring himself that Dejah Thoris was not a captive there.

During the period of our incarceration Kantos Kan and I became well acquainted, and formed a warm personal friendship. A few days only elapsed, however, before we were dragged forth from our dungeon for the great games. We were conducted early one morning to an enormous amphitheater, which instead of having been built upon the surface of the ground was excavated below the surface. It had partially filled with debris so that how large it had originally been was difficult to say. In its present condition it held the entire twenty thousand Warhoons of the assembled hordes.

The arena was immense but extremely uneven and unkempt. Around it the Warhoons had piled building stone from some of the ruined edifices of the ancient city to prevent the animals and the captives from escaping into the audience, and at each end had been constructed cages to hold them until their turns came to meet some horrible death upon the arena.

Kantos Kan and I were confined together in one of the cages. In the others were wild calots, thoats, mad zitidars, green warriors, and women of other hordes, and many strange and ferocious wild beasts of Barsoom which I had never before seen. The din of their roaring, growling and squealing was deafening and the formidable appearance of any one of them was enough to make the stoutest heart feel grave forebodings.

Kantos Kan explained to me that at the end of the day one of these prisoners would gain freedom and the others would lie dead about the arena. The winners in the various contests of the day would be pitted against each other until only two remained alive; the victor in the last encounter being set free, whether animal or man. The following morning the cages would be filled with a new consignment of victims, and so on throughout the ten days of the games.

Shortly after we had been caged the amphitheater began to fill and within an hour every available part of the seating space was occupied. Dak Kova, with his jeds and chieftains, sat at the center of one side of the arena upon a large raised platform.

At a signal from Dak Kova the doors of two cages were thrown open and a dozen green Martian females were driven to the center of the arena. Each was given a dagger and then, at the far end, a pack of twelve calots, or wild dogs were loosed upon them.

As the brutes, growling and foaming, rushed upon the almost defenseless women I turned my head that I might not see the horrid sight. The yells and laughter of the green horde bore witness to the excellent quality of the sport and when I turned back to the arena, as Kantos Kan told me it was over, I saw three victorious calots, snarling and growling over the bodies of their prey. The women had given a good account of themselves.

Next a mad zitidar was loosed among the remaining dogs, and so it went throughout the long, hot, horrible day.

During the day I was pitted against first men and then beasts, but as I was armed with a long-sword and always outclassed my adversary in agility and generally in strength as well, it proved but child's play to me. Time and time again I won the applause of the bloodthirsty multitude, and toward the end there were cries that I be taken from the arena and be made a member of the hordes of Warhoon.

Finally there were but three of us left, a great green warrior of some far northern horde, Kantos Kan, and myself.

The other two were to battle and then I to fight the conqueror for the liberty which was accorded the final winner.

Kantos Kan had fought several times during the day and like myself had always proven victorious, but occasionally by the smallest of margins, especially when pitted against the green warriors. I had little hope that he could best his giant adversary who had mowed down all before him during the day. The fellow towered nearly sixteen feet in height, while Kantos Kan was some inches under six feet. As they advanced to meet one another I saw for the first time a trick of Martian swordsmanship which centered Kantos Kan's every hope of victory and life on one cast of the dice, for, as he came to within about twenty feet of the huge fellow he threw his sword arm far behind him over his shoulder and with a mighty sweep hurled his weapon point foremost at the green warrior. It flew true as an arrow and piercing the poor devil's heart laid him dead upon the arena.

Kantos Kan and I were now pitted against each other but as we approached to the encounter I whispered to him to prolong the battle until nearly dark in the hope that we might find some means of escape. The horde evidently guessed that we had no hearts to fight each other and so they howled in rage as neither of us placed a fatal thrust. Just as I saw the sudden coming of dark I whispered to Kantos Kan to thrust his sword between my left arm and my body. As he did so I staggered back clasping the sword tightly with my arm and thus fell to the ground with his weapon apparently protruding from my chest. Kantos Kan perceived my coup and stepping quickly to my side he placed his foot upon my neck and withdrawing his sword from my body gave me the final death blow through the neck which is supposed to sever the jugular vein, but in this instance the cold blade slipped harmlessly into the sand of the arena. In the darkness which had now fallen none could tell but that he had really finished me. I whispered to him to go and claim his freedom and then look for me in the hills east of the city, and so he left me.

When the amphitheater had cleared I crept stealthily to the top and as the great excavation lay far from the plaza and in an untenanted portion of the great dead city I had little trouble in reaching the hills beyond.

CHAPTER TWENTY

In the Atmosphere Factory

FOR TWO DAYS I waited there for Kantos Kan, but as he did not come I started off on foot in a northwesterly direction toward a point where he had told me lay the nearest waterway. My only food consisted of vegetable milk from the plants which gave so bounteously of this priceless fluid.

Through two long weeks I wandered, stumbling through the nights guided only by the stars and hiding during the days behind some protruding rock or among the occasional hills I traversed. Several times I was attacked by wild beasts; strange, uncouth monstrosities that leaped upon me in the dark, so that I had ever to grasp my long-sword in my hand that I might be ready for them. Usually my strange, newly acquired telepathic power warned me in ample time, but once I was down with vicious fangs at my jugular and a hairy face pressed close to mine before I knew that I was even threatened.

What manner of thing was upon me I did not know, but that it was large and heavy and many-legged I could feel. My hands were at its throat before the fangs had a chance to bury themselves in my neck, and slowly I forced the hairy face from me and closed my fingers, vise-like, upon its windpipe.

Without sound we lay there, the beast exerting every effort to reach me with those awful fangs, and I straining to maintain my grip and choke the life from it as I kept it from my throat. Slowly my arms gave to the unequal struggle, and inch by inch the burning eyes and gleaming tusks of my antagonist crept toward me, until, as the hairy face touched mine again, I realized that all was over. And then a living mass of destruction sprang from the surrounding darkness full upon the creature that held me pinioned to the ground. The two rolled growling upon the moss, tearing and rending one another in a frightful manner, but it was soon over and my preserver stood with lowered head above the throat of the dead thing which would have killed me.

The nearer moon, hurtling suddenly above the horizon and lighting up the Barsoomian scene, showed me that my preserver was Woola, but from whence he had come, or how found me, I was at a loss to know. That I was glad of his companionship it is needless to say, but my pleasure at seeing him was tempered by anxiety as to the reason of his leaving Dejah Thoris. Only her death I felt sure, could account for his absence from her, so faithful I knew him to be to my commands.

By the light of the now brilliant moons I saw that he was but a shadow of his former self, and as he turned from my caress and commenced greedily to devour the dead carcass at my feet I realized that the poor fellow was more than half starved. I, myself, was in but little better plight but I could not bring myself to eat the uncooked flesh and I had no means of making a fire. When Woola had finished his meal I again took up my weary and seemingly endless wandering in quest of the elusive waterway.

At daybreak of the fifteenth day of my search I was overjoyed to see the high trees that denoted the object of my search. About noon I dragged myself wearily to the portals of a huge building which covered perhaps four square miles and towered two hundred feet in the air. It showed no aperture in the mighty walls other than the tiny door at which I sank exhausted, nor was there any sign of life about it.

I could find no bell or other method of making my presence known to the inmates of the place, unless a small round role in the wall near the door was for that purpose. It was of about the bigness of a lead pencil and thinking that it might be in the nature of a speaking tube I put my mouth to it and was about to call into it when a voice issued from it asking me whom I might be, where from, and the nature of my errand.

I explained that I had escaped from the Warhoons and was dying of starvation and exhaustion.

"You wear the metal of a green warrior and are followed by a calot, yet you are of the figure of a red man. In color you are neither green nor red. In the name of the ninth day, what manner of creature are you?"

"I am a friend of the red men of Barsoom and I am starving. In the name of humanity open to us," I replied.

Presently the door commenced to recede before me until it had sunk into the wall fifty feet, then it stopped and slid easily to the left, exposing a short, narrow corridor of concrete, at the further end of which was another door, similar in every respect to the one I had just passed. No one was in sight, yet immediately we passed the first door it slid gently into place behind us and receded rapidly to its original position in the front wall of the building. As the door had slipped aside I had noted its great thickness, fully twenty feet, and as it reached its place once more after closing behind us, great cylinders of steel had dropped from the ceiling behind it and fitted their lower ends into apertures countersunk in the floor.

A second and third door receded before me and slipped to one side as the first, before I reached a large inner chamber where I found food and drink set out upon a great stone table. A voice directed me to satisfy my hunger and to feed my calot, and while I was thus engaged my invisible host put me through a severe and searching cross-examination.

"Your statements are most remarkable," said the voice, on concluding its questioning, "but you are evidently speaking the truth, and it is equally evident that you are not of Barsoom. I can tell that by the conformation of your brain and the strange location of your internal organs and the shape and size of your heart."

"Can you see through me?" I exclaimed.

"Yes, I can see all but your thoughts, and were you a Barsoomian I could read those."

Then a door opened at the far side of the chamber and a strange, dried up, little mummy of a man came toward me. He wore but a single article of clothing or adornment, a small collar of gold from which depended upon his chest a great ornament as large as a dinner plate set solid with huge diamonds, except for the exact center which was occupied by a strange stone, an inch in diameter, that scintillated nine different and distinct rays; the seven colors of our earthly prism and two beautiful rays which, to me, were new and nameless. I cannot describe them any more than you could describe red to a blind man. I only know that they were beautiful in the extreme.

The old man sat and talked with me for hours, and the strangest part of our intercourse was that I could read his every thought while he could not fathom an iota from my mind unless I spoke.

I did not apprise him of my ability to sense his mental operations, and thus I learned a great deal which proved of immense value to me later and which I would never have known had he suspected my strange power, for the Martians have such perfect control of their mental machinery that they are able to direct their thoughts with absolute precision.

The building in which I found myself contained the machinery which produces that artificial atmosphere which sustains life on Mars. The secret of the entire process hinges on the use of the ninth ray, one of the beautiful scintillations which I had noted emanating from the great stone in my host's diadem.

This ray is separated from the other rays of the sun by means of finely adjusted instruments placed upon the roof of the huge build-ing, three-quarters of which is used for reservoirs in which the ninth ray is stored. This product is then treated electrically, or rather certain proportions of refined electric vibrations are incorporated with it, and the result is then pumped to the five principal air centers of the planet where, as it is released, contact with the ether of space transforms it into atmosphere.

There is always sufficient reserve of the ninth ray stored in the great building to maintain the present Martian atmosphere for a thousand years, and the only fear, as my new friend told me, was that some ac-cident might befall the pumping apparatus.

He led me to an inner chamber where I beheld a battery of twenty radium pumps any one of which was equal to the task of furnishing all Mars with the atmosphere compound. For eight hundred years, he told me, he had watched these pumps which are used alternately a day each at a stretch, or a little over twenty-four and one-half Earth hours. He has one assistant who divides the watch with him. Half a Martian year, about three hundred and forty-four of our days, each of these men spend alone in this huge, isolated plant.

Every red Martian is taught during earliest childhood the principles of the manufacture of atmosphere, but only two at one time ever hold the secret of ingress to the great building, which, built as it is with walls a hundred and fifty feet thick, is absolutely unassailable, even the roof being guarded from assault by air craft by a glass covering five feet thick.

The only fear they entertain of attack is from the green Martians or some demented red man, as all Barsoomians realize that the very existence of every form of life of Mars is dependent upon the uninterrupted working of this plant.

One curious fact I discovered as I watched his thoughts was that the outer doors are manipulated by telepathic means. The locks are so finely adjusted that the doors are released by the action of a certain combination of thought waves. To experiment with my new-found toy I thought to surprise him into revealing this combination and so I asked him in a casual manner how he had managed to unlock the massive doors for me from the inner chambers of the building. As quick as a flash there leaped to his mind nine Martian sounds, but as quickly faded as he answered that this was a secret he must not divulge.

From then on his manner toward me changed as though he feared that he had been surprised into divulging his great secret, and I read suspicion and fear in his looks and thoughts, though his words were still fair.

Before I retired for the night he promised to give me a letter to a nearby agricultural officer who would help me on my way to Zodanga, which he said, was the nearest Martian city.

"But be sure that you do not let them know you are bound for Helium as they are at war with that country. My assistant and I are of no country, we belong to all Barsoom and this talisman which we wear protects us in all lands, even among the green men – though we do not trust ourselves to their hands if we can avoid it," he added.

"And so good-night, my friend," he continued, "may you have a long and restful sleep – yes, a long sleep."

And though he smiled pleasantly I saw in his thoughts the wish that he had never admitted me, and then a picture of him standing over me in the night, and the swift thrust of a long dagger and the half formed words, "I am sorry, but it is for the best good of Barsoom."

As he closed the door of my chamber behind him his thoughts were cut off from me as was the sight of him, which seemed strange to me in my little knowledge of thought transference.

What was I to do? How could I escape through these mighty walls? Easily could I kill him now that I was warned, but once he was dead I could no more escape, and with the stopping of the machinery of the great plant I should die with all the other inhabitants of the planet – all, even Dejah Thoris were she not already dead. For the others I did not give the snap of my finger, but the thought of Dejah Thoris drove from my mind all desire to kill my mistaken host.

Cautiously I opened the door of my apartment and, followed by Woola, sought the inner of the great doors. A wild scheme had come to me; I would attempt to force the great locks by the nine thought waves I had read in my host's mind.

Creeping stealthily through corridor after corridor and down winding runways which turned hither and thither I finally reached the great hall in which I had broken my long fast that morning. Nowhere had I seen my host, nor did I know where he kept himself by night.

I was on the point of stepping boldly out into the room when a slight noise behind me warned me back into the shadows of a recess in the corridor. Dragging Woola after me I crouched low in the darkness.

Presently the old man passed close by me, and as he entered the dimly lighted chamber which I had been about to pass through I saw that he held a long thin dagger in his hand and that he was sharpening it upon a stone. In his mind was the decision to inspect the radium pumps, which would take about thirty minutes, and then return to my bed chamber and finish me.

As he passed through the great hall and disappeared down the runway which led to the pump-room, I stole stealthily from my hiding place and crossed to the great door, the inner of the three which stood between me and liberty.

Concentrating my mind upon the massive lock I hurled the nine thought waves against it. In breathless expectancy I waited, when finally the great door moved softly toward me and slid quietly to one side. One after the other the remaining mighty portals opened at my command and Woola and I stepped forth into the darkness, free, but little better off than we had been before, other than that we had full stomachs.

Hastening away from the shadows of the formidable pile I made for the first crossroad, intending to strike the central turnpike as quickly as possible. This I reached about morning and entering the first enclosure I came to I searched for some evidences of a habitation.

There were low rambling buildings of concrete barred with heavy impassable doors, and no amount of hammering and hallooing brought any response. Weary and exhausted from sleeplessness I threw myself upon the ground commanding Woola to stand guard.

Some time later I was awakened by his frightful growlings and opened my eyes to see three red Martians standing a short distance from us and covering me with their rifles.

"I am unarmed and no enemy," I hastened to explain. "I have been a prisoner among the green men and am on my way to Zodanga. All I ask is food and rest for myself and my calot and the proper directions for reaching my destination."

They lowered their rifles and advanced pleasantly toward me placing their right hands upon my left shoulder, after the manner of their custom of salute, and asking me many questions about myself and my wanderings. They then took me to the house of one of them which was only a short distance away.

The buildings I had been hammering at in the early morning were occupied only by stock and farm produce, the house proper standing among a grove of enormous trees, and, like all red-Martian homes, had been raised at night some forty or fifty feet from the ground on a large round metal shaft which slid up or down within a sleeve sunk in the ground, and was operated by a tiny radium engine in the entrance hall of the building. Instead of bothering with bolts and bars for their dwellings, the red Martians simply run them up out of harm's way during the night. They also have private means for lowering or raising them from the ground without if they wish to go away and leave them.

These brothers, with their wives and children, occupied three similar houses on this farm. They did no work themselves, being government officers in charge. The labor was performed by convicts, prisoners of war, delinquent debtors and confirmed bachelors who were too poor to pay the high celibate tax which all red-Martian governments impose.

They were the personification of cordiality and hospitality and I spent several days with them, resting and recuperating from my long and arduous experiences.

When they had heard my story – I omitted all reference to Dejah Thoris and the old man of the atmosphere plant – they advised me to color my body to more nearly resemble their own race and then attempt to find employment in Zodanga, either in the army or the navy.

"The chances are small that your tale will be believed until after you have proven your trustworthiness and won friends among the higher nobles of the court. This you can most easily do through military service, as we are a warlike people on Barsoom," explained one of them, "and save our richest favors for the fighting man."

When I was ready to depart they furnished me with a small domestic bull thoat, such as is used for saddle purposes by all red Martians. The animal is about the size of a horse and quite gentle, but in color and shape an exact replica of his huge and fierce cousin of the wilds.

The brothers had supplied me with a reddish oil with which I anointed my entire body and one of them cut my hair, which had grown quite long, in the prevailing fashion of the time, square at the back and banged in front, so that I could have passed anywhere upon Barsoom as a full-fledged red Martian. My metal and ornaments were also renewed in the style of a Zodangan gentleman, attached to the house of Ptor, which was the family name of my benefactors.

They filled a little sack at my side with Zodangan money. The medium of exchange upon Mars is not dissimilar from our own except that the coins are oval. Paper money is issued by individuals as they require it and redeemed twice yearly. If a man issues more than he can redeem, the government pays his creditors in full and the debtor works out the amount upon the farms or in mines, which are all owned by the government. This suits everybody except the debtor as it has been a difficult thing to obtain sufficient voluntary labor to work the great isolated farm lands of Mars, stretching as they do like narrow ribbons from pole to pole, through wild stretches peopled by wild animals and wilder men.

When I mentioned my inability to repay them for their kindness to me they assured me that I would have ample opportunity if I lived long upon Barsoom, and bidding me farewell they watched me until I was out of sight upon the broad white turnpike.

CHAPTER TWENTY ONE

An Air Scout for Zodanga

As I proceeded on my journey toward Zodanga many strange and interesting sights arrested my attention, and at the several farm houses where I stopped I learned a number of new and instructive things concerning the methods and manners of Barsoom.

The water which supplies the farms of Mars is collected in immense underground reservoirs at either pole from the melting ice caps, and pumped through long conduits to the various populated centers. Along either side of these conduits, and extending their entire length, lie the cultivated districts. These are divided into tracts of about the same size, each tract being under the supervision of one or more government officers.

Instead of flooding the surface of the fields, and thus wasting immense quantities of water by evaporation, the precious liquid is carried underground through a vast network of small pipes directly to the roots of the vegetation. The crops upon Mars are always uniform, for there are no droughts, no rains, no high winds, and no insects, or destroying birds.

On this trip I tasted the first meat I had eaten since leaving Earth – large, juicy steaks and chops from the well-fed domestic animals of the farms. Also I enjoyed luscious fruits and vegetables, but not a single article of food which was exactly similar to anything on Earth. Every plant and flower and vegetable and animal has been so refined by ages of careful, scientific cultivation and breeding that the like of them on Earth dwindled into pale, gray, characterless nothingness by comparison.

At a second stop I met some highly cultivated people of the noble class and while in conversation we chanced to speak of Helium. One of the older men had been there on a diplomatic mission several years before and spoke with regret of the conditions which seemed destined ever to keep these two countries at war.

"Helium," he said, "rightly boasts the most beautiful women of Barsoom, and of all her treasures the wondrous daughter of Mors Kajak, Dejah Thoris, is the most exquisite flower.

"Why," he added, "the people really worship the ground she walks upon and since her loss on that ill-starred expedition all Helium has been draped in mourning.

"That our ruler should have attacked the disabled fleet as it was returning to Helium was but another of his awful blunders which I fear will sooner or later compel Zodanga to elevate a wiser man to his place."

"Even now, though our victorious armies are surrounding Helium, the people of Zodanga are voicing their displeasure, for the war is not a popular one, since it is not based on right or justice. Our forces took advantage of the absence of the principal fleet of Helium on their search for the princess, and so we have been able easily to reduce the city to a sorry plight. It is said she will fall within the next few passages of the further moon."

"And what, think you, may have been the fate of the princess, Dejah Thoris?" I asked as casually as possible.

"She is dead," he answered. "This much was learned from a green warrior recently captured by our forces in the south. She escaped from the hordes of Thark with a strange creature of another world, only to fall into the hands of the Warhoons. Their thoats were found wandering upon the sea bottom and evidences of a bloody conflict were discovered nearby."

While this information was in no way reassuring, neither was it at all conclusive proof of the death of Dejah Thoris, and so I determined to make every effort possible to reach Helium as quickly as I could and carry to Tardos Mors such news of his granddaughter's possible whereabouts as lay in my power.

Ten days after leaving the three Ptor brothers I arrived at Zodanga. From the moment that I had come in contact with the red inhabitants of Mars I had noticed that Woola drew a great amount of unwelcome attention to me, since the huge brute belonged to a species which is never domesticated by the red men. Were one to stroll down Broadway with a Numidian lion at his heels the effect would be somewhat similar to that which I should have produced had I entered Zodanga with Woola.

The very thought of parting with the faithful fellow caused me so great regret and genuine sorrow that I put it off until just before we arrived at the city's gates; but then, finally, it became imperative that we separate. Had nothing further than my own safety or pleasure been at stake no argument could have prevailed upon me to turn away the one creature upon Barsoom that had never failed in a demonstration of affection and loyalty; but as I would willingly have offered my life in the service of her in search of whom I was about to challenge the unknown dangers of this, to me, mysterious city, I could not permit even Woola's life to threaten the success of my venture, much less his momentary happiness, for I doubted not he soon would forget me. And so I bade the poor beast an affectionate farewell, promising him, however, that if I came through my adventure in safety that in some way I should find the means to search him out.

He seemed to understand me fully, and when I pointed back in the direction of Thark he turned sorrowfully away, nor could I bear to watch him go; but resolutely set my face toward Zodanga and with a touch of heartsickness approached her frowning walls.

The letter I bore from them gained me immediate entrance to the vast, walled city. It was still very early in the morning and the streets were practically deserted. The residences, raised high upon their metal columns, resembled huge rookeries, while the uprights themselves presented the appearance of steel tree trunks. The shops as a rule were not raised from the ground nor were their doors bolted or barred, since thievery is practically unknown upon Barsoom. Assassination is the ever-present fear of all Barsoomians, and for this reason alone their homes are raised high above the ground at night, or in times of danger.

The Ptor brothers had given me explicit directions for reaching the point of the city where I could find living accommodations and be near the offices of the government agents to whom they had given me letters. My way led to the central square or plaza, which is a characteristic of all Martian cities.

The plaza of Zodanga covers a square mile and is bounded by the palaces of the jeddak, the jeds, and other members of the royalty and nobility of Zodanga, as well as by the principal public buildings, cafes, and shops.

As I was crossing the great square lost in wonder and admiration of the magnificent architecture and the gorgeous scarlet vegetation which carpeted the broad lawns I discovered a red Martian walking briskly toward me from one of the avenues. He paid not the slightest attention to me, but as he came abreast I recognized him, and turning I placed my hand upon his shoulder, calling out:

"Kaor, Kantos Kan!"

Like lightning he wheeled and before I could so much as lower my hand the point of his long-sword was at my breast.

"Who are you?" he growled, and then as a backward leap carried me fifty feet from his sword he dropped the point to the ground and exclaimed, laughing,

"I do not need a better reply, there is but one man upon all Barsoom who can bounce about like a rubber ball. By the mother of the further moon, John Carter, how came you here, and have you become a Darseen that you can change your color at will?"

"You gave me a bad half minute my friend," he continued, after I had briefly outlined my adventures since parting with him in the arena at Warhoon. "Were my name and city known to the Zodangans I would shortly be sitting on the banks of the lost sea of Korus with my revered and departed ancestors. I am here in the interest of Tardos Mors, Jeddak of Helium, to discover the whereabouts of Dejah Thoris, our princess. Sab Than, prince of Zodanga, has her hidden in the city and has fallen madly in love with her. His father, Than Kosis, Jeddak of Zodanga, has made her voluntary marriage to his son the price of peace between our countries, but Tardos Mors will not accede to the demands and has sent word that he and his people would rather look upon the dead face of their princess than see her wed to any than her own choice, and that personally he would prefer being engulfed in the ashes of a lost and burning Helium to joining the metal of his house with that of Than Kosis. His reply was the deadliest affront he could have put upon Than Kosis and the Zodangans, but his people love him the more for it and his strength in Helium is greater today than ever.

"I have been here three days," continued Kantos Kan, "but I have not yet found where Dejah Thoris is imprisoned. Today I join the Zodangan navy as an air scout and I hope in this way to win the confidence of Sab Than, the prince, who is commander of this division of the navy, and thus learn the whereabouts of Dejah Thoris. I am glad that you are here, John Carter, for I know your loyalty to my princess and two of us working together should be able to accomplish much."

The plaza was now commencing to fill with people going and coming upon the daily activities of their duties. The shops were opening and the cafes filling with early morning patrons. Kantos Kan led me to one of these gorgeous eating places where we were served entirely by mechanical apparatus. No hand touched the food from the time it entered the building in its raw state until it emerged hot and delicious upon the tables before the guests, in response to the touching of tiny buttons to indicate their desires.

After our meal, Kantos Kan took me with him to the headquarters of the air-scout squadron and introducing me to his superior asked that I be enrolled as a member of the corps. In accordance with custom an examination was necessary, but Kantos Kan had told me to have no fear on this score as he would attend to that part of the matter. He accomplished this by taking my order for examination to the examining officer and representing himself as John Carter.

"This ruse will be discovered later," he cheerfully explained, "when they check up my weights, measurements, and other personal identification data, but it will be several months before this is done and our mission should be accomplished or have failed long before that time."

The next few days were spent by Kantos Kan in teaching me the intricacies of flying and of repairing the dainty little contrivances which the Martians use for this purpose. The body of the one-man air craft is about sixteen feet long, two feet wide and three inches thick, tapering to a point at each end. The driver sits on top of this plane upon a seat constructed over the small, noiseless radium engine which propels it. The medium of buoyancy is contained within the thin metal walls of the body and consists of the eighth Barsoomian ray, or ray of propulsion, as it may be termed in view of its properties.

This ray, like the ninth ray, is unknown on Earth, but the Martians have discovered that it is an inherent property of all light no matter from what source it emanates. They have learned that it is the solar eighth ray which propels the light of the sun to the various planets, and that it is the individual eighth ray of each planet which "reflects," or propels the light thus obtained out into space once more. The solar eighth ray would be absorbed by the surface of Barsoom, but the Barsoomian eighth ray, which tends to propel light from Mars into space, is constantly streaming out from the planet constituting a force of repulsion of gravity which when confined is able to lift enormous weights from the surface of the ground.

It is this ray which has enabled them to so perfect aviation that battle ships far outweighing anything known upon Earth sail as gracefully and lightly through the thin air of Barsoom as a toy balloon in the heavy atmosphere of Earth.

During the early years of the discovery of this ray many strange accidents occurred before the Martians learned to measure and control the wonderful power they had found. In one instance, some nine hundred years before, the first great battle ship to be built with eighth ray reservoirs was stored with too great a quantity of the rays and she had sailed up from Helium with five hundred officers and men, never to return.

Her power of repulsion for the planet was so great that it had carried her far into space, where she can be seen today, by the aid of powerful telescopes, hurtling through the heavens ten thousand miles from Mars; a tiny satellite that will thus encircle Barsoom to the end of time.

The fourth day after my arrival at Zodanga I made my first flight, and as a result of it I won a promotion which included quarters in the palace of Than Kosis.

As I rose above the city I circled several times, as I had seen Kantos Kan do, and then throwing my engine into top speed I raced at terrific velocity toward the south, following one of the great waterways which enter Zodanga from that direction.

I had traversed perhaps two hundred miles in a little less than an hour when I descried far below me a party of three green warriors racing madly toward a small figure on foot which seemed to be trying to reach the confines of one of the walled fields.

Dropping my machine rapidly toward them, and circling to the rear of the warriors, I soon saw that the object of their pursuit was a red Martian wearing the metal of the scout squadron to which I was attached. A short distance away lay his tiny flier, surrounded by the tools with which he had evidently been occupied in repairing some damage when surprised by the green warriors.

They were now almost upon him; their flying mounts charging down on the relatively puny figure at terrific speed, while the warriors leaned low to the right, with their great metal-shod spears. Each seemed striving to be the first to impale the poor Zodangan and in another moment his fate would have been sealed had it not been for my timely arrival.

Driving my fleet air craft at high speed directly behind the warriors I soon overtook them and without diminishing my speed I rammed the prow of my little flier between the shoulders of the nearest. The impact sufficient to have torn through inches of solid steel, hurled the fellow's headless body into the air over the head of his thoat, where it fell sprawling upon the moss. The mounts of the other two warriors turned squealing in terror, and bolted in opposite directions.

Reducing my speed I circled and came to the ground at the feet of the astonished Zodangan. He was warm in his thanks for my timely aid and promised that my day's work would bring the reward it merited, for it was none other than a cousin of the jeddak of Zodanga whose life I had saved.

We wasted no time in talk as we knew that the warriors would surely return as soon as they had gained control of their mounts. Hastening to his damaged machine we were bending every effort to finish the needed repairs and had almost completed them when we saw the two green monsters returning at top speed from opposite sides of us. When they had approached within a hundred yards their thoats again became unmanageable and absolutely refused to advance further toward the air craft which had frightened them.

The warriors finally dismounted and hobbling their animals advanced toward us on foot with drawn long-swords.

I advanced to meet the larger, telling the Zodangan to do the best he could with the other. Finishing my man with almost no effort, as had now from much practice become habitual with me, I hastened to return to my new acquaintance whom I found indeed in desperate straits.

He was wounded and down with the huge foot of his antagonist upon his throat and the great long-sword raised to deal the final thrust. With a bound I cleared the fifty feet intervening between us, and with outstretched point drove my sword completely through the body of the green warrior. His sword fell, harmless, to the ground and he sank limply upon the prostrate form of the Zodangan.

A cursory examination of the latter revealed no mortal injuries and after a brief rest he asserted that he felt fit to attempt the return voyage. He would have to pilot his own craft, however, as these frail vessels are not intended to convey but a single person.

Quickly completing the repairs we rose together into the still, cloudless Martian sky, and at great speed and without further mishap returned to Zodanga.

As we neared the city we discovered a mighty concourse of civilians and troops assembled upon the plain before the city. The sky was black with naval vessels and private and public pleasure craft, flying long streamers of gay-colored silks, and banners and flags of odd and picturesque design.

My companion signaled that I slow down, and running his machine close beside mine suggested that we approach and watch the ceremony, which, he said, was for the purpose of conferring honors on individual officers and men for bravery and other distinguished service. He then unfurled a little ensign which denoted that his craft bore a member of the royal family of Zodanga, and together we made our way through the maze of low-lying air vessels until we hung directly over the jeddak of Zodanga and his staff. All were mounted upon the small domestic bull thoats of the red Martians, and their trappings and ornamentation bore such a quantity of gorgeously colored feathers that I could not but be struck with the startling resemblance the concourse bore to a band of the red Indians of my own Earth.

One of the staff called the attention of Than Kosis to the presence of my companion above them and the ruler motioned for him to descend. As they waited for the troops to move into position facing the jeddak the two talked earnestly together, the jeddak and his staff occasionally glancing up at me. I could not hear their conversation and presently it ceased and all dismounted, as the last body of troops had wheeled into position before their emperor. A member of the staff advanced toward the troops, and calling the name of a soldier commanded him to advance. The officer then recited the nature of the heroic act which had won the approval of the jeddak, and the latter advanced and placed a metal ornament upon the left arm of the lucky man.

Ten men had been so decorated when the aide called out,

"John Carter, air scout!"

Never in my life had I been so surprised, but the habit of military discipline is strong within me, and I dropped my little machine lightly to the ground and advanced on foot as I had seen the others do. As I halted before the officer, he addressed me in a voice audible to the entire assemblage of troops and spectators.

"In recognition, John Carter," he said, "of your remarkable courage and skill in defending the person of the cousin of the jeddak Than Kosis and, singlehanded, vanquishing three green warriors, it is the pleasure of our jeddak to confer on you the mark of his esteem."

Than Kosis then advanced toward me and placing an ornament upon me, said:

"My cousin has narrated the details of your wonderful achievement, which seems little short of miraculous, and if you can so well defend a cousin of the jeddak how much better could you defend the person of the jeddak himself. You are therefore appointed a padwar of The Guards and will be quartered in my palace hereafter."

I thanked him, and at his direction joined the members of his staff. After the ceremony I returned my machine to its quarters on the roof of the barracks of the air-scout squadron, and with an orderly from the palace to guide me I reported to the officer in charge of the palace.

CHAPTER TWENTY TWO

I Find Dejah

THE MAJOR-DOMO to whom I reported had been given instructions to station me near the person of the jeddak, who, in time of war, is always in great danger of assassination, as the rule that all is fair in war seems to constitute the entire ethics of Martian conflict.

He therefore escorted me immediately to the apartment in which Than Kosis then was. The ruler was engaged in conversation with his son, Sab Than, and several courtiers of his household, and did not perceive my entrance.

The walls of the apartment were completely hung with splendid tapestries which hid any windows or doors which may have pierced them. The room was lighted by imprisoned rays of sunshine held between the ceiling proper and what appeared to be a ground-glass false ceiling a few inches below.

My guide drew aside one of the tapestries, disclosing a passage which encircled the room, between the hangings and the walls of the chamber. Within this passage I was to remain, he said, so long as Than Kosis was in the apartment. When he left I was to follow. My only duty was to guard the ruler and keep out of sight as much as possible. I would be relieved after a period of four hours. The major-domo then left me.

The tapestries were of a strange weaving which gave the appearance of heavy solidity from one side, but from my hiding place I could perceive all that took place within the room as readily as though there had been no curtain intervening.

Scarcely had I gained my post than the tapestry at the opposite end of the chamber separated and four soldiers of The Guard entered, surrounding a female figure. As they approached Than Kosis the soldiers fell to either side and there standing before the jeddak and not ten feet from me, her beautiful face radiant with smiles, was Dejah Thoris.

Sab Than, Prince of Zodanga, advanced to meet her, and hand in hand they approached close to the jeddak. Than Kosis looked up in surprise, and, rising, saluted her.

"To what strange freak do I owe this visit from the Princess of Helium, who, two days ago, with rare consideration for my pride, assured me that she would prefer Tal Hajus, the green Thark, to my son?"

Dejah Thoris only smiled the more and with the roguish dimples playing at the corners of her mouth she made answer:

"From the beginning of time upon Barsoom it has been the prerogative of woman to change her mind as she listed and to dissemble in matters concerning her heart. That you will forgive, Than Kosis, as has your son. Two days ago I was not sure of his love for me, but now I am, and I have come to beg of you to forget my rash words and to accept the assurance of the Princess of Helium that when the time comes she will wed Sab Than, Prince of Zodanga."

"I am glad that you have so decided," replied Than Kosis. "It is far from my desire to push war further against the people of Helium, and, your promise shall be recorded and a proclamation to my people issued forthwith."

"It were better, Than Kosis," interrupted Dejah Thoris, "that the proclamation wait the ending of this war. It would look strange indeed to my people and to yours were the Princess of Helium to give herself to her country's enemy in the midst of hostilities."

"Cannot the war be ended at once?" spoke Sab Than. "It requires but the word of Than Kosis to bring peace. Say it, my father, say the word that will hasten my happiness, and end this unpopular strife."

"We shall see," replied Than Kosis, "how the people of Helium take to peace. I shall at least offer it to them."

Dejah Thoris, after a few words, turned and left the apartment, still followed by her guards.

Thus was the edifice of my brief dream of happiness dashed, broken, to the ground of reality. The woman for whom I had offered my life, and from whose lips I had so recently heard a declaration of love for me, had lightly forgotten my very existence and smilingly given herself to the son of her people's most hated enemy.

Although I had heard it with my own ears I could not believe it. I must search out her apartments and force her to repeat the cruel truth to me alone before I would be convinced, and so I deserted my post and hastened through the passage behind the tapestries toward the door by which she had left the chamber. Slipping quietly through this opening I discovered a maze of winding corridors, branching and turning in every direction.

Running rapidly down first one and then another of them I soon became hopelessly lost and was standing panting against a side wall when I heard voices near me. Apparently they were coming from the opposite side of the partition against which I leaned and presently I made out the tones of Dejah Thoris. I could not hear the words but I knew that I could not possibly be mistaken in the voice.

Moving on a few steps I discovered another passageway at the end of which lay a door. Walking boldly forward I pushed into the room only to find myself in a small antechamber in which were the four guards who had accompanied her. One of them instantly arose and accosted me, asking the nature of my business.

"I am from Than Kosis," I replied, "and wish to speak privately with Dejah Thoris, Princess of Helium."

"And your order?" asked the fellow.

I did not know what he meant, but replied that I was a member of The Guard, and without waiting for a reply from him I strode toward the opposite door of the antechamber, behind which I could hear Dejah Thoris conversing.

But my entrance was not to be so easily accomplished. The guardsman stepped before me, saying,

"No one comes from Than Kosis without carrying an order or the password. You must give me one or the other before you may pass."

"The only order I require, my friend, to enter where I will, hangs at my side," I answered, tapping my long-sword; "will you let me pass in peace or no?"

For reply he whipped out his own sword, calling to the others to join him, and thus the four stood, with drawn weapons, barring my further progress.

"You are not here by the order of Than Kosis," cried the one who had first addressed me, "and not only shall you not enter the apartments of the Princess of Helium but you shall go back to Than Kosis under guard to explain this unwarranted temerity. Throw down your sword; you cannot hope to overcome four of us," he added with a grim smile.

My reply was a quick thrust which left me but three antagonists and I can assure you that they were worthy of my metal. They had me backed against the wall in no time, fighting for my life. Slowly I worked my way to a corner of the room where I could force them to come at me only one at a time, and thus we fought upward of twenty minutes; the clanging of steel on steel producing a veritable bedlam in the little room.

The noise had brought Dejah Thoris to the door of her apartment, and there she stood throughout the conflict with Sola at her back peering over her shoulder. Her face was set and emotionless and I knew that she did not recognize me, nor did Sola.

Finally a lucky cut brought down a second guardsman and then, with only two opposing me, I changed my tactics and rushed them down after the fashion of my fighting that had won me many a victory. The third fell within ten seconds after the second, and the last lay dead upon the bloody floor a few moments later. They were brave men and noble fighters, and it grieved me that I had been forced to kill them, but I would have willingly depopulated all Barsoom could I have reached the side of my Dejah Thoris in no other way.

Sheathing my bloody blade I advanced toward my Martian Princess, who still stood mutely gazing at me without sign of recognition.

"Who are you, Zodangan?" she whispered. "Another enemy to harass me in my misery?"

"I am a friend," I answered, "a once cherished friend."

"No friend of Helium's princess wears that metal," she replied, "and yet the voice! I have heard it before; it is not – it cannot be – no, for he is dead."

"It is, though, my Princess, none other than John Carter," I said. "Do you not recognize, even through paint and strange metal, the heart of your chieftain?"

As I came close to her she swayed toward me with outstretched hands, but as I reached to take her in my arms she drew back with a shudder and a little moan of misery.

"Too late, too late," she grieved. "O my chieftain that was, and whom I thought dead, had you but returned one little hour before – but now it is too late, too late."

"What do you mean, Dejah Thoris?" I cried. "That you would not have promised yourself to the Zodangan prince had you known that I lived?"

"Think you, John Carter, that I would give my heart to you yesterday and today to another? I thought that it lay buried with your ashes in the pits of Warhoon, and so today I have promised my body to another to save my people from the curse of a victorious Zodangan army."

"But I am not dead, my princess. I have come to claim you, and all Zodanga cannot prevent it."

"It is too late, John Carter, my promise is given, and on Barsoom that is final. The ceremonies which follow later are but meaningless formalities. They make the fact of marriage no more certain than does the funeral cortege of a jeddak again place the seal of death upon him. I am as good as married, John Carter. No longer may you call me your princess. No longer are you my chieftain."

"I know but little of your customs here upon Barsoom, Dejah Thoris, but I do know that I love you, and if you meant the last words you spoke to me that day as the hordes of Warhoon were charging down upon us, no other man shall ever claim you as his bride. You meant them then, my princess, and you mean them still! Say that it is true."

"I meant them, John Carter," she whispered. "I cannot repeat them now for I have given myself to another. Ah, if you had only known our ways, my friend," she continued, half to herself, "the promise would have been yours long months ago, and you could have claimed me before all others. It might have meant the fall of Helium, but I would have given my empire for my Tharkian chief."

Then aloud she said: "Do you remember the night when you offended me? You called me your princess without having asked my hand of me, and then you boasted that you had fought for me. You did not know, and I should not have been offended; I see that now. But there was no one to tell you what I could not, that upon Barsoom there are two kinds of women in the cities of the red men. The one they fight for that they may ask them in marriage; the other kind they fight for also, but never ask their hands. When a man has won a woman he may address her as his princess, or in any of the several terms which signify possession. You had fought for me, but had never asked me in marriage, and so when you called me your princess, you see," she faltered, "I was hurt, but even then, John Carter, I did not repulse you, as I should have done, until you made it doubly worse by taunting me with having won me through combat."

"I do not need ask your forgiveness now, Dejah Thoris," I cried. "You must know that my fault was of ignorance of your Barsoomian customs. What I failed to do, through implicit belief that my petition would be presumptuous and unwelcome, I do now, Dejah Thoris; I ask you to be my wife, and by all the Virginian fighting blood that flows in my veins you shall be."

"No, John Carter, it is useless," she cried, hopelessly, "I may never be yours while Sab Than lives."

"You have sealed his death warrant, my princess – Sab Than dies."

"Nor that either," she hastened to explain. "I may not wed the man who slays my husband, even in self-defense. It is custom. We are ruled by custom upon Barsoom. It is useless, my friend. You must bear the sorrow with me. That at least we may share in common. That, and the memory of the brief days among the Tharks. You must go now, nor ever see me again. Good-bye, my chieftain that was."

Disheartened and dejected, I withdrew from the room, but I was not entirely discouraged, nor would I admit that Dejah Thoris was lost to me until the ceremony had actually been performed.

As I wandered along the corridors, I was as absolutely lost in the mazes of winding passageways as I had been before I discovered Dejah Thoris' apartments.

I knew that my only hope lay in escape from the city of Zodanga, for the matter of the four dead guardsmen would have to be explained, and as I could never reach my original post without a guide, suspicion would surely rest on me so soon as I was discovered wandering aimlessly through the palace.

Presently I came upon a spiral runway leading to a lower floor, and this I followed downward for several stories until I reached the doorway of a large apartment in which were a number of guardsmen. The walls of this room were hung with transparent tapestries behind which I secreted myself without being apprehended.

The conversation of the guardsmen was general, and awakened no interest in me until an officer entered the room and ordered four of the men to relieve the detail who were guarding the Princess of Helium. Now, I knew, my troubles would commence in earnest and indeed they were upon me all too soon, for it seemed that the squad had scarcely left the guardroom before one of their number burst in again breathlessly, crying that they had found their four comrades butchered in the antechamber.

In a moment the entire palace was alive with people. Guardsmen, officers, courtiers, servants, and slaves ran helter-skelter through the corridors and apartments carrying messages and orders, and searching for signs of the assassin.

This was my opportunity and slim as it appeared I grasped it, for as a number of soldiers came hurrying past my hiding place I fell in behind them and followed through the mazes of the palace until, in passing through a great hall, I saw the blessed light of day coming in through a series of larger windows.

Here I left my guides, and, slipping to the nearest window, sought for an avenue of escape. The windows opened upon a great balcony which overlooked one of the broad avenues of Zodanga. The ground was about thirty feet below, and at a like distance from the building was a wall fully twenty feet high, constructed of polished glass about a foot in thickness. To a red Martian escape by this path would have appeared impossible, but to me, with my earthly strength and agility, it seemed already accomplished. My only fear was in being detected before darkness fell, for I could not make the leap in broad daylight while the court below and the avenue beyond were crowded with Zodangans.

Accordingly I searched for a hiding place and finally found one by accident, inside a huge hanging ornament which swung from the ceiling of the hall, and about ten feet from the floor. Into the capacious bowl-like vase I sprang with ease, and scarcely had I settled down within it than I heard a number of people enter the apartment. The group stopped beneath my hiding place and I could plainly overhear their every word.

"It is the work of Heliumites," said one of the men.

"Yes, O Jeddak, but how had they access to the palace? I could believe that even with the diligent care of your guardsmen a single enemy might reach the inner chambers, but how a force of six or eight fighting men could have done so unobserved is beyond me. We shall soon know, however, for here comes the royal psychologist."

Another man now joined the group, and, after making his formal greetings to his ruler, said:

"O mighty Jeddak, it is a strange tale I read in the dead minds of your faithful guardsmen. They were felled not by a number of fighting men, but by a single opponent."

He paused to let the full weight of this announcement impress his hearers, and that his statement was scarcely credited was evidenced by the impatient exclamation of incredulity which escaped the lips of Than Kosis.

"What manner of weird tale are you bringing me, Notan?" he cried.

"It is the truth, my Jeddak," replied the psychologist. "In fact the impressions were strongly marked on the brain of each of the four guardsmen. Their antagonist was a very tall man, wearing the metal of one of your own guardsmen, and his fighting ability was little short of marvelous for he fought fair against the entire four and vanquished them by his surpassing skill and superhuman strength and endurance. Though he wore the metal of Zodanga, my Jeddak, such a man was never seen before in this or any other country upon Barsoom.

"The mind of the Princess of Helium whom I have examined and questioned was a blank to me, she has perfect control, and I could not read one iota of it. She said that she witnessed a portion of the encounter, and that when she looked there was but one man engaged with the guardsmen; a man whom she did not recognize as ever having seen."

"Where is my erstwhile savior?" spoke another of the party, and I recognized the voice of the cousin of Than Kosis, whom I had rescued from the green warriors. "By the metal of my first ancestor," he went on, "but the description fits him to perfection, especially as to his fighting ability."

"Where is this man?" cried Than Kosis. "Have him brought to me at once. What know you of him, cousin? It seemed strange to me now that I think upon it that there should have been such a fighting man in Zodanga, of whose name, even, we were ignorant before today. And his name too, John Carter, who ever heard of such a name upon Barsoom!"

Word was soon brought that I was nowhere to be found, either in the palace or at my former quarters in the barracks of the air-scout squadron. Kantos Kan, they had found and questioned, but he knew nothing of my whereabouts, and as to my past, he had told them he knew as little, since he had but recently met me during our captivity among the Warhoons.

"Keep your eyes on this other one," commanded Than Kosis. "He also is a stranger and likely as not they both hail from Helium, and where one is we shall sooner or later find the other. Quadruple the air patrol, and let every man who leaves the city by air or ground be subjected to the closest scrutiny."

Another messenger now entered with word that I was still within the palace walls.

"The likeness of every person who has entered or left the palace grounds today has been carefully examined," concluded the fellow, "and not one approaches the likeness of this new padwar of the guards, other than that which was recorded of him at the time he entered."

"Then we will have him shortly," commented Than Kosis contentedly, "and in the meanwhile we will repair to the apartments of the Princess of Helium and question her in regard to the affair. She may know more than she cared to divulge to you, Notan. Come."

They left the hall, and, as darkness had fallen without, I slipped lightly from my hiding place and hastened to the balcony. Few were in sight, and choosing a moment when none seemed near I sprang quickly to the top of the glass wall and from there to the avenue beyond the palace grounds.

CHAPTER TWENTY THREE
Lost in the Sky

WITHOUT EFFORT AT CONCEALMENT I hastened to the vicinity of our quarters, where I felt sure I should find Kantos Kan. As I neared the building I became more careful, as I judged, and rightly, that the place would be guarded. Several men in civilian metal loitered near the front entrance and in the rear were others. My only means of reaching, unseen, the upper story where our apartments were situated was through an adjoining building, and after considerable maneuvering I managed to attain the roof of a shop several doors away.

Leaping from roof to roof, I soon reached an open window in the building where I hoped to find the Heliumite, and in another moment I stood in the room before him. He was alone and showed no surprise at my coming, saying he had expected me much earlier, as my tour of duty must have ended some time since.

I saw that he knew nothing of the events of the day at the palace, and when I had enlightened him he was all excitement. The news that Dejah Thoris had promised her hand to Sab Than filled him with dismay.

"It cannot be," he exclaimed. "It is impossible! Why no man in all Helium but would prefer death to the selling of our loved princess to the ruling house of Zodanga. She must have lost her mind to have assented to such an atrocious bargain. You, who do not know how we of Helium love the members of our ruling house, cannot appreciate the horror with which I contemplate such an unholy alliance."

"What can be done, John Carter?" he continued. "You are a resourceful man. Can you not think of some way to save Helium from this disgrace?"

"If I can come within sword's reach of Sab Than," I answered, "I can solve the difficulty in so far as Helium is concerned, but for personal reasons I would prefer that another struck the blow that frees Dejah Thoris."

Kantos Kan eyed me narrowly before he spoke.

"You love her!" he said. "Does she know it?"

"She knows it, Kantos Kan, and repulses me only because she is promised to Sab Than."

The splendid fellow sprang to his feet, and grasping me by the shoulder raised his sword on high, exclaiming:

"And had the choice been left to me I could not have chosen a more fitting mate for the first princess of Barsoom. Here is my hand upon your shoulder, John Carter, and my word that Sab Than shall go out at the point of my sword for the sake of my love for Helium, for Dejah Thoris, and for you. This very night I shall try to reach his quarters in the palace."

"How?" I asked. "You are strongly guarded and a quadruple force patrols the sky."

He bent his head in thought a moment, then raised it with an air of confidence.

"I only need to pass these guards and I can do it," he said at last. "I know a secret entrance to the palace through the pinnacle of the highest tower. I fell upon it by chance one day as I was passing above the palace on patrol duty. In this work it is required that we investigate any unusual occurrence we may witness, and a face peering from the pinnacle of the high tower of the palace was, to me, most unusual. I therefore drew near and discovered that the possessor of the peering face was none other than Sab Than. He was slightly put out at being detected and commanded me to keep the matter to myself, explaining that the passage from the tower led directly to his apartments, and was known only to him. If I can reach the roof of the barracks and get my machine I can be in Sab Than's quarters in five minutes; but how am I to escape from this building, guarded as you say it is?"

"How well are the machine sheds at the barracks guarded?" I asked.

"There is usually but one man on duty there at night upon the roof."

"Go to the roof of this building, Kantos Kan, and wait me there."

Without stopping to explain my plans I retraced my way to the street and hastened to the barracks. I did not dare to enter the building, filled as it was with members of the air-scout squadron, who, in common with all Zodanga, were on the lookout for me.

The building was an enormous one, rearing its lofty head fully a thousand feet into the air. But few buildings in Zodanga were higher than these barracks, though several topped it by a few hundred feet; the docks of the great battleships of the line standing some fifteen hundred feet from the ground, while the freight and passenger stations of the merchant squadrons rose nearly as high.

It was a long climb up the face of the building, and one fraught with much danger, but there was no other way, and so I essayed the task. The fact that Barsoomian architecture is extremely ornate made the feat much simpler than I had anticipated, since I found ornamental ledges and projections which fairly formed a perfect ladder for me all the way to the eaves of the building. Here I met my first real obstacle. The eaves projected nearly twenty feet from the wall to which I clung, and though I encircled the great building I could find no opening through them.

The top floor was alight, and filled with soldiers engaged in the pastimes of their kind; I could not, therefore, reach the roof through the building.

There was one slight, desperate chance, and that I decided I must take – it was for Dejah Thoris, and no man has lived who would not risk a thousand deaths for such as she.

Clinging to the wall with my feet and one hand, I unloosened one of the long leather straps of my trappings at the end of which dangled a great hook by which air sailors are hung to the sides and bottoms of their craft for various purposes of repair, and by means of which landing parties are lowered to the ground from the battleships.

I swung this hook cautiously to the roof several times before it finally found lodgment; gently I pulled on it to strengthen its hold, but whether it would bear the weight of my body I did not know. It might be barely caught upon the very outer verge of the roof, so that as my body swung out at the end of the strap it would slip off and launch me to the pavement a thousand feet below.

An instant I hesitated, and then, releasing my grasp upon the supporting ornament, I swung out into space at the end of the strap. Far below me lay the brilliantly lighted streets, the hard pavements, and death. There was a little jerk at the top of the supporting eaves, and a nasty slipping, grating sound which turned me cold with apprehension; then the hook caught and I was safe.

Clambering quickly aloft I grasped the edge of the eaves and drew myself to the surface of the roof above. As I gained my feet I was confronted by the sentry on duty, into the muzzle of whose revolver I found myself looking.

"Who are you and whence came you?" he cried.

"I am an air scout, friend, and very near a dead one, for just by the merest chance I escaped falling to the avenue below," I replied.

"But how came you upon the roof, man? No one has landed or come up from the building for the past hour. Quick, explain yourself, or I call the guard."

"Look you here, sentry, and you shall see how I came and how close a shave I had to not coming at all," I answered, turning toward the edge of the roof, where, twenty feet below, at the end of my strap, hung all my weapons.

The fellow, acting on impulse of curiosity, stepped to my side and to his undoing, for as he leaned to peer over the eaves I grasped him by his throat and his pistol arm and threw him heavily to the roof. The weapon dropped from his grasp, and my fingers choked off his attempted cry for assistance. I gagged and bound him and then hung him over the edge of the roof as I myself had hung a few moments before. I knew it would be morning before he would be discovered, and I needed all the time that I could gain.

Donning my trappings and weapons I hastened to the sheds, and soon had out both my machine and Kantos Kan's. Making his fast behind mine I started my engine, and skimming over the edge of the roof I dove down into the streets of the city far below the plane usually occupied by the air patrol. In less than a minute I was settling safely upon the roof of our apartment beside the astonished Kantos Kan.

I lost no time in explanation, but plunged immediately into a discussion of our plans for the immediate future. It was decided that I was to try to make Helium while Kantos Kan was to enter the palace and dispatch Sab Than. If successful he was then to follow me. He set my compass for me, a clever little device which will remain steadfastly fixed upon any given point on the surface of Barsoom, and bidding each other farewell we rose together and sped in the direction of the palace which lay in the route which I must take to reach Helium.

As we neared the high tower a patrol shot down from above, throwing its piercing searchlight full upon my craft, and a voice roared out a command to halt, following with a shot as I paid no attention to his hail. Kantos Kan dropped quickly into the darkness, while I rose steadily and at terrific speed raced through the Martian sky followed by a dozen of the air-scout craft which had joined the pursuit, and later by a swift cruiser carrying a hundred men and a battery of rapid-fire guns. By twisting and turning my little machine, now rising and now falling, I managed to elude their search-lights most of the time, but I was also losing ground by these tactics, and so I decided to hazard everything on a straight-away course and leave the result to fate and the speed of my machine.

Kantos Kan had shown me a trick of gearing, which is known only to the navy of Helium, that greatly increased the speed of our machines, so that I felt sure I could distance my pursuers if I could dodge their projectiles for a few moments.

As I sped through the air the screeching of the bullets around me convinced me that only by a miracle could I escape, but the die was cast, and throwing on full speed I raced a straight course toward Helium. Gradually I left my pursuers further and further behind, and I was just congratulating myself on my lucky escape, when a well-directed shot from the cruiser exploded at the prow of my little craft. The concussion nearly capsized her, and with a sickening plunge she hurtled downward through the dark night.

How far I fell before I regained control of the plane I do not know, but I must have been very close to the ground when I started to rise again, as I plainly heard the squealing of animals below me. Rising again I scanned the heavens for my pursuers, and finally making out their lights far behind me, saw that they were landing, evidently in search of me.

Not until their lights were no longer discernible did I venture to flash my little lamp upon my compass, and then I found to my consternation that a fragment of the projectile had utterly destroyed my only guide, as well as my speedometer. It was true I could follow the stars in the general direction of Helium, but without knowing the exact location of the city or the speed at which I was traveling my chances for finding it were slim.

Helium lies a thousand miles southwest of Zodanga, and with my compass intact I should have made the trip, barring accidents, in between four and five hours. As it turned out, however, morning found me speeding over a vast expanse of dead sea bottom after nearly six hours of continuous flight at high speed. Presently a great city showed below me, but it was not Helium, as that alone of all Barsoomian metropolises consists in two immense circular walled cities about seventy-five miles apart and would have been easily distinguishable from the altitude at which I was flying.

Believing that I had come too far to the north and west, I turned back in a southeasterly direction, passing during the forenoon several other large cities, but none resembling the description which Kantos Kan had given me of Helium. In addition to the twin-city formation of Helium, another distinguishing feature is the two immense towers, one of vivid scarlet rising nearly a mile into the air from the center of one of the cities, while the other, of bright yellow and of the same height, marks her sister.

CHAPTER TWENTY FOUR
Tars Tarkas Finds a Friend

About noon I passed low over a great dead city of ancient Mars, and as I skimmed out across the plain beyond I came full upon several thousand green warriors engaged in a terrific battle. Scarcely had I seen them than a volley of shots was directed at me, and with the almost unfailing accuracy of their aim my little craft was instantly a ruined wreck, sinking erratically to the ground.

I fell almost directly in the center of the fierce combat, among warriors who had not seen my approach so busily were they engaged in life and death struggles. The men were fighting on foot with long-swords, while an occasional shot from a sharpshooter on the outskirts of the conflict would bring down a warrior who might for an instant separate himself from the entangled mass.

As my machine sank among them I realized that it was fight or die, with good chances of dying in any event, and so I struck the ground with drawn long-sword ready to defend myself as I could.

I fell beside a huge monster who was engaged with three antagonists, and as I glanced at his fierce face, filled with the light of battle, I recognized Tars Tarkas the Thark. He did not see me, as I was a trifle behind him, and just then the three warriors opposing him, and whom I recognized as Warhoons, charged simultaneously. The mighty fellow made quick work of one of them, but in stepping back for another thrust he fell over a dead body behind him and was down and at the mercy of his foes in an instant. Quick as lightning they were upon him, and Tars Tarkas would have been gathered to his fathers in short order had I not sprung before his prostrate form and engaged his adversaries. I had accounted for one of them when the mighty Thark regained his feet and quickly settled the other.

He gave me one look, and a slight smile touched his grim lip as, touching my shoulder, he said,

"I would scarcely recognize you, John Carter, but there is no other mortal upon Barsoom who would have done what you have for me. I think I have learned that there is such a thing as friendship, my friend."

He said no more, nor was there opportunity, for the Warhoons were closing in about us, and together we fought, shoulder to shoulder, during all that long, hot afternoon, until the tide of battle turned and the remnant of the fierce Warhoon horde fell back upon their thoats, and fled into the gathering darkness.

Ten thousand men had been engaged in that titanic struggle, and upon the field of battle lay three thousand dead. Neither side asked or gave quarter, nor did they attempt to take prisoners.

On our return to the city after the battle we had gone directly to Tars Tarkas' quarters, where I was left alone while the chieftain attended the customary council which immediately follows an engagement.

As I sat awaiting the return of the green warrior I heard something move in an adjoining apartment, and as I glanced up there rushed suddenly upon me a huge and hideous creature which bore me backward upon the pile of silks and furs upon which I had been reclining. It was Woola – faithful, loving Woola. He had found his way back to Thark and, as Tars Tarkas later told me, had gone immediately to my former quarters where he had taken up his pathetic and seemingly hopeless watch for my return.

"Tal Hajus knows that you are here, John Carter," said Tars Tarkas, on his return from the jeddak's quarters; "Sarkoja saw and recognized you as we were returning. Tal Hajus has ordered me to bring you before him tonight. I have ten thoats, John Carter; you may take your choice from among them, and I will accompany you to the nearest waterway that leads to Helium. Tars Tarkas may be a cruel green warrior, but he can be a friend as well. Come, we must start."

"And when you return, Tars Tarkas?" I asked.

"The wild calots, possibly, or worse," he replied. "Unless I should chance to have the opportunity I have so long waited of battling with Tal Hajus."

"We will stay, Tars Tarkas, and see Tal Hajus tonight. You shall not sacrifice yourself, and it may be that tonight you can have the chance you wait."

He objected strenuously, saying that Tal Hajus often flew into wild fits of passion at the mere thought of the blow I had dealt him, and that if ever he laid his hands upon me I would be subjected to the most horrible tortures.

While we were eating I repeated to Tars Tarkas the story which Sola had told me that night upon the sea bottom during the march to Thark.

He said but little, but the great muscles of his face worked in passion and in agony at recollection of the horrors which had been heaped upon the only thing he had ever loved in all his cold, cruel, terrible existence.

He no longer demurred when I suggested that we go before Tal Hajus, only saying that he would like to speak to Sarkoja first. At his request I accompanied him to her quarters, and the look of venomous hatred she cast upon me was almost adequate recompense for any future misfortunes this accidental return to Thark might bring me.

"Sarkoja," said Tars Tarkas, "forty years ago you were instrumental in bringing about the torture and death of a woman named Gozava. I have just discovered that the warrior who loved that woman has learned of your part in the transaction. He may not kill you, Sarkoja, it is not our custom, but there is nothing to prevent him tying one end of a strap about your neck and the other end to a wild thoat, merely to test your fitness to survive and help perpetuate our race. Having heard that he would do this on the morrow, I thought it only right to warn you, for I am a just man. The river Iss is but a short pilgrimage, Sarkoja. Come, John Carter."

The next morning Sarkoja was gone, nor was she ever seen after.

In silence we hastened to the jeddak's palace, where we were immediately admitted to his presence; in fact, he could scarcely wait to see me and was standing erect upon his platform glowering at the entrance as I came in.

"Strap him to that pillar," he shrieked. "We shall see who it is dares strike the mighty Tal Hajus. Heat the irons; with my own hands I shall burn the eyes from his head that he may not pollute my person with his vile gaze."

"Chieftains of Thark," I cried, turning to the assembled council and ignoring Tal Hajus, "I have been a chief among you, and today I have fought for Thark shoulder to shoulder with her greatest warrior. You owe me, at least, a hearing. I have won that much today. You claim to be just people – "

"Silence," roared Tal Hajus. "Gag the creature and bind him as I command."

"Justice, Tal Hajus," exclaimed Lorquas Ptomel. "Who are you to set aside the customs of ages among the Tharks."

"Yes, justice!" echoed a dozen voices, and so, while Tal Hajus fumed and frothed, I continued.

"You are a brave people and you love bravery, but where was your mighty jeddak during the fighting today? I did not see him in the thick of battle; he was not there. He rends defenseless women and little children in his lair, but how recently has one of you seen him fight with men? Why, even I, a midget beside him, felled him with a single blow of my fist. Is it of such that the Tharks fashion their jeddaks? There stands beside me now a great Thark, a mighty warrior and a noble man. Chieftains, how sounds, Tars Tarkas, Jeddak of Thark?"

A roar of deep-toned applause greeted this suggestion.

"It but remains for this council to command, and Tal Hajus must prove his fitness to rule. Were he a brave man he would invite Tars Tarkas to combat, for he does not love him, but Tal Hajus is afraid; Tal Hajus, your jeddak, is a coward. With my bare hands I could kill him, and he knows it."

After I ceased there was tense silence, as all eyes were riveted upon Tal Hajus. He did not speak or move, but the blotchy green of his countenance turned livid, and the froth froze upon his lips.

"Tal Hajus," said Lorquas Ptomel in a cold, hard voice, "never in my long life have I seen a jeddak of the Tharks so humiliated. There could be but one answer to this arraignment. We wait it." And still Tal Hajus stood as though electrified.

"Chieftains," continued Lorquas Ptomel, "shall the jeddak, Tal Hajus, prove his fitness to rule over Tars Tarkas?"

There were twenty chieftains about the rostrum, and twenty swords flashed high in assent.

There was no alternative. That decree was final, and so Tal Hajus drew his long-sword and advanced to meet Tars Tarkas.

The combat was soon over, and, with his foot upon the neck of the dead monster, Tars Tarkas became jeddak among the Tharks.

His first act was to make me a full-fledged chieftain with the rank I had won by my combats the first few weeks of my captivity among them.

Seeing the favorable disposition of the warriors toward Tars Tarkas, as well as toward me, I grasped the opportunity to enlist them in my cause against Zodanga. I told Tars Tarkas the story of my adventures, and in a few words had explained to him the thought I had in mind.

"John Carter has made a proposal," he said, addressing the council, "which meets with my sanction. I shall put it to you briefly. Dejah Thoris, the Princess of Helium, who was our prisoner, is now held by the jeddak of Zodanga, whose son she must wed to save her country from devastation at the hands of the Zodangan forces.

"John Carter suggests that we rescue her and return her to Helium. The loot of Zodanga would be magnificent, and I have often thought that had we an alliance with the people of Helium we could obtain sufficient assurance of sustenance to permit us to increase the size and frequency of our hatchings, and thus become unquestionably supreme among the green men of all Barsoom. What say you?"

It was a chance to fight, an opportunity to loot, and they rose to the bait as a speckled trout to a fly.

For Tharks they were wildly enthusiastic, and before another half hour had passed twenty mounted messengers were speeding across dead sea bottoms to call the hordes together for the expedition.

In three days we were on the march toward Zodanga, one hundred thousand strong, as Tars Tarkas had been able to enlist the services of three smaller hordes on the promise of the great loot of Zodanga.

At the head of the column I rode beside the great Thark while at the heels of my mount trotted my beloved Woola.

We traveled entirely by night, timing our marches so that we camped during the day at deserted cities where, even to the beasts, we were all kept indoors during the daylight hours. On the march Tars Tarkas, through his remarkable ability and statesmanship, enlisted fifty thousand more warriors from various hordes, so that, ten days after we set out we halted at midnight outside the great walled city of Zodanga, one hundred and fifty thousand strong.

The fighting strength and efficiency of this horde of ferocious green monsters was equivalent to ten times their number of red men. Never in the history of Barsoom, Tars Tarkas told me, had such a force of green warriors marched to battle together. It was a monstrous task to keep even a semblance of harmony among them, and it was a marvel to me that he got them to the city without a mighty battle among themselves.

But as we neared Zodanga their personal quarrels were submerged by their greater hatred for the red men, and especially for the Zodangans, who had for years waged a ruthless campaign of extermination against the green men, directing special attention toward despoiling their incubators.

Now that we were before Zodanga the task of obtaining entry to the city devolved upon me, and directing Tars Tarkas to hold his forces in two divisions out of earshot of the city, with each division opposite a large gateway, I took twenty dismounted warriors and approached one of the small gates that pierced the walls at short intervals. These gates have no regular guard, but are covered by sentries, who patrol the avenue that encircles the city just within the walls as our metropolitan police patrol their beats.

The walls of Zodanga are seventy-five feet in height and fifty feet thick. They are built of enormous blocks of carborundum, and the task of entering the city seemed, to my escort of green warriors, an impossibility. The fellows who had been detailed to accompany me were of one of the smaller hordes, and therefore did not know me.

Placing three of them with their faces to the wall and arms locked, I commanded two more to mount to their shoulders, and a sixth I ordered to climb upon the shoulders of the upper two. The head of the topmost warrior towered over forty feet from the ground.

In this way, with ten warriors, I built a series of three steps from the ground to the shoulders of the topmost man. Then starting from a short distance behind them I ran swiftly up from one tier to the next, and with a final bound from the broad shoulders of the highest I clutched the top of the great wall and quietly drew myself to its broad expanse. After me I dragged six lengths of leather from an equal number of my warriors. These lengths we had previously fastened together, and passing one end to the topmost warrior I lowered the other end cautiously over the opposite side of the wall toward the avenue below. No one was in sight, so, lowering myself to the end of my leather strap, I dropped the remaining thirty feet to the pavement below.

I had learned from Kantos Kan the secret of opening these gates, and in another moment my twenty great fighting men stood within the doomed city of Zodanga.

I found to my delight that I had entered at the lower boundary of the enormous palace grounds. The building itself showed in the distance a blaze of glorious light, and on the instant I determined to lead a detachment of warriors directly within the palace itself, while the balance of the great horde was attacking the barracks of the soldiery.

Dispatching one of my men to Tars Tarkas for a detail of fifty Tharks, with word of my intentions, I ordered ten warriors to capture and open one of the great gates while with the nine remaining I took the other. We were to do our work quietly, no shots were to be fired and no general advance made until I had reached the palace with my fifty Tharks. Our plans worked to perfection. The two sentries we met were dispatched to their fathers upon the banks of the lost sea of Korus, and the guards at both gates followed them in silence.

CHAPTER TWENTY FIVE

The Looting of Zodanga

AS THE GREAT GATE where I stood swung open my fifty Tharks, headed by Tars Tarkas himself, rode in upon their mighty thoats. I led them to the palace walls, which I negotiated easily without assistance. Once inside, however, the gate gave me considerable trouble, but I finally was rewarded by seeing it swing upon its huge hinges, and soon my fierce escort was riding across the gardens of the jeddak of Zodanga.

As we approached the palace I could see through the great windows of the first floor into the brilliantly illuminated audience chamber of Than Kosis. The immense hall was crowded with nobles and their women, as though some important function was in progress. There was not a guard in sight without the palace, due, I presume, to the fact that the city and palace walls were considered impregnable, and so I came close and peered within.

At one end of the chamber, upon massive golden thrones encrusted with diamonds, sat Than Kosis and his consort, surrounded by officers and dignitaries of state. Before them stretched a broad aisle lined on either side with soldiery, and as I looked there entered this aisle at the far end of the hall, the head of a procession which advanced to the foot of the throne.

First there marched four officers of the jeddak's Guard bearing a huge salver on which reposed, upon a cushion of scarlet silk, a great golden chain with a collar and padlock at each end. Directly behind these officers came four others carrying a similar salver which supported the magnificent ornaments of a prince and princess of the reigning house of Zodanga.

At the foot of the throne these two parties separated and halted, facing each other at opposite sides of the aisle. Then came more dignitaries, and the officers of the palace and of the army, and finally two figures entirely muffled in scarlet silk, so that not a feature of either was discernible. These two stopped at the foot of the throne, facing Than Kosis. When the balance of the procession had entered and assumed their stations Than Kosis addressed the couple standing before him. I could not hear his words, but presently two officers advanced and removed the scarlet robe from one of the figures, and I saw that Kantos Kan had failed in his mission, for it was Sab Than, Prince of Zodanga, who stood revealed before me.

Than Kosis now took a set of the ornaments from one of the salvers and placed one of the collars of gold about his son's neck, springing the padlock fast. After a few more words addressed to Sab Than he turned to the other figure, from which the officers now removed the enshrouding silks, disclosing to my now comprehending view Dejah Thoris, Princess of Helium.

The object of the ceremony was clear to me; in another moment Dejah Thoris would be joined forever to the Prince of Zodanga. It was an impressive and beautiful ceremony, I presume, but to me it seemed the most fiendish sight I had ever witnessed, and as the ornaments were adjusted upon her beautiful figure and her collar of gold swung open in the hands of Than Kosis I raised my long-sword above my head, and, with the heavy hilt, I shattered the glass of the great window and sprang into the midst of the astonished assemblage. With a bound I was on the steps of the platform beside Than Kosis, and as he stood riveted with surprise I brought my long-sword down upon the golden chain that would have bound Dejah Thoris to another.

In an instant all was confusion; a thousand drawn swords menaced me from every quarter, and Sab Than sprang upon me with a jeweled dagger he had drawn from his nuptial ornaments. I could have killed him as easily as I might a fly, but the age-old custom of Barsoom stayed my hand, and grasping his wrist as the dagger flew toward my heart I held him as though in a vise and with my long-sword pointed to the far end of the hall.

"Zodanga has fallen," I cried. "Look!"

All eyes turned in the direction I had indicated, and there, forging through the portals of the entranceway rode Tars Tarkas and his fifty warriors on their great thoats.

A cry of alarm and amazement broke from the assemblage, but no word of fear, and in a moment the soldiers and nobles of Zodanga were hurling themselves upon the advancing Tharks.

Thrusting Sab Than headlong from the platform, I drew Dejah Thoris to my side. Behind the throne was a narrow doorway and in this Than Kosis now stood facing me, with drawn long-sword. In an instant we were engaged, and I found no mean antagonist.

As we circled upon the broad platform I saw Sab Than rushing up the steps to aid his father, but, as he raised his hand to strike, Dejah Thoris sprang before him and then my sword found the spot that made Sab Than jeddak of Zodanga. As his father rolled dead upon the floor the new jeddak tore himself free from Dejah Thoris' grasp, and again we faced each other. He was soon joined by a quartet of officers, and, with my back against a golden throne, I fought once again for Dejah Thoris. I was hard pressed to defend myself and yet not strike down Sab Than and, with him, my last chance to win the woman I loved. My blade was swinging with the rapidity of lightning as I sought to parry the thrusts and cuts of my opponents. Two I had disarmed, and one was down, when several more rushed to the aid of their new ruler, and to avenge the death of the old.

As they advanced there were cries of "The woman! The woman! Strike her down; it is her plot. Kill her! Kill her!"

Calling to Dejah Thoris to get behind me I worked my way toward the little doorway back of the throne, but the officers realized my intentions, and three of them sprang in behind me and blocked my chances for gaining a position where I could have defended Dejah Thoris against any army of swordsmen.

The Tharks were having their hands full in the center of the room, and I began to realize that nothing short of a miracle could save Dejah Thoris and myself, when I saw Tars Tarkas surging through the crowd of pygmies that swarmed about him. With one swing of his mighty longsword he laid a dozen corpses at his feet, and so he hewed a pathway before him until in another moment he stood upon the platform beside me, dealing death and destruction right and left.

The bravery of the Zodangans was awe-inspiring, not one attempted to escape, and when the fighting ceased it was because only Tharks remained alive in the great hall, other than Dejah Thoris and myself.

Sab Than lay dead beside his father, and the corpses of the flower of Zodangan nobility and chivalry covered the floor of the bloody shambles.

My first thought when the battle was over was for Kantos Kan, and leaving Dejah Thoris in charge of Tars Tarkas I took a dozen warriors and hastened to the dungeons beneath the palace. The jailers had all left to join the fighters in the throne room, so we searched the labyrinthine prison without opposition.

I called Kantos Kan's name aloud in each new corridor and compartment, and finally I was rewarded by hearing a faint response. Guided by the sound, we soon found him helpless in a dark recess.

He was overjoyed at seeing me, and to know the meaning of the fight, faint echoes of which had reached his prison cell. He told me that the air patrol had captured him before he reached the high tower of the palace, so that he had not even seen Sab Than.

We discovered that it would be futile to attempt to cut away the bars and chains which held him prisoner, so, at his suggestion I returned to search the bodies on the floor above for keys to open the padlocks of his cell and of his chains.

Fortunately among the first I examined I found his jailer, and soon we had Kantos Kan with us in the throne room.

The sounds of heavy firing, mingled with shouts and cries, came to us from the city's streets, and Tars Tarkas hastened away to direct the fighting without. Kantos Kan accompanied him to act as guide, the green warriors commencing a thorough search of the palace for other Zodangans and for loot, and Dejah Thoris and I were left alone.

She had sunk into one of the golden thrones, and as I turned to her she greeted me with a wan smile.

"Was there ever such a man!" she exclaimed. "I know that Barsoom has never before seen your like. Can it be that all Earth men are as you? Alone, a stranger, hunted, threatened, persecuted, you have done in a few short months what in all the past ages of Barsoom no man has ever done: joined together the wild hordes of the sea bottoms and brought them to fight as allies of a red Martian people."

"The answer is easy, Dejah Thoris," I replied smiling. "It was not I who did it, it was love, love for Dejah Thoris, a power that would work greater miracles than this you have seen."

A pretty flush overspread her face and she answered,

"You may say that now, John Carter, and I may listen, for I am free."

"And more still I have to say, ere it is again too late," I returned. "I have done many strange things in my life, many things that wiser men would not have dared, but never in my wildest fancies have I dreamed of winning a Dejah Thoris for myself – for never had I dreamed that in all the universe dwelt such a woman as the Princess of Helium. That you are a princess does not abash me, but that you are you is enough to make me doubt my sanity as I ask you, my princess, to be mine."

"He does not need to be abashed who so well knew the answer to his plea before the plea were made," she replied, rising and placing her dear hands upon my shoulders, and so I took her in my arms and kissed her.

And thus in the midst of a city of wild conflict, filled with the alarms of war; with death and destruction reaping their terrible harvest around her, did Dejah Thoris, Princess of Helium, true daughter of Mars, the God of War, promise herself in marriage to John Carter, Gentleman of Virginia.

CHAPTER TWENTY SIX

Through Carnage to Joy

SOMETIME LATER Tars Tarkas and Kantos Kan returned to report that Zodanga had been completely reduced. Her forces were entirely destroyed or captured, and no further resistance was to be expected from within. Several battleships had escaped, but there were thousands of war and merchant vessels under guard of Thark warriors.

The lesser hordes had commenced looting and quarreling among themselves, so it was decided that we collect what warriors we could, man as many vessels as possible with Zodangan prisoners and make for Helium without further loss of time.

Five hours later we sailed from the roofs of the dock buildings with a fleet of two hundred and fifty battleships, carrying nearly one hundred thousand green warriors, followed by a fleet of transports with our thoats.

Behind us we left the stricken city in the fierce and brutal clutches of some forty thousand green warriors of the lesser hordes. They were looting, murdering, and fighting amongst themselves. In a hundred places they had applied the torch, and columns of dense smoke were rising above the city as though to blot out from the eye of heaven the horrid sights beneath.

In the middle of the afternoon we sighted the scarlet and yellow towers of Helium, and a short time later a great fleet of Zodangan battleships rose from the camps of the besiegers without the city, and advanced to meet us.

The banners of Helium had been strung from stem to stern of each of our mighty craft, but the Zodangans did not need this sign to realize that we were enemies, for our green Martian warriors had opened fire upon them almost as they left the ground. With their uncanny marksmanship they raked the on-coming fleet with volley after volley.

The twin cities of Helium, perceiving that we were friends, sent out hundreds of vessels to aid us, and then began the first real air battle I had ever witnessed.

The vessels carrying our green warriors were kept circling above the contending fleets of Helium and Zodanga, since their batteries were useless in the hands of the Tharks who, having no navy, have no skill in naval gunnery. Their small-arm fire, however, was most effective, and the final outcome of the engagement was strongly influenced, if not wholly determined, by their presence.

At first the two forces circled at the same altitude, pouring broadside after broadside into each other. Presently a great hole was torn in the hull of one of the immense battle craft from the Zodangan camp; with a lurch she turned completely over, the little figures of her crew plunging, turning and twisting toward the ground a thousand feet below; then with sickening velocity she tore after them, almost completely burying herself in the soft loam of the ancient sea bottom.

A wild cry of exultation arose from the Heliumite squadron, and with redoubled ferocity they fell upon the Zodangan fleet. By a pretty maneuver two of the vessels of Helium gained a position above their adversaries, from which they poured upon them from their keel bomb batteries a perfect torrent of exploding bombs.

Then, one by one, the battleships of Helium succeeded in rising above the Zodangans, and in a short time a number of the beleaguering battleships were drifting hopeless wrecks toward the high scarlet tower of greater Helium. Several others attempted to escape, but they were soon surrounded by thousands of tiny individual fliers, and above each hung a monster battleship of Helium ready to drop boarding parties upon their decks.

Within but little more than an hour from the moment the victorious Zodangan squadron had risen to meet us from the camp of the besiegers the battle was over, and the remaining vessels of the conquered Zodangans were headed toward the cities of Helium under prize crews.

There was an extremely pathetic side to the surrender of these mighty fliers, the result of an age-old custom which demanded that surrender should be signalized by the voluntary plunging to earth of the commander of the vanquished vessel. One after another the brave fellows, holding their colors high above their heads, leaped from the towering bows of their mighty craft to an awful death.

Not until the commander of the entire fleet took the fearful plunge, thus indicating the surrender of the remaining vessels, did the fighting cease, and the useless sacrifice of brave men come to an end.

We now signaled the flagship of Helium's navy to approach, and when she was within hailing distance I called out that we had the Princess Dejah Thoris on board, and that we wished to transfer her to the flagship that she might be taken immediately to the city.

As the full import of my announcement bore in upon them a great cry arose from the decks of the flagship, and a moment later the colors of the Princess of Helium broke from a hundred points upon her upper works. When the other vessels of the squadron caught the meaning of the signals flashed them they took up the wild acclaim and unfurled her colors in the gleaming sunlight.

The flagship bore down upon us, and as she swung gracefully to and touched our side a dozen officers sprang upon our decks. As their astonished gaze fell upon the hundreds of green warriors, who now came forth from the fighting shelters, they stopped aghast, but at sight of Kantos Kan, who advanced to meet them, they came forward, crowding about him.

Dejah Thoris and I then advanced, and they had no eyes for other than her. She received them gracefully, calling each by name, for they were men high in the esteem and service of her grandfather, and she knew them well.

"Lay your hands upon the shoulder of John Carter," she said to them, turning toward me, "the man to whom Helium owes her princess as well as her victory today."

They were very courteous to me and said many kind and complimentary things, but what seemed to impress them most was that I had won the aid of the fierce Tharks in my campaign for the liberation of Dejah Thoris, and the relief of Helium.

"You owe your thanks more to another man than to me," I said, "and here he is; meet one of Barsoom's greatest soldiers and statesmen, Tars Tarkas, Jeddak of Thark."

With the same polished courtesy that had marked their manner toward me they extended their greetings to the great Thark, nor, to my surprise, was he much behind them in ease of bearing or in courtly speech. Though not a garrulous race, the Tharks are extremely formal, and their ways lend themselves amazingly well to dignified and courtly manners.

Dejah Thoris went aboard the flagship, and was much put out that I would not follow, but, as I explained to her, the battle was but partly won; we still had the land forces of the besieging Zodangans to account for, and I would not leave Tars Tarkas until that had been accomplished.

The commander of the naval forces of Helium promised to arrange to have the armies of Helium attack from the city in conjunction with our land attack, and so the vessels separated and Dejah Thoris was borne in triumph back to the court of her grandfather, Tardos Mors, Jeddak of Helium.

In the distance lay our fleet of transports, with the thoats of the green warriors, where they had remained during the battle. Without landing stages it was to be a difficult matter to unload these beasts upon the open plain, but there was nothing else for it, and so we put out for a point about ten miles from the city and began the task.

It was necessary to lower the animals to the ground in slings and this work occupied the remainder of the day and half the night. Twice we were attacked by parties of Zodangan cavalry, but with little loss, however, and after darkness shut down they withdrew.

As soon as the last thoat was unloaded Tars Tarkas gave the command to advance, and in three parties we crept upon the Zodangan camp from the north, the south and the east.

About a mile from the main camp we encountered their outposts and, as had been prearranged, accepted this as the signal to charge. With wild, ferocious cries and amidst the nasty squealing of battle-enraged thoats we bore down upon the Zodangans.

We did not catch them napping, but found a well-entrenched battle line confronting us. Time after time we were repulsed until, toward noon, I began to fear for the result of the battle.

The Zodangans numbered nearly a million fighting men, gathered from pole to pole, wherever stretched their ribbon-like waterways, while pitted against them were less than a hundred thousand green warriors. The forces from Helium had not arrived, nor could we receive any word from them.

Just at noon we heard heavy firing all along the line between the Zodangans and the cities, and we knew then that our much-needed reinforcements had come.

Again Tars Tarkas ordered the charge, and once more the mighty thoats bore their terrible riders against the ramparts of the enemy. At the same moment the battle line of Helium surged over the opposite breastworks of the Zodangans and in another moment they were being crushed as between two millstones. Nobly they fought, but in vain.

The plain before the city became a veritable shambles ere the last Zodangan surrendered, but finally the carnage ceased, the prisoners were marched back to Helium, and we entered the greater city's gates, a huge triumphal procession of conquering heroes.

The broad avenues were lined with women and children, among which were the few men whose duties necessitated that they remain within the city during the battle. We were greeted with an endless round of applause and showered with ornaments of gold, platinum, silver, and precious jewels. The city had gone mad with joy.

My fierce Tharks caused the wildest excitement and enthusiasm. Never before had an armed body of green warriors entered the gates of Helium, and that they came now as friends and allies filled the red men with rejoicing.

That my poor services to Dejah Thoris had become known to the Heliumites was evidenced by the loud crying of my name, and by the loads of ornaments that were fastened upon me and my huge thoat as we passed up the avenues to the palace, for even in the face of the ferocious appearance of Woola the populace pressed close about me.

As we approached this magnificent pile we were met by a party of officers who greeted us warmly and requested that Tars Tarkas and his jeds with the jeddaks and jeds of his wild allies, together with myself, dismount and accompany them to receive from Tardos Mors an expression of his gratitude for our services.

At the top of the great steps leading up to the main portals of the palace stood the royal party, and as we reached the lower steps one of their number descended to meet us.

He was an almost perfect specimen of manhood; tall, straight as an arrow, superbly muscled and with the carriage and bearing of a ruler of men. I did not need to be told that he was Tardos Mors, Jeddak of Helium.

The first member of our party he met was Tars Tarkas and his first words sealed forever the new friendship between the races.

"That Tardos Mors," he said, earnestly, "may meet the greatest living warrior of Barsoom is a priceless honor, but that he may lay his hand on the shoulder of a friend and ally is a far greater boon."

"Jeddak of Helium," returned Tars Tarkas, "it has remained for a man of another world to teach the green warriors of Barsoom the meaning of friendship; to him we owe the fact that the hordes of Thark can understand you; that they can appreciate and reciprocate the sentiments so graciously expressed."

Tardos Mors then greeted each of the green jeddaks and jeds, and to each spoke words of friendship and appreciation.

As he approached me he laid both hands upon my shoulders.

"Welcome, my son," he said; "that you are granted, gladly, and without one word of opposition, the most precious jewel in all Helium, yes, on all Barsoom, is sufficient earnest of my esteem."

We were then presented to Mors Kajak, Jed of lesser Helium, and father of Dejah Thoris. He had followed close behind Tardos Mors and seemed even more affected by the meeting than had his father.

He tried a dozen times to express his gratitude to me, but his voice choked with emotion and he could not speak, and yet he had, as I was to later learn, a reputation for ferocity and fearlessness as a fighter that was remarkable even upon warlike Barsoom. In common with all Helium he worshiped his daughter, nor could he think of what she had escaped without deep emotion.

CHAPTER TWENTY SEVEN

From Joy to Death

FOR TEN DAYS the hordes of Thark and their wild allies were feasted and entertained, and, then, loaded with costly presents and escorted by ten thousand soldiers of Helium commanded by Mors Kajak, they started on the return journey to their own lands. The jed of lesser Helium with a small party of nobles accompanied them all the way to Thark to cement more closely the new bonds of peace and friendship.

Sola also accompanied Tars Tarkas, her father, who before all his chieftains had acknowledged her as his daughter.

Three weeks later, Mors Kajak and his officers, accompanied by Tars Tarkas and Sola, returned upon a battleship that had been dispatched to Thark to fetch them in time for the ceremony which made Dejah Thoris and John Carter one.

For nine years I served in the councils and fought in the armies of Helium as a prince of the house of Tardos Mors. The people seemed never to tire of heaping honors upon me, and no day passed that did not bring some new proof of their love for my princess, the incomparable Dejah Thoris.

In a golden incubator upon the roof of our palace lay a snow-white egg. For nearly five years ten soldiers of the jeddak's Guard had constantly stood over it, and not a day passed when I was in the city that Dejah Thoris and I did not stand hand in hand before our little shrine planning for the future, when the delicate shell should break.

Vivid in my memory is the picture of the last night as we sat there talking in low tones of the strange romance which had woven our lives together and of this wonder which was coming to augment our happiness and fulfill our hopes.

In the distance we saw the bright-white light of an approaching airship, but we attached no special significance to so common a sight. Like a bolt of lightning it raced toward Helium until its very speed bespoke the unusual.

Flashing the signals which proclaimed it a dispatch bearer for the jeddak, it circled impatiently awaiting the tardy patrol boat which must convoy it to the palace docks.

Ten minutes after it touched at the palace a message called me to the council chamber, which I found filling with the members of that body.

On the raised platform of the throne was Tardos Mors, pacing back and forth with tense-drawn face. When all were in their seats he turned toward us.

"This morning," he said, "word reached the several governments of Barsoom that the keeper of the atmosphere plant had made no wireless report for two days, nor had almost ceaseless calls upon him from a score of capitals elicited a sign of response.

"The ambassadors of the other nations asked us to take the matter in hand and hasten the assistant keeper to the plant. All day a thousand cruisers have been searching for him until just now one of them returns bearing his dead body, which was found in the pits beneath his house horribly mutilated by some assassin.

"I do not need to tell you what this means to Barsoom. It would take months to penetrate those mighty walls, in fact the work has already commenced, and there would be little to fear were the engine of the pumping plant to run as it should and as they all have for hundreds of years now; but the worst, we fear, has happened. The instruments show a rapidly decreasing air pressure on all parts of Barsoom – the engine has stopped."

"My gentlemen," he concluded, "we have at best three days to live."

There was absolute silence for several minutes, and then a young noble arose, and with his drawn sword held high above his head addressed Tardos Mors.

"The men of Helium have prided themselves that they have ever shown Barsoom how a nation of red men should live, now is our opportunity to show them how they should die. Let us go about our duties as though a thousand useful years still lay before us."

The chamber rang with applause and as there was nothing better to do than to allay the fears of the people by our example we went our ways with smiles upon our faces and sorrow gnawing at our hearts.

When I returned to my palace I found that the rumor already had reached Dejah Thoris, so I told her all that I had heard.

"We have been very happy, John Carter," she said, "and I thank whatever fate overtakes us that it permits us to die together."

The next two days brought no noticeable change in the supply of air, but on the morning of the third day breathing became difficult at the higher altitudes of the rooftops. The avenues and plazas of Helium were filled with people. All business had ceased. For the most part the people looked bravely into the face of their unalterable doom. Here and there, however, men and women gave way to quiet grief.

Toward the middle of the day many of the weaker commenced to succumb and within an hour the people of Barsoom were sinking by thousands into the unconsciousness which precedes death by asphyxiation.

Dejah Thoris and I with the other members of the royal family had collected in a sunken garden within an inner courtyard of the palace. We conversed in low tones, when we conversed at all, as the awe of the grim shadow of death crept over us. Even Woola seemed to feel the weight of the impending calamity, for he pressed close to Dejah Thoris and to me, whining pitifully.

The little incubator had been brought from the roof of our palace at request of Dejah Thoris and now she sat gazing longingly upon the unknown little life that now she would never know.

As it was becoming perceptibly difficult to breathe Tardos Mors arose, saying,

"Let us bid each other farewell. The days of the greatness of Barsoom are over. Tomorrow's sun will look down upon a dead world which through all eternity must go swinging through the heavens peopled not even by memories. It is the end."

He stooped and kissed the women of his family, and laid his strong hand upon the shoulders of the men.

As I turned sadly from him my eyes fell upon Dejah Thoris. Her head was drooping upon her breast, to all appearances she was lifeless. With a cry I sprang to her and raised her in my arms.

Her eyes opened and looked into mine.

"Kiss me, John Carter," she murmured. "I love you! I love you! It is cruel that we must be torn apart who were just starting upon a life of love and happiness."

As I pressed her dear lips to mine the old feeling of unconquerable power and authority rose in me. The fighting blood of Virginia sprang to life in my veins.

"It shall not be, my princess," I cried. "There is, there must be some way, and John Carter, who has fought his way through a strange world for love of you, will find it."

And with my words there crept above the threshold of my conscious mind a series of nine long forgotten sounds. Like a flash of lightning in the darkness their full purport dawned upon me – the key to the three great doors of the atmosphere plant!

Turning suddenly toward Tardos Mors as I still clasped my dying love to my breast I cried.

"A flier, Jeddak! Quick! Order your swiftest flier to the palace top. I can save Barsoom yet."

He did not wait to question, but in an instant a guard was racing to the nearest dock and though the air was thin and almost gone at the rooftop they managed to launch the fastest one-man, air-scout machine that the skill of Barsoom had ever produced.

Kissing Dejah Thoris a dozen times and commanding Woola, who would have followed me, to remain and guard her, I bounded with my old agility and strength to the high ramparts of the palace, and in another moment I was headed toward the goal of the hopes of all Barsoom.

I had to fly low to get sufficient air to breathe, but I took a straight course across an old sea bottom and so had to rise only a few feet above the ground.

I traveled with awful velocity for my errand was a race against time with death. The face of Dejah Thoris hung always before me. As I turned for a last look as I left the palace garden I had seen her stagger and sink upon the ground beside the little incubator. That she had dropped into the last coma which would end in death, if the air supply remained unreplenished, I well knew, and so, throwing caution to the winds, I flung overboard everything but the engine and compass, even to my ornaments, and lying on my belly along the deck with one hand on the steering wheel and the other pushing the speed lever to its last notch I split the thin air of dying Mars with the speed of a meteor.

An hour before dark the great walls of the atmosphere plant loomed suddenly before me, and with a sickening thud I plunged to the ground before the small door which was withholding the spark of life from the inhabitants of an entire planet.

Beside the door a great crew of men had been laboring to pierce the wall, but they had scarcely scratched the flint-like surface, and now most of them lay in the last sleep from which not even air would awaken them.

Conditions seemed much worse here than at Helium, and it was with difficulty that I breathed at all. There were a few men still conscious, and to one of these I spoke.

"If I can open these doors is there a man who can start the engines?" I asked.

"I can," he replied, "if you open quickly. I can last but a few moments more. But it is useless, they are both dead and no one else upon Barsoom knew the secret of these awful locks. For three days men crazed with fear have surged about this portal in vain attempts to solve its mystery."

I had no time to talk, I was becoming very weak and it was with difficulty that I controlled my mind at all.

But, with a final effort, as I sank weakly to my knees I hurled the nine thought waves at that awful thing before me. The Martian had crawled to my side and with staring eyes fixed on the single panel before us we waited in the silence of death.

Slowly the mighty door receded before us. I attempted to rise and follow it but I was too weak.

"After it," I cried to my companion, "and if you reach the pump room turn loose all the pumps. It is the only chance Barsoom has to exist tomorrow!"

From where I lay I opened the second door, and then the third, and as I saw the hope of Barsoom crawling weakly on hands and knees through the last doorway I sank unconscious upon the ground.

At the Arizona Cave

IT WAS DARK when I opened my eyes again. Strange, stiff garments were upon my body; garments that cracked and powdered away from me as I rose to a sitting posture.

I felt myself over from head to foot and from head to foot I was clothed, though when I fell unconscious at the little doorway I had been naked. Before me was a small patch of moonlit sky which showed through a ragged aperture.

As my hands passed over my body they came in contact with pockets and in one of these a small parcel of matches wrapped in oiled paper. One of these matches I struck, and its dim flame lighted up what appeared to be a huge cave, toward the back of which I discovered a strange, still figure huddled over a tiny bench. As I approached it I saw that it was the dead and mummified remains of a little old woman with long black hair, and the thing it leaned over was a small charcoal burner upon which rested a round copper vessel containing a small quantity of greenish powder.

Behind her, depending from the roof upon rawhide thongs, and stretching entirely across the cave, was a row of human skeletons. From the thong which held them stretched another to the dead hand of the little old woman; as I touched the cord the skeletons swung to the motion with a noise as of the rustling of dry leaves.

It was a most grotesque and horrid tableau and I hastened out into the fresh air; glad to escape from so gruesome a place.

The sight that met my eyes as I stepped out upon a small ledge which ran before the entrance of the cave filled me with consternation.

A new heaven and a new landscape met my gaze. The silvered mountains in the distance, the almost stationary moon hanging in the sky, the cacti-studded valley below me were not of Mars. I could scarcely believe my eyes, but the truth slowly forced itself upon me – I was looking upon Arizona from the same ledge from which ten years before I had gazed with longing upon Mars.

Burying my head in my arms I turned, broken, and sorrowful, down the trail from the cave.

Above me shone the red eye of Mars holding her awful secret, forty-eight million miles away.

Did the Martian reach the pump room? Did the vitalizing air reach the people of that distant planet in time to save them? Was my Dejah Thoris alive, or did her beautiful body lie cold in death beside the tiny golden incubator in the sunken garden of the inner courtyard of the palace of Tardos Mors, the jeddak of Helium?

For ten years I have waited and prayed for an answer to my questions. For ten years I have waited and prayed to be taken back to the world of my lost love. I would rather lie dead beside her there than live on Earth all those millions of terrible miles from her.

The old mine, which I found untouched, has made me fabulously wealthy; but what care I for wealth!

As I sit here tonight in my little study overlooking the Hudson, just twenty years have elapsed since I first opened my eyes upon Mars.

I can see her shining in the sky through the little window by my desk, and tonight she seems calling to me again as she has not called before since that long dead night, and I think I can see, across that awful abyss of space, a beautiful black-haired woman standing in the garden of a palace, and at her side is a little boy who puts his arm around her as she points into the sky toward the planet Earth, while at their feet is a huge and hideous creature with a heart of gold.

I believe that they are waiting there for me, and something tells me that I shall soon know.

THE GODS
OF MARS
BOOK TWO

FOREWORD

TWELVE YEARS HAD PASSED since I had laid the body of my great-uncle, Captain John Carter, of Virginia, away from the sight of men in that strange mausoleum in the old cemetery at Richmond.

Often had I pondered on the odd instructions he had left me governing the construction of his mighty tomb, and especially those parts which directed that he be laid in an *open* casket and that the ponderous mechanism which controlled the bolts of the vault's huge door be accessible *only from the inside.*

Twelve years had passed since I had read the remarkable manuscript of this remarkable man; this man who remembered no childhood and who could not even offer a vague guess as to his age; who was always young and yet who had dandled my grandfather's great-grandfather upon his knee; this man who had spent ten years upon the planet Mars; who had fought for the green men of Barsoom and fought against them; who had fought for and against the red men and who had won the ever beautiful Dejah Thoris, Princess of Helium, for his wife, and for nearly ten years had been a prince of the house of Tardos Mors, Jeddak of Helium.

Twelve years had passed since his body had been found upon the bluff before his cottage overlooking the Hudson, and oft-times during these long years I had wondered if John Carter were really dead, or if he again roamed the dead sea bottoms of that dying planet; if he had returned to Barsoom to find that he had opened the frowning portals of the mighty atmosphere plant in time to save the countless millions who were dying of asphyxiation on that far-gone day that had seen him hurtled ruthlessly through forty-eight million miles of space back to Earth once more. I had wondered if he had found his black-haired Princess and the slender son he had dreamed was with her in the royal gardens of Tardos Mors, awaiting his return.

Or, had he found that he had been too late, and thus gone back to a living death upon a dead world? Or was he really dead after all, never to return either to his mother Earth or his beloved Mars?

Thus was I lost in useless speculation one sultry August evening when old Ben, my body servant, handed me a telegram. Tearing it open I read:

'Meet me to-morrow hotel Raleigh Richmond.
'*John Carter*'

Early the next morning I took the first train for Richmond and within two hours was being ushered into the room occupied by John Carter.

As I entered he rose to greet me, his old-time cordial smile of welcome lighting his handsome face. Apparently he had not aged a minute, but was still the straight, clean-limbed fighting-man of thirty. His keen grey eyes were undimmed, and the only lines upon his face were the lines of iron character and determination that always had been there since first I remembered him, nearly thirty-five years before.

'Well, nephew,' he greeted me, 'do you feel as though you were seeing a ghost, or suffering from the effects of too many of Uncle Ben's juleps?'

'Juleps, I reckon,' I replied, 'for I certainly feel mighty good; but maybe it's just the sight of you again that affects me. You have been back to Mars? Tell me. And Dejah Thoris? You found her well and awaiting you?'

'Yes, I have been to Barsoom again, and – but it's a long story, too long to tell in the limited time I have before I must return. I have learned the secret, nephew, and I may traverse the trackless void at my will, coming and going between the countless planets as I list; but my heart is always in Barsoom, and while it is there in the keeping of my Martian Princess, I doubt that I shall ever again leave the dying world that is my life.

'I have come now because my affection for you prompted me to see you once more before you pass over for ever into that other life that I shall never know, and which though I have died thrice and shall die again to-night, as you know death, I am as unable to fathom as are you.

'Even the wise and mysterious therns of Barsoom, that ancient cult which for countless ages has been credited with holding the secret of life and death in their impregnable fastnesses upon the hither slopes of the Mountains of Otz, are as ignorant as we. I have proved it, though I near lost my life in the doing of it; but you shall read it all in the notes I have been making during the last three months that I have been back upon Earth.'

He patted a swelling portfolio that lay on the table at his elbow.

'I know that you are interested and that you believe, and I know that the world, too, is interested, though they will not believe for many years; yes, for many ages, since they cannot understand. Earth men have not yet progressed to a point where they can comprehend the things that I have written in those notes.

'Give them what you wish of it, what you think will not harm them, but do not feel aggrieved if they laugh at you.'

That night I walked down to the cemetery with him. At the door of his vault he turned and pressed my hand.

'Good-bye, nephew,' he said. 'I may never see you again, for I doubt that I can ever bring myself to leave my wife and boy while they live, and the span of life upon Barsoom is often more than a thousand years.'

He entered the vault. The great door swung slowly to. The ponderous bolts grated into place. The lock clicked. I have never seen Captain John Carter, of Virginia, since.

But here is the story of his return to Mars on that other occasion, as I have gleaned it from the great mass of notes which he left for me upon the table of his room in the hotel at Richmond.

There is much which I have left out; much which I have not dared to tell; but you will find the story of his second search for Dejah Thoris, Princess of Helium, even more remarkable than was his first manuscript which I gave to an unbelieving world a short time since and through which we followed the fighting Virginian across dead sea bottoms under the moons of Mars.

E. R. B.

CHAPTER ONE

The Plant Men

As I STOOD UPON THE BLUFF before my cottage on that clear cold night in the early part of March, 1886, the noble Hudson flowing like the grey and silent spectre of a dead river below me, I felt again the strange, compelling influence of the mighty god of war, my beloved Mars, which for ten long and lonesome years I had implored with outstretched arms to carry me back to my lost love.

Not since that other March night in 1866, when I had stood without that Arizona cave in which my still and lifeless body lay wrapped in the similitude of earthly death had I felt the irresistible attraction of the god of my profession.

With arms outstretched toward the red eye of the great star I stood praying for a return of that strange power which twice had drawn me through the immensity of space, praying as I had prayed on a thousand nights before during the long ten years that I had waited and hoped.

Suddenly a qualm of nausea swept over me, my senses swam, my knees gave beneath me and I pitched headlong to the ground upon the very verge of the dizzy bluff.

Instantly my brain cleared and there swept back across the threshold of my memory the vivid picture of the horrors of that ghostly Arizona cave; again, as on that far-gone night, my muscles refused to respond to my will and again, as though even here upon the banks of the placid Hudson, I could hear the awful moans and rustling of the fearsome thing which had lurked and threatened me from the dark recesses of the cave, I made the same mighty and superhuman effort to break the bonds of the strange anaesthesia which held me, and again came the sharp click as of the sudden parting of a taut wire, and I stood naked and free beside the staring, lifeless thing that had so recently pulsed with the warm, red life-blood of John Carter.

With scarcely a parting glance I turned my eyes again toward Mars, lifted my hands toward his lurid rays, and waited.

Nor did I have long to wait; for scarce had I turned ere I shot with the rapidity of thought into the awful void before me. There was the same instant of unthinkable cold and utter darkness that I had experienced twenty years before, and then I opened my eyes in another world, beneath the burning rays of a hot sun, which beat through a tiny opening in the dome of the mighty forest in which I lay.

The scene that met my eyes was so un-Martian that my heart sprang to my throat as the sudden fear swept through me that I had been aimlessly tossed upon some strange planet by a cruel fate.

Why not? What guide had I through the trackless waste of interplanetary space? What assurance that I might not as well be hurtled to some far-distant star of another solar system, as to Mars?

I lay upon a close-cropped sward of red grasslike vegetation, and about me stretched a grove of strange and beautiful trees, covered with huge and gorgeous blossoms and filled with brilliant, voiceless birds. I call them birds since they were winged, but mortal eye ne'er rested on such odd, unearthly shapes.

The vegetation was similar to that which covers the lawns of the red Martians of the great waterways, but the trees and birds were unlike anything that I had ever seen upon Mars, and then through the further trees I could see that most un-Martian of all sights – an open sea, its blue waters shimmering beneath the brazen sun.

As I rose to investigate further I experienced the same ridiculous catastrophe that had met my first attempt to walk under Martian conditions. The lesser attraction of this smaller planet and the reduced air pressure of its greatly rarefied atmosphere, afforded so little resistance to my earthly muscles that the ordinary exertion of the mere act of rising sent me several feet into the air and precipitated me upon my face in the soft and brilliant grass of this strange world.

This experience, however, gave me some slightly increased assurance that, after all, I might indeed be in some, to me, unknown corner of Mars, and this was very possible since during my ten years' residence upon the planet I had explored but a comparatively tiny area of its vast expanse.

I arose again, laughing at my forgetfulness, and soon had mastered once more the art of attuning my earthly sinews to these changed conditions.

As I walked slowly down the imperceptible slope toward the sea I could not help but note the park-like appearance of the sward and trees. The grass was as close-cropped and carpet-like as some old English lawn and the trees themselves showed evidence of careful pruning to a uniform height of about fifteen feet from the ground, so that as one turned his glance in any direction the forest had the appearance at a little distance of a vast, high-ceiled chamber.

All these evidences of careful and systematic cultivation convinced me that I had been fortunate enough to make my entry into Mars on this second occasion through the domain of a civilized people and that when I should find them I would be accorded the courtesy and protection that my rank as a Prince of the house of Tardos Mors entitled me to.

The trees of the forest attracted my deep admiration as I proceeded toward the sea. Their great stems, some of them fully a hundred feet in diameter, attested their prodigious height, which I could only guess at, since at no point could I penetrate their dense foliage above me to more than sixty or eighty feet.

As far aloft as I could see the stems and branches and twigs were as smooth and as highly polished as the newest of American-made pianos. The wood of some of the trees was as black as ebony, while their nearest neighbours might perhaps gleam in the subdued light of the forest as clear and white as the finest china, or, again, they were azure, scarlet, yellow, or deepest purple.

And in the same way was the foliage as gay and variegated as the stems, while the blooms that clustered thick upon them may not be described in any earthly tongue, and indeed might challenge the language of the gods.

As I neared the confines of the forest I beheld before me and between the grove and the open sea, a broad expanse of meadow land, and as I was about to emerge from the shadows of the trees a sight met my eyes that banished all romantic and poetic reflection upon the beauties of the strange landscape.

To my left the sea extended as far as the eye could reach, before me only a vague, dim line indicated its further shore, while at my right a mighty river, broad, placid, and majestic, flowed between scarlet banks to empty into the quiet sea before me.

At a little distance up the river rose mighty perpendicular bluffs, from the very base of which the great river seemed to rise.

But it was not these inspiring and magnificent evidences of Nature's grandeur that took my immediate attention from the beauties of the forest. It was the sight of a score of figures moving slowly about the meadow near the bank of the mighty river.

Odd, grotesque shapes they were; unlike anything that I had ever seen upon Mars, and yet, at a distance, most manlike in appearance. The larger specimens appeared to be about ten or twelve feet in height when they stood erect, and to be proportioned as to torso and lower extremities precisely as is earthly man.

Their arms, however, were very short, and from where I stood seemed as though fashioned much after the manner of an elephant's trunk, in that they moved in sinuous and snakelike undulations, as though entirely without bony structure, or if there were bones it seemed that they must be vertebral in nature.

As I watched them from behind the stem of a huge tree, one of the creatures moved slowly in my direction, engaged in the occupation that seemed to be the principal business of each of them, and which consisted in running their oddly shaped hands over the surface of the sward, for what purpose I could not determine.

As he approached quite close to me I obtained an excellent view of him, and though I was later to become better acquainted with his kind, I may say that that single cursory examination of this awful travesty on Nature would have proved quite sufficient to my desires had I been a free agent. The fastest flier of the Heliumetic Navy could not quickly enough have carried me far from this hideous creature.

Its hairless body was a strange and ghoulish blue, except for a broad band of white which encircled its protruding, single eye: an eye that was all dead white – pupil, iris, and ball.

Its nose was a ragged, inflamed, circular hole in the centre of its blank face; a hole that resembled more closely nothing that I could think of other than a fresh bullet wound which has not yet commenced to bleed.

Below this repulsive orifice the face was quite blank to the chin, for the thing had no mouth that I could discover.

The head, with the exception of the face, was covered by a tangled mass of jet-black hair some eight or ten inches in length. Each hair was about the bigness of a large angleworm, and as the thing moved the muscles of its scalp this awful head-covering seemed to writhe and wriggle and crawl about the fearsome face as though indeed each separate hair was endowed with independent life.

The body and the legs were as symmetrically human as Nature could have fashioned them, and the feet, too, were human in shape, but of monstrous proportions. From heel to toe they were fully three feet long, and very flat and very broad.

As it came quite close to me I discovered that its strange movements, running its odd hands over the surface of the turf, were the result of its peculiar method of feeding, which consists in cropping off the tender vegetation with its razorlike talons and sucking it up from its two mouths, which lie one in the palm of each hand, through its arm-like throats.

In addition to the features which I have already described, the beast was equipped with a massive tail about six feet in length, quite round where it joined the body, but tapering to a flat, thin blade toward the end, which trailed at right angles to the ground.

By far the most remarkable feature of this most remarkable creature, however, were the two tiny replicas of it, each about six inches in length, which dangled, one on either side, from its armpits. They were suspended by a small stem which seemed to grow from the exact tops of their heads to where it connected them with the body of the adult.

Whether they were the young, or merely portions of a composite creature, I did not know.

As I had been scrutinizing this weird monstrosity the balance of the herd had fed quite close to me and I now saw that while many had the smaller specimens dangling from them, not all were thus equipped, and I further noted that the little ones varied in size from what appeared to be but tiny unopened buds an inch in diameter through various stages of development to the full-fledged and perfectly formed creature of ten to twelve inches in length.

Feeding with the herd were many of the little fellows not much larger than those which remained attached to their parents, and from the young of that size the herd graded up to the immense adults.

Fearsome-looking as they were, I did not know whether to fear them or not, for they did not seem to be particularly well equipped for fighting, and I was on the point of stepping from my hiding-place and revealing myself to them to note the effect upon them of the sight of a man when my rash resolve was, fortunately for me, nipped in the bud by a strange shrieking wail, which seemed to come from the direction of the bluffs at my right.

Naked and unarmed, as I was, my end would have been both speedy and horrible at the hands of these cruel creatures had I had time to put my resolve into execution, but at the moment of the shriek each member of the herd turned in the direction from which the sound seemed to come, and at the same instant every particular snake-like hair upon their heads rose stiffly perpendicular as if each had been a sentient organism looking or listening for the source or meaning of the wail. And indeed the latter proved to be the truth, for this strange growth upon the craniums of the plant men of Barsoom represents the thousand ears of these hideous creatures, the last remnant of the strange race which sprang from the original Tree of Life.

Instantly every eye turned toward one member of the herd, a large fellow who evidently was the leader. A strange purring sound issued from the mouth in the palm of one of his hands, and at the same time he started rapidly toward the bluff, followed by the entire herd.

Their speed and method of locomotion were both remarkable, springing as they did in great leaps of twenty or thirty feet, much after the manner of a kangaroo.

They were rapidly disappearing when it occurred to me to follow them, and so, hurling caution to the winds, I sprang across the meadow in their wake with leaps and bounds even more prodigious than their own, for the muscles of an athletic Earth man produce remarkable results when pitted against the lesser gravity and air pressure of Mars.

Their way led directly towards the apparent source of the river at the base of the cliffs, and as I neared this point I found the meadow dotted with huge boulders that the ravages of time had evidently dislodged from the towering crags above.

For this reason I came quite close to the cause of the disturbance before the scene broke upon my horrified gaze. As I topped a great boulder I saw the herd of plant men surrounding a little group of perhaps five or six green men and women of Barsoom.

That I was indeed upon Mars I now had no doubt, for here were members of the wild hordes that people the dead sea bottoms and deserted cities of that dying planet.

Here were the great males towering in all the majesty of their imposing height; here were the gleaming white tusks protruding from their massive lower jaws to a point near the centre of their foreheads, the laterally placed, protruding eyes with which they could look forward or backward, or to either side without turning their heads, here the strange antennae-like ears rising from the tops of their foreheads; and the additional pair of arms extending from midway between the shoulders and the hips.

Even without the glossy green hide and the metal ornaments which denoted the tribes to which they belonged, I would have known them on the instant for what they were, for where else in all the universe is their like duplicated?

There were two men and four females in the party and their ornaments denoted them as members of different hordes, a fact which tended to puzzle me infinitely, since the various hordes of green men of Barsoom are eternally at deadly war with one another, and never, except on that single historic instance when the great Tars Tarkas of Thark gathered a hundred and fifty thousand green warriors from several hordes to march upon the doomed city of Zodanga to rescue Dejah Thoris, Princess of Helium, from the clutches of Than Kosis, had I seen green Martians of different hordes associated in other than mortal combat.

But now they stood back to back, facing, in wide-eyed amazement, the very evidently hostile demonstrations of a common enemy.

Both men and women were armed with long-swords and daggers, but no firearms were in evidence, else it had been short shrift for the gruesome plant men of Barsoom.

Presently the leader of the plant men charged the little party, and his method of attack was as remarkable as it was effective, and by its very strangeness was the more potent, since in the science of the green warriors there was no defence for this singular manner of attack, the like of which it soon was evident to me they were as unfamiliar with as they were with the monstrosities which confronted them.

The plant man charged to within a dozen feet of the party and then, with a bound, rose as though to pass directly above their heads. His powerful tail was raised high to one side, and as he passed close above them he brought it down in one terrific sweep that crushed a green warrior's skull as though it had been an eggshell.

The balance of the frightful herd was now circling rapidly and with bewildering speed about the little knot of victims. Their prodigious bounds and the shrill, screeching purr of their uncanny mouths were well calculated to confuse and terrorize their prey, so that as two of them leaped simultaneously from either side, the mighty sweep of those awful tails met with no resistance and two more green Martians went down to an ignoble death.

There were now but one warrior and two females left, and it seemed that it could be but a matter of seconds ere these, also, lay dead upon the scarlet sward.

But as two more of the plant men charged, the warrior, who was now prepared by the experiences of the past few minutes, swung his mighty long-sword aloft and met the hurtling bulk with a clean cut that clove one of the plant men from chin to groin.

The other, however, dealt a single blow with his cruel tail that laid both of the females crushed corpses upon the ground.

As the green warrior saw the last of his companions go down and at the same time perceived that the entire herd was charging him in a body, he rushed boldly to meet them, swinging his long-sword in the terrific manner that I had so often seen the men of his kind wield it in their ferocious and almost continual warfare among their own race.

Cutting and hewing to right and left, he laid an open path straight through the advancing plant men, and then commenced a mad race for the forest, in the shelter of which he evidently hoped that he might find a haven of refuge.

He had turned for that portion of the forest which abutted on the cliffs, and thus the mad race was taking the entire party farther and farther from the boulder where I lay concealed.

As I had watched the noble fight which the great warrior had put up against such enormous odds my heart had swelled in admiration for him, and acting as I am wont to do, more upon impulse than after mature deliberation, I instantly sprang from my sheltering rock and bounded quickly toward the bodies of the dead green Martians, a well-defined plan of action already formed.

Half a dozen great leaps brought me to the spot, and another instant saw me again in my stride in quick pursuit of the hideous monsters that were rapidly gaining on the fleeing warrior, but this time I grasped a mighty long-sword in my hand and in my heart was the old blood lust of the fighting man, and a red mist swam before my eyes and I felt my lips respond to my heart in the old smile that has ever marked me in the midst of the joy of battle.

Swift as I was I was none too soon, for the green warrior had been overtaken ere he had made half the distance to the forest, and now he stood with his back to a boulder, while the herd, temporarily balked, hissed and screeched about him.

With their single eyes in the centre of their heads and every eye turned upon their prey, they did not note my soundless approach, so that I was upon them with my great long-sword and four of them lay dead ere they knew that I was among them.

For an instant they recoiled before my terrific onslaught, and in that instant the green warrior rose to the occasion and, springing to my side, laid to the right and left of him as I had never seen but one other warrior do, with great circling strokes that formed a figure eight about him and that never stopped until none stood living to oppose him, his keen blade passing through flesh and bone and metal as though each had been alike thin air.

As we bent to the slaughter, far above us rose that shrill, weird cry which I had heard once before, and which had called the herd to the attack upon their victims. Again and again it rose, but we were too much engaged with the fierce and powerful creatures about us to attempt to search out even with our eyes the author of the horrid notes.

Great tails lashed in frenzied anger about us, razor-like talons cut our limbs and bodies, and a green and sticky syrup, such as oozes from a crushed caterpillar, smeared us from head to foot, for every cut and thrust of our longswords brought spurts of this stuff upon us from the severed arteries of the plant men, through which it courses in its sluggish viscidity in lieu of blood.

Once I felt the great weight of one of the monsters upon my back and as keen talons sank into my flesh I experienced the frightful sensation of moist lips sucking the lifeblood from the wounds to which the claws still clung.

I was very much engaged with a ferocious fellow who was endeavouring to reach my throat from in front, while two more, one on either side, were lashing viciously at me with their tails.

The green warrior was much put to it to hold his own, and I felt that the unequal struggle could last but a moment longer when the huge fellow discovered my plight, and tearing himself from those that surrounded him, he raked the assailant from my back with a single sweep of his blade, and thus relieved I had little difficulty with the others.

Once together, we stood almost back to back against the great boulder, and thus the creatures were prevented from soaring above us to deliver their deadly blows, and as we were easily their match while they remained upon the ground, we were making great headway in dispatching what remained of them when our attention was again attracted by the shrill wail of the caller above our heads.

This time I glanced up, and far above us upon a little natural balcony on the face of the cliff stood a strange figure of a man shrieking out his shrill signal, the while he waved one hand in the direction of the river's mouth as though beckoning to some one there, and with the other pointed and gesticulated toward us.

A glance in the direction toward which he was looking was sufficient to apprise me of his aims and at the same time to fill me with the dread of dire apprehension, for, streaming in from all directions across the meadow, from out of the forest, and from the far distance of the flat land across the river, I could see converging upon us a hundred different lines of wildly leaping creatures such as we were now engaged with, and with them some strange new monsters which ran with great swiftness, now erect and now upon all fours.

"It will be a great death," I said to my companion. "Look!"

As he shot a quick glance in the direction I indicated he smiled.

"We may at least die fighting and as great warriors should, John Carter," he replied.

We had just finished the last of our immediate antagonists as he spoke, and I turned in surprised wonderment at the sound of my name.

And there before my astonished eyes I beheld the greatest of the green men of Barsoom; their shrewdest statesman, their mightiest general, my great and good friend, Tars Tarkas, Jeddak of Thark.

CHAPTER TWO
A Forest Battle

Tars Tarkas and I found no time for an exchange of experiences as we stood there before the great boulder surrounded by the corpses of our grotesque assailants, for from all directions down the broad valley was streaming a perfect torrent of terrifying creatures in response to the weird call of the strange figure far above us.

"Come," cried Tars Tarkas, "we must make for the cliffs. There lies our only hope of even temporary escape; there we may find a cave or a narrow ledge which two may defend for ever against this motley, unarmed horde."

Together we raced across the scarlet sward, I timing my speed that I might not outdistance my slower companion. We had, perhaps, three hundred yards to cover between our boulder and the cliffs, and then to search out a suitable shelter for our stand against the terrifying things that were pursuing us.

They were rapidly overhauling us when Tars Tarkas cried to me to hasten ahead and discover, if possible, the sanctuary we sought. The suggestion was a good one, for thus many valuable minutes might be saved to us, and, throwing every ounce of my earthly muscles into the effort, I cleared the remaining distance between myself and the cliffs in great leaps and bounds that put me at their base in a moment.

The cliffs rose perpendicular directly from the almost level sward of the valley. There was no accumulation of fallen debris, forming a more or less rough ascent to them, as is the case with nearly all other cliffs I have ever seen. The scattered boulders that had fallen from above and lay upon or partly buried in the turf, were the only indication that any disintegration of the massive, towering pile of rocks ever had taken place.

My first cursory inspection of the face of the cliffs filled my heart with forebodings, since nowhere could I discern, except where the weird herald stood still shrieking his shrill summons, the faintest indication of even a bare foothold upon the lofty escarpment.

To my right the bottom of the cliff was lost in the dense foliage of the forest, which terminated at its very foot, rearing its gorgeous foliage fully a thousand feet against its stern and forbidding neighbour.

To the left the cliff ran, apparently unbroken, across the head of the broad valley, to be lost in the outlines of what appeared to be a range of mighty mountains that skirted and confined the valley in every direction.

Perhaps a thousand feet from me the river broke, as it seemed, directly from the base of the cliffs, and as there seemed not the remotest chance for escape in that direction I turned my attention again toward the forest.

The cliffs towered above me a good five thousand feet. The sun was not quite upon them and they loomed a dull yellow in their own shade. Here and there they were broken with streaks and patches of dusky red, green, and occasional areas of white quartz.

Altogether they were very beautiful, but I fear that I did not regard them with a particularly appreciative eye on this, my first inspection of them.

Just then I was absorbed in them only as a medium of escape, and so, as my gaze ran quickly, time and again, over their vast expanse in search of some cranny or crevice, I came suddenly to loathe them as the prisoner must loathe the cruel and impregnable walls of his dungeon.

Tars Tarkas was approaching me rapidly, and still more rapidly came the awful horde at his heels.

It seemed the forest now or nothing, and I was just on the point of motioning Tars Tarkas to follow me in that direction when the sun passed the cliff's zenith, and as the bright rays touched the dull surface it burst out into a million scintillant lights of burnished gold, of flaming red, of soft greens, and gleaming whites – a more gorgeous and inspiring spectacle human eye has never rested upon.

The face of the entire cliff was, as later inspection conclusively proved, so shot with veins and patches of solid gold as to quite present the appearance of a solid wall of that precious metal except where it was broken by outcroppings of ruby, emerald, and diamond boulders – a faint and alluring indication of the vast and unguessable riches which lay deeply buried behind the magnificent surface.

But what caught my most interested attention at the moment that the sun's rays set the cliff's face a-shimmer, was the several black spots which now appeared quite plainly in evidence high across the gorgeous wall close to the forest's top, and extending apparently below and behind the branches.

Almost immediately I recognised them for what they were, the dark openings of caves entering the solid walls – possible avenues of escape or temporary shelter, could we but reach them.

There was but a single way, and that led through the mighty, towering trees upon our right. That I could scale them I knew full well, but Tars Tarkas, with his mighty bulk and enormous weight, would find it a task possibly quite beyond his prowess or his skill, for Martians are at best but poor climbers. Upon the entire surface of that ancient planet I never before had seen a hill or mountain that exceeded four thousand feet in height above the dead sea bottoms, and as the ascent was usually gradual, nearly to their summits they presented but few opportunities for the practice of climbing. Nor would the Martians have embraced even such opportunities as might present themselves, for they could always find a circuitous route about the base of any eminence, and these roads they preferred and followed in preference to the shorter but more arduous ways.

However, there was nothing else to consider than an attempt to scale the trees contiguous to the cliff in an effort to reach the caves above.

The Thark grasped the possibilities and the difficulties of the plan at once, but there was no alternative, and so we set out rapidly for the trees nearest the cliff.

Our relentless pursuers were now close to us, so close that it seemed that it would be an utter impossibility for the Jeddak of Thark to reach the forest in advance of them, nor was there any considerable will in the efforts that Tars Tarkas made, for the green men of Barsoom do not relish flight, nor ever before had I seen one fleeing from death in whatsoever form it might have confronted him. But that Tars Tarkas was the bravest of the brave he had proven thousands of times; yes, tens of thousands in countless mortal combats with men and beasts. And so I knew that there was another reason than fear of death behind his flight, as he knew that a greater power than pride or honour spurred me to escape these fierce destroyers. In my case it was love – love of the divine Dejah Thoris; and the cause of the Thark's great and sudden love of life I could not fathom, for it is oftener that they seek death than life – these strange, cruel, loveless, unhappy people.

At length, however, we reached the shadows of the forest, while right behind us sprang the swiftest of our pursuers – a giant plant man with claws outreaching to fasten his bloodsucking mouths upon us.

He was, I should say, a hundred yards in advance of his closest companion, and so I called to Tars Tarkas to ascend a great tree that brushed the cliff's face while I dispatched the fellow, thus giving the less agile Thark an opportunity to reach the higher branches before the entire horde should be upon us and every vestige of escape cut off.

But I had reckoned without a just appreciation either of the cunning of my immediate antagonist or the swiftness with which his fellows were covering the distance which had separated them from me.

As I raised my long-sword to deal the creature its death thrust it halted in its charge and, as my sword cut harmlessly through the empty air, the great tail of the thing swept with the power of a grizzly's arm across the sward and carried me bodily from my feet to the ground. In an instant the brute was upon me, but ere it could fasten its hideous mouths into my breast and throat I grasped a writhing tentacle in either hand.

The plant man was well muscled, heavy, and powerful but my earthly sinews and greater agility, in conjunction with the deathly strangle hold I had upon him, would have given me, I think, an eventual victory had we had time to discuss the merits of our relative prowess uninterrupted. But as we strained and struggled about the tree into which Tars Tarkas was clambering with infinite difficulty, I suddenly caught a glimpse over the shoulder of my antagonist of the great swarm of pursuers that now were fairly upon me.

Now, at last, I saw the nature of the other monsters who had come with the plant men in response to the weird calling of the man upon the cliff's face. They were that most dreaded of Martian creatures – great white apes of Barsoom.

My former experiences upon Mars had familiarized me thoroughly with them and their methods, and I may say that of all the fearsome and terrible, weird and grotesque inhabitants of that strange world, it is the white apes that come nearest to familiarizing me with the sensation of fear.

I think that the cause of this feeling which these apes engender within me is due to their remarkable resemblance in form to our Earth men, which gives them a human appearance that is most uncanny when coupled with their enormous size.

They stand fifteen feet in height and walk erect upon their hind feet. Like the green Martians, they have an intermediary set of arms midway between their upper and lower limbs. Their eyes are very close set, but do not protrude as do those of the green men of Mars; their ears are high set, but more laterally located than are the green men's, while their snouts and teeth are much like those of our African gorilla. Upon their heads grows an enormous shock of bristly hair.

It was into the eyes of such as these and the terrible plant men that I gazed above the shoulder of my foe, and then, in a mighty wave of snarling, snapping, screaming, purring rage, they swept over me – and of all the sounds that assailed my ears as I went down beneath them, to me the most hideous was the horrid purring of the plant men.

Instantly a score of cruel fangs and keen talons were sunk into my flesh; cold, sucking lips fastened themselves upon my arteries. I struggled to free myself, and even though weighed down by these immense bodies, I succeeded in struggling to my feet, where, still grasping my long-sword, and shortening my grip upon it until I could use it as a dagger, I wrought such havoc among them that at one time I stood for an instant free.

What it has taken minutes to write occurred in but a few seconds, but during that time Tars Tarkas had seen my plight and had dropped from the lower branches, which he had reached with such infinite labour, and as I flung the last of my immediate antagonists from me the great Thark leaped to my side, and again we fought, back to back, as we had done a hundred times before.

Time and again the ferocious apes sprang in to close with us, and time and again we beat them back with our swords. The great tails of the plant men lashed with tremendous power about us as they charged from various directions or sprang with the agility of greyhounds above our heads; but every attack met a gleaming blade in sword hands that had been reputed for twenty years the best that Mars ever had known; for Tars Tarkas and John Carter were names that the fighting men of the world of warriors loved best to speak.

But even the two best swords in a world of fighters can avail not for ever against overwhelming numbers of fierce and savage brutes that know not what defeat means until cold steel teaches their hearts no longer to beat, and so, step by step, we were forced back. At length we stood against the giant tree that we had chosen for our ascent, and then, as charge after charge hurled its weight upon us, we gave back again and again, until we had been forced half-way around the huge base of the colossal trunk.

Tars Tarkas was in the lead, and suddenly I heard a little cry of exultation from him.

"Here is shelter for one at least, John Carter," he said, and, glancing down, I saw an opening in the base of the tree about three feet in diameter.

"In with you, Tars Tarkas," I cried, but he would not go; saying that his bulk was too great for the little aperture, while I might slip in easily.

"We shall both die if we remain without, John Carter; here is a slight chance for one of us. Take it and you may live to avenge me, it is useless for me to attempt to worm my way into so small an opening with this horde of demons besetting us on all sides."

"Then we shall die together, Tars Tarkas," I replied, "for I shall not go first. Let me defend the opening while you get in, then my smaller stature will permit me to slip in with you before they can prevent."

We still were fighting furiously as we talked in broken sentences, punctured with vicious cuts and thrusts at our swarming enemy.

At length he yielded, for it seemed the only way in which either of us might be saved from the ever-increasing numbers of our assailants, who were still swarming upon us from all directions across the broad valley.

"It was ever your way, John Carter, to think last of your own life," he said; "but still more your way to command the lives and actions of others, even to the greatest of Jeddaks who rule upon Barsoom."

There was a grim smile upon his cruel, hard face, as he, the greatest Jeddak of them all, turned to obey the dictates of a creature of another world – of a man whose stature was less than half his own.

"If you fail, John Carter," he said, "know that the cruel and heartless Thark, to whom you taught the meaning of friendship, will come out to die beside you."

"As you will, my friend," I replied; "but quickly now, head first, while I cover your retreat."

He hesitated a little at that word, for never before in his whole life of continual strife had he turned his back upon aught than a dead or defeated enemy.

"Haste, Tars Tarkas," I urged, "or we shall both go down to profitless defeat; I cannot hold them for ever alone."

As he dropped to the ground to force his way into the tree, the whole howling pack of hideous devils hurled themselves upon me. To right and left flew my shimmering blade, now green with the sticky juice of a plant man, now red with the crimson blood of a great white ape; but always flying from one opponent to another, hesitating but the barest fraction of a second to drink the lifeblood in the centre of some savage heart.

And thus I fought as I never had fought before, against such frightful odds that I cannot realize even now that human muscles could have withstood that awful onslaught, that terrific weight of hurtling tons of ferocious, battling flesh.

With the fear that we would escape them, the creatures redoubled their efforts to pull me down, and though the ground about me was piled high with their dead and dying comrades, they succeeded at last in overwhelming me, and I went down beneath them for the second time that day, and once again felt those awful sucking lips against my flesh.

But scarce had I fallen ere I felt powerful hands grip my ankles, and in another second I was being drawn within the shelter of the tree's interior. For a moment it was a tug of war between Tars Tarkas and a great plant man, who clung tenaciously to my breast, but presently I got the point of my long-sword beneath him and with a mighty thrust pierced his vitals.

Torn and bleeding from many cruel wounds, I lay panting upon the ground within the hollow of the tree, while Tars Tarkas defended the opening from the furious mob without.

For an hour they howled about the tree, but after a few attempts to reach us they confined their efforts to terrorizing shrieks and screams, to horrid growling on the part of the great white apes, and the fearsome and indescribable purring by the plant men.

At length, all but a score, who had apparently been left to prevent our escape, had left us, and our adventure seemed destined to result in a siege, the only outcome of which could be our death by starvation; for even should we be able to slip out after dark, whither in this unknown and hostile valley could we hope to turn our steps toward possible escape?

As the attacks of our enemies ceased and our eyes became accustomed to the semi-darkness of the interior of our strange retreat, I took the opportunity to explore our shelter.

The tree was hollow to an extent of about fifty feet in diameter, and from its flat, hard floor I judged that it had often been used to domicile others before our occupancy. As I raised my eyes toward its roof to note the height I saw far above me a faint glow of light.

There was an opening above. If we could but reach it we might still hope to make the shelter of the cliff caves. My eyes had now become quite used to the subdued light of the interior, and as I pursued my investigation I presently came upon a rough ladder at the far side of the cave.

Quickly I mounted it, only to find that it connected at the top with the lower of a series of horizontal wooden bars that spanned the now narrow and shaft-like interior of the tree's stem. These bars were set one above another about three feet apart, and formed a perfect ladder as far above me as I could see.

Dropping to the floor once more, I detailed my discovery to Tars Tarkas, who suggested that I explore aloft as far as I could go in safety while he guarded the entrance against a possible attack.

As I hastened above to explore the strange shaft I found that the ladder of horizontal bars mounted always as far above me as my eyes could reach, and as I ascended, the light from above grew brighter and brighter.

For fully five hundred feet I continued to climb, until at length I reached the opening in the stem which admitted the light. It was of about the same diameter as the entrance at the foot of the tree, and opened directly upon a large flat limb, the well worn surface of which testified to its long continued use as an avenue for some creature to and from this remarkable shaft.

I did not venture out upon the limb for fear that I might be discovered and our retreat in this direction cut off; but instead hurried to retrace my steps to Tars Tarkas.

I soon reached him and presently we were both ascending the long ladder toward the opening above.

Tars Tarkas went in advance and as I reached the first of the horizontal bars I drew the ladder up after me and, handing it to him, he carried it a hundred feet further aloft, where he wedged it safely between one of the bars and the side of the shaft. In like manner I dislodged the lower bars as I passed them, so that we soon had the interior of the tree denuded of all possible means of ascent for a distance of a hundred feet from the base; thus precluding possible pursuit and attack from the rear.

As we were to learn later, this precaution saved us from dire predicament, and was eventually the means of our salvation.

When we reached the opening at the top Tars Tarkas drew to one side that I might pass out and investigate, as, owing to my lesser weight and greater agility, I was better fitted for the perilous threading of this dizzy, hanging pathway.

The limb upon which I found myself ascended at a slight angle toward the cliff, and as I followed it I found that it terminated a few feet above a narrow ledge which protruded from the cliff's face at the entrance to a narrow cave.

As I approached the slightly more slender extremity of the branch it bent beneath my weight until, as I balanced perilously upon its outer tip, it swayed gently on a level with the ledge at a distance of a couple of feet.

Five hundred feet below me lay the vivid scarlet carpet of the valley; nearly five thousand feet above towered the mighty, gleaming face of the gorgeous cliffs.

The cave that I faced was not one of those that I had seen from the ground, and which lay much higher, possibly a thousand feet. But so far as I might know it was as good for our purpose as another, and so I returned to the tree for Tars Tarkas.

Together we wormed our way along the waving pathway, but when we reached the end of the branch we found that our combined weight so depressed the limb that the cave's mouth was now too far above us to be reached.

We finally agreed that Tars Tarkas should return along the branch, leaving his longest leather harness strap with me, and that when the limb had risen to a height that would permit me to enter the cave I was to do so, and on Tars Tarkas' return I could then lower the strap and haul him up to the safety of the ledge.

This we did without mishap and soon found ourselves together upon the verge of a dizzy little balcony, with a magnificent view of the valley spreading out below us.

As far as the eye could reach gorgeous forest and crimson sward skirted a silent sea, and about all towered the brilliant monster guardian cliffs. Once we thought we discerned a gilded minaret gleaming in the sun amidst the waving tops of far-distant trees, but we soon abandoned the idea in the belief that it was but an hallucination born of our great desire to discover the haunts of civilized men in this beautiful, yet forbidding, spot.

Below us upon the river's bank the great white apes were devouring the last remnants of Tars Tarkas' former companions, while great herds of plant men grazed in ever-widening circles about the sward which they kept as close clipped as the smoothest of lawns.

Knowing that attack from the tree was now improbable, we determined to explore the cave, which we had every reason to believe was but a continuation of the path we had already traversed, leading the gods alone knew where, but quite evidently away from this valley of grim ferocity.

As we advanced we found a well-proportioned tunnel cut from the solid cliff. Its walls rose some twenty feet above the floor, which was about five feet in width. The roof was arched. We had no means of making a light, and so groped our way slowly into the ever-increasing darkness, Tars Tarkas keeping in touch with one wall while I felt along the other, while, to prevent our wandering into diverging branches and becoming separated or lost in some intricate and labyrinthine maze, we clasped hands.

How far we traversed the tunnel in this manner I do not know, but presently we came to an obstruction which blocked our further progress. It seemed more like a partition than a sudden ending of the cave, for it was constructed not of the material of the cliff, but of something which felt like very hard wood.

Silently I groped over its surface with my hands, and presently was rewarded by the feel of the button which as commonly denotes a door on Mars as does a door knob on Earth.

Gently pressing it, I had the satisfaction of feeling the door slowly give before me, and in another instant we were looking into a dimly lighted apartment, which, so far as we could see, was unoccupied.

Without more ado I swung the door wide open and, followed by the huge Thark, stepped into the chamber. As we stood for a moment in silence gazing about the room a slight noise behind caused me to turn quickly, when, to my astonishment, I saw the door close with a sharp click as though by an unseen hand.

Instantly I sprang toward it to wrench it open again, for something in the uncanny movement of the thing and the tense and almost palpable silence of the chamber seemed to portend a lurking evil lying hidden in this rock-bound chamber within the bowels of the Golden Cliffs.

My fingers clawed futilely at the unyielding portal, while my eyes sought in vain for a duplicate of the button which had given us ingress.

And then, from unseen lips, a cruel and mocking peal of laughter rang through the desolate place.

CHAPTER THREE

The Chamber of Mystery

FOR MOMENTS AFTER that awful laugh had ceased reverberating through the rocky room, Tars Tarkas and I stood in tense and expectant silence. But no further sound broke the stillness, nor within the range of our vision did aught move.

At length Tars Tarkas laughed softly, after the manner of his strange kind when in the presence of the horrible or terrifying. It is not an hysterical laugh, but rather the genuine expression of the pleasure they derive from the things that move Earth men to loathing or to tears.

Often and again have I seen them roll upon the ground in mad fits of uncontrollable mirth when witnessing the death agonies of women and little children beneath the torture of that hellish green Martian fete – the Great Games.

I looked up at the Thark, a smile upon my own lips, for here in truth was greater need for a smiling face than a trembling chin.

"What do you make of it all?" I asked. "Where in the deuce are we?"

He looked at me in surprise.

"Where are we?" he repeated. "Do you tell me, John Carter, that you know not where you be?"

"That I am upon Barsoom is all that I can guess, and but for you and the great white apes I should not even guess that, for the sights I have seen this day are as unlike the things of my beloved Barsoom as I knew it ten long years ago as they are unlike the world of my birth."

"No, Tars Tarkas, I know not where we be."

"Where have you been since you opened the mighty portals of the atmosphere plant years ago, after the keeper had died and the engines stopped and all Barsoom was dying, that had not already died, of asphyxiation? Your body even was never found, though the men of a whole world sought after it for years, though the Jeddak of Helium and his granddaughter, your princess, offered such fabulous rewards that even princes of royal blood joined in the search.

"There was but one conclusion to reach when all efforts to locate you had failed, and that, that you had taken the long, last pilgrimage down the mysterious River Iss, to await in the Valley Dor upon the shores of the Lost Sea of Korus the beautiful Dejah Thoris, your princess.

"Why you had gone none could guess, for your princess still lived – "

"Thank God," I interrupted him. "I did not dare to ask you, for I feared I might have been too late to save her – she was very low when I left her in the royal gardens of Tardos Mors that long-gone night; so very low that I scarcely hoped even then to reach the atmosphere plant ere her dear spirit had fled from me for ever. And she lives yet?"

"She lives, John Carter."

"You have not told me where we are," I reminded him.

"We are where I expected to find you, John Carter – and another. Many years ago you heard the story of the woman who taught me the thing that green Martians are reared to hate, the woman who taught me to love. You know the cruel tortures and the awful death her love won for her at the hands of the beast, Tal Hajus.

"She, I thought, awaited me by the Lost Sea of Korus.

"You know that it was left for a man from another world, for yourself, John Carter, to teach this cruel Thark what friendship is; and you, I thought, also roamed the care-free Valley Dor.

"Thus were the two I most longed for at the end of the long pilgrimage I must take some day, and so as the time had elapsed which Dejah Thoris had hoped might bring you once more to her side, for she has always tried to believe that you had but temporarily returned to your own planet, I at last gave way to my great yearning and a month since I started upon the journey, the end of which you have this day witnessed. Do you understand now where you be, John Carter?"

"And that was the River Iss, emptying into the Lost Sea of Korus in the Valley Dor?" I asked.

"This is the valley of love and peace and rest to which every Barsoomian since time immemorial has longed to pilgrimage at the end of a life of hate and strife and bloodshed," he replied. "This, John Carter, is Heaven."

His tone was cold and ironical; its bitterness but reflecting the terrible disappointment he had suffered. Such a fearful disillusionment, such a blasting of life-long hopes and aspirations, such an uprooting of age-old tradition might have excused a vastly greater demonstration on the part of the Thark.

I laid my hand upon his shoulder.

"I am sorry," I said, nor did there seem aught else to say.

"Think, John Carter, of the countless billions of Barsoomians who have taken the voluntary pilgrimage down this cruel river since the beginning of time, only to fall into the ferocious clutches of the terrible creatures that to-day assailed us.

"There is an ancient legend that once a red man returned from the banks of the Lost Sea of Korus, returned from the Valley Dor, back through the mysterious River Iss, and the legend has it that he narrated a fearful blasphemy of horrid brutes that inhabited a valley of wondrous loveliness, brutes that pounced upon each Barsoomian as he terminated his pilgrimage and devoured him upon the banks of the Lost Sea where he had looked to find love and peace and happiness; but the ancients killed the blasphemer, as tradition has ordained that any shall be killed who return from the bosom of the River of Mystery.

"But now we know that it was no blasphemy, that the legend is a true one, and that the man told only of what he saw; but what does it profit us, John Carter, since even should we escape, we also would be treated as blasphemers? We are between the wild thoat of certainty and the mad zitidar of fact – we can escape neither."

"As Earth men say, we are between the devil and the deep sea, Tars Tarkas," I replied, nor could I help but smile at our dilemma.

"There is naught that we can do but take things as they come, and at least have the satisfaction of knowing that whoever slays us eventually will have far greater numbers of their own dead to count than they will get in return. White ape or plant man, green Barsoomian or red man, whosoever it shall be that takes the last toll from us will know that it is costly in lives to wipe out John Carter, Prince of the House of Tardos Mors, and Tars Tarkas, Jeddak of Thark, at the same time."

I could not help but laugh at his grim humour, and he joined in with me in one of those rare laughs of real enjoyment which was one of the attributes of this fierce Tharkian chief which marked him from the others of his kind.

"But about yourself, John Carter," he cried at last. "If you have not been here all these years where indeed have you been, and how is it that I find you here to-day?"

"I have been back to Earth," I replied. "For ten long Earth years I have been praying and hoping for the day that would carry me once more to this grim old planet of yours, for which, with all its cruel and terrible customs, I feel a bond of sympathy and love even greater than for the world that gave me birth.

"For ten years have I been enduring a living death of uncertainty and doubt as to whether Dejah Thoris lived, and now that for the first time in all these years my prayers have been answered and my doubt relieved I find myself, through a cruel whim of fate, hurled into the one tiny spot of all Barsoom from which there is apparently no escape, and if there were, at a price which would put out for ever the last flickering hope which I may cling to of seeing my princess again in this life – and you have seen to-day with what pitiful futility man yearns toward a material hereafter.

"Only a bare half-hour before I saw you battling with the plant men I was standing in the moonlight upon the banks of a broad river that taps the eastern shore of Earth's most blessed land. I have answered you, my friend. Do you believe?"

"I believe," replied Tars Tarkas, "though I cannot understand."

As we talked I had been searching the interior of the chamber with my eyes. It was, perhaps, two hundred feet in length and half as broad, with what appeared to be a doorway in the centre of the wall directly opposite that through which we had entered.

The apartment was hewn from the material of the cliff, showing mostly dull gold in the dim light which a single minute radium illuminator in the centre of the roof diffused throughout its great dimensions. Here and there polished surfaces of ruby, emerald, and diamond patched the golden walls and ceiling. The floor was of another material, very hard, and worn by much use to the smoothness of glass. Aside from the two doors I could discern no sign of other aperture, and as one we knew to be locked against us I approached the other.

As I extended my hand to search for the controlling button, that cruel and mocking laugh rang out once more, so close to me this time that I involuntarily shrank back, tightening my grip upon the hilt of my great sword.

And then from the far corner of the great chamber a hollow voice chanted: "There is no hope, there is no hope; the dead return not, the dead return not; nor is there any resurrection. Hope not, for there is no hope."

Though our eyes instantly turned toward the spot from which the voice seemed to emanate, there was no one in sight, and I must admit that cold shivers played along my spine and the short hairs at the base of my head stiffened and rose up, as do those upon a hound's neck when in the night his eyes see those uncanny things which are hidden from the sight of man.

Quickly I walked toward the mournful voice, but it had ceased ere I reached the further wall, and then from the other end of the chamber came another voice, shrill and piercing:

"Fools! Fools!" it shrieked. "Thinkest thou to defeat the eternal laws of life and death? Wouldst cheat the mysterious Issus, Goddess of Death, of her just dues? Did not her mighty messenger, the ancient Iss, bear you upon her leaden bosom at your own behest to the Valley Dor?

"Thinkest thou, O fools, that Issus wilt give up her own? Thinkest thou to escape from whence in all the countless ages but a single soul has fled?

"Go back the way thou camest, to the merciful maws of the children of the Tree of Life or the gleaming fangs of the great white apes, for there lies speedy surcease from suffering; but insist in your rash purpose to thread the mazes of the Golden Cliffs of the Mountains of Otz, past the ramparts of the impregnable fortresses of the Holy Therns, and upon your way Death in its most frightful form will overtake you – a death so horrible that even the Holy Therns themselves, who conceived both Life and Death, avert their eyes from its fiendishness and close their ears against the hideous shrieks of its victims.

"Go back, O fools, the way thou camest."

And then the awful laugh broke out from another part of the chamber.

"Most uncanny," I remarked, turning to Tars Tarkas.

"What shall we do?" he asked. "We cannot fight empty air; I would almost sooner return and face foes into whose flesh I may feel my blade bite and know that I am selling my carcass dearly before I go down to that eternal oblivion which is evidently the fairest and most desirable eternity that mortal man has the right to hope for."

"If, as you say, we cannot fight empty air, Tars Tarkas," I replied, "neither, on the other hand, can empty air fight us. I, who have faced and conquered in my time thousands of sinewy warriors and tempered blades, shall not be turned back by wind; nor no more shall you, Thark."

"But unseen voices may emanate from unseen and unseeable creatures who wield invisible blades," answered the green warrior.

"Rot, Tars Tarkas," I cried, "those voices come from beings as real as you or as I. In their veins flows lifeblood that may be let as easily as ours, and the fact that they remain invisible to us is the best proof to my mind that they are mortal; nor overly courageous mortals at that. Think you, Tars Tarkas, that John Carter will fly at the first shriek of a cowardly foe who dare not come out into the open and face a good blade?"

I had spoken in a loud voice that there might be no question that our would-be terrorizers should hear me, for I was tiring of this nerve-racking fiasco. It had occurred to me, too, that the whole business was but a plan to frighten us back into the valley of death from which we had escaped, that we might be quickly disposed of by the savage creatures there.

For a long period there was silence, then of a sudden a soft, stealthy sound behind me caused me to turn suddenly to behold a great many-legged banth creeping sinuously upon me.

The banth is a fierce beast of prey that roams the low hills surrounding the dead seas of ancient Mars. Like nearly all Martian animals it is almost hairless, having only a great bristly mane about its thick neck.

Its long, lithe body is supported by ten powerful legs, its enormous jaws are equipped, like those of the calot, or Martian hound, with several rows of long needle-like fangs; its mouth reaches to a point far back of its tiny ears, while its enormous, protruding eyes of green add the last touch of terror to its awful aspect.

As it crept toward me it lashed its powerful tail against its yellow sides, and when it saw that it was discovered it emitted the terrifying roar which often freezes its prey into momentary paralysis in the instant that it makes its spring.

And so it launched its great bulk toward me, but its mighty voice had held no paralysing terrors for me, and it met cold steel instead of the tender flesh its cruel jaws gaped so widely to engulf.

An instant later I drew my blade from the still heart of this great Barsoomian lion, and turning toward Tars Tarkas was surprised to see him facing a similar monster.

No sooner had he dispatched his than I, turning, as though drawn by the instinct of my guardian subconscious mind, beheld another of the savage denizens of the Martian wilds leaping across the chamber toward me.

From then on for the better part of an hour one hideous creature after another was launched upon us, springing apparently from the empty air about us.

Tars Tarkas was satisfied; here was something tangible that he could cut and slash with his great blade, while I, for my part, may say that the diversion was a marked improvement over the uncanny voices from unseen lips.

That there was nothing supernatural about our new foes was well evidenced by their howls of rage and pain as they felt the sharp steel at their vitals, and the very real blood which flowed from their severed arteries as they died the real death.

I noticed during the period of this new persecution that the beasts appeared only when our backs were turned; we never saw one really materialize from thin air, nor did I for an instant sufficiently lose my excellent reasoning faculties to be once deluded into the belief that the beasts came into the room other than through some concealed and well-contrived doorway.

Among the ornaments of Tars Tarkas' leather harness, which is the only manner of clothing worn by Martians other than silk capes and robes of silk and fur for protection from the cold after dark, was a small mirror, about the bigness of a lady's hand glass, which hung midway between his shoulders and his waist against his broad back.

Once as he stood looking down at a newly fallen antagonist my eyes happened to fall upon this mirror and in its shiny surface I saw pictured a sight that caused me to whisper:

"Move not, Tars Tarkas! Move not a muscle!"

He did not ask why, but stood like a graven image while my eyes watched the strange thing that meant so much to us.

What I saw was the quick movement of a section of the wall behind me. It was turning upon pivots, and with it a section of the floor directly in front of it was turning. It was as though you placed a visiting-card upon end on a silver dollar that you had laid flat upon a table, so that the edge of the card perfectly bisected the surface of the coin.

The card might represent the section of the wall that turned and the silver dollar the section of the floor. Both were so nicely fitted into the adjacent portions of the floor and wall that no crack had been noticeable in the dim light of the chamber.

As the turn was half completed a great beast was revealed sitting upon its haunches upon that part of the revolving floor that had been on the opposite side before the wall commenced to move; when the section stopped, the beast was facing toward me on our side of the partition – it was very simple.

But what had interested me most was the sight that the half-turned section had presented through the opening that it had made. A great chamber, well lighted, in which were several men and women chained to the wall, and in front of them, evidently directing and operating the movement of the secret doorway, a wicked-faced man, neither red as are the red men of Mars, nor green as are the green men, but white, like myself, with a great mass of flowing yellow hair.

The prisoners behind him were red Martians. Chained with them were a number of fierce beasts, such as had been turned upon us, and others equally as ferocious.

As I turned to meet my new foe it was with a heart considerably lightened.

"Watch the wall at your end of the chamber, Tars Tarkas," I cautioned, "it is through secret doorways in the wall that the brutes are loosed upon us." I was very close to him and spoke in a low whisper that my knowledge of their secret might not be disclosed to our tormentors.

As long as we remained each facing an opposite end of the apartment no further attacks were made upon us, so it was quite clear to me that the partitions were in some way pierced that our actions might be observed from without.

At length a plan of action occurred to me, and backing quite close to Tars Tarkas I unfolded my scheme in a low whisper, keeping my eyes still glued upon my end of the room.

The great Thark grunted his assent to my proposition when I had done, and in accordance with my plan commenced backing toward the wall which I faced while I advanced slowly ahead of him.

When we had reached a point some ten feet from the secret doorway I halted my companion, and cautioning him to remain absolutely motionless until I gave the prearranged signal I quickly turned my back to the door through which I could almost feel the burning and baleful eyes of our would be executioner.

Instantly my own eyes sought the mirror upon Tars Tarkas' back and in another second I was closely watching the section of the wall which had been disgorging its savage terrors upon us.

I had not long to wait, for presently the golden surface commenced to move rapidly. Scarcely had it started than I gave the signal to Tars Tarkas, simultaneously springing for the receding half of the pivoting door. In like manner the Thark wheeled and leaped for the opening being made by the inswinging section.

A single bound carried me completely through into the adjoining room and brought me face to face with the fellow whose cruel face I had seen before. He was about my own height and well muscled and in every outward detail moulded precisely as are Earth men.

At his side hung a long-sword, a short-sword, a dagger, and one of the destructive radium revolvers that are common upon Mars.

The fact that I was armed only with a long-sword, and so according to the laws and ethics of battle everywhere upon Barsoom should only have been met with a similar or lesser weapon, seemed to have no effect upon the moral sense of my enemy, for he whipped out his revolver ere I scarce had touched the floor by his side, but an uppercut from my long-sword sent it flying from his grasp before he could discharge it.

Instantly he drew his long-sword, and thus evenly armed we set to in earnest for one of the closest battles I ever have fought.

The fellow was a marvellous swordsman and evidently in practice, while I had not gripped the hilt of a sword for ten long years before that morning.

But it did not take me long to fall easily into my fighting stride, so that in a few minutes the man began to realize that he had at last met his match.

His face became livid with rage as he found my guard impregnable, while blood flowed from a dozen minor wounds upon his face and body.

"Who are you, white man?" he hissed. "That you are no Barsoomian from the outer world is evident from your colour. And you are not of us."

His last statement was almost a question.

"What if I were from the Temple of Issus?" I hazarded on a wild guess.

"Fate forfend!" he exclaimed, his face going white under the blood that now nearly covered it.

I did not know how to follow up my lead, but I carefully laid the idea away for future use should circumstances require it. His answer indicated that for all he KNEW I might be from the Temple of Issus and in it were men like unto myself, and either this man feared the inmates of the temple or else he held their persons or their power in such reverence that he trembled to think of the harm and indignities he had heaped upon one of them.

But my present business with him was of a different nature than that which requires any considerable abstract reasoning; it was to get my sword between his ribs, and this I succeeded in doing within the next few seconds, nor was I an instant too soon.

The chained prisoners had been watching the combat in tense silence; not a sound had fallen in the room other than the clashing of our contending blades, the soft shuffling of our naked feet and the few whispered words we had hissed at each other through clenched teeth the while we continued our mortal duel.

But as the body of my antagonist sank an inert mass to the floor a cry of warning broke from one of the female prisoners.

"Turn! Turn! Behind you!" she shrieked, and as I wheeled at the first note of her shrill cry I found myself facing a second man of the same race as he who lay at my feet.

The fellow had crept stealthily from a dark corridor and was almost upon me with raised sword ere I saw him. Tars Tarkas was nowhere in sight and the secret panel in the wall, through which I had come, was closed.

How I wished that he were by my side now! I had fought almost continuously for many hours; I had passed through such experiences and adventures as must sap the vitality of man, and with all this I had not eaten for nearly twenty-four hours, nor slept.

I was fagged out, and for the first time in years felt a question as to my ability to cope with an antagonist; but there was naught else for it than to engage my man, and that as quickly and ferociously as lay in me, for my only salvation was to rush him off his feet by the impetuosity of my attack – I could not hope to win a long-drawn-out battle.

But the fellow was evidently of another mind, for he backed and parried and parried and sidestepped until I was almost completely fagged from the exertion of attempting to finish him.

He was a more adroit swordsman, if possible, than my previous foe, and I must admit that he led me a pretty chase and in the end came near to making a sorry fool of me – and a dead one into the bargain.

I could feel myself growing weaker and weaker, until at length objects commenced to blur before my eyes and I staggered and blundered about more asleep than awake, and then it was that he worked his pretty little coup that came near to losing me my life.

He had backed me around so that I stood in front of the corpse of his fellow, and then he rushed me suddenly so that I was forced back upon it, and as my heel struck it the impetus of my body flung me backward across the dead man.

My head struck the hard pavement with a resounding whack, and to that alone I owe my life, for it cleared my brain and the pain roused my temper, so that I was equal for the moment to tearing my enemy to pieces with my bare hands, and I verily believe that I should have attempted it had not my right hand, in the act of raising my body from the ground, come in contact with a bit of cold metal.

As the eyes of the layman so is the hand of the fighting man when it comes in contact with an implement of his vocation, and thus I did not need to look or reason to know that the dead man's revolver, lying where it had fallen when I struck it from his grasp, was at my disposal.

The fellow whose ruse had put me down was springing toward me, the point of his gleaming blade directed straight at my heart, and as he came there rang from his lips the cruel and mocking peal of laughter that I had heard within the Chamber of Mystery.

And so he died, his thin lips curled in the snarl of his hateful laugh, and a bullet from the revolver of his dead companion bursting in his heart.

His body, borne by the impetus of his headlong rush, plunged upon me. The hilt of his sword must have struck my head, for with the impact of the corpse I lost consciousness.

CHAPTER FOUR

Thuvia

IT WAS THE SOUND of conflict that aroused me once more to the realities of life. For a moment I could neither place my surroundings nor locate the sounds which had aroused me. And then from beyond the blank wall beside which I lay I heard the shuffling of feet, the snarling of grim beasts, the clank of metal accoutrements, and the heavy breathing of a man.

As I rose to my feet I glanced hurriedly about the chamber in which I had just encountered such a warm reception. The prisoners and the savage brutes rested in their chains by the opposite wall eyeing me with varying expressions of curiosity, sullen rage, surprise, and hope.

The latter emotion seemed plainly evident upon the handsome and intelligent face of the young red Martian woman whose cry of warning had been instrumental in saving my life.

She was the perfect type of that remarkably beautiful race whose outward appearance is identical with the more god-like races of Earth men, except that this higher race of Martians is of a light reddish copper colour. As she was entirely unadorned I could not even guess her station in life, though it was evident that she was either a prisoner or slave in her present environment.

It was several seconds before the sounds upon the opposite side of the partition jolted my slowly returning faculties into a realization of their probable import, and then of a sudden I grasped the fact that they were caused by Tars Tarkas in what was evidently a desperate struggle with wild beasts or savage men.

With a cry of encouragement I threw my weight against the secret door, but as well have assayed the down-hurling of the cliffs themselves. Then I sought feverishly for the secret of the revolving panel, but my search was fruitless, and I was about to raise my longsword against the sullen gold when the young woman prisoner called out to me.

"Save thy sword, O Mighty Warrior, for thou shalt need it more where it will avail to some purpose – shatter it not against senseless metal which yields better to the lightest finger touch of one who knows its secret."

"Know you the secret of it then?" I asked.

"Yes; release me and I will give you entrance to the other horror chamber, if you wish. The keys to my fetters are upon the first dead of thy foemen. But why would you return to face again the fierce banth, or whatever other form of destruction they have loosed within that awful trap?"

"Because my friend fights there alone," I answered, as I hastily sought and found the keys upon the carcass of the dead custodian of this grim chamber of horrors.

There were many keys upon the oval ring, but the fair Martian maid quickly selected that which sprung the great lock at her waist, and freed she hurried toward the secret panel.

Again she sought out a key upon the ring. This time a slender, needle-like affair which she inserted in an almost invisible hole in the wall. Instantly the door swung upon its pivot, and the contiguous section of the floor upon which I was standing carried me with it into the chamber where Tars Tarkas fought.

The great Thark stood with his back against an angle of the walls, while facing him in a semi-circle a half-dozen huge monsters crouched waiting for an opening. Their blood-streaked heads and shoulders testified to the cause of their wariness as well as to the swordsmanship of the green warrior whose glossy hide bore the same mute but eloquent witness to the ferocity of the attacks that he had so far withstood.

Sharp talons and cruel fangs had torn leg, arm, and breast literally to ribbons. So weak was he from continued exertion and loss of blood that but for the supporting wall I doubt that he even could have stood erect. But with the tenacity and indomitable courage of his kind he still faced his cruel and relentless foes – the personification of that ancient proverb of his tribe: "Leave to a Thark his head and one hand and he may yet conquer."

As he saw me enter, a grim smile touched those grim lips of his, but whether the smile signified relief or merely amusement at the sight of my own bloody and dishevelled condition I do not know.

As I was about to spring into the conflict with my sharp long-sword I felt a gentle hand upon my shoulder and turning found, to my surprise, that the young woman had followed me into the chamber.

"Wait," she whispered, "leave them to me," and pushing me advanced, all defenceless and unarmed, upon the snarling banths.

When quite close to them she spoke a single Martian word in low but peremptory tones. Like lightning the great beasts wheeled upon her, and I looked to see her torn to pieces before I could reach her side, but instead the creatures slunk to her feet like puppies that expect a merited whipping.

Again she spoke to them, but in tones so low I could not catch the words, and then she started toward the opposite side of the chamber with the six mighty monsters trailing at heel. One by one she sent them through the secret panel into the room beyond, and when the last had passed from the chamber where we stood in wide-eyed amazement she turned and smiled at us and then herself passed through, leaving us alone.

For a moment neither of us spoke. Then Tars Tarkas said:

"I heard the fighting beyond the partition through which you passed, but I did not fear for you, John Carter, until I heard the report of a revolver shot. I knew that there lived no man upon all Barsoom who could face you with naked steel and live, but the shot stripped the last vestige of hope from me, since you I knew to be without firearms. Tell me of it."

I did as he bade, and then together we sought the secret panel through which I had just entered the apartment – the one at the opposite end of the room from that through which the girl had led her savage companions.

To our disappointment the panel eluded our every effort to negotiate its secret lock. We felt that once beyond it we might look with some little hope of success for a passage to the outside world.

The fact that the prisoners within were securely chained led us to believe that surely there must be an avenue of escape from the terrible creatures which inhabited this unspeakable place.

Again and again we turned from one door to another, from the baffling golden panel at one end of the chamber to its mate at the other – equally baffling.

When we had about given up all hope one of the panels turned silently toward us, and the young woman who had led away the banths stood once more beside us.

"Who are you?" she asked, "and what your mission, that you have the temerity to attempt to escape from the Valley Dor and the death you have chosen?"

"I have chosen no death, maiden," I replied. "I am not of Barsoom, nor have I taken yet the voluntary pilgrimage upon the River Iss. My friend here is Jeddak of all the Tharks, and though he has not yet expressed a desire to return to the living world, I am taking him with me from the living lie that hath lured him to this frightful place.

"I am of another world. I am John Carter, Prince of the House of Tardos Mors, Jeddak of Helium. Perchance some faint rumour of me may have leaked within the confines of your hellish abode."

She smiled.

"Yes," she replied, "naught that passes in the world we have left is unknown here. I have heard of you, many years ago. The therns have ofttimes wondered whither you had flown, since you had neither taken the pilgrimage, nor could be found upon the face of Barsoom."

"Tell me," I said, "and who be you, and why a prisoner, yet with power over the ferocious beasts of the place that denotes familiarity and authority far beyond that which might be expected of a prisoner or a slave?"

"Slave I am," she answered. "For fifteen years a slave in this terrible place, and now that they have tired of me and become fearful of the power which my knowledge of their ways has given me I am but recently condemned to die the death."

She shuddered.

"What death?" I asked.

"The Holy Therns eat human flesh," she answered me; "but only that which has died beneath the sucking lips of a plant man – flesh from which the defiling blood of life has been drawn. And to this cruel end I have been condemned. It was to be within a few hours, had your advent not caused an interruption of their plans."

"Was it then Holy Therns who felt the weight of John Carter's hand?" I asked.

"Oh, no; those whom you laid low are lesser therns; but of the same cruel and hateful race. The Holy Therns abide upon the outer slopes of these grim hills, facing the broad world from which they harvest their victims and their spoils.

"Labyrinthine passages connect these caves with the luxurious palaces of the Holy Therns, and through them pass upon their many duties the lesser therns, and hordes of slaves, and prisoners, and fierce beasts; the grim inhabitants of this sunless world.

"There be within this vast network of winding passages and countless chambers men, women, and beasts who, born within its dim and gruesome underworld, have never seen the light of day – nor ever shall.

"They are kept to do the bidding of the race of therns; to furnish at once their sport and their sustenance.

"Now and again some hapless pilgrim, drifting out upon the silent sea from the cold Iss, escapes the plant men and the great white apes that guard the Temple of Issus and falls into the remorseless clutches of the therns; or, as was my misfortune, is coveted by the Holy Thern who chances to be upon watch in the balcony above the river where it issues from the bowels of the mountains through the cliffs of gold to empty into the Lost Sea of Korus.

"All who reach the Valley Dor are, by custom, the rightful prey of the plant men and the apes, while their arms and ornaments become the portion of the therns; but if one escapes the terrible denizens of the valley for even a few hours the therns may claim such a one as their own. And again the Holy Thern on watch, should he see a victim he covets, often tramples upon the rights of the unreasoning brutes of the valley and takes his prize by foul means if he cannot gain it by fair.

"It is said that occasionally some deluded victim of Barsoomian superstition will so far escape the clutches of the countless enemies that beset his path from the moment that he emerges from the subterranean passage through which the Iss flows for a thousand miles before it enters the Valley Dor as to reach the very walls of the Temple of Issus; but what fate awaits one there not even the Holy Therns may guess, for who has passed within those gilded walls never has returned to unfold the mysteries they have held since the beginning of time.

"The Temple of Issus is to the therns what the Valley Dor is imagined by the peoples of the outer world to be to them; it is the ultimate haven of peace, refuge, and happiness to which they pass after this life and wherein an eternity of eternities is spent amidst the delights of the flesh which appeal most strongly to this race of mental giants and moral pygmies."

"The Temple of Issus is, I take it, a heaven within a heaven," I said. "Let us hope that there it will be meted to the therns as they have meted it here unto others."

"Who knows?" the girl murmured.

"The therns, I judge from what you have said, are no less mortal than we; and yet have I always heard them spoken of with the utmost awe and reverence by the people of Barsoom, as one might speak of the gods themselves."

"The therns are mortal," she replied. "They die from the same causes as you or I might: those who do not live their allotted span of life, one thousand years, when by the authority of custom they may take their way in happiness through the long tunnel that leads to Issus.

"Those who die before are supposed to spend the balance of their allotted time in the image of a plant man, and it is for this reason that the plant men are held sacred by the therns, since they believe that each of these hideous creatures was formerly a thern."

"And should a plant man die?" I asked.

"Should he die before the expiration of the thousand years from the birth of the thern whose immortality abides within him then the soul passes into a great white ape, but should the ape die short of the exact hour that terminates the thousand years the soul is for ever lost and passes for all eternity into the carcass of the slimy and fearsome silians whose wriggling thousands seethe the silent sea beneath the hurtling moons when the sun has gone and strange shapes walk through the Valley Dor."

"We sent several Holy Therns to the silians to-day, then," said Tars Tarkas, laughing.

"And so will your death be the more terrible when it comes," said the maiden. "And come it will – you cannot escape."

"One has escaped, centuries ago," I reminded her, "and what has been done may be done again."

"It is useless even to try," she answered hopelessly.

"But try we shall," I cried, "and you shall go with us, if you wish."

"To be put to death by mine own people, and render my memory a disgrace to my family and my nation? A Prince of the House of Tardos Mors should know better than to suggest such a thing."

Tars Tarkas listened in silence, but I could feel his eyes riveted upon me and I knew that he awaited my answer as one might listen to the reading of his sentence by the foreman of a jury.

What I advised the girl to do would seal our fate as well, since if I bowed to the inevitable decree of age-old superstition we must all remain and meet our fate in some horrible form within this awful abode of horror and cruelty.

"We have the right to escape if we can," I answered. "Our own moral senses will not be offended if we succeed, for we know that the fabled life of love and peace in the blessed Valley of Dor is a rank and wicked deception. We know that the valley is not sacred; we know that the Holy Therns are not holy; that they are a race of cruel and heartless mortals, knowing no more of the real life to come than we do.

"Not only is it our right to bend every effort to escape – it is a solemn duty from which we should not shrink even though we know that we should be reviled and tortured by our own peoples when we returned to them.

"Only thus may we carry the truth to those without, and though the likelihood of our narrative being given credence is, I grant you, remote, so wedded are mortals to their stupid infatuation for impossible superstitions, we should be craven cowards indeed were we to shirk the plain duty which confronts us.

"Again there is a chance that with the weight of the testimony of several of us the truth of our statements may be accepted, and at least a compromise effected which will result in the dispatching of an expedition of investigation to this hideous mockery of heaven."

Both the girl and the green warrior stood silent in thought for some moments. The former it was who eventually broke the silence.

"Never had I considered the matter in that light before," she said. "Indeed would I give my life a thousand times if I could but save a single soul from the awful life that I have led in this cruel place. Yes, you are right, and I will go with you as far as we can go; but I doubt that we ever shall escape."

I turned an inquiring glance toward the Thark.

"To the gates of Issus, or to the bottom of Korus," spoke the green warrior; "to the snows to the north or to the snows to the south, Tars Tarkas follows where John Carter leads. I have spoken."

"Come, then," I cried, "we must make the start, for we could not be further from escape than we now are in the heart of this mountain and within the four walls of this chamber of death."

"Come, then," said the girl, "but do not flatter yourself that you can find no worse place than this within the territory of the therns."

So saying she swung the secret panel that separated us from the apartment in which I had found her, and we stepped through once more into the presence of the other prisoners.

There were in all ten red Martians, men and women, and when we had briefly explained our plan they decided to join forces with us, though it was evident that it was with some considerable misgivings that they thus tempted fate by opposing an ancient superstition, even though each knew through cruel experience the fallacy of its entire fabric.

Thuvia, the girl whom I had first freed, soon had the others at liberty. Tars Tarkas and I stripped the bodies of the two therns of their weapons, which included swords, daggers, and two revolvers of the curious and deadly type manufactured by the red Martians.

We distributed the weapons as far as they would go among our followers, giving the firearms to two of the women; Thuvia being one so armed.

With the latter as our guide we set off rapidly but cautiously through a maze of passages, crossing great chambers hewn from the solid metal of the cliff, following winding corridors, ascending steep inclines, and now and again concealing ourselves in dark recesses at the sound of approaching footsteps.

Our destination, Thuvia said, was a distant storeroom where arms and ammunition in plenty might be found. From there she was to lead us to the summit of the cliffs, from where it would require both wondrous wit and mighty fighting to win our way through the very heart of the stronghold of the Holy Therns to the world without.

"And even then, O Prince," she cried, "the arm of the Holy Thern is long. It reaches to every nation of Barsoom. His secret temples are hidden in the heart of every community. Wherever we go should we escape we shall find that word of our coming has preceded us, and death awaits us before we may pollute the air with our blasphemies."

We had proceeded for possibly an hour without serious interruption, and Thuvia had just whispered to me that we were approaching our first destination, when on entering a great chamber we came upon a man, evidently a thern.

He wore in addition to his leathern trappings and jewelled ornaments a great circlet of gold about his brow in the exact centre of which was set an immense stone, the exact counterpart of that which I had seen upon the breast of the little old man at the atmosphere plant nearly twenty years before.

It is the one priceless jewel of Barsoom. Only two are known to exist, and these were worn as the insignia of their rank and position by the two old men in whose charge was placed the operation of the great engines which pump the artificial atmosphere to all parts of Mars from the huge atmosphere plant, the secret to whose mighty portals placed in my possession the ability to save from immediate extinction the life of a whole world.

The stone worn by the thern who confronted us was of about the same size as that which I had seen before; an inch in diameter I should say. It scintillated nine different and distinct rays; the seven primary colours of our earthly prism and the two rays which are unknown upon Earth, but whose wondrous beauty is indescribable.

As the thern saw us his eyes narrowed to two nasty slits.

"Stop!" he cried. "What means this, Thuvia?"

For answer the girl raised her revolver and fired point-blank at him. Without a sound he sank to the earth, dead.

"Beast!" she hissed. "After all these years I am at last revenged."

Then as she turned toward me, evidently with a word of explanation on her lips, her eyes suddenly widened as they rested upon me, and with a little exclamation she started toward me.

"O Prince," she cried, "Fate is indeed kind to us. The way is still difficult, but through this vile thing upon the floor we may yet win to the outer world. Notest thou not the remarkable resemblance between this Holy Thern and thyself?"

The man was indeed of my precise stature, nor were his eyes and features unlike mine; but his hair was a mass of flowing yellow locks, like those of the two I had killed, while mine is black and close cropped.

"What of the resemblance?" I asked the girl Thuvia. "Do you wish me with my black, short hair to pose as a yellow-haired priest of this infernal cult?"

She smiled, and for answer approached the body of the man she had slain, and kneeling beside it removed the circlet of gold from the forehead, and then to my utter amazement lifted the entire scalp bodily from the corpse's head.

Rising, she advanced to my side and placing the yellow wig over my black hair, crowned me with the golden circlet set with the magnificent gem.

"Now don his harness, Prince," she said, "and you may pass where you will in the realms of the therns, for Sator Throg was a Holy Thern of the Tenth Cycle, and mighty among his kind."

As I stooped to the dead man to do her bidding I noted that not a hair grew upon his head, which was quite as bald as an egg.

"They are all thus from birth," explained Thuvia noting my surprise. "The race from which they sprang were crowned with a luxuriant growth of golden hair, but for many ages the present race has been entirely bald. The wig, however, has come to be a part of their apparel, and so important a part do they consider it that it is cause for the deepest disgrace were a thern to appear in public without it."

In another moment I stood garbed in the habiliments of a Holy Thern.

At Thuvia's suggestion two of the released prisoners bore the body of the dead thern upon their shoulders with us as we continued our journey toward the storeroom, which we reached without further mishap.

Here the keys which Thuvia bore from the dead thern of the prison vault were the means of giving us immediate entrance to the chamber, and very quickly we were thoroughly outfitted with arms and ammunition.

By this time I was so thoroughly fagged out that I could go no further, so I threw myself upon the floor, bidding Tars Tarkas to do likewise, and cautioning two of the released prisoners to keep careful watch.

In an instant I was asleep.

CHAPTER FIVE

Corridors of Peril

How long I slept upon the floor of the storeroom I do not know, but it must have been many hours.

I was awakened with a start by cries of alarm, and scarce were my eyes opened, nor had I yet sufficiently collected my wits to quite realize where I was, when a fusillade of shots rang out, reverberating through the subterranean corridors in a series of deafening echoes.

In an instant I was upon my feet. A dozen lesser therns confronted us from a large doorway at the opposite end of the storeroom from which we had entered. About me lay the bodies of my companions, with the exception of Thuvia and Tars Tarkas, who, like myself, had been asleep upon the floor and thus escaped the first raking fire.

As I gained my feet the therns lowered their wicked rifles, their faces distorted in mingled chagrin, consternation, and alarm.

Instantly I rose to the occasion.

"What means this?" I cried in tones of fierce anger. "Is Sator Throg to be murdered by his own vassals?"

"Have mercy, O Master of the Tenth Cycle!" cried one of the fellows, while the others edged toward the doorway as though to attempt a surreptitious escape from the presence of the mighty one.

"Ask them their mission here," whispered Thuvia at my elbow.

"What do you here, fellows?" I cried.

"Two from the outer world are at large within the dominions of the therns. We sought them at the command of the Father of Therns. One was white with black hair, the other a huge green warrior," and here the fellow cast a suspicious glance toward Tars Tarkas.

"Here, then, is one of them," spoke Thuvia, indicating the Thark, "and if you will look upon this dead man by the door perhaps you will recognize the other. It was left for Sator Throg and his poor slaves to accomplish what the lesser therns of the guard were unable to do – we have killed one and captured the other; for this had Sator Throg given us our liberty. And now in your stupidity have you come and killed all but myself, and like to have killed the mighty Sator Throg himself."

The men looked very sheepish and very scared.

"Had they not better throw these bodies to the plant men and then return to their quarters, O Mighty One?" asked Thuvia of me.

"Yes; do as Thuvia bids you," I said.

As the men picked up the bodies I noticed that the one who stooped to gather up the late Sator Throg started as his closer scrutiny fell upon the upturned face, and then the fellow stole a furtive, sneaking glance in my direction from the corner of his eye.

That he suspicioned something of the truth I could have sworn; but that it was only a suspicion which he did not dare voice was evidenced by his silence.

Again, as he bore the body from the room, he shot a quick but searching glance toward me, and then his eyes fell once more upon the bald and shiny dome of the dead man in his arms. The last fleeting glimpse that I obtained of his profile as he passed from my sight without the chamber revealed a cunning smile of triumph upon his lips.

Only Tars Tarkas, Thuvia, and I were left. The fatal marksmanship of the therns had snatched from our companions whatever slender chance they had of gaining the perilous freedom of the world without.

So soon as the last of the gruesome procession had disappeared the girl urged us to take up our flight once more.

She, too, had noted the questioning attitude of the thern who had borne Sator Throg away.

"It bodes no good for us, O Prince," she said. "For even though this fellow dared not chance accusing you in error, there be those above with power sufficient to demand a closer scrutiny, and that, Prince, would indeed prove fatal."

I shrugged my shoulders. It seemed that in any event the outcome of our plight must end in death. I was refreshed from my sleep, but still weak from loss of blood. My wounds were painful. No medicinal aid seemed possible. How I longed for the almost miraculous healing power of the strange salves and lotions of the green Martian women. In an hour they would have had me as new.

I was discouraged. Never had a feeling of such utter hopelessness come over me in the face of danger. Then the long flowing, yellow locks of the Holy Thern, caught by some vagrant draught, blew about my face.

Might they not still open the way of freedom? If we acted in time, might we not even yet escape before the general alarm was sounded? We could at least try.

"What will the fellow do first, Thuvia?" I asked. "How long will it be before they may return for us?"

"He will go directly to the Father of Therns, old Matai Shang. He may have to wait for an audience, but since he is very high among the lesser therns, in fact as a thorian among them, it will not be long that Matai Shang will keep him waiting.

"Then if the Father of Therns puts credence in his story, another hour will see the galleries and chambers, the courts and gardens, filled with searchers."

"What we do then must be done within an hour. What is the best way, Thuvia, the shortest way out of this celestial Hades?"

"Straight to the top of the cliffs, Prince," she replied, "and then through the gardens to the inner courts. From there our way will lie within the temples of the therns and across them to the outer court. Then the ramparts – O Prince, it is hopeless. Ten thousand warriors could not hew a way to liberty from out this awful place.

"Since the beginning of time, little by little, stone by stone, have the therns been ever adding to the defences of their stronghold. A continuous line of impregnable fortifications circles the outer slopes of the Mountains of Otz.

"Within the temples that lie behind the ramparts a million fighting-men are ever ready. The courts and gardens are filled with slaves, with women and with children.

"None could go a stone's throw without detection."

"If there is no other way, Thuvia, why dwell upon the difficulties of this. We must face them."

"Can we not better make the attempt after dark?" asked Tars Tarkas. "There would seem to be no chance by day."

"There would be a little better chance by night, but even then the ramparts are well guarded; possibly better than by day. There are fewer abroad in the courts and gardens, though," said Thuvia.

"What is the hour?" I asked.

"It was midnight when you released me from my chains," said Thuvia. "Two hours later we reached the storeroom. There you slept for fourteen hours. It must now be nearly sundown again. Come, we will go to some nearby window in the cliff and make sure."

So saying, she led the way through winding corridors until at a sudden turn we came upon an opening which overlooked the Valley Dor.

At our right the sun was setting, a huge red orb, below the western range of Otz. A little below us stood the Holy Thern on watch upon his balcony. His scarlet robe of office was pulled tightly about him in anticipation of the cold that comes so suddenly with darkness as the sun sets. So rare is the atmosphere of Mars that it absorbs very little heat from the sun. During the daylight hours it is always extremely hot; at night it is intensely cold. Nor does the thin atmosphere refract the sun's rays or diffuse its light as upon Earth. There is no twilight on Mars. When the great orb of day disappears beneath the horizon the effect is precisely as that of the extinguishing of a single lamp within a chamber. From brilliant light you are plunged without warning into utter darkness. Then the moons come; the mysterious, magic moons of Mars, hurtling like monster meteors low across the face of the planet.

The declining sun lighted brilliantly the eastern banks of Korus, the crimson sward, the gorgeous forest. Beneath the trees we saw feeding many herds of plant men. The adults stood aloft upon their toes and their mighty tails, their talons pruning every available leaf and twig. It was then that I understood the careful trimming of the trees which had led me to form the mistaken idea when first I opened my eyes upon the grove that it was the playground of a civilized people.

As we watched, our eyes wandered to the rolling Iss, which issued from the base of the cliffs beneath us. Presently there emerged from the mountain a canoe laden with lost souls from the outer world. There were a dozen of them. All were of the highly civilized and cultured race of red men who are dominant on Mars.

The eyes of the herald upon the balcony beneath us fell upon the doomed party as soon as did ours. He raised his head and leaning far out over the low rail that rimmed his dizzy perch, voiced the shrill, weird wail that called the demons of this hellish place to the attack.

For an instant the brutes stood with stiffly erected ears, then they poured from the grove toward the river's bank, covering the distance with great, ungainly leaps.

The party had landed and was standing on the sward as the awful horde came in sight. There was a brief and futile effort of defence. Then silence as the huge, repulsive shapes covered the bodies of their victims and scores of sucking mouths fastened themselves to the flesh of their prey.

I turned away in disgust.

"Their part is soon over," said Thuvia. "The great white apes get the flesh when the plant men have drained the arteries. Look, they are coming now."

As I turned my eyes in the direction the girl indicated, I saw a dozen of the great white monsters running across the valley toward the river bank. Then the sun went down and darkness that could almost be felt engulfed us.

Thuvia lost no time in leading us toward the corridor which winds back and forth up through the cliffs toward the surface thousands of feet above the level on which we had been.

Twice great banths, wandering loose through the galleries, blocked our progress, but in each instance Thuvia spoke a low word of command and the snarling beasts slunk sullenly away.

"If you can dissolve all our obstacles as easily as you master these fierce brutes I can see no difficulties in our way," I said to the girl, smiling. "How do you do it?"

She laughed, and then shuddered.

"I do not quite know," she said. "When first I came here I angered Sator Throg, because I repulsed him. He ordered me to be thrown into one of the great pits in the inner gardens. It was filled with banths. In my own country I had been accustomed to command. Something in my voice, I do not know what, cowed the beasts as they sprang to attack me.

"Instead of tearing me to pieces, as Sator Throg had desired, they fawned at my feet. So greatly were Sator Throg and his friends amused by the sight that they kept me to train and handle the terrible creatures. I know them all by name. There are many of them wandering through these lower regions. They are the scavengers. Many prisoners die here in their chains. The banths solve the problem of sanitation, at least in this respect.

"In the gardens and temples above they are kept in pits. The therns fear them. It is because of the banths that they seldom venture below ground except as their duties call them."

An idea occurred to me, suggested by what Thuvia had just said.

"Why not take a number of banths and set them loose before us above ground?" I asked.

Thuvia laughed.

"It would distract attention from us, I am sure," she said.

She commenced calling in a low singsong voice that was half purr. She continued this as we wound our tedious way through the maze of subterranean passages and chambers.

Presently soft, padded feet sounded close behind us, and as I turned I saw a pair of great, green eyes shining in the dark shadows at our rear. From a diverging tunnel a sinuous, tawny form crept stealthily toward us.

Low growls and angry snarls assailed our ears on every side as we hastened on and one by one the ferocious creatures answered the call of their mistress.

She spoke a word to each as it joined us. Like well-schooled terriers, they paced the corridors with us, but I could not help but note the lathering jowls, nor the hungry expressions with which they eyed Tars Tarkas and myself.

Soon we were entirely surrounded by some fifty of the brutes. Two walked close on either side of Thuvia, as guards might walk. The sleek sides of others now and then touched my own naked limbs. It was a strange experience; the almost noiseless passage of naked human feet and padded paws; the golden walls splashed with precious stones; the dim light cast by the tiny radium bulbs set at considerable distances along the roof; the huge, maned beasts of prey crowding with low growls about us; the mighty green warrior towering high above us all; myself crowned with the priceless diadem of a Holy Thern; and leading the procession the beautiful girl, Thuvia.

I shall not soon forget it.

Presently we approached a great chamber more brightly lighted than the corridors. Thuvia halted us. Quietly she stole toward the entrance and glanced within. Then she motioned us to follow her.

The room was filled with specimens of the strange beings that inhabit this underworld; a heterogeneous collection of hybrids – the offspring of the prisoners from the outside world; red and green Martians and the white race of therns.

Constant confinement below ground had wrought odd freaks upon their skins. They more resemble corpses than living beings. Many are deformed, others maimed, while the majority, Thuvia explained, are sightless.

As they lay sprawled about the floor, sometimes overlapping one another, again in heaps of several bodies, they suggested instantly to me the grotesque illustrations that I had seen in copies of Dante's *Inferno*, and what more fitting comparison? Was this not indeed a veritable hell, peopled by lost souls, dead and damned beyond all hope?

Picking our way carefully we threaded a winding path across the chamber, the great banths sniffing hungrily at the tempting prey spread before them in such tantalizing and defenceless profusion.

Several times we passed the entrances to other chambers similarly peopled, and twice again we were compelled to cross directly through them. In others were chained prisoners and beasts.

"Why is it that we see no therns?" I asked of Thuvia.

"They seldom traverse the underworld at night, for then it is that the great banths prowl the dim corridors seeking their prey. The therns fear the awful denizens of this cruel and hopeless world that they have fostered and allowed to grow beneath their feet. The prisoners even sometimes turn upon them and rend them. The thern can never tell from what dark shadow an assassin may spring upon his back.

"By day it is different. Then the corridors and chambers are filled with guards passing to and fro; slaves from the temples above come by hundreds to the granaries and storerooms. All is life then. You did not see it because I led you not in the beaten tracks, but through roundabout passages seldom used. Yet it is possible that we may meet a thern even yet. They do occasionally find it necessary to come here after the sun has set. Because of this I have moved with such great caution."

But we reached the upper galleries without detection and presently Thuvia halted us at the foot of a short, steep ascent.

"Above us," she said, "is a doorway which opens on to the inner gardens. I have brought you thus far. From here on for four miles to the outer ramparts our way will be beset by countless dangers. Guards patrol the courts, the temples, the gardens. Every inch of the ramparts themselves is beneath the eye of a sentry."

I could not understand the necessity for such an enormous force of armed men about a spot so surrounded by mystery and superstition that not a soul upon Barsoom would have dared to approach it even had they known its exact location. I questioned Thuvia, asking her what enemies the therns could fear in their impregnable fortress.

We had reached the doorway now and Thuvia was opening it.

"They fear the black pirates of Barsoom, O Prince," she said, "from whom may our first ancestors preserve us."

The door swung open; the smell of growing things greeted my nostrils; the cool night air blew against my cheek. The great banths sniffed the unfamiliar odours, and then with a rush they broke past us with low growls, swarming across the gardens beneath the lurid light of the nearer moon.

Suddenly a great cry arose from the roofs of the temples; a cry of alarm and warning that, taken up from point to point, ran off to the east and to the west, from temple, court, and rampart, until it sounded as a dim echo in the distance.

The great Thark's long-sword leaped from its scabbard; Thuvia shrank shuddering to my side.

CHAPTER SIX

The Black Pirates of Barsoom

"WHAT IS IT?" I asked of the girl.

For answer she pointed to the sky.

I looked, and there, above us, I saw shadowy bodies flitting hither and thither high over temple, court, and garden.

Almost immediately flashes of light broke from these strange objects. There was a roar of musketry, and then answering flashes and roars from temple and rampart.

"The black pirates of Barsoom, O Prince," said Thuvia.

In great circles the air craft of the marauders swept lower and lower toward the defending forces of the therns.

Volley after volley they vomited upon the temple guards; volley on volley crashed through the thin air toward the fleeting and illusive fliers.

As the pirates swooped closer toward the ground, thern soldiery poured from the temples into the gardens and courts. The sight of them in the open brought a score of fliers darting toward us from all directions.

The therns fired upon them through shields affixed to their rifles, but on, steadily on, came the grim, black craft. They were small fliers for the most part, built for two to three men. A few larger ones there were, but these kept high aloft dropping bombs upon the temples from their keel batteries.

At length, with a concerted rush, evidently in response to a signal of command, the pirates in our immediate vicinity dashed recklessly to the ground in the very midst of the thern soldiery.

Scarcely waiting for their craft to touch, the creatures manning them leaped among the therns with the fury of demons. Such fighting! Never had I witnessed its like before. I had thought the green Martians the most ferocious warriors in the universe, but the awful abandon with which the black pirates threw themselves upon their foes transcended everything I ever before had seen.

Beneath the brilliant light of Mars' two glorious moons the whole scene presented itself in vivid distinctness. The golden-haired, white-skinned therns battling with desperate courage in hand-to-hand conflict with their ebony-skinned foemen.

Here a little knot of struggling warriors trampled a bed of gorgeous pimalia; there the curved sword of a black man found the heart of a thern and left its dead foeman at the foot of a wondrous statue carved from a living ruby; yonder a dozen therns pressed a single pirate back upon a bench of emerald, upon whose iridescent surface a strangely beautiful Barsoomian design was traced out in inlaid diamonds.

A little to one side stood Thuvia, the Thark, and I. The tide of battle had not reached us, but the fighters from time to time swung close enough that we might distinctly note them.

The black pirates interested me immensely. I had heard vague rumours, little more than legends they were, during my former life on Mars; but never had I seen them, nor talked with one who had.

They were popularly supposed to inhabit the lesser moon, from which they descended upon Barsoom at long intervals. Where they visited they wrought the most horrible atrocities, and when they left carried away with them firearms and ammunition, and young girls as prisoners. These latter, the rumour had it, they sacrificed to some terrible god in an orgy which ended in the eating of their victims.

I had an excellent opportunity to examine them, as the strife occasionally brought now one and now another close to where I stood. They were large men, possibly six feet and over in height. Their features were clear cut and handsome in the extreme; their eyes were well set and large, though a slight narrowness lent them a crafty appearance; the iris, as well as I could determine by moonlight, was of extreme blackness, while the eyeball itself was quite white and clear. The physical structure of their bodies seemed identical with those of the therns, the red men, and my own. Only in the colour of their skin did they differ materially from us; that is of the appearance of polished ebony, and odd as it may seem for a Southerner to say it, adds to rather than detracts from their marvellous beauty.

But if their bodies are divine, their hearts, apparently, are quite the reverse. Never did I witness such a malign lust for blood as these demons of the outer air evinced in their mad battle with the therns.

All about us in the garden lay their sinister craft, which the therns for some reason, then unaccountable to me, made no effort to injure. Now and again a black warrior would rush from a near by temple bearing a young woman in his arms. Straight for his flier he would leap while those of his comrades who fought near by would rush to cover his escape.

The therns on their side would hasten to rescue the girl, and in an instant the two would be swallowed in the vortex of a maelstrom of yelling devils, hacking and hewing at one another, like fiends incarnate.

But always, it seemed, were the black pirates of Barsoom victorious, and the girl, brought miraculously unharmed through the conflict, borne away into the outer darkness upon the deck of a swift flier.

Fighting similar to that which surrounded us could be heard in both directions as far as sound carried, and Thuvia told me that the attacks of the black pirates were usually made simultaneously along the entire ribbon-like domain of the therns, which circles the Valley Dor on the outer slopes of the Mountains of Otz.

As the fighting receded from our position for a moment, Thuvia turned toward me with a question.

"Do you understand now, O Prince," she said, "why a million warriors guard the domains of the Holy Therns by day and by night?"

"The scene you are witnessing now is but a repetition of what I have seen enacted a score of times during the fifteen years I have been a prisoner here. From time immemorial the black pirates of Barsoom have preyed upon the Holy Therns.

"Yet they never carry their expeditions to a point, as one might readily believe it was in their power to do, where the extermination of the race of therns is threatened. It is as though they but utilized the race as playthings, with which they satisfy their ferocious lust for fighting; and from whom they collect toll in arms and ammunition and in prisoners."

"Why don't they jump in and destroy these fliers?" I asked. "That would soon put a stop to the attacks, or at least the blacks would scarce be so bold. Why, see how perfectly unguarded they leave their craft, as though they were lying safe in their own hangars at home."

"The therns do not dare. They tried it once, ages ago, but the next night and for a whole moon thereafter a thousand great black battleships circled the Mountains of Otz, pouring tons of projectiles upon the temples, the gardens, and the courts, until every thern who was not killed was driven for safety into the subterranean galleries.

"The therns know that they live at all only by the sufferance of the black men. They were near to extermination that once and they will not venture risking it again."

As she ceased talking a new element was instilled into the conflict. It came from a source equally unlooked for by either thern or pirate. The great banths which we had liberated in the garden had evidently been awed at first by the sound of the battle, the yelling of the warriors and the loud report of rifle and bomb.

But now they must have become angered by the continuous noise and excited by the smell of new blood, for all of a sudden a great form shot from a clump of low shrubbery into the midst of a struggling mass of humanity. A horrid scream of bestial rage broke from the banth as he felt warm flesh beneath his powerful talons.

As though his cry was but a signal to the others, the entire great pack hurled themselves among the fighters. Panic reigned in an instant. Thern and black man turned alike against the common enemy, for the banths showed no partiality toward either.

The awful beasts bore down a hundred men by the mere weight of their great bodies as they hurled themselves into the thick of the fight. Leaping and clawing, they mowed down the warriors with their powerful paws, turning for an instant to rend their victims with frightful fangs.

The scene was fascinating in its terribleness, but suddenly it came to me that we were wasting valuable time watching this conflict, which in itself might prove a means of our escape.

The therns were so engaged with their terrible assailants that now, if ever, escape should be comparatively easy. I turned to search for an opening through the contending hordes. If we could but reach the ramparts we might find that the pirates somewhere had thinned the guarding forces and left a way open to us to the world without.

As my eyes wandered about the garden, the sight of the hundreds of air craft lying unguarded around us suggested the simplest avenue to freedom. Why it had not occurred to me before! I was thoroughly familiar with the mechanism of every known make of flier on Barsoom. For nine years I had sailed and fought with the navy of Helium. I had raced through space on the tiny one-man air scout and I had commanded the greatest battleship that ever had floated in the thin air of dying Mars.

To think, with me, is to act. Grasping Thuvia by the arm, I whispered to Tars Tarkas to follow me. Quickly we glided toward a small flier which lay furthest from the battling warriors. Another instant found us huddled on the tiny deck. My hand was on the starting lever. I pressed my thumb upon the button which controls the ray of repulsion, that splendid discovery of the Martians which permits them to navigate the

thin atmosphere of their planet in huge ships that dwarf the dreadnoughts of our earthly navies into pitiful significance.

The craft swayed slightly but she did not move. Then a new cry of
warning broke upon our ears. Turning, I saw a dozen black pirates dashing toward us from the melee. We had been discovered. With shrieks of
rage the demons sprang for us. With frenzied insistence I continued to
press the little button which should have sent us racing out into space,
but still the vessel refused to budge. Then it came to me – the reason
that she would not rise.

We had stumbled upon a two-man flier. Its ray tanks were charged
only with sufficient repulsive energy to lift two ordinary men. The
Thark's great weight was anchoring us to our doom.

The blacks were nearly upon us. There was not an instant to be lost
in hesitation or doubt.

I pressed the button far in and locked it. Then I set the lever at high
speed and as the blacks came yelling upon us I slipped from the craft's
deck and with drawn long-sword met the attack.

At the same moment a girl's shriek rang out behind me and an
instant later, as the blacks fell upon me. I heard far above my head,
and faintly, in Thuvia's voice: "My Prince, O my Prince; I would rather
remain and die with – " But the rest was lost in the noise of my assailants.

I knew though that my ruse had worked and that temporarily at
least Thuvia and Tars Tarkas were safe, and the means of escape was
theirs.

For a moment it seemed that I could not withstand the weight of
numbers that confronted me, but again, as on so many other occasions
when I had been called upon to face fearful odds upon this planet of
warriors and fierce beasts, I found that my earthly strength so far transcended that of my opponents that the odds were not so greatly against
me as they appeared.

My seething blade wove a net of death about me. For an instant the
blacks pressed close to reach me with their shorter swords, but presently they gave back, and the esteem in which they suddenly had learned
to hold my sword arm was writ large upon each countenance.

I knew though that it was but a question of minutes before their
greater numbers would wear me down, or get around my guard. I must
go down eventually to certain death before them. I shuddered at the
thought of it, dying thus in this terrible place where no word of my
end ever could reach my Dejah Thoris. Dying at the hands of nameless
black men in the gardens of the cruel therns.

Then my old-time spirit reasserted itself. The fighting blood of my Virginian sires coursed hot through my veins. The fierce blood lust and the joy of battle surged over me. The fighting smile that has brought consternation to a thousand foemen touched my lips. I put the thought of death out of my mind, and fell upon my antagonists with fury that those who escaped will remember to their dying day.

That others would press to the support of those who faced me I knew, so even as I fought I kept my wits at work, searching for an avenue of escape.

It came from an unexpected quarter out of the black night behind me. I had just disarmed a huge fellow who had given me a desperate struggle, and for a moment the blacks stood back for a breathing spell.

They eyed me with malignant fury, yet withal there was a touch of respect in their demeanour.

"Thern," said one, "you fight like a Dator. But for your detestable yellow hair and your white skin you would be an honour to the First Born of Barsoom."

"I am no thern," I said, and was about to explain that I was from another world, thinking that by patching a truce with these fellows and fighting with them against the therns I might enlist their aid in regaining my liberty. But just at that moment a heavy object smote me a resounding whack between my shoulders that nearly felled me to the ground.

As I turned to meet this new enemy an object passed over my shoulder, striking one of my assailants squarely in the face and knocking him senseless to the sward. At the same instant I saw that the thing that had struck us was the trailing anchor of a rather fair-sized air vessel; possibly a ten man cruiser.

The ship was floating slowly above us, not more than fifty feet over our heads. Instantly the one chance for escape that it offered presented itself to me. The vessel was slowly rising and now the anchor was beyond the blacks who faced me and several feet above their heads.

With a bound that left them gaping in wide-eyed astonishment I sprang completely over them. A second leap carried me just high enough to grasp the now rapidly receding anchor.

But I was successful, and there I hung by one hand, dragging through the branches of the higher vegetation of the gardens, while my late foemen shrieked and howled beneath me.

Presently the vessel veered toward the west and then swung gracefully to the south. In another instant I was carried beyond the crest of the Golden Cliffs, out over the Valley Dor, where, six thousand feet below me, the Lost Sea of Korus lay shimmering in the moonlight.

Carefully I climbed to a sitting posture across the anchor's arms. I wondered if by chance the vessel might be deserted. I hoped so. Or possibly it might belong to a friendly people, and have wandered by accident almost within the clutches of the pirates and the therns. The fact that it was retreating from the scene of battle lent colour to this hypothesis.

But I decided to know positively, and at once, so, with the greatest caution, I commenced to climb slowly up the anchor chain toward the deck above me.

One hand had just reached for the vessel's rail and found it when a fierce black face was thrust over the side and eyes filled with triumphant hate looked into mine.

CHAPTER SEVEN
A Fair Goddess

FOR AN INSTANT the black pirate and I remained motionless, glaring into each other's eyes. Then a grim smile curled the handsome lips above me, as an ebony hand came slowly in sight from above the edge of the deck and the cold, hollow eye of a revolver sought the centre of my forehead.

Simultaneously my free hand shot out for the black throat, just within reach, and the ebony finger tightened on the trigger. The pirate's hissing, "Die, cursed thern," was half choked in his windpipe by my clutching fingers. The hammer fell with a futile click upon an empty chamber.

Before he could fire again I had pulled him so far over the edge of the deck that he was forced to drop his firearm and clutch the rail with both hands.

My grasp upon his throat effectually prevented any outcry, and so we struggled in grim silence; he to tear away from my hold, I to drag him over to his death.

His face was taking on a livid hue, his eyes were bulging from their sockets. It was evident to him that he soon must die unless he tore loose from the steel fingers that were choking the life from him. With a final effort he threw himself further back upon the deck, at the same instant releasing his hold upon the rail to tear frantically with both hands at my fingers in an effort to drag them from his throat.

That little second was all that I awaited. With one mighty downward surge I swept him clear of the deck. His falling body came near to tearing me from the frail hold that my single free hand had upon the anchor chain and plunging me with him to the waters of the sea below.

I did not relinquish my grasp upon him, however, for I knew that a single shriek from those lips as he hurtled to his death in the silent waters of the sea would bring his comrades from above to avenge him.

Instead I held grimly to him, choking, ever choking, while his frantic struggles dragged me lower and lower toward the end of the chain.

Gradually his contortions became spasmodic, lessening by degrees until they ceased entirely. Then I released my hold upon him and in an instant he was swallowed by the black shadows far below.

Again I climbed to the ship's rail. This time I succeeded in raising my eyes to the level of the deck, where I could take a careful survey of the conditions immediately confronting me.

The nearer moon had passed below the horizon, but the clear effulgence of the further satellite bathed the deck of the cruiser, bringing into sharp relief the bodies of six or eight black men sprawled about in sleep.

Huddled close to the base of a rapid fire gun was a young white girl, securely bound. Her eyes were widespread in an expression of horrified anticipation and fixed directly upon me as I came in sight above the edge of the deck.

Unutterable relief instantly filled them as they fell upon the mystic jewel which sparkled in the centre of my stolen headpiece. She did not speak. Instead her eyes warned me to beware the sleeping figures that surrounded her.

Noiselessly I gained the deck. The girl nodded to me to approach her. As I bent low she whispered to me to release her.

"I can aid you," she said, "and you will need all the aid available when they awaken."

"Some of them will awake in Korus," I replied smiling.

She caught the meaning of my words, and the cruelty of her answering smile horrified me. One is not astonished by cruelty in a hideous face, but when it touches the features of a goddess whose fine-chiselled lineaments might more fittingly portray love and beauty, the contrast is appalling.

Quickly I released her.

"Give me a revolver," she whispered. "I can use that upon those your sword does not silence in time."

I did as she bid. Then I turned toward the distasteful work that lay before me. This was no time for fine compunctions, nor for a chivalry that these cruel demons would neither appreciate nor reciprocate.

Stealthily I approached the nearest sleeper. When he awoke he was well on his journey to the bosom of Korus. His piercing shriek as consciousness returned to him came faintly up to us from the black depths beneath.

The second awoke as I touched him, and, though I succeeded in hurling him from the cruiser's deck, his wild cry of alarm brought the remaining pirates to their feet. There were five of them.

As they arose the girl's revolver spoke in sharp staccato and one sank back to the deck again to rise no more.

The others rushed madly upon me with drawn swords. The girl evidently dared not fire for fear of wounding me, but I saw her sneak stealthily and cat-like toward the flank of the attackers. Then they were on me.

For a few minutes I experienced some of the hottest fighting I had ever passed through. The quarters were too small for foot work. It was stand your ground and give and take. At first I took considerably more than I gave, but presently I got beneath one fellow's guard and had the satisfaction of seeing him collapse upon the deck.

The others redoubled their efforts. The crashing of their blades upon mine raised a terrific din that might have been heard for miles through the silent night. Sparks flew as steel smote steel, and then there was the dull and sickening sound of a shoulder bone parting beneath the keen edge of my Martian sword.

Three now faced me, but the girl was working her way to a point that would soon permit her to reduce the number by one at least. Then things happened with such amazing rapidity that I can scarce comprehend even now all that took place in that brief instant.

The three rushed me with the evident purpose of forcing me back the few steps that would carry my body over the rail into the void below. At the same instant the girl fired and my sword arm made two moves. One man dropped with a bullet in his brain; a sword flew clattering across the deck and dropped over the edge beyond as I disarmed one of my opponents and the third went down with my blade buried to the hilt in his breast and three feet of it protruding from his back, and falling wrenched the sword from my grasp.

Disarmed myself, I now faced my remaining foeman, whose own sword lay somewhere thousands of feet below us, lost in the Lost Sea.

The new conditions seemed to please my adversary, for a smile of satisfaction bared his gleaming teeth as he rushed at me bare-handed. The great muscles which rolled beneath his glossy black hide evidently assured him that here was easy prey, not worth the trouble of drawing the dagger from his harness.

I let him come almost upon me. Then I ducked beneath his outstretched arms, at the same time sidestepping to the right. Pivoting on my left toe, I swung a terrific right to his jaw, and, like a felled ox, he dropped in his tracks.

A low, silvery laugh rang out behind me.

"You are no thern," said the sweet voice of my companion, "for all your golden locks or the harness of Sator Throg. Never lived there upon all Barsoom before one who could fight as you have fought this night. Who are you?"

"I am John Carter, Prince of the House of Tardos Mors, Jeddak of Helium," I replied. "And whom," I added, "has the honour of serving been accorded me?"

She hesitated a moment before speaking. Then she asked:

"You are no thern. Are you an enemy of the therns?"

"I have been in the territory of the therns for a day and a half. During that entire time my life has been in constant danger. I have been harassed and persecuted. Armed men and fierce beasts have been set upon me. I had no quarrel with the therns before, but can you wonder that I feel no great love for them now? I have spoken."

She looked at me intently for several minutes before she replied. It was as though she were attempting to read my inmost soul, to judge my character and my standards of chivalry in that long-drawn, searching gaze.

Apparently the inventory satisfied her.

"I am Phaidor, daughter of Matai Shang, Holy Hekkador of the Holy Therns, Father of Therns, Master of Life and Death upon Barsoom, Brother of Issus, Prince of Life Eternal."

At that moment I noticed that the black I had dropped with my fist was commencing to show signs of returning consciousness. I sprang to his side. Stripping his harness from him I securely bound his hands behind his back, and after similarly fastening his feet tied him to a heavy gun carriage.

"Why not the simpler way?" asked Phaidor.

"I do not understand. What 'simpler way'?" I replied.

With a slight shrug of her lovely shoulders she made a gesture with her hands personating the casting of something over the craft's side.

"I am no murderer," I said. "I kill in self-defence only."

She looked at me narrowly. Then she puckered those divine brows of hers, and shook her head. She could not comprehend.

Well, neither had my own Dejah Thoris been able to understand what to her had seemed a foolish and dangerous policy toward enemies. Upon Barsoom, quarter is neither asked nor given, and each dead man means so much more of the waning resources of this dying planet to be divided amongst those who survive.

But there seemed a subtle difference here between the manner in which this girl contemplated the dispatching of an enemy and the tender-hearted regret of my own princess for the stern necessity which demanded it.

I think that Phaidor regretted the thrill that the spectacle would have afforded her rather than the fact that my decision left another enemy alive to threaten us.

The man had now regained full possession of his faculties, and was regarding us intently from where he lay bound upon the deck. He was a handsome fellow, clean limbed and powerful, with an intelligent face and features of such exquisite chiselling that Adonis himself might have envied him.

The vessel, unguided, had been moving slowly across the valley; but now I thought it time to take the helm and direct her course. Only in a very general way could I guess the location of the Valley Dor. That it was far south of the equator was evident from the constellations, but I was not sufficiently a Martian astronomer to come much closer than a rough guess without the splendid charts and delicate instruments with which, as an officer in the Heliumite Navy, I had formerly reckoned the positions of the vessels on which I sailed.

That a northerly course would quickest lead me toward the more settled portions of the planet immediately decided the direction that I should steer. Beneath my hand the cruiser swung gracefully about. Then the button which controlled the repulsive rays sent us soaring far out into space. With speed lever pulled to the last notch, we raced toward the north as we rose ever farther and farther above that terrible valley of death.

As we passed at a dizzy height over the narrow domains of the therns the flash of powder far below bore mute witness to the ferocity of the battle that still raged along that cruel frontier. No sound of conflict reached our ears, for in the rarefied atmosphere of our great altitude no sound wave could penetrate; they were dissipated in thin air far below us.

It became intensely cold. Breathing was difficult. The girl, Phaidor, and the black pirate kept their eyes glued upon me. At length the girl spoke.

"Unconsciousness comes quickly at this altitude," she said quietly. "Unless you are inviting death for us all you had best drop, and that quickly."

There was no fear in her voice. It was as one might say: "You had better carry an umbrella. It is going to rain."

I dropped the vessel quickly to a lower level. Nor was I a moment too soon. The girl had swooned.

The black, too, was unconscious, while I, myself, retained my senses, I think, only by sheer will. The one on whom all responsibility rests is apt to endure the most.

We were swinging along low above the foothills of the Otz. It was comparatively warm and there was plenty of air for our starved lungs, so I was not surprised to see the black open his eyes, and a moment later the girl also.

"It was a close call," she said.

"It has taught me two things though," I replied.

"What?"

"That even Phaidor, daughter of the Master of Life and Death, is mortal," I said smiling.

"There is immortality only in Issus," she replied. "And Issus is for the race of therns alone. Thus am I immortal."

I caught a fleeting grin passing across the features of the black as he heard her words. I did not then understand why he smiled. Later I was to learn, and she, too, in a most horrible manner.

"If the other thing you have just learned," she continued, "has led to as erroneous deductions as the first you are little richer in knowledge than you were before."

"The other," I replied, "is that our dusky friend here does not hail from the nearer moon – he was like to have died at a few thousand feet above Barsoom. Had we continued the five thousand miles that lie between Thuria and the planet he would have been but the frozen memory of a man."

Phaidor looked at the black in evident astonishment.

"If you are not of Thuria, then where?" she asked.

He shrugged his shoulders and turned his eyes elsewhere, but did not reply.

The girl stamped her little foot in a peremptory manner.

"The daughter of Matai Shang is not accustomed to having her queries remain unanswered," she said. "One of the lesser breed should feel honoured that a member of the holy race that was born to inherit life eternal should deign even to notice him."

Again the black smiled that wicked, knowing smile.

"Xodar, Dator of the First Born of Barsoom, is accustomed to give commands, not to receive them," replied the black pirate. Then, turning to me, "What are your intentions concerning me?"

"I intend taking you both back to Helium," I said. "No harm will come to you. You will find the red men of Helium a kindly and magnanimous race, but if they listen to me there will be no more voluntary pilgrimages down the river Iss, and the impossible belief that they have cherished for ages will be shattered into a thousand pieces."

"Are you of Helium?" he asked.

"I am a Prince of the House of Tardos Mors, Jeddak of Helium," I replied, "but I am not of Barsoom. I am of another world."

Xodar looked at me intently for a few moments.

"I can well believe that you are not of Barsoom," he said at length. "None of this world could have bested eight of the First Born single-handed. But how is it that you wear the golden hair and the jewelled circlet of a Holy Thern?" He emphasized the word holy with a touch of irony.

"I had forgotten them," I said. "They are the spoils of conquest," and with a sweep of my hand I removed the disguise from my head.

When the black's eyes fell on my close-cropped black hair they opened in astonishment. Evidently he had looked for the bald pate of a thern.

"You are indeed of another world," he said, a touch of awe in his voice. "With the skin of a thern, the black hair of a First Born and the muscles of a dozen Dators it was no disgrace even for Xodar to acknowledge your supremacy. A thing he could never do were you a Barsoomian," he added.

"You are travelling several laps ahead of me, my friend," I interrupted. "I glean that your name is Xodar, but whom, pray, are the First Born, and what a Dator, and why, if you were conquered by a Barsoomian, could you not acknowledge it?"

"The First Born of Barsoom," he explained, "are the race of black men of which I am a Dator, or, as the lesser Barsoomians would say, Prince. My race is the oldest on the planet. We trace our lineage, unbroken, direct to the Tree of Life which flourished in the centre of the Valley Dor twenty-three million years ago.

"For countless ages the fruit of this tree underwent the gradual changes of evolution, passing by degrees from true plant life to a combination of plant and animal. In the first stages the fruit of the tree possessed only the power of independent muscular action, while the stem remained attached to the parent plant; later a brain developed in the fruit, so that hanging there by their long stems they thought and moved as individuals.

"Then, with the development of perceptions came a comparison of them; judgments were reached and compared, and thus reason and the power to reason were born upon Barsoom.

"Ages passed. Many forms of life came and went upon the Tree of Life, but still all were attached to the parent plant by stems of varying lengths. At length the fruit tree consisted in tiny plant men, such as we now see reproduced in such huge dimensions in the Valley Dor, but still hanging to the limbs and branches of the tree by the stems which grew from the tops of their heads.

"The buds from which the plant men blossomed resembled large nuts about a foot in diameter, divided by double partition walls into four sections. In one section grew the plant man, in another a sixteen-legged worm, in the third the progenitor of the white ape and in the fourth the primaeval black man of Barsoom.

"When the bud burst the plant man remained dangling at the end of his stem, but the three other sections fell to the ground, where the efforts of their imprisoned occupants to escape sent them hopping about in all directions.

"Thus as time went on, all Barsoom was covered with these imprisoned creatures. For countless ages they lived their long lives within their hard shells, hopping and skipping about the broad planet; falling into rivers, lakes, and seas, to be still further spread about the surface of the new world.

"Countless billions died before the first black man broke through his prison walls into the light of day. Prompted by curiosity, he broke open other shells and the peopling of Barsoom commenced.

"The pure strain of the blood of this first black man has remained untainted by admixture with other creatures in the race of which I am a member; but from the sixteen-legged worm, the first ape and renegade black man has sprung every other form of animal life upon Barsoom.

"The therns," and he smiled maliciously as he spoke, "are but the result of ages of evolution from the pure white ape of antiquity. They are a lower order still. There is but one race of true and immortal humans on Barsoom. It is the race of black men.

"The Tree of Life is dead, but before it died the plant men learned to detach themselves from it and roam the face of Barsoom with the other children of the First Parent.

"Now their bisexuality permits them to reproduce themselves after the manner of true plants, but otherwise they have progressed but little in all the ages of their existence. Their actions and movements are largely matters of instinct and not guided to any great extent by reason, since the brain of a plant man is but a trifle larger than the end of your smallest finger. They live upon vegetation and the blood of animals, and their brain is just large enough to direct their movements in the direction of food, and to translate the food sensations which are carried to it from their eyes and ears. They have no sense of self-preservation and so are entirely without fear in the face of danger. That is why they are such terrible antagonists in combat."

I wondered why the black man took such pains to discourse thus at length to enemies upon the genesis of life Barsoomian. It seemed a strangely inopportune moment for a proud member of a proud race to unbend in casual conversation with a captor. Especially in view of the fact that the black still lay securely bound upon the deck.

It was the faintest straying of his eye beyond me for the barest fraction of a second that explained his motive for thus dragging out my interest in his truly absorbing story.

He lay a little forward of where I stood at the levers, and thus he faced the stern of the vessel as he addressed me. It was at the end of his description of the plant men that I caught his eye fixed momentarily upon something behind me.

Nor could I be mistaken in the swift gleam of triumph that brightened those dark orbs for an instant.

Some time before I had reduced our speed, for we had left the Valley Dor many miles astern, and I felt comparatively safe.

I turned an apprehensive glance behind me, and the sight that I saw froze the new-born hope of freedom that had been springing up within me.

A great battleship, forging silent and unlighted through the dark night, loomed close astern.

CHAPTER EIGHT

The Depths of Omean

Now I REALIZED why the black pirate had kept me engrossed with his strange tale. For miles he had sensed the approach of succour, and but for that single tell-tale glance the battleship would have been directly above us in another moment, and the boarding party which was doubtless even now swinging in their harness from the ship's keel, would have swarmed our deck, placing my rising hope of escape in sudden and total eclipse.

I was too old a hand in aerial warfare to be at a loss now for the right manoeuvre. Simultaneously I reversed the engines and dropped the little vessel a sheer hundred feet.

Above my head I could see the dangling forms of the boarding party as the battleship raced over us. Then I rose at a sharp angle, throwing my speed lever to its last notch.

Like a bolt from a crossbow my splendid craft shot its steel prow straight at the whirring propellers of the giant above us. If I could but touch them the huge bulk would be disabled for hours and escape once more possible.

At the same instant the sun shot above the horizon, disclosing a hundred grim, black faces peering over the stern of the battleship upon us.

At sight of us a shout of rage went up from a hundred throats. Orders were shouted, but it was too late to save the giant propellers, and with a crash we rammed them.

Instantly with the shock of impact I reversed my engine, but my prow was wedged in the hole it had made in the battleship's stern. Only a second I hung there before tearing away, but that second was amply long to swarm my deck with black devils.

There was no fight. In the first place there was no room to fight. We were simply submerged by numbers. Then as swords menaced me a command from Xodar stayed the hands of his fellows.

"Secure them," he said, "but do not injure them."

Several of the pirates already had released Xodar. He now personally attended to my disarming and saw that I was properly bound. At least he thought that the binding was secure. It would have been had I been a Martian, but I had to smile at the puny strands that confined my wrists. When the time came I could snap them as they had been cotton string.

The girl they bound also, and then they fastened us together. In the meantime they had brought our craft alongside the disabled battleship, and soon we were transported to the latter's deck.

Fully a thousand black men manned the great engine of destruction. Her decks were crowded with them as they pressed forward as far as discipline would permit to get a glimpse of their captives.

The girl's beauty elicited many brutal comments and vulgar jests. It was evident that these self-thought supermen were far inferior to the red men of Barsoom in refinement and in chivalry.

My close-cropped black hair and thern complexion were the subjects of much comment. When Xodar told his fellow nobles of my fighting ability and strange origin they crowded about me with numerous questions.

The fact that I wore the harness and metal of a thern who had been killed by a member of my party convinced them that I was an enemy of their hereditary foes, and placed me on a better footing in their estimation.

Without exception the blacks were handsome men, and well built. The officers were conspicuous through the wondrous magnificence of their resplendent trappings. Many harnesses were so encrusted with gold, platinum, silver and precious stones as to entirely hide the leather beneath.

The harness of the commanding officer was a solid mass of diamonds. Against the ebony background of his skin they blazed out with a peculiarly accentuated effulgence. The whole scene was enchanting. The handsome men; the barbaric splendour of the accoutrements; the polished skeel wood of the deck; the gloriously grained sorapus of the cabins, inlaid with priceless jewels and precious metals in intricate and beautiful design; the burnished gold of hand rails; the shining metal of the guns.

Phaidor and I were taken below decks, where, still fast bound, we were thrown into a small compartment which contained a single porthole. As our escort left us they barred the door behind them.

We could hear the men working on the broken propellers, and from the port-hole we could see that the vessel was drifting lazily toward the south.

For some time neither of us spoke. Each was occupied with his own thoughts. For my part I was wondering as to the fate of Tars Tarkas and the girl, Thuvia.

Even if they succeeded in eluding pursuit they must eventually fall into the hands of either red men or green, and as fugitives from the Valley Dor they could look for but little else than a swift and terrible death.

How I wished that I might have accompanied them. It seemed to me that I could not fail to impress upon the intelligent red men of Barsoom the wicked deception that a cruel and senseless superstition had foisted upon them.

Tardos Mors would believe me. Of that I was positive. And that he would have the courage of his convictions my knowledge of his character assured me. Dejah Thoris would believe me. Not a doubt as to that entered my head. Then there were a thousand of my red and green warrior friends whom I knew would face eternal damnation gladly for my sake. Like Tars Tarkas, where I led they would follow.

My only danger lay in that should I ever escape the black pirates it might be to fall into the hands of unfriendly red or green men. Then it would mean short shrift for me.

Well, there seemed little to worry about on that score, for the likelihood of my ever escaping the blacks was extremely remote.

The girl and I were linked together by a rope which permitted us to move only about three or four feet from each other. When we had entered the compartment we had seated ourselves upon a low bench beneath the porthole. The bench was the only furniture of the room. It was of sorapus wood. The floor, ceiling and walls were of carborundum aluminum, a light, impenetrable composition extensively utilized in the construction of Martian fighting ships.

As I had sat meditating upon the future my eyes had been riveted upon the port-hole which was just level with them as I sat. Suddenly I looked toward Phaidor. She was regarding me with a strange expression I had not before seen upon her face. She was very beautiful then.

Instantly her white lids veiled her eyes, and I thought I discovered a delicate flush tingeing her cheek. Evidently she was embarrassed at having been detected in the act of staring at a lesser creature, I thought.

"Do you find the study of the lower orders interesting?" I asked, laughing.

She looked up again with a nervous but relieved little laugh.

"Oh very," she said, "especially when they have such excellent profiles."

It was my turn to flush, but I did not. I felt that she was poking fun at me, and I admired a brave heart that could look for humour on the road to death, and so I laughed with her.

"Do you know where we are going?" she said.

"To solve the mystery of the eternal hereafter, I imagine," I replied.

"I am going to a worse fate than that," she said, with a little shudder. "What do you mean?"

"I can only guess," she replied, "since no thern damsel of all the millions that have been stolen away by black pirates during the ages they have raided our domains has ever returned to narrate her experiences among them. That they never take a man prisoner lends strength to the belief that the fate of the girls they steal is worse than death."

"Is it not a just retribution?" I could not help but ask.

"What do you mean?"

"Do not the therns themselves do likewise with the poor creatures who take the voluntary pilgrimage down the River of Mystery? Was not Thuvia for fifteen years a plaything and a slave? Is it less than just that you should suffer as you have caused others to suffer?"

"You do not understand," she replied. "We therns are a holy race. It is an honour to a lesser creature to be a slave among us. Did we not occasionally save a few of the lower orders that stupidly float down an unknown river to an unknown end all would become the prey of the plant men and the apes."

"But do you not by every means encourage the superstition among those of the outside world?" I argued. "That is the wickedest of your deeds. Can you tell me why you foster the cruel deception?"

"All life on Barsoom," she said, "is created solely for the support of the race of therns. How else could we live did the outer world not furnish our labour and our food? Think you that a thern would demean himself by labour?"

"It is true then that you eat human flesh?" I asked in horror.

She looked at me in pitying commiseration for my ignorance.

"Truly we eat the flesh of the lower orders. Do not you also?"

"The flesh of beasts, yes," I replied, "but not the flesh of man."

"As man may eat of the flesh of beasts, so may gods eat of the flesh of man. The Holy Therns are the gods of Barsoom."

I was disgusted and I imagine that I showed it.

"You are an unbeliever now," she continued gently, "but should we be fortunate enough to escape the clutches of the black pirates and come again to the court of Matai Shang I think that we shall find an argument to convince you of the error of your ways. And – ," she hesitated, "perhaps we shall find a way to keep you as – as – one of us."

Again her eyes dropped to the floor, and a faint colour suffused her cheek. I could not understand her meaning; nor did I for a long time. Dejah Thoris was wont to say that in some things I was a veritable simpleton, and I guess that she was right.

"I fear that I would ill requite your father's hospitality," I answered, "since the first thing that I should do were I a thern would be to set an armed guard at the mouth of the River Iss to escort the poor deluded voyagers back to the outer world. Also should I devote my life to the extermination of the hideous plant men and their horrible companions, the great white apes."

She looked at me really horror struck.

"No, no," she cried, "you must not say such terribly sacrilegious things – you must not even think them. Should they ever guess that you entertained such frightful thoughts, should we chance to regain the temples of the therns, they would mete out a frightful death to you. Not even my – my – " Again she flushed, and started over. "Not even I could save you."

I said no more. Evidently it was useless. She was even more steeped in superstition than the Martians of the outer world. They only worshipped a beautiful hope for a life of love and peace and happiness in the hereafter. The therns worshipped the hideous plant men and the apes, or at least they reverenced them as the abodes of the departed spirits of their own dead.

At this point the door of our prison opened to admit Xodar.

He smiled pleasantly at me, and when he smiled his expression was kindly – anything but cruel or vindictive.

"Since you cannot escape under any circumstances," he said, "I cannot see the necessity for keeping you confined below. I will cut your bonds and you may come on deck. You will witness something very interesting, and as you never shall return to the outer world it will do no harm to permit you to see it. You will see what no other than the First Born and their slaves know the existence of – the subterranean entrance to the Holy Land, to the real heaven of Barsoom.

"It will be an excellent lesson for this daughter of the therns," he added, "for she shall see the Temple of Issus, and Issus, perchance, shall embrace her."

Phaidor's head went high.

"What blasphemy is this, dog of a pirate?" she cried. "Issus would wipe out your entire breed an' you ever came within sight of her temple."

"You have much to learn, thern," replied Xodar, with an ugly smile, "nor do I envy you the manner in which you will learn it."

As we came on deck I saw to my surprise that the vessel was passing over a great field of snow and ice. As far as the eye could reach in any direction naught else was visible.

There could be but one solution to the mystery. We were above the south polar ice cap. Only at the poles of Mars is there ice or snow upon the planet. No sign of life appeared below us. Evidently we were too far south even for the great fur-bearing animals which the Martians so delight in hunting.

Xodar was at my side as I stood looking out over the ship's rail.

"What course?" I asked him.

"A little west of south," he replied. "You will see the Otz Valley directly. We shall skirt it for a few hundred miles."

"The Otz Valley!" I exclaimed; "but, man, is not there where lie the domains of the therns from which I but just escaped?"

"Yes," answered Xodar. "You crossed this ice field last night in the long chase that you led us. The Otz Valley lies in a mighty depression at the south pole. It is sunk thousands of feet below the level of the surrounding country, like a great round bowl. A hundred miles from its northern boundary rise the Otz Mountains which circle the inner Valley of Dor, in the exact centre of which lies the Lost Sea of Korus. On the shore of this sea stands the Golden Temple of Issus in the Land of the First Born. It is there that we are bound."

As I looked I commenced to realize why it was that in all the ages only one had escaped from the Valley Dor. My only wonder was that even the one had been successful. To cross this frozen, wind-swept waste of bleak ice alone and on foot would be impossible.

"Only by air boat could the journey be made," I finished aloud.

"It was thus that one did escape the therns in bygone times; but none has ever escaped the First Born," said Xodar, with a touch of pride in his voice.

We had now reached the southernmost extremity of the great ice barrier. It ended abruptly in a sheer wall thousands of feet high at the base of which stretched a level valley, broken here and there by low rolling hills and little clumps of forest, and with tiny rivers formed by the melting of the ice barrier at its base.

Once we passed far above what seemed to be a deep canyon-like rift stretching from the ice wall on the north across the valley as far as the eye could reach. "That is the bed of the River Iss," said Xodar. "It runs far beneath the ice field, and below the level of the Valley Otz, but its canyon is open here."

Presently I descried what I took to be a village, and pointing it out to Xodar asked him what it might be.

"It is a village of lost souls," he answered, laughing. "This strip between the ice barrier and the mountains is considered neutral ground.

Some turn off from their voluntary pilgrimage down the Iss, and, scaling the awful walls of its canyon below us, stop in the valley. Also a slave now and then escapes from the therns and makes his way hither.

"They do not attempt to recapture such, since there is no escape from this outer valley, and as a matter of fact they fear the patrolling cruisers of the First Born too much to venture from their own domains.

"The poor creatures of this outer valley are not molested by us since they have nothing that we desire, nor are they numerically strong enough to give us an interesting fight – so we too leave them alone.

"There are several villages of them, but they have increased in numbers but little in many years since they are always warring among themselves."

Now we swung a little north of west, leaving the valley of lost souls, and shortly I discerned over our starboard bow what appeared to be a black mountain rising from the desolate waste of ice. It was not high and seemed to have a flat top.

Xodar had left us to attend to some duty on the vessel, and Phaidor and I stood alone beside the rail. The girl had not once spoken since we had been brought to the deck.

"Is what he has been telling me true?" I asked her.

"In part, yes," she answered. "That about the outer valley is true, but what he says of the location of the Temple of Issus in the centre of his country is false. If it is not false – " she hesitated. "Oh it cannot be true, it cannot be true. For if it were true then for countless ages have my people gone to torture and ignominious death at the hands of their cruel enemies, instead of to the beautiful Life Eternal that we have been taught to believe Issus holds for us."

"As the lesser Barsoomians of the outer world have been lured by you to the terrible Valley Dor, so may it be that the therns themselves have been lured by the First Born to an equally horrid fate," I suggested. "It would be a stern and awful retribution, Phaidor; but a just one."

"I cannot believe it," she said.

"We shall see," I answered, and then we fell silent again for we were rapidly approaching the black mountains, which in some indefinable way seemed linked with the answer to our problem.

As we neared the dark, truncated cone the vessel's speed was diminished until we barely moved. Then we topped the crest of the mountain and below us I saw yawning the mouth of a huge circular well, the bottom of which was lost in inky blackness.

The diameter of this enormous pit was fully a thousand feet. The walls were smooth and appeared to be composed of a black, basaltic rock.

For a moment the vessel hovered motionless directly above the centre of the gaping void, then slowly she began to settle into the black chasm. Lower and lower she sank until as darkness enveloped us her lights were thrown on and in the dim halo of her own radiance the monster battleship dropped on and on down into what seemed to me must be the very bowels of Barsoom.

For quite half an hour we descended and then the shaft terminated abruptly in the dome of a mighty subterranean world. Below us rose and fell the billows of a buried sea. A phosphorescent radiance illuminated the scene. Thousands of ships dotted the bosom of the ocean. Little islands rose here and there to support the strange and colourless vegetation of this strange world.

Slowly and with majestic grace the battleship dropped until she rested on the water. Her great propellers had been drawn and housed during our descent of the shaft and in their place had been run out the smaller but more powerful water propellers. As these commenced to revolve the ship took up its journey once more, riding the new element as buoyantly and as safely as she had the air.

Phaidor and I were dumbfounded. Neither had either heard or dreamed that such a world existed beneath the surface of Barsoom.

Nearly all the vessels we saw were war craft. There were a few lighters and barges, but none of the great merchantmen such as ply the upper air between the cities of the outer world.

"Here is the harbour of the navy of the First Born," said a voice behind us, and turning we saw Xodar watching us with an amused smile on his lips.

"This sea," he continued, "is larger than Korus. It receives the waters of the lesser sea above it. To keep it from filling above a certain level we have four great pumping stations that force the oversupply back into the reservoirs far north from which the red men draw the water which irrigates their farm lands."

A new light burst on me with this explanation. The red men had always considered it a miracle that caused great columns of water to spurt from the solid rock of their reservoir sides to increase the supply of the precious liquid which is so scarce in the outer world of Mars.

Never had their learned men been able to fathom the secret of the source of this enormous volume of water. As ages passed they had simply come to accept it as a matter of course and ceased to question its origin.

We passed several islands on which were strangely shaped circular buildings, apparently roofless, and pierced midway between the ground and their tops with small, heavily barred windows. They bore the earmarks of prisons, which were further accentuated by the armed guards who squatted on low benches without, or patrolled the short beach lines.

Few of these islets contained over an acre of ground, but presently we sighted a much larger one directly ahead. This proved to be our destination, and the great ship was soon made fast against the steep shore.

Xodar signalled us to follow him and with a half-dozen officers and men we left the battleship and approached a large oval structure a couple of hundred yards from the shore.

"You shall soon see Issus," said Xodar to Phaidor. "The few prisoners we take are presented to her. Occasionally she selects slaves from among them to replenish the ranks of her handmaidens. None serves Issus above a single year," and there was a grim smile on the black's lips that lent a cruel and sinister meaning to his simple statement.

Phaidor, though loath to believe that Issus was allied to such as these, had commenced to entertain doubts and fears. She clung very closely to me, no longer the proud daughter of the Master of Life and Death upon Barsoom, but a young and frightened girl in the power of relentless enemies.

The building which we now entered was entirely roofless. In its centre was a long tank of water, set below the level of the floor like the swimming pool of a natatorium. Near one side of the pool floated an odd-looking black object. Whether it were some strange monster of these buried waters, or a queer raft, I could not at once perceive.

We were soon to know, however, for as we reached the edge of the pool directly above the thing, Xodar cried out a few words in a strange tongue. Immediately a hatch cover was raised from the surface of the object, and a black seaman sprang from the bowels of the strange craft.

Xodar addressed the seaman.

"Transmit to your officer," he said, "the commands of Dator Xodar. Say to him that Dator Xodar, with officers and men, escorting two prisoners, would be transported to the gardens of Issus beside the Golden Temple."

"Blessed be the shell of thy first ancestor, most noble Dator," replied the man. "It shall be done even as thou sayest," and raising both hands, palms backward, above his head after the manner of salute which is common to all races of Barsoom, he disappeared once more into the entrails of his ship.

A moment later an officer resplendent in the gorgeous trappings of his rank appeared on deck and welcomed Xodar to the vessel, and in the latter's wake we filed aboard and below.

The cabin in which we found ourselves extended entirely across the ship, having port-holes on either side below the water line. No sooner were all below than a number of commands were given, in accordance with which the hatch was closed and secured, and the vessel commenced to vibrate to the rhythmic purr of its machinery.

"Where can we be going in such a tiny pool of water?" asked Phaidor.

"Not up," I replied, "for I noticed particularly that while the building is roofless it is covered with a strong metal grating."

"Then where?" she asked again.

"From the appearance of the craft I judge we are going down," I replied.

Phaidor shuddered. For such long ages have the waters of Barsoom's seas been a thing of tradition only that even this daughter of the therns, born as she had been within sight of Mars' only remaining sea, had the same terror of deep water as is a common attribute of all Martians.

Presently the sensation of sinking became very apparent. We were going down swiftly. Now we could hear the water rushing past the port-holes, and in the dim light that filtered through them to the water beyond the swirling eddies were plainly visible.

Phaidor grasped my arm.

"Save me!" she whispered. "Save me and your every wish shall be granted. Anything within the power of the Holy Therns to give will be yours. Phaidor – " she stumbled a little here, and then in a very low voice, "Phaidor already is yours."

I felt very sorry for the poor child, and placed my hand over hers where it rested on my arm. I presume my motive was misunderstood, for with a swift glance about the apartment to assure herself that we were alone, she threw both her arms about my neck and dragged my face down to hers.

CHAPTER NINE

Issus, Goddess of Life Eternal

THE CONFESSION OF LOVE which the girl's fright had wrung from her touched me deeply; but it humiliated me as well, since I felt that in some thoughtless word or act I had given her reason to believe that I reciprocated her affection.

Never have I been much of a ladies' man, being more concerned with fighting and kindred arts which have ever seemed to me more befitting a man than mooning over a scented glove four sizes too small for him, or kissing a dead flower that has begun to smell like a cabbage. So I was quite at a loss as to what to do or say. A thousand times rather face the wild hordes of the dead sea bottoms than meet the eyes of this beautiful young girl and tell her the thing that I must tell her.

But there was nothing else to be done, and so I did it. Very clumsily too, I fear.

Gently I unclasped her hands from about my neck, and still holding them in mine I told her the story of my love for Dejah Thoris. That of all the women of two worlds that I had known and admired during my long life she alone had I loved.

The tale did not seem to please her. Like a tigress she sprang, panting, to her feet. Her beautiful face was distorted in an expression of horrible malevolence. Her eyes fairly blazed into mine.

"Dog," she hissed. "Dog of a blasphemer! Think you that Phaidor, daughter of Matai Shang, supplicates? She commands. What to her is your puny outer world passion for the vile creature you chose in your other life?

"Phaidor has glorified you with her love, and you have spurned her. Ten thousand unthinkably atrocious deaths could not atone for the affront that you have put upon me. The thing that you call Dejah Thoris shall die the most horrible of them all. You have sealed the warrant for her doom.

"And you! You shall be the meanest slave in the service of the goddess you have attempted to humiliate. Tortures and ignominies shall be heaped upon you until you grovel at my feet asking the boon of death.

"In my gracious generosity I shall at length grant your prayer, and from the high balcony of the Golden Cliffs I shall watch the great white apes tear you asunder."

She had it all fixed up. The whole lovely programme from start to finish. It amazed me to think that one so divinely beautiful could at the same time be so fiendishly vindictive. It occurred to me, however, that she had overlooked one little factor in her revenge, and so, without any intent to add to her discomfiture, but rather to permit her to rearrange her plans along more practical lines, I pointed to the nearest port-hole.

Evidently she had entirely forgotten her surroundings and her present circumstances, for a single glance at the dark, swirling waters without sent her crumpled upon a low bench, where with her face buried in her arms she sobbed more like a very unhappy little girl than a proud and all-powerful goddess.

Down, down we continued to sink until the heavy glass of the portholes became noticeably warm from the heat of the water without. Evidently we were very far beneath the surface crust of Mars.

Presently our downward motion ceased, and I could hear the propellers swirling through the water at our stern and forcing us ahead at high speed. It was very dark down there, but the light from our port-holes, and the reflection from what must have been a powerful searchlight on the submarine's nose showed that we were forging through a narrow passage, rock-lined, and tube-like.

After a few minutes the propellers ceased their whirring. We came to a full stop, and then commenced to rise swiftly toward the surface. Soon the light from without increased and we came to a stop.

Xodar entered the cabin with his men.

"Come," he said, and we followed him through the hatchway which had been opened by one of the seamen.

We found ourselves in a small subterranean vault, in the centre of which was the pool in which lay our submarine, floating as we had first seen her with only her black back showing.

Around the edge of the pool was a level platform, and then the walls of the cave rose perpendicularly for a few feet to arch toward the centre of the low roof. The walls about the ledge were pierced with a number of entrances to dimly lighted passageways.

Toward one of these our captors led us, and after a short walk halted before a steel cage which lay at the bottom of a shaft rising above us as far as one could see.

The cage proved to be one of the common types of elevator cars that I had seen in other parts of Barsoom. They are operated by means of enormous magnets which are suspended at the top of the shaft. By an electrical device the volume of magnetism generated is regulated and the speed of the car varied.

In long stretches they move at a sickening speed, especially on the upward trip, since the small force of gravity inherent to Mars results in very little opposition to the powerful force above.

Scarcely had the door of the car closed behind us than we were slowing up to stop at the landing above, so rapid was our ascent of the long shaft.

When we emerged from the little building which houses the upper terminus of the elevator, we found ourselves in the midst of a veritable fairyland of beauty. The combined languages of Earth men hold no words to convey to the mind the gorgeous beauties of the scene.

One may speak of scarlet sward and ivory-stemmed trees decked with brilliant purple blooms; of winding walks paved with crushed rubies, with emerald, with turquoise, even with diamonds themselves; of a magnificent temple of burnished gold, hand-wrought with marvellous designs; but where are the words to describe the glorious colours that are unknown to earthly eyes? where the mind or the imagination that can grasp the gorgeous scintillations of unheard-of rays as they emanate from the thousand nameless jewels of Barsoom?

Even my eyes, for long years accustomed to the barbaric splendours of a Martian Jeddak's court, were amazed at the glory of the scene.

Phaidor's eyes were wide in amazement.

"The Temple of Issus," she whispered, half to herself.

Xodar watched us with his grim smile, partly of amusement and partly malicious gloating.

The gardens swarmed with brilliantly trapped black men and women. Among them moved red and white females serving their every want. The places of the outer world and the temples of the therns had been robbed of their princesses and goddesses that the blacks might have their slaves.

Through this scene we moved toward the temple. At the main entrance we were halted by a cordon of armed guards. Xodar spoke a few words to an officer who came forward to question us. Together they entered the temple, where they remained for some time.

When they returned it was to announce that Issus desired to look upon the daughter of Matai Shang, and the strange creature from another world who had been a Prince of Helium.

Slowly we moved through endless corridors of unthinkable beauty; through magnificent apartments, and noble halls. At length we were halted in a spacious chamber in the centre of the temple. One of the officers who had accompanied us advanced to a large door in the further end of the chamber. Here he must have made some sort of signal for immediately the door opened and another richly trapped courtier emerged.

We were then led up to the door, where we were directed to get down on our hands and knees with our backs toward the room we were to enter. The doors were swung open and after being cautioned not to turn our heads under penalty of instant death we were commanded to back into the presence of Issus.

Never have I been in so humiliating a position in my life, and only my love for Dejah Thoris and the hope which still clung to me that I might again see her kept me from rising to face the goddess of the First Born and go down to my death like a gentleman, facing my foes and with their blood mingling with mine.

After we had crawled in this disgusting fashion for a matter of a couple of hundred feet we were halted by our escort.

"Let them rise," said a voice behind us; a thin, wavering voice, yet one that had evidently been accustomed to command for many years.

"Rise," said our escort, "but do not face toward Issus."

"The woman pleases me," said the thin, wavering voice again after a few moments of silence. "She shall serve me the allotted time. The man you may return to the Isle of Shador which lies against the northern shore of the Sea of Omean. Let the woman turn and look upon Issus, knowing that those of the lower orders who gaze upon the holy vision of her radiant face survive the blinding glory but a single year."

I watched Phaidor from the corner of my eye. She paled to a ghastly hue. Slowly, very slowly she turned, as though drawn by some invisible yet irresistible force. She was standing quite close to me, so close that her bare arm touched mine as she finally faced Issus, Goddess of Life Eternal.

I could not see the girl's face as her eyes rested for the first time on the Supreme Deity of Mars, but felt the shudder that ran through her in the trembling flesh of the arm that touched mine.

"It must be dazzling loveliness indeed," thought I, "to cause such emotion in the breast of so radiant a beauty as Phaidor, daughter of Matai Shang."

"Let the woman remain. Remove the man. Go." Thus spoke Issus, and the heavy hand of the officer fell upon my shoulder. In accordance with his instructions I dropped to my hands and knees once more and crawled from the Presence. It had been my first audience with deity, but I am free to confess that I was not greatly impressed – other than with the ridiculous figure I cut scrambling about on my marrow bones.

Once without the chamber the doors closed behind us and I was bid to rise. Xodar joined me and together we slowly retraced our steps toward the gardens.

"You spared my life when you easily might have taken it," he said after we had proceeded some little way in silence, "and I would aid you if I might. I can help to make your life here more bearable, but your fate is inevitable. You may never hope to return to the outer world."

"What will be my fate?" I asked.

"That will depend largely upon Issus. So long as she does not send for you and reveal her face to you, you may live on for years in as mild a form of bondage as I can arrange for you."

"Why should she send for me?" I asked.

"The men of the lower orders she often uses for various purposes of amusement. Such a fighter as you, for example, would render fine sport in the monthly rites of the temple. There are men pitted against men, and against beasts for the edification of Issus and the replenishment of her larder."

"She eats human flesh?" I asked. Not in horror, however, for since my recently acquired knowledge of the Holy Therns I was prepared for anything in this still less accessible heaven, where all was evidently dictated by a single omnipotence; where ages of narrow fanaticism and self-worship had eradicated all the broader humanitarian instincts that the race might once have possessed.

They were a people drunk with power and success, looking upon the other inhabitants of Mars as we look upon the beasts of the field and the forest. Why then should they not eat of the flesh of the lower orders whose lives and characters they no more understood than do we the inmost thoughts and sensibilities of the cattle we slaughter for our earthly tables.

"She eats only the flesh of the best bred of the Holy Therns and the red Barsoomians. The flesh of the others goes to our boards. The animals are eaten by the slaves. She also eats other dainties."

I did not understand then that there lay any special significance in his reference to other dainties. I thought the limit of ghoulishness already had been reached in the recitation of Issus' menu. I still had much to learn as to the depths of cruelty and bestiality to which omnipotence may drag its possessor.

We had about reached the last of the many chambers and corridors which led to the gardens when an officer overtook us.

"Issus would look again upon this man," he said. "The girl has told her that he is of wondrous beauty and of such prowess that alone he slew seven of the First Born, and with his bare hands took Xodar captive, binding him with his own harness."

Xodar looked uncomfortable. Evidently he did not relish the thought that Issus had learned of his inglorious defeat.

Without a word he turned and we followed the officer once again to the closed doors before the audience chamber of Issus, Goddess of Life Eternal.

Here the ceremony of entrance was repeated. Again Issus bid me rise. For several minutes all was silent as the tomb. The eyes of deity were appraising me.

Presently the thin wavering voice broke the stillness, repeating in a singsong drone the words which for countless ages had sealed the doom of numberless victims.

"Let the man turn and look upon Issus, knowing that those of the lower orders who gaze upon the holy vision of her radiant face survive the blinding glory but a single year."

I turned as I had been bid, expecting such a treat as only the revealment of divine glory to mortal eyes might produce. What I saw was a solid phalanx of armed men between myself and a dais supporting a great bench of carved sorapus wood. On this bench, or throne, squatted a female black. She was evidently very old. Not a hair remained upon her wrinkled skull. With the exception of two yellow fangs she was entirely toothless. On either side of her thin, hawk-like nose her eyes burned from the depths of horribly sunken sockets. The skin of her face was seamed and creased with a million deepcut furrows. Her body was as wrinkled as her face, and as repulsive.

Emaciated arms and legs attached to a torso which seemed to be mostly distorted abdomen completed the "holy vision of her radiant beauty."

Surrounding her were a number of female slaves, among them Phaidor, white and trembling.

"This is the man who slew seven of the First Born and, bare-handed, bound Dator Xodar with his own harness?" asked Issus.

"Most glorious vision of divine loveliness, it is," replied the officer who stood at my side.

"Produce Dator Xodar," she commanded.

Xodar was brought from the adjoining room.

Issus glared at him, a baleful light in her hideous eyes.

"And such as you are a Dator of the First Born?" she squealed. "For the disgrace you have brought upon the Immortal Race you shall be degraded to a rank below the lowest. No longer be you a Dator, but for evermore a slave of slaves, to fetch and carry for the lower orders that serve in the gardens of Issus. Remove his harness. Cowards and slaves wear no trappings."

Xodar stood stiffly erect. Not a muscle twitched, nor a tremor shook his giant frame as a soldier of the guard roughly stripped his gorgeous trappings from him.

"Begone," screamed the infuriated little old woman. "Begone, but instead of the light of the gardens of Issus let you serve as a slave of this slave who conquered you in the prison on the Isle of Shador in the Sea of Omean. Take him away out of the sight of my divine eyes."

Slowly and with high held head the proud Xodar turned and stalked from the chamber. Issus rose and turned to leave the room by another exit.

Turning to me, she said: "You shall be returned to Shador for the present. Later Issus will see the manner of your fighting. Go." Then she disappeared, followed by her retinue. Only Phaidor lagged behind, and as I started to follow my guard toward the gardens, the girl came running after me.

"Oh, do not leave me in this terrible place," she begged. "Forgive the things I said to you, my Prince. I did not mean them. Only take me away with you. Let me share your imprisonment on Shador." Her words were an almost incoherent volley of thoughts, so rapidly she spoke. "You did not understand the honour that I did you. Among the therns there is no marriage or giving in marriage, as among the lower orders of the outer world. We might have lived together for ever in love and happiness. We have both looked upon Issus and in a year we die. Let us live that year at least together in what measure of joy remains for the doomed."

"If it was difficult for me to understand you, Phaidor," I replied, "can you not understand that possibly it is equally difficult for you to understand the motives, the customs and the social laws that guide me? I do not wish to hurt you, nor to seem to undervalue the honour which you have done me, but the thing you desire may not be. Regardless of the foolish belief of the peoples of the outer world, or of Holy Thern, or ebon First Born, I am not dead. While I live my heart beats for but one woman – the incomparable Dejah Thoris, Princess of Helium. When death overtakes me my heart shall have ceased to beat; but what comes after that I know not. And in that I am as wise as Matai Shang, Master of Life and Death upon Barsoom; or Issus, Goddess of Life Eternal."

Phaidor stood looking at me intently for a moment. No anger showed in her eyes this time, only a pathetic expression of hopeless sorrow.

"I do not understand," she said, and turning walked slowly in the direction of the door through which Issus and her retinue had passed. A moment later she had passed from my sight.

CHAPTER TEN

The Prison Isle of Shador

IN THE OUTER GARDENS to which the guard now escorted me, I found Xodar surrounded by a crowd of noble blacks. They were reviling and cursing him. The men slapped his face. The women spat upon him.

When I appeared they turned their attentions toward me.

"Ah," cried one, "so this is the creature who overcame the great Xodar bare-handed. Let us see how it was done."

"Let him bind Thurid," suggested a beautiful woman, laughing. "Thurid is a noble Dator. Let Thurid show the dog what it means to face a real man."

"Yes, Thurid! Thurid!" cried a dozen voices.

"Here he is now," exclaimed another, and turning in the direction indicated I saw a huge black weighed down with resplendent ornaments and arms advancing with noble and gallant bearing toward us.

"What now?" he cried. "What would you of Thurid?"

Quickly a dozen voices explained.

Thurid turned toward Xodar, his eyes narrowing to two nasty slits.

"Calot!" he hissed. "Ever did I think you carried the heart of a sorak in your putrid breast. Often have you bested me in the secret councils of Issus, but now in the field of war where men are truly gauged your scabby heart hath revealed its sores to all the world. Calot, I spurn you with my foot," and with the words he turned to kick Xodar.

My blood was up. For minutes it had been boiling at the cowardly treatment they had been according this once powerful comrade because he had fallen from the favour of Issus. I had no love for Xodar, but I cannot stand the sight of cowardly injustice and persecution without seeing red as through a haze of bloody mist, and doing things on the impulse of the moment that I presume I never should do after mature deliberation.

I was standing close beside Xodar as Thurid swung his foot for the cowardly kick. The degraded Dator stood erect and motionless as a carven image. He was prepared to take whatever his former comrades had to offer in the way of insults and reproaches, and take them in manly silence and stoicism.

But as Thurid's foot swung so did mine, and I caught him a painful blow upon the shin bone that saved Xodar from this added ignominy.

For a moment there was tense silence, then Thurid, with a roar of rage sprang for my throat; just as Xodar had upon the deck of the cruiser. The results were identical. I ducked beneath his outstretched arms, and as he lunged past me planted a terrific right on the side of his jaw.

The big fellow spun around like a top, his knees gave beneath him and he crumpled to the ground at my feet.

The blacks gazed in astonishment, first at the still form of the proud Dator lying there in the ruby dust of the pathway, then at me as though they could not believe that such a thing could be.

"You asked me to bind Thurid," I cried; "behold!" And then I stooped beside the prostrate form, tore the harness from it, and bound the fellow's arms and legs securely.

"As you have done to Xodar, now do you likewise to Thurid. Take him before Issus, bound in his own harness, that she may see with her own eyes that there be one among you now who is greater than the First Born."

"Who are you?" whispered the woman who had first suggested that I attempt to bind Thurid.

"I am a citizen of two worlds; Captain John Carter of Virginia, Prince of the House of Tardos Mors, Jeddak of Helium. Take this man to your goddess, as I have said, and tell her, too, that as I have done to Xodar and Thurid, so also can I do to the mightiest of her Dators. With naked hands, with long-sword or with short-sword, I challenge the flower of her fighting-men to combat."

"Come," said the officer who was guarding me back to Shador; "my orders are imperative; there is to be no delay. Xodar, come you also."

There was little of disrespect in the tone that the man used in addressing either Xodar or myself. It was evident that he felt less contempt for the former Dator since he had witnessed the ease with which I disposed of the powerful Thurid.

That his respect for me was greater than it should have been for a slave was quite apparent from the fact that during the balance of the return journey he walked or stood always behind me, a drawn short-sword in his hand.

The return to the Sea of Omean was uneventful. We dropped down the awful shaft in the same car that had brought us to the surface. There we entered the submarine, taking the long dive to the tunnel far beneath the upper world. Then through the tunnel and up again to the pool from which we had had our first introduction to the wonderful passageway from Omean to the Temple of Issus.

From the island of the submarine we were transported on a small cruiser to the distant Isle of Shador. Here we found a small stone prison and a guard of half a dozen blacks. There was no ceremony wasted in completing our incarceration. One of the blacks opened the door of the prison with a huge key, we walked in, the door closed behind us, the lock grated, and with the sound there swept over me again that terrible feeling of hopelessness that I had felt in the Chamber of Mystery in the Golden Cliffs beneath the gardens of the Holy Therns.

Then Tars Tarkas had been with me, but now I was utterly alone in so far as friendly companionship was concerned. I fell to wondering about the fate of the great Thark, and of his beautiful companion, the girl, Thuvia. Even should they by some miracle have escaped and been received and spared by a friendly nation, what hope had I of the succour which I knew they would gladly extend if it lay in their power.

They could not guess my whereabouts or my fate, for none on all Barsoom even dream of such a place as this. Nor would it have advantaged me any had they known the exact location of my prison, for who could hope to penetrate to this buried sea in the face of the mighty navy of the First Born? No: my case was hopeless.

Well, I would make the best of it, and, rising, I swept aside the brooding despair that had been endeavouring to claim me. With the idea of exploring my prison, I started to look around.

Xodar sat, with bowed head, upon a low stone bench near the centre of the room in which we were. He had not spoken since Issus had degraded him.

The building was roofless, the walls rising to a height of about thirty feet. Half-way up were a couple of small, heavily barred windows. The prison was divided into several rooms by partitions twenty feet high. There was no one in the room which we occupied, but two doors which led to other rooms were opened. I entered one of these rooms, but found it vacant. Thus I continued through several of the chambers until in the last one I found a young red Martian boy sleeping upon the stone bench which constituted the only furniture of any of the prison cells.

Evidently he was the only other prisoner. As he slept I leaned over and looked at him. There was something strangely familiar about his face, and yet I could not place him.

His features were very regular and, like the proportions of his graceful limbs and body, beautiful in the extreme. He was very light in colour for a red man, but in other respects he seemed a typical specimen of this handsome race.

I did not awaken him, for sleep in prison is such a priceless boon that I have seen men transformed into raging brutes when robbed by one of their fellow-prisoners of a few precious moments of it.

Returning to my own cell, I found Xodar still sitting in the same position in which I had left him.

"Man," I cried, "it will profit you nothing to mope thus. It were no disgrace to be bested by John Carter. You have seen that in the ease with which I accounted for Thurid. You knew it before when on the cruiser's deck you saw me slay three of your comrades."

"I would that you had dispatched me at the same time," he said.

"Come, come!" I cried. "There is hope yet. Neither of us is dead. We are great fighters. Why not win to freedom?"

He looked at me in amazement.

"You know not of what you speak," he replied. "Issus is omnipotent. Issus is omniscient. She hears now the words you speak. She knows the thoughts you think. It is sacrilege even to dream of breaking her commands."

"Rot, Xodar," I ejaculated impatiently.

He sprang to his feet in horror.

"The curse of Issus will fall upon you," he cried. "In another instant you will be smitten down, writhing to your death in horrible agony."

"Do you believe that, Xodar?" I asked.

"Of course; who would dare doubt?"

"I doubt; yes, and further, I deny," I said. "Why, Xodar, you tell me that she even knows my thoughts. The red men have all had that power for ages. And another wonderful power. They can shut their minds so that none may read their thoughts. I learned the first secret years ago; the other I never had to learn, since upon all Barsoom is none who can read what passes in the secret chambers of my brain.

"Your goddess cannot read my thoughts; nor can she read yours when you are out of sight, unless you will it. Had she been able to read mine, I am afraid that her pride would have suffered a rather severe shock when I turned at her command to 'gaze upon the holy vision of her radiant face.'"

"What do you mean?" he whispered in an affrighted voice, so low that I could scarcely hear him.

"I mean that I thought her the most repulsive and vilely hideous creature my eyes ever had rested upon."

For a moment he eyed me in horror-stricken amazement, and then with a cry of "Blasphemer" he sprang upon me.

I did not wish to strike him again, nor was it necessary, since he was unarmed and therefore quite harmless to me.

As he came I grasped his left wrist with my left hand, and, swinging my right arm about his left shoulder, caught him beneath the chin with my elbow and bore him backward across my thigh.

There he hung helpless for a moment, glaring up at me in impotent rage.

"Xodar," I said, "let us be friends. For a year, possibly, we may be forced to live together in the narrow confines of this tiny room. I am sorry to have offended you, but I could not dream that one who had suffered from the cruel injustice of Issus still could believe her divine.

"I will say a few more words, Xodar, with no intent to wound your feelings further, but rather that you may give thought to the fact that while we live we are still more the arbiters of our own fate than is any god.

"Issus, you see, has not struck me dead, nor is she rescuing her faithful Xodar from the clutches of the unbeliever who defamed her fair beauty. No, Xodar, your Issus is a mortal old woman. Once out of her clutches and she cannot harm you.

"With your knowledge of this strange land, and my knowledge of the outer world, two such fighting-men as you and I should be able to win our way to freedom. Even though we died in the attempt, would not our memories be fairer than as though we remained in servile fear to be butchered by a cruel and unjust tyrant – call her goddess or mortal, as you will."

As I finished I raised Xodar to his feet and released him. He did not renew the attack upon me, nor did he speak. Instead, he walked toward the bench, and, sinking down upon it, remained lost in deep thought for hours.

A long time afterward I heard a soft sound at the doorway leading to one of the other apartments, and, looking up, beheld the red Martian youth gazing intently at us.

"Kaor," I cried, after the red Martian manner of greeting.

"Kaor," he replied. "What do you here?"

"I await my death, I presume," I replied with a wry smile.

He too smiled, a brave and winning smile.

"I also," he said. "Mine will come soon. I looked upon the radiant beauty of Issus nearly a year since. It has always been a source of keen wonder to me that I did not drop dead at the first sight of that hideous countenance. And her belly! By my first ancestor, but never was there so grotesque a figure in all the universe. That they should call such a one Goddess of Life Eternal, Goddess of Death, Mother of the Nearer Moon, and fifty other equally impossible titles, is quite beyond me."

"How came you here?" I asked.

"It is very simple. I was flying a one-man air scout far to the south when the brilliant idea occurred to me that I should like to search for the Lost Sea of Korus which tradition places near to the south pole. I must have inherited from my father a wild lust for adventure, as well as a hollow where my bump of reverence should be.

"I had reached the area of eternal ice when my port propeller jammed, and I dropped to the ground to make repairs. Before I knew it the air was black with fliers, and a hundred of these First Born devils were leaping to the ground all about me.

"With drawn swords they made for me, but before I went down beneath them they had tasted of the steel of my father's sword, and I had given such an account of myself as I know would have pleased my sire had he lived to witness it."

"Your father is dead?" I asked.

"He died before the shell broke to let me step out into a world that has been very good to me. But for the sorrow that I had never the honour to know my father, I have been very happy. My only sorrow now is that my mother must mourn me as she has for ten long years mourned my father."

"Who was your father?" I asked.

He was about to reply when the outer door of our prison opened and a burly guard entered and ordered him to his own quarters for the night, locking the door after him as he passed through into the further chamber.

"It is Issus' wish that you two be confined in the same room," said the guard when he had returned to our cell. "This cowardly slave of a slave is to serve you well," he said to me, indicating Xodar with a wave of his hand. "If he does not, you are to beat him into submission. It is Issus' wish that you heap upon him every indignity and degradation of which you can conceive."

With these words he left us.

Xodar still sat with his face buried in his hands. I walked to his side and placed my hand upon his shoulder.

"Xodar," I said, "you have heard the commands of Issus, but you need not fear that I shall attempt to put them into execution. You are a brave man, Xodar. It is your own affair if you wish to be persecuted and humiliated; but were I you I should assert my manhood and defy my enemies."

"I have been thinking very hard, John Carter," he said, "of all the new ideas you gave me a few hours since. Little by little I have been piecing together the things that you said which sounded blasphemous to me then with the things that I have seen in my past life and dared not even think about for fear of bringing down upon me the wrath of Issus.

"I believe now that she is a fraud; no more divine than you or I. More I am willing to concede – that the First Born are no holier than the Holy Therns, nor the Holy Therns more holy than the red men.

"The whole fabric of our religion is based on superstitious belief in lies that have been foisted upon us for ages by those directly above us, to whose personal profit and aggrandizement it was to have us continue to believe as they wished us to believe.

"I am ready to cast off the ties that have bound me. I am ready to defy Issus herself; but what will it avail us? Be the First Born gods or mortals, they are a powerful race, and we are as fast in their clutches as though we were already dead. There is no escape."

"I have escaped from bad plights in the past, my friend," I replied; "nor while life is in me shall I despair of escaping from the Isle of Shador and the Sea of Omean."

"But we cannot escape even from the four walls of our prison," urged Xodar. "Test this flint-like surface," he cried, smiting the solid rock that confined us. "And look upon this polished surface; none could cling to it to reach the top."

I smiled.

"That is the least of our troubles, Xodar," I replied. "I will guarantee to scale the wall and take you with me, if you will help with your knowledge of the customs here to appoint the best time for the attempt, and guide me to the shaft that lets from the dome of this abysmal sea to the light of God's pure air above."

"Night time is the best and offers the only slender chance we have, for then men sleep, and only a dozing watch nods in the tops of the battleships. No watch is kept upon the cruisers and smaller craft. The watchers upon the larger vessels see to all about them. It is night now."

"But," I exclaimed, "it is not dark! How can it be night, then?"

He smiled.

"You forget," he said, "that we are far below ground. The light of the sun never penetrates here. There are no moons and no stars reflected in the bosom of Omean. The phosphorescent light you now see pervading this great subterranean vault emanates from the rocks that form its dome; it is always thus upon Omean, just as the billows are always as you see them – rolling, ever rolling over a windless sea.

"At the appointed hour of night upon the world above, the men whose duties hold them here sleep, but the light is ever the same."

"It will make escape more difficult," I said, and then I shrugged my shoulders; for what, pray, is the pleasure of doing an easy thing?

"Let us sleep on it to-night," said Xodar. "A plan may come with our awakening."

So we threw ourselves upon the hard stone floor of our prison and slept the sleep of tired men.

CHAPTER ELEVEN

When Hell Broke Loose

EARLY THE NEXT MORNING Xodar and I commenced work upon our plans for escape. First I had him sketch upon the stone floor of our cell as accurate a map of the south polar regions as was possible with the crude instruments at our disposal – a buckle from my harness, and the sharp edge of the wondrous gem I had taken from Sator Throg.

From this I computed the general direction of Helium and the distance at which it lay from the opening which led to Omean.

Then I had him draw a map of Omean, indicating plainly the position of Shador and of the opening in the dome which led to the outer world.

These I studied until they were indelibly imprinted in my memory. From Xodar I learned the duties and customs of the guards who patrolled Shador. It seemed that during the hours set aside for sleep only one man was on duty at a time. He paced a beat that passed around the prison, at a distance of about a hundred feet from the building.

The pace of the sentries, Xodar said, was very slow, requiring nearly ten minutes to make a single round. This meant that for practically five minutes at a time each side of the prison was unguarded as the sentry pursued his snail like pace upon the opposite side.

"This information you ask," said Xodar, "will be all very valuable *after* we get out, but nothing that you have asked has any bearing on that first and most important consideration."

"We will get out all right," I replied, laughing. "Leave that to me."

"When shall we make the attempt?" he asked.

"The first night that finds a small craft moored near the shore of Shador," I replied.

"But how will you know that any craft is moored near Shador? The windows are far beyond our reach."

"Not so, friend Xodar; look!"

With a bound I sprang to the bars of the window opposite us, and took a quick survey of the scene without.

Several small craft and two large battleships lay within a hundred yards of Shador.

"To-night," I thought, and was just about to voice my decision to Xodar, when, without warning, the door of our prison opened and a guard stepped in.

If the fellow saw me there our chances of escape might quickly go glimmering, for I knew that they would put me in irons if they had the slightest conception of the wonderful agility which my earthly muscles gave me upon Mars.

The man had entered and was standing facing the centre of the room, so that his back was toward me. Five feet above me was the top of a partition wall separating our cell from the next.

There was my only chance to escape detection. If the fellow turned, I was lost; nor could I have dropped to the floor undetected, since he was no nearly below me that I would have struck him had I done so.

"Where is the white man?" cried the guard of Xodar. "Issus commands his presence." He started to turn to see if I were in another part of the cell.

I scrambled up the iron grating of the window until I could catch a good footing on the sill with one foot; then I let go my hold and sprang for the partition top.

"What was that?" I heard the deep voice of the black bellow as my metal grated against the stone wall as I slipped over. Then I dropped lightly to the floor of the cell beyond.

"Where is the white slave?" again cried the guard.

"I know not," replied Xodar. "He was here even as you entered. I am not his keeper – go find him."

The black grumbled something that I could not understand, and then I heard him unlocking the door into one of the other cells on the further side. Listening intently, I caught the sound as the door closed behind him. Then I sprang once more to the top of the partition and dropped into my own cell beside the astonished Xodar.

"Do you see now how we will escape?" I asked him in a whisper.

"I see how you may," he replied, "but I am no wiser than before as to how I am to pass these walls. Certain it is that I cannot bounce over them as you do."

We heard the guard moving about from cell to cell, and finally, his rounds completed, he again entered ours. When his eyes fell upon me they fairly bulged from his head.

"By the shell of my first ancestor!" he roared. "Where have you been?" "I have been in prison since you put me here yesterday," I answered. "I was in this room when you entered. You had better look to your eyesight."

He glared at me in mingled rage and relief.

"Come," he said. "Issus commands your presence."

He conducted me outside the prison, leaving Xodar behind. There we found several other guards, and with them the red Martian youth who occupied another cell upon Shador.

The journey I had taken to the Temple of Issus on the preceding day was repeated. The guards kept the red boy and myself separated, so that we had no opportunity to continue the conversation that had been interrupted the previous night.

The youth's face had haunted me. Where had I seen him before. There was something strangely familiar in every line of him; in his carriage, his manner of speaking, his gestures. I could have sworn that I knew him, and yet I knew too that I had never seen him before.

When we reached the gardens of Issus we were led away from the temple instead of toward it. The way wound through enchanted parks to a mighty wall that towered a hundred feet in air.

Massive gates gave egress upon a small plain, surrounded by the same gorgeous forests that I had seen at the foot of the Golden Cliffs.

Crowds of blacks were strolling in the same direction that our guards were leading us, and with them mingled my old friends the plant men and great white apes.

The brutal beasts moved among the crowd as pet dogs might. If they were in the way the blacks pushed them roughly to one side, or whacked them with the flat of a sword, and the animals slunk away as in great fear.

Presently we came upon our destination, a great amphitheatre situated at the further edge of the plain, and about half a mile beyond the garden walls.

Through a massive arched gateway the blacks poured in to take their seats, while our guards led us to a smaller entrance near one end of the structure.

Through this we passed into an enclosure beneath the seats, where we found a number of other prisoners herded together under guard. Some of them were in irons, but for the most part they seemed sufficiently awed by the presence of their guards to preclude any possibility of attempted escape.

During the trip from Shador I had had no opportunity to talk with my fellow-prisoner, but now that we were safely within the barred paddock our guards abated their watchfulness, with the result that I found myself able to approach the red Martian youth for whom I felt such a strange attraction.

"What is the object of this assembly?" I asked him. "Are we to fight for the edification of the First Born, or is it something worse than that?"

"It is a part of the monthly rites of Issus," he replied, "in which black men wash the sins from their souls in the blood of men from the outer world. If, perchance, the black is killed, it is evidence of his disloyalty to Issus – the unpardonable sin. If he lives through the contest he is held acquitted of the charge that forced the sentence of the rites, as it is called, upon him.

"The forms of combat vary. A number of us may be pitted together against an equal number, or twice the number of blacks; or singly we may be sent forth to face wild beasts, or some famous black warrior."

"And if we are victorious," I asked, "what then – freedom?"

He laughed.

"Freedom, forsooth. The only freedom for us death. None who enters the domains of the First Born ever leave. If we prove able fighters we are permitted to fight often. If we are not mighty fighters – " He shrugged his shoulders. "Sooner or later we die in the arena."

"And you have fought often?" I asked.

"Very often," he replied. "It is my only pleasure. Some hundred black devils have I accounted for during nearly a year of the rites of Issus. My mother would be very proud could she only know how well I have maintained the traditions of my father's prowess."

"Your father must have been a mighty warrior!" I said. "I have known most of the warriors of Barsoom in my time; doubtless I knew him. Who was he?"

"My father was – "

"Come, calots!" cried the rough voice of a guard. "To the slaughter with you," and roughly we were hustled to the steep incline that led to the chambers far below which let out upon the arena.

The amphitheatre, like all I had ever seen upon Barsoom, was built in a large excavation. Only the highest seats, which formed the low wall surrounding the pit, were above the level of the ground. The arena itself was far below the surface.

Just beneath the lowest tier of seats was a series of barred cages on a level with the surface of the arena. Into these we were herded. But, unfortunately, my youthful friend was not of those who occupied a cage with me.

Directly opposite my cage was the throne of Issus. Here the horrid creature squatted, surrounded by a hundred slave maidens sparkling in jewelled trappings. Brilliant cloths of many hues and strange patterns formed the soft cushion covering of the dais upon which they reclined about her.

On four sides of the throne and several feet below it stood three solid ranks of heavily armed soldiery, elbow to elbow. In front of these were the high dignitaries of this mock heaven – gleaming blacks bedecked with precious stones, upon their foreheads the insignia of their rank set in circles of gold.

On both sides of the throne stretched a solid mass of humanity from top to bottom of the amphitheatre. There were as many women as men, and each was clothed in the wondrously wrought harness of his station and his house. With each black was from one to three slaves, drawn from the domains of the therns and from the outer world. The blacks are all "noble." There is no peasantry among the First Born. Even the lowest soldier is a god, and has his slaves to wait upon him.

The First Born do no work. The men fight – that is a sacred privilege and duty; to fight and die for Issus. The women do nothing, absolutely nothing. Slaves wash them, slaves dress them, slaves feed them. There are some, even, who have slaves that talk for them, and I saw one who sat during the rites with closed eyes while a slave narrated to her the events that were transpiring within the arena.

The first event of the day was the Tribute to Issus. It marked the end of those poor unfortunates who had looked upon the divine glory of the goddess a full year before. There were ten of them – splendid beauties from the proud courts of mighty Jeddaks and from the temples of the Holy Therns. For a year they had served in the retinue of Issus; to-day they were to pay the price of this divine preferment with their lives; to-morrow they would grace the tables of the court functionaries.

A huge black entered the arena with the young women. Carefully he inspected them, felt of their limbs and poked them in the ribs. Presently he selected one of their number whom he led before the throne of Issus. He addressed some words to the goddess which I could not hear. Issus nodded her head. The black raised his hands above his head in token of salute, grasped the girl by the wrist, and dragged her from the arena through a small doorway below the throne.

"Issus will dine well to-night," said a prisoner beside me.

"What do you mean?" I asked.

"That was her dinner that old Thabis is taking to the kitchens. Didst not note how carefully he selected the plumpest and tenderest of the lot?"

I growled out my curses on the monster sitting opposite us on the gorgeous throne.

"Fume not," admonished my companion; "you will see far worse than that if you live even a month among the First Born."

I turned again in time to see the gate of a nearby cage thrown open and three monstrous white apes spring into the arena. The girls shrank in a frightened group in the centre of the enclosure.

One was on her knees with imploring hands outstretched toward Issus; but the hideous deity only leaned further forward in keener anticipation of the entertainment to come. At length the apes spied the huddled knot of terror-stricken maidens and with demoniacal shrieks of bestial frenzy, charged upon them.

A wave of mad fury surged over me. The cruel cowardliness of the power-drunk creature whose malignant mind conceived such frightful forms of torture stirred to their uttermost depths my resentment and my manhood. The blood-red haze that presaged death to my foes swam before my eyes.

The guard lolled before the unbarred gate of the cage which confined me. What need of bars, indeed, to keep those poor victims from rushing into the arena which the edict of the gods had appointed as their death place!

A single blow sent the black unconscious to the ground. Snatching up his long-sword, I sprang into the arena. The apes were almost upon the maidens, but a couple of mighty bounds were all my earthly muscles required to carry me to the centre of the sand-strewn floor.

For an instant silence reigned in the great amphitheatre, then a wild shout arose from the cages of the doomed. My long-sword circled whirring through the air, and a great ape sprawled, headless, at the feet of the fainting girls.

The other apes turned now upon me, and as I stood facing them a sullen roar from the audience answered the wild cheers from the cages. From the tail of my eye I saw a score of guards rushing across the glistening sand toward me. Then a figure broke from one of the cages behind them. It was the youth whose personality so fascinated me.

He paused a moment before the cages, with upraised sword.

"Come, men of the outer world!" he shouted. "Let us make our deaths worth while, and at the back of this unknown warrior turn this day's Tribute to Issus into an orgy of revenge that will echo through the ages and cause black skins to blanch at each repetition of the rites of Issus. Come! The racks without your cages are filled with blades."

Without waiting to note the outcome of his plea, he turned and bounded toward me. From every cage that harboured red men a thunderous shout went up in answer to his exhortation. The inner guards went down beneath howling mobs, and the cages vomited forth their inmates hot with the lust to kill.

The racks that stood without were stripped of the swords with which the prisoners were to have been armed to enter their allotted combats, and a swarm of determined warriors sped to our support.

The great apes, towering in all their fifteen feet of height, had gone down before my sword while the charging guards were still some distance away. Close behind them pursued the youth. At my back were the young girls, and as it was in their service that I fought, I remained standing there to meet my inevitable death, but with the determination to give such an account of myself as would long be remembered in the land of the First Born.

I noted the marvellous speed of the young red man as he raced after the guards. Never had I seen such speed in any Martian. His leaps and bounds were little short of those which my earthly muscles had produced to create such awe and respect on the part of the green Martians into whose hands I had fallen on that long-gone day that had seen my first advent upon Mars.

The guards had not reached me when he fell upon them from the rear, and as they turned, thinking from the fierceness of his onslaught that a dozen were attacking them, I rushed them from my side.

In the rapid fighting that followed I had little chance to note aught else than the movements of my immediate adversaries, but now and again I caught a fleeting glimpse of a purring sword and a lightly springing figure of sinewy steel that filled my heart with a strange yearning and a mighty but unaccountable pride.

On the handsome face of the boy a grim smile played, and ever and anon he threw a taunting challenge to the foes that faced him. In this and other ways his manner of fighting was similar to that which had always marked me on the field of combat.

Perhaps it was this vague likeness which made me love the boy, while the awful havoc that his sword played amongst the blacks filled my soul with a tremendous respect for him.

For my part, I was fighting as I had fought a thousand times before – now sidestepping a wicked thrust, now stepping quickly in to let my sword's point drink deep in a foeman's heart, before it buried itself in the throat of his companion.

We were having a merry time of it, we two, when a great body of Issus' own guards were ordered into the arena. On they came with fierce cries, while from every side the armed prisoners swarmed upon them.

For half an hour it was as though all hell had broken loose. In the walled confines of the arena we fought in an inextricable mass – howling, cursing, blood-streaked demons; and ever the sword of the young red man flashed beside me.

Slowly and by repeated commands I had succeeded in drawing the prisoners into a rough formation about us, so that at last we fought formed into a rude circle in the centre of which were the doomed maids.

Many had gone down on both sides, but by far the greater havoc had been wrought in the ranks of the guards of Issus. I could see messengers running swiftly through the audience, and as they passed the nobles there unsheathed their swords and sprang into the arena. They were going to annihilate us by force of numbers – that was quite evidently their plan.

I caught a glimpse of Issus leaning far forward upon her throne, her hideous countenance distorted in a horrid grimace of hate and rage, in which I thought I could distinguish an expression of fear. It was that face that inspired me to the thing that followed.

Quickly I ordered fifty of the prisoners to drop back behind us and form a new circle about the maidens.

"Remain and protect them until I return," I commanded.

Then, turning to those who formed the outer line, I cried, "Down with Issus! Follow me to the throne; we will reap vengeance where vengeance is deserved."

The youth at my side was the first to take up the cry of "Down with Issus!" and then at my back and from all sides rose a hoarse shout, "To the throne! To the throne!"

As one man we moved, an irresistible fighting mass, over the bodies of dead and dying foes toward the gorgeous throne of the Martian deity. Hordes of the doughtiest fighting-men of the First Born poured from the audience to check our progress. We mowed them down before us as they had been paper men.

"To the seats, some of you!" I cried as we approached the arena's barrier wall. "Ten of us can take the throne," for I had seen that Issus' guards had for the most part entered the fray within the arena.

On both sides of me the prisoners broke to left and right for the seats, vaulting the low wall with dripping swords lusting for the crowded victims who awaited them.

In another moment the entire amphitheatre was filled with the shrieks of the dying and the wounded, mingled with the clash of arms and triumphant shouts of the victors.

Side by side the young red man and I, with perhaps a dozen others, fought our way to the foot of the throne. The remaining guards, reinforced by the high dignitaries and nobles of the First Born, closed in between us and Issus, who sat leaning far forward upon her carved sorapus bench, now screaming high-pitched commands to her following, now hurling blighting curses upon those who sought to desecrate her godhood.

The frightened slaves about her trembled in wide-eyed expectancy, knowing not whether to pray for our victory or our defeat. Several among them, proud daughters no doubt of some of Barsoom's noblest warriors, snatched swords from the hands of the fallen and fell upon the guards of Issus, but they were soon cut down; glorious martyrs to a hopeless cause.

The men with us fought well, but never since Tars Tarkas and I fought out that long, hot afternoon shoulder to shoulder against the hordes of Warhoon in the dead sea bottom before Thark, had I seen two men fight to such good purpose and with such unconquerable ferocity as the young red man and I fought that day before the throne of Issus, Goddess of Death, and of Life Eternal.

Man by man those who stood between us and the carven sorapus wood bench went down before our blades. Others swarmed in to fill the breach, but inch by inch, foot by foot we won nearer and nearer to our goal.

Presently a cry went up from a section of the stands near by – "Rise slaves!" "Rise slaves!" it rose and fell until it swelled to a mighty volume of sound that swept in great billows around the entire amphitheatre.

For an instant, as though by common assent, we ceased our fighting to look for the meaning of this new note nor did it take but a moment to translate its significance. In all parts of the structure the female slaves were falling upon their masters with whatever weapon came first to hand. A dagger snatched from the harness of her mistress was waved aloft by some fair slave, its shimmering blade crimson with the lifeblood of its owner; swords plucked from the bodies of the dead about them; heavy ornaments which could be turned into bludgeons – such were the implements with which these fair women wreaked the long-pent vengeance which at best could but partially recompense them for the unspeakable cruelties and indignities which their black masters had heaped upon them. And those who could find no other weapons used their strong fingers and their gleaming teeth.

It was at once a sight to make one shudder and to cheer; but in a brief second we were engaged once more in our own battle with only the unquenchable battle cry of the women to remind us that they still fought – "Rise slaves!" "Rise slaves!"

Only a single thin rank of men now stood between us and Issus. Her face was blue with terror. Foam flecked her lips. She seemed too para-lysed with fear to move. Only the youth and I fought now. The others all had fallen, and I was like to have gone down too from a nasty long-sword cut had not a hand reached out from behind my adversary and clutched his elbow as the blade was falling upon me. The youth sprang to my side and ran his sword through the fellow before he could recover to deliver another blow.

I should have died even then but for that as my sword was tight wedged in the breastbone of a Dator of the First Born. As the fellow went down I snatched his sword from him and over his prostrate body looked into the eyes of the one whose quick hand had saved me from the first cut of his sword – it was Phaidor, daughter of Matai Shang.

"Fly, my Prince!" she cried. "It is useless to fight them longer. All with-in the arena are dead. All who charged the throne are dead but you and this youth. Only among the seats are there left any of your fighting-men, and they and the slave women are fast being cut down. Listen! You can scarce hear the battle-cry of the women now for nearly all are dead. For each one of you there are ten thousand blacks within the domains of the First Born. Break for the open and the sea of Korus. With your mighty sword arm you may yet win to the Golden Cliffs and the templed gardens of the Holy Therns. There tell your story to Matai Shang, my father. He will keep you, and together you may find a way to rescue me. Fly while there is yet a bare chance for flight."

But that was not my mission, nor could I see much to be preferred in the cruel hospitality of the Holy Therns to that of the First Born.

"Down with Issus!" I shouted, and together the boy and I took up the fight once more. Two blacks went down with our swords in their vitals, and we stood face to face with Issus. As my sword went up to end her horrid career her paralysis left her, and with an ear-piercing shriek she turned to flee. Directly behind her a black gulf suddenly yawned in the flooring of the dais. She sprang for the opening with the youth and I close at her heels. Her scattered guard rallied at her cry and rushed for us. A blow fell upon the head of the youth. He staggered and would have fallen, but I caught him in my left arm and turned to face an infuriated mob of religious fanatics crazed by the affront I had put upon their goddess, just as Issus disappeared into the black depths beneath me.

CHAPTER TWELVE

Doomed to Die

For an instant I stood there before they fell upon me, but the first rush of them forced me back a step or two. My foot felt for the floor but found only empty space. I had backed into the pit which had received Issus. For a second I toppled there upon the brink. Then I too with the boy still tightly clutched in my arms pitched backward into the black abyss.

We struck a polished chute, the opening above us closed as magically as it had opened, and we shot down, unharmed, into a dimly lighted apartment far below the arena.

As I rose to my feet the first thing I saw was the malignant countenance of Issus glaring at me through the heavy bars of a grated door at one side of the chamber.

"Rash mortal!" she shrilled. "You shall pay the awful penalty for your blasphemy in this secret cell. Here you shall lie alone and in darkness with the carcass of your accomplice festering in its rottenness by your side, until crazed by loneliness and hunger you feed upon the crawling maggots that were once a man."

That was all. In another instant she was gone, and the dim light which had filled the cell faded into Cimmerian blackness.

"Pleasant old lady," said a voice at my side.

"Who speaks?" I asked.

"'Tis I, your companion, who has had the honour this day of fighting shoulder to shoulder with the greatest warrior that ever wore metal upon Barsoom."

"I thank God that you are not dead," I said. "I feared for that nasty cut upon your head."

"It but stunned me," he replied. "A mere scratch."

"Maybe it were as well had it been final," I said. "We seem to be in a pretty fix here with a splendid chance of dying of starvation and thirst."

"Where are we?"

"Beneath the arena," I replied. "We tumbled down the shaft that swallowed Issus as she was almost at our mercy."

He laughed a low laugh of pleasure and relief, and then reaching out through the inky blackness he sought my shoulder and pulled my ear close to his mouth.

"Nothing could be better," he whispered. "There are secrets within the secrets of Issus of which Issus herself does not dream."

"What do you mean?"

"I laboured with the other slaves a year since in the remodelling of these subterranean galleries, and at that time we found below these an ancient system of corridors and chambers that had been sealed up for ages. The blacks in charge of the work explored them, taking several of us along to do whatever work there might be occasion for. I know the entire system perfectly.

"There are miles of corridors honeycombing the ground beneath the gardens and the temple itself, and there is one passage that leads down to and connects with the lower regions that open on the water shaft that gives passage to Omean.

"If we can reach the submarine undetected we may yet make the sea in which there are many islands where the blacks never go. There we may live for a time, and who knows what may transpire to aid us to escape?"

He had spoken all in a low whisper, evidently fearing spying ears even here, and so I answered him in the same subdued tone.

"Lead back to Shador, my friend," I whispered. "Xodar, the black, is there. We were to attempt our escape together, so I cannot desert him."

"No," said the boy, "one cannot desert a friend. It were better to be recaptured ourselves than that."

Then he commenced groping his way about the floor of the dark chamber searching for the trap that led to the corridors beneath. At length he summoned me by a low, "S-s-t," and I crept toward the sound of his voice to find him kneeling on the brink of an opening in the floor.

"There is a drop here of about ten feet," he whispered. "Hang by your hands and you will alight safely on a level floor of soft sand."

Very quietly I lowered myself from the inky cell above into the inky pit below. So utterly dark was it that we could not see our hands at an inch from our noses. Never, I think, have I known such complete absence of light as existed in the pits of Issus.

For an instant I hung in mid air. There is a strange sensation connected with an experience of that nature which is quite difficult to describe. When the feet tread empty air and the distance below is shrouded in darkness there is a feeling akin to panic at the thought of releasing the hold and taking the plunge into unknown depths.

Although the boy had told me that it was but ten feet to the floor below I experienced the same thrills as though I were hanging above a bottomless pit. Then I released my hold and dropped – four feet to a soft cushion of sand.

The boy followed me.

"Raise me to your shoulders," he said, "and I will replace the trap."

This done he took me by the hand, leading me very slowly, with much feeling about and frequent halts to assure himself that he did not stray into wrong passageways.

Presently we commenced the descent of a very steep incline.

"It will not be long," he said, "before we shall have light. At the lower levels we meet the same strata of phosphorescent rock that illuminates Omean."

Never shall I forget that trip through the pits of Issus. While it was devoid of important incidents yet it was filled for me with a strange charm of excitement and adventure which I think I must have hinged principally on the unguessable antiquity of these long-forgotten corridors. The things which the Stygian darkness hid from my objective eye could not have been half so wonderful as the pictures which my imagination wrought as it conjured to life again the ancient peoples of this dying world and set them once more to the labours, the intrigues, the mysteries and the cruelties which they had practised to make their last stand against the swarming hordes of the dead sea bottoms that had driven them step by step to the uttermost pinnacle of the world where they were now intrenched behind an impenetrable barrier of superstition.

In addition to the green men there had been three principal races upon Barsoom. The blacks, the whites, and a race of yellow men. As the waters of the planet dried and the seas receded, all other resources dwindled until life upon the planet became a constant battle for survival.

The various races had made war upon one another for ages, and the three higher types had easily bested the green savages of the water places of the world, but now that the receding seas necessitated constant abandonment of their fortified cities and forced upon them a more or less nomadic life in which they became separated into smaller communities they soon fell prey to the fierce hordes of green men. The result was a partial amalgamation of the blacks, whites and yellows, the result of which is shown in the present splendid race of red men.

I had always supposed that all traces of the original races had disappeared from the face of Mars, yet within the past four days I had found both whites and blacks in great multitudes. Could it be possible that in some far-off corner of the planet there still existed a remnant of the ancient race of yellow men?

My reveries were broken in upon by a low exclamation from the boy.

"At last, the lighted way," he cried, and looking up I beheld at a long distance before us a dim radiance.

As we advanced the light increased until presently we emerged into well-lighted passageways. From then on our progress was rapid until we came suddenly to the end of a corridor that let directly upon the ledge surrounding the pool of the submarine.

The craft lay at her moorings with uncovered hatch. Raising his finger to his lips and then tapping his sword in a significant manner, the youth crept noiselessly toward the vessel. I was close at his heels.

Silently we dropped to the deserted deck, and on hands and knees crawled toward the hatchway. A stealthy glance below revealed no guard in sight, and so with the quickness and the soundlessness of cats we dropped together into the main cabin of the submarine. Even here was no sign of life. Quickly we covered and secured the hatch.

Then the boy stepped into the pilot house, touched a button and the boat sank amid swirling waters toward the bottom of the shaft. Even then there was no scurrying of feet as we had expected, and while the boy remained to direct the boat I slid from cabin to cabin in futile search for some member of the crew. The craft was entirely deserted. Such good fortune seemed almost unbelievable.

When I returned to the pilot house to report the good news to my companion he handed me a paper.

"This may explain the absence of the crew," he said.

It was a radio-aerial message to the commander of the submarine:

"The slaves have risen. Come with what men you have and those that you can gather on the way. Too late to get aid from Omean. They are massacring all within the amphitheatre. Issus is threatened. Haste.

"*Zithad*"

"Zithad is Dator of the guards of Issus," explained the youth. "We gave them a bad scare – one that they will not soon forget."

"Let us hope that it is but the beginning of the end of Issus," I said.

"Only our first ancestor knows," he replied.

We reached the submarine pool in Omean without incident. Here we debated the wisdom of sinking the craft before leaving her, but finally decided that it would add nothing to our chances for escape. There were plenty of blacks on Omean to thwart us were we apprehended; however many more might come from the temples and gardens of Issus would not in any decrease our chances.

We were now in a quandary as to how to pass the guards who patrolled the island about the pool. At last I hit upon a plan.

"What is the name or title of the officer in charge of these guards?" I asked the boy.

"A fellow named Torith was on duty when we entered this morning," he replied.

"Good. And what is the name of the commander of the submarine?"

"Yersted."

I found a dispatch blank in the cabin and wrote the following order:

"Dator Torith: Return these two slaves at once to Shador.

"*Yersted*"

"That will be the simpler way to return," I said, smiling, as I handed the forged order to the boy. "Come, we shall see now how well it works."

"But our swords!" he exclaimed. "What shall we say to explain them?"

"Since we cannot explain them we shall have to leave them behind us," I replied.

"Is it not the extreme of rashness to thus put ourselves again, unarmed, in the power of the First Born?"

"It is the only way," I answered. "You may trust me to find a way out of the prison of Shador, and I think, once out, that we shall find no great difficulty in arming ourselves once more in a country which abounds so plentifully in armed men."

"As you say," he replied with a smile and shrug. "I could not follow another leader who inspired greater confidence than you. Come, let us put your ruse to the test."

Boldly we emerged from the hatchway of the craft, leaving our swords behind us, and strode to the main exit which led to the sentry's post and the office of the Dator of the guard.

At sight of us the members of the guard sprang forward in surprise, and with levelled rifles halted us. I held out the message to one of them. He took it and seeing to whom it was addressed turned and handed it to Torith who was emerging from his office to learn the cause of the commotion.

The black read the order, and for a moment eyed us with evident suspicion.

"Where is Dator Yersted?" he asked, and my heart sank within me, as I cursed myself for a stupid fool in not having sunk the submarine to make good the lie that I must tell.

"His orders were to return immediately to the temple landing," I replied.

Torith took a half step toward the entrance to the pool as though to corroborate my story. For that instant everything hung in the balance, for had he done so and found the empty submarine still lying at her wharf the whole weak fabric of my concoction would have tumbled about our heads; but evidently he decided the message must be genuine, nor indeed was there any good reason to doubt it since it would scarce have seemed credible to him that two slaves would voluntarily have given themselves into custody in any such manner as this. It was the very boldness of the plan which rendered it successful.

"Were you connected with the rising of the slaves?" asked Torith. "We have just had meagre reports of some such event."

"All were involved," I replied. "But it amounted to little. The guards quickly overcame and killed the majority of us."

He seemed satisfied with this reply. "Take them to Shador," he ordered, turning to one of his subordinates. We entered a small boat lying beside the island, and in a few minutes were disembarking upon Shador. Here we were returned to our respective cells; I with Xodar, the boy by himself; and behind locked doors we were again prisoners of the First Born.

CHAPTER THIRTEEN

A Break for Liberty

XODAR LISTENED in incredulous astonishment to my narration of the events which had transpired within the arena at the rites of Issus. He could scarce conceive, even though he had already professed his doubt as to the deity of Issus, that one could threaten her with sword in hand and not be blasted into a thousand fragments by the mere fury of her divine wrath.

"It is the final proof," he said, at last. "No more is needed to completely shatter the last remnant of my superstitious belief in the divinity of Issus. She is only a wicked old woman, wielding a mighty power for evil through machinations that have kept her own people and all Barsoom in religious ignorance for ages."

"She is still all-powerful here, however," I replied. "So it behooves us to leave at the first moment that appears at all propitious."

"I hope that you may find a propitious moment," he said, with a laugh, "for it is certain that in all my life I have never seen one in which a prisoner of the First Born might escape."

"To-night will do as well as any," I replied.

"It will soon be night," said Xodar. "How may I aid in the adventure?"

"Can you swim?" I asked him.

"No slimy silian that haunts the depths of Korus is more at home in water than is Xodar," he replied.

"Good. The red one in all probability cannot swim," I said, "since there is scarce enough water in all their domains to float the tiniest craft. One of us therefore will have to support him through the sea to the craft we select. I had hoped that we might make the entire distance below the surface, but I fear that the red youth could not thus perform the trip. Even the bravest of the brave among them are terrorized at the mere thought of deep water, for it has been ages since their forebears saw a lake, a river or a sea."

"The red one is to accompany us?" asked Xodar.

"Yes."

"It is well. Three swords are better than two. Especially when the third is as mighty as this fellow's. I have seen him battle in the arena at the rites of Issus many times. Never, until I saw you fight, had I seen one who seemed unconquerable even in the face of great odds. One might think you two master and pupil, or father and son. Come to recall his face there is a resemblance between you. It is very marked when you fight – there is the same grim smile, the same maddening contempt for your adversary apparent in every movement of your bodies and in every changing expression of your faces."

"Be that as it may, Xodar, he is a great fighter. I think that we will make a trio difficult to overcome, and if my friend Tars Tarkas, Jeddak of Thark, were but one of us we could fight our way from one end of Barsoom to the other even though the whole world were pitted against us."

"It will be," said Xodar, "when they find from whence you have come. That is but one of the superstitions which Issus has foisted upon a credulous humanity. She works through the Holy Therns who are as ignorant of her real self as are the Barsoomians of the outer world. Her decrees are borne to the therns written in blood upon a strange parchment. The poor deluded fools think that they are receiving the revelations of a goddess through some supernatural agency, since they find these messages upon their guarded altars to which none could have access without detection. I myself have borne these messages for Issus for many years. There is a long tunnel from the temple of Issus to the principal temple of Matai Shang. It was dug ages ago by the slaves of the First Born in such utter secrecy that no thern ever guessed its existence.

"The therns for their part have temples dotted about the entire civilized world. Here priests whom the people never see communicate the doctrine of the Mysterious River Iss, the Valley Dor, and the Lost Sea of Korus to persuade the poor deluded creatures to take the voluntary pilgrimage that swells the wealth of the Holy Therns and adds to the numbers of their slaves.

"Thus the therns are used as the principal means for collecting the wealth and labour that the First Born wrest from them as they need it. Occasionally the First Born themselves make raids upon the outer world. It is then that they capture many females of the royal houses of the red men, and take the newest in battleships and the trained artisans who build them, that they may copy what they cannot create.

"We are a non-productive race, priding ourselves upon our non-productiveness. It is criminal for a First Born to labour or invent. That is the work of the lower orders, who live merely that the First Born may enjoy long lives of luxury and idleness. With us fighting is all that counts; were it not for that there would be more of the First Born than all the creatures of Barsoom could support, for in so far as I know none of us ever dies a natural death. Our females would live for ever but for the fact that we tire of them and remove them to make place for others. Issus alone of all is protected against death. She has lived for countless ages."

"Would not the other Barsoomians live for ever but for the doctrine of the voluntary pilgrimage which drags them to the bosom of Iss at or before their thousandth year?" I asked him.

"I feel now that there is no doubt but that they are precisely the same species of creature as the First Born, and I hope that I shall live to fight for them in atonement of the sins I have committed against them through the ignorance born of generations of false teaching."

As he ceased speaking a weird call rang out across the waters of Omean. I had heard it at the same time the previous evening and knew that it marked the ending of the day, when the men of Omean spread their silks upon the deck of battleship and cruiser and fall into the dreamless sleep of Mars.

Our guard entered to inspect us for the last time before the new day broke upon the world above. His duty was soon performed and the heavy door of our prison closed behind him – we were alone for the night.

I gave him time to return to his quarters, as Xodar said he probably would do, then I sprang to the grated window and surveyed the nearby waters. At a little distance from the island, a quarter of a mile perhaps, lay a monster battleship, while between her and the shore were a number of smaller cruisers and one-man scouts. Upon the battleship alone was there a watch. I could see him plainly in the upper works of the ship, and as I watched I saw him spread his sleeping silks upon the tiny platform in which he was stationed. Soon he threw himself at full length upon his couch. The discipline on Omean was lax indeed. But it is not to be wondered at since no enemy guessed the existence upon Barsoom of such a fleet, or even of the First Born, or the Sea of Omean. Why indeed should they maintain a watch?

Presently I dropped to the floor again and talked with Xodar, describing the various craft I had seen.

"There is one there," he said, "my personal property, built to carry five men, that is the swiftest of the swift. If we can board her we can at least make a memorable run for liberty," and then he went on to describe to me the equipment of the boat; her engines, and all that went to make her the flier that she was.

In his explanation I recognized a trick of gearing that Kantos Kan had taught me that time we sailed under false names in the navy of Zodanga beneath Sab Than, the Prince. And I knew then that the First Born had stolen it from the ships of Helium, for only they are thus geared. And I knew too that Xodar spoke the truth when he lauded the speed of his little craft, for nothing that cleaves the thin air of Mars can approximate the speed of the ships of Helium.

We decided to wait for an hour at least until all the stragglers had sought their silks. In the meantime I was to fetch the red youth to our cell so that we would be in readiness to make our rash break for freedom together.

I sprang to the top of our partition wall and pulled myself up on to it. There I found a flat surface about a foot in width and along this I walked until I came to the cell in which I saw the boy sitting upon his bench. He had been leaning back against the wall looking up at the glowing dome above Omean, and when he spied me balancing upon the partition wall above him his eyes opened wide in astonishment. Then a wide grin of appreciative understanding spread across his countenance.

As I stooped to drop to the floor beside him he motioned me to wait, and coming close below me whispered: "Catch my hand; I can almost leap to the top of that wall myself. I have tried it many times, and each day I come a little closer. Some day I should have been able to make it."

I lay upon my belly across the wall and reached my hand far down toward him. With a little run from the centre of the cell he sprang up until I grasped his outstretched hand, and thus I pulled him to the wall's top beside me.

"You are the first jumper I ever saw among the red men of Barsoom," I said.

He smiled. "It is not strange. I will tell you why when we have more time."

Together we returned to the cell in which Xodar sat; descending to talk with him until the hour had passed.

There we made our plans for the immediate future, binding ourselves by a solemn oath to fight to the death for one another against whatsoever enemies should confront us, for we knew that even should we succeed in escaping the First Born we might still have a whole world against us – the power of religious superstition is mighty.

It was agreed that I should navigate the craft after we had reached her, and that if we made the outer world in safety we should attempt to reach Helium without a stop.

"Why Helium?" asked the red youth.

"I am a prince of Helium," I replied.

He gave me a peculiar look, but said nothing further on the subject. I wondered at the time what the significance of his expression might be, but in the press of other matters it soon left my mind, nor did I have occasion to think of it again until later.

"Come," I said at length, "now is as good a time as any. Let us go."

Another moment found me at the top of the partition wall again with the boy beside me. Unbuckling my harness I snapped it together with a single long strap which I lowered to the waiting Xodar below. He grasped the end and was soon sitting beside us.

"How simple," he laughed.

"The balance should be even simpler," I replied. Then I raised myself to the top of the outer wall of the prison, just so that I could peer over and locate the passing sentry. For a matter of five minutes I waited and then he came in sight on his slow and snail-like beat about the structure.

I watched him until he had made the turn at the end of the building which carried him out of sight of the side of the prison that was to witness our dash for freedom. The moment his form disappeared I grasped Xodar and drew him to the top of the wall. Placing one end of my harness strap in his hands I lowered him quickly to the ground below. Then the boy grasped the strap and slid down to Xodar's side.

In accordance with our arrangement they did not wait for me, but walked slowly toward the water, a matter of a hundred yards, directly past the guard-house filled with sleeping soldiers.

They had taken scarce a dozen steps when I too dropped to the ground and followed them leisurely toward the shore. As I passed the guard-house the thought of all the good blades lying there gave me pause, for if ever men were to have need of swords it was my companions and I on the perilous trip upon which we were about to embark.

I glanced toward Xodar and the youth and saw that they had slipped over the edge of the dock into the water. In accordance with our plan they were to remain there clinging to the metal rings which studded the concrete-like substance of the dock at the water's level, with only their mouths and noses above the surface of the sea, until I should join them.

The lure of the swords within the guard-house was strong upon me, and I hesitated a moment, half inclined to risk the attempt to take the few we needed. That he who hesitates is lost proved itself a true aphorism in this instance, for another moment saw me creeping stealthily toward the door of the guard-house.

Gently I pressed it open a crack; enough to discover a dozen blacks stretched upon their silks in profound slumber. At the far side of the room a rack held the swords and firearms of the men. Warily I pushed the door a trifle wider to admit my body. A hinge gave out a resentful groan. One of the men stirred, and my heart stood still. I cursed myself for a fool to have thus jeopardized our chances for escape; but there was nothing for it now but to see the adventure through.

With a spring as swift and as noiseless as a tiger's I lit beside the guardsman who had moved. My hands hovered about his throat awaiting the moment that his eyes should open. For what seemed an eternity to my overwrought nerves I remained poised thus. Then the fellow turned again upon his side and resumed the even respiration of deep slumber.

Carefully I picked my way between and over the soldiers until I had gained the rack at the far side of the room. Here I turned to survey the sleeping men. All were quiet. Their regular breathing rose and fell in a soothing rhythm that seemed to me the sweetest music I ever had heard.

Gingerly I drew a long-sword from the rack. The scraping of the scabbard against its holder as I withdrew it sounded like the filing of cast iron with a great rasp, and I looked to see the room immediately filled with alarmed and attacking guardsmen. But none stirred.

The second sword I withdrew noiselessly, but the third clanked in its scabbard with a frightful din. I knew that it must awaken some of the men at least, and was on the point of forestalling their attack by a rapid charge for the doorway, when again, to my intense surprise, not a black moved. Either they were wondrous heavy sleepers or else the noises that I made were really much less than they seemed to me.

I was about to leave the rack when my attention was attracted by the revolvers. I knew that I could not carry more than one away with me, for I was already too heavily laden to move quietly with any degree of safety or speed. As I took one of them from its pin my eye fell for the first time on an open window beside the rack. Ah, here was a splendid means of escape, for it let directly upon the dock, not twenty feet from the water's edge.

And as I congratulated myself, I heard the door opposite me open, and there looking me full in the face stood the officer of the guard. He evidently took in the situation at a glance and appreciated the gravity of it as quickly as I, for our revolvers came up simultaneously and the sounds of the two reports were as one as we touched the buttons on the grips that exploded the cartridges.

I felt the wind of his bullet as it whizzed past my ear, and at the same instant I saw him crumple to the ground. Where I hit him I do not know, nor if I killed him, for scarce had he started to collapse when I was through the window at my rear. In another second the waters of Omean closed above my head, and the three of us were making for the little flier a hundred yards away.

Xodar was burdened with the boy, and I with the three long-swords. The revolver I had dropped, so that while we were both strong swimmers it seemed to me that we moved at a snail's pace through the water. I was swimming entirely beneath the surface, but Xodar was compelled to rise often to let the youth breathe, so it was a wonder that we were not discovered long before we were.

In fact we reached the boat's side and were all aboard before the watch upon the battleship, aroused by the shots, detected us. Then an alarm gun bellowed from a ship's bow, its deep boom reverberating in deafening tones beneath the rocky dome of Omean.

Instantly the sleeping thousands were awake. The decks of a thousand monster craft teemed with fighting-men, for an alarm on Omean was a thing of rare occurrence.

We cast away before the sound of the first gun had died, and another second saw us rising swiftly from the surface of the sea. I lay at full length along the deck with the levers and buttons of control before me. Xodar and the boy were stretched directly behind me, prone also that we might offer as little resistance to the air as possible.

"Rise high," whispered Xodar. "They dare not fire their heavy guns toward the dome – the fragments of the shells would drop back among their own craft. If we are high enough our keel plates will protect us from rifle fire."

I did as he bade. Below us we could see the men leaping into the water by hundreds, and striking out for the small cruisers and one-man fliers that lay moored about the big ships. The larger craft were getting under way, following us rapidly, but not rising from the water.

"A little to your right," cried Xodar, for there are no points of compass upon Omean where every direction is due north.

The pandemonium that had broken out below us was deafening. Rifles cracked, officers shouted orders, men yelled directions to one another from the water and from the decks of myriad boats, while through all ran the purr of countless propellers cutting water and air.

I had not dared pull my speed lever to the highest for fear of overrunning the mouth of the shaft that passed from Omean's dome to the world above, but even so we were hitting a clip that I doubt has ever been equalled on the windless sea.

The smaller fliers were commencing to rise toward us when Xodar shouted: "The shaft! The shaft! Dead ahead," and I saw the opening, black and yawning in the glowing dome of this underworld.

A ten-man cruiser was rising directly in front to cut off our escape. It was the only vessel that stood in our way, but at the rate that it was traveling it would come between us and the shaft in plenty of time to thwart our plans.

It was rising at an angle of about forty-five degrees dead ahead of us, with the evident intention of combing us with grappling hooks from above as it skimmed low over our deck.

There was but one forlorn hope for us, and I took it. It was useless to try to pass over her, for that would have allowed her to force us against the rocky dome above, and we were already too near that as it was. To have attempted to dive below her would have put us entirely at her mercy, and precisely where she wanted us. On either side a hundred other menacing craft were hastening toward us. The alternative was filled with risk – in fact it was all risk, with but a slender chance of success.

As we neared the cruiser I rose as though to pass above her, so that she would do just what she did do, rise at a steeper angle to force me still higher. Then as we were almost upon her I yelled to my companions to hold tight, and throwing the little vessel into her highest speed I deflected her bows at the same instant until we were running horizontally and at terrific velocity straight for the cruiser's keel.

Her commander may have seen my intentions then, but it was too late. Almost at the instant of impact I turned my bows upward, and then with a shattering jolt we were in collision. What I had hoped for happened. The cruiser, already tilted at a perilous angle, was carried completely over backward by the impact of my smaller vessel. Her crew fell twisting and screaming through the air to the water far below, while the cruiser, her propellers still madly churning, dived swiftly headforemost after them to the bottom of the Sea of Omean.

The collision crushed our steel bows, and notwithstanding every effort on our part came near to hurling us from the deck. As it was we landed in a wildly clutching heap at the very extremity of the flier, where Xodar and I succeeded in grasping the hand-rail, but the boy would have plunged overboard had I not fortunately grasped his ankle as he was already partially over.

Unguided, our vessel careened wildly in its mad flight, rising ever nearer the rocks above. It took but an instant, however, for me to regain the levers, and with the roof barely fifty feet above I turned her nose once more into the horizontal plane and headed her again for the black mouth of the shaft.

The collision had retarded our progress and now a hundred swift scouts were close upon us. Xodar had told me that ascending the shaft by virtue of our repulsive rays alone would give our enemies their best chance to overtake us, since our propellers would be idle and in rising we would be outclassed by many of our pursuers. The swifter craft are seldom equipped with large buoyancy tanks, since the added bulk of them tends to reduce a vessel's speed.

As many boats were now quite close to us it was inevitable that we would be quickly overhauled in the shaft, and captured or killed in short order.

To me there always seems a way to gain the opposite side of an obstacle. If one cannot pass over it, or below it, or around it, why then there is but a single alternative left, and that is to pass through it. I could not get around the fact that many of these other boats could rise faster than ours by the fact of their greater buoyancy, but I was none the less determined to reach the outer world far in advance of them or die a death of my own choosing in event of failure.

"Reverse?" screamed Xodar, behind me. "For the love of your first ancestor, reverse. We are at the shaft."

"Hold tight!" I screamed in reply. "Grasp the boy and hold tight – we are going straight up the shaft."

The words were scarce out of my mouth as we swept beneath the pitch-black opening. I threw the bow hard up, dragged the speed lever to its last notch, and clutching a stanchion with one hand and the steering-wheel with the other hung on like grim death and consigned my soul to its author.

I heard a little exclamation of surprise from Xodar, followed by a grim laugh. The boy laughed too and said something which I could not catch for the whistling of the wind of our awful speed.

I looked above my head, hoping to catch the gleam of stars by which I could direct our course and hold the hurtling thing that bore us true to the centre of the shaft. To have touched the side at the speed we were making would doubtless have resulted in instant death for us all. But not a star showed above – only utter and impenetrable darkness.

Then I glanced below me, and there I saw a rapidly diminishing circle of light – the mouth of the opening above the phosphorescent radiance of Omean. By this I steered, endeavouring to keep the circle of light below me ever perfect. At best it was but a slender cord that held us from destruction, and I think that I steered that night more by intuition and blind faith than by skill or reason.

We were not long in the shaft, and possibly the very fact of our enormous speed saved us, for evidently we started in the right direction and so quickly were we out again that we had no time to alter our course. Omean lies perhaps two miles below the surface crust of Mars. Our speed must have approximated two hundred miles an hour, for Martian fliers are swift, so that at most we were in the shaft not over forty seconds.

We must have been out of it for some seconds before I realised that we had accomplished the impossible. Black darkness enshrouded all about us. There were neither moons nor stars. Never before had I seen such a thing upon Mars, and for the moment I was nonplussed. Then the explanation came to me. It was summer at the south pole. The ice cap was melting and those meteoric phenomena, clouds, unknown upon the greater part of Barsoom, were shutting out the light of heaven from this portion of the planet.

Fortunate indeed it was for us, nor did it take me long to grasp the opportunity for escape which this happy condition offered us. Keeping the boat's nose at a stiff angle I raced her for the impenetrable curtain which Nature had hung above this dying world to shut us out from the sight of our pursuing enemies.

We plunged through the cold damp fog without diminishing our speed, and in a moment emerged into the glorious light of the two moons and the million stars. I dropped into a horizontal course and headed due north. Our enemies were a good half-hour behind us with no conception of our direction. We had performed the miraculous and come through a thousand dangers unscathed – we had escaped from the land of the First Born. No other prisoners in all the ages of Barsoom had done this thing, and now as I looked back upon it it did not seem to have been so difficult after all.

I said as much to Xodar, over my shoulder.

"It is very wonderful, nevertheless," he replied. "No one else could have accomplished it but John Carter."

At the sound of that name the boy jumped to his feet.

"John Carter!" he cried. "John Carter! Why, man, John Carter, Prince of Helium, has been dead for years. I am his son."

CHAPTER FOURTEEN

The Eyes in the Dark

My son! I could not believe my ears. Slowly I rose and faced the handsome youth. Now that I looked at him closely I commenced to see why his face and personality had attracted me so strongly. There was much of his mother's incomparable beauty in his clear-cut features, but it was strongly masculine beauty, and his grey eyes and the expression of them were mine.

The boy stood facing me, half hope and half uncertainty in his look.

"Tell me of your mother," I said. "Tell me all you can of the years that I have been robbed by a relentless fate of her dear companionship."

With a cry of pleasure he sprang toward me and threw his arms about my neck, and for a brief moment as I held my boy close to me the tears welled to my eyes and I was like to have choked after the manner of some maudlin fool – but I do not regret it, nor am I ashamed. A long life has taught me that a man may seem weak where women and children are concerned and yet be anything but a weakling in the sterner avenues of life.

"Your stature, your manner, the terrible ferocity of your swordsmanship," said the boy, "are as my mother has described them to me a thousand times – but even with such evidence I could scarce credit the truth of what seemed so improbable to me, however much I desired it to be true. Do you know what thing it was that convinced me more than all the others?"

"What, my boy?" I asked.

"Your first words to me – they were of my mother. None else but the man who loved her as she has told me my father did would have thought first of her."

"For long years, my son, I can scarce recall a moment that the radiant vision of your mother's face has not been ever before me. Tell me of her."

"Those who have known her longest say that she has not changed, unless it be to grow more beautiful – were that possible. Only, when she thinks I am not about to see her, her face grows very sad, and, oh, so wistful. She thinks ever of you, my father, and all Helium mourns with her and for her. Her grandfather's people love her. They loved you also, and fairly worship your memory as the saviour of Barsoom.

"Each year that brings its anniversary of the day that saw you racing across a near dead world to unlock the secret of that awful portal behind which lay the mighty power of life for countless millions a great festival is held in your honour; but there are tears mingled with the thanksgiving – tears of real regret that the author of the happiness is not with them to share the joy of living he died to give them. Upon all Barsoom there is no greater name than John Carter."

"And by what name has your mother called you, my boy?" I asked.

"The people of Helium asked that I be named with my father's name, but my mother said no, that you and she had chosen a name for me together, and that your wish must be honoured before all others, so the name that she called me is the one that you desired, a combination of hers and yours – Carthoris."

Xodar had been at the wheel as I talked with my son, and now he called me.

"She is dropping badly by the head, John Carter," he said. "So long as we were rising at a stiff angle it was not noticeable, but now that I am trying to keep a horizontal course it is different. The wound in her bow has opened one of her forward ray tanks."

It was true, and after I had examined the damage I found it a much graver matter than I had anticipated. Not only was the forced angle at which we were compelled to maintain the bow in order to keep a horizontal course greatly impeding our speed, but at the rate that we were losing our repulsive rays from the forward tanks it was but a question of an hour or more when we would be floating stern up and helpless.

We had slightly reduced our speed with the dawning of a sense of security, but now I took the helm once more and pulled the noble little engine wide open, so that again we raced north at terrific velocity. In the meantime Carthoris and Xodar with tools in hand were puttering with the great rent in the bow in a hopeless endeavour to stem the tide of escaping rays.

It was still dark when we passed the northern boundary of the ice cap and the area of clouds. Below us lay a typical Martian landscape. Rolling ochre sea bottom of long dead seas, low surrounding hills, with here and there the grim and silent cities of the dead past; great piles of mighty architecture tenanted only by age-old memories of a once powerful race, and by the great white apes of Barsoom.

It was becoming more and more difficult to maintain our little vessel in a horizontal position. Lower and lower sagged the bow until it became necessary to stop the engine to prevent our flight terminating in a swift dive to the ground.

As the sun rose and the light of a new day swept away the darkness of night our craft gave a final spasmodic plunge, turned half upon her side, and then with deck tilting at a sickening angle swung in a slow circle, her bow dropping further below her stern each moment.

To hand-rail and stanchion we clung, and finally as we saw the end approaching, snapped the buckles of our harness to the rings at her sides. In another moment the deck reared at an angle of ninety degrees and we hung in our leather with feet dangling a thousand yards above the ground.

I was swinging quite close to the controlling devices, so I reached out to the lever that directed the rays of repulsion. The boat responded to the touch, and very gently we began to sink toward the ground.

It was fully half an hour before we touched. Directly north of us rose a rather lofty range of hills, toward which we decided to make our way, since they afforded greater opportunity for concealment from the pursuers we were confident might stumble in this direction.

An hour later found us in the time-rounded gullies of the hills, amid the beautiful flowering plants that abound in the arid waste places of Barsoom. There we found numbers of huge milk-giving shrubs – that strange plant which serves in great part as food and drink for the wild hordes of green men. It was indeed a boon to us, for we all were nearly famished.

Beneath a cluster of these which afforded perfect concealment from wandering air scouts, we lay down to sleep – for me the first time in many hours. This was the beginning of my fifth day upon Barsoom since I had found myself suddenly translated from my cottage on the Hudson to Dor, the valley beautiful, the valley hideous. In all this time I had slept but twice, though once the clock around within the storehouse of the therns.

It was mid-afternoon when I was awakened by some one seizing my hand and covering it with kisses. With a start I opened my eyes to look into the beautiful face of Thuvia.

"My Prince! My Prince!" she cried, in an ecstasy of happiness. "'Tis you whom I had mourned as dead. My ancestors have been good to me; I have not lived in vain."

The girl's voice awoke Xodar and Carthoris. The boy gazed upon the woman in surprise, but she did not seem to realize the presence of another than I. She would have thrown her arms about my neck and smothered me with caresses, had I not gently but firmly disengaged myself.

"Come, come, Thuvia," I said soothingly; "you are overwrought by the danger and hardships you have passed through. You forget yourself, as you forget that I am the husband of the Princess of Helium."

"I forget nothing, my Prince," she replied. "You have spoken no word of love to me, nor do I expect that you ever shall; but nothing can prevent me loving you. I would not take the place of Dejah Thoris. My greatest ambition is to serve you, my Prince, for ever as your slave. No greater boon could I ask, no greater honour could I crave, no greater happiness could I hope."

As I have before said, I am no ladies' man, and I must admit that I seldom have felt so uncomfortable and embarrassed as I did that moment. While I was quite familiar with the Martian custom which allows female slaves to Martian men, whose high and chivalrous honour is always ample protection for every woman in his household, yet I had never myself chosen other than men as my body servants.

"And I ever return to Helium, Thuvia," I said, "you shall go with me, but as an honoured equal, and not as a slave. There you shall find plenty of handsome young nobles who would face Issus herself to win a smile from you, and we shall have you married in short order to one of the best of them. Forget your foolish gratitude-begotten infatuation, which your innocence has mistaken for love. I like your friendship better, Thuvia."

"You are my master; it shall be as you say," she replied simply, but there was a note of sadness in her voice.

"How came you here, Thuvia?" I asked. "And where is Tars Tarkas?"

"The great Thark, I fear, is dead," she replied sadly. "He was a mighty fighter, but a multitude of green warriors of another horde than his overwhelmed him. The last that I saw of him they were bearing him, wounded and bleeding, to the deserted city from which they had sallied to attack us."

"You are not sure that he is dead, then?" I asked. "And where is this city of which you speak?"

"It is just beyond this range of hills. The vessel in which you so nobly resigned a place that we might find escape defied our small skill in navigation, with the result that we drifted aimlessly about for two days. Then we decided to abandon the craft and attempt to make our way on foot to the nearest waterway. Yesterday we crossed these hills and came upon the dead city beyond. We had passed within its streets and were walking toward the central portion, when at an intersecting avenue we saw a body of green warriors approaching.

"Tars Tarkas was in advance, and they saw him, but me they did not see. The Thark sprang back to my side and forced me into an adjacent doorway, where he told me to remain in hiding until I could escape, making my way to Helium if possible.

"'There will be no escape for me now,' he said, 'for these be the Warhoon of the South. When they have seen my metal it will be to the death.'

"Then he stepped out to meet them. Ah, my Prince, such fighting! For an hour they swarmed about him, until the Warhoon dead formed a hill where he had stood; but at last they overwhelmed him, those behind pushing the foremost upon him until there remained no space to swing his great sword. Then he stumbled and went down and they rolled over him like a huge wave. When they carried him away toward the heart of the city, he was dead, I think, for I did not see him move."

"Before we go farther we must be sure," I said. "I cannot leave Tars Tarkas alive among the Warhoons. To-night I shall enter the city and make sure."

"And I shall go with you," spoke Carthoris.

"And I," said Xodar.

"Neither one of you shall go," I replied. "It is work that requires stealth and strategy, not force. One man alone may succeed where more would invite disaster. I shall go alone. If I need your help, I will return for you."

They did not like it, but both were good soldiers, and it had been agreed that I should command. The sun already was low, so that I did not have long to wait before the sudden darkness of Barsoom engulfed us.

With a parting word of instructions to Carthoris and Xodar, in case I should not return, I bade them all farewell and set forth at a rapid dogtrot toward the city.

As I emerged from the hills the nearer moon was winging its wild flight through the heavens, its bright beams turning to burnished silver the barbaric splendour of the ancient metropolis. The city had been built upon the gently rolling foothills that in the dim and distant past had sloped down to meet the sea. It was due to this fact that I had no difficulty in entering the streets unobserved.

The green hordes that use these deserted cities seldom occupy more than a few squares about the central plaza, and as they come and go always across the dead sea bottoms that the cities face, it is usually a matter of comparative ease to enter from the hillside.

Once within the streets, I kept close in the dense shadows of the walls. At intersections I halted a moment to make sure that none was in sight before I sprang quickly to the shadows of the opposite side. Thus I made the journey to the vicinity of the plaza without detection. As I approached the purlieus of the inhabited portion of the city I was made aware of the proximity of the warriors' quarters by the squealing and grunting of the thoats and zitidars corralled within the hollow court-yards formed by the buildings surrounding each square.

These old familiar sounds that are so distinctive of green Martian life sent a thrill of pleasure surging through me. It was as one might feel on coming home after a long absence. It was amid such sounds that I had first courted the incomparable Dejah Thoris in the age-old marble halls of the dead city of Korad.

As I stood in the shadows at the far corner of the first square which housed members of the horde, I saw warriors emerging from several of the buildings. They all went in the same direction, toward a great building which stood in the centre of the plaza. My knowledge of green Martian customs convinced me that this was either the quarters of the principal chieftain or contained the audience chamber wherein the Jed-dak met his jeds and lesser chieftains. In either event, it was evident that something was afoot which might have a bearing on the recent capture of Tars Tarkas.

To reach this building, which I now felt it imperative that I do, I must needs traverse the entire length of one square and cross a broad avenue and a portion of the plaza. From the noises of the animals which came from every courtyard about me, I knew that there were many people in the surrounding buildings – probably several communities of the great horde of the Warhoons of the South.

To pass undetected among all these people was in itself a difficult task, but if I was to find and rescue the great Thark I must expect even more formidable obstacles before success could be mine. I had entered the city from the south and now stood on the corner of the avenue through which I had passed and the first intersecting avenue south of the plaza. The buildings upon the south side of this square did not ap-pear to be inhabited, as I could see no lights, and so I decided to gain the inner courtyard through one of them.

Nothing occurred to interrupt my progress through the deserted pile I chose, and I came into the inner court close to the rear walls of the east buildings without detection. Within the court a great herd of tho-ats and zitidars moved restlessly about, cropping the moss-like ochre vegetation which overgrows practically the entire uncultivated area of

Mars. What breeze there was came from the north-west, so there was little danger that the beasts would scent me. Had they, their squealing and grunting would have grown to such a volume as to attract the attention of the warriors within the buildings.

Close to the east wall, beneath the overhanging balconies of the second floors, I crept in dense shadows the full length of the courtyard, until I came to the buildings at the north end. These were lighted for about three floors up, but above the third floor all was dark.

To pass through the lighted rooms was, of course, out of the question, since they swarmed with green Martian men and women. My only path lay through the upper floors, and to gain these it was necessary to scale the face of the wall. The reaching of the balcony of the second floor was a matter of easy accomplishment – an agile leap gave my hands a grasp upon the stone hand-rail above. In another instant I had drawn myself upon the balcony.

Here through the open windows I saw the green folk squatting upon their sleeping silks and furs, grunting an occasional monosyllable, which, in connection with their wondrous telepathic powers, is ample for their conversational requirements. As I drew closer to listen to their words a warrior entered the room from the hall beyond.

"Come, Tan Gama," he cried, "we are to take the Thark before Kab Kadja. Bring another with you."

The warrior addressed arose and, beckoning to a fellow squatting near, the three turned and left the apartment.

If I could but follow them the chance might come to free Tars Tarkas at once. At least I would learn the location of his prison.

At my right was a door leading from the balcony into the building. It was at the end of an unlighted hall, and on the impulse of the moment I stepped within. The hall was broad and led straight through to the front of the building. On either side were the doorways of the various apartments which lined it.

I had no more than entered the corridor than I saw the three warriors at the other end – those whom I had just seen leaving the apartment. Then a turn to the right took them from my sight again. Quickly I hastened along the hallway in pursuit. My gait was reckless, but I felt that Fate had been kind indeed to throw such an opportunity within my grasp, and I could not afford to allow it to elude me now.

At the far end of the corridor I found a spiral stairway leading to the floors above and below. The three had evidently left the floor by this avenue. That they had gone down and not up I was sure from my knowledge of these ancient buildings and the methods of the Warhoons.

I myself had once been a prisoner of the cruel hordes of northern Warhoon, and the memory of the underground dungeon in which I lay still is vivid in my memory. And so I felt certain that Tars Tarkas lay in the dark pits beneath some nearby building, and that in that direction I should find the trail of the three warriors leading to his cell.

Nor was I wrong. At the bottom of the runway, or rather at the landing on the floor below, I saw that the shaft descended into the pits beneath, and as I glanced down the flickering light of a torch revealed the presence of the three I was trailing.

Down they went toward the pits beneath the structure, and at a safe distance behind I followed the flicker of their torch. The way led through a maze of tortuous corridors, unlighted save for the wavering light they carried. We had gone perhaps a hundred yards when the party turned abruptly through a doorway at their right. I hastened on as rapidly as I dared through the darkness until I reached the point at which they had left the corridor. There, through an open door, I saw them removing the chains that secured the great Thark, Tars Tarkas, to the wall.

Hustling him roughly between them, they came immediately from the chamber, so quickly in fact that I was near to being apprehended. But I managed to run along the corridor in the direction I had been going in my pursuit of them far enough to be without the radius of their meagre light as they emerged from the cell.

I had naturally assumed that they would return with Tars Tarkas the same way that they had come, which would have carried them away from me; but, to my chagrin, they wheeled directly in my direction as they left the room. There was nothing for me but to hasten on in advance and keep out of the light of their torch. I dared not attempt to halt in the darkness of any of the many intersecting corridors, for I knew nothing of the direction they might take. Chance was as likely as not to carry me into the very corridor they might choose to enter.

The sensation of moving rapidly through these dark passages was far from reassuring. I knew not at what moment I might plunge headlong into some terrible pit or meet with some of the ghoulish creatures that inhabit these lower worlds beneath the dead cities of dying Mars. There filtered to me a faint radiance from the torch of the men behind – just enough to permit me to trace the direction of the winding passageways directly before me, and so keep me from dashing myself against the walls at the turns.

Presently I came to a place where five corridors diverged from a common point. I had hastened along one of them for some little distance when suddenly the faint light of the torch disappeared from behind me. I paused to listen for sounds of the party behind me, but the silence was as utter as the silence of the tomb.

Quickly I realized that the warriors had taken one of the other corridors with their prisoner, and so I hastened back with a feeling of considerable relief to take up a much safer and more desirable position behind them. It was much slower work returning, however, than it had been coming, for now the darkness was as utter as the silence.

It was necessary to feel every foot of the way back with my hand against the side wall, that I might not pass the spot where the five roads radiated. After what seemed an eternity to me, I reached the place and recognized it by groping across the entrances to the several corridors until I had counted five of them. In not one, however, showed the faintest sign of light.

I listened intently, but the naked feet of the green men sent back no guiding echoes, though presently I thought I detected the clank of side arms in the far distance of the middle corridor. Up this, then, I hastened, searching for the light, and stopping to listen occasionally for a repetition of the sound; but soon I was forced to admit that I must have been following a blind lead, as only darkness and silence rewarded my efforts.

Again I retraced my steps toward the parting of the ways, when to my surprise I came upon the entrance to three diverging corridors, any one of which I might have traversed in my hasty dash after the false clue I had been following. Here was a pretty fix, indeed! Once back at the point where the five passageways met, I might wait with some assurance for the return of the warriors with Tars Tarkas. My knowledge of their customs lent colour to the belief that he was but being escorted to the audience chamber to have sentence passed upon him. I had not the slightest doubt but that they would preserve so doughty a warrior as the great Thark for the rare sport he would furnish at the Great Games.

But unless I could find my way back to that point the chances were most excellent that I would wander for days through the awful blackness, until, overcome by thirst and hunger, I lay down to die, or – What was that!

A faint shuffling sounded behind me, and as I cast a hasty glance over my shoulder my blood froze in my veins for the thing I saw there. It was not so much fear of the present danger as it was the horrifying memories it recalled of that time I near went mad over the corpse of the man I had killed in the dungeons of the Warhoons, when blazing eyes came out of the dark recesses and dragged the thing that had been a man from my clutches and I heard it scraping over the stone of my prison as they bore it away to their terrible feast.

And now in these black pits of the other Warhoons I looked into those same fiery eyes, blazing at me through the terrible darkness, revealing no sign of the beast behind them. I think that the most fearsome attribute of these awesome creatures is their silence and the fact that one never sees them – nothing but those baleful eyes glaring unblinkingly out of the dark void behind.

Grasping my long-sword tightly in my hand, I backed slowly along the corridor away from the thing that watched me, but ever as I retreated the eyes advanced, nor was there any sound, not even the sound of breathing, except the occasional shuffling sound as of the dragging of a dead limb, that had first attracted my attention.

On and on I went, but I could not escape my sinister pursuer. Suddenly I heard the shuffling noise at my right, and, looking, saw another pair of eyes, evidently approaching from an intersecting corridor. As I started to renew my slow retreat I heard the noise repeated behind me, and then before I could turn I heard it again at my left.

The things were all about me. They had me surrounded at the intersection of two corridors. Retreat was cut off in all directions, unless I chose to charge one of the beasts. Even then I had no doubt but that the others would hurl themselves upon my back. I could not even guess the size or nature of the weird creatures. That they were of goodly proportions I guessed from the fact that the eyes were on a level with my own.

Why is it that darkness so magnifies our dangers? By day I would have charged the great banth itself, had I thought it necessary, but hemmed in by the darkness of these silent pits I hesitated before a pair of eyes.

Soon I saw that the matter shortly would be taken entirely from my hands, for the eyes at my right were moving slowly nearer me, as were those at my left and those behind and before me. Gradually they were closing in upon me – but still that awful stealthy silence!

For what seemed hours the eyes approached gradually closer and closer, until I felt that I should go mad for the horror of it. I had been constantly turning this way and that to prevent any sudden rush from behind, until I was fairly worn out. At length I could endure it no longer, and, taking a fresh grasp upon my long-sword, I turned suddenly and charged down upon one of my tormentors.

As I was almost upon it the thing retreated before me, but a sound from behind caused me to wheel in time to see three pairs of eyes rushing at me from the rear. With a cry of rage I turned to meet the cowardly beasts, but as I advanced they retreated as had their fellow.

Another glance over my shoulder discovered the first eyes sneaking on me again. And again I charged, only to see the eyes retreat before me and hear the muffled rush of the three at my back.

Thus we continued, the eyes always a little closer in the end than they had been before, until I thought that I should go mad with the terrible strain of the ordeal. That they were waiting to spring upon my back seemed evident, and that it would not be long before they succeeded was equally apparent, for I could not endure the wear of this repeated charge and countercharge indefinitely. In fact, I could feel myself weakening from the mental and physical strain I had been undergoing.

At that moment I caught another glimpse from the corner of my eye of the single pair of eyes at my back making a sudden rush upon me. I turned to meet the charge; there was a quick rush of the three from the other direction; but I determined to pursue the single pair until I should have at least settled my account with one of the beasts and thus be relieved of the strain of meeting attacks from both directions.

There was no sound in the corridor, only that of my own breathing, yet I knew that those three uncanny creatures were almost upon me. The eyes in front were not retreating so rapidly now; I was almost within sword reach of them. I raised my sword arm to deal the blow that should free me, and then I felt a heavy body upon my back. A cold, moist, slimy something fastened itself upon my throat. I stumbled and went down.

CHAPTER FIFTEEN

Flight and Pursuit

I COULD NOT HAVE BEEN unconscious more than a few seconds, and yet I know that I was unconscious, for the next thing I realized was that a growing radiance was illuminating the corridor about me and the eyes were gone.

I was unharmed except for a slight bruise upon my forehead where it had struck the stone flagging as I fell.

I sprang to my feet to ascertain the cause of the light. It came from a torch in the hand of one of a party of four green warriors, who were coming rapidly down the corridor toward me. They had not yet seen me, and so I lost no time in slipping into the first intersecting corridor that I could find. This time, however, I did not advance so far away from the main corridor as on the other occasion that had resulted in my losing Tars Tarkas and his guards.

The party came rapidly toward the opening of the passageway in which I crouched against the wall. As they passed by I breathed a sigh of relief. I had not been discovered, and, best of all, the party was the same that I had followed into the pits. It consisted of Tars Tarkas and his three guards.

I fell in behind them and soon we were at the cell in which the great Thark had been chained. Two of the warriors remained without while the man with the keys entered with the Thark to fasten his irons upon him once more. The two outside started to stroll slowly in the direction of the spiral runway which led to the floors above, and in a moment were lost to view beyond a turn in the corridor.

The torch had been stuck in a socket beside the door, so that its rays illuminated both the corridor and the cell at the same time. As I saw the two warriors disappear I approached the entrance to the cell, with a well-defined plan already formulated.

While I disliked the thought of carrying out the thing that I had de-cided upon, there seemed no alternative if Tars Tarkas and I were to go back together to my little camp in the hills.

Keeping near the wall, I came quite close to the door to Tars Tarkas' cell, and there I stood with my longsword above my head, grasped with both hands, that I might bring it down in one quick cut upon the skull of the jailer as he emerged.

I dislike to dwell upon what followed after I heard the footsteps of the man as he approached the doorway. It is enough that within anoth-er minute or two, Tars Tarkas, wearing the metal of a Warhoon chief, was hurrying down the corridor toward the spiral runway, bearing the Warhoon's torch to light his way. A dozen paces behind him followed John Carter, Prince of Helium.

The two companions of the man who lay now beside the door of the cell that had been Tars Tarkas' had just started to ascend the runway as the Thark came in view.

"Why so long, Tan Gama?" cried one of the men.

"I had trouble with a lock," replied Tars Tarkas. "And now I find that I have left my short-sword in the Thark's cell. Go you on, I'll return and fetch it."

"As you will, Tan Gama," replied he who had before spoken. "We shall see you above directly."

"Yes," replied Tars Tarkas, and turned as though to retrace his steps to the cell, but he only waited until the two had disappeared at the floor above. Then I joined him, we extinguished the torch, and together we crept toward the spiral incline that led to the upper floors of the building.

At the first floor we found that the hallway ran but halfway through, necessitating the crossing of a rear room full of green folk, ere we could reach the inner courtyard, so there was but one thing left for us to do, and that was to gain the second floor and the hallway through which I had traversed the length of the building.

Cautiously we ascended. We could hear the sounds of conversa-tion coming from the room above, but the hall still was unlighted, nor was any one in sight as we gained the top of the runway. Together we threaded the long hall and reached the balcony overlooking the court-yard, without being detected.

At our right was the window letting into the room in which I had seen Tan Gama and the other warriors as they started to Tars Tarkas' cell earlier in the evening. His companions had returned here, and we now overheard a portion of their conversation.

"What can be detaining Tan Gama?" asked one.

"He certainly could not be all this time fetching his shortsword from the Thark's cell," spoke another.

"His short-sword?" asked a woman. "What mean you?"

"Tan Gama left his short-sword in the Thark's cell," explained the first speaker, "and left us at the runway, to return and get it."

"Tan Gama wore no short-sword this night," said the woman. "It was broken in to-day's battle with the Thark, and Tan Gama gave it to me to repair. See, I have it here," and as she spoke she drew Tan Gama's short-sword from beneath her sleeping silks and furs.

The warriors sprang to their feet.

"There is something amiss here," cried one.

"'Tis even what I myself thought when Tan Gama left us at the runway," said another. "Methought then that his voice sounded strangely."

"Come! let us hasten to the pits."

We waited to hear no more. Slinging my harness into a long single strap, I lowered Tars Tarkas to the courtyard beneath, and an instant later dropped to his side.

We had spoken scarcely a dozen words since I had felled Tan Gama at the cell door and seen in the torch's light the expression of utter bewilderment upon the great Thark's face.

"By this time," he had said, "I should have learned to wonder at nothing which John Carter accomplishes." That was all. He did not need to tell me that he appreciated the friendship which had prompted me to risk my life to rescue him, nor did he need to say that he was glad to see me.

This fierce green warrior had been the first to greet me that day, now twenty years gone, which had witnessed my first advent upon Mars. He had met me with levelled spear and cruel hatred in his heart as he charged down upon me, bending low at the side of his mighty thoat as I stood beside the incubator of his horde upon the dead sea bottom beyond Korad. And now among the inhabitants of two worlds I counted none a better friend than Tars Tarkas, Jeddak of the Tharks.

As we reached the courtyard we stood in the shadows beneath the balcony for a moment to discuss our plans.

"There be five now in the party, Tars Tarkas," I said; "Thuvia, Xodar, Carthoris, and ourselves. We shall need five thoats to bear us."

"Carthoris!" he cried. "Your son?"

"Yes. I found him in the prison of Shador, on the Sea of Omean, in the land of the First Born."

"I know not any of these places, John Carter. Be they upon Barsoom?"

"Upon and below, my friend; but wait until we shall have made good our escape, and you shall hear the strangest narrative that ever a Barsoomian of the outer world gave ear to. Now we must steal our thoats and be well away to the north before these fellows discover how we have tricked them."

In safety we reached the great gates at the far end of the courtyard, through which it was necessary to take our thoats to the avenue beyond. It is no easy matter to handle five of these great, fierce beasts, which by nature are as wild and ferocious as their masters and held in subjection by cruelty and brute force alone.

As we approached them they sniffed our unfamiliar scent and with squeals of rage circled about us. Their long, massive necks upreared raised their great, gaping mouths high above our heads. They are fearsome appearing brutes at best, but when they are aroused they are fully as dangerous as they look. The thoat stands a good ten feet at the shoulder. His hide is sleek and hairless, and of a dark slate colour on back and sides, shading down his eight legs to a vivid yellow at the huge, padded, nailless feet; the belly is pure white. A broad, flat tail, larger at the tip than at the root, completes the picture of this ferocious green Martian mount – a fit war steed for these warlike people.

As the thoats are guided by telepathic means alone, there is no need for rein or bridle, and so our object now was to find two that would obey our unspoken commands. As they charged about us we succeeded in mastering them sufficiently to prevent any concerted attack upon us, but the din of their squealing was certain to bring investigating warriors into the courtyard were it to continue much longer.

At length I was successful in reaching the side of one great brute, and ere he knew what I was about I was firmly seated astride his glossy back. A moment later Tars Tarkas had caught and mounted another, and then between us we herded three or four more toward the great gates.

Tars Tarkas rode ahead and, leaning down to the latch, threw the barriers open, while I held the loose thoats from breaking back to the herd. Then together we rode through into the avenue with our stolen mounts and, without waiting to close the gates, hurried off toward the southern boundary of the city.

Thus far our escape had been little short of marvellous, nor did our good fortune desert us, for we passed the outer purlieus of the dead city and came to our camp without hearing even the faintest sound of pursuit.

Here a low whistle, the prearranged signal, apprised the balance of our party that I was returning, and we were met by the three with every manifestation of enthusiastic rejoicing.

But little time was wasted in narration of our adventure. Tars Tarkas and Carthoris exchanged the dignified and formal greetings common upon Barsoom, but I could tell intuitively that the Thark loved my boy and that Carthoris reciprocated his affection.

Xodar and the green Jeddak were formally presented to each other. Then Thuvia was lifted to the least fractious thoat, Xodar and Carthoris mounted two others, and we set out at a rapid pace toward the east. At the far extremity of the city we circled toward the north, and under the glorious rays of the two moons we sped noiselessly across the dead sea bottom, away from the Warhoons and the First Born, but to what new dangers and adventures we knew not.

Toward noon of the following day we halted to rest our mounts and ourselves. The beasts we hobbled, that they might move slowly about cropping the ochre moss-like vegetation which constitutes both food and drink for them on the march. Thuvia volunteered to remain on watch while the balance of the party slept for an hour.

It seemed to me that I had but closed my eyes when I felt her hand upon my shoulder and heard her soft voice warning me of a new danger.

"Arise, O Prince," she whispered. "There be that behind us which has the appearance of a great body of pursuers."

The girl stood pointing in the direction from whence we had come, and as I arose and looked, I, too, thought that I could detect a thin dark line on the far horizon. I awoke the others. Tars Tarkas, whose giant stature towered high above the rest of us, could see the farthest.

"It is a great body of mounted men," he said, "and they are travelling at high speed."

There was no time to be lost. We sprang to our hobbled thoats, freed them, and mounted. Then we turned our faces once more toward the north and took our flight again at the highest speed of our slowest beast.

For the balance of the day and all the following night we raced across that ochre wilderness with the pursuers at our back ever gaining upon us. Slowly but surely they were lessening the distance between us. Just before dark they had been close enough for us to plainly distinguish that they were green Martians, and all during the long night we distinctly heard the clanking of their accoutrements behind us.

As the sun rose on the second day of our flight it disclosed the pursuing horde not a half-mile in our rear. As they saw us a fiendish shout of triumph rose from their ranks.

Several miles in advance lay a range of hills – the farther shore of the dead sea we had been crossing. Could we but reach these hills our chances of escape would be greatly enhanced, but Thuvia's mount, although carrying the lightest burden, already was showing signs of exhaustion. I was riding beside her when suddenly her animal staggered and lurched against mine. I saw that he was going down, but ere he fell I snatched the girl from his back and swung her to a place upon my own thoat, behind me, where she clung with her arms about me.

This double burden soon proved too much for my already overtaxed beast, and thus our speed was terribly diminished, for the others would proceed no faster than the slowest of us could go. In that little party there was not one who would desert another; yet we were of different countries, different colours, different races, different religions – and one of us was of a different world.

We were quite close to the hills, but the Warhoons were gaining so rapidly that we had given up all hope of reaching them in time. Thuvia and I were in the rear, for our beast was lagging more and more. Suddenly I felt the girl's warm lips press a kiss upon my shoulder. "For thy sake, O my Prince," she murmured. Then her arms slipped from about my waist and she was gone.

I turned and saw that she had deliberately slipped to the ground in the very path of the cruel demons who pursued us, thinking that by lightening the burden of my mount it might thus be enabled to bear me to the safety of the hills. Poor child! She should have known John Carter better than that.

Turning my thoat, I urged him after her, hoping to reach her side and bear her on again in our hopeless flight. Carthoris must have glanced behind him at about the same time and taken in the situation, for by the time I had reached Thuvia's side he was there also, and, springing from his mount, he threw her upon its back and, turning the animal's head toward the hills, gave the beast a sharp crack across the rump with the flat of his sword. Then he attempted to do the same with mine.

The brave boy's act of chivalrous self-sacrifice filled me with pride, nor did I care that it had wrested from us our last frail chance for escape. The Warhoons were now close upon us. Tars Tarkas and Xodar had discovered our absence and were charging rapidly to our support. Everything pointed toward a splendid ending of my second journey to Barsoom. I hated to go out without having seen my divine Princess, and held her in my arms once again; but if it were not writ upon the book of Fate that such was to be, then would I take the most that was coming to me, and in these last few moments that were to be vouchsafed me before I passed over into that unguessed future I could at least give such an account of myself in my chosen vocation as would leave the Warhoons of the South food for discourse for the next twenty generations.

As Carthoris was not mounted, I slipped from the back of my own mount and took my place at his side to meet the charge of the howling devils bearing down upon us. A moment later Tars Tarkas and Xodar ranged themselves on either hand, turning their thoats loose that we might all be on an equal footing.

The Warhoons were perhaps a hundred yards from us when a loud explosion sounded from above and behind us, and almost at the same instant a shell burst in their advancing ranks. At once all was confusion. A hundred warriors toppled to the ground. Riderless thoats plunged hither and thither among the dead and dying. Dismounted warriors were trampled underfoot in the stampede which followed. All semblance of order had left the ranks of the green men, and as they looked far above our heads to trace the origin of this unexpected attack, disorder turned to retreat and retreat to a wild panic. In another moment they were racing as madly away from us as they had before been charging down upon us.

We turned to look in the direction from whence the first report had come, and there we saw, just clearing the tops of the nearer hills, a great battleship swinging majestically through the air. Her bow gun spoke again even as we looked, and another shell burst among the fleeing Warhoons.

As she drew nearer I could not repress a wild cry of elation, for upon her bows I saw the device of Helium.

CHAPTER SIXTEEN
Under Arrest

As CARTHORIS, Xodar, Tars Tarkas, and I stood gazing at the magnificent vessel which meant so much to all of us, we saw a second and then a third top the summit of the hills and glide gracefully after their sister.

Now a score of one-man air scouts were launching from the upper decks of the nearer vessel, and in a moment more were speeding in long, swift dives to the ground about us.

In another instant we were surrounded by armed sailors, and an officer had stepped forward to address us, when his eyes fell upon Carthoris. With an exclamation of surprised pleasure he sprang forward, and, placing his hands upon the boy's shoulder, called him by name.

"Carthoris, my Prince," he cried, "Kaor! Kaor! Hor Vastus greets the son of Dejah Thoris, Princess of Helium, and of her husband, John Carter. Where have you been, O my Prince? All Helium has been plunged in sorrow. Terrible have been the calamities that have befallen your great-grandsire's mighty nation since the fatal day that saw you leave our midst."

"Grieve not, my good Hor Vastus," cried Carthoris, "since I bring not back myself alone to cheer my mother's heart and the hearts of my beloved people, but also one whom all Barsoom loved best – her greatest warrior and her saviour – John Carter, Prince of Helium!"

Hor Vastus turned in the direction indicated by Carthoris, and as his eyes fell upon me he was like to have collapsed from sheer surprise.

"John Carter!" he exclaimed, and then a sudden troubled look came into his eyes. "My Prince," he started, "where hast thou – " and then he stopped, but I knew the question that his lips dared not frame. The loyal fellow would not be the one to force from mine a confession of the terrible truth that I had returned from the bosom of the Iss, the River of Mystery, back from the shore of the Lost Sea of Korus, and the Valley Dor.

"Ah, my Prince," he continued, as though no thought had inter-rupted his greeting, "that you are back is sufficient, and let Hor Vastus' sword have the high honour of being first at thy feet." With these words the noble fellow unbuckled his scabbard and flung his sword upon the ground before me.

Could you know the customs and the character of red Martians you would appreciate the depth of meaning that that simple act conveyed to me and to all about us who witnessed it. The thing was equivalent to saying, "My sword, my body, my life, my soul are yours to do with as you wish. Until death and after death I look to you alone for authority for my every act. Be you right or wrong, your word shall be my only truth. Whoso raises his hand against you must answer to my sword."

It is the oath of fealty that men occasionally pay to a Jeddak whose high character and chivalrous acts have inspired the enthusiastic love of his followers. Never had I known this high tribute paid to a lesser mortal. There was but one response possible. I stooped and lifted the sword from the ground, raised the hilt to my lips, and then, stepping to Hor Vastus, I buckled the weapon upon him with my own hands.

"Hor Vastus," I said, placing my hand upon his shoulder, "you know best the promptings of your own heart. That I shall need your sword I have little doubt, but accept from John Carter upon his sacred honour the assurance that he will never call upon you to draw this sword other than in the cause of truth, justice, and righteousness."

"That I knew, my Prince," he replied, "ere ever I threw my beloved blade at thy feet."

As we spoke other fliers came and went between the ground and the battleship, and presently a larger boat was launched from above, one capable of carrying a dozen persons, perhaps, and dropped lightly near us. As she touched, an officer sprang from her deck to the ground, and, advancing to Hor Vastus, saluted.

"Kantos Kan desires that this party whom we have rescued be brought immediately to the deck of the Xavarian," he said.

As we approached the little craft I looked about for the members of my party and for the first time noticed that Thuvia was not among them. Questioning elicited the fact that none had seen her since Car-thoris had sent her thoat galloping madly toward the hills, in the hope of carrying her out of harm's way.

Immediately Hor Vastus dispatched a dozen air scouts in as many di-rections to search for her. It could not be possible that she had gone far since we had last seen her. We others stepped to the deck of the craft that had been sent to fetch us, and a moment later were upon the Xavarian.

The first man to greet me was Kantos Kan himself. My old friend had won to the highest place in the navy of Helium, but he was still to me the same brave comrade who had shared with me the privations of a Warhoon dungeon, the terrible atrocities of the Great Games, and later the dangers of our search for Dejah Thoris within the hostile city of Zodanga.

Then I had been an unknown wanderer upon a strange planet, and he a simple padwar in the navy of Helium. To-day he commanded all Helium's great terrors of the skies, and I was a Prince of the House of Tardos Mors, Jeddak of Helium.

He did not ask me where I had been. Like Hor Vastus, he too dreaded the truth and would not be the one to wrest a statement from me. That it must come some time he well knew, but until it came he seemed satisfied to but know that I was with him once more. He greeted Carthoris and Tars Tarkas with the keenest delight, but he asked neither where he had been. He could scarcely keep his hands off the boy.

"You do not know, John Carter," he said to me, "how we of Helium love this son of yours. It is as though all the great love we bore his noble father and his poor mother had been centred in him. When it became known that he was lost, ten million people wept."

"What mean you, Kantos Kan," I whispered, "by 'his poor mother'?" for the words had seemed to carry a sinister meaning which I could not fathom.

He drew me to one side.

"For a year," he said, "Ever since Carthoris disappeared, Dejah Thoris has grieved and mourned for her lost boy. The blow of years ago, when you did not return from the atmosphere plant, was lessened to some extent by the duties of motherhood, for your son broke his white shell that very night."

"That she suffered terribly then, all Helium knew, for did not all Helium suffer with her the loss of her lord! But with the boy gone there was nothing left, and after expedition upon expedition returned with the same hopeless tale of no clue as to his whereabouts, our beloved Princess drooped lower and lower, until all who saw her felt that it could be but a matter of days ere she went to join her loved ones within the precincts of the Valley Dor.

"As a last resort, Mors Kajak, her father, and Tardos Mors, her grandfather, took command of two mighty expeditions, and a month ago sailed away to explore every inch of ground in the northern hemisphere of Barsoom. For two weeks no word has come back from them, but rumours were rife that they had met with a terrible disaster and that all were dead.

"About this time Zat Arras renewed his importunities for her hand in marriage. He has been for ever after her since you disappeared. She hated him and feared him, but with both her father and grandfather gone, Zat Arras was very powerful, for he is still Jed of Zodanga, to which position, you will remember, Tardos Mors appointed him after you had refused the honour.

"He had a secret audience with her six days ago. What took place none knows, but the next day Dejah Thoris had disappeared, and with her had gone a dozen of her household guard and body servants, including Sola the green woman – Tars Tarkas' daughter, you recall. No word left they of their intentions, but it is always thus with those who go upon the voluntary pilgrimage from which none returns. We cannot think aught than that Dejah Thoris has sought the icy bosom of Iss, and that her devoted servants have chosen to accompany her.

"Zat Arras was at Helium when she disappeared. He commands this fleet which has been searching for her since. No trace of her have we found, and I fear that it be a futile quest."

While we talked, Hor Vastus' fliers were returning to the Xavarian. Not one, however, had discovered a trace of Thuvia. I was much depressed over the news of Dejah Thoris' disappearance, and now there was added the further burden of apprehension concerning the fate of this girl whom I believed to be the daughter of some proud Barsoomian house, and it had been my intention to make every effort to return her to her people.

I was about to ask Kantos Kan to prosecute a further search for her when a flier from the flagship of the fleet arrived at the Xavarian with an officer bearing a message to Kantos Kan from Arras.

My friend read the dispatch and then turned to me.

"Zat Arras commands me to bring our 'prisoners' before him. There is naught else to do. He is supreme in Helium, yet it would be far more in keeping with chivalry and good taste were he to come hither and greet the saviour of Barsoom with the honours that are his due."

"You know full well, my friend," I said, smiling, "that Zat Arras has good cause to hate me. Nothing would please him better than to humiliate me and then to kill me. Now that he has so excellent an excuse, let us go and see if he has the courage to take advantage of it."

Summoning Carthoris, Tars Tarkas, and Xodar, we entered the small flier with Kantos Kan and Zat Arras' officer, and in a moment were stepping to the deck of Zat Arras' flagship.

As we approached the Jed of Zodanga no sign of greeting or recognition crossed his face; not even to Carthoris did he vouchsafe a friendly word. His attitude was cold, haughty, and uncompromising.

"Kaor, Zat Arras," I said in greeting, but he did not respond.

"Why were these prisoners not disarmed?" he asked to Kantos Kan.

"They are not prisoners, Zat Arras," replied the officer.

"Two of them are of Helium's noblest family. Tars Tarkas, Jeddak of Thark, is Tardos Mors' best beloved ally. The other is a friend and companion of the Prince of Helium – that is enough for me to know."

"It is not enough for me, however," retorted Zat Arras. "More must I hear from those who have taken the pilgrimage than their names. Where have you been, John Carter?"

"I have just come from the Valley Dor and the Land of the First Born, Zat Arras," I replied.

"Ah!" he exclaimed in evident pleasure, "you do not deny it, then? You have returned from the bosom of Iss?"

"I have come back from a land of false hope, from a valley of torture and death; with my companions I have escaped from the hideous clutches of lying fiends. I have come back to the Barsoom that I saved from a painless death to again save her, but this time from death in its most frightful form."

"Cease, blasphemer!" cried Zat Arras. "Hope not to save thy cowardly carcass by inventing horrid lies to – " But he got no further. One does not call John Carter "coward" and "liar" thus lightly, and Zat Arras should have known it. Before a hand could be raised to stop me, I was at his side and one hand grasped his throat.

"Come I from heaven or hell, Zat Arras, you will find me still the same John Carter that I have always been; nor did ever man call me such names and live – without apologizing." And with that I commenced to bend him back across my knee and tighten my grip upon his throat.

"Seize him!" cried Zat Arras, and a dozen officers sprang forward to assist him.

Kantos Kan came close and whispered to me.

"Desist, I beg of you. It will but involve us all, for I cannot see these men lay hands upon you without aiding you. My officers and men will join me and we shall have a mutiny then that may lead to the revolution. For the sake of Tardos Mors and Helium, desist."

At his words I released Zat Arras and, turning my back upon him, walked toward the ship's rail.

"Come, Kantos Kan," I said, "the Prince of Helium would return to the Xavarian."

None interfered. Zat Arras stood white and trembling amidst his officers. Some there were who looked upon him with scorn and drew toward me, while one, a man long in the service and confidence of Tardos Mors, spoke to me in a low tone as I passed him.

"You may count my metal among your fighting-men, John Carter," he said.

I thanked him and passed on. In silence we embarked, and shortly after stepped once more upon the deck of the Xavarian. Fifteen minutes later we received orders from the flagship to proceed toward Helium.

Our journey thither was uneventful. Carthoris and I were wrapped in the gloomiest of thoughts. Kantos Kan was sombre in contemplation of the further calamity that might fall upon Helium should Zat Arras attempt to follow the age-old precedent that allotted a terrible death to fugitives from the Valley Dor. Tars Tarkas grieved for the loss of his daughter. Xodar alone was care-free – a fugitive and outlaw, he could be no worse off in Helium than elsewhere.

"Let us hope that we may at least go out with good red blood upon our blades," he said. It was a simple wish and one most likely to be gratified.

Among the officers of the Xavarian I thought I could discern division into factions ere we had reached Helium. There were those who gathered about Carthoris and myself whenever the opportunity presented, while about an equal number held aloof from us. They offered us only the most courteous treatment, but were evidently bound by their superstitious belief in the doctrine of Dor and Iss and Korus. I could not blame them, for I knew how strong a hold a creed, however ridiculous it may be, may gain upon an otherwise intelligent people.

By returning from Dor we had committed a sacrilege; by recounting our adventures there, and stating the facts as they existed we had outraged the religion of their fathers. We were blasphemers – lying heretics. Even those who still clung to us from personal love and loyalty I think did so in the face of the fact that at heart they questioned our veracity – it is very hard to accept a new religion for an old, no matter how alluring the promises of the new may be; but to reject the old as a tissue of falsehoods without being offered anything in its stead is indeed a most difficult thing to ask of any people.

Kantos Kan would not talk of our experiences among the therns and the First Born.

"It is enough," he said, "that I jeopardize my life here and hereafter by countenancing you at all – do not ask me to add still further to my sins by listening to what I have always been taught was the rankest heresy."

I knew that sooner or later the time must come when our friends and enemies would be forced to declare themselves openly. When we reached Helium there must be an accounting, and if Tardos Mors had not returned I feared that the enmity of Zat Arras might weigh heavily against us, for he represented the government of Helium. To take sides against him were equivalent to treason. The majority of the troops would doubtless follow the lead of their officers, and I knew that many of the highest and most powerful men of both land and air forces would cleave to John Carter in the face of god, man, or devil.

On the other hand, the majority of the populace unquestionably would demand that we pay the penalty of our sacrilege. The outlook seemed dark from whatever angle I viewed it, but my mind was so torn with anguish at the thought of Dejah Thoris that I realize now that I gave the terrible question of Helium's plight but scant attention at that time.

There was always before me, day and night, a horrible nightmare of the frightful scenes through which I knew my Princess might even then be passing – the horrid plant men – the ferocious white apes. At times I would cover my face with my hands in a vain effort to shut out the fearful thing from my mind.

It was in the forenoon that we arrived above the mile-high scarlet tower which marks greater Helium from her twin city. As we descended in great circles toward the navy docks a mighty multitude could be seen surging in the streets beneath. Helium had been notified by radio-aerogram of our approach.

From the deck of the Xavarian we four, Carthoris, Tars Tarkas, Xodar, and I, were transferred to a lesser flier to be transported to quarters within the Temple of Reward. It is here that Martian justice is meted to benefactor and malefactor. Here the hero is decorated. Here the felon is condemned. We were taken into the temple from the landing stage upon the roof, so that we did not pass among the people at all, as is customary. Always before I had seen prisoners of note, or returned wanderers of eminence, paraded from the Gate of Jeddaks to the Temple of Reward up the broad Avenue of Ancestors through dense crowds of jeering or cheering citizens.

I knew that Zat Arras dared not trust the people near to us, for he feared that their love for Carthoris and myself might break into a demonstration which would wipe out their superstitious horror of the crime we were to be charged with. What his plans were I could only guess, but that they were sinister was evidenced by the fact that only his most trusted servitors accompanied us upon the flier to the Temple of Reward.

We were lodged in a room upon the south side of the temple, overlooking the Avenue of Ancestors down which we could see the full length to the Gate of Jeddaks, five miles away. The people in the temple plaza and in the streets for a distance of a full mile were standing as close packed as it was possible for them to get. They were very orderly – there were neither scoffs nor plaudits, and when they saw us at the window above them there were many who buried their faces in their arms and wept.

Late in the afternoon a messenger arrived from Zat Arras to inform us that we would be tried by an impartial body of nobles in the great hall of the temple at the 1st zode* on the following day, or about 8:40 A.M. Earth time.

*Wherever Captain Carter has used Martian measurements of time, distance, weight, and the like I have translated them into as nearly their equivalent in earthly values as is possible. His notes contain many Martian tables, and a great volume of scientific data, but since the International Astronomic Society is at present engaged in classifying, investigating, and verifying this vast fund of remarkable and valuable information, I have felt that it will add nothing to the interest of Captain Carter's story or to the sum total of human knowledge to maintain a strict adherence to the original manuscript in these matters, while it might readily confuse the reader and detract from the interest of the history. For those who may be interested, however, I will explain that the Martian day is a trifle over 24 hours 37 minutes duration (Earth time). This the Martians divide into ten equal parts, commencing the day at about 6 A.M. Earth time. The zodes are divided into fifty shorter periods, each of which in turn is composed of 200 brief periods of time, about equivalent to the earthly second. The Barsoomian Table of Time as here given is but a part of the full table appearing in Captain Carter's notes.

TABLE

200 tals 1 xat
50 xats 1 zode
10 zodes 1 revolution of Mars upon its axis.

CHAPTER SEVENTEEN
The Death Sentence

A FEW MOMENTS before the appointed time on the following morning a strong guard of Zat Arras' officers appeared at our quarters to conduct us to the great hall of the temple.

In twos we entered the chamber and marched down the broad Aisle of Hope, as it is called, to the platform in the centre of the hall. Before and behind us marched armed guards, while three solid ranks of Zodangan soldiery lined either side of the aisle from the entrance to the rostrum.

As we reached the raised enclosure I saw our judges. As is the custom upon Barsoom there were thirty-one, supposedly selected by lot from men of the noble class, for nobles were on trial. But to my amazement I saw no single friendly face among them. Practically all were Zodangans, and it was I to whom Zodanga owed her defeat at the hands of the green hordes and her subsequent vassalage to Helium. There could be little justice here for John Carter, or his son, or for the great Thark who had commanded the savage tribesmen who overran Zodanga's broad avenues, looting, burning, and murdering.

About us the vast circular coliseum was packed to its full capacity. All classes were represented – all ages, and both sexes. As we entered the hall the hum of subdued conversation ceased until as we halted upon the platform, or Throne of Righteousness, the silence of death enveloped the ten thousand spectators.

The judges were seated in a great circle about the periphery of the circular platform. We were assigned seats with our backs toward a small platform in the exact centre of the larger one. This placed us facing the judges and the audience. Upon the smaller platform each would take his place while his case was being heard.

Zat Arras himself sat in the golden chair of the presiding magistrate. As we were seated and our guards retired to the foot of the stairway leading to the platform, he arose and called my name.

"John Carter," he cried, "take your place upon the Pedestal of Truth to be judged impartially according to your acts and here to know the reward you have earned thereby." Then turning to and fro toward the audience he narrated the acts upon the value of which my reward was to be determined.

"Know you, O judges and people of Helium," he said, "that John Carter, one time Prince of Helium, has returned by his own statement from the Valley Dor and even from the Temple of Issus itself. That, in the presence of many men of Helium he has blasphemed against the Sacred Iss, and against the Valley Dor, and the Lost Sea of Korus, and the Holy Therns themselves, and even against Issus, Goddess of Death, and of Life Eternal. And know you further by witness of thine own eyes that see him here now upon the Pedestal of Truth that he has indeed returned from these sacred precincts in the face of our ancient customs, and in violation of the sanctity of our ancient religion.

"He who be once dead may not live again. He who attempts it must be made dead for ever. Judges, your duty lies plain before you – here can be no testimony in contravention of truth. What reward shall be meted to John Carter in accordance with the acts he has committed?"

"Death!" shouted one of the judges.

And then a man sprang to his feet in the audience, and raising his hand on high, cried: "Justice! Justice! Justice!" It was Kantos Kan, and as all eyes turned toward him he leaped past the Zodangan soldiery and sprang upon the platform.

"What manner of justice be this?" he cried to Zat Arras. "The defendant has not been heard, nor has he had an opportunity to call others in his behalf. In the name of the people of Helium I demand fair and impartial treatment for the Prince of Helium."

A great cry arose from the audience then: "Justice! Justice! Justice!" and Zat Arras dared not deny them.

"Speak, then," he snarled, turning to me; "but blaspheme not against the things that are sacred upon Barsoom."

"Men of Helium," I cried, turning to the spectators, and speaking over the heads of my judges, "how can John Carter expect justice from the men of Zodanga? He cannot nor does he ask it. It is to the men of Helium that he states his case; nor does he appeal for mercy to any. It is not in his own cause that he speaks now – it is in thine. In the cause of your wives and daughters, and of wives and daughters yet unborn. It is to save them from the unthinkably atrocious indignities that I have seen heaped upon the fair women of Barsoom in the place men call the Temple of Issus. It is to save them from the sucking embrace of the plant men, from the fangs of the great white apes of Dor, from the cruel lust of the Holy Therns, from all that the cold, dead Iss carries them to from homes of love and life and happiness.

"Sits there no man here who does not know the history of John Carter. How he came among you from another world and rose from a prisoner among the green men, through torture and persecution, to a place high among the highest of Barsoom. Nor ever did you know John Carter to lie in his own behalf, or to say aught that might harm the people of Barsoom, or to speak lightly of the strange religion which he respected without understanding.

"There be no man here, or elsewhere upon Barsoom to-day who does not owe his life directly to a single act of mine, in which I sacrificed myself and the happiness of my Princess that you might live. And so, men of Helium, I think that I have the right to demand that I be heard, that I be believed, and that you let me serve you and save you from the false hereafter of Dor and Issus as I saved you from the real death that other day.

"It is to you of Helium that I speak now. When I am done let the men of Zodanga have their will with me. Zat Arras has taken my sword from me, so the men of Zodanga no longer fear me. Will you listen?"

"Speak, John Carter, Prince of Helium," cried a great noble from the audience, and the multitude echoed his permission, until the building rocked with the noise of their demonstration.

Zat Arras knew better than to interfere with such a sentiment as was expressed that day in the Temple of Reward, and so for two hours I talked with the people of Helium.

But when I had finished, Zat Arras arose and, turning to the judges, said in a low tone: "My nobles, you have heard John Carter's plea; every opportunity has been given him to prove his innocence if he be not guilty; but instead he has but utilized the time in further blasphemy. What, gentlemen, is your verdict?"

"Death to the blasphemer!" cried one, springing to his feet, and in an instant the entire thirty-one judges were on their feet with upraised swords in token of the unanimity of their verdict.

If the people did not hear Zat Arras' charge, they certainly did hear the verdict of the tribunal. A sullen murmur rose louder and louder about the packed coliseum, and then Kantos Kan, who had not left the platform since first he had taken his place near me, raised his hand for silence. When he could be heard he spoke to the people in a cool and level voice.

"You have heard the fate that the men of Zodanga would mete to Helium's noblest hero. It may be the duty of the men of Helium to accept the verdict as final. Let each man act according to his own heart. Here is the answer of Kantos Kan, head of the navy of Helium, to Zat Arras and his judges," and with that he unbuckled his scabbard and threw his sword at my feet.

In an instant soldiers and citizens, officers and nobles were crowding past the soldiers of Zodanga and forcing their way to the Throne of Righteousness. A hundred men surged upon the platform, and a hundred blades rattled and clanked to the floor at my feet. Zat Arras and his officers were furious, but they were helpless. One by one I raised the swords to my lips and buckled them again upon their owners.

"Come," said Kantos Kan, "we will escort John Carter and his party to his own palace," and they formed about us and started toward the stairs leading to the Aisle of Hope.

"Stop!" cried Zat Arras. "Soldiers of Helium, let no prisoner leave the Throne of Righteousness."

The soldiery from Zodanga were the only organized body of Heliumetic troops within the temple, so Zat Arras was confident that his orders would be obeyed, but I do not think that he looked for the opposition that was raised the moment the soldiers advanced toward the throne.

From every quarter of the coliseum swords flashed and men rushed threateningly upon the Zodangans. Some one raised a cry: "Tardos Mors is dead – a thousand years to John Carter, Jeddak of Helium." As I heard that and saw the ugly attitude of the men of Helium toward the soldiers of Zat Arras, I knew that only a miracle could avert a clash that would end in civil war.

"Hold!" I cried, leaping to the Pedestal of Truth once more. "Let no man move till I am done. A single sword thrust here to-day may plunge Helium into a bitter and bloody war the results of which none can foresee. It will turn brother against brother and father against son. No man's life is worth that sacrifice. Rather would I submit to the biased judgment of Zat Arras than be the cause of civil strife in Helium.

"Let us each give in a point to the other, and let this entire matter rest until Tardos Mors returns, or Mors Kajak, his son. If neither be back at the end of a year a second trial may be held – the thing has a precedent." And then turning to Zat Arras, I said in a low voice: "Unless you be a bigger fool than I take you to be, you will grasp the chance I am offering you ere it is too late. Once that multitude of swords below is drawn against your soldiery no man upon Barsoom – not even Tardos Mors himself – can avert the consequences. What say you? Speak quickly."

The Jed of Zodangan Helium raised his voice to the angry sea beneath us.

"Stay your hands, men of Helium," he shouted, his voice trembling with rage. "The sentence of the court is passed, but the day of retribution has not been set. I, Zat Arras, Jed of Zodanga, appreciating the royal connections of the prisoner and his past services to Helium and Barsoom, grant a respite of one year, or until the return of Mors Kajak, or Tardos Mors to Helium. Disperse quietly to your houses. Go."

No one moved. Instead, they stood in tense silence with their eyes fastened upon me, as though waiting for a signal to attack.

"Clear the temple," commanded Zat Arras, in a low tone to one of his officers.

Fearing the result of an attempt to carry out this order by force, I stepped to the edge of the platform and, pointing toward the main entrance, bid them pass out. As one man they turned at my request and filed, silent and threatening, past the soldiers of Zat Arras, Jed of Zodanga, who stood scowling in impotent rage.

Kantos Kan with the others who had sworn allegiance to me still stood upon the Throne of Righteousness with me.

"Come," said Kantos Kan to me, "we will escort you to your palace, my Prince. Come, Carthoris and Xodar. Come, Tars Tarkas." And with a haughty sneer for Zat Arras upon his handsome lips, he turned and strode to the throne steps and up the Aisle of Hope. We four and the hundred loyal ones followed behind him, nor was a hand raised to stay us, though glowering eyes followed our triumphal march through the temple.

In the avenues we found a press of people, but they opened a pathway for us, and many were the swords that were flung at my feet as I passed through the city of Helium toward my palace upon the outskirts. Here my old slaves fell upon their knees and kissed my hands as I greeted them. They cared not where I had been. It was enough that I had returned to them.

"Ah, master," cried one, "if our divine Princess were but here this would be a day indeed."

Tears came to my eyes, so that I was forced to turn away that I might hide my emotions. Carthoris wept openly as the slaves pressed about him with expressions of affection, and words of sorrow for our common loss. It was now that Tars Tarkas for the first time learned that his daughter, Sola, had accompanied Dejah Thoris upon the last long pilgrimage. I had not had the heart to tell him what Kantos Kan had told me. With the stoicism of the green Martian he showed no sign of suffering, yet I knew that his grief was as poignant as my own. In marked contrast to his kind, he had in well-developed form the kindlier human characteristics of love, friendship, and charity.

It was a sad and sombre party that sat at the feast of welcome in the great dining hall of the palace of the Prince of Helium that day. We were over a hundred strong, not counting the members of my little court, for Dejah Thoris and I had maintained a household consistent with our royal rank.

The board, according to red Martian custom, was triangular, for there were three in our family. Carthoris and I presided in the centre of our sides of the table – midway of the third side Dejah Thoris' high-backed, carven chair stood vacant except for her gorgeous wedding trappings and jewels which were draped upon it. Behind stood a slave as in the days when his mistress had occupied her place at the board, ready to do her bidding. It was the way upon Barsoom, so I endured the anguish of it, though it wrung my heart to see that silent chair where should have been my laughing and vivacious Princess keeping the great hall ringing with her merry gaiety.

At my right sat Kantos Kan, while to the right of Dejah Thoris' empty place Tars Tarkas sat in a huge chair before a raised section of the board which years ago I had had constructed to meet the requirements of his mighty bulk. The place of honour at a Martian hoard is always at the hostess's right, and this place was ever reserved by Dejah Thoris for the great Thark upon the occasions that he was in Helium.

Hor Vastus sat in the seat of honour upon Carthoris' side of the table. There was little general conversation. It was a quiet and saddened party. The loss of Dejah Thoris was still fresh in the minds of all, and to this was added fear for the safety of Tardos Mors and Mors Kajak, as well as doubt and uncertainty as to the fate of Helium, should it prove true that she was permanently deprived of her great Jeddak.

Suddenly our attention was attracted by the sound of distant shouting, as of many people raising their voices at once, but whether in anger or rejoicing, we could not tell. Nearer and nearer came the tumult. A slave rushed into the dining hall to cry that a great concourse of people was swarming through the palace gates. A second burst upon the heels of the first alternately laughing and shrieking as a madman.

"Dejah Thoris is found!" he cried. "A messenger from Dejah Thoris!"

I waited to hear no more. The great windows of the dining hall overlooked the avenue leading to the main gates – they were upon the opposite side of the hall from me with the table intervening. I did not waste time in circling the great board – with a single leap I cleared table and diners and sprang upon the balcony beyond. Thirty feet below lay the scarlet sward of the lawn and beyond were many people crowding about a great thoat which bore a rider headed toward the palace. I vaulted to the ground below and ran swiftly toward the advancing party.

As I came near to them I saw that the figure on the thoat was Sola.

"Where is the Princess of Helium?" I cried.

The green girl slid from her mighty mount and ran toward me.

"O my Prince! My Prince!" she cried. "She is gone for ever. Even now she may be a captive upon the lesser moon. The black pirates of Barsoom have stolen her."

CHAPTER EIGHTEEN
Sola's Story

ONCE WITHIN THE PALACE, I drew Sola to the dining hall, and, when she had greeted her father after the formal manner of the green men, she told the story of the pilgrimage and capture of Dejah Thoris.

"Seven days ago, after her audience with Zat Arras, Dejah Thoris attempted to slip from the palace in the dead of night. Although I had not heard the outcome of her interview with Zat Arras I knew that something had occurred then to cause her the keenest mental agony, and when I discovered her creeping from the palace I did not need to be told her destination.

"Hastily arousing a dozen of her most faithful guards, I explained my fears to them, and as one they enlisted with me to follow our beloved Princess in her wanderings, even to the Sacred Iss and the Valley Dor. We came upon her but a short distance from the palace. With her was faithful Woola the hound, but none other. When we overtook her she feigned anger, and ordered us back to the palace, but for once we disobeyed her, and when she found that we would not let her go upon the last long pilgrimage alone, she wept and embraced us, and together we went out into the night toward the south.

"The following day we came upon a herd of small thoats, and thereafter we were mounted and made good time. We travelled very fast and very far due south until the morning of the fifth day we sighted a great fleet of battleships sailing north. They saw us before we could seek shelter, and soon we were surrounded by a horde of black men. The Princess's guard fought nobly to the end, but they were soon overcome and slain. Only Dejah Thoris and I were spared.

"When she realized that she was in the clutches of the black pirates, she attempted to take her own life, but one of the blacks tore her dagger from her, and then they bound us both so that we could not use our hands.

"The fleet continued north after capturing us. There were about twenty large battleships in all, besides a number of small swift cruisers. That evening one of the smaller cruisers that had been far in advance of the fleet returned with a prisoner – a young red woman whom they had picked up in a range of hills under the very noses, they said, of a fleet of three red Martian battleships.

"From scraps of conversation which we overheard it was evident that the black pirates were searching for a party of fugitives that had escaped them several days prior. That they considered the capture of the young woman important was evident from the long and earnest interview the commander of the fleet held with her when she was brought to him. Later she was bound and placed in the compartment with Dejah Thoris and myself.

"The new captive was a very beautiful girl. She told Dejah Thoris that many years ago she had taken the voluntary pilgrimage from the court of her father, the Jeddak of Ptarth. She was Thuvia, the Princess of Ptarth. And then she asked Dejah Thoris who she might be, and when she heard she fell upon her knees and kissed Dejah Thoris' fettered hands, and told her that that very morning she had been with John Carter, Prince of Helium, and Carthoris, her son.

"Dejah Thoris could not believe her at first, but finally when the girl had narrated all the strange adventures that had befallen her since she had met John Carter, and told her of the things John Carter, and Carthoris, and Xodar had narrated of their adventures in the Land of the First Born, Dejah Thoris knew that it could be none other than the Prince of Helium; 'For who,' she said, 'upon all Barsoom other than John Carter could have done the deeds you tell of.' And when Thuvia told Dejah Thoris of her love for John Carter, and his loyalty and devotion to the Princess of his choice, Dejah Thoris broke down and wept – cursing Zat Arras and the cruel fate that had driven her from Helium but a few brief days before the return of her beloved lord.

"'I do not blame you for loving him, Thuvia,' she said; 'and that your affection for him is pure and sincere I can well believe from the candour of your avowal of it to me.'

"The fleet continued north nearly to Helium, but last night they evidently realized that John Carter had indeed escaped them and so they turned toward the south once more. Shortly thereafter a guard entered our compartment and dragged me to the deck.

"'There is no place in the Land of the First Born for a green one,' he said, and with that he gave me a terrific shove that carried me toppling from the deck of the battleship. Evidently this seemed to him the easiest way of ridding the vessel of my presence and killing me at the same time.

"But a kind fate intervened, and by a miracle I escaped with but slight bruises. The ship was moving slowly at the time, and as I lunged overboard into the darkness beneath I shuddered at the awful plunge I thought awaited me, for all day the fleet had sailed thousands of feet above the ground; but to my utter surprise I struck upon a soft mass of vegetation not twenty feet from the deck of the ship. In fact, the keel of the vessel must have been grazing the surface of the ground at the time.

"I lay all night where I had fallen and the next morning brought an explanation of the fortunate coincidence that had saved me from a terrible death. As the sun rose I saw a vast panorama of sea bottom and distant hills lying far below me. I was upon the highest peak of a lofty range. The fleet in the darkness of the preceding night had barely grazed the crest of the hills, and in the brief span that they hovered close to the surface the black guard had pitched me, as he supposed, to my death.

"A few miles west of me was a great waterway. When I reached it I found to my delight that it belonged to Helium. Here a thoat was procured for me – the rest you know."

For many minutes none spoke. Dejah Thoris in the clutches of the First Born! I shuddered at the thought, but of a sudden the old fire of unconquerable self-confidence surged through me. I sprang to my feet, and with back-thrown shoulders and upraised sword took a solemn vow to reach, rescue, and revenge my Princess.

A hundred swords leaped from a hundred scabbards, and a hundred fighting-men sprang to the table-top and pledged me their lives and fortunes to the expedition. Already my plans were formulated. I thanked each loyal friend, and leaving Carthoris to entertain them, withdrew to my own audience chamber with Kantos Kan, Tars Tarkas, Xodar, and Hor Vastus.

Here we discussed the details of our expedition until long after dark. Xodar was positive that Issus would choose both Dejah Thoris and Thuvia to serve her for a year.

"For that length of time at least they will be comparatively safe," he said, "and we will at least know where to look for them."

In the matter of equipping a fleet to enter Omean the details were left to Kantos Kan and Xodar. The former agreed to take such vessels as we required into dock as rapidly as possible, where Xodar would direct their equipment with water propellers.

For many years the black had been in charge of the refitting of captured battleships that they might navigate Omean, and so was familiar with the construction of the propellers, housings, and the auxiliary gearing required.

It was estimated that it would require six months to complete our preparations in view of the fact that the utmost secrecy must be maintained to keep the project from the ears of Zat Arras. Kantos Kan was confident now that the man's ambitions were fully aroused and that nothing short of the title of Jeddak of Helium would satisfy him.

"I doubt," he said, "if he would even welcome Dejah Thoris' return, for it would mean another nearer the throne than he. With you and Carthoris out of the way there would be little to prevent him from assuming the title of Jeddak, and you may rest assured that so long as he is supreme here there is no safety for either of you."

"There is a way," cried Hor Vastus, "to thwart him effectually and for ever."

"What?" I asked.

He smiled.

"I shall whisper it here, but some day I shall stand upon the dome of the Temple of Reward and shout it to cheering multitudes below."

"What do you mean?" asked Kantos Kan.

"John Carter, Jeddak of Helium," said Hor Vastus in a low voice.

The eyes of my companions lighted, and grim smiles of pleasure and anticipation overspread their faces, as each eye turned toward me questioningly. But I shook my head.

"No, my friends," I said, smiling, "I thank you, but it cannot be. Not yet, at least. When we know that Tardos Mors and Mors Kajak are gone to return no more; if I be here, then I shall join you all to see that the people of Helium are permitted to choose fairly their next Jeddak. Whom they choose may count upon the loyalty of my sword, nor shall I seek the honour for myself. Until then Tardos Mors is Jeddak of Helium, and Zat Arras is his representative."

"As you will, John Carter," said Hor Vastus, "but – What was that?" he whispered, pointing toward the window overlooking the gardens.

The words were scarce out of his mouth ere he had sprung to the balcony without.

"There he goes!" he cried excitedly. "The guards! Below there! The guards!"

We were close behind him, and all saw the figure of a man run quickly across a little piece of sward and disappear in the shrubbery beyond.

"He was on the balcony when I first saw him," cried Hor Vastus. "Quick! Let us follow him!"

Together we ran to the gardens, but even though we scoured the grounds with the entire guard for hours, no trace could we find of the night marauder.

"What do you make of it, Kantos Kan?" asked Tars Tarkas.

"A spy sent by Zat Arras," he replied. "It was ever his way."

"He will have something interesting to report to his master then," laughed Hor Vastus.

"I hope he heard only our references to a new Jeddak," I said. "If he overheard our plans to rescue Dejah Thoris, it will mean civil war, for he will attempt to thwart us, and in that I will not be thwarted. There would I turn against Tardos Mors himself, were it necessary. If it throws all Helium into a bloody conflict, I shall go on with these plans to save my Princess. Nothing shall stay me now short of death, and should I die, my friends, will you take oath to prosecute the search for her and bring her back in safety to her grandfather's court?"

Upon the hilt of his sword each of them swore to do as I had asked.

It was agreed that the battleships that were to be remodelled should be ordered to Hastor, another Heliumetic city, far to the south-west. Kantos Kan thought that the docks there, in addition to their regular work, would accommodate at least six battleships at a time. As he was commander-in-chief of the navy, it would be a simple matter for him to order the vessels there as they could be handled, and thereafter keep the remodelled fleet in remote parts of the empire until we should be ready to assemble it for the dash upon Omean.

It was late that night before our conference broke up, but each man there had his particular duties outlined, and the details of the entire plan had been mapped out.

Kantos Kan and Xodar were to attend to the remodelling of the ships. Tars Tarkas was to get into communication with Thark and learn the sentiments of his people toward his return from Dor. If favourable, he was to repair immediately to Thark and devote his time to the assembling of a great horde of green warriors whom it was our plan to send in transports directly to the Valley Dor and the Temple of Issus, while the fleet entered Omean and destroyed the vessels of the First Born.

Upon Hor Vastus devolved the delicate mission of organising a secret force of fighting-men sworn to follow John Carter wherever he might lead. As we estimated that it would require over a million men to man the thousand great battleships we intended to use on Omean and the transports for the green men as well as the ships that were to convoy the transports, it was no trifling job that Hor Vastus had before him.

After they had left I bid Carthoris good-night, for I was very tired, and going to my own apartments, bathed and lay down upon my sleeping silks and furs for the first good night's sleep I had had an opportunity to look forward to since I had returned to Barsoom. But even now I was to be disappointed.

How long I slept I do not know. When I awoke suddenly it was to find a half-dozen powerful men upon me, a gag already in my mouth, and a moment later my arms and legs securely bound. So quickly had they worked and to such good purpose, that I was utterly beyond the power to resist them by the time I was fully awake.

Never a word spoke they, and the gag effectually prevented me speaking. Silently they lifted me and bore me toward the door of my chamber. As they passed the window through which the farther moon was casting its brilliant beams, I saw that each of the party had his face swathed in layers of silk – I could not recognize one of them.

When they had come into the corridor with me, they turned toward a secret panel in the wall which led to the passage that terminated in the pits beneath the palace. That any knew of this panel outside my own household, I was doubtful. Yet the leader of the band did not hesitate a moment. He stepped directly to the panel, touched the concealed button, and as the door swung open he stood aside while his companions entered with me. Then he closed the panel behind him and followed us.

Down through the passageways to the pits we went. The leader rapped upon it with the hilt of his sword – three quick, sharp blows, a pause, then three more, another pause, and then two. A second later the wall swung in, and I was pushed within a brilliantly lighted chamber in which sat three richly trapped men.

One of them turned toward me with a sardonic smile upon his thin, cruel lips – it was Zat Arras.

CHAPTER NINETEEN

Black Despair

"Ah," said Zat Arras, "to what kindly circumstance am I indebted for the pleasure of this unexpected visit from the Prince of Helium?"

While he was speaking, one of my guards had removed the gag from my mouth, but I made no reply to Zat Arras: simply standing there in silence with level gaze fixed upon the Jed of Zodanga. And I doubt not that my expression was coloured by the contempt I felt for the man.

The eyes of those within the chamber were fixed first upon me and then upon Zat Arras, until finally a flush of anger crept slowly over his face.

"You may go," he said to those who had brought me, and when only his two companions and ourselves were left in the chamber, he spoke to me again in a voice of ice – very slowly and deliberately, with many pauses, as though he would choose his words cautiously.

"John Carter," he said, "by the edict of custom, by the law of our religion, and by the verdict of an impartial court, you are condemned to die. The people cannot save you – I alone may accomplish that. You are absolutely in my power to do with as I wish – I may kill you, or I may free you, and should I elect to kill you, none would be the wiser.

"Should you go free in Helium for a year, in accordance with the conditions of your reprieve, there is little fear that the people would ever insist upon the execution of the sentence imposed upon you.

"You may go free within two minutes, upon one condition. Tardos Mors will never return to Helium. Neither will Mors Kajak, nor Dejah Thoris. Helium must select a new Jeddak within the year. Zat Arras would be Jeddak of Helium. Say that you will espouse my cause. This is the price of your freedom. I am done."

I knew it was within the scope of Zat Arras' cruel heart to destroy me, and if I were dead I could see little reason to doubt that he might easily become Jeddak of Helium. Free, I could prosecute the search for Dejah Thoris. Were I dead, my brave comrades might not be able to carry out our plans. So, by refusing to accede to his request, it was quite probable that not only would I not prevent him from becoming Jeddak of Helium, but that I would be the means of sealing Dejah Thoris' fate – of consigning her, through my refusal, to the horrors of the arena of Issus.

For a moment I was perplexed, but for a moment only. The proud daughter of a thousand Jeddaks would choose death to a dishonorable alliance such as this, nor could John Carter do less for Helium than his Princess would do.

Then I turned to Zat Arras.

"There can be no alliance," I said, "between a traitor to Helium and a prince of the House of Tardos Mors. I do not believe, Zat Arras, that the great Jeddak is dead."

Zat Arras shrugged his shoulders.

"It will not be long, John Carter," he said, "that your opinions will be of interest even to yourself, so make the best of them while you can. Zat Arras will permit you in due time to reflect further upon the magnanimous offer he has made you. Into the silence and darkness of the pits you will enter upon your reflection this night with the knowledge that should you fail within a reasonable time to agree to the alternative which has been offered you, never shall you emerge from the darkness and the silence again. Nor shall you know at what minute the hand will reach out through the darkness and the silence with the keen dagger that shall rob you of your last chance to win again the warmth and the freedom and joyousness of the outer world."

Zat Arras clapped his hands as he ceased speaking. The guards returned. Zat Arras waved his hand in my direction.

"To the pits," he said. That was all. Four men accompanied me from the chamber, and with a radium hand-light to illumine the way, escorted me through seemingly interminable tunnels, down, ever down beneath the city of Helium.

At length they halted within a fair-sized chamber. There were rings set in the rocky walls. To them chains were fastened, and at the ends of many of the chains were human skeletons. One of these they kicked aside, and, unlocking the huge padlock that had held a chain about what had once been a human ankle, they snapped the iron band about my own leg. Then they left me, taking the light with them.

Utter darkness prevailed. For a few minutes I could hear the clanking of accoutrements, but even this grew fainter and fainter, until at last the silence was as complete as the darkness. I was alone with my gruesome companions – with the bones of dead men whose fate was likely but the index of my own.

How long I stood listening in the darkness I do not know, but the silence was unbroken, and at last I sunk to the hard floor of my prison, where, leaning my head against the stony wall, I slept.

It must have been several hours later that I awakened to find a young man standing before me. In one hand he bore a light, in the other a receptacle containing a gruel-like mixture – the common prison fare of Barsoom.

"Zat Arras sends you greetings," said the young man, "and commands me to inform you that though he is fully advised of the plot to make you Jeddak of Helium, he is, however, not inclined to withdraw the offer which he has made you. To gain your freedom you have but to request me to advise Zat Arras that you accept the terms of his proposition."

I but shook my head. The youth said no more, and, after placing the food upon the floor at my side, returned up the corridor, taking the light with him.

Twice a day for many days this youth came to my cell with food, and ever the same greetings from Zat Arras. For a long time I tried to engage him in conversation upon other matters, but he would not talk, and so, at length, I desisted.

For months I sought to devise methods to inform Carthoris of my whereabouts. For months I scraped and scraped upon a single link of the massive chain which held me, hoping eventually to wear it through, that I might follow the youth back through the winding tunnels to a point where I could make a break for liberty.

I was beside myself with anxiety for knowledge of the progress of the expedition which was to rescue Dejah Thoris. I felt that Carthoris would not let the matter drop, were he free to act, but in so far as I knew, he also might be a prisoner in Zat Arras' pits.

That Zat Arras' spy had overheard our conversation relative to the selection of a new Jeddak, I knew, and scarcely a half-dozen minutes prior we had discussed the details of the plan to rescue Dejah Thoris. The chances were that that matter, too, was well known to him. Carthoris, Kantos Kan, Tars Tarkas, Hor Vastus, and Xodar might even now be the victims of Zat Arras' assassins, or else his prisoners.

I determined to make at least one more effort to learn something, and to this end I adopted strategy when next the youth came to my cell. I had noticed that he was a handsome fellow, about the size and age of Carthoris. And I had also noticed that his shabby trappings but illy comported with his dignified and noble bearing.

It was with these observations as a basis that I opened my negotiations with him upon his next subsequent visit.

"You have been very kind to me during my imprisonment here," I said to him, "and as I feel that I have at best but a very short time to live,

I wish, ere it is too late, to furnish substantial testimony of my appreciation of all that you have done to render my imprisonment bearable.

"Promptly you have brought my food each day, seeing that it was pure and of sufficient quantity. Never by word or deed have you attempted to take advantage of my defenceless condition to insult or torture me. You have been uniformly courteous and considerate – it is this more than any other thing which prompts my feeling of gratitude and my desire to give you some slight token of it.

"In the guard-room of my palace are many fine trappings. Go thou there and select the harness which most pleases you – it shall be yours. All I ask is that you wear it, that I may know that my wish has been realized. Tell me that you will do it."

The boy's eyes had lighted with pleasure as I spoke, and I saw him glance from his rusty trappings to the magnificence of my own. For a moment he stood in thought before he spoke, and for that moment my heart fairly ceased beating – so much for me there was which hung upon the substance of his answer.

"And I went to the palace of the Prince of Helium with any such demand, they would laugh at me and, into the bargain, would more than likely throw me headforemost into the avenue. No, it cannot be, though I thank you for the offer. Why, if Zat Arras even dreamed that I contemplated such a thing he would have my heart cut out of me."

"There can be no harm in it, my boy," I urged. "By night you may go to my palace with a note from me to Carthoris, my son. You may read the note before you deliver it, that you may know that it contains nothing harmful to Zat Arras. My son will be discreet, and so none but us three need know. It is very simple, and such a harmless act that it could be condemned by no one."

Again he stood silently in deep thought.

"And there is a jewelled short-sword which I took from the body of a northern Jeddak. When you get the harness, see that Carthoris gives you that also. With it and the harness which you may select there will be no more handsomely accoutred warrior in all Zodanga.

"Bring writing materials when you come next to my cell, and within a few hours we shall see you garbed in a style befitting your birth and carriage."

Still in thought, and without speaking, he turned and left me. I could not guess what his decision might be, and for hours I sat fretting over the outcome of the matter.

If he accepted a message to Carthoris it would mean to me that Carthoris still lived and was free. If the youth returned wearing the harness and the sword, I would know that Carthoris had received my note and that he knew that I still lived. That the bearer of the note was a Zodangan would be sufficient to explain to Carthoris that I was a prisoner of Zat Arras.

It was with feelings of excited expectancy which I could scarce hide that I heard the youth's approach upon the occasion of his next regular visit. I did not speak beyond my accustomed greeting of him. As he placed the food upon the floor by my side he also deposited writing materials at the same time.

My heart fairly bounded for joy. I had won my point. For a moment I looked at the materials in feigned surprise, but soon I permitted an expression of dawning comprehension to come into my face, and then, picking them up, I penned a brief order to Carthoris to deliver to Parthak a harness of his selection and the short-sword which I described. That was all. But it meant everything to me and to Carthoris.

I laid the note open upon the floor. Parthak picked it up and, without a word, left me.

As nearly as I could estimate, I had at this time been in the pits for three hundred days. If anything was to be done to save Dejah Thoris it must be done quickly, for, were she not already dead, her end must soon come, since those whom Issus chose lived but a single year.

The next time I heard approaching footsteps I could scarce await to see if Parthak wore the harness and the sword, but judge, if you can, my chagrin and disappointment when I saw that he who bore my food was not Parthak.

"What has become of Parthak?" I asked, but the fellow would not answer, and as soon as he had deposited my food, turned and retraced his steps to the world above.

Days came and went, and still my new jailer continued his duties, nor would he ever speak a word to me, either in reply to the simplest question or of his own initiative.

I could only speculate on the cause of Parthak's removal, but that it was connected in some way directly with the note I had given him was most apparent to me. After all my rejoicing, I was no better off than before, for now I did not even know that Carthoris lived, for if Parthak had wished to raise himself in the estimation of Zat Arras he would have permitted me to go on precisely as I did, so that he could carry my note to his master, in proof of his own loyalty and devotion.

Thirty days had passed since I had given the youth the note. Three hundred and thirty days had passed since my incarceration. As closely as I could figure, there remained a bare thirty days ere Dejah Thoris would be ordered to the arena for the rites of Issus.

As the terrible picture forced itself vividly across my imagination, I buried my face in my arms, and only with the greatest difficulty was it that I repressed the tears that welled to my eyes despite my every effort. To think of that beautiful creature torn and rended by the cruel fangs of the hideous white apes! It was unthinkable. Such a horrid fact could not be; and yet my reason told me that within thirty days my incomparable Princess would be fought over in the arena of the First Born by those very wild beasts; that her bleeding corpse would be dragged through the dirt and the dust, until at last a part of it would be rescued to be served as food upon the tables of the black nobles.

I think that I should have gone crazy but for the sound of my approaching jailer. It distracted my attention from the terrible thoughts that had been occupying my entire mind. Now a new and grim determination came to me. I would make one super-human effort to escape. Kill my jailer by a ruse, and trust to fate to lead me to the outer world in safety.

With the thought came instant action. I threw myself upon the floor of my cell close by the wall, in a strained and distorted posture, as though I were dead after a struggle or convulsions. When he should stoop over me I had but to grasp his throat with one hand and strike him a terrific blow with the slack of my chain, which I gripped firmly in my right hand for the purpose.

Nearer and nearer came the doomed man. Now I heard him halt before me. There was a muttered exclamation, and then a step as he came to my side. I felt him kneel beside me. My grip tightened upon the chain. He leaned close to me. I must open my eyes to find his throat, grasp it, and strike one mighty final blow all at the same instant.

The thing worked just as I had planned. So brief was the interval between the opening of my eyes and the fall of the chain that I could not check it, though it that minute interval I recognized the face so close to mine as that of my son, Carthoris.

God! What cruel and malign fate had worked to such a frightful end! What devious chain of circumstances had led my boy to my side at this one particular minute of our lives when I could strike him down and kill him, in ignorance of his identity! A benign though tardy Providence blurred my vision and my mind as I sank into unconsciousness across the lifeless body of my only son.

When I regained consciousness it was to feel a cool, firm hand pressed upon my forehead. For an instant I did not open my eyes. I was endeavouring to gather the loose ends of many thoughts and memories which flitted elusively through my tired and overwrought brain.

At length came the cruel recollection of the thing that I had done in my last conscious act, and then I dared not to open my eyes for fear of what I should see lying beside me. I wondered who it could be who ministered to me. Carthoris must have had a companion whom I had not seen. Well, I must face the inevitable some time, so why not now, and with a sigh I opened my eyes.

Leaning over me was Carthoris, a great bruise upon his forehead where the chain had struck, but alive, thank God, alive! There was no one with him. Reaching out my arms, I took my boy within them, and if ever there arose from any planet a fervent prayer of gratitude, it was there beneath the crust of dying Mars as I thanked the Eternal Mystery for my son's life.

The brief instant in which I had seen and recognized Carthoris before the chain fell must have been ample to check the force of the blow. He told me that he had lain unconscious for a time – how long he did not know.

"How came you here at all?" I asked, mystified that he had found me without a guide.

"It was by your wit in apprising me of your existence and imprisonment through the youth, Parthak. Until he came for his harness and his sword, we had thought you dead. When I had read your note I did as you had bid, giving Parthak his choice of the harnesses in the guardroom, and later bringing the jewelled short-sword to him; but the minute that I had fulfilled the promise you evidently had made him, my obligation to him ceased. Then I commenced to question him, but he would give me no information as to your whereabouts. He was intensely loyal to Zat Arras.

"Finally I gave him a fair choice between freedom and the pits beneath the palace – the price of freedom to be full information as to where you were imprisoned and directions which would lead us to you; but still he maintained his stubborn partisanship. Despairing, I had him removed to the pits, where he still is.

"No threats of torture or death, no bribes, however fabulous, would move him. His only reply to all our importunities was that whenever Parthak died, were it to-morrow or a thousand years hence, no man could truly say, 'A traitor is gone to his deserts.'

"Finally, Xodar, who is a fiend for subtle craftiness, evolved a plan whereby we might worm the information from him. And so I caused Hor Vastus to be harnessed in the metal of a Zodangan soldier and chained in Parthak's cell beside him. For fifteen days the noble Hor Vastus has languished in the darkness of the pits, but not in vain. Little by little he won the confidence and friendship of the Zodangan, until only to-day Parthak, thinking that he was speaking not only to a countryman, but to a dear friend, revealed that Hor Vastus the exact cell in which you lay.

"It took me but a short time to locate the plans of the pits of Helium among thy official papers. To come to you, though, was a trifle more difficult matter. As you know, while all the pits beneath the city are connected, there are but single entrances from those beneath each section and its neighbour, and that at the upper level just underneath the ground.

"Of course, these openings which lead from contiguous pits to those beneath government buildings are always guarded, and so, while I easily came to the entrance to the pits beneath the palace which Zat Arras is occupying, I found there a Zodangan soldier on guard. There I left him when I had gone by, but his soul was no longer with him.

"And here I am, just in time to be nearly killed by you," he ended, laughing.

As he talked Carthoris had been working at the lock which held my fetters, and now, with an exclamation of pleasure, he dropped the end of the chain to the floor, and I stood up once more, freed from the galling irons I had chafed in for almost a year.

He had brought a long-sword and a dagger for me, and thus armed we set out upon the return journey to my palace.

At the point where we left the pits of Zat Arras we found the body of the guard Carthoris had slain. It had not yet been discovered, and, in order to still further delay search and mystify the jed's people, we carried the body with us for a short distance, hiding it in a tiny cell off the main corridor of the pits beneath an adjoining estate.

Some half-hour later we came to the pits beneath our own palace, and soon thereafter emerged into the audience chamber itself, where we found Kantos Kan, Tars Tarkas, Hor Vastus, and Xodar awaiting us most impatiently.

No time was lost in fruitless recounting of my imprisonment. What I desired to know was how well the plans we had laid nearly a year ago and had been carried out.

"It has taken much longer than we had expected," replied Kantos Kan. "The fact that we were compelled to maintain utter secrecy has handicapped us terribly. Zat Arras' spies are everywhere. Yet, to the best of my knowledge, no word of our real plans has reached the villain's ear.

"To-night there lies about the great docks at Hastor a fleet of a thousand of the mightiest battleships that ever sailed above Barsoom, and each equipped to navigate the air of Omean and the waters of Omean itself. Upon each battleship there are five ten-man cruisers, and ten five-man scouts, and a hundred one-man scouts; in all, one hundred and sixteen thousand craft fitted with both air and water propellers.

"At Thark lie the transports for the green warriors of Tars Tarkas, nine hundred large troopships, and with them their convoys. Seven days ago all was in readiness, but we waited in the hope that by so doing your rescue might be encompassed in time for you to command the expedition. It is well we waited, my Prince."

"How is it, Tars Tarkas," I asked, "that the men of Thark take not the accustomed action against one who returns from the bosom of Iss?"

"They sent a council of fifty chieftains to talk with me here," replied the Thark. "We are a just people, and when I had told them the entire story they were as one man in agreeing that their action toward me would be guided by the action of Helium toward John Carter. In the meantime, at their request, I was to resume my throne as Jeddak of Thark, that I might negotiate with neighboring hordes for warriors to compose the land forces of the expedition. I have done that which I agreed. Two hundred and fifty thousand fighting men, gathered from the ice cap at the north to the ice cap at the south, and representing a thousand different communities, from a hundred wild and warlike hordes, fill the great city of Thark tonight. They are ready to sail for the Land of the First Born when I give the word and fight there until I bid them stop. All they ask is the loot they take and transportation to their own territories when the fighting and the looting are over. I am done."

"And thou, Hor Vastus," I asked, "what has been thy success?"

"A million veteran fighting-men from Helium's thin waterways man the battleships, the transports, and the convoys," he replied. "Each is sworn to loyalty and secrecy, nor were enough recruited from a single district to cause suspicion."

"Good!" I cried. "Each has done his duty, and now, Kantos Kan, may we not repair at once to Hastor and get under way before to-morrow's sun?"

"We should lose no time, Prince," replied Kantos Kan. "Already the people of Hastor are questioning the purpose of so great a fleet fully manned with fighting-men. I wonder much that word of it has not before reached Zat Arras. A cruiser awaits above at your own dock; let us leave at – " A fusillade of shots from the palace gardens just without cut short his further words.

Together we rushed to the balcony in time to see a dozen members of my palace guard disappear in the shadows of some distant shrubbery as in pursuit of one who fled. Directly beneath us upon the scarlet sward a handful of guardsmen were stooping above a still and prostrate form.

While we watched they lifted the figure in their arms and at my command bore it to the audience chamber where we had been in council. When they stretched the body at our feet we saw that it was that of a red man in the prime of life – his metal was plain, such as common soldiers wear, or those who wish to conceal their identity.

"Another of Zat Arras' spies," said Hor Vastus.

"So it would seem," I replied, and then to the guard: "You may remove the body."

"Wait!" said Xodar. "If you will, Prince, ask that a cloth and a little thoat oil be brought."

I nodded to one of the soldiers, who left the chamber, returning presently with the things that Xodar had requested. The black kneeled beside the body and, dipping a corner of the cloth in the thoat oil, rubbed for a moment on the dead face before him, Then he turned to me with a smile, pointing to his work. I looked and saw that where Xodar had applied the thoat oil the face was white, as white as mine, and then Xodar seized the black hair of the corpse and with a sudden wrench tore it all away, revealing a hairless pate beneath.

Guardsmen and nobles pressed close about the silent witness upon the marble floor. Many were the exclamations of astonishment and questioning wonder as Xodar's acts confirmed the suspicion which he had held.

"A thern!" whispered Tars Tarkas.

"Worse than that, I fear," replied Xodar. "But let us see."

With that he drew his dagger and cut open a locked pouch which had dangled from the thern's harness, and from it he brought forth a circlet of gold set with a large gem – it was the mate to that which I had taken from Sator Throg.

"He was a Holy Thern," said Xodar. "Fortunate indeed it is for us that he did not escape."

The officer of the guard entered the chamber at this juncture.

"My Prince," he said, "I have to report that this fellow's companion escaped us. I think that it was with the connivance of one or more of the men at the gate. I have ordered them all under arrest."

Xodar handed him the thoat oil and cloth.

"With this you may discover the spy among you," he said.

I at once ordered a secret search within the city, for every Martian noble maintains a secret service of his own.

A half-hour later the officer of the guard came again to report. This time it was to confirm our worst fears – half the guards at the gate that night had been therns disguised as red men.

"Come!" I cried. "We must lose no time. On to Hastor at once. Should the therns attempt to check us at the southern verge of the ice cap it may result in the wrecking of all our plans and the total destruction of the expedition."

Ten minutes later we were speeding through the night toward Hastor, prepared to strike the first blow for the preservation of Dejah Thoris.

CHAPTER TWENTY

The Air Battle

TWO HOURS AFTER LEAVING my palace at Helium, or about midnight, Kantos Kan, Xodar, and I arrived at Hastor. Carthoris, Tars Tarkas, and Hor Vastus had gone directly to Thark upon another cruiser.

The transports were to get under way immediately and move slowly south. The fleet of battleships would overtake them on the morning of the second day.

At Hastor we found all in readiness, and so perfectly had Kantos Kan planned every detail of the campaign that within ten minutes of our arrival the first of the fleet had soared aloft from its dock, and thereafter, at the rate of one a second, the great ships floated gracefully out into the night to form a long, thin line which stretched for miles toward the south.

It was not until after we had entered the cabin of Kantos Kan that I thought to ask the date, for up to now I was not positive how long I had lain in the pits of Zat Arras. When Kantos Kan told me, I realized with a pang of dismay that I had misreckoned the time while I lay in the utter darkness of my cell. Three hundred and sixty-five days had passed – it was too late to save Dejah Thoris.

The expedition was no longer one of rescue but of revenge. I did not remind Kantos Kan of the terrible fact that ere we could hope to enter the Temple of Issus, the Princess of Helium would be no more. In so far as I knew she might be already dead, for I did not know the exact date on which she first viewed Issus.

What now the value of burdening my friends with my added personal sorrows – they had shared quite enough of them with me in the past. Hereafter I would keep my grief to myself, and so I said nothing to any other of the fact that we were too late. The expedition could yet do much if it could but teach the people of Barsoom the facts of the cruel deception that had been worked upon them for countless ages, and thus save thousands each year from the horrid fate that awaited them at the conclusion of the voluntary pilgrimage.

If it could open to the red men the fair Valley Dor it would have accomplished much, and in the Land of Lost Souls between the Mountains of Otz and the ice barrier were many broad acres that needed no irrigation to bear rich harvests.

Here at the bottom of a dying world was the only naturally productive area upon its surface. Here alone were dews and rains, here alone was an open sea, here was water in plenty; and all this was but the stamping ground of fierce brutes and from its beauteous and fertile expanse the wicked remnants of two once mighty races barred all the other millions of Barsoom. Could I but succeed in once breaking down the barrier of religious superstition which had kept the red races from this El Dorado it would be a fitting memorial to the immortal virtues of my Princess – I should have again served Barsoom and Dejah Thoris' martyrdom would not have been in vain.

On the morning of the second day we raised the great fleet of transports and their consorts at the first flood of dawn, and soon were near enough to exchange signals. I may mention here that radio-aerograms are seldom if ever used in war time, or for the transmission of secret dispatches at any time, for as often as one nation discovers a new cipher, or invents a new instrument for wireless purposes its neighbours bend every effort until they are able to intercept and translate the messages. For so long a time has this gone on that practically every possibility of wireless communication has been exhausted and no nation dares transmit dispatches of importance in this way.

Tars Tarkas reported all well with the transports. The battleships passed through to take an advanced position, and the combined fleets moved slowly over the ice cap, hugging the surface closely to prevent detection by the therns whose land we were approaching.

Far in advance of all a thin line of one-man air scouts protected us from surprise, and on either side they flanked us, while a smaller number brought up the rear some twenty miles behind the transports. In this formation we had progressed toward the entrance to Omean for several hours when one of our scouts returned from the front to report that the cone-like summit of the entrance was in sight. At almost the same instant another scout from the left flank came racing toward the flagship.

His very speed bespoke the importance of his information. Kantos Kan and I awaited him upon the little forward deck which corresponds with the bridge of earthly battleships. Scarcely had his tiny flier come to rest upon the broad landing-deck of the flagship ere he was bounding up the stairway to the deck where we stood.

"A great fleet of battleships south-south-east, my Prince," he cried. "There must be several thousands and they are bearing down directly upon us."

"The thern spies were not in the palace of John Carter for nothing," said Kantos Kan to me. "Your orders, Prince."

"Dispatch ten battleships to guard the entrance to Omean, with orders to let no hostile enter or leave the shaft. That will bottle up the great fleet of the First Born.

"Form the balance of the battleships into a great V with the apex pointing directly south-south-east. Order the transports, surrounded by their convoys, to follow closely in the wake of the battleships until the point of the V has entered the enemies' line, then the V must open outward at the apex, the battleships of each leg engage the enemy fiercely and drive him back to form a lane through his line into which the transports with their convoys must race at top speed that they may gain a position above the temples and gardens of the therns.

"Here let them land and teach the Holy Therns such a lesson in ferocious warfare as they will not forget for countless ages. It had not been my intention to be distracted from the main issue of the campaign, but we must settle this attack with the therns once and for all, or there will be no peace for us while our fleet remains near Dor, and our chances of ever returning to the outer world will be greatly minimized."

Kantos Kan saluted and turned to deliver my instructions to his waiting aides. In an incredibly short space of time the formation of the battleships changed in accordance with my commands, the ten that were to guard the way to Omean were speeding toward their destination, and the troopships and convoys were closing up in preparation for the spurt through the lane.

The order of full speed ahead was given, the fleet sprang through the air like coursing greyhounds, and in another moment the ships of the enemy were in full view. They formed a ragged line as far as the eye could reach in either direction and about three ships deep. So sudden was our onslaught that they had no time to prepare for it. It was as unexpected as lightning from a clear sky.

Every phase of my plan worked splendidly. Our huge ships mowed their way entirely through the line of thern battlecraft; then the V opened up and a broad lane appeared through which the transports leaped toward the temples of the therns which could now be plainly seen glistening in the sunlight. By the time the therns had rallied from the attack a hundred thousand green warriors were already pouring through their courts and gardens, while a hundred and fifty thousand others leaned from low swinging transports to direct their almost un-canny marksmanship upon the thern soldiery that manned the ram-parts, or attempted to defend the temples.

Now the two great fleets closed in a titanic struggle far above the fiendish din of battle in the gorgeous gardens of the therns. Slowly the two lines of Helium's battleships joined their ends, and then com-menced the circling within the line of the enemy which is so marked a characteristic of Barsoomian naval warfare.

Around and around in each other's tracks moved the ships under Kantos Kan, until at length they formed nearly a perfect circle. By this time they were moving at high speed so that they presented a difficult target for the enemy. Broadside after broadside they delivered as each vessel came in line with the ships of the therns. The latter attempted to rush in and break up the formation, but it was like stopping a buzz saw with the bare hand.

From my position on the deck beside Kantos Kan I saw ship after ship of the enemy take the awful, sickening dive which proclaims its total destruction. Slowly we manoeuvered our circle of death until we hung above the gardens where our green warriors were engaged. The order was passed down for them to embark. Then they rose slowly to a position within the centre of the circle.

In the meantime the therns' fire had practically ceased. They had had enough of us and were only too glad to let us go on our way in peace. But our escape was not to be encompassed with such ease, for scarcely had we gotten under way once more in the direction of the entrance to Omean than we saw far to the north a great black line topping the horizon. It could be nothing other than a fleet of war.

Whose or whither bound, we could not even conjecture. When they had come close enough to make us out at all, Kantos Kan's operator received a radio-aerogram, which he immediately handed to my com-panion. He read the thing and handed it to me.

"Kantos Kan:" it read. "Surrender, in the name of the Jeddak of He-lium, for you cannot escape," and it was signed, "Zat Arras."

The therns must have caught and translated the message almost as soon as did we, for they immediately renewed hostilities when they realized that we were soon to be set upon by other enemies.

Before Zat Arras had approached near enough to fire a shot we were again hotly engaged with the thern fleet, and as soon as he drew near he too commenced to pour a terrific fusillade of heavy shot into us. Ship after ship reeled and staggered into uselessness beneath the pitiless fire that we were undergoing.

The thing could not last much longer. I ordered the transports to descend again into the gardens of the therns.

"Wreak your vengeance to the utmost," was my message to the green allies, "for by night there will be none left to avenge your wrongs."

Presently I saw the ten battleships that had been ordered to hold the shaft of Omean. They were returning at full speed, firing their stern batteries almost continuously. There could be but one explanation. They were being pursued by another hostile fleet. Well, the situation could be no worse. The expedition already was doomed. No man that had embarked upon it would return across that dreary ice cap. How I wished that I might face Zat Arras with my longsword for just an instant before I died! It was he who had caused our failure.

As I watched the oncoming ten I saw their pursuers race swiftly into sight. It was another great fleet; for a moment I could not believe my eyes, but finally I was forced to admit that the most fatal calamity had overtaken the expedition, for the fleet I saw was none other than the fleet of the First Born, that should have been safely bottled up in Omean. What a series of misfortunes and disasters! What awful fate hovered over me, that I should have been so terribly thwarted at every angle of my search for my lost love! Could it be possible that the curse of Issus was upon me! That there was, indeed, some malign divinity in that hideous carcass! I would not believe it, and, throwing back my shoulders, I ran to the deck below to join my men in repelling boarders from one of the thern craft that had grappled us broadside. In the wild lust of hand-to-hand combat my old dauntless hopefulness returned. And as thern after thern went down beneath my blade, I could almost feel that we should win success in the end, even from apparent failure.

My presence among the men so greatly inspirited them that they fell upon the luckless whites with such terrible ferocity that within a few moments we had turned the tables upon them and a second later as we swarmed their own decks I had the satisfaction of seeing their commander take the long leap from the bows of his vessel in token of surrender and defeat.

Then I joined Kantos Kan. He had been watching what had taken place on the deck below, and it seemed to have given him a new thought. Immediately he passed an order to one of his officers, and presently the colours of the Prince of Helium broke from every point of the flagship.

A great cheer arose from the men of our own ship, a cheer that was taken up by every other vessel of our expedition as they in turn broke my colours from their upper works.

Then Kantos Kan sprang his coup. A signal legible to every sailor of all the fleets engaged in that fierce struggle was strung aloft upon the flagship.

"Men of Helium for the Prince of Helium against all his enemies," it read. Presently my colours broke from one of Zat Arras' ships. Then from another and another. On some we could see fierce battles waging between the Zodangan soldiery and the Heliumetic crews, but eventually the colours of the Prince of Helium floated above every ship that had followed Zat Arras upon our trail – only his flagship flew them not.

Zat Arras had brought five thousand ships. The sky was black with the three enormous fleets. It was Helium against the field now, and the fight had settled to countless individual duels. There could be little or no manoeuvering of fleets in that crowded, fire-split sky.

Zat Arras' flagship was close to my own. I could see the thin features of the man from where I stood. His Zodangan crew was pouring broadside after broadside into us and we were returning their fire with equal ferocity. Closer and closer came the two vessels until but a few yards intervened. Grapplers and boarders lined the contiguous rails of each. We were preparing for the death struggle with our hated enemy.

There was but a yard between the two mighty ships as the first grappling irons were hurled. I rushed to the deck to be with my men as they boarded. Just as the vessels came together with a slight shock, I forced my way through the lines and was the first to spring to the deck of Zat Arras' ship. After me poured a yelling, cheering, cursing throng of Helium's best fighting-men. Nothing could withstand them in the fever of battle lust which enthralled them.

Down went the Zodangans before that surging tide of war, and as my men cleared the lower decks I sprang to the forward deck where stood Zat Arras.

"You are my prisoner, Zat Arras," I cried. "Yield and you shall have quarter."

For a moment I could not tell whether he contemplated acceding to my demand or facing me with drawn sword. For an instant he stood hesitating, and then throwing down his arms he turned and rushed to the opposite side of the deck. Before I could overtake him he had sprung to the rail and hurled himself headforemost into the awful depths below.

And thus came Zat Arras, Jed of Zodanga, to his end.

On and on went that strange battle. The therns and blacks had not combined against us. Wherever thern ship met ship of the First Born was a battle royal, and in this I thought I saw our salvation. Wherever messages could be passed between us that could not be intercepted by our enemies I passed the word that all our vessels were to withdraw from the fight as rapidly as possible, taking a position to the west and south of the combatants. I also sent an air scout to the fighting green men in the gardens below to re-embark, and to the transports to join us.

My commanders were further instructed that when engaged with an enemy to draw him as rapidly as possible toward a ship of his hereditary foeman, and by careful manoeuvring to force the two to engage, thus leaving him-self free to withdraw. This stratagem worked to perfection, and just before the sun went down I had the satisfaction of seeing all that was left of my once mighty fleet gathered nearly twenty miles southwest of the still terrific battle between the blacks and whites.

I now transferred Xodar to another battleship and sent him with all the transports and five thousand battleships directly overhead to the Temple of Issus. Carthoris and I, with Kantos Kan, took the remaining ships and headed for the entrance to Omean.

Our plan now was to attempt to make a combined assault upon Issus at dawn of the following day. Tars Tarkas with his green warriors and Hor Vastus with the red men, guided by Xodar, were to land within the garden of Issus or the surrounding plains; while Carthoris, Kantos Kan, and I were to lead our smaller force from the sea of Omean through the pits beneath the temple, which Carthoris knew so well.

I now learned for the first time the cause of my ten ships' retreat from the mouth of the shaft. It seemed that when they had come upon the shaft the navy of the First Born were already issuing from its mouth. Fully twenty vessels had emerged, and though they gave battle immediately in an effort to stem the tide that rolled from the black pit, the odds against them were too great and they were forced to flee.

With great caution we approached the shaft, under cover of darkness. At a distance of several miles I caused the fleet to be halted, and from there Carthoris went ahead alone upon a one-man flier to reconnoitre. In perhaps half an hour he returned to report that there was no sign of a patrol boat or of the enemy in any form, and so we moved swiftly and noiselessly forward once more toward Omean.

At the mouth of the shaft we stopped again for a moment for all the vessels to reach their previously appointed stations, then with the flagship I dropped quickly into the black depths, while one by one the other vessels followed me in quick succession.

We had decided to stake all on the chance that we would be able to reach the temple by the subterranean way and so we left no guard of vessels at the shaft's mouth. Nor would it have profited us any to have done so, for we did not have sufficient force all told to have withstood the vast navy of the First Born had they returned to engage us.

For the safety of our entrance upon Omean we depended largely upon the very boldness of it, believing that it would be some little time before the First Born on guard there would realize that it was an enemy and not their own returning fleet that was entering the vault of the buried sea.

And such proved to be the case. In fact, four hundred of my fleet of five hundred rested safely upon the bosom of Omean before the first shot was fired. The battle was short and hot, but there could have been but one outcome, for the First Born in the carelessness of fancied security had left but a handful of ancient and obsolete hulks to guard their mighty harbour.

It was at Carthoris' suggestion that we landed our prisoners under guard upon a couple of the larger islands, and then towed the ships of the First Born to the shaft, where we managed to wedge a number of them securely in the interior of the great well. Then we turned on the buoyance rays in the balance of them and let them rise by themselves to further block the passage to Omean as they came into contact with the vessels already lodged there.

We now felt that it would be some time at least before the returning First Born could reach the surface of Omean, and that we would have ample opportunity to make for the subterranean passages which lead to Issus. One of the first steps I took was to hasten personally with a good-sized force to the island of the submarine, which I took without resistance on the part of the small guard there.

I found the submarine in its pool, and at once placed a strong guard upon it and the island, where I remained to wait the coming of Carthoris and the others.

Among the prisoners was Yersted, commander of the submarine. He recognized me from the three trips that I had taken with him during my captivity among the First Born.

"How does it seem," I asked him, "to have the tables turned? To be prisoner of your erstwhile captive?"

He smiled, a very grim smile pregnant with hidden meaning.

"It will not be for long, John Carter," he replied. "We have been expecting you and we are prepared."

"So it would appear," I answered, "for you were all ready to become my prisoners with scarce a blow struck on either side."

"The fleet must have missed you," he said, "but it will return to Omean, and then that will be a very different matter – for John Carter."

"I do not know that the fleet has missed me as yet," I said, but of course he did not grasp my meaning, and only looked puzzled.

"Many prisoners travel to Issus in your grim craft, Yersted?" I asked.

"Very many," he assented.

"Might you remember one whom men called Dejah Thoris?"

"Well, indeed, for her great beauty, and then, too, for the fact that she was wife to the first mortal that ever escaped from Issus through all the countless ages of her godhood. And the way that Issus remembers her best as the wife of one and the mother of another who raised their hands against the Goddess of Life Eternal."

I shuddered for fear of the cowardly revenge that I knew Issus might have taken upon the innocent Dejah Thoris for the sacrilege of her son and her husband.

"And where is Dejah Thoris now?" I asked, knowing that he would say the words I most dreaded, but yet I loved her so that I could not refrain from hearing even the worst about her fate so that it fell from the lips of one who had seen her but recently. It was to me as though it brought her closer to me.

"Yesterday the monthly rites of Issus were held," replied Yersted, "and I saw her then sitting in her accustomed place at the foot of Issus."

"What," I cried, "she is not dead, then?"

"Why, no," replied the black, "it has been no year since she gazed upon the divine glory of the radiant face of – "

"No year?" I interrupted.

"Why, no," insisted Yersted. "It cannot have been upward of three hundred and seventy or eighty days."

A great light burst upon me. How stupid I had been! I could scarcely retain an outward exhibition of my great joy. Why had I forgotten the great difference in the length of Martian and Earthly years! The ten Earth years I had spent upon Barsoom had encompassed but five years and ninety-six days of Martian time, whose days are forty-one minutes longer than ours, and whose years number six hundred and eighty-seven days.

I am in time! I am in time! The words surged through my brain again and again, until at last I must have voiced them audibly, for Yersted shook his head.

"In time to save your Princess?" he asked, and then without waiting for my reply, "No, John Carter, Issus will not give up her own. She knows that you are coming, and ere ever a vandal foot is set within the precincts of the Temple of Issus, if such a calamity should befall, Dejah Thoris will be put away for ever from the last faint hope of rescue."

"You mean that she will be killed merely to thwart me?" I asked.

"Not that, other than as a last resort," he replied. "Hast ever heard of the Temple of the Sun? It is there that they will put her. It lies far within the inner court of the Temple of Issus, a little temple that raises a thin spire far above the spires and minarets of the great temple that surrounds it. Beneath it, in the ground, there lies the main body of the temple consisting in six hundred and eighty-seven circular chambers, one below another. To each chamber a single corridor leads through solid rock from the pits of Issus.

"As the entire Temple of the Sun revolves once with each revolution of Barsoom about the sun, but once each year does the entrance to each separate chamber come opposite the mouth of the corridor which forms its only link to the world without.

"Here Issus puts those who displease her, but whom she does not care to execute forthwith. Or to punish a noble of the First Born she may cause him to be placed within a chamber of the Temple of the Sun for a year. Ofttimes she imprisons an executioner with the condemned, that death may come in a certain horrible form upon a given day, or again but enough food is deposited in the chamber to sustain life but the number of days that Issus has allotted for mental anguish.

"Thus will Dejah Thoris die, and her fate will be sealed by the first alien foot that crosses the threshold of Issus."

So I was to be thwarted in the end, although I had performed the miraculous and come within a few short moments of my divine Princess, yet was I as far from her as when I stood upon the banks of the Hudson forty-eight million miles away.

CHAPTER TWENTY ONE

Through Flood and Flame

YERSTED'S INFORMATION convinced me that there was no time to be lost. I must reach the Temple of Issus secretly before the forces under Tars Tarkas assaulted at dawn. Once within its hated walls I was positive that I could overcome the guards of Issus and bear away my Princess, for at my back I would have a force ample for the occasion.

No sooner had Carthoris and the others joined me than we commenced the transportation of our men through the submerged passage to the mouth of the gangways which lead from the submarine pool at the temple end of the watery tunnel to the pits of Issus.

Many trips were required, but at last all stood safely together again at the beginning of the end of our quest. Five thousand strong we were, all seasoned fighting-men of the most warlike race of the red men of Barsoom.

As Carthoris alone knew the hidden ways of the tunnels we could not divide the party and attack the temple at several points at once as would have been most desirable, and so it was decided that he lead us all as quickly as possible to a point near the temple's centre.

As we were about to leave the pool and enter the corridor, an officer called my attention to the waters upon which the submarine floated. At first they seemed to be merely agitated as from the movement of some great body beneath the surface, and I at once conjectured that another submarine was rising to the surface in pursuit of us; but presently it became apparent that the level of the waters was rising, not with extreme rapidity, but very surely, and that soon they would overflow the sides of the pool and submerge the floor of the chamber.

For a moment I did not fully grasp the terrible import of the slowly rising water. It was Carthoris who realized the full meaning of the thing – its cause and the reason for it.

"Haste!" he cried. "If we delay, we all are lost. The pumps of Omean have been stopped. They would drown us like rats in a trap. We must reach the upper levels of the pits in advance of the flood or we shall never reach them. Come."

"Lead the way, Carthoris," I cried. "We will follow."

At my command, the youth leaped into one of the corridors, and in column of twos the soldiers followed him in good order, each company entering the corridor only at the command of its dwar, or captain.

Before the last company filed from the chamber the water was ankle deep, and that the men were nervous was quite evident. Entirely unaccustomed to water except in quantities sufficient for drinking and bathing purposes the red Martians instinctively shrank from it in such formidable depths and menacing activity. That they were undaunted while it swirled and eddied about their ankles, spoke well for their bravery and their discipline.

I was the last to leave the chamber of the submarine, and as I followed the rear of the column toward the corridor, I moved through water to my knees. The corridor, too, was flooded to the same depth, for its floor was on a level with the floor of the chamber from which it led, nor was there any perceptible rise for many yards.

The march of the troops through the corridor was as rapid as was consistent with the number of men that moved through so narrow a passage, but it was not ample to permit us to gain appreciably on the pursuing tide. As the level of the passage rose, so, too, did the waters rise until it soon became apparent to me, who brought up the rear, that they were gaining rapidly upon us. I could understand the reason for this, as with the narrowing expanse of Omean as the waters rose toward the apex of its dome, the rapidity of its rise would increase in inverse ratio to the ever-lessening space to be filled.

Long ere the last of the column could hope to reach the upper pits which lay above the danger point I was convinced that the waters would surge after us in overwhelming volume, and that fully half the expedition would be snuffed out.

As I cast about for some means of saving as many as possible of the doomed men, I saw a diverging corridor which seemed to rise at a steep angle at my right. The waters were now swirling about my waist. The men directly before me were quickly becoming panic-stricken. Something must be done at once or they would rush forward upon their fellows in a mad stampede that would result in trampling down hundreds beneath the flood and eventually clogging the passage beyond any hope of retreat for those in advance.

Raising my voice to its utmost, I shouted my command to the dwars ahead of me.

"Call back the last twenty-five utans," I shouted. "Here seems a way of escape. Turn back and follow me."

My orders were obeyed by nearer thirty utans, so that some three thousand men came about and hastened into the teeth of the flood to reach the corridor up which I directed them.

As the first dwar passed in with his utan I cautioned him to listen closely for my commands, and under no circumstances to venture into the open, or leave the pits for the temple proper until I should have come up with him, "or you know that I died before I could reach you."

The officer saluted and left me. The men filed rapidly past me and entered the diverging corridor which I hoped would lead to safety. The water rose breast high. Men stumbled, floundered, and went down. Many I grasped and set upon their feet again, but alone the work was greater than I could cope with. Soldiers were being swept beneath the boiling torrent, never to rise. At length the dwar of the 10th utan took a stand beside me. He was a valorous soldier, Gur Tus by name, and together we kept the now thoroughly frightened troops in the semblance of order and rescued many that would have drowned otherwise.

Djor Kantos, son of Kantos Kan, and a padwar of the fifth utan joined us when his utan reached the opening through which the men were fleeing. Thereafter not a man was lost of all the hundreds that remained to pass from the main corridor to the branch.

As the last utan was filing past us the waters had risen until they surged about our necks, but we clasped hands and stood our ground until the last man had passed to the comparative safety of the new passageway. Here we found an immediate and steep ascent, so that within a hundred yards we had reached a point above the waters.

For a few minutes we continued rapidly up the steep grade, which I hoped would soon bring us quickly to the upper pits that let into the Temple of Issus. But I was to meet with a cruel disappointment.

Suddenly I heard a cry of "fire" far ahead, followed almost at once by cries of terror and the loud commands of dwars and padwars who were evidently attempting to direct their men away from some grave danger. At last the report came back to us. "They have fired the pits ahead." "We are hemmed in by flames in front and flood behind." "Help, John Carter; we are suffocating," and then there swept back upon us at the rear a wave of dense smoke that sent us, stumbling and blinded, into a choking retreat.

There was naught to do other than seek a new avenue of escape. The fire and smoke were to be feared a thousand times over the water, and so I seized upon the first gallery which led out of and up from the suffocating smoke that was engulfing us.

Again I stood to one side while the soldiers hastened through on the new way. Some two thousand must have passed at a rapid run, when the stream ceased, but I was not sure that all had been rescued who had not passed the point of origin of the flames, and so to assure myself that no poor devil was left behind to die a horrible death, unsuccoured, I ran quickly up the gallery in the direction of the flames which I could now see burning with a dull glow far ahead.

It was hot and stifling work, but at last I reached a point where the fire lit up the corridor sufficiently for me to see that no soldier of Helium lay between me and the conflagration – what was in it or upon the far side I could not know, nor could any man have passed through that seething hell of chemicals and lived to learn.

Having satisfied my sense of duty, I turned and ran rapidly back to the corridor through which my men had passed. To my horror, however, I found that my retreat in this direction had been blocked – across the mouth of the corridor stood a massive steel grating that had evidently been lowered from its resting-place above for the purpose of effectually cutting off my escape.

That our principal movements were known to the First Born I could not have doubted, in view of the attack of the fleet upon us the day before, nor could the stopping of the pumps of Omean at the psychological moment have been due to chance, nor the starting of a chemical combustion within the one corridor through which we were advancing upon the Temple of Issus been due to aught than well-calculated design.

And now the dropping of the steel gate to pen me effectually between fire and flood seemed to indicate that invisible eyes were upon us at every moment. What chance had I, then, to rescue Dejah Thoris were I to be compelled to fight foes who never showed themselves. A thousand times I berated myself for being drawn into such a trap as I might have known these pits easily could be. Now I saw that it would have been much better to have kept our force intact and made a concerted attack upon the temple from the valley side, trusting to chance and our great fighting ability to have overwhelmed the First Born and compelled the safe delivery of Dejah Thoris to me.

The smoke from the fire was forcing me further and further back down the corridor toward the waters which I could hear surging through the darkness. With my men had gone the last torch, nor was this corridor lighted by the radiance of phosphorescent rock as were those of the lower levels. It was this fact that assured me that I was not far from the upper pits which lie directly beneath the temple.

Finally I felt the lapping waters about my feet. The smoke was thick behind me. My suffering was intense. There seemed but one thing to do, and that to choose the easier death which confronted me, and so I moved on down the corridor until the cold waters of Omean closed about me, and I swam on through utter blackness toward – what?

The instinct of self-preservation is strong even when one, unafraid and in the possession of his highest reasoning faculties, knows that death – positive and unalterable – lies just ahead. And so I swam slowly on, waiting for my head to touch the top of the corridor, which would mean that I had reached the limit of my flight and the point where I must sink for ever to an unmarked grave.

But to my surprise I ran against a blank wall before I reached a point where the waters came to the roof of the corridor. Could I be mistaken? I felt around. No, I had come to the main corridor, and still there was a breathing space between the surface of the water and the rocky ceiling above. And then I turned up the main corridor in the direction that Carthoris and the head of the column had passed a half-hour before. On and on I swam, my heart growing lighter at every stroke, for I knew that I was approaching closer and closer to the point where there would be no chance that the waters ahead could be deeper than they were about me. I was positive that I must soon feel the solid floor beneath my feet again and that once more my chance would come to reach the Temple of Issus and the side of the fair prisoner who languished there.

But even as hope was at its highest I felt the sudden shock of contact as my head struck the rocks above. The worst, then, had come to me. I had reached one of those rare places where a Martian tunnel dips suddenly to a lower level. Somewhere beyond I knew that it rose again, but of what value was that to me, since I did not know how great the distance that it maintained a level entirely beneath the surface of the water!

There was but a single forlorn hope, and I took it. Filling my lungs with air, I dived beneath the surface and swam through the inky, icy blackness on and on along the submerged gallery. Time and time again I rose with upstretched hand, only to feel the disappointing rocks close above me.

Not for much longer would my lungs withstand the strain upon them. I felt that I must soon succumb, nor was there any retreating now that I had gone this far. I knew positively that I could never endure to retrace my path now to the point from which I had felt the waters close above my head. Death stared me in the face, nor ever can I recall a time that I so distinctly felt the icy breath from his dead lips upon my brow.

One more frantic effort I made with my fast ebbing strength. Weakly I rose for the last time – my tortured lungs gasped for the breath that would fill them with a strange and numbing element, but instead I felt the revivifying breath of life-giving air surge through my starving nostrils into my dying lungs. I was saved.

A few more strokes brought me to a point where my feet touched the floor, and soon thereafter I was above the water level entirely, and racing like mad along the corridor searching for the first doorway that would lead me to Issus. If I could not have Dejah Thoris again I was at least determined to avenge her death, nor would any life satisfy me other than that of the fiend incarnate who was the cause of such immeasurable suffering upon Barsoom.

Sooner than I had expected I came to what appeared to me to be a sudden exit into the temple above. It was at the right side of the corridor, which ran on, probably, to other entrances to the pile above.

To me one point was as good as another. What knew I where any of them led! And so without waiting to be again discovered and thwarted, I ran quickly up the short, steep incline and pushed open the doorway at its end.

The portal swung slowly in, and before it could be slammed against me I sprang into the chamber beyond. Although not yet dawn, the room was brilliantly lighted. Its sole occupant lay prone upon a low couch at the further side, apparently in sleep. From the hangings and sumptuous furniture of the room I judged it to be a living-room of some priestess, possibly of Issus herself.

At the thought the blood tingled through my veins. What, indeed, if fortune had been kind enough to place the hideous creature alone and unguarded in my hands. With her as hostage I could force acquiescence to my every demand. Cautiously I approached the recumbent figure, on noiseless feet. Closer and closer I came to it, but I had crossed but little more than half the chamber when the figure stirred, and, as I sprang, rose and faced me.

At first an expression of terror overspread the features of the woman who confronted me – then startled incredulity – hope – thanksgiving.

My heart pounded within my breast as I advanced toward her – tears came to my eyes – and the words that would have poured forth in a perfect torrent choked in my throat as I opened my arms and took into them once more the woman I loved – Dejah Thoris, Princess of Helium.

CHAPTER TWENTY TWO

Victory and Defeat

"JOHN CARTER, John Carter," she sobbed, with her dear head upon my shoulder; "even now I can scarce believe the witness of my own eyes. When the girl, Thuvia, told me that you had returned to Barsoom, I listened, but I could not understand, for it seemed that such happiness would be impossible for one who had suffered so in silent loneliness for all these long years. At last, when I realized that it was truth, and then came to know the awful place in which I was held prisoner, I learned to doubt that even you could reach me here.

"As the days passed, and moon after moon went by without bringing even the faintest rumour of you, I resigned myself to my fate. And now that you have come, scarce can I believe it. For an hour I have heard the sounds of conflict within the palace. I knew not what they meant, but I have hoped against hope that it might be the men of Helium headed by my Prince.

"And tell me, what of Carthoris, our son?"

"He was with me less than an hour since, Dejah Thoris," I replied. "It must have been he whose men you have heard battling within the precincts of the temple.

"Where is Issus?" I asked suddenly.

Dejah Thoris shrugged her shoulders.

"She sent me under guard to this room just before the fighting began within the temple halls. She said that she would send for me later. She seemed very angry and somewhat fearful. Never have I seen her act in so uncertain and almost terrified a manner. Now I know that it must have been because she had learned that John Carter, Prince of Helium, was approaching to demand an accounting of her for the imprisonment of his Princess."

The sounds of conflict, the clash of arms, the shouting and the hurrying of many feet came to us from various parts of the temple. I knew that I was needed there, but I dared not leave Dejah Thoris, nor dared I take her with me into the turmoil and danger of battle.

At last I bethought me of the pits from which I had just emerged. Why not secrete her there until I could return and fetch her away in safety and for ever from this awful place. I explained my plan to her.

For a moment she clung more closely to me.

"I cannot bear to be parted from you now, even for a moment, John Carter," she said. "I shudder at the thought of being alone again where that terrible creature might discover me. You do not know her. None can imagine her ferocious cruelty who has not witnessed her daily acts for over half a year. It has taken me nearly all this time to realize even the things that I have seen with my own eyes."

"I shall not leave you, then, my Princess," I replied.

She was silent for a moment, then she drew my face to hers and kissed me.

"Go, John Carter," she said. "Our son is there, and the soldiers of Helium, fighting for the Princess of Helium. Where they are you should be. I must not think of myself now, but of them and of my husband's duty. I may not stand in the way of that. Hide me in the pits, and go."

I led her to the door through which I had entered the chamber from below. There I pressed her dear form to me, and then, though it tore my heart to do it, and filled me only with the blackest shadows of terrible foreboding, I guided her across the threshold, kissed her once again, and closed the door upon her.

Without hesitating longer, I hurried from the chamber in the direction of the greatest tumult. Scarce half a dozen chambers had I traversed before I came upon the theatre of a fierce struggle. The blacks were massed at the entrance to a great chamber where they were attempting to block the further progress of a body of red men toward the inner sacred precincts of the temple.

Coming from within as I did, I found myself behind the blacks, and, without waiting to even calculate their numbers or the foolhardiness of my venture, I charged swiftly across the chamber and fell upon them from the rear with my keen long-sword.

As I struck the first blow I cried aloud, "For Helium!" And then I rained cut after cut upon the surprised warriors, while the reds without took heart at the sound of my voice, and with shouts of "John Carter! John Carter!" redoubled their efforts so effectually that before the blacks could recover from their temporary demoralization their ranks were broken and the red men had burst into the chamber.

The fight within that room, had it had but a competent chronicler, would go down in the annals of Barsoom as a historic memorial to the grim ferocity of her warlike people. Five hundred men fought there that day, the black men against the red. No man asked quarter or gave it. As though by common assent they fought, as though to determine once and for all their right to live, in accordance with the law of the survival of the fittest.

I think we all knew that upon the outcome of this battle would hinge for ever the relative positions of these two races upon Barsoom. It was a battle between the old and the new, but not for once did I question the outcome of it. With Carthoris at my side I fought for the red men of Barsoom and for their total emancipation from the throttling bondage of a hideous superstition.

Back and forth across the room we surged, until the floor was ankle deep in blood, and dead men lay so thickly there that half the time we stood upon their bodies as we fought. As we swung toward the great windows which overlooked the gardens of Issus a sight met my gaze which sent a wave of exultation over me.

"Look!" I cried. "Men of the First Born, look!"

For an instant the fighting ceased, and with one accord every eye turned in the direction I had indicated, and the sight they saw was one no man of the First Born had ever imagined could be.

Across the gardens, from side to side, stood a wavering line of black warriors, while beyond them and forcing them ever back was a great horde of green warriors astride their mighty thoats. And as we watched, one, fiercer and more grimly terrible than his fellows, rode forward from the rear, and as he came he shouted some fierce command to his terrible legion.

It was Tars Tarkas, Jeddak of Thark, and as he couched his great forty-foot metal-shod lance we saw his warriors do likewise. Then it was that we interpreted his command. Twenty yards now separated the green men from the black line. Another word from the great Thark, and with a wild and terrifying battle-cry the green warriors charged. For a moment the black line held, but only for a moment – then the fearsome beasts that bore equally terrible riders passed completely through it.

After them came utan upon utan of red men. The green horde broke to surround the temple. The red men charged for the interior, and then we turned to continue our interrupted battle; but our foes had vanished.

My first thought was of Dejah Thoris. Calling to Carthoris that I had found his mother, I started on a run toward the chamber where I had left her, with my boy close beside me. After us came those of our little force who had survived the bloody conflict.

The moment I entered the room I saw that some one had been there since I had left. A silk lay upon the floor. It had not been there before. There were also a dagger and several metal ornaments strewn about as though torn from their wearer in a struggle. But worst of all, the door leading to the pits where I had hidden my Princess was ajar.

With a bound I was before it, and, thrusting it open, rushed within. Dejah Thoris had vanished. I called her name aloud again and again, but there was no response. I think in that instant I hovered upon the verge of insanity. I do not recall what I said or did, but I know that for an instant I was seized with the rage of a maniac.

"Issus!" I cried. "Issus! Where is Issus? Search the temple for her, but let no man harm her but John Carter. Carthoris, where are the apartments of Issus?"

"This way," cried the boy, and, without waiting to know that I had heard him, he dashed off at breakneck speed, further into the bowels of the temple. As fast as he went, however, I was still beside him, urging him on to greater speed.

At last we came to a great carved door, and through this Carthoris dashed, a foot ahead of me. Within, we came upon such a scene as I had witnessed within the temple once before – the throne of Issus, with the reclining slaves, and about it the ranks of soldiery.

We did not even give the men a chance to draw, so quickly were we upon them. With a single cut I struck down two in the front rank. And then by the mere weight and momentum of my body, I rushed completely through the two remaining ranks and sprang upon the dais beside the carved sorapus throne.

The repulsive creature, squatting there in terror, attempted to escape me and leap into a trap behind her. But this time I was not to be outwitted by any such petty subterfuge. Before she had half arisen I had grasped her by the arm, and then, as I saw the guard starting to make a concerted rush upon me from all sides, I whipped out my dagger and, holding it close to that vile breast, ordered them to halt.

"Back!" I cried to them. "Back! The first black foot that is planted upon this platform sends my dagger into Issus' heart."

For an instant they hesitated. Then an officer ordered them back, while from the outer corridor there swept into the throne room at the heels of my little party of survivors a full thousand red men under Kantos Kan, Hor Vastus, and Xodar.

"Where is Dejah Thoris?" I cried to the thing within my hands.

For a moment her eyes roved wildly about the scene beneath her. I think that it took a moment for the true condition to make any impression upon her – she could not at first realize that the temple had fallen before the assault of men of the outer world. When she did, there must have come, too, a terrible realization of what it meant to her – the loss of power – humiliation – the exposure of the fraud and imposture which she had for so long played upon her own people.

There was just one thing needed to complete the reality of the picture she was seeing, and that was added by the highest noble of her realm – the high priest of her religion – the prime minister of her government.

"Issus, Goddess of Death, and of Life Eternal," he cried, "arise in the might of thy righteous wrath and with one single wave of thy omnipotent hand strike dead thy blasphemers! Let not one escape. Issus, thy people depend upon thee. Daughter of the Lesser Moon, thou only art all-powerful. Thou only canst save thy people. I am done. We await thy will. Strike!"

And then it was that she went mad. A screaming, gibbering maniac writhed in my grasp. It bit and clawed and scratched in impotent fury. And then it laughed a weird and terrible laughter that froze the blood. The slave girls upon the dais shrieked and cowered away. And the thing jumped at them and gnashed its teeth and then spat upon them from frothing lips. God, but it was a horrid sight.

Finally, I shook the thing, hoping to recall it for a moment to rationality.

"Where is Dejah Thoris?" I cried again.

The awful creature in my grasp mumbled inarticulately for a moment, then a sudden gleam of cunning shot into those hideous, close-set eyes.

"Dejah Thoris? Dejah Thoris?" and then that shrill, unearthly laugh pierced our ears once more.

"Yes, Dejah Thoris – I know. And Thuvia, and Phaidor, daughter of Matai Shang. They each love John Carter. Ha-ah! but it is droll. Together for a year they will meditate within the Temple of the Sun, but ere the year is quite gone there will be no more food for them. Ho-oh! what divine entertainment," and she licked the froth from her cruel lips. "There will be no more food – except each other. Ha-ah! Ha-ah!"

The horror of the suggestion nearly paralysed me. To this awful fate the creature within my power had condemned my Princess. I trembled in the ferocity of my rage. As a terrier shakes a rat I shook Issus, Goddess of Life Eternal.

"Countermand your orders!" I cried. "Recall the condemned. Haste, or you die!"

"It is too late. Ha-ah! Ha-ah!" and then she commenced her gibbering and shrieking again.

Almost of its own volition, my dagger flew up above that putrid heart. But something stayed my hand, and I am now glad that it did. It were a terrible thing to have struck down a woman with one's own hand. But a fitter fate occurred to me for this false deity.

"First Born," I cried, turning to those who stood within the chamber, "you have seen to-day the impotency of Issus – the gods are impotent. Issus is no god. She is a cruel and wicked old woman, who has deceived and played upon you for ages. Take her. John Carter, Prince of Helium, would not contaminate his hand with her blood," and with that I pushed the raving beast, whom a short half-hour before a whole world had worshipped as divine, from the platform of her throne into the waiting clutches of her betrayed and vengeful people.

Spying Xodar among the officers of the red men, I called him to lead me quickly to the Temple of the Sun, and, without waiting to learn what fate the First Born would wreak upon their goddess, I rushed from the chamber with Xodar, Carthoris, Hor Vastus, Kantos Kan, and a score of other red nobles.

The black led us rapidly through the inner chambers of the temple, until we stood within the central court – a great circular space paved with a transparent marble of exquisite whiteness. Before us rose a golden temple wrought in the most wondrous and fanciful designs, inlaid with diamond, ruby, sapphire, turquoise, emerald, and the thousand nameless gems of Mars, which far transcend in loveliness and purity of ray the most priceless stones of Earth.

"This way," cried Xodar, leading us toward the entrance to a tunnel which opened in the courtyard beside the temple. Just as we were on the point of descending we heard a deep-toned roar burst from the Temple of Issus, which we had but just quitted, and then a red man, Djor Kantos, padwar of the fifth utan, broke from a nearby gate, crying to us to return.

"The blacks have fired the temple," he cried. "In a thousand places it is burning now. Haste to the outer gardens, or you are lost."

As he spoke we saw smoke pouring from a dozen windows looking out upon the courtyard of the Temple of the Sun, and far above the highest minaret of Issus hung an ever-growing pall of smoke.

"Go back! Go back!" I cried to those who had accompanied me. "The way! Xodar; point the way and leave me. I shall reach my Princess yet."

"Follow me, John Carter," replied Xodar, and without waiting for my reply he dashed down into the tunnel at our feet. At his heels I ran down through a half-dozen tiers of galleries, until at last he led me along a level floor at the end of which I discerned a lighted chamber.

Massive bars blocked our further progress, but beyond I saw her – my incomparable Princess, and with her were Thuvia and Phaidor. When she saw me she rushed toward the bars that separated us. Already the chamber had turned upon its slow way so far that but a portion of the opening in the temple wall was opposite the barred end of the corridor. Slowly the interval was closing. In a short time there would be but a tiny crack, and then even that would be closed, and for a long Barsoomian year the chamber would slowly revolve until once more for a brief day the aperture in its wall would pass the corridor's end.

But in the meantime what horrible things would go on within that chamber!

"Xodar!" I cried. "Can no power stop this awful revolving thing? Is there none who holds the secret of these terrible bars?"

"None, I fear, whom we could fetch in time, though I shall go and make the attempt. Wait for me here."

After he had left I stood and talked with Dejah Thoris, and she stretched her dear hand through those cruel bars that I might hold it until the last moment.

Thuvia and Phaidor came close also, but when Thuvia saw that we would be alone she withdrew to the further side of the chamber. Not so the daughter of Matai Shang.

"John Carter," she said, "this be the last time that you shall see any of us. Tell me that you love me, that I may die happy."

"I love only the Princess of Helium," I replied quietly. "I am sorry, Phaidor, but it is as I have told you from the beginning."

She bit her lip and turned away, but not before I saw the black and ugly scowl she turned upon Dejah Thoris. Thereafter she stood a little way apart, but not so far as I should have desired, for I had many little confidences to impart to my long-lost love.

For a few minutes we stood thus talking in low tones. Ever smaller and smaller grew the opening. In a short time now it would be too small even to permit the slender form of my Princess to pass. Oh, why did not Xodar haste. Above we could hear the faint echoes of a great tumult. It was the multitude of black and red and green men fighting their way through the fire from the burning Temple of Issus.

A draught from above brought the fumes of smoke to our nostrils. As we stood waiting for Xodar the smoke became thicker and thicker. Presently we heard shouting at the far end of the corridor, and hurrying feet.

"Come back, John Carter, come back!" cried a voice, "even the pits are burning."

In a moment a dozen men broke through the now blinding smoke to my side. There was Carthoris, and Kantos Kan, and Hor Vastus, and Xodar, with a few more who had followed me to the temple court.

"There is no hope, John Carter," cried Xodar. "The keeper of the keys is dead and his keys are not upon his carcass. Our only hope is to quench this conflagration and trust to fate that a year will find your Princess alive and well. I have brought sufficient food to last them. When this crack closes no smoke can reach them, and if we hasten to extinguish the flames I believe they will be safe."

"Go, then, yourself and take these others with you," I replied. "I shall remain here beside my Princess until a merciful death releases me from my anguish. I care not to live."

As I spoke Xodar had been tossing a great number of tiny cans within the prison cell. The remaining crack was not over an inch in width a moment later. Dejah Thoris stood as close to it as she could, whispering words of hope and courage to me, and urging me to save myself.

Suddenly beyond her I saw the beautiful face of Phaidor contorted into an expression of malign hatred. As my eyes met hers she spoke.

"Think not, John Carter, that you may so lightly cast aside the love of Phaidor, daughter of Matai Shang. Nor ever hope to hold thy Dejah Thoris in thy arms again. Wait you the long, long year; but know that when the waiting is over it shall be Phaidor's arms which shall welcome you – not those of the Princess of Helium. Behold, she dies!"

And as she finished speaking I saw her raise a dagger on high, and then I saw another figure. It was Thuvia's. As the dagger fell toward the unprotected breast of my love, Thuvia was almost between them. A blinding gust of smoke blotted out the tragedy within that fearsome cell – a shriek rang out, a single shriek, as the dagger fell.

The smoke cleared away, but we stood gazing upon a blank wall. The last crevice had closed, and for a long year that hideous chamber would retain its secret from the eyes of men.

They urged me to leave.

"In a moment it will be too late," cried Xodar. "There is, in fact, but a bare chance that we can come through to the outer garden alive even now. I have ordered the pumps started, and in five minutes the pits will be flooded. If we would not drown like rats in a trap we must hasten above and make a dash for safety through the burning temple."

"Go," I urged them. "Let me die here beside my Princess – there is no hope or happiness elsewhere for me. When they carry her dear body from that terrible place a year hence let them find the body of her lord awaiting her."

Of what happened after that I have only a confused recollection. It seems as though I struggled with many men, and then that I was picked bodily from the ground and borne away. I do not know. I have never asked, nor has any other who was there that day intruded on my sorrow or recalled to my mind the occurrences which they know could but at best reopen the terrible wound within my heart.

Ah! If I could but know one thing, what a burden of suspense would be lifted from my shoulders! But whether the assassin's dagger reached one fair bosom or another, only time will divulge.

THE WARLORD OF MARS

BOOK THREE

CHAPTER ONE

On the River Iss

IN THE SHADOWS of the forest that flanks the crimson plain by the side of the Lost Sea of Korus in the Valley Dor, beneath the hurtling moons of Mars, speeding their meteoric way close above the bosom of the dying planet, I crept stealthily along the trail of a shadowy form that hugged the darker places with a persistency that proclaimed the sinister nature of its errand.

For six long Martian months I had haunted the vicinity of the hateful Temple of the Sun, within whose slow-revolving shaft, far beneath the surface of Mars, my princess lay entombed – but whether alive or dead I knew not. Had Phaidor's slim blade found that beloved heart? Time only would reveal the truth.

Six hundred and eighty-seven Martian days must come and go before the cell's door would again come opposite the tunnel's end where last I had seen my ever-beautiful Dejah Thoris.

Half of them had passed, or would on the morrow, yet vivid in my memory, obliterating every event that had come before or after, there remained the last scene before the gust of smoke blinded my eyes and the narrow slit that had given me sight of the interior of her cell closed between me and the Princess of Helium for a long Martian year.

As if it were yesterday, I still saw the beautiful face of Phaidor, daughter of Matai Shang, distorted with jealous rage and hatred as she sprang forward with raised dagger upon the woman I loved.

I saw the red girl, Thuvia of Ptarth, leap forward to prevent the hideous deed.

The smoke from the burning temple had come then to blot out the tragedy, but in my ears rang the single shriek as the knife fell. Then silence, and when the smoke had cleared, the revolving temple had shut off all sight or sound from the chamber in which the three beautiful women were imprisoned.

Much there had been to occupy my attention since that terrible moment; but never for an instant had the memory of the thing faded, and all the time that I could spare from the numerous duties that had devolved upon me in the reconstruction of the government of the First Born since our victorious fleet and land forces had overwhelmed them, had been spent close to the grim shaft that held the mother of my boy, Carthoris of Helium.

The race of blacks that for ages had worshiped Issus, the false deity of Mars, had been left in a state of chaos by my revealment of her as naught more than a wicked old woman. In their rage they had torn her to pieces.

From the high pinnacle of their egotism the First Born had been plunged to the depths of humiliation. Their deity was gone, and with her the whole false fabric of their religion. Their vaunted navy had fallen in defeat before the superior ships and fighting men of the red men of Helium.

Fierce green warriors from the ocher sea bottoms of outer Mars had ridden their wild thoats across the sacred gardens of the Temple of Issus, and Tars Tarkas, Jeddak of Thark, fiercest of them all, had sat upon the throne of Issus and ruled the First Born while the allies were deciding the conquered nation's fate.

Almost unanimous was the request that I ascend the ancient throne of the black men, even the First Born themselves concurring in it; but I would have none of it. My heart could never be with the race that had heaped indignities upon my princess and my son.

At my suggestion Xodar became Jeddak of the First Born. He had been a dator, or prince, until Issus had degraded him, so that his fitness for the high office bestowed was unquestioned.

The peace of the Valley Dor thus assured, the green warriors dispersed to their desolate sea bottoms, while we of Helium returned to our own country. Here again was a throne offered me, since no word had been received from the missing Jeddak of Helium, Tardos Mors, grandfather of Dejah Thoris, or his son, Mors Kajak, Jed of Helium, her father.

Over a year had elapsed since they had set out to explore the northern hemisphere in search of Carthoris, and at last their disheartened people had accepted as truth the vague rumors of their death that had filtered in from the frozen region of the pole.

Once again I refused a throne, for I would not believe that the mighty Tardos Mors, or his no less redoubtable son, was dead.

"Let one of their own blood rule you until they return," I said to the assembled nobles of Helium, as I addressed them from the Pedestal of Truth beside the Throne of Righteousness in the Temple of Reward, from the very spot where I had stood a year before when Zat Arras pronounced the sentence of death upon me.

As I spoke I stepped forward and laid my hand upon the shoulder of Carthoris where he stood in the front rank of the circle of nobles about me.

As one, the nobles and the people lifted their voices in a long cheer of approbation. Ten thousand swords sprang on high from as many scabbards, and the glorious fighting men of ancient Helium hailed Carthoris Jeddak of Helium.

His tenure of office was to be for life or until his great-grandfather, or grandfather, should return. Having thus satisfactorily arranged this important duty for Helium, I started the following day for the Valley Dor that I might remain close to the Temple of the Sun until the fateful day that should see the opening of the prison cell where my lost love lay buried.

Hor Vastus and Kantos Kan, with my other noble lieutenants, I left with Carthoris at Helium, that he might have the benefit of their wisdom, bravery, and loyalty in the performance of the arduous duties which had devolved upon him. Only Woola, my Martian hound, accompanied me.

At my heels tonight the faithful beast moved softly in my tracks. As large as a Shetland pony, with hideous head and frightful fangs, he was indeed an awesome spectacle, as he crept after me on his ten short, muscular legs; but to me he was the embodiment of love and loyalty.

The figure ahead was that of the black dator of the First Born, Thurid, whose undying enmity I had earned that time I laid him low with my bare hands in the courtyard of the Temple of Issus, and bound him with his own harness before the noble men and women who had but a moment before been extolling his prowess.

Like many of his fellows, he had apparently accepted the new order of things with good grace, and had sworn fealty to Xodar, his new ruler; but I knew that he hated me, and I was sure that in his heart he envied and hated Xodar, so I had kept a watch upon his comings and goings, to the end that of late I had become convinced that he was occupied with some manner of intrigue.

Several times I had observed him leaving the walled city of the First Born after dark, taking his way out into the cruel and horrible Valley Dor, where no honest business could lead any man.

Tonight he moved quickly along the edge of the forest until well beyond sight or sound of the city, then he turned across the crimson sward toward the shore of the Lost Sea of Korus.

The rays of the nearer moon, swinging low across the valley, touched his jewel-incrusted harness with a thousand changing lights and glanced from the glossy ebony of his smooth hide. Twice he turned his head back toward the forest, after the manner of one who is upon an evil errand, though he must have felt quite safe from pursuit.

I did not dare follow him there beneath the moonlight, since it best suited my plans not to interrupt his – I wished him to reach his destination unsuspecting, that I might learn just where that destination lay and the business that awaited the night prowler there.

So it was that I remained hidden until after Thurid had disappeared over the edge of the steep bank beside the sea a quarter of a mile away. Then, with Woola following, I hastened across the open after the black dator.

The quiet of the tomb lay upon the mysterious valley of death, crouching deep in its warm nest within the sunken area at the south pole of the dying planet. In the far distance the Golden Cliffs raised their mighty barrier faces far into the starlit heavens, the precious metals and scintillating jewels that composed them sparkling in the brilliant light of Mars's two gorgeous moons.

At my back was the forest, pruned and trimmed like the sward to parklike symmetry by the browsing of the ghoulish plant men.

Before me lay the Lost Sea of Korus, while farther on I caught the shimmering ribbon of Iss, the River of Mystery, where it wound out from beneath the Golden Cliffs to empty into Korus, to which for countless ages had been borne the deluded and unhappy Martians of the outer world upon the voluntary pilgrimage to this false heaven.

The plant men, with their blood-sucking hands, and the monstrous white apes that make Dor hideous by day, were hidden in their lairs for the night.

There was no longer a Holy Thern upon the balcony in the Golden Cliffs above the Iss to summon them with weird cry to the victims floating down to their maws upon the cold, broad bosom of ancient Iss.

The navies of Helium and the First Born had cleared the fortresses and the temples of the therns when they had refused to surrender and accept the new order of things that had swept their false religion from long-suffering Mars.

In a few isolated countries they still retained their age-old power; but Matai Shang, their hekkador, Father of Therns, had been driven from his temple. Strenuous had been our endeavors to capture him; but with a few of the faithful he had escaped, and was in hiding – where we knew not.

As I came cautiously to the edge of the low cliff overlooking the Lost Sea of Korus I saw Thurid pushing out upon the bosom of the shimmering water in a small skiff – one of those strangely wrought craft of unthinkable age which the Holy Therns, with their organization of priests and lesser therns, were wont to distribute along the banks of the Iss, that the long journey of their victims might be facilitated.

Drawn up on the beach below me were a score of similar boats, each with its long pole, at one end of which was a pike, at the other a paddle. Thurid was hugging the shore, and as he passed out of sight round a near-by promontory I shoved one of the boats into the water and, calling Woola into it, pushed out from shore.

The pursuit of Thurid carried me along the edge of the sea toward the mouth of the Iss. The farther moon lay close to the horizon, casting a dense shadow beneath the cliffs that fringed the water. Thuria, the nearer moon, had set, nor would it rise again for near four hours, so that I was ensured concealing darkness for that length of time at least.

On and on went the black warrior. Now he was opposite the mouth of the Iss. Without an instant's hesitation he turned up the grim river, paddling hard against the strong current.

After him came Woola and I, closer now, for the man was too intent upon forcing his craft up the river to have any eyes for what might be transpiring behind him. He hugged the shore where the current was less strong.

Presently he came to the dark cavernous portal in the face of the Golden Cliffs, through which the river poured. On into the Stygian darkness beyond he urged his craft.

It seemed hopeless to attempt to follow him here where I could not see my hand before my face, and I was almost on the point of giving up the pursuit and drifting back to the mouth of the river, there to await his return, when a sudden bend showed a faint luminosity ahead.

My quarry was plainly visible again, and in the increasing light from the phosphorescent rock that lay embedded in great patches in the roughly arched roof of the cavern I had no difficulty in following him.

It was my first trip upon the bosom of Iss, and the things I saw there will live forever in my memory.

Terrible as they were, they could not have commenced to approximate the horrible conditions which must have obtained before Tars Tarkas, the great green warrior, Xodar, the black dator, and I brought the light of truth to the outer world and stopped the mad rush of millions upon the voluntary pilgrimage to what they believed would end in a beautiful valley of peace and happiness and love.

Even now the low islands which dotted the broad stream were choked with the skeletons and half devoured carcasses of those who, through fear or a sudden awakening to the truth, had halted almost at the completion of their journey.

In the awful stench of these frightful charnel isles haggard maniacs screamed and gibbered and fought among the torn remnants of their grisly feasts; while on those which contained but clean-picked bones they battled with one another, the weaker furnishing sustenance for the stronger; or with clawlike hands clutched at the bloated bodies that drifted down with the current.

Thurid paid not the slightest attention to the screaming things that either menaced or pleaded with him as the mood directed them – evidently he was familiar with the horrid sights that surrounded him. He continued up the river for perhaps a mile; and then, crossing over to the left bank, drew his craft up on a low ledge that lay almost on a level with the water.

I dared not follow across the stream, for he most surely would have seen me. Instead I stopped close to the opposite wall beneath an overhanging mass of rock that cast a dense shadow beneath it. Here I could watch Thurid without danger of discovery.

The black was standing upon the ledge beside his boat, looking up the river, as though he were awaiting one whom he expected from that direction.

As I lay there beneath the dark rocks I noticed that a strong current seemed to flow directly toward the center of the river, so that it was difficult to hold my craft in its position. I edged farther into the shadow that I might find a hold upon the bank; but, though I proceeded several yards, I touched nothing; and then, finding that I would soon reach a point from where I could no longer see the black man, I was compelled to remain where I was, holding my position as best I could by paddling strongly against the current which flowed from beneath the rocky mass behind me.

I could not imagine what might cause this strong lateral flow, for the main channel of the river was plainly visible to me from where I sat, and I could see the rippling junction of it and the mysterious current which had aroused my curiosity.

While I was still speculating upon the phenomenon, my attention was suddenly riveted upon Thurid, who had raised both palms forward above his head in the universal salute of Martians, and a moment later his "Kaor!" the Barsoomian word of greeting, came in low but distinct tones.

I turned my eyes up the river in the direction that his were bent, and presently there came within my limited range of vision a long boat, in which were six men. Five were at the paddles, while the sixth sat in the seat of honor.

The white skins, the flowing yellow wigs which covered their bald pates, and the gorgeous diadems set in circlets of gold about their heads marked them as Holy Therns.

As they drew up beside the ledge upon which Thurid awaited them, he in the bow of the boat arose to step ashore, and then I saw that it was none other than Matai Shang, Father of Therns.

The evident cordiality with which the two men exchanged greetings filled me with wonder, for the black and white men of Barsoom were hereditary enemies – nor ever before had I known of two meeting other than in battle.

Evidently the reverses that had recently overtaken both peoples had resulted in an alliance between these two individuals – at least against the common enemy – and now I saw why Thurid had come so often out into the Valley Dor by night, and that the nature of his conspiring might be such as to strike very close to me or to my friends.

I wished that I might have found a point closer to the two men from which to have heard their conversation; but it was out of the question now to attempt to cross the river, and so I lay quietly watching them, who would have given so much to have known how close I lay to them, and how easily they might have overcome and killed me with their superior force.

Several times Thurid pointed across the river in my direction, but that his gestures had any reference to me I did not for a moment believe. Presently he and Matai Shang entered the latter's boat, which turned out into the river and, swinging round, forged steadily across in my direction.

As they advanced I moved my boat farther and farther in beneath the overhanging wall, but at last it became evident that their craft was holding the same course. The five paddlers sent the larger boat ahead at a speed that taxed my energies to equal.

Every instant I expected to feel my prow crash against solid rock. The light from the river was no longer visible, but ahead I saw the faint tinge of a distant radiance, and still the water before me was open.

At last the truth dawned upon me – I was following a subterranean river which emptied into the Iss at the very point where I had hidden.

The rowers were now quite close to me. The noise of their own paddles drowned the sound of mine, but in another instant the growing light ahead would reveal me to them.

There was no time to be lost. Whatever action I was to take must be taken at once. Swinging the prow of my boat toward the right, I sought the river's rocky side, and there I lay while Matai Shang and Thurid approached up the center of the stream, which was much narrower than the Iss.

As they came nearer I heard the voices of Thurid and the Father of Therns raised in argument.

"I tell you, Thern," the black dator was saying, "that I wish only vengeance upon John Carter, Prince of Helium. I am leading you into no trap. What could I gain by betraying you to those who have ruined my nation and my house?"

"Let us stop here a moment that I may hear your plans," replied the hekkador, "and then we may proceed with a better understanding of our duties and obligations."

To the rowers he issued the command that brought their boat in toward the bank not a dozen paces beyond the spot where I lay.

Had they pulled in below me they must surely have seen me against the faint glow of light ahead, but from where they finally came to rest I was as secure from detection as though miles separated us.

The few words I had already overheard whetted my curiosity, and I was anxious to learn what manner of vengeance Thurid was planning against me. Nor had I long to wait. I listened intently.

"There are no obligations, Father of Therns," continued the First Born. "Thurid, Dator of Issus, has no price. When the thing has been accomplished I shall be glad if you will see to it that I am well received, as is befitting my ancient lineage and noble rank, at some court that is yet loyal to thy ancient faith, for I cannot return to the Valley Dor or elsewhere within the power of the Prince of Helium; but even that I do not demand – it shall be as your own desire in the matter directs."

"It shall be as you wish, Dator," replied Matai Shang; "nor is that all – power and riches shall be yours if you restore my daughter, Phaidor, to me, and place within my power Dejah Thoris, Princess of Helium.

"Ah," he continued with a malicious snarl, "but the Earth man shall suffer for the indignities he has put upon the holy of holies, nor shall any vileness be too vile to inflict upon his princess. Would that it were in my power to force him to witness the humiliation and degradation of the red woman."

"You shall have your way with her before another day has passed, Matai Shang," said Thurid, "if you but say the word."

"I have heard of the Temple of the Sun, Dator," replied Matai Shang, "but never have I heard that its prisoners could be released before the allotted year of their incarceration had elapsed. How, then, may you accomplish the impossible?"

"Access may be had to any cell of the temple at any time," replied Thurid. "Only Issus knew this; nor was it ever Issus' way to divulge more of her secrets than were necessary. By chance, after her death, I came upon an ancient plan of the temple, and there I found, plainly writ, the most minute directions for reaching the cells at any time.

"And more I learned – that many men had gone thither for Issus in the past, always on errands of death and torture to the prisoners; but those who thus learned the secret way were wont to die mysteriously immediately they had returned and made their reports to cruel Issus."

"Let us proceed, then," said Matai Shang at last. "I must trust you, yet at the same time you must trust me, for we are six to your one."

"I do not fear," replied Thurid, "nor need you. Our hatred of the common enemy is sufficient bond to insure our loyalty to each other, and after we have defiled the Princess of Helium there will be still greater reason for the maintenance of our allegiance – unless I greatly mistake the temper of her lord."

Matai Shang spoke to the paddlers. The boat moved on up the tributary.

It was with difficulty that I restrained myself from rushing upon them and slaying the two vile plotters; but quickly I saw the mad rashness of such an act, which would cut down the only man who could lead the way to Dejah Thoris' prison before the long Martian year had swung its interminable circle.

If he should lead Matai Shang to that hollowed spot, then, too, should he lead John Carter, Prince of Helium.

With silent paddle I swung slowly into the wake of the larger craft.

CHAPTER TWO

Under the Mountains

As WE ADVANCED up the river which winds beneath the Golden Cliffs out of the bowels of the Mountains of Otz to mingle its dark waters with the grim and mysterious Iss the faint glow which had appeared before us grew gradually into an all-enveloping radiance.

The river widened until it presented the aspect of a large lake whose vaulted dome, lighted by glowing phosphorescent rock, was splashed with the vivid rays of the diamond, the sapphire, the ruby, and the countless, nameless jewels of Barsoom which lay incrusted in the virgin gold which forms the major portion of these magnificent cliffs.

Beyond the lighted chamber of the lake was darkness – what lay behind the darkness I could not even guess.

To have followed the thern boat across the gleaming water would have been to invite instant detection, and so, though I was loath to permit Thurid to pass even for an instant beyond my sight, I was forced to wait in the shadows until the other boat had passed from my sight at the far extremity of the lake.

Then I paddled out upon the brilliant surface in the direction they had taken.

When, after what seemed an eternity, I reached the shadows at the upper end of the lake I found that the river issued from a low aperture, to pass beneath which it was necessary that I compel Woola to lie flat in the boat, and I, myself, must need bend double before the low roof cleared my head.

Immediately the roof rose again upon the other side, but no longer was the way brilliantly lighted. Instead only a feeble glow emanated from small and scattered patches of phosphorescent rock in wall and roof.

Directly before me the river ran into this smaller chamber through three separate arched openings.

Thurid and the therns were nowhere to be seen – into which of the dark holes had they disappeared? There was no means by which I might know, and so I chose the center opening as being as likely to lead me in the right direction as another.

Here the way was through utter darkness. The stream was narrow – so narrow that in the blackness I was constantly bumping first one rock wall and then another as the river wound hither and thither along its flinty bed.

Far ahead I presently heard a deep and sullen roar which increased in volume as I advanced, and then broke upon my ears with all the intensity of its mad fury as I swung round a sharp curve into a dimly lighted stretch of water.

Directly before me the river thundered down from above in a mighty waterfall that filled the narrow gorge from side to side, rising far above me several hundred feet – as magnificent a spectacle as I ever had seen.

But the roar – the awful, deafening roar of those tumbling waters penned in the rocky, subterranean vault! Had the fall not entirely blocked my further passage and shown me that I had followed the wrong course I believe that I should have fled anyway before the maddening tumult.

Thurid and the therns could not have come this way. By stumbling upon the wrong course I had lost the trail, and they had gained so much ahead of me that now I might not be able to find them before it was too late, if, in fact, I could find them at all.

It had taken several hours to force my way up to the falls against the strong current, and other hours would be required for the descent, although the pace would be much swifter.

With a sigh I turned the prow of my craft down stream, and with mighty strokes hastened with reckless speed through the dark and tortuous channel until once again I came to the chamber into which flowed the three branches of the river.

Two unexplored channels still remained from which to choose; nor was there any means by which I could judge which was the more likely to lead me to the plotters.

Never in my life, that I can recall, have I suffered such an agony of indecision. So much depended upon a correct choice; so much depended upon haste.

The hours that I had already lost might seal the fate of the incomparable Dejah Thoris were she not already dead – to sacrifice other hours, and maybe days in a fruitless exploration of another blind lead would unquestionably prove fatal.

Several times I essayed the right-hand entrance only to turn back as though warned by some strange intuitive sense that this was not the way. At last, convinced by the oft-recurring phenomenon, I cast my all upon the left-hand archway; yet it was with a lingering doubt that I turned a parting look at the sullen waters which rolled, dark and forbidding, from beneath the grim, low archway on the right.

And as I looked there came bobbing out upon the current from the Stygian darkness of the interior the shell of one of the great, succulent fruits of the sorapus tree.

I could scarce restrain a shout of elation as this silent, insensate messenger floated past me, on toward the Iss and Korus, for it told me that journeying Martians were above me on that very stream.

They had eaten of this marvelous fruit which nature concentrates within the hard shell of the sorapus nut, and having eaten had cast the husk overboard. It could have come from no others than the party I sought.

Quickly I abandoned all thought of the left-hand passage, and a moment later had turned into the right. The stream soon widened, and recurring areas of phosphorescent rock lighted my way.

I made good time, but was convinced that I was nearly a day behind those I was tracking. Neither Woola nor I had eaten since the previous day, but in so far as he was concerned it mattered but little, since practically all the animals of the dead sea bottoms of Mars are able to go for incredible periods without nourishment.

Nor did I suffer. The water of the river was sweet and cold, for it was unpolluted by decaying bodies – like the Iss – and as for food, why the mere thought that I was nearing my beloved princess raised me above every material want.

As I proceeded, the river became narrower and the current swift and turbulent – so swift in fact that it was with difficulty that I forced my craft upward at all. I could not have been making to exceed a hundred yards an hour when, at a bend, I was confronted by a series of rapids through which the river foamed and boiled at a terrific rate.

My heart sank within me. The sorapus nutshell had proved a false prophet, and, after all, my intuition had been correct – it was the left-hand channel that I should have followed.

Had I been a woman I should have wept. At my right was a great, slow-moving eddy that circled far beneath the cliff's overhanging side, and to rest my tired muscles before turning back I let my boat drift into its embrace.

I was almost prostrated by disappointment. It would mean another half-day's loss of time to retrace my way and take the only passage that yet remained unexplored. What hellish fate had led me to select from three possible avenues the two that were wrong?

As the lazy current of the eddy carried me slowly about the periphery of the watery circle my boat twice touched the rocky side of the river in the dark recess beneath the cliff. A third time it struck, gently as it had before, but the contact resulted in a different sound – the sound of wood scraping upon wood.

In an instant I was on the alert, for there could be no wood within that buried river that had not been man brought. Almost coincidentally with my first apprehension of the noise, my hand shot out across the boat's side, and a second later I felt my fingers gripping the gunwale of another craft.

As though turned to stone I sat in tense and rigid silence, straining my eyes into the utter darkness before me in an effort to discover if the boat were occupied.

It was entirely possible that there might be men on board it who were still ignorant of my presence, for the boat was scraping gently against the rocks upon one side, so that the gentle touch of my boat upon the other easily could have gone unnoticed.

Peer as I would I could not penetrate the darkness, and then I listened intently for the sound of breathing near me; but except for the noise of the rapids, the soft scraping of the boats, and the lapping of the water at their sides I could distinguish no sound. As usual, I thought rapidly.

A rope lay coiled in the bottom of my own craft. Very softly I gathered it up, and making one end fast to the bronze ring in the prow I stepped gingerly into the boat beside me. In one hand I grasped the rope, in the other my keen long-sword.

For a full minute, perhaps, I stood motionless after entering the strange craft. It had rocked a trifle beneath my weight, but it had been the scraping of its side against the side of my own boat that had seemed most likely to alarm its occupants, if there were any.

But there was no answering sound, and a moment later I had felt from stem to stern and found the boat deserted.

Groping with my hands along the face of the rocks to which the craft was moored, I discovered a narrow ledge which I knew must be the avenue taken by those who had come before me. That they could be none other than Thurid and his party I was convinced by the size and build of the boat I had found.

Calling to Woola to follow me I stepped out upon the ledge. The great, savage brute, agile as a cat, crept after me.

As he passed through the boat that had been occupied by Thurid and the therns he emitted a single low growl, and when he came beside me upon the ledge and my hand rested upon his neck I felt his short mane bristling with anger. I think he sensed telepathically the recent presence of an enemy, for I had made no effort to impart to him the nature of our quest or the status of those we tracked.

This omission I now made haste to correct, and, after the manner of green Martians with their beasts, I let him know partially by the weird and uncanny telepathy of Barsoom and partly by word of mouth that we were upon the trail of those who had recently occupied the boat through which we had just passed.

A soft purr, like that of a great cat, indicated that Woola understood, and then, with a word to him to follow, I turned to the right along the ledge, but scarcely had I done so than I felt his mighty fangs tugging at my leathern harness.

As I turned to discover the cause of his act he continued to pull me steadily in the opposite direction, nor would he desist until I had turned about and indicated that I would follow him voluntarily.

Never had I known him to be in error in a matter of tracking, so it was with a feeling of entire security that I moved cautiously in the huge beast's wake. Through Cimmerian darkness he moved along the narrow ledge beside the boiling rapids.

As we advanced, the way led from beneath the overhanging cliffs out into a dim light, and then it was that I saw that the trail had been cut from the living rock, and that it ran up along the river's side beyond the rapids.

For hours we followed the dark and gloomy river farther and farther into the bowels of Mars. From the direction and distance I knew that we must be well beneath the Valley Dor, and possibly beneath the Sea of Omean as well – it could not be much farther now to the Temple of the Sun.

Even as my mind framed the thought, Woola halted suddenly before a narrow, arched doorway in the cliff by the trail's side. Quickly he crouched back away from the entrance, at the same time turning his eyes toward me.

Words could not have more plainly told me that danger of some sort lay near by, and so I pressed quietly forward to his side, and passing him looked into the aperture at our right.

Before me was a fair-sized chamber that, from its appointments, I knew must have at one time been a guardroom. There were racks for weapons, and slightly raised platforms for the sleeping silks and furs of the warriors, but now its only occupants were two of the therns who had been of the party with Thurid and Matai Shang.

The men were in earnest conversation, and from their tones it was apparent that they were entirely unaware that they had listeners.

"I tell you," one of them was saying, "I do not trust the black one. There was no necessity for leaving us here to guard the way. Against what, pray, should we guard this long-forgotten, abysmal path? It was but a ruse to divide our numbers.

"He will have Matai Shang leave others elsewhere on some pretext or other, and then at last he will fall upon us with his confederates and slay us all."

"I believe you, Lakor," replied the other, "there can never be aught else than deadly hatred between thern and First Born. And what think you of the ridiculous matter of the light? 'Let the light shine with the intensity of three radium units for fifty tals, and for one xat let it shine with the intensity of one radium unit, and then for twenty-five tals with nine units.' Those were his very words, and to think that wise old Matai Shang should listen to such foolishness."

"Indeed, it is silly," replied Lakor. "It will open nothing other than the way to a quick death for us all. He had to make some answer when Matai Shang asked him flatly what he should do when he came to the Temple of the Sun, and so he made his answer quickly from his imagination – I would wager a hekkador's diadem that he could not now repeat it himself."

"Let us not remain here longer, Lakor," spoke the other thern. "Perchance if we hasten after them we may come in time to rescue Matai Shang, and wreak our own vengeance upon the black dator. What say you?"

"Never in a long life," answered Lakor, "have I disobeyed a single command of the Father of Therns. I shall stay here until I rot if he does not return to bid me elsewhere."

Lakor's companion shook his head.

"You are my superior," he said; "I cannot do other than you sanction, though I still believe that we are foolish to remain."

I, too, thought that they were foolish to remain, for I saw from Woola's actions that the trail led through the room where the two therns held guard. I had no reason to harbor any considerable love for this race of self-deified demons, yet I would have passed them by were it possible without molesting them.

It was worth trying anyway, for a fight might delay us considerably, or even put an end entirely to my search – better men than I have gone down before fighters of meaner ability than that possessed by the fierce thern warriors.

Signaling Woola to heel I stepped suddenly into the room before the two men. At sight of me their long-swords flashed from the harness at their sides, but I raised my hand in a gesture of restraint.

"I seek Thurid, the black dator," I said. "My quarrel is with him, not with you. Let me pass then in peace, for if I mistake not he is as much your enemy as mine, and you can have no cause to protect him."

They lowered their swords and Lakor spoke.

"I know not whom you may be, with the white skin of a thern and the black hair of a red man; but were it only Thurid whose safety were at stake you might pass, and welcome, in so far as we be concerned.

"Tell us who you be, and what mission calls you to this unknown world beneath the Valley Dor, then maybe we can see our way to let you pass upon the errand which we should like to undertake would our orders permit."

I was surprised that neither of them had recognized me, for I thought that I was quite sufficiently well known either by personal experience or reputation to every thern upon Barsoom as to make my identity immediately apparent in any part of the planet. In fact, I was the only white man upon Mars whose hair was black and whose eyes were gray, with the exception of my son, Carthoris.

To reveal my identity might be to precipitate an attack, for every thern upon Barsoom knew that to me they owed the fall of their age-old spiritual supremacy. On the other hand my reputation as a fighting man might be sufficient to pass me by these two were their livers not of the right complexion to welcome a battle to the death.

To be quite candid I did not attempt to delude myself with any such sophistry, since I knew well that upon war-like Mars there are few cowards, and that every man, whether prince, priest, or peasant, glories in deadly strife. And so I gripped my long-sword the tighter as I replied to Lakor.

"I believe that you will see the wisdom of permitting me to pass unmolested," I said, "for it would avail you nothing to die uselessly in the rocky bowels of Barsoom merely to protect a hereditary enemy, such as Thurid, Dator of the First Born.

"That you shall die should you elect to oppose me is evidenced by the moldering corpses of all the many great Barsoomian warriors who have gone down beneath this blade – I am John Carter, Prince of Helium."

For a moment that name seemed to paralyze the two men; but only for a moment, and then the younger of them, with a vile name upon his lips, rushed toward me with ready sword.

He had been standing a little behind his companion, Lakor, during our parley, and now, ere he could engage me, the older man grasped his harness and drew him back.

"Hold!" commanded Lakor. "There will be plenty of time to fight if we find it wise to fight at all. There be good reasons why every thern upon Barsoom should yearn to spill the blood of the blasphemer, the sacrilegist; but let us mix wisdom with our righteous hate. The Prince of Helium is bound upon an errand which we ourselves, but a moment since, were wishing that we might undertake.

"Let him go then and slay the black. When he returns we shall still be here to bar his way to the outer world, and thus we shall have rid ourselves of two enemies, nor have incurred the displeasure of the Father of Therns."

As he spoke I could not but note the crafty glint in his evil eyes, and while I saw the apparent logic of his reasoning I felt, subconsciously perhaps, that his words did but veil some sinister intent. The other thern turned toward him in evident surprise, but when Lakor had whispered a few brief words into his ear he, too, drew back and nodded acquiescence to his superior's suggestion.

"Proceed, John Carter," said Lakor; "but know that if Thurid does not lay you low there will be those awaiting your return who will see that you never pass again into the sunlight of the upper world. Go!"

During our conversation Woola had been growling and bristling close to my side. Occasionally he would look up into my face with a low, pleading whine, as though begging for the word that would send him headlong at the bare throats before him. He, too, sensed the villainy behind the smooth words.

Beyond the therns several doorways opened off the guardroom, and toward the one upon the extreme right Lakor motioned.

"That way leads to Thurid," he said.

But when I would have called Woola to follow me there the beast whined and held back, and at last ran quickly to the first opening at the left, where he stood emitting his coughing bark, as though urging me to follow him upon the right way.

I turned a questioning look upon Lakor.

"The brute is seldom wrong," I said, "and while I do not doubt your superior knowledge, Thern, I think that I shall do well to listen to the voice of instinct that is backed by love and loyalty."

As I spoke I smiled grimly that he might know without words that I distrusted him.

"As you will," the fellow replied with a shrug. "In the end it shall be all the same."

I turned and followed Woola into the left-hand passage, and though my back was toward my enemies, my ears were on the alert; yet I heard no sound of pursuit. The passageway was dimly lighted by occasional radium bulbs, the universal lighting medium of Barsoom.

These same lamps may have been doing continuous duty in these subterranean chambers for ages, since they require no attention and are so compounded that they give off but the minutest of their substance in the generation of years of luminosity.

We had proceeded for but a short distance when we commenced to pass the mouths of diverging corridors, but not once did Woola hesitate. It was at the opening to one of these corridors upon my right that I presently heard a sound that spoke more plainly to John Carter, fighting man, than could the words of my mother tongue – it was the clank of metal – the metal of a warrior's harness – and it came from a little distance up the corridor upon my right.

Woola heard it, too, and like a flash he had wheeled and stood facing the threatened danger, his mane all abristle and all his rows of glistening fangs bared by snarling, backdrawn lips. With a gesture I silenced him, and together we drew aside into another corridor a few paces farther on.

Here we waited; nor did we have long to wait, for presently we saw the shadows of two men fall upon the floor of the main corridor athwart the doorway of our hiding place. Very cautiously they were moving now – the accidental clank that had alarmed me was not repeated.

Presently they came opposite our station; nor was I surprised to see that the two were Lakor and his companion of the guardroom.

They walked very softly, and in the right hand of each gleamed a keen long-sword. They halted quite close to the entrance of our retreat, whispering to each other.

"Can it be that we have distanced them already?" said Lakor.

"Either that or the beast has led the man upon a wrong trail," replied the other, "for the way which we took is by far the shorter to this point – for him who knows it. John Carter would have found it a short road to death had he taken it as you suggested to him."

"Yes," said Lakor, "no amount of fighting ability would have saved him from the pivoted flagstone. He surely would have stepped upon it, and by now, if the pit beneath it has a bottom, which Thurid denies, he should have been rapidly approaching it. Curses on that calot of his that warned him toward the safer avenue!"

"There be other dangers ahead of him, though," spoke Lakor's fellow, "which he may not so easily escape – should he succeed in escaping our two good swords. Consider, for example, what chance he will have, coming unexpectedly into the chamber of – "

I would have given much to have heard the balance of that conversation that I might have been warned of the perils that lay ahead, but fate intervened, and just at the very instant of all other instants that I would not have elected to do it, I sneezed.

CHAPTER THREE

The Temple of the Sun

THERE WAS NOTHING for it now other than to fight; nor did I have any advantage as I sprang, sword in hand, into the corridor before the two therns, for my untimely sneeze had warned them of my presence and they were ready for me.

There were no words, for they would have been a waste of breath. The very presence of the two proclaimed their treachery. That they were following to fall upon me unawares was all too plain, and they, of course, must have known that I understood their plan.

In an instant I was engaged with both, and though I loathe the very name of thern, I must in all fairness admit that they are mighty swordsmen; and these two were no exception, unless it were that they were even more skilled and fearless than the average among their race.

While it lasted it was indeed as joyous a conflict as I ever had experienced. Twice at least I saved my breast from the mortal thrust of piercing steel only by the wondrous agility with which my earthly muscles endow me under the conditions of lesser gravity and air pressure upon Mars.

Yet even so I came near to tasting death that day in the gloomy corridor beneath Mars's southern pole, for Lakor played a trick upon me that in all my experience of fighting upon two planets I never before had witnessed the like of.

The other thern was engaging me at the time, and I was forcing him back – touching him here and there with my point until he was bleeding from a dozen wounds, yet not being able to penetrate his marvelous guard to reach a vulnerable spot for the brief instant that would have been sufficient to send him to his ancestors.

It was then that Lakor quickly unslung a belt from his harness, and as I stepped back to parry a wicked thrust he lashed one end of it about my left ankle so that it wound there for an instant, while he jerked suddenly upon the other end, throwing me heavily upon my back.

Then, like leaping panthers, they were upon me; but they had reckoned without Woola, and before ever a blade touched me, a roaring embodiment of a thousand demons hurtled above my prostrate form and my loyal Martian calot was upon them.

Imagine, if you can, a huge grizzly with ten legs armed with mighty talons and an enormous froglike mouth splitting his head from ear to ear, exposing three rows of long, white tusks. Then endow this creature of your imagination with the agility and ferocity of a half-starved Bengal tiger and the strength of a span of bulls, and you will have some faint conception of Woola in action.

Before I could call him off he had crushed Lakor into a jelly with a single blow of one mighty paw, and had literally torn the other thern to ribbons; yet when I spoke to him sharply he cowed sheepishly as though he had done a thing to deserve censure and chastisement.

Never had I had the heart to punish Woola during the long years that had passed since that first day upon Mars when the green jed of the Tharks had placed him on guard over me, and I had won his love and loyalty from the cruel and loveless masters of his former life, yet I believe he would have submitted to any cruelty that I might have inflicted upon him, so wondrous was his affection for me.

The diadem in the center of the circlet of gold upon the brow of Lakor proclaimed him a Holy Thern, while his companion, not thus adorned, was a lesser thern, though from his harness I gleaned that he had reached the Ninth Cycle, which is but one below that of the Holy Therns.

As I stood for a moment looking at the gruesome havoc Woola had wrought, there recurred to me the memory of that other occasion upon which I had masqueraded in the wig, diadem, and harness of Sator Throg, the Holy Thern whom Thuvia of Ptarth had slain, and now it occurred to me that it might prove of worth to utilize Lakor's trappings for the same purpose.

A moment later I had torn his yellow wig from his bald pate and transferred it and the circlet, as well as all his harness, to my own person.

Woola did not approve of the metamorphosis. He sniffed at me and growled ominously, but when I spoke to him and patted his huge head he at length became reconciled to the change, and at my command trotted off along the corridor in the direction we had been going when our progress had been interrupted by the therns.

We moved cautiously now, warned by the fragment of conversation I had overheard. I kept abreast of Woola that we might have the benefit of all our eyes for what might appear suddenly ahead to menace us, and well it was that we were forewarned.

At the bottom of a flight of narrow steps the corridor turned sharply back upon itself, immediately making another turn in the original direction, so that at that point it formed a perfect letter S, the top leg of which debouched suddenly into a large chamber, illy lighted, and the floor of which was completely covered by venomous snakes and loathsome reptiles.

To have attempted to cross that floor would have been to court instant death, and for a moment I was almost completely discouraged. Then it occurred to me that Thurid and Matai Shang with their party must have crossed it, and so there was a way.

Had it not been for the fortunate accident by which I overheard even so small a portion of the therns' conversation we should have blundered at least a step or two into that wriggling mass of destruction, and a single step would have been all-sufficient to have sealed our doom.

These were the only reptiles I had ever seen upon Barsoom, but I knew from their similarity to the fossilized remains of supposedly extinct species I had seen in the museums of Helium that they comprised many of the known prehistoric reptilian genera, as well as others undiscovered.

A more hideous aggregation of monsters had never before assailed my vision. It would be futile to attempt to describe them to Earth men, since substance is the only thing which they possess in common with any creature of the past or present with which you are familiar – even their venom is of an unearthly virulence that, by comparison, would make the cobra de capello seem quite as harmless as an angleworm.

As they spied me there was a concerted rush by those nearest the entrance where we stood, but a line of radium bulbs inset along the threshold of their chamber brought them to a sudden halt – evidently they dared not cross that line of light.

I had been quite sure that they would not venture beyond the room in which I had discovered them, though I had not guessed at what deterred them. The simple fact that we had found no reptiles in the corridor through which we had just come was sufficient assurance that they did not venture there.

I drew Woola out of harm's way, and then began a careful survey of as much of the Chamber of Reptiles as I could see from where I stood. As my eyes became accustomed to the dim light of its interior I gradually made out a low gallery at the far end of the apartment from which opened several exits.

Coming as close to the threshold as I dared, I followed this gallery with my eyes, discovering that it circled the room as far as I could see. Then I glanced above me along the upper edge of the entrance to which we had come, and there, to my delight, I saw an end of the gallery not a foot above my head. In an instant I had leaped to it and called Woola after me.

Here there were no reptiles – the way was clear to the opposite side of the hideous chamber – and a moment later Woola and I dropped down to safety in the corridor beyond.

Not ten minutes later we came into a vast circular apartment of white marble, the walls of which were inlaid with gold in the strange hieroglyphics of the First Born.

From the high dome of this mighty apartment a huge circular column extended to the floor, and as I watched I saw that it slowly revolved.

I had reached the base of the Temple of the Sun!

Somewhere above me lay Dejah Thoris, and with her were Phaidor, daughter of Matai Shang, and Thuvia of Ptarth. But how to reach them, now that I had found the only vulnerable spot in their mighty prison, was still a baffling riddle.

Slowly I circled the great shaft, looking for a means of ingress. Part way around I found a tiny radium flash torch, and as I examined it in mild curiosity as to its presence there in this almost inaccessible and unknown spot, I came suddenly upon the insignia of the house of Thurid jewel-inset in its metal case.

I am upon the right trail, I thought, as I slipped the bauble into the pocket-pouch which hung from my harness. Then I continued my search for the entrance, which I knew must be somewhere about; nor had I long to search, for almost immediately thereafter I came upon a small door so cunningly inlaid in the shaft's base that it might have passed unnoticed by a less keen or careful observer.

There was the door that would lead me within the prison, but where was the means to open it? No button or lock were visible. Again and again I went carefully over every square inch of its surface, but the most that I could find was a tiny pinhole a little above and to the right of the door's center – a pinhole that seemed only an accident of manufacture or an imperfection of material.

Into this minute aperture I attempted to peer, but whether it was but a fraction of an inch deep or passed completely through the door I could not tell – at least no light showed beyond it. I put my ear to it next and listened, but again my efforts brought negligible results.

During these experiments Woola had been standing at my side gazing intently at the door, and as my glance fell upon him it occurred to me to test the correctness of my hypothesis, that this portal had been the means of ingress to the temple used by Thurid, the black dator, and Matai Shang, Father of Therns.

Turning away abruptly, I called to him to follow me. For a moment he hesitated, and then leaped after me, whining and tugging at my harness to draw me back. I walked on, however, some distance from the door before I let him have his way, that I might see precisely what he would do. Then I permitted him to lead me wherever he would.

Straight back to that baffling portal he dragged me, again taking up his position facing the blank stone, gazing straight at its shining surface. For an hour I worked to solve the mystery of the combination that would open the way before me.

Carefully I recalled every circumstance of my pursuit of Thurid, and my conclusion was identical with my original belief – that Thurid had come this way without other assistance than his own knowledge and passed through the door that barred my progress, unaided from within. But how had he accomplished it?

I recalled the incident of the Chamber of Mystery in the Golden Cliffs that time I had freed Thuvia of Ptarth from the dungeon of the therns, and she had taken a slender, needle-like key from the keyring of her dead jailer to open the door leading back into the Chamber of Mystery where Tars Tarkas fought for his life with the great banths. Such a tiny keyhole as now defied me had opened the way to the intricate lock in that other door.

Hastily I dumped the contents of my pocket-pouch upon the ground before me. Could I but find a slender bit of steel I might yet fashion a key that would give me ingress to the temple prison.

As I examined the heterogeneous collection of odds and ends that is always to be found in the pocket-pouch of a Martian warrior my hand fell upon the emblazoned radium flash torch of the black dator.

As I was about to lay the thing aside as of no value in my present predicament my eyes chanced upon a few strange characters roughly and freshly scratched upon the soft gold of the case.

Casual curiosity prompted me to decipher them, but what I read carried no immediate meaning to my mind. There were three sets of characters, one below another:

3 | – | 50 T
1 | – | 1 X
9 | – | 25 T

For only an instant my curiosity was piqued, and then I replaced the torch in my pocket-pouch, but my fingers had not unclasped from it when there rushed to my memory the recollection of the conversation between Lakor and his companion when the lesser thern had quoted the words of Thurid and scoffed at them: "And what think you of the ridiculous matter of the light? Let the light shine with the intensity of three radium units for fifty tals" – ah, there was the first line of characters upon the torch's metal case – 3 – 50 T; "and for one xat let it shine with the intensity of one radium unit" – there was the second line; "and then for twenty-five tals with nine units."

The formula was complete; but – what did it mean?

I thought I knew, and, seizing a powerful magnifying glass from the litter of my pocket-pouch, I applied myself to a careful examination of the marble immediately about the pinhole in the door. I could have cried aloud in exultation when my scrutiny disclosed the almost invisible incrustation of particles of carbonized electrons which are thrown off by these Martian torches.

It was evident that for countless ages radium torches had been applied to this pinhole, and for what purpose there could be but a single answer – the mechanism of the lock was actuated by light rays; and I, John Carter, Prince of Helium, held the combination in my hand – scratched by the hand of my enemy upon his own torch case.

In a cylindrical bracelet of gold about my wrist was my Barsoomian chronometer – a delicate instrument that records the tals and xats and zodes of Martian time, presenting them to view beneath a strong crystal much after the manner of an earthly odometer.

Timing my operations carefully, I held the torch to the small aperture in the door, regulating the intensity of the light by means of the thumb-lever upon the side of the case.

For fifty tals I let three units of light shine full in the pinhole, then one unit for one xat, and for twenty-five tals nine units. Those last twenty-five tals were the longest twenty-five seconds of my life. Would the lock click at the end of those seemingly interminable intervals of time?

Twenty-three! Twenty-four! Twenty-five!

I shut off the light with a snap. For seven tals I waited – there had been no appreciable effect upon the lock's mechanism. Could it be that my theory was entirely wrong?

Hold! Had the nervous strain resulted in a hallucination, or did the door really move? Slowly the solid stone sank noiselessly back into the wall – there was no hallucination here.

Back and back it slid for ten feet until it had disclosed at its right a narrow doorway leading into a dark and narrow corridor that paralleled the outer wall. Scarcely was the entrance uncovered than Woola and I had leaped through – then the door slipped quietly back into place.

Down the corridor at some distance I saw the faint reflection of a light, and toward this we made our way. At the point where the light shone was a sharp turn, and a little distance beyond this a brilliantly lighted chamber.

Here we discovered a spiral stairway leading up from the center of the circular room.

Immediately I knew that we had reached the center of the base of the Temple of the Sun – the spiral runway led upward past the inner walls of the prison cells. Somewhere above me was Dejah Thoris, unless Thurid and Matai Shang had already succeeded in stealing her.

We had scarcely started up the runway when Woola suddenly displayed the wildest excitement. He leaped back and forth, snapping at my legs and harness, until I thought that he was mad, and finally when I pushed him from me and started once more to ascend he grasped my sword arm between his jaws and dragged me back.

No amount of scolding or cuffing would suffice to make him release me, and I was entirely at the mercy of his brute strength unless I cared to use my dagger upon him with my left hand; but, mad or no, I had not the heart to run the sharp blade into that faithful body.

Down into the chamber he dragged me, and across it to the side opposite that at which we had entered. Here was another doorway leading into a corridor which ran directly down a steep incline. Without a moment's hesitation Woola jerked me along this rocky passage.

Presently he stopped and released me, standing between me and the way we had come, looking up into my face as though to ask if I would now follow him voluntarily or if he must still resort to force.

Looking ruefully at the marks of his great teeth upon my bare arm I decided to do as he seemed to wish me to do. After all, his strange instinct might be more dependable than my faulty human judgment.

And well it was that I had been forced to follow him. But a short distance from the circular chamber we came suddenly into a brilliantly lighted labyrinth of crystal glass partitioned passages.

At first I thought it was one vast, unbroken chamber, so clear and transparent were the walls of the winding corridors, but after I had nearly brained myself a couple of times by attempting to pass through solid vitreous walls I went more carefully.

We had proceeded but a few yards along the corridor that had given us entrance to this strange maze when Woola gave mouth to a most frightful roar, at the same time dashing against the clear partition at our left.

The resounding echoes of that fearsome cry were still reverberating through the subterranean chambers when I saw the thing that had startled it from the faithful beast.

Far in the distance, dimly through the many thicknesses of intervening crystal, as in a haze that made them seem unreal and ghostly, I discerned the figures of eight people – three females and five men.

At the same instant, evidently startled by Woola's fierce cry, they halted and looked about. Then, of a sudden, one of them, a woman, held her arms out toward me, and even at that great distance I could see that her lips moved – it was Dejah Thoris, my ever beautiful and ever youthful Princess of Helium.

With her were Thuvia of Ptarth, Phaidor, daughter of Matai Shang, and Thurid, and the Father of Therns, and the three lesser therns that had accompanied them.

Thurid shook his fist at me, and then two of the therns grasped Dejah Thoris and Thuvia roughly by their arms and hurried them on. A moment later they had disappeared into a stone corridor beyond the labyrinth of glass.

They say that love is blind; but so great a love as that of Dejah Thoris that knew me even beneath the thern disguise I wore and across the misty vista of that crystal maze must indeed be far from blind.

CHAPTER FOUR
The Secret Tower

I HAVE NO STOMACH to narrate the monotonous events of the tedious days that Woola and I spent ferreting our way across the labyrinth of glass, through the dark and devious ways beyond that led beneath the Valley Dor and Golden Cliffs to emerge at last upon the flank of the Otz Mountains just above the Valley of Lost Souls – that pitiful purgatory peopled by the poor unfortunates who dare not continue their abandoned pilgrimage to Dor, or return to the various lands of the outer world from whence they came.

Here the trail of Dejah Thoris' abductors led along the mountains' base, across steep and rugged ravines, by the side of appalling precipices, and sometimes out into the valley, where we found fighting aplenty with the members of the various tribes that make up the population of this vale of hopelessness.

But through it all we came at last to where the way led up a narrow gorge that grew steeper and more impracticable at every step until before us loomed a mighty fortress buried beneath the side of an overhanging cliff.

Here was the secret hiding place of Matai Shang, Father of Therns. Here, surrounded by a handful of the faithful, the hekkador of the ancient faith, who had once been served by millions of vassals and dependents, dispensed the spiritual words among the half dozen nations of Barsoom that still clung tenaciously to their false and discredited religion.

Darkness was just falling as we came in sight of the seemingly impregnable walls of this mountain stronghold, and lest we be seen I drew back with Woola behind a jutting granite promontory, into a clump of the hardy, purple scrub that thrives upon the barren sides of Otz.

Here we lay until the quick transition from daylight to darkness had passed. Then I crept out to approach the fortress walls in search of a way within.

Either through carelessness or over-confidence in the supposed inaccessibility of their hiding place, the triple-barred gate stood ajar. Beyond were a handful of guards, laughing and talking over one of their incomprehensible Barsoomian games.

I saw that none of the guardsmen had been of the party that accompanied Thurid and Matai Shang; and so, relying entirely upon my disguise, I walked boldly through the gateway and up to the thern guard.

The men stopped their game and looked up at me, but there was no sign of suspicion. Similarly they looked at Woola, growling at my heel.

"Kaor!" I said in true Martian greeting, and the warriors arose and saluted me. "I have but just found my way hither from the Golden Cliffs," I continued, "and seek audience with the hekkador, Matai Shang, Father of Therns. Where may he be found?"

"Follow me," said one of the guard, and, turning, led me across the outer courtyard toward a second buttressed wall.

Why the apparent ease with which I seemingly deceived them did not rouse my suspicions I know not, unless it was that my mind was still so full of that fleeting glimpse of my beloved princess that there was room in it for naught else. Be that as it may, the fact is that I marched buoyantly behind my guide straight into the jaws of death.

Afterward I learned that thern spies had been aware of my coming for hours before I reached the hidden fortress.

The gate had been purposely left ajar to tempt me on. The guards had been schooled well in their part of the conspiracy; and I, more like a schoolboy than a seasoned warrior, ran headlong into the trap.

At the far side of the outer court a narrow door let into the angle made by one of the buttresses with the wall. Here my guide produced a key and opened the way within; then, stepping back, he motioned me to enter.

"Matai Shang is in the temple court beyond," he said; and as Woola and I passed through, the fellow closed the door quickly upon us.

The nasty laugh that came to my ears through the heavy planking of the door after the lock clicked was my first intimation that all was not as it should be.

I found myself in a small, circular chamber within the buttress. Before me a door opened, presumably, upon the inner court beyond. For a moment I hesitated, all my suspicions now suddenly, though tardily, aroused; then, with a shrug of my shoulders, I opened the door and stepped out into the glare of torches that lighted the inner court.

Directly opposite me a massive tower rose to a height of three hundred feet. It was of the strangely beautiful modern Barsoomian style of architecture, its entire surface hand carved in bold relief with intricate and fanciful designs. Thirty feet above the courtyard and overlooking it was a broad balcony, and there, indeed, was Matai Shang, and with him were Thurid and Phaidor, Thuvia, and Dejah Thoris – the last two heavily ironed. A handful of thern warriors stood just behind the little party.

As I entered the enclosure the eyes of those in the balcony were full upon me.

An ugly smile distorted the cruel lips of Matai Shang. Thurid hurled a taunt at me and placed a familiar hand upon the shoulder of my princess. Like a tigress she turned upon him, striking the beast a heavy blow with the manacles upon her wrist.

He would have struck back had not Matai Shang interfered, and then I saw that the two men were not over-friendly; for the manner of the thern was arrogant and domineering as he made it plain to the First Born that the Princess of Helium was the personal property of the Father of Therns. And Thurid's bearing toward the ancient hekkador savored not at all of liking or respect.

When the altercation in the balcony had subsided Matai Shang turned again to me.

"Earth man," he cried, "you have earned a more ignoble death than now lies within our weakened power to inflict upon you; but that the death you die tonight may be doubly bitter, know you that when you have passed, your widow becomes the wife of Matai Shang, Hekkador of the Holy Therns, for a Martian year.

"At the end of that time, as you know, she shall be discarded, as is the law among us, but not, as is usual, to lead a quiet and honored life as high priestess of some hallowed shrine. Instead, Dejah Thoris, Princess of Helium, shall become the plaything of my lieutenants – perhaps of thy most hated enemy, Thurid, the black dator."

As he ceased speaking he awaited in silence evidently for some outbreak of rage upon my part – something that would have added to the spice of his revenge. But I did not give him the satisfaction that he craved.

Instead, I did the one thing of all others that might rouse his anger and increase his hatred of me; for I knew that if I died Dejah Thoris, too, would find a way to die before they could heap further tortures or indignities upon her.

Of all the holy of holies which the thern venerates and worships none is more revered than the yellow wig which covers his bald pate, and next thereto comes the circlet of gold and the great diadem, whose scintillant rays mark the attainment of the Tenth Cycle.

And, knowing this, I removed the wig and circlet from my head, tossing them carelessly upon the flagging of the court. Then I wiped my feet upon the yellow tresses; and as a groan of rage arose from the balcony I spat full upon the holy diadem.

Matai Shang went livid with anger, but upon the lips of Thurid I could see a grim smile of amusement, for to him these things were not holy; so, lest he should derive too much amusement from my act, I cried: "And thus did I with the holies of Issus, Goddess of Life Eternal, ere I threw Issus herself to the mob that once had worshiped her, to be torn to pieces in her own temple."

That put an end to Thurid's grinning, for he had been high in the favor of Issus.

"Let us have an end to this blaspheming!" he cried, turning to the Father of Therns.

Matai Shang rose and, leaning over the edge of the balcony, gave voice to the weird call that I had heard from the lips of the priests upon the tiny balcony upon the face of the Golden Cliffs overlooking the Valley Dor, when, in times past, they called the fearsome white apes and the hideous plant men to the feast of victims floating down the broad bosom of the mysterious Iss toward the silian-infested waters of the Lost Sea of Korus. "Let loose the death!" he cried, and immediately a dozen doors in the base of the tower swung open, and a dozen grim and terrible banths sprang into the arena.

This was not the first time that I had faced the ferocious Barsoomian lion, but never had I been pitted, single-handed, against a full dozen of them. Even with the assistance of the fierce Woola, there could be but a single outcome to so unequal a struggle.

For a moment the beasts hesitated beneath the brilliant glare of the torches; but presently their eyes, becoming accustomed to the light, fell upon Woola and me, and with bristling manes and deep-throated roars they advanced, lashing their tawny sides with their powerful tails.

In the brief interval of life that was left me I shot a last, parting glance toward my Dejah Thoris. Her beautiful face was set in an expression of horror; and as my eyes met hers she extended both arms toward me as, struggling with the guards who now held her, she endeavored to cast herself from the balcony into the pit beneath, that she might share my death with me. Then, as the banths were about to close upon me, she turned and buried her dear face in her arms.

Suddenly my attention was drawn toward Thuvia of Ptarth. The beautiful girl was leaning far over the edge of the balcony, her eyes bright with excitement.

In another instant the banths would be upon me, but I could not force my gaze from the features of the red girl, for I knew that her expression meant anything but the enjoyment of the grim tragedy that would so soon be enacted below her; there was some deeper, hidden meaning which I sought to solve.

For an instant I thought of relying on my earthly muscles and agility to escape the banths and reach the balcony, which I could easily have done, but I could not bring myself to desert the faithful Woola and leave him to die alone beneath the cruel fangs of the hungry banths; that is not the way upon Barsoom, nor was it ever the way of John Carter.

Then the secret of Thuvia's excitement became apparent as from her lips there issued the purring sound I had heard once before; that time that, within the Golden Cliffs, she called the fierce banths about her and led them as a shepherdess might lead her flock of meek and harmless sheep.

At the first note of that soothing sound the banths halted in their tracks, and every fierce head went high as the beasts sought the origin of the familiar call. Presently they discovered the red girl in the balcony above them, and, turning, roared out their recognition and their greeting.

Guards sprang to drag Thuvia away, but ere they had succeeded she had hurled a volley of commands at the listening brutes, and as one they turned and marched back into their dens.

"You need not fear them now, John Carter!" cried Thuvia, before they could silence her. "Those banths will never harm you now, nor Woola, either."

It was all I cared to know. There was naught to keep me from that balcony now, and with a long, running leap I sprang far aloft until my hands grasped its lowest sill.

In an instant all was wild confusion. Matai Shang shrank back. Thurid sprang forward with drawn sword to cut me down.

Again Dejah Thoris wielded her heavy irons and fought him back. Then Matai Shang grasped her about the waist and dragged her away through a door leading within the tower.

For an instant Thurid hesitated, and then, as though fearing that the Father of Therns would escape him with the Princess of Helium, he, too, dashed from the balcony in their wake.

Phaidor alone retained her presence of mind. Two of the guards she ordered to bear away Thuvia of Ptarth; the others she commanded to remain and prevent me from following. Then she turned toward me.

"John Carter," she cried, "for the last time I offer you the love of Phaidor, daughter of the Holy Hekkador. Accept and your princess shall be returned to the court of her grandfather, and you shall live in peace and happiness. Refuse and the fate that my father has threatened shall fall upon Dejah Thoris.

"You cannot save her now, for by this time they have reached a place where even you may not follow. Refuse and naught can save you; for, though the way to the last stronghold of the Holy Therns was made easy for you, the way hence hath been made impossible. What say you?"

"You knew my answer, Phaidor," I replied, "before ever you spoke. Make way," I cried to the guards, "for John Carter, Prince of Helium, would pass!"

With that I leaped over the low baluster that surrounded the balcony, and with drawn long-sword faced my enemies.

There were three of them; but Phaidor must have guessed what the outcome of the battle would be, for she turned and fled from the balcony the moment she saw that I would have none of her proposition.

The three guardsmen did not wait for my attack. Instead, they rushed me – the three of them simultaneously; and it was that which gave me an advantage, for they fouled one another in the narrow precincts of the balcony, so that the foremost of them stumbled full upon my blade at the first onslaught.

The red stain upon my point roused to its full the old blood-lust of the fighting man that has ever been so strong within my breast, so that my blade flew through the air with a swiftness and deadly accuracy that threw the two remaining therns into wild despair.

When at last the sharp steel found the heart of one of them the other turned to flee, and, guessing that his steps would lead him along the way taken by those I sought, I let him keep ever far enough ahead to think that he was safely escaping my sword.

Through several inner chambers he raced until he came to a spiral runway. Up this he dashed, I in close pursuit. At the upper end we came out into a small chamber, the walls of which were blank except for a single window overlooking the slopes of Otz and the Valley of Lost Souls beyond.

Here the fellow tore frantically at what appeared to be but a piece of the blank wall opposite the single window. In an instant I guessed that it was a secret exit from the room, and so I paused that he might have an opportunity to negotiate it, for I cared nothing to take the life of this poor servitor – all I craved was a clear road in pursuit of Dejah Thoris, my long-lost princess.

But, try as he would, the panel would yield neither to cunning nor force, so that eventually he gave it up and turned to face me.

"Go thy way, Thern," I said to him, pointing toward the entrance to the runway up which we had but just come. "I have no quarrel with you, nor do I crave your life. Go!"

For answer he sprang upon me with his sword, and so suddenly, at that, that I was like to have gone down before his first rush. So there was nothing for it but to give him what he sought, and that as quickly as might be, that I might not be delayed too long in this chamber while Matai Shang and Thurid made way with Dejah Thoris and Thuvia of Ptarth.

The fellow was a clever swordsman – resourceful and extremely tricky. In fact, he seemed never to have heard that there existed such a thing as a code of honor, for he repeatedly outraged a dozen Barsoomian fighting customs that an honorable man would rather die than ignore.

He even went so far as to snatch his holy wig from his head and throw it in my face, so as to blind me for a moment while he thrust at my unprotected breast.

When he thrust, however, I was not there, for I had fought with therns before; and while none had ever resorted to precisely that same expedient, I knew them to be the least honorable and most treacherous fighters upon Mars, and so was ever on the alert for some new and devilish subterfuge when I was engaged with one of their race.

But at length he overdid the thing; for, drawing his shortsword, he hurled it, javelinwise, at my body, at the same instant rushing upon me with his long-sword. A single sweeping circle of my own blade caught the flying weapon and hurled it clattering against the far wall, and then, as I sidestepped my antagonist's impetuous rush, I let him have my point full in the stomach as he hurtled by.

Clear to the hilt my weapon passed through his body, and with a frightful shriek he sank to the floor, dead.

Halting only for the brief instant that was required to wrench my sword from the carcass of my late antagonist, I sprang across the chamber to the blank wall beyond, through which the thern had attempted to pass. Here I sought for the secret of its lock, but all to no avail.

In despair I tried to force the thing, but the cold, unyielding stone might well have laughed at my futile, puny endeavors. In fact, I could have sworn that I caught the faint suggestion of taunting laughter from beyond the baffling panel.

In disgust I desisted from my useless efforts and stepped to the chamber's single window.

The slopes of Otz and the distant Valley of Lost Souls held nothing to compel my interest then; but, towering far above me, the tower's carved wall riveted my keenest attention.

Somewhere within that massive pile was Dejah Thoris. Above me I could see windows. There, possibly, lay the only way by which I could reach her. The risk was great, but not too great when the fate of a world's most wondrous woman was at stake.

I glanced below. A hundred feet beneath lay jagged granite boulders at the brink of a frightful chasm upon which the tower abutted; and if not upon the boulders, then at the chasm's bottom, lay death, should a foot slip but once, or clutching fingers loose their hold for the fraction of an instant.

But there was no other way and with a shrug, which I must admit was half shudder, I stepped to the window's outer sill and began my perilous ascent.

To my dismay I found that, unlike the ornamentation upon most Heliumetic structures, the edges of the carvings were quite generally rounded, so that at best my every hold was most precarious.

Fifty feet above me commenced a series of projecting cylindrical stones some six inches in diameter. These apparently circled the tower at six-foot intervals, in bands six feet apart; and as each stone cylinder protruded some four or five inches beyond the surface of the other ornamentation, they presented a comparatively easy mode of ascent could I but reach them.

Laboriously I climbed toward them by way of some windows which lay below them, for I hoped that I might find ingress to the tower through one of these, and thence an easier avenue along which to prosecute my search.

At times so slight was my hold upon the rounded surfaces of the carving's edges that a sneeze, a cough, or even a slight gust of wind would have dislodged me and sent me hurtling to the depths below.

But finally I reached a point where my fingers could just clutch the sill of the lowest window, and I was on the point of breathing a sigh of relief when the sound of voices came to me from above through the open window.

"He can never solve the secret of that lock." The voice was Matai Shang's. "Let us proceed to the hangar above that we may be far to the south before he finds another way – should that be possible."

"All things seem possible to that vile calot," replied another voice, which I recognized as Thurid's.

"Then let us haste," said Matai Shang. "But to be doubly sure, I will leave two who shall patrol this runway. Later they may follow us upon another flier – overtaking us at Kaol."

My upstretched fingers never reached the window's sill. At the first sound of the voices I drew back my hand and clung there to my perilous perch, flattened against the perpendicular wall, scarce daring to breathe.

What a horrible position, indeed, in which to be discovered by Thurid! He had but to lean from the window to push me with his sword's point into eternity.

Presently the sound of the voices became fainter, and once again I took up my hazardous ascent, now more difficult, since more circuitous, for I must climb so as to avoid the windows.

Matai Shang's reference to the hangar and the fliers indicated that my destination lay nothing short of the roof of the tower, and toward this seemingly distant goal I set my face.

The most difficult and dangerous part of the journey was accomplished at last, and it was with relief that I felt my fingers close about the lowest of the stone cylinders.

It is true that these projections were too far apart to make the balance of the ascent anything of a sinecure, but I at least had always within my reach a point of safety to which I might cling in case of accident.

Some ten feet below the roof, the wall inclined slightly inward possibly a foot in the last ten feet, and here the climbing was indeed immeasurably easier, so that my fingers soon clutched the eaves.

As I drew my eyes above the level of the tower's top I saw a flier all but ready to rise.

Upon her deck were Matai Shang, Phaidor, Dejah Thoris, Thuvia of Ptarth, and a few thern warriors, while near her was Thurid in the act of clambering aboard.

He was not ten paces from me, facing in the opposite direction; and what cruel freak of fate should have caused him to turn about just as my eyes topped the roof's edge I may not even guess.

But turn he did; and when his eyes met mine his wicked face lighted with a malignant smile as he leaped toward me, where I was hastening to scramble to the secure footing of the roof.

Dejah Thoris must have seen me at the same instant, for she screamed a useless warning just as Thurid's foot, swinging in a mighty kick, landed full in my face.

Like a felled ox, I reeled and tumbled backward over the tower's side.

CHAPTER FIVE

On the Kaolian Road

IF THERE BE A FATE that is sometimes cruel to me, there surely is a kind and merciful Providence which watches over me.

As I toppled from the tower into the horrid abyss below I counted myself already dead; and Thurid must have done likewise, for he evidently did not even trouble himself to look after me, but must have turned and mounted the waiting flier at once.

Ten feet only I fell, and then a loop of my tough, leathern harness caught upon one of the cylindrical stone projections in the tower's surface – and held. Even when I had ceased to fall I could not believe the miracle that had preserved me from instant death, and for a moment I hung there, cold sweat exuding from every pore of my body.

But when at last I had worked myself back to a firm position I hesitated to ascend, since I could not know that Thurid was not still awaiting me above.

Presently, however, there came to my ears the whirring of the propellers of a flier, and as each moment the sound grew fainter I realized that the party had proceeded toward the south without assuring themselves as to my fate.

Cautiously I retraced my way to the roof, and I must admit that it was with no pleasant sensation that I raised my eyes once more above its edge; but, to my relief, there was no one in sight, and a moment later I stood safely upon its broad surface.

To reach the hangar and drag forth the only other flier which it contained was the work of but an instant; and just as the two thern warriors whom Matai Shang had left to prevent this very contingency emerged upon the roof from the tower's interior, I rose above them with a taunting laugh.

Then I dived rapidly to the inner court where I had last seen Woola, and to my immense relief found the faithful beast still there.

The twelve great banths lay in the doorways of their lairs, eyeing him and growling ominously, but they had not disobeyed Thuvia's injunction; and I thanked the fate that had made her their keeper within the Golden Cliffs, and endowed her with the kind and sympathetic nature that had won the loyalty and affection of these fierce beasts for her.

Woola leaped in frantic joy when he discovered me; and as the flier touched the pavement of the court for a brief instant he bounded to the deck beside me, and in the bearlike manifestation of his exuberant happiness all but caused me to wreck the vessel against the courtyard's rocky wall.

Amid the angry shouting of thern guardsmen we rose high above the last fortress of the Holy Therns, and then raced straight toward the northeast and Kaol, the destination which I had heard from the lips of Matai Shang.

Far ahead, a tiny speck in the distance, I made out another flier late in the afternoon. It could be none other than that which bore my lost love and my enemies.

I had gained considerably on the craft by night; and then, knowing that they must have sighted me and would show no lights after dark, I set my destination compass upon her – that wonderful little Martian mechanism which, once attuned to the object of destination, points away toward it, irrespective of every change in its location.

All that night we raced through the Barsoomian void, passing over low hills and dead sea bottoms; above long-deserted cities and populous centers of red Martian habitation upon the ribbon-like lines of cultivated land which border the globe-encircling waterways, which Earth men call the canals of Mars.

Dawn showed that I had gained appreciably upon the flier ahead of me. It was a larger craft than mine, and not so swift; but even so, it had covered an immense distance since the flight began.

The change in vegetation below showed me that we were rapidly nearing the equator. I was now near enough to my quarry to have used my bow gun; but, though I could see that Dejah Thoris was not on deck, I feared to fire upon the craft which bore her.

Thurid was deterred by no such scruples; and though it must have been difficult for him to believe that it was really I who followed them, he could not very well doubt the witness of his own eyes; and so he trained their stern gun upon me with his own hands, and an instant later an explosive radium projectile whizzed perilously close above my deck.

The black's next shot was more accurate, striking my flier full upon the prow and exploding with the instant of contact, ripping wide open the bow buoyancy tanks and disabling the engine.

So quickly did my bow drop after the shot that I scarce had time to lash Woola to the deck and buckle my own harness to a gunwale ring before the craft was hanging stern up and making her last long drop to ground.

Her stern buoyancy tanks prevented her dropping with great rapidity; but Thurid was firing rapidly now in an attempt to burst these also, that I might be dashed to death in the swift fall that would instantly follow a successful shot.

Shot after shot tore past or into us, but by a miracle neither Woola nor I was hit, nor were the after tanks punctured. This good fortune could not last indefinitely, and, assured that Thurid would not again leave me alive, I awaited the bursting of the next shell that hit; and then, throwing my hands above my head, I let go my hold and crumpled, limp and inert, dangling in my harness like a corpse.

The ruse worked, and Thurid fired no more at us. Presently I heard the diminishing sound of whirring propellers and realized that again I was safe.

Slowly the stricken flier sank to the ground, and when I had freed myself and Woola from the entangling wreckage I found that we were upon the verge of a natural forest – so rare a thing upon the bosom of dying Mars that, outside of the forest in the Valley Dor beside the Lost Sea of Korus, I never before had seen its like upon the planet.

From books and travelers I had learned something of the little-known land of Kaol, which lies along the equator almost halfway round the planet to the east of Helium.

It comprises a sunken area of extreme tropical heat, and is inhabited by a nation of red men varying but little in manners, customs, and appearance from the balance of the red men of Barsoom.

I knew that they were among those of the outer world who still clung tenaciously to the discredited religion of the Holy Therns, and that Matai Shang would find a ready welcome and safe refuge among them; while John Carter could look for nothing better than an ignoble death at their hands.

The isolation of the Kaolians is rendered almost complete by the fact that no waterway connects their land with that of any other nation, nor have they any need of a waterway since the low, swampy land which comprises the entire area of their domain self-waters their abundant tropical crops.

For great distances in all directions rugged hills and arid stretches of dead sea bottom discourage intercourse with them, and since there is practically no such thing as foreign commerce upon warlike Barsoom, where each nation is sufficient to itself, really little has been known relative to the court of the Jeddak of Kaol and the numerous strange, but interesting, people over whom he rules.

Occasional hunting parties have traveled to this out-of-the-way corner of the globe, but the hostility of the natives has usually brought disaster upon them, so that even the sport of hunting the strange and savage creatures which haunt the jungle fastnesses of Kaol has of later years proved insufficient lure even to the most intrepid warriors.

It was upon the verge of the land of the Kaols that I now knew myself to be, but in what direction to search for Dejah Thoris, or how far into the heart of the great forest I might have to penetrate I had not the faintest idea.

But not so Woola.

Scarcely had I disentangled him than he raised his head high in air and commenced circling about at the edge of the forest. Presently he halted, and, turning to see if I were following, set off straight into the maze of trees in the direction we had been going before Thurid's shot had put an end to our flier.

As best I could, I stumbled after him down a steep declivity beginning at the forest's edge.

Immense trees reared their mighty heads far above us, their broad fronds completely shutting off the slightest glimpse of the sky. It was easy to see why the Kaolians needed no navy; their cities, hidden in the midst of this towering forest, must be entirely invisible from above, nor could a landing be made by any but the smallest fliers, and then only with the greatest risk of accident.

How Thurid and Matai Shang were to land I could not imagine, though later I was to learn that to the level of the forest top there rises in each city of Kaol a slender watchtower which guards the Kaolians by day and by night against the secret approach of a hostile fleet. To one of these the hekkador of the Holy Therns had no difficulty in approaching, and by its means the party was safely lowered to the ground.

As Woola and I approached the bottom of the declivity the ground became soft and mushy, so that it was with the greatest difficulty that we made any headway whatever.

Slender purple grasses topped with red and yellow fern-like fronds grew rankly all about us to the height of several feet above my head.

Myriad creepers hung festooned in graceful loops from tree to tree, and among them were several varieties of the Martian "man-flower," whose blooms have eyes and hands with which to see and seize the insects which form their diet.

The repulsive calot tree was, too, much in evidence. It is a carnivorous plant of about the bigness of a large sage-brush such as dots our western plains. Each branch ends in a set of strong jaws, which have been known to drag down and devour large and formidable beasts of prey.

Both Woola and I had several narrow escapes from these greedy, arboreous monsters.

Occasional areas of firm sod gave us intervals of rest from the arduous labor of traversing this gorgeous, twilight swamp, and it was upon one of these that I finally decided to make camp for the night which my chronometer warned me would soon be upon us.

Many varieties of fruit grew in abundance about us; and as Martian calots are omnivorous, Woola had no difficulty in making a square meal after I had brought down the viands for him. Then, having eaten, too, I lay down with my back to that of my faithful hound, and dropped into a deep and dreamless sleep.

The forest was shrouded in impenetrable darkness when a low growl from Woola awakened me. All about us I could hear the stealthy movement of great, padded feet, and now and then the wicked gleam of green eyes upon us. Arising, I drew my long-sword and waited.

Suddenly a deep-toned, horrid roar burst from some savage throat almost at my side. What a fool I had been not to have found safer lodgings for myself and Woola among the branches of one of the countless trees that surrounded us!

By daylight it would have been comparatively easy to have hoisted Woola aloft in one manner or another, but now it was too late. There was nothing for it but to stand our ground and take our medicine, though, from the hideous racket which now assailed our ears, and for which that first roar had seemed to be the signal, I judged that we must be in the midst of hundreds, perhaps thousands, of the fierce, man-eating denizens of the Kaolian jungle.

All the balance of the night they kept up their infernal din, but why they did not attack us I could not guess, nor am I sure to this day, unless it is that none of them ever venture upon the patches of scarlet sward which dot the swamp.

When morning broke they were still there, walking about as in a circle, but always just beyond the edge of the sward. A more terrifying aggregation of fierce and blood-thirsty monsters it would be difficult to imagine.

Singly and in pairs they commenced wandering off into the jungle shortly after sunrise, and when the last of them had departed Woola and I resumed our journey.

Occasionally we caught glimpses of horrid beasts all during the day; but, fortunately, we were never far from a sward island, and when they saw us their pursuit always ended at the verge of the solid sod.

Toward noon we stumbled upon a well-constructed road running in the general direction we had been pursuing. Everything about this highway marked it as the work of skilled engineers, and I was confident, from the indications of antiquity which it bore, as well as from the very evident signs of its being still in everyday use, that it must lead to one of the principal cities of Kaol.

Just as we entered it from one side a huge monster emerged from the jungle upon the other, and at sight of us charged madly in our direction.

Imagine, if you can, a bald-faced hornet of your earthly experience grown to the size of a prize Hereford bull, and you will have some faint conception of the ferocious appearance and awesome formidability of the winged monster that bore down upon me.

Frightful jaws in front and mighty, poisoned sting behind made my relatively puny long-sword seem a pitiful weapon of defense indeed. Nor could I hope to escape the lightning-like movements or hide from those myriad facet eyes which covered three-fourths of the hideous head, permitting the creature to see in all directions at one and the same time.

Even my powerful and ferocious Woola was as helpless as a kitten before that frightful thing. But to flee were useless, even had it ever been to my liking to turn my back upon a danger; so I stood my ground, Woola snarling at my side, my only hope to die as I had always lived – fighting.

The creature was upon us now, and at the instant there seemed to me a single slight chance for victory. If I could but remove the terrible menace of certain death hidden in the poison sacs that fed the sting the struggle would be less unequal.

At the thought I called to Woola to leap upon the creature's head and hang there, and as his mighty jaws closed upon that fiendish face, and glistening fangs buried themselves in the bone and cartilage and lower part of one of the huge eyes, I dived beneath the great body as the creature rose, dragging Woola from the ground, that it might bring its sting beneath and pierce the body of the thing hanging to its head.

To put myself in the path of that poison-laden lance was to court instant death, but it was the only way; and as the thing shot lightning-like toward me I swung my long-sword in a terrific cut that severed the deadly member close to the gorgeously marked body.

Then, like a battering-ram, one of the powerful hind legs caught me full in the chest and hurled me, half stunned and wholly winded, clear across the broad highway and into the underbrush of the jungle that fringes it.

Fortunately, I passed between the boles of trees; had I struck one of them I should have been badly injured, if not killed, so swiftly had I been catapulted by that enormous hind leg.

Dazed though I was, I stumbled to my feet and staggered back to Woola's assistance, to find his savage antagonist circling ten feet above the ground, beating madly at the clinging calot with all six powerful legs.

Even during my sudden flight through the air I had not once released my grip upon my long-sword, and now I ran beneath the two battling monsters, jabbing the winged terror repeatedly with its sharp point.

The thing might easily have risen out of my reach, but evidently it knew as little concerning retreat in the face of danger as either Woola or I, for it dropped quickly toward me, and before I could escape had grasped my shoulder between its powerful jaws.

Time and again the now useless stub of its giant sting struck futilely against my body, but the blows alone were almost as effective as the kick of a horse; so that when I say futilely, I refer only to the natural function of the disabled member – eventually the thing would have hammered me to a pulp. Nor was it far from accomplishing this when an interruption occurred that put an end forever to its hostilities.

From where I hung a few feet above the road I could see along the highway a few hundred yards to where it turned toward the east, and just as I had about given up all hope of escaping the perilous position in which I now was I saw a red warrior come into view from around the bend.

He was mounted on a splendid thoat, one of the smaller species used by red men, and in his hand was a wondrous long, light lance.

His mount was walking sedately when I first perceived them, but the instant that the red man's eyes fell upon us a word to the thoat brought the animal at full charge down upon us. The long lance of the warrior dipped toward us, and as thoat and rider hurtled beneath, the point passed through the body of our antagonist.

With a convulsive shudder the thing stiffened, the jaws relaxed, dropping me to the ground, and then, careening once in mid air, the creature plunged headforemost to the road, full upon Woola, who still clung tenaciously to its gory head.

By the time I had regained my feet the red man had turned and ridden back to us. Woola, finding his enemy inert and lifeless, released his hold at my command and wriggled from beneath the body that had covered him, and together we faced the warrior looking down upon us.

I started to thank the stranger for his timely assistance, but he cut me off peremptorily.

"Who are you," he asked, "who dare enter the land of Kaol and hunt in the royal forest of the jeddak?"

Then, as he noted my white skin through the coating of grime and blood that covered me, his eyes went wide and in an altered tone he whispered: "Can it be that you are a Holy Thern?"

I might have deceived the fellow for a time, as I had deceived others, but I had cast away the yellow wig and the holy diadem in the presence of Matai Shang, and I knew that it would not be long ere my new acquaintance discovered that I was no thern at all.

"I am not a thern," I replied, and then, flinging caution to the winds, I said: "I am John Carter, Prince of Helium, whose name may not be entirely unknown to you."

If his eyes had gone wide when he thought that I was a Holy Thern, they fairly popped now that he knew that I was John Carter. I grasped my long-sword more firmly as I spoke the words which I was sure would precipitate an attack, but to my surprise they precipitated nothing of the kind.

"John Carter, Prince of Helium," he repeated slowly, as though he could not quite grasp the truth of the statement. "John Carter, the mightiest warrior of Barsoom!"

And then he dismounted and placed his hand upon my shoulder after the manner of most friendly greeting upon Mars.

"It is my duty, and it should be my pleasure, to kill you, John Carter," he said, "but always in my heart of hearts have I admired your prowess and believed in your sincerity the while I have questioned and disbelieved the therns and their religion.

"It would mean my instant death were my heresy to be suspected in the court of Kulan Tith, but if I may serve you, Prince, you have but to command Torkar Bar, Dwar of the Kaolian Road."

Truth and honesty were writ large upon the warrior's noble countenance, so that I could not but have trusted him, enemy though he should have been. His title of Captain of the Kaolian Road explained his timely presence in the heart of the savage forest, for every highway upon Barsoom is patrolled by doughty warriors of the noble class, nor is there any service more honorable than this lonely and dangerous duty in the less frequented sections of the domains of the red men of Barsoom.

"Torkar Bar has already placed a great debt of gratitude upon my shoulders," I replied, pointing to the carcass of the creature from whose heart he was dragging his long spear.

The red man smiled.

"It was fortunate that I came when I did," he said. "Only this poisoned spear pricking the very heart of a sith can kill it quickly enough to save its prey. In this section of Kaol we are all armed with a long sith spear, whose point is smeared with the poison of the creature it is intended to kill; no other virus acts so quickly upon the beast as its own.

"Look," he continued, drawing his dagger and making an incision in the carcass a foot above the root of the sting, from which he presently drew forth two sacs, each of which held fully a gallon of the deadly liquid.

"Thus we maintain our supply, though were it not for certain commercial uses to which the virus is put, it would scarcely be necessary to add to our present store, since the sith is almost extinct.

"Only occasionally do we now run upon one. Of old, however, Kaol was overrun with the frightful monsters that often came in herds of twenty or thirty, darting down from above into our cities and carrying away women, children, and even warriors."

As he spoke I had been wondering just how much I might safely tell this man of the mission which brought me to his land, but his next words anticipated the broaching of the subject on my part, and rendered me thankful that I had not spoken too soon.

"And now as to yourself, John Carter," he said, "I shall not ask your business here, nor do I wish to hear it. I have eyes and ears and ordinary intelligence, and yesterday morning I saw the party that came to the city of Kaol from the north in a small flier. But one thing I ask of you, and that is: the word of John Carter that he contemplates no overt act against either the nation of Kaol or its jeddak."

"You may have my word as to that, Torkar Bar," I replied.

"My way leads along the Kaolian road, away from the city of Kaol," he continued. "I have seen no one – John Carter least of all. Nor have you seen Torkar Bar, nor ever heard of him. You understand?"

"Perfectly," I replied.

He laid his hand upon my shoulder.

"This road leads directly into the city of Kaol," he said. "I wish you fortune," and vaulting to the back of his thoat he trotted away without even a backward glance.

It was after dark when Woola and I spied through the mighty forest the great wall which surrounds the city of Kaol.

We had traversed the entire way without mishap or adventure, and though the few we had met had eyed the great calot wonderingly, none had pierced the red pigment with which I had smoothly smeared every square inch of my body.

But to traverse the surrounding country, and to enter the guarded city of Kulan Tith, Jeddak of Kaol, were two very different things. No man enters a Martian city without giving a very detailed and satisfactory account of himself, nor did I delude myself with the belief that I could for a moment impose upon the acumen of the officers of the guard to whom I should be taken the moment I applied at any one of the gates.

My only hope seemed to lie in entering the city surreptitiously under cover of the darkness, and once in, trust to my own wits to hide myself in some crowded quarter where detection would be less liable to occur.

With this idea in view I circled the great wall, keeping within the fringe of the forest, which is cut away for a short distance from the wall all about the city, that no enemy may utilize the trees as a means of ingress.

Several times I attempted to scale the barrier at different points, but not even my earthly muscles could overcome that cleverly constructed rampart. To a height of thirty feet the face of the wall slanted outward, and then for almost an equal distance it was perpendicular, above which it slanted in again for some fifteen feet to the crest.

And smooth! Polished glass could not be more so. Finally I had to admit that at last I had discovered a Barsoomian fortification which I could not negotiate.

Discouraged, I withdrew into the forest beside a broad highway which entered the city from the east, and with Woola beside me lay down to sleep.

CHAPTER SIX

A Hero in Kaol

IT WAS DAYLIGHT when I was awakened by the sound of stealthy movement near by.

As I opened my eyes Woola, too, moved and, coming up to his haunches, stared through the intervening brush toward the road, each hair upon his neck stiffly erect.

At first I could see nothing, but presently I caught a glimpse of a bit of smooth and glossy green moving among the scarlet and purple and yellow of the vegetation.

Motioning Woola to remain quietly where he was, I crept forward to investigate, and from behind the bole of a great tree I saw a long line of the hideous green warriors of the dead sea bottoms hiding in the dense jungle beside the road.

As far as I could see, the silent line of destruction and death stretched away from the city of Kaol. There could be but one explanation. The green men were expecting an exodus of a body of red troops from the nearest city gate, and they were lying there in ambush to leap upon them.

I owed no fealty to the Jeddak of Kaol, but he was of the same race of noble red men as my own princess, and I would not stand supinely by and see his warriors butchered by the cruel and heartless demons of the waste places of Barsoom.

Cautiously I retraced my steps to where I had left Woola, and warning him to silence, signaled him to follow me. Making a considerable detour to avoid the chance of falling into the hands of the green men, I came at last to the great wall.

A hundred yards to my right was the gate from which the troops were evidently expected to issue, but to reach it I must pass the flank of the green warriors within easy sight of them, and, fearing that my plan to warn the Kaolians might thus be thwarted, I decided upon hastening toward the left, where another gate a mile away would give me ingress to the city.

I knew that the word I brought would prove a splendid passport to Kaol, and I must admit that my caution was due more to my ardent desire to make my way into the city than to avoid a brush with the green men. As much as I enjoy a fight, I cannot always indulge myself, and just now I had more weighty matters to occupy my time than spilling the blood of strange warriors.

Could I but win beyond the city's wall, there might be opportunity in the confusion and excitement which were sure to follow my announcement of an invading force of green warriors to find my way within the palace of the jeddak, where I was sure Matai Shang and his party would be quartered.

But scarcely had I taken a hundred steps in the direction of the farther gate when the sound of marching troops, the clank of metal, and the squealing of thoats just within the city apprised me of the fact that the Kaolians were already moving toward the other gate.

There was no time to be lost. In another moment the gate would be opened and the head of the column pass out upon the death-bordered highway.

Turning back toward the fateful gate, I ran rapidly along the edge of the clearing, taking the ground in the mighty leaps that had first made me famous upon Barsoom. Thirty, fifty, a hundred feet at a bound are nothing for the muscles of an athletic Earth man upon Mars.

As I passed the flank of the waiting green men they saw my eyes turned upon them, and in an instant, knowing that all secrecy was at an end, those nearest me sprang to their feet in an effort to cut me off before I could reach the gate.

At the same instant the mighty portal swung wide and the head of the Kaolian column emerged. A dozen green warriors had succeeded in reaching a point between me and the gate, but they had but little idea who it was they had elected to detain.

I did not slacken my speed an iota as I dashed among them, and as they fell before my blade I could not but recall the happy memory of those other battles when Tars Tarkas, Jeddak of Thark, mightiest of Martian green men, had stood shoulder to shoulder with me through long, hot Martian days, as together we hewed down our enemies until the pile of corpses about us rose higher than a tall man's head.

When several pressed me too closely, there before the carved gateway of Kaol, I leaped above their heads, and fashioning my tactics after those of the hideous plant men of Dor, struck down upon my enemies' heads as I passed above them.

From the city the red warriors were rushing toward us, and from the jungle the savage horde of green men were coming to meet them. In a moment I was in the very center of as fierce and bloody a battle as I had ever passed through.

These Kaolians are most noble fighters, nor are the green men of the equator one whit less warlike than their cold, cruel cousins of the temperate zone. There were many times when either side might have withdrawn without dishonor and thus ended hostilities, but from the mad abandon with which each invariably renewed hostilities I soon came to believe that what need not have been more than a trifling skirmish would end only with the complete extermination of one force or the other.

With the joy of battle once roused within me, I took keen delight in the fray, and that my fighting was noted by the Kaolians was often evidenced by the shouts of applause directed at me.

If I sometimes seem to take too great pride in my fighting ability, it must be remembered that fighting is my vocation. If your vocation be shoeing horses, or painting pictures, and you can do one or the other better than your fellows, then you are a fool if you are not proud of your ability. And so I am very proud that upon two planets no greater fighter has ever lived than John Carter, Prince of Helium.

And I outdid myself that day to impress the fact upon the natives of Kaol, for I wished to win a way into their hearts – and their city. Nor was I to be disappointed in my desire.

All day we fought, until the road was red with blood and clogged with corpses. Back and forth along the slippery highway the tide of battle surged, but never once was the gateway to Kaol really in danger.

There were breathing spells when I had a chance to converse with the red men beside whom I fought, and once the jeddak, Kulan Tith himself, laid his hand upon my shoulder and asked my name.

"I am Dotar Sojat," I replied, recalling a name given me by the Tharks many years before, from the surnames of the first two of their warriors I had killed, which is the custom among them.

"You are a mighty warrior, Dotar Sojat," he replied, "and when this day is done I shall speak with you again in the great audience chamber."

And then the fight surged upon us once more and we were separated, but my heart's desire was attained, and it was with renewed vigor and a joyous soul that I laid about me with my long-sword until the last of the green men had had enough and had withdrawn toward their distant sea bottom.

Not until the battle was over did I learn why the red troops had sallied forth that day. It seemed that Kulan Tith was expecting a visit from a mighty jeddak of the north – a powerful and the only ally of the Kaolians, and it had been his wish to meet his guest a full day's journey from Kaol.

But now the march of the welcoming host was delayed until the following morning, when the troops again set out from Kaol. I had not been bidden to the presence of Kulan Tith after the battle, but he had sent an officer to find me and escort me to comfortable quarters in that part of the palace set aside for the officers of the royal guard.

There, with Woola, I had spent a comfortable night, and rose much refreshed after the arduous labors of the past few days. Woola had fought with me through the battle of the previous day, true to the instincts and training of a Martian war dog, great numbers of which are often to be found with the savage green hordes of the dead sea bottoms.

Neither of us had come through the conflict unscathed, but the marvelous, healing salves of Barsoom had sufficed, overnight, to make us as good as new.

I breakfasted with a number of the Kaolian officers, whom I found as courteous and delightful hosts as even the nobles of Helium, who are renowned for their ease of manners and excellence of breeding. The meal was scarcely concluded when a messenger arrived from Kulan Tith summoning me before him.

As I entered the royal presence the jeddak rose, and stepping from the dais which supported his magnificent throne, came forward to meet me – a mark of distinction that is seldom accorded to other than a visiting ruler.

"Kaor, Dotar Sojat!" he greeted me. "I have summoned you to receive the grateful thanks of the people of Kaol, for had it not been for your heroic bravery in daring fate to warn us of the ambuscade we must surely have fallen into the well-laid trap. Tell me more of yourself – from what country you come, and what errand brings you to the court of Kulan Tith."

"I am from Hastor," I said, for in truth I had a small palace in that southern city which lies within the far-flung dominions of the Heliumetic nation.

"My presence in the land of Kaol is partly due to accident, my flier being wrecked upon the southern fringe of your great forest. It was while seeking entrance to the city of Kaol that I discovered the green horde lying in wait for your troops."

If Kulan Tith wondered what business brought me in a flier to the very edge of his domain he was good enough not to press me further for an explanation, which I should indeed have had difficulty in rendering.

During my audience with the jeddak another party entered the chamber from behind me, so that I did not see their faces until Kulan Tith stepped past me to greet them, commanding me to follow and be presented.

As I turned toward them it was with difficulty that I controlled my features, for there, listening to Kulan Tith's eulogistic words concerning me, stood my arch-enemies, Matai Shang and Thurid.

"Holy Hekkador of the Holy Therns," the jeddak was saying, "shower thy blessings upon Dotar Sojat, the valorous stranger from distant Hastor, whose wondrous heroism and marvelous ferocity saved the day for Kaol yesterday."

Matai Shang stepped forward and laid his hand upon my shoulder. No slightest indication that he recognized me showed upon his countenance – my disguise was evidently complete.

He spoke kindly to me and then presented me to Thurid. The black, too, was evidently entirely deceived. Then Kulan Tith regaled them, much to my amusement, with details of my achievements upon the field of battle.

The thing that seemed to have impressed him most was my remarkable agility, and time and again he described the wondrous way in which I had leaped completely over an antagonist, cleaving his skull wide open with my long-sword as I passed above him.

I thought that I saw Thurid's eyes widen a bit during the narrative, and several times I surprised him gazing intently into my face through narrowed lids. Was he commencing to suspect? And then Kulan Tith told of the savage calot that fought beside me, and after that I saw suspicion in the eyes of Matai Shang – or did I but imagine it?

At the close of the audience Kulan Tith announced that he would have me accompany him upon the way to meet his royal guest, and as I departed with an officer who was to procure proper trappings and a suitable mount for me, both Matai Shang and Thurid seemed most sincere in professing their pleasure at having had an opportunity to know me. It was with a sigh of relief that I quitted the chamber, convinced that nothing more than a guilty conscience had prompted my belief that either of my enemies suspected my true identity.

A half-hour later I rode out of the city gate with the column that accompanied Kulan Tith upon the way to meet his friend and ally. Though my eyes and ears had been wide open during my audience with the jeddak and my various passages through the palace, I had seen or heard nothing of Dejah Thoris or Thuvia of Ptarth. That they must be somewhere within the great rambling edifice I was positive, and I should have given much to have found a way to remain behind during Kulan Tith's absence, that I might search for them.

Toward noon we came in touch with the head of the column we had set out to meet.

It was a gorgeous train that accompanied the visiting jeddak, and for miles it stretched along the wide, white road to Kaol. Mounted troops, their trappings of jewel and metal-incrusted leather glistening in the sunlight, formed the vanguard of the body, and then came a thousand gorgeous chariots drawn by huge zitidars.

These low, commodious wagons moved two abreast, and on either side of them marched solid ranks of mounted warriors, for in the chariots were the women and children of the royal court. Upon the back of each monster zitidar rode a Martian youth, and the whole scene carried me back to my first days upon Barsoom, now twenty-two years in the past, when I had first beheld the gorgeous spectacle of a caravan of the green horde of Tharks.

Never before today had I seen zitidars in the service of red men. These brutes are huge mastodonian animals that tower to an immense height even beside the giant green men and their giant thoats; but when compared to the relatively small red man and his breed of thoats they assume Brobdingnagian proportions that are truly appalling.

The beasts were hung with jeweled trappings and saddlepads of gay silk, embroidered in fanciful designs with strings of diamonds, pearls, rubies, emeralds, and the countless unnamed jewels of Mars, while from each chariot rose a dozen standards from which streamers, flags, and pennons fluttered in the breeze.

Just in front of the chariots the visiting jeddak rode alone upon a pure white thoat – another unusual sight upon Barsoom – and after them came interminable ranks of mounted spearmen, riflemen, and swordsmen. It was indeed a most imposing sight.

Except for the clanking of accouterments and the occasional squeal of an angry thoat or the low guttural of a zitidar, the passage of the cavalcade was almost noiseless, for neither thoat nor zitidar is a hoofed animal, and the broad tires of the chariots are of an elastic composition, which gives forth no sound.

Now and then the gay laughter of a woman or the chatter of children could be heard, for the red Martians are a social, pleasure-loving people – in direct antithesis to the cold and morbid race of green men.

The forms and ceremonials connected with the meeting of the two jeddaks consumed an hour, and then we turned and retraced our way toward the city of Kaol, which the head of the column reached just

before dark, though it must have been nearly morning before the rear guard passed through the gateway.

Fortunately, I was well up toward the head of the column, and after the great banquet, which I attended with the officers of the royal guard, I was free to seek repose. There was so much activity and bustle about the palace all during the night with the constant arrival of the noble officers of the visiting jeddak's retinue that I dared not attempt to prosecute a search for Dejah Thoris, and so, as soon as it was seemly for me to do so, I returned to my quarters.

As I passed along the corridors between the banquet hall and the apartments that had been allotted me, I had a sudden feeling that I was under surveillance, and, turning quickly in my tracks, caught a glimpse of a figure which darted into an open doorway the instant I wheeled about.

Though I ran quickly back to the spot where the shadower had disappeared I could find no trace of him, yet in the brief glimpse that I had caught I could have sworn that I had seen a white face surmounted by a mass of yellow hair.

The incident gave me considerable food for speculation, since if I were right in the conclusion induced by the cursory glimpse I had had of the spy, then Matai Shang and Thurid must suspect my identity, and if that were true not even the service I had rendered Kulan Tith could save me from his religious fanaticism.

But never did vague conjecture or fruitless fears for the future lie with sufficient weight upon my mind to keep me from my rest, and so tonight I threw myself upon my sleeping silks and furs and passed at once into dreamless slumber.

Calots are not permitted within the walls of the palace proper, and so I had had to relegate poor Woola to quarters in the stables where the royal thoats are kept. He had comfortable, even luxurious apartments, but I would have given much to have had him with me; and if he had been, the thing which happened that night would not have come to pass.

I could not have slept over a quarter of an hour when I was suddenly awakened by the passing of some cold and clammy thing across my forehead. Instantly I sprang to my feet, clutching in the direction I thought the presence lay. For an instant my hand touched against human flesh, and then, as I lunged headforemost through the darkness to seize my nocturnal visitor, my foot became entangled in my sleeping silks and I fell sprawling to the floor.

By the time I had resumed my feet and found the button which controlled the light my caller had disappeared. Careful search of the room revealed nothing to explain either the identity or business of the person who had thus secretly sought me in the dead of night.

That the purpose might be theft I could not believe, since thieves are practically unknown upon Barsoom. Assassination, however, is rampant, but even this could not have been the motive of my stealthy friend, for he might easily have killed me had he desired.

I had about given up fruitless conjecture and was on the point of returning to sleep when a dozen Kaolian guardsmen entered my apartment. The officer in charge was one of my genial hosts of the morning, but now upon his face was no sign of friendship.

"Kulan Tith commands your presence before him," he said. "Come!"

CHAPTER SEVEN

New Allies

Surrounded by guardsmen I marched back along the corridors of the palace of Kulan Tith, Jeddak of Kaol, to the great audience chamber in the center of the massive structure.

As I entered the brilliantly lighted apartment, filled with the nobles of Kaol and the officers of the visiting jeddak, all eyes were turned upon me. Upon the great dais at the end of the chamber stood three thrones, upon which sat Kulan Tith and his two guests, Matai Shang, and the visiting jeddak.

Up the broad center aisle we marched beneath deadly silence, and at the foot of the thrones we halted.

"Prefer thy charge," said Kulan Tith, turning to one who stood among the nobles at his right; and then Thurid, the black dator of the First Born, stepped forward and faced me.

"Most noble Jeddak," he said, addressing Kulan Tith, "from the first I suspected this stranger within thy palace. Your description of his fiendish prowess tallied with that of the arch-enemy of truth upon Barsoom.

"But that there might be no mistake I despatched a priest of your own holy cult to make the test that should pierce his disguise and reveal the truth. Behold the result!" and Thurid pointed a rigid finger at my forehead.

All eyes followed the direction of that accusing digit – I alone seemed at a loss to guess what fatal sign rested upon my brow.

The officer beside me guessed my perplexity; and as the brows of Kulan Tith darkened in a menacing scowl as his eyes rested upon me, the noble drew a small mirror from his pocket-pouch and held it before my face.

One glance at the reflection it gave back to me was sufficient.

From my forehead the hand of the sneaking thern had reached out through the concealing darkness of my bed-chamber and wiped away a patch of the disguising red pigment as broad as my palm. Beneath showed the tanned texture of my own white skin.

For a moment Thurid ceased speaking, to enhance, I suspect, the dramatic effect of his disclosure. Then he resumed.

"Here, O Kulan Tith," he cried, "is he who has desecrated the temples of the Gods of Mars, who has violated the persons of the Holy Therns themselves and turned a world against its age-old religion. Before you, in your power, Jeddak of Kaol, Defender of the Holies, stands John Carter, Prince of Helium!"

Kulan Tith looked toward Matai Shang as though for corroboration of these charges. The Holy Thern nodded his head.

"It is indeed the arch-blasphemer," he said. "Even now he has followed me to the very heart of thy palace, Kulan Tith, for the sole purpose of assassinating me. He – "

"He lies!" I cried. "Kulan Tith, listen that you may know the truth. Listen while I tell you why John Carter has followed Matai Shang to the heart of thy palace. Listen to me as well as to them, and then judge if my acts be not more in accord with true Barsoomian chivalry and honor than those of these revengeful devotees of the spurious creeds from whose cruel bonds I have freed your planet."

"Silence!" roared the jeddak, leaping to his feet and laying his hand upon the hilt of his sword. "Silence, blasphemer! Kulan Tith need not permit the air of his audience chamber to be defiled by the heresies that issue from your polluted throat to judge you.

"You stand already self-condemned. It but remains to determine the manner of your death. Even the service that you rendered the arms of Kaol shall avail you naught; it was but a base subterfuge whereby you might win your way into my favor and reach the side of this holy man whose life you craved. To the pits with him!" he concluded, addressing the officer of my guard.

Here was a pretty pass, indeed! What chance had I against a whole nation? What hope for me of mercy at the hands of the fanatical Kulan Tith with such advisers as Matai Shang and Thurid. The black grinned malevolently in my face.

"You shall not escape this time, Earth man," he taunted.

The guards closed toward me. A red haze blurred my vision. The fighting blood of my Virginian sires coursed hot through my veins. The lust of battle in all its mad fury was upon me.

With a leap I was beside Thurid, and ere the devilish smirk had faded from his handsome face I had caught him full upon the mouth with my clenched fist; and as the good, old American blow landed, the black dator shot back a dozen feet, to crumple in a heap at the foot of Kulan Tith's throne, spitting blood and teeth from his hurt mouth.

Then I drew my sword and swung round, on guard, to face a nation.

In an instant the guardsmen were upon me, but before a blow had been struck a mighty voice rose above the din of shouting warriors, and a giant figure leaped from the dais beside Kulan Tith and, with drawn long-sword, threw himself between me and my adversaries.

It was the visiting jeddak.

"Hold!" he cried. "If you value my friendship, Kulan Tith, and the age-old peace that has existed between our peoples, call off your swordsmen; for wherever or against whomsoever fights John Carter, Prince of Helium, there beside him and to the death fights Thuvan Dihn, Jeddak of Ptarth."

The shouting ceased and the menacing points were lowered as a thousand eyes turned first toward Thuvan Dihn in surprise and then toward Kulan Tith in question. At first the Jeddak of Kaol went white in rage, but before he spoke he had mastered himself, so that his tone was calm and even as befitted intercourse between two great jeddaks.

"Thuvan Dihn," he said slowly, "must have great provocation thus to desecrate the ancient customs which inspire the deportment of a guest within the palace of his host. Lest I, too, should forget myself as has my royal friend, I should prefer to remain silent until the Jeddak of Ptarth has won from me applause for his action by relating the causes which provoked it."

I could see that the Jeddak of Ptarth was of half a mind to throw his metal in Kulan Tith's face, but he controlled himself even as well as had his host.

"None knows better than Thuvan Dihn," he said, "the laws which govern the acts of men in the domains of their neighbors; but Thuvan Dihn owes allegiance to a higher law than these – the law of gratitude. Nor to any man upon Barsoom does he owe a greater debt of gratitude than to John Carter, Prince of Helium.

"Years ago, Kulan Tith," he continued, "upon the occasion of your last visit to me, you were greatly taken with the charms and graces of my only daughter, Thuvia. You saw how I adored her, and later you learned that, inspired by some unfathomable whim, she had taken the last, long, voluntary pilgrimage upon the cold bosom of the mysterious Iss, leaving me desolate.

"Some months ago I first heard of the expedition which John Carter had led against Issus and the Holy Therns. Faint rumors of the atrocities reported to have been committed by the therns upon those who for countless ages have floated down the mighty Iss came to my ears.

"I heard that thousands of prisoners had been released, few of whom dared to return to their own countries owing to the mandate of terrible death which rests against all who return from the Valley Dor.

"For a time I could not believe the heresies which I heard, and I prayed that my daughter Thuvia might have died before she ever committed the sacrilege of returning to the outer world. But then my father's love asserted itself, and I vowed that I would prefer eternal damnation to further separation from her if she could be found.

"So I sent emissaries to Helium, and to the court of Xodar, Jeddak of the First Born, and to him who now rules those of the thern nation that have renounced their religion; and from each and all I heard the same story of unspeakable cruelties and atrocities perpetrated upon the poor defenseless victims of their religion by the Holy Therns.

"Many there were who had seen or known my daughter, and from therns who had been close to Matai Shang I learned of the indignities that he personally heaped upon her; and I was glad when I came here to find that Matai Shang was also your guest, for I should have sought him out had it taken a lifetime.

"More, too, I heard, and that of the chivalrous kindness that John Carter had accorded my daughter. They told me how he fought for her and rescued her, and how he spurned escape from the savage Warhoons of the south, sending her to safety upon his own thoat and remaining upon foot to meet the green warriors.

"Can you wonder, Kulan Tith, that I am willing to jeopardize my life, the peace of my nation, or even your friendship, which I prize more than aught else, to champion the Prince of Helium?"

For a moment Kulan Tith was silent. I could see by the expression of his face that he was sore perplexed. Then he spoke.

"Thuvan Dihn," he said, and his tone was friendly though sad, "who am I to judge my fellow-man? In my eyes the Father of Therns is still holy, and the religion which he teaches the only true religion, but were I faced by the same problem that has vexed you I doubt not that I should feel and act precisely as you have.

"In so far as the Prince of Helium is concerned I may act, but between you and Matai Shang my only office can be one of conciliation. The Prince of Helium shall be escorted in safety to the boundary of my domain ere the sun has set again, where he shall be free to go whither he will; but upon pain of death must he never again enter the land of Kaol.

"If there be a quarrel between you and the Father of Therns, I need not ask that the settlement of it be deferred until both have passed beyond the limits of my power. Are you satisfied, Thuvan Dihn?"

The Jeddak of Ptarth nodded his assent, but the ugly scowl that he bent upon Matai Shang harbored ill for that pasty-faced godling.

"The Prince of Helium is far from satisfied," I cried, breaking rudely in upon the beginnings of peace, for I had no stomach for peace at the price that had been named.

"I have escaped death in a dozen forms to follow Matai Shang and overtake him, and I do not intend to be led, like a decrepit thoat to the slaughter, from the goal that I have won by the prowess of my sword arm and the might of my muscles.

"Nor will Thuvan Dihn, Jeddak of Ptarth, be satisfied when he has heard me through. Do you know why I have followed Matai Shang and Thurid, the black dator, from the forests of the Valley Dor across half a world through almost insurmountable difficulties?

"Think you that John Carter, Prince of Helium, would stoop to assassination? Can Kulan Tith be such a fool as to believe that lie, whispered in his ear by the Holy Thern or Dator Thurid?

"I do not follow Matai Shang to kill him, though the God of mine own planet knows that my hands itch to be at his throat. I follow him, Thuvan Dihn, because with him are two prisoners – my wife, Dejah Thoris, Princess of Helium, and your daughter, Thuvia of Ptarth.

"Now think you that I shall permit myself to be led beyond the walls of Kaol unless the mother of my son accompanies me, and thy daughter be restored?"

Thuvan Dihn turned upon Kulan Tith. Rage flamed in his keen eyes; but by the masterfulness of his self-control he kept his tones level as he spoke.

"Knew you this thing, Kulan Tith?" he asked. "Knew you that my daughter lay a prisoner in your palace?"

"He could not know it," interrupted Matai Shang, white with what I am sure was more fear than rage. "He could not know it, for it is a lie."

I would have had his life for that upon the spot, but even as I sprang toward him Thuvan Dihn laid a heavy hand upon my shoulder.

"Wait," he said to me, and then to Kulan Tith. "It is not a lie. This much have I learned of the Prince of Helium – he does not lie. Answer me, Kulan Tith – I have asked you a question."

"Three women came with the Father of Therns," replied Kulan Tith. "Phaidor, his daughter, and two who were reported to be her slaves. If these be Thuvia of Ptarth and Dejah Thoris of Helium I did not know it – I have seen neither. But if they be, then shall they be returned to you on the morrow."

As he spoke he looked straight at Matai Shang, not as a devotee should look at a high priest, but as a ruler of men looks at one to whom he issues a command.

It must have been plain to the Father of Therns, as it was to me, that the recent disclosures of his true character had done much already to weaken the faith of Kulan Tith, and that it would require but little more to turn the powerful jeddak into an avowed enemy; but so strong are the seeds of superstition that even the great Kaolian still hesitated to cut the final strand that bound him to his ancient religion.

Matai Shang was wise enough to seem to accept the mandate of his follower, and promised to bring the two slave women to the audience chamber on the morrow.

"It is almost morning now," he said, "and I should dislike to break in upon the slumber of my daughter, or I would have them fetched at once that you might see that the Prince of Helium is mistaken," and he emphasized the last word in an effort to affront me so subtlely that I could not take open offense.

I was about to object to any delay, and demand that the Princess of Helium be brought to me forthwith, when Thuvan Dihn made such insistence seem unnecessary.

"I should like to see my daughter at once," he said, "but if Kulan Tith will give me his assurance that none will be permitted to leave the palace this night, and that no harm shall befall either Dejah Thoris or Thuvia of Ptarth between now and the moment they are brought into our presence in this chamber at daylight I shall not insist."

"None shall leave the palace tonight," replied the Jeddak of Kaol, "and Matai Shang will give us assurance that no harm will come to the two women?"

The thern assented with a nod. A few moments later Kulan Tith indicated that the audience was at an end, and at Thuvan Dihn's invitation I accompanied the Jeddak of Ptarth to his own apartments, where we sat until daylight, while he listened to the account of my experiences upon his planet and to all that had befallen his daughter during the time that we had been together.

I found the father of Thuvia a man after my own heart, and that night saw the beginning of a friendship which has grown until it is second only to that which obtains between Tars Tarkas, the green Jeddak of Thark, and myself.

The first burst of Mars's sudden dawn brought messengers from Kulan Tith, summoning us to the audience chamber where Thuvan Dihn was to receive his daughter after years of separation, and I was to be reunited with the glorious daughter of Helium after an almost unbroken separation of twelve years.

My heart pounded within my bosom until I looked about me in embarrassment, so sure was I that all within the room must hear. My arms ached to enfold once more the divine form of her whose eternal youth and undying beauty were but outward manifestations of a perfect soul.

At last the messenger despatched to fetch Matai Shang returned. I craned my neck to catch the first glimpse of those who should be following, but the messenger was alone.

Halting before the throne he addressed his jeddak in a voice that was plainly audible to all within the chamber.

"O Kulan Tith, Mightiest of Jeddaks," he cried, after the fashion of the court, "your messenger returns alone, for when he reached the apartments of the Father of Therns he found them empty, as were those occupied by his suite."

Kulan Tith went white.

A low groan burst from the lips of Thuvan Dihn who stood next me, not having ascended the throne which awaited him beside his host. For a moment the silence of death reigned in the great audience chamber of Kulan Tith, Jeddak of Kaol. It was he who broke the spell.

Rising from his throne he stepped down from the dais to the side of Thuvan Dihn. Tears dimmed his eyes as he placed both his hands upon the shoulders of his friend.

"O Thuvan Dihn," he cried, "that this should have happened in the palace of thy best friend! With my own hands would I have wrung the neck of Matai Shang had I guessed what was in his foul heart. Last night my life-long faith was weakened – this morning it has been shattered; but too late, too late.

"To wrest your daughter and the wife of this royal warrior from the clutches of these archfiends you have but to command the resources of a mighty nation, for all Kaol is at your disposal. What may be done? Say the word!"

"First," I suggested, "let us find those of your people who be responsible for the escape of Matai Shang and his followers. Without assistance on the part of the palace guard this thing could not have come to pass.

Seek the guilty, and from them force an explanation of the manner of their going and the direction they have taken."

Before Kulan Tith could issue the commands that would initiate the investigation a handsome young officer stepped forward and addressed his jeddak.

"O Kulan Tith, Mightiest of Jeddaks," he said, "I alone be responsible for this grievous error. Last night it was I who commanded the palace guard. I was on duty in other parts of the palace during the audience of the early morning, and knew nothing of what transpired then, so that when the Father of Therns summoned me and explained that it was your wish that his party be hastened from the city because of the presence here of a deadly enemy who sought the Holy Hekkador's life I did only what a lifetime of training has taught me was the proper thing to do – I obeyed him whom I believed to be the ruler of us all, mightier even than thou, mightiest of jeddaks.

"Let the consequences and the punishment fall on me alone, for I alone am guilty. Those others of the palace guard who assisted in the flight did so under my instructions."

Kulan Tith looked first at me and then at Thuvan Dihn, as though to ask our judgment upon the man, but the error was so evidently excusable that neither of us had any mind to see the young officer suffer for a mistake that any might readily have made.

"How left they," asked Thuvan Dihn, "and what direction did they take?"

"They left as they came," replied the officer, "upon their own flier. For some time after they had departed I watched the vessel's lights, which vanished finally due north."

"Where north could Matai Shang find an asylum?" asked Thuvan Dihn of Kulan Tith.

For some moments the Jeddak of Kaol stood with bowed head, apparently deep in thought. Then a sudden light brightened his countenance.

"I have it!" he cried. "Only yesterday Matai Shang let drop a hint of his destination, telling me of a race of people unlike ourselves who dwell far to the north. They, he said, had always been known to the Holy Therns and were devout and faithful followers of the ancient cult. Among them would he find a perpetual haven of refuge, where no 'lying heretics' might seek him out. It is there that Matai Shang has gone."

"And in all Kaol there be no flier wherein to follow," I cried.

"Nor nearer than Ptarth," replied Thuvan Dihn.

"Wait!" I exclaimed, "beyond the southern fringe of this great forest lies the wreck of the thern flier which brought me that far upon my way. If you will loan me men to fetch it, and artificers to assist me, I can repair it in two days, Kulan Tith."

I had been more than half suspicious of the seeming sincerity of the Kaolian jeddak's sudden apostasy, but the alacrity with which he embraced my suggestion, and the despatch with which a force of officers and men were placed at my disposal entirely removed the last vestige of my doubts.

Two days later the flier rested upon the top of the watchtower, ready to depart. Thuvan Dihn and Kulan Tith had offered me the entire resources of two nations – millions of fighting men were at my disposal; but my flier could hold but one other than myself and Woola.

As I stepped aboard her, Thuvan Dihn took his place beside me. I cast a look of questioning surprise upon him. He turned to the highest of his own officers who had accompanied him to Kaol.

"To you I entrust the return of my retinue to Ptarth," he said. "There my son rules ably in my absence. The Prince of Helium shall not go alone into the land of his enemies. I have spoken. Farewell!"

CHAPTER EIGHT

Through the Carrion Caves

STRAIGHT TOWARD THE NORTH, day and night, our destination compass led us after the fleeing flier upon which it had remained set since I first attuned it after leaving the thern fortress.

Early in the second night we noticed the air becoming perceptibly colder, and from the distance we had come from the equator were assured that we were rapidly approaching the north arctic region.

My knowledge of the efforts that had been made by countless expeditions to explore that unknown land bade me to caution, for never had flier returned who had passed to any considerable distance beyond the mighty ice-barrier that fringes the southern hem of the frigid zone.

What became of them none knew – only that they passed forever out of the sight of man into that grim and mysterious country of the pole.

The distance from the barrier to the pole was no more than a swift flier should cover in a few hours, and so it was assumed that some frightful catastrophe awaited those who reached the "forbidden land," as it had come to be called by the Martians of the outer world.

Thus it was that I went more slowly as we approached the barrier, for it was my intention to move cautiously by day over the ice-pack that I might discover, before I had run into a trap, if there really lay an inhabited country at the north pole, for there only could I imagine a spot where Matai Shang might feel secure from John Carter, Prince of Helium.

We were flying at a snail's pace but a few feet above the ground – literally feeling our way along through the darkness, for both moons had set, and the night was black with the clouds that are to be found only at Mars's two extremities.

Suddenly a towering wall of white rose directly in our path, and though I threw the helm hard over, and reversed our engine, I was too late to avoid collision. With a sickening crash we struck the high looming obstacle three-quarters on.

The flier reeled half over; the engine stopped; as one, the patched buoyancy tanks burst, and we plunged, headforemost, to the ground twenty feet beneath.

Fortunately none of us was injured, and when we had disentangled ourselves from the wreckage, and the lesser moon had burst again from below the horizon, we found that we were at the foot of a mighty ice-barrier, from which outcropped great patches of the granite hills which hold it from encroaching farther toward the south.

What fate! With the journey all but completed to be thus wrecked upon the wrong side of that precipitous and unscalable wall of rock and ice!

I looked at Thuvan Dihn. He but shook his head dejectedly.

The balance of the night we spent shivering in our inadequate sleeping silks and furs upon the snow that lies at the foot of the ice-barrier.

With daylight my battered spirits regained something of their accustomed hopefulness, though I must admit that there was little enough for them to feed upon.

"What shall we do?" asked Thuvan Dihn. "How may we pass that which is impassable?"

"First we must disprove its impassability," I replied. "Nor shall I admit that it is impassable before I have followed its entire circle and stand again upon this spot, defeated. The sooner we start, the better, for I see no other way, and it will take us more than a month to travel the weary, frigid miles that lie before us."

For five days of cold and suffering and privation we traversed the rough and frozen way which lies at the foot of the ice-barrier. Fierce, fur-bearing creatures attacked us by daylight and by dark. Never for a moment were we safe from the sudden charge of some huge demon of the north.

The apt was our most consistent and dangerous foe.

It is a huge, white-furred creature with six limbs, four of which, short and heavy, carry it swiftly over the snow and ice; while the other two, growing forward from its shoulders on either side of its long, powerful neck, terminate in white, hairless hands, with which it seizes and holds its prey.

Its head and mouth are more similar in appearance to those of a hippopotamus than to any other earthly animal, except that from the sides of the lower jawbone two mighty horns curve slightly downward toward the front.

Its two huge eyes inspired my greatest curiosity. They extend in two vast, oval patches from the center of the top of the cranium down either side of the head to below the roots of the horns, so that these weapons really grow out from the lower part of the eyes, which are composed of several thousand ocelli each.

This eye structure seemed remarkable in a beast whose haunts were upon a glaring field of ice and snow, and though I found upon minute examination of several that we killed that each ocellus is furnished with its own lid, and that the animal can at will close as many of the facets of his huge eyes as he chooses, yet I was positive that nature had thus equipped him because much of his life was to be spent in dark, subterranean recesses.

Shortly after this we came upon the hugest apt that we had seen. The creature stood fully eight feet at the shoulder, and was so sleek and clean and glossy that I could have sworn that he had but recently been groomed.

He stood head-on eyeing us as we approached him, for we had found it a waste of time to attempt to escape the perpetual bestial rage which seems to possess these demon creatures, who rove the dismal north attacking every living thing that comes within the scope of their far-seeing eyes.

Even when their bellies are full and they can eat no more, they kill purely for the pleasure which they derive from taking life, and so when this particular apt failed to charge us, and instead wheeled and trotted away as we neared him, I should have been greatly surprised had I not chanced to glimpse the sheen of a golden collar about its neck.

Thuvan Dihn saw it, too, and it carried the same message of hope to us both. Only man could have placed that collar there, and as no race of Martians of which we knew aught ever had attempted to domesticate the ferocious apt, he must belong to a people of the north of whose very existence we were ignorant – possibly to the fabled yellow men of Barsoom; that once powerful race which was supposed to be extinct, though sometimes, by theorists, thought still to exist in the frozen north.

Simultaneously we started upon the trail of the great beast. Woola was quickly made to understand our desires, so that it was unnecessary to attempt to keep in sight of the animal whose swift flight over the rough ground soon put him beyond our vision.

For the better part of two hours the trail paralleled the barrier, and then suddenly turned toward it through the roughest and seemingly most impassable country I ever had beheld.

Enormous granite boulders blocked the way on every hand; deep rifts in the ice threatened to engulf us at the least misstep; and from the north a slight breeze wafted to our nostrils an unspeakable stench that almost choked us.

For another two hours we were occupied in traversing a few hundred yards to the foot of the barrier.

Then, turning about the corner of a wall-like outcropping of granite, we came upon a smooth area of two or three acres before the base of the towering pile of ice and rock that had baffled us for days, and before us beheld the dark and cavernous mouth of a cave.

From this repelling portal the horrid stench was emanating, and as Thuvan Dihn espied the place he halted with an exclamation of profound astonishment.

"By all my ancestors!" he ejaculated. "That I should have lived to witness the reality of the fabled Carrion Caves! If these indeed be they, we have found a way beyond the ice-barrier.

"The ancient chronicles of the first historians of Barsoom – so ancient that we have for ages considered them mythology – record the passing of the yellow men from the ravages of the green hordes that overran Barsoom as the drying up of the great oceans drove the dominant races from their strongholds.

"They tell of the wanderings of the remnants of this once powerful race, harassed at every step, until at last they found a way through the ice-barrier of the north to a fertile valley at the pole.

"At the opening to the subterranean passage that led to their haven of refuge a mighty battle was fought in which the yellow men were victorious, and within the caves that gave ingress to their new home they piled the bodies of the dead, both yellow and green, that the stench might warn away their enemies from further pursuit.

"And ever since that long-gone day have the dead of this fabled land been carried to the Carrion Caves, that in death and decay they might serve their country and warn away invading enemies. Here, too, is brought, so the fable runs, all the waste stuff of the nation – everything that is subject to rot, and that can add to the foul stench that assails our nostrils.

"And death lurks at every step among rotting dead, for here the fierce apts lair, adding to the putrid accumulation with the fragments of their own prey which they cannot devour. It is a horrid avenue to our goal, but it is the only one."

"You are sure, then, that we have found the way to the land of the yellow men?" I cried.

"As sure as may be," he replied; "having only ancient legend to support my belief. But see how closely, so far, each detail tallies with the world-old story of the hegira of the yellow race. Yes, I am sure that we have discovered the way to their ancient hiding place."

"If it be true, and let us pray that such may be the case," I said, "then here may we solve the mystery of the disappearance of Tardos Mors, Jeddak of Helium, and Mors Kajak, his son, for no other spot upon Barsoom has remained unexplored by the many expeditions and the countless spies that have been searching for them for nearly two years. The last word that came from them was that they sought Carthoris, my own brave son, beyond the ice-barrier."

As we talked we had been approaching the entrance to the cave, and as we crossed the threshold I ceased to wonder that the ancient green enemies of the yellow men had been halted by the horrors of that awful way.

The bones of dead men lay man high upon the broad floor of the first cave, and over all was a putrid mush of decaying flesh, through which the apts had beaten a hideous trail toward the entrance to the second cave beyond.

The roof of this first apartment was low, like all that we traversed subsequently, so that the foul odors were confined and condensed to such an extent that they seemed to possess tangible substance. One was almost tempted to draw his short-sword and hew his way through in search of pure air beyond.

"Can man breathe this polluted air and live?" asked Thuvan Dihn, choking.

"Not for long, I imagine," I replied; "so let us make haste. I will go first, and you bring up the rear, with Woola between. Come," and with the words I dashed forward, across the fetid mass of putrefaction.

It was not until we had passed through seven caves of different sizes and varying but little in the power and quality of their stenches that we met with any physical opposition. Then, within the eighth cave, we came upon a lair of apts.

A full score of the mighty beasts were disposed about the chamber. Some were sleeping, while others tore at the fresh-killed carcasses of new-brought prey, or fought among themselves in their love-making.

Here in the dim light of their subterranean home the value of their great eyes was apparent, for these inner caves are shrouded in perpetual gloom that is but little less than utter darkness.

To attempt to pass through the midst of that fierce herd seemed, even to me, the height of folly, and so I proposed to Thuvan Dihn that he return to the outer world with Woola, that the two might find their way to civilization and come again with a sufficient force to overcome not only the apts, but any further obstacles that might lie between us and our goal.

"In the meantime," I continued, "I may discover some means of winning my way alone to the land of the yellow men, but if I am unsuccessful one life only will have been sacrificed. Should we all go on and perish, there will be none to guide a succoring party to Dejah Thoris and your daughter."

"I shall not return and leave you here alone, John Carter," replied Thuvan Dihn. "Whether you go on to victory or death, the Jeddak of Ptarth remains at your side. I have spoken."

I knew from his tone that it were useless to attempt to argue the question, and so I compromised by sending Woola back with a hastily penned note enclosed in a small metal case and fastened about his neck. I commanded the faithful creature to seek Carthoris at Helium, and though half a world and countless dangers lay between I knew that if the thing could be done Woola would do it.

Equipped as he was by nature with marvelous speed and endurance, and with frightful ferocity that made him a match for any single enemy of the way, his keen intelligence and wondrous instinct should easily furnish all else that was needed for the successful accomplishment of his mission.

It was with evident reluctance that the great beast turned to leave me in compliance with my command, and ere he had gone I could not resist the inclination to throw my arms about his great neck in a parting hug. He rubbed his cheek against mine in a final caress, and a moment later was speeding through the Carrion Caves toward the outer world.

In my note to Carthoris I had given explicit directions for locating the Carrion Caves, impressing upon him the necessity for making entrance to the country beyond through this avenue, and not to attempt under any circumstances to cross the ice-barrier with a fleet. I told him that what lay beyond the eighth cave I could not even guess; but I was sure that somewhere upon the other side of the ice-barrier his mother lay in the power of Matai Shang, and that possibly his grandfather and great-grandfather as well, if they lived.

Further, I advised him to call upon Kulan Tith and the son of Thuvan Dihn for warriors and ships that the expedition might be sufficiently strong to insure success at the first blow.

"And," I concluded, "if there be time bring Tars Tarkas with you, for if I live until you reach me I can think of few greater pleasures than to fight once more, shoulder to shoulder, with my old friend."

When Woola had left us Thuvan Dihn and I, hiding in the seventh cave, discussed and discarded many plans for crossing the eighth chamber. From where we stood we saw that the fighting among the apts was growing less, and that many that had been feeding had ceased and lain down to sleep.

Presently it became apparent that in a short time all the ferocious monsters might be peacefully slumbering, and thus a hazardous opportunity be presented to us to cross through their lair.

One by one the remaining brutes stretched themselves upon the bubbling decomposition that covered the mass of bones upon the floor of their den, until but a single apt remained awake. This huge fellow roamed restlessly about, nosing among his companion and the abhorrent litter of the cave.

Occasionally he would stop to peer intently toward first one of the exits from the chamber and then the other. His whole demeanor was as of one who acts as sentry.

We were at last forced to the belief that he would not sleep while the other occupants of the lair slept, and so cast about in our minds for some scheme whereby we might trick him. Finally I suggested a plan to Thuvan Dihn, and as it seemed as good as any that we had discussed we decided to put it to the test.

To this end Thuvan Dihn placed himself close against the cave's wall, beside the entrance to the eighth chamber, while I deliberately showed myself to the guardian apt as he looked toward our retreat. Then I sprang to the opposite side of the entrance, flattening my body close to the wall.

Without a sound the great beast moved rapidly toward the seventh cave to see what manner of intruder had thus rashly penetrated so far within the precincts of his habitation.

As he poked his head through the narrow aperture that connects the two caves a heavy long-sword was awaiting him upon either hand, and before he had an opportunity to emit even a single growl his severed head rolled at our feet.

Quickly we glanced into the eighth chamber – not an apt had moved. Crawling over the carcass of the huge beast that blocked the doorway Thuvan Dihn and I cautiously entered the forbidding and dangerous den.

Like snails we wound our silent and careful way among the huge, recumbent forms. The only sound above our breathing was the sucking noise of our feet as we lifted them from the ooze of decaying flesh through which we crept.

Halfway across the chamber and one of the mighty beasts directly before me moved restlessly at the very instant that my foot was poised above his head, over which I must step.

Breathlessly I waited, balancing upon one foot, for I did not dare move a muscle. In my right hand was my keen short-sword, the point hovering an inch above the thick fur beneath which beat the savage heart.

Finally the apt relaxed, sighing, as with the passing of a bad dream, and resumed the regular respiration of deep slumber. I planted my raised foot beyond the fierce head and an instant later had stepped over the beast.

Thuvan Dihn followed directly after me, and another moment found us at the further door, undetected.

The Carrion Caves consist of a series of twenty-seven connecting chambers, and present the appearance of having been eroded by running water in some far-gone age when a mighty river found its way to the south through this single breach in the barrier of rock and ice that hems the country of the pole.

Thuvan Dihn and I traversed the remaining nineteen caverns without adventure or mishap.

We were afterward to learn that but once a month is it possible to find all the apts of the Carrion Caves in a single chamber.

At other times they roam singly or in pairs in and out of the caves, so that it would have been practically impossible for two men to have passed through the entire twenty-seven chambers without encountering an apt in nearly every one of them. Once a month they sleep for a full day, and it was our good fortune to stumble by accident upon one of these occasions.

Beyond the last cave we emerged into a desolate country of snow and ice, but found a well-marked trail leading north. The way was boulder-strewn, as had been that south of the barrier, so that we could see but a short distance ahead of us at any time.

After a couple of hours we passed round a huge boulder to come to a steep declivity leading down into a valley.

Directly before us we saw a half dozen men – fierce, black-bearded fellows, with skins the color of a ripe lemon.

"The yellow men of Barsoom!" ejaculated Thuvan Dihn, as though even now that he saw them he found it scarce possible to believe that the very race we expected to find hidden in this remote and inaccessible land did really exist.

We withdrew behind an adjacent boulder to watch the actions of the little party, which stood huddled at the foot of another huge rock, their backs toward us.

One of them was peering round the edge of the granite mass as though watching one who approached from the opposite side.

Presently the object of his scrutiny came within the range of my vision and I saw that it was another yellow man. All were clothed in magnificent furs – the six in the black and yellow striped hide of the orluk, while he who approached alone was resplendent in the pure white skin of an apt.

The yellow men were armed with two swords, and a short javelin was slung across the back of each, while from their left arms hung cuplike shields no larger than a dinner plate, the concave sides of which turned outward toward an antagonist.

They seemed puny and futile implements of safety against an even ordinary swordsman, but I was later to see the purpose of them and with what wondrous dexterity the yellow men manipulate them.

One of the swords which each of the warriors carried caught my immediate attention. I call it a sword, but really it was a sharp-edged blade with a complete hook at the far end.

The other sword was of about the same length as the hooked instrument, and somewhere between that of my long-sword and my short-sword. It was straight and two-edged. In addition to the weapons I have enumerated each man carried a dagger in his harness.

As the white-furred one approached, the six grasped their swords more firmly – the hooked instrument in the left hand, the straight sword in the right, while above the left wrist the small shield was held rigid upon a metal bracelet.

As the lone warrior came opposite them the six rushed out upon him with fiendish yells that resembled nothing more closely than the savage war cry of the Apaches of the South-west.

Instantly the attacked drew both his swords, and as the six fell upon him I witnessed as pretty fighting as one might care to see.

With their sharp hooks the combatants attempted to take hold of an adversary, but like lightning the cupshaped shield would spring before the darting weapon and into its hollow the hook would plunge.

Once the lone warrior caught an antagonist in the side with his hook, and drawing him close ran his sword through him.

But the odds were too unequal, and, though he who fought alone was by far the best and bravest of them all, I saw that it was but a question of time before the remaining five would find an opening through his marvelous guard and bring him down.

Now my sympathies have ever been with the weaker side of an argument, and though I knew nothing of the cause of the trouble I could not stand idly by and see a brave man butchered by superior numbers.

As a matter of fact I presume I gave little attention to seeking an excuse, for I love a good fight too well to need any other reason for joining in when one is afoot.

So it was that before Thuvan Dihn knew what I was about he saw me standing by the side of the white-clad yellow man, battling like mad with his five adversaries.

CHAPTER NINE

With the Yellow Men

THUVAN DIHN was not long in joining me; and, though we found the hooked weapon a strange and savage thing with which to deal, the three of us soon despatched the five black-bearded warriors who opposed us.

When the battle was over our new acquaintance turned to me, and removing the shield from his wrist, held it out. I did not know the significance of his act, but judged that it was but a form of expressing his gratitude to me.

I afterward learned that it symbolized the offering of a man's life in return for some great favor done him; and my act of refusing, which I had immediately done, was what was expected of me.

"Then accept from Talu, Prince of Marentina," said the yellow man, "this token of my gratitude," and reaching beneath one of his wide sleeves he withdrew a bracelet and placed it upon my arm. He then went through the same ceremony with Thuvan Dihn.

Next he asked our names, and from what land we hailed. He seemed quite familiar with the geography of the outerworld, and when I said I was from Helium he raised his brows.

"Ah," he said, "you seek your ruler and his company?"

"Know you of them?" I asked.

"But little more than that they were captured by my uncle, Salensus Oll, Jeddak of Jeddaks, Ruler of Okar, land of the yellow men of Barsoom. As to their fate I know nothing, for I am at war with my uncle, who would crush my power in the principality of Marentina.

"These from whom you have just saved me are warriors he has sent out to find and slay me, for they know that often I come alone to hunt and kill the sacred apt which Salensus Oll so much reveres. It is partly because I hate his religion that Salensus Oll hates me; but mostly does he fear my growing power and the great faction which has arisen throughout Okar that would be glad to see me ruler of Okar and Jeddak of Jeddaks in his place.

"He is a cruel and tyrannous master whom all hate, and were it not for the great fear they have of him I could raise an army overnight that would wipe out the few that might remain loyal to him. My own people are faithful to me, and the little valley of Marentina has paid no tribute to the court of Salensus Oll for a year.

"Nor can he force us, for a dozen men may hold the narrow way to Marentina against a million. But now, as to thine own affairs. How may I aid you? My palace is at your disposal, if you wish to honor me by coming to Marentina."

"When our work is done we shall be glad to accept your invitation," I replied. "But now you can assist us most by directing us to the court of Salensus Oll, and suggesting some means by which we may gain admission to the city and the palace, or whatever other place we find our friends to be confined."

Talu gazed ruefully at our smooth faces and at Thuvan Dihn's red skin and my white one.

"First you must come to Marentina," he said, "for a great change must be wrought in your appearance before you can hope to enter any city in Okar. You must have yellow faces and black beards, and your apparel and trappings must be those least likely to arouse suspicion. In my palace is one who can make you appear as truly yellow men as does Salensus Oll himself."

His counsel seemed wise; and as there was apparently no other way to insure a successful entry to Kadabra, the capital city of Okar, we set out with Talu, Prince of Marentina, for his little, rock-bound country.

The way was over some of the worst traveling I have ever seen, and I do not wonder that in this land where there are neither thoats nor fliers that Marentina is in little fear of invasion; but at last we reached our destination, the first view of which I had from a slight elevation a half-mile from the city.

Nestled in a deep valley lay a city of Martian concrete, whose every street and plaza and open space was roofed with glass. All about lay snow and ice, but there was none upon the rounded, domelike, crystal covering that enveloped the whole city.

Then I saw how these people combated the rigors of the arctic, and lived in luxury and comfort in the midst of a land of perpetual ice. Their cities were veritable hothouses, and when I had come within this one my respect and admiration for the scientific and engineering skill of this buried nation was unbounded.

The moment we entered the city Talu threw off his outer garments of fur, as did we, and I saw that his apparel differed but little from that of the red races of Barsoom. Except for his leathern harness, covered thick with jewels and metal, he was naked, nor could one have comfortably worn apparel in that warm and humid atmosphere.

For three days we remained the guests of Prince Talu, and during that time he showered upon us every attention and courtesy within his power. He showed us all that was of interest in his great city.

The Marentina atmosphere plant will maintain life indefinitely in the cities of the north pole after all life upon the balance of dying Mars is extinct through the failure of the air supply, should the great central plant again cease functioning as it did upon that memorable occasion that gave me the opportunity of restoring life and happiness to the strange world that I had already learned to love so well.

He showed us the heating system that stores the sun's rays in great reservoirs beneath the city, and how little is necessary to maintain the perpetual summer heat of the glorious garden spot within this arctic paradise.

Broad avenues of sod sewn with the seed of the ocher vegetation of the dead sea bottoms carried the noiseless traffic of light and airy ground fliers that are the only form of artificial transportation used north of the gigantic ice-barrier.

The broad tires of these unique fliers are but rubber-like gas bags filled with the eighth Barsoomian ray, or ray of propulsion – that remarkable discovery of the Martians that has made possible the great fleets of mighty airships that render the red man of the outer world supreme. It is this ray which propels the inherent or reflected light of the planet off into space, and when confined gives to the Martian craft their airy buoyancy.

The ground fliers of Marentina contain just sufficient buoyancy in their automobile-like wheels to give the cars traction for steering purposes; and though the hind wheels are geared to the engine, and aid in driving the machine, the bulk of this work is carried by a small propeller at the stern.

I know of no more delightful sensation than that of riding in one of these luxuriously appointed cars which skim, light and airy as feathers, along the soft, mossy avenues of Marentina. They move with absolute noiselessness between borders of crimson sward and beneath arching trees gorgeous with the wondrous blooms that mark so many of the highly cultivated varieties of Barsoomian vegetation.

By the end of the third day the court barber – I can think of no other earthly appellation by which to describe him – had wrought so remarkable a transformation in both Thuvan Dihn and myself that our own wives would never have known us. Our skins were of the same lemon color as his own, and great, black beards and mustaches had been deftly affixed to our smooth faces. The trappings of warriors of Okar aided in the deception; and for wear beyond the hothouse cities we each had suits of the black- and yellow-striped orluk.

Talu gave us careful directions for the journey to Kadabra, the capital city of the Okar nation, which is the racial name of the yellow men. This good friend even accompanied us part way, and then, promising to aid us in any way that he found possible, bade us adieu.

On parting he slipped upon my finger a curiously wrought ring set with a dead-black, lusterless stone, which appeared more like a bit of bituminous coal than the priceless Barsoomian gem which in reality it is.

"There had been but three others cut from the mother stone," he said, "which is in my possession. These three are worn by nobles high in my confidence, all of whom have been sent on secret missions to the court of Salensus Oll.

"Should you come within fifty feet of any of these three you will feel a rapid, pricking sensation in the finger upon which you wear this ring. He who wears one of its mates will experience the same feeling; it is caused by an electrical action that takes place the moment two of these gems cut from the same mother stone come within the radius of each other's power. By it you will know that a friend is at hand upon whom you may depend for assistance in time of need.

"Should another wearer of one of these gems call upon you for aid do not deny him, and should death threaten you swallow the ring rather than let it fall into the hands of enemies. Guard it with your life, John Carter, for some day it may mean more than life to you."

With this parting admonition our good friend turned back toward Marentina, and we set our faces in the direction of the city of Kadabra and the court of Salensus Oll, Jeddak of Jeddaks.

That very evening we came within sight of the walled and glass-roofed city of Kadabra. It lies in a low depression near the pole, surrounded by rocky, snow-clad hills. From the pass through which we entered the valley we had a splendid view of this great city of the north. Its crystal domes sparkled in the brilliant sunlight gleaming above the frost-covered outer wall that circles the entire one hundred miles of its circumference.

At regular intervals great gates give entrance to the city; but even at the distance from which we looked upon the massive pile we could see that all were closed, and, in accordance with Talu's suggestion, we deferred attempting to enter the city until the following morning.

As he had said, we found numerous caves in the hillsides about us, and into one of these we crept for the night. Our warm orluk skins kept us perfectly comfortable, and it was only after a most refreshing sleep that we awoke shortly after daylight on the following morning.

Already the city was astir, and from several of the gates we saw parties of yellow men emerging. Following closely each detail of the instructions given us by our good friend of Marentina, we remained concealed for several hours until one party of some half dozen warriors had passed along the trail below our hiding place and entered the hills by way of the pass along which we had come the previous evening.

After giving them time to get well out of sight of our cave, Thuvan Dihn and I crept out and followed them, overtaking them when they were well into the hills.

When we had come almost to them I called aloud to their leader, when the whole party halted and turned toward us. The crucial test had come. Could we but deceive these men the rest would be comparatively easy.

"Kaor!" I cried as I came closer to them.

"Kaor!" responded the officer in charge of the party.

"We be from Illall," I continued, giving the name of the most remote city of Okar, which has little or no intercourse with Kadabra. "Only yesterday we arrived, and this morning the captain of the gate told us that you were setting out to hunt orluks, which is a sport we do not find in our own neighborhood. We have hastened after you to pray that you allow us to accompany you."

The officer was entirely deceived, and graciously permitted us to go with them for the day. The chance guess that they were bound upon an orluk hunt proved correct, and Talu had said that the chances were ten to one that such would be the mission of any party leaving Kadabra by the pass through which we entered the valley, since that way leads directly to the vast plains frequented by this elephantine beast of prey.

In so far as the hunt was concerned, the day was a failure, for we did not see a single orluk; but this proved more than fortunate for us, since the yellow men were so chagrined by their misfortune that they would not enter the city by the same gate by which they had left it in the morning, as it seemed that they had made great boasts to the captain of that gate about their skill at this dangerous sport.

We, therefore, approached Kadabra at a point several miles from that at which the party had quitted it in the morning, and so were relieved of the danger of embarrassing questions and explanations on the part of the gate captain, whom we had said had directed us to this particular hunting party.

We had come quite close to the city when my attention was attracted toward a tall, black shaft that reared its head several hundred feet into the air from what appeared to be a tangled mass of junk or wreckage, now partially snow-covered.

I did not dare venture an inquiry for fear of arousing suspicion by evident ignorance of something which as a yellow man I should have known; but before we reached the city gate I was to learn the purpose of that grim shaft and the meaning of the mighty accumulation beneath it.

We had come almost to the gate when one of the party called to his fellows, at the same time pointing toward the distant southern horizon. Following the direction he indicated, my eyes descried the hull of a large flier approaching rapidly from above the crest of the encircling hills.

"Still other fools who would solve the mysteries of the forbidden north," said the officer, half to himself. "Will they never cease their fatal curiosity?"

"Let us hope not," answered one of the warriors, "for then what should we do for slaves and sport?"

"True; but what stupid beasts they are to continue to come to a region from whence none of them ever has returned."

"Let us tarry and watch the end of this one," suggested one of the men.

The officer looked toward the city.

"The watch has seen him," he said; "we may remain, for we may be needed."

I looked toward the city and saw several hundred warriors issuing from the nearest gate. They moved leisurely, as though there were no need for haste – nor was there, as I was presently to learn.

Then I turned my eyes once more toward the flier. She was moving rapidly toward the city, and when she had come close enough I was surprised to see that her propellers were idle.

Straight for that grim shaft she bore. At the last minute I saw the great blades move to reverse her, yet on she came as though drawn by some mighty, irresistible power.

Intense excitement prevailed upon her deck, where men were running hither and thither, manning the guns and preparing to launch the small, one-man fliers, a fleet of which is part of the equipment of every Martian war vessel. Closer and closer to the black shaft the ship sped. In another instant she must strike, and then I saw the familiar signal flown that sends the lesser boats in a great flock from the deck of the mother ship.

Instantly a hundred tiny fliers rose from her deck, like a swarm of huge dragon flies; but scarcely were they clear of the battleship than the nose of each turned toward the shaft, and they, too, rushed on at frightful speed toward the same now seemingly inevitable end that menaced the larger vessel.

A moment later the collision came. Men were hurled in every direction from the ship's deck, while she, bent and crumpled, took the last, long plunge to the scrap-heap at the shaft's base.

With her fell a shower of her own tiny fliers, for each of them had come in violent collision with the solid shaft.

I noticed that the wrecked fliers scraped down the shaft's side, and that their fall was not as rapid as might have been expected; and then suddenly the secret of the shaft burst upon me, and with it an explanation of the cause that prevented a flier that passed too far across the ice-barrier ever returning.

The shaft was a mighty magnet, and when once a vessel came within the radius of its powerful attraction for the aluminum steel that enters so largely into the construction of all Barsoomian craft, no power on earth could prevent such an end as we had just witnessed.

I afterward learned that the shaft rests directly over the magnetic pole of Mars, but whether this adds in any way to its incalculable power of attraction I do not know. I am a fighting man, not a scientist.

Here, at last, was an explanation of the long absence of Tardos Mors and Mors Kajak. These valiant and intrepid warriors had dared the mysteries and dangers of the frozen north to search for Carthoris, whose long absence had bowed in grief the head of his beautiful mother, Dejah Thoris, Princess of Helium.

The moment that the last of the fliers came to rest at the base of the shaft the black-bearded, yellow warriors swarmed over the mass of wreckage upon which they lay, making prisoners of those who were uninjured and occasionally despatching with a sword-thrust one of the wounded who seemed prone to resent their taunts and insults.

A few of the uninjured red men battled bravely against their cruel foes, but for the most part they seemed too overwhelmed by the horror of the catastrophe that had befallen them to do more than submit supinely to the golden chains with which they were manacled.

When the last of the prisoners had been confined, the party returned to the city, at the gate of which we met a pack of fierce, gold-collared apts, each of which marched between two warriors, who held them with strong chains of the same metal as their collars.

Just beyond the gate the attendants loosened the whole terrible herd, and as they bounded off toward the grim, black shaft I did not need to ask to know their mission. Had there not been those within the cruel city of Kadabra who needed succor far worse than the poor unfortunate dead and dying out there in the cold upon the bent and broken carcasses of a thousand fliers I could not have restrained my desire to hasten back and do battle with those horrid creatures that had been despatched to rend and devour them.

As it was I could but follow the yellow warriors, with bowed head, and give thanks for the chance that had given Thuvan Dihn and me such easy ingress to the capital of Salensus Oll.

Once within the gates, we had no difficulty in eluding our friends of the morning, and presently found ourselves in a Martian hostelry.

CHAPTER TEN

In Durance

The public houses of Barsoom, I have found, vary but little. There is no privacy for other than married couples.

Men without their wives are escorted to a large chamber, the floor of which is usually of white marble or heavy glass, kept scrupulously clean. Here are many small, raised platforms for the guest's sleeping silks and furs, and if he have none of his own clean, fresh ones are furnished at a nominal charge.

Once a man's belongings have been deposited upon one of these platforms he is a guest of the house, and that platform his own until he leaves. No one will disturb or molest his belongings, as there are no thieves upon Mars.

As assassination is the one thing to be feared, the proprietors of the hostelries furnish armed guards, who pace back and forth through the sleeping-rooms day and night. The number of guards and gorgeousness of their trappings quite usually denote the status of the hotel.

No meals are served in these houses, but generally a public eating place adjoins them. Baths are connected with the sleeping chambers, and each guest is required to bathe daily or depart from the hotel.

Usually on a second or third floor there is a large sleeping-room for single women guests, but its appointments do not vary materially from the chamber occupied by men. The guards who watch the women remain in the corridor outside the sleeping chamber, while female slaves pace back and forth among the sleepers within, ready to notify the warriors should their presence be required.

I was surprised to note that all the guards with the hotel at which we stopped were red men, and on inquiring of one of them I learned that they were slaves purchased by the proprietors of the hotels from the government. The man whose post was past my sleeping platform had been commander of the navy of a great Martian nation; but fate had carried his flagship across the ice-barrier within the radius of power of the magnetic shaft, and now for many tedious years he had been a slave of the yellow men.

He told me that princes, jeds, and even jeddaks of the outer world, were among the menials who served the yellow race; but when I asked him if he had heard of the fate of Mors Kajak or Tardos Mors he shook his head, saying that he never had heard of their being prisoners here, though he was very familiar with the reputations and fame they bore in the outer world.

Neither had he heard any rumor of the coming of the Father of Therns and the black dator of the First Born, but he hastened to explain that he knew little of what took place within the palace. I could see that he wondered not a little that a yellow man should be so inquisitive about certain red prisoners from beyond the ice-barrier, and that I should be so ignorant of customs and conditions among my own race.

In fact, I had forgotten my disguise upon discovering a red man pacing before my sleeping platform; but his growing expression of surprise warned me in time, for I had no mind to reveal my identity to any unless some good could come of it, and I did not see how this poor fellow could serve me yet, though I had it in my mind that later I might be the means of serving him and all the other thousands of prisoners who do the bidding of their stern masters in Kadabra.

Thuvan Dihn and I discussed our plans as we sat together among our sleeping silks and furs that night in the midst of the hundreds of yellow men who occupied the apartment with us. We spoke in low whispers, but, as that is only what courtesy demands in a public sleeping place, we roused no suspicion.

At last, determining that all must be but idle speculation until after we had had a chance to explore the city and attempt to put into execution the plan Talu had suggested, we bade each other good night and turned to sleep.

After breakfasting the following morning we set out to see Kadabra, and as, through the generosity of the prince of Marentina, we were well supplied with the funds current in Okar we purchased a handsome ground flier. Having learned to drive them while in Marentina, we spent a delightful and profitable day exploring the city, and late in the afternoon at the hour Talu told us we would find government officials in their offices, we stopped before a magnificent building on the plaza opposite the royal grounds and the palace.

Here we walked boldly in past the armed guard at the door, to be met by a red slave within who asked our wishes.

"Tell Sorav, your master, that two warriors from Illall wish to take service in the palace guard," I said.

Sorav, Talu had told us, was the commander of the forces of the palace, and as men from the further cities of Okar – and especially Illall – were less likely to be tainted with the germ of intrigue which had for years infected the household of Salensus Oll, he was sure that we would be welcomed and few questions asked us.

He had primed us with such general information as he thought would be necessary for us to pass muster before Sorav, after which we would have to undergo a further examination before Salensus Oll that he might determine our physical fitness and our ability as warriors.

The little experience we had had with the strange hooked sword of the yellow man and his cuplike shield made it seem rather unlikely that either of us could pass this final test, but there was the chance that we might be quartered in the palace of Salensus Oll for several days after being accepted by Sorav before the Jeddak of Jeddaks would find time to put us to the final test.

After a wait of several minutes in an ante-chamber we were summoned into the private office of Sorav, where we were courteously greeted by this ferocious-appearing, black-bearded officer. He asked us our names and stations in our own city, and having received replies that were evidently satisfactory to him, he put certain questions to us that Talu had foreseen and prepared us for.

The interview could not have lasted over ten minutes when Sorav summoned an aid whom he instructed to record us properly, and then escort us to the quarters in the palace which are set aside for aspirants to membership in the palace guard.

The aid took us to his own office first, where he measured and weighed and photographed us simultaneously with a machine ingeniously devised for that purpose, five copies being instantly reproduced in five different offices of the government, two of which are located in other cities miles distant. Then he led us through the palace grounds to the main guardroom of the palace, there turning us over to the officer in charge.

This individual again questioned us briefly, and finally despatched a soldier to guide us to our quarters. These we found located upon the second floor of the palace in a semi-detached tower at the rear of the edifice.

When we asked our guide why we were quartered so far from the guardroom he replied that the custom of the older members of the guard of picking quarrels with aspirants to try their metal had resulted in so many deaths that it was found difficult to maintain the guard at its full strength while this custom prevailed. Salensus Oll had, therefore, set apart these quarters for aspirants, and here they were securely locked against the danger of attack by members of the guard.

This unwelcome information put a sudden check to all our well-laid plans, for it meant that we should virtually be prisoners in the palace of Salensus Oll until the time that he should see fit to give us the final examination for efficiency.

As it was this interval upon which we had banked to accomplish so much in our search for Dejah Thoris and Thuvia of Ptarth, our chagrin was unbounded when we heard the great lock click behind our guide as he had quitted us after ushering us into the chambers we were to occupy.

With a wry face I turned to Thuvan Dihn. My companion but shook his head disconsolately and walked to one of the windows upon the far side of the apartment.

Scarcely had he gazed beyond them than he called to me in a tone of suppressed excitement and surprise. In an instant I was by his side.

"Look!" said Thuvan Dihn, pointing toward the courtyard below.

As my eyes followed the direction indicated I saw two women pacing back and forth in an enclosed garden.

At the same moment I recognized them – they were Dejah Thoris and Thuvia of Ptarth!

There were they whom I had trailed from one pole to another, the length of a world. Only ten feet of space and a few metal bars separated me from them.

With a cry I attracted their attention, and as Dejah Thoris looked up full into my eyes I made the sign of love that the men of Barsoom make to their women.

To my astonishment and horror her head went high, and as a look of utter contempt touched her finely chiseled features she turned her back full upon me. My body is covered with the scars of a thousand conflicts, but never in all my long life have I suffered such anguish from a wound, for this time the steel of a woman's look had entered my heart.

With a groan I turned away and buried my face in my arms. I heard Thuvan Dihn call aloud to Thuvia, but an instant later his exclamation of surprise betokened that he, too, had been repulsed by his own daughter.

"They will not even listen," he cried to me. "They have put their hands over their ears and walked to the farther end of the garden. Ever heard you of such mad work, John Carter? The two must be bewitched."

Presently I mustered the courage to return to the window, for even though she spurned me I loved her, and could not keep my eyes from feasting upon her divine face and figure, but when she saw me looking she again turned away.

I was at my wit's end to account for her strange actions, and that Thuvia, too, had turned against her father seemed incredible. Could it be that my incomparable princess still clung to the hideous faith from which I had rescued her world? Could it be that she looked upon me with loathing and contempt because I had returned from the Valley Dor, or because I had desecrated the temples and persons of the Holy Therns?

To naught else could I ascribe her strange deportment, yet it seemed far from possible that such could be the case, for the love of Dejah Thoris for John Carter had been a great and wondrous love – far above racial distinctions, creed, or religion.

As I gazed ruefully at the back of her haughty, royal head a gate at the opposite end of the garden opened and a man entered. As he did so he turned and slipped something into the hand of the yellow guardsman beyond the gate, nor was the distance too great that I might not see that money had passed between them.

Instantly I knew that this newcomer had bribed his way within the garden. Then he turned in the direction of the two women, and I saw that he was none other than Thurid, the black dator of the First Born.

He approached quite close to them before he spoke, and as they turned at the sound of his voice I saw Dejah Thoris shrink from him.

There was a nasty leer upon his face as he stepped close to her and spoke again. I could not hear his words, but her answer came clearly.

"The granddaughter of Tardos Mors can always die," she said, "but she could never live at the price you name."

Then I saw the black scoundrel go upon his knees beside her, fairly groveling in the dirt, pleading with her. Only part of what he said came to me, for though he was evidently laboring under the stress of passion and excitement, it was equally apparent that he did not dare raise his voice for fear of detection.

"I would save you from Matai Shang," I heard him say. "You know the fate that awaits you at his hands. Would you not choose me rather than the other?"

"I would choose neither," replied Dejah Thoris, "even were I free to choose, as you know well I am not."

"You *are* free!" he cried. "John Carter, Prince of Helium, is dead."

"I know better than that; but even were he dead, and I must needs choose another mate, it should be a plant man or a great white ape in preference to either Matai Shang or you, black calot," she answered with a sneer of contempt.

Of a sudden the vicious beast lost all control of himself, as with a vile oath he leaped at the slender woman, gripping her tender throat in his brute clutch. Thuvia screamed and sprang to aid her fellow-prisoner, and at the same instant I, too, went mad, and tearing at the bars that spanned my window I ripped them from their sockets as they had been but copper wire.

Hurling myself through the aperture I reached the garden, but a hundred feet from where the black was choking the life from my Dejah Thoris, and with a single great bound I was upon him. I spoke no word as I tore his defiling fingers from that beautiful throat, nor did I utter a sound as I hurled him twenty feet from me.

Foaming with rage, Thurid regained his feet and charged me like a mad bull.

"Yellow man," he shrieked, "you knew not upon whom you had laid your vile hands, but ere I am done with you, you will know well what it means to offend the person of a First Born."

Then he was upon me, reaching for my throat, and precisely as I had done that day in the courtyard of the Temple of Issus I did here in the garden of the palace of Salensus Oll. I ducked beneath his outstretched arms, and as he lunged past me I planted a terrific right upon the side of his jaw.

Just as he had done upon that other occasion he did now. Like a top he spun round, his knees gave beneath him, and he crumpled to the ground at my feet. Then I heard a voice behind me.

It was the deep voice of authority that marks the ruler of men, and when I turned to face the resplendent figure of a giant yellow man I did not need to ask to know that it was Salensus Oll. At his right stood Matai Shang, and behind them a score of guardsmen.

"Who are you," he cried, "and what means this intrusion within the precincts of the women's garden? I do not recall your face. How came you here?"

But for his last words I should have forgotten my disguise entirely and told him outright that I was John Carter, Prince of Helium; but his question recalled me to myself. I pointed to the dislodged bars of the window above.

"I am an aspirant to membership in the palace guard," I said, "and from yonder window in the tower where I was confined awaiting the final test for fitness I saw this brute attack the – this woman. I could not stand idly by, O Jeddak, and see this thing done within the very palace grounds, and yet feel that I was fit to serve and guard your royal person."

I had evidently made an impression upon the ruler of Okar by my fair words, and when he had turned to Dejah Thoris and Thuvia of Ptarth, and both had corroborated my statements it began to look pretty dark for Thurid.

I saw the ugly gleam in Matai Shang's evil eyes as Dejah Thoris narrated all that had passed between Thurid and herself, and when she came to that part which dealt with my interference with the dator of the First Born her gratitude was quite apparent, though I could see by her eyes that something puzzled her strangely.

I did not wonder at her attitude toward me while others were present; but that she should have denied me while she and Thuvia were the only occupants of the garden still cut me sorely.

As the examination proceeded I cast a glance at Thurid and startled him looking wide-eyed and wonderingly at me, and then of a sudden he laughed full in my face.

A moment later Salensus Oll turned toward the black.

"What have you to say in explanation of these charges?" he asked in a deep and terrible voice. "Dare you aspire to one whom the Father of Therns has chosen – one who might even be a fit mate for the Jeddak of Jeddaks himself?"

And then the black-bearded tyrant turned and cast a sudden greedy look upon Dejah Thoris, as though with the words a new thought and a new desire had sprung up within his mind and breast.

Thurid had been about to reply and, with a malicious grin upon his face, was pointing an accusing finger at me, when Salensus Oll's words and the expression of his face cut him short.

A cunning look crept into his eyes, and I knew from the expression of his face that his next words were not the ones he had intended to speak.

"O Mightiest of Jeddaks," he said, "the man and the women do not speak the truth. The fellow had come into the garden to assist them to escape. I was beyond and overheard their conversation, and when I entered, the woman screamed and the man sprang upon me and would have killed me.

"What know you of this man? He is a stranger to you, and I dare say that you will find him an enemy and a spy. Let him be put on trial, Salensus Oll, rather than your friend and guest, Thurid, Dator of the First Born."

Salensus Oll looked puzzled. He turned again and looked upon Dejah Thoris, and then Thurid stepped quite close to him and whispered something in his ear – what, I know not.

Presently the yellow ruler turned to one of his officers.

"See that this man be securely confined until we have time to go deeper into this affair," he commanded, "and as bars alone seem inadequate to restrain him, let chains be added."

Then he turned and left the garden, taking Dejah Thoris with him – his hand upon her shoulder. Thurid and Matai Shang went also, and as they reached the gateway the black turned and laughed again aloud in my face.

What could be the meaning of his sudden change toward me? Could he suspect my true identity? It must be that, and the thing that had betrayed me was the trick and blow that had laid him low for the second time.

As the guards dragged me away my heart was very sad and bitter indeed, for now to the two relentless enemies that had hounded her for so long another and a more powerful one had been added, for I would have been but a fool had I not recognized the sudden love for Dejah Thoris that had just been born in the terrible breast of Salensus Oll, Jeddak of Jeddaks, ruler of Okar.

CHAPTER ELEVEN

The Pit of Plenty

I DID NOT LANGUISH long within the prison of Salensus Oll. During the short time that I lay there, fettered with chains of gold, I often wondered as to the fate of Thuvan Dihn, Jeddak of Ptarth.

My brave companion had followed me into the garden as I attacked Thurid, and when Salensus Oll had left with Dejah Thoris and the others, leaving Thuvia of Ptarth behind, he, too, had remained in the garden with his daughter, apparently unnoticed, for he was appareled similarly to the guards.

The last I had seen of him he stood waiting for the warriors who escorted me to close the gate behind them, that he might be alone with Thuvia. Could it be possible that they had escaped? I doubted it, and yet with all my heart I hoped that it might be true.

The third day of my incarceration brought a dozen warriors to escort me to the audience chamber, where Salensus Oll himself was to try me. A great number of nobles crowded the room, and among them I saw Thurid, but Matai Shang was not there.

Dejah Thoris, as radiantly beautiful as ever, sat upon a small throne beside Salensus Oll. The expression of sad hopelessness upon her dear face cut deep into my heart.

Her position beside the Jeddak of Jeddaks boded ill for her and me, and on the instant that I saw her there, there sprang to my mind the firm intention never to leave that chamber alive if I must leave her in the clutches of this powerful tyrant.

I had killed better men than Salensus Oll, and killed them with my bare hands, and now I swore to myself that I should kill him if I found that the only way to save the Princess of Helium. That it would mean almost instant death for me I cared not, except that it would remove me from further efforts in behalf of Dejah Thoris, and for this reason alone I would have chosen another way, for even though I should kill Salensus Oll that act would not restore my beloved wife to her own people. I determined to wait the final outcome of the trial, that I might learn all that I could of the Okarian ruler's intentions, and then act accordingly.

Scarcely had I come before him than Salensus Oll summoned Thurid also.

"Dator Thurid," he said, "you have made a strange request of me; but, in accordance with your wishes and your promise that it will result only to my interests, I have decided to accede.

"You tell me that a certain announcement will be the means of convicting this prisoner and, at the same time, open the way to the gratification of my dearest wish."

Thurid nodded.

"Then shall I make the announcement here before all my nobles," continued Salensus Oll. "For a year no queen has sat upon the throne beside me, and now it suits me to take to wife one who is reputed the most beautiful woman upon Barsoom. A statement which none may truthfully deny.

"Nobles of Okar, unsheathe your swords and do homage to Dejah Thoris, Princess of Helium and future Queen of Okar, for at the end of the allotted ten days she shall become the wife of Salensus Oll."

As the nobles drew their blades and lifted them on high, in accordance with the ancient custom of Okar when a jeddak announces his intention to wed, Dejah Thoris sprang to her feet and, raising her hand aloft, cried in a loud voice that they desist.

"I may not be the wife of Salensus Oll," she pleaded, "for already I be a wife and mother. John Carter, Prince of Helium, still lives. I know it to be true, for I overheard Matai Shang tell his daughter Phaidor that he had seen him in Kaor, at the court of Kulan Tith, Jeddak. A jeddak does not wed a married woman, nor will Salensus Oll thus violate the bonds of matrimony."

Salensus Oll turned upon Thurid with an ugly look.

"Is this the surprise you held in store for me?" he cried. "You assured me that no obstacle which might not be easily overcome stood between me and this woman, and now I find that the one insuperable obstacle intervenes. What mean you, man? What have you to say?"

"And should I deliver John Carter into your hands, Salensus Oll, would you not feel that I had more than satisfied the promise that I made you?" answered Thurid.

"Talk not like a fool," cried the enraged jeddak. "I am no child to be thus played with."

"I am talking only as a man who knows," replied Thurid. "Knows that he can do all that he claims."

"Then turn John Carter over to me within ten days or yourself suffer the end that I should mete out to him were he in my power!" snapped the Jeddak of Jeddaks, with an ugly scowl.

"You need not wait ten days, Salensus Oll," replied Thurid; and then, turning suddenly upon me as he extended a pointing finger, he cried: "There stands John Carter, Prince of Helium!"

"Fool!" shrieked Salensus Oll. "Fool! John Carter is a white man. This fellow be as yellow as myself. John Carter's face is smooth – Matai Shang has described him to me. This prisoner has a beard and mustache as large and black as any in Okar. Quick, guardsmen, to the pits with the black maniac who wishes to throw his life away for a poor joke upon your ruler!"

"Hold!" cried Thurid, and springing forward before I could guess his intention, he had grasped my beard and ripped the whole false fabric from my face and head, revealing my smooth, tanned skin beneath and my close-cropped black hair.

Instantly pandemonium reigned in the audience chamber of Salensus Oll. Warriors pressed forward with drawn blades, thinking that I might be contemplating the assassination of the Jeddak of Jeddaks; while others, out of curiosity to see one whose name was familiar from pole to pole, crowded behind their fellows.

As my identity was revealed I saw Dejah Thoris spring to her feet – amazement writ large upon her face – and then through that jam of armed men she forced her way before any could prevent. A moment only and she was before me with outstretched arms and eyes filled with the light of her great love.

"John Carter! John Carter!" she cried as I folded her to my breast, and then of a sudden I knew why she had denied me in the garden beneath the tower.

What a fool I had been! Expecting that she would penetrate the marvelous disguise that had been wrought for me by the barber of Marentina! She had not known me, that was all; and when she saw the sign of love from a stranger she was offended and righteously indignant. Indeed, but I had been a fool.

"And it was you," she cried, "who spoke to me from the tower! How could I dream that my beloved Virginian lay behind that fierce beard and that yellow skin?"

She had been wont to call me her Virginian as a term of endearment, for she knew that I loved the sound of that beautiful name, made a thousand times more beautiful and hallowed by her dear lips, and as I heard it again after all those long years my eyes became dimmed with tears and my voice choked with emotion.

But an instant did I crush that dear form to me ere Salensus Oll, trembling with rage and jealousy, shouldered his way to us.

"Seize the man," he cried to his warriors, and a hundred ruthless hands tore us apart.

Well it was for the nobles of the court of Okar that John Carter had been disarmed. As it was, a dozen of them felt the weight of my clenched fists, and I had fought my way half up the steps before the throne to which Salensus Oll had carried Dejah Thoris ere ever they could stop me.

Then I went down, fighting, beneath a half-hundred warriors; but before they had battered me into unconsciousness I heard that from the lips of Dejah Thoris that made all my suffering well worth while.

Standing there beside the great tyrant, who clutched her by the arm, she pointed to where I fought alone against such awful odds.

"Think you, Salensus Oll, that the wife of such as he is," she cried, "would ever dishonor his memory, were he a thousand times dead, by mating with a lesser mortal? Lives there upon any world such another as John Carter, Prince of Helium? Lives there another man who could fight his way back and forth across a warlike planet, facing savage beasts and hordes of savage men, for the love of a woman?

"I, Dejah Thoris, Princess of Helium, am his. He fought for me and won me. If you be a brave man you will honor the bravery that is his, and you will not kill him. Make him a slave if you will, Salensus Oll; but spare his life. I would rather be a slave with such as he than be Queen of Okar."

"Neither slave nor queen dictates to Salensus Oll," replied the Jeddak of Jeddaks. "John Carter shall die a natural death in the Pit of Plenty, and the day he dies Dejah Thoris shall become my queen."

I did not hear her reply, for it was then that a blow upon my head brought unconsciousness, and when I recovered my senses only a handful of guardsmen remained in the audience chamber with me. As I opened my eyes they goaded me with the points of their swords and bade me rise.

Then they led me through long corridors to a court far toward the center of the palace.

In the center of the court was a deep pit, near the edge of which stood half a dozen other guardsmen, awaiting me. One of them carried a long rope in his hands, which he commenced to make ready as we approached.

We had come to within fifty feet of these men when I felt a sudden strange and rapid pricking sensation in one of my fingers.

For a moment I was nonplused by the odd feeling, and then there came to me recollection of that which in the stress of my adventure I had entirely forgotten – the gift ring of Prince Talu of Marentina.

Instantly I looked toward the group we were nearing, at the same time raising my left hand to my forehead, that the ring might be visible to one who sought it. Simultaneously one of the waiting warriors raised his left hand, ostensibly to brush back his hair, and upon one of his fingers I saw the duplicate of my own ring.

A quick look of intelligence passed between us, after which I kept my eyes turned away from the warrior and did not look at him again, for fear that I might arouse the suspicion of the Okarians. When we reached the edge of the pit I saw that it was very deep, and presently I realized I was soon to judge just how far it extended below the surface of the court, for he who held the rope passed it about my body in such a way that it could be released from above at any time; and then, as all the warriors grasped it, he pushed me forward, and I fell into the yawning abyss.

After the first jerk as I reached the end of the rope that had been paid out to let me fall below the pit's edge they lowered me quickly but smoothly. The moment before the plunge, while two or three of the men had been assisting in adjusting the rope about me, one of them had brought his mouth close to my cheek, and in the brief interval before I was cast into the forbidding hole he breathed a single word into my ear:

"Courage!"

The pit, which my imagination had pictured as bottomless, proved to be not more than a hundred feet in depth; but as its walls were smoothly polished it might as well have been a thousand feet, for I could never hope to escape without outside assistance.

For a day I was left in darkness; and then, quite suddenly, a brilliant light illumined my strange cell. I was reasonably hungry and thirsty by this time, not having tasted food or drink since the day prior to my incarceration.

To my amazement I found the sides of the pit, that I had thought smooth, lined with shelves, upon which were the most delicious viands and liquid refreshments that Okar afforded.

With an exclamation of delight I sprang forward to partake of some of the welcome food, but ere ever I reached it the light was extinguished, and, though I groped my way about the chamber, my hands came in contact with nothing beside the smooth, hard wall that I had felt on my first examination of my prison.

Immediately the pangs of hunger and thirst began to assail me. Where before I had had but a mild craving for food and drink, I now actually suffered for want of it, and all because of the tantalizing sight that I had had of food almost within my grasp.

Once more darkness and silence enveloped me, a silence that was broken only by a single mocking laugh.

For another day nothing occurred to break the monotony of my imprisonment or relieve the suffering superinduced by hunger and thirst. Slowly the pangs became less keen, as suffering deadened the activity of certain nerves; and then the light flashed on once again, and before me stood an array of new and tempting dishes, with great bottles of clear water and flagons of refreshing wine, upon the outside of which the cold sweat of condensation stood.

Again, with the hunger madness of a wild beast, I sprang forward to seize those tempting dishes; but, as before, the light went out and I came to a sudden stop against a hard wall.

Then the mocking laugh rang out for a second time.

The Pit of Plenty!

Ah, what a cruel mind must have devised this exquisite, hellish torture! Day after day was the thing repeated, until I was on the verge of madness; and then, as I had done in the pits of the Warhoons, I took a new, firm hold upon my reason and forced it back into the channels of sanity.

By sheer will-power I regained control over my tottering mentality, and so successful was I that the next time that the light came I sat quite still and looked indifferently at the fresh and tempting food almost within my reach. Glad I was that I had done so, for it gave me an opportunity to solve the seeming mystery of those vanishing banquets.

As I made no move to reach the food, the torturers left the light turned on in the hope that at last I could refrain no longer from giving them the delicious thrill of enjoyment that my former futile efforts to obtain it had caused.

And as I sat scrutinizing the laden shelves I presently saw how the thing was accomplished, and so simple was it that I wondered I had not guessed it before. The wall of my prison was of clearest glass – behind the glass were the tantalizing viands.

After nearly an hour the light went out, but this time there was no mocking laughter – at least not upon the part of my tormentors; but I, to be at quits with them, gave a low laugh that none might mistake for the cackle of a maniac.

Nine days passed, and I was weak from hunger and thirst, but no longer suffering – I was past that. Then, down through the darkness above, a little parcel fell to the floor at my side.

Indifferently I groped for it, thinking it but some new invention of my jailers to add to my sufferings.

At last I found it – a tiny package wrapped in paper, at the end of a strong and slender cord. As I opened it a few lozenges fell to the floor. As I gathered them up, feeling of them and smelling of them, I discovered that they were tablets of concentrated food such as are quite common in all parts of Barsoom.

Poison! I thought.

Well, what of it? Why not end my misery now rather than drag out a few more wretched days in this dark pit? Slowly I raised one of the little pellets to my lips.

"Good-bye, my Dejah Thoris!" I breathed. "I have lived for you and fought for you, and now my next dearest wish is to be realized, for I shall die for you," and, taking the morsel in my mouth, I devoured it.

One by one I ate them all, nor ever did anything taste better than those tiny bits of nourishment, within which I knew must lie the seeds of death – possibly of some hideous, torturing death.

As I sat quietly upon the floor of my prison, waiting for the end, my fingers by accident came in contact with the bit of paper in which the things had been wrapped; and as I idly played with it, my mind roaming far back into the past, that I might live again for a few brief moments before I died some of the many happy moments of a long and happy life, I became aware of strange protuberances upon the smooth surface of the parchment-like substance in my hands.

For a time they carried no special significance to my mind – I merely was mildly wondrous that they were there; but at last they seemed to take form, and then I realized that there was but a single line of them, like writing.

Now, more interestedly, my fingers traced and retraced them. There were four separate and distinct combinations of raised lines. Could it be that these were four words, and that they were intended to carry a message to me?

The more I thought of it the more excited I became, until my fingers raced madly back and forth over those bewildering little hills and valleys upon that bit of paper.

But I could make nothing of them, and at last I decided that my very haste was preventing me from solving the mystery. Then I took it more slowly. Again and again my forefinger traced the first of those four combinations.

Martian writing is rather difficult to explain to an Earth man – it is something of a cross between shorthand and picture-writing, and is an entirely different language from the spoken language of Mars.

Upon Barsoom there is but a single oral language.

It is spoken today by every race and nation, just as it was at the beginning of human life upon Barsoom. It has grown with the growth of the planet's learning and scientific achievements, but so ingenious a thing it is that new words to express new thoughts or describe new conditions or discoveries form themselves – no other word could explain the thing that a new word is required for other than the word that naturally falls to it, and so, no matter how far removed two nations or races, their spoken languages are identical.

Not so their written languages, however. No two nations have the same written language, and often cities of the same nation have a written language that differs greatly from that of the nation to which they belong.

Thus it was that the signs upon the paper, if in reality they were words, baffled me for some time; but at last I made out the first one.

It was "courage," and it was written in the letters of Marentina.

Courage!

That was the word the yellow guardsman had whispered in my ear as I stood upon the verge of the Pit of Plenty.

The message must be from him, and he I knew was a friend.

With renewed hope I bent my every energy to the deciphering of the balance of the message, and at last success rewarded my endeavor – I had read the four words:

"Courage! Follow the rope."

CHAPTER TWELVE
"Follow the Rope"

WHAT COULD it mean?

"Follow the rope." What rope?

Presently I recalled the cord that had been attached to the parcel when it fell at my side, and after a little groping my hand came in contact with it again. It depended from above, and when I pulled upon it I discovered that it was rigidly fastened, possibly at the pit's mouth.

Upon examination I found that the cord, though small, was amply able to sustain the weight of several men. Then I made another discovery – there was a second message knotted in the rope at about the height of my head. This I deciphered more easily, now that the key was mine.

"Bring the rope with you. Beyond the knots lies danger."

That was all there was to this message. It was evidently hastily formed – an afterthought.

I did not pause longer than to learn the contents of the second message, and, though I was none too sure of the meaning of the final admonition, "Beyond the knots lies danger," yet I was sure that here before me lay an avenue of escape, and that the sooner I took advantage of it the more likely was I to win to liberty.

At least, I could be but little worse off than I had been in the Pit of Plenty.

I was to find, however, ere I was well out of that damnable hole that I might have been very much worse off had I been compelled to remain there another two minutes.

It had taken me about that length of time to ascend some fifty feet above the bottom when a noise above attracted my attention. To my chagrin I saw that the covering of the pit was being removed far above me, and in the light of the courtyard beyond I saw a number of yellow warriors.

Could it be that I was laboriously working my way into some new trap? Were the messages spurious, after all? And then, just as my hope and courage had ebbed to their lowest, I saw two things.

One was the body of a huge, struggling, snarling apt being lowered over the side of the pit toward me, and the other was an aperture in the side of the shaft – an aperture larger than a man's body, into which my rope led.

Just as I scrambled into the dark hole before me the apt passed me, reaching out with his mighty hands to clutch me, and snapping, growling, and roaring in a most frightful manner.

Plainly now I saw the end for which Salensus Oll had destined me. After first torturing me with starvation he had caused this fierce beast to be lowered into my prison to finish the work that the jeddak's hellish imagination had conceived.

And then another truth flashed upon me – I had lived nine days of the allotted ten which must intervene before Salensus Oll could make Dejah Thoris his queen. The purpose of the apt was to insure my death before the tenth day.

I almost laughed aloud as I thought how Salensus Oll's measure of safety was to aid in defeating the very end he sought, for when they discovered that the apt was alone in the Pit of Plenty they could not know but that he had completely devoured me, and so no suspicion of my escape would cause a search to be made for me.

Coiling the rope that had carried me thus far upon my strange journey, I sought for the other end, but found that as I followed it forward it extended always before me. So this was the meaning of the words: "Follow the rope."

The tunnel through which I crawled was low and dark. I had followed it for several hundred yards when I felt a knot beneath my fingers. "Beyond the knots lies danger."

Now I went with the utmost caution, and a moment later a sharp turn in the tunnel brought me to an opening into a large, brilliantly lighted chamber.

The trend of the tunnel I had been traversing had been slightly upward, and from this I judged that the chamber into which I now found myself looking must be either on the first floor of the palace or directly beneath the first floor.

Upon the opposite wall were many strange instruments and devices, and in the center of the room stood a long table, at which two men were seated in earnest conversation.

He who faced me was a yellow man – a little, wizened-up, pasty-faced old fellow with great eyes that showed the white round the entire circumference of the iris.

His companion was a black man, and I did not need to see his face to know that it was Thurid, for there was no other of the First Born north of the ice-barrier.

Thurid was speaking as I came within hearing of the men's voices.

"Solan," he was saying, "there is no risk and the reward is great. You know that you hate Salensus Oll and that nothing would please you more than to thwart him in some cherished plan. There be nothing that he more cherishes today than the idea of wedding the beautiful Princess of Helium; but I, too, want her, and with your help I may win her.

"You need not more than step from this room for an instant when I give you the signal. I will do the rest, and then, when I am gone, you may come and throw the great switch back into its place, and all will be as before. I need but an hour's start to be safe beyond the devilish power that you control in this hidden chamber beneath the palace of your master. See how easy," and with the words the black dator rose from his seat and, crossing the room, laid his hand upon a large, burnished lever that protruded from the opposite wall.

"No! No!" cried the little old man, springing after him, with a wild shriek. "Not that one! Not that one! That controls the sunray tanks, and should you pull it too far down, all Kadabra would be consumed by heat before I could replace it. Come away! Come away! You know not with what mighty powers you play. This is the lever that you seek. Note well the symbol inlaid in white upon its ebon surface."

Thurid approached and examined the handle of the lever.

"Ah, a magnet," he said. "I will remember. It is settled then I take it," he continued.

The old man hesitated. A look of combined greed and apprehension overspread his none too beautiful features.

"Double the figure," he said. "Even that were all too small an amount for the service you ask. Why, I risk my life by even entertaining you here within the forbidden precincts of my station. Should Salensus Oll learn of it he would have me thrown to the apts before the day was done."

"He dare not do that, and you know it full well, Solan," contradicted the black. "Too great a power of life and death you hold over the people of Kadabra for Salensus Oll ever to risk threatening you with death. Before ever his minions could lay their hands upon you, you might seize this very lever from which you have just warned me and wipe out the entire city."

"And myself into the bargain," said Solan, with a shudder.

"But if you were to die, anyway, you would find the nerve to do it," replied Thurid.

"Yes," muttered Solan, "I have often thought upon that very thing. Well, First Born, is your red princess worth the price I ask for my services, or will you go without her and see her in the arms of Salensus Oll tomorrow night?"

"Take your price, yellow man," replied Thurid, with an oath. "Half now and the balance when you have fulfilled your contract."

With that the dator threw a well-filled money-pouch upon the table.

Solan opened the pouch and with trembling fingers counted its contents. His weird eyes assumed a greedy expression, and his unkempt beard and mustache twitched with the muscles of his mouth and chin. It was quite evident from his very mannerism that Thurid had keenly guessed the man's weakness – even the clawlike, clutching movement of the fingers betokened the avariciousness of the miser.

Having satisfied himself that the amount was correct, Solan replaced the money in the pouch and rose from the table.

"Now," he said, "are you quite sure that you know the way to your destination? You must travel quickly to cover the ground to the cave and from thence beyond the Great Power, all within a brief hour, for no more dare I spare you."

"Let me repeat it to you," said Thurid, "that you may see if I be letter-perfect."

"Proceed," replied Solan.

"Through yonder door," he commenced, pointing to a door at the far end of the apartment, "I follow a corridor, passing three diverging corridors upon my right; then into the fourth right-hand corridor straight to where three corridors meet; here again I follow to the right, hugging the left wall closely to avoid the pit.

"At the end of this corridor I shall come to a spiral runway, which I must follow down instead of up; after that the way is along but a single branchless corridor. Am I right?"

"Quite right, Dator," answered Solan; "and now begone. Already have you tempted fate too long within this forbidden place."

"Tonight, or tomorrow, then, you may expect the signal," said Thurid, rising to go.

"Tonight, or tomorrow," repeated Solan, and as the door closed behind his guest the old man continued to mutter as he turned back to the table, where he again dumped the contents of the money-pouch, running his fingers through the heap of shining metal; piling the coins into little towers; counting, recounting, and fondling the wealth the while he muttered on and on in a crooning undertone.

Presently his fingers ceased their play; his eyes popped wider than ever as they fastened upon the door through which Thurid had disappeared. The croon changed to a querulous muttering, and finally to an ugly growl.

Then the old man rose from the table, shaking his fist at the closed door. Now he raised his voice, and his words came distinctly.

"Fool!" he muttered. "Think you that for your happiness Solan will give up his life? If you escaped, Salensus Oll would know that only through my connivance could you have succeeded. Then would he send for me. What would you have me do? Reduce the city and myself to ashes? No, fool, there is a better way – a better way for Solan to keep thy money and be revenged upon Salensus Oll."

He laughed in a nasty, cackling note.

"Poor fool! You may throw the great switch that will give you the freedom of the air of Okar, and then, in fatuous security, go on with thy red princess to the freedom of – death. When you have passed beyond this chamber in your flight, what can prevent Solan replacing the switch as it was before your vile hand touched it? Nothing; and then the Guardian of the North will claim you and your woman, and Salensus Oll, when he sees your dead bodies, will never dream that the hand of Solan had aught to do with the thing."

Then his voice dropped once more into mutterings that I could not translate, but I had heard enough to cause me to guess a great deal more, and I thanked the kind Providence that had led me to this chamber at a time so filled with importance to Dejah Thoris and myself as this.

But how to pass the old man now! The cord, almost invisible upon the floor, stretched straight across the apartment to a door upon the far side.

There was no other way of which I knew, nor could I afford to ignore the advice to "follow the rope." I must cross this room, but however I should accomplish it undetected with that old man in the very center of it baffled me.

Of course I might have sprung in upon him and with my bare hands silenced him forever, but I had heard enough to convince me that with him alive the knowledge that I had gained might serve me at some future moment, while should I kill him and another be stationed in his place Thurid would not come hither with Dejah Thoris, as was quite evidently his intention.

As I stood in the dark shadow of the tunnel's end racking my brain for a feasible plan the while I watched, catlike, the old man's every move, he took up the money-pouch and crossed to one end of the apartment, where, bending to his knees, he fumbled with a panel in the wall.

Instantly I guessed that here was the hiding place in which he hoarded his wealth, and while he bent there, his back toward me, I entered the chamber upon tiptoe, and with the utmost stealth essayed to reach the opposite side before he should complete his task and turn again toward the room's center.

Scarcely thirty steps, all told, must I take, and yet it seemed to my overwrought imagination that that farther wall was miles away; but at last I reached it, nor once had I taken my eyes from the back of the old miser's head.

He did not turn until my hand was upon the button that controlled the door through which my way led, and then he turned away from me as I passed through and gently closed the door.

For an instant I paused, my ear close to the panel, to learn if he had suspected aught, but as no sound of pursuit came from within I wheeled and made my way along the new corridor, following the rope, which I coiled and brought with me as I advanced.

But a short distance farther on I came to the rope's end at a point where five corridors met. What was I to do? Which way should I turn? I was nonplused.

A careful examination of the end of the rope revealed the fact that it had been cleanly cut with some sharp instrument. This fact and the words that had cautioned me that danger lay beyond the KNOTS convinced me that the rope had been severed since my friend had placed it as my guide, for I had but passed a single knot, whereas there had evidently been two or more in the entire length of the cord.

Now, indeed, was I in a pretty fix, for neither did I know which avenue to follow nor when danger lay directly in my path; but there was nothing else to be done than follow one of the corridors, for I could gain nothing by remaining where I was.

So I chose the central opening, and passed on into its gloomy depths with a prayer upon my lips.

The floor of the tunnel rose rapidly as I advanced, and a moment later the way came to an abrupt end before a heavy door.

I could hear nothing beyond, and, with my accustomed rashness, pushed the portal wide to step into a room filled with yellow warriors.

The first to see me opened his eyes wide in astonishment, and at the same instant I felt the tingling sensation in my finger that denoted the presence of a friend of the ring.

Then others saw me, and there was a concerted rush to lay hands upon me, for these were all members of the palace guard – men familiar with my face.

The first to reach me was the wearer of the mate to my strange ring, and as he came close he whispered: "Surrender to me!" then in a loud voice shouted: "You are my prisoner, white man," and menaced me with his two weapons.

And so John Carter, Prince of Helium, meekly surrendered to a single antagonist. The others now swarmed about us, asking many questions, but I would not talk to them, and finally my captor announced that he would lead me back to my cell.

An officer ordered several other warriors to accompany him, and a moment later we were retracing the way I had just come. My friend walked close beside me, asking many silly questions about the country from which I had come, until finally his fellows paid no further attention to him or his gabbling.

Gradually, as he spoke, he lowered his voice, so that presently he was able to converse with me in a low tone without attracting attention. His ruse was a clever one, and showed that Talu had not misjudged the man's fitness for the dangerous duty upon which he was detailed.

When he had fully assured himself that the other guardsmen were not listening, he asked me why I had not followed the rope, and when I told him that it had ended at the five corridors he said that it must have been cut by someone in need of a piece of rope, for he was sure that "the stupid Kadabrans would never have guessed its purpose."

Before we had reached the spot from which the five corridors diverge my Marentinian friend had managed to drop to the rear of the little column with me, and when we came in sight of the branching ways he whispered:

"Run up the first upon the right. It leads to the watchtower upon the south wall. I will direct the pursuit up the next corridor," and with that he gave me a great shove into the dark mouth of the tunnel, at the same time crying out in simulated pain and alarm as he threw himself upon the floor as though I had felled him with a blow.

From behind the voices of the excited guardsmen came reverberating along the corridor, suddenly growing fainter as Talu's spy led them up the wrong passageway in fancied pursuit.

As I ran for my life through the dark galleries beneath the palace of Salensus Oll I must indeed have presented a remarkable appearance had there been any to note it, for though death loomed large about me, my face was split by a broad grin as I thought of the resourcefulness of the nameless hero of Marentina to whom I owed my life.

Of such stuff are the men of my beloved Helium, and when I meet another of their kind, of whatever race or color, my heart goes out to him as it did now to my new friend who had risked his life for me simply because I wore the mate to the ring his ruler had put upon his finger.

The corridor along which I ran led almost straight for a considerable distance, terminating at the foot of a spiral runway, up which I proceeded to emerge presently into a circular chamber upon the first floor of a tower.

In this apartment a dozen red slaves were employed polishing or repairing the weapons of the yellow men. The walls of the room were lined with racks in which were hundreds of straight and hooked swords, javelins, and daggers. It was evidently an armory. There were but three warriors guarding the workers.

My eyes took in the entire scene at a glance. Here were weapons in plenty! Here were sinewy red warriors to wield them!

And here now was John Carter, Prince of Helium, in need both of weapons and warriors!

As I stepped into the apartment, guards and prisoners saw me simultaneously.

Close to the entrance where I stood was a rack of straight swords, and as my hand closed upon the hilt of one of them my eyes fell upon the faces of two of the prisoners who worked side by side.

One of the guards started toward me. "Who are you?" he demanded. "What do you here?"

"I come for Tardos Mors, Jeddak of Helium, and his son, Mors Kajak," I cried, pointing to the two red prisoners, who had now sprung to their feet, wide-eyed in astonished recognition.

"Rise, red men! Before we die let us leave a memorial in the palace of Okar's tyrant that will stand forever in the annals of Kadabra to the honor and glory of Helium," for I had seen that all the prisoners there were men of Tardos Mors's navy.

Then the first guardsman was upon me and the fight was on, but scarce did we engage ere, to my horror, I saw that the red slaves were shackled to the floor.

CHAPTER THIRTEEN

The Magnet Switch

The guardsmen paid not the slightest attention to their wards, for the red men could not move over two feet from the great rings to which they were padlocked, though each had seized a weapon upon which he had been engaged when I entered the room, and stood ready to join me could they have but done so.

The yellow men devoted all their attention to me, nor were they long in discovering that the three of them were none too many to defend the armory against John Carter. Would that I had had my own good long-sword in my hand that day; but, as it was, I rendered a satisfactory ac-count of myself with the unfamiliar weapon of the yellow man.

At first I had a time of it dodging their villainous hook-swords, but after a minute or two I had succeeded in wresting a second straight sword from one of the racks along the wall, and thereafter, using it to parry the hooks of my antagonists, I felt more evenly equipped.

The three of them were on me at once, and but for a lucky circum-stance my end might have come quickly. The foremost guardsman made a vicious lunge for my side with his hook after the three of them had backed me against the wall, but as I sidestepped and raised my arm his weapon but grazed my side, passing into a rack of javelins, where it became entangled.

Before he could release it I had run him through, and then, fall-ing back upon the tactics that have saved me a hundred times in tight pinches, I rushed the two remaining warriors, forcing them back with a perfect torrent of cuts and thrusts, weaving my sword in and out about their guards until I had the fear of death upon them.

Then one of them commenced calling for help, but it was too late to save them.

They were as putty in my hands now, and I backed them about the armory as I would until I had them where I wanted them – within reach of the swords of the shackled slaves. In an instant both lay dead upon the floor. But their cries had not been entirely fruitless, for now I heard answering shouts and the footfalls of many men running and the clank of accouterments and the commands of officers.

"The door! Quick, John Carter, bar the door!" cried Tardos Mors.

Already the guard was in sight, charging across the open court that was visible through the doorway.

A dozen seconds would bring them into the tower. A single leap carried me to the heavy portal. With a resounding bang I slammed it shut.

"The bar!" shouted Tardos Mors.

I tried to slip the huge fastening into place, but it defied my every attempt.

"Raise it a little to release the catch," cried one of the red men.

I could hear the yellow warriors leaping along the flagging just beyond the door. I raised the bar and shot it to the right just as the foremost of the guardsmen threw himself against the opposite side of the massive panels.

The barrier held – I had been in time, but by the fraction of a second only.

Now I turned my attention to the prisoners. To Tardos Mors I went first, asking where the keys might be which would unfasten their fetters.

"The officer of the guard has them," replied the Jeddak of Helium, "and he is among those without who seek entrance. You will have to force them."

Most of the prisoners were already hacking at their bonds with the swords in their hands. The yellow men were battering at the door with javelins and axes.

I turned my attention to the chains that held Tardos Mors. Again and again I cut deep into the metal with my sharp blade, but ever faster and faster fell the torrent of blows upon the portal.

At last a link parted beneath my efforts, and a moment later Tardos Mors was free, though a few inches of trailing chain still dangled from his ankle.

A splinter of wood falling inward from the door announced the headway that our enemies were making toward us.

The mighty panels trembled and bent beneath the furious onslaught of the enraged yellow men.

What with the battering upon the door and the hacking of the red men at their chains the din within the armory was appalling. No sooner was Tardos Mors free than he turned his attention to another of the prisoners, while I set to work to liberate Mors Kajak.

We must work fast if we would have all those fetters cut before the door gave way. Now a panel crashed inward upon the floor, and Mors Kajak sprang to the opening to defend the way until we should have time to release the others.

With javelins snatched from the wall he wrought havoc among the foremost of the Okarians while we battled with the insensate metal that stood between our fellows and freedom.

At length all but one of the prisoners were freed, and then the door fell with a mighty crash before a hastily improvised battering-ram, and the yellow horde was upon us.

"To the upper chambers!" shouted the red man who was still fettered to the floor. "To the upper chambers! There you may defend the tower against all Kadabra. Do not delay because of me, who could pray for no better death than in the service of Tardos Mors and the Prince of Helium."

But I would have sacrificed the life of every man of us rather than desert a single red man, much less the lion-hearted hero who begged us to leave him.

"Cut his chains," I cried to two of the red men, "while the balance of us hold off the foe."

There were ten of us now to do battle with the Okarian guard, and I warrant that that ancient watchtower never looked down upon a more hotly contested battle than took place that day within its own grim walls.

The first inrushing wave of yellow warriors recoiled from the slashing blades of ten of Helium's veteran fighting men. A dozen Okarian corpses blocked the doorway, but over the gruesome barrier a score more of their fellows dashed, shouting their hoarse and hideous war-cry.

Upon the bloody mound we met them, hand to hand, stabbing where the quarters were too close to cut, thrusting when we could push a foeman to arm's length; and mingled with the wild cry of the Okarian there rose and fell the glorious words: "For Helium! For Helium!" that for countless ages have spurred on the bravest of the brave to those deeds of valor that have sent the fame of Helium's heroes broadcast throughout the length and breadth of a world.

Now were the fetters struck from the last of the red men, and thirteen strong we met each new charge of the soldiers of Salensus Oll. Scarce one of us but bled from a score of wounds, yet none had fallen.

From without we saw hundreds of guardsmen pouring into the courtyard, and along the lower corridor from which I had found my way to the armory we could hear the clank of metal and the shouting of men.

In a moment we should be attacked from two sides, and with all our prowess we could not hope to withstand the unequal odds which would thus divide our attention and our small numbers.

"To the upper chambers!" cried Tardos Mors, and a moment later we fell back toward the runway that led to the floors above.

Here another bloody battle was waged with the force of yellow men who charged into the armory as we fell back from the doorway. Here we lost our first man, a noble fellow whom we could ill spare; but at length all had backed into the runway except myself, who remained to hold back the Okarians until the others were safe above.

In the mouth of the narrow spiral but a single warrior could attack me at a time, so that I had little difficulty in holding them all back for the brief moment that was necessary. Then, backing slowly before them, I commenced the ascent of the spiral.

All the long way to the tower's top the guardsmen pressed me closely. When one went down before my sword another scrambled over the dead man to take his place; and thus, taking an awful toll with each few feet gained, I came to the spacious glass-walled watchtower of Kadabra.

Here my companions clustered ready to take my place, and for a moment's respite I stepped to one side while they held the enemy off.

From the lofty perch a view could be had for miles in every direction. Toward the south stretched the rugged, ice-clad waste to the edge of the mighty barrier. Toward the east and west, and dimly toward the north I descried other Okarian cities, while in the immediate foreground, just beyond the walls of Kadabra, the grim guardian shaft reared its somber head.

Then I cast my eyes down into the streets of Kadabra, from which a sudden tumult had arisen, and there I saw a battle raging, and beyond the city's walls I saw armed men marching in great columns toward a near-by gate.

Eagerly I pressed forward against the glass wall of the observatory, scarce daring to credit the testimony of my own eyes. But at last I could doubt no longer, and with a shout of joy that rose strangely in the midst of the cursing and groaning of the battling men at the entrance to the chamber, I called to Tardos Mors.

As he joined me I pointed down into the streets of Kadabra and to the advancing columns beyond, above which floated bravely in the arctic air the flags and banners of Helium.

An instant later every red man in the lofty chamber had seen the inspiring sight, and such a shout of thanksgiving arose as I warrant never before echoed through that age-old pile of stone.

But still we must fight on, for though our troops had entered Kadabra, the city was yet far from capitulation, nor had the palace been even assaulted. Turn and turn about we held the top of the runway while the others feasted their eyes upon the sight of our valiant countrymen battling far beneath us.

Now they have rushed the palace gate! Great battering-rams are dashed against its formidable surface. Now they are repulsed by a deadly shower of javelins from the wall's top!

Once again they charge, but a sortie by a large force of Okarians from an intersecting avenue crumples the head of the column, and the men of Helium go down, fighting, beneath an overwhelming force.

The palace gate flies open and a force of the jeddak's own guard, picked men from the flower of the Okarian army, sallies forth to shatter the broken regiments. For a moment it looks as though nothing could avert defeat, and then I see a noble figure upon a mighty thoat – not the tiny thoat of the red man, but one of his huge cousins of the dead sea bottoms.

The warrior hews his way to the front, and behind him rally the disorganized soldiers of Helium. As he raises his head aloft to fling a challenge at the men upon the palace walls I see his face, and my heart swells in pride and happiness as the red warriors leap to the side of their leader and win back the ground that they had but just lost – the face of him upon the mighty thoat is the face of my son – Carthoris of Helium.

At his side fights a huge Martian war-hound, nor did I need a second look to know that it was Woola – my faithful Woola who had thus well performed his arduous task and brought the succoring legions in the nick of time.

"In the nick of time?"

Who yet might say that they were not too late to save, but surely they could avenge! And such retribution as that unconquered army would deal out to the hateful Okarians! I sighed to think that I might not be alive to witness it.

Again I turned to the windows. The red men had not yet forced the outer palace wall, but they were fighting nobly against the best that Okar afforded – valiant warriors who contested every inch of the way.

Now my attention was caught by a new element without the city wall – a great body of mounted warriors looming large above the red men. They were the huge green allies of Helium – the savage hordes from the dead sea bottoms of the far south.

In grim and terrible silence they sped on toward the gate, the padded hoofs of their frightful mounts giving forth no sound. Into the doomed city they charged, and as they wheeled across the wide plaza before the palace of the Jeddak of Jeddaks I saw, riding at their head, the mighty figure of their mighty leader – Tars Tarkas, Jeddak of Thark.

My wish, then, was to be gratified, for I was to see my old friend battling once again, and though not shoulder to shoulder with him, I, too, would be fighting in the same cause here in the high tower of Okar.

Nor did it seem that our foes would ever cease their stubborn attacks, for still they came, though the way to our chamber was often clogged with the bodies of their dead. At times they would pause long enough to drag back the impeding corpses, and then fresh warriors would forge upward to taste the cup of death.

I had been taking my turn with the others in defending the approach to our lofty retreat when Mors Kajak, who had been watching the battle in the street below, called aloud in sudden excitement. There was a note of apprehension in his voice that brought me to his side the instant that I could turn my place over to another, and as I reached him he pointed far out across the waste of snow and ice toward the southern horizon.

"Alas!" he cried, "that I should be forced to witness cruel fate betray them without power to warn or aid; but they be past either now."

As I looked in the direction he indicated I saw the cause of his perturbation. A mighty fleet of fliers was approaching majestically toward Kadabra from the direction of the ice-barrier. On and on they came with ever increasing velocity.

"The grim shaft that they call the Guardian of the North is beckoning to them," said Mors Kajak sadly, "just as it beckoned to Tardos Mors and his great fleet; see where they lie, crumpled and broken, a grim and terrible monument to the mighty force of destruction which naught can resist."

I, too, saw; but something else I saw that Mors Kajak did not; in my mind's eye I saw a buried chamber whose walls were lined with strange instruments and devices.

In the center of the chamber was a long table, and before it sat a little, pop-eyed old man counting his money; but, plainest of all, I saw upon the wall a great switch with a small magnet inlaid within the surface of its black handle.

Then I glanced out at the fast-approaching fleet. In five minutes that mighty armada of the skies would be bent and worthless scrap, lying at the base of the shaft beyond the city's wall, and yellow hordes would be loosed from another gate to rush out upon the few survivors stumbling blindly down through the mass of wreckage; then the apts would come. I shuddered at the thought, for I could vividly picture the whole horrible scene.

Quick have I always been to decide and act. The impulse that moves me and the doing of the thing seem simultaneous; for if my mind goes through the tedious formality of reasoning, it must be a subconscious act of which I am not objectively aware. Psychologists tell me that, as the subconscious does not reason, too close a scrutiny of my mental activities might prove anything but flattering; but be that as it may, I have often won success while the thinker would have been still at the endless task of comparing various judgments.

And now celerity of action was the prime essential to the success of the thing that I had decided upon.

Grasping my sword more firmly in my hand, I called to the red man at the opening to the runway to stand aside.

"Way for the Prince of Helium!" I shouted; and before the astonished yellow man whose misfortune it was to be at the fighting end of the line at that particular moment could gather his wits together my sword had decapitated him, and I was rushing like a mad bull down upon those behind him.

"Way for the Prince of Helium!" I shouted as I cut a path through the astonished guardsmen of Salensus Oll.

Hewing to right and left, I beat my way down that warrior-choked spiral until, near the bottom, those below, thinking that an army was descending upon them, turned and fled.

The armory at the first floor was vacant when I entered it, the last of the Okarians having fled into the courtyard, so none saw me continue down the spiral toward the corridor beneath.

Here I ran as rapidly as my legs would carry me toward the five corners, and there plunged into the passageway that led to the station of the old miser.

Without the formality of a knock, I burst into the room. There sat the old man at his table; but as he saw me he sprang to his feet, drawing his sword.

With scarce more than a glance toward him I leaped for the great switch; but, quick as I was, that wiry old fellow was there before me.

How he did it I shall never know, nor does it seem credible that any Martian-born creature could approximate the marvelous speed of my earthly muscles.

Like a tiger he turned upon me, and I was quick to see why Solan had been chosen for this important duty.

Never in all my life have I seen such wondrous swordsmanship and such uncanny agility as that ancient bag of bones displayed. He was in forty places at the same time, and before I had half a chance to awaken to my danger he was like to have made a monkey of me, and a dead monkey at that.

It is strange how new and unexpected conditions bring out unguessed ability to meet them.

That day in the buried chamber beneath the palace of Salensus Oll I learned what swordsmanship meant, and to what heights of sword mastery I could achieve when pitted against such a wizard of the blade as Solan.

For a time he liked to have bested me; but presently the latent possibilities that must have been lying dormant within me for a lifetime came to the fore, and I fought as I had never dreamed a human being could fight.

That that duel-royal should have taken place in the dark recesses of a cellar, without a single appreciative eye to witness it has always seemed to me almost a world calamity – at least from the viewpoint Barsoomian, where bloody strife is the first and greatest consideration of individuals, nations, and races.

I was fighting to reach the switch, Solan to prevent me; and, though we stood not three feet from it, I could not win an inch toward it, for he forced me back an inch for the first five minutes of our battle.

I knew that if I were to throw it in time to save the oncoming fleet it must be done in the next few seconds, and so I tried my old rushing tactics; but I might as well have rushed a brick wall for all that Solan gave way.

In fact, I came near to impaling myself upon his point for my pains; but right was on my side, and I think that that must give a man greater confidence than though he knew himself to be battling in a wicked cause.

At least, I did not want in confidence; and when I next rushed Solan it was to one side with implicit confidence that he must turn to meet my new line of attack, and turn he did, so that now we fought with our sides towards the coveted goal – the great switch stood within my reach upon my right hand.

To uncover my breast for an instant would have been to court sudden death, but I saw no other way than to chance it, if by so doing I might rescue that oncoming, succoring fleet; and so, in the face of a wicked sword-thrust, I reached out my point and caught the great switch a sudden blow that released it from its seating.

So surprised and horrified was Solan that he forgot to finish his thrust; instead, he wheeled toward the switch with a loud shriek – a shriek which was his last, for before his hand could touch the lever it sought, my sword's point had passed through his heart.

CHAPTER FOURTEEN

The Tide of Battle

BUT SOLAN'S LAST LOUD CRY had not been without effect, for a moment later a dozen guardsmen burst into the chamber, though not before I had so bent and demolished the great switch that it could not be again used to turn the powerful current into the mighty magnet of destruction it controlled.

The result of the sudden coming of the guardsmen had been to compel me to seek seclusion in the first passageway that I could find, and that to my disappointment proved to be not the one with which I was familiar, but another upon its left.

They must have either heard or guessed which way I went, for I had proceeded but a short distance when I heard the sound of pursuit. I had no mind to stop and fight these men here when there was fighting aplenty elsewhere in the city of Kadabra – fighting that could be of much more avail to me and mine than useless life-taking far below the palace.

But the fellows were pressing me; and as I did not know the way at all, I soon saw that they would overtake me unless I found a place to conceal myself until they had passed, which would then give me an opportunity to return the way I had come and regain the tower, or possibly find a way to reach the city streets.

The passageway had risen rapidly since leaving the apartment of the switch, and now ran level and well lighted straight into the distance as far as I could see. The moment that my pursuers reached this straight stretch I would be in plain sight of them, with no chance to escape from the corridor undetected.

Presently I saw a series of doors opening from either side of the corridor, and as they all looked alike to me I tried the first one that I reached. It opened into a small chamber, luxuriously furnished, and was evidently an ante-chamber off some office or audience chamber of the palace.

On the far side was a heavily curtained doorway beyond which I heard the hum of voices. Instantly I crossed the small chamber, and, parting the curtains, looked within the larger apartment.

Before me were a party of perhaps fifty gorgeously clad nobles of the court, standing before a throne upon which sat Salensus Oll. The Jeddak of Jeddaks was addressing them.

"The allotted hour has come," he was saying as I entered the apartment; "and though the enemies of Okar be within her gates, naught may stay the will of Salensus Oll. The great ceremony must be omitted that no single man may be kept from his place in the defenses other than the fifty that custom demands shall witness the creation of a new queen in Okar.

"In a moment the thing shall have been done and we may return to the battle, while she who is now the Princess of Helium looks down from the queen's tower upon the annihilation of her former countrymen and witnesses the greatness which is her husband's."

Then, turning to a courtier, he issued some command in a low voice.

The addressed hastened to a small door at the far end of the chamber and, swinging it wide, cried: "Way for Dejah Thoris, future Queen of Okar!"

Immediately two guardsmen appeared dragging the unwilling bride toward the altar. Her hands were still manacled behind her, evidently to prevent suicide.

Her disheveled hair and panting bosom betokened that, chained though she was, still had she fought against the thing that they would do to her.

At sight of her Salensus Oll rose and drew his sword, and the sword of each of the fifty nobles was raised on high to form an arch, beneath which the poor, beautiful creature was dragged toward her doom.

A grim smile forced itself to my lips as I thought of the rude awakening that lay in store for the ruler of Okar, and my itching fingers fondled the hilt of my bloody sword.

As I watched the procession that moved slowly toward the throne – a procession which consisted of but a handful of priests, who followed Dejah Thoris and the two guardsmen – I caught a fleeting glimpse of a black face peering from behind the draperies that covered the wall back of the dais upon which stood Salensus Oll awaiting his bride.

Now the guardsmen were forcing the Princess of Helium up the few steps to the side of the tyrant of Okar, and I had no eyes and no thoughts for aught else. A priest opened a book and, raising his hand, commenced to drone out a sing-song ritual. Salensus Oll reached for the hand of his bride.

I had intended waiting until some circumstance should give me a reasonable hope of success; for, even though the entire ceremony should be completed, there could be no valid marriage while I lived.

What I was most concerned in, of course, was the rescuing of Dejah Thoris – I wished to take her from the palace of Salensus Oll, if such a thing were possible; but whether it were accomplished before or after the mock marriage was a matter of secondary import.

When, however, I saw the vile hand of Salensus Oll reach out for the hand of my beloved princess I could restrain myself no longer, and before the nobles of Okar knew that aught had happened I had leaped through their thin line and was upon the dais beside Dejah Thoris and Salensus Oll.

With the flat of my sword I struck down his polluting hand; and grasping Dejah Thoris round the waist, I swung her behind me as, with my back against the draperies of the dais, I faced the tyrant of the north and his roomful of noble warriors.

The Jeddak of Jeddaks was a great mountain of a man – a coarse, brutal beast of a man – and as he towered above me there, his fierce black whiskers and mustache bristling in rage, I can well imagine that a less seasoned warrior might have trembled before him.

With a snarl he sprang toward me with naked sword, but whether Salensus Oll was a good swordsman or a poor I never learned; for with Dejah Thoris at my back I was no longer human – I was a superman, and no man could have withstood me then.

With a single, low: "For the Princess of Helium!" I ran my blade straight through the rotten heart of Okar's rotten ruler, and before the white, drawn faces of his nobles Salensus Oll rolled, grinning in horrible death, to the foot of the steps below his marriage throne.

For a moment tense silence reigned in the nuptial-room. Then the fifty nobles rushed upon me. Furiously we fought, but the advantage was mine, for I stood upon a raised platform above them, and I fought for the most glorious woman of a glorious race, and I fought for a great love and for the mother of my boy.

And from behind my shoulder, in the silvery cadence of that dear voice, rose the brave battle anthem of Helium which the nation's women sing as their men march out to victory.

That alone was enough to inspire me to victory over even greater odds, and I verily believe that I should have bested the entire roomful of yellow warriors that day in the nuptial chamber of the palace at Kadabra had not interruption come to my aid.

Fast and furious was the fighting as the nobles of Salensus Oll sprang, time and again, up the steps before the throne only to fall back before a sword hand that seemed to have gained a new wizardry from its experience with the cunning Solan.

Two were pressing me so closely that I could not turn when I heard a movement behind me, and noted that the sound of the battle anthem had ceased. Was Dejah Thoris preparing to take her place beside me?

Heroic daughter of a heroic world! It would not be unlike her to have seized a sword and fought at my side, for, though the women of Mars are not trained in the arts of war, the spirit is theirs, and they have been known to do that very thing upon countless occasions.

But she did not come, and glad I was, for it would have doubled my burden in protecting her before I should have been able to force her back again out of harm's way. She must be contemplating some cunning strategy, I thought, and so I fought on secure in the belief that my divine princess stood close behind me.

For half an hour at least I must have fought there against the nobles of Okar ere ever a one placed a foot upon the dais where I stood, and then of a sudden all that remained of them formed below me for a last, mad, desperate charge; but even as they advanced the door at the far end of the chamber swung wide and a wild-eyed messenger sprang into the room.

"The Jeddak of Jeddaks!" he cried. "Where is the Jeddak of Jeddaks? The city has fallen before the hordes from beyond the barrier, and but now the great gate of the palace itself has been forced and the warriors of the south are pouring into its sacred precincts.

"Where is Salensus Oll? He alone may revive the flagging courage of our warriors. He alone may save the day for Okar. Where is Salensus Oll?"

The nobles stepped back from about the dead body of their ruler, and one of them pointed to the grinning corpse.

The messenger staggered back in horror as though from a blow in the face.

"Then fly, nobles of Okar!" he cried, "for naught can save you. Hark! They come!"

As he spoke we heard the deep roar of angry men from the corridor without, and the clank of metal and the clang of swords.

Without another glance toward me, who had stood a spectator of the tragic scene, the nobles wheeled and fled from the apartment through another exit.

Almost immediately a force of yellow warriors appeared in the doorway through which the messenger had come. They were backing toward the apartment, stubbornly resisting the advance of a handful of red men who faced them and forced them slowly but inevitably back.

Above the heads of the contestants I could see from my elevated station upon the dais the face of my old friend Kantos Kan. He was leading the little party that had won its way into the very heart of the palace of Salensus Oll.

In an instant I saw that by attacking the Okarians from the rear I could so quickly disorganize them that their further resistance would be short-lived, and with this idea in mind I sprang from the dais, casting a word of explanation to Dejah Thoris over my shoulder, though I did not turn to look at her.

With myself ever between her enemies and herself, and with Kantos Kan and his warriors winning to the apartment, there could be no danger to Dejah Thoris standing there alone beside the throne.

I wanted the men of Helium to see me and to know that their beloved princess was here, too, for I knew that this knowledge would inspire them to even greater deeds of valor than they had performed in the past, though great indeed must have been those which won for them a way into the almost impregnable palace of the tyrant of the north.

As I crossed the chamber to attack the Kadabrans from the rear a small doorway at my left opened, and, to my surprise, revealed the figures of Matai Shang, Father of Therns and Phaidor, his daughter, peering into the room.

A quick glance about they took. Their eyes rested for a moment, wide in horror, upon the dead body of Salensus Oll, upon the blood that crimsoned the floor, upon the corpses of the nobles who had fallen thick before the throne, upon me, and upon the battling warriors at the other door.

They did not essay to enter the apartment, but scanned its every corner from where they stood, and then, when their eyes had sought its entire area, a look of fierce rage overspread the features of Matai Shang, and a cold and cunning smile touched the lips of Phaidor.

Then they were gone, but not before a taunting laugh was thrown directly in my face by the woman.

I did not understand then the meaning of Matai Shang's rage or Phaidor's pleasure, but I knew that neither boded good for me.

A moment later I was upon the backs of the yellow men, and as the red men of Helium saw me above the shoulders of their antagonists a great shout rang through the corridor, and for a moment drowned the noise of battle.

"For the Prince of Helium!" they cried. "For the Prince of Helium!" and, like hungry lions upon their prey, they fell once more upon the weakening warriors of the north.

The yellow men, cornered between two enemies, fought with the desperation that utter hopelessness often induces. Fought as I should have fought had I been in their stead, with the determination to take as many of my enemies with me when I died as lay within the power of my sword arm.

It was a glorious battle, but the end seemed inevitable, when presently from down the corridor behind the red men came a great body of reenforcing yellow warriors.

Now were the tables turned, and it was the men of Helium who seemed doomed to be ground between two millstones. All were compelled to turn to meet this new assault by a greatly superior force, so that to me was left the remnants of the yellow men within the throneroom.

They kept me busy, too; so busy that I began to wonder if indeed I should ever be done with them. Slowly they pressed me back into the room, and when they had all passed in after me, one of them closed and bolted the door, effectually barring the way against the men of Kantos Kan.

It was a clever move, for it put me at the mercy of a dozen men within a chamber from which assistance was locked out, and it gave the red men in the corridor beyond no avenue of escape should their new antagonists press them too closely.

But I have faced heavier odds myself than were pitted against me that day, and I knew that Kantos Kan had battled his way from a hundred more dangerous traps than that in which he now was. So it was with no feelings of despair that I turned my attention to the business of the moment.

Constantly my thoughts reverted to Dejah Thoris, and I longed for the moment when, the fighting done, I could fold her in my arms, and hear once more the words of love which had been denied me for so many years.

During the fighting in the chamber I had not even a single chance to so much as steal a glance at her where she stood behind me beside the throne of the dead ruler. I wondered why she no longer urged me on with the strains of the martial hymn of Helium; but I did not need more than the knowledge that I was battling for her to bring out the best that is in me.

It would be wearisome to narrate the details of that bloody struggle; of how we fought from the doorway, the full length of the room to the very foot of the throne before the last of my antagonists fell with my blade piercing his heart.

And then, with a glad cry, I turned with outstretched arms to seize my princess, and as my lips smothered hers to reap the reward that would be thrice ample payment for the bloody encounters through which I had passed for her dear sake from the south pole to the north.

The glad cry died, frozen upon my lips; my arms dropped limp and lifeless to my sides; as one who reels beneath the burden of a mortal wound I staggered up the steps before the throne.

Dejah Thoris was gone.

CHAPTER FIFTEEN
Rewards

WITH THE REALIZATION that Dejah Thoris was no longer within the throneroom came the belated recollection of the dark face that I had glimpsed peering from behind the draperies that backed the throne of Salensus Oll at the moment that I had first come so unexpectedly upon the strange scene being enacted within the chamber.

Why had the sight of that evil countenance not warned me to greater caution? Why had I permitted the rapid development of new situations to efface the recollection of that menacing danger? But, alas, vain regret would not erase the calamity that had befallen.

Once again had Dejah Thoris fallen into the clutches of that archfiend, Thurid, the black dator of the First Born. Again was all my arduous labor gone for naught. Now I realized the cause of the rage that had been writ so large upon the features of Matai Shang and the cruel pleasure that I had seen upon the face of Phaidor.

They had known or guessed the truth, and the hekkador of the Holy Therns, who had evidently come to the chamber in the hope of thwarting Salensus Oll in his contemplated perfidy against the high priest who coveted Dejah Thoris for himself, realized that Thurid had stolen the prize from beneath his very nose.

Phaidor's pleasure had been due to her realization of what this last cruel blow would mean to me, as well as to a partial satisfaction of her jealous hatred for the Princess of Helium.

My first thought was to look beyond the draperies at the back of the throne, for there it was that I had seen Thurid. With a single jerk I tore the priceless stuff from its fastenings, and there before me was revealed a narrow doorway behind the throne.

No question entered my mind but that here lay the opening of the avenue of escape which Thurid had followed, and had there been it would have been dissipated by the sight of a tiny, jeweled ornament which lay a few steps within the corridor beyond.

As I snatched up the bauble I saw that it bore the device of the Princess of Helium, and then pressing it to my lips I dashed madly along the winding way that led gently downward toward the lower galleries of the palace.

I had followed but a short distance when I came upon the room in which Solan formerly had held sway. His dead body still lay where I had left it, nor was there any sign that another had passed through the room since I had been there; but I knew that two had done so – Thurid, the black dator, and Dejah Thoris.

For a moment I paused uncertain as to which of the several exits from the apartment would lead me upon the right path. I tried to recollect the directions which I had heard Thurid repeat to Solan, and at last, slowly, as though through a heavy fog, the memory of the words of the First Born came to me:

"Follow a corridor, passing three diverging corridors upon the right; then into the fourth right-hand corridor to where three corridors meet; here again follow to the right, hugging the left wall closely to avoid the pit. At the end of this corridor I shall come to a spiral runway which I must follow down instead of up; after that the way is along but a single branchless corridor."

And I recalled the exit at which he had pointed as he spoke.

It did not take me long to start upon that unknown way, nor did I go with caution, although I knew that there might be grave dangers before me.

Part of the way was black as sin, but for the most it was fairly well lighted. The stretch where I must hug the left wall to avoid the pits was darkest of them all, and I was nearly over the edge of the abyss before I knew that I was near the danger spot. A narrow ledge, scarce a foot wide, was all that had been left to carry the initiated past that frightful cavity into which the unknowing must surely have toppled at the first step. But at last I had won safely beyond it, and then a feeble light made the balance of the way plain, until, at the end of the last corridor, I came suddenly out into the glare of day upon a field of snow and ice.

Clad for the warm atmosphere of the hothouse city of Kadabra, the sudden change to arctic frigidity was anything but pleasant; but the worst of it was that I knew I could not endure the bitter cold, almost naked as I was, and that I would perish before ever I could overtake Thurid and Dejah Thoris.

To be thus blocked by nature, who had had all the arts and wiles of cunning man pitted against him, seemed a cruel fate, and as I staggered back into the warmth of the tunnel's end I was as near hopelessness as I ever have been.

I had by no means given up my intention of continuing the pursuit, for if needs be I would go ahead though I perished ere ever I reached my goal, but if there were a safer way it were well worth the delay to attempt to discover it, that I might come again to the side of Dejah Thoris in fit condition to do battle for her.

Scarce had I returned to the tunnel than I stumbled over a portion of a fur garment that seemed fastened to the floor of the corridor close to the wall. In the darkness I could not see what held it, but by groping with my hands I discovered that it was wedged beneath the bottom of a closed door.

Pushing the portal aside, I found myself upon the threshold of a small chamber, the walls of which were lined with hooks from which depended suits of the complete outdoor apparel of the yellow men.

Situated as it was at the mouth of a tunnel leading from the palace, it was quite evident that this was the dressing-room used by the nobles leaving and entering the hothouse city, and that Thurid, having knowledge of it, had stopped here to outfit himself and Dejah Thoris before venturing into the bitter cold of the arctic world beyond.

In his haste he had dropped several garments upon the floor, and the telltale fur that had fallen partly within the corridor had proved the means of guiding me to the very spot he would least have wished me to have knowledge of.

It required but the matter of a few seconds to don the necessary or-luk-skin clothing, with the heavy, fur-lined boots that are so essential a part of the garmenture of one who would successfully contend with the frozen trails and the icy winds of the bleak northland.

Once more I stepped beyond the tunnel's mouth to find the fresh tracks of Thurid and Dejah Thoris in the new-fallen snow. Now, at last, was my task an easy one, for though the going was rough in the extreme, I was no longer vexed by doubts as to the direction I should follow, or harassed by darkness or hidden dangers.

Through a snow-covered canyon the way led up toward the summit of low hills. Beyond these it dipped again into another canyon, only to rise a quarter-mile farther on toward a pass which skirted the flank of a rocky hill.

I could see by the signs of those who had gone before that when Dejah Thoris had walked she had been continually holding back, and that the black man had been compelled to drag her. For other stretches only his foot-prints were visible, deep and close together in the heavy snow, and I knew from these signs that then he had been forced to carry her, and I could well imagine that she had fought him fiercely every step of the way.

As I came round the jutting promontory of the hill's shoulder I saw that which quickened my pulses and set my heart to beating high, for within a tiny basin between the crest of this hill and the next stood four people before the mouth of a great cave, and beside them upon the gleaming snow rested a flier which had evidently but just been dragged from its hiding place.

The four were Dejah Thoris, Phaidor, Thurid, and Matai Shang. The two men were engaged in a heated argument – the Father of Therns threatening, while the black scoffed at him as he went about the work at which he was engaged.

As I crept toward them cautiously that I might come as near as possible before being discovered, I saw that finally the men appeared to have reached some sort of a compromise, for with Phaidor's assistance they both set about dragging the resisting Dejah Thoris to the flier's deck.

Here they made her fast, and then both again descended to the ground to complete the preparations for departure. Phaidor entered the small cabin upon the vessel's deck.

I had come to within a quarter of a mile of them when Matai Shang espied me. I saw him seize Thurid by the shoulder, wheeling him around in my direction as he pointed to where I was now plainly visible, for the moment that I knew I had been perceived I cast aside every attempt at stealth and broke into a mad race for the flier.

The two redoubled their efforts at the propeller at which they were working, and which very evidently was being replaced after having been removed for some purpose of repair.

They had the thing completed before I had covered half the distance that lay between me and them, and then both made a rush for the boarding-ladder.

Thurid was the first to reach it, and with the agility of a monkey clambered swiftly to the boat's deck, where a touch of the button controlling the buoyancy tanks sent the craft slowly upward, though not with the speed that marks the well-conditioned flier.

I was still some hundred yards away as I saw them rising from my grasp.

Back by the city of Kadabra lay a great fleet of mighty fliers – the ships of Helium and Ptarth that I had saved from destruction earlier in the day; but before ever I could reach them Thurid could easily make good his escape.

As I ran I saw Matai Shang clambering up the swaying, swinging ladder toward the deck, while above him leaned the evil face of the First Born. A trailing rope from the vessel's stern put new hope in me, for if I could but reach it before it whipped too high above my head there was yet a chance to gain the deck by its slender aid.

That there was something radically wrong with the flier was evident from its lack of buoyancy, and the further fact that though Thurid had turned twice to the starting lever the boat still hung motionless in the air, except for a slight drifting with a low breeze from the north.

Now Matai Shang was close to the gunwale. A long, claw-like hand was reaching up to grasp the metal rail.

Thurid leaned farther down toward his co-conspirator.

Suddenly a raised dagger gleamed in the upflung hand of the black. Down it drove toward the white face of the Father of Therns. With a loud shriek of fear the Holy Hekkador grasped frantically at that menacing arm.

I was almost to the trailing rope by now. The craft was still rising slowly, the while it drifted from me. Then I stumbled on the icy way, striking my head upon a rock as I fell sprawling but an arm's length from the rope, the end of which was now just leaving the ground.

With the blow upon my head came unconsciousness.

It could not have been more than a few seconds that I lay senseless there upon the northern ice, while all that was dearest to me drifted farther from my reach in the clutches of that black fiend, for when I opened my eyes Thurid and Matai Shang yet battled at the ladder's top, and the flier drifted but a hundred yards farther to the south – but the end of the trailing rope was now a good thirty feet above the ground.

Goaded to madness by the cruel misfortune that had tripped me when success was almost within my grasp, I tore frantically across the intervening space, and just beneath the rope's dangling end I put my earthly muscles to the supreme test.

With a mighty, catlike bound I sprang upward toward that slender strand – the only avenue which yet remained that could carry me to my vanishing love.

A foot above its lowest end my fingers closed. Tightly as I clung I felt the rope slipping, slipping through my grasp. I tried to raise my free hand to take a second hold above my first, but the change of position that resulted caused me to slip more rapidly toward the end of the rope.

Slowly I felt the tantalizing thing escaping me. In a moment all that I had gained would be lost – then my fingers reached a knot at the very end of the rope and slipped no more.

With a prayer of gratitude upon my lips I scrambled upward toward the boat's deck. I could not see Thurid and Matai Shang now, but I heard the sounds of conflict and thus knew that they still fought – the thern for his life and the black for the increased buoyancy that relief from the weight of even a single body would give the craft.

Should Matai Shang die before I reached the deck my chances of ever reaching it would be slender indeed, for the black dator need but cut the rope above me to be freed from me forever, for the vessel had drifted across the brink of a chasm into whose yawning depths my body would drop to be crushed to a shapeless pulp should Thurid reach the rope now.

At last my hand closed upon the ship's rail and that very instant a horrid shriek rang out below me that sent my blood cold and turned my horrified eyes downward to a shrieking, hurtling, twisting thing that shot downward into the awful chasm beneath me.

It was Matai Shang, Holy Hekkador, Father of Therns, gone to his last accounting.

Then my head came above the deck and I saw Thurid, dagger in hand, leaping toward me. He was opposite the forward end of the cabin, while I was attempting to clamber aboard near the vessel's stern. But a few paces lay between us. No power on earth could raise me to that deck before the infuriated black would be upon me.

My end had come. I knew it; but had there been a doubt in my mind the nasty leer of triumph upon that wicked face would have convinced me. Beyond Thurid I could see my Dejah Thoris, wide-eyed and horrified, struggling at her bonds. That she should be forced to witness my awful death made my bitter fate seem doubly cruel.

I ceased my efforts to climb across the gunwale. Instead I took a firm grasp upon the rail with my left hand and drew my dagger.

I should at least die as I had lived – fighting.

As Thurid came opposite the cabin's doorway a new element projected itself into the grim tragedy of the air that was being enacted upon the deck of Matai Shang's disabled flier.

It was Phaidor.

With flushed face and disheveled hair, and eyes that betrayed the recent presence of mortal tears – above which this proud goddess had always held herself – she leaped to the deck directly before me.

In her hand was a long, slim dagger. I cast a last look upon my beloved princess, smiling, as men should who are about to die. Then I turned my face up toward Phaidor – waiting for the blow.

Never have I seen that beautiful face more beautiful than it was at that moment. It seemed incredible that one so lovely could yet harbor within her fair bosom a heart so cruel and relentless, and today there was a new expression in her wondrous eyes that I never before had seen there – an unfamiliar softness, and a look of suffering.

Thurid was beside her now – pushing past to reach me first, and then what happened happened so quickly that it was all over before I could realize the truth of it.

Phaidor's slim hand shot out to close upon the black's dagger wrist. Her right hand went high with its gleaming blade.

"That for Matai Shang!" she cried, and she buried her blade deep in the dator's breast. "That for the wrong you would have done Dejah Thoris!" and again the sharp steel sank into the bloody flesh.

"And that, and that, and that!" she shrieked, "for John Carter, Prince of Helium," and with each word her sharp point pierced the vile heart of the great villain. Then, with a vindictive shove she cast the carcass of the First Born from the deck to fall in awful silence after the body of his victim.

I had been so paralyzed by surprise that I had made no move to reach the deck during the awe-inspiring scene which I had just witnessed, and now I was to be still further amazed by her next act, for Phaidor extended her hand to me and assisted me to the deck, where I stood gazing at her in unconcealed and stupefied wonderment.

A wan smile touched her lips – it was not the cruel and haughty smile of the goddess with which I was familiar. "You wonder, John Carter," she said, "what strange thing has wrought this change in me? I will tell you. It is love – love of you," and when I darkened my brows in disapproval of her words she raised an appealing hand.

"Wait," she said. "It is a different love from mine – it is the love of your princess, Dejah Thoris, for you that has taught me what true love may be – what it should be, and how far from real love was my selfish and jealous passion for you.

"Now I am different. Now could I love as Dejah Thoris loves, and so my only happiness can be to know that you and she are once more united, for in her alone can you find true happiness.

"But I am unhappy because of the wickedness that I have wrought. I have many sins to expiate, and though I be deathless, life is all too short for the atonement.

"But there is another way, and if Phaidor, daughter of the Holy Hekkador of the Holy Therns, has sinned she has this day already made partial reparation, and lest you doubt the sincerity of her protestations and her avowal of a new love that embraces Dejah Thoris also, she will prove her sincerity in the only way that lies open – having saved you for another, Phaidor leaves you to her embraces."

With her last word she turned and leaped from the vessel's deck into the abyss below.

With a cry of horror I sprang forward in a vain attempt to save the life that for two years I would so gladly have seen extinguished. I was too late.

With tear-dimmed eyes I turned away that I might not see the awful sight beneath.

A moment later I had struck the bonds from Dejah Thoris, and as her dear arms went about my neck and her perfect lips pressed to mine I forgot the horrors that I had witnessed and the suffering that I had endured in the rapture of my reward.

CHAPTER SIXTEEN

The New Ruler

THE FLIER UPON WHOSE deck Dejah Thoris and I found ourselves after twelve long years of separation proved entirely useless. Her buoyancy tanks leaked badly. Her engine would not start. We were helpless there in mid air above the arctic ice.

The craft had drifted across the chasm which held the corpses of Matai Shang, Thurid, and Phaidor, and now hung above a low hill. Opening the buoyancy escape valves I permitted her to come slowly to the ground, and as she touched, Dejah Thoris and I stepped from her deck and, hand in hand, turned back across the frozen waste toward the city of Kadabra.

Through the tunnel that had led me in pursuit of them we passed, walking slowly, for we had much to say to each other.

She told me of that last terrible moment months before when the door of her prison cell within the Temple of the Sun was slowly closing between us. Of how Phaidor had sprung upon her with uplifted dagger, and of Thuvia's shriek as she had realized the foul intention of the thern goddess.

It had been that cry that had rung in my ears all the long, weary months that I had been left in cruel doubt as to my princess' fate; for I had not known that Thuvia had wrested the blade from the daughter of Matai Shang before it had touched either Dejah Thoris or herself.

She told me, too, of the awful eternity of her imprisonment. Of the cruel hatred of Phaidor, and the tender love of Thuvia, and of how even when despair was the darkest those two red girls had clung to the same hope and belief – that John Carter would find a way to release them.

Presently we came to the chamber of Solan. I had been proceeding without thought of caution, for I was sure that the city and the palace were both in the hands of my friends by this time.

And so it was that I bolted into the chamber full into the midst of a dozen nobles of the court of Salensus Oll. They were passing through on their way to the outside world along the corridors we had just traversed.

At sight of us they halted in their tracks, and then an ugly smile overspread the features of their leader.

"The author of all our misfortunes!" he cried, pointing at me. "We shall have the satisfaction of a partial vengeance at least when we leave behind us here the dead and mutilated corpses of the Prince and Princess of Helium.

"When they find them," he went on, jerking his thumb upward toward the palace above, "they will realize that the vengeance of the yellow man costs his enemies dear. Prepare to die, John Carter, but that your end may be the more bitter, know that I may change my intention as to meting a merciful death to your princess – possibly she shall be preserved as a plaything for my nobles."

I stood close to the instrument-covered wall – Dejah Thoris at my side. She looked up at me wonderingly as the warriors advanced upon us with drawn swords, for mine still hung within its scabbard at my side, and there was a smile upon my lips.

The yellow nobles, too, looked in surprise, and then as I made no move to draw they hesitated, fearing a ruse; but their leader urged them on. When they had come almost within sword's reach of me I raised my hand and laid it upon the polished surface of a great lever, and then, still smiling grimly, I looked my enemies full in the face.

As one they came to a sudden stop, casting affrighted glances at me and at one another.

"Stop!" shrieked their leader. "You dream not what you do!"

"Right you are," I replied. "John Carter does not dream. He knows – knows that should one of you take another step toward Dejah Thoris, Princess of Helium, I pull this lever wide, and she and I shall die together; but we shall not die alone."

The nobles shrank back, whispering together for a few moments. At last their leader turned to me.

"Go your way, John Carter," he said, "and we shall go ours."

"Prisoners do not go their own way," I answered, "and you are prisoners – prisoners of the Prince of Helium."

Before they could make answer a door upon the opposite side of the apartment opened and a score of yellow men poured into the apartment. For an instant the nobles looked relieved, and then as their eyes fell upon the leader of the new party their faces fell, for he was Talu, rebel Prince of Marentina, and they knew that they could look for neither aid nor mercy at his hands.

"Well done, John Carter," he cried. "You turn their own mighty power against them. Fortunate for Okar is it that you were here to prevent their escape, for these be the greatest villains north of the ice-barrier, and this one" – pointing to the leader of the party – "would have made himself Jeddak of Jeddaks in the place of the dead Salensus Oll. Then indeed would we have had a more villainous ruler than the hated tyrant who fell before your sword."

The Okarian nobles now submitted to arrest, since nothing but death faced them should they resist, and, escorted by the warriors of Talu, we made our way to the great audience chamber that had been Salensus Oll's. Here was a vast concourse of warriors.

Red men from Helium and Ptarth, yellow men of the north, rubbing elbows with the blacks of the First Born who had come under my friend Xodar to help in the search for me and my princess. There were savage, green warriors from the dead sea bottoms of the south, and a handful of white-skinned therns who had renounced their religion and sworn allegiance to Xodar.

There was Tardos Mors and Mors Kajak, and tall and mighty in his gorgeous warrior trappings, Carthoris, my son. These three fell upon Dejah Thoris as we entered the apartment, and though the lives and training of royal Martians tend not toward vulgar demonstration, I thought that they would suffocate her with their embraces.

And there were Tars Tarkas, Jeddak of Thark, and Kantos Kan, my old-time friends, and leaping and tearing at my harness in the exuberance of his great love was dear old Woola – frantic mad with happiness.

Long and loud was the cheering that burst forth at sight of us; deafening was the din of ringing metal as the veteran warriors of every Martian clime clashed their blades together on high in token of success and victory, but as I passed among the throng of saluting nobles and warriors, jeds and jeddaks, my heart still was heavy, for there were two faces missing that I would have given much to have seen there – Thuvan Dihn and Thuvia of Ptarth were not to be found in the great chamber.

I made inquiries concerning them among men of every nation, and at last from one of the yellow prisoners of war I learned that they had been apprehended by an officer of the palace as they sought to reach the Pit of Plenty while I lay imprisoned there.

I did not need to ask to know what had sent them thither – the courageous jeddak and his loyal daughter. My informer said that they lay now in one of the many buried dungeons of the palace where they had been placed pending a decision as to their fate by the tyrant of the north.

A moment later searching parties were scouring the ancient pile in search of them, and my cup of happiness was full when I saw them being escorted into the room by a cheering guard of honor.

Thuvia's first act was to rush to the side of Dejah Thoris, and I needed no better proof of the love these two bore for each other than the sincerity with which they embraced.

Looking down upon that crowded chamber stood the silent and empty throne of Okar.

Of all the strange scenes it must have witnessed since that long-dead age that had first seen a Jeddak of Jeddaks take his seat upon it, none might compare with that upon which it now looked down, and as I pondered the past and future of that long-buried race of black-bearded yellow men I thought that I saw a brighter and more useful existence for them among the great family of friendly nations that now stretched from the south pole almost to their very doors.

Twenty-two years before I had been cast, naked and a stranger, into this strange and savage world. The hand of every race and nation was raised in continual strife and warring against the men of every other land and color. Today, by the might of my sword and the loyalty of the friends my sword had made for me, black man and white, red man and green rubbed shoulders in peace and good-fellowship. All the nations of Barsoom were not yet as one, but a great stride forward toward that goal had been taken, and now if I could but cement the fierce yellow race into this solidarity of nations I should feel that I had rounded out a great lifework, and repaid to Mars at least a portion of the immense debt of gratitude I owed her for having given me my Dejah Thoris.

And as I thought, I saw but one way, and a single man who could insure the success of my hopes. As is ever the way with me, I acted then as I always act – without deliberation and without consultation.

Those who do not like my plans and my ways of promoting them have always their swords at their sides wherewith to back up their disapproval; but now there seemed to be no dissenting voice, as, grasping Talu by the arm, I sprang to the throne that had once been Salensus Oll's.

"Warriors of Barsoom," I cried, "Kadabra has fallen, and with her the hateful tyrant of the north; but the integrity of Okar must be preserved. The red men are ruled by red jeddaks, the green warriors of the ancient seas acknowledge none but a green ruler, the First Born of the south pole take their law from black Xodar; nor would it be to the interests of either yellow or red man were a red jeddak to sit upon the throne of Okar.

"There be but one warrior best fitted for the ancient and mighty title of Jeddak of Jeddaks of the North. Men of Okar, raise your swords to your new ruler – Talu, the rebel prince of Marentina!"

And then a great cry of rejoicing rose among the free men of Marentina and the Kadabran prisoners, for all had thought that the red men would retain that which they had taken by force of arms, for such had been the way upon Barsoom, and that they should be ruled henceforth by an alien Jeddak.

The victorious warriors who had followed Carthoris joined in the mad demonstration, and amidst the wild confusion and the tumult and the cheering, Dejah Thoris and I passed out into the gorgeous garden of the jeddaks that graces the inner courtyard of the palace of Kadabra.

At our heels walked Woola, and upon a carved seat of wondrous beauty beneath a bower of purple blooms we saw two who had preceded us – Thuvia of Ptarth and Carthoris of Helium.

The handsome head of the handsome youth was bent low above the beautiful face of his companion. I looked at Dejah Thoris, smiling, and as I drew her close to me I whispered: "Why not?"

Indeed, why not? What matter ages in this world of perpetual youth?

We remained at Kadabra, the guests of Talu, until after his formal induction into office, and then, upon the great fleet which I had been so fortunate to preserve from destruction, we sailed south across the ice-barrier; but not before we had witnessed the total demolition of the grim Guardian of the North under orders of the new Jeddak of Jeddaks.

"Henceforth," he said, as the work was completed, "the fleets of the red men and the black are free to come and go across the ice-barrier as over their own lands.

"The Carrion Caves shall be cleansed, that the green men may find an easy way to the land of the yellow, and the hunting of the sacred apt shall be the sport of my nobles until no single specimen of that hideous creature roams the frozen north."

We bade our yellow friends farewell with real regret, as we set sail for Ptarth. There we remained, the guest of Thuvan Dihn, for a month; and I could see that Carthoris would have remained forever had he not been a Prince of Helium.

Above the mighty forests of Kaol we hovered until word from Kulan Tith brought us to his single landing-tower, where all day and half a night the vessels disembarked their crews. At the city of Kaol we visited, cementing the new ties that had been formed between Kaol and Helium, and then one long-to-be-remembered day we sighted the tall, thin towers of the twin cities of Helium.

The people had long been preparing for our coming. The sky was gorgeous with gaily trimmed fliers. Every roof within both cities was spread with costly silks and tapestries.

Gold and jewels were scattered over roof and street and plaza, so that the two cities seemed ablaze with the fires of the hearts of the magnificent stones and burnished metal that reflected the brilliant sunlight, changing it into countless glorious hues.

At last, after twelve years, the royal family of Helium was reunited in their own mighty city, surrounded by joy-mad millions before the palace gates. Women and children and mighty warriors wept in gratitude for the fate that had restored their beloved Tardos Mors and the divine princess whom the whole nation idolized. Nor did any of us who had been upon that expedition of indescribable danger and glory lack for plaudits.

That night a messenger came to me as I sat with Dejah Thoris and Carthoris upon the roof of my city palace, where we had long since caused a lovely garden to be made that we three might find seclusion and quiet happiness among ourselves, far from the pomp and ceremony of court, to summon us to the Temple of Reward – "where one is to be judged this night," the summons concluded.

I racked my brain to try and determine what important case there might be pending which could call the royal family from their palaces on the eve of their return to Helium after years of absence; but when the jeddak summons no man delays.

As our flier touched the landing stage at the temple's top we saw countless other craft arriving and departing. In the streets below a great multitude surged toward the great gates of the temple.

Slowly there came to me the recollection of the deferred doom that awaited me since that time I had been tried here in the Temple by Zat Arras for the sin of returning from the Valley Dor and the Lost Sea of Korus.

Could it be possible that the strict sense of justice which dominates the men of Mars had caused them to overlook the great good that had come out of my heresy? Could they ignore the fact that to me, and me alone, was due the rescue of Carthoris, of Dejah Thoris, of Mors Kajak, of Tardos Mors?

I could not believe it, and yet for what other purpose could I have been summoned to the Temple of Reward immediately upon the return of Tardos Mors to his throne?

My first surprise as I entered the temple and approached the Throne of Righteousness was to note the men who sat there as judges. There was

Kulan Tith, Jeddak of Kaol, whom we had but just left within his own palace a few days since; there was Thuvan Dihn, Jeddak of Ptarth – how came he to Helium as soon as we?

There was Tars Tarkas, Jeddak of Thark, and Xodar, Jeddak of the First Born; there was Talu, Jeddak of Jeddaks of the North, whom I could have sworn was still in his ice-bound hothouse city beyond the northern barrier, and among them sat Tardos Mors and Mors Kajak, with enough lesser jeds and jeddaks to make up the thirty-one who must sit in judgment upon their fellow-man.

A right royal tribunal indeed, and such a one, I warrant, as never before sat together during all the history of ancient Mars.

As I entered, silence fell upon the great concourse of people that packed the auditorium. Then Tardos Mors arose.

"John Carter," he said in his deep, martial voice, "take your place upon the Pedestal of Truth, for you are to be tried by a fair and impartial tribunal of your fellow-men."

With level eye and high-held head I did as he bade, and as I glanced about that circle of faces that a moment before I could have sworn contained the best friends I had upon Barsoom, I saw no single friendly glance – only stern, uncompromising judges, there to do their duty.

A clerk rose and from a great book read a long list of the more notable deeds that I had thought to my credit, covering a long period of twenty-two years since first I had stepped the ocher sea bottom beside the incubator of the Tharks. With the others he read of all that I had done within the circle of the Otz Mountains where the Holy Therns and the First Born had held sway.

It is the way upon Barsoom to recite a man's virtues with his sins when he is come to trial, and so I was not surprised that all that was to my credit should be read there to my judges – who knew it all by heart – even down to the present moment. When the reading had ceased Tardos Mors arose.

"Most righteous judges," he exclaimed, "you have heard recited all that is known of John Carter, Prince of Helium – the good with the bad. What is your judgment?"

Then Tars Tarkas came slowly to his feet, unfolding all his mighty, towering height until he loomed, a green-bronze statue, far above us all. He turned a baleful eye upon me – he, Tars Tarkas, with whom I had fought through countless battles; whom I loved as a brother.

I could have wept had I not been so mad with rage that I almost whipped my sword out and had at them all upon the spot.

"Judges," he said, "there can be but one verdict. No longer may John Carter be Prince of Helium" – he paused – "but instead let him be Jeddak of Jeddaks, Warlord of Barsoom!"

As the thirty-one judges sprang to their feet with drawn and upraised swords in unanimous concurrence in the verdict, the storm broke throughout the length and breadth and height of that mighty building until I thought the roof would fall from the thunder of the mad shouting.

Now, at last, I saw the grim humor of the method they had adopted to do me this great honor, but that there was any hoax in the reality of the title they had conferred upon me was readily disproved by the sincerity of the congratulations that were heaped upon me by the judges first and then the nobles.

Presently fifty of the mightiest nobles of the greatest courts of Mars marched down the broad Aisle of Hope bearing a splendid car upon their shoulders, and as the people saw who sat within, the cheers that had rung out for me paled into insignificance beside those which thundered through the vast edifice now, for she whom the nobles carried was Dejah Thoris, beloved Princess of Helium.

Straight to the Throne of Righteousness they bore her, and there Tardos Mors assisted her from the car, leading her forward to my side.

"Let a world's most beautiful woman share the honor of her husband," he said.

Before them all I drew my wife close to me and kissed her upon the lips.

THUVIA, MAID OF MARS
BOOK FOUR

CHAPTER ONE

Carthoris and Thuvia

UPON A MASSIVE BENCH of polished ersite beneath the gorgeous blooms of a giant pimalia a woman sat. Her shapely, sandalled foot tapped impatiently upon the jewel-strewn walk that wound beneath the stately sorapus trees across the scarlet sward of the royal gardens of Thuvan Dihn, Jeddak of Ptarth, as a dark-haired, red-skinned warrior bent low toward her, whispering heated words close to her ear.

"Ah, Thuvia of Ptarth," he cried, "you are cold even before the fiery blasts of my consuming love! No harder than your heart, nor colder is the hard, cold ersite of this thrice happy bench which supports your divine and fadeless form! Tell me, O Thuvia of Ptarth, that I may still hope – that though you do not love me now, yet some day, some day, my princess, I – "

The girl sprang to her feet with an exclamation of surprise and displeasure. Her queenly head was poised haughtily upon her smooth red shoulders. Her dark eyes looked angrily into those of the man.

"You forget yourself, and the customs of Barsoom, Astok," she said. "I have given you no right thus to address the daughter of Thuvan Dihn, nor have you won such a right."

The man reached suddenly forth and grasped her by the arm.

"You shall be my princess!" he cried. "By the breast of Issus, thou shalt, nor shall any other come between Astok, Prince of Dusar, and his heart's desire. Tell me that there is another, and I shall cut out his foul heart and fling it to the wild calots of the dead sea-bottoms!"

At touch of the man's hand upon her flesh the girl went pallid beneath her coppery skin, for the persons of the royal women of the courts of Mars are held but little less than sacred. The act of Astok, Prince of Dusar, was profanation. There was no terror in the eyes of Thuvia of Ptarth – only horror for the thing the man had done and for its possible consequences.

"Release me." Her voice was level – frigid.

The man muttered incoherently and drew her roughly toward him.

"Release me!" she repeated sharply, "or I call the guard, and the Prince of Dusar knows what that will mean."

Quickly he threw his right arm about her shoulders and strove to draw her face to his lips. With a little cry she struck him full in the mouth with the massive bracelets that circled her free arm.

"Calot!" she exclaimed, and then: "The guard! The guard! Hasten in protection of the Princess of Ptarth!"

In answer to her call a dozen guardsmen came racing across the scarlet sward, their gleaming long-swords naked in the sun, the metal of their accoutrements clanking against that of their leathern harness, and in their throats hoarse shouts of rage at the sight which met their eyes.

But before they had passed half across the royal garden to where Astok of Dusar still held the struggling girl in his grasp, another figure sprang from a cluster of dense foliage that half hid a golden fountain close at hand. A tall, straight youth he was, with black hair and keen grey eyes; broad of shoulder and narrow of hip; a clean-limbed fighting man. His skin was but faintly tinged with the copper colour that marks the red men of Mars from the other races of the dying planet – he was like them, and yet there was a subtle difference greater even than that which lay in his lighter skin and his grey eyes.

There was a difference, too, in his movements. He came on in great leaps that carried him so swiftly over the ground that the speed of the guardsmen was as nothing by comparison.

Astok still clutched Thuvia's wrist as the young warrior confronted him. The new-comer wasted no time and he spoke but a single word.

"Calot!" he snapped, and then his clenched fist landed beneath the other's chin, lifting him high into the air and depositing him in a crumpled heap within the centre of the pimalia bush beside the ersite bench.

Her champion turned toward the girl. "Kaor, Thuvia of Ptarth!" he cried. "It seems that fate timed my visit well."

"Kaor, Carthoris of Helium!" the princess returned the young man's greeting, "and what less could one expect of the son of such a sire?"

He bowed his acknowledgment of the compliment to his father, John Carter, Warlord of Mars. And then the guardsmen, panting from their charge, came up just as the Prince of Dusar, bleeding at the mouth, and with drawn sword, crawled from the entanglement of the pimalia.

Astok would have leaped to mortal combat with the son of Dejah Thoris, but the guardsmen pressed about him, preventing, though it was clearly evident that naught would have better pleased Carthoris of Helium.

"But say the word, Thuvia of Ptarth," he begged, "and naught will give me greater pleasure than meting to this fellow the punishment he has earned."

"It cannot be, Carthoris," she replied. "Even though he has forfeited all claim upon my consideration, yet is he the guest of the jeddak, my father, and to him alone may he account for the unpardonable act he has committed."

"As you say, Thuvia," replied the Heliumite. "But afterward he shall account to Carthoris, Prince of Helium, for this affront to the daughter of my father's friend." As he spoke, though, there burned in his eyes a fire that proclaimed a nearer, dearer cause for his championship of this glorious daughter of Barsoom.

The maid's cheek darkened beneath the satin of her transparent skin, and the eyes of Astok, Prince of Dusar, darkened, too, as he read that which passed unspoken between the two in the royal gardens of the jeddak.

"And thou to me," he snapped at Carthoris, answering the young man's challenge.

The guard still surrounded Astok. It was a difficult position for the young officer who commanded it. His prisoner was the son of a mighty jeddak; he was the guest of Thuvan Dihn – until but now an honoured guest upon whom every royal dignity had been showered. To arrest him forcibly could mean naught else than war, and yet he had done that which in the eyes of the Ptarth warrior merited death.

The young man hesitated. He looked toward his princess. She, too, guessed all that hung upon the action of the coming moment. For many years Dusar and Ptarth had been at peace with each other. Their great merchant ships plied back and forth between the larger cities of the two nations. Even now, far above the gold-shot scarlet dome of the jeddak's palace, she could see the huge bulk of a giant freighter taking its majestic way through the thin Barsoomian air toward the west and Dusar.

By a word she might plunge these two mighty nations into a bloody conflict that would drain them of their bravest blood and their incalculable riches, leaving them all helpless against the inroads of their envious and less powerful neighbors, and at last a prey to the savage green hordes of the dead sea-bottoms.

No sense of fear influenced her decision, for fear is seldom known to the children of Mars. It was rather a sense of the responsibility that she, the daughter of their jeddak, felt for the welfare of her father's people.

"I called you, Padwar," she said to the lieutenant of the guard, "to protect the person of your princess, and to keep the peace that must not be violated within the royal gardens of the jeddak. That is all. You will escort me to the palace, and the Prince of Helium will accompany me."

Without another glance in the direction of Astok she turned, and taking Carthoris' proffered hand, moved slowly toward the massive marble pile that housed the ruler of Ptarth and his glittering court. On either side marched a file of guardsmen. Thus Thuvia of Ptarth found a way out of a dilemma, escaping the necessity of placing her father's royal guest under forcible restraint, and at the same time separating the two princes, who otherwise would have been at each other's throat the moment she and the guard had departed.

Beside the pimalia stood Astok, his dark eyes narrowed to mere slits of hate beneath his lowering brows as he watched the retreating forms of the woman who had aroused the fiercest passions of his nature and the man whom he now believed to be the one who stood between his love and its consummation.

As they disappeared within the structure Astok shrugged his shoulders, and with a murmured oath crossed the gardens toward another wing of the building where he and his retinue were housed.

That night he took formal leave of Thuvan Dihn, and though no mention was made of the happening within the garden, it was plain to see through the cold mask of the jeddak's courtesy that only the customs of royal hospitality restrained him from voicing the contempt he felt for the Prince of Dusar.

Carthoris was not present at the leave-taking, nor was Thuvia. The ceremony was as stiff and formal as court etiquette could make it, and when the last of the Dusarians clambered over the rail of the battleship that had brought them upon this fateful visit to the court of Ptarth, and the mighty engine of destruction had risen slowly from the ways of the landing-stage, a note of relief was apparent in the voice of Thuvan Dihn as he turned to one of his officers with a word of comment upon a subject foreign to that which had been uppermost in the minds of all for hours.

But, after all, was it so foreign?

"Inform Prince Sovan," he directed, "that it is our wish that the fleet which departed for Kaol this morning be recalled to cruise to the west of Ptarth."

As the warship, bearing Astok back to the court of his father, turned toward the west, Thuvia of Ptarth, sitting upon the same bench where the Prince of Dusar had affronted her, watched the twinkling lights of the craft growing smaller in the distance. Beside her, in the brilliant light of the nearer moon, sat Carthoris. His eyes were not upon the dim bulk of the battleship, but on the profile of the girl's upturned face.

"Thuvia," he whispered.

The girl turned her eyes toward his. His hand stole out to find hers, but she drew her own gently away.

"Thuvia of Ptarth, I love you!" cried the young warrior. "Tell me that it does not offend."

She shook her head sadly. "The love of Carthoris of Helium," she said simply, "could be naught but an honour to any woman; but you must not speak, my friend, of bestowing upon me that which I may not reciprocate."

The young man got slowly to his feet. His eyes were wide in astonishment. It never had occurred to the Prince of Helium that Thuvia of Ptarth might love another.

"But at Kadabra!" he exclaimed. "And later here at your father's court, what did you do, Thuvia of Ptarth, that might have warned me that you could not return my love?"

"And what did I do, Carthoris of Helium," she returned, "that might lead you to believe that I *did* return it?"

He paused in thought, and then shook his head. "Nothing, Thuvia, that is true; yet I could have sworn you loved me. Indeed, you well knew how near to worship has been my love for you."

"And how might I know it, Carthoris?" she asked innocently. "Did you ever tell me as much? Ever before have words of love for me fallen from your lips?"

"But you *must* have known it!" he exclaimed. "I am like my father – witless in matters of the heart, and of a poor way with women; yet the jewels that strew these royal garden paths – the trees, the flowers, the sward – all must have read the love that has filled my heart since first my eyes were made new by imaging your perfect face and form; so how could you alone have been blind to it?"

"Do the maids of Helium pay court to their men?" asked Thuvia.

"You are playing with me!" exclaimed Carthoris. "Say that you are but playing, and that after all you love me, Thuvia!"

"I cannot tell you that, Carthoris, for I am promised to another."

Her tone was level, but was there not within it the hint of an infinite depth of sadness? Who may say?

"Promised to another?" Carthoris scarcely breathed the words. His face went almost white, and then his head came up as befitted him in whose veins flowed the blood of the overlord of a world.

"Carthoris of Helium wishes you every happiness with the man of your choice," he said. "With – " and then he hesitated, waiting for her to fill in the name.

"Kulan Tith, Jeddak of Kaol," she replied. "My father's friend and Ptarth's most puissant ally."

The young man looked at her intently for a moment before he spoke again.

"You love him, Thuvia of Ptarth?" he asked.

"I am promised to him," she replied simply.

He did not press her. "He is of Barsoom's noblest blood and mightiest fighters," mused Carthoris. "My father's friend and mine – would that it might have been another!" he muttered almost savagely. What the girl thought was hidden by the mask of her expression, which was tinged only by a little shadow of sadness that might have been for Carthoris, herself, or for them both.

Carthoris of Helium did not ask, though he noted it, for his loyalty to Kulan Tith was the loyalty of the blood of John Carter of Virginia for a friend, greater than which could be no loyalty.

He raised a jewel-encrusted bit of the girl's magnificent trappings to his lips.

"To the honour and happiness of Kulan Tith and the priceless jewel that has been bestowed upon him," he said, and though his voice was husky there was the true ring of sincerity in it. "I told you that I loved you, Thuvia, before I knew that you were promised to another. I may not tell you it again, but I am glad that you know it, for there is no dishonour in it either to you or to Kulan Tith or to myself. My love is such that it may embrace as well Kulan Tith – if you love him." There was almost a question in the statement.

"I am promised to him," she replied.

Carthoris backed slowly away. He laid one hand upon his heart, the other upon the pommel of his long-sword.

"These are yours – always," he said. A moment later he had entered the palace, and was gone from the girl's sight.

Had he returned at once he would have found her prone upon the ersite bench, her face buried in her arms. Was she weeping? There was none to see.

Carthoris of Helium had come all unannounced to the court of his father's friend that day. He had come alone in a small flier, sure of the same welcome that always awaited him at Ptarth. As there had been no formality in his coming there was no need of formality in his going.

To Thuvan Dihn he explained that he had been but testing an invention of his own with which his flier was equipped – a clever improvement of the ordinary Martian air compass, which, when set for a certain destination, will remain constantly fixed thereon, making it only necessary to keep a vessel's prow always in the direction of the compass needle to reach any given point upon Barsoom by the shortest route.

Carthoris' improvement upon this consisted of an auxiliary device which steered the craft mechanically in the direction of the compass, and upon arrival directly over the point for which the compass was set, brought the craft to a standstill and lowered it, also automatically, to the ground.

"You readily discern the advantages of this invention," he was saying to Thuvan Dihn, who had accompanied him to the landing-stage upon the palace roof to inspect the compass and bid his young friend farewell.

A dozen officers of the court with several body servants were grouped behind the jeddak and his guest, eager listeners to the conversation – so eager on the part of one of the servants that he was twice rebuked by a noble for his forwardness in pushing himself ahead of his betters to view the intricate mechanism of the wonderful "controlling destination compass," as the thing was called.

"For example," continued Carthoris, "I have an all-night trip before me, as to-night. I set the pointer here upon the right-hand dial which represents the eastern hemisphere of Barsoom, so that the point rests upon the exact latitude and longitude of Helium. Then I start the engine, roll up in my sleeping silks and furs, and with lights burning, race through the air toward Helium, confident that at the appointed hour I shall drop gently toward the landing-stage upon my own palace, whether I am still asleep or no."

"Provided," suggested Thuvan Dihn, "you do not chance to collide with some other night wanderer in the meanwhile."

Carthoris smiled. "No danger of that," he replied. "See here," and he indicated a device at the right of the destination compass. "This is my 'obstruction evader,' as I call it. This visible device is the switch which throws the mechanism on or off. The instrument itself is below deck, geared both to the steering apparatus and the control levers.

"It is quite simple, being nothing more than a radium generator diffusing radio-activity in all directions to a distance of a hundred yards or so from the flier. Should this enveloping force be interrupted in any direction a delicate instrument immediately apprehends the irregularity, at the same time imparting an impulse to a magnetic device which in turn actuates the steering mechanism, diverting the bow of the flier away from the obstacle until the craft's radio-activity sphere is no longer in contact with the obstruction, then she falls once more into her normal course. Should the disturbance approach from the rear, as in case of a faster-moving craft overhauling me, the mechanism actuates the speed control as well as the steering gear, and the flier shoots ahead and either up or down, as the oncoming vessel is upon a lower or higher plane than herself.

"In aggravated cases, that is when the obstructions are many, or of such a nature as to deflect the bow more than forty-five degrees in any direction, or when the craft has reached its destination and dropped to within a hundred yards of the ground, the mechanism brings her to a full stop, at the same time sounding a loud alarm which will instantly awaken the pilot. You see I have anticipated almost every contingency."

Thuvan Dihn smiled his appreciation of the marvellous device. The forward servant pushed almost to the flier's side. His eyes were narrowed to slits.

"All but one," he said.

The nobles looked at him in astonishment, and one of them grasped the fellow none too gently by the shoulder to push him back to his proper place. Carthoris raised his hand.

"Wait," he urged. "Let us hear what the man has to say – no creation of mortal mind is perfect. Perchance he has detected a weakness that it will be well to know at once. Come, my good fellow, and what may be the one contingency I have overlooked?"

As he spoke Carthoris observed the servant closely for the first time. He saw a man of giant stature and handsome, as are all those of the race of Martian red men; but the fellow's lips were thin and cruel, and across one cheek was the faint, white line of a sword-cut from the right temple to the corner of the mouth.

"Come," urged the Prince of Helium. "Speak!"

The man hesitated. It was evident that he regretted the temerity that had made him the centre of interested observation. But at last, seeing no alternative, he spoke.

"It might be tampered with," he said, "by an enemy."

Carthoris drew a small key from his leathern pocket-pouch.

"Look at this," he said, handing it to the man. "If you know aught of locks, you will know that the mechanism which this unlooses is beyond the cunning of a picker of locks. It guards the vitals of the instrument from crafty tampering. Without it an enemy must half wreck the device to reach its heart, leaving his handiwork apparent to the most casual observer."

The servant took the key, glanced at it shrewdly, and then as he made to return it to Carthoris dropped it upon the marble flagging. Turning to look for it he planted the sole of his sandal full upon the glittering object. For an instant he bore all his weight upon the foot that covered the key, then he stepped back and with an exclamation as of pleasure that he had found it, stooped, recovered it, and returned it to the Heliumite. Then he dropped back to his station behind the nobles and was forgotten.

A moment later Carthoris had made his adieux to Thuvan Dihn and his nobles, and with lights twinkling had risen into the star-shot void of the Martian night.

CHAPTER TWO

Slavery

As THE RULER OF PTARTH, followed by his courtiers, descended from the landing-stage above the palace, the servants dropped into their places in the rear of their royal or noble masters, and behind the others one lingered to the last. Then quickly stooping he snatched the sandal from his right foot, slipping it into his pocket-pouch.

When the party had come to the lower levels, and the jeddak had dispersed them by a sign, none noticed that the forward fellow who had drawn so much attention to himself before the Prince of Helium departed, was no longer among the other servants.

To whose retinue he had been attached none had thought to inquire, for the followers of a Martian noble are many, coming and going at the whim of their master, so that a new face is scarcely ever questioned, as the fact that a man has passed within the palace walls is considered proof positive that his loyalty to the jeddak is beyond question, so rigid is the examination of each who seeks service with the nobles of the court.

A good rule that, and only relaxed by courtesy in favour of the retinue of visiting royalty from a friendly foreign power.

It was late in the morning of the next day that a giant serving man in the harness of the house of a great Ptarth noble passed out into the city from the palace gates. Along one broad avenue and then another he strode briskly until he had passed beyond the district of the nobles and had come to the place of shops. Here he sought a pretentious building that rose spire-like toward the heavens, its outer walls elaborately wrought with delicate carvings and intricate mosaics.

It was the Palace of Peace in which were housed the representatives of the foreign powers, or rather in which were located their embassies;

for the ministers themselves dwelt in gorgeous palaces within the district occupied by the nobles.

Here the man sought the embassy of Dusar. A clerk arose questioningly as he entered, and at his request to have a word with the minister asked his credentials. The visitor slipped a plain metal armlet from above his elbow, and pointing to an inscription upon its inner surface, whispered a word or two to the clerk.

The latter's eyes went wide, and his attitude turned at once to one of deference. He bowed the stranger to a seat, and hastened to an inner room with the armlet in his hand. A moment later he reappeared and conducted the caller into the presence of the minister.

For a long time the two were closeted together, and when at last the giant serving man emerged from the inner office his expression was cast in a smile of sinister satisfaction. From the Palace of Peace he hurried directly to the palace of the Dusarian minister.

That night two swift fliers left the same palace top. One sped its rapid course toward Helium; the other –

Thuvia of Ptarth strolled in the gardens of her father's palace, as was her nightly custom before retiring. Her silks and furs were drawn about her, for the air of Mars is chill after the sun has taken his quick plunge beneath the planet's western verge.

The girl's thoughts wandered from her impending nuptials, that would make her empress of Kaol, to the person of the trim young Heliumite who had laid his heart at her feet the preceding day.

Whether it was pity or regret that saddened her expression as she gazed toward the southern heavens where she had watched the lights of his flier disappear the previous night, it would be difficult to say.

So, too, is it impossible to conjecture just what her emotions may have been as she discerned the lights of a flier speeding rapidly out of the distance from that very direction, as though impelled toward her garden by the very intensity of the princess' thoughts.

She saw it circle lower above the palace until she was positive that it but hovered in preparation for a landing.

Presently the powerful rays of its searchlight shot downward from the bow. They fell upon the landing-stage for a brief instant, revealing the figures of the Ptarthian guard, picking into brilliant points of fire the gems upon their gorgeous harnesses.

Then the blazing eye swept onward across the burnished domes and graceful minarets, down into court and park and garden to pause at last upon the ersite bench and the girl standing there beside it, her face upturned full toward the flier.

For but an instant the searchlight halted upon Thuvia of Ptarth, then it was extinguished as suddenly as it had come to life. The flier passed on above her to disappear beyond a grove of lofty skeel trees that grew within the palace grounds.

The girl stood for some time as it had left her, except that her head was bent and her eyes downcast in thought.

Who but Carthoris could it have been? She tried to feel anger that he should have returned thus, spying upon her; but she found it difficult to be angry with the young prince of Helium.

What mad caprice could have induced him so to transgress the etiquette of nations? For lesser things great powers had gone to war.

The princess in her was shocked and angered – but what of the girl! And the guard – what of them? Evidently they, too, had been so much surprised by the unprecedented action of the stranger that they had not even challenged; but that they had no thought to let the thing go unnoticed was quickly evidenced by the skirring of motors upon the landing-stage and the quick shooting airward of a long-lined patrol boat.

Thuvia watched it dart swiftly eastward. So, too, did other eyes watch.

Within the dense shadows of the skeel grove, in a wide avenue beneath o'erspreading foliage, a flier hung a dozen feet above the ground. From its deck keen eyes watched the far-fanning searchlight of the patrol boat. No light shone from the enshadowed craft. Upon its deck was the silence of the tomb. Its crew of a half-dozen red warriors watched the lights of the patrol boat diminishing in the distance.

"The intellects of our ancestors are with us to-night," said one in a low tone.

"No plan ever carried better," returned another. "They did precisely as the prince foretold."

He who had first spoken turned toward the man who squatted before the control board.

"Now!" he whispered. There was no other order given. Every man upon the craft had evidently been well schooled in each detail of that night's work. Silently the dark hull crept beneath the cathedral arches of the dark and silent grove.

Thuvia of Ptarth, gazing toward the east, saw the blacker blot against the blackness of the trees as the craft topped the buttressed garden wall. She saw the dim bulk incline gently downward toward the scarlet sward of the garden.

She knew that men came not thus with honourable intent. Yet she did not cry aloud to alarm the near-by guardsmen, nor did she flee to the safety of the palace.

Why?

I can see her shrug her shapely shoulders in reply as she voices the age-old, universal answer of the woman: Because!

Scarce had the flier touched the ground when four men leaped from its deck. They ran forward toward the girl.

Still she made no sign of alarm, standing as though hypnotized. Or could it have been as one who awaited a welcome visitor?

Not until they were quite close to her did she move. Then the nearer moon, rising above the surrounding foliage, touched their faces, lighting all with the brilliancy of her silver rays.

Thuvia of Ptarth saw only strangers – warriors in the harness of Dusar. Now she took fright, but too late!

Before she could voice but a single cry, rough hands seized her. A heavy silken scarf was wound about her head. She was lifted in strong arms and borne to the deck of the flier. There was the sudden whirl of propellers, the rushing of air against her body, and, from far beneath the shouting and the challenge from the guard.

Racing toward the south another flier sped toward Helium. In its cabin a tall red man bent over the soft sole of an upturned sandal. With delicate instruments he measured the faint imprint of a small object which appeared there. Upon a pad beside him was the outline of a key, and here he noted the results of his measurements.

A smile played upon his lips as he completed his task and turned to one who waited at the opposite side of the table.

"The man is a genius," he remarked.

"Only a genius could have evolved such a lock as this is designed to spring. Here, take the sketch, Larok, and give all thine own genius full and unfettered freedom in reproducing it in metal."

The warrior-artificer bowed. "Man builds naught," he said, "that man may not destroy." Then he left the cabin with the sketch.

As dawn broke upon the lofty towers which mark the twin cities of Helium – the scarlet tower of one and the yellow tower of its sister – a flier floated lazily out of the north.

Upon its bow was emblazoned the signia of a lesser noble of a far city of the empire of Helium. Its leisurely approach and the evident confidence with which it moved across the city aroused no suspicion in the minds of the sleepy guard. Their round of duty nearly done, they had little thought beyond the coming of those who were to relieve them.

Peace reigned throughout Helium. Stagnant, emasculating peace. Helium had no enemies. There was naught to fear.

Without haste the nearest air patrol swung sluggishly about and approached the stranger. At easy speaking distance the officer upon her deck hailed the incoming craft.

The cheery "Kaor!" and the plausible explanation that the owner had come from distant parts for a few days of pleasure in gay Helium sufficed. The air-patrol boat sheered off, passing again upon its way. The stranger continued toward a public landing-stage, where she dropped into the ways and came to rest.

At about the same time a warrior entered her cabin.

"It is done, Vas Kor," he said, handing a small metal key to the tall noble who had just risen from his sleeping silks and furs.

"Good!" exclaimed the latter. "You must have worked upon it all during the night, Larok."

The warrior nodded.

"Now fetch me the Heliumetic metal you wrought some days since," commanded Vas Kor.

This done, the warrior assisted his master to replace the handsome jewelled metal of his harness with the plainer ornaments of an ordinary fighting man of Helium, and with the insignia of the same house that appeared upon the bow of the flier.

Vas Kor breakfasted on board. Then he emerged upon the aerial dock, entered an elevator, and was borne quickly to the street below, where he was soon engulfed by the early morning throng of workers hastening to their daily duties.

Among them his warrior trappings were no more remarkable than is a pair of trousers upon Broadway. All Martian men are warriors, save those physically unable to bear arms. The tradesman and his clerk clank with their martial trappings as they pursue their vocations. The schoolboy, coming into the world, as he does, almost adult from the snowy shell that has encompassed his development for five long years, knows so little of life without a sword at his hip that he would feel the same discomfiture at going abroad unarmed that an Earth boy would experience in walking the streets knicker-bockerless.

Vas Kor's destination lay in Greater Helium, which lies some seventy-five miles across the level plain from Lesser Helium. He had landed at the latter city because the air patrol is less suspicious and alert than that above the larger metropolis where lies the palace of the jeddak.

As he moved with the throng in the parklike canyon of the thoroughfare the life of an awakening Martian city was in evidence about him. Houses, raised high upon their slender metal columns for the night were dropping gently toward the ground. Among the flowers upon the scarlet sward which lies about the buildings children were already playing, and comely women laughing and chatting with their neighbours as they culled gorgeous blossoms for the vases within doors.

The pleasant "kaor" of the Barsoomian greeting fell continually upon the ears of the stranger as friends and neighbours took up the duties of a new day.

The district in which he had landed was residential – a district of merchants of the more prosperous sort. Everywhere were evidences of luxury and wealth. Slaves appeared upon every housetop with gorgeous silks and costly furs, laying them in the sun for airing. Jewel-encrusted women lolled even thus early upon the carven balconies before their sleeping apartments. Later in the day they would repair to the roofs when the slaves had arranged couches and pitched silken canopies to shade them from the sun.

Strains of inspiring music broke pleasantly from open windows, for the Martians have solved the problem of attuning the nerves pleasantly to the sudden transition from sleep to waking that proves so difficult a thing for most Earth folk.

Above him raced the long, light passenger fliers, plying, each in its proper plane, between the numerous landing-stages for internal passenger traffic. Landing-stages that tower high into the heavens are for the great international passenger liners. Freighters have other landing-stages at various lower levels, to within a couple of hundred feet of the ground; nor dare any flier rise or drop from one plane to another except in certain restricted districts where horizontal traffic is forbidden.

Along the close-cropped sward which paves the avenue ground fliers were moving in continuous lines in opposite directions. For the greater part they skimmed along the surface of the sward, soaring gracefully into the air at times to pass over a slower-going driver ahead, or at intersections, where the north and south traffic has the right of way and the east and west must rise above it.

From private hangars upon many a roof top fliers were darting into the line of traffic. Gay farewells and parting admonitions mingled with the whirring of motors and the subdued noises of the city.

Yet with all the swift movement and the countless thousands rushing hither and thither, the predominant suggestion was that of luxurious ease and soft noiselessness.

Martians dislike harsh, discordant clamour. The only loud noises they can abide are the martial sounds of war, the clash of arms, the collision of two mighty dreadnoughts of the air. To them there is no sweeter music than this.

At the intersection of two broad avenues Vas Kor descended from the street level to one of the great pneumatic stations of the city. Here he paid before a little wicket the fare to his destination with a couple of the dull, oval coins of Helium.

Beyond the gatekeeper he came to a slowly moving line of what to Earthly eyes would have appeared to be conical-nosed, eight-foot projectiles for some giant gun. In slow procession the things moved in single file along a grooved track. A half dozen attendants assisted passengers to enter, or directed these carriers to their proper destination.

Vas Kor approached one that was empty. Upon its nose was a dial and a pointer. He set the pointer for a certain station in Greater Helium, raised the arched lid of the thing, stepped in and lay down upon the upholstered bottom. An attendant closed the lid, which locked with a little click, and the carrier continued its slow way.

Presently it switched itself automatically to another track, to enter, a moment later, one of the series of dark-mouthed tubes.

The instant that its entire length was within the black aperture it sprang forward with the speed of a rifle ball. There was an instant of whizzing – a soft, though sudden, stop, and slowly the carrier emerged upon another platform, another attendant raised the lid and Vas Kor stepped out at the station beneath the centre of Greater Helium, seventy-five miles from the point at which he had embarked.

Here he sought the street level, stepping immediately into a waiting ground flier. He spoke no word to the slave sitting in the driver's seat. It was evident that he had been expected, and that the fellow had received his instructions before his coming.

Scarcely had Vas Kor taken his seat when the flier went quickly into the fast-moving procession, turning presently from the broad and crowded avenue into a less congested street. Presently it left the thronged district behind to enter a section of small shops, where it stopped before the entrance to one which bore the sign of a dealer in foreign silks.

Vas Kor entered the low-ceiling room. A man at the far end motioned him toward an inner apartment, giving no further sign of recognition until he had passed in after the caller and closed the door.

Then he faced his visitor, saluting deferentially.

"Most noble – " he commenced, but Vas Kor silenced him with a gesture.

"No formalities," he said. "We must forget that I am aught other than your slave. If all has been as carefully carried out as it has been planned, we have no time to waste. Instead we should be upon our way to the slave market. Are you ready?"

The merchant nodded, and, turning to a great chest, produced the unemblazoned trappings of a slave. These Vas Kor immediately donned. Then the two passed from the shop through a rear door, traversed a winding alley to an avenue beyond, where they entered a flier which awaited them.

Five minutes later the merchant was leading his slave to the public market, where a great concourse of people filled the great open space in the centre of which stood the slave block.

The crowds were enormous to-day, for Carthoris, Prince of Helium, was to be the principal bidder.

One by one the masters mounted the rostrum beside the slave block upon which stood their chattels. Briefly and clearly each recounted the virtues of his particular offering.

When all were done, the major-domo of the Prince of Helium re-called to the block such as had favourably impressed him. For such he had made a fair offer.

There was little haggling as to price, and none at all when Vas Kor was placed upon the block. His merchant-master accepted the first offer that was made for him, and thus a Dusarian noble entered the household of Carthoris.

CHAPTER THREE

Treachery

THE DAY FOLLOWING the coming of Vas Kor to the palace of the Prince of Helium great excitement reigned throughout the twin cities, reaching its climax in the palace of Carthoris. Word had come of the abduction of Thuvia of Ptarth from her father's court, and with it the veiled hint that the Prince of Helium might be suspected of considerable knowledge of the act and the whereabouts of the princess.

In the council chamber of John Carter, Warlord of Mars, was Tardos Mors, Jeddak of Helium; Mors Kajak, his son, Jed of Lesser Helium; Carthoris, and a score of the great nobles of the empire.

"There must be no war between Ptarth and Helium, my son," said John Carter. "That you are innocent of the charge that has been placed against you by insinuation, we well know; but Thuvan Dihn must know it well, too.

"There is but one who may convince him, and that one be you. You must hasten at once to the court of Ptarth, and by your presence there as well as by your words assure him that his suspicions are groundless. Bear with you the authority of the Warlord of Barsoom, and of the Jeddak of Helium to offer every resource of the allied powers to assist Thuvan Dihn to recover his daughter and punish her abductors, whomsoever they may be.

"Go! I know that I do not need to urge upon you the necessity for haste."

Carthoris left the council chamber, and hastened to his palace.

Here slaves were busy in a moment setting things to rights for the departure of their master. Several worked about the swift flier that would bear the Prince of Helium rapidly toward Ptarth.

At last all was done. But two armed slaves remained on guard. The setting sun hung low above the horizon. In a moment darkness would envelop all.

One of the guardsmen, a giant of a fellow across whose right cheek there ran a thin scar from temple to mouth, approached his companion. His gaze was directed beyond and above his comrade. When he had come quite close he spoke.

"What strange craft is that?" he asked.

The other turned about quickly to gaze heavenward. Scarce was his back turned toward the giant than the short-sword of the latter was plunged beneath his left shoulder blade, straight through his heart.

Voiceless, the soldier sank in his tracks – stone dead. Quickly the murderer dragged the corpse into the black shadows within the hangar. Then he returned to the flier.

Drawing a cunningly wrought key from his pocket-pouch, he removed the cover of the right-hand dial of the controlling destination compass. For a moment he studied the construction of the mechanism beneath. Then he returned the dial to its place, set the pointer, and removed it again to note the resultant change in the position of the parts affected by the act.

A smile crossed his lips. With a pair of cutters he snipped off the projection which extended through the dial from the external pointer – now the latter might be moved to any point upon the dial without affecting the mechanism below. In other words, the eastern hemisphere dial was useless.

Now he turned his attention to the western dial. This he set upon a certain point. Afterward he removed the cover of this dial also, and with keen tool cut the steel finger from the under side of the pointer.

As quickly as possible he replaced the second dial cover, and resumed his place on guard. To all intents and purposes the compass was as efficient as before; but, as a matter of fact, the moving of the pointers upon the dials resulted now in no corresponding shift of the mechanism beneath – and the device was set, immovably, upon a destination of the slave's own choosing.

Presently came Carthoris, accompanied by but a handful of his gentlemen. He cast but a casual glance upon the single slave who stood guard. The fellow's thin, cruel lips, and the sword-cut that ran from temple to mouth aroused the suggestion of an unpleasant memory within him. He wondered where Saran Tal had found the man – then the matter faded from his thoughts, and in another moment the Prince of Helium was laughing and chatting with his companions, though below the surface his heart was cold with dread, for what contingencies confronted Thuvia of Ptarth he could not even guess.

First to his mind, naturally, had sprung the thought that Astok of Dusar had stolen the fair Ptarthian; but almost simultaneously with the report of the abduction had come news of the great fetes at Dusar in honour of the return of the jeddak's son to the court of his father.

It could not have been he, thought Carthoris, for on the very night that Thuvia was taken Astok had been in Dusar, and yet –

He entered the flier, exchanging casual remarks with his companions as he unlocked the mechanism of the compass and set the pointer upon the capital city of Ptarth.

With a word of farewell he touched the button which controlled the repulsive rays, and as the flier rose lightly into the air, the engine purred in answer to the touch of his finger upon a second button, the propellers whirred as his hand drew back the speed lever, and Carthoris, Prince of Helium, was off into the gorgeous Martian night beneath the hurtling moons and the million stars.

Scarce had the flier found its speed ere the man, wrapping his sleeping silks and furs about him, stretched at full length upon the narrow deck to sleep.

But sleep did not come at once at his bidding.

Instead, his thoughts ran riot in his brain, driving sleep away. He recalled the words of Thuvia of Ptarth, words that had half assured him that she loved him; for when he had asked her if she loved Kulan Tith, she had answered only that she was promised to him.

Now he saw that her reply was open to more than a single construction. It might, of course, mean that she did not love Kulan Tith; and so, by inference, be taken to mean that she loved another.

But what assurance was there that the other was Carthoris of Helium?

The more he thought upon it the more positive he became that not only was there no assurance in her words that she loved him, but none either in any act of hers. No, the fact was, she did not love him. She loved another. She had not been abducted – she had fled willingly with her lover.

With such pleasant thoughts filling him alternately with despair and rage, Carthoris at last dropped into the sleep of utter mental exhaustion.

The breaking of the sudden dawn found him still asleep. His flier was rushing swiftly above a barren, ochre plain – the world-old bottom of a long-dead Martian sea.

In the distance rose low hills. Toward these the craft was headed. As it approached them, a great promontory might have been seen from its deck, stretching out into what had once been a mighty ocean, and circling back once more to enclose the forgotten harbour of a forgotten city, which still stretched back from its deserted quays, an imposing pile of wondrous architecture of a long-dead past.

The countless dismal windows, vacant and forlorn, stared, sightless, from their marble walls; the whole sad city taking on the semblance of scattered mounds of dead men's sun-bleached skulls – the casements having the appearance of eyeless sockets, the portals, grinning jaws.

Closer came the flier, but now its speed was diminishing – yet this was not Ptarth.

Above the central plaza it stopped, slowly settling Marsward. Within a hundred yards of the ground it came to rest, floating gently in the light air, and at the same instant an alarm sounded at the sleeper's ear.

Carthoris sprang to his feet. Below him he looked to see the teeming metropolis of Ptarth. Beside him, already, there should have been an air patrol.

He gazed about in bewildered astonishment. There indeed was a great city, but it was not Ptarth. No multitudes surged through its broad avenues. No signs of life broke the dead monotony of its deserted roof tops. No gorgeous silks, no priceless furs lent life and colour to the cold marble and the gleaming ersite.

No patrol boat lay ready with its familiar challenge. Silent and empty lay the great city – empty and silent the surrounding air.

What had happened?

Carthoris examined the dial of his compass. The pointer was set upon Ptarth. Could the creature of his genius have thus betrayed him? He would not believe it.

Quickly he unlocked the cover, turning it back upon its hinge. A single glance showed him the truth, or at least a part of it – the steel projection that communicated the movement of the pointer upon the dial to the heart of the mechanism beneath had been severed.

Who could have done the thing – and why?

Carthoris could not hazard even a faint guess. But the thing now was to learn in what portion of the world he was, and then take up his interrupted journey once more.

If it had been the purpose of some enemy to delay him, he had succeeded well, thought Carthoris, as he unlocked the cover of the second dial the first having shown that its pointer had not been set at all.

Beneath the second dial he found the steel pin severed as in the other, but the controlling mechanism had first been set for a point upon the western hemisphere.

He had just time to judge his location roughly at some place south-west of Helium, and at a considerable distance from the twin cities, when he was startled by a woman's scream beneath him.

Leaning over the side of the flier, he saw what appeared to be a red woman being dragged across the plaza by a huge green warrior – one of those fierce, cruel denizens of the dead sea-bottoms and deserted cities of dying Mars.

Carthoris waited to see no more. Reaching for the control board, he sent his craft racing plummet-like toward the ground.

The green man was hurrying his captive toward a huge thoat that browsed upon the ochre vegetation of the once scarlet-gorgeous plaza. At the same instant a dozen red warriors leaped from the entrance of a nearby ersite palace, pursuing the abductor with naked swords and shouts of rageful warning.

Once the woman turned her face upward toward the falling flier, and in the single swift glance Carthoris saw that it was Thuvia of Ptarth!

CHAPTER FOUR
A Green Man's Captive

WHEN THE LIGHT OF DAY broke upon the little craft to whose deck the Princess of Ptarth had been snatched from her father's garden, Thuvia saw that the night had wrought a change in her abductors.

No longer did their trappings gleam with the metal of Dusar, but instead there was emblazoned there the insignia of the Prince of Helium.

The girl felt renewed hope, for she could not believe that in the heart of Carthoris could lie intent to harm her.

She spoke to the warrior squatting before the control board.

"Last night you wore the trappings of a Dusarian," she said. "Now your metal is that of Helium. What means it?"

The man looked at her with a grin.

"The Prince of Helium is no fool," he said.

Just then an officer emerged from the tiny cabin. He reprimanded the warrior for conversing with the prisoner, nor would he himself reply to any of her inquiries.

No harm was offered her during the journey, and so they came at last to their destination with the girl no wiser as to her abductors or their purpose than at first.

Here the flier settled slowly into the plaza of one of those mute monuments of Mars' dead and forgotten past – the deserted cities that fringe the sad ochre sea-bottoms where once rolled the mighty floods upon whose bosoms moved the maritime commerce of the peoples that are gone for ever.

Thuvia of Ptarth was no stranger to such places. During her wanderings in search of the River Iss, that time she had set out upon what, for countless ages, had been the last, long pilgrimage of Martians, toward the Valley Dor, where lies the Lost Sea of Korus, she had encountered several of these sad reminders of the greatness and the glory of ancient Barsoom.

And again, during her flight from the temples of the Holy Therns with Tars Tarkas, Jeddak of Thark, she had seen them, with their weird and ghostly inmates, the great white apes of Barsoom.

She knew, too, that many of them were used now by the nomadic tribes of green men, but that among them all was no city that the red men did not shun, for without exception they stood amidst vast, waterless tracts, unsuited for the continued sustenance of the dominant race of Martians.

Why, then, should they be bringing her to such a place? There was but a single answer. Such was the nature of their work that they must needs seek the seclusion that a dead city afforded. The girl trembled at thought of her plight.

For two days her captors kept her within a huge palace that even in decay reflected the splendour of the age which its youth had known.

Just before dawn on the third day she had been aroused by the voices of two of her abductors.

"He should be here by dawn," one was saying. "Have her in readiness upon the plaza – else he will never land. The moment he finds that he is in a strange country he will turn about – methinks the prince's plan is weak in this one spot."

"There was no other way," replied the other. "It is wondrous work to get them both here at all, and even if we do not succeed in luring him to the ground, we shall have accomplished much."

Just then the speaker caught the eyes of Thuvia upon him, revealed by the quick-moving patch of light cast by Thuria in her mad race through the heavens.

With a quick sign to the other, he ceased speaking, and advancing toward the girl, motioned her to rise. Then he led her out into the night toward the centre of the great plaza.

"Stand here," he commanded, "until we come for you. We shall be watching, and should you attempt to escape it will go ill with you – much worse than death. Such are the prince's orders."

Then he turned and retraced his steps toward the palace, leaving her alone in the midst of the unseen terrors of the haunted city, for in truth these places are haunted in the belief of many Martians who still cling to an ancient superstition which teaches that the spirits of Holy Therns who die before their allotted one thousand years, pass, on occasions, into the bodies of the great white apes.

To Thuvia, however, the real danger of attack by one of these ferocious, manlike beasts was quite sufficient. She no longer believed in the weird soul transmigration that the therns had taught her before she was rescued from their clutches by John Carter; but she well knew the horrid fate that awaited her should one of the terrible beasts chance to spy her during its nocturnal prowlings.

What was that?

Surely she could not be mistaken. Something had moved, stealthily, in the shadow of one of the great monoliths that line the avenue where it entered the plaza opposite her!

Thar Ban, jed among the hordes of Torquas, rode swiftly across the ochre vegetation of the dead sea-bottom toward the ruins of ancient Aaanthor.

He had ridden far that night, and fast, for he had but come from the despoiling of the incubator of a neighbouring green horde with which the hordes of Torquas were perpetually warring.

His giant thoat was far from jaded, yet it would be well, thought Thar Ban, to permit him to graze upon the ochre moss which grows to greater height within the protected courtyards of deserted cities, where the soil is richer than on the sea-bottoms, and the plants partly shaded from the sun during the cloudless Martian day.

Within the tiny stems of this dry-seeming plant is sufficient moisture for the needs of the huge bodies of the mighty thoats, which can exist for months without water, and for days without even the slight moisture which the ochre moss contains.

As Thar Ban rode noiselessly up the broad avenue which leads from the quays of Aaanthor to the great central plaza, he and his mount might have been mistaken for spectres from a world of dreams, so grotesque the man and beast, so soundless the great thoat's padded, nailless feet upon the moss-grown flagging of the ancient pavement.

The man was a splendid specimen of his race. Fully fifteen feet towered his great height from sole to pate. The moonlight glistened against his glossy green hide, sparkling the jewels of his heavy harness and the ornaments that weighted his four muscular arms, while the upcurving tusks that protruded from his lower jaw gleamed white and terrible.

At the side of his thoat were slung his long radium rifle and his great, forty-foot, metal-shod spear, while from his own harness depended his long-sword and his short-sword, as well as his lesser weapons.

His protruding eyes and antennae-like ears were turning constantly hither and thither, for Thar Ban was yet in the country of the enemy, and, too, there was always the menace of the great white apes, which,

John Carter was wont to say, are the only creatures that can arouse in the breasts of these fierce denizens of the dead sea-bottoms even the remotest semblance of fear.

As the rider neared the plaza, he reined suddenly in. His slender, tubular ears pointed rigidly forward. An unwonted sound had reached them. Voices! And where there were voices, outside of Torquas, there, too, were enemies. All the world of wide Barsoom contained naught but enemies for the fierce Torquasians.

Thar Ban dismounted. Keeping in the shadows of the great monoliths that line the Avenue of Quays of sleeping Aaanthor, he approached the plaza. Directly behind him, as a hound at heel, came the slate-grey thoat, his white belly shadowed by his barrel, his vivid yellow feet merging into the yellow of the moss beneath them.

In the centre of the plaza Thar Ban saw the figure of a red woman. A red warrior was conversing with her. Now the man turned and retraced his steps toward the palace at the opposite side of the plaza.

Thar Ban watched until he had disappeared within the yawning portal. Here was a captive worth having! Seldom did a female of their hereditary enemies fall to the lot of a green man. Thar Ban licked his thin lips.

Thuvia of Ptarth watched the shadow behind the monolith at the opening to the avenue opposite her. She hoped that it might be but the figment of an overwrought imagination.

But no! Now, clearly and distinctly, she saw it move. It came from behind the screening shelter of the ersite shaft.

The sudden light of the rising sun fell upon it. The girl trembled. The *thing* was a huge green warrior!

Swiftly it sprang toward her. She screamed and tried to flee; but she had scarce turned toward the palace when a giant hand fell upon her arm, she was whirled about, and half dragged, half carried toward a huge thoat that was slowly grazing out of the avenue's mouth on to the ochre moss of the plaza.

At the same instant she turned her face upward toward the whirring sound of something above her, and there she saw a swift flier dropping toward her, the head and shoulders of a man leaning far over the side; but the man's features were deeply shadowed, so that she did not recognize them.

Now from behind her came the shouts of her red abductors. They were racing madly after him who dared to steal what they already had stolen.

As Thar Ban reached the side of his mount he snatched his long radium rifle from its boot, and, wheeling, poured three shots into the oncoming red men.

Such is the uncanny marksmanship of these Martian savages that three red warriors dropped in their tracks as three projectiles exploded in their vitals.

The others halted, nor did they dare return the fire for fear of wounding the girl.

Then Thar Ban vaulted to the back of his thoat, Thuvia of Ptarth still in his arms, and with a savage cry of triumph disappeared down the black canyon of the Avenue of Quays between the sullen palaces of forgotten Aaanthor.

Carthoris' flier had not touched the ground before he had sprung from its deck to race after the swift thoat, whose eight long legs were sending it down the avenue at the rate of an express train; but the men of Dusar who still remained alive had no mind to permit so valuable a capture to escape them.

They had lost the girl. That would be a difficult thing to explain to Astok; but some leniency might be expected could they carry the Prince of Helium to their master instead.

So the three who remained set upon Carthoris with their long-swords, crying to him to surrender; but they might as successfully have cried aloud to Thuria to cease her mad hurtling through the Barsoomian sky, for Carthoris of Helium was a true son of the Warlord of Mars and his incomparable Dejah Thoris.

Carthoris' long-sword had been already in his hand as he leaped from the deck of the flier, so the instant that he realized the menace of the three red warriors, he wheeled to face them, meeting their onslaught as only John Carter himself might have done.

So swift his sword, so mighty and agile his half-earthly muscles, that one of his opponents was down, crimsoning the ochre moss with his life-blood, when he had scarce made a single pass at Carthoris.

Now the two remaining Dusarians rushed simultaneously upon the Heliumite. Three long-swords clashed and sparkled in the moonlight, until the great white apes, roused from their slumbers, crept to the lowering windows of the dead city to view the bloody scene beneath them.

Thrice was Carthoris touched, so that the red blood ran down his face, blinding him and dyeing his broad chest. With his free hand he wiped the gore from his eyes, and with the fighting smile of his father touching his lips, leaped upon his antagonists with renewed fury.

A single cut of his heavy sword severed the head of one of them, and then the other, backing away clear of that point of death, turned and fled toward the palace at his back.

Carthoris made no step to pursue. He had other concern than the meting of even well-deserved punishment to strange men who masqueraded in the metal of his own house, for he had seen that these men were tricked out in the insignia that marked his personal followers.

Turning quickly toward his flier, he was soon rising from the plaza in pursuit of Thar Ban.

The red warrior whom he had put to flight turned in the entrance to the palace, and, seeing Carthoris' intent, snatched a rifle from those that he and his fellows had left leaning against the wall as they had rushed out with drawn swords to prevent the theft of their prisoner.

Few red men are good shots, for the sword is their chosen weapon; so now as the Dusarian drew bead upon the rising flier, and touched the button upon his rifle's stock, it was more to chance than proficiency that he owed the partial success of his aim.

The projectile grazed the flier's side, the opaque coating breaking sufficiently to permit daylight to strike in upon the powder phial within the bullet's nose. There was a sharp explosion. Carthoris felt his craft reel drunkenly beneath him, and the engine stopped.

The momentum the air boat had gained carried her on over the city toward the sea-bottom beyond.

The red warrior in the plaza fired several more shots, none of which scored. Then a lofty minaret shut the drifting quarry from his view.

In the distance before him Carthoris could see the green warrior bearing Thuvia of Ptarth away upon his mighty thoat. The direction of his flight was toward the north-west of Aaanthor, where lay a mountainous country little known to red men.

The Heliumite now gave his attention to his injured craft. A close examination revealed the fact that one of the buoyancy tanks had been punctured, but the engine itself was uninjured.

A splinter from the projectile had damaged one of the control levers beyond the possibility of repair outside a machine shop; but after considerable tinkering, Carthoris was able to propel his wounded flier at low speed, a rate which could not approach the rapid gait of the thoat, whose eight long, powerful legs carried it over the ochre vegetation of the dead sea-bottom at terrific speed.

The Prince of Helium chafed and fretted at the slowness of his pursuit, yet he was thankful that the damage was no worse, for now he could at least move more rapidly than on foot.

But even this meagre satisfaction was soon to be denied him, for presently the flier commenced to sag toward the port and by the bow. The damage to the buoyancy tanks had evidently been more grievous than he had at first believed.

All the balance of that long day Carthoris crawled erratically through the still air, the bow of the flier sinking lower and lower, and the list to port becoming more and more alarming, until at last, near dark, he was floating almost bowdown, his harness buckled to a heavy deck ring to keep him from being precipitated to the ground below.

His forward movement was now confined to a slow drifting with the gentle breeze that blew out of the south-east, and when this died down with the setting of the sun, he let the flier sink gently to the mossy carpet beneath.

Far before him loomed the mountains toward which the green man had been fleeing when last he had seen him, and with dogged resolution the son of John Carter, endowed with the indomitable will of his mighty sire, took up the pursuit on foot.

All that night he forged ahead until, with the dawning of a new day, he entered the low foothills that guard the approach to the fastness of the mountains of Torquas.

Rugged, granitic walls towered before him. Nowhere could he discern an opening through the formidable barrier; yet somewhere into this inhospitable world of stone the green warrior had borne the woman of the red man's heart's desire.

Across the yielding moss of the sea-bottom there had been no spoor to follow, for the soft pads of the thoat but pressed down in his swift passage the resilient vegetation which sprang up again behind his fleeting feet, leaving no sign.

But here in the hills, where loose rock occasionally strewed the way; where black loam and wild flowers partially replaced the sombre monotony of the waste places of the lowlands, Carthoris hoped to find some sign that would lead him in the right direction.

Yet, search as he would, the baffling mystery of the trail seemed likely to remain for ever unsolved.

It was drawing toward the day's close once more when the keen eyes of the Heliumite discerned the tawny yellow of a sleek hide moving among the boulders several hundred yards to his left.

Crouching quickly behind a large rock, Carthoris watched the thing before him. It was a huge banth, one of those savage Barsoomian lions that roam the desolate hills of the dying planet.

The creature's nose was close to the ground. It was evident that he was following the spoor of meat by scent.

As Carthoris watched him, a great hope leaped into the man's heart. Here, possibly, might lie the solution to the mystery he had been endeavouring to solve. This hungry carnivore, keen always for the flesh of man, might even now be trailing the two whom Carthoris sought.

Cautiously the youth crept out upon the trail of the man-eater. Along the foot of the perpendicular cliff the creature moved, sniffing at the invisible spoor, and now and then emitting the low moan of the hunting banth.

Carthoris had followed the creature for but a few minutes when it disappeared as suddenly and mysteriously as though dissolved into thin air.

The man leaped to his feet. Not again was he to be cheated as the man had cheated him. He sprang forward at a reckless pace to the spot at which he last had seen the great, skulking brute.

Before him loomed the sheer cliff, its face unbroken by any aperture into which the huge banth might have wormed its great carcass. Beside him was a small, flat boulder, not larger than the deck of a ten-man flier, nor standing to a greater height than twice his own stature.

Perhaps the banth was in hiding behind this? The brute might have discovered the man upon his trail, and even now be lying in wait for his easy prey.

Cautiously, with drawn long-sword, Carthoris crept around the corner of the rock. There was no banth there, but something which surprised him infinitely more than would the presence of twenty banths.

Before him yawned the mouth of a dark cave leading downward into the ground. Through this the banth must have disappeared. Was it his lair? Within its dark and forbidding interior might there not lurk not one but many of the fearsome creatures?

Carthoris did not know, nor, with the thought that had been spurring him onward upon the trail of the creature uppermost in his mind, did he much care; for into this gloomy cavern he was sure the banth had trailed the green man and his captive, and into it he, too, would follow, content to give his life in the service of the woman he loved.

Not an instant did he hesitate, nor yet did he advance rashly; but with ready sword and cautious steps, for the way was dark, he stole on. As he advanced, the obscurity became impenetrable blackness.

CHAPTER FIVE

The Fair Race

Downward along a smooth, broad floor led the strange tunnel, for such Carthoris was now convinced was the nature of the shaft he at first had thought but a cave.

Before him he could hear the occasional low moans of the banth, and presently from behind came a similar uncanny note. Another banth had entered the passageway on *his* trail!

His position was anything but pleasant. His eyes could not penetrate the darkness even to the distinguishing of his hand before his face, while the banths, he knew, could see quite well, though absence of light were utter.

No other sounds came to his ears than the dismal, bloodthirsty moanings of the beast ahead and the beast behind.

The tunnel had led straight, from where he had entered it beneath the side of the rock furthest from the unscaleable cliffs, toward the mighty barrier that had baffled him so long.

Now it was running almost level, and presently he noted a gradual ascent.

The beast behind him was gaining upon him, crowding him perilously close upon the heels of the beast in front. Presently he should have to do battle with one, or both. More firmly he gripped his weapon.

Now he could hear the breathing of the banth at his heels. Not for much longer could he delay the encounter.

Long since he had become assured that the tunnel led beneath the cliffs to the opposite side of the barrier, and he had hoped that he might reach the moonlit open before being compelled to grapple with either of the monsters.

The sun had been setting as he entered the tunnel, and the way had been sufficiently long to assure him that darkness now reigned upon the world without. He glanced behind him. Blazing out of the darkness, seemingly not ten paces behind, glared two flaming points of fire. As the savage eyes met his, the beast emitted a frightful roar and then he charged.

To face that savage mountain of onrushing ferocity, to stand unshaken before the hideous fangs that he knew were bared in slavering blood-thirstiness, though he could not see them, required nerves of steel; but of such were the nerves of Carthoris of Helium.

He had the brute's eyes to guide his point, and, as true as the sword hand of his mighty sire, his guided the keen point to one of those blazing orbs, even as he leaped lightly to one side.

With a hideous scream of pain and rage, the wounded banth hurtled, clawing, past him. Then it turned to charge once more; but this time Carthoris saw but a single gleaming point of fiery hate directed upon him.

Again the needle point met its flashing target. Again the horrid cry of the stricken beast reverberated through the rocky tunnel, shocking in its torture-laden shrillness, deafening in its terrific volume.

But now, as it turned to charge again, the man had no guide whereby to direct his point. He heard the scraping of the padded feet upon the rocky floor. He knew the thing was charging down upon him once again, but he could see nothing.

Yet, if he could not see his antagonist, neither could his antagonist now see him.

Leaping, as he thought, to the exact centre of the tunnel, he held his sword point ready on a line with the beast's chest. It was all that he could do, hoping that chance might send the point into the savage heart as he went down beneath the great body.

So quickly was the thing over that Carthoris could scarce believe his senses as the mighty body rushed madly past him. Either he had not placed himself in the centre of the tunnel, or else the blinded banth had erred in its calculations.

However, the huge body missed him by a foot, and the creature continued on down the tunnel as though in pursuit of the prey that had eluded him.

Carthoris, too, followed the same direction, nor was it long before his heart was gladdened by the sight of the moonlit exit from the long, dark passage.

Before him lay a deep hollow, entirely surrounded by gigantic cliffs. The surface of the valley was dotted with enormous trees, a strange sight so far from a Martian waterway. The ground itself was clothed in brilliant scarlet sward, picked out with innumerable patches of gorgeous wild flowers.

Beneath the glorious effulgence of the two moons the scene was one of indescribable loveliness, tinged with the weirdness of strange enchantment.

For only an instant, however, did his gaze rest upon the natural beauties outspread before him. Almost immediately they were riveted upon the figure of a great banth standing across the carcass of a new-killed thoat.

The huge beast, his tawny mane bristling around his hideous head, kept his eyes fixed upon another banth that charged erratically hither and thither, with shrill screams of pain, and horrid roars of hate and rage.

Carthoris quickly guessed that the second brute was the one he had blinded during the fight in the tunnel, but it was the dead thoat that centred his interest more than either of the savage carnivores.

The harness was still upon the body of the huge Martian mount, and Carthoris could not doubt but that this was the very animal upon which the green warrior had borne away Thuvia of Ptarth.

But where were the rider and his prisoner? The Prince of Helium shuddered as he thought upon the probability of the fate that had overtaken them.

Human flesh is the food most craved by the fierce Barsoomian lion, whose great carcass and giant thews require enormous quantities of meat to sustain them.

Two human bodies would have but whetted the creature's appetite, and that he had killed and eaten the green man and the red girl seemed only too likely to Carthoris. He had left the carcass of the mighty thoat to be devoured after having consumed the more tooth-some portion of his banquet.

Now the sightless banth, in its savage, aimless charging and counter-charging, had passed beyond the kill of its fellow, and there the light breeze that was blowing wafted the scent of new blood to its nostrils.

No longer were its movements erratic. With outstretched tail and foaming jaws it charged straight as an arrow, for the body of the thoat and the mighty creature of destruction that stood with forepaws upon the slate-grey side, waiting to defend its meat.

When the charging banth was twenty paces from the dead thoat the killer gave vent to its hideous challenge, and with a mighty spring leaped forward to meet it.

The battle that ensued awed even the warlike Barsoomian. The mad rending, the hideous and deafening roaring, the implacable savagery of the blood-stained beasts held him in the paralysis of fascination, and when it was over and the two creatures, their heads and shoulders torn to ribbons, lay with their dead jaws still buried in each other's bodies, Carthoris tore himself from the spell only by an effort of the will.

Hurrying to the side of the dead thoat, he searched for traces of the girl he feared had shared the thoat's fate, but nowhere could he discover anything to confirm his fears.

With slightly lightened heart he started out to explore the valley, but scarce a dozen steps had he taken when the glistening of a jewelled bauble lying on the sward caught his eye.

As he picked it up his first glance showed him that it was a woman's hair ornament, and emblazoned upon it was the insignia of the royal house of Ptarth.

But, sinister discovery, blood, still wet, splotched the magnificent jewels of the setting.

Carthoris half choked as the dire possibilities which the thing suggested presented themselves to his imagination. Yet he could not, would not believe it.

It was impossible that that radiant creature could have met so hideous an end. It was incredible that the glorious Thuvia should ever cease to be.

Upon his already jewel-encrusted harness, to the strap that crossed his great chest beneath which beat his loyal heart, Carthoris, Prince of Helium, fastened the gleaming thing that Thuvia of Ptarth had worn, and wearing, had made holy to the Heliumite.

Then he proceeded upon his way into the heart of the unknown valley.

For the most part the giant trees shut off his view to any but the most limited distances. Occasionally he caught glimpses of the towering hills that bounded the valley upon every side, and though they stood out clear beneath the light of the two moons, he knew that they were far off, and that the extent of the valley was immense.

For half the night he continued his search, until presently he was brought to a sudden halt by the distant sound of squealing thoats.

Guided by the noise of these habitually angry beasts, he stole forward through the trees until at last he came upon a level, treeless plain, in the centre of which a mighty city reared its burnished domes and vividly coloured towers.

About the walled city the red man saw a huge encampment of the green warriors of the dead sea-bottoms, and as he let his eyes rove carefully over the city he realized that here was no deserted metropolis of a dead past.

But what city could it be? His studies had taught him that in this little-explored portion of Barsoom the fierce tribe of Torquasian green men ruled supreme, and that as yet no red man had succeeded in piercing to the heart of their domain to return again to the world of civilization.

The men of Torquas had perfected huge guns with which their uncanny marksmanship had permitted them to repulse the few determined efforts that near-by red nations had made to explore their country by means of battle fleets of airships.

That he was within the boundary of Torquas, Carthoris was sure, but that there existed there such a wondrous city he never had dreamed, nor had the chronicles of the past even hinted at such a possibility, for the Torquasians were known to live, as did the other green men of Mars, within the deserted cities that dotted the dying planet, nor ever had any green horde built so much as a single edifice, other than the low-walled incubators where their young are hatched by the sun's heat.

The encircling camp of green warriors lay about five hundred yards from the city's walls. Between it and the city was no semblance of breastwork or other protection against rifle or cannon fire; yet distinctly now in the light of the rising sun Carthoris could see many figures moving along the summit of the high wall, and upon the roof tops beyond.

That they were beings like himself he was sure, though they were at too great distance from him for him to be positive that they were red men.

Almost immediately after sunrise the green warriors commenced firing upon the little figures upon the wall. To Carthoris' surprise the fire was not returned, but presently the last of the city's inhabitants had sought shelter from the weird marksmanship of the green men, and no further sign of life was visible beyond the wall.

Then Carthoris, keeping within the shelter of the trees that fringed the plain, began circling the rear of the besiegers' line, hoping against hope that somewhere he would obtain sight of Thuvia of Ptarth, for even now he could not believe that she was dead.

That he was not discovered was a miracle, for mounted warriors were constantly riding back and forth from the camp into the forest; but the long day wore on and still he continued his seemingly fruitless quest, until, near sunset, he came opposite a mighty gate in the city's western wall.

Here seemed to be the principal force of the attacking horde. Here a great platform had been erected whereon Carthoris could see squatting a huge green warrior, surrounded by others of his kind.

This, then, must be the notorious Hortan Gur, Jeddak of Torquas, the fierce old ogre of the south-western hemisphere, as only for a jeddak are platforms raised in temporary camps or upon the march by the green hordes of Barsoom.

As the Heliumite watched he saw another green warrior push his way forward toward the rostrum. Beside him he dragged a captive, and as the surrounding warriors parted to let the two pass, Carthoris caught a fleeting glimpse of the prisoner.

His heart leaped in rejoicing. Thuvia of Ptarth still lived!

It was with difficulty that Carthoris restrained the impulse to rush forward to the side of the Ptarthian princess; but in the end his better judgment prevailed, for in the face of such odds he knew that he should have been but throwing away, uselessly, any future opportunity he might have to succour her.

He saw her dragged to the foot of the rostrum. He saw Hortan Gur address her. He could not hear the creature's words, nor Thuvia's reply; but it must have angered the green monster, for Carthoris saw him leap toward the prisoner, striking her a cruel blow across the face with his metal-banded arm.

Then the son of John Carter, Jeddak of Jeddaks, Warlord of Barsoom, went mad. The old, blood-red haze through which his sire had glared at countless foes, floated before his eyes.

His half-Earthly muscles, responding quickly to his will, sent him in enormous leaps and bounds toward the green monster that had struck the woman he loved.

The Torquasians were not looking in the direction of the forest. All eyes had been upon the figures of the girl and their jeddak, and loud was the hideous laughter that rang out in appreciation of the wit of the green emperor's reply to his prisoner's appeal for liberty.

Carthoris had covered about half the distance between the forest and the green warriors, when a new factor succeeded in still further directing the attention of the latter from him.

Upon a high tower within the beleaguered city a man appeared. From his upturned mouth there issued a series of frightful shrieks; uncanny shrieks that swept, shrill and terrifying, across the city's walls, over the heads of the besiegers, and out across the forest to the uttermost confines of the valley.

Once, twice, thrice the fearsome sound smote upon the ears of the listening green men and then far, far off across the broad woods came sharp and clear from the distance an answering shriek.

It was but the first. From every point rose similar savage cries, until the world seemed to tremble to their reverberations.

The green warriors looked nervously this way and that. They knew not fear, as Earth men may know it; but in the face of the unusual their wonted self-assurance deserted them.

And then the great gate in the city wall opposite the platform of Hortan Gur swung suddenly wide. From it issued as strange a sight as Carthoris ever had witnessed, though at the moment he had time to cast but a single fleeting glance at the tall bowmen emerging through the portal behind their long, oval shields; to note their flowing auburn hair; and to realize that the growling things at their side were fierce Barsoomian lions.

Then he was in the midst of the astonished Torquasians. With drawn long-sword he was among them, and to Thuvia of Ptarth, whose startled eyes were the first to fall upon him, it seemed that she was looking upon John Carter himself, so strangely similar to the fighting of the father was that of the son.

Even to the famous fighting smile of the Virginian was the resemblance true. And the sword arm! Ah, the subtleness of it, and the speed!

All about was turmoil and confusion. Green warriors were leaping to the backs of their restive, squealing thoats. Calots were growling out their savage gutturals, whining to be at the throats of the oncoming foemen.

Thar Ban and another by the side of the rostrum had been the first to note the coming of Carthoris, and it was with them he battled for possession of the red girl, while the others hastened to meet the host advancing from the beleaguered city.

Carthoris sought both to defend Thuvia of Ptarth and reach the side of the hideous Hortan Gur that he might avenge the blow the creature had struck the girl.

He succeeded in reaching the rostrum, over the dead bodies of two warriors who had turned to join Thar Ban and his companion in repulsing this adventurous red man, just as Hortan Gur was about to leap from it to the back of his thoat.

The attention of the green warriors turned principally upon the bowmen advancing upon them from the city, and upon the savage banths that paced beside them – cruel beasts of war, infinitely more terrible than their own savage calots.

As Carthoris leaped to the rostrum he drew Thuvia up beside him, and then he turned upon the departing jeddak with an angry challenge and a sword thrust.

As the Heliumite's point pricked his green hide, Hortan Gur turned upon his adversary with a snarl, but at the same instant two of his chieftains called to him to hasten, for the charge of the fair-skinned inhabitants of the city was developing into a more serious matter than the Torquasians had anticipated.

Instead of remaining to battle with the red man, Hortan Gur promised him his attention after he had disposed of the presumptuous citizens of the walled city, and, leaping astride his thoat, galloped off to meet the rapidly advancing bowmen.

The other warriors quickly followed their jeddak, leaving Thuvia and Carthoris alone upon the platform.

Between them and the city raged a terrific battle. The fair-skinned warriors, armed only with their long bows and a kind of short-handled war-axe, were almost helpless beneath the savage mounted green men at close quarters; but at a distance their sharp arrows did fully as much execution as the radium projectiles of the green men.

But if the warriors themselves were outclassed, not so their savage companions, the fierce banths. Scarce had the two lines come together when hundreds of these appalling creatures had leaped among the Torquasians, dragging warriors from their thoats – dragging down the huge thoats themselves, and bringing consternation to all before them.

The numbers of the citizenry, too, was to their advantage, for it seemed that scarce a warrior fell but his place was taken by a score more, in such a constant stream did they pour from the city's great gate.

And so it came, what with the ferocity of the banths and the numbers of the bowmen, that at last the Torquasians fell back, until presently the platform upon which stood Carthoris and Thuvia lay directly in the centre of the fight.

That neither was struck by a bullet or an arrow seemed a miracle to both; but at last the tide had rolled completely past them, so that they were alone between the fighters and the city, except for the dying and the dead, and a score or so of growling banths, less well trained than their fellows, who prowled among the corpses seeking meat.

To Carthoris the strangest part of the battle had been the terrific toll taken by the bowmen with their relatively puny weapons. Nowhere that he could see was there a single wounded green man, but the corpses of their dead lay thick upon the field of battle.

Death seemed to follow instantly the slightest pinprick of a bowman's arrow, nor apparently did one ever miss its goal. There could be but one explanation: the missiles were poison-tipped.

Presently the sounds of conflict died in the distant forest. Quiet reigned, broken only by the growling of the devouring banths. Carthoris turned toward Thuvia of Ptarth. As yet neither had spoken.

"Where are we, Thuvia?" he asked.

The girl looked at him questioningly. His very presence had seemed to proclaim a guilty knowledge of her abduction. How else might he have known the destination of the flier that brought her!

"Who should know better than the Prince of Helium?" she asked in return. "Did he not come hither of his own free will?"

"From Aaanthor I came voluntarily upon the trail of the green man who had stolen you, Thuvia," he replied; "but from the time I left Helium until I awoke above Aaanthor I thought myself bound for Ptarth.

"It had been intimated that I had guilty knowledge of your abduction," he explained simply, "and I was hastening to the jeddak, your father, to convince him of the falsity of the charge, and to give my service to your recovery. Before I left Helium some one tampered with my compass, so that it bore me to Aaanthor instead of to Ptarth. That is all. You believe me?"

"But the warriors who stole me from the garden!" she exclaimed. "After we arrived at Aaanthor they wore the metal of the Prince of Helium. When they took me they were trapped in Dusarian harness. There seemed but a single explanation. Whoever dared the outrage wished to put the onus upon another, should he be detected in the act; but once safely away from Ptarth he felt safe in having his minions return to their own harness."

"You believe that I did this thing, Thuvia?" he asked.

"Ah, Carthoris," she replied sadly, "I did not wish to believe it; but when everything pointed to you – even then I would not believe it."

"I did not do it, Thuvia," he said. "But let me be entirely honest with you. As much as I love your father, as much as I respect Kulan Tith, to whom you are betrothed, as well as I know the frightful consequences that must have followed such an act of mine, hurling into war, as it would, three of the greatest nations of Barsoom – yet, notwithstanding all this, I should not have hesitated to take you thus, Thuvia of Ptarth, had you even hinted that it would not have displeased YOU.

"But you did nothing of the kind, and so I am here, not in my own service, but in yours, and in the service of the man to whom you are promised, to save you for him, if it lies within the power of man to do so," he concluded, almost bitterly.

Thuvia of Ptarth looked into his face for several moments. Her breast was rising and falling as though to some resistless emotion. She half took a step toward him. Her lips parted as though to speak – swiftly and impetuously.

And then she conquered whatever had moved her.

"The future acts of the Prince of Helium," she said coldly, "must constitute the proof of his past honesty of purpose."

Carthoris was hurt by the girl's tone, as much as by the doubt as to his integrity which her words implied.

He had half hoped that she might hint that his love would be acceptable – certainly there was due him at least a little gratitude for his recent acts in her behalf; but the best he received was cold skepticism.

The Prince of Helium shrugged his broad shoulders. The girl noted it, and the little smile that touched his lips, so that it became her turn to be hurt.

Of course she had not meant to hurt him. He might have known that after what he had said she could not do anything to encourage him! But he need not have made his indifference quite so palpable. The men of Helium were noted for their gallantry – not for boorishness. Possibly it was the Earth blood that flowed in his veins.

How could she know that the shrug was but Carthoris' way of attempting, by physical effort, to cast blighting sorrow from his heart, or that the smile upon his lips was the fighting smile of his father with which the son gave outward evidence of the determination he had reached to submerge his own great love in his efforts to save Thuvia of Ptarth for another, because he believed that she loved this other!

He reverted to his original question.

"Where are we?" he asked. "I do not know."

"Nor I," replied the girl. "Those who stole me from Ptarth spoke among themselves of Aaanthor, so that I thought it possible that the ancient city to which they took me was that famous ruin; but where we may be now I have no idea."

"When the bowmen return we shall doubtless learn all that there is to know," said Carthoris. "Let us hope that they prove friendly. What race may they be? Only in the most ancient of our legends and in the mural paintings of the deserted cities of the dead sea-bottoms are depicted such a race of auburn-haired, fair-skinned people. Can it be that we have stumbled upon a surviving city of the past which all Barsoom believes buried beneath the ages?"

Thuvia was looking toward the forest into which the green men and the pursuing bowmen had disappeared. From a great distance came the hideous cries of banths, and an occasional shot.

"It is strange that they do not return," said the girl.

"One would expect to see the wounded limping or being carried back to the city," replied Carthoris, with a puzzled frown. "But how about the wounded nearer the city? Have they carried them within?"

Both turned their eyes toward the field between them and the walled city, where the fighting had been most furious.

There were the banths, still growling about their hideous feast.

Carthoris looked at Thuvia in astonishment. Then he pointed toward the field.

"Where are they?" he whispered. "*What has become of their dead and wounded?*"

CHAPTER SIX

The Jeddak of Lothar

THE GIRL LOOKED her incredulity.

"They lay in piles," she murmured. "There were thousands of them but a minute ago."

"And now," continued Carthoris, "there remain but the banths and the carcasses of the green men."

"They must have sent forth and carried the dead bowmen away while we were talking," said the girl.

"It is impossible!" replied Carthoris. "Thousands of dead lay there upon the field but a moment since. It would have required many hours to have removed them. The thing is uncanny."

"I had hoped," said Thuvia, "that we might find an asylum with these fair-skinned people. Notwithstanding their valour upon the field of battle, they did not strike me as a ferocious or warlike people. I had been about to suggest that we seek entrance to the city, but now I scarce know if I care to venture among people whose dead vanish into thin air."

"Let us chance it," replied Carthoris. "We can be no worse off within their walls than without. Here we may fall prey to the banths or the no less fierce Torquasians. There, at least, we shall find beings moulded after our own images.

"All that causes me to hesitate," he added, "is the danger of taking you past so many banths. A single sword would scarce prevail were even a couple of them to charge simultaneously."

"Do not fear on that score," replied the girl, smiling. "The banths will not harm us."

As she spoke she descended from the platform, and with Carthoris at her side stepped fearlessly out upon the bloody field in the direction of the walled city of mystery.

They had advanced but a short distance when a banth, looking up from its gory feast, descried them. With an angry roar the beast walked quickly in their direction, and at the sound of its voice a score of others followed its example.

Carthoris drew his long-sword. The girl stole a quick glance at his face. She saw the smile upon his lips, and it was as wine to sick nerves; for even upon warlike Barsoom where all men are brave, woman reacts quickly to quiet indifference to danger – to dare-deviltry that is without bombast.

"You may return your sword," she said. "I told you that the banths would not harm us. Look!" and as she spoke she stepped quickly toward the nearest animal.

Carthoris would have leaped after her to protect her, but with a gesture she motioned him back. He heard her calling to the banths in a low, singsong voice that was half purr.

Instantly the great heads went up and all the wicked eyes were riveted upon the figure of the girl. Then, stealthily, they commenced moving toward her. She had stopped now and was standing waiting them.

One, closer to her than the others, hesitated. She spoke to him imperiously, as a master might speak to a refractory hound.

The great carnivore let its head droop, and with tail between its legs came slinking to the girl's feet, and after it came the others until she was entirely surrounded by the savage maneaters.

Turning she led them to where Carthoris stood. They growled a little as they neared the man, but a few sharp words of command put them in their places.

"How do you do it?" exclaimed Carthoris.

"Your father once asked me that same question in the galleries of the Golden Cliffs within the Otz Mountains, beneath the temples of the therns. I could not answer him, nor can I answer you. I do not know whence comes my power over them, but ever since the day that Sator Throg threw me among them in the banth pit of the Holy Therns, and the great creatures fawned upon instead of devouring me, I ever have had the same strange power over them. They come at my call and do my bidding, even as the faithful Woola does the bidding of your mighty sire."

With a word the girl dispersed the fierce pack. Roaring, they returned to their interrupted feast, while Carthoris and Thuvia passed among them toward the walled city.

As they advanced the man looked with wonder upon the dead bodies of those of the green men that had not been devoured or mauled by the banths.

He called the girl's attention to them. No arrows protruded from the great carcasses. Nowhere upon any of them was the sign of mortal wound, nor even slightest scratch or abrasion.

Before the bowmen's dead had disappeared the corpses of the Torquasians had bristled with the deadly arrows of their foes. Where had the slender messengers of death departed? What unseen hand had plucked them from the bodies of the slain?

Despite himself Carthoris could scarce repress a shudder of apprehension as he glanced toward the silent city before them. No longer was sign of life visible upon wall or roof top. All was quiet – brooding, ominous quiet.

Yet he was sure that eyes watched them from somewhere behind that blank wall.

He glanced at Thuvia. She was advancing with wide eyes fixed upon the city gate. He looked in the direction of her gaze, but saw nothing.

His gaze upon her seemed to arouse her as from a lethargy. She glanced up at him, a quick, brave smile touching her lips, and then, as though the act was involuntary, she came close to his side and placed one of her hands in his.

He guessed that something within her that was beyond her conscious control was appealing to him for protection. He threw an arm about her, and thus they crossed the field. She did not draw away from him. It is doubtful that she realized that his arm was there, so engrossed was she in the mystery of the strange city before them.

They stopped before the gate. It was a mighty thing. From its construction Carthoris could but dimly speculate upon its unthinkable antiquity.

It was circular, closing a circular aperture, and the Heliumite knew from his study of ancient Barsoomian architecture that it rolled to one side, like a huge wheel, into an aperture in the wall.

Even such world-old cities as ancient Aaanthor were as yet undreamed of when the races lived that built such gates as these.

As he stood speculating upon the identity of this forgotten city, a voice spoke to them from above. Both looked up. There, leaning over the edge of the high wall, was a man.

His hair was auburn, his skin fair – fairer even than that of John Carter, the Virginian. His forehead was high, his eyes large and intelligent.

The language that he used was intelligible to the two below, yet there was a marked difference between it and their Barsoomian tongue.

"Who are you?" he asked. "And what do you here before the gate of Lothar?"

"We are friends," replied Carthoris. "This be the princess, Thuvia of Ptarth, who was captured by the Torquasian horde. I am Carthoris of Helium, Prince of the house of Tardos Mors, Jeddak of Helium, and son of John Carter, Warlord of Mars, and of his wife, Dejah Thoris."

"'Ptarth'?" repeated the man. "'Helium'?" He shook his head. "I never have heard of these places, nor did I know that there dwelt upon Barsoom a race of thy strange colour. Where may these cities lie, of which you speak? From our loftiest tower we have never seen another city than Lothar."

Carthoris pointed toward the north-east.

"In that direction lie Helium and Ptarth," he said. "Helium is over eight thousand haads from Lothar, while Ptarth lies nine thousand five hundred haads north-east of Helium."[*1]

Still the man shook his head.

"I know of nothing beyond the Lotharian hills," he said. "Naught may live there beside the hideous green hordes of Torquas. They have conquered all Barsoom except this single valley and the city of Lothar. Here we have defied them for countless ages, though periodically they renew their attempts to destroy us. From whence you come I cannot guess unless you be descended from the slaves the Torquasians captured in early times when they reduced the outer world to their vassalage; but we had heard that they destroyed all other races but their own."

Carthoris tried to explain that the Torquasians ruled but a relatively tiny part of the surface of Barsoom, and even this only because their domain held nothing to attract the red race; but the Lotharian could not seem to conceive of anything beyond the valley of Lothar other than a trackless waste peopled by the ferocious green hordes of Torquas.

After considerable parleying he consented to admit them to the city, and a moment later the wheel-like gate rolled back within its niche, and Thuvia and Carthoris entered the city of Lothar.

---

1   On Barsoom the ad is the basis of linear measurement. It is the equivalent of an Earthly foot, measuring about 11.694 Earth inches. As has been my custom in the past, I have generally translated Barsoomian symbols of time, distance, etc., into their Earthly equivalent, as being more easily understood by Earth readers. For those of a more studious turn of mind it may be interesting to know the Martian table of linear measurement, and so I give it here:

    10 sofads = 1 ad

    200 ads = 1 haad

    100 haads = 1 karad

    360 karads = 1 circumference of Mars at equator.

  A haad, or Barsoomian mile, contains about 2,339 Earth feet. A karad is one degree. A sofad about 1.17 Earth inches.

All about them were evidences of fabulous wealth. The facades of the buildings fronting upon the avenue within the wall were richly carven, and about the windows and doors were ofttimes set foot-wide borders of precious stones, intricate mosaics, or tablets of beaten gold bearing bas-reliefs depicting what may have been bits of the history of this forgotten people.

He with whom they had conversed across the wall was in the avenue to receive them. About him were a hundred or more men of the same race. All were clothed in flowing robes and all were beardless.

Their attitude was more of fearful suspicion than antagonism. They followed the new-comers with their eyes; but spoke no word to them.

Carthoris could not but notice the fact that though the city had been but a short time before surrounded by a horde of bloodthirsty demons yet none of the citizens appeared to be armed, nor was there sign of soldiery about.

He wondered if all the fighting men had sallied forth in one supreme effort to rout the foe, leaving the city all unguarded. He asked their host.

The man smiled.

"No creature other than a score or so of our sacred banths has left Lothar to-day," he replied.

"But the soldiers – the bowmen!" exclaimed Carthoris. "We saw thousands emerge from this very gate, overwhelming the hordes of Torquas and putting them to rout with their deadly arrows and their fierce banths."

Still the man smiled his knowing smile.

"Look!" he cried, and pointed down a broad avenue before him.

Carthoris and Thuvia followed the direction indicated, and there, marching bravely in the sunlight, they saw advancing toward them a great army of bowmen.

"Ah!" exclaimed Thuvia. "They have returned through another gate, or perchance these be the troops that remained to defend the city?"

Again the fellow smiled his uncanny smile.

"There are no soldiers in Lothar," he said. "Look!"

Both Carthoris and Thuvia had turned toward him while he spoke, and now as they turned back again toward the advancing regiments their eyes went wide in astonishment, for the broad avenue before them was as deserted as the tomb.

"And those who marched out upon the hordes to-day?" whispered Carthoris. "They, too, were unreal?"

The man nodded.

"But their arrows slew the green warriors," insisted Thuvia.

"Let us go before Tario," replied the Lotharian. "He will tell you that which he deems it best you know. I might tell you too much."

"Who is Tario?" asked Carthoris.

"Jeddak of Lothar," replied the guide, leading them up the broad avenue down which they had but a moment since seen the phantom army marching.

For half an hour they walked along lovely avenues between the most gorgeous buildings that the two had ever seen. Few people were in evidence. Carthoris could not but note the deserted appearance of the mighty city.

At last they came to the royal palace. Carthoris saw it from a distance, and guessing the nature of the magnificent pile wondered that even here there should be so little sign of activity and life.

Not even a single guard was visible before the great entrance gate, nor in the gardens beyond, into which he could see, was there sign of the myriad life that pulses within the precincts of the royal estates of the red jeddaks.

"Here," said their guide, "is the palace of Tario."

As he spoke Carthoris again let his gaze rest upon the wondrous palace. With a startled exclamation he rubbed his eyes and looked again. No! He could not be mistaken. Before the massive gate stood a score of sentries. Within, the avenue leading to the main building was lined on either side by ranks of bowmen. The gardens were dotted with officers and soldiers moving quickly to and fro, as though bent upon the duties of the minute.

What manner of people were these who could conjure an army out of thin air? He glanced toward Thuvia. She, too, evidently had witnessed the transformation.

With a little shudder she pressed more closely toward him.

"What do you make of it?" she whispered. "It is most uncanny."

"I cannot account for it," replied Carthoris, "unless we have gone mad."

Carthoris turned quickly toward the Lotharian. The fellow was smiling broadly.

"I thought that you just said that there were no soldiers in Lothar," said the Heliumite, with a gesture toward the guardsmen. "What are these?"

"Ask Tario," replied the other. "We shall soon be before him."

Nor was it long before they entered a lofty chamber at one end of which a man reclined upon a rich couch that stood upon a high dais.

As the trio approached, the man turned dreamy eyes sleepily upon them. Twenty feet from the dais their conductor halted, and, whispering

to Thuvia and Carthoris to follow his example, threw himself headlong to the floor. Then rising to hands and knees, he commenced crawling toward the foot of the throne, swinging his head to and fro and wiggling his body as you have seen a hound do when approaching its master.

Thuvia glanced quickly toward Carthoris. He was standing erect, with high-held head and arms folded across his broad chest. A haughty smile curved his lips.

The man upon the dais was eyeing him intently, and Carthoris of Helium was looking straight in the other's face.

"Who be these, Jav?" asked the man of him who crawled upon his belly along the floor.

"O Tario, most glorious Jeddak," replied Jav, "these be strangers who came with the hordes of Torquas to our gates, saying that they were prisoners of the green men. They tell strange tales of cities far beyond Lothar."

"Arise, Jav," commanded Tario, "and ask these two why they show not to Tario the respect that is his due."

Jav arose and faced the strangers. At sight of their erect positions his face went livid. He leaped toward them.

"Creatures!" he screamed. "Down! Down upon your bellies before the last of the jeddaks of Barsoom!"

CHAPTER SEVEN

The Phantom Bowmen

As Jav leaped toward him Carthoris laid his hand upon the hilt of his long-sword. The Lotharian halted. The great apartment was empty save for the four at the dais, yet as Jav stepped back from the menace of the Heliumite's threatening attitude the latter found himself surrounded by a score of bowmen.

From whence had they sprung? Both Carthoris and Thuvia looked their astonishment.

Now the former's sword leaped from its scabbard, and at the same instant the bowmen drew back their slim shafts.

Tario had half raised himself upon one elbow. For the first time he saw the full figure of Thuvia, who had been concealed behind the person of Carthoris.

"Enough!" cried the jeddak, raising a protesting hand, but at that very instant the sword of the Heliumite cut viciously at its nearest antagonist.

As the keen edge reached its goal Carthoris let the point fall to the floor, as with wide eyes he stepped backward in consternation, throwing the back of his left hand across his brow. His steel had cut but empty air – his antagonist had vanished – there were no bowmen in the room!

"It is evident that these are strangers," said Tario to Jav. "Let us first determine that they knowingly affronted us before we take measures for punishment."

Then he turned to Carthoris, but ever his gaze wandered to the perfect lines of Thuvia's glorious figure, which the harness of a Barsoomian princess accentuated rather than concealed.

"Who are you," he asked, "who knows not the etiquette of the court of the last of jeddaks?"

"I am Carthoris, Prince of Helium," replied the Heliumite. "And this is Thuvia, Princess of Ptarth. In the courts of our fathers men do not prostrate themselves before royalty. Not since the First Born tore their immortal goddess limb from limb have men crawled upon their bellies to any throne upon Barsoom. Now think you that the daughter of one mighty jeddak and the son of another would so humiliate themselves?"

Tario looked at Carthoris for a long time. At last he spoke.

"There is no other jeddak upon Barsoom than Tario," he said. "There is no other race than that of Lothar, unless the hordes of Torquas may be dignified by such an appellation. Lotharians are white; your skins are red. There are no women left upon Barsoom. Your companion is a woman."

He half rose from the couch, leaning far forward and pointing an accusing finger at Carthoris.

"You are a lie!" he shrieked. "You are both lies, and you dare to come before Tario, last and mightiest of the jeddaks of Barsoom, and assert your reality. Some one shall pay well for this, Jav, and unless I mistake it is yourself who has dared thus flippantly to trifle with the good nature of your jeddak.

"Remove the man. Leave the woman. We shall see if both be lies. And later, Jav, you shall suffer for your temerity. There be few of us left, but – Komal must be fed. Go!"

Carthoris could see that Jav trembled as he prostrated himself once more before his ruler, and then, rising, turned toward the Prince of Helium.

"Come!" he said.

"And leave the Princess of Ptarth here alone?" cried Carthoris.

Jav brushed closely past him, whispering:

"Follow me – he cannot harm her, except to kill; and that he can do whether you remain or not. We had best go now – trust me."

Carthoris did not understand, but something in the urgency of the other's tone assured him, and so he turned away, but not without a glance toward Thuvia in which he attempted to make her understand that it was in her own interest that he left her.

For answer she turned her back full upon him, but not without first throwing him such a look of contempt that brought the scarlet to his cheek.

Then he hesitated, but Jav seized him by the wrist.

"Come!" he whispered. "Or he will have the bowmen upon you, and this time there will be no escape. Did you not see how futile is your steel against thin air!"

Carthoris turned unwillingly to follow. As the two left the room he turned to his companion.

"If I may not kill thin air," he asked, "how, then, shall I fear that thin air may kill me?"

"You saw the Torquasians fall before the bowmen?" asked Jav.

Carthoris nodded.

"So would you fall before them, and without one single chance for self-defence or revenge."

As they talked Jav led Carthoris to a small room in one of the numerous towers of the palace. Here were couches, and Jav bid the Heliumite be seated.

For several minutes the Lotharian eyed his prisoner, for such Carthoris now realized himself to be.

"I am half convinced that you are real," he said at last.

Carthoris laughed.

"Of course I am real," he said. "What caused you to doubt it? Can you not see me, feel me?"

"So may I see and feel the bowmen," replied Jav, "and yet we all know that they, at least, are not real."

Carthoris showed by the expression of his face his puzzlement at each new reference to the mysterious bowmen – the vanishing soldiery of Lothar.

"What, then, may they be?" he asked.

"You really do not know?" asked Jav.

Carthoris shook his head negatively.

"I can almost believe that you have told us the truth and that you are really from another part of Barsoom, or from another world. But tell me, in your own country have you no bowmen to strike terror to the hearts of the green hordesmen as they slay in company with the fierce banths of war?"

"We have soldiers," replied Carthoris. "We of the red race are all soldiers, but we have no bowmen to defend us, such as yours. We defend ourselves."

"You go out and get killed by your enemies!" cried Jav incredulously.

"Certainly," replied Carthoris. "How do the Lotharians?"

"You have seen," replied the other. "We send out our deathless archers – deathless because they are lifeless, existing only in the imaginations of our enemies. It is really our giant minds that defend us, sending out legions of imaginary warriors to materialize before the mind's eye of the foe.

"They see them – they see their bows drawn back – they see their slender arrows speed with unerring precision toward their hearts. And they die – killed by the power of suggestion."

"But the archers that are slain?" exclaimed Carthoris. "You call them deathless, and yet I saw their dead bodies piled high upon the battle-field. How may that be?"

"It is but to lend reality to the scene," replied Jav. "We picture many of our own defenders killed that the Torquasians may not guess that there are really no flesh and blood creatures opposing them.

"Once that truth became implanted in their minds, it is the theory of many of us, no longer would they fall prey to the suggestion of the deadly arrows, for greater would be the suggestion of the truth, and the more powerful suggestion would prevail – it is law."

"And the banths?" questioned Carthoris. "They, too, were but creatures of suggestion?"

"Some of them were real," replied Jav. "Those that accompanied the archers in pursuit of the Torquasians were unreal. Like the archers, they never returned, but, having served their purpose, vanished with the bowmen when the rout of the enemy was assured.

"Those that remained about the field were real. Those we loosed as scavengers to devour the bodies of the dead of Torquas. This thing is de-manded by the realists among us. I am a realist. Tario is an etherealist.

"The etherealists maintain that there is no such thing as matter – that all is mind. They say that none of us exists, except in the imagination of his fellows, other than as an intangible, invisible mentality.

"According to Tario, it is but necessary that we all unite in imagining that there are no dead Torquasians beneath our walls, and there will be none, nor any need of scavenging banths."

"You, then, do not hold Tario's beliefs?" asked Carthoris.

"In part only," replied the Lotharian. "I believe, in fact I know, that there are some truly ethereal creatures. Tario is one, I am convinced. He has no existence except in the imaginations of his people.

"Of course, it is the contention of all us realists that all ethereal-ists are but figments of the imagination. They contend that no food is necessary, nor do they eat; but any one of the most rudimentary intelligence must realize that food is a necessity to creatures having actual existence."

"Yes," agreed Carthoris, "not having eaten to-day I can readily agree with you."

"Ah, pardon me," exclaimed Jav. "Pray be seated and satisfy your hunger," and with a wave of his hand he indicated a bountifully laden table that had not been there an instant before he spoke. Of that Car-thoris was positive, for he had searched the room diligently with his eyes several times.

"It is well," continued Jav, "that you did not fall into the hands of an etherealist. Then, indeed, would you have gone hungry."

"But," exclaimed Carthoris, "this is not real food – it was not here an instant since, and real food does not materialize out of thin air."

Jav looked hurt.

"There is no real food or water in Lothar," he said; "nor has there been for countless ages. Upon such as you now see before you have we existed since the dawn of history. Upon such, then, may you exist."

"But I thought you were a realist," exclaimed Carthoris.

"Indeed," cried Jav, "what more realistic than this bounteous feast? It is just here that we differ most from the etherealists. They claim that it is unnecessary to imagine food; but we have found that for the maintenance of life we must thrice daily sit down to hearty meals.

"The food that one eats is supposed to undergo certain chemical changes during the process of digestion and assimilation, the result, of course, being the rebuilding of wasted tissue.

"Now we all know that mind is all, though we may differ in the interpretation of its various manifestations. Tario maintains that there is no such thing as substance, all being created from the substanceless matter of the brain.

"We realists, however, know better. We know that mind has the power to maintain substance even though it may not be able to create substance – the latter is still an open question. And so we know that in order to maintain our physical bodies we must cause all our organs properly to function.

"This we accomplish by materializing food-thoughts, and by partaking of the food thus created. We chew, we swallow, we digest. All our organs function precisely as if we had partaken of material food. And what is the result? What must be the result? The chemical changes take place through both direct and indirect suggestion, and we live and thrive."

Carthoris eyed the food before him. It seemed real enough. He lifted a morsel to his lips. There was substance indeed. And flavour as well. Yes, even his palate was deceived.

Jav watched him, smiling, as he ate.

"Is it not entirely satisfying?" he asked.

"I must admit that it is," replied Carthoris. "But tell me, how does Tario live, and the other etherealists who maintain that food is unnecessary?"

Jav scratched his head.

"That is a question we often discuss," he replied. "It is the strongest evidence we have of the non-existence of the etherealists; but who may know other than Komal?"

"Who is Komal?" asked Carthoris. "I heard your jeddak speak of him."

Jav bent low toward the ear of the Heliumite, looking fearfully about before he spoke.

"Komal is the essence," he whispered. "Even the etherealists admit that mind itself must have substance in order to transmit to imaginings the appearance of substance. For if there really was no such thing as substance it could not be suggested – what never has been cannot be imagined. Do you follow me?"

"I am groping," replied Carthoris dryly.

"So the essence must be substance," continued Jav. "Komal is the essence of the All, as it were. He is maintained by substance. He eats. He eats the real. To be explicit, he eats the realists. That is Tario's work.

"He says that inasmuch as we maintain that we alone are real we should, to be consistent, admit that we alone are proper food for Komal. Sometimes, as to-day, we find other food for him. He is very fond of Torquasians."

"And Komal is a man?" asked Carthoris.

"He is All, I told you," replied Jav. "I know not how to explain him in words that you will understand. He is the beginning and the end. All life emanates from Komal, since the substance which feeds the brain with imaginings radiates from the body of Komal.

"Should Komal cease to eat, all life upon Barsoom would cease to be. He cannot die, but he might cease to eat, and, thus, to radiate."

"And he feeds upon the men and women of your belief?" cried Carthoris.

"Women!" exclaimed Jav. "There are no women in Lothar. The last of the Lotharian females perished ages since, upon that cruel and terrible journey across the muddy plains that fringed the half-dried seas, when the green hordes scourged us across the world to this our last hiding-place – our impregnable fortress of Lothar.

"Scarce twenty thousand men of all the countless millions of our race lived to reach Lothar. Among us were no women and no children. All these had perished by the way.

"As time went on, we, too, were dying and the race fast approaching extinction, when the Great Truth was revealed to us, that mind is all. Many more died before we perfected our powers, but at last we were able to defy death when we fully understood that death was merely a state of mind.

"Then came the creation of mind-people, or rather the materialization of imaginings. We first put these to practical use when the Torquasians discovered our retreat, and fortunate for us it was that it required ages of search upon their part before they found the single tiny entrance to the valley of Lothar.

"That day we threw our first bowmen against them. The intention was purely to frighten them away by the vast numbers of bowmen which we could muster upon our walls. All Lothar bristled with the bows and arrows of our ethereal host.

"But the Torquasians did not frighten. They are lower than the beasts – they know no fear. They rushed upon our walls, and standing upon the shoulders of others they built human approaches to the wall tops, and were on the very point of surging in upon us and overwhelming us.

"Not an arrow had been discharged by our bowmen – we did but cause them to run to and fro along the wall top, screaming taunts and threats at the enemy.

"Presently I thought to attempt the thing – *the great thing*. I centred all my mighty intellect upon the bowmen of my own creation – each of us produces and directs as many bowmen as his mentality and imagination is capable of.

"I caused them to fit arrows to their bows for the first time. I made them take aim at the hearts of the green men. I made the green men see all this, and then I made them see the arrows fly, and I made them think that the points pierced their hearts.

"It was all that was necessary. By hundreds they toppled from our walls, and when my fellows saw what I had done they were quick to follow my example, so that presently the hordes of Torquas had retreated beyond the range of our arrows.

"We might have killed them at any distance, but one rule of war we have maintained from the first – the rule of realism. We do nothing, or rather we cause our bowmen to do nothing within sight of the enemy that is beyond the understanding of the foe. Otherwise they might guess the truth, and that would be the end of us.

"But after the Torquasians had retreated beyond bowshot, they turned upon us with their terrible rifles, and by constant popping at us made life miserable within our walls.

"So then I bethought the scheme to hurl our bowmen through the gates upon them. You have seen this day how well it works. For ages they have come down upon us at intervals, but always with the same results."

"And all this is due to your intellect, Jav?" asked Carthoris. "I should think that you would be high in the councils of your people."

"I am," replied Jav, proudly. "I am next to Tario."

"But why, then, your cringing manner of approaching the throne?"

"Tario demands it. He is jealous of me. He only awaits the slightest excuse to feed me to Komal. He fears that I may some day usurp his power."

Carthoris suddenly sprang from the table.

"Jav!" he exclaimed. "I am a beast! Here I have been eating my fill, while the Princess of Ptarth may perchance be still without food. Let us return and find some means of furnishing her with nourishment."

The Lotharian shook his head.

"Tario would not permit it," he said. "He will, doubtless, make an etherealist of her."

"But I must go to her," insisted Carthoris. "You say that there are no women in Lothar. Then she must be among men, and if this be so I intend to be near where I may defend her if the need arises."

"Tario will have his way," insisted Jav. "He sent you away and you may not return until he sends for you."

"Then I shall go without waiting to be sent for."

"Do not forget the bowmen," cautioned Jav.

"I do not forget them," replied Carthoris, but he did not tell Jav that he remembered something else that the Lotharian had let drop – something that was but a conjecture, possibly, and yet one well worth pinning a forlorn hope to, should necessity arise.

Carthoris started to leave the room. Jav stepped before him, barring his way.

"I have learned to like you, red man," he said; "but do not forget that Tario is still my jeddak, and that Tario has commanded that you remain here."

Carthoris was about to reply, when there came faintly to the ears of both a woman's cry for help.

With a sweep of his arm the Prince of Helium brushed the Lotharian aside, and with drawn sword sprang into the corridor without.

CHAPTER EIGHT

The Hall of Doom

As Thuvia of Ptarth saw Carthoris depart from the presence of Tario, leaving her alone with the man, a sudden qualm of terror seized her.

There was an air of mystery pervading the stately chamber. Its furnishings and appointments bespoke wealth and culture, and carried the suggestion that the room was often the scene of royal functions which filled it to its capacity.

And yet nowhere about her, in antechamber or corridor, was there sign of any other being than herself and the recumbent figure of Tario, the jeddak, who watched her through half-closed eyes from the gorgeous trappings of his regal couch.

For a time after the departure of Jav and Carthoris the man eyed her intently. Then he spoke.

"Come nearer," he said, and, as she approached: "Whose creature are you? Who has dared materialize his imaginings of woman? It is contrary to the customs and the royal edicts of Lothar. Tell me, woman, from whose brain have you sprung? Jav's? No, do not deny it. I know that it could be no other than that envious realist. He seeks to tempt me. He would see me fall beneath the spell of your charms, and then he, your master, would direct my destiny and – my end. I see it all! I see it all!"

The blood of indignation and anger had been rising to Thuvia's face. Her chin was up, a haughty curve upon her perfect lips.

"I know naught," she cried, "of what you are prating! I am Thuvia, Princess of Ptarth. I am no man's 'creature.' Never before to-day did I lay eyes upon him you call Jav, nor upon your ridiculous city, of which even the greatest nations of Barsoom have never dreamed.

"My charms are not for you, nor such as you. They are not for sale or barter, even though the price were a real throne. And as for using them to win your worse than futile power – " She ended her sentence with a shrug of her shapely shoulders, and a little scornful laugh.

When she had finished Tario was sitting upon the edge of his couch, his feet upon the floor. He was leaning forward with eyes no longer half closed, but wide with a startled expression in them.

He did not seem to note the *lèse majesté* of her words and manner. There was evidently something more startling and compelling about her speech than that.

Slowly he came to his feet.

"By the fangs of Komal!" he muttered. "But you are *real! A real* woman! No dream! No vain and foolish figment of the mind!"

He took a step toward her, with hands outstretched.

"Come!" he whispered. "Come, woman! For countless ages have I dreamed that some day you would come. And now that you are here I can scarce believe the testimony of my eyes. Even now, knowing that you are real, I still half dread that you may be a lie."

Thuvia shrank back. She thought the man mad. Her hand stole to the jewelled hilt of her dagger. The man saw the move, and stopped. A cunning expression entered his eyes. Then they became at once dreamy and penetrating as they fairly bored into the girl's brain.

Thuvia suddenly felt a change coming over her. What the cause of it she did not guess; but somehow the man before her began to assume a new relationship within her heart.

No longer was he a strange and mysterious enemy, but an old and trusted friend. Her hand slipped from the dagger's hilt. Tario came closer. He spoke gentle, friendly words, and she answered him in a voice that seemed hers and yet another's.

He was beside her now. His hand was up her shoulder. His eyes were down-bent toward hers. She looked up into his face. His gaze seemed to bore straight through her to some hidden spring of sentiment within her.

Her lips parted in sudden awe and wonder at the strange revealment of her inner self that was being laid bare before her consciousness. She had known Tario for ever. He was more than friend to her. She moved a little closer to him. In one swift flood of light she knew the truth. She loved Tario, Jeddak of Lothar! She had always loved him.

The man, seeing the success of his strategy, could not restrain a faint smile of satisfaction. Whether there was something in the expression of his face, or whether from Carthoris of Helium in a far chamber of the palace came a more powerful suggestion, who may say? But something there was that suddenly dispelled the strange, hypnotic influence of the man.

As though a mask had been torn from her eyes, Thuvia suddenly saw Tario as she had formerly seen him, and, accustomed as she was to the strange manifestations of highly developed mentality which are common upon Barsoom, she quickly guessed enough of the truth to know that she was in grave danger.

Quickly she took a step backward, tearing herself from his grasp. But the momentary contact had aroused within Tario all the long-buried passions of his loveless existence.

With a muffled cry he sprang upon her, throwing his arms about her and attempting to drag her lips to his.

"Woman!" he cried. "Lovely woman! Tario would make you queen of Lothar. Listen to me! Listen to the love of the last jeddaks of Barsoom."

Thuvia struggled to free herself from his embrace.

"Stop, creature!" she cried. "Stop! I do not love you. Stop, or I shall scream for help!"

Tario laughed in her face.

"'Scream for help,'" he mimicked. "And who within the halls of Lothar is there who might come in answer to your call? Who would dare enter the presence of Tario, unsummoned?"

"There is one," she replied, "who would come, and, coming, dare to cut you down upon your own throne, if he thought that you had offered affront to Thuvia of Ptarth!"

"Who, Jav?" asked Tario.

"Not Jav, nor any other soft-skinned Lotharian," she replied; "but a real man, a real warrior – Carthoris of Helium!"

Again the man laughed at her.

"You forget the bowmen," he reminded her. "What could your red warrior accomplish against my fearless legions?"

Again he caught her roughly to him, dragging her towards his couch.

"If you will not be my queen," he said, "you shall be my slave."

"Neither!" cried the girl.

As she spoke the single word there was a quick move of her right hand; Tario, releasing her, staggered back, both hands pressed to his side. At the same instant the room filled with bowmen, and then the jeddak of Lothar sank senseless to the marble floor.

At the instant that he lost consciousness the bowmen were about to release their arrows into Thuvia's heart. Involuntarily she gave a single cry for help, though she knew that not even Carthoris of Helium could save her now.

Then she closed her eyes and waited for the end. No slender shafts pierced her tender side. She raised her lids to see what stayed the hand of her executioners.

The room was empty save for herself and the still form of the jeddak of Lothar lying at her feet, a little pool of crimson staining the white marble of the floor beside him. Tario was unconscious.

Thuvia was amazed. Where were the bowmen? Why had they not loosed their shafts? What could it all mean?

An instant before the room had been mysteriously filled with armed men, evidently called to protect their jeddak; yet now, with the evidence of her deed plain before them, they had vanished as mysteriously as they had come, leaving her alone with the body of their ruler, into whose side she had slipped her long, keen blade.

The girl glanced apprehensively about, first for signs of the return of the bowmen, and then for some means of escape.

The wall behind the dais was pierced by two small doorways, hidden by heavy hangings. Thuvia was running quickly towards one of these when she heard the clank of a warrior's metal at the end of the apartment behind her.

Ah, if she had but an instant more of time she could have reached that screening arras and, perchance, have found some avenue of escape behind it; but now it was too late – she had been discovered!

With a feeling that was akin to apathy she turned to meet her fate, and there, before her, running swiftly across the broad chamber to her side, was Carthoris, his naked long-sword gleaming in his hand.

For days she had doubted his intentions of the Heliumite. She had thought him a party to her abduction. Since Fate had thrown them together she had scarce favoured him with more than the most perfunctory replies to his remarks, unless at such times as the weird and uncanny happenings at Lothar had surprised her out of her reserve.

She knew that Carthoris of Helium would fight for her; but whether to save her for himself or another, she was in doubt.

He knew that she was promised to Kulan Tith, Jeddak of Kaol, but if he had been instrumental in her abduction, his motives could not be prompted by loyalty to his friend, or regard for her honour.

And yet, as she saw him coming across the marble floor of the audience chamber of Tario of Lothar, his fine eyes filled with apprehension for her safety, his splendid figure personifying all that is finest in the fighting men of martial Mars, she could not believe that any faintest trace of perfidy lurked beneath so glorious an exterior.

Never, she thought, in all her life had the sight of any man been so welcome to her. It was with difficulty that she refrained from rushing forward to meet him.

She knew that he loved her; but, in time, she recalled that she was promised to Kulan Tith. Not even might she trust herself to show too great gratitude to the Heliumite, lest he misunderstand.

Carthoris was by her side now. His quick glance had taken in the scene within the room – the still figure of the jeddak sprawled upon the floor – the girl hastening toward a shrouded exit.

"Did he harm you, Thuvia?" he asked.

She held up her crimsoned blade that he might see it.

"No," she said, "he did not harm me."

A grim smile lighted Carthoris' face.

"Praised be our first ancestor!" he murmured. "And now let us see if we may not make good our escape from this accursed city before the Lotharians discover that their jeddak is no more."

With the firm authority that sat so well upon him in whose veins flowed the blood of John Carter of Virginia and Dejah Thoris of Helium, he grasped her hand and, turning back across the hall, strode toward the great doorway through which Jav had brought them into the presence of the jeddak earlier in the day.

They had almost reached the threshold when a figure sprang into the apartment through another entrance. It was Jav. He, too, took in the scene within at a glance.

Carthoris turned to face him, his sword ready in his hand, and his great body shielding the slender figure of the girl.

"Come, Jav of Lothar!" he cried. "Let us face the issue at once, for only one of us may leave this chamber alive with Thuvia of Ptarth." Then, seeing that the man wore no sword, he exclaimed: "Bring on your bowmen, then, or come with us as my prisoner until we have safely passed the outer portals of thy ghostly city."

"You have killed Tario!" exclaimed Jav, ignoring the other's challenge. "You have killed Tario! I see his blood upon the floor – real blood – real death. Tario was, after all, as real as I. Yet he was an etherealist. He would not materialize his sustenance. Can it be that they are right? Well, we, too, are right. And all these ages we have been quarrelling – each saying that the other was wrong!

"However, he is dead now. Of that I am glad. Now shall Jav come into his own. Now shall Jav be Jeddak of Lothar!"

As he finished, Tario opened his eyes and then quickly sat up.

"Traitor! Assassin!" he screamed, and then: "Kadar! Kadar!" which is the Barsoomian for guard.

Jav went sickly white. He fell upon his belly, wriggling toward Tario.

"Oh, my Jeddak, my Jeddak!" he whimpered. "Jav had no hand in this. Jav, your faithful Jav, but just this instant entered the apartment to find you lying prone upon the floor and these two strangers about to leave. How it happened I know not. Believe me, most glorious Jeddak!"

"Cease, knave!" cried Tario. "I heard your words: 'However, he is dead now. Of that I am glad. Now shall Jav come into his own. Now shall Jav be Jeddak of Lothar.'

"At last, traitor, I have found you out. Your own words have condemned you as surely as the acts of these red creatures have sealed their fates – unless – " He paused. "Unless the woman – "

But he got no further. Carthoris guessed what he would have said, and before the words could be uttered he had sprung forward and struck the man across the mouth with his open palm.

Tario frothed in rage and mortification.

"And should you again affront the Princess of Ptarth," warned the Heliumite, "I shall forget that you wear no sword – not for ever may I control my itching sword hand."

Tario shrank back toward the little doorways behind the dais. He was trying to speak, but so hideously were the muscles of his face working that he could utter no word for several minutes. At last he managed to articulate intelligibly.

"Die!" he shrieked. "Die!" and then he turned toward the exit at his back.

Jav leaped forward, screaming in terror.

"Have pity, Tario! Have pity! Remember the long ages that I have served you faithfully. Remember all that I have done for Lothar. Do not condemn me now to the death hideous. Save me! Save me!"

But Tario only laughed a mocking laugh and continued to back toward the hangings that hid the little doorway.

Jav turned toward Carthoris.

"Stop him!" he screamed. "Stop him! If you love life, let him not leave this room," and as he spoke he leaped in pursuit of his jeddak.

Carthoris followed Jav's example, but the "last of the jeddaks of Barsoom" was too quick for them. By the time they reached the arras behind which he had disappeared, they found a heavy stone door blocking their further progress.

Jav sank to the floor in a spasm of terror.

"Come, man!" cried Carthoris. "We are not dead yet. Let us hasten to the avenues and make an attempt to leave the city. We are still alive, and while we live we may yet endeavour to direct our own destinies. Of what avail, to sink spineless to the floor? Come, be a man!"

Jav but shook his head.

"Did you not hear him call the guards?" he moaned. "Ah, if we could have but intercepted him! Then there might have been hope; but, alas, he was too quick for us."

"Well, well," exclaimed Carthoris impatiently. "What if he did call the guards? There will be time enough to worry about that after they come – at present I see no indication that they have any idea of over-exerting themselves to obey their jeddak's summons."

Jav shook his head mournfully.

"You do not understand," he said. "The guards have already come – and gone. They have done their work and we are lost. Look to the various exits."

Carthoris and Thuvia turned their eyes in the direction of the several doorways which pierced the walls of the great chamber. Each was tightly closed by huge stone doors.

"Well?" asked Carthoris.

"We are to die the death," whispered Jav faintly.

Further than that he would not say. He just sat upon the edge of the jeddak's couch and waited.

Carthoris moved to Thuvia's side, and, standing there with naked sword, he let his brave eyes roam ceaselessly about the great chamber, that no foe might spring upon them unseen.

For what seemed hours no sound broke the silence of their living tomb. No sign gave their executioners of the time or manner of their death. The suspense was terrible. Even Carthoris of Helium began to feel the terrible strain upon his nerves. If he could but know how and whence the hand of death was to strike, he could meet it unafraid, but to suffer longer the hideous tension of this blighting ignorance of the plans of their assassins was telling upon him grievously.

Thuvia of Ptarth drew quite close to him. She felt safer with the feel of his arm against hers, and with the contact of her the man took a new grip upon himself. With his old-time smile he turned toward her.

"It would seem that they are trying to frighten us to death," he said, laughing; "and, shame be upon me that I should confess it, I think they were close to accomplishing their designs upon me."

She was about to make some reply when a fearful shriek broke from the lips of the Lotharian.

"The end is coming!" he cried. "The end is coming! The floor! The floor! Oh, Komal, be merciful!"

Thuvia and Carthoris did not need to look at the floor to be aware of the strange movement that was taking place.

Slowly the marble flagging was sinking in all directions toward the centre. At first the movement, being gradual, was scarce noticeable; but presently the angle of the floor became such that one might stand easily only by bending one knee considerably.

Jav was shrieking still, and clawing at the royal couch that had already commenced to slide toward the centre of the room, where both Thuvia and Carthoris suddenly noted a small orifice which grew in diameter as the floor assumed more closely a funnel-like contour.

Now it became more and more difficult to cling to the dizzy inclination of the smooth and polished marble.

Carthoris tried to support Thuvia, but himself commenced to slide and slip toward the ever-enlarging aperture.

Better to cling to the smooth stone he kicked off his sandals of zitidar hide and with his bare feet braced himself against the sickening tilt, at the same time throwing his arms supportingly about the girl.

In her terror her own hands clasped about the man's neck. Her cheek was close to his. Death, unseen and of unknown form, seemed close upon them, and because unseen and unknowable infinitely more terrifying.

"Courage, my princess," he whispered.

She looked up into his face to see smiling lips above hers and brave eyes, untouched by terror, drinking deeply of her own.

Then the floor sagged and tilted more swiftly. There was a sudden slipping rush as they were precipitated toward the aperture.

Jav's screams rose weird and horrible in their ears, and then the three found themselves piled upon the royal couch of Tario, which had stuck within the aperture at the base of the marble funnel.

For a moment they breathed more freely, but presently they discovered that the aperture was continuing to enlarge. The couch slipped downward. Jav shrieked again. There was a sickening sensation as they felt all let go beneath them, as they fell through darkness to an unknown death.

CHAPTER NINE

The Battle in the Plain

THE DISTANCE FROM THE BOTTOM of the funnel to the floor of the chamber beneath it could not have been great, for all three of the victims of Tario's wrath alighted unscathed.

Carthoris, still clasping Thuvia tightly to his breast, came to the ground catlike, upon his feet, breaking the shock for the girl. Scarce had his feet touched the rough stone flagging of this new chamber than his sword flashed out ready for instant use. But though the room was lighted, there was no sign of enemy about.

Carthoris looked toward Jav. The man was pasty white with fear.

"What is to be our fate?" asked the Heliumite. "Tell me, man! Shake off your terror long enough to tell me, so I may be prepared to sell my life and that of the Princess of Ptarth as dearly as possible."

"Komal!" whispered Jav. "We are to be devoured by Komal!"

"Your deity?" asked Carthoris.

The Lotharian nodded his head. Then he pointed toward a low doorway at one end of the chamber.

"From thence will he come upon us. Lay aside your puny sword, fool. It will but enrage him the more and make our sufferings the worse."

Carthoris smiled, gripping his long-sword the more firmly.

Presently Jav gave a horrified moan, at the same time pointing toward the door.

"He has come," he whimpered.

Carthoris and Thuvia looked in the direction the Lotharian had indicated, expecting to see some strange and fearful creature in human form; but to their astonishment they saw the broad head and great-maned shoulders of a huge banth, the largest that either ever had seen.

Slowly and with dignity the mighty beast advanced into the room. Jav had fallen to the floor, and was wriggling his body in the same servile manner that he had adopted toward Tario. He spoke to the fierce beast as he would have spoken to a human being, pleading with it for mercy.

Carthoris stepped between Thuvia and the banth, his sword ready to contest the beast's victory over them. Thuvia turned toward Jav.

"Is this Komal, your god?" she asked.

Jav nodded affirmatively. The girl smiled, and then, brushing past Carthoris, she stepped swiftly toward the growling carnivore.

In low, firm tones she spoke to it as she had spoken to the banths of the Golden Cliffs and the scavengers before the walls of Lothar.

The beast ceased its growling. With lowered head and catlike purr, it came slinking to the girl's feet. Thuvia turned toward Carthoris.

"It is but a banth," she said. "We have nothing to fear from it."

Carthoris smiled.

"I did not fear it," he replied, "for I, too, believed it to be only a banth, and I have my long-sword."

Jav sat up and gazed at the spectacle before him – the slender girl weaving her fingers in the tawny mane of the huge creature that he had thought divine, while Komal rubbed his hideous snout against her side.

"So this is your god!" laughed Thuvia.

Jav looked bewildered. He scarce knew whether he dare chance offending Komal or not, for so strong is the power of superstition that even though we know that we have been reverencing a sham, yet still we hesitate to admit the validity of our new-found convictions.

"Yes," he said, "this is Komal. For ages the enemies of Tario have been hurled to this pit to fill his maw, for Komal must be fed."

"Is there any way out of this chamber to the avenues of the city?" asked Carthoris.

Jav shrugged.

"I do not know," he replied. "Never have I been here before, nor ever have I cared to do so."

"Come," suggested Thuvia, "let us explore. There must be a way out."

Together the three approached the doorway through which Komal had entered the apartment that was to have witnessed their deaths. Beyond was a low-roofed lair, with a small door at the far end.

This, to their delight, opened to the lifting of an ordinary latch, letting them into a circular arena, surrounded by tiers of seats.

"Here is where Komal is fed in public," explained Jav. "Had Tario dared it would have been here that our fates had been sealed; but he feared too much thy keen blade, red man, and so he hurled us all downward to the pit. I did not know how closely connected were the two chambers. Now we may easily reach the avenues and the city gates. Only the bowmen may dispute the right of way, and, knowing their secret, I doubt that they have power to harm us."

Another door led to a flight of steps that rose from the arena level upward through the seats to an exit at the back of the hall. Beyond this was a straight, broad corridor, running directly through the palace to the gardens at the side.

No one appeared to question them as they advanced, mighty Komal pacing by the girl's side.

"Where are the people of the palace – the jeddak's retinue?" asked Carthoris. "Even in the city streets as we came through I scarce saw sign of a human being, yet all about are evidences of a mighty population."

Jav sighed.

"Poor Lothar," he said. "It is indeed a city of ghosts. There are scarce a thousand of us left, who once were numbered in the millions. Our great city is peopled by the creatures of our own imaginings. For our own needs we do not take the trouble to materialize these peoples of our brain, yet they are apparent to us.

"Even now I see great throngs lining the avenue, hastening to and fro in the round of their duties. I see women and children laughing on the balconies – these we are forbidden to materialize; but yet I see them – they are here. . . . But why not?" he mused. "No longer need I fear Tario – he has done his worst, and failed. Why not indeed?

"Stay, friends," he continued. "Would you see Lothar in all her glory?"

Carthoris and Thuvia nodded their assent, more out of courtesy than because they fully grasped the import of his mutterings.

Jav gazed at them penetratingly for an instant, then, with a wave of his hand, cried: "Look!"

The sight that met them was awe-inspiring. Where before there had been naught but deserted pavements and scarlet swards, yawning windows and tenantless doors, now swarmed a countless multitude of happy, laughing people.

"It is the past," said Jav in a low voice. "They do not see us – they but live the old dead past of ancient Lothar – the dead and crumbled Lothar of antiquity, which stood upon the shore of Throxus, mightiest of the five oceans.

"See those fine, upstanding men swinging along the broad avenue? See the young girls and the women smile upon them? See the men greet them with love and respect? Those be seafarers coming up from their ships which lie at the quays at the city's edge.

"Brave men, they – ah, but the glory of Lothar has faded! See their weapons. They alone bore arms, for they crossed the five seas to strange places where dangers were. With their passing passed the martial spirit of the Lotharians, leaving, as the ages rolled by, a race of spineless cowards.

"We hated war, and so we trained not our youth in warlike ways. Thus followed our undoing, for when the seas dried and the green hordes encroached upon us we could do naught but flee. But we remembered the seafaring bowmen of the days of our glory – it is the memory of these which we hurl upon our enemies."

As Jav ceased speaking, the picture faded, and once more, the three took up their way toward the distant gates, along deserted avenues.

Twice they sighted Lotharians of flesh and blood. At sight of them and the huge banth which they must have recognized as Komal, the citizens turned and fled.

"They will carry word of our flight to Tario," cried Jav, "and soon he will send his bowmen after us. Let us hope that our theory is correct, and that their shafts are powerless against minds cognizant of their unreality. Otherwise we are doomed.

"Explain, red man, to the woman the truths that I have explained to you, that she may meet the arrows with a stronger counter-suggestion of immunity."

Carthoris did as Jav bid him; but they came to the great gates without sign of pursuit developing. Here Jav set in motion the mechanism that rolled the huge, wheel-like gate aside, and a moment later the three, accompanied by the banth, stepped out into the plain before Lothar.

Scarce had they covered a hundred yards when the sound of many men shouting arose behind them. As they turned they saw a company of bowmen debouching upon the plain from the gate through which they had but just passed.

Upon the wall above the gate were a number of Lotharians, among whom Jav recognized Tario. The jeddak stood glaring at them, evidently concentrating all the forces of his trained mind upon them. That he was making a supreme effort to render his imaginary creatures deadly was apparent.

Jav turned white, and commenced to tremble. At the crucial moment he appeared to lose the courage of his conviction. The great banth turned back toward the advancing bowmen and growled. Carthoris placed himself between Thuvia and the enemy and, facing them, awaited the outcome of their charge.

Suddenly an inspiration came to Carthoris.

"Hurl your own bowmen against Tario's!" he cried to Jav. "Let us see a materialized battle between two mentalities."

The suggestion seemed to hearten the Lotharian, and in another moment the three stood behind solid ranks of huge bowmen who hurled taunts and menaces at the advancing company emerging from the walled city.

Jav was a new man the moment his battalions stood between him and Tario. One could almost have sworn the man believed these creatures of his strange hypnotic power to be real flesh and blood.

With hoarse battle cries they charged the bowmen of Tario. Barbed shafts flew thick and fast. Men fell, and the ground was red with gore.

Carthoris and Thuvia had difficulty in reconciling the reality of it all with their knowledge of the truth. They saw utan after utan march from the gate in perfect step to reinforce the outnumbered company which Tario had first sent forth to arrest them.

They saw Jav's forces grow correspondingly until all about them rolled a sea of fighting, cursing warriors, and the dead lay in heaps about the field.

Jav and Tario seemed to have forgotten all else beside the struggling bowmen that surged to and fro, filling the broad field between the forest and the city.

The wood loomed close behind Thuvia and Carthoris. The latter cast a glance toward Jav.

"Come!" he whispered to the girl. "Let them fight out their empty battle – neither, evidently, has power to harm the other. They are like two controversialists hurling words at one another. While they are engaged we may as well be devoting our energies to an attempt to find the passage through the cliffs to the plain beyond."

As he spoke, Jav, turning from the battle for an instant, caught his words. He saw the girl move to accompany the Heliumite. A cunning look leaped to the Lotharian's eyes.

The thing that lay beyond that look had been deep in his heart since first he had laid eyes upon Thuvia of Ptarth. He had not recognized it, however, until now that she seemed about to pass out of his existence.

He centred his mind upon the Heliumite and the girl for an instant.

Carthoris saw Thuvia of Ptarth step forward with outstretched hand. He was surprised at this sudden softening toward him, and it was with a full heart that he let his fingers close upon hers, as together they turned away from forgotten Lothar, into the woods, and bent their steps toward the distant mountains.

As the Lotharian had turned toward them, Thuvia had been surprised to hear Carthoris suddenly voice a new plan.

"Remain here with Jav," she had heard him say, "while I go to search for the passage through the cliffs."

She had dropped back in surprise and disappointment, for she knew that there was no reason why she should not have accompanied him. Certainly she should have been safer with him than left here alone with the Lotharian.

And Jav watched the two and smiled his cunning smile.

When Carthoris had disappeared within the wood, Thuvia seated herself apathetically upon the scarlet sward to watch the seemingly interminable struggles of the bowmen.

The long afternoon dragged its weary way toward darkness, and still the imaginary legions charged and retreated. The sun was about to set when Tario commenced to withdraw his troops slowly toward the city.

His plan for cessation of hostilities through the night evidently met with Jav's entire approval, for he caused his forces to form themselves in orderly utans and march just within the edge of the wood, where they were soon busily engaged in preparing their evening meal, and spreading down their sleeping silks and furs for the night.

Thuvia could scarce repress a smile as she noted the scrupulous care with which Jav's imaginary men attended to each tiny detail of deportment as truly as if they had been real flesh and blood.

Sentries were posted between the camp and the city. Officers clanked hither and thither issuing commands and seeing to it that they were properly carried out.

Thuvia turned toward Jav.

"Why is it," she asked, "that you observe such careful nicety in the regulation of your creatures when Tario knows quite as well as you that they are but figments of your brain? Why not permit them simply to dissolve into thin air until you again require their futile service?"

"You do not understand them," replied Jav. "While they exist they are real. I do but call them into being now, and in a way direct their general actions. But thereafter, until I dissolve them, they are as actual as you or I. Their officers command them, under my guidance. I am the general – that is all. And the psychological effect upon the enemy is far greater than were I to treat them merely as substanceless vagaries.

"Then, too," continued the Lotharian, "there is always the hope, which with us is little short of belief, that some day these materializations will merge into the real – that they will remain, some of them, after we have dissolved their fellows, and that thus we shall have discovered a means for perpetuating our dying race.

"Some there are who claim already to have accomplished the thing. It is generally supposed that the etherealists have quite a few among their number who are permanent materializations. It is even said that such is Tario, but that cannot be, for he existed before we had discovered the full possibilities of suggestion.

"There are others among us who insist that none of us is real. That we could not have existed all these ages without material food and water had we ourselves been material. Although I am a realist, I rather incline toward this belief myself.

"It seems well and sensibly based upon the belief that our ancient forbears developed before their extinction such wondrous mentalities that some of the stronger minds among them lived after the death of their bodies – that we are but the deathless minds of individuals long dead.

"It would appear possible, and yet in so far as I am concerned I have all the attributes of corporeal existence. I eat, I sleep" – he paused, casting a meaning look upon the girl – "I love!"

Thuvia could not mistake the palpable meaning of his words and expression. She turned away with a little shrug of disgust that was not lost upon the Lotharian.

He came close to her and seized her arm.

"Why not Jav?" he cried. "Who more honourable than the second of the world's most ancient race? Your Heliumite? He has gone. He has deserted you to your fate to save himself. Come, be Jav's!"

Thuvia of Ptarth rose to her full height, her lifted shoulder turned toward the man, her haughty chin upraised, a scornful twist to her lips.

"You lie!" she said quietly, "the Heliumite knows less of disloyalty than he knows of fear, and of fear he is as ignorant as the unhatched young."

"Then where is he?" taunted the Lotharian. "I tell you he has fled the valley. He has left you to your fate. But Jav will see that it is a pleasant one. To-morrow we shall return into Lothar at the head of my victorious army, and I shall be jeddak and you shall be my consort. Come!" And he attempted to crush her to his breast.

The girl struggled to free herself, striking at the man with her metal armlets. Yet still he drew her toward him, until both were suddenly startled by a hideous growl that rumbled from the dark wood close behind them.

CHAPTER TEN

Kar Komak, the Bowman

As CARTHORIS MOVED through the forest toward the distant cliffs with Thuvia's hand still tight pressed in his, he wondered a little at the girl's continued silence, yet the contact of her cool palm against his was so pleasant that he feared to break the spell of her new-found reliance in him by speaking.

Onward through the dim wood they passed until the shadows of the quick coming Martian night commenced to close down upon them. Then it was that Carthoris turned to speak to the girl at his side.

They must plan together for the future. It was his idea to pass through the cliffs at once if they could locate the passage, and he was quite positive that they were now close to it; but he wanted her assent to the proposition.

As his eyes rested upon her, he was struck by her strangely ethereal appearance. She seemed suddenly to have dissolved into the tenuous substance of a dream, and as he continued to gaze upon her, she faded slowly from his sight.

For an instant he was dumbfounded, and then the whole truth flashed suddenly upon him. Jav had caused him to believe that Thuvia was accompanying him through the wood while, as a matter of fact, he had detained the girl for himself!

Carthoris was horrified. He cursed himself for his stupidity, and yet he knew that the fiendish power which the Lotharian had invoked to confuse him might have deceived any.

Scarce had he realized the truth than he had started to retrace his steps toward Lothar, but now he moved at a trot, the Earthly thews that he had inherited from his father carrying him swiftly over the soft carpet of fallen leaves and rank grass.

Thuria's brilliant light flooded the plain before the walled city of Lothar as Carthoris broke from the wood opposite the great gate that had given the fugitives egress from the city earlier in the day.

At first he saw no indication that there was another than himself anywhere about. The plain was deserted. No myriad bowmen camped now beneath the overhanging verdure of the giant trees. No gory heaps of tortured dead defaced the beauty of the scarlet sward. All was silence. All was peace.

The Heliumite, scarce pausing at the forest's verge, pushed on across the plain toward the city, when presently he descried a huddled form in the grass at his feet.

It was the body of a man, lying prone. Carthoris turned the figure over upon its back. It was Jav, but torn and mangled almost beyond recognition.

The prince bent low to note if any spark of life remained, and as he did so the lids raised and dull, suffering eyes looked up into his.

"The Princess of Ptarth!" cried Carthoris. "Where is she? Answer me, man, or I complete the work that another has so well begun."

"Komal," muttered Jav. "He sprang upon me . . . and would have devoured me but for the girl. Then they went away together into the wood – the girl and the great banth . . . her fingers twined in his tawny mane."

"Which way went they?" asked Carthoris.

"There," replied Jav faintly, "toward the passage through the cliffs."

The Prince of Helium waited to hear no more, but springing to his feet, raced back again into the forest.

It was dawn when he reached the mouth of the dark tunnel that would lead him to the other world beyond this valley of ghostly memories and strange hypnotic influences and menaces.

Within the long, dark passages he met with no accident or obstacle, coming at last into the light of day beyond the mountains, and no great distance from the southern verge of the domains of the Torquasians, not more than one hundred and fifty haad at the most.

From the boundary of Torquas to the city of Aaanthor is a distance of some two hundred haads, so that the Heliumite had before him a journey of more than one hundred and fifty Earth miles between him and Aaanthor.

He could at best but hazard a chance guess that toward Aaanthor Thuvia would take her flight. There lay the nearest water, and there might be expected some day a rescuing party from her father's empire; for Carthoris knew Thuvan Dihn well enough to know that he would leave no stone unturned until he had tracked down the truth as to his daughter's abduction, and learned all that there might be to learn of her whereabouts.

He realized, of course, that the trick which had laid suspicion upon him would greatly delay the discovery of the truth, but little did he guess to what vast proportions had the results of the villainy of Astok of Dusar already grown.

Even as he emerged from the mouth of the passage to look across the foothills in the direction of Aaanthor, a Ptarth battle fleet was winging its majestic way slowly toward the twin cities of Helium, while from far distant Kaol raced another mighty armada to join forces with its ally.

He did not know that in the face of the circumstantial evidence against him even his own people had commenced to entertain suspicions that he might have stolen the Ptarthian princess.

He did not know of the lengths to which the Dusarians had gone to disrupt the friendship and alliance which existed between the three great powers of the eastern hemisphere – Helium, Ptarth and Kaol.

How Dusarian emissaries had found employment in important posts in the foreign offices of the three great nations, and how, through these men, messages from one jeddak to another were altered and garbled until the patience and pride of the three rulers and former friends could no longer endure the humiliations and insults contained in these falsified papers – not any of this he knew.

Nor did he know how even to the last John Carter, Warlord of Mars, had refused to permit the jeddak of Helium to declare war against either Ptarth or Kaol, because of his implicit belief in his son, and that eventually all would be satisfactorily explained.

And now two great fleets were moving upon Helium, while the Dusarian spies at the court of Tardos Mors saw to it that the twin cities remained in ignorance of their danger.

War had been declared by Thuvan Dihn, but the messenger who had been dispatched with the proclamation had been a Dusarian who had seen to it that no word of warning reached the twin cities of the approach of a hostile fleet.

For several days diplomatic relations had been severed between Helium and her two most powerful neighbors, and with the departure of the ministers had come a total cessation of wireless communication between the disputants, as is usual upon Barsoom.

But of all this Carthoris was ignorant. All that interested him at present was the finding of Thuvia of Ptarth. Her trail beside that of the huge banth had been well marked to the tunnel, and was once more visible leading southward into the foothills.

As he followed rapidly downward toward the dead sea-bottom, where he knew he must lose the spoor in the resilient ochre vegetation, he was suddenly surprised to see a naked man approaching him from the north-east.

As the fellow drew closer, Carthoris halted to await his coming. He knew that the man was unarmed, and that he was apparently a Lotharian, for his skin was white and his hair auburn.

He approached the Heliumite without sign of fear, and when quite close called out the cheery Barsoomian "kaor" of greeting.

"Who are you?" asked Carthoris.

"I am Kar Komak, odwar of the bowmen," replied the other. "A strange thing has happened to me. For ages Tario has been bringing me into existence as he needed the services of the army of his mind. Of all the bowmen it has been Kar Komak who has been oftenest materialized.

"For a long time Tario has been concentrating his mind upon my permanent materialization. It has been an obsession with him that some day this thing could be accomplished and the future of Lothar assured. He asserted that matter was nonexistent except in the imagination of man – that all was mental, and so he believed that by persisting in his suggestion he could eventually make of me a permanent suggestion in the minds of all creatures.

"Yesterday he succeeded, but at such a time! It must have come all unknown to him, as it came to me without my knowledge, as, with my horde of yelling bowmen, I pursued the fleeing Torquasians back to their ochre plains.

"As darkness settled and the time came for us to fade once more into thin air, I suddenly found myself alone upon the edge of the great plain which lies yonder at the foot of the low hills.

"My men were gone back to the nothingness from which they had sprung, but I remained – naked and unarmed.

"At first I could not understand, but at last came a realization of what had occurred. Tario's long suggestions had at last prevailed, and Kar Komak had become a reality in the world of men; but my harness and my weapons had faded away with my fellows, leaving me naked and unarmed in a hostile country far from Lothar."

"You wish to return to Lothar?" asked Carthoris.

"No!" replied Kar Komak quickly. "I have no love for Tario. Being a creature of his mind, I know him too well. He is cruel and tyrannical – a master I have no desire to serve. Now that he has succeeded in accomplishing my permanent materialization, he will be unbearable, and he will go on until he has filled Lothar with his creatures. I wonder if he has succeeded as well with the maid of Lothar."

"I thought there were no women there," said Carthoris.

"In a hidden apartment in the palace of Tario," replied Kar Komak, "the jeddak has maintained the suggestion of a beautiful girl, hoping that some day she would become permanent. I have seen her there. She is wonderful! But for her sake I hope that Tario succeeds not so well with her as he has with me.

"Now, red man, I have told you of myself – what of you?"

Carthoris liked the face and manner of the bowman. There had been no sign of doubt or fear in his expression as he had approached the heavily-armed Heliumite, and he had spoken directly and to the point.

So the Prince of Helium told the bowman of Lothar who he was and what adventure had brought him to this far country.

"Good!" exclaimed the other, when he had done. "Kar Komak will accompany you. Together we shall find the Princess of Ptarth and with you Kar Komak will return to the world of men – such a world as he knew in the long-gone past when the ships of mighty Lothar ploughed angry Throxus, and the roaring surf beat against the barrier of these parched and dreary hills."

"What mean you?" asked Carthoris. "Had you really a former actual existence?"

"Most assuredly," replied Kar Komak. "In my day I commanded the fleets of Lothar – mightiest of all the fleets that sailed the five salt seas.

"Wherever men lived upon Barsoom there was the name of Kar Komak known and respected. Peaceful were the land races in those distant days – only the seafarers were warriors; but now has the glory of the past faded, nor did I think until I met you that there remained upon Barsoom a single person of our own mould who lived and loved and fought as did the ancient seafarers of my time.

"Ah, but it will seem good to see men once again – real men! Never had I much respect for the landsmen of my day. They remained in their walled cities wasting their time in play, depending for their protection entirely upon the sea race. And the poor creatures who remain, the Tarios and Javs of Lothar, are even worse than their ancient forbears."

Carthoris was a trifle skeptical as to the wisdom of permitting the stranger to attach himself to him. There was always the chance that he was but the essence of some hypnotic treachery which Tario or Jav was attempting to exert upon the Heliumite; and yet, so sincere had been the manner and the words of the bowman, so much the fighting man did he seem, but Carthoris could not find it in his heart to doubt him.

The outcome of the matter was that he gave the naked odwar leave to accompany him, and together they set out upon the spoor of Thuvia and Komal.

Down to the ochre sea-bottom the trail led. There it disappeared, as Carthoris had known that it would; but where it entered the plain its direction had been toward Aaanthor and so toward Aaanthor the two turned their faces.

It was a long and tedious journey, fraught with many dangers. The bowman could not travel at the pace set by Carthoris, whose muscles carried him with great rapidity over the face of the small planet, the force of gravity of which exerts so much less retarding power than that of the Earth. Fifty miles a day is a fair average for a Barsoomian, but the son of John Carter might easily have covered a hundred or more miles had he cared to desert his new-found comrade.

All the way they were in constant danger of discovery by roving bands of Torquasians, and especially was this true before they reached the boundary of Torquas.

Good fortune was with them, however, and although they sighted two detachments of the savage green men, they were not themselves seen.

And so they came, upon the morning of the third day, within sight of the glistening domes of distant Aaanthor. Throughout the journey Carthoris had ever strained his eyes ahead in search of Thuvia and the great banth; but not till now had he seen aught to give him hope.

This morning, far ahead, half-way between themselves and Aaanthor, the men saw two tiny figures moving toward the city. For a moment they watched them intently. Then Carthoris, convinced, leaped forward at a rapid run, Kar Komak following as swiftly as he could.

The Heliumite shouted to attract the girl's attention, and presently he was rewarded by seeing her turn and stand looking toward him. At her side the great banth stood with up-pricked ears, watching the approaching man.

Not yet could Thuvia of Ptarth have recognized Carthoris, though that it was he she must have been convinced, for she waited there for him without sign of fear.

Presently he saw her point toward the northwest, beyond him. Without slackening his pace, he turned his eyes in the direction she indicated.

Racing silently over the thick vegetation, not half a mile behind, came a score of fierce green warriors, charging him upon their mighty thoats.

To their right was Kar Komak, naked and unarmed, yet running valiantly toward Carthoris and shouting warning as though he, too, had but just discovered the silent, menacing company that moved so swiftly forward with couched spears and ready long-swords.

Carthoris shouted to the Lotharian, warning him back, for he knew that he could but uselessly sacrifice his life by placing himself, all unarmed, in the path of the cruel and relentless savages.

But Kar Komak never hesitated. With shouts of encouragement to his new friend, he hurried onward toward the Prince of Helium. The red man's heart leaped in response to this exhibition of courage and self-sacrifice. He regretted now that he had not thought to give Kar Komak one of his swords; but it was too late to attempt it, for should he wait for the Lotharian to overtake him or return to meet him, the Torquasians would reach Thuvia of Ptarth before he could do so.

Even as it was, it would be nip and tuck as to who came first to her side.

Again he turned his face in her direction, and now, from Aaanthor way, he saw a new force hastening toward them – two medium-sized war craft – and even at the distance they still were from him he discerned the device of Dusar upon their bows.

Now, indeed, seemed little hope for Thuvia of Ptarth. With savage warriors of the hordes of Torquas charging toward her from one direction, and no less implacable enemies, in the form of the creatures of Astok, Prince of Dusar, bearing down upon her from another, while only a banth, a red warrior, and an unarmed bowman were near to defend her, her plight was quite hopeless and her cause already lost ere ever it was contested.

As Thuvia saw Carthoris approaching, she felt again that unaccountable sensation of entire relief from responsibility and fear that she had experienced upon a former occasion. Nor could she account for it while her mind still tried to convince her heart that the Prince of Helium had been instrumental in her abduction from her father's court. She only knew that she was glad when he was by her side, and that with him there all things seemed possible – even such impossible things as escape from her present predicament.

Now had he stopped, panting, before her. A brave smile of encouragement lit his face.

"Courage, my princess," he whispered.

To the girl's memory flashed the occasion upon which he had used those same words – in the throne-room of Tario of Lothar as they had commenced to slip down the sinking marble floor toward an unknown fate.

Then she had not chidden him for the use of that familiar salutation, nor did she chide him now, though she was promised to another. She wondered at herself – flushing at her own turpitude; for upon Barsoom it is a shameful thing for a woman to listen to those two words from another than her husband or her betrothed.

Carthoris saw her flush of mortification, and in an instant regretted his words. There was but a moment before the green warriors would be upon them.

"Forgive me!" said the man in a low voice. "Let my great love be my excuse – that, and the belief that I have but a moment more of life," and with the words he turned to meet the foremost of the green warriors.

The fellow was charging with couched spear, but Carthoris leaped to one side, and as the great thoat and its rider hurtled harmlessly past him he swung his long-sword in a mighty cut that clove the green carcass in twain.

At the same moment Kar Komak leaped with bare hands clawing at the leg of another of the huge riders; the balance of the horde raced in to close quarters, dismounting the better to wield their favourite long-swords; the Dusarian fliers touched the soft carpet of the ochre-clad sea-bottom, disgorging fifty fighting men from their bowels; and into the swirling sea of cutting, slashing swords sprang Komal, the great banth.

CHAPTER ELEVEN

Green Men and White Apes

A Torquasian sword smote a glancing blow across the forehead of Carthoris. He had a fleeting vision of soft arms about his neck, and warm lips close to his before he lost consciousness.

How long he lay there senseless he could not guess; but when he opened his eyes again he was alone, except for the bodies of the dead green men and Dusarians, and the carcass of a great banth that lay half across his own.

Thuvia was gone, nor was the body of Kar Komak among the dead.

Weak from loss of blood, Carthoris made his way slowly toward Aaanthor, reaching its outskirts at dark.

He wanted water more than any other thing, and so he kept on up a broad avenue toward the great central plaza, where he knew the precious fluid was to be found in a half-ruined building opposite the great palace of the ancient jeddak, who once had ruled this mighty city.

Disheartened and discouraged by the strange sequence of events that seemed fore-ordained to thwart his every attempt to serve the Princess of Ptarth, he paid little or no attention to his surroundings, moving through the deserted city as though no great white apes lurked in the black shadows of the mystery-haunted piles that flanked the broad avenues and the great plaza.

But if Carthoris was careless of his surroundings, not so other eyes that watched his entrance into the plaza, and followed his slow footsteps toward the marble pile that housed the tiny, half-choked spring whose water one might gain only by scratching a deep hole in the red sand that covered it.

And as the Heliumite entered the small building a dozen mighty, grotesque figures emerged from the doorway of the palace to speed noiselessly across the plaza toward him.

For half an hour Carthoris remained in the building, digging for water and gaining the few much-needed drops which were the fruits of his labour. Then he rose and slowly left the structure. Scarce had he stepped beyond the threshold than twelve Torquasian warriors leaped upon him.

No time then to draw long-sword; but swift from his harness flew his long, slim dagger, and as he went down beneath them more than a single green heart ceased beating at the bite of that keen point.

Then they overpowered him and took his weapons away; but only nine of the twelve warriors who had crossed the plaza returned with their prize.

They dragged their prisoner roughly to the palace pits, where in utter darkness they chained him with rusty links to the solid masonry of the wall.

"To-morrow Thar Ban will speak with you," they said. "Now he sleeps. But great will be his pleasure when he learns who has wandered amongst us – and great will be the pleasure of Hortan Gur when Thar Ban drags before him the mad fool who dared prick the great jeddak with his sword."

Then they left him to the silence and the darkness.

For what seemed hours Carthoris squatted upon the stone floor of his prison, his back against the wall in which was sunk the heavy eyebolt that secured the chain which held him.

Then, from out of the mysterious blackness before him, there came to his ears the sound of naked feet moving stealthily upon stone – approaching nearer and nearer to where he lay, unarmed and defenceless.

Minutes passed – minutes that seemed hours – during which time periods of sepulchral silence would be followed by a repetition of the uncanny scraping of naked feet slinking warily upon him.

At last he heard a sudden rush of unshod soles across the empty blackness, and at a little distance a scuffling sound, heavy breathing, and once what he thought the muttered imprecation of a man battling against great odds. Then the clanging of a chain, and a noise as of the snapping back against stone of a broken link.

Again came silence. But for a moment only. Now he heard once more the soft feet approaching him. He thought that he discerned wicked eyes gleaming fearfully at him through the darkness. He knew that he could hear the heavy breathing of powerful lungs.

Then came the rush of many feet toward him, and the *things* were upon him.

Hands terminating in manlike fingers clutched at his throat and arms and legs. Hairy bodies strained and struggled against his own smooth hide as he battled in grim silence against these horrid foemen in the darkness of the pits of ancient Aaanthor.

Thewed like some giant god was Carthoris of Helium, yet in the clutches of these unseen creatures of the pit's Stygian night he was helpless as a frail woman.

Yet he battled on, striking futile blows against great, hispid breasts he could not see; feeling thick, squat throats beneath his fingers; the drool of saliva upon his cheek, and hot, foul breath in his nostrils.

Fangs, too, mighty fangs, he knew were close, and why they did not sink into his flesh he could not guess.

At last he became aware of the mighty surging of a number of his antagonists back and forth upon the great chain that held him, and presently came the same sound that he had heard at a little distance from him a short time before he had been attacked – his chain had parted and the broken end snapped back against the stone wall.

Now he was seized upon either side and dragged at a rapid pace through the dark corridors – toward what fate he could not even guess.

At first he had thought his foes might be of the tribe of Torquas, but their hairy bodies belied that belief. Now he was at last quite sure of their identity, though why they had not killed and devoured him at once he could not imagine.

After half an hour or more of rapid racing through the underground passages that are a distinguishing feature of all Barsoomian cities, modern as well as ancient, his captors suddenly emerged into the moonlight of a courtyard, far from the central plaza.

Immediately Carthoris saw that he was in the power of a tribe of the great white apes of Barsoom. All that had caused him doubt before as to the identity of his attackers was the hairiness of their breasts, for the white apes are entirely hairless except for a great shock bristling from their heads.

Now he saw the cause of that which had deceived him – across the chest of each of them were strips of hairy hide, usually of banth, in imitation of the harness of the green warriors who so often camped at their deserted city.

Carthoris had read of the existence of tribes of apes that seemed to be progressing slowly toward higher standards of intelligence. Into the hands of such, he realized, he had fallen; but – what were their intentions toward him?

As he glanced about the courtyard, he saw fully fifty of the hideous beasts, squatting on their haunches, and at a little distance from him another human being, closely guarded.

As his eyes met those of his fellow-captive a smile lit the other's face, and: "Kaor, red man!" burst from his lips. It was Kar Komak, the bowman.

"Kaor!" cried Carthoris, in response. "How came you here, and what befell the princess?"

"Red men like yourself descended in mighty ships that sailed the air, even as the great ships of my distant day sailed the five seas," replied Kar Komak. "They fought with the green men of Torquas. They slew Komal, god of Lothar. I thought they were your friends, and I was glad when finally those of them who survived the battle carried the red girl to one of the ships and sailed away with her into the safety of the high air.

"Then the green men seized me, and carried me to a great, empty city, where they chained me to a wall in a black pit. Afterward came these and dragged me hither. And what of you, red man?"

Carthoris related all that had befallen him, and as the two men talked the great apes squatted about them watching them intently.

"What are we to do now?" asked the bowman.

"Our case looks rather hopeless," replied Carthoris ruefully. "These creatures are born man-eaters. Why they have not already devoured us I cannot imagine – there!" he whispered. "See? The end is coming."

Kar Komak looked in the direction Carthoris indicated to see a huge ape advancing with a mighty bludgeon.

"It is thus they like best to kill their prey," said Carthoris.

"Must we die without a struggle?" asked Kar Komak.

"Not I," replied Carthoris, "though I know how futile our best defence must be against these mighty brutes! Oh, for a long-sword!"

"Or a good bow," added Kar Komak, "and a utan of bowmen."

At the words Carthoris half sprang to his feet, only to be dragged roughly down by his guard.

"Kar Komak!" he cried. "Why cannot you do what Tario and Jav did? They had no bowmen other than those of their own creation. You must know the secret of their power. Call forth your own utan, Kar Komak!"

The Lotharian looked at Carthoris in wide-eyed astonishment as the full purport of the suggestion bore in upon his understanding.

"Why not?" he murmured.

The savage ape bearing the mighty bludgeon was slinking toward Carthoris. The Heliumite's fingers were working as he kept his eyes upon his executioner. Kar Komak bent his gaze penetratingly upon the apes. The effort of his mind was evidenced in the sweat upon his contracted brows.

The creature that was to slay the red man was almost within arm's reach of his prey when Carthoris heard a hoarse shout from the opposite side of the courtyard. In common with the squatting apes and the demon with the club he turned in the direction of the sound, to see a company of sturdy bowmen rushing from the doorway of a near-by building.

With screams of rage the apes leaped to their feet to meet the charge. A volley of arrows met them half-way, sending a dozen rolling lifeless to the ground. Then the apes closed with their adversaries. All their attention was occupied by the attackers – even the guard had deserted the prisoners to join in the battle.

"Come!" whispered Kar Komak. "Now may we escape while their attention is diverted from us by my bowmen."

"And leave those brave fellows leaderless?" cried Carthoris, whose loyal nature revolted at the merest suggestion of such a thing.

Kar Komak laughed.

"You forget," he said, "that they are but thin air – figments of my brain. They will vanish, unscathed, when we have no further need for them. Praised be your first ancestor, redman, that you thought of this chance in time! It would never have occurred to me to imagine that I might wield the same power that brought me into existence."

"You are right," said Carthoris. "Still, I hate to leave them, though there is naught else to do," and so the two turned from the courtyard, and making their way into one of the broad avenues, crept stealthily in the shadows of the building toward the great central plaza upon which were the buildings occupied by the green warriors when they visited the deserted city.

When they had come to the plaza's edge Carthoris halted.

"Wait here," he whispered. "I go to fetch thoats, since on foot we may never hope to escape the clutches of these green fiends."

To reach the courtyard where the thoats were kept it was necessary for Carthoris to pass through one of the buildings which surrounded the square. Which were occupied and which not he could not even guess, so he was compelled to take considerable chances to gain the enclosure in which he could hear the restless beasts squealing and quarrelling among themselves.

Chance carried him through a dark doorway into a large chamber in which lay a score or more green warriors wrapped in their sleeping silks and furs. Scarce had Carthoris passed through the short hallway that connected the door of the building and the great room beyond it than he became aware of the presence of something or some one in the hallway through which he had but just passed.

He heard a man yawn, and then, behind him, he saw the figure of a sentry rise from where the fellow had been dozing, and stretching himself resume his wakeful watchfulness.

Carthoris realized that he must have passed within a foot of the warrior, doubtless rousing him from his slumber. To retreat now would be impossible. Yet to cross through that roomful of sleeping warriors seemed almost equally beyond the pale of possibility.

Carthoris shrugged his broad shoulders and chose the lesser evil. Warily he entered the room. At his right, against the wall, leaned several swords and rifles and spears – extra weapons which the warriors had stacked here ready to their hands should there be a night alarm calling them suddenly from slumber. Beside each sleeper lay his weapon – these were never far from their owners from childhood to death.

The sight of the swords made the young man's palm itch. He stepped quickly to them, selecting two short-swords – one for Kar Komak, the other for himself; also some trappings for his naked comrade.

Then he started directly across the centre of the apartment among the sleeping Torquasians.

Not a man of them moved until Carthoris had completed more than half of the short though dangerous journey. Then a fellow directly in his path turned restlessly upon his sleeping silks and furs.

The Heliumite paused above him, one of the short-swords in readiness should the warrior awaken. For what seemed an eternity to the young prince the green man continued to move uneasily upon his couch, then, as though actuated by springs, he leaped to his feet and faced the red man.

Instantly Carthoris struck, but not before a savage grunt escaped the other's lips. In an instant the room was in turmoil. Warriors leaped to their feet, grasping their weapons as they rose, and shouting to one another for an explanation of the disturbance.

To Carthoris all within the room was plainly visible in the dim light reflected from without, for the further moon stood directly at zenith; but to the eyes of the newly-awakened green men objects as yet had not taken on familiar forms – they but saw vaguely the figures of warriors moving about their apartment.

Now one stumbled against the corpse of him whom Carthoris had slain. The fellow stooped and his hand came in contact with the cleft skull. He saw about him the giant figures of other green men, and so he jumped to the only conclusion that was open to him.

"The Thurds!" he cried. "The Thurds are upon us! Rise, warriors of Torquas, and drive home your swords within the hearts of Torquas' ancient enemies!"

Instantly the green men began to fall upon one another with naked swords. Their savage lust of battle was aroused. To fight, to kill, to die with cold steel buried in their vitals! Ah, that to them was Nirvana.

Carthoris was quick to guess their error and take advantage of it. He knew that in the pleasure of killing they might fight on long after they had discovered their mistake, unless their attention was distracted by sight of the real cause of the altercation, and so he lost no time in continuing across the room to the doorway upon the opposite side, which opened into the inner court, where the savage thoats were squealing and fighting among themselves.

Once here he had no easy task before him. To catch and mount one of these habitually rageful and intractable beasts was no child's play under the best of conditions; but now, when silence and time were such important considerations, it might well have seemed quite hopeless to a less resourceful and optimistic man than the son of the great warlord.

From his father he had learned much concerning the traits of these mighty beasts, and from Tars Tarkas, also, when he had visited that great green jeddak among his horde at Thark. So now he centred upon the work in hand all that he had ever learned about them from others and from his own experience, for he, too, had ridden and handled them many times.

The temper of the thoats of Torquas appeared even shorter than their vicious cousins among the Tharks and Warhoons, and for a time it seemed unlikely that he should escape a savage charge on the part of a couple of old bulls that circled, squealing, about him; but at last he managed to get close enough to one of them to touch the beast. With the feel of his hand upon the sleek hide the creature quieted, and in answer to the telepathic command of the red man sank to its knees.

In a moment Carthoris was upon its back, guiding it toward the great gate that leads from the courtyard through a large building at one end into an avenue beyond.

The other bull, still squealing and enraged, followed after his fellow. There was no bridle upon either, for these strange creatures are controlled entirely by suggestion – when they are controlled at all.

Even in the hands of the giant green men bridle reins would be hopelessly futile against the mad savagery and mastodonic strength of the thoat, and so they are guided by that strange telepathic power with which the men of Mars have learned to communicate in a crude way with the lower orders of their planet.

With difficulty Carthoris urged the two beasts to the gate, where, leaning down, he raised the latch. Then the thoat that he was riding placed his great shoulder to the skeel-wood planking, pushed through, and a moment later the man and the two beasts were swinging silently down the avenue to the edge of the plaza, where Kar Komak hid.

Here Carthoris found considerable difficulty in subduing the second thoat, and as Kar Komak had never before ridden one of the beasts, it seemed a most hopeless job; but at last the bowman managed to scramble to the sleek back, and again the two beasts fled softly down the moss-grown avenues toward the open sea-bottom beyond the city.

All that night and the following day and the second night they rode toward the north-east. No indication of pursuit developed, and at dawn of the second day Carthoris saw in the distance the waving ribbon of great trees that marked one of the long Barsoomian water-ways.

Immediately they abandoned their thoats and approached the culti-vated district on foot. Carthoris also discarded the metal from his har-ness, or such of it as might serve to identify him as a Heliumite, or of royal blood, for he did not know to what nation belonged this water-way, and upon Mars it is always well to assume every man and nation your enemy until you have learned the contrary.

It was mid-forenoon when the two at last entered one of the roads that cut through the cultivated districts at regular intervals, joining the arid wastes on either side with the great, white, central highway that follows through the centre from end to end of the far-reaching, threadlike farm lands.

The high wall surrounding the fields served as a protection against surprise by raiding green hordes, as well as keeping the savage banths and other carnivora from the domestic animals and the human beings upon the farms.

Carthoris stopped before the first gate he came to, pounding for ad-mission. The young man who answered his summons greeted the two hospitably, though he looked with considerable wonder upon the white skin and auburn hair of the bowman.

After he had listened for a moment to a partial narration of their escape from the Torquasians, he invited them within, took them to his house and bade the servants there prepare food for them.

As they waited in the low-ceiled, pleasant living room of the farm-house until the meal should be ready, Carthoris drew his host into con-versation that he might learn his nationality, and thus the nation under whose dominion lay the waterway where circumstance had placed him.

"I am Hal Vas," said the young man, "son of Vas Kor, of Dusar, a noble in the retinue of Astok, Prince of Dusar. At present I am Dwar of the Road for this district."

Carthoris was very glad that he had not disclosed his identity, for though he had no idea of anything that had transpired since he had left Helium, or that Astok was at the bottom of all his misfortunes, he well knew that the Dusarian had no love for him, and that he could hope for no assistance within the dominions of Dusar.

"And who are you?" asked Hal Vas. "By your appearance I take you for a fighting man, but I see no insignia upon your harness. Can it be that you are a panthan?"

Now, these wandering soldiers of fortune are common upon Barsoom, where most men love to fight. They sell their services wherever war exists, and in the occasional brief intervals when there is no organized warfare between the red nations, they join one of the numerous expeditions that are constantly being dispatched against the green men in protection of the waterways that traverse the wilder portions of the globe.

When their service is over they discard the metal of the nation they have been serving until they shall have found a new master. In the intervals they wear no insignia, their war-worn harness and grim weapons being sufficient to attest their calling.

The suggestion was a happy one, and Carthoris embraced the chance it afforded to account satisfactorily for himself. There was, however, a single drawback. In times of war such panthans as happened to be within the domain of a belligerent nation were compelled to don the insignia of that nation and fight with her warriors.

As far as Carthoris knew Dusar was not at war with any other nation, but there was never any telling when one red nation would be flying at the throat of a neighbour, even though the great and powerful alliance at the head of which was his father, John Carter, had managed to maintain a long peace upon the greater portion of Barsoom.

A pleasant smile lighted Hal Vas' face as Carthoris admitted his vocation.

"It is well," exclaimed the young man, "that you chanced to come hither, for here you will find the means of obtaining service in short order. My father, Vas Kor, is even now with me, having come hither to recruit a force for the new war against Helium."

CHAPTER TWELVE

To Save Dusar

THUVIA OF PTARTH, battling for more than life against the lust of Jav, cast a quick glance over her shoulder toward the forest from which had rumbled the fierce growl. Jav looked, too.

What they saw filled each with apprehension. It was Komal, the banth-god, rushing wide-jawed upon them!

Which had he chosen for his prey? Or was it to be both?

They had not long to wait, for though the Lotharian attempted to hold the girl between himself and the terrible fangs, the great beast found him at last.

Then, shrieking, he attempted to fly toward Lothar, after pushing Thuvia bodily into the face of the man-eater. But his flight was of short duration. In a moment Komal was upon him, rending his throat and chest with demoniacal fury.

The girl reached their side a moment later, but it was with difficulty that she tore the mad beast from its prey. Still growling and casting hungry glances back upon Jav, the banth at last permitted itself to be led away into the wood.

With her giant protector by her side Thuvia set forth to find the passage through the cliffs, that she might attempt the seemingly impossible feat of reaching far-distant Ptarth across the more than seventeen thousand haads of savage Barsoom.

She could not believe that Carthoris had deliberately deserted her, and so she kept a constant watch for him; but as she bore too far to the north in her search for the tunnel she passed the Heliumite as he was returning to Lothar in search of her.

Thuvia of Ptarth was having difficulty in determining the exact status of the Prince of Helium in her heart. She could not admit even to herself that she loved him, and yet she had permitted him to apply to her that term of endearment and possession to which a Barsoomian maid should turn deaf ears when voiced by other lips than those of her husband or fiance – "my princess."

Kulan Tith, Jeddak of Kaol, to whom she was affianced, commanded her respect and admiration. Had it been that she had surrendered to her father's wishes because of pique that the handsome Heliumite had not taken advantage of his visits to her father's court to push the suit for her hand that she had been quite sure he had contemplated since that distant day the two had sat together upon the carved seat within the gorgeous Garden of the Jeddaks that graced the inner courtyard of the palace of Salensus Oll at Kadabra?

Did she love Kulan Tith? Bravely she tried to believe that she did; but all the while her eyes wandered through the coming darkness for the figure of a clean-limbed fighting man – black-haired and grey-eyed. Black was the hair of Kulan Tith; but his eyes were brown.

It was almost dark when she found the entrance to the tunnel. Safely she passed through to the hills beyond, and here, under the bright light of Mars' two moons, she halted to plan her future action.

Should she wait here in the hope that Carthoris would return in search of her? Or should she continue her way north-east toward Ptarth? Where, first, would Carthoris have gone after leaving the valley of Lothar?

Her parched throat and dry tongue gave her the answer – toward Aaanthor and water. Well, she, too, would go first to Aaanthor, where she might find more than the water she needed.

With Komal by her side she felt little fear, for he would protect her from all other savage beasts. Even the great white apes would flee the mighty banth in terror. Men only need she fear, but she must take this and many other chances before she could hope to reach her father's court again.

When at last Carthoris found her, only to be struck down by the long-sword of a green man, Thuvia prayed that the same fate might overtake her.

The sight of the red warriors leaping from their fliers had, for a moment, filled her with renewed hope – hope that Carthoris of Helium might be only stunned and that they would rescue him; but when she saw the Dusarian metal upon their harness, and that they sought only to escape with her alone from the charging Torquasians, she gave up.

Komal, too, was dead – dead across the body of the Heliumite. She was, indeed, alone now. There was none to protect her.

The Dusarian warriors dragged her to the deck of the nearest flier. All about them the green warriors surged in an attempt to wrest her from the red.

At last those who had not died in the conflict gained the decks of the two craft. The engines throbbed and purred – the propellers whirred. Quickly the swift boats shot heavenward.

Thuvia of Ptarth glanced about her. A man stood near, smiling down into her face. With a gasp of recognition she looked full into his eyes, and then with a little moan of terror and understanding she buried her face in her hands and sank to the polished skeel-wood deck. It was Astok, Prince of Dusar, who bent above her.

Swift were the fliers of Astok of Dusar, and great the need for reaching his father's court as quickly as possible, for the fleets of war of Helium and Ptarth and Kaol were scattered far and wide above Barsoom. Nor would it go well with Astok or Dusar should any one of them discover Thuvia of Ptarth a prisoner upon his own vessel.

Aaanthor lies in fifty south latitude, and forty east of Horz, the deserted seat of ancient Barsoomian culture and learning, while Dusar lies fifteen degrees north of the equator and twenty degrees east from Horz.

Great though the distance is, the fliers covered it without a stop. Long before they had reached their destination Thuvia of Ptarth had learned several things that cleared up the doubts that had assailed her mind for many days. Scarce had they risen above Aaanthor than she recognized one of the crew as a member of the crew of that other flier that had borne her from her father's gardens to Aaanthor. The presence of Astok upon the craft settled the whole question. She had been stolen by emissaries of the Dusarian prince – Carthoris of Helium had had nothing to do with it.

Nor did Astok deny the charge when she accused him. He only smiled and pleaded his love for her.

"I would sooner mate with a white ape!" she cried, when he would have urged his suit.

Astok glowered sullenly upon her.

"You shall mate with me, Thuvia of Ptarth," he growled, "or, by your first ancestor, you shall have your preference – and mate with a white ape."

The girl made no reply, nor could he draw her into conversation during the balance of the journey.

As a matter of fact Astok was a trifle awed by the proportions of the conflict which his abduction of the Ptarthian princess had induced, nor was he over comfortable with the weight of responsibility which the possession of such a prisoner entailed.

His one thought was to get her to Dusar, and there let his father assume the responsibility. In the meantime he would be as careful as possible to do nothing to affront her, lest they all might be captured and he have to account for his treatment of the girl to one of the great jeddaks whose interest centred in her.

And so at last they came to Dusar, where Astok hid his prisoner in a secret room high in the east tower of his own palace. He had sworn his men to silence in the matter of the identity of the girl, for until he had seen his father, Nutus, Jeddak of Dusar, he dared not let any one know whom he had brought with him from the south.

But when he appeared in the great audience chamber before the cruel-lipped man who was his sire, he found his courage oozing, and he dared not speak of the princess hid within his palace. It occurred to him to test his father's sentiments upon the subject, and so he told a tale of capturing one who claimed to know the whereabouts of Thuvia of Ptarth.

"And if you command it, Sire," he said, "I will go and capture her – fetching her here to Dusar."

Nutus frowned and shook his head.

"You have done enough already to set Ptarth and Kaol and Helium all three upon us at once should they learn your part in the theft of the Ptarth princess. That you succeeded in shifting the guilt upon the Prince of Helium was fortunate, and a masterly move of strategy; but were the girl to know the truth and ever return to her father's court, all Dusar would have to pay the penalty, and to have her here a prisoner amongst us would be an admission of guilt from the consequences of which naught could save us. It would cost me my throne, Astok, and that I have no mind to lose.

"If we had her here – " the elder man suddenly commenced to muse, repeating the phrase again and again. "If we had her here, Astok," he exclaimed fiercely. "Ah, if we but had her here and none knew that she was here! Can you not guess, man? The guilt of Dusar might be for ever buried with her bones," he concluded in a low, savage whisper.

Astok, Prince of Dusar, shuddered.

Weak he was; yes, and wicked, too; but the suggestion that his father's words implied turned him cold with horror.

Cruel to their enemies are the men of Mars; but the word "enemies" is commonly interpreted to mean men only. Assassination runs riot in the great Barsoomian cities; yet to murder a woman is a crime so unthinkable that even the most hardened of the paid assassins would shrink from you in horror should you suggest such a thing to him.

Nutus was apparently oblivious to his son's all-too-patent terror at his suggestion. Presently he continued:

"You say that you know where the girl lies hid, since she was stolen from your people at Aaanthor. Should she be found by any one of the three powers, her unsupported story would be sufficient to turn them all against us.

"There is but one way, Astok," cried the older man. "You must return at once to her hiding-place and fetch her hither in all secrecy. And, look you here! Return not to Dusar without her, upon pain of death!"

Astok, Prince of Dusar, well knew his royal father's temper. He knew that in the tyrant's heart there pulsed no single throb of love for any creature.

Astok's mother had been a slave woman. Nutus had never loved her. He had never loved another. In youth he had tried to find a bride at the courts of several of his powerful neighbours, but their women would have none of him.

After a dozen daughters of his own nobility had sought self-destruction rather than wed him he had given up. And then it had been that he had legally wed one of his slaves that he might have a son to stand among the jeds when Nutus died and a new jeddak was chosen.

Slowly Astok withdrew from the presence of his father. With white face and shaking limbs he made his way to his own palace. As he crossed the courtyard his glance chanced to wander to the great east tower looming high against the azure of the sky.

At sight of it beads of sweat broke out upon his brow.

Issus! No other hand than his could be trusted to do the horrid thing. With his own fingers he must crush the life from that perfect throat, or plunge the silent blade into the red, red heart.

Her heart! The heart that he had hoped would brim with love for him!

But had it done so? He recalled the haughty contempt with which his protestations of love had been received. He went cold and then hot to the memory of it. His compunctions cooled as the self-satisfaction of a near revenge crowded out the finer instincts that had for a moment asserted themselves – the good that he had inherited from the slave woman was once again submerged in the bad blood that had come down to him from his royal sire; as, in the end, it always was.

A cold smile supplanted the terror that had dilated his eyes. He turned his steps toward the tower. He would see her before he set out upon the journey that was to blind his father to the fact that the girl was already in Dusar.

Quietly he passed in through the secret way, ascending a spiral run-way to the apartment in which the Princess of Ptarth was immured.

As he entered the room he saw the girl leaning upon the sill of the east casement, gazing out across the roof tops of Dusar toward distant Ptarth. He hated Ptarth. The thought of it filled him with rage. Why not finish her now and have it done with?

At the sound of his step she turned quickly toward him. Ah, how beautiful she was! His sudden determination faded beneath the glorious light of her wondrous beauty. He would wait until he had returned from his little journey of deception – maybe there might be some other way then. Some other hand to strike the blow – with that face, with those eyes before him, he could never do it. Of that he was positive. He had always gloried in the cruelty of his nature, but, Issus! he was not that cruel. No, another must be found – one whom he could trust.

He was still looking at her as she stood there before him meeting his gaze steadily and unafraid. He felt the hot passion of his love mounting higher and higher.

Why not sue once more? If she would relent, all might yet be well. Even if his father could not be persuaded, they could fly to Ptarth, laying all the blame of the knavery and intrigue that had thrown four great nations into war, upon the shoulders of Nutus. And who was there that would doubt the justice of the charge?

"Thuvia," he said, "I come once again, for the last time, to lay my heart at your feet. Ptarth and Kaol and Dusar are battling with Helium because of you. Wed me, Thuvia, and all may yet be as it should be."

The girl shook her head.

"Wait!" he commanded, before she could speak. "Know the truth before you speak words that may seal, not only your own fate, but that of the thousands of warriors who battle because of you.

"Refuse to wed me willingly, and Dusar would be laid waste should ever the truth be known to Ptarth and Kaol and Helium. They would raze our cities, leaving not one stone upon another. They would scatter our peoples across the face of Barsoom from the frozen north to the frozen south, hunting them down and slaying them, until this great nation remained only as a hated memory in the minds of men.

"But while they are exterminating the Dusarians, countless thousands of their own warriors must perish – and all because of the stubbornness of a single woman who would not wed the prince who loves her.

"Refuse, Thuvia of Ptarth, and there remains but a single alternative – no man must ever know your fate. Only a handful of loyal servitors besides my royal father and myself know that you were stolen from the gardens of Thuvan Dihn by Astok, Prince of Dusar, or that to-day you be imprisoned in my palace.

"Refuse, Thuvia of Ptarth, and you must die to save Dusar – there is no other way. Nutus, the jeddak, has so decreed. I have spoken."

For a long moment the girl let her level gaze rest full upon the face of Astok of Dusar. Then she spoke, and though the words were few, the unimpassioned tone carried unfathomable depths of cold contempt.

"Better all that you have threatened," she said, "than you."

Then she turned her back upon him and went to stand once more before the east window, gazing with sad eyes toward distant Ptarth.

Astok wheeled and left the room, returning after a short interval of time with food and drink.

"Here," he said, "is sustenance until I return again. The next to enter this apartment will be your executioner. Commend yourself to your ancestors, Thuvia of Ptarth, for within a few days you shall be with them."

Then he was gone.

Half an hour later he was interviewing an officer high in the navy of Dusar.

"Whither went Vas Kor?" he asked. "He is not at his palace."

"South, to the great waterway that skirts Torquas," replied the other. "His son, Hal Vas, is Dwar of the Road there, and thither has Vas Kor gone to enlist recruits among the workers on the farms."

"Good," said Astok, and a half-hour more found him rising above Dusar in his swiftest flier.

CHAPTER THIRTEEN
Turjun, the Panthan

THE FACE OF CARTHORIS of Helium gave no token of the emotions that convulsed him inwardly as he heard from the lips of Hal Vas that Helium was at war with Dusar, and that fate had thrown him into the service of the enemy.

That he might utilize this opportunity to the good of Helium scarce sufficed to outweigh the chagrin he felt that he was not fighting in the open at the head of his own loyal troops.

To escape the Dusarians might prove an easy matter; and then again it might not. Should they suspect his loyalty (and the loyalty of an impressed panthan was always open to suspicion), he might not find an opportunity to elude their vigilance until after the termination of the war, which might occur within days, or, again, only after long and weary years of bloodshed.

He recalled that history recorded wars in which actual military operations had been carried on without cessation for five or six hundred years, and even now there were nations upon Barsoom with which Helium had made no peace within the history of man.

The outlook was not cheering. He could not guess that within a few hours he would be blessing the fate that had thrown him into the service of Dusar.

"Ah!" exclaimed Hal Vas. "Here is my father now. Kaor! Vas Kor. Here is one you will be glad to meet – a doughty panthan – " He hesitated.

"Turjun," interjected Carthoris, seizing upon the first appellation that occurred to him.

As he spoke his eyes crossed quickly to the tall warrior who was entering the room. Where before had he seen that giant figure, that taciturn countenance, and the livid sword-cut from temple to mouth?

"Vas Kor," repeated Carthoris mentally. "Vas Kor!" Where had he seen the man before?

And then the noble spoke, and like a flash it all came back to Carthoris – the forward servant upon the landing-stage at Ptarth that time that
he had been explaining the intricacies of his new compass to Thuvan
Dihn; the lone slave that had guarded his own hangar that night he had
left upon his ill-fated journey for Ptarth – the journey that had brought
him so mysteriously to far Aaanthor.

"Vas Kor," he repeated aloud, "blessed be your ancestors for this
meeting," nor did the Dusarian guess the wealth of meaning that lay beneath that hackneyed phrase with which a Barsoomian acknowledges
an introduction.

"And blessed be yours, Turjun," replied Vas Kor.

Now came the introduction of Kar Komak to Vas Kor, and as Carthoris went through the little ceremony there came to him the only
explanation he might make to account for the white skin and auburn
hair of the bowman; for he feared that the truth might not be believed
and thus suspicion be cast upon them both from the beginning.

"Kar Komak," he explained, "is, as you can see, a thern. He has wandered far from his icebound southern temples in search of adventure. I
came upon him in the pits of Aaanthor; but though I have known him
so short a time, I can vouch for his bravery and loyalty."

Since the destruction of the fabric of their false religion by John
Carter, the majority of the therns had gladly accepted the new order of
things, so that it was now no longer uncommon to see them mingling
with the multitudes of red men in any of the great cities of the outer
world, so Vas Kor neither felt nor expressed any great astonishment.

All during the interview Carthoris watched, catlike, for some indication
that Vas Kor recognized in the battered panthan the erstwhile gorgeous
Prince of Helium; but the sleepless nights, the long days of marching and
fighting, the wounds and the dried blood had evidently sufficed to obliter-
ate the last remnant of his likeness to his former self; and then Vas Kor had
seen him but twice in all his life. Little wonder that he did not know him.

During the evening Vas Kor announced that on the morrow they
should depart north toward Dusar, picking up recruits at various stations along the way.

In a great field behind the house a flier lay – a fair-sized cruiser-transport that would accommodate many men, yet swift and well armed
also. Here Carthoris slept, and Kar Komak, too, with the other recruits,
under guard of the regular Dusarian warriors that manned the craft.

Toward midnight Vas Kor returned to the vessel from his son's house,
repairing at once to his cabin. Carthoris, with one of the Dusarians,
was on watch. It was with difficulty that the Heliumite repressed a cold

smile as the noble passed within a foot of him – within a foot of the long, slim, Heliumitic blade that swung in his harness.

How easy it would have been! How easy to avenge the cowardly trick that had been played upon him – to avenge Helium and Ptarth and Thuvia!

But his hand moved not toward the dagger's hilt, for first Vas Kor must serve a better purpose – he might know where Thuvia of Ptarth lay hidden now, if it had truly been Dusarians that had spirited her away during the fight before Aaanthor.

And then, too, there was the instigator of the entire foul plot. *He* must pay the penalty; and who better than Vas Kor could lead the Prince of Helium to Astok of Dusar?

Faintly out of the night there came to Carthoris's ears the purring of a distant motor. He scanned the heavens.

Yes, there it was far in the north, dimly outlined against the dark void of space that stretched illimitably beyond it, the faint suggestion of a flier passing, unlighted, through the Barsoomian night.

Carthoris, knowing not whether the craft might be friend or foe of Dusar, gave no sign that he had seen, but turned his eyes in another direction, leaving the matter to the Dusarian who stood watch with him.

Presently the fellow discovered the oncoming craft, and sounded the low alarm which brought the balance of the watch and an officer from their sleeping silks and furs upon the deck near by.

The cruiser-transport lay without lights, and, resting as she was upon the ground, must have been entirely invisible to the oncoming flier, which all presently recognized as a small craft.

It soon became evident that the stranger intended making a landing, for she was now spiraling slowly above them, dropping lower and lower in each graceful curve.

"It is the Thuria," whispered one of the Dusarian warriors. "I would know her in the blackness of the pits among ten thousand other craft."

"Right you are!" exclaimed Vas Kor, who had come on deck. And then he hailed:

"Kaor, Thuria!"

"Kaor!" came presently from above after a brief silence. Then: "What ship?"

"Cruiser-transport Kalksus, Vas Kor of Dusar."

"Good!" came from above. "Is there safe landing alongside?"

"Yes, close in to starboard. Wait, we will show our lights," and a moment later the smaller craft settled close beside the Kalksus, and the lights of the latter were immediately extinguished once more.

Several figures could be seen slipping over the side of the Thuria and advancing toward the Kalksus. Ever suspicious, the Dusarians stood ready to receive the visitors as friends or foes as closer inspection might prove them. Carthoris stood quite near the rail, ready to take sides with the new-comers should chance have it that they were Heliumites playing a bold stroke of strategy upon this lone Dusarian ship. He had led like parties himself, and knew that such a contingency was quite possible.

But the face of the first man to cross the rail undeceived him with a shock that was not at all unpleasurable – it was the face of Astok, Prince of Dusar.

Scarce noticing the others upon the deck of the Kalksus, Astok strode forward to accept Vas Kor's greeting, then he summoned the noble below. The warriors and officers returned to their sleeping silks and furs, and once more the deck was deserted except for the Dusarian warrior and Turjun, the panthan, who stood guard.

The latter walked quietly to and fro. The former leaned across the rail, wishing for the hour that would bring him relief. He did not see his companion approach the lights of the cabin of Vas Kor. He did not see him stoop with ear close pressed to a tiny ventilator.

"May the white apes take us all," cried Astok ruefully, "if we are not in as ugly a snarl as you have ever seen! Nutus thinks that we have her in hiding far away from Dusar. He has bidden me bring her here."

He paused. No man should have heard from his lips the thing he was trying to tell. It should have been for ever the secret of Nutus and Astok, for upon it rested the safety of a throne. With that knowledge any man could wrest from the Jeddak of Dusar whatever he listed.

But Astok was afraid, and he wanted from this older man the sugges-tion of an alternative. He went on.

"I am to kill her," he whispered, looking fearfully around. "Nutus merely wishes to see the body that he may know his commands have been executed. I am now supposed to be gone to the spot where we have her hidden that I may fetch her in secrecy to Dusar. None is to know that she has ever been in the keeping of a Dusarian. I do not need to tell you what would befall Dusar should Ptarth and Helium and Kaol ever learn the truth."

The jaws of the listener at the ventilator clicked together with a vi-cious snap. Before he had but guessed at the identity of the subject of this conversation. Now he knew. And they were to kill her! His muscu-lar fingers clenched until the nails bit into the palms.

"And you wish me to go with you while you fetch her to Dusar," Vas Kor was saying. "Where is she?"

Astok bent close and whispered into the other's ear. The suggestion of a smile crossed the cruel features of Vas Kor. He realized the power that lay within his grasp. He should be a jed at least.

"And how may I help you, my Prince?" asked the older man suavely.

"I cannot kill her," said Astok. "Issus! I cannot do it! When she turns those eyes upon me my heart becomes water."

Vas Kor's eyes narrowed.

"And you wish – " He paused, the interrogation unfinished, yet complete.

Astok nodded.

"YOU do not love her," he said.

"But I love my life – though I am only a lesser noble," he concluded meaningly.

"You shall be a greater noble – a noble of the first rank!" exclaimed Astok.

"I would be a jed," said Vas Kor bluntly.

Astok hesitated.

"A jed must die before there can be another jed," he pleaded.

"Jeds have died before," snapped Vas Kor. "It would doubtless be not difficult for you to find a jed you do not love, Astok – there are many who do not love you."

Already Vas Kor was commencing to presume upon his power over the young prince. Astok was quick to note and appreciate the subtle change in his lieutenant. A cunning scheme entered his weak and wicked brain.

"As you say, Vas Kor!" he exclaimed. "You shall be a jed when the thing is done," and then, to himself: "Nor will it then be difficult for me to find a jed I do not love."

"When shall we return to Dusar?" asked the noble.

"At once," replied Astok. "Let us get under way now – there is naught to keep you here?"

"I had intended sailing on the morrow, picking up such recruits as the various Dwars of the Roads might have collected for me, as we returned to Dusar."

"Let the recruits wait," said Astok. "Or, better still, come you to Dusar upon the Thuria, leaving the Kalksus to follow and pick up the recruits."

"Yes," acquiesced Vas Kor; "that is the better plan. Come; I am ready," and he rose to accompany Astok to the latter's flier.

The listener at the ventilator came to his feet slowly, like an old man. His face was drawn and pinched and very white beneath the light copper of his skin. She was to die! And he helpless to avert the tragedy. He did not even know where she was imprisoned.

The two men were ascending from the cabin to the deck. Turjun, the panthan, crept close to the companionway, his sinuous fingers closing tightly upon the hilt of his dagger. Could he despatch them both before he was overpowered? He smiled. He could slay an entire utan of her enemies in his present state of mind.

They were almost abreast of him now. Astok was speaking.

"Bring a couple of your men along, Vas Kor," he said. "We are short-handed upon the Thuria, so quickly did we depart."

The panthan's fingers dropped from the dagger's hilt. His quick mind had grasped here a chance for succouring Thuvia of Ptarth. He might be chosen as one to accompany the assassins, and once he had learned where the captive lay he could dispatch Astok and Vas Kor as well as now. To kill them before he knew where Thuvia was hid was simply to leave her to death at the hands of others; for sooner or later Nutus would learn her whereabouts, and Nutus, Jeddak of Dusar, could not afford to let her live.

Turjun put himself in the path of Vas Kor that he might not be overlooked. The noble aroused the men sleeping upon the deck, but always before him the strange panthan whom he had recruited that same day found means for keeping himself to the fore.

Vas Kor turned to his lieutenant, giving instruction for the bringing of the Kalksus to Dusar, and the gathering up of the recruits; then he signed to two warriors who stood close behind the padwar.

"You two accompany us to the Thuria," he said, "and put yourselves at the disposal of her dwar."

It was dark upon the deck of the Kalksus, so Vas Kor had not a good look at the faces of the two he chose; but that was of no moment, for they were but common warriors to assist with the ordinary duties upon a flier, and to fight if need be.

One of the two was Kar Komak, the bowman. The other was not Carthoris.

The Heliumite was mad with disappointment. He snatched his dagger from his harness; but already Astok had left the deck of the Kalksus, and he knew that before he could overtake him, should he dispatch Vas Kor, he would be killed by the Dusarian warriors, who now were thick upon the deck. With either one of the two alive Thuvia was in as great danger as though both lived – it must be both!

As Vas Kor descended to the ground Carthoris boldly followed him, nor did any attempt to halt him, thinking, doubtless, that he was one of the party.

After him came Kar Komak and the Dusarian warrior who had been detailed to duty upon the Thuria. Carthoris walked close to the left side of the latter. Now they came to the dense shadow under the side of the Thuria. It was very dark there, so that they had to grope for the ladder.

Kar Komak preceded the Dusarian. The latter reached upward for the swinging rounds, and as he did so steel fingers closed upon his windpipe and a steel blade pierced the very centre of his heart.

Turjun, the panthan, was the last to clamber over the rail of the Thuria, drawing the rope ladder in after him.

A moment later the flier was rising rapidly, headed for the north.

At the rail Kar Komak turned to speak to the warrior who had been detailed to accompany him. His eyes went wide as they rested upon the face of the young man whom he had met beside the granite cliffs that guard mysterious Lothar. How had he come in place of the Dusarian?

A quick sign, and Kar Komak turned once more to find the Thuria's dwar that he might report himself for duty. Behind him followed the panthan.

Carthoris blessed the chance that had caused Vas Kor to choose the bowman of all others, for had it been another Dusarian there would have been questions to answer as to the whereabouts of the warrior who lay so quietly in the field beyond the residence of Hal Vas, Dwar of the Southern Road; and Carthoris had no answer to that question other than his sword point, which alone was scarce adequate to convince the entire crew of the Thuria.

The journey to Dusar seemed interminable to the impatient Carthoris, though as a matter of fact it was quickly accomplished. Some time before they reached their destination they met and spoke with another Dusarian war flier. From it they learned that a great battle was soon to be fought south-east of Dusar.

The combined navies of Dusar, Ptarth and Kaol had been intercepted in their advance toward Helium by the mighty Heliumitic navy – the most formidable upon Barsoom, not alone in numbers and armament, but in the training and courage of its officers and warriors, and the zitidaric proportions of many of its monster battleships.

Not for many a day had there been the promise of such a battle. Four jeddaks were in direct command of their own fleets – Kulan Tith of Kaol, Thuvan Dihn of Ptarth, and Nutus of Dusar upon one side; while upon the other was Tardos Mors, Jeddak of Helium. With the latter was John Carter, Warlord of Mars.

From the far north another force was moving south across the barrier cliffs – the new navy of Talu, Jeddak of Okar, coming in response to the call from the warlord. Upon the decks of the sullen ships of war black-bearded yellow men looked over eagerly toward the south. Gorgeous were they in their splendid cloaks of orluk and apt. Fierce, formidable fighters from the hothouse cities of the frozen north.

And from the distant south, from the sea of Omean and the cliffs of gold, from the temples of the therns and the garden of Issus, other thousands sailed into the north at the call of the great man they all had learned to respect, and, respecting, love. Pacing the flagship of this mighty fleet, second only to the navy of Helium, was the ebon Xodar, Jeddak of the First Born, his heart beating strong in anticipation of the coming moment when he should hurl his savage crews and the weight of his mighty ships upon the enemies of the warlord.

But would these allies reach the theatre of war in time to be of avail to Helium? Or, would Helium need them?

Carthoris, with the other members of the crew of the Thuria, heard the gossip and the rumours. None knew of the two fleets, the one from the south and the other from the north, that were coming to support the ships of Helium, and all of Dusar were convinced that nothing now could save the ancient power of Helium from being wiped for ever from the upper air of Barsoom.

Carthoris, too, loyal son of Helium that he was, felt that even his beloved navy might not be able to cope successfully with the combined forces of three great powers.

Now the Thuria touched the landing-stage above the palace of Astok. Hurriedly the prince and Vas Kor disembarked and entered the drop that would carry them to the lower levels of the palace.

Close beside it was another drop that was utilized by common warriors. Carthoris touched Kar Komak upon the arm.

"Come!" he whispered. "You are my only friend among a nation of enemies. Will you stand by me?"

"To the death," replied Kar Komak.

The two approached the drop. A slave operated it.

"Where are your passes?" he asked.

Carthoris fumbled in his pocket pouch as though in search of them, at the same time entering the cage. Kar Komak followed him, closing the door. The slave did not start the cage downward. Every second counted. They must reach the lower level as soon as possible after Astok and Vas Kor if they would know whither the two went.

Carthoris turned suddenly upon the slave, hurling him to the opposite side of the cage.

"Bind and gag him, Kar Komak!" he cried.

Then he grasped the control lever, and as the cage shot downward at sickening speed, the bowman grappled with the slave. Carthoris could not leave the control to assist his companion, for should they touch the lowest level at the speed at which they were going, all would be dashed to instant death.

Below him he could now see the top of Astok's cage in the parallel shaft, and he reduced the speed of his to that of the other. The slave commenced to scream.

"Silence him!" cried Carthoris.

A moment later a limp form crumpled to the floor of the cage.

"He is silenced," said Kar Komak.

Carthoris brought the cage to a sudden stop at one of the higher levels of the palace. Opening the door, he grasped the still form of the slave and pushed it out upon the floor. Then he banged the gate and resumed the downward drop.

Once more he sighted the top of the cage that held Astok and Vas Kor. An instant later it had stopped, and as he brought his car to a halt, he saw the two men disappear through one of the exits of the corridor beyond.

CHAPTER FOURTEEN

Kulan Tith's Sacrifice

THE MORNING OF THE second day of her incarceration in the east tower of the palace of Astok, Prince of Dusar, found Thuvia of Ptarth waiting in dull apathy the coming of the assassin.

She had exhausted every possibility of escape, going over and over again the door and the windows, the floor and the walls.

The solid ersite slabs she could not even scratch; the tough Barsoomian glass of the windows would have shattered to nothing less than a heavy sledge in the hands of a strong man. The door and the lock were impregnable. There was no escape. And they had stripped her of her weapons so that she could not even anticipate the hour of her doom, thus robbing them of the satisfaction of witnessing her last moments.

When would they come? Would Astok do the deed with his own hands? She doubted that he had the courage for it. At heart he was a coward – she had known it since first she had heard him brag as, a visitor at the court of her father, he had sought to impress her with his valour.

She could not help but compare him with another. And with whom would an affianced bride compare an unsuccessful suitor? With her betrothed? And did Thuvia of Ptarth now measure Astok of Dusar by the standards of Kulan Tith, Jeddak of Kaol?

She was about to die; her thoughts were her own to do with as she pleased; yet furthest from them was Kulan Tith. Instead the figure of the tall and comely Heliumite filled her mind, crowding therefrom all other images.

She dreamed of his noble face, the quiet dignity of his bearing, the smile that lit his eyes as he conversed with his friends, and the smile that touched his lips as he fought with his enemies – the fighting smile of his Virginian sire.

And Thuvia of Ptarth, true daughter of Barsoom, found her breath quickening and heart leaping to the memory of this other smile – the smile that she would never see again. With a little half-sob the girl sank to the pile of silks and furs that were tumbled in confusion beneath the east windows, burying her face in her arms.

In the corridor outside her prison-room two men had paused in heated argument.

"I tell you again, Astok," one was saying, "that I shall not do this thing unless you be present in the room."

There was little of the respect due royalty in the tone of the speaker's voice. The other, noting it, flushed.

"Do not impose too far upon my friendship for you, Vas Kor," he snapped. "There is a limit to my patience."

"There is no question of royal prerogative here," returned Vas Kor. "You ask me to become an assassin in your stead, and against your jeddak's strict injunctions. You are in no position, Astok, to dictate to me; but rather should you be glad to accede to my reasonable request that you be present, thus sharing the guilt with me. Why should I bear it all?"

The younger man scowled, but he advanced toward the locked door, and as it swung in upon its hinges, he entered the room beyond at the side of Vas Kor.

Across the chamber the girl, hearing them enter, rose to her feet and faced them. Under the soft copper of her skin she blanched just a trifle; but her eyes were brave and level, and the haughty tilt of her firm little chin was eloquent of loathing and contempt.

"You still prefer death?" asked Astok.

"To *you*, yes," replied the girl coldly.

The Prince of Dusar turned to Vas Kor and nodded. The noble drew his short-sword and crossed the room toward Thuvia.

"Kneel!" he commanded.

"I prefer to die standing," she replied.

"As you will," said Vas Kor, feeling the point of his blade with his left thumb. "In the name of Nutus, Jeddak of Dusar!" he cried, and ran quickly toward her.

"In the name of Carthoris, Prince of Helium!" came in low tones from the doorway.

Vas Kor turned to see the panthan he had recruited at his son's house leaping across the floor toward him. The fellow brushed past Astok with an: "After him, you – calot!"

Vas Kor wheeled to meet the charging man.

"What means this treason?" he cried.

Astok, with bared sword, leaped to Vas Kor's assistance. The panthan's sword clashed against that of the noble, and in the first encounter Vas Kor knew that he faced a master swordsman.

Before he half realized the stranger's purpose he found the man between himself and Thuvia of Ptarth, at bay facing the two swords of the Dusarians. But he fought not like a man at bay. Ever was he the aggressor, and though always he kept his flashing blade between the girl and her enemies, yet he managed to force them hither and thither about the room, calling to the girl to follow close behind him.

Until it was too late neither Vas Kor nor Astok dreamed of that which lay in the panthan's mind; but at last as the fellow stood with his back toward the door, both understood – they were penned in their own prison, and now the intruder could slay them at his will, for Thuvia of Ptarth was bolting the door at the man's direction, first taking the key from the opposite side, where Astok had left it when they had entered.

Astok, as was his way, finding that the enemy did not fall immediately before their swords, was leaving the brunt of the fighting to Vas Kor, and now as his eyes appraised the panthan carefully they presently went wider and wider, for slowly he had come to recognize the features of the Prince of Helium.

The Heliumite was pressing close upon Vas Kor. The noble was bleeding from a dozen wounds. Astok saw that he could not for long withstand the cunning craft of that terrible sword hand.

"Courage, Vas Kor!" he whispered in the other's ear. "I have a plan. Hold him but a moment longer and all will be well," but the balance of the sentence, "with Astok, Prince of Dusar," he did not voice aloud.

Vas Kor, dreaming no treachery, nodded his head, and for a moment succeeded in holding Carthoris at bay. Then the Heliumite and the girl saw the Dusarian prince run swiftly to the opposite side of the chamber, touch something in the wall that sent a great panel swinging inward, and disappear into the black vault beyond.

It was done so quickly that by no possibility could they have intercepted him. Carthoris, fearful lest Vas Kor might similarly elude him, or Astok return immediately with reinforcements, sprang viciously in upon his antagonist, and a moment later the headless body of the Dusarian noble rolled upon the ersite floor.

"Come!" cried Carthoris. "There is no time to be lost. Astok will be back in a moment with enough warriors to overpower me."

But Astok had no such plan in mind, for such a move would have meant the spreading of the fact among the palace gossips that the Ptarthian princess was a prisoner in the east tower. Quickly would the word have come to his father, and no amount of falsifying could have explained away the facts that the jeddak's investigation would have brought to light.

Instead Astok was racing madly through a long corridor to reach the door of the tower-room before Carthoris and Thuvia left the apartment. He had seen the girl remove the key and place it in her pocket-pouch, and he knew that a dagger point driven into the keyhole from the opposite side would imprison them in the secret chamber till eight dead worlds circled a cold, dead sun.

As fast as he could run Astok entered the main corridor that led to the tower chamber. Would he reach the door in time? What if the Heliumite should have already emerged and he should run upon him in the passageway? Astok felt a cold chill run up his spine. He had no stomach to face that uncanny blade.

He was almost at the door. Around the next turn of the corridor it stood. No, they had not left the apartment. Evidently Vas Kor was still holding the Heliumite!

Astok could scarce repress a grin at the clever manner in which he had outwitted the noble and disposed of him at the same time. And then he rounded the turn and came face to face with an auburn-haired, white giant.

The fellow did not wait to ask the reason for his coming; instead he leaped upon him with a long-sword, so that Astok had to parry a dozen vicious cuts before he could disengage himself and flee back down the runway.

A moment later Carthoris and Thuvia entered the corridor from the secret chamber.

"Well, Kar Komak?" asked the Heliumite.

"It is fortunate that you left me here, red man," said the bowman. "I but just now intercepted one who seemed over-anxious to reach this door – it was he whom they call Astok, Prince of Dusar."

Carthoris smiled.

"Where is he now?" he asked.

"He escaped my blade, and ran down this corridor," replied Kar Komak.

"We must lose no time, then!" exclaimed Carthoris. "He will have the guard upon us yet!"

Together the three hastened along the winding passages through which Carthoris and Kar Komak had tracked the Dusarians by the marks of the latter's sandals in the thin dust that overspread the floors of these seldom-used passage-ways.

They had come to the chamber at the entrances to the lifts before they met with opposition. Here they found a handful of guardsmen, and an officer, who, seeing that they were strangers, questioned their presence in the palace of Astok.

Once more Carthoris and Kar Komak had recourse to their blades, and before they had won their way to one of the lifts the noise of the conflict must have aroused the entire palace, for they heard men shouting, and as they passed the many levels on their quick passage to the landing-stage they saw armed men running hither and thither in search of the cause of the commotion.

Beside the stage lay the Thuria, with three warriors on guard. Again the Heliumite and the Lotharian fought shoulder to shoulder, but the battle was soon over, for the Prince of Helium alone would have been a match for any three that Dusar could produce.

Scarce had the Thuria risen from the ways ere a hundred or more fighting men leaped to view upon the landing-stage. At their head was Astok of Dusar, and as he saw the two he had thought so safely in his power slipping from his grasp, he danced with rage and chagrin, shaking his fists and hurling abuse and vile insults at them.

With her bow inclined upward at a dizzy angle, the Thuria shot meteor-like into the sky. From a dozen points swift patrol boats darted after her, for the scene upon the landing-stage above the palace of the Prince of Dusar had not gone unnoticed.

A dozen times shots grazed the Thuria's side, and as Carthoris could not leave the control levers, Thuvia of Ptarth turned the muzzles of the craft's rapid-fire guns upon the enemy as she clung to the steep and slippery surface of the deck.

It was a noble race and a noble fight. One against a score now, for other Dusarian craft had joined in the pursuit; but Astok, Prince of Dusar, had built well when he built the Thuria. None in the navy of his sire possessed a swifter flier; no other craft so well armoured or so well armed.

One by one the pursuers were distanced, and as the last of them fell out of range behind, Carthoris dropped the Thuria's nose to a horizontal plane, as with lever drawn to the last notch, she tore through the thin air of dying Mars toward the east and Ptarth.

Thirteen and a half thousand haads away lay Ptarth – a stiff thirty-hour journey for the swiftest of fliers, and between Dusar and Ptarth might lie half the navy of Dusar, for in this direction was the reported seat of the great naval battle that even now might be in progress.

Could Carthoris have known precisely where the great fleets of the contending nations lay, he would have hastened to them without delay, for in the return of Thuvia to her sire lay the greatest hope of peace.

Half the distance they covered without sighting a single warship, and then Kar Komak called Carthoris's attention to a distant craft that rested upon the ochre vegetation of the great dead sea-bottom, above which the Thuria was speeding.

About the vessel many figures could be seen swarming. With the aid of powerful glasses, the Heliumite saw that they were green warriors, and that they were repeatedly charging down upon the crew of the stranded airship. The nationality of the latter he could not make out at so great a distance.

It was not necessary to change the course of the Thuria to permit of passing directly above the scene of battle, but Carthoris dropped his craft a few hundred feet that he might have a better and closer view.

If the ship was of a friendly power, he could do no less than stop and direct his guns upon her enemies, though with the precious freight he carried he scarcely felt justified in landing, for he could offer but two swords in reinforcement – scarce enough to warrant jeopardizing the safety of the Princess of Ptarth.

As they came close above the stricken ship, they could see that it would be but a question of minutes before the green horde would swarm across the armoured bulwarks to glut the ferocity of their blood-lust upon the defenders.

"It would be futile to descend," said Carthoris to Thuvia. "The craft may even be of Dusar – she shows no insignia. All that we may do is fire upon the hordesmen"; and as he spoke he stepped to one of the guns and deflected its muzzle toward the green warriors at the ship's side.

At the first shot from the Thuria those upon the vessel below evidently discovered her for the first time. Immediately a device fluttered from the bow of the warship on the ground. Thuvia of Ptarth caught her breath quickly, glancing at Carthoris.

The device was that of Kulan Tith, Jeddak of Kaol – the man to whom the Princess of Ptarth was betrothed!

How easy for the Heliumite to pass on, leaving his rival to the fate that could not for long be averted! No man could accuse him of cowardice or treachery, for Kulan Tith was in arms against Helium, and, further, upon the Thuria were not enough swords to delay even temporarily the outcome that already was a foregone conclusion in the minds of the watchers.

What would Carthoris, Prince of Helium, do?

Scarce had the device broken to the faint breeze ere the bow of the Thuria dropped at a sharp angle toward the ground.

"Can you navigate her?" asked Carthoris of Thuvia.

The girl nodded.

"I am going to try to take the survivors aboard," he continued. "It will need both Kar Komak and myself to man the guns while the Kaolians take to the boarding tackle. Keep her bow depressed against the rifle fire. She can bear it better in her forward armour, and at the same time the propellers will be protected."

He hurried to the cabin as Thuvia took the control. A moment later the boarding tackle dropped from the keel of the Thuria, and from a dozen points along either side stout, knotted leathern lines trailed downward. At the same time a signal broke from her bow:

"Prepare to board us."

A shout arose from the deck of the Kaolian warship. Carthoris, who by this time had returned from the cabin, smiled sadly. He was about to snatch from the jaws of death the man who stood between himself and the woman he loved.

"Take the port bow gun, Kar Komak," he called to the bowman, and himself stepped to the gun upon the starboard bow.

They could now feel the sharp shock of the explosions of the green warriors' projectiles against the armored sides of the staunch *Thuria*.

It was a forlorn hope at best. At any moment the repulsive ray tanks might be pierced. The men upon the Kaolian ship were battling with renewed hope. In the bow stood Kulan Tith, a brave figure fighting beside his brave warriors, beating back the ferocious green men.

The Thuria came low above the other craft. The Kaolians were forming under their officers in readiness to board, and then a sudden fierce fusillade from the rifles of the green warriors vomited their hail of death and destruction into the side of the brave flier.

Like a wounded bird she dived suddenly Marsward careening drunkenly. Thuvia turned the bow upward in an effort to avert the imminent tragedy, but she succeeded only in lessening the shock of the flier's impact as she struck the ground beside the Kaolian ship.

When the green men saw only two warriors and a woman upon the deck of the Thuria, a savage shout of triumph arose from their ranks, while an answering groan broke from the lips of the Kaolians.

The former now turned their attention upon the new arrival, for they saw her defenders could soon be overcome and that from her deck they could command the deck of the better-manned ship.

As they charged a shout of warning came from Kulan Tith, upon the bridge of his own ship, and with it an appreciation of the valour of the act that had put the smaller vessel in these sore straits.

"Who is it," he cried, "that offers his life in the service of Kulan Tith? Never was wrought a nobler deed of self-sacrifice upon Barsoom!"

The green horde was scrambling over the Thuria's side as there broke from the bow the device of Carthoris, Prince of Helium, in reply to the query of the jeddak of Kaol. None upon the smaller flier had opportunity to note the effect of this announcement upon the Kaolians, for their attention was claimed slowly now by that which was transpiring upon their own deck.

Kar Komak stood behind the gun he had been operating, staring with wide eyes at the onrushing hideous green warriors. Carthoris, seeing him thus, felt a pang of regret that, after all, this man that he had thought so valorous should prove, in the hour of need, as spineless as Jav or Tario.

"Kar Komak – the man!" he shouted. "Grip yourself! Remember the days of the glory of the seafarers of Lothar. Fight! Fight, man! Fight as never man fought before. All that remains to us is to die fighting."

Kar Komak turned toward the Heliumite, a grim smile upon his lips.

"Why should we fight," he asked. "Against such fearful odds? There is another way – a better way. Look!" He pointed toward the companion-way that led below deck.

The green men, a handful of them, had already reached the Thuria's deck, as Carthoris glanced in the direction the Lotharian had indicated. The sight that met his eyes set his heart to thumping in joy and relief – Thuvia of Ptarth might yet be saved? For from below there poured a stream of giant bowmen, grim and terrible. Not the bowmen of Tario or Jav, but the bowmen of an odwar of bowmen – savage fighting men, eager for the fray.

The green warriors paused in momentary surprise and consternation, but only for a moment. Then with horrid war-cries they leaped forward to meet these strange, new foemen.

A volley of arrows stopped them in their tracks. In a moment the only green warriors upon the deck of the Thuria were dead warriors, and the bowmen of Kar Komak were leaping over the vessel's sides to charge the hordesmen upon the ground.

Utan after utan tumbled from the bowels of the Thuria to launch themselves upon the unfortunate green men. Kulan Tith and his Kaolians stood wide-eyed and speechless with amazement as they saw thousands of these strange, fierce warriors emerge from the companion-way of the small craft that could not comfortably have accommodated more than fifty.

At last the green men could withstand the onslaught of overwhelming numbers no longer. Slowly, at first, they fell back across the ochre plain. The bowmen pursued them. Kar Komak, standing upon the deck of the Thuria, trembled with excitement.

At the top of his lungs he voiced the savage war-cry of his forgotten day. He roared encouragement and commands at his battling utans, and then, as they charged further and further from the Thuria, he could no longer withstand the lure of battle.

Leaping over the ship's side to the ground, he joined the last of his bowmen as they raced off over the dead sea-bottom in pursuit of the fleeing green horde.

Beyond a low promontory of what once had been an island the green men were disappearing toward the west. Close upon their heels raced the fleet bowmen of a bygone day, and forging steadily ahead among

them Carthoris and Thuvia could see the mighty figure of Kar Komak, brandishing aloft the Torquasian short-sword with which he was armed, as he urged his creatures after the retreating enemy.

As the last of them disappeared behind the promontory, Carthoris turned toward Thuvia of Ptarth.

"They have taught me a lesson, these vanishing bowmen of Lothar," he said. "When they have served their purpose they remain not to embarrass their masters by their presence. Kulan Tith and his warriors are here to protect you. My acts have constituted the proof of my honesty of purpose. Good-bye," and he knelt at her feet, raising a bit of her harness to his lips.

The girl reached out a hand and laid it upon the thick black hair of the head bent before her. Softly she asked:

"Where are you going, Carthoris?"

"With Kar Komak, the bowman," he replied. "There will be fighting and forgetfulness."

The girl put her hands before her eyes, as though to shut out some mighty temptation from her sight.

"May my ancestors have mercy upon me," she cried, "if I say the thing I have no right to say; but I cannot see you cast your life away, Carthoris, Prince of Helium! Stay, my chieftain. Stay – I love you!"

A cough behind them brought both about, and there they saw standing, not two paces from them Kulan Tith, Jeddak of Kaol.

For a long moment none spoke. Then Kulan Tith cleared his throat.

"I could not help hearing all that passed," he said. "I am no fool, to be blind to the love that lies between you. Nor am I blind to the lofty honour that has caused you, Carthoris, to risk your life and hers to save mine, though you thought that that very act would rob you of the chance to keep her for your own.

"Nor can I fail to appreciate the virtue that has kept your lips sealed against words of love for this Heliumite, Thuvia, for I know that I have but just heard the first declaration of your passion for him. I do not condemn you. Rather should I have condemned you had you entered a loveless marriage with me.

"Take back your liberty, Thuvia of Ptarth," he cried, "and bestow it where your heart already lies enchained, and when the golden collars are clasped about your necks you will see that Kulan Tith's is the first sword to be raised in declaration of eternal friendship for the new Princess of Helium and her royal mate!"

THE CHESSMEN OF MARS

BOOK FIVE

John Carter Comes to Earth

SHEA HAD JUST BEATEN ME at chess, as usual, and, also as usual, I had gleaned what questionable satisfaction I might by twitting him with this indication of failing mentality by calling his attention to the nth time to that theory, propounded by certain scientists, which is based upon the assertion that phenomenal chess players are always found to be from the ranks of children under twelve, adults over seventy-two or the mentally defective – a theory that is lightly ignored upon those rare occasions that I win. Shea had gone to bed and I should have followed suit, for we are always in the saddle here before sunrise; but instead I sat there before the chess table in the library, idly blowing smoke at the dishonored head of my defeated king.

While thus profitably employed I heard the east door of the living-room open and someone enter. I thought it was Shea returning to speak with me on some matter of tomorrow's work; but when I raised my eyes to the doorway that connects the two rooms I saw framed there the figure of a bronzed giant, his otherwise naked body trapped with a jewel-encrusted harness from which there hung at one side an ornate short-sword and at the other a pistol of strange pattern. The black hair, the steel-gray eyes, brave and smiling, the noble features – I recognized them at once, and leaping to my feet I advanced with outstretched hand.

"John Carter!" I cried. "You?"

"None other, my son," he replied, taking my hand in one of his and placing the other upon my shoulder.

"And what are you doing here?" I asked. "It has been long years since you revisited Earth, and never before in the trappings of Mars. Lord! but it is good to see you – and not a day older in appearance than when you trotted me on your knee in my babyhood. How do you explain it, John Carter, Warlord of Mars, or do you try to explain it?"

"Why attempt to explain the inexplicable?" he replied. "As I have told you before, I am a very old man. I do not know how old I am. I recall no childhood; but recollect only having been always as you see me now and as you saw me first when you were five years old. You, yourself, have aged, though not as much as most men in a corresponding number of years, which may be accounted for by the fact that the same blood runs in our veins; but I have not aged at all. I have discussed the question with a noted Martian scientist, a friend of mine; but his theories are still only theories. However, I am content with the fact – I never age, and I love life and the vigor of youth.

"And now as to your natural question as to what brings me to Earth again and in this, to earthly eyes, strange habiliment. We may thank Kar Komak, the bowman of Lothar. It was he who gave me the idea upon which I have been experimenting until at last I have achieved success. As you know I have long possessed the power to cross the void in spirit, but never before have I been able to impart to inanimate things a similar power. Now, however, you see me for the first time precisely as my Martian fellows see me – you see the very short-sword that has tasted the blood of many a savage foeman; the harness with the devices of Helium and the insignia of my rank; the pistol that was presented to me by Tars Tarkas, Jeddak of Thark.

"Aside from seeing you, which is my principal reason for being here, and satisfying myself that I can transport inanimate things from Mars to Earth, and therefore animate things if I so desire, I have no purpose. Earth is not for me. My every interest is upon Barsoom – my wife, my children, my work; all are there. I will spend a quiet evening with you and then back to the world I love even better than I love life."

As he spoke he dropped into the chair upon the opposite side of the chess table.

"You spoke of children," I said. "Have you more than Carthoris?"

"A daughter," he replied, "only a little younger than Carthoris, and, barring one, the fairest thing that ever breathed the thin air of dying Mars. Only Dejah Thoris, her mother, could be more beautiful than Tara of Helium."

For a moment he fingered the chessmen idly. "We have a game on Mars similar to chess," he said, "very similar. And there is a race there that plays it grimly with men and naked swords. We call the game jetan. It is played on a board like yours, except that there are a hundred squares and we use twenty pieces on each side. I never see it played without thinking of Tara of Helium and what befell her among the chessmen of Barsoom. Would you like to hear her story?"

I said that I would and so he told it to me, and now I shall try to re-tell it for you as nearly in the words of The Warlord of Mars as I can recall them, but in the third person. If there be inconsistencies and errors, let the blame fall not upon John Carter, but rather upon my faulty memory, where it belongs. It is a strange tale and utterly Barsoomian.

CHAPTER ONE

Tara in a Tantrum

TARA OF HELIUM rose from the pile of silks and soft furs upon which she had been reclining, stretched her lithe body languidly, and crossed toward the center of the room, where, above a large table, a bronze disc depended from the low ceiling. Her carriage was that of health and physical perfection – the effortless harmony of faultless coordination. A scarf of silken gossamer crossing over one shoulder was wrapped about her body; her black hair was piled high upon her head. With a wooden stick she tapped upon the bronze disc, lightly, and presently the summons was answered by a slave girl, who entered, smiling, to be greeted similarly by her mistress.

"Are my father's guests arriving?" asked the princess.

"Yes, Tara of Helium, they come," replied the slave. "I have seen Kantos Kan, Overlord of the Navy, and Prince Soran of Ptarth, and Djor Kantos, son of Kantos Kan," she shot a roguish glance at her mistress as she mentioned Djor Kantos' name, "and – oh, there were others, many have come."

"The bath, then, Uthia," said her mistress. "And why, Uthia," she added, "do you look thus and smile when you mention the name of Djor Kantos?"

The slave girl laughed gaily. "It is so plain to all that he worships you," she replied.

"It is not plain to me," said Tara of Helium. "He is the friend of my brother, Carthoris, and so he is here much; but not to see me. It is his friendship for Carthoris that brings him thus often to the palace of my father."

"But Carthoris is hunting in the north with Talu, Jeddak of Okar," Uthia reminded her.

"My bath, Uthia!" cried Tara of Helium. "That tongue of yours will bring you to some misadventure yet."

"The bath is ready, Tara of Helium," the girl responded, her eyes still twinkling with merriment, for she well knew that in the heart of her mistress was no anger that could displace the love of the princess for her slave. Preceding the daughter of The Warlord she opened the door of an adjoining room where lay the bath – a gleaming pool of scented water in a marble basin. Golden stanchions supported a chain of gold encircling it and leading down into the water on either side of marble steps. A glass dome let in the sun-light, which flooded the interior, glancing from the polished white of the marble walls and the procession of bathers and fishes, which, in conventional design, were inlaid with gold in a broad band that circled the room.

Tara of Helium removed the scarf from about her and handed it to the slave. Slowly she descended the steps to the water, the temperature of which she tested with a symmetrical foot, undeformed by tight shoes and high heels – a lovely foot, as God intended that feet should be and seldom are. Finding the water to her liking, the girl swam leisurely to and fro about the pool. With the silken ease of the seal she swam, now at the surface, now below, her smooth muscles rolling softly beneath her clear skin – a wordless song of health and happiness and grace. Presently she emerged and gave herself into the hands of the slave girl, who rubbed the body of her mistress with a sweet smelling semi-liquid substance contained in a golden urn, until the glowing skin was covered with a foamy lather, then a quick plunge into the pool, a drying with soft towels, and the bath was over. Typical of the life of the princess was the simple elegance of her bath – no retinue of useless slaves, no pomp, no idle waste of precious moments. In another half hour her hair was dried and built into the strange, but becoming, coiffure of her station; her leathern trappings, encrusted with gold and jewels, had been adjusted to her figure and she was ready to mingle with the guests that had been bidden to the midday function at the palace of The Warlord.

As she left her apartments to make her way to the gardens where the guests were congregating, two warriors, the insignia of the House of the Prince of Helium upon their harness, followed a few paces behind her, grim reminders that the assassin's blade may never be ignored upon Barsoom, where, in a measure, it counterbalances the great natural span of human life, which is estimated at not less than a thousand years.

As they neared the entrance to the garden another woman, similarly guarded, approached them from another quarter of the great palace. As she neared them Tara of Helium turned toward her with a smile and a happy greeting, while her guards knelt with bowed heads in willing and voluntary adoration of the beloved of Helium. Thus always, solely at the command of their own hearts, did the warriors of Helium greet Dejah Thoris, whose deathless beauty had more than once brought them to bloody warfare with other nations of Barsoom. So great was the love of the people of Helium for the mate of John Carter it amounted practically to worship, as though she were indeed the goddess that she looked.

The mother and daughter exchanged the gentle, Barsoomian, "kaor" of greeting and kissed. Then together they entered the gardens where the guests were. A huge warrior drew his short-sword and struck his metal shield with the flat of it, the brazen sound ringing out above the laughter and the speech.

"The Princess comes!" he cried. "Dejah Thoris! The Princess comes! Tara of Helium!" Thus always is royalty announced. The guests arose; the two women inclined their heads; the guards fell back upon either side of the entrance-way; a number of nobles advanced to pay their respects; the laughing and the talking were resumed and Dejah Thoris and her daughter moved simply and naturally among their guests, no suggestion of differing rank apparent in the bearing of any who were there, though there was more than a single Jeddak and many common warriors whose only title lay in brave deeds, or noble patriotism. Thus it is upon Mars where men are judged upon their own merits rather than upon those of their grandsires, even though pride of lineage be great.

Tara of Helium let her slow gaze wander among the throng of guests until presently it halted upon one she sought. Was the faint shadow of a frown that crossed her brow an indication of displeasure at the sight that met her eyes, or did the brilliant rays of the noonday sun distress her? Who may say! She had been reared to believe that one day she should wed Djor Kantos, son of her father's best friend. It had been the dearest wish of Kantos Kan and The Warlord that this should be, and Tara of Helium had accepted it as a matter of all but accomplished fact. Djor Kantos had seemed to accept the matter in the same way. They had spoken of it casually as something that would, as a matter of course, take place in the indefinite future, as, for instance, his promotion in the navy, in which he was now a padwar; or the set functions of the court of her grandfather, Tardos Mors, Jeddak of Helium; or Death. They had never spoken of love and that had puzzled Tara of Helium upon the rare occasions she gave it thought, for she knew that people who were to wed were usually much occupied with the matter of love and she had all of a woman's curiosity – she wondered what love was like. She was very fond of Djor Kantos and she knew that he was very fond of her. They liked to be together, for they liked the same things and the same people and the same books and their dancing was a joy, not only to themselves but to those who watched them. She could not imagine wanting to marry anyone other than Djor Kantos.

So perhaps it was only the sun that made her brows contract just the tiniest bit at the same instant that she discovered Djor Kantos sitting in earnest conversation with Olvia Marthis, daughter of the Jed of Hastor. It was Djor Kantos' duty immediately to pay his respects to Dejah Thoris and Tara of Helium; but he did not do so and presently the daughter of The Warlord frowned indeed. She looked long at Olvia Marthis, and though she had seen her many times before and knew her well, she looked at her today through new eyes that saw, apparently for the first time, that the girl from Hastor was noticeably beautiful even among those other beautiful women of Helium. Tara of Helium was disturbed. She attempted to analyze her emotions; but found it difficult. Olvia Marthis was her friend – she was very fond of her and she felt no anger toward her. Was she angry with Djor Kantos? No, she finally decided that she was not. It was merely surprise, then, that she felt – surprise that Djor Kantos could be more interested in another than in herself. She was about to cross the garden and join them when she heard her father's voice directly behind her.

"Tara of Helium!" he called, and she turned to see him approaching with a strange warrior whose harness and metal bore devices with which she was unfamiliar. Even among the gorgeous trappings of the men of Helium and the visitors from distant empires those of the stranger were remarkable for their barbaric splendor. The leather of his harness was completely hidden beneath ornaments of platinum thickly set with brilliant diamonds, as were the scabbards of his swords and the ornate holster that held his long, Martian pistol. Moving through the sunlit garden at the side of the great Warlord, the scintillant rays of his countless gems enveloping him as in an aureole of light imparted to his noble figure a suggestion of godliness.

"Tara of Helium, I bring you Gahan, Jed of Gathol," said John Carter, after the simple Barsoomian custom of presentation.

"Kaor! Gahan, Jed of Gathol," returned Tara of Helium.

"My sword is at your feet, Tara of Helium," said the young chieftain.

The Warlord left them and the two seated themselves upon an ersite bench beneath a spreading sorapus tree.

"Far Gathol," mused the girl. "Ever in my mind has it been connected with mystery and romance and the half-forgotten lore of the ancients. I cannot think of Gathol as existing today, possibly because I have never before seen a Gatholian."

"And perhaps too because of the great distance that separates Helium and Gathol, as well as the comparative insignificance of my little free city, which might easily be lost in one corner of mighty Helium," added Gahan. "But what we lack in power we make up in pride," he continued, laughing. "We believe ours the oldest inhabited city upon Barsoom. It is one of the few that has retained its freedom, and this despite the fact that its ancient diamond mines are the richest known and, unlike practically all the other fields, are today apparently as inexhaustible as ever."

"Tell me of Gathol," urged the girl. "The very thought fills me with interest," nor was it likely that the handsome face of the young jed detracted anything from the glamour of far Gathol.

Nor did Gahan seem displeased with the excuse for further monopolizing the society of his fair companion. His eyes seemed chained to her exquisite features, from which they moved no further than to a rounded breast, part hid beneath its jeweled covering, a naked shoulder or the symmetry of a perfect arm, resplendent in bracelets of barbaric magnificence.

"Your ancient history has doubtless told you that Gathol was built upon an island in Throxeus, mightiest of the five oceans of old Barsoom. As the ocean receded Gathol crept down the sides of the mountain, the summit of which was the island upon which she had been built, until today she covers the slopes from summit to base, while the bowels of the great hill are honeycombed with the galleries of her mines. Entirely surrounding us is a great salt marsh, which protects us from invasion by land, while the rugged and ofttimes vertical topography of our mountain renders the landing of hostile airships a precarious undertaking."

"That, and your brave warriors?" suggested the girl.

Gahan smiled. "We do not speak of that except to enemies," he said, "and then with tongues of steel rather than of flesh."

"But what practice in the art of war has a people which nature has thus protected from attack?" asked Tara of Helium, who had liked the young jed's answer to her previous question, but yet in whose mind persisted a vague conviction of the possible effeminacy of her companion, induced, doubtless, by the magnificence of his trappings and weapons which carried a suggestion of splendid show rather than grim utility.

"Our natural barriers, while they have doubtless saved us from defeat on countless occasions, have not by any means rendered us immune from attack," he explained, "for so great is the wealth of Gathol's diamond treasury that there yet may be found those who will risk almost certain defeat in an effort to loot our unconquered city; so thus we find occasional practice in the exercise of arms; but there is more to Gathol than the mountain city. My country extends from Polodona (Equator) north ten karads and from the tenth karad west of Horz to the twentieth west, including thus a million square haads, the greater proportion of which is fine grazing land where run our great herds of thoats and zitidars.

"Surrounded as we are by predatory enemies our herdsmen must indeed be warriors or we should have no herds, and you may be assured they get plenty of fighting. Then there is our constant need of workers in the mines. The Gatholians consider themselves a race of warriors and as such prefer not to labor in the mines. The law is, however, that each male Gatholian shall give an hour a day in labor to the government. That is practically the only tax that is levied upon them. They prefer however, to furnish a substitute to perform this labor, and as our own people will not hire out for labor in the mines it has been necessary to obtain slaves, and I do not need to tell you that slaves are not won without fighting. We sell these slaves in the public market, the proceeds going, half and half, to the government and the warriors who bring them in. The purchasers are credited with the amount of labor performed by their particular slaves. At the end of a year a good slave will have performed the labor tax of his master for six years, and if slaves are plentiful he is freed and permitted to return to his own people."

"You fight in platinum and diamonds?" asked Tara, indicating his gorgeous trappings with a quizzical smile.

Gahan laughed. "We are a vain people," he admitted, good-naturedly, "and it is possible that we place too much value on personal appearances. We vie with one another in the splendor of our accoutrements when trapped for the observance of the lighter duties of life, though when we take the field our leather is the plainest I ever have seen worn by fighting men of Barsoom. We pride ourselves, too, upon our physical beauty, and especially upon the beauty of our women. May I dare to say, Tara of Helium, that I am hoping for the day when you will visit Gathol that my people may see one who is really beautiful?"

"The women of Helium are taught to frown with displeasure upon the tongue of the flatterer," rejoined the girl, but Gahan, Jed of Gathol, observed that she smiled as she said it.

A bugle sounded, clear and sweet, above the laughter and the talk. "The Dance of Barsoom!" exclaimed the young warrior. "I claim you for it, Tara of Helium."

The girl glanced in the direction of the bench where she had last seen Djor Kantos. He was not in sight. She inclined her head in assent to the claim of the Gatholian. Slaves were passing among the guests, distributing small musical instruments of a single string. Upon each instrument were characters which indicated the pitch and length of its tone. The instruments were of skeel, the string of gut, and were shaped to fit the left forearm of the dancer, to which it was strapped. There was also a ring wound with gut which was worn between the first and second joints of the index finger of the right hand and which, when passed over the string of the instrument, elicited the single note required of the dancer.

The guests had risen and were slowly making their way toward the expanse of scarlet sward at the south end of the gardens where the dance was to be held, when Djor Kantos came hurriedly toward Tara of Helium. "I claim – " he exclaimed as he neared her; but she interrupted him with a gesture.

"You are too late, Djor Kantos," she cried in mock anger. "No laggard may claim Tara of Helium; but haste now lest thou lose also Olvia Marthis, whom I have never seen wait long to be claimed for this or any other dance."

"I have already lost her," admitted Djor Kantos ruefully.

"And you mean to say that you came for Tara of Helium only after having lost Olvia Marthis?" demanded the girl, still simulating displeasure.

"Oh, Tara of Helium, you know better than that," insisted the young man. "Was it not natural that I should assume that you would expect me, who alone has claimed you for the Dance of Barsoom for at least twelve times past?"

"And sit and play with my thumbs until you saw fit to come for me?" she questioned. "Ah, no, Djor Kantos; Tara of Helium is for no laggard," and she threw him a sweet smile and passed on toward the assembling dancers with Gahan, Jed of far Gathol.

The Dance of Barsoom bears a relation similar to the more formal dancing functions of Mars that The Grand March does to ours, though it is infinitely more intricate and more beautiful. Before a Martian youth of either sex may attend an important social function where there is dancing, he must have become proficient in at least three dances – The Dance of Barsoom, his national dance, and the dance of his city. In these three dances the dancers furnish their own music, which never varies; nor do the steps or figures vary, having been handed down from time immemorial. All Barsoomian dances are stately and beautiful, but The Dance of Barsoom is a wondrous epic of motion and harmony – there is no grotesque posturing, no vulgar or suggestive movements. It has been described as the interpretation of the highest ideals of a world that aspired to grace and beauty and chastity in woman, and strength and dignity and loyalty in man.

Today, John Carter, Warlord of Mars, with Dejah Thoris, his mate, led in the dancing, and if there was another couple that vied with them in possession of the silent admiration of the guests it was the resplendent Jed of Gathol and his beautiful partner. In the ever-changing figures of the dance the man found himself now with the girl's hand in his and again with an arm about the lithe body that the jeweled harness but inadequately covered, and the girl, though she had danced a thousand dances in the past, realized for the first time the personal contact of a man's arm against her naked flesh. It troubled her that she should notice it, and she looked up questioningly and almost with displeasure at the man as though it was his fault. Their eyes met and she saw in his that which she had never seen in the eyes of Djor Kantos. It was at the very end of the dance and they both stopped suddenly with the music and stood there looking straight into each other's eyes. It was Gahan of Gathol who spoke first.

"Tara of Helium, I love you!" he said.

The girl drew herself to her full height. "The Jed of Gathol forgets himself," she exclaimed haughtily.

"The Jed of Gathol would forget everything but you, Tara of Helium," he replied. Fiercely he pressed the soft hand that he still retained from the last position of the dance. "I love you, Tara of Helium," he repeated. "Why should your ears refuse to hear what your eyes but just now did not refuse to see – and answer?"

"What meanest thou?" she cried. "Are the men of Gathol such boors, then?"

"They are neither boors nor fools," he replied, quietly. "They know when they love a woman – and when she loves them."

Tara of Helium stamped her little foot in anger. "Go!" she said, "before it is necessary to acquaint my father with the dishonor of his guest."

She turned and walked away. "Wait!" cried the man. "Just another word."

"Of apology?" she asked.

"Of prophecy," he said.

"I do not care to hear it," replied Tara of Helium, and left him standing there. She was strangely unstrung and shortly thereafter returned to her own quarter of the palace, where she stood for a long time by a window looking out beyond the scarlet tower of Greater Helium toward the northwest.

Presently she turned angrily away. "I hate him!" she exclaimed aloud.

"Whom?" inquired the privileged Uthia.

Tara of Helium stamped her foot. "That ill-mannered boor, the Jed of Gathol," she replied.

Uthia raised her slim brows.

At the stamping of the little foot, a great beast rose from the corner of the room and crossed to Tara of Helium where it stood looking up into her face. She placed her hand upon the ugly head. "Dear old Woola," she said; "no love could be deeper than yours, yet it never offends. Would that men might pattern themselves after you!"

CHAPTER TWO

At the Gale's Mercy

TARA OF HELIUM did not return to her father's guests, but awaited in her own apartments the word from Djor Kantos which she knew must come, begging her to return to the gardens. She would then refuse, haughtily. But no appeal came from Djor Kantos. At first Tara of Helium was angry, then she was hurt, and always she was puzzled. She could not understand. Occasionally she thought of the Jed of Gathol and then she would stamp her foot, for she was very angry indeed with Gahan. The presumption of the man! He had insinuated that he read love for him in her eyes. Never had she been so insulted and humiliated. Never had she so thoroughly hated a man. Suddenly she turned toward Uthia.

"My flying leather!" she commanded.

"But the guests!" exclaimed the slave girl. "Your father, The Warlord, will expect you to return."

"He will be disappointed," snapped Tara of Helium.

The slave hesitated. "He does not approve of your flying alone," she reminded her mistress.

The young princess sprang to her feet and seized the unhappy slave by the shoulders, shaking her. "You are becoming unbearable, Uthia," she cried. "Soon there will be no alternative than to send you to the public slave-market. Then possibly you will find a master to your liking."

Tears came to the soft eyes of the slave girl. "It is because I love you, my princess," she said softly. Tara of Helium melted. She took the slave in her arms and kissed her.

"I have the disposition of a thoat, Uthia," she said. "Forgive me! I love you and there is nothing that I would not do for you and nothing would I do to harm you. Again, as I have so often in the past, I offer you your freedom."

"I do not wish my freedom if it will separate me from you, Tara of Helium," replied Uthia. "I am happy here with you – I think that I should die without you."

Again the girls kissed. "And you will not fly alone, then?" questioned the slave.

Tara of Helium laughed and pinched her companion. "You persistent little pest," she cried. "Of course I shall fly – does not Tara of Helium always do that which pleases her?"

Uthia shook her head sorrowfully. "Alas! she does," she admitted. "Iron is the Warlord of Barsoom to the influences of all but two. In the hands of Dejah Thoris and Tara of Helium he is as potters' clay."

"Then run and fetch my flying leather like the sweet slave you are," directed the mistress.

Far out across the ochre sea-bottoms beyond the twin cities of Helium raced the swift flier of Tara of Helium. Thrilling to the speed and the buoyancy and the obedience of the little craft the girl drove toward the northwest. Why she should choose that direction she did not pause to consider. Perhaps because in that direction lay the least known areas of Barsoom, and, ergo, Romance, Mystery, and Adventure. In that direction also lay far Gathol; but to that fact she gave no conscious thought.

She did, however, think occasionally of the jed of that distant kingdom, but the reaction to these thoughts was scarcely pleasurable. They still brought a flush of shame to her cheeks and a surge of angry blood to her heart. She was very angry with the Jed of Gathol, and though she should never see him again she was quite sure that hate of him would remain fresh in her memory forever. Mostly her thoughts revolved about another – Djor Kantos. And when she thought of him she thought also of Olvia Marthis of Hastor. Tara of Helium thought that she was jealous of the fair Olvia and it made her very angry to think that. She was angry with Djor Kantos and herself, but she was not angry at all with Olvia Marthis, whom she loved, and so of course she was not jealous really. The trouble was, that Tara of Helium had failed for once to have her own way. Djor Kantos had not come running like a willing slave when she had expected him, and, ah, here was the nub of the whole thing! Gahan, Jed of Gathol, a stranger, had been a witness to her humiliation. He had seen her unclaimed at the beginning of a great function and he had had to come to her rescue to save her, as he doubtless thought, from the inglorious fate of a wall-flower. At the recurring thought, Tara of

Helium could feel her whole body burning with scarlet shame and then she went suddenly white and cold with rage; whereupon she turned her flier about so abruptly that she was all but torn from her lashings upon the flat, narrow deck. She reached home just before dark. The guests had departed. Quiet had descended upon the palace. An hour later she joined her father and mother at the evening meal.

"You deserted us, Tara of Helium," said John Carter. "It is not what the guests of John Carter should expect."

"They did not come to see me," replied Tara of Helium. "I did not ask them."

"They were no less your guests," replied her father.

The girl rose, and came and stood beside him and put her arms about his neck.

"My proper old Virginian," she cried, rumpling his shock of black hair.

"In Virginia you would be turned over your father's knee and spanked," said the man, smiling.

She crept into his lap and kissed him. "You do not love me any more," she announced. "No one loves me," but she could not compose her features into a pout because bubbling laughter insisted upon breaking through.

"The trouble is there are too many who love you," he said. "And now there is another."

"Indeed!" she cried. "What do you mean?"

"Gahan of Gathol has asked permission to woo you."

The girl sat up very straight and tilted her chin in the air. "I would not wed with a walking diamond-mine," she said. "I will not have him."

"I told him as much," replied her father, "and that you were as good as betrothed to another. He was very courteous about it; but at the same time he gave me to understand that he was accustomed to getting what he wanted and that he wanted you very much. I suppose it will mean another war. Your mother's beauty kept Helium at war for many years, and – well, Tara of Helium, if I were a young man I should doubtless be willing to set all Barsoom afire to win you, as I still would to keep your divine mother," and he smiled across the sorapus table and its golden service at the undimmed beauty of Mars' most beautiful woman.

"Our little girl should not yet be troubled with such matters," said Dejah Thoris. "Remember, John Carter, that you are not dealing with an Earth child, whose span of life would be more than half completed before a daughter of Barsoom reached actual maturity."

"But do not the daughters of Barsoom sometimes marry as early as twenty?" he insisted.

"Yes, but they will still be desirable in the eyes of men after forty generations of Earth folk have returned to dust – there is no hurry, at least, upon Barsoom. We do not fade and decay here as you tell me those of your planet do, though you, yourself, belie your own words. When the time seems proper Tara of Helium shall wed with Djor Kantos, and until then let us give the matter no further thought."

"No," said the girl, "the subject irks me, and I shall not marry Djor Kantos, or another – I do not intend to wed."

Her father and mother looked at her and smiled. "When Gahan of Gathol returns he may carry you off," said the former.

"He has gone?" asked the girl.

"His flier departs for Gathol in the morning," John Carter replied.

"I have seen the last of him then," remarked Tara of Helium with a sigh of relief.

"He says not," returned John Carter.

The girl dismissed the subject with a shrug and the conversation passed to other topics. A letter had arrived from Thuvia of Ptarth, who was visiting at her father's court while Carthoris, her mate, hunted in Okar. Word had been received that the Tharks and Warhoons were again at war, or rather that there had been an engagement, for war was their habitual state. In the memory of man there had been no peace between these two savage green hordes – only a single temporary truce. Two new battleships had been launched at Hastor. A little band of holy therns was attempting to revive the ancient and discredited religion of Issus, who they claimed still lived in spirit and had communicated with them. There were rumors of war from Dusar. A scientist claimed to have discovered human life on the further moon. A madman had attempted to destroy the atmosphere plant. Seven people had been assassinated in Greater Helium during the last ten zodes, (the equivalent of an Earth day).

Following the meal Dejah Thoris and The Warlord played at jetan, the Barsoomian game of chess, which is played upon a board of a hundred alternate black and orange squares. One player has twenty black pieces, the other, twenty orange pieces. A brief description of the game may interest those Earth readers who care for chess, and will not be lost upon those who pursue this narrative to its conclusion, since before they are done they will find that a knowledge of jetan will add to the interest and the thrills that are in store for them.

The men are placed upon the board as in chess upon the first two rows next the players. In order from left to right on the line of squares nearest the players, the jetan pieces are Warrior, Padwar, Dwar, Flier, Chief, Princess, Flier, Dwar, Padwar, Warrior. In the next line all are Panthans except the end pieces, which are called Thoats, and represent mounted warriors.

The Panthans, which are represented as warriors with one feather, may move one space in any direction except backward; the Thoats, mounted warriors with three feathers, may move one straight and one diagonal, and may jump intervening pieces; Warriors, foot soldiers with two feathers, straight in any direction, or diagonally, two spaces; Padwars, lieutenants wearing two feathers, two diagonal in any direction, or combination; Dwars, captains wearing three feathers, three spaces straight in any direction, or combination; Fliers, represented by a propellor with three blades, three spaces in any direction, or combination, diagonally, and may jump intervening pieces; the Chief, indicated by a diadem with ten jewels, three spaces in any direction, straight, or diagonal; Princess, diadem with a single jewel, same as Chief, and can jump intervening pieces.

The game is won when a player places any of his pieces on the same square with his opponent's Princess, or when a Chief takes a Chief. It is drawn when a Chief is taken by any opposing piece other than the opposing Chief; or when both sides have been reduced to three pieces, or less, of equal value, and the game is not terminated in the following ten moves, five apiece. This is but a general outline of the game, briefly stated.

It was this game that Dejah Thoris and John Carter were playing when Tara of Helium bid them good night, retiring to her own quarters and her sleeping silks and furs. "Until morning, my beloved," she called back to them as she passed from the apartment, nor little did she guess, nor her parents, that this might indeed be the last time that they would ever set eyes upon her.

The morning broke dull and gray. Ominous clouds billowed restlessly and low. Beneath them torn fragments scudded toward the northwest. From her window Tara of Helium looked out upon this unusual scene. Dense clouds seldom overcast the Barsoomian sky. At this hour of the day it was her custom to ride one of those small thoats that are the saddle animals of the red Martians, but the sight of the billowing clouds lured her to a new adventure. Uthia still slept and the girl did not disturb her. Instead, she dressed quietly and went to the hangar upon the roof of the palace directly above her quarters where her own swift flier was housed. She had never driven through the clouds. It was an adventure that always she had longed to experience. The wind was strong and it was with difficulty that she maneuvered the craft from the hangar without accident, but once away it raced swiftly out above the twin cities. The buffeting winds caught and tossed it, and the girl laughed aloud in sheer joy of the resultant thrills. She handled the little ship like a veteran, though few veterans would have faced the menace of such a storm in so light a craft. Swiftly she rose toward the clouds, racing with the scudding streamers of the storm-swept fragments, and a moment later she was swallowed by the dense masses billowing above. Here was a new world, a world of chaos unpeopled except for herself; but it was a cold, damp, lonely world and she found it depressing after the novelty of it had been dissipated, by an overpowering sense of the magnitude of the forces surging about her. Suddenly she felt very lonely and very cold and very little. Hurriedly, therefore, she rose until presently her craft broke through into the glorious sunlight that transformed the upper surface of the somber element into rolling masses of burnished silver. Here it was still cold, but without the dampness of the clouds, and in the eye of the brilliant sun her spirits rose with the mounting needle of her altimeter. Gazing at the clouds, now far beneath, the girl experienced the sensation of hanging stationary in mid-heaven; but the whirring of her propellor, the wind beating upon her, the high figures that rose and fell beneath the glass of her speedometer, these told her that her speed was terrific. It was then that she determined to turn back.

The first attempt she made above the clouds, but it was unsuccessful. To her surprise she discovered that she could not even turn against the high wind, which rocked and buffeted the frail craft. Then she dropped swiftly to the dark and wind-swept zone between the hurtling clouds and the gloomy surface of the shadowed ground. Here she tried again to force the nose of the flier back toward Helium, but the tempest seized the frail thing and hurled it remorselessly about, rolling it over and over and tossing it as it were a cork in a cataract. At last the girl succeeded in righting the flier, perilously close to the ground. Never before had she been so close to death, yet she was not terrified. Her coolness had saved her, that and the strength of the deck lashings that held her. Traveling with the storm she was safe, but where was it bearing her? She pictured the apprehension of her father and mother when she failed to appear at the morning meal. They would find her flier missing and they would guess that somewhere in the path of the storm it lay a wrecked and tangled mass upon her dead body, and then brave men would go out in search of her, risking their lives; and that lives would be lost in the search, she knew, for she realized now that never in her life-time had such a tempest raged upon Barsoom.

She must turn back! She must reach Helium before her mad lust for thrills had cost the sacrifice of a single courageous life! She determined that greater safety and likelihood of success lay above the clouds, and once again she rose through the chilling, wind-tossed vapor. Her speed again was terrific, for the wind seemed to have increased rather than to have lessened. She sought gradually to check the swift flight of her craft, but though she finally succeeded in reversing her motor the wind but carried her on as it would. Then it was that Tara of Helium lost her temper. Had her world not always bowed in acquiescence to her every wish? What were these elements that they dared to thwart her? She would demonstrate to them that the daughter of The Warlord was not to be denied! They would learn that Tara of Helium might not be ruled even by the forces of nature!

And so she drove her motor forward again and then with her firm, white teeth set in grim determination she drove the steering lever far down to port with the intention of forcing the nose of her craft straight into the teeth of the wind, and the wind seized the frail thing and toppled it over upon its back, and twisted and turned it and hurled it over and over; the propellor raced for an instant in an air pocket and then the tempest seized it again and twisted it from its shaft, leaving the girl helpless upon an unmanageable atom that rose and fell, and rolled and tumbled – the sport of the elements she had defied. Tara of Helium's first sensation was one of surprise – that she had failed to have her own way. Then she commenced to feel concern – not for her own safety but for the anxiety of her parents and the dangers that the inevitable searchers must face. She reproached herself for the thoughtless selfishness that had jeopardized the peace and safety of others. She realized her own grave danger, too; but she was still unterrified, as befitted the daughter of Dejah Thoris and John Carter. She knew that her buoyancy tanks might keep her afloat indefinitely, but she had neither food nor water, and she was being borne toward the least-known area of Barsoom. Perhaps it would be better to land immediately and await the coming of the searchers, rather than to allow herself to be carried still further from Helium, thus greatly reducing the chances of early discovery; but when she dropped toward the ground she discovered that the violence of the wind rendered an attempt to land tantamount to destruction and she rose again, rapidly.

Carried along a few hundred feet above the ground she was better able to appreciate the Titanic proportions of the storm than when she had flown in the comparative serenity of the zone above the clouds, for now she could distinctly see the effect of the wind upon the surface of Barsoom. The air was filled with dust and flying bits of vegetation and when the storm carried her across an irrigated area of farm land she saw great trees and stone walls and buildings lifted high in air and scattered broadcast over the devastated country; and then she was carried swiftly on to other sights that forced in upon her consciousness a rapidly growing conviction that after all Tara of Helium was a very small and insignificant and helpless person. It was quite a shock to her self-pride while it lasted, and toward evening she was ready to believe that it was going to last forever. There had been no abatement in the ferocity of the tempest, nor was there indication of any. She could only guess at the distance she had been carried for she could not believe in the correctness of the high figures that had been piled upon the record of her odometer. They seemed unbelievable and yet, had she known it, they were quite true – in twelve hours she had flown and been carried by the storm full seven thousand haads. Just before dark she was carried over one of the deserted cities of ancient Mars. It was Torquas, but she did not know it. Had she, she might readily have been forgiven for abandoning the last vestige of hope, for to the people of Helium Torquas seems as remote as do the South Sea Islands to us. And still the tempest, its fury unabated, bore her on.

All that night she hurtled through the dark beneath the clouds, or rose to race through the moonlit void beneath the glory of Barsoom's two satellites. She was cold and hungry and altogether miserable, but her brave little spirit refused to admit that her plight was hopeless even though reason proclaimed the truth. Her reply to reason, sometime spoken aloud in sudden defiance, recalled the Spartan stubbornness of her sire in the face of certain annihilation: "I still live!"

That morning there had been an early visitor at the palace of The Warlord. It was Gahan, Jed of Gathol. He had arrived shortly after the absence of Tara of Helium had been noted, and in the excitement he had remained unannounced until John Carter had happened upon him in the great reception corridor of the palace as The Warlord was hurrying out to arrange for the dispatch of ships in search of his daughter.

Gahan read the concern upon the face of The Warlord. "Forgive me if I intrude, John Carter," he said. "I but came to ask the indulgence of another day since it would be fool-hardy to attempt to navigate a ship in such a storm."

"Remain, Gahan, a welcome guest until you choose to leave us," replied The Warlord; "but you must forgive any seeming inattention upon the part of Helium until my daughter is restored to us."

"You daughter! Restored! What do you mean?" exclaimed the Gatholian. "I do not understand."

"She is gone, together with her light flier. That is all we know. We can only assume that she decided to fly before the morning meal and was caught in the clutches of the tempest. You will pardon me, Gahan, if I leave you abruptly – I am arranging to send ships in search of her;" but Gahan, Jed of Gathol, was already speeding in the direction of the palace gate. There he leaped upon a waiting thoat and followed by two warriors in the metal of Gathol, he dashed through the avenues of Helium toward the palace that had been set aside for his entertainment.

CHAPTER THREE

The Headless Humans

ABOVE THE ROOF of the palace that housed the Jed of Gathol and his entourage, the cruiser Vanator tore at her stout moorings. The groaning tackle bespoke the mad fury of the gale, while the worried faces of those members of the crew whose duties demanded their presence on the straining craft gave corroborative evidence of the gravity of the situation. Only stout lashings prevented these men from being swept from the deck, while those upon the roof below were constantly compelled to cling to rails and stanchions to save themselves from being carried away by each new burst of meteoric fury. Upon the prow of the Vanator was painted the device of Gathol, but no pennants were displayed in the upper works since the storm had carried away several in rapid succession, just as it seemed to the watching men that it must carry away the ship itself. They could not believe that any tackle could withstand for long this Titanic force. To each of the twelve lashings clung a brawny warrior with drawn short-sword. Had but a single mooring given to the power of the tempest eleven short-swords would have cut the others; since, partially moored, the ship was doomed, while free in the tempest it stood at least some slight chance for life.

"By the blood of Issus, I believe they will hold!" screamed one warrior to another.

"And if they do not hold may the spirits of our ancestors reward the brave warriors upon the Vanator," replied another of those upon the roof of the palace, "for it will not be long from the moment her cables part before her crew dons the leather of the dead; but yet, Tanus, I believe they will hold. Give thanks at least that we did not sail before the tempest fell, since now each of us has a chance to live."

"Yes," replied Tanus, "I should hate to be abroad today upon the stoutest ship that sails the Barsoomian sky."

It was then that Gahan the Jed appeared upon the roof. With him were the balance of his own party and a dozen warriors of Helium. The young chief turned to his followers.

"I sail at once upon the Vanator," he said, "in search of Tara of Helium who is thought to have been carried away upon a one-man flier by the storm. I do not need to explain to you the slender chances the Vanator has to withstand the fury of the tempest, nor will I order you to your deaths. Let those who wish remain behind without dishonor. The others will follow me," and he leaped for the rope ladder that lashed wildly in the gale.

The first man to follow him was Tanus and when the last reached the deck of the cruiser there remained upon the palace roof only the twelve warriors of Helium, who, with naked swords, had taken the posts of the Gatholians at the moorings.

Not a single warrior who had remained aboard the Vanator would leave her now.

"I expected no less," said Gahan, as with the help of those already on the deck he and the others found secure lashings. The commander of the Vanator shook his head. He loved his trim craft, the pride of her class in the little navy of Gathol. It was of her he thought – not of himself. He saw her lying torn and twisted upon the ochre vegetation of some distant sea-bottom, to be presently overrun and looted by some savage, green horde. He looked at Gahan.

"Are you ready, San Tothis?" asked the jed.

"All is ready."

"Then cut away!"

Word was passed across the deck and over the side to the Heliumetic warriors below that at the third gun they were to cut away. Twelve keen swords must strike simultaneously and with equal power, and each must sever completely and instantly three strands of heavy cable that no loose end fouling a block bring immediate disaster upon the Vanator.

Boom! The voice of the signal gun rolled down through the screaming wind to the twelve warriors upon the roof. Boom! Twelve swords were raised above twelve brawny shoulders. Boom! Twelve keen edges severed twelve complaining moorings, clean and as one.

The Vanator, her propellors whirling, shot forward with the storm. The tempest struck her in the stern as with a mailed fist and stood the great ship upon her nose, and then it caught her and spun her as a child's top spins; and upon the palace roof the twelve men looked on in silent helplessness and prayed for the souls of the brave warriors who were going to their death. And others saw, from Helium's lofty landing stages and from a thousand hangars upon a thousand roofs; but only for an instant did the preparations stop that would send other brave men into the frightful maelstrom of that apparently hopeless search, for such is the courage of the warriors of Barsoom.

But the Vanator did not fall to the ground, within sight of the city at least, though as long as the watchers could see her never for an instant did she rest upon an even keel. Sometimes she lay upon one side or the other, or again she hurtled along keel up, or rolled over and over, or stood upon her nose or her tail at the caprice of the great force that carried her along. And the watchers saw that this great ship was merely being blown away with the other bits of debris great and small that filled the sky. Never in the memory of man or the annals of recorded history had such a storm raged across the face of Barsoom.

And in another instant was the Vanator forgotten as the lofty, scarlet tower that had marked Lesser Helium for ages crashed to ground, carrying death and demolition upon the city beneath. Panic reigned. A fire broke out in the ruins. The city's every force seemed crippled, and it was then that The Warlord ordered the men that were about to set forth in search of Tara of Helium to devote their energies to the salvation of the city, for he too had witnessed the start of the Vanator and realized the futility of wasting men who were needed sorely if Lesser Helium was to be saved from utter destruction.

Shortly after noon of the second day the storm commenced to abate, and before the sun went down, the little craft upon which Tara of Helium had hovered between life and death these many hours drifted slowly before a gentle breeze above a landscape of rolling hills that once had been lofty mountains upon a Martian continent. The girl was exhausted from loss of sleep, from lack of food and drink, and from the nervous reaction consequent to the terrifying experiences through which she had passed. In the near distance, just topping an intervening hill, she caught a momentary glimpse of what appeared to be a dome-capped tower. Quickly she dropped the flier until the hill shut it off from the view of the possible occupants of the structure she had seen. The tower meant to her the habitation of man, suggesting the presence of water and, perhaps, of food. If the tower was the deserted relic of a bygone age she would scarcely find food there, but there was still a chance that there might be water. If it was inhabited, then must her approach be cautious, for only enemies might be expected to abide in so far distant a land. Tara of Helium knew that she must be far from the twin cities of her grandfather's empire, but had she guessed within even a thousand haads of the reality, she had been stunned by realization of the utter hopelessness of her state.

Keeping the craft low, for the buoyancy tanks were still intact, the girl skimmed the ground until the gently-moving wind had carried her to the side of the last hill that intervened between her and the structure she had thought a man-built tower. Here she brought the flier to the ground among some stunted trees, and dragging it beneath one where it might be somewhat hidden from craft passing above, she made it fast and set forth to reconnoiter. Like most women of her class she was armed only with a single slender blade, so that in such an emergency as now confronted her she must depend almost solely upon her cleverness in remaining undiscovered by enemies. With utmost caution she crept warily toward the crest of the hill, taking advantage of every natural screen that the landscape afforded to conceal her approach from possible observers ahead, while momentarily she cast quick glances rearward lest she be taken by surprise from that quarter.

She came at last to the summit, where, from the concealment of a low bush, she could see what lay beyond. Beneath her spread a beautiful valley surrounded by low hills. Dotting it were numerous circular towers, dome-capped, and surrounding each tower was a stone wall enclosing several acres of ground. The valley appeared to be in a high state of cultivation. Upon the opposite side of the hill and just beneath her was a tower and enclosure. It was the roof of the former that had first attracted her attention. In all respects it seemed identical in construction with those further out in the valley – a high, plastered wall of massive construction surrounding a similarly constructed tower, upon whose gray surface was painted in vivid colors a strange device. The towers were about forty sofads in diameter, approximately forty earth-feet, and sixty in height to the base of the dome. To an Earth man they would have immediately suggested the silos in which dairy farmers store ensilage for their herds; but closer scrutiny, revealing an occasional embrasured opening together with the strange construction of the domes, would have altered such a conclusion. Tara of Helium saw that the domes seemed to be faced with innumerable prisms of glass, those that were exposed to the declining sun scintillating so gorgeously as to remind her suddenly of the magnificent trappings of Gahan of Gathol. As she thought of the man she shook her head angrily, and moved cautiously forward a foot or two that she might get a less obstructed view of the nearer tower and its enclosure.

As Tara of Helium looked down into the enclosure surrounding the nearest tower, her brows contracted momentarily in frowning surprise, and then her eyes went wide in an expression of incredulity tinged with horror, for what she saw was a score or two of human bodies – naked and headless. For a long moment she watched, breathless; unable to believe the evidence of her own eyes – that these grewsome things moved and had life! She saw them crawling about on hands and knees over and across one another, searching about with their fingers. And she saw some of them at troughs, for which the others seemed to be searching, and those at the troughs were taking something from these receptacles and apparently putting it in a hole where their necks should have been. They were not far beneath her – she could see them distinctly and she saw that there were the bodies of both men and women, and that they were beautifully proportioned, and that their skin was similar to hers, but of a slightly lighter red. At first she had thought that she was looking upon a shambles and that the bodies, but recently decapitated, were moving under the impulse of muscular reaction; but presently she realized that this was their normal condition. The horror of them fascinated her, so that she could scarce take her eyes from them. It was evident from their groping hands that they were eyeless, and their sluggish movements suggested a rudimentary nervous system and a correspondingly minute brain. The girl wondered how they subsisted for she could not, even by the wildest stretch of imagination, picture these imperfect creatures as intelligent tillers of the soil. Yet that the soil of the valley was tilled was evident and that these things had food was equally so. But who tilled the soil? Who kept and fed these unhappy things, and for what purpose? It was an enigma beyond her powers of deduction.

The sight of food aroused again a consciousness of her own gnawing hunger and the thirst that parched her throat. She could see both food and water within the enclosure; but would she dare enter even should she find means of ingress? She doubted it, since the very thought of possible contact with these grewsome creatures sent a shudder through her frame.

Then her eyes wandered again out across the valley until presently they picked out what appeared to be a tiny stream winding its way through the center of the farm lands – a strange sight upon Barsoom. Ah, if it were but water! Then might she hope with a real hope, for the fields would give her sustenance which she could gain by night, while by day she hid among the surrounding hills, and sometime, yes, sometime she knew, the searchers would come, for John Carter, Warlord of Barsoom, would never cease to search for his daughter until every square haad of the planet had been combed again and again. She knew him and she knew the warriors of Helium and so she knew that could she but manage to escape harm until they came, they would indeed come at last.

She would have to wait until dark before she dare venture into the valley, and in the meantime she thought it well to search out a place of safety nearby where she might be reasonably safe from savage beasts. It was possible that the district was free from carnivora, but one might never be sure in a strange land. As she was about to withdraw be hind the brow of the hill her attention was again attracted to the enclosure below. Two figures had emerged from the tower. Their beautiful bodies seemed identical with those of the headless creatures among which they moved, but the newcomers were not headless. Upon their shoulders were heads that seemed human, yet which the girl intuitively sensed were not human. They were just a trifle too far away for her to see them distinctly in the waning light of the dying day, but she knew that they were too large, they were out of proportion to the perfectly proportioned bodies, and they were oblate in form. She could see that the men wore some manner of harness to which were slung the customary long-sword and short-sword of the Barsoomian warrior, and that about their short necks were massive leather collars cut to fit closely over the shoulders and snugly to the lower part of the head. Their features were scarce discernible, but there was a suggestion of grotesqueness about them that carried to her a feeling of revulsion.

The two carried a long rope to which were fastened, at intervals of about two sofads, what she later guessed were light manacles, for she saw the warriors passing among the poor creatures in the enclosure and about the right wrist of each they fastened one of the manacles. When all had been thus fastened to the rope one of the warriors commenced to pull and tug at the loose end as though attempting to drag the headless company toward the tower, while the other went among them with a long, light whip with which he flicked them upon the naked skin. Slowly, dully, the creatures rose to their feet and between the tugging of the warrior in front and the lashing of him behind the hopeless band was finally herded within the tower. Tara of Helium shuddered as she turned away. What manner of creatures were these?

Suddenly it was night. The Barsoomian day had ended, and then the brief period of twilight that renders the transition from daylight to darkness almost as abrupt as the switching off of an electric light, and Tara of Helium had found no sanctuary. But perhaps there were no beasts to fear, or rather to avoid – Tara of Helium liked not the word fear. She would have been glad, however, had there been a cabin, even a very tiny cabin, upon her small flier; but there was no cabin. The interior of the hull was completely taken up by the buoyancy tanks. Ah, she had it! How stupid of her not to have thought of it before! She could moor the craft to the tree beneath which it rested and let it rise the length of the rope. Lashed to the deck rings she would then be safe from any roaming beast of prey that chanced along. In the morning she could drop to the ground again before the craft was discovered.

As Tara of Helium crept over the brow of the hill down toward the valley, her presence was hidden by the darkness of the night from the sight of any chance observer who might be loitering by a window in the nearby tower. Cluros, the farther moon, was just rising above the horizon to commence his leisurely journey through the heavens. Eight zodes later he would set – a trifle over nineteen and a half Earth hours – and during that time Thuria, his vivacious mate, would have circled the planet twice and be more than half way around on her third trip. She had but just set. It would be more than three and a half hours before she shot above the opposite horizon to hurtle, swift and low, across the face of the dying planet. During this temporary absence of the mad moon Tara of Helium hoped to find both food and water, and gain again the safety of her flier's deck.

She groped her way through the darkness, giving the tower and its enclosure as wide a berth as possible. Sometimes she stumbled, for in the long shadows cast by the rising Cluros objects were grotesquely distorted though the light from the moon was still not sufficient to be of much assistance to her. Nor, as a matter of fact, did she want light. She could find the stream in the dark, by the simple expedient of going down hill until she walked into it and she had seen that bearing trees and many crops grew throughout the valley, so that she would pass food in plenty ere she reached the stream. If the moon showed her the way more clearly and thus saved her from an occasional fall, he would, too, show her more clearly to the strange denizens of the towers, and that, of course, must not be. Could she have waited until the following night conditions would have been better, since Cluros would not appear in the heavens at all and so, during Thuria's absence, utter darkness would reign; but the pangs of thirst and the gnawing of hunger could be endured no longer with food and drink both in sight, and so she had decided to risk discovery rather than suffer longer.

Safely past the nearest tower, she moved as rapidly as she felt consistent with safety, choosing her way wherever possible so that she might take advantage of the shadows of the trees that grew at intervals and at the same time discover those which bore fruit. In this latter she met with almost immediate success, for the very third tree beneath which she halted was heavy with ripe fruit. Never, thought Tara of Helium, had aught so delicious impinged upon her palate, and yet it was naught else than the almost tasteless usa, which is considered to be palatable only after having been cooked and highly spiced. It grows easily with little irrigation and the trees bear abundantly. The fruit, which ranks high in food value, is one of the staple foods of the less well-to-do, and because of its cheapness and nutritive value forms one of the principal rations of both armies and navies upon Barsoom, a use which has won for it a Martian sobriquet which, freely translated into English, would be, The Fighting Potato. The girl was wise enough to eat but sparingly, but she filled her pocket-pouch with the fruit before she continued upon her way.

Two towers she passed before she came at last to the stream, and here again was she temperate, drinking but little and that very slowly, contenting herself with rinsing her mouth frequently and bathing her face, her hands, and her feet; and even though the night was cold, as Martian nights are, the sensation of refreshment more than compensated for the physical discomfort of the low temperature. Replacing her sandals she sought among the growing track near the stream for whatever edible berries or tubers might be planted there, and found a couple of varieties that could be eaten raw. With these she replaced some of the usa in her pocket-pouch, not only to insure a variety but because she found them more palatable. Occasionally she returned to the stream to drink, but each time moderately. Always were her eyes and ears alert for the first signs of danger, but she had neither seen nor heard aught to disturb her. And presently the time approached when she felt she must return to her flier lest she be caught in the revealing light of low swinging Thuria. She dreaded leaving the water for she knew that she must become very thirsty before she could hope to come again to the stream. If she only had some little receptacle in which to carry water, even a small amount would tide her over until the following night; but she had nothing and so she must content herself as best she could with the juices of the fruit and tubers she had gathered.

After a last drink at the stream, the longest and deepest she had allowed herself, she rose to retrace her steps toward the hills; but even as she did so she became suddenly tense with apprehension. What was that? She could have sworn that she saw something move in the shadows beneath a tree not far away. For a long minute the girl did not move – she scarce breathed. Her eyes remained fixed upon the dense shadows below the tree, her ears strained through the silence of the night. A low moaning came down from the hills where her flier was hidden. She knew it well – the weird note of the hunting banth. And the great carnivore lay directly in her path. But he was not so close as this other thing, hiding there in the shadows just a little way off. What was it? It was the strain of uncertainty that weighed heaviest upon her. Had she known the nature of the creature lurking there half its menace would have vanished. She cast quickly about her in search of some haven of refuge should the thing prove dangerous.

Again arose the moaning from the hills, but this time closer. Almost immediately it was answered from the opposite side of the valley, behind her, and then from the distance to the right of her, and twice upon her left. Her eyes had found a tree, quite near. Slowly, and without taking her eyes from the shadows of that other tree, she moved toward the overhanging branches that might afford her sanctuary in the event of need, and at her first move a low growl rose from the spot she had been watching and she heard the sudden moving of a big body. Simultaneously the creature shot into the moonlight in full charge upon her, its tail erect, its tiny ears laid flat, its great mouth with its multiple rows of sharp and powerful fangs already yawning for its prey, its ten legs carrying it forward in great leaps, and now from the beast's throat issued the frightful roar with which it seeks to paralyze its prey. It was a banth – the great, maned lion of Barsoom. Tara of Helium saw it coming and leaped for the tree toward which she had been moving, and the banth realized her intention and redoubled his speed. As his hideous roar awakened the echoes in the hills, so too it awakened echoes in the valley; but these echoes came from the living throats of others of his kind, until it seemed to the girl that Fate had thrown her into the midst of a countless multitude of these savage beasts.

Almost incredibly swift is the speed of a charging banth, and fortunate it was that the girl had not been caught farther in the open. As it was, her margin of safety was next to negligible, for as she swung nimbly to the lower branches the creature in pursuit of her crashed among the foliage almost upon her as it sprang upward to seize her. It was only a combination of good fortune and agility that saved her. A stout branch deflected the raking talons of the carnivore, but so close was the call that a giant forearm brushed her flesh in the instant before she scrambled to the higher branches.

Baffled, the banth gave vent to his rage and disappointment in a series of frightful roars that caused the very ground to tremble, and to these were added the roarings and the growlings and the moanings of his fellows as they approached from every direction, in the hope of wresting from him whatever of his kill they could take by craft or prowess. And now he turned snarling upon them as they circled the tree, while the girl, huddled in a crotch above them, looked down upon the gaunt, yellow monsters padding on noiseless feet in a restless circle about her. She wondered now at the strange freak of fate that had permitted her to come down this far into the valley by night unharmed, but even more she wondered how she was to return to the hills. She knew that she would not dare venture it by night and she guessed, too, that by day she might be confronted by even graver perils. To depend upon this valley for sustenance she now saw to be beyond the pale of possibility because of the banths that would keep her from food and water by night, while the dwellers in the towers would doubtless make it equally impossible for her to forage by day. There was but one solution of her difficulty and that was to return to her flier and pray that the wind would waft her to some less terrorful land; but when might she return to the flier? The banths gave little evidence of relinquishing hope of her, and even if they wandered out of sight would she dare risk the attempt? She doubted it.

Hopeless indeed seemed her situation – hopeless it was.

CHAPTER FOUR

Captured

As THURIA, swift racer of the night, shot again into the sky the scene changed. As by magic a new aspect fell athwart the face of Nature. It was as though in the instant one had been transported from one planet to another. It was the age-old miracle of the Martian nights that is always new, even to Martians – two moons resplendent in the heavens, where one had been but now; conflicting, fast-changing shadows that altered the very hills themselves; far Cluros, stately, majestic, almost stationary, shedding his steady light upon the world below; Thuria, a great and glorious orb, swinging swift across the vaulted dome of the blue-black night, so low that she seemed to graze the hills, a gorgeous spectacle that held the girl now beneath the spell of its enchantment as it always had and always would.

"Ah, Thuria, mad queen of heaven!" murmured Tara of Helium. "The hills pass in stately procession, their bosoms rising and falling; the trees move in restless circles; the little grasses describe their little arcs; and all is movement, restless, mysterious movement without sound, while Thuria passes." The girl sighed and let her gaze fall again to the stern realities beneath. There was no mystery in the huge banths. He who had discovered her squatted there looking hungrily up at her. Most of the others had wandered away in search of other prey, but a few remained hoping yet to bury their fangs in that soft body.

The night wore on. Again Thuria left the heavens to her lord and master, hurrying on to keep her tryst with the Sun in other skies. But a single banth waited impatiently beneath the tree which harbored Tara of Helium. The others had left, but their roars, and growls, and moans thundered or rumbled, or floated back to her from near and far. What prey found they in this little valley? There must be something that they were accustomed to find here that they should be drawn in so great numbers. The girl wondered what it could be.

How long the night! Numb, cold, and exhausted, Tara of Helium clung to the tree in growing desperation, for once she had dozed and almost fallen. Hope was low in her brave little heart. How much more could she endure? She asked herself the question and then, with a brave shake of her head, she squared her shoulders. "I still live!" she said aloud.

The banth looked up and growled.

Came Thuria again and after awhile the great Sun – a flaming lover, pursuing his heart's desire. And Cluros, the cold husband, continued his serene way, as placid as before his house had been violated by this hot Lothario. And now the Sun and both Moons rode together in the sky, lending their far mysteries to make weird the Martian dawn. Tara of Helium looked out across the fair valley that spread upon all sides of her. It was rich and beautiful, but even as she looked upon it she shuddered, for to her mind came a picture of the headless things that the towers and the walls hid. Those by day and the banths by night! Ah, was it any wonder that she shuddered?

With the coming of the Sun the great Barsoomian lion rose to his feet. He turned angry eyes upon the girl above him, voiced a single ominous growl, and slunk away toward the hills. The girl watched him, and she saw that he gave the towers as wide a berth as possible and that he never took his eyes from one of them while he was passing it. Evidently the inmates had taught these savage creatures to respect them. Presently he passed from sight in a narrow defile, nor in any direction that she could see was there another. Momentarily at least the landscape was deserted. The girl wondered if she dared to attempt to regain the hills and her flier. She dreaded the coming of the workmen to the fields as she was sure they would come. She shrank from again seeing the headless bodies, and found herself wondering if these things would come out into the fields and work. She looked toward the nearest tower. There was no sign of life there. The valley lay quiet now and deserted. She lowered herself stiffly to the ground. Her muscles were cramped and every move brought a twinge of pain. Pausing a moment to drink again at the stream she felt refreshed and then turned without more delay toward the hills. To cover the distance as quickly as possible seemed the only plan to pursue. The trees no longer offered concealment and so she did not go out of her way to be near them. The hills seemed very far away. She had not thought, the night before, that she had traveled so far. Really it had not been far, but now, with the three towers to pass in broad daylight, the distance seemed great indeed.

The second tower lay almost directly in her path. To make a detour would not lessen the chance of detection, it would only lengthen the period of her danger, and so she laid her course straight for the hill where her flier was, regardless of the tower. As she passed the first enclosure she thought that she heard the sound of movement within, but the gate did not open and she breathed more easily when it lay behind her. She came then to the second enclosure, the outer wall of which she must circle, as it lay across her route. As she passed close along it she distinctly heard not only movement within, but voices. In the world-language of Barsoom she heard a man issuing instructions – so many were to pick usa, so many were to irrigate this field, so many to cultivate that, and so on, as a foreman lay out the day's work for his crew.

Tara of Helium had just reached the gate in the outer wall. Without warning it swung open toward her. She saw that for a moment it would hide her from those within and in that moment she turned and ran, keeping close to the wall, until, passing out of sight beyond the curve of the structure, she came to the opposite side of the enclosure. Here, panting from her exertion and from the excitement of her narrow escape, she threw herself among some tall weeds that grew close to the foot of the wall. There she lay trembling for some time, not even daring to raise her head and look about. Never before had Tara of Helium felt the paralyzing effects of terror. She was shocked and angry at herself, that she, daughter of John Carter, Warlord of Barsoom, should exhibit fear. Not even the fact that there had been none there to witness it lessened her shame and anger, and the worst of it was she knew that under similar circumstances she would again be equally as craven. It was not the fear of death – she knew that. No, it was the thought of those headless bodies and that she might see them and that they might even touch her – lay hands upon her – seize her. She shuddered and trembled at the thought.

After a while she gained sufficient command of herself to raise her head and look about. To her horror she discovered that everywhere she looked she saw people working in the fields or preparing to do so. Workmen were coming from other towers. Little bands were passing to this field and that. They were even some already at work within thirty ads of her – about a hundred yards. There were ten, perhaps, in the party nearest her, both men and women, and all were beautiful of form and grotesque of face. So meager were their trappings that they were practically naked; a fact that was in no way remarkable among the tillers of the fields of Mars. Each wore the peculiar, high leather collar that completely hid the neck, and each wore sufficient other leather to support a single

sword and a pocket-pouch. The leather was very old and worn, showing long, hard service, and was absolutely plain with the exception of a
single device upon the left shoulder. The heads, however, were covered
with ornaments of precious metals and jewels, so that little more than
eyes, nose, and mouth were discernible. These were hideously inhuman
and yet grotesquely human at the same time. The eyes were far apart and
protruding, the nose scarce more than two small, parallel slits set verti-
cally above a round hole that was the mouth. The heads were peculiarly
repulsive – so much so that it seemed unbelievable to the girl that they
formed an integral part of the beautiful bodies below them.

So fascinated was Tara of Helium that she could scarce take her eyes
from the strange creatures – a fact that was to prove her undoing, for
in order that she might see them she was forced to expose a part of
her own head and presently, to her consternation, she saw that one of
the creatures had stopped his work and was staring directly at her. She
did not dare move, for it was still possible that the thing had not seen
her, or at least was only suspicious that some creature lay hid among
the weeds. If she could allay this suspicion by remaining motionless
the creature might believe that he had been mistaken and return to his
work; but, alas, such was not to be the case. She saw the thing call the
attention of others to her and almost immediately four or five of them
started to move in her direction.

It was impossible now to escape discovery. Her only hope lay in
flight. If she could elude them and reach the hills and the flier ahead
of them she might escape, and that could be accomplished in but one
way – flight, immediate and swift. Leaping to her feet she darted along
the base of the wall which she must skirt to the opposite side, beyond
which lay the hill that was her goal. Her act was greeted by strange
whistling sounds from the things behind her, and casting a glance over
her shoulder she saw them all in rapid pursuit.

There were also shrill commands that she halt, but to these she paid
no attention. Before she had half circled the enclosure she discovered
that her chances for successful escape were great, since it was evident
to her that her pursuers were not so fleet as she. High indeed then
were her hopes as she came in sight of the hill, but they were soon
dashed by what lay before her, for there, in the fields that lay between,
were fully a hundred creatures similar to those behind her and all
were on the alert, evidently warned by the whistling of their fellows.
Instructions and commands were shouted to and fro, with the result
that those before her spread roughly into a great half circle to intercept
her, and when she turned to the right, hoping to elude the net, she saw

others coming from fields beyond, and to the left the same was true. But Tara of Helium would not admit defeat. Without once pausing she turned directly toward the center of the advancing semi-circle, beyond which lay her single chance of escape, and as she ran she drew her long, slim dagger. Like her valiant sire, if die she must, she would die fighting. There were gaps in the thin line confronting her and toward the widest of one of these she directed her course. The things on either side of the opening guessed her intent for they closed in to place themselves in her path. This widened the openings on either side of them and as the girl appeared almost to rush into their arms she turned suddenly at right angles, ran swiftly in the new direction for a few yards, and then dashed quickly toward the hill again. Now only a single warrior, with a wide gap on either side of him, barred her clear way to freedom, though all the others were speeding as rapidly as they could to intercept her. If she could pass this one without too much delay she could escape, of that she was certain. Her every hope hinged on this. The creature before her realized it, too, for he moved cautiously, though swiftly, to intercept her, as a Rugby fullback might maneuver in the realization that he alone stood between the opposing team and a touchdown.

At first Tara of Helium had hoped that she might dodge him, for she could not but guess that she was not only more fleet but infinitely more agile than these strange creatures; but soon there came to her the realization that in the time consumed in an attempt to elude his grasp his nearer fellows would be upon her and escape then impossible, so she chose instead to charge straight for him, and when he guessed her decision he stood, half crouching and with outstretched arms, awaiting her. In one hand was his sword, but a voice arose, crying in tones of authority. "Take her alive! Do not harm her!" Instantly the fellow returned his sword to its scabbard and then Tara of Helium was upon him. Straight for that beautiful body she sprang and in the instant that the arms closed to seize her her sharp blade drove deep into the naked chest. The impact hurled them both to the ground and as Tara of Helium sprang to her feet again she saw, to her horror, that the loathsome head had rolled from the body and was now crawling away from her on six short, spider-like legs. The body struggled spasmodically and lay still. As brief as had been the delay caused by the encounter, it still had been of sufficient duration to undo her, for even as she rose two more of the things fell upon her and instantly thereafter she was surrounded. Her blade sank once more into naked flesh and once more a head rolled free and crawled away. Then they overpowered her and in another moment she was surrounded by fully a hundred of the creatures, all seeking to lay hands upon her. At first she thought that they wished to tear her to pieces in revenge for her having slain two of their fellows, but presently she realized that they were prompted more by curiosity than by any sinister motive.

"Come!" said one of her captors, both of whom had retained a hold upon her. As he spoke he tried to lead her away with him toward the nearest tower.

"She belongs to me," cried the other. "Did not I capture her? She will come with me to the tower of Moak."

"Never!" insisted the first. "She is Luud's. To Luud I will take her, and whosoever interferes may feel the keenness of my sword – in the head!" He almost shouted the last three words.

"Come! Enough of this," cried one who spoke with some show of authority. "She was captured in Luud's fields – she will go to Luud."

"She was discovered in Moak's fields, at the very foot of the tower of Moak," insisted he who had claimed her for Moak.

"You have heard the Nolach speak," cried the Luud. "It shall be as he says."

"Not while this Moak holds a sword," replied the other. "Rather will I cut her in twain and take my half to Moak than to relinquish her all to Luud," and he drew his sword, or rather he laid his hand upon its hilt in a threatening gesture; but before ever he could draw it the Luud had whipped his out and with a fearful blow cut deep into the head of his adversary. Instantly the big, round head collapsed, almost as a punctured balloon collapses, as a grayish, semi-fluid matter spurted from it. The protruding eyes, apparently lidless, merely stared, the sphincter-like muscle of the mouth opened and closed, and then the head toppled from the body to the ground. The body stood dully for a moment and then slowly started to wander aimlessly about until one of the others seized it by the arm.

One of the two heads crawling about on the ground now approached. "This rykor belongs to Moak," it said. "I am a Moak. I will take it," and without further discussion it commenced to crawl up the front of the headless body, using its six short, spiderlike legs and two stout chelae which grew just in front of its legs and strongly resembled those of an Earthly lobster, except that they were both of the same size. The body in the meantime stood in passive indifference, its arms hanging idly at its sides. The head climbed to the shoulders and settled itself inside the leather collar that now hid its chelae and legs. Almost immediately the body gave evidence of intelligent animation. It raised its hands and adjusted the collar more comfortably, it took the head between its palms and settled it in place and when it moved around it did not wander aimlessly, but instead its steps were firm and to some purpose.

The girl watched all these things in growing wonder, and presently, no other of the Moaks seeming inclined to dispute the right of the Luud to her, she was led off by her captor toward the nearest tower. Several accompanied them, including one who carried the loose head under his arm. The head that was being carried conversed with the head upon the shoulders of the thing that carried it. Tara of Helium shivered. It was horrible! All that she had seen of these frightful creatures was horrible. And to be a prisoner, wholly in their power. Shadow of her first ancestor! What had she done to deserve so cruel a fate?

At the wall enclosing the tower they paused while one opened the gate and then they passed within the enclosure, which, to the girl's horror, she found filled with headless bodies. The creature who carried the bodiless head now set its burden upon the ground and the latter immediately crawled toward one of the bodies that was lying near by. Some wandered stupidly to and fro, but this one lay still. It was a female. The head crawled to it and made its way to the shoulders where it settled itself. At once the body sprang lightly erect. Another of those who had accompanied them from the fields approached with the harness and collar that had been taken from the dead body that the head had formerly topped. The new body now appropriated these and the hands deftly adjusted them. The creature was now as good as before Tara of Helium had struck down its former body with her slim blade. But there was a difference. Before it had been male – now it was female. That, however, seemed to make no difference to the head. In fact, Tara of Helium had noticed during the scramble and the fight about her that sex differences seemed of little moment to her captors. Males and females had taken equal part in her pursuit, both were identically harnessed and both carried swords, and she had seen as many females as males draw their weapons at the moment that a quarrel between the two factions seemed imminent.

The girl was given but brief opportunity for further observation of the pitiful creatures in the enclosure as her captor, after having directed the others to return to the fields, led her toward the tower, which they entered, passing into an apartment about ten feet wide and twenty long, in one end of which was a stairway leading to an upper level and in the other an opening to a similar stairway leading downward. The chamber, though on a level with the ground, was brilliantly lighted by windows in its inner wall, the light coming from a circular court in the center of the tower. The walls of this court appeared to be faced with what resembled glazed, white tile and the whole interior of it was flooded with dazzling light, a fact which immediately explained to the girl the purpose of the glass prisms of which the domes were constructed. The stairways themselves were sufficient to cause remark, since in nearly all Barsoomian architecture inclined runways are utilized for purposes of communication between different levels, and especially is this true of the more ancient forms and of those of remote districts where fewer changes have come to alter the customs of antiquity.

Down the stairway her captor led Tara of Helium. Down and down through chambers still lighted from the brilliant well. Occasionally they passed others going in the opposite direction and these always stopped to examine the girl and ask questions of her captor.

"I know nothing but that she was found in the fields and that I caught her after a fight in which she slew two rykors and in which I slew a Moak, and that I take her to Luud, to whom, of course, she belongs. If Luud wishes to question her that is for Luud to do – not for me." Thus always he answered the curious.

Presently they reached a room from which a circular tunnel led away from the tower, and into this the creature conducted her. The tunnel was some seven feet in diameter and flattened on the bottom to form a walk. For a hundred feet from the tower it was lined with the same tile-like material of the light well and amply illuminated by reflected light from that source. Beyond it was faced with stone of various shapes and sizes, neatly cut and fitted together – a very fine mosaic without a pattern. There were branches, too, and other tunnels which crossed this, and occasionally openings not more than a foot in diameter; these latter being usually close to the floor. Above each of these smaller openings was painted a different device, while upon the walls of the larger tunnels at all intersections and points of convergence hieroglyphics appeared. These the girl could not read though she guessed that they were the names of the tunnels, or notices indicating the points to which they led. She tried to study some of them out, but there was not a character that was familiar to her, which seemed strange, since, while the written languages of the various nations of Barsoom differ, it still is true that they have many characters and words in common.

She had tried to converse with her guard but he had not seemed inclined to talk with her and she had finally desisted. She could not but note that he had offered her no indignities, nor had he been either unnecessarily rough or in any way cruel. The fact that she had slain two of the bodies with her dagger had apparently aroused no animosity or desire for revenge in the minds of the strange heads that surmounted the bodies – even those whose bodies had been killed. She did not try to understand it, since she could not approach the peculiar relationship between the heads and the bodies of these creatures from the basis of any past knowledge or experience of her own. So far their treatment of her seemed to augur naught that might arouse her fears. Perhaps, after all, she had been fortunate to fall into the hands of these strange people, who might not only protect her from harm, but even aid her in returning to Helium. That they were repulsive and uncanny she could not forget, but if they meant her no harm she could, at least, overlook their repulsiveness. Renewed hope aroused within her a spirit of greater cheerfulness, and it was almost blithely now that she moved at the side of her weird companion. She even caught herself humming a gay little tune that was then popular in Helium. The creature at her side turned its expressionless eyes upon her.

"What is that noise that you are making?" it asked.

"I was but humming an air," she replied.

"'Humming an air,'" he repeated. "I do not know what you mean; but do it again, I like it."

This time she sang the words, while her companion listened intently. His face gave no indication of what was passing in that strange head. It was as devoid of expression as that of a spider. It reminded her of a spider. When she had finished he turned toward her again.

"That was different," he said. "I liked that better, even, than the other. How do you do it?"

"Why," she said, "it is singing. Do you not know what song is?"

"No," he replied. "Tell me how you do it."

"It is difficult to explain," she told him, "since any explanation of it presupposes some knowledge of melody and of music, while your very question indicates that you have no knowledge of either."

"No," he said, "I do not know what you are talking about; but tell me how you do it."

"It is merely the melodious modulations of my voice," she explained. "Listen!" and again she sang.

"I do not understand," he insisted; "but I like it. Could you teach me to do it?"

"I do not know, but I shall be glad to try."

"We will see what Luud does with you," he said. "If he does not want you I will keep you and you shall teach me to make sounds like that."

At his request she sang again as they continued their way along the winding tunnel, which was now lighted by occasional bulbs which appeared to be similar to the radium bulbs with which she was familiar and which were common to all the nations of Barsoom, insofar as she knew, having been perfected at so remote a period that their very origin was lost in antiquity. They consist, usually, of a hemispherical bowl of heavy glass in which is packed a compound containing what, according to John Carter, must be radium. The bowl is then cemented into a metal plate with a heavily insulated back and the whole affair set in the masonry of wall or ceiling as desired, where it gives off light of greater or less intensity, according to the composition of the filling material, for an almost incalculable period of time.

As they proceeded they met a greater number of the inhabitants of this underground world, and the girl noted that among many of these the metal and harness were more ornate than had been those of the workers in the fields above. The heads and bodies, however, were similar, even identical, she thought. No one offered her harm and she was now experiencing a feeling of relief almost akin to happiness, when her guide turned suddenly into an opening on the right side of the tunnel and she found herself in a large, well lighted chamber.

CHAPTER FIVE

The Perfect Brain

THE SONG THAT HAD BEEN upon her lips as she entered died there – frozen by the sight of horror that met her eyes. In the center of the chamber a headless body lay upon the floor – a body that had been partially devoured – while over and upon it crawled a half a dozen heads upon their short, spider legs, and they tore at the flesh of the woman with their chelae and carried the bits to their awful mouths. They were eating human flesh – eating it raw!

Tara of Helium gasped in horror and turning away covered her eyes with her palms.

"Come!" said her captor. "What is the matter?"

"They are eating the flesh of the woman," she whispered in tones of horror.

"Why not?" he inquired. "Did you suppose that we kept the rykor for labor alone? Ah, no. They are delicious when kept and fattened. Fortunate, too, are those that are bred for food, since they are never called upon to do aught but eat."

"It is hideous!" she cried.

He looked at her steadily for a moment, but whether in surprise, in anger, or in pity his expressionless face did not reveal. Then he led her on across the room past the frightful thing, from which she turned away her eyes. Lying about the floor near the walls were half a dozen headless bodies in harness. These she guessed had been abandoned temporarily by the feasting heads until they again required their services. In the walls of this room there were many of the small, round openings she had noticed in various parts of the tunnels, the purpose of which she could not guess.

They passed through another corridor and then into a second chamber, larger than the first and more brilliantly illuminated. Within were several of the creatures with heads and bodies assembled, while many headless bodies lay about near the walls. Here her captor halted and spoke to one of the occupants of the chamber.

"I seek Luud," he said. "I bring to Luud a creature that I captured in the fields above."

The others crowded about to examine Tara of Helium. One of them whistled, whereupon the girl learned something of the smaller openings in the walls, for almost immediately there crawled from them, like giant spiders, a score or more of the hideous heads. Each sought one of the recumbent bodies and fastened itself in place. Immediately the bodies reacted to the intelligent direction of the heads. They arose, the hands adjusted the leather collars and put the balance of the harness in order, then the creatures crossed the room to where Tara of Helium stood. She noted that their leather was more highly ornamented than that worn by any of the others she had previously seen, and so she guessed that these must be higher in authority than the others. Nor was she mistaken. The demeanor of her captor indicated it. He addressed them as one who holds intercourse with superiors.

Several of those who examined her felt her flesh, pinching it gently between thumb and forefinger, a familiarity that the girl resented. She struck down their hands. "Do not touch me!" she cried, imperiously, for was she not a princess of Helium? The expression on those terrible faces did not change. She could not tell whether they were angry or amused, whether her action had filled them with respect for her, or contempt. Only one of them spoke immediately.

"She will have to be fattened more," he said.

The girl's eyes went wide with horror. She turned upon her captor. "Do these frightful creatures intend to devour me?" she cried.

"That is for Luud to say," he replied, and then he leaned closer so that his mouth was near her ear. "That noise you made which you called song pleased me," he whispered, "and I will repay you by warning you not to antagonize these kaldanes. They are very powerful. Luud listens to them. Do not call them frightful. They are very handsome. Look at their wonderful trappings, their gold, their jewels."

"Thank you," she said. "You called them kaldanes – what does that mean?"

"We are all kaldanes," he replied.

"You, too?" and she pointed at him, her slim finger directed toward his chest.

"No, not this," he explained, touching his body; "this is a rykor; but this," and he touched his head, "is a kaldane. It is the brain, the intellect, the power that directs all things. The rykor," he indicated his body, "is nothing. It is not so much even as the jewels upon our harness; no, not so much as the harness itself. It carries us about. It is true that we would find difficulty getting along without it; but it has less value than harness or jewels because it is less difficult to reproduce." He turned again to the other kaldanes. "Will you notify Luud that I am here?" he asked.

"Sept has already gone to Luud. He will tell him," replied one. "Where did you find this rykor with the strange kaldane that cannot detach itself?"

The girl's captor narrated once more the story of her capture. He stated facts just as they had occurred, without embellishment, his voice as expressionless as his face, and his story was received in the same manner that it was delivered. The creatures seemed totally lacking in emotion, or, at least, the capacity to express it. It was impossible to judge what impression the story made upon them, or even if they heard it. Their protruding eyes simply stared and occasionally the muscles of their mouths opened and closed. Familiarity did not lessen the horror the girl felt for them. The more she saw of them the more repulsive they seemed. Often her body was shaken by convulsive shudders as she looked at the kaldanes, but when her eyes wandered to the beautiful bodies and she could for a moment expunge the heads from her consciousness the effect was soothing and refreshing, though when the bodies lay, headless, upon the floor they were quite as shocking as the heads mounted on bodies. But by far the most grewsome and uncanny sight of all was that of the heads crawling about upon their spider legs. If one of these should approach and touch her Tara of Helium was positive that she should scream, while should one attempt to crawl up her person – ugh! the very idea induced a feeling of faintness.

Sept returned to the chamber. "Luud will see you and the captive. Come!" he said, and turned toward a door opposite that through which Tara of Helium had entered the chamber. "What is your name?" His question was directed to the girl's captor.

"I am Ghek, third foreman of the fields of Luud," he answered.

"And hers?"

"I do not know."

"It makes no difference. Come!"

The patrician brows of Tara of Helium went high. It made no difference, indeed! She, a princess of Helium; only daughter of The Warlord of Barsoom!

"Wait!" she cried. "It makes much difference who I am. If you are conducting me into the presence of your jed you may announce The Princess Tara of Helium, daughter of John Carter, The Warlord of Barsoom."

"Hold your peace!" commanded Sept. "Speak when you are spoken to. Come with me!"

The anger of Tara of Helium all but choked her. "Come," admonished Ghek, and took her by the arm, and Tara of Helium came. She was naught but a prisoner. Her rank and titles meant nothing to these inhuman monsters. They led her through a short, S-shaped passageway into a chamber entirely lined with the white, tile-like material with which the interior of the light wall was faced. Close to the base of the walls were numerous smaller apertures, circular in shape, but larger than those of similar aspect that she had noted elsewhere. The majority of these apertures were sealed. Directly opposite the entrance was one framed in gold, and above it a peculiar device was inlaid in the same precious metal.

Sept and Ghek halted just within the room, the girl between them, and all three stood silently facing the opening in the opposite wall. On the floor beside the aperture lay a headless male body of almost heroic proportions, and on either side of this stood a heavily armed warrior, with drawn sword. For perhaps five minutes the three waited and then something appeared in the opening. It was a pair of large chelae and immediately thereafter there crawled forth a hideous kaldane of enormous proportions. He was half again as large as any that Tara of Helium had yet seen and his whole aspect infinitely more terrible. The skin of the others was a bluish gray – this one was of a little bluer tinge and the eyes were ringed with bands of white and scarlet, as was its mouth.

From each nostril a band of white and one of scarlet extended outward horizontally the width of the face.

No one spoke or moved. The creature crawled to the prostrate body and affixed itself to the neck. Then the two rose as one and approached the girl. He looked at her and then he spoke to her captor.

"You are the third foreman of the fields of Luud?" he asked.

"Yes, Luud; I am called Ghek."

"Tell me what you know of this," and he nodded toward Tara of Helium. Ghek did as he was bid and then Luud addressed the girl.

"What were you doing within the borders of Bantoom?" he asked.

"I was blown hither in a great storm that injured my flier and carried me I knew not where. I came down into the valley at night for food and drink. The banths came and drove me to the safety of a tree, and then your people caught me as I was trying to leave the valley. I do not know why they took me. I was doing no harm. All I ask is that you let me go my way in peace."

"None who enters Bantoom ever leaves," replied Luud.

"But my people are not at war with yours. I am a princess of Helium; my great-grandfather is a jeddak; my grandfather a jed; and my father is Warlord of all Barsoom. You have no right to keep me and I demand that you liberate me at once."

"None who enters Bantoom ever leaves," repeated the creature without expression. "I know nothing of the lesser creatures of Barsoom, of whom you speak. There is but one high race – the race of Bantoomians. All Nature exists to serve them. You shall do your share, but not yet – you are too skinny. We shall have to put some fat upon it, Sept. I tire of rykor. Perhaps this will have a different flavor. The banths are too rank and it is seldom that any other creature enters the valley. And you, Ghek; you shall be rewarded. I shall promote you from the fields to the burrows. Hereafter you shall remain underground as every Bantoomian longs to. No more shall you be forced to endure the hated sun, or look upon the hideous sky, or the hateful growing things that defile the surface. For the present you shall look after this thing that you have brought me, seeing that it sleeps and eats – and does nothing else. You understand me, Ghek; nothing else!"

"I understand, Luud," replied the other.

"Take it away!" commanded the creature.

Ghek turned and led Tara of Helium from the apartment. The girl was horrified by contemplation of the fate that awaited her – a fate from which it seemed, there was no escape. It was only too evident that these creatures possessed no gentle or chivalric sentiments to which she could appeal, and that she might escape from the labyrinthine mazes of their underground burrows appeared impossible.

Outside the audience chamber Sept overtook them and conversed with Ghek for a brief period, then her keeper led her through a confusing web of winding tunnels until they came to a small apartment.

"We are to remain here for a while. It may be that Luud will send for you again. If he does you will probably not be fattened – he will use you for another purpose." It was fortunate for the girl's peace of mind that she did not realize what he meant. "Sing for me," said Ghek, presently.

Tara of Helium did not feel at all like singing, but she sang, nevertheless, for there was always the hope that she might escape if given the opportunity and if she could win the friendship of one of the creatures, her chances would be increased proportionately. All during the ordeal, for such it was to the overwrought girl, Ghek stood with his eyes fixed upon her.

"It is wonderful," he said, when she had finished; "but I did not tell Luud – you noticed that I did not tell Luud about it. Had he known, he would have had you sing to him and that would have resulted in your being kept with him that he might hear you sing whenever he wished; but now I can have you all the time."

"How do you know he would like my singing?" she asked.

"He would have to," replied Ghek. "If I like a thing he has to like it, for are we not identical – all of us?"

"The people of my race do not all like the same things," said the girl.

"How strange!" commented Ghek. "All kaldanes like the same things and dislike the same things. If I discover something new and like it I know that all kaldanes will like it. That is how I know that Luud would like your singing. You see we are all exactly alike."

"But you do not look like Luud," said the girl.

"Luud is king. He is larger and more gorgeously marked; but otherwise he and I are identical, and why not? Did not Luud produce the egg from which I hatched?"

"What?" queried the girl; "I do not understand you."

"Yes," explained Ghek, "all of us are from Luud's eggs, just as all the swarm of Moak are from Moak's eggs."

"Oh!" exclaimed Tara of Helium understandingly; "you mean that Luud has many wives and that you are the offspring of one of them."

"No, not that at all," replied Ghek. "Luud has no wife. He lays the eggs himself. You do not understand."

Tara of Helium admitted that she did not.

"I will try to explain, then," said Ghek, "if you will promise to sing to me later."

"I promise," she said.

"We are not like the rykors," he began. "They are creatures of a low order, like yourself and the banths and such things. We have no sex – not one of us except our king, who is bi-sexual. He produces many eggs from which we, the workers and the warriors, are hatched; and one in every thousand eggs is another king egg, from which a king is hatched. Did you notice the sealed openings in the room where you saw Luud? Sealed in each of those is another king. If one of them escaped he would fall upon Luud and try to kill him and if he succeeded we should have a new king; but there would be no difference. His name would be Luud and all would go on as before, for are we not all alike? Luud has lived a long time and has produced many kings, so he lets only a few live that there may be a successor to him when he dies. The others he kills."

"Why does he keep more than one?" queried the girl.

"Sometimes accidents occur," replied Ghek, "and all the kings that a swarm has saved are killed. When this happens the swarm comes and obtains another king from a neighboring swarm."

"Are all of you the children of Luud?" she asked.

"All but a few, who are from the eggs of the preceding king, as was Luud; but Luud has lived a long time and not many of the others are left."

"You live a long time, or short?" Tara asked.

"A very long time."

"And the rykors, too; they live a long time?"

"No; the rykors live for ten years, perhaps," he said, "if they remain strong and useful. When they can no longer be of service to us, either through age or sickness, we leave them in the fields and the banths come at night and get them."

"How horrible!" she exclaimed.

"Horrible?" he repeated. "I see nothing horrible about that. The rykors are but brainless flesh. They neither see, nor feel, nor hear. They can scarce move but for us. If we did not bring them food they would starve to death. They are less deserving of thought than our leather. All that they can do for themselves is to take food from a trough and put it in their mouths, but with us – look at them!" and he proudly exhibited the noble figure that he surmounted, palpitant with life and energy and feeling.

"How do you do it?" asked Tara of Helium. "I do not understand it at all."

"I will show you," he said, and lay down upon the floor. Then he detached himself from the body, which lay as a thing dead. On his spider legs he walked toward the girl. "Now look," he admonished her. "Do you see this thing?" and he extended what appeared to be a bundle of tentacles from the posterior part of his head. "There is an aperture just back of the rykor's mouth and directly over the upper end of his spinal column. Into this aperture I insert my tentacles and seize the spinal cord. Immediately I control every muscle of the rykor's body – it becomes my own, just as you direct the movement of the muscles of your body. I feel what the rykor would feel if he had a head and brain. If he is hurt, I would suffer if I remained connected with him; but the instant one of them is injured or becomes sick we desert it for another. As we would suffer the pains of their physical injuries, similarly do we enjoy the physical pleasures of the rykors. When your body becomes fatigued you are comparatively useless; it is sick, you are sick; if it is killed, you die. You are the slave of a mass of stupid flesh and bone and blood. There is nothing more wonderful about your carcass than there is about the carcass of a banth. It is only your brain that makes you superior to the banth, but your brain is bound by the limitations of your body. Not so, ours. With us brain is everything. Ninety per centum of our volume is brain. We have only the simplest of vital organs and they are very small for they do not have to assist in the support of a complicated system of nerves, muscles, flesh and bone. We have no lungs, for we do not require air. Far below the levels to which we can take the rykors is a vast network of burrows where the real life of the kaldane is lived. There the air-breathing rykor would perish as you would perish. There we have stored vast quantities of food in hermetically sealed chambers. It will last forever. Far beneath the surface is water that will flow for countless ages after the surface water is exhausted. We are preparing for the time we know must come – the time when the last vestige of the Barsoomian atmosphere is spent – when the waters and the food are gone. For this purpose were we created, that there might not perish from the planet Nature's divinest creation – the perfect brain."

"But what purpose can you serve when that time comes?" asked the girl.

"You do not understand," he said. "It is too big for you to grasp, but I will try to explain it. Barsoom, the moons, the sun, the stars, were created for a single purpose. From the beginning of time Nature has labored arduously toward the consummation of this purpose. At the very beginning things existed with life, but with no brain. Gradually rudimentary nervous systems and minute brains evolved. Evolution proceeded. The brains became larger and more powerful. In us you see the highest development; but there are those of us who believe that there is yet another step – that some time in the far future our race shall develop into the super-thing – just brain. The incubus of legs and chelae and vital organs will be removed. The future kaldane will be nothing but a great brain. Deaf, dumb, and blind it will lie sealed in its buried vault far beneath the surface of Barsoom – just a great, wonderful, beautiful brain with nothing to distract it from eternal thought."

"You mean it will just lie there and think?" cried Tara of Helium.

"Just that!" he exclaimed. "Could aught be more wonderful?"

"Yes," replied the girl, "I can think of a number of things that would be infinitely more wonderful."

CHAPTER SIX

In the Toils of Horror

WHAT THE CREATURE had told her gave Tara of Helium food for thought. She had been taught that every created thing fulfilled some useful purpose, and she tried conscientiously to discover just what was the rightful place of the kaldane in the universal scheme of things. She knew that it must have its place but what that place was it was beyond her to conceive. She had to give it up. They recalled to her mind a little group of people in Helium who had forsworn the pleasures of life in the pursuit of knowledge. They were rather patronizing in their relations with those whom they thought not so intellectual. They considered themselves quite superior. She smiled at recollection of a remark her father had once made concerning them, to the effect that if one of them ever dropped his egotism and broke it it would take a week to fumigate Helium. Her father liked normal people – people who knew too little and people who knew too much were equally a bore. Tara of Helium was like her father in this respect and like him, too, she was both sane and normal.

Outside of her personal danger there was much in this strange world that interested her. The rykors aroused her keenest pity, and vast conjecture. How and from what form had they evolved? She asked Ghek.

"Sing to me again and I will tell you," he said. "If Luud would let me have you, you should never die. I should keep you always to sing to me."

The girl marvelled at the effect her voice had upon the creature. Somewhere in that enormous brain there was a chord that was touched by melody. It was the sole link between herself and the brain when detached from the rykor. When it dominated the rykor it might have other human instincts; but these she dreaded even to think of. After she had sung she waited for Ghek to speak. For a long time he was silent, just looking at her through those awful eyes.

"I wonder," he said presently, "if it might not be pleasant to be of your race. Do you all sing?"

"Nearly all, a little," she said; "but we do many other interesting and enjoyable things. We dance and play and work and love and sometimes we fight, for we are a race of warriors."

"Love!" said the kaldane. "I think I know what you mean; but we, fortunately, are above sentiment – when we are detached. But when we dominate the rykor – ah, that is different, and when I hear you sing and look at your beautiful body I know what you mean by love. I could love you."

The girl shrank from him. "You promised to tell me the origin of the rykor," she reminded him.

"Ages ago," he commenced, "our bodies were larger and our heads smaller. Our legs were very weak and we could not travel fast or far. There was a stupid creature that went upon four legs. It lived in a hole in the ground, to which it brought its food, so we ran our burrows into this hole and ate the food it brought; but it did not bring enough for all – for itself and all the kaldanes that lived upon it, so we had also to go abroad and get food. This was hard work for our weak legs. Then it was that we commenced to ride upon the backs of these primitive rykors. It took many ages, undoubtedly, but at last came the time when the kaldane had found means to guide the rykor, until presently the latter depended entirely upon the superior brain of his master to guide him to food. The brain of the rykor grew smaller as time went on. His ears went and his eyes, for he no longer had use for them – the kaldane saw and heard for him. By similar steps the rykor came to go upon its hind feet that the kaldane might be able to see farther. As the brain shrank, so did the head. The mouth was the only feature of the head that was used and so the mouth alone remains. Members of the red race fell into the hands of our ancestors from time to time. They saw the beauties and the advantages of the form that nature had given the red race over that which the rykor was developing into. By intelligent crossing the present rykor was achieved. He is really solely the product of the super-intelligence of the kaldane – he is our body, to do with as we see fit, just as you do what you see fit with your body, only we have the advantage of possessing an unlimited supply of bodies. Do you not wish that you were a kaldane?"

For how long they kept her in the subterranean chamber Tara of Helium did not know. It seemed a very long time. She ate and slept and watched the interminable lines of creatures that passed the entrance to her prison. There was a laden line passing from above carrying food, food, food. In the other line they returned empty handed. When she saw them she knew that it was daylight above. When they did not pass she knew it was night, and that the banths were about devouring the rykors that had been abandoned in the fields the previous day. She commenced to grow pale and thin. She did not like the food they gave her – it was not suited to her kind – nor would she have eaten overmuch palatable food, for the fear of becoming fat. The idea of plumpness had a new significance here – a horrible significance.

Ghek noted that she was growing thin and white. He spoke to her about it and she told him that she could not thrive thus beneath the ground – that she must have fresh air and sunshine, or she would wither and die. Evidently he carried her words to Luud, since it was not long after that he told her that the king had ordered that she be confined in the tower and to the tower she was taken. She had hoped against hope that this very thing might result from her conversation with Ghek. Even to see the sun again was something, but now there sprang to her breast a hope that she had not dared to nurse before, while she lay in the terrible labyrinth from which she knew she could never have found her way to the outer world; but now there was some slight reason to hope. At least she could see the hills and if she could see them might there not come also the opportunity to reach them? If she could have but ten minutes – just ten little minutes! The flier was still there – she knew that it must be. Just ten minutes and she would be free – free forever from this frightful place; but the days wore on and she was never alone, not even for half of ten minutes. Many times she planned her escape. Had it not been for the banths it had been easy of accomplishment by night. Ghek always detached his body then and sank into what seemed a semi-comatose condition. It could not be said that he slept, or at least it did not appear like sleep, since his lidless eyes were unchanged; but he lay quietly in a corner. Tara of Helium enacted a thousand times in her mind the scene of her escape. She would rush to the side of the rykor and seize the sword that hung in its harness. Before Ghek knew what she purposed, she would have this and then before he could give an alarm she would drive the blade through his hideous head. It would take but a moment to reach the enclosure. The rykors could not stop her, for they had no brains to tell them that she was escaping. She had watched from her window the opening and closing of the gate that led from the enclosure out into the fields and she knew how the great latch operated. She would pass through and make a quick dash for the hill. It was so near that they could not overtake her. It was so easy! Or it would have been but for the banths! The banths at night and the workers in the fields by day.

Confined to the tower and without proper exercise or food, the girl failed to show the improvement that her captors desired. Ghek questioned her in an effort to learn why it was that she did not grow round and plump; that she did not even look as well as when they had captured her. His concern was prompted by repeated inquiries on the part of Luud and finally resulted in suggesting to Tara of Helium a plan whereby she might find a new opportunity of escape.

"I am accustomed to walking in the fresh air and the sunlight," she told Ghek. "I cannot become as I was before if I am to be always shut away in this one chamber, breathing poor air and getting no proper exercise. Permit me to go out in the fields every day and walk about while the sun is shining. Then, I am sure, I shall become nice and fat."

"You would run away," he said.

"But how could I if you were always with me?" she asked. "And even if I wished to run away where could I go? I do not know even the direction of Helium. It must be very far. The very first night the banths would get me, would they not?"

"They would," said Ghek. "I will ask Luud about it."

The following day he told her that Luud had said that she was to be taken into the fields. He would try that for a time and see if she improved.

"If you do not grow fatter he will send for you anyway," said Ghek; "but he will not use you for food."

Tara of Helium shuddered.

That day and for many days thereafter she was taken from the tower, through the enclosure and out into the fields. Always was she alert for an opportunity to escape; but Ghek was always close by her side. It was not so much his presence that deterred her from making the attempt as the number of workers that were always between her and the hills where the flier lay. She could easily have eluded Ghek, but there were too many of the others. And then, one day, Ghek told her as he accompanied her into the open that this would be the last time.

"Tonight you go to Luud," he said. "I am sorry as I shall not hear you sing again."

"Tonight!" She scarce breathed the word, yet it was vibrant with horror.

She glanced quickly toward the hills. They were so close! Yet between were the inevitable workers – perhaps a score of them.

"Let us walk over there?" she said, indicating them. "I should like to see what they are doing."

"It is too far," said Ghek. "I hate the sun. It is much pleasanter here where I can stand beneath the shade of this tree."

"All right," she agreed; "then you stay here and I will walk over. It will take me but a minute."

"No," he answered. "I will go with you. You want to escape; but you are not going to."

"I cannot escape," she said.

"I know it," agreed Ghek; "but you might try. I do not wish you to try. Possibly it will be better if we return to the tower at once. It would go hard with me should you escape."

Tara of Helium saw her last chance fading into oblivion. There would never be another after today. She cast about for some pretext to lure him even a little nearer to the hills.

"It is very little that I ask," she said. "Tonight you will want me to sing to you. It will be the last time, if you do not let me go and see what those kaldanes are doing I shall never sing to you again."

Ghek hesitated. "I will hold you by the arm all the time, then," he said.

"Why, of course, if you wish," she assented. "Come!"

The two moved toward the workers and the hills. The little party was digging tubers from the ground. She had noted this and that nearly always they were stooped low over their work, the hideous eyes bent upon the upturned soil. She led Ghek quite close to them, pretending that she wished to see exactly how they did the work, and all the time he held her tightly by her left wrist.

"It is very interesting," she said, with a sigh, and then, suddenly; "Look, Ghek!" and pointed quickly back in the direction of the tower. The kaldane, still holding her turned half away from her to look in the direction she had indicated and simultaneously, with the quickness of a banth, she struck him with her right fist, backed by every ounce of strength she possessed – struck the back of the pulpy head just above the collar. The blow was sufficient to accomplish her design, dislodging the kaldane from its rykor and tumbling it to the ground. Instantly the grasp upon her wrist relaxed as the body, no longer controlled by the brain of Ghek, stumbled aimlessly about for an instant before it sank to its knees and then rolled over on its back; but Tara of Helium waited not to note the full results of her act. The instant the fingers loosened upon her wrist she broke away and dashed toward the hills. Simultaneously a warning whistle broke from Ghek's lips and in instant response the workers leaped to their feet, one almost in the girl's path. She dodged the outstretched arms and was away again toward the hills and freedom, when her foot caught in one of the hoe-like instruments with which the soil had been upturned and which had been left, half imbedded in the ground. For an instant she ran on, stumbling, in a mad effort to regain her equilibrium, but the upturned furrows caught her feet – again she stumbled and this time went down, and as she scrambled to rise again a heavy body fell upon her and seized her arms. A moment later she was surrounded and dragged to her feet and as she looked around she saw Ghek crawling to his prostrate rykor. A moment later he advanced to her side.

The hideous face, incapable of registering emotion, gave no clue to what was passing in the enormous brain. Was he nursing thoughts of anger, of hate, of revenge? Tara of Helium could not guess, nor did she care. The worst had happened. She had tried to escape and she had failed. There would never be another opportunity.

"Come!" said Ghek. "We will return to the tower." The deadly monotone of his voice was unbroken. It was worse than anger, for it revealed nothing of his intentions. It but increased her horror of these great brains that were beyond the possibility of human emotions.

And so she was dragged back to her prison in the tower and Ghek took up his vigil again, squatting by the doorway, but now he carried a naked sword in his hand and did not quit his rykor, only to change to another that he had brought to him when the first gave indications of weariness. The girl sat looking at him. He had not been unkind to her, but she felt no sense of gratitude, nor, on the other hand, any sense of hatred. The brains, incapable themselves of any of the finer sentiments, awoke none in her. She could not feel gratitude, or affection, or hatred of them. There was only the same unceasing sense of horror in their presence. She had heard great scientists discuss the future of the red race and she recalled that some had maintained that eventually the brain would entirely dominate the man. There would be no more instinctive acts or emotions, nothing would be done on impulse; but on the contrary reason would direct our every act. The propounder of the theory regretted that he might never enjoy the blessings of such a state, which, he argued, would result in the ideal life for mankind.

Tara of Helium wished with all her heart that this learned scientist might be here to experience to the full the practical results of the fulfillment of his prophecy. Between the purely physical rykor and the purely mental kaldane there was little choice; but in the happy medium of normal, and imperfect man, as she knew him, lay the most desirable state of existence. It would have been a splendid object lesson, she thought, to all those idealists who seek mass perfection in any phase of human endeavor, since here they might discover the truth that absolute perfection is as little to be desired as is its antithesis.

Gloomy were the thoughts that filled the mind of Tara of Helium as she awaited the summons from Luud – the summons that could mean for her but one thing; death. She guessed why he had sent for her and she knew that she must find the means for self-destruction before the night was over; but still she clung to hope and to life. She would not give up until there was no other way. She startled Ghek once by exclaiming aloud, almost fiercely: "I still live!"

"What do you mean?" asked the kaldane.

"I mean just what I say," she replied. "I still live and while I live I may still find a way. Dead, there is no hope."

"Find a way to what?" he asked.

"To life and liberty and mine own people," she responded.

"None who enters Bantoom ever leaves," he droned.

She did not reply and after a time he spoke again. "Sing to me," he said.

It was while she was singing that four warriors came to take her to Luud. They told Ghek that he was to remain where he was.

"Why?" asked Ghek.

"You have displeased Luud," replied one of the warriors.

"How?" demanded Ghek.

"You have demonstrated a lack of uncontaminated reasoning power. You have permitted sentiment to influence you, thus demonstrating that you are a defective. You know the fate of defectives."

"I know the fate of defectives, but I am no defective," insisted Ghek.

"You permitted the strange noises which issue from her throat to please and soothe you, knowing well that their origin and purpose had nothing whatever to do with logic or the powers of reason. This in itself constitutes an unimpeachable indictment of weakness. Then, influenced doubtless by an illogical feeling of sentiment, you permitted her to walk abroad in the fields to a place where she was able to make an almost successful attempt to escape. Your own reasoning power, were it not defective, would convince you that you are unfit. The natural, and reasonable, consequence is destruction. Therefore you will be destroyed in such a way that the example will be beneficial to all other kaldanes of the swarm of Luud. In the meantime you will remain where you are."

"You are right," said Ghek. "I will remain here until Luud sees fit to destroy me in the most reasonable manner."

Tara of Helium shot a look of amazement at him as they led her from the chamber. Over her shoulder she called back to him: "Remember, Ghek, you still live!" Then they led her along the interminable tunnels to where Luud awaited her.

When she was conducted into his presence he was squatting in a corner of the chamber upon his six spidery legs. Near the opposite wall lay his rykor, its beautiful form trapped in gorgeous harness – a dead thing without a guiding kaldane. Luud dismissed the warriors who had accompanied the prisoner. Then he sat with his terrible eyes fixed upon her and without speaking for some time. Tara of Helium could but wait. What was to come she could only guess. When it came would be sufficiently the time to meet it. There was no necessity for anticipating the end. Presently Luud spoke.

"You think to escape," he said, in the deadly, expressionless monotone of his kind – the only possible result of orally expressing reason uninfluenced by sentiment. "You will not escape. You are merely the embodiment of two imperfect things – an imperfect brain and an imperfect body. The two cannot exist together in perfection. There you see a perfect body." He pointed toward the rykor. "It has no brain. Here," and he raised one of his chelae to his head, "is the perfect brain. It needs no body to function perfectly and properly as a brain. You would pit your feeble intellect against mine! Even now you are planning to slay me. If you are thwarted in that you expect to slay yourself. You will learn the power of mind over matter. I am the mind. You are the matter. What brain you have is too weak and ill-developed to deserve the name of brain. You have permitted it to be weakened by impulsive acts dictated by sentiment. It has no value. It has practically no control over your existence. You will not kill me. You will not kill yourself. When I am through with you you shall be killed if it seems the logical thing to do. You have no conception of the possibilities for power which lie in a perfectly developed brain. Look at that rykor. He has no brain. He can move but slightly of his own volition. An inherent mechanical instinct that we have permitted to remain in him allows him to carry food to his mouth; but he could not find food for himself. We have to place it within his reach and always in the same place. Should we put food at his feet and leave him alone he would starve to death. But now watch what a real brain may accomplish."

He turned his eyes upon the rykor and squatted there glaring at the insensate thing. Presently, to the girl's horror, the headless body moved. It rose slowly to its feet and crossed the room to Luud; it stooped and took the hideous head in its hands; it raised the head and set it on its shoulders.

"What chance have you against such power?" asked Luud. "As I did with the rykor so can I do with you."

Tara of Helium made no reply. Evidently no vocal reply was necessary.

"You doubt my ability!" stated Luud, which was precisely the fact, though the girl had only thought it – she had not said it.

Luud crossed the room and lay down. Then he detached himself from the body and crawled across the floor until he stood directly in front of the circular opening through which she had seen him emerge the day that she had first been brought to his presence. He stopped there and fastened his terrible eyes upon her. He did not speak, but his eyes seemed to be boring straight to the center of her brain. She felt an almost irresistible force urging her toward the kaldane. She fought to resist it; she tried to turn away her eyes, but she could not. They were held as in horrid fascination upon the glittering, lidless orbs of the great brain that faced her.

Slowly, every step a painful struggle of resistance, she moved toward the horrific monster. She tried to cry aloud in an effort to awaken her numbing faculties, but no sound passed her lips. If those eyes would but turn away, just for an instant, she felt that she might regain the power to control her steps; but the eyes never left hers. They seemed but to burn deeper and deeper, gathering up every vestige of control of her entire nervous system.

As she approached the thing it backed slowly away upon its spider legs. She noticed that its chelae waved slowly to and fro before it as it backed, backed, backed, through the round aperture in the wall. Must she follow it there, too? What new and nameless horror lay concealed in that hidden chamber? No! she would not do it. Yet before she reached the wall she found herself down and crawling upon her hands and knees straight toward the hole from which the two eyes still clung to hers. At the very threshold of the opening she made a last, heroic stand, battling against the force that drew her on; but in the end she succumbed. With a gasp that ended in a sob Tara of Helium passed through the aperture into the chamber beyond.

The opening was but barely large enough to admit her. Upon the opposite side she found herself in a small chamber. Before her squatted Luud. Against the opposite wall lay a large and beautiful male rykor. He was without harness or other trappings.

"You see now," said Luud, "the futility of revolt."

The words seemed to release her momentarily from the spell. Quickly she turned away her eyes.

"Look at me!" commanded Luud.

Tara of Helium kept her eyes averted. She felt a new strength, or at least a diminution of the creature's power over her. Had she stumbled upon the secret of its uncanny domination over her will? She dared not hope. With eyes averted she turned toward the aperture through which those baleful eyes had drawn her. Again Luud commanded her to stop, but the voice alone lacked all authority to influence her. It was not like the eyes. She heard the creature whistle and knew that it was summoning assistance, but because she did not dare look toward it she did not see it turn and concentrate its gaze upon the great, headless body lying by the further wall.

The girl was still slightly under the spell of the creature's influence – she had not regained full and independent domination of her powers. She moved as one in the throes of some hideous nightmare – slowly, painfully, as though each limb was hampered by a great weight, or as she were dragging her body through a viscous fluid. The aperture was close, ah, so close, yet, struggle as she would, she seemed to be making no appreciable progress toward it.

Behind her, urged on by the malevolent power of the great brain, the headless body crawled upon all-fours toward her. At last she had reached the aperture. Something seemed to tell her that once beyond it the domination of the kaldane would be broken. She was almost through into the adjoining chamber when she felt a heavy hand close upon her ankle. The rykor had reached forth and seized her, and though she struggled the thing dragged her back into the room with Luud. It held her tight and drew her close, and then, to her horror, it commenced to caress her.

"You see now," she heard Luud's dull voice, "the futility of revolt – and its punishment."

Tara of Helium fought to defend herself, but pitifully weak were her muscles against this brainless incarnation of brute power. Yet she fought, fought on in the face of hopeless odds for the honor of the proud name she bore – fought alone, she whom the fighting men of a mighty empire, the flower of Martian chivalry, would gladly have lain down their lives to save.

CHAPTER SEVEN
A Repellent Sight

THE CRUISER VANATOR careened through the tempest. That she had not been dashed to the ground, or twisted by the force of the elements into tangled wreckage, was due entirely to the caprice of Nature. For all the duration of the storm she rode, a helpless derelict, upon those storm-tossed waves of wind. But for all the dangers and vicissitudes they underwent, she and her crew might have borne charmed lives up to within an hour of the abating of the hurricane. It was then that the catastrophe occurred – a catastrophe indeed to the crew of the Vanator and the kingdom of Gathol.

The men had been without food or drink since leaving Helium, and they had been hurled about and buffeted in their lashings until all were worn to exhaustion. There was a brief lull in the storm during which one of the crew attempted to reach his quarters, after releasing the lashings which had held him to the precarious safety of the deck. The act in itself was a direct violation of orders and, in the eyes of the other members of the crew, the effect, which came with startling suddenness, took the form of a swift and terrible retribution. Scarce had the man released the safety snaps ere a swift arm of the storm-monster encircled the ship, rolling it over and over, with the result that the foolhardy warrior went overboard at the first turn.

Unloosed from their lashing by the constant turning and twisting of the ship and the force of the wind, the boarding and landing tackle had been trailing beneath the keel, a tangled mass of cordage and leather. Upon the occasions that the Vanator rolled completely over, these things would be wrapped around her until another revolution in the opposite direction, or the wind itself, carried them once again clear of the deck to trail, whipping in the storm, beneath the hurtling ship.

Into this fell the body of the warrior, and as a drowning man clutches at a straw so the fellow clutched at the tangled cordage that caught him and arrested his fall. With the strength of desperation he clung to the cordage, seeking frantically to entangle his legs and body in it. With each jerk of the ship his hand holds were all but torn loose, and though he knew that eventually they would be and that he must be dashed to the ground beneath, yet he fought with the madness that is born of hopelessness for the pitiful second which but prolonged his agony.

It was upon this sight then that Gahan of Gathol looked, over the edge of the careening deck of the Vanator, as he sought to learn the fate of his warrior. Lashed to the gunwale close at hand a single landing leather that had not fouled the tangled mass beneath whipped free from the ship's side, the hook snapping at its outer end. The Jed of Gathol grasped the situation in a single glance. Below him one of his people looked into the eyes of Death. To the jed's hand lay the means for succor.

There was no instant's hesitation. Casting off his deck lashings, he seized the landing leather and slipped over the ship's side. Swinging like a bob upon a mad pendulum he swung far out and back again, turning and twisting three thousand feet above the surface of Barsoom, and then, at last, the thing he had hoped for occurred. He was carried within reach of the cordage where the warrior still clung, though with rapidly diminishing strength. Catching one leg on a loop of the tangled strands Gahan pulled himself close enough to seize another quite near to the fellow. Clinging precariously to this new hold the jed slowly drew in the landing leather, down which he had clambered until he could grasp the hook at its end. This he fastened to a ring in the warrior's harness, just before the man's weakened fingers slipped from their hold upon the cordage.

Temporarily, at least, he had saved the life of his subject, and now he turned his attention toward insuring his own safety. Inextricably entangled in the mess to which he was clinging were numerous other landing hooks such as he had attached to the warrior's harness, and with one of these he sought to secure himself until the storm should abate sufficiently to permit him to climb to the deck, but even as he reached for one that swung near him the ship was caught in a renewed burst of the storm's fury, the thrashing cordage whipped and snapped to the lunging of the great craft and one of the heavy metal hooks, lashing through the air, struck the Jed of Gathol fair between the eyes.

Momentarily stunned, Gahan's fingers slipped from their hold upon the cordage and the man shot downward through the thin air of dying Mars toward the ground three thousand feet beneath, while upon the deck of the rolling Vanator his faithful warriors clung to their lashings all unconscious of the fate of their beloved leader; nor was it until more than an hour later, after the storm had materially subsided, that they realized he was lost, or knew the self-sacrificing heroism of the act that had sealed his doom. The Vanator now rested upon an even keel as she was carried along by a strong, though steady, wind. The warriors had cast off their deck lashings and the officers were taking account of losses and damage when a weak cry was heard from oversides, attracting their attention to the man hanging in the cordage beneath the keel. Strong arms hoisted him to the deck and then it was that the crew of the Vanator learned of the heroism of their jed and his end. How far they had traveled since his loss they could only vaguely guess, nor could they return in search of him in the disabled condition of the ship. It was a saddened company that drifted onward through the air toward whatever destination Fate was to choose for them.

And Gahan, Jed of Gathol – what of him? Plummet-like he fell for a thousand feet and then the storm seized him in its giant clutch and bore him far aloft again. As a bit of paper borne upon a gale he was tossed about in mid-air, the sport and plaything of the wind. Over and over it turned him and upward and downward it carried him, but after each new sally of the element he was brought nearer to the ground. The freaks of cyclonic storms are the rule of cyclonic storms, demolish giant trees, and in the same gust they transport frail infants for miles and deposit them unharmed in their wake.

And so it was with Gahan of Gathol. Expecting momentarily to be dashed to destruction he presently found himself deposited gently upon the soft, ochre moss of a dead sea-bottom, bodily no worse off for his harrowing adventure than in the possession of a slight swelling upon his forehead where the metal hook had struck him. Scarcely able to believe that Fate had dealt thus gently with him, the jed arose slowly, as though more than half convinced that he should discover crushed and splintered bones that would not support his weight. But he was intact. He looked about him in a vain effort at orientation. The air was filled with flying dust and debris. The Sun was obliterated. His vision was confined to a radius of a few hundred yards of ochre moss and dust-filled air. Five hundred yards away in any direction there might have arisen the walls of a great city and he not known it. It was useless to move from where he was until the air cleared, since he could not know in what direction he was moving, and so he stretched himself upon the moss and waited, pondering the fate of his warriors and his ship, but giving little thought to his own precarious situation.

Lashed to his harness were his swords, his pistols, and a dagger, and in his pocket-pouch a small quantity of the concentrated rations that form a part of the equipment of the fighting men of Barsoom. These things together with trained muscles, high courage, and an undaunted spirit sufficed him for whatever misadventures might lie between him and Gathol, which lay in what direction he knew not, nor at what distance.

The wind was falling rapidly and with it the dust that obscured the landscape. That the storm was over he was convinced, but he chafed at the inactivity the low visibility put upon him, nor did conditions better materially before night fell, so that he was forced to await the new day at the very spot at which the tempest had deposited him. Without his sleeping silks and furs he spent a far from comfortable night, and it was with feelings of unmixed relief that he saw the sudden dawn burst upon him. The air was now clear and in the light of the new day he saw an undulating plain stretching in all directions about him, while to the northwest there were barely discernible the outlines of low hills. Toward the southeast of Gathol was such a country, and as Gahan surmised the direction and the velocity of the storm to have carried him somewhere in the vicinity of the country he thought he recognized, he assumed that Gathol lay behind the hills he now saw, whereas, in reality, it lay far to the northeast.

It was two days before Gahan had crossed the plain and reached the summit of the hills from which he hoped to see his own country, only to meet at last with disappointment. Before him stretched another plain, of even greater proportions than that he had but just crossed, and beyond this other hills. In one material respect this plain differed from that behind him in that it was dotted with occasional isolated hills. Convinced, however, that Gathol lay somewhere in the direction of his search he descended into the valley and bent his steps toward the northwest.

For weeks Gahan of Gathol crossed valleys and hills in search of some familiar landmark that might point his way toward his native land, but the summit of each succeeding ridge revealed but another unfamiliar view. He saw few animals and no men, until he finally came to the belief that he had fallen upon that fabled area of ancient Barsoom which lay under the curse of her olden gods – the once rich and fertile country whose people in their pride and arrogance had denied the deities, and whose punishment had been extermination.

And then, one day, he scaled low hills and looked into an inhabited valley – a valley of trees and cultivated fields and plots of ground enclosed by stone walls surrounding strange towers. He saw people working in the fields, but he did not rush down to greet them. First he must know more of them and whether they might be assumed to be friends or enemies. Hidden by concealing shrubbery he crawled to a vantage point upon a hill that projected further into the valley, and here he lay upon his belly watching the workers closest to him. They were still quite a distance from him and he could not be quite sure of them, but there was something verging upon the unnatural about them. Their heads seemed out of proportion to their bodies – too large.

For a long time he lay watching them and ever more forcibly it was borne in upon his consciousness that they were not as he, and that it would be rash to trust himself among them. Presently he saw a couple appear from the nearest enclosure and slowly approach those who were working nearest to the hill where he lay in hiding. Immediately he was aware that one of these differed from all the others. Even at the greater distance he noted that the head was smaller and as they approached, he was confident that the harness of one of them was not as the harness of its companion or of that of any of those who tilled the fields.

The two stopped often, apparently in argument, as though one would proceed in the direction that they were going while the other demurred. But each time the smaller won reluctant consent from the other, and so they came closer and closer to the last line of workers toiling between the enclosure from which they had come and the hill where Gahan of Gathol lay watching, and then suddenly the smaller figure struck its companion full in the face. Gahan, horrified, saw the latter's head topple from its body, saw the body stagger and fall to the ground. The man half rose from his concealment the better to view the happening in the valley below. The creature that had felled its companion was dashing madly in the direction of the hill upon which he was hidden, it dodged one of the workers that sought to seize it. Gahan hoped that it would gain its liberty, why he did not know other than at closer range it had every appearance of being a creature of his own race. Then he saw it stumble and go down and instantly its pursuers were upon it. Then it was that Gahan's eyes chanced to return to the figure of the creature the fugitive had felled.

What horror was this that he was witnessing? Or were his eyes playing some ghastly joke upon him? No, impossible though it was – it was true – the head was moving slowly to the fallen body. It placed itself upon the shoulders, the body rose, and the creature, seemingly as good as new, ran quickly to where its fellows were dragging the hapless captive to its feet.

The watcher saw the creature take its prisoner by the arm and lead it back to the enclosure, and even across the distance that separated them from him he could note dejection and utter hopelessness in the bearing of the prisoner, and, too, he was half convinced that it was a woman, perhaps a red Martian of his own race. Could he be sure that this was true he must make some effort to rescue her even though the customs of his strange world required it only in case she was of his own country; but he was not sure; she might not be a red Martian at all, or, if she were, it was as possible that she sprang from an enemy people as not. His first duty was to return to his own people with as little personal risk as possible, and though the thought of adventure stirred his blood he put the temptation aside with a sigh and turned away from the peaceful and beautiful valley that he longed to enter, for it was his intention to skirt its eastern edge and continue his search for Gathol beyond.

As Gahan of Gathol turned his steps along the southern slopes of the hills that bound Bantoom upon the south and east, his attention was attracted toward a small cluster of trees a short distance to his right. The low sun was casting long shadows. It would soon be night. The trees were off the path that he had chosen and he had little mind to be diverted from his way; but as he looked again he hesitated. There was something there besides boles of trees, and underbrush. There were suggestions of familiar lines of the handicraft of man. Gahan stopped and strained his eyes in the direction of the thing that had arrested his attention. No, he must be mistaken – the branches of the trees and a low bush had taken on an unnatural semblance in the horizontal rays of the setting sun. He turned and continued upon his way; but as he cast another side glance in the direction of the object of his interest, the sun's rays were shot back into his eyes from a glistening point of radiance among the trees.

Gahan shook his head and walked quickly toward the mystery, determined now to solve it. The shining object still lured him on and when he had come closer to it his eyes went wide in surprise, for the thing they saw was naught else than the jewel-encrusted emblem upon the prow of a small flier. Gahan, his hand upon his short-sword, moved silently forward, but as he neared the craft he saw that he had naught to fear, for it was deserted. Then he turned his attention toward the emblem. As its significance was flashed to his understanding his face paled and his heart went cold – it was the insignia of the house of The Warlord of Barsoom. Instantly he saw the dejected figure of the captive being led back to her prison in the valley just beyond the hills. Tara of Helium! And he had been so near to deserting her to her fate. The cold sweat stood in beads upon his brow.

A hasty examination of the deserted craft unfolded to the young jed the whole tragic story. The same tempest that had proved his undoing had borne Tara of Helium to this distant country. Here, doubtless, she had landed in hope of obtaining food and water since, without a propellor, she could not hope to reach her native city, or any other friendly port, other than by the merest caprice of Fate. The flier seemed intact except for the missing propellor and the fact that it had been carefully moored in the shelter of the clump of trees indicated that the girl had expected to return to it, while the dust and leaves upon its deck spoke of the long days, and even weeks, since she had landed. Mute yet eloquent proofs, these things, that Tara of Helium was a prisoner, and that she was the very prisoner whose bold dash for liberty he had so recently witnessed he now had not the slightest doubt.

The question now revolved solely about her rescue. He knew to which tower she had been taken – that much and no more. Of the number, the kind, or the disposition of her captors he knew nothing; nor did he care – for Tara of Helium he would face a hostile world alone. Rapidly he considered several plans for succoring her; but the one that appealed most strongly to him was that which offered the greatest chance of escape for the girl should he be successful in reaching her. His decision reached he turned his attention quickly toward the flier. Casting off its lashings he dragged it out from beneath the trees, and, mounting to the deck tested out the various controls. The motor started at a touch and purred sweetly, the buoyancy tanks were well stocked, and the ship answered perfectly to the controls which regulated her altitude. There was nothing needed but a propellor to make her fit for the long voyage to Helium. Gahan shrugged impatiently – there must not be a propellor within a thousand haads. But what mattered it? The craft even without a propellor would still answer the purpose his plan required of it – provided the captors of Tara of Helium were a people without ships, and he had seen nothing to suggest that they had ships. The architecture of their towers and enclosures assured him that they had not.

The sudden Barsoomian night had fallen. Cluros rode majestically the high heavens. The rumbling roar of a banth reverberated among the hills. Gahan of Gathol let the ship rise a few feet from the ground, then, seizing a bow rope, he dropped over the side. To tow the little craft was now a thing of ease, and as Gahan moved rapidly toward the brow of the hill above Bantoom the flier floated behind him as lightly as a swan upon a quiet lake. Now down the hill toward the tower dimly visible in the moonlight the Gatholian turned his steps. Closer behind him sounded the roar of the hunting banth. He wondered if the beast sought him or was following some other spoor. He could not be delayed now by any hungry beast of prey, for what might that very instant be befalling Tara of Helium he could not guess; and so he hastened his steps. But closer and closer came the horrid screams of the great carnivore, and now he heard the swift fall of padded feet upon the hillside behind him. He glanced back just in time to see the beast break into a rapid charge. His hand leaped to the hilt of his long-sword, but he did not draw, for in the same instant he saw the futility of armed resistance, since behind the first banth came a herd of at least a dozen others. There was but a single alternative to a futile stand and that he grasped in the instant that he saw the overwhelming numbers of his antagonists.

Springing lightly from the ground he swarmed up the rope toward the bow of the flier. His weight drew the craft slightly lower and at the very instant that the man drew himself to the deck at the bow of the vessel, the leading banth sprang for the stern. Gahan leaped to his feet and rushed toward the great beast in the hope of dislodging it before it had succeeded in clambering aboard. At the same instant he saw that others of the banths were racing toward them with the quite evident intention of following their leader to the ship's deck. Should they reach it in any numbers he would be lost. There was but a single hope. Leaping for the altitude control Gahan pulled it wide. Simultaneously three banths leaped for the deck. The craft rose swiftly. Gahan felt the impact of a body against the keel, followed by the soft thuds of the great bodies as they struck the ground beneath. His act had not been an instant too soon. And now the leader had gained the deck and stood at the stern with glaring eyes and snarling jaws. Gahan drew his sword. The beast, possibly disconcerted by the novelty of its position, did not charge. Instead it crept slowly toward its intended prey. The craft was rising and Gahan placed a foot upon the control and stopped the ascent. He did not wish to chance rising to some higher air current that would bear him away. Already the craft was moving slowly toward the tower, carried thither by the impetus of the banth's heavy body leaping upon it from astern.

The man watched the slow approach of the monster, the slavering jowls, the malignant expression of the devilish face. The creature, finding the deck stable, appeared to be gaining confidence, and then the man leaped suddenly to one side of the deck and the tiny flier heeled as suddenly in response. The banth slipped and clutched frantically at the deck. Gahan leaped in with his naked sword; the great beast caught itself and reared upon its hind legs to reach forth and seize this presumptuous mortal that dared question its right to the flesh it craved; and then the man sprang to the opposite side of the deck. The banth toppled sideways at the same instant that it attempted to spring; a raking talon passed close to Gahan's head at the moment that his sword lunged through the savage heart, and as the warrior wrenched his blade from the carcass it slipped silently over the side of the ship.

A glance below showed that the vessel was drifting in the direction of the tower to which Gahan had seen the prisoner led. In another moment or two it would be directly over it. The man sprang to the control and let the craft drop quickly toward the ground where followed the banths, still hot for their prey. To land outside the enclosure spelled certain death, while inside he could see many forms huddled upon the ground as in sleep. The ship floated now but a few feet above the wall of the enclosure. There was nothing for it but to risk all on a bold bid for fortune, or drift helplessly past without hope of returning through the banth-infested valley, from many points of which he could now hear the roars and growls of these fierce Barsoomian lions.

Slipping over the side Gahan descended by the trailing anchor-rope until his feet touched the top of the wall, where he had no difficulty in arresting the slow drifting of the ship. Then he drew up the anchor and lowered it inside the enclosure. Still there was no movement upon the part of the sleepers beneath – they lay as dead men. Dull lights shone from openings in the tower; but there was no sign of guard or waking inmate. Clinging to the rope Gahan lowered himself within the enclosure, where he had his first close view of the creatures lying there in what he had thought sleep. With a half smothered exclamation of horror the man drew back from the headless bodies of the rykors. At first he thought them the corpses of decapitated humans like himself, which was quite bad enough; but when he saw them move and realized that they were endowed with life, his horror and disgust became even greater.

Here then was the explanation of the thing he had witnessed that afternoon, when Tara of Helium had struck the back to its body. And to think that the pearl of Helium was in the power of such hideous things as these. Again the man shuddered, but he hastened to make fast the flier, clamber again to its deck and lower it to the floor of the enclosure. Then he strode toward a door in the base of the tower, stepping lightly over the recumbent forms of the unconscious rykors, and crossing the threshold disappeared within.

CHAPTER EIGHT

Close Work

GHEK, IN HIS HAPPIER DAYS third foreman of the fields of Luud, sat nursing his anger and his humiliation. Recently something had awakened within him the existence of which he had never before even dreamed. Had the influence of the strange captive woman aught to do with this unrest and dissatisfaction? He did not know. He missed the soothing influence of the noise she called singing. Could it be that there were other things more desirable than cold logic and undefiled brain power? Was well balanced imperfection more to be sought after then, than the high development of a single characteristic? He thought of the great, ultimate brain toward which all kaldanes were striving. It would be deaf, and dumb, and blind. A thousand beautiful strangers might sing and dance about it, but it could derive no pleasure from the singing or the dancing since it would possess no perceptive faculties. Already had the kaldanes shut themselves off from most of the gratifications of the senses. Ghek wondered if much was to be gained by denying themselves still further, and with the thought came a question as to the whole fabric of their theory. After all perhaps the girl was right; what purpose could a great brain serve sealed in the bowels of the earth?

And he, Ghek, was to die for this theory. Luud had decreed it. The injustice of it overwhelmed him with rage. But he was helpless. There was no escape. Beyond the enclosure the banths awaited him; within, his own kind, equally as merciless and ferocious. Among them there was no such thing as love, or loyalty, or friendship – they were just brains. He might kill Luud; but what would that profit him? Another king would be loosed from his sealed chamber and Ghek would be killed. He did not know it but he would not even have the poor satisfaction of satisfied revenge, since he was not capable of feeling so abstruse a sentiment.

Ghek, mounted upon his rykor, paced the floor of the tower chamber in which he had been ordered to remain. Ordinarily he would have accepted the sentence of Luud with perfect equanimity, since it was but the logical result of reason; but now it seemed different. The stranger woman had bewitched him. Life appeared a pleasant thing – there were great possibilities in it. The dream of the ultimate brain had receded into a tenuous haze far in the background of his thoughts.

At that moment there appeared in the doorway of the chamber a red warrior with naked sword. He was a male counterpart of the prisoner whose sweet voice had undermined the cold, calculating reason of the kaldane.

"Silence!" admonished the newcomer, his straight brows gathered in an ominous frown and the point of his longsword playing menacingly before the eyes of the kaldane. "I seek the woman, Tara of Helium. Where is she? If you value your life speak quickly and speak the truth."

If he valued his life! It was a truth that Ghek had but just learned. He thought quickly. After all, a great brain is not without its uses. Perhaps here lay escape from the sentence of Luud.

"You are of her kind?" he asked. "You come to rescue her?"

"Yes."

"Listen, then. I have befriended her, and because of this I am to die. If I help you to liberate her, will you take me with you?"

Gahan of Gathol eyed the weird creature from crown to foot – the perfect body, the grotesque head, the expressionless face. Among such as these had the beautiful daughter of Helium been held captive for days and weeks.

"If she lives and is unharmed," he said, "I will take you with us."

"When they took her from me she was alive and unharmed," replied Ghek. "I cannot say what has befallen her since. Luud sent for her."

"Who is Luud? Where is he? Lead me to him." Gahan spoke quickly in tones vibrant with authority.

"Come, then," said Ghek, leading the way from the apartment and down a stairway toward the underground burrows of the kaldanes. "Luud is my king. I will take you to his chambers."

"Hasten!" urged Gahan.

"Sheathe your sword," warned Ghek, "so that should we pass others of my kind I may say to them that you are a new prisoner with some likelihood of winning their belief."

Gahan did as he was bid, but warning the kaldane that his hand was ever ready at his dagger's hilt.

"You need have no fear of treachery," said Ghek "My only hope of life lies in you."

"And if you fail me," Gahan admonished him, "I can promise you as sure a death as even your king might guarantee you."

Ghek made no reply, but moved rapidly through the winding subterranean corridors until Gahan began to realize how truly was he in the hands of this strange monster. If the fellow should prove false it would profit Gahan nothing to slay him, since without his guidance the red man might never hope to retrace his way to the tower and freedom.

Twice they met and were accosted by other kaldanes; but in both instances Ghek's simple statement that he was taking a new prisoner to Luud appeared to allay all suspicion, and then at last they came to the ante-chamber of the king.

"Here, now, red man, thou must fight, if ever," whispered Ghek. "Enter there!" and he pointed to a doorway before them.

"And you?" asked Gahan, still fearful of treachery.

"My rykor is powerful," replied the kaldane. "I shall accompany you and fight at your side. As well die thus as in torture later at the will of Luud. Come!"

But Gahan had already crossed the room and entered the chamber beyond. Upon the opposite side of the room was a circular opening guarded by two warriors. Beyond this opening he could see two figures struggling upon the floor, and the fleeting glimpse he had of one of the faces suddenly endowed him with the strength of ten warriors and the ferocity of a wounded banth. It was Tara of Helium, fighting for her honor or her life.

The warriors, startled by the unexpected appearance of a red man, stood for a moment in dumb amazement, and in that moment Gahan of Gathol was upon them, and one was down, a sword-thrust through its heart.

"Strike at the heads," whispered the voice of Ghek in Gahan's ear. The latter saw the head of the fallen warrior crawl quickly within the aperture leading to the chamber where he had seen Tara of Helium in the clutches of a headless body. Then the sword of Ghek struck the kaldane of the remaining warrior from its rykor and Gahan ran his sword through the repulsive head.

Instantly the red warrior leaped for the aperture, while close behind him came Ghek.

"Look not upon the eyes of Luud," warned the kaldane, "or you are lost."

Within the chamber Gahan saw Tara of Helium in the clutches of a mighty body, while close to the wall upon the opposite side of the apartment crouched the hideous, spider-like Luud. Instantly the king realized the menace to himself and sought to fasten his eyes upon the eyes of

Gahan, and in doing so he was forced to relax his concentration upon the rykor in whose embraces Tara struggled, so that almost immediately the girl found herself able to tear away from the awful, headless thing.

As she rose quickly to her feet she saw for the first time the cause of the interruption of Luud's plans. A red warrior! Her heart leaped in rejoicing and thanksgiving. What miracle of fate had sent him to her? She did not recognize him, though, this travel-worn warrior in the plain harness which showed no single jewel. How could she have guessed him the same as the scintillant creature of platinum and diamonds that she had seen for a brief hour under such different circumstances at the court of her august sire?

Luud saw Ghek following the strange warrior into the chamber. "Strike him down, Ghek!" commanded the king. "Strike down the stranger and your life shall be yours."

Gahan glanced at the hideous face of the king.

"Seek not his eyes," screamed Tara in warning; but it was too late. Already the horrid hypnotic gaze of the king kaldane had seized upon the eyes of Gahan. The red warrior hesitated in his stride. His sword point drooped slowly toward the floor. Tara glanced toward Ghek. She saw the creature glaring with his expressionless eyes upon the broad back of the stranger. She saw the hand of the creature's rykor creeping stealthily toward the hilt of its dagger.

And then Tara of Helium raised her eyes aloft and poured forth the notes of Mars' most beautiful melody, The Song of Love.

Ghek drew his dagger from its sheath. His eyes turned toward the singing girl. Luud's glance wavered from the eyes of the man to the face of Tara, and the instant that the latter's song distracted his attention from his victim, Gahan of Gathol shook himself and as with a supreme effort of will forced his eyes to the wall above Luud's hideous head. Ghek raised his dagger above his right shoulder, took a single quick step forward, and struck. The girl's song ended in a stifled scream as she leaped forward with the evident intention of frustrating the kaldane's purpose; but she was too late, and well it was, for an instant later she realized the purpose of Ghek's act as she saw the dagger fly from his hand, pass Gahan's shoulder, and sink full to the guard in the soft face of Luud.

"Come!" cried the assassin, "we have no time to lose," and started for the aperture through which they had entered the chamber; but in his stride he paused as his glance was arrested by the form of the mighty rykor lying prone upon the floor – a king's rykor; the most beautiful, the most powerful, that the breeders of Bantoom could produce. Ghek realized that in his escape he could take with him but a single rykor, and there was none in Bantoom that could give him better service than this giant lying here. Quickly he transferred himself to the shoulders of the great, inert hulk. Instantly the latter was transformed to a sentient creature, filled with pulsing life and alert energy.

"Now," said the kaldane, "we are ready. Let whoso would revert to nothingness impede me." Even as he spoke he stooped and crawled into the chamber beyond, while Gahan, taking Tara by the arm, motioned her to follow. The girl looked him full in the eyes for the first time. "The Gods of my people have been kind," she said; "you came just in time. To the thanks of Tara of Helium shall be added those of The Warlord of Barsoom and his people. Thy reward shall surpass thy greatest desires."

Gahan of Gathol saw that she did not recognize him, and quickly he checked the warm greeting that had been upon his lips.

"Be thou Tara of Helium or another," he replied, "is immaterial, to serve thus a red woman of Barsoom is in itself sufficient reward."

As they spoke the girl was making her way through the aperture after Ghek, and presently all three had quitted the apartments of Luud and were moving rapidly along the winding corridors toward the tower. Ghek repeatedly urged them to greater speed, but the red men of Barsoom were never keen for retreat, and so the two that followed him moved all too slowly for the kaldane.

"There are none to impede our progress," urged Gahan, "so why tax the strength of the Princess by needless haste?"

"I fear not so much opposition ahead, for there are none there who know the thing that has been done in Luud's chambers this night; but the kaldane of one of the warriors who stood guard before Luud's apartment escaped, and you may count it a truth that he lost no time in seeking aid. That it did not come before we left is due solely to the rapidity with which events transpired in the king's[2] room. Long before we reach the tower they will be upon us from behind, and that they will come in numbers far superior to ours and with great and powerful rykors I well know."

Nor was Ghek's prophecy long in fulfilment. Presently the sounds of pursuit became audible in the distant clanking of accouterments and the whistling call to arms of the kaldanes.

2   I have used the word king in describing the rulers or chiefs of the Bantoomian swarms, since the word itself is unpronounceable in English, nor does jed or jeddak of the red Martian tongue have quite the same meaning as the Bantoomian word, which has practically the same significance as the English word queen as applied to the leader of a swarm of bees. – J. C.

"The tower is but a short distance now," cried Ghek. "Make haste while yet you may, and if we can barricade it until the sun rises we may yet escape."

"We shall need no barricades for we shall not linger in the tower," replied Gahan, moving more rapidly as he realized from the volume of sound behind them the great number of their pursuers.

"But we may not go further than the tower tonight," insisted Ghek. "Beyond the tower await the banths and certain death."

Gahan smiled. "Fear not the banths," he assured them. "Can we but reach the enclosure a little ahead of our pursuers we have naught to fear from any evil power within this accursed valley."

Ghek made no reply, nor did his expressionless face denote either belief or skepticism. The girl looked into the face of the man questioningly. She did not understand.

"Your flier," he said. "It is moored before the tower."

Her face lighted with pleasure and relief. "You found it!" she exclaimed. "What fortune!"

"It was fortune indeed," he replied. "Since it not only told that you were a prisoner here; but it saved me from the banths as I was crossing the valley from the hills to this tower into which I saw them take you this afternoon after your brave attempt at escape."

"How did you know it was I?" she asked, her puzzled brows scanning his face as though she sought to recall from past memories some scene in which he figured.

"Who is there but knows of the loss of the Princess Tara of Helium?" he replied. "And when I saw the device upon your flier I knew at once, though I had not known when I saw you among them in the fields a short time earlier. Too great was the distance for me to make certain whether the captive was man or woman. Had chance not divulged the hiding place of your flier I had gone my way, Tara of Helium. I shudder to think how close was the chance at that. But for the momentary shining of the sun upon the emblazoned device on the prow of your craft, I had passed on unknowing."

The girl shuddered. "The Gods sent you," she whispered reverently.

"The Gods sent me, Tara of Helium," he replied.

"But I do not recognize you," she said. "I have tried to recall you, but I have failed. Your name, what may it be?"

"It is not strange that so great a princess should not recall the face of every roving panthan of Barsoom," he replied with a smile.

"But your name?" insisted the girl.

"Call me Turan," replied the man, for it had come to him that if Tara of Helium recognized him as the man whose impetuous avowal of love had angered her that day in the gardens of The Warlord, her situation might be rendered infinitely less bearable than were she to believe him a total stranger. Then, too, as a simple panthan[3] he might win a greater degree of her confidence by his loyalty and faithfulness and a place in her esteem that seemed to have been closed to the resplendent Jed of Gathol.

They had reached the tower now, and as they entered it from the subterranean corridor a backward glance revealed the van of their pursuers – hideous kaldanes mounted upon swift and powerful rykors. As rapidly as might be the three ascended the stairways leading to the ground level, but after them, even more rapidly, came the minions of Luud. Ghek led the way, grasping one of Tara's hands the more easily to guide and assist her, while Gahan of Gathol followed a few paces in their rear, his bared sword ready for the assault that all realized must come upon them now before ever they reached the enclosure and the flier.

"Let Ghek drop behind to your side," said Tara, "and fight with you."

"There is but room for a single blade in these narrow corridors," replied the Gatholian. "Hasten on with Ghek and win to the deck of the flier. Have your hand upon the control, and if I come far enough ahead of these to reach the dangling cable you can rise at my word and I can clamber to the deck at my leisure; but if one of them emerges first into the enclosure you will know that I shall never come, and you will rise quickly and trust to the Gods of our ancestors to give you a fair breeze in the direction of a more hospitable people."

Tara of Helium shook her head. "We will not desert you, panthan," she said.

Gahan, ignoring her reply, spoke above her head to Ghek. "Take her to the craft moored within the enclosure," he commanded. "It is our only hope. Alone, I may win to its deck; but have I to wait upon you two at the last moment the chances are that none of us will escape. Do as I bid." His tone was haughty and arrogant – the tone of a man who has commanded other men from birth, and whose will has been law. Tara of Helium was both angered and vexed. She was not accustomed to being either commanded or ignored, but with all her royal pride she was no fool, and she knew the man was right, that he was risking his life to save hers, so she hastened on with Ghek as she was bid, and after the first flush of anger she smiled, for the realization came to her that this fellow was but a rough untutored warrior, skilled not in the

3   Soldier of Fortune; free-lance warrior.

finer usages of cultured courts. His heart was right, though; a brave and loyal heart, and gladly she forgave him the offense of his tone and manner. But what a tone! Recollection of it gave her sudden pause. Panthans were rough and ready men. Often they rose to positions of high command, so it was not the note of authority in the fellow's voice that seemed remarkable; but something else – a quality that was indefinable, yet as distinct as it was familiar. She had heard it before when the voice of her great-grandsire, Tardos Mors, Jeddak of Helium, had risen in command; and in the voice of her grandfather, Mors Kajak, the jed; and in the ringing tones of her illustrious sire, John Carter, Warlord of Barsoom, when he addressed his warriors.

But now she had no time to speculate upon so trivial a thing, for behind her came the sudden clash of arms and she knew that Turan, the panthan, had crossed swords with the first of their pursuers. As she glanced back he was still visible beyond a turn in the stairway, so that she could see the quick swordplay that ensued. Daughter of a world's greatest swordsman, she knew well the finest points of the art. She saw the clumsy attack of the kaldane and the quick, sure return of the panthan. As she looked down from above upon his almost naked body, trapped only in the simplest of unadorned harness, and saw the play of the lithe muscles beneath the red-bronze skin, and witnessed the quick and delicate play of his sword point, to her sense of obligation was added a spontaneous admission of admiration that was but the natural tribute of a woman to skill and bravery and, perchance, some trifle to manly symmetry and strength.

Three times the panthan's blade changed its position – once to fend a savage cut; once to feint; and once to thrust. And as he withdrew it from the last position the kaldane rolled lifeless from its stumbling rykor and Turan sprang quickly down the steps to engage the next behind, and then Ghek had drawn Tara upward and a turn in the stairway shut the battling panthan from her view; but still she heard the ring of steel on steel, the clank of accouterments and the shrill whistling of the kaldanes. Her heart moved her to turn back to the side of her brave defender; but her judgment told her that she could serve him best by being ready at the control of the flier at the moment he reached the enclosure.

CHAPTER NINE

Adrift Over Strange Regions

PRESENTLY GHEK PUSHED ASIDE a door that opened from the stairway, and before them Tara saw the moonlight flooding the walled court where the headless rykors lay beside their feeding-troughs. She saw the perfect bodies, muscled as the best of her father's fighting men, and the females whose figures would have been the envy of many of Helium's most beautiful women. Ah, if she could but endow these with the power to act! Then indeed might the safety of the panthan be assured; but they were only poor lumps of clay, nor had she the power to quicken them to life. Ever must they lie thus until dominated by the cold, heartless brain of the kaldane. The girl sighed in pity even as she shuddered in disgust as she picked her way over and among the sprawled creatures toward the flier.

Quickly she and Ghek mounted to the deck after the latter had cast off the moorings. Tara tested the control, raising and lowering the ship a few feet within the walled space. It responded perfectly. Then she lowered it to the ground again and waited. From the open doorway came the sounds of conflict, now nearing them, now receding. The girl, having witnessed her champion's skill, had little fear of the outcome. Only a single antagonist could face him at a time upon the narrow stairway, he had the advantage of position and of the defensive, and he was a master of the sword while they were clumsy bunglers by comparison. Their sole advantage was in their numbers, unless they might find a way to come upon him from behind.

She paled at the thought. Could she have seen him she might have been further perturbed, for he took no advantage of many opportunities to win nearer the enclosure. He fought coolly, but with a savage persistence that bore little semblance to purely defensive action. Often he clambered over the body of a fallen foe to leap against the next be-

hind, and once there lay five dead kaldanes behind him, so far had he pushed back his antagonists. They did not know it; these kaldanes that he fought, nor did the girl awaiting him upon the flier, but Gahan of Gathol was engaged in a more alluring sport than winning to freedom, for he was avenging the indignities that had been put upon the woman he loved; but presently he realized that he might be jeopardizing her safety uselessly, and so he struck down another before him and turning leaped quickly up the stairway, while the leading kaldanes slipped upon the brain-covered floor and stumbled in pursuit.

Gahan reached the enclosure twenty paces ahead of them and raced toward the flier. "Rise!" he shouted to the girl. "I will ascend the cable."

Slowly the small craft rose from the ground as Gahan leaped the inert bodies of the rykors lying in his path. The first of the pursuers sprang from the tower just as Gahan seized the trailing rope.

"Faster!" he shouted to the girl above, "or they will drag us down!" But the ship seemed scarcely to move, though in reality she was rising as rapidly as might have been expected of a one-man flier carrying a load of three. Gahan swung free above the top of the wall, but the end of the rope still dragged the ground as the kaldanes reached it. They were pouring in a steady stream from the tower into the enclosure. The leader seized the rope.

"Quick!" he cried. "Lay hold and we will drag them down."

It needed but the weight of a few to accomplish his design. The ship was stopped in its flight and then, to the horror of the girl, she felt it being dragged steadily downward. Gahan, too, realized the danger and the necessity for instant action. Clinging to the rope with his left hand, he had wound a leg about it, leaving his right hand free for his long-sword which he had not sheathed. A downward cut clove the soft head of a kaldane, and another severed the taut rope beneath the panthan's feet. The girl heard a sudden renewal of the shrill whistling of her foes, and at the same time she realized that the craft was rising again. Slowly it drifted upward, out of reach of the enemy, and a moment later she saw the figure of Turan clamber over the side. For the first time in many weeks her heart was filled with the joy of thanksgiving; but her first thought was of another.

"You are not wounded?" she asked.

"No, Tara of Helium," he replied. "They were scarce worth the effort of my blade, and never were they a menace to me because of their swords."

"They should have slain you easily," said Ghek. "So great and highly developed is the power of reason among us that they should have known before you struck just where, logically, you must seek to strike, and so they should have been able to parry your every thrust and easily find an opening to your heart."

"But they did not, Ghek," Gahan reminded him. "Their theory of development is wrong, for it does not tend toward a perfectly balanced whole. You have developed the brain and neglected the body and you can never do with the hands of another what you can do with your own hands. Mine are trained to the sword – every muscle responds instantly and accurately, and almost mechanically, to the need of the instant. I am scarcely objectively aware that I think when I fight, so quickly does my point take advantage of every opening, or spring to my defense if I am threatened that it is almost as though the cold steel had eyes and brains.

You, with your kaldane brain and your rykor body, never could hope to achieve in the same degree of perfection those things that I can achieve. Development of the brain should not be the sum total of human endeavor. The richest and happiest peoples will be those who attain closest to well-balanced perfection of both mind and body, and even these must always be short of perfection. In absolute and general perfection lies stifling monotony and death. Nature must have contrasts; she must have shadows as well as highlights; sorrow with happiness; both wrong and right; and sin as well as virtue."

"Always have I been taught differently," replied Ghek; "but since I have known this woman and you, of another race, I have come to believe that there may be other standards fully as high and desirable as those of the kaldanes. At least I have had a glimpse of the thing you call happiness and I realize that it may be good even though I have no means of expressing it. I cannot laugh nor smile, and yet within me is a sense of contentment when this woman sings – a sense that seems to open before me wondrous vistas of beauty and unguessed pleasure that far transcend the cold joys of a perfectly functioning brain. I would that I had been born of thy race."

Caught by a gentle current of air the flier was drifting slowly toward the northeast across the valley of Bantoom. Below them lay the cultivated fields, and one after another they passed over the strange towers of Moak and Nolach and the other kings of the swarms that inhabited this weird and terrible land. Within each enclosure surrounding the towers grovelled the rykors, repellent, headless things, beautiful yet hideous.

"A lesson, those," remarked Gahan, indicating the rykors in an enclosure above which they were drifting at the time, "to that fortunately small minority of our race which worships the flesh and makes a god of appetite. You know them, Tara of Helium; they can tell you exactly what they had at the midday meal two weeks ago, and how the loin of the thoat should be prepared, and what drink should be served with the rump of the zitidar."

Tara of Helium laughed. "But not one of them could tell you the name of the man whose painting took the Jeddak's Award in The Temple of Beauty this year," she said. "Like the rykors, their development has not been balanced."

"Fortunate indeed are those in which there is combined a little good and a little bad, a little knowledge of many things outside their own callings, a capacity for love and a capacity for hate, for such as these can look with tolerance upon all, unbiased by the egotism of him whose head is so heavy on one side that all his brains run to that point."

As Gahan ceased speaking Ghek made a little noise in his throat as one does who would attract attention. "You speak as one who has thought much upon many subjects. Is it, then, possible that you of the red race have pleasure in thought? Do you know aught of the joys of introspection? Do reason and logic form any part of your lives?"

"Most assuredly," replied Gahan, "but not to the extent of occupying all our time – at least not objectively. You, Ghek, are an example of the egotism of which I spoke. Because you and your kind devote your lives to the worship of mind, you believe that no other created beings think. And possibly we do not in the sense that you do, who think only of yourselves and your great brains. We think of many things that concern the welfare of a world. Had it not been for the red men of Barsoom even the kaldanes had perished from the planet, for while you may live without air the things upon which you depend for existence cannot, and there had been no air in sufficient quantities upon Barsoom these many ages had not a red man planned and built the great atmosphere plant which gave new life to a dying world.

"What have all the brains of all the kaldanes that have ever lived done to compare with that single idea of a single red man?"

Ghek was stumped. Being a kaldane he knew that brains spelled the sum total of universal achievement, but it had never occurred to him that they should be put to use in practical and profitable ways. He turned away and looked down upon the valley of his ancestors across which he was slowly drifting, into what unknown world? He should be a veritable god among the underlings, he knew; but somehow a doubt assailed him. It was evident that these two from that other world were ready to question his preeminence. Even through his great egotism was filtering a suspicion that they patronized him; perhaps even pitied him. Then he began to wonder what was to become of him. No longer would he have many rykors to do his bidding. Only this single one and when it died there could not be another. When it tired, Ghek must lie almost helpless while it rested. He wished that he had never seen this red woman. She had brought him only discontent and dishonor and now exile. Presently Tara of Helium commenced to hum a tune and Ghek, the kaldane, was content.

Gently they drifted beneath the hurtling moons above the mad shadows of a Martian night. The roaring of the banths came in diminishing volume to their ears as their craft passed on beyond the boundaries of Bantoom, leaving behind the terrors of that unhappy land. But to what were they being borne? The girl looked at the man sitting cross-legged upon the deck of the tiny flier, gazing off into the night ahead, apparently absorbed in thought.

"Where are we?" she asked. "Toward what are we drifting?"

Turan shrugged his broad shoulders. "The stars tell me that we are drifting toward the northeast," he replied, "but where we are, or what lies in our path I cannot even guess. A week since I could have sworn that I knew what lay behind each succeeding ridge that I approached; but now I admit in all humility that I have no conception of what lies a mile in any direction. Tara of Helium, I am lost, and that is all that I can tell you."

He was smiling and the girl smiled back at him. There was a slightly puzzled expression on her face – there was something tantalizingly familiar about that smile of his. She had met many a panthan – they came and went, following the fighting of a world – but she could not place this one.

"From what country are you, Turan?" she asked suddenly.

"Know you not, Tara of Helium," he countered, "that a panthan has no country? Today he fights beneath the banner of one master, tomorrow beneath that of another."

"But you must own allegiance to some country when you are not fighting," she insisted. "What banner, then, owns you now?"

He rose and stood before her, then, bowing low. "And I am acceptable," he said, "I serve beneath the banner of the daughter of The Warlord now – and forever."

She reached forth and touched his arm with a slim brown hand. "Your services are accepted," she said; "and if ever we reach Helium I promise that your reward shall be all that your heart could desire."

"I shall serve faithfully, hoping for that reward," he said; but Tara of Helium did not guess what was in his mind, thinking rather that he was mercenary. For how could the proud daughter of The Warlord guess that a simple panthan aspired to her hand and heart?

The dawn found them moving rapidly over an unfamiliar landscape. The wind had increased during the night and had borne them far from Bantoom. The country below them was rough and inhospitable. No water was visible and the surface of the ground was cut by deep gorges, while nowhere was any but the most meager vegetation discernible. They saw no life of any nature, nor was there any indication that the country could support life. For two days they drifted over this horrid wasteland. They were without food or water and suffered accordingly. Ghek had temporarily abandoned his rykor after enlisting Turan's assistance in lashing it safely to the deck. The less he used it the less would its vitality be spent. Already it was showing the effects of privation. Ghek crawled about the vessel like a great spider – over the side, down beneath the keel, and up over the opposite rail. He seemed equally at home one place as another. For his companions, however, the quarters were cramped, for the deck of a one-man flier is not intended for three.

Turan sought always ahead for signs of water. Water they must have, or that water-giving plant which makes life possible upon many of the seemingly arid areas of Mars; but there was neither the one nor the other for these two days and now the third night was upon them. The girl did not complain, but Turan knew that she must be suffering and his heart was heavy within him. Ghek suffered least of all, and he explained to them that his kind could exist for long periods without food or water. Turan almost cursed him as he saw the form of Tara of Helium slowly wasting away before his eyes, while the hideous kaldane seemed as full of vitality as ever.

"There are circumstances," remarked Ghek, "under which a gross and material body is less desirable than a highly developed brain."

Turan looked at him, but said nothing. Tara of Helium smiled faintly. "One cannot blame him," she said, "were we not a bit boastful in the pride of our superiority? When our stomachs were filled," she added.

"Perhaps there is something to be said for their system," Turan admitted. "If we could but lay aside our stomachs when they cried for food and water I have no doubt but that we should do so."

"I should never miss mine now," assented Tara; "it is mighty poor company."

A new day had dawned, revealing a less desolate country and renewing again the hope that had been low within them. Suddenly Turan leaned forward, pointing ahead.

"Look, Tara of Helium!" he cried. "A city! As I am Ga – as I am Turan the panthan, a city."

Far in the distance the domes and walls and slender towers of a city shone in the rising sun. Quickly the man seized the control and the ship dropped rapidly behind a low range of intervening hills, for well Turan knew that they must not be seen until they could discover whether friend or foe inhabited the strange city. Chances were that they were far from the abode of friends and so must the panthan move with the utmost caution; but there was a city and where a city was, was water, even though it were a deserted city, and food if it were inhabited.

To the red man food and water, even in the citadel of an enemy, meant food and drink for Tara of Helium. He would accept it from friends or he would take it from enemies. Just so long as it was there he would have it – and there was shown the egotism of the fighting man, though Turan did not see it, nor Tara who came from a long line of fighting men; but Ghek might have smiled had he known how.

Turan permitted the flier to drift closer behind the screening hills, and then when he could advance no farther without fear of discovery, he dropped the craft gently to ground in a little ravine, and leaping over the side made her fast to a stout tree. For several moments they discussed their plans – whether it would be best to wait where they were until darkness hid their movements and then approach the city in search of food and water, or approach it now, taking advantage of what cover they could, until they could glean something of the nature of its inhabitants.

It was Turan's plan which finally prevailed. They would approach as close as safety dictated in the hope of finding water outside the city; food, too, perhaps. If they did not they could at least reconnoiter the ground by daylight, and then when night came Turan could quickly come close to the city and in comparative safety prosecute his search for food and drink.

Following the ravine upward they finally topped the summit of the ridge, from which they had an excellent view of that part of the city which lay nearest them, though themselves hidden by the brush behind which they crouched. Ghek had resumed his rykor, which had suffered less than either Tara or Turan through their enforced fast.

The first glance at the city, now much closer than when they had first discovered it, revealed the fact that it was inhabited. Banners and pennons broke from many a staff. People were moving about the gate before them. The high white walls were paced by sentinels at far intervals. Upon the roofs of higher buildings the women could be seen airing the sleeping silks and furs. Turan watched it all in silence for some time.

"I do not know them," he said at last. "I cannot guess what city this may be. But it is an ancient city. Its people have no fliers and no firearms. It must be old indeed."

"How do you know they have not these things?" asked the girl.

"There are no landing-stages upon the roofs – not one that can be seen from here; while were we looking similarly at Helium we would see hundreds. And they have no firearms because their defenses are all built to withstand the attack of spear and arrow, with spear and arrow. They are an ancient people."

"If they are ancient perhaps they are friendly," suggested the girl. "Did we not learn as children in the history of our planet that it was once peopled by a friendly, peace-loving race?"

"But I fear they are not as ancient as that," replied Turan, laughing. "It has been long ages since the men of Barsoom loved peace."

"My father loves peace," returned the girl.

"And yet he is always at war," said the man.

She laughed. "But he says he likes peace."

"We all like peace," he rejoined; "peace with honor; but our neighbors will not let us have it, and so we must fight."

"And to fight well men must like to fight," she added.

"And to like to fight they must know how to fight," he said, "for no man likes to do the thing that he does not know how to do well."

"Or that some other man can do better than he."

"And so always there will be wars and men will fight," he concluded, "for always the men with hot blood in their veins will practice the art of war."

"We have settled a great question," said the girl, smiling; "but our stomachs are still empty."

"Your panthan is neglecting his duty," replied Turan; "and how can he with the great reward always before his eyes!"

She did not guess in what literal a sense he spoke.

"I go forthwith," he continued, "to wrest food and drink from the ancients."

"No," she cried, laying a hand upon his arm, "not yet. They would slay you or make you prisoner. You are a brave panthan and a mighty one, but you cannot overcome a city singlehanded."

She smiled up into his face and her hand still lay upon his arm. He felt the thrill of hot blood coursing through his veins. He could have seized her in his arms and crushed her to him. There was only Ghek the kaldane there, but there was something stronger within him that restrained his hand. Who may define it – that inherent chivalry that renders certain men the natural protectors of women?

From their vantage point they saw a body of armed warriors ride forth from the gate, and winding along a well-beaten road pass from sight about the foot of the hill from which they watched. The men were red, like themselves, and they rode the small saddle thoats of the red race. Their trappings were barbaric and magnificent, and in their head-dress were many feathers as had been the custom of ancients. They were armed with swords and long spears and they rode almost naked, their bodies being painted in ochre and blue and white. There were, perhaps, a score of them in the party and as they galloped away on their tireless mounts they presented a picture at once savage and beautiful.

"They have the appearance of splendid warriors," said Turan. "I have a great mind to walk boldly into their city and seek service."

Tara shook her head. "Wait," she admonished. "What would I do without you, and if you were captured how could you collect your reward?"

"I should escape," he said. "At any rate I shall try it," and he started to rise.

"You shall not," said the girl, her tone all authority.

The man looked at her quickly – questioningly.

"You have entered my service," she said, a trifle haughtily.

"You have entered my service for hire and you shall do as I bid you."

Turan sank down beside her again with a half smile upon his lips. "It is yours to command, Princess," he said.

The day passed. Ghek, tiring of the sunlight, had deserted his rykor and crawled down a hole he had discovered close by. Tara and Turan reclined beneath the scant shade of a small tree. They watched the people coming and going through the gate. The party of horsemen did not return. A small herd of zitidars was driven into the city during the day, and once a caravan of broad-wheeled carts drawn by these huge animals wound out of the distant horizon and came down to the city. It, too, passed from their sight within the gateway. Then darkness came and Tara of Helium bid her panthan search for food and drink; but she cautioned him against attempting to enter the city. Before he left her he bent and kissed her hand as a warrior may kiss the hand of his queen.

CHAPTER TEN

Entrapped

TURAN THE PANTHAN approached the strange city under cover of the darkness. He entertained little hope of finding either food or water outside the wall, but he would try and then, if he failed, he would attempt to make his way into the city, for Tara of Helium must have sustenance and have it soon. He saw that the walls were poorly sentineled, but they were sufficiently high to render an attempt to scale them foredoomed to failure. Taking advantage of underbrush and trees, Turan managed to reach the base of the wall without detection. Silently he moved north past the gateway which was closed by a massive gate which effectively barred even the slightest glimpse within the city beyond. It was Turan's hope to find upon the north side of the city away from the hills a level plain where grew the crops of the inhabitants, and here too water from their irrigating system, but though he traveled far along that seemingly interminable wall he found no fields nor any water. He searched also for some means of ingress to the city, yet here, too, failure was his only reward, and now as he went keen eyes watched him from above and a silent stalker kept pace with him for a time upon the summit of the wall; but presently the shadower descended to the pavement within and hurrying swiftly raced ahead of the stranger without.

He came presently to a small gate beside which was a low building and before the doorway of the building a warrior standing guard. He spoke a few quick words to the warrior and then entered the building only to return almost immediately to the street, followed by fully forty warriors. Cautiously opening the gate the fellow peered carefully along the wall upon the outside in the direction from which he had come. Evidently satisfied, he issued a few words of instruction to those behind him, whereupon half the warriors returned to the interior of the building, while the other half followed the man stealthily through the gateway where they crouched low among the shrubbery in a half circle just north of the gateway which they had left open. Here they waited in utter silence, nor had they long to wait before Turan the panthan came cautiously along the base of the wall. To the very gate he came and when he found it and that it was open he paused for a moment, listening; then he approached and looked within. Assured that there was none within sight to apprehend him he stepped through the gateway into the city.

He found himself in a narrow street that paralleled the wall. Upon the opposite side rose buildings of an architecture unknown to him, yet strangely beautiful. While the buildings were packed closely together there seemed to be no two alike and their fronts were of all shapes and heights and of many hues. The skyline was broken by spire and dome and minaret and tall, slender towers, while the walls supported many a balcony and in the soft light of Cluros, the farther moon, now low in the west, he saw, to his surprise and consternation, the figures of people upon the balconies. Directly opposite him were two women and a man. They sat leaning upon the rail of the balcony looking, apparently, directly at him; but if they saw him they gave no sign.

Turan hesitated a moment in the face of almost certain discovery and then, assured that they must take him for one of their own people, he moved boldly into the avenue. Having no idea of the direction in which he might best hope to find what he sought, and not wishing to arouse suspicion by further hesitation, he turned to the left and stepped briskly along the pavement with the intention of placing himself as quickly as possible beyond the observation of those nocturnal watchers. He knew that the night must be far spent; and so he could not but wonder why people should sit upon their balconies when they should have been asleep among their silks and furs. At first he had thought them the late guests of some convivial host; but the windows behind them were shrouded in darkness and utter quiet prevailed, quite upsetting such a theory. And as he proceeded he passed many another group sitting silently upon other balconies. They paid no attention to him, seeming not even to note his passing. Some leaned with a single elbow upon the rail, their chins resting in their palms; others leaned upon both arms across the balcony, looking down into the street, while several that he saw held musical instruments in their hands, but their fingers moved not upon the strings.

And then Turan came to a point where the avenue turned to the right, to skirt a building that jutted from the inside of the city wall, and as he rounded the corner he came full upon two warriors standing upon either side of the entrance to a building upon his right. It was impossible for them not to be aware of his presence, yet neither moved, nor gave other evidence that they had seen him. He stood there waiting, his hand upon the hilt of his long-sword, but they neither challenged nor halted him. Could it be that these also thought him one of their own kind? Indeed upon no other grounds could he explain their inaction.

As Turan had passed through the gateway into the city and taken his unhindered way along the avenue, twenty warriors had entered the city and closed the gate behind them, and then one had taken to the wall and followed along its summit in the rear of Turan, and another had followed him along the avenue, while a third had crossed the street and entered one of the buildings upon the opposite side.

The balance of them, with the exception of a single sentinel beside the gate, had re-entered the building from which they had been summoned. They were well built, strapping, painted fellows, their naked figures covered now by gorgeous robes against the chill of night. As they spoke of the stranger they laughed at the ease with which they had tricked him, and were still laughing as they threw themselves upon their sleeping silks and furs to resume their broken slumber. It was evident that they constituted a guard detailed for the gate beside which they slept, and it was equally evident that the gates were guarded and the city watched much more carefully than Turan had believed. Chagrined indeed had been the Jed of Gathol had he dreamed that he was being so neatly tricked.

As Turan proceeded along the avenue he passed other sentries beside other doors but now he gave them small heed, since they neither challenged nor otherwise outwardly noted his passing; but while at nearly every turn of the erratic avenue he passed one or more of these silent sentinels he could not guess that he had passed one of them many times and that his every move was watched by silent, clever stalkers. Scarce had he passed a certain one of these rigid guardsmen before the fellow awoke to sudden life, bounded across the avenue, entered a narrow opening in the outer wall where he swiftly followed a corridor built within the wall itself until presently he emerged a little distance ahead of Turan, where he assumed the stiff and silent attitude of a soldier upon guard. Nor did Turan know that a second followed in the shadows of the buildings behind him, nor of the third who hastened ahead of him upon some urgent mission.

And so the panthan moved through the silent streets of the strange city in search of food and drink for the woman he loved. Men and women looked down upon him from shadowy balconies, but spoke not; and sentinels saw him pass and did not challenge. Presently from along the avenue before him came the familiar sound of clanking accouterments, the herald of marching warriors, and almost simultaneously he saw upon his right an open doorway dimly lighted from within. It was the only available place where he might seek to hide from the approaching company, and while he had passed several sentries unquestioned he could scarce hope to escape scrutiny and questioning from a patrol, as he naturally assumed this body of men to be.

Inside the doorway he discovered a passage turning abruptly to the right and almost immediately thereafter to the left. There was none in sight within and so he stepped cautiously around the second turn the more effectually to be hidden from the street. Before him stretched a long corridor, dimly lighted like the entrance. Waiting there he heard the party approach the building, he heard someone at the entrance to his hiding place, and then he heard the door past which he had come slam to. He laid his hand upon his sword, expecting momentarily to hear footsteps approaching along the corridor; but none came. He approached the turn and looked around it; the corridor was empty to the closed door. Whoever had closed it had remained upon the outside.

Turan waited, listening. He heard no sound. Then he advanced to the door and placed an ear against it. All was silence in the street beyond. A sudden draft must have closed the door, or perhaps it was the duty of the patrol to see to such things. It was immaterial. They had evidently passed on and now he would return to the street and continue upon his way. Somewhere there would be a public fountain where he could obtain water, and the chance of food lay in the strings of dried vegetables and meat which hung before the doorways of nearly every Barsoomian home of the poorer classes that he had ever seen. It was this district he was seeking, and it was for this reason his search had led him away from the main gate of the city which he knew would not be located in a poor district.

He attempted to open the door only to find that it resisted his every effort – it was locked upon the outside. Here indeed was a sorry contretemps. Turan the panthan scratched his head. "Fortune frowns upon me," he murmured; but beyond the door, Fate, in the form of a painted warrior, stood smiling. Neatly had he tricked the unwary stranger. The lighted doorway, the marching patrol – these had been planned and timed to a nicety by the third warrior who had sped ahead of Turan along another avenue, and the stranger had done precisely what the fellow had thought he would do – no wonder, then, that he smiled.

This exit barred to him Turan turned back into the corridor. He followed it cautiously and silently. Occasionally there was a door on one side or the other. These he tried only to find each securely locked. The corridor wound more erratically the farther he advanced. A locked door barred his way at its end, but a door upon his right opened and he stepped into a dimly-lighted chamber, about the walls of which were three other doors, each of which he tried in turn. Two were locked; the other opened upon a runway leading downward. It was spiral and he could see no farther than the first turn. A door in the corridor he had quitted opened after he had passed, and the third warrior stepped out and followed after him. A faint smile still lingered upon the fellow's grim lips.

Turan drew his short-sword and cautiously descended. At the bottom was a short corridor with a closed door at the end. He approached the single heavy panel and listened. No sound came to him from beyond the mysterious portal. Gently he tried the door, which swung easily toward him at his touch. Before him was a low-ceiled chamber with a dirt floor. Set in its walls were several other doors and all were closed. As Turan stepped cautiously within, the third warrior descended the spiral runway behind him. The panthan crossed the room quickly and tried a door. It was locked. He heard a muffled click behind him and turned about with ready sword. He was alone; but the door through which he had entered was closed – it was the click of its lock that he had heard.

With a bound he crossed the room and attempted to open it; but to no avail. No longer did he seek silence, for he knew now that the thing had gone beyond the sphere of chance. He threw his weight against the wooden panel; but the thick skeel of which it was constructed would have withstood a battering ram. From beyond came a low laugh.

Rapidly Turan examined each of the other doors. They were all locked. A glance about the chamber revealed a wooden table and a bench. Set in the walls were several heavy rings to which rusty chains were attached – all too significant of the purpose to which the room was dedicated. In the dirt floor near the wall were two or three holes resembling the mouths of burrows – doubtless the habitat of the giant Martian rat. He had observed this much when suddenly the dim light was extinguished, leaving him in darkness utter and complete. Turan, groping about, sought the table and the bench. Placing the latter against the wall he drew the table in front of him and sat down upon the bench, his long-sword gripped in readiness before him. At least they should fight before they took him.

For some time he sat there waiting for he knew not what. No sound penetrated to his subterranean dungeon. He slowly revolved in his mind the incidents of the evening – the open, unguarded gate; the lighted doorway – the only one he had seen thus open and lighted along the avenue he had followed; the advance of the warriors at precisely the moment that he could find no other avenue of escape or concealment; the corridors and chambers that led past many locked doors to this underground prison leaving no other path for him to pursue.

"By my first ancestor!" he swore; "but it was simple and I a simpleton. They tricked me neatly and have taken me without exposing themselves to a scratch; but for what purpose?"

He wished that he might answer that question and then his thoughts turned to the girl waiting there on the hill beyond the city for him – and he would never come. He knew the ways of the more savage peoples of Barsoom. No, he would never come, now. He had disobeyed her. He smiled at the sweet recollection of those words of command that had fallen from her dear lips. He had disobeyed her and now he had lost the reward.

But what of her? What now would be her fate – starving before a hostile city with only an inhuman kaldane for company? Another thought – a horrid thought – obtruded itself upon him. She had told him of the hideous sights she had witnessed in the burrows of the kaldanes and he knew that they ate human flesh. Ghek was starving. Should he eat his rykor he would be helpless; but – there was sustenance there for them both, for the rykor and the kaldane. Turan cursed himself for a fool. Why had he left her? Far better to have remained and died with her, ready always to protect her, than to have left her at the mercy of the hideous Bantoomian.

Now Turan detected a heavy odor in the air. It oppressed him with a feeling of drowsiness. He would have risen to fight off the creeping lethargy, but his legs seemed weak, so that he sank again to the bench. Presently his sword slipped from his fingers and he sprawled forward upon the table his head resting upon his arms.

Tara of Helium, as the night wore on and Turan did not return, became more and more uneasy, and when dawn broke with no sign of him she guessed that he had failed. Something more than her own unhappy predicament brought a feeling of sorrow to her heart – of sorrow and loneliness. She realized now how she had come to depend upon this panthan not only for protection but for companionship as well. She missed him, and in missing him realized suddenly that he had meant more to her than a mere hired warrior. It was as though a friend had been taken from her – an old and valued friend. She rose from her place of concealment that she might have a better view of the city.

U-Dor, dwar of the 8th Utan of O-Tar, Jeddak of Manator, rode back in the early dawn toward Manator from a brief excursion to a neighboring village. As he was rounding the hills south of the city, his keen eyes were attracted by a slight movement among the shrubbery close to the summit of the nearest hill. He halted his vicious mount and watched more closely. He saw a figure rise facing away from him and peer down toward Manator beyond the hill.

"Come!" he signalled to his followers, and with a word to this thoat turned the beast at a rapid gallop up the hillside. In his wake swept his twenty savage warriors, the padded feet of their mounts soundless upon the soft turf. It was the rattle of sidearms and harness that brought Tara of Helium suddenly about, facing them. She saw a score of warriors with couched lances bearing down upon her.

She glanced at Ghek. What would the spiderman do in this emergency? She saw him crawl to his rykor and attach himself. Then he arose, the beautiful body once again animated and alert. She thought that the creature was preparing for flight. Well, it made little difference to her. Against such as were streaming up the hill toward them a single mediocre swordsman such as Ghek was worse than no defense at all.

"Hurry, Ghek!" she admonished him. "Back into the hills! You may find there a hiding-place;" but the creature only stepped between her and the oncoming riders, drawing his long-sword.

"It is useless, Ghek," she said, when she saw that he intended to defend her. "What can a single sword accomplish against such odds?"

"I can die but once," replied the kaldane. "You and your panthan saved me from Luud and I but do what your panthan would do were he here to protect you."

"It is brave, but it is useless," she replied. "Sheathe your sword. They may not intend us harm."

Ghek let the point of his weapon drop to the ground, but he did not sheathe it, and thus the two stood waiting as U-Dor the dwar stopped his thoat before them while his twenty warriors formed a rough circle about. For a long minute U-Dor sat his mount in silence, looking searchingly first at Tara of Helium and then at her hideous companion.

"What manner of creature are you?" he asked presently. "And what do you before the gates of Manator?"

"We are from far countries," replied the girl, "and we are lost and starving. We ask only food and rest and the privilege to go our way seeking our own homes."

U-Dor smiled a grim smile. "Manator and the hills which guard it alone know the age of Manator," he said; "yet in all the ages that have rolled by since Manator first was, there be no record in the annals of Manator of a stranger departing from Manator."

"But I am a princess," cried the girl haughtily, "and my country is not at war with yours. You must give me and my companions aid and assist us to return to our own land. It is the law of Barsoom."

"Manator knows only the laws of Manator," replied U-Dor; "but come. You shall go with us to the city, where you, being beautiful, need have no fear. I, myself, will protect you if O-Tar so decrees. And as for your companion – but hold! You said 'companions' – there are others of your party then?"

"You see what you see," replied Tara haughtily.

"Be that as it may," said U-Dor. "If there be more they shall not escape Manator; but as I was saying, if your companion fights well he too may live, for O-Tar is just, and just are the laws of Manator. Come!"

Ghek demurred.

"It is useless," said the girl, seeing that he would have stood his ground and fought them. "Let us go with them. Why pit your puny blade against their mighty ones when there should lie in your great brain the means to outwit them?" She spoke in a low whisper, rapidly.

"You are right, Tara of Helium," he replied and sheathed his sword.

And so they moved down the hillside toward the gates of Manator – Tara, Princess of Helium, and Ghek, the kaldane of Bantoom – and surrounding them rode the savage, painted warriors of U-Dor, dwar of the 8th Utan of O-Tar, Jeddak of Manator.

CHAPTER ELEVEN

The Choice of Tara

THE DAZZLING SUNLIGHT of Barsoom clothed Manator in an aureole of splendor as the girl and her captors rode into the city through The Gate of Enemies. Here the wall was some fifty feet thick, and the sides of the passageway within the gate were covered with parallel shelves of masonry from bottom to top. Within these shelves, or long, horizontal niches, stood row upon row of small figures, appearing like tiny, grotesque statuettes of men, their long, black hair falling below their feet and sometimes trailing to the shelf beneath. The figures were scarce a foot in height and but for their diminutive proportions might have been the mummified bodies of once living men. The girl noticed that as they passed, the warriors saluted the figures with their spears after the manner of Barsoomian fighting men in extending a military courtesy, and then they rode on into the avenue beyond, which ran, wide and stately, through the city toward the east.

On either side were great buildings wondrously wrought. Paintings of great beauty and antiquity covered many of the walls, their colors softened and blended by the suns of ages. Upon the pavement the life of the newly-awakened city was already afoot. Women in brilliant trappings, befeathered warriors, their bodies daubed with paint; artisans, armed but less gaily caparisoned, took their various ways upon the duties of the day. A giant zitidar, magnificent in rich harness, rumbled its broad-wheeled cart along the stone pavement toward The Gate of Enemies. Life and color and beauty wrought together a picture that filled the eyes of Tara of Helium with wonder and with admiration, for here was a scene out of the dead past of dying Mars. Such had been the cities of the founders of her race before Throxeus, mightiest of oceans, had disappeared from the face of a world. And from balconies on either side men and women looked down in silence upon the scene below.

The people in the street looked at the two prisoners, especially at the hideous Ghek, and called out in question or comment to their guard; but the watchers upon the balconies spoke not, nor did one so much as turn a head to note their passing. There were many balconies on each building and not a one that did not hold its silent party of richly trapped men and women, with here and there a child or two, but even the children maintained the uniform silence and immobility of their elders. As they approached the center of the city the girl saw that even the roofs bore companies of these idle watchers, harnessed and bejeweled as for some gala-day of laughter and music, but no laughter broke from those silent lips, nor any music from the strings of the instruments that many of them held in jeweled fingers.

And now the avenue widened into an immense square, at the far end of which rose a stately edifice gleaming white in virgin marble among the gaily painted buildings surrounding it and its scarlet sward and gaily-flowering, green-foliaged shrubbery. Toward this U-Dor led his prisoners and their guard to the great arched entrance before which a line of fifty mounted warriors barred the way. When the commander of the guard recognized U-Dor the guardsmen fell back to either side leaving a broad avenue through which the party passed. Directly inside the entrance were inclined runways leading upward on either side. U-Dor turned to the left and led them upward to the second floor and down a long corridor. Here they passed other mounted men and in chambers upon either side they saw more. Occasionally there was another runway leading either up or down. A warrior, his steed at full gallop, dashed into sight from one of these and raced swiftly past them upon some errand.

Nowhere as yet had Tara of Helium seen a man afoot in this great building; but when at a turn, U-Dor led them to the third floor she caught glimpses of chambers in which many riderless thoats were penned and others adjoining where dismounted warriors lolled at ease or played games of skill or chance and many there were who played at jetan, and then the party passed into a long, wide hall of state, as magnificent an apartment as even a princess of mighty Helium ever had seen. The length of the room ran an arched ceiling ablaze with countless radium bulbs. The mighty spans extended from wall to wall leaving the vast floor unbroken by a single column. The arches were of white marble, apparently quarried in single, huge blocks from which each arch was cut complete. Between the arches, the ceiling was set solid about the radium bulbs with precious stones whose scintillant fire and color and beauty filled the whole apartment. The stones were carried down the walls in an irregular fringe for a few feet, where they appeared to hang like a beautiful and gorgeous drapery against the white marble of the wall. The marble ended some six or seven feet from the floor, the walls from that point down being wainscoted in solid gold. The floor itself was of marble richly inlaid with gold. In that single room was a vast treasure equal to the wealth of many a large city.

But what riveted the girl's attention even more than the fabulous treasure of decorations were the files of gorgeously harnessed warriors who sat their thoats in grim silence and immobility on either side of the central aisle, rank after rank of them to the farther walls, and as the party passed between them she could not note so much as the flicker of an eyelid, or the twitching of a thoat's ear.

"The Hall of Chiefs," whispered one of her guard, evidently noting her interest. There was a note of pride in the fellow's voice and something of hushed awe. Then they passed through a great doorway into the chamber beyond, a large, square room in which a dozen mounted warriors lolled in their saddles.

As U-Dor and his party entered the room, the warriors came quickly erect in their saddles and formed a line before another door upon the opposite side of the wall. The padwar commanding them saluted U-Dor who, with his party, had halted facing the guard.

"Send one to O-Tar announcing that U-Dor brings two prisoners worthy of the observation of the great jeddak," said U-Dor; "one because of her extreme beauty, the other because of his extreme ugliness."

"O-Tar sits in council with the lesser chiefs," replied the lieutenant; "but the words of U-Dor the dwar shall be carried to him," and he turned and gave instructions to one who sat his thoat behind him.

"What manner of creature is the male?" he asked of U-Dor. "It cannot be that both are of one race."

"They were together in the hills south of the city," explained U-Dor, "and they say that they are lost and starving."

"The woman is beautiful," said the padwar. "She will not long go begging in the city of Manator," and then they spoke of other matters – of the doings of the palace, of the expedition of U-Dor, until the messenger returned to say that O-Tar bade them bring the prisoners to him.

They passed then through a massive doorway, which, when opened, revealed the great council chamber of O-Tar, Jeddak of Manator, beyond. A central aisle led from the doorway the full length of the great hall, terminating at the steps of a marble dais upon which a man sat in a great throne-chair. Upon either side of the aisle were ranged rows of highly carved desks and chairs of skeel, a hard wood of great beauty. Only a few of the desks were occupied – those in the front row, just below the rostrum.

At the entrance U-Dor dismounted with four of his followers who formed a guard about the two prisoners who were then conducted toward the foot of the throne, following a few paces behind U-Dor. As they halted at the foot of the marble steps, the proud gaze of Tara of Helium rested upon the enthroned figure of the man above her. He sat erect without stiffness – a commanding presence trapped in the barbaric splendor that the Barsoomian chieftain loves. He was a large man, the perfection of whose handsome face was marred only by the hauteur of his cold eyes and the suggestion of cruelty imparted by too thin lips. It needed no second glance to assure the least observing that here indeed was a ruler of men – a fighting jeddak whose people might worship but not love, and for whose slightest favor warriors would vie with one another to go forth and die. This was O-Tar, Jeddak of Manator, and as Tara of Helium saw him for the first time she could not but acknowledge a certain admiration for this savage chieftain who so virilely personified the ancient virtues of the God of War.

U-Dor and the jeddak interchanged the simple greetings of Barsoom, and then the former recounted the details of the discovery and capture of the prisoners. O-Tar scrutinized them both intently during U-Dor's narration of events, his expression revealing naught of what passed in the brain behind those inscrutable eyes. When the officer had finished the jeddak fastened his gaze upon Ghek.

"And you," he asked, "what manner of thing are you? From what country? Why are you in Manator?"

"I am a kaldane," replied Ghek; "the highest type of created creature upon the face of Barsoom; I am mind, you are matter. I come from Bantoom. I am here because we were lost and starving."

"And you!" O-Tar turned suddenly on Tara. "You, too, are a kaldane?"

"I am a princess of Helium," replied the girl. "I was a prisoner in Bantoom. This kaldane and a warrior of my own race rescued me. The warrior left us to search for food and water. He has doubtless fallen into the hands of your people. I ask you to free him and give us food and drink and let us go upon our way. I am a granddaughter of a jeddak, the daughter of a jeddak of jeddaks, The Warlord of Barsoom. I ask only the treatment that my people would accord you or yours."

"Helium," repeated O-Tar. "I know naught of Helium, nor does the Jeddak of Helium rule Manator. I, O-Tar, am Jeddak of Manator. I alone rule. I protect my own. You have never seen a woman or a warrior of Manator captive in Helium! Why should I protect the people of another jeddak? It is his duty to protect them. If he cannot, he is weak, and his people must fall into the hands of the strong. I, O-Tar, am strong. I will keep you. That – " he pointed at Ghek – "can it fight?"

"It is brave," replied Tara of Helium, "but it has not the skill at arms which my people possess."

"There is none then to fight for you?" asked O-Tar. "We are a just people," he continued without waiting for a reply, "and had you one to fight for you he might win to freedom for himself and you as well."

"But U-Dor assured me that no stranger ever had departed from Manator," she answered.

O-Tar shrugged. "That does not disprove the justice of the laws of Manator," replied O-Tar, "but rather that the warriors of Manator are invincible. Had there come one who could defeat our warriors that one had won to liberty."

"And you fetch my warrior," cried Tara haughtily, "you shall see such swordplay as doubtless the crumbling walls of your decaying city never have witnessed, and if there be no trick in your offer we are already as good as free."

O-Tar smiled more broadly than before and U-Dor smiled, too, and the chiefs and warriors who looked on nudged one another and whispered, laughing. And Tara of Helium knew then that there was trickery in their justice; but though her situation seemed hopeless she did not cease to hope, for was she not the daughter of John Carter, Warlord of Barsoom, whose famous challenge to Fate, "I still live!" remained the one irreducible defense against despair? At thought of her noble sire the patrician chin of Tara of Helium rose a shade higher. Ah! if he but knew where she was there were little to fear then. The hosts of Helium would batter at the gates of Manator, the great green warriors of John Carter's savage allies would swarm up from the dead sea bottoms lusting for pillage and for loot, the stately ships of her beloved navy would soar above the unprotected towers and minarets of the doomed city which only capitulation and heavy tribute could then save.

But John Carter did not know! There was only one other to whom she might hope to look – Turan the panthan; but where was he? She had seen his sword in play and she knew that it had been wielded by a master hand, and who should know swordplay better than Tara of Helium, who had learned it well under the constant tutorage of John Carter himself. Tricks she knew that discounted even far greater physical prowess than her own, and a method of attack that might have been at once the envy and despair of the cleverest of warriors. And so it was that her thoughts turned to Turan the panthan, though not alone because of the protection he might afford her. She had realized, since he had left her in search of food, that there had grown between them a certain comradeship that she now missed. There had been that about him which seemed to have bridged the gulf between their stations in life. With him she had failed to consider that he was a panthan or that she was a princess – they had been comrades. Suddenly she realized that she missed him for himself more than for his sword. She turned toward O-Tar.

"Where is Turan, my warrior?" she demanded.

"You shall not lack for warriors," replied the jeddak. "One of your beauty will find plenty ready to fight for her. Possibly it shall not be necessary to look farther than the jeddak of Manator. You please me, woman. What say you to such an honor?"

Through narrowed lids the Princess of Helium scrutinized the Jeddak of Manator, from feathered headdress to sandaled foot and back to feathered headdress.

"'Honor'!" she mimicked in tones of scorn. "I please thee, do I? Then know, swine, that thou pleaseth me not – that the daughter of John Carter is not for such as thou!"

A sudden, tense silence fell upon the assembled chiefs. Slowly the blood receded from the sinister face of O-Tar, Jeddak of Manator, leaving him a sickly purple in his wrath. His eyes narrowed to two thin slits, his lips were compressed to a bloodless line of malevolence. For a long moment there was no sound in the throne room of the palace at Manator. Then the jeddak turned toward U-Dor.

"Take her away," he said in a level voice that belied his appearance of rage. "Take her away, and at the next games let the prisoners and the common warriors play at Jetan for her."

"And this?" asked U-Dor, pointing at Ghek.

"To the pits until the next games," replied O-Tar.

"So this is your vaunted justice!" cried Tara of Helium; "that two strangers who have not wronged you shall be sentenced without trial? And one of them is a woman. The swine of Manator are as just as they are brave."

"Away with her!" shouted O-Tar, and at a sign from U-Dor the guards formed about the two prisoners and conducted them from the chamber.

Outside the palace, Ghek and Tara of Helium were separated. The girl was led through long avenues toward the center of the city and finally into a low building, topped by lofty towers of massive construction. Here she was turned over to a warrior who wore the insignia of a dwar, or captain.

"It is O-Tar's wish," explained U-Dor to this one, "that she be kept until the next games, when the prisoners and the common warriors shall play for her. Had she not the tongue of a thoat she had been a worthy stake for our noblest steel," and U-Dor sighed. "Perhaps even yet I may win a pardon for her. It were too bad to see such beauty fall to the lot of some common fellow. I would have honored her myself."

"If I am to be imprisoned, imprison me," said the girl. "I do not recall that I was sentenced to listen to the insults of every low-born boor who chanced to admire me."

"You see, A-Kor," cried U-Dor, "the tongue that she has. Even so and worse spoke she to O-Tar the jeddak."

"I see," replied A-Kor, whom Tara saw was with difficulty restraining a smile. "Come, then, with me, woman," he said, "and we shall find a safe place within The Towers of Jetan – but stay! what ails thee?"

The girl had staggered and would have fallen had not the man caught her in his arms. She seemed to gather herself then and bravely sought to stand erect without support. A-Kor glanced at U-Dor. "Knew you the woman was ill?" he asked.

"Possibly it is lack of food," replied the other. "She mentioned, I believe, that she and her companions had not eaten for several days."

"Brave are the warriors of O-Tar," sneered A-Kor; "lavish their hospitality. U-Dor, whose riches are uncounted, and the brave O-Tar, whose squealing thoats are stabled within marble halls and fed from troughs of gold, can spare no crust to feed a starving girl."

The black haired U-Dor scowled. "Thy tongue will yet pierce thy heart, son of a slave!" he cried. "Once too often mayst thus try the patience of the just O-Tar. Hereafter guard thy speech as well as thy towers."

"Think not to taunt me with my mother's state," said A-Kor. "'Tis the blood of the slave woman that fills my veins with pride, and my only shame is that I am also the son of thy jeddak."

"And O-Tar heard this?" queried U-Dor.

"O-Tar has already heard it from my own lips," replied A-Kor; "this, and more."

He turned upon his heel, a supporting arm still around the waist of Tara of Helium and thus he half led, half carried her into The Towers of Jetan, while U-Dor wheeled his thoat and galloped back in the direction of the palace.

Within the main entrance to The Tower of Jetan lolled a half-dozen warriors. To one of these spoke A-Kor, keeper of the towers. "Fetch Lan-O, the slave girl, and bid her bring food and drink to the upper level of the Thurian tower," then he lifted the half-fainting girl in his arms and bore her along the spiral, inclined runway that led upward within the tower.

Somewhere in the long ascent Tara lost consciousness. When it returned she found herself in a large, circular chamber, the stone walls of which were pierced by windows at regular intervals about the entire circumference of the room. She was lying upon a pile of sleeping silks and furs while there knelt above her a young woman who was forcing drops of some cooling beverage between her parched lips. Tara of Helium half rose upon an elbow and looked about. In the first moments of returning consciousness there were swept from the screen of recollection the happenings of many weeks. She thought that she awoke in the palace of The Warlord at Helium. Her brows knit as she scrutinized the strange face bending over her.

"Who are you?" she asked, and, "Where is Uthia?"

"I am Lan-O the slave girl," replied the other. "I know none by the name of Uthia."

Tara of Helium sat erect and looked about her. This rough stone was not the marble of her father's halls. "Where am I?" she asked.

"In The Thurian Tower," replied the girl, and then seeing that the other still did not understand she guessed the truth. "You are a prisoner in The Towers of Jetan in the city of Manator," she explained. "You were brought to this chamber, weak and fainting, by A-Kor, Dwar of The Towers of Jetan, who sent me to you with food and drink, for kind is the heart of A-Kor."

"I remember, now," said Tara, slowly. "I remember; but where is Turan, my warrior? Did they speak of him?"

"I heard naught of another," replied Lan-O; "you alone were brought to the towers. In that you are fortunate, for there be no nobler man in Manator than A-Kor. It is his mother's blood that makes him so. She was a slave girl from Gathol."

"Gathol!" exclaimed Tara of Helium. "Lies Gathol close by Manator?"

"Not close, yet still the nearest country," replied Lan-O. "About twenty-two degrees[4] east, it lies."

"Gathol!" murmured Tara, "Far Gathol!"

"But you are not from Gathol," said the slave girl; "your harness is not of Gathol."

"I am from Helium," said Tara

"It is far from Helium to Gathol;" said the slave girl, "but in our studies we learned much of the greatness of Helium, we of Gathol, so it seems not so far away."

"You, too, are from Gathol?" asked Tara.

4   Approximately 814 Earth Miles.

"Many of us are from Gathol who are slaves in Manator," replied the girl. "It is to Gathol, nearest country, that the Manatorians look for slaves most often. They go in great numbers at intervals of three or seven years and haunt the roads that lead to Gathol, and thus they capture whole caravans leaving none to bear warning to Gathol of their fate. Nor do any ever escape from Manator to carry word of us back to Gahan our jed."

Tara of Helium ate slowly and in silence. The girl's words aroused memories of the last hours she had spent in her father's palace and the great midday function at which she had met Gahan of Gathol. Even now she flushed as she recalled his daring words.

Upon her reveries the door opened and a burly warrior appeared in the opening – a hulking fellow, with thick lips and an evil, leering face. The slave girl sprang to her feet, facing him.

"What does this mean, E-Med?" she cried, "was it not the will of A-Kor that this woman be not disturbed?"

"The will of A-Kor, indeed!" and the man sneered. "The will of A-Kor is without power in The Towers of Jetan, or elsewhere, for A-Kor lies now in the pits of O-Tar, and E-Med is dwar of the Towers."

Tara of Helium saw the face of the slave girl pale and the terror in her eyes.

CHAPTER TWELVE

Ghek Plays Pranks

While Tara of Helium was being led to The Towers of Jetan, Ghek was escorted to the pits beneath the palace where he was imprisoned in a dimly-lighted chamber. Here he found a bench and a table standing upon the dirt floor near the wall, and set in the wall several rings from which depended short lengths of chain. At the base of the walls were several holes in the dirt floor. These, alone, of the several things he saw, interested him. Ghek sat down upon the bench and waited in silence, listening. Presently the lights were extinguished. If Ghek could have smiled he would have then, for Ghek could see as well in the dark as in the light – better, perhaps. He watched the dark openings of the holes in the floor and waited. Presently he detected a change in the air about him – it grew heavy with a strange odor, and once again might Ghek have smiled, could he have smiled.

Let them replace all the air in the chamber with their most deadly fumes; it would be all the same to Ghek, the kaldane, who, having no lungs, required no air. With the rykor it might be different. Deprived of air it would die; but if only a sufficient amount of the gas was introduced to stupefy an ordinary creature it would have no effect upon the rykor, who had no objective mind to overcome. So long as the excess of carbon dioxide in the blood was not sufficient to prevent heart action, the rykor would suffer only a diminution of vitality; but would still respond to the exciting agency of the kaldane's brain.

Ghek caused the rykor to assume a sitting position with its back against the wall where it might remain without direction from his brain. Then he released his contact with its spinal cord; but remained in position upon its shoulders, waiting and watching, for the kaldane's curiosity was aroused. He had not long to wait before the lights were flashed on and one of the locked doors opened to admit a half-dozen warriors. They approached him rapidly and worked quickly. First they removed all his weapons and then, snapping a fetter about one of the rykor's ankles, secured him to the end of one of the chains hanging from the walls. Next they dragged the long table to a new position and there bolted it to the floor so that an end, instead of the middle, was directly before the prisoner. On the table before him they set food and water and upon the opposite end of the table they laid the key to the fetter. Then they unlocked and opened all the doors and departed.

When Turan the panthan regained consciousness it was to the realization of a sharp pain in one of his forearms. The effects of the gas departed as rapidly as they had overcome him so that as he opened his eyes he was in full possession of all his faculties. The lights were on again and in their glow there was revealed to the man the figure of a giant Martian rat crouching upon the table and gnawing upon his arm. Snatching his arm away he reached for his short-sword, while the rat, growling, sought to seize his arm again. It was then that Turan discovered that his weapons had been removed – short-sword, long-sword, dagger, and pistol. The rat charged him then and striking the creature away with his hand the man rose and backed off, searching for something with which to strike a harder blow. Again the rat charged and as Turan stepped quickly back to avoid the menacing jaws, something seemed to jerk suddenly upon his right ankle, and as he drew his left foot back to regain his equilibrium his heel caught upon a taut chain and he fell heavily backward to the floor just as the rat leaped upon his breast and sought his throat.

The Martian rat is a fierce and unlovely thing. It is many-legged and hairless, its hide resembling that of a newborn mouse in repulsiveness. In size and weight it is comparable to a large Airedale terrier. Its eyes are small and close-set, and almost hidden in deep, fleshy apertures. But its most ferocious and repulsive feature is its jaws, the entire bony structure of which protrudes several inches beyond the flesh, revealing five sharp, spadelike teeth in the upper jaw and the same number of similar teeth in the lower, the whole suggesting the appearance of a rotting face from which much of the flesh has sloughed away.

It was such a thing that leaped upon the breast of the panthan to tear at his jugular. Twice Turan struck it away as he sought to regain his feet, but both times it returned with increased ferocity to renew the attack. Its only weapons are its jaws since its broad, splay feet are armed with

blunt talons. With its protruding jaws it excavates its winding burrows and with its broad feet it pushes the dirt behind it. To keep the jaws from his flesh then was Turan's only concern and this he succeeded in doing until chance gave him a hold upon the creature's throat. After that the end was but a matter of moments. Rising at last he flung the lifeless thing from him with a shudder of disgust.

Now he turned his attention to a hurried inventory of the new conditions which surrounded him since the moment of his incarceration. He realized vaguely what had happened. He had been anaesthetized and stripped of his weapons, and as he rose to his feet he saw that one ankle was fettered to a chain in the wall. He looked about the room. All the doors swung wide open! His captors would render his imprisonment the more cruel by leaving ever before him tempting glimpses of open aisles to the freedom he could not attain. Upon the end of the table and within easy reach was food and drink. This at least was attainable and at sight of it his starved stomach seemed almost to cry aloud for sustenance. It was with difficulty that he ate and drank in moderation.

As he devoured the food his eyes wandered about the confines of his prison until suddenly they seized upon a thing that lay on the table at the end farthest from him. It was a key. He raised his fettered ankle and examined the lock. There could be no doubt of it! The key that lay there on the table before him was the key to that very lock. A careless warrior had laid it there and departed, forgetting.

Hope surged high in the breast of Gahan of Gathol, of Turan the panthan. Furtively his eyes sought the open doorways. There was no one in sight. Ah, if he could but gain his freedom! He would find some way from this odious city back to her side and never again would he leave her until he had won safety for her or death for himself.

He rose and moved cautiously toward the opposite end of the table where lay the coveted key. The fettered ankle halted his first step, but he stretched at full length along the table, extending eager fingers toward the prize. They almost laid hold upon it – a little more and they would touch it. He strained and stretched, but still the thing lay just beyond his reach. He hurled himself forward until the iron fetter bit deep into his flesh, but all futilely. He sat back upon the bench then and glared at the open doors and the key, realizing now that they were part of a well-laid scheme of refined torture, none the less demoralizing because it inflicted no physical suffering.

For just a moment the man gave way to useless regret and foreboding, then he gathered himself together, his brows cleared, and he returned to his unfinished meal. At least they should not have the satisfaction of knowing how sorely they had hit him. As he ate it occurred to him that by dragging the table along the floor he could bring the key within his reach, but when he essayed to do so, he found that the table had been securely bolted to the floor during the period of his unconsciousness. Again Gahan smiled and shrugged and resumed his eating.

When the warriors had departed from the prison in which Ghek was confined, the kaldane crawled from the shoulders of the rykor to the table. Here he drank a little water and then directed the hands of the rykor to the balance of it and to the food, upon which the brainless thing fell with avidity. While it was thus engaged Ghek took his spider-like way along the table to the opposite end where lay the key to the fetter. Seizing it in a chela he leaped to the floor and scurried rapidly toward the mouth of one of the burrows against the wall, into which he disappeared. For long had the brain been contemplating these burrow entrances. They appealed to his kaldanean tastes, and further, they pointed a hiding place for the key and a lair for the only kind of food that the kaldane relished – flesh and blood.

Ghek had never seen an ulsio, since these great Martian rats had long ago disappeared from Bantoom, their flesh and blood having been greatly relished by the kaldanes; but Ghek had inherited, almost unimpaired, every memory of every ancestor, and so he knew that ulsio inhabited these lairs and that ulsio was good to eat, and he knew what ulsio looked like and what his habits were, though he had never seen him nor any picture of him. As we breed animals for the transmission of physical attributes, so the Kaldanes breed themselves for the transmission of attributes of the mind, including memory and the power of recollection, and thus have they raised what we term instinct, above the level of the threshold of the objective mind where it may be commanded and utilized by recollection. Doubtless in our own subjective minds lie many of the impressions and experiences of our forebears. These may impinge upon our consciousness in dreams only, or in vague, haunting suggestions that we have before experienced some transient phase of our present existence. Ah, if we had but the power to recall them! Before us would unfold the forgotten story of the lost eons that have preceded us. We might even walk with God in the garden of His stars while man was still but a budding idea within His mind.

Ghek descended into the burrow at a steep incline for some ten feet, when he found himself in an elaborate and delightful network of burrows! The kaldane was elated. This indeed was life! He moved rapidly and fearlessly and he went as straight to his goal as you could to the kitchen of your own home. This goal lay at a low level in a spheroidal cavity about the size of a large barrel. Here, in a nest of torn bits of silk and fur lay six baby ulsios.

When the mother returned there were but five babies and a great spider-like creature, which she immediately sprang to attack only to be met by powerful chelae which seized and held her so that she could not move. Slowly they dragged her throat toward a hideous mouth and in a little moment she was dead.

Ghek might have remained in the nest for a long time, since there was ample food for many days; but he did not do so. Instead he explored the burrows. He followed them into many subterranean chambers of the city of Manator, and upward through walls to rooms above the ground. He found many ingeniously devised traps, and he found poisoned food and other signs of the constant battle that the inhabitants of Manator waged against these repulsive creatures that dwelt beneath their homes and public buildings.

His exploration revealed not only the vast proportions of the network of runways that apparently traversed every portion of the city, but the great antiquity of the majority of them. Tons upon tons of dirt must have been removed, and for a long time he wondered where it had been deposited, until in following downward a tunnel of great size and length he sensed before him the thunderous rush of subterranean waters, and presently came to the bank of a great, underground river, tumbling onward, no doubt, the length of a world to the buried sea of Omean. Into this torrential sewer had unthinkable generations of ulsios pushed their few handsful of dirt in the excavating of their vast labyrinth.

For only a moment did Ghek tarry by the river, for his seemingly aimless wanderings were in reality prompted by a definite purpose, and this he pursued with vigor and singleness of design. He followed such runways as appeared to terminate in the pits or other chambers of the inhabitants of the city, and these he explored, usually from the safety of a burrow's mouth, until satisfied that what he sought was not there. He moved swiftly upon his spider legs and covered remarkable distances in short periods of time.

His search not being rewarded with immediate success, he decided to return to the pit where his rykor lay chained and look to its wants. As he approached the end of the burrow that terminated in the pit he slackened his pace, stopping just within the entrance of the runway that he might scan the interior of the chamber before entering it. As he did so he saw the figure of a warrior appear suddenly in an opposite doorway. The rykor sprawled upon the table, his hands groping blindly for more food. Ghek saw the warrior pause and gaze in sudden astonishment at the rykor; he saw the fellow's eyes go wide and an ashen hue replace the copper bronze of his cheek. He stepped back as though someone had struck him in the face. For an instant only he stood thus as in a paralysis of fear, then he uttered a smothered shriek and turned and fled. Again was it a catastrophe that Ghek, the kaldane, could not smile.

Quickly entering the room he crawled to the table top and affixed himself to the shoulders of his rykor, and there he waited; and who may say that Ghek, though he could not smile, possessed not a sense of humor? For a half-hour he sat there, and then there came to him the sound of men approaching along corridors of stone. He could hear their arms clank against the rocky walls and he knew that they came at a rapid pace; but just before they reached the entrance to his prison they paused and advanced more slowly. In the lead was an officer, and just behind him, wide-eyed and perhaps still a little ashen, the warrior who had so recently departed in haste. At the doorway they halted and the officer turned sternly upon the warrior. With upraised finger he pointed at Ghek.

"There sits the creature! Didst thou dare lie, then, to thy dwar?"

"I swear," cried the warrior, "that I spoke the truth. But a moment since the thing groveled, headless, upon this very table! And may my first ancestor strike me dead upon the spot if I speak other than a true word!"

The officer looked puzzled. The men of Mars seldom if ever lie. He scratched his head. Then he addressed Ghek. "How long have you been here?" he asked.

"Who knows better than those who placed me here and chained me to a wall?" he returned in reply.

"Saw you this warrior enter here a few minutes since?"

"I saw him," replied Ghek.

"And you sat there where you sit now?" continued the officer.

"Look thou to my chain and tell me then where else might I sit!" cried Ghek. "Art the people of thy city all fools?"

Three other warriors pressed behind the two in front, craning their necks to view the prisoner while they grinned at the discomfiture of their fellow. The officer scowled at Ghek.

"Thy tongue is as venomous as that of the she-banth O-Tar sent to The Towers of Jetan," he said.

"You speak of the young woman who was captured with me?" asked Ghek, his expressionless monotone and face revealing naught of the interest he felt.

"I speak of her," replied the dwar, and then turning to the warrior who had summoned him: "return to thy quarters and remain there until the next games. Perhaps by that time thy eyes may have learned not to deceive thee."

The fellow cast a venomous glance at Ghek and turned away. The officer shook his head. "I do not understand it," he muttered. "Always has U-Van been a true and dependable warrior. Could it be – ?" he glanced piercingly at Ghek. "Thou hast a strange head that misfits thy body, fellow," he cried. "Our legends tell us of those ancient creatures that placed hallucinations upon the mind of their fellows. If thou be such then maybe U-Van suffered from thy forbidden powers. If thou be such O-Tar will know well how to deal with thee." He wheeled about and motioned his warriors to follow him.

"Wait!" cried Ghek. "Unless I am to be starved, send me food."

"You have had food," replied the warrior.

"Am I to be fed but once a day?" asked Ghek. "I require food oftener than that. Send me food."

"You shall have food," replied the officer. "None may say that the prisoners of Manator are ill-fed. Just are the laws of Manator," and he departed.

No sooner had the sounds of their passing died away in the distance than Ghek clambered from the shoulders of his rykor, and scurried to the burrow where he had hidden the key. Fetching it he unlocked the fetter from about the creature's ankle, locked it empty and carried the key farther down into the burrow. Then he returned to his place upon his brainless servitor. After a while he heard footsteps approaching, whereupon he rose and passed into another corridor from that down which he knew the warrior was coming. Here he waited out of sight, listening. He heard the man enter the chamber and halt. He heard a muttered exclamation, followed by the jangle of metal dishes as a salver was slammed upon a table; then rapidly retreating footsteps, which quickly died away in the distance.

Ghek lost no time in returning to the chamber, recovering the key, relocking the rykor to his chain. Then he replaced the key in the burrow and squatting on the table beside his headless body, directed its hands toward the food. While the rykor ate Ghek sat listening for the scraping sandals and clattering arms that he knew soon would come. Nor had he long to wait. Ghek scrambled to the shoulders of his rykor as he heard them coming. Again it was the officer who had been summoned by U-Van and with him were three warriors. The one directly behind him was evidently the same who had brought the food, for his eyes went wide when he saw Ghek sitting at the table and he looked very foolish as the dwar turned his stern glance upon him.

"It is even as I said," he cried. "He was not here when I brought his food."

"But he is here now," said the officer grimly, "and his fetter is locked about his ankle. Look! it has not been opened – but where is the key? It should be upon the table at the end opposite him. Where is the key, creature?" he shouted at Ghek.

"How should I, a prisoner, know better than my jailer the where-abouts of the key to my fetters?" he retorted.

"But it lay here," cried the officer, pointing to the other end of the table.

"Did you see it?" asked Ghek.

The officer hesitated. "No but it must have been there," he parried.

"Did you see the key lying there?" asked Ghek, pointing to another warrior.

The fellow shook his head negatively. "And you? and you?" contin-ued the kaldane addressing the others.

They both admitted that they never had seen the key. "And if it had been there how could I have reached it?" he continued.

"No, he could not have reached it," admitted the officer; "but there shall be no more of this! I-Zav, you will remain here on guard with this prisoner until you are relieved."

I-Zav looked anything but happy as this intelligence was transmitted to him, and he eyed Ghek suspiciously as the dwar and the other war-riors turned and left him to his unhappy lot.

CHAPTER THIRTEEN

A Desperate Deed

E-MED CROSSED THE tower chamber toward Tara of Helium and the slave girl, Lan-O. He seized the former roughly by a shoulder. "Stand!" he commanded. Tara struck his hand from her and rising, backed away.

"Lay not your hand upon the person of a princess of Helium, beast!" she warned.

E-Med laughed. "Think you that I play at jetan for you without first knowing something of the stake for which I play?" he demanded. "Come here!"

The girl drew herself to her full height, folding her arms across her breast, nor did E-Med note that the slim fingers of her right hand were inserted beneath the broad leather strap of her harness where it passed over her left shoulder.

"And O-Tar learns of this you shall rue it, E-Med," cried the slave girl; "there be no law in Manator that gives you this girl before you shall have won her fairly."

"What cares O-Tar for her fate?" replied E-Med. "Have I not heard? Did she not flout the great jeddak, heaping abuse upon him? By my first ancestor, I think O-Tar might make a jed of the man who subdued her," and again he advanced toward Tara.

"Wait!" said the girl in low, even tone. "Perhaps you know not what you do. Sacred to the people of Helium are the persons of the women of Helium. For the honor of the humblest of them would the great jeddak himself unsheathe his sword. The greatest nations of Barsoom have trembled to the thunders of war in defense of the person of Dejah Thoris, my mother. We are but mortal and so may die; but we may not be defiled. You may play at jetan for a princess of Helium, but though you may win the match, never may you claim the reward. If thou wouldst possess a dead body press me too far, but know, man of Manator, that the blood of The Warlord flows not in the veins of Tara of Helium for naught. I have spoken."

"I know naught of Helium and O-Tar is our warlord," replied E-Med; "but I do know that I would examine more closely the prize that I shall play for and win. I would test the lips of her who is to be my slave after the next games; nor is it well, woman, to drive me too far to anger." His eyes narrowed as he spoke, his visage taking on the semblance of that of a snarling beast. "If you doubt the truth of my words ask Lan-O, the slave girl."

"He speaks truly, O woman of Helium," interjected Lan-O. "Try not the temper of E-Med, if you value your life."

But Tara of Helium made no reply. Already had she spoken. She stood in silence now facing the burly warrior who approached her. He came close and then quite suddenly he seized her and, bending, tried to draw her lips to his.

Lan-O saw the woman from Helium half turn, and with a quick movement jerk her right hand from where it had lain upon her breast. She saw the hand shoot from beneath the arm of E-Med and rise behind his shoulder and she saw in the hand a long, slim blade. The lips of the warrior were drawing closer to those of the woman, but they never touched them, for suddenly the man straightened, stiffly, a shriek upon his lips, and then he crumpled like an empty fur and lay, a shrunken heap, upon the floor. Tara of Helium stooped and wiped her blade upon his harness.

Lan-O, wide-eyed, looked with horror upon the corpse. "For this we shall both die," she cried.

"And who would live a slave in Manator?" asked Tara of Helium.

"I am not so brave as thou," said the slave girl, "and life is sweet and there is always hope."

"Life is sweet," agreed Tara of Helium, "but honor is sacred. But do not fear. When they come I shall tell them the truth – that you had no hand in this and no opportunity to prevent it."

For a moment the slave girl seemed to be thinking deeply. Suddenly her eyes lighted. "There is a way, perhaps," she said, "to turn suspicion from us. He has the key to this chamber upon him. Let us open the door and drag him out – maybe we shall find a place to hide him."

"Good!" exclaimed Tara of Helium, and the two immediately set about the matter Lan-O had suggested. Quickly they found the key and unlatched the door and then, between them, they half carried, half dragged, the corpse of E-Med from the room and down the stairway to the next level where Lan-O said there were vacant chambers. The first door they tried was unlatched, and through this the two bore their grisly burden into a small room lighted by a single window. The apartment bore evidence of having been utilized as a living-room rather than as a cell, being furnished with a degree of comfort and even luxury. The walls were paneled to a height of about seven feet from the floor, while the plaster above and the ceiling were decorated with faded paintings of another day.

As Tara's eyes ran quickly over the interior her attention was drawn to a section of paneling that seemed to be separated at one edge from the piece next adjoining it. Quickly she crossed to it, discovering that one vertical edge of an entire panel projected a half-inch beyond the others. There was a possible explanation which piqued her curiosity, and acting upon its suggestion she seized upon the projecting edge and pulled outward. Slowly the panel swung toward her, revealing a dark aperture in the wall behind.

"Look, Lan-O!" she cried. "See what I have found – a hole in which we may hide the thing upon the floor."

Lan-O joined her and together the two investigated the dark aperture, finding a small platform from which a narrow runway led downward into Stygian darkness. Thick dust covered the floor within the doorway, indicating that a great period of time had elapsed since human foot had trod it – a secret way, doubtless, unknown to living Manatorians. Here they dragged the corpse of E-Med, leaving it upon the platform, and as they left the dark and forbidden closet Lan-O would have slammed to the panel had not Tara prevented.

"Wait!" she said, and fell to examining the door frame and the stile.

"Hurry!" whispered the slave girl. "If they come we are lost."

"It may serve us well to know how to open this place again," replied Tara of Helium, and then suddenly she pressed a foot against a section of the carved base at the right of the open panel. "Ah!" she breathed, a note of satisfaction in her tone, and closed the panel until it fitted snugly in its place. "Come!" she said and turned toward the outer doorway of the chamber.

They reached their own cell without detection, and closing the door Tara locked it from the inside and placed the key in a secret pocket in her harness.

"Let them come," she said. "Let them question us! What could two poor prisoners know of the whereabouts of their noble jailer? I ask you, Lan-O, what could they?"

"Nothing," admitted Lan-O, smiling with her companion.

"Tell me of these men of Manator," said Tara presently. "Are they all like E-Med, or are some of them like A-Kor, who seemed a brave and chivalrous character?"

"They are not unlike the peoples of other countries," replied Lan-O. "There be among them both good and bad. They are brave warriors and mighty. Among themselves they are not without chivalry and honor, but in their dealings with strangers they know but one law – the law of might. The weak and unfortunate of other lands fill them with contempt and arouse all that is worst in their natures, which doubtless accounts for their treatment of us, their slaves."

"But why should they feel contempt for those who have suffered the misfortune of falling into their hands?" queried Tara.

"I do not know," said Lan-O; "A-Kor says that he believes that it is because their country has never been invaded by a victorious foe. In their stealthy raids never have they been defeated, because they have never waited to face a powerful force; and so they have come to believe themselves invincible, and the other peoples are held in contempt as inferior in valor and the practice of arms."

"Yet A-Kor is one of them," said Tara.

"He is a son of O-Tar, the jeddak," replied Lan-O; "but his mother was a high born Gatholian, captured and made slave by O-Tar, and A-Kor boasts that in his veins runs only the blood of his mother, and indeed is he different from the others. His chivalry is of a gentler form, though not even his worst enemy has dared question his courage, while his skill with the sword, and the spear, and the thoat is famous throughout the length and breadth of Manator."

"What think you they will do with him?" asked Tara of Helium.

"Sentence him to the games," replied Lan-O. "If O-Tar be not greatly angered he may be sentenced to but a single game, in which case he may come out alive; but if O-Tar wishes really to dispose of him he will be sentenced to the entire series, and no warrior has ever survived the full ten, or rather none who was under a sentence from O-Tar."

"What are the games? I do not understand," said Tara "I have heard them speak of playing at jetan, but surely no one can be killed at jetan. We play it often at home."

"But not as they play it in the arena at Manator," replied Lan-O. "Come to the window," and together the two approached an aperture facing toward the east.

Below her Tara of Helium saw a great field entirely surrounded by the low building, and the lofty towers of which that in which she was imprisoned was but a unit. About the arena were tiers of seats; but the a thing that caught her attention was a gigantic jetan board laid out upon the floor of the arena in great squares of alternate orange and black.

"Here they play at jetan with living pieces. They play for great stakes and usually for a woman – some slave of exceptional beauty. O-Tar himself might have played for you had you not angered him, but now you will be played for in an open game by slaves and criminals, and you will belong to the side that wins – not to a single warrior, but to all who survive the game."

The eyes of Tara of Helium flashed, but she made no comment.

"Those who direct the play do not necessarily take part in it," continued the slave girl, "but sit in those two great thrones which you see at either end of the board and direct their pieces from square to square."

"But where lies the danger?" asked Tara of Helium. "If a piece be taken it is merely removed from the board – this is a rule of jetan as old almost as the civilization of Barsoom."

"But here in Manator, when they play in the great arena with living men, that rule is altered," explained Lan-O. "When a warrior is moved to a square occupied by an opposing piece, the two battle to the death for possession of the square and the one that is successful advantages by the move. Each is caparisoned to simulate the piece he represents and in addition he wears that which indicates whether he be slave, a warrior serving a sentence, or a volunteer. If serving a sentence the number of games he must play is also indicated, and thus the one directing the moves knows which pieces to risk and which to conserve, and further than this, a man's chances are affected by the position that is assigned him for the game. Those whom they wish to die are always Panthans in the game, for the Panthan has the least chance of surviving."

"Do those who direct the play ever actually take part in it?" asked Tara.

"Oh, yes," said Lan-O. "Often when two warriors, even of the highest class, hold a grievance against one another O-Tar compels them to settle it upon the arena. Then it is that they take active part and with drawn swords direct their own players from the position of Chief. They pick their own players, usually the best of their own warriors and slaves, if they be powerful men who possess such, or their friends may volunteer, or they may obtain prisoners from the pits. These are games indeed – the very best that are seen. Often the great chiefs themselves are slain."

"It is within this amphitheater that the justice of Manator is meted, then?" asked Tara.

"Very largely," replied Lan-O.

"How, then, through such justice, could a prisoner win his liberty?" continued the girl from Helium.

"If a man, and he survived ten games his liberty would be his," replied Lan-O.

"But none ever survives?" queried Tara. "And if a woman?"

"No stranger within the gates of Manator ever has survived ten games," replied the slave girl. "They are permitted to offer themselves into perpetual slavery if they prefer that to fighting at jetan. Of course they may be called upon, as any warrior, to take part in a game, but their chances then of surviving are increased, since they may never again have the chance of winning to liberty."

"But a woman," insisted Tara; "how may a woman win her freedom?"

Lan-O laughed. "Very simply," she cried, derisively. "She has but to find a warrior who will fight through ten consecutive games for her and survive."

"'Just are the laws of Manator,'" quoted Tara, scornfully.

Then it was that they heard footsteps outside their cell and a moment later a key turned in the lock and the door opened. A warrior faced them.

"Hast seen E-Med the dwar?" he asked.

"Yes," replied Tara, "he was here some time ago."

The man glanced quickly about the bare chamber and then searchingly first at Tara of Helium and then at the slave girl, Lan-O. The puzzled expression upon his face increased. He scratched his head. "It is strange," he said. "A score of men saw him ascend into this tower; and though there is but a single exit, and that well guarded, no man has seen him pass out."

Tara of Helium hid a yawn with the back of a shapely hand. "The Princess of Helium is hungry, fellow," she drawled; "tell your master that she would eat."

It was an hour later that food was brought, an officer and several warriors accompanying the bearer. The former examined the room carefully, but there was no sign that aught amiss had occurred there. The wound that had sent E-Med the dwar to his ancestors had not bled, fortunately for Tara of Helium.

"Woman," cried the officer, turning upon Tara, "you were the last to see E-Med the dwar. Answer me now and answer me truthfully. Did you see him leave this room?"

"I did," answered Tara of Helium.

"Where did he go from here?"

"How should I know? Think you that I can pass through a locked door of skeel?" the girl's tone was scornful.

"Of that we do not know," said the officer. "Strange things have happened in the cell of your companion in the pits of Manator. Perhaps you could pass through a locked door of skeel as easily as he performs seemingly more impossible feats."

"Whom do you mean," she cried; "Turan the panthan? He lives, then? Tell me, is he here in Manator unharmed?"

"I speak of that thing which calls itself Ghek the kaldane," replied the officer.

"But Turan! Tell me, padwar, have you heard aught of him?" Tara's tone was insistent and she leaned a little forward toward the officer, her lips slightly parted in expectancy.

Into the eyes of the slave girl, Lan-O, who was watching her, there crept a soft light of understanding; but the officer ignored Tara's question – what was the fate of another slave to him? "Men do not disappear into thin air," he growled, "and if E-Med be not found soon O-Tar himself may take a hand in this. I warn you, woman, if you be one of those horrid Corphals that by commanding the spirits of the wicked dead gains evil mastery over the living, as many now believe the thing called Ghek to be, that lest you return E-Med, O-Tar will have no mercy on you."

"What foolishness is this?" cried the girl. "I am a princess of Helium, as I have told you all a score of times. Even if the fabled Corphals existed, as none but the most ignorant now believes, the lore of the ancients tells us that they entered only into the bodies of wicked criminals of the lowest class. Man of Manator, thou art a fool, and thy jeddak and all his people," and she turned her royal back upon the padwar, and gazed through the window across the Field of Jetan and the roofs of Manator through the low hills and the rolling country and freedom.

"And you know so much of Corphals, then," he cried, "you know that while no common man dare harm them they may be slain by the hand of a jeddak with impunity!"

The girl did not reply, nor would she speak again, for all his threats and rage, for she knew now that none in all Manator dared harm her save O-Tar, the jeddak, and after a while the padwar left, taking his men with him. And after they had gone Tara stood for long looking out upon the city of Manator, and wondering what more of cruel wrongs Fate held in store for her. She was standing thus in silent meditation when there rose to her the strains of martial music from the city below – the deep, mellow tones of the long war trumpets of mounted troops, the clear, ringing notes of foot-soldiers' music. The girl raised her head and looked about, listening, and Lan-O, standing at an opposite window, looking toward the west, motioned Tara to join her. Now they could see across roofs and avenues to The Gate of Enemies, through which troops were marching into the city.

"The Great Jed is coming," said Lan-O, "none other dares enter thus, with blaring trumpets, the city of Manator. It is U-Thor, Jed of Manatos, second city of Manator. They call him The Great Jed the length and breadth of Manator, and because the people love him, O-Tar hates him. They say, who know, that it would need but slight provocation to inflame the two to war. How such a war would end no one could guess; for the people of Manator worship the great O-Tar, though they do not love him. U-Thor they love, but he is not the jeddak," and Tara understood, as only a Martian may, how much that simple statement encompassed.

The loyalty of a Martian to his jeddak is almost an instinct, and second not even to the instinct of self-preservation at that. Nor is this strange in a race whose religion includes ancestor worship, and where families trace their origin back into remote ages and a jeddak sits upon the same throne that his direct progenitors have occupied for, perhaps, hundreds of thousands of years, and rules the descendants of the same people that his forebears ruled. Wicked jeddaks have been dethroned, but seldom are they replaced by other than members of the imperial house, even though the law gives to the jeds the right to select whom they please.

"U-Thor is a just man and good, then?" asked Tara of Helium.

"There be none nobler," replied Lan-O. "In Manatos none but wicked criminals who deserve death are forced to play at jetan, and even then the play is fair and they have their chance for freedom. Volunteers may play, but the moves are not necessarily to the death – a wound, and even sometimes points in swordplay, deciding the issue. There they look upon jetan as a martial sport – here it is but butchery. And U-Thor is opposed to the ancient slave raids and to the policy that keeps Manator forever isolated from the other nations of Barsoom; but U-Thor is not jeddak and so there is no change."

The two girls watched the column moving up the broad avenue from The Gate of Enemies toward the palace of O-Tar. A gorgeous, barbaric procession of painted warriors in jewel-studded harness and waving feathers; vicious, squealing thoats caparisoned in rich trappings; far above their heads the long lances of their riders bore fluttering pennons; foot-soldiers swinging easily along the stone pavement, their sandals of zitidar hide giving forth no sound; and at the rear of each utan a train of painted chariots, drawn by mammoth zitidars, carrying the equipment of the company to which they were attached. Utan after utan entered through the great gate, and even when the head of the column reached the palace of O-Tar they were not all within the city.

"I have been here many years," said the girl, Lan-O; "but never have I seen even The Great Jed bring so many fighting men into the city of Manator."

Through half-closed eyes Tara of Helium watched the warriors marching up the broad avenue, trying to imagine them the fighting men of her beloved Helium coming to the rescue of their princess. That splendid figure upon the great thoat might be John Carter, himself, Warlord of Barsoom, and behind him utan after utan of the veterans of the empire, and then the girl opened her eyes again and saw the host of painted, be-feathered barbarians, and sighed. But yet she watched, fascinated by the martial scene, and now she noted again the groups of silent figures upon the balconies. No waving silks; no cries of welcome; no showers of flowers and jewels such as would have marked the entry of such a splendid, friendly pageant into the twin cities of her birth.

"The people do not seem friendly to the warriors of Manatos," she remarked to Lan-O; "I have not seen a single welcoming sign from the people on the balconies."

The slave girl looked at her in surprise. "It cannot be that you do not know!" she exclaimed. "Why, they are – " but she got no further. The door swung open and an officer stood before them.

"The slave girl, Tara, is summoned to the presence of O-Tar, the jeddak!" he announced.

CHAPTER FOURTEEN

At Ghek's Command

TURAN THE PANTHAN CHAFED in his chains. Time dragged; silence and monotony prolonged minutes into hours. Uncertainty of the fate of the woman he loved turned each hour into an eternity of hell. He listened impatiently for the sound of approaching footsteps that he might see and speak to some living creature and learn, perchance, some word of Tara of Helium. After torturing hours his ears were rewarded by the rattle of harness and arms. Men were coming! He waited breathlessly. Perhaps they were his executioners; but he would welcome them notwithstanding. He would question them. But if they knew naught of Tara he would not divulge the location of the hiding place in which he had left her.

Now they came – a half-dozen warriors and an officer, escorting an unarmed man; a prisoner, doubtless. Of this Turan was not left long in doubt, since they brought the newcomer and chained him to an adjoining ring. Immediately the panthan commenced to question the officer in charge of the guard.

"Tell me," he demanded, "why I have been made prisoner, and if other strangers were captured since I entered your city."

"What other prisoners?" asked the officer.

"A woman, and a man with a strange head," replied Turan.

"It is possible," said the officer; "but what were their names?"

"The woman was Tara, Princess of Helium, and the man was Ghek, a kaldane, of Bantoom."

"These were your friends?" asked the officer.

"Yes," replied Turan.

"It is what I would know," said the officer, and with a curt command to his men to follow him he turned and left the cell.

"Tell me of them!" cried Turan after him. "Tell me of Tara of Helium! Is she safe?" but the man did not answer and soon the sound of their departure died in the distance.

"Tara of Helium was safe, but a short time since," said the prisoner chained at Turan's side.

The panthan turned toward the speaker, seeing a large man, handsome of face and with a manner both stately and dignified. "You have seen her?" he asked. "They captured her then? She is in danger?"

"She is being held in The Towers of Jetan as a prize for the next games," replied the stranger.

"And who are you?" asked Turan. "And why are you here, a prisoner?"

"I am A-Kor the dwar, keeper of The Towers of Jetan," replied the other. "I am here because I dared speak the truth of O-Tar the jeddak, to one of his officers."

"And your punishment?" asked Turan.

"I do not know. O-Tar has not yet spoken. Doubtless the games – perhaps the full ten, for O-Tar does not love A-Kor, his son."

"You are the jeddak's son?" asked Turan.

"I am the son of O-Tar and of a slave, Haja of Gathol, who was a princess in her own land."

Turan looked searchingly at the speaker. A son of Haja of Gathol! A son of his mother's sister, this man, then, was his own cousin. Well did Gahan remember the mysterious disappearance of the Princess Haja and an entire utan of her personal troops. She had been upon a visit far from the city of Gathol and returning home had vanished with her whole escort from the sight of man. So this was the secret of the seeming mystery? Doubtless it explained many other similar disappearances that extended nearly as far back as the history of Gathol. Turan scrutinized his companion, discovering many evidences of resemblance to his mother's people. A-Kor might have been ten years younger than he, but such differences in age are scarce accounted among a people who seldom or never age outwardly after maturity and whose span of life may be a thousand years.

"And where lies Gathol?" asked Turan.

"Almost due east of Manator," replied A-Kor.

"And how far?"

"Some twenty-one degrees it is from the city of Manator to the city of Gathol," replied A-Kor; "but little more than ten degrees between the boundaries of the two countries. Between them, though, there lies a country of torn rocks and yawning chasms."

Well did Gahan know this country that bordered his upon the west – even the ships of the air avoided it because of the treacherous currents that rose from the deep chasms, and the almost total absence of safe landings. He knew now where Manator lay and for the first time in long weeks the way to his own Gathol, and here was a man, a fellow prisoner, in whose veins flowed the blood of his own ancestors – a man who knew Manator; its people, its customs and the country surrounding it – one who could aid him, with advice at least, to find a plan for the rescue of Tara of Helium and for escape. But would A-Kor – could he dare broach the subject? He could do no less than try.

"And O-Tar you think will sentence you to death?" he asked; "and why?"

"He would like to," replied A-Kor, "for the people chafe beneath his iron hand and their loyalty is but the loyalty of a people to the long line of illustrious jeddaks from which he has sprung. He is a jealous man and has found the means of disposing of most of those whose blood might entitle them to a claim upon the throne, and whose place in the affections of the people endowed them with any political significance. The fact that I was the son of a slave relegated me to a position of minor importance in the consideration of O-Tar, yet I am still the son of a jeddak and might sit upon the throne of Manator with as perfect congruity as O-Tar himself. Combined with this is the fact that of recent years the people, and especially many of the younger warriors, have evinced a growing affection for me, which I attribute to certain virtues of character and training derived from my mother, but which O-Tar assumes to be the result of an ambition upon my part to occupy the throne of Manator.

"And now, I am firmly convinced, he has seized upon my criticism of his treatment of the slave girl Tara as a pretext for ridding himself of me."

"But if you could escape and reach Gathol," suggested Turan.

"I have thought of that," mused A-Kor; "but how much better off would I be? In the eyes of the Gatholians I would be, not a Gatholian; but a stranger and doubtless they would accord me the same treatment that we of Manator accord strangers."

"Could you convince them that you are the son of the Princess Haja your welcome would be assured," said Turan; "while on the other hand you could purchase your freedom and citizenship with a brief period of labor in the diamond mines."

"How know you all these things?" asked A-Kor. "I thought you were from Helium."

"I am a panthan," replied Turan, "and I have served many countries, among them Gathol."

"It is what the slaves from Gathol have told me," said A-Kor, thoughtfully, "and my mother, before O-Tar sent her to live at Manatos. I think he must have feared her power and influence among the slaves from Gathol and their descendants, who number perhaps a million people throughout the land of Manator."

"Are these slaves organized?" asked Turan.

A-Kor looked straight into the eyes of the panthan for a long moment before he replied. "You are a man of honor," he said; "I read it in your face, and I am seldom mistaken in my estimate of a man; but – " and he leaned closer to the other – "even the walls have ears," he whispered, and Turan's question was answered.

It was later in the evening that warriors came and unlocked the fetter from Turan's ankle and led him away to appear before O-Tar, the jeddak. They conducted him toward the palace along narrow, winding streets and broad avenues; but always from the balconies there looked down upon them in endless ranks the silent people of the city. The palace itself was filled with life and activity. Mounted warriors galloped through the corridors and up and down the runways connecting adjacent floors. It seemed that no one walked within the palace other than a few slaves. Squealing, fighting thoats were stabled in magnificent halls while their riders, if not upon some duty of the palace, played at jetan with small figures carved from wood.

Turan noted the magnificence of the interior architecture of the palace, the lavish expenditure of precious jewels and metals, the gorgeous mural decorations which depicted almost exclusively martial scenes, and principally duels which seemed to be fought upon jetan boards of heroic size. The capitals of many of the columns supporting the ceilings of the corridors and chambers through which they passed were wrought into formal likenesses of jetan pieces – everywhere there seemed a suggestion of the game. Along the same path that Tara of Helium had been led Turan was conducted toward the throne room of O-Tar the jeddak, and when he entered the Hall of Chiefs his interest turned to wonder and admiration as he viewed the ranks of statuesque thoatmen decked in their gorgeous, martial panoply. Never, he thought, had he seen upon Barsoom more soldierly figures or thoats so perfectly trained to perfection of immobility as these. Not a muscle quivered, not a tail lashed, and the riders were as motionless as their mounts – each warlike eye straight to the front, the great spears inclined at the same angle. It was a picture to fill the breast of a fighting man with awe and reverence. Nor did it fail in its effect upon Turan as they conducted him the length of the chamber, where he waited before great doors until he should be summoned into the presence of the ruler of Manator.

When Tara of Helium was ushered into the throne room of O-Tar she found the great hall filled with the chiefs and officers of O-Tar and U-Thor, the latter occupying the place of honor at the foot of the throne, as was his due. The girl was conducted to the foot of the aisle and halted before the jeddak, who looked down upon her from his high throne with scowling brows and fierce, cruel eyes.

"The laws of Manator are just," said O-Tar, addressing her; "thus is it that you have been summoned here again to be judged by the highest authority of Manator. Word has reached me that you are suspected of being a Corphal. What word have you to say in refutation of the charge?"

Tara of Helium could scarce restrain a sneer as she answered the ridiculous accusation of witchcraft. "So ancient is the culture of my people," she said, "that authentic history reveals no defense for that which we know existed only in the ignorant and superstitious minds of the most primitive peoples of the past. To those who are yet so untutored as to believe in the existence of Corphals, there can be no argument that will convince them of their error – only long ages of refinement and culture can accomplish their release from the bondage of ignorance. I have spoken."

"Yet you do not deny the accusation," said O-Tar.

"It is not worthy the dignity of a denial," she responded haughtily.

"And I were you, woman," said a deep voice at her side, "I should, nevertheless, deny it."

Tara of Helium turned to see the eyes of U-Thor, the great jed of Manatos, upon her. Brave eyes they were, but neither cold nor cruel. O-Tar rapped impatiently upon the arm of his throne. "U-Thor forgets," he cried, "that O-Tar is the jeddak."

"U-Thor remembers," replied the jed of Manatos, "that the laws of Manator permit any who may be accused to have advice and counsel before their judge."

Tara of Helium saw that for some reason this man would have assisted her, and so she acted upon his advice.

"I deny the charge," she said, "I am no Corphal."

"Of that we shall learn," snapped O-Tar. "U-Dor, where are those who have knowledge of the powers of this woman?"

And U-Dor brought several who recounted the little that was known of the disappearance of E-Med, and others who told of the capture of Ghek and Tara, suggesting by deduction that having been found together they had sufficient in common to make it reasonably certain that one was as bad as the other, and that, therefore, it remained but to convict one of them of Corphalism to make certain the guilt of both.

And then O-Tar called for Ghek, and immediately the hideous kaldane was dragged before him by warriors who could not conceal the fear in which they held this creature.

"And you!" said O-Tar in cold accusing tones. "Already have I been told enough of you to warrant me in passing through your heart the jeddak's steel – of how you stole the brains from the warrior U-Van so that he thought he saw your headless body still endowed with life; of how you caused another to believe that you had escaped, making him to see naught but an empty bench and a blank wall where you had been."

"Ah, O-Tar, but that is as nothing!" cried a young padwar who had come in command of the escort that brought Ghek. "The thing which he did to I-Zav, here, would prove his guilt alone."

"What did he to the warrior I-Zav?" demanded O-Tar. "Let I-Zav speak!"

The warrior I-Zav, a great fellow of bulging muscles and thick neck, advanced to the foot of the throne. He was pale and still trembling visibly as from a nervous shock.

"Let my first ancestor be my witness, O-Tar, that I speak the truth," he began. "I was left to guard this creature, who sat upon a bench, shackled to the wall. I stood by the open doorway at the opposite side of the chamber. He could not reach me, yet, O-Tar, may Iss engulf me if he did not drag me to him helpless as an unhatched egg. He dragged me to him, greatest of jeddaks, with his eyes! With his eyes he seized upon my eyes and dragged me to him and he made me lay my swords and dagger upon the table and back off into a corner, and still keeping his eyes upon my eyes his head quitted his body and crawling upon six short legs it descended to the floor and backed part way into the hole of an ulsio, but not so far that the eyes were not still upon me and then it returned with the key to its fetter and after resuming its place upon its own shoulders it unlocked the fetter and again dragged me across the room and made me to sit upon the bench where it had been and there it fastened the fetter about my ankle, and I could do naught for the power of its eyes and the fact that it wore my two swords and my dagger. And then the head disappeared down the hole of the ulsio with the key, and when it returned, it resumed its body and stood guard over me at the doorway until the padwar came to fetch it hither."

"It is enough!" said O-Tar, sternly. "Both shall receive the jeddak's steel," and rising from his throne he drew his long sword and descended the marble steps toward them, while two brawny warriors seized Tara by either arm and two seized Ghek, holding them facing the naked blade of the jeddak.

"Hold, just O-Tar!" cried U-Dor. "There be yet another to be judged. Let us confront him who calls himself Turan with these his fellows before they die."

"Good!" exclaimed O-Tar, pausing half way down the steps. "Fetch Turan, the slave!"

When Turan had been brought into the chamber he was placed a little to Tara's left and a step nearer the throne. O-Tar eyed him menacingly.

"You are Turan," he asked, "friend and companion of these?"

The panthan was about to reply when Tara of Helium spoke. "I know not this fellow," she said. "Who dares say that he be a friend and companion of the Princess Tara of Helium?"

Turan and Ghek looked at her in surprise, but at Turan she did not look, and to Ghek she passed a quick glance of warning, as to say: "Hold thy peace."

The panthan tried not to fathom her purpose for the head is useless when the heart usurps its functions, and Turan knew only that the woman he loved had denied him, and though he tried not even to think it his foolish heart urged but a single explanation – that she refused to recognize him lest she be involved in his difficulties.

O-Tar looked first at one and then at another of them; but none of them spoke.

"Were they not captured together?" he asked of U-Dor.

"No," replied the dwar. "He who is called Turan was found seeking entrance to the city and was enticed to the pits. The following morning I discovered the other two upon the hill beyond The Gate of Enemies."

"But they are friends and companions," said a young padwar, "for this Turan inquired of me concerning these two, calling them by name and saying that they were his friends."

"It is enough," stated O-Tar, "all three shall die," and he took another step downward from the throne.

"For what shall we die?" asked Ghek. "Your people prate of the just laws of Manator, and yet you would slay three strangers without telling them of what crime they are accused."

"He is right," said a deep voice. It was the voice of U-Thor, the great jed of Manatos. O-Tar looked at him and scowled; but there came voices from other portions of the chamber seconding the demand for justice.

"Then know, though you shall die anyway," cried O-Tar, "that all three are convicted of Corphalism and that as only a jeddak may slay such as you in safety you are about to be honored with the steel of O-Tar."

"Fool!" cried Turan. "Know you not that in the veins of this woman flows the blood of ten thousand jeddaks – that greater than yours is her power in her own land? She is Tara, Princess of Helium, great-granddaughter of Tardos Mors, daughter of John Carter, Warlord of Barsoom. She cannot be a Corphal. Nor is this creature Ghek, nor am I. And you would know more, I can prove my right to be heard and to be believed if I may have word with the Princess Haja of Gathol, whose son is my fellow prisoner in the pits of O-Tar, his father."

At this U-Thor rose to his feet and faced O-Tar. "What means this?" he asked. "Speaks the man the truth? Is the son of Haja a prisoner in thy pits, O-Tar?"

"And what is it to the jed of Manatos who be the prisoners in the pits of his jeddak?" demanded O-Tar, angrily.

"It is this to the jed of Manatos," replied U-Thor in a voice so low as to be scarce more than a whisper and yet that was heard the whole length and breadth of the great throne room of O-Tar, Jeddak of Manator. "You gave me a slave woman, Haja, who had been a princess in Gathol, because you feared her influence among the slaves from Gathol. I have made of her a free woman, and I have married her and made her thus a princess of Manatos. Her son is my son, O-Tar, and though thou be my jeddak, I say to you that for any harm that befalls A-Kor you shall answer to U-Thor of Manatos."

O-Tar looked long at U-Thor, but he made no reply. Then he turned again to Turan. "If one be a Corphal," he said, "then all of you be Corphals, and we know well from the things that this creature has done," he pointed at Ghek, "that he is a Corphal, for no mortal has such powers as he. And as you are all Corphals you must all die." He took another step downward, when Ghek spoke.

"These two have no such powers as I," he said. "They are but ordinary, brainless things such as yourself. I have done all the things that your poor, ignorant warriors have told you; but this only demonstrates that I am of a higher order than yourselves, as is indeed the fact. I am a kaldane, not a Corphal. There is nothing supernatural or mysterious about me, other than that to the ignorant all things which they cannot understand are mysterious. Easily might I have eluded your warriors and escaped your pits; but I remained in the hope that I might help these two foolish creatures who have not the brains to escape without help. They befriended me and saved my life. I owe them this debt. Do not slay them – they are harmless. Slay me if you will. I offer my life if it will appease your ignorant wrath. I cannot return to Bantoom and so I might as well die, for there is no pleasure in intercourse with the feeble intellects that cumber the face of the world outside the valley of Bantoom."

"Hideous egotist," said O-Tar, "prepare to die and assume not to dictate to O-Tar the jeddak. He has passed sentence and all three of you shall feel the jeddak's naked steel. I have spoken!"

He took another step downward and then a strange thing happened. He paused, his eyes fixed upon the eyes of Ghek. His sword slipped from nerveless fingers, and still he stood there swaying forward and back. A jed rose to rush to his side; but Ghek stopped him with a word.

"Wait!" he cried. "The life of your jeddak is in my hands. You believe me a Corphal and so you believe, too, that only the sword of a jeddak may slay me, therefore your blades are useless against me. Offer harm to any one of us, or seek to approach your jeddak until I have spoken, and he shall sink lifeless to the marble. Release the two prisoners and let them come to my side – I would speak to them, privately. Quick! do as I say; I would as lief as not slay O-Tar. I but let him live that I may gain freedom for my friends – obstruct me and he dies."

The guards fell back, releasing Tara and Turan, who came close to Ghek's side.

"Do as I tell you and do it quickly," whispered the kaldane. "I cannot hold this fellow long, nor could I kill him thus. There are many minds working against mine and presently mine will tire and O-Tar will be himself again. You must make the best of your opportunity while you may. Behind the arras that you see hanging in the rear of the throne above you is a secret opening. From it a corridor leads to the pits of the palace, where there are storerooms containing food and drink. Few people go there. From these pits lead others to all parts of the city. Follow one that runs due west and it will bring you to The Gate of Enemies. The rest will then lie with you. I can do no more; hurry before my waning powers fail me – I am not as Luud, who was a king. He could have held this creature forever. Make haste! Go!"

CHAPTER FIFTEEN

The Old Man of the Pits

"I SHALL NOT DESERT YOU, Ghek," said Tara of Helium, simply.

"Go! Go!" whispered the kaldane. "You can do me no good. Go, or all I have done is for naught."

Tara shook her head. "I cannot," she said.

"They will slay her," said Ghek to Turan, and the panthan, torn between loyalty to this strange creature who had offered its life for him, and love of the woman, hesitated but a moment, then he swept Tara from her feet and lifting her in his arms leaped up the steps that led to the throne of Manator. Behind the throne he parted the arras and found the secret opening. Into this he bore the girl and down a long, narrow corridor and winding runways that led to lower levels until they came to the pits of the palace of O-Tar. Here was a labyrinth of passages and chambers presenting a thousand hiding-places.

As Turan bore Tara up the steps toward the throne a score of warriors rose as though to rush forward to intercept them. "Stay!" cried Ghek, "or your jeddak dies," and they halted in their tracks, waiting the will of this strange, uncanny creature.

Presently Ghek took his eyes from the eyes of O-Tar and the jeddak shook himself as one who would be rid of a bad dream and straightened up, half dazed still.

"Look," said Ghek, then, "I have given your jeddak his life, nor have I harmed one of those whom I might easily have slain when they were in my power. No harm have I or my friends done in the city of Manator. Why then should you persecute us? Give us our lives. Give us our liberty."

O-Tar, now in command of his faculties, stooped and regained his sword. In the room was silence as all waited to hear the jeddak's answer.

"Just are the laws of Manator," he said at last. "Perhaps, after all, there is truth in the words of the stranger. Return him then to the pits and pursue the others and capture them. Through the mercy of O-Tar they shall be permitted to win their freedom upon the Field of Jetan, in the coming games."

Still ashen was the face of the jeddak as Ghek was led away and his appearance was that of a man who had been snatched from the brink of eternity into which he has gazed, not with the composure of great courage, but with fear. There were those in the throne room who knew that the execution of the three prisoners had but been delayed and the responsibility placed upon the shoulders of others, and one of those who knew was U-Thor, the great jed of Manatos. His curling lip betokened his scorn of the jeddak who had chosen humiliation rather than death. He knew that O-Tar had lost more of prestige in those few moments than he could regain in a lifetime, for the Martians are jealous of the courage of their chiefs – there can be no evasions of stern duty, no temporizing with honor. That there were others in the room who shared U-Thor's belief was evidenced by the silence and the grim scowls.

O-Tar glanced quickly around. He must have sensed the hostility and guessed its cause, for he went suddenly angry, and as one who seeks by the vehemence of his words to establish the courage of his heart he roared forth what could be considered as naught other than a challenge.

"The will of O-Tar, the jeddak, is the law of Manator," he cried, "and the laws of Manator are just – they cannot err. U-Dor, dispatch those who will search the palace, the pits, and the city, and return the fugitives to their cells.

"And now for you, U-Thor of Manatos! Think you with impunity to threaten your jeddak – to question his right to punish traitors and instigators of treason? What am I to think of your own loyalty, who takes to wife a woman I have banished from my court because of her intrigues against the authority of her jeddak and her master? But O-Tar is just. Make your explanations and your peace, then, before it is too late."

"U-Thor has nothing to explain," replied the jed of Manatos; "nor is he at war with his jeddak; but he has the right that every jed and every warrior enjoys, of demanding justice at the hands of the jeddak for whomsoever he believes to be persecuted. With increasing rigor has the jeddak of Manator persecuted the slaves from Gathol since he took to himself the unwilling Princess Haja. If the slaves from Gathol have harbored thoughts of vengeance and escape 'tis no more than might be expected from a proud and courageous people. Ever have I counselled greater fairness in our treatment of our slaves, many of whom, in their own lands, are people of great distinction and power; but always has O-Tar, the jeddak, flouted with arrogance my every suggestion. Though it has been through none of my seeking that the question has arisen now I am glad that it has, for the time was bound to come when the jeds of Manator would demand from O-Tar the respect and consideration that is their due from the man who holds his high office at their pleasure. Know, then, O-Tar, that you must free A-Kor, the dwar, forthwith or bring him to fair trial before the assembled jeds of Manator. I have spoken."

"You have spoken well and to the point, U-Thor," cried O-Tar, "for you have revealed to your jeddak and your fellow jeds the depth of the disloyalty that I have long suspected. A-Kor already has been tried and sentenced by the supreme tribunal of Manator – O-Tar, the jeddak; and you too shall receive justice from the same unfailing source. In the meantime you are under arrest. To the pits with him! To the pits with U-Thor the false jed!" He clapped his hands to summon the surrounding warriors to do his bidding. A score leaped forward to seize U-Thor. They were warriors of the palace, mostly; but two score leaped to defend U-Thor, and with ringing steel they fought at the foot of the steps to the throne of Manator where stood O-Tar, the jeddak, with drawn sword ready to take his part in the melee.

At the clash of steel, palace guards rushed to the scene from other parts of the great building until those who would have defended U-Thor were outnumbered two to one, and then the jed of Manatos slowly withdrew with his forces, and fighting his way through the corridors and chambers of the palace came at last to the avenue. Here he was reinforced by the little army that had marched with him into Manator. Slowly they retreated toward The Gate of Enemies between the rows of silent people looking down upon them from the balconies and there, within the city walls, they made their stand.

In a dimly-lighted chamber beneath the palace of O-Tar the jeddak, Turan the panthan lowered Tara of Helium from his arms and faced her. "I am sorry, Princess," he said, "that I was forced to disobey your commands, or to abandon Ghek; but there was no other way. Could he have saved you I would have stayed in his place. Tell me that you forgive me."

"How could I do less?" she replied graciously. "But it seemed cowardly to abandon a friend."

"Had we been three fighting men it had been different," he said. "We could only have remained and died together, fighting; but you know, Tara of Helium, that we may not jeopardize a woman's safety even though we risk the loss of honor."

"I know that, Turan," she said; "but no one may say that you have risked honor, who knows the honor and bravery that are yours."

He heard her with surprise for these were the first words that she had spoken to him that did not savor of the attitude of a princess to a panthan – though it was more in her tone than the actual words that he apprehended the difference. How at variance were they to her recent repudiation of him! He could not fathom her, and so he blurted out the question that had been in his mind since she had told O-Tar that she did not know him.

"Tara of Helium," he said, "your words are balm to the wound you gave me in the throne room of O-Tar. Tell me, Princess, why you denied me."

She turned her great, deep eyes up to his and in them was a little of reproach.

"You did not guess," she asked, "that it was my lips alone and not my heart that denied you? O-Tar had ordered that I die, more because I was a companion of Ghek than because of any evidence against me, and so I knew that if I acknowledged you as one of us, you would be slain, too."

"It was to save me, then?" he cried, his face suddenly lighting.

"It was to save my brave panthan," she said in a low voice.

"Tara of Helium," said the warrior, dropping to one knee, "your words are as food to my hungry heart," and he took her fingers in his and pressed them to his lips.

Gently she raised him to his feet. "You need not tell me, kneeling," she said, softly.

Her hand was still in his as he rose and they were very close, and the man was still flushed with the contact of her body since he had carried her from the throne room of O-Tar. He felt his heart pounding in his breast and the hot blood surging through his veins as he looked at her beautiful face, with its downcast eyes and the half-parted lips that he would have given a kingdom to possess, and then he swept her to him and as he crushed her against his breast his lips smothered hers with kisses.

But only for an instant. Like a tigress the girl turned upon him, striking him, and thrusting him away. She stepped back, her head high and her eyes flashing fire. "You would dare?" she cried. "You would dare thus defile a princess of Helium?"

His eyes met hers squarely and there was no shame and no remorse in them.

"Yes, I would dare," he said. "I would dare love Tara of Helium; but I would not dare defile her or any woman with kisses that were not prompted by love of her alone." He stepped closer to her and laid his hands upon her shoulders. "Look into my eyes, daughter of The Warlord," he said, "and tell me that you do not wish the love of Turan, the panthan."

"I do not wish your love," she cried, pulling away. "I hate you!" and then turning away she bent her head into the hollow of her arm, and wept.

The man took a step toward her as though to comfort her when he was arrested by the sound of a crackling laugh behind him. Wheeling about, he discovered a strange figure of a man standing in a doorway. It was one of those rarities occasionally to be seen upon Barsoom – an old man with the signs of age upon him. Bent and wrinkled, he had more the appearance of a mummy than a man.

"Love in the pits of O-Tar!" he cried, and again his thin laughter jarred upon the silence of the subterranean vaults. "A strange place to woo! A strange place to woo, indeed! When I was a young man we roamed in the gardens beneath giant pimalias and stole our kisses in the brief shadows of hurtling Thuria. We came not to the gloomy pits to speak of love; but times have changed and ways have changed, though I had never thought to live to see the time when the way of a man with a maid, or a maid with a man would change. Ah, but we kissed them then! And what if they objected, eh? What if they objected? Why, we kissed them more. Ey, ey, those were the days!" and he cackled again. "Ey, well do I recall the first of them I ever kissed, and I've kissed an army of them since; she was a fine girl, but she tried to slip a dagger into me while I was kissing her. Ey, ey, those were the days! But I kissed her. She's been dead over a thousand years now, but she was never kissed again like that while she lived, I'll swear, not since she's been dead, either. And then there was that other – " but Turan, seeing a thousand or more years of osculatory memoirs portending, interrupted.

"Tell me, ancient one," he said, "not of thy loves but of thyself. Who are you? What do you here in the pits of O-Tar?"

"I might ask you the same, young man," replied the other. "Few there are who visit the pits other than the dead, except my pupils – ey! That is it – you are new pupils! Good! But never before have they sent a woman to learn the great art from the greatest artist. But times have changed. Now, in my day the women did no work – they were just for kissing and loving. Ey, those were the women. I mind the one we captured in the south – ey! she was a devil, but how she could love. She had breasts of marble and a heart of fire. Why, she – "

"Yes, yes," interrupted Turan; "we are pupils, and we are anxious to get to work. Lead on and we will follow."

"Ey, yes! Ey, yes! Come! All is rush and hurry as though there were not another countless myriad of ages ahead. Ey, yes! as many as lie behind. Two thousand years have passed since I broke my shell and always rush, rush, rush, yet I cannot see that aught has been accomplished. Manator is the same today as it was then – except the girls. We had the girls then. There was one that I gained upon The Fields of Jetan. Ey, but you should have seen – "

"Lead on!" cried Turan. "After we are at work you shall tell us of her."

"Ey, yes," said the old fellow and shuffled off down a dimly lighted passage. "Follow me!"

"You are going with him?" asked Tara.

"Why not?" replied Turan. "We know not where we are, or the way from these pits; for I know not east from west; but he doubtless knows and if we are shrewd we may learn from him that which we would know. At least we cannot afford to arouse his suspicions"; and so they followed him – followed along winding corridors and through many chambers, until they came at last to a room in which there were several marble slabs raised upon pedestals some three feet above the floor and upon each slab lay a human corpse.

"Here we are," exclaimed the old man. "These are fresh and we shall have to get to work upon them soon. I am working now on one for The Gate of Enemies. He slew many of our warriors. Truly is he entitled to a place in The Gate. Come, you shall see him."

He led them to an adjoining apartment. Upon the floor were many fresh, human bones and upon a marble slab a mass of shapeless flesh.

"You will learn this later," announced the old man; "but it will not harm you to watch me now, for there are not many thus prepared, and it may be long before you will have the opportunity to see another prepared for The Gate of Enemies. First, you see, I remove all the bones, carefully that the skin may be damaged as little as possible. The skull is the most difficult, but it can be removed by a skilful artist. You see, I have made but a single opening. This I now sew up, and that done, the body is hung so," and he fastened a piece of rope to the hair of the corpse and swung the horrid thing to a ring in the ceiling. Directly below it was a circular manhole in the floor from which he removed the cover revealing a well partially filled with a reddish liquid. "Now we lower it into this, the formula for which you shall learn in due time. We fasten it thus to the bottom of the cover, which we now replace. In a year it will be ready; but it must be examined often in the meantime and the liquid kept above the level of its crown. It will be a very beautiful piece, this one, when it is ready.

"And you are fortunate again, for there is one to come out today." He crossed to the opposite side of the room and raised another cover, reached in and dragged a grotesque looking figure from the hole. It was a human body, shrunk by the action of the chemical in which it had been immersed, to a little figure scarce a foot high.

"Ey! is it not fine?" cried the little old man. "Tomorrow it will take its place in The Gate of Enemies." He dried it off with cloths and packed it away carefully in a basket. "Perhaps you would like to see some of my life work," he suggested, and without waiting for their assent led them to another apartment, a large chamber in which were forty or fifty people. All were sitting or standing quietly about the walls, with the exception of one huge warrior who bestrode a great thoat in the very center of the room, and all were motionless. Instantly there sprang to the minds of Tara and Turan the rows of silent people upon the balconies that lined the avenues of the city, and the noble array of mounted warriors in The Hall of Chiefs, and the same explanation came to both but neither dared voice the question that was in his mind, for fear of revealing by his ignorance the fact that they were strangers in Manator and therefore impostors in the guise of pupils.

"It is very wonderful," said Turan. "It must require great skill and patience and time."

"That it does," replied the old man, "though having done it so long I am quicker than most; but mine are the most natural. Why, I would defy the wife of that warrior to say that insofar as appearances are concerned he does not live," and he pointed at the man upon the thoat. "Many of them, of course, are brought here wasted or badly wounded and these I have to repair. That is where great skill is required, for everyone wants his dead to look as they did at their best in life; but you shall learn – to mount them and paint them and repair them and sometimes to make an ugly one look beautiful. And it will be a great comfort to be able to mount your own. Why, for fifteen hundred years no one has mounted my own dead but myself.

"I have many, my balconies are crowded with them; but I keep a great room for my wives. I have them all, as far back as the first one, and many is the evening I spend with them – quiet evenings and very pleasant. And then the pleasure of preparing them and making them even more beautiful than in life partially recompenses one for their loss. I take my time with them, looking for a new one while I am working on the old. When I am not sure about a new one I bring her to the chamber where my wives are, and compare her charms with theirs, and there is always a great satisfaction at such times in knowing that they will not object. I love harmony."

"Did you prepare all the warriors in The Hall of Chiefs?" asked Turan.

"Yes, I prepare them and repair them," replied the old man. "O-Tar will trust no other. Even now I have two in another room who were damaged in some way and brought down to me. O-Tar does not like to have them gone long, since it leaves two riderless thoats in the Hall; but I shall have them ready presently. He wants them all there in the event any momentous question arises upon which the living jeds cannot agree, or do not agree with O-Tar. Such questions he carries to the jeds in The Hall of Chiefs. There he shuts himself up alone with the great chiefs who have attained wisdom through death. It is an excellent plan and there is never any friction or misunderstandings. O-Tar has said that it is the finest deliberative body upon Barsoom – much more intelligent than that composed of the living jeds. But come, we must get to work; come into the next chamber and I will begin your instruction."

He led the way into the chamber in which lay the several corpses upon their marble slabs, and going to a cabinet he donned a pair of huge spectacles and commenced to select various tools from little compartments. This done he turned again toward his two pupils.

"Now let me have a look at you," he said. "My eyes are not what they once were, and I need these powerful lenses for my work, or to see distinctly the features of those around me."

He turned his eyes upon the two before him. Turan held his breath for he knew that now the man must discover that they wore not the harness or insignia of Manator. He had wondered before why the old fellow had not noticed it, for he had not known that he was half blind. The other examined their faces, his eyes lingering long upon the beauty of Tara of Helium, and then they drifted to the harness of the two. Turan thought that he noted an appreciable start of surprise on the part of the taxidermist, but if the old man noticed anything his next words did not reveal it.

"Come with I-Gos," he said to Turan, "I have materials in the next room that I would have you fetch hither. Remain here, woman, we shall be gone but a moment."

He led the way to one of the numerous doors opening into the chamber and entered ahead of Turan. Just inside the door he stopped, and pointing to a bundle of silks and furs upon the opposite side of the room directed Turan to fetch them. The latter had crossed the room and was stooping to raise the bundle when he heard the click of a lock behind him. Wheeling instantly he saw that he was alone in the room and that the single door was closed. Running rapidly to it he strove to open it, only to find that he was a prisoner.

I-Gos, stepping out and locking the door behind him, turned toward Tara.

"Your leather betrayed you," he said, laughing his cackling laugh. "You sought to deceive old I-Gos, but you found that though his eyes are weak his brain is not. But it shall not go ill with you. You are beautiful and I-Gos loves beautiful women. I might not have you elsewhere in Manator, but here there is none to deny old I-Gos. Few come to the pits of the dead – only those who bring the dead and they hasten away as fast as they can. No one will know that I-Gos has a beautiful woman locked with his dead. I shall ask you no questions and then I will not have to give you up, for I will not know to whom you belong, eh? And when you die I shall mount you beautifully and place you in the chamber with my other women. Will not that be fine, eh?" He had approached until he stood close beside the horrified girl. "Come!" he cried, seizing her by the wrist. "Come to I-Gos!"

CHAPTER SIXTEEN

Another Change of Name

TURAN DASHED HIMSELF against the door of his prison in a vain effort to break through the solid skeel to the side of Tara whom he knew to be in grave danger, but the heavy panels held and he succeeded only in bruising his shoulders and his arms. At last he desisted and set about searching his prison for some other means of escape. He found no other opening in the stone walls, but his search revealed a heterogeneous collection of odds and ends of arms and apparel, of harness and ornaments and insignia, and sleeping silks and furs in great quantities. There were swords and spears and several large, two-bladed battle-axes, the heads of which bore a striking resemblance to the propellor of a small flier. Seizing one of these he attacked the door once more with great fury. He expected to hear something from I-Gos at this ruthless destruction, but no sound came to him from beyond the door, which was, he thought, too thick for the human voice to penetrate; but he would have wagered much that I-Gos heard him. Bits of the hard wood splintered at each impact of the heavy axe, but it was slow work and heavy. Presently he was compelled to rest, and so it went for what seemed hours – working almost to the verge of exhaustion and then resting for a few minutes; but ever the hole grew larger though he could see nothing of the interior of the room beyond because of the hanging that I-Gos had drawn across it after he had locked Turan within.

At last, however, the panthan had hewn an opening through which his body could pass, and seizing a long-sword that he had brought close to the door for the purpose he crawled through into the next room. Flinging aside the arras he stood ready, sword in hand, to fight his way to the side of Tara of Helium – but she was not there. In the center of the room lay I-Gos, dead upon the floor; but Tara of Helium was nowhere to be seen.

Turan was nonplussed. It must have been her hand that had struck down the old man, yet she had made no effort to release Turan from his prison. And then he thought of those last words of hers: "I do not want your love! I hate you," and the truth dawned upon him – she had seized upon this first opportunity to escape him. With downcast heart Turan turned away. What should he do? There could be but one answer. While he lived and she lived he must still leave no stone unturned to effect her escape and safe return to the land of her people. But how? How was he even to find his way from this labyrinth? How was he to find her again? He walked to the nearest doorway. It chanced to be that which led into the room containing the mounted dead, awaiting transportation to balcony or grim room or whatever place was to receive them. His eyes travelled to the great, painted warrior on the thoat and as they ran over the splendid trappings and the serviceable arms a new light came into the pain-dulled eyes of the panthan. With a quick step he crossed to the side of the dead warrior and dragged him from his mount. With equal celerity he stripped him of his harness and his arms, and tearing off his own, donned the regalia of the dead man. Then he hastened back to the room in which he had been trapped, for there he had seen that which he needed to make his disguise complete. In a cabinet he found them – pots of paint that the old taxidermist had used to place the war-paint in its wide bands across the cold faces of dead warriors.

A few moments later Gahan of Gathol emerged from the room a warrior of Manator in every detail of harness, equipment, and ornamentation. He had removed from the leather of the dead man the insignia of his house and rank so that he might pass, with the least danger of arousing suspicion, as a common warrior.

To search for Tara of Helium in the vast, dim labyrinth of the pits of O-Tar seemed to the Gatholian a hopeless quest, foredoomed to failure. It would be wiser to seek the streets of Manator where he might hope to learn first if she had been recaptured and, if not, then he could return to the pits and pursue the hunt for her. To find egress from the maze he must perforce travel a considerable distance through the winding corridors and chambers, since he had no idea as to the location or direction of any exit. In fact, he could not have retraced his steps a hundred yards toward the point at which he and Tara had entered the gloomy caverns, and so he set out in the hope that he might find by accident either Tara of Helium or a way to the street level above.

For a time he passed room after room filled with the cunningly preserved dead of Manator, many of which were piled in tiers after the manner that firewood is corded, and as he moved through corridor and chamber he noticed hieroglyphics painted upon the walls above every opening and at each fork or crossing of corridors, until by observation he reached the conclusion that these indicated the designations of passageways, so that one who understood them might travel quickly and surely through the pits; but Turan did not understand them. Even could he have read the language of Manator they might not materially have aided one unfamiliar with the city; but he could not read them at all since, though there is but one spoken language upon Barsoom, there are as many different written languages as there are nations. One thing, however, soon became apparent to him – the hieroglyphic of a corridor remained the same until the corridor ended.

It was not long before Turan realized from the distance that he had traveled that the pits were part of a vast system undermining, possibly, the entire city. At least he was convinced that he had passed beyond the precincts of the palace. The corridors and chambers varied in appearance and architecture from time to time. All were lighted, though usually quite dimly, with radium bulbs. For a long time he saw no signs of life other than an occasional ulsio, then quite suddenly he came face to face with a warrior at one of the numerous crossings. The fellow looked at him, nodded, and passed on. Turan breathed a sigh of relief as he realized that his disguise was effective, but he was caught in the middle of it by a hail from the warrior who had stopped and turned toward him. The panthan was glad that a sword hung at his side, and glad too that they were buried in the dim recesses of the pits and that there would be but a single antagonist, for time was precious.

"Heard you any word of the other?" called the warrior to him.

"No," replied Turan, who had not the faintest idea to whom or what the fellow referred.

"He cannot escape," continued the warrior. "The woman ran directly into our arms, but she swore that she knew not where her companion might be found."

"They took her back to O-Tar?" asked Turan, for now he knew whom the other meant, and he would know more.

"They took her back to The Towers of Jetan," replied the warrior. "Tomorrow the games commence and doubtless she will be played for, though I doubt if any wants her, beautiful as she is. She fears not even O-Tar. By Cluros! but she would make a hard slave to subdue – a regular she-banth she is. Not for me," and he continued on his way shaking his head.

Turan hurried on searching for an avenue that led to the level of the streets above when suddenly he came to the open doorway of a small chamber in which sat a man who was chained to the wall. Turan voiced a low exclamation of surprise and pleasure as he recognized that the man was A-Kor, and that he had stumbled by accident upon the very cell in which he had been imprisoned. A-Kor looked at him questioningly. It was evident that he did not recognize his fellow prisoner. Turan crossed to the table and leaning close to the other whispered to him.

"I am Turan the panthan," he said, "who was chained beside you."

A-Kor looked at him closely. "Your own mother would never know you!" he said; "but tell me, what has transpired since they took you away?"

Turan recounted his experiences in the throne room of O-Tar and in the pits beneath, "and now," he continued, "I must find these Towers of Jetan and see what may be done toward liberating the Princess of Helium."

A-Kor shook his head. "Long was I dwar of the Towers," he said, "and I can say to you, stranger, that you might as well attempt to reduce Manator, single handed, as to rescue a prisoner from The Towers of Jetan."

"But I must," replied Turan.

"Are you better than a good swordsman?" asked A-Kor presently.

"I am accounted so," replied Turan.

"Then there is a way – sst!" he was suddenly silent and pointing toward the base of the wall at the end of the room.

Turan looked in the direction the other's forefinger indicated, to see projecting from the mouth of an ulsio's burrow two large chelae and a pair of protruding eyes.

"Ghek!" he cried and immediately the hideous kaldane crawled out upon the floor and approached the table. A-Kor drew back with a half-stifled ejaculation of repulsion. "Do not fear," Turan reassured him. "It is my friend – he whom I told you held O-Tar while Tara and I escaped."

Ghek climbed to the table top and squatted between the two warriors. "You are safe in assuming," he said addressing A-Kor, "that Turan the panthan has no master in all Manator where the art of sword-play is concerned. I overheard your conversation – go on."

"You are his friend," continued A-Kor, "and so I may explain safely in your presence the only plan I know whereby he may hope to rescue the Princess of Helium. She is to be the stake of one of the games and it is O-Tar's desire that she be won by slaves and common warriors, since she repulsed him. Thus would he punish her. Not a single man, but all who survive upon the winning side are to possess her. With money, however, one may buy off the others before the game. That you could do, and if your side won and you survived she would become your slave."

"But how may a stranger and a hunted fugitive accomplish this?" asked Turan.

"No one will recognize you. You will go tomorrow to the keeper of the Towers and enlist in that game for which the girl is to be the stake, telling the keeper that you are from Manataj, the farthest city of Manator. If he questions you, you may say that you saw her when she was brought into the city after her capture. If you win her, you will find thoats stabled at my palace and you will carry from me a token that will place all that is mine at your disposal."

"But how can I buy off the others in the game without money?" asked Turan. "I have none – not even of my own country."

A-Kor opened his pocket-pouch and drew forth a packet of Manatorian money.

"Here is sufficient to buy them off twice over," he said, handing a portion of it to Turan.

"But why do you do this for a stranger?" asked the panthan.

"My mother was a captive princess here," replied A-Kor. "I but do for the Princess of Helium what my mother would have me do."

"Under the circumstances, then, Manatorian," replied Turan, "I cannot but accept your generosity on behalf of Tara of Helium and live in hope that some day I may do for you something in return."

"Now you must be gone," advised A-Kor. "At any minute a guard may come and discover you here. Go directly to the Avenue of Gates, which circles the city just within the outer wall. There you will find many places devoted to the lodging of strangers. You will know them by the thoat's head carved above the doors. Say that you are here from Manataj to witness the games. Take the name of U-Kal – it will arouse no suspicion, nor will you if you can avoid conversation. Early in the morning seek the keeper of The Towers of Jetan. May the strength and fortune of all your ancestors be with you!"

Bidding good-bye to Ghek and A-Kor, the panthan, following directions given him by A-Kor, set out to find his way to the Avenue of Gates, nor had he any great difficulty. On the way he met several warriors, but beyond a nod they gave him no heed. With ease he found a lodging place where there were many strangers from other cities of Manator. As he had had no sleep since the previous night he threw himself among the silks and furs of his couch to gain the rest which he must have, was he to give the best possible account of himself in the service of Tara of Helium the following day.

It was already morning when he awoke, and rising he paid for his lodgings, sought a place to eat, and a short time later was on his way toward The Towers of Jetan, which he had no difficulty in finding owing to the great crowds that were winding along the avenues toward the games.

The new keeper of The Towers who had succeeded E-Med was too busy to scrutinize entries closely, for in addition to the many volunteer players there were scores of slaves and prisoners being forced into the games by their owners or the government. The name of each must be recorded as well as the position he was to play and the game or games in which he was to be entered, and then there were the substitutes for each that was entered in more than a single game – one for each additional game that an individual was entered for, that no succeeding game might be delayed by the death or disablement of a player.

"Your name?" asked a clerk as Turan presented himself.

"U-Kal," replied the panthan.

"Your city?"

"Manataj."

The keeper, who was standing beside the clerk, looked at Turan. "You have come a great way to play at jetan," he said. "It is seldom that the men of Manataj attend other than the decennial games. Tell me of O-Zar! Will he attend next year? Ah, but he was a noble fighter. If you be half the swordsman, U-Kal, the fame of Manataj will increase this day. But tell me, what of O-Zar?"

"He is well," replied Turan, glibly, "and he sent greetings to his friends in Manator."

"Good!" exclaimed the keeper, "and now in what game would you enter?"

"I would play for the Heliumetic princess, Tara," replied Turan.

"But man, she is to be the stake of a game for slaves and criminals," cried the keeper. "You would not volunteer for such a game!"

"But I would," replied Turan. "I saw here when she was brought into the city and even then I vowed to possess her."

"But you will have to share her with the survivors even if your color wins," objected the other.

"They may be brought to reason," insisted Turan.

"And you will chance incurring the wrath of O-Tar, who has no love for this savage barbarian," explained the keeper.

"And I win her O-Tar will be rid of her," said Turan.

The keeper of The Towers of Jetan shook his head. "You are rash," he said. "I would that I might dissuade the friend of my friend O-Zar from such madness."

"Would you favor the friend of O-Zar?" asked Turan.

"Gladly!" exclaimed the other. "What may I do for him?"

"Make me chief of the Black and give me for my pieces all slaves from Gathol, for I understand that those be excellent warriors," replied the panthan.

"It is a strange request," said the keeper, "but for my friend O-Zar I would do even more, though of course – " he hesitated – "it is customary for one who would be chief to make some slight payment."

"Certainly," Turan hastened to assure him; "I had not forgotten that. I was about to ask you what the customary amount is."

"For the friend of my friend it shall be nominal," replied the keeper, naming a figure that Gahan, accustomed to the high price of wealthy Gathol, thought ridiculously low.

"Tell me," he said, handing the money to the keeper, "when the game for the Heliumite is to be played."

"It is the second in order of the day's games; and now if you will come with me you may select your pieces."

Turan followed the keeper to a large court which lay between the towers and the jetan field, where hundreds of warriors were assembled. Already chiefs for the games of the day were selecting their pieces and assigning them to positions, though for the principal games these matters had been arranged for weeks before. The keeper led Turan to a part of the courtyard where the majority of the slaves were assembled.

"Take your choice of those not assigned," said the keeper, "and when you have your quota conduct them to the field. Your place will be assigned you by an officer there, and there you will remain with your pieces until the second game is called. I wish you luck, U-Kal, though from what I have heard you will be more lucky to lose than to win the slave from Helium."

After the fellow had departed Turan approached the slaves. "I seek the best swordsmen for the second game," he announced. "Men from Gathol I wish, for I have heard that these be noble fighters."

A slave rose and approached him. "It is all the same in which game we die," he said. "I would fight for you as a panthan in the second game."

Another came. "I am not from Gathol," he said. "I am from Helium, and I would fight for the honor of a princess of Helium."

"Good!" exclaimed Turan. "Art a swordsman of repute in Helium?"

"I was a dwar under the great Warlord, and I have fought at his side in a score of battles from The Golden Cliffs to The Carrion Caves. My name is Val Dor. Who knows Helium, knows my prowess."

The name was well known to Gahan, who had heard the man spoken of on his last visit to Helium, and his mysterious disappearance discussed as well as his renown as a fighter.

"How could I know aught of Helium?" asked Turan; "but if you be such a fighter as you say no position could suit you better than that of Flier. What say you?"

The man's eyes denoted sudden surprise. He looked keenly at Turan, his eyes running quickly over the other's harness. Then he stepped quite close so that his words might not be overheard.

"Methinks you may know more of Helium than of Manator," he whispered.

"What mean you, fellow?" demanded Turan, seeking to cudgel his brains for the source of this man's knowledge, guess, or inspiration.

"I mean," replied Val Dor, "that you are not of Manator and that if you wish to hide the fact it is well that you speak not to a Manatorian as you did just speak to me of – Fliers! There be no Fliers in Manator and no piece in their game of Jetan bearing that name. Instead they call him who stands next to the Chief or Princess, Odwar. The piece has the same moves and power that the Flier has in the game as played outside Manator. Remember this then and remember, too, that if you have a secret it be safe in the keeping of Val Dor of Helium."

Turan made no reply but turned to the task of selecting the remainder of his pieces. Val Dor, the Heliumite, and Floran, the volunteer from Gathol, were of great assistance to him, since one or the other of them knew most of the slaves from whom his selection was to be made. The pieces all chosen, Turan led them to the place beside the playing field where they were to wait their turn, and here he passed the word around that they were to fight for more than the stake he offered for the princess should they win. This stake they accepted, so that Turan was sure of possessing Tara if his side was victorious, but he knew that these men would fight even more valorously for chivalry than for money, nor was it difficult to enlist the interest even of the Gatholians in the service of the princess. And now he held out the possibility of a still further reward.

"I cannot promise you," he explained, "but I may say I have heard that this day which makes it possible that should we win this game we may even win your freedom!"

They leaped to their feet and crowded around him with many questions.

"It may not be spoken of aloud," he said; "but Floran and Val Dor know and they assure me that you may all be trusted. Listen! What I would tell you places my life in your hands, but you must know that every man will realize that he is fighting today the greatest battle of his life – for the honor and the freedom of Barsoom's most wondrous princess and for his own freedom as well – for the chance to return each to his own country and to the woman who awaits him there.

"First, then, is my secret. I am not of Manator. Like yourselves I am a slave, though for the moment disguised as a Manatorian from Manataj.

My country and my identity must remain undisclosed for reasons that have no bearing upon our game today. I, then, am one of you. I fight for the same things that you will fight for.

"And now for that which I have but just learned. U-Thor, the great jed of Manatos, quarreled with O-Tar in the palace the day before yesterday and their warriors set upon one another. U-Thor was driven as far as The Gate of Enemies, where he now lies encamped. At any moment the fight may be renewed; but it is thought that U-Thor has sent to Manatos for reinforcements. Now, men of Gathol, here is the thing that interests you. U-Thor has recently taken to wife the Princess Haja of Gathol, who was slave to O-Tar and whose son, A-Kor, was dwar of The Towers of Jetan. Haja's heart is filled with loyalty for Gathol and compassion for her sons who are here enslaved, and this latter sentiment she has to some extent transmitted to U-Thor. Aid me, therefore, in freeing the Princess Tara of Helium and I believe that I can aid you and her and myself to escape the city. Bend close your ears, slaves of O-Tar, that no cruel enemy may hear my words," and Gahan of Gathol whispered in low tones the daring plan he had conceived. "And now," he demanded, when he had finished, "let him who does not dare speak now." None replied. "Is there none?"

"And it would not betray you should I cast my sword at thy feet, it had been done ere this," said one in low tones pregnant with suppressed feeling.

"And I!" "And I!" "And I!" chorused the others in vibrant whispers.

CHAPTER SEVENTEEN

A Play to the Death

CLEAR AND SWEET a trumpet spoke across The Fields of Jetan. From The High Tower its cool voice floated across the city of Manator and above the babel of human discords rising from the crowded mass that filled the seats of the stadium below. It called the players for the first game, and simultaneously there fluttered to the peaks of a thousand staffs on tower and battlement and the great wall of the stadium the rich, gay pennons of the fighting chiefs of Manator. Thus was marked the opening of The Jeddak's Games, the most important of the year and second only to the Grand Decennial Games.

Gahan of Gathol watched every play with eagle eye. The match was an unimportant one, being but to settle some petty dispute between two chiefs, and was played with professional jetan players for points only. No one was killed and there was but little blood spilled. It lasted about an hour and was terminated by the chief of the losing side deliberately permitting himself to be out-pointed, that the game might be called a draw.

Again the trumpet sounded, this time announcing the second and last game of the afternoon. While this was not considered an important match, those being reserved for the fourth and fifth days of the games, it promised to afford sufficient excitement since it was a game to the death. The vital difference between the game played with living men and that in which inanimate pieces are used, lies in the fact that while in the latter the mere placing of a piece upon a square occupied by an opponent piece terminates the move, in the former the two pieces thus brought together engage in a duel for possession of the square. Therefore there enters into the former game not only the strategy of jetan but the personal prowess and bravery of each individual piece, so that a knowledge not only of one's own men but of each player upon the opposing side is of vast value to a chief.

In this respect was Gahan handicapped, though the loyalty of his players did much to offset his ignorance of them, since they aided him in arranging the board to the best advantage and told him honestly the faults and virtues of each. One fought best in a losing game; another was too slow; another too impetuous; this one had fire and a heart of steel, but lacked endurance. Of the opponents, though, they knew little or nothing, and now as the two sides took their places upon the black and orange squares of the great jetan board Gahan obtained, for the first time, a close view of those who opposed him. The Orange Chief had not yet entered the field, but his men were all in place. Val Dor turned to Gahan. "They are all criminals from the pits of Manator," he said. "There is no slave among them. We shall not have to fight against a single fellow-countryman and every life we take will be the life of an enemy."

"It is well," replied Gahan; "but where is their Chief, and where the two Princesses?"

"They are coming now, see?" and he pointed across the field to where two women could be seen approaching under guard.

As they came nearer Gahan saw that one was indeed Tara of Helium, but the other he did not recognize, and then they were brought to the center of the field midway between the two sides and there waited until the Orange Chief arrived.

Floran voiced an exclamation of surprise when he recognized him. "By my first ancestor if it is not one of their great chiefs," he said, "and we were told that slaves and criminals were to play for the stake of this game."

His words were interrupted by the keeper of The Towers whose duty it was not only to announce the games and the stakes, but to act as referee as well.

"Of this, the second game of the first day of the Jeddak's Games in the four hundred and thirty-third year of O-Tar, Jeddak of Manator, the Princesses of each side shall be the sole stakes and to the survivors of the winning side shall belong both the Princesses, to do with as they shall see fit. The Orange Princess is the slave woman Lan-O of Gathol; the Black Princess is the slave woman Tara, a princess of Helium. The Black Chief is U-Kal of Manataj, a volunteer player; the Orange Chief is the dwar U-Dor of the 8th Utan of the jeddak of Manator, also a volunteer player. The squares shall be contested to the death. Just are the laws of Manator! I have spoken."

The initial move was won by U-Dor, following which the two Chiefs escorted their respective Princesses to the square each was to occupy. It was the first time Gahan had been alone with Tara since she had been brought upon the field. He saw her scrutinizing him closely as he approached to lead her to her place and wondered if she recognized him: but if she did she gave no sign of it. He could not but remember her last words – "I hate you!" and her desertion of him when he had been locked in the room beneath the palace by I-Gos, the taxidermist, and so he did not seek to enlighten her as to his identity. He meant to fight for her – to die for her, if necessary – and if he did not die to go on fighting to the end for her love. Gahan of Gathol was not easily to be discouraged, but he was compelled to admit that his chances of winning the love of Tara of Helium were remote. Already had she repulsed him twice. Once as jed of Gathol and again as Turan the panthan. Before his love, however, came her safety and the former must be relegated to the background until the latter had been achieved.

Passing among the players already at their stations the two took their places upon their respective squares. At Tara's left was the Black Chief, Gahan of Gathol; directly in front of her the Princess' Panthan, Floran of Gathol; and at her right the Princess' Odwar, Val Dor of Helium. And each of these knew the part that he was to play, win or lose, as did each of the other Black players. As Tara took her place Val Dor bowed low. "My sword is at your feet, Tara of Helium," he said.

She turned and looked at him, an expression of surprise and incredulity upon her face. "Val Dor, the dwar!" she exclaimed. "Val Dor of Helium – one of my father's trusted captains! Can it be possible that my eyes speak the truth?"

"It is Val Dor, Princess," the warrior replied, "and here to die for you if need be, as is every wearer of the Black upon this field of jetan today. Know Princess," he whispered, "that upon this side is no man of Manator, but each and every is an enemy of Manator."

She cast a quick, meaning glance toward Gahan. "But what of him?" she whispered, and then she caught her breath quickly in surprise. "Shade of the first jeddak!" she exclaimed. "I did but just recognize him through his disguise."

"And you trust him?" asked Val Dor. "I know him not; but he spoke fairly, as an honorable warrior, and we have taken him at his word."

"You have made no mistake," replied Tara of Helium. "I would trust him with my life – with my soul; and you, too, may trust him."

Happy indeed would have been Gahan of Gathol could he have heard those words; but Fate, who is usually unkind to the lover in such matters, ordained it otherwise, and then the game was on.

U-Dor moved his Princess' Odwar three squares diagonally to the right, which placed the piece upon the Black Chief's Odwar's seventh. The move was indicative of the game that U-Dor intended playing – a game of blood, rather than of science – and evidenced his contempt for his opponents.

Gahan followed with his Odwar's Panthan one square straight forward, a more scientific move, which opened up an avenue for himself through his line of Panthans, as well as announcing to the players and spectators that he intended having a hand in the fighting himself even before the exigencies of the game forced it upon him. The move elicited a ripple of applause from those sections of seats reserved for the common warriors and their women, showing perhaps that U-Dor was none too popular with these, and, too, it had its effect upon the morale of Gahan's pieces. A Chief may, and often does, play almost an entire game without leaving his own square, where, mounted upon a thoat, he may overlook the entire field and direct each move, nor may he be reproached for lack of courage should he elect thus to play the game since, by the rules, were he to be slain or so badly wounded as to be compelled to withdraw, a game that might otherwise have been won by the science of his play and the prowess of his men would be drawn. To invite personal combat, therefore, denotes confidence in his own swordsmanship, and great courage, two attributes that were calculated to fill the Black players with hope and valor when evinced by their Chief thus early in the game.

U-Dor's next move placed Lan-O's Odwar upon Tara's Odwar's fourth – within striking distance of the Black Princess.

Another move and the game would be lost to Gahan unless the Orange Odwar was overthrown, or Tara moved to a position of safety; but to move his Princess now would be to admit his belief in the superiority of the Orange. In the three squares allowed him he could not place himself squarely upon the square occupied by the Odwar of U-Dor's Princess. There was only one player upon the Black side that might dispute the square with the enemy and that was the Chief's Odwar, who stood upon Gahan's left. Gahan turned upon his thoat and looked at the man. He was a splendid looking fellow, resplendent in the gorgeous trappings of an Odwar, the five brilliant feathers which denoted his position rising defiantly erect from his thick, black hair. In common with every player upon the field and every spectator in the crowded stands he knew what was passing in his Chief's mind. He dared not speak, the ethics of the game forbade it, but what his lips might not voice his eyes expressed in martial fire, and eloquently: "The honor of the Black and the safety of our Princess are secure with me!"

Gahan hesitated no longer. "Chief's Odwar to Princess' Odwar's fourth!" he commanded. It was the courageous move of a leader who had taken up the gauntlet thrown down by his opponent.

The warrior sprang forward and leaped into the square occupied by U-Dor's piece. It was the first disputed square of the game. The eyes of the players were fastened upon the contestants, the spectators leaned forward in their seats after the first applause that had greeted the move, and silence fell upon the vast assemblage. If the Black went down to defeat, U-Dor could move his victorious piece on to the square occupied by Tara of Helium and the game would be over – over in four moves and lost to Gahan of Gathol. If the Orange lost U-Dor would have sacrificed one of his most important pieces and more than lost what advantage the first move might have given him.

Physically the two men appeared perfectly matched and each was fighting for his life, but from the first it was apparent that the Black Odwar was the better swordsman, and Gahan knew that he had another and perhaps a greater advantage over his antagonist. The latter was fighting for his life only, without the spur of chivalry or loyalty. The Black Odwar had these to strengthen his arm, and besides these the knowledge of the thing that Gahan had whispered into the ears of his players before the game, and so he fought for what is more than life to the man of honor.

It was a duel that held those who witnessed it in spellbound silence. The weaving blades gleamed in the brilliant sunlight, ringing to the parries of cut and thrust. The barbaric harness of the duelists lent splendid color to the savage, martial scene. The Orange Odwar, forced upon the defensive, was fighting madly for his life. The Black, with cool and terrible efficiency, was forcing him steadily, step by step, into a corner of the square – a position from which there could be no escape. To abandon the square was to lose it to his opponent and win for himself ignoble and immediate death before the jeering populace. Spurred on by the seeming hopelessness of his plight, the Orange Odwar burst into a sudden fury of offense that forced the Black back a half dozen steps, and then the sword of U-Dor's piece leaped in and drew first blood, from the shoulder of his merciless opponent. An ill-smothered cry of encouragement went up from U-Dor's men; the Orange Odwar, encouraged by his single success, sought to bear down the Black by the rapidity of his attack. There was a moment in which the swords moved with a rapidity that no man's eye might follow, and then the Black Odwar made a lightning parry of a vicious thrust, leaned quickly forward into the opening he had effected, and drove his sword through the heart of the Orange Odwar – to the hilt he drove it through the body of the Orange Odwar.

A shout arose from the stands, for wherever may have been the favor of the spectators, none there was who could say that it had not been a pretty fight, or that the better man had not won. And from the Black players came a sigh of relief as they relaxed from the tension of the past moments.

I shall not weary you with the details of the game – only the high features of it are necessary to your understanding of the outcome. The fourth move after the victory of the Black Odwar found Gahan upon U-Dor's fourth; an Orange Panthan was on the adjoining square diagonally to his right and the only opposing piece that could engage him other than U-Dor himself.

It had been apparent to both players and spectators for the past two moves, that Gahan was moving straight across the field into the enemy's country to seek personal combat with the Orange Chief – that he was staking all upon his belief in the superiority of his own swordsmanship, since if the two Chiefs engage, the outcome decides the game. U-Dor could move out and engage Gahan, or he could move his Princess' Panthan upon the square occupied by Gahan in he hope that the former would defeat the Black Chief and thus draw the game, which is the outcome if any other than a Chief slays the opposing Chief, or he could move away and escape, temporarily, the necessity for personal combat, or at least that is evidently what he had in mind as was obvious to all who saw him scanning the board about him; and his disappointment was apparent when he finally discovered that Gahan had so placed himself that there was no square to which U-Dor could move that it was not within Gahan's power to reach at his own next move.

U-Dor had placed his own Princess four squares east of Gahan when her position had been threatened, and he had hoped to lure the Black Chief after her and away from U-Dor; but in that he had failed. He now discovered that he might play his own Odwar into personal combat with Gahan; but he had already lost one Odwar and could ill spare the other. His position was a delicate one, since he did not wish to engage Gahan personally, while it appeared that there was little likelihood of his being able to escape. There was just one hope and that lay in his Princess' Panthan, so, without more deliberation he ordered the piece onto the square occupied by the Black Chief.

The sympathies of the spectators were all with Gahan now. If he lost, the game would be declared a draw, nor do they think better of drawn games upon Barsoom than do Earth men. If he won, it would doubtless mean a duel between the two Chiefs, a development for which they all were hoping. The game already bade fair to be a short one and it would be an angry crowd should it be decided a draw with only two men slain.

There were great, historic games on record where of the forty pieces on the field when the game opened only three survived – the two Princesses and the victorious Chief.

They blamed U-Dor, though in fact he was well within his rights in directing his play as he saw fit, nor was a refusal on his part to engage the Black Chief necessarily an imputation of cowardice. He was a great chief who had conceived a notion to possess the slave Tara. There was no honor that could accrue to him from engaging in combat with slaves and criminals, or an unknown warrior from Manataj, nor was the stake of sufficient import to warrant the risk.

But now the duel between Gahan and the Orange Panthan was on and the decision of the next move was no longer in other hands than theirs. It was the first time that these Manatorians had seen Gahan of Gathol fight, but Tara of Helium knew that he was master of his sword. Could he have seen the proud light in her eyes as he crossed blades with the wearer of the Orange, he might easily have wondered if they were the same eyes that had flashed fire and hatred at him that time he had covered her lips with mad kisses, in the pits of the palace of O-Tar. As she watched him she could not but compare his swordplay with that of the greatest swordsman of two worlds – her father, John Carter, of Virginia, a Prince of Helium, Warlord of Barsoom – and she knew that the skill of the Black Chief suffered little by the comparison.

Short and to the point was the duel that decided possession of the Orange Chief's fourth. The spectators had settled themselves for an interesting engagement of at least average duration when they were brought almost standing by a brilliant flash of rapid swordplay that was over ere one could catch his breath. They saw the Black Chief step quickly back, his point upon the ground, while his opponent, his sword slipping from his fingers, clutched his breast, sank to his knees and then lunged forward upon his face.

And then Gahan of Gathol turned his eyes directly upon U-Dor of Manator, three squares away. Three squares is a Chief's move – three squares in any direction or combination of directions, only provided that he does not cross the same square twice in a given move. The people saw and guessed Gahan's intention. They rose and roared forth their approval as he moved deliberately across the intervening squares toward the Orange Chief.

O-Tar, in the royal enclosure, sat frowning upon the scene. O-Tar was angry. He was angry with U-Dor for having entered this game for possession of a slave, for whom it had been his wish only slaves and criminals should strive. He was angry with the warrior from Manataj for having so far out-generaled and out-fought the men from Manator. He was angry with the populace because of their open hostility toward one who had basked in the sunshine of his favor for long years. O-Tar the jeddak had not enjoyed the afternoon. Those who surrounded him were equally glum – they, too, scowled upon the field, the players, and the people. Among them was a bent and wrinkled old man who gazed through weak and watery eyes upon the field and the players.

As Gahan entered his square, U-Dor leaped toward him with drawn sword with such fury as might have overborne a less skilled and powerful swordsman. For a minute the fighting was fast and furious and by comparison reducing to insignificance all that had gone before. Here indeed were two magnificent swordsmen, and here was to be a battle that bade fair to make up for whatever the people felt they had been defrauded of by the shortness of the game. Nor had it continued long before many there were who would have prophesied that they were witnessing a duel that was to become historic in the annals of jetan at Manator. Every trick, every subterfuge, known to the art of fence these men employed. Time and again each scored a point and brought blood to his opponent's copper hide until both were red with gore; but neither seemed able to administer the coup de grace.

From her position upon the opposite side of the field Tara of Helium watched the long-drawn battle. Always it seemed to her that the Black Chief fought upon the defensive, or when he assumed to push his opponent, he neglected a thousand openings that her practiced eye beheld. Never did he seem in real danger, nor never did he appear to exert himself to quite the pitch needful for victory. The duel already had been long contested and the day was drawing to a close. Presently the sudden transition from daylight to darkness which, owing to the tenuity of the air upon Barsoom, occurs almost without the warning twilight of Earth, would occur. Would the fight never end? Would the game be called a draw after all? What ailed the Black Chief?

Tara wished that she might answer at least the last of these questions for she was sure that Turan the panthan, as she knew him, while fighting brilliantly, was not giving of himself all that he might. She could not believe that fear was restraining his hand, but that there was something beside inability to push U-Dor more fiercely she was confident. What it was, however, she could not guess.

Once she saw Gahan glance quickly up toward the sinking sun. In thirty minutes it would be dark. And then she saw and all those others saw a strange transition steal over the swordplay of the Black Chief. It was as though he had been playing with the great dwar, U-Dor, all

these hours, and now he still played with him but there was a difference. He played with him terribly as a carnivore plays with its victim
in the instant before the kill. The Orange Chief was helpless now in the
hands of a swordsman so superior that there could be no comparison,
and the people sat in open-mouthed wonder and awe as Gahan of
Gathol cut his foe to ribbons and then struck him down with a blow
that cleft him to the chin.

In twenty minutes the sun would set. But what of that?

CHAPTER EIGHTEEN

A Task for Loyalty

LONG AND LOUD was the applause that rose above the Field of Jetan at Manator, as The Keeper of the Towers summoned the two Princesses and the victorious Chief to the center of the field and presented to the latter the fruits of his prowess, and then, as custom demanded, the victorious players, headed by Gahan and the two Princesses, formed in procession behind The Keeper of the Towers and were conducted to the place of victory before the royal enclosure that they might receive the commendation of the jeddak. Those who were mounted gave up their thoats to slaves as all must be on foot for this ceremony. Directly beneath the royal enclosure are the gates to one of the tunnels that, passing beneath the seats, give ingress or egress to or from the Field. Before this gate the party halted while O-Tar looked down upon them from above. Val Dor and Floran, passing quietly ahead of the others, went directly to the gates, where they were hidden from those who occupied the enclosure with O-Tar. The Keeper of the Towers may have noticed them, but so occupied was he with the formality of presenting the victorious Chief to the jeddak that he paid no attention to them.

"I bring you, O-Tar, Jeddak of Manator, U-Kal of Manataj," he cried in a loud voice that might be heard by as many as possible, "victor over the Orange in the second of the Jeddak's Games of the four hundred and thirty-third year of O-Tar, and the slave woman Tara and the slave woman Lan-O that you may bestow these, the stakes, upon U-Kal."

As he spoke, a little, wrinkled, old man peered over the rail of the enclosure down upon the three who stood directly behind The Keeper, and strained his weak and watery eyes in an effort to satisfy the curiosity of old age in a matter of no particular import, for what were two slaves and a common warrior from Manataj to any who sat with O-Tar the jeddak?

"U-Kal of Manataj," said O-Tar, "you have deserved the stakes. Seldom have we looked upon more noble swordplay. And you tire of Manataj there be always here in the city of Manator a place for you in The Jeddak's Guard."

While the jeddak was speaking the little, old man, failing clearly to discern the features of the Black Chief, reached into his pocket-pouch and drew forth a pair of thick-lensed spectacles, which he placed upon his nose. For a moment he scrutinized Gahan closely, then he leaped to his feet and addressing O-Tar pointed a shaking finger it Gahan. As he rose Tara of Helium clutched the Black Chief's arm.

"Turan!" she whispered. "It is I-Gos, whom I thought to have slain in the pits of O-Tar. It is I-Gos and he recognizes you and will – "

But what I-Gos would do was already transpiring. In his falsetto voice he fairly screamed: "It is the slave Turan who stole the woman Tara from your throne room, O-Tar. He desecrated the dead chief I-Mal and wears his harness now!"

Instantly all was pandemonium. Warriors drew their swords and leaped to their feet. Gahan's victorious players rushed forward in a body, sweeping The Keeper of the Towers from his feet. Val Dor and Floran threw open the gates beneath the royal enclosure, opening the tunnel that led to the avenue in the city beyond the Towers. Gahan, surrounded by his men, drew Tara and Lan-O into the passageway, and at a rapid pace the party sought to reach the opposite end of the tunnel before their escape could be cut off. They were successful and when they emerged into the city the sun had set and darkness had come, relieved only by an antiquated and ineffective lighting system, which cast but a pale glow over the shadowy streets.

Now it was that Tara of Helium guessed why the Black Chief had drawn out his duel with U-Dor and realized that he might have slain his man at almost any moment he had elected. The whole plan that Gahan had whispered to his players before the game was thoroughly understood. They were to make their way to The Gate of Enemies and there offer their services to U-Thor, the great Jed of Manatos. The fact that most of them were Gatholians and that Gahan could lead rescuers to the pit where A-Kor, the son of U-Thor's wife, was confined, convinced the Jed of Gathol that they would meet with no rebuff at the hands of U-Thor. But even should he refuse them, still were they bound together to go on toward freedom, if necessary cutting their way through the forces of U-Thor at The Gate of Enemies – twenty men against a small army; but of such stuff are the warriors of Barsoom.

They had covered a considerable distance along the almost deserted avenue before signs of pursuit developed and then there came upon them suddenly from behind a dozen warriors mounted on thoats – a detachment, evidently, from The Jeddak's Guard. Instantly the avenue was a pandemonium of clashing blades, cursing warriors, and squealing thoats. In the first onslaught life blood was spilled upon both sides. Two of Gahan's men went down, and upon the enemies' side three riderless thoats attested at least a portion of their casualties.

Gahan was engaged with a fellow who appeared to have been selected to account for him only, since he rode straight for him and sought to cut him down without giving the slightest heed to several who slashed at him as he passed them. The Gatholian, practiced in the art of combating a mounted warrior from the ground, sought to reach the left side of the fellow's thoat a little to the rider's rear, the only position in which he would have any advantage over his antagonist, or rather the position that would most greatly reduce the advantage of the mounted man, and, similarly, the Manatorian strove to thwart his design. And so the guardsman wheeled and turned his vicious, angry mount while Gahan leaped in and out in an effort to reach the coveted vantage point, but always seeking some other opening in his foe's defense.

And while they jockeyed for position a rider swept swiftly past them. As he passed behind Gahan the latter heard a cry of alarm.

"Turan, they have me!" came to his ears in the voice of Tara of Helium.

A quick glance across his shoulder showed him the galloping thoatman in the act of dragging Tara to the withers of the beast, and then, with the fury of a demon, Gahan of Gathol leaped for his own man, dragged him from his mount and as he fell smote his head from his shoulders with a single cut of his keen sword. Scarce had the body touched the pavement when the Gatholian was upon the back of the dead warrior's mount, and galloping swiftly down the avenue after the diminishing figures of Tara and her abductor, the sounds of the fight waning in the distance as he pursued his quarry along the avenue that passes the palace of O-Tar and leads to The Gate of Enemies.

Gahan's mount, carrying but a single rider, gained upon that of the Manatorian, so that as they neared the palace Gahan was scarce a hundred yards behind, and now, to his consternation, he saw the fellow turn into the great entrance-way. For a moment only was he halted by the guards and then he disappeared within. Gahan was almost upon him then, but evidently he had warned the guards, for they leaped out to intercept the Gatholian. But no! the fellow could not have known that he was pursued, since he had not seen Gahan seize a mount, nor would he have thought that pursuit would come so soon. If he had passed then, so could Gahan pass, for did he not wear the trappings of a Manatorian? The Gatholian thought quickly, and stopping his thoat called to the guardsmen to let him pass, "In the name of O-Tar!" They hesitated a moment.

"Aside!" cried Gahan. "Must the jeddak's messenger parley for the right to deliver his message?"

"To whom would you deliver it?" asked the padwar of the guard.

"Saw you not him who just entered?" cried Gahan, and without waiting for a reply urged his thoat straight past them into the palace, and while they were deliberating what was best to be done, it was too late to do anything – which is not unusual.

Along the marble corridors Gahan guided his thoat, and because he had gone that way before, rather than because he knew which way Tara had been taken, he followed the runways and passed through the chambers that led to the throne room of O-Tar. On the second level he met a slave.

"Which way went he who carried the woman before him?" he asked.

The slave pointed toward a nearby runway that led to the third level and Gahan dashed rapidly on in pursuit. At the same moment a thoat-man, riding at a furious pace, approached the palace and halted his mount at the gate.

"Saw you aught of a warrior pursuing one who carried a woman before him on his thoat?" he shouted to the guard.

"He but just passed in," replied the padwar, "saying that he was O-Tar's messenger."

"He lied," cried the newcomer. "He was Turan, the slave, who stole the woman from the throne room two days since. Arouse the palace! He must be seized, and alive if possible. It is O-Tar's command."

Instantly warriors were dispatched to search for the Gatholian and warn the inmates of the palace to do likewise. Owing to the games there were comparatively few retainers in the great building, but those whom they found were immediately enlisted in the search, so that presently at least fifty warriors were seeking through the countless chambers and corridors of the palace of O-Tar.

As Gahan's thoat bore him to the third Level the man glimpsed the hind quarters of another thoat disappearing at the turn of a corridor far ahead. Urging his own animal forward he raced swiftly in pursuit and making the turn discovered only an empty corridor ahead. Along this he hurried to discover near its farther end a runway to the fourth level, which he followed upward. Here he saw that he had gained upon his quarry who was just turning through a doorway fifty yards ahead. As Gahan reached the opening he saw that the warrior had dismounted and was dragging Tara toward a small door on the opposite side of the chamber. At the same instant the clank of harness to his rear caused him to cast a glance behind where, along the corridor he had just traversed, he saw three warriors approaching on foot at a run. Leaping from his thoat Gahan sprang into the chamber where Tara was struggling to free herself from the grasp of her captor, slammed the door behind him, shot the great bolt into its seat, and drawing his sword crossed the room at a run to engage the Manatorian. The fellow, thus menaced, called aloud to Gahan to halt, at the same time thrusting Tara at arm's length and threatening her heart with the point of his short-sword.

"Stay!" he cried, "or the woman dies, for such is the command of O-Tar, rather than that she again fall into your hands."

Gahan stopped. But a few feet separated him from Tara and her captor, yet he was helpless to aid her. Slowly the warrior backed toward the open doorway behind him, dragging Tara with him. The girl struggled and fought, but the warrior was a powerful man and having seized her by the harness from behind was able to hold her in a position of helplessness.

"Save me, Turan!" she cried. "Let them not drag me to a fate worse than death. Better that I die now while my eyes behold a brave friend than later, fighting alone among enemies in defense of my honor."

He took a step nearer. The warrior made a threatening gesture with his sword close to the soft, smooth skin of the princess, and Gahan halted.

"I cannot, Tara of Helium," he cried. "Think not ill of me that I am weak – that I cannot see you die. Too great is my love for you, daughter of Helium."

The Manatorian warrior, a derisive grin upon his lips, backed steadily away. He had almost reached the doorway when Gahan saw another warrior in the chamber toward which Tara was being borne – a fellow who moved silently, almost stealthily, across the marble floor as he approached Tara's captor from behind. In his right hand he grasped a long-sword.

"Two to one," thought Gahan, and a grim smile touched his lips, for he had no doubt that once they had Tara safely in the adjoining chamber the two would set upon him. If he could not save her, he could at least die for her.

And then, suddenly, Gahan's eyes fastened with amazement upon the figure of the warrior behind the grinning fellow who held Tara and was forcing her to the doorway. He saw the newcomer step almost within arm's reach of the other. He saw him stop, an expression of malevolent hatred upon his features. He saw the great sword swing through the arc of a great circle, gathering swift and terrific momentum from its own weight backed by the brawn of the steel thews that guided it; he saw it pass through the feathered skull of the Manatorian, splitting his sardonic grin in twain, and open him to the middle of his breast bone.

As the dead hand relaxed its grasp upon Tara's wrist the girl leaped forward, without a backward glance, to Gahan's side. His left arm encircled her, nor did she draw away, as with ready sword the Gatholian awaited Fate's next decree. Before them Tara's deliverer was wiping the blood from his sword upon the hair of his victim. He was evidently a Manatorian, his trappings those of the Jeddak's Guard, and so his act was inexplicable to Gahan and to Tara. Presently he sheathed his sword and approached them.

"When a man chooses to hide his identity behind an assumed name," he said, looking straight into Gahan's eyes, "whatever friend pierces the deception were no friend if he divulged the other's secret."

He paused as though awaiting a reply.

"Your integrity has perceived and your lips voiced an unalterable truth," replied Gahan, whose mind was filled with wonder if the implication could by any possibility be true – that this Manatorian had guessed his identity.

"We are thus agreed," continued the other, "and I may tell you that though I am here known as A-Sor, my real name is Tasor." He paused and watched Gahan's face intently for any sign of the effect of this knowledge and was rewarded with a quick, though guarded expression of recognition.

Tasor! Friend of his youth. The son of that great Gatholian noble who had given his life so gloriously, however futilely, in an attempt to defend Gahan's sire from the daggers of the assassins. Tasor an under-padwar in the guard of O-Tar, Jeddak of Manator! It was inconceivable – and yet it was he; there could be no doubt of it. "Tasor," Gahan repeated aloud. "But it is no Manatorian name." The statement was half interrogatory, for Gahan's curiosity was aroused. He would know how his friend and loyal subject had become a Manatorian. Long years had passed since Tasor had disappeared as mysteriously as the Princess Haja and many other of Gahan's subjects. The Jed of Gathol had long supposed him dead.

"No," replied Tasor, "nor is it a Manatorian name. Come, while I search for a hiding place for you in some forgotten chamber in one of the untenanted portions of the palace, and as we go I will tell you briefly how Tasor the Gatholian became A-Sor the Manatorian."

"It befell that as I rode with a dozen of my warriors along the western border of Gathol searching for zitidars that had strayed from my herds, we were set upon and surrounded by a great company of Manatorians. They overpowered us, though not before half our number was slain and the balance helpless from wounds. And so I was brought a prisoner to Manataj, a distant city of Manator, and there sold into slavery. A woman bought me – a princess of Manataj whose wealth and position were un-equaled in the city of her birth. She loved me and when her husband dis-covered her infatuation she beseeched me to slay him, and when I refused she hired another to do it. Then she married me; but none would have aught to do with her in Manataj, for they suspected her guilty knowledge of her husband's murder. And so we set out from Manataj for Manatos accompanied by a great caravan bearing all her worldly goods and jewels and precious metals, and on the way she caused the rumor to be spread that she and I had died. Then we came to Manator instead, she taking a new name and I the name A-Sor, that we might not be traced through our names. With her great wealth she bought me a post in The Jeddak's Guard and none knows that I am not a Manatorian, for she is dead. She was beautiful, but she was a devil."

"And you never sought to return to your native city?" asked Gahan.

"Never has the hope been absent from my heart, or my mind empty of a plan," replied Tasor. "I dream of it by day and by night, but always must I return to the same conclusion – that there can be but a single means for escape. I must wait until Fortune favors me with a place in a raiding party to Gathol. Then, once within the boundaries of my own country, they shall see me no more."

"Perhaps your opportunity lies already within your grasp," said Gahan, "has not your fealty to your own Jed been undermined by years of association with the men of Manator." The statement was half challenge.

"And my Jed stood before me now," cried Tasor, "and my avowal could be made without violating his confidence, I should cast my sword at his feet and beg the high privilege of dying for him as my sire died for his sire."

There could be no doubt of his sincerity nor any that he was cog-nizant of Gahan's identity. The Jed of Gathol smiled. "And if your Jed were here there is little doubt but that he would command you to de-vote your talents and your prowess to the rescue of the Princess Tara of Helium," he said, meaningly. "And he possessed the knowledge I have gained during my captivity he would say to you, 'Go, Tasor, to the pit where A-kor, son of Haja of Gathol, is confined and set him free and with him arouse the slaves from Gathol and march to The Gate of Enemies and offer your services to U-Thor of Manataj, who is wed to Haja of Gathol, and ask of him in return that he attack the palace of O-Tar and rescue Tara of Helium and when that thing is accomplished that he free the slaves of Gathol and furnish them with the arms and the means to return to their own country.' That, Tasor of Gathol, is what Gahan your Jed would demand of you."

"And that, Turan the slave, is what I shall bend my every effort to accomplish after I have found a safe refuge for Tara of Helium and her panthan," replied Tasor.

Gahan's glance carried to Tasor an intimation of his Jed's gratification and filled him with a chivalrous determination to do the thing required of him, or die, for he considered that he had received from the lips of his beloved ruler a commission that placed upon his shoulders a responsibility that encompassed not alone the life of Gahan and Tara but the welfare, perhaps the whole future, of Gathol. And so he hastened them onward through the musty corridors of the old palace where the dust of ages lay undisturbed upon the marble tiles. Now and again he tried a door until he found one that was unlocked. Opening it he ushered them into a chamber, heavy with dust. Crumbling silks and furs adorned the walls, with ancient weapons, and great paintings whose colors were toned by age to wondrous softness.

"This be as good as any place," he said. "No one comes here. Never have I been here before, so I know no more of the other chambers than you; but this one, at least, I can find again when I bring you food and drink. O-Mai the Cruel occupied this portion of the palace during his reign, five thousand years before O-Tar. In one of these apartments he was found dead, his face contorted in an expression of fear so horrible that it drove to madness those who looked upon it; yet there was no mark of violence upon him. Since then the quarters of O-Mai have been shunned for the legends have it that the ghosts of Corphals pursue the spirit of the wicked Jeddak nightly through these chambers, shrieking and moaning as they go. But," he added, as though to reassure himself as well as his companions, "such things may not be countenanced by the culture of Gathol or Helium."

Gahan laughed. "And if all who looked upon him were driven mad, who then was there to perform the last rites or prepare the body of the Jeddak for them?"

"There was none," replied Tasor. "Where they found him they left him and there to this very day his mouldering bones lie hid in some forgotten chamber of this forbidden suite."

Tasor left them then assuring them that he would seek the first opportunity to speak with A-Kor, and upon the following day he would bring them food and drink.[5]

After Tasor had gone Tara turned to Gahan and approaching laid a hand upon his arm. "So swiftly have events transpired since I recognized you beneath your disguise," she said, "that I have had no opportunity to assure you of my gratitude and the high esteem that your valor has won for you in my consideration. Let me now acknowledge my indebtedness; and if promises be not vain from one whose life and liberty are in grave jeopardy, accept my assurance of the great reward that awaits you at the hand of my father in Helium."

"I desire no reward," he replied, "other than the happiness of knowing that the woman I love is happy."

For an instant the eyes of Tara of Helium blazed as she drew herself haughtily to her full height, and then they softened and her attitude relaxed as she shook her head sadly.

"I have it not in my heart to reprimand you, Turan," she said, "however great your fault, for you have been an honorable and a loyal friend to Tara of Helium; but you must not say what my ears must not hear."

"You mean," he asked, "that the ears of a Princess must not listen to words of love from a panthan?"

"It is not that, Turan," she replied; "but rather that I may not in honor listen to words of love from another than him to whom I am betrothed – a fellow countryman, Djor Kantos."

"You mean, Tara of Helium," he cried, "that were it not for that you would – "

"Stop!" she commanded. "You have no right to assume aught else than my lips testify."

"The eyes are ofttimes more eloquent than the lips, Tara," he replied; "and in yours I have read that which is neither hatred nor contempt for Turan the panthan, and my heart tells me that your lips bore false witness when they cried in anger: 'I hate you!'"

"I do not hate you, Turan, nor yet may I love you," said the girl, simply.

"When I broke my way out from the chamber of I-Gos I was indeed upon the verge of believing that you did hate me," he said, "for only hatred, it seemed to me, could account for the fact that you had gone without making an effort to liberate me; but presently both my heart

5   Those who have read John Carter's description of the Green Martians in A Princess of Mars will recall that these strange people could exist for considerable periods of time without food or water, and to a lesser degree is the same true of all Martians.

and my judgment told me that Tara of Helium could not have deserted a companion in distress, and though I still am in ignorance of the facts I know that it was beyond your power to aid me."

"It was indeed," said the girl. "Scarce had I-Gos fallen at the bite of my dagger than I heard the approach of warriors. I ran then to hide until they had passed, thinking to return and liberate you; but in seeking to elude the party I had heard I ran full into the arms of another. They questioned me as to your whereabouts, and I told them that you had gone ahead and that I was following you and thus I led them from you."

"I knew," was Gahan's only comment, but his heart was glad with elation, as a lover's must be who has heard from the lips of his divinity an avowal of interest and loyalty, however little tinged by a suggestion of warmer regard it may be. To be abused, even, by the mistress of one's heart is better than to be ignored.

As the two conversed in the ill-lit chamber, the dim bulbs of which were encrusted with the accumulated dust of centuries, a bent and withered figure traversed slowly the gloomy corridors without, his weak and watery eyes peering through thick lenses at the signs of passage written upon the dusty floor.

CHAPTER NINETEEN

The Menace of the Dead

THE NIGHT WAS STILL YOUNG when there came one to the entrance of the banquet hall where O-Tar of Manator dined with his chiefs, and brushing past the guards entered the great room with the insolence of a privileged character, as in truth he was. As he approached the head of the long board O-Tar took notice of him.

"Well, hoary one!" he cried. "What brings you out of your beloved and stinking burrow again this day. We thought that the sight of the multitude of living men at the games would drive you back to your corpses as quickly as you could go."

The cackling laugh of I-Gos acknowledged the royal sally. "Ey, ey, O-Tar," squeaked the ancient one, "I-Gos goes out not upon pleasure bound; but when one does ruthlessly desecrate the dead of I-Gos, vengeance must be had!"

"You refer to the act of the slave Turan?" demanded O-Tar.

"Turan, yes, and the slave Tara, who slipped beneath my hide a murderous blade. Another fraction of an inch, O-Tar, and I-Gos' ancient and wrinkled covering were even now in some apprentice tanner's hands, ey, ey!"

"But they have again eluded us," cried O-Tar. "Even in the palace of the great jeddak twice have they escaped the stupid knaves I call The Jeddak's Guard." O-Tar had risen and was angrily emphasizing his words with heavy blows upon the table, dealt with a golden goblet.

"Ey, O-Tar, they elude thy guard but not the wise old calot, I-Gos."

"What mean you? Speak!" commanded O-Tar.

"I know where they are hid," said the ancient taxidermist. "In the dust of unused corridors their feet have betrayed them."

"You followed them? You have seen them?" demanded the jeddak.

"I followed them and I heard them speaking beyond a closed door," replied I-Gos; "but I did not see them."

"Where is that door?" cried O-Tar. "We will send at once and fetch them," he looked about the table as though to decide to whom he would entrust this duty. A dozen warrior chiefs arose and laid their hands upon their swords.

"To the chambers of O-Mai the Cruel I traced them," squeaked I-Gos. "There you will find them where the moaning Corphals pursue the shrieking ghost of O-Mai; ey!" and he turned his eyes from O-Tar toward the warriors who had arisen, only to discover that, to a man, they were hurriedly resuming their seats.

The cackling laughter of I-Gos broke derisively the hush that had fallen on the room. The warriors looked sheepishly at the food upon their plates of gold. O-Tar snapped his fingers impatiently.

"Be there only cravens among the chiefs of Manator?" he cried. "Repeatedly have these presumptuous slaves flouted the majesty of your jeddak. Must I command one to go and fetch them?"

Slowly a chief arose and two others followed his example, though with ill-concealed reluctance. "All, then, are not cowards," commented O-Tar. "The duty is distasteful. Therefore all three of you shall go, taking as many warriors as you wish."

"But do not ask for volunteers," interrupted I-Gos, "or you will go alone."

The three chiefs turned and left the banquet hall, walking slowly like doomed men to their fate.

Gahan and Tara remained in the chamber to which Tasor had led them, the man brushing away the dust from a deep and comfortable bench where they might rest in comparative comfort. He had found the ancient sleeping silks and furs too far gone to be of any service, crumbling to powder at a touch, thus removing any chance of making a comfortable bed for the girl, and so the two sat together, talking in low tones, of the adventures through which they already had passed and speculating upon the future; planning means of escape and hoping Tasor would not be long gone. They spoke of many things – of Hastor, and Helium, and Ptarth, and finally the conversation reminded Tara of Gathol.

"You have served there?" she asked.

"Yes," replied Turan.

"I met Gahan the Jed of Gathol at my father's palace," she said, "the very day before the storm snatched me from Helium – he was a presumptuous fellow, magnificently trapped in platinum and diamonds. Never in my life saw I so gorgeous a harness as his, and you must well know, Turan, that the splendor of all Barsoom passes through the court at Helium; but in my mind I could not see so resplendent a creature drawing that jeweled sword in mortal combat. I fear me that the Jed of Gathol, though a pretty picture of a man, is little else."

In the dim light Tara did not perceive the wry expression upon the half-averted face of her companion.

"You thought little then of the Jed of Gathol?" he asked.

"Then or now," she replied, and with a little laugh; "how it would pique his vanity to know, if he might, that a poor panthan had won a higher place in the regard of Tara of Helium," and she laid her fingers gently upon his knee.

He seized the fingers in his and carried them to his lips. "O, Tara of Helium," he cried. "Think you that I am a man of stone?" One arm slipped about her shoulders and drew the yielding body toward him.

"May my first ancestor forgive me my weakness," she cried, as her arms stole about his neck and she raised her panting lips to his. For long they clung there in love's first kiss and then she pushed him away, gently. "I love you, Turan," she half sobbed; "I love you so! It is my only poor excuse for having done this wrong to Djor Kantos, whom now I know I never loved, who knew not the meaning of love. And if you love me as you say, Turan, your love must protect me from greater dishonor, for I am but as clay in your hands."

Again he crushed her to him and then as suddenly released her, and rising, strode rapidly to and fro across the chamber as though he endeavored by violent exercise to master and subdue some evil spirit that had laid hold upon him. Ringing through his brain and heart and soul like some joyous paean were those words that had so altered the world for Gahan of Gathol: "I love you, Turan; I love you so!" And it had come so suddenly. He had thought that she felt for him only gratitude for his loyalty and then, in an instant, her barriers were all down, she was no longer a princess; but instead a – his reflections were interrupted by a sound from beyond the closed door. His sandals of zitidar hide had given forth no sound upon the marble floor he strode, and as his rapid pacing carried him past the entrance to the chamber there came faintly from the distance of the long corridor the sound of metal on metal – the unmistakable herald of the approach of armed men.

For a moment Gahan listened intently, close to the door, until there could be no doubt but that a party of warriors was approaching. From what Tasor had told him he guessed correctly that they would be coming to this portion of the palace but for a single purpose – to search for Tara and himself – and it behooved him therefore to seek immediate means for eluding them. The chamber in which they were had other doorways beside that at which they had entered, and to one of these he must look for some safer hiding place. Crossing to Tara he acquainted her with his suspicion, leading her to one of the doors which they found unsecured. Beyond it lay a dimly-lighted chamber at the threshold of which they halted in consternation, drawing back quickly into the chamber they had just quitted, for their first glance revealed four warriors seated around a jetan board.

That their entrance had not been noted was attributed by Gahan to the absorption of the two players and their friends in the game. Quietly closing the door the fugitives moved silently to the next, which they found locked. There was now but another door which they had not tried, and this they approached quickly as they knew that the searching party must be close to the chamber. To their chagrin they found this avenue of escape barred.

Now indeed were they in a sorry plight, for should the searchers have information leading them to this room they were lost. Again leading Tara to the door behind which were the jetan players Gahan drew his sword and waited, listening. The sound of the party in the corridor came distinctly to their ears – they must be quite close, and doubtless they were coming in force. Beyond the door were but four warriors who might be readily surprised. There could, then, be but one choice and acting upon it Gahan quietly opened the door again, stepped through into the adjoining chamber, Tara's hand in his, and closed the door behind them. The four at the jetan board evidently failed to hear them. One player had either just made or was contemplating a move, for his fingers grasped a piece that still rested upon the board. The other three were watching his move. For an instant Gahan looked at them, playing jetan there in the dim light of this forgotten and forbidden chamber, and then a slow smile of understanding lighted his face.

"Come!" he said to Tara. "We have nothing to fear from these. For more than five thousand years they have sat thus, a monument to the handiwork of some ancient taxidermist."

As they approached more closely they saw that the lifelike figures were coated with dust, but that otherwise the skin was in as fine a state of preservation as the most recent of I-Gos' groups, and then they heard the door of the chamber they had quitted open and knew that the searchers were close upon them. Across the room they saw the opening of what appeared to be a corridor and which investigation proved to be a short passageway, terminating in a chamber in the center of which was an ornate sleeping dais. This room, like the others, was but poorly lighted, time having dimmed the radiance of its bulbs and coated them with dust. A glance showed that it was hung with heavy goods and contained considerable massive furniture in addition to the sleeping platform, a second glance at which revealed what appeared to be the form of a man lying partially on the floor and partially on the dais. No doorways were visible other than that at which they had entered, though both knew that others might be concealed by the hangings.

Gahan, his curiosity aroused by the legends surrounding this portion of the palace, crossed to the dais to examine the figure that apparently had fallen from it, to find the dried and shrivelled corpse of a man lying upon his back on the floor with arms outstretched and fingers stiffly outspread. One of his feet was doubled partially beneath him, while the other was still entangled in the sleeping silks and furs upon the dais. After five thousand years the expression of the withered face and the eyeless sockets retained the aspect of horrid fear to such an extent, that Gahan knew that he was looking upon the body of O-Mai the Cruel.

Suddenly Tara, who stood close beside him, clutched his arm and pointed toward a far corner of the room. Gahan looked and looking felt the hairs upon his neck rising. He threw his left arm about the girl and with bared sword stood between her and the hangings that they watched, and then slowly Gahan of Gathol backed away, for in this grim and somber chamber, which no human foot had trod for five thousand years and to which no breath of wind might enter, the heavy hangings in the far corner had moved. Not gently had they moved as a draught might have moved them had there been a draught, but suddenly they had bulged out as though pushed against from behind. To the opposite corner backed Gahan until they stood with their backs against the hangings there, and then hearing the approach of their pursuers across the chamber beyond Gahan pushed Tara through the hangings and, following her, kept open with his left hand, which he had disengaged from the girl's grasp, a tiny opening through which he could view the apartment and the doorway upon the opposite side through which the pursuers would enter, if they came this far.

Behind the hangings there was a space of about three feet in width between them and the wall, making a passageway entirely around the room, broken only by the single entrance opposite them; this being a common arrangement especially in the sleeping apartments of the rich and powerful upon Barsoom. The purposes of this arrangement were several. The passageway afforded a station for guards in the same room with their master without intruding entirely upon his privacy; it concealed secret exits from the chamber; it permitted the occupant of the room to hide eavesdroppers and assassins for use against enemies that he might lure to his chamber.

The three chiefs with a dozen warriors had had no difficulty in following the tracks of the fugitives through the dust of the corridors and chambers they had traversed. To enter this portion of the palace at all had required all the courage they possessed, and now that they were within the very chambers of O-Mai their nerves were pitched to the highest key – another turn and they would snap; for the people of Manator are filled with weird superstitions. As they entered the outer chamber they moved slowly, with drawn swords, no one seeming anxious to take the lead, and the twelve warriors hanging back in unconcealed and shameless terror, while the three chiefs, spurred on by fear of O-Tar and by pride, pressed together for mutual encouragement as they slowly crossed the dimly-lighted room.

Following the tracks of Gahan and Tara they found that though each doorway had been approached only one threshold had been crossed and this door they gingerly opened, revealing to their astonished gaze the four warriors at the jetan table. For a moment they were on the verge of flight, for though they knew what they were, coming as they did upon them in this mysterious and haunted suite, they were as startled as though they had beheld the very ghosts of the departed. But they presently regained their courage sufficiently to cross this chamber too and enter the short passageway that led to the ancient sleeping apartment of O-Mai the Cruel. They did not know that this awful chamber lay just before them, or it were doubtful that they would have proceeded farther; but they saw that those they sought had come this way and so they followed, but within the gloomy interior of the chamber they halted, the three chiefs urging their followers, in low whispers, to close in behind them, and there just within the entrance they stood until, their eyes becoming accustomed to the dim light, one of them pointed suddenly to the thing lying upon the floor with one foot tangled in the coverings of the dais.

"Look!" he gasped. "It is the corpse of O-Mai! Ancestor of ancestors! we are in the forbidden chamber." Simultaneously there came from behind the hangings beyond the grewsome dead a hollow moan followed by a piercing scream, and the hangings shook and bellied before their eyes.

With one accord, chieftains and warriors, they turned and bolted for the doorway; a narrow doorway, where they jammed, fighting and screaming in an effort to escape. They threw away their swords and clawed at one another to make a passage for escape; those behind climbed upon the shoulders of those in front; and some fell and were trampled upon; but at last they all got through, and, the swiftest first, they bolted across the two intervening chambers to the outer corridor beyond, nor did they halt their mad retreat before they stumbled, weak and trembling, into the banquet hall of O-Tar. At sight of them the warriors who had remained with the jeddak leaped to their feet with drawn swords, thinking that their fellows were pursued by many enemies; but no one followed them into the room, and the three chieftains came and stood before O-Tar with bowed heads and trembling knees.

"Well?" demanded the jeddak. "What ails you? Speak!"

"O-Tar," cried one of them when at last he could master his voice. "When have we three failed you in battle or combat? Have our swords been not always among the foremost in defense of your safety and your honor?"

"Have I denied this?" demanded O-Tar.

"Listen, then, O Jeddak, and judge us with leniency. We followed the two slaves to the apartments of O-Mai the Cruel. We entered the accursed chambers and still we did not falter. We came at last to that horrid chamber no human eye had scanned before in fifty centuries and we looked upon the dead face of O-Mai lying as he has lain for all this time. To the very death chamber of O-Mai the Cruel we came and yet we were ready to go farther; when suddenly there broke upon our horrified ears the moans and the shrieking that mark these haunted chambers and the hangings moved and rustled in the dead air. O-Tar, it was more than human nerves could endure. We turned and fled. We threw away our swords and fought with one another to escape. With sorrow, but without shame, I tell it, for there be no man in all Manator that would not have done the same. If these slaves be Corphals they are safe among their fellow ghosts. If they be not Corphals, then already are they dead in the chambers of O-Mai, and there may they rot for all of me, for I would not return to that accursed spot for the harness of a jeddak and the half of Barsoom for an empire. I have spoken."

O-Tar knitted his scowling brows. "Are all my chieftains cowards and cravens?" he demanded presently in sneering tones.

From among those who had not been of the searching party a chieftain arose and turned a scowling face upon O-Tar.

"The jeddak knows," he said, "that in the annals of Manator her jeddaks have ever been accounted the bravest of her warriors. Where my jeddak leads I will follow, nor may any jeddak call me a coward or a craven unless I refuse to go where he dares to go. I have spoken."

After he had resumed his seat there was a painful silence, for all knew that the speaker had challenged the courage of O-Tar the Jeddak of Manator and all awaited the reply of their ruler. In every mind was the same thought – O-Tar must lead them at once to the chamber of O-Mai the Cruel, or accept forever the stigma of cowardice, and there could be no coward upon the throne of Manator. That they all knew and that O-Tar knew, as well.

But O-Tar hesitated. He looked about upon the faces of those around him at the banquet board; but he saw only the grim visages of relentless warriors. There was no trace of leniency in the face of any. And then his eyes wandered to a small entrance at one side of the great chamber. An expression of relief expunged the scowl of anxiety from his features.

"Look!" he exclaimed. "See who has come!"

CHAPTER TWENTY

The Charge of Cowardice

GAHAN, WATCHING THROUGH the aperture between the hangings, saw the frantic flight of their pursuers. A grim smile rested upon his lips as he viewed the mad scramble for safety and saw them throw away their swords and fight with one another to be first from the chamber of fear, and when they were all gone he turned back toward Tara, the smile still upon his lips; but the smile died the instant that he turned, for he saw that Tara had disappeared.

"Tara!" he called in a loud voice, for he knew that there was no danger that their pursuers would return; but there was no response, unless it was a faint sound as of cackling laughter from afar. Hurriedly he searched the passageway behind the hangings finding several doors, one of which was ajar. Through this he entered the adjoining chamber which was lighted more brilliantly for the moment by the soft rays of hurtling Thuria taking her mad way through the heavens. Here he found the dust upon the floor disturbed, and the imprint of sandals. They had come this way – Tara and whatever the creature was that had stolen her.

But what could it have been? Gahan, a man of culture and high intelligence, held few if any superstitions. In common with nearly all races of Barsoom he clung, more or less inherently, to a certain exalted form of ancestor worship, though it was rather the memory or legends of the virtues and heroic deeds of his forebears that he deified rather than themselves. He never expected any tangible evidence of their existence after death; he did not believe that they had the power either for good or for evil other than the effect that their example while living might have had upon following generations; he did not believe therefore in the materialization of dead spirits. If there was a life hereafter he knew nothing of it, for he knew that science had demonstrated the existence of some material cause for every seemingly supernatural phenomenon of ancient religions and superstitions. Yet he was at a loss to know what power might have removed Tara so suddenly and mysteriously from his side in a chamber that had not known the presence of man for five thousand years.

In the darkness he could not see whether there were the imprints of other sandals than Tara's – only that the dust was disturbed – and when it led him into gloomy corridors he lost the trail altogether. A perfect labyrinth of passages and apartments were now revealed to him as he hurried on through the deserted quarters of O-Mai. Here was an ancient bath – doubtless that of the jeddak himself, and again he passed through a room in which a meal had been laid upon a table five thousand years before – the untasted breakfast of O-Mai, perhaps. There passed before his eyes in the brief moments that he traversed the chambers, a wealth of ornaments and jewels and precious metals that surprised even the Jed of Gathol whose harness was of diamonds and platinum and whose riches were the envy of a world. But at last his search of O-Mai's chambers ended in a small closet in the floor of which was the opening to a spiral runway leading straight down into Stygian darkness. The dust at the entrance of the closet had been freshly disturbed, and as this was the only possible indication that Gahan had of the direction taken by the abductor of Tara it seemed as well to follow on as to search elsewhere. So, without hesitation, he descended into the utter darkness below. Feeling with a foot before taking a forward step his descent was necessarily slow, but Gahan was a Barsoomian and so knew the pitfalls that might await the unwary in such dark, forbidden portions of a jeddak's palace.

He had descended for what he judged might be three full levels and was pausing, as he occasionally did, to listen, when he distinctly heard a peculiar shuffling, scraping sound approaching him from below. Whatever the thing was it was ascending the runway at a steady pace and would soon be near him. Gahan laid his hand upon the hilt of his sword and drew it slowly from its scabbard that he might make no noise that would apprise the creature of his presence. He wished that there might be even the slightest lessening of the darkness. If he could see but the outline of the thing that approached him he would feel that he had a fairer chance in the meeting; but he could see nothing, and then because he could see nothing the end of his scabbard struck the stone side of the runway, giving off a sound that the stillness and the narrow confines of the passage and the darkness seemed to magnify to a terrific clatter.

Instantly the shuffling sound of approach ceased. For a moment Gahan stood in silent waiting, then casting aside discretion he moved on again down the spiral. The thing, whatever it might be, gave forth no sound now by which Gahan might locate it. At any moment it might be upon him and so he kept his sword in readiness. Down, ever downward the steep spiral led. The darkness and the silence of the tomb surrounded him, yet somewhere ahead was something. He was not alone in that horrid place – another presence that he could not hear or see hovered before him – of that he was positive. Perhaps it was the thing that had stolen Tara. Perhaps Tara herself, still in the clutches of some nameless horror, was just ahead of him. He quickened his pace – it became almost a run at the thought of the danger that threatened the woman he loved, and then he collided with a wooden door that swung open to the impact. Before him was a lighted corridor. On either side were chambers. He had advanced but a short distance from the bottom of the spiral when he recognized that he was in the pits below the palace. A moment later he heard behind him the shuffling sound that had attracted his attention in the spiral runway. Wheeling about he saw the author of the sound emerging from a doorway he had just passed. It was Ghek the kaldane.

"Ghek!" exclaimed Gahan. "It was you in the runway? Have you seen Tara of Helium?"

"It was I in the spiral," replied the kaldane; "but I have not seen Tara of Helium. I have been searching for her. Where is she?"

"I do not know," replied the Gatholian; "but we must find her and take her from this place."

"We may find her," said Ghek; "but I doubt our ability to take her away. It is not so easy to leave Manator as it is to enter it. I may come and go at will, through the ancient burrows of the ulsios; but you are too large for that and your lungs need more air than may be found in some of the deeper runways."

"But U-Thor!" exclaimed Gahan. "Have you heard aught of him or his intentions?"

"I have heard much," replied Ghek. "He camps at The Gate of Enemies. That spot he holds and his warriors lie just beyond The Gate; but he has not sufficient force to enter the city and take the palace. An hour since and you might have made your way to him; but now every avenue is strongly guarded since O-Tar learned that A-Kor had escaped to U-Thor."

"A-Kor has escaped and joined U-Thor!" exclaimed Gahan.

"But little more than an hour since. I was with him when a warrior came – a man whose name is Tasor – who brought a message from you. It was decided that Tasor should accompany A-Kor in an attempt to reach the camp of U-Thor, the great jed of Manatos, and exact from him the assurances you required. Then U-Thor was to return and take food to you and the Princess of Helium. I accompanied them. We won through easily and found U-Thor more than willing to respect your every wish, but when Tasor would have returned to you the way was blocked by the warriors of O-Tar. Then it was that I volunteered to come to you and report and find food and drink and then go forth among the Gatholian slaves of Manator and prepare them for their part in the plan that U-Thor and Tasor conceived."

"And what was this plan?"

"U-Thor has sent for reinforcements. To Manatos he has sent and to all the outlying districts that are his. It will take a month to collect and bring them hither and in the meantime the slaves within the city are to organize secretly, stealing and hiding arms against the day that the reinforcements arrive. When that day comes the forces of U-Thor will enter the Gate of Enemies and as the warriors of O-Tar rush to repulse them the slaves from Gathol will fall upon them from the rear with the majority of their numbers, while the balance will assault the palace. They hope thus to divert so many from The Gate that U-Thor will have little difficulty in forcing an entrance to the city."

"Perhaps they will succeed," commented Gahan; "but the warriors of O-Tar are many, and those who fight in defense of their homes and their jeddak have always an advantage. Ah, Ghek, would that we had the great warships of Gathol or of Helium to pour their merciless fire into the streets of Manator while U-Thor marched to the palace over the corpses of the slain." He paused, deep in thought, and then turned his gaze again upon the kaldane. "Heard you aught of the party that escaped with me from The Field of Jetan – of Floran, Val Dor, and the others? What of them?"

"Ten of these won through to U-Thor at The Gate of Enemies and were well received by him. Eight fell in the fighting upon the way. Val Dor and Floran live, I believe, for I am sure that I heard U-Thor address two warriors by these names."

"Good!" exclaimed Gahan. "Go then, through the burrows of the ulsios, to The Gate of Enemies and carry to Floran the message that I shall write in his own language. Come, while I write the message."

In a nearby room they found a bench and table and there Gahan sat and wrote in the strange, stenographic characters of Martian script a message to Floran of Gathol. "Why," he asked, when he had finished it, "did you search for Tara through the spiral runway where we nearly met?"

"Tasor told me where you were to be found, and as I have explored the greater part of the palace by means of the ulsio runways and the darker and less frequented passages I knew precisely where you were and how to reach you. This secret spiral ascends from the pits to the roof of the loftiest of the palace towers. It has secret openings at every level; but there is no living Manatorian, I believe, who knows of its existence. At least never have I met one within it and I have used it many times. Thrice have I been in the chamber where O-Mai lies, though I knew nothing of his identity or the story of his death until Tasor told it to us in the camp of U-Thor."

"You know the palace thoroughly then?" Gahan interrupted.

"Better than O-Tar himself or any of his servants."

"Good! And you would serve the Princess Tara, Ghek, you may serve her best by accompanying Floran and following his instructions. I will write them here at the close of my message to him, for the walls have ears, Ghek, while none but a Gatholian may read what I have written to Floran. He will transmit it to you. Can I trust you?"

"I may never return to Bantoom," replied Ghek. "Therefore I have but two friends in all Barsoom. What better may I do than serve them faithfully? You may trust me, Gatholian, who with a woman of your kind has taught me that there be finer and nobler things than perfect mentality uninfluenced by the unreasoning tuitions of the heart. I go."

As O-Tar pointed to the little doorway all eyes turned in the direction he indicated and surprise was writ large upon the faces of the warriors when they recognized the two who had entered the banquet hall. There was I-Gos, and he dragged behind him one who was gagged and whose hands were fastened behind with a ribbon of tough silk. It was the slave girl. I-Gos' cackling laughter rose above the silence of the room.

"Ey, ey!" he shrilled. "What the young warriors of O-Tar cannot do, old I-Gos does alone."

"Only a Corphal may capture a Corphal," growled one of the chiefs who had fled from the chambers of O-Mai.

I-Gos laughed. "Terror turned your heart to water," he replied; "and shame your tongue to libel. This be no Corphal, but only a woman of Helium; her companion a warrior who can match blades with the best of you and cut your putrid hearts. Not so in the days of I-Gos' youth. Ah, then were there men in Manator. Well do I recall that day that I – "

"Peace, doddering fool!" commanded O-Tar. "Where is the man?"

"Where I found the woman – in the death chamber of O-Mai. Let your wise and brave chieftains go thither and fetch him. I am an old man, and could bring but one."

"You have done well, I-Gos," O-Tar hastened to assure him, for when he learned that Gahan might still be in the haunted chambers he wished to appease the wrath of I-Gos, knowing well the vitriolic tongue and temper of the ancient one. "You think she is no Corphal, then, I-Gos?" he asked, wishing to carry the subject from the man who was still at large.

"No more than you," replied the ancient taxidermist.

O-Tar looked long and searchingly at Tara of Helium. All the beauty that was hers seemed suddenly to be carried to every fibre of his consciousness. She was still garbed in the rich harness of a Black Princess of Jetan, and as O-Tar the Jeddak gazed upon her he realized that never before had his eyes rested upon a more perfect figure – a more beautiful face.

"She is no Corphal," he murmured to himself. "She is no Corphal and she is a princess – a princess of Helium, and, by the golden hair of the Holy Hekkador, she is beautiful. Take the gag from her mouth and release her hands," he commanded aloud. "Make room for the Princess Tara of Helium at the side of O-Tar of Manator. She shall dine as becomes a princess."

Slaves did as O-Tar bid and Tara of Helium stood with flashing eyes behind the chair that was offered her. "Sit!" commanded O-Tar.

The girl sank into the chair. "I sit as a prisoner," she said; "not as a guest at the board of my enemy, O-Tar of Manator."

O-Tar motioned his followers from the room. "I would speak alone with the Princess of Helium," he said. The company and the slaves withdrew and once more the Jeddak of Manator turned toward the girl. "O-Tar of Manator would be your friend," he said.

Tara of Helium sat with arms folded upon her small, firm breasts, her eyes flashing from behind narrowed lids, nor did she deign to answer his overture. O-Tar leaned closer to her. He noted the hostility of her bearing and he recalled his first encounter with her. She was a she-banth, but she was beautiful. She was by far the most desirable woman that O-Tar had ever looked upon and he was determined to possess her. He told her so.

"I could take you as my slave," he said to her; "but it pleases me to make you my wife. You shall be Jeddara of Manator. You shall have seven days in which to prepare for the great honor that O-Tar is conferring upon you, and at this hour of the seventh day you shall become an empress and the wife of O-Tar in the throne room of the jeddaks of Manator." He struck a gong that stood beside him upon the table and when a slave appeared he bade him recall the company. Slowly the chiefs filed in and took their places at the table. Their faces were grim and scowling, for there was still unanswered the question of their jeddak's courage. If O-Tar had hoped they would forget he had been mistaken in his men.

O-Tar arose. "In seven days," he announced, "there will be a great feast in honor of the new Jeddara of Manator," and he waved his hand toward Tara of Helium. "The ceremony will occur at the beginning of the seventh zode[6] in the throne room. In the meantime the Princess of Helium will be cared for in the tower of the women's quarters of the palace. Conduct her thither, E-Thas, with a suitable guard of honor and see to it that slaves and eunuchs be placed at her disposal, who shall attend upon all her wants and guard her carefully from harm."

Now E-Thas knew that the real meaning concealed in these fine words was that he should conduct the prisoner under a strong guard to the women's quarters and confine her there in the tower for seven days, placing about her trustworthy guards who would prevent her escape or frustrate any attempted rescue.

As Tara was departing from the chamber with E-Thas and the guard, O-Tar leaned close to her ear and whispered: "Consider well during these seven days the high honor I have offered you, and – its sole alternative." As though she had not heard him the girl passed out of the banquet hall, her head high and her eyes straight to the front.

After Ghek had left him Gahan roamed the pits and the ancient corridors of the deserted portions of the palace seeking some clue to the whereabouts or the fate of Tara of Helium. He utilized the spiral runway in passing from level to level until he knew every foot of it from the pits to the summit of the high tower, and into what apartments it opened at the various levels as well as the ingenious and hidden mechanism that operated the locks of the cleverly concealed doors leading to it. For food he drew upon the stores he found in the pits and when he slept he lay upon the royal couch of O-Mai in the forbidden chamber sharing the dais with the dead foot of the ancient jeddak.

In the palace about him seethed, all unknown to Gahan, a vast unrest. Warriors and chieftains pursued the duties of their vocations with dour faces, and little knots of them were collecting here and there and with frowns of anger discussing some subject that was uppermost in the

6   About 8:30 P. M. Earth Time.

minds of all. It was upon the fourth day following Tara's incarceration in the tower that E-Thas, the major-domo of the palace and one of O-Tar's creatures, came to his master upon some trivial errand. O-Tar was alone in one of the smaller chambers of his personal suite when the major-domo was announced, and after the matter upon which E-Thas had come was disposed of the jeddak signed him to remain.

"From the position of an obscure warrior I have elevated you, E-Thas, to the honors of a chief. Within the confines of the palace your word is second only to mine. You are not loved for this, E-Thas, and should another jeddak ascend the throne of Manator what would become of you, whose enemies are among the most powerful of Manator?"

"Speak not of it, O-Tar," begged E-Thas. "These last few days I have thought upon it much and I would forget it; but I have sought to appease the wrath of my worst enemies. I have been very kind and indulgent with them."

"You, too, read the voiceless message in the air?" demanded the jeddak.

E-Thas was palpably uneasy and he did not reply.

"Why did you not come to me with your apprehensions?" demanded O-Tar. "Be this loyalty?"

"I feared, O mighty jeddak!" replied E-Thas. "I feared that you would not understand and that you would be angry."

"What know you? Speak the whole truth!" commanded O-Tar.

"There is much unrest among the chieftains and the warriors," replied E-Thas. "Even those who were your friends fear the power of those who speak against you."

"What say they?" growled the jeddak.

"They say that you are afraid to enter the apartments of O-Mai in search of the slave Turan – oh, do not be angry with me, Jeddak; it is but what they say that I repeat. I, your loyal E-Thas, believe no such foul slander."

"No, no; why should I fear?" demanded O-Tar. "We do not know that he is there. Did not my chiefs go thither and see nothing of him?"

"But they say that you did not go," pursued E-Thas, "and that they will have none of a coward upon the throne of Manator."

"They said that treason?" O-Tar almost shouted.

"They said that and more, great jeddak," answered the major-domo. "They said that not only did you fear to enter the chambers of O-Mai, but that you feared the slave Turan, and they blame you for your treatment of A-Kor, whom they all believe to have been murdered at your command. They were fond of A-Kor and there are many now who say aloud that A-Kor would have made a wondrous jeddak."

"They dare?" screamed O-Tar. "They dare suggest the name of a slave's bastard for the throne of O-Tar!"

"He is your son, O-Tar," E-Thas reminded him, "nor is there a more beloved man in Manator – I but speak to you of facts which may not be ignored, and I dare do so because only when you realize the truth may you seek a cure for the ills that draw about your throne."

O-Tar had slumped down upon his bench – suddenly he looked shrunken and tired and old. "Cursed be the day," he cried, "that saw those three strangers enter the city of Manator. Would that U-Dor had been spared to me. He was strong – my enemies feared him; but he is gone – dead at the hands of that hateful slave, Turan; may the curse of Issus be upon him!"

"My jeddak, what shall we do?" begged E-Thas. "Cursing the slave will not solve your problems."

"But the great feast and the marriage is but three days off," plead O-Tar. "It shall be a great gala occasion. The warriors and the chiefs all know that – it is the custom. Upon that day gifts and honors shall be bestowed. Tell me, who are most bitter against me? I will send you among them and let it be known that I am planning rewards for their past services to the throne. We will make jeds of chiefs and chiefs of warriors, and grant them palaces and slaves. Eh, E-Thas?"

The other shook his head. "It will not do, O-Tar. They will have nothing of your gifts or honors. I have heard them say as much."

"What do they want?" demanded O-Tar.

"They want a jeddak as brave as the bravest," replied E-Thas, though his knees shook as he said it.

"They think I am a coward?" cried the jeddak.

"They say you are afraid to go to the apartments of O-mai the Cruel."

For a long time O-Tar sat, his head sunk upon his breast, staring blankly at the floor.

"Tell them," he said at last in a hollow voice that sounded not at all like the voice of a great jeddak; "tell them that I will go to the chambers of O-Mai and search for Turan the slave."

CHAPTER TWENTY ONE

A Risk for Love

"EY, EY, HE IS A CRAVEN and he called me 'doddering fool'!" The speaker was I-Gos and he addressed a knot of chieftains in one of the chambers of the palace of O-Tar, Jeddak of Manator: "If A-Kor was alive there were a jeddak for us!"

"Who says that A-Kor is dead?" demanded one of the chiefs.

"Where is he then?" asked I-Gos. "Have not others disappeared whom O-Tar thought too well beloved for men so near the throne as they?"

The chief shook his head. "And I thought that, or knew it, rather; I'd join U-Thor at The Gate of Enemies."

"S-s-st," cautioned one; "here comes the licker of feet," and all eyes were turned upon the approaching E-Thas.

"Kaor, friends!" he exclaimed as he stopped among them, but his friendly greeting elicited naught but a few surly nods. "Have you heard the news?" he continued, unabashed by treatment to which he was becoming accustomed.

"What – has O-Tar seen an ulsio and fainted?" demanded I-Gos with broad sarcasm.

"Men have died for less than that, ancient one," E-Thas reminded him.

"I am safe," retorted I-Gos, "for I am not a brave and popular son of the jeddak of Manator."

This was indeed open treason, but E-Thas feigned not to hear it. He ignored I-Gos and turned to the others. "O-Tar goes to the chamber of O-Mai this night in search of Turan the slave," he said. "He sorrows that his warriors have not the courage for so mean a duty and that their jeddak is thus compelled to arrest a common slave," with which taunt E-Thas passed on to spread the word in other parts of the palace. As a matter of fact the latter part of his message was purely original with himself, and he took great delight in delivering it to the discomfiture of his enemies. As he was leaving the little group of men I-Gos called after him. "At what hour does O-Tar intend visiting the chambers of O-Mai?" he asked.

"Toward the end of the eighth zode[7]," replied the major-domo, and went his way.

"We shall see," stated I-Gos.

"What shall we see?" asked a warrior.

"We shall see whether O-Tar visits the chamber of O-Mai."

"How?"

"I shall be there myself and if I see him I will know that he has been there. If I don't see him I will know that he has not," explained the old taxidermist.

"Is there anything there to fill an honest man with fear?" asked a chieftain. "What have you seen?"

"It was not so much what I saw, though that was bad enough, as what I heard," said I-Gos.

"Tell us! What heard and saw you?"

"I saw the dead O-Mai," said I-Gos. The others shuddered.

"And you went not mad?" they asked.

"Am I mad?" retorted I-Gos.

"And you will go again?"

"Yes."

"Then indeed you are mad," cried one.

"You saw the dead O-Mai; but what heard you that was worse?" whispered another.

"I saw the dead O-Mai lying upon the floor of his sleeping chamber with one foot tangled in the sleeping silks and furs upon his couch. I heard horrid moans and frightful screams."

"And you are not afraid to go there again?" demanded several.

"The dead cannot harm me," said I-Gos. "He has lain thus for five thousand years. Nor can a sound harm me. I heard it once and live – I can hear it again. It came from almost at my side where I hid behind the hangings and watched the slave Turan before I snatched the woman away from him."

"I-Gos, you are a very brave man," said a chieftain.

"O-Tar called me 'doddering fool' and I would face worse dangers than lie in the forbidden chambers of O-Mai to know it if he does not visit the chamber of O-Mai. Then indeed shall O-Tar fall!"

7   About 1:00 A.M. Earth Time.

The night came and the zodes dragged and the time approached when O-Tar, Jeddak of Manator, was to visit the chamber of O-Mai in search of the slave Turan. To us, who may doubt the existence of malignant spirits, his fear may seem unbelievable, for he was a strong man, an excellent swordsman, and a warrior of great repute; but the fact remained that O-Tar of Manator was nervous with apprehension as he strode the corridors of his palace toward the deserted halls of O-Mai and when he stood at last with his hand upon the door that opened from the dusty corridor to the very apartments themselves he was almost paralyzed with terror. He had come alone for two very excellent reasons, the first of which was that thus none might note his terror-stricken state nor his defection should he fail at the last moment, and the other was that should he accomplish the thing alone or be able to make his chiefs believe that he had, the credit would be far greater than were he to be accompanied by warriors.

But though he had started alone he had become aware that he was being followed, and he knew that it was because his people had no faith in either his courage or his veracity. He did not believe that he would find the slave Turan. He did not very much want to find him, for though O-Tar was an excellent swordsman and a brave warrior in physical combat, he had seen how Turan had played with U-Dor and he had no stomach for a passage at arms with one whom he knew outclassed him.

And so O-Tar stood with his hand upon the door – afraid to enter; afraid not to. But at last his fear of his own warriors, watching behind him, grew greater than the fear of the unknown behind the ancient door and he pushed the heavy skeel aside and entered.

Silence and gloom and the dust of centuries lay heavy upon the chamber. From his warriors he knew the route that he must take to the horrid chamber of O-Mai and so he forced his unwilling feet across the room before him, across the room where the jetan players sat at their eternal game, and came to the short corridor that led into the room of O-Mai. His naked sword trembled in his grasp. He paused after each forward step to listen and when he was almost at the door of the ghost-haunted chamber, his heart stood still within his breast and the cold sweat broke from the clammy skin of his forehead, for from within there came to his affrighted ears the sound of muffled breathing. Then it was that O-Tar of Manator came near to fleeing from the nameless horror that he could not see, but that he knew lay waiting for him in that chamber just ahead. But again came the fear of the wrath and contempt of his warriors and his chiefs. They would degrade him and they would slay him into the bargain. There was no doubt of what his fate would be should he flee the apartments of O-Mai in terror. His only hope, therefore, lay in daring the unknown in preference to the known.

He moved forward. A few steps took him to the doorway. The chamber before him was darker than the corridor, so that he could just indistinctly make out the objects in the room. He saw a sleeping dais near the center, with a darker blotch of something lying on the marble floor beside it. He moved a step farther into the doorway and the scabbard of his sword scraped against the stone frame. To his horror he saw the sleeping silks and furs upon the central dais move. He saw a figure slowly arising to a sitting posture from the death bed of O-Mai the Cruel. His knees shook, but he gathered all his moral forces, and gripping his sword more tightly in his trembling fingers prepared to leap across the chamber upon the horrid apparition. He hesitated just a moment. He felt eyes upon him – ghoulish eyes that bored through the darkness into his withering heart – eyes that he could not see. He gathered himself for the rush – and then there broke from the thing upon the couch an awful shriek, and O-Tar sank senseless to the floor.

Gahan rose from the couch of O-Mai, smiling, only to swing quickly about with drawn sword as the shadow of a noise impinged upon his keen ears from the shadows behind him. Between the parted hangings he saw a bent and wrinkled figure. It was I-Gos.

"Sheathe your sword, Turan," said the old man. "You have naught to fear from I-Gos."

"What do you here?" demanded Gahan.

"I came to make sure that the great coward did not cheat us. Ey, and he called me 'doddering fool;' but look at him now! Stricken insensible by terror, but, ey, one might forgive him that who had heard your uncanny scream. It all but blasted my own courage. And it was you, then, who moaned and screamed when the chiefs came the day that I stole Tara from you?"

"It was you, then, old scoundrel?" demanded Gahan, moving threateningly toward I-Gos.

"Come, come!" expostulated the old man; "it was I, but then I was your enemy. I would not do it now. Conditions have changed."

"How have they changed? What has changed them?" asked Gahan.

"Then I did not fully realize the cowardice of my jeddak, or the bravery of you and the girl. I am an old man from another age and I love courage. At first I resented the girl's attack upon me, but later I came to see the bravery of it and it won my admiration, as have all her acts. She feared not O-tar, she feared not me, she feared not all the warriors of

Manator. And you! Blood of a million sires! how you fight! I am sorry that I exposed you at The Fields of Jetan. I am sorry that I dragged the girl Tara back to O-Tar. I would make amends. I would be your friend. Here is my sword at your feet," and drawing his weapon I-Gos cast it to the floor in front of Gahan.

The Gatholian knew that scarce the most abandoned of knaves would repudiate this solemn pledge, and so he stooped, and picking up the old man's sword returned it to him, hilt first, in acceptance of his friendship.

"Where is the Princess Tara of Helium?" asked Gahan. "Is she safe?"

"She is confined in the tower of the women's quarters awaiting the ceremony that is to make her Jeddara of Manator," replied I-Gos.

"This thing dared think that Tara of Helium would mate with him?" growled Gahan. "I will make short work of him if he is not already dead from fright," and he stepped toward the fallen O-Tar to run his sword through the jeddak's heart.

"No!" cried I-Gos. "Slay him not and pray that he be not dead if you would save your princess."

"How is that?" asked Gahan.

"If word of O-Tar's death reached the quarters of the women the Princess Tara would be lost. They know O-Tar's intention of taking her to wife and making her Jeddara of Manator, so you may rest assured that they all hate her with the hate of jealous women. Only O-Tar's power protects her now from harm. Should O-Tar die they would turn her over to the warriors and the male slaves, for there would be none to avenge her."

Gahan sheathed his sword. "Your point is well taken; but what shall we do with him?"

"Leave him where he lies," counseled I-Gos. "He is not dead. When he revives he will return to his quarters with a fine tale of his bravery and there will be none to impugn his boasts – none but I-Gos. Come! he may revive at any moment and he must not find us here."

I-Gos crossed to the body of his jeddak, knelt beside it for an instant, and then returned past the couch to Gahan. The two quit the chamber of O-Mai and took their way toward the spiral runway. Here I-Gos led Gahan to a higher level and out upon the roof of that portion of the palace from where he pointed to a high tower quite close by. "There," he said, "lies the Princess of Helium, and quite safe she will be until the time of the ceremony."

"Safe, possibly, from other hands, but not from her own," said Gahan. "She will never become Jeddara of Manator – first will she destroy herself."

"She would do that?" asked I-Gos.

"She will, unless you can get word to her that I still live and that there is yet hope," replied Gahan.

"I cannot get word to her," said I-Gos. "The quarters of his women O-Tar guards with jealous hand. Here are his most trusted slaves and warriors, yet even so, thick among them are countless spies, so that no man knows which be which. No shadow falls within those chambers that is not marked by a hundred eyes."

Gahan stood gazing at the lighted windows of the high tower in the upper chambers of which Tara of Helium was confined. "I will find a way, I-Gos," he said.

"There is no way," replied the old man.

For some time they stood upon the roof beneath the brilliant stars and hurtling moons of dying Mars, laying their plans against the time that Tara of Helium should be brought from the high tower to the throne room of O-Tar. It was then, and then alone, argued I-Gos, that any hope of rescuing her might be entertained. Just how far he might trust the other Gahan did not know, and so he kept to himself the knowledge of the plan that he had forwarded to Floran and Val Dor by Ghek, but he assured the ancient taxidermist that if he were sincere in his oft-repeated declaration that O-Tar should be denounced and superseded he would have his opportunity on the night that the jeddak sought to wed the Heliumetic princess.

"Your time shall come then, I-Gos," Gahan assured the other, "and if you have any party that thinks as you do, prepare them for the eventuality that will succeed O-Tar's presumptuous attempt to wed the daughter of The Warlord. Where shall I see you again, and when? I go now to speak with Tara, Princess of Helium."

"I like your boldness," said I-Gos; "but it will avail you naught. You will not speak with Tara, Princess of Helium, though doubtless the blood of many Manatorians will drench the floors of the women's quarters before you are slain."

Gahan smiled. "I shall not be slain. Where and when shall we meet? But you may find me in O-Mai's chamber at night. That seems the safest retreat in all Manator for an enemy of the jeddak in whose palace it lies. I go!"

"And may the spirits of your ancestors surround you," said I-Gos.

After the old man had left him Gahan made his way across the roof to the high tower, which appeared to have been constructed of concrete and afterward elaborately carved, its entire surface being covered with intricate designs cut deep into the stone-like material of which it was composed. Though wrought ages since, it was but little weather-worn owing to the aridity of the Martian atmosphere, the infrequency of rains, and the rarity of dust storms. To scale it, though, presented difficulties and danger that might have deterred the bravest of men – that would, doubtless, have deterred Gahan, had he not felt that the life of the woman he loved depended upon his accomplishing the hazardous feat.

Removing his sandals and laying aside all of his harness and weapons other than a single belt supporting a dagger, the Gatholian essayed the dangerous ascent. Clinging to the carvings with hands and feet he worked himself slowly aloft, avoiding the windows and keeping upon the shadowy side of the tower, away from the light of Thuria and Cluros. The tower rose some fifty feet above the roof of the adjacent part of the palace, comprising five levels or floors with windows looking in every direction. A few of the windows were balconied, and these more than the others he sought to avoid, although, it being now near the close of the ninth zode, there was little likelihood that many were awake within the tower.

His progress was noiseless and he came at last, undetected, to the windows of the upper level. These, like several of the others he had passed at lower levels, were heavily barred, so that there was no possibility of his gaining ingress to the apartment where Tara was confined. Darkness hid the interior behind the first window that he approached. The second opened upon a lighted chamber where he could see a guard sleeping at his post outside a door. Here also was the top of the runway leading to the next level below. Passing still farther around the tower Gahan approached another window, but now he clung to that side of the tower which ended in a courtyard a hundred feet below and in a short time the light of Thuria would reach him. He realized that he must hasten and he prayed that behind the window he now approached he would find Tara of Helium.

Coming to the opening he looked in upon a small chamber dimly lighted. In the center was a sleeping dais upon which a human form lay beneath silks and furs. A bare arm, protruding from the coverings, lay exposed against a black and yellow striped orluk skin – an arm of wondrous beauty about which was clasped an armlet that Gahan knew. No other creature was visible within the chamber, all of which was exposed to Gahan's view. Pressing his face to the bars the Gatholian whispered her dear name. The girl stirred, but did not awaken. Again he called, but this time louder. Tara sat up and looked about and at the same instant a huge eunuch leaped to his feet from where he had been lying on

the floor close by that side of the dais farthest from Gahan. Simultaneously the brilliant light of Thuria flashed full upon the window where Gahan clung silhouetting him plainly to the two within.

Both sprang to their feet. The eunuch drew his sword and leaped for the window where the helpless Gahan would have fallen an easy victim to a single thrust of the murderous weapon the fellow bore, had not Tara of Helium leaped upon her guard dragging him back. At the same time she drew the slim dagger from its hiding place in her harness and even as the eunuch sought to hurl her aside its keen point found his heart. Without a sound he died and lunged forward to the floor. Then Tara ran to the window.

"Turan, my chief!" she cried. "What awful risk is this you take to seek me here, where even your brave heart is powerless to aid me."

"Be not so sure of that, heart of my heart," he replied. "While I bring but words to my love, they be the forerunner of deeds, I hope, that will give her back to me forever. I feared that you might destroy yourself, Tara of Helium, to escape the dishonor that O-Tar would do you, and so I came to give you new hope and to beg that you live for me through whatever may transpire, in the knowledge that there is yet a way and that if all goes well we shall be freed at last. Look for me in the throne room of O-Tar the night that he would wed you. And now, how may we dispose of this fellow?" He pointed to the dead eunuch upon the floor.

"We need not concern ourselves about that," she replied. "None dares harm me for fear of the wrath of O-Tar – otherwise I should have been dead so soon as ever I entered this portion of the palace, for the women hate me. O-Tar alone may punish me, and what cares O-Tar for the life of a eunuch? No, fear not upon this score."

Their hands were clasped between the bars and now Gahan drew her nearer to him.

"One kiss," he said, "before I go, my princess," and the proud daughter of Dejah Thoris, Princess of Helium, and The Warlord of Barsoom whispered: "My chieftain!" and pressed her lips to the lips of Turan, the common panthan.

CHAPTER TWENTY TWO

At the Moment of Marriage

THE SILENCE OF THE TOMB lay heavy about him as O-Tar, Jeddak of Manator, opened his eyes in the chamber of O-Mai. Recollection of the frightful apparition that had confronted him swept to his consciousness. He listened, but heard naught. Within the range of his vision there was nothing apparent that might cause alarm. Slowly he lifted his head and looked about. Upon the floor beside the couch lay the thing that had at first attracted his attention and his eyes closed in terror as he recognized it for what it was; but it moved not, nor spoke. O-Tar opened his eyes again and rose to his feet. He was trembling in every limb. There was nothing on the dais from which he had seen the thing arise.

O-Tar backed slowly from the room. At last he gained the outer corridor. It was empty. He did not know that it had emptied rapidly as the loud scream with which his own had mingled had broken upon the startled ears of the warriors who had been sent to spy upon him. He looked at the timepiece set in a massive bracelet upon his left forearm. The ninth zode was nearly half gone. O-Tar had lain for an hour unconscious. He had spent an hour in the chamber of O-Mai and he was not dead! He had looked upon the face of his predecessor and was still sane! He shook himself and smiled. Rapidly he subdued his rebelliously shaking nerves, so that by the time he reached the tenanted portion of the palace he had gained control of himself. He walked with chin high and something of a swagger. To the banquet hall he went, knowing that his chiefs awaited him there and as he entered they arose and upon the faces of many were incredulity and amaze, for they had not thought to see O-Tar the jeddak again after what the spies had told them of the horrid sounds issuing from the chamber of O-Mai. Thankful was O-Tar that he had gone alone to that chamber of fright, for now no one could deny the tale that he should tell.

E-Thas rushed forward to greet him, for E-Thas had seen black looks directed toward him as the tals slipped by and his benefactor failed to return.

"O brave and glorious jeddak!" cried the major-domo. "We rejoice at your safe return and beg of you the story of your adventure."

"It was naught," exclaimed O-Tar. "I searched the chambers carefully and waited in hiding for the return of the slave, Turan, if he were temporarily away; but he came not. He is not there and I doubt if he ever goes there. Few men would choose to remain long in such a dismal place."

"You were not attacked?" asked E-Thas. "You heard no screams, nor moans?"

"I heard hideous noises and saw phantom figures; but they fled before me so that never could I lay hold of one, and I looked upon the face of O-Mai and I am not mad. I even rested in the chamber beside his corpse."

In a far corner of the room a bent and wrinkled old man hid a smile behind a golden goblet of strong brew.

"Come! Let us drink!" cried O-Tar and reached for the dagger, the pommel of which he was accustomed to use to strike the gong which summoned slaves, but the dagger was not in its scabbard. O-Tar was puzzled. He knew that it had been there just before he entered the chamber of O-Mai, for he had carefully felt of all his weapons to make sure that none was missing. He seized instead a table utensil and struck the gong, and when the slaves came bade them bring the strongest brew for O-Tar and his chiefs. Before the dawn broke many were the expressions of admiration bellowed from drunken lips – admiration for the courage of their jeddak; but some there were who still looked glum.

Came at last the day that O-Tar would take the Princess Tara of Helium to wife. For hours slaves prepared the unwilling bride. Seven perfumed baths occupied three long and weary hours, then her whole body was anointed with the oil of pimalia blossoms and massaged by the deft fingers of a slave from distant Dusar. Her harness, all new and wrought for the occasion was of the white hide of the great white apes of Barsoom, hung heavily with platinum and diamonds – fairly encrusted with them. The glossy mass of her jet hair had been built into a coiffure of stately and becoming grandeur, into which diamond-headed pins were stuck until the whole scintillated as the stars in heaven upon a moonless night.

But it was a sullen and defiant bride that they led from the high tower toward the throne room of O-Tar. The corridors were filled with slaves and warriors, and the women of the palace and the city who had been commanded to attend the ceremony. All the power and pride, wealth and beauty of Manator were there.

Slowly Tara, surrounded by a heavy guard of honor, moved along the marble corridors filled with people. At the entrance to The Hall of Chiefs E-Thas, the major-domo, received her. The Hall was empty except for its ranks of dead chieftains upon their dead mounts. Through this long chamber E-Thas escorted her to the throne room which also was empty, the marriage ceremony in Manator differing from that of other countries of Barsoom. Here the bride would await the groom at the foot of the steps leading to the throne. The guests followed her in and took their places, leaving the central aisle from The Hall of Chiefs to the throne clear, for up this O-Tar would approach his bride alone after a short solitary communion with the dead behind closed doors in The Hall of Chiefs. It was the custom.

The guests had all filed through The Hall of Chiefs; the doors at both ends had been closed. Presently those at the lower end of the hall opened and O-Tar entered. His black harness was ornamented with rubies and gold; his face was covered by a grotesque mask of the precious metal in which two enormous rubies were set for eyes, though below them were narrow slits through which the wearer could see. His crown was a fillet supporting carved feathers of the same metal as the mask. To the least detail his regalia was that demanded of a royal bridegroom by the customs of Manator, and now in accordance with that same custom he came alone to The Hall of Chiefs to receive the blessings and the council of the great ones of Manator who had preceded him.

As the doors at the lower end of the Hall closed behind him O-Tar the Jeddak stood alone with the great dead. By the dictates of ages no mortal eye might look upon the scene enacted within that sacred chamber. As the mighty of Manator respected the traditions of Manator, let us, too, respect those traditions of a proud and sensitive people. Of what concern to us the happenings in that solemn chamber of the dead?

Five minutes passed. The bride stood silently at the foot of the throne. The guests spoke together in low whispers until the room was filled with the hum of many voices. At length the doors leading into The Hall of Chiefs swung open, and the resplendent bridegroom stood framed for a moment in the massive opening. A hush fell upon the wedding guests. With measured and impressive step the groom approached the bride. Tara felt the muscles of her heart contract with the apprehension that had been growing upon her as the coils of Fate settled more closely about her and no sign came from Turan. Where was he? What, indeed, could he accomplish now to save her? Surrounded by the power of O-Tar with never a friend among them, her position seemed at last without vestige of hope.

"I still live!" she whispered inwardly in a last brave attempt to combat the terrible hopelessness that was overwhelming her, but her fingers stole for reassurance to the slim blade that she had managed to transfer, undetected, from her old harness to the new. And now the groom was at her side and taking her hand was leading her up the steps to the throne, before which they halted and stood facing the gathering below. Came then, from the back of the room a procession headed by the high dignitary whose office it was to make these two man and wife, and directly behind him a richly-clad youth bearing a silken pillow on which lay the golden handcuffs connected by a short length of chain-of-gold with which the ceremony would be concluded when the dignitary clasped a handcuff about the wrist of each symbolizing their indissoluble union in the holy bonds of wedlock.

Would Turan's promised succor come too late? Tara listened to the long, monotonous intonation of the wedding service. She heard the virtues of O-Tar extolled and the beauties of the bride. The moment was approaching and still no sign of Turan. But what could he accomplish should he succeed in reaching the throne room, other than to die with her? There could be no hope of rescue.

The dignitary lifted the golden handcuffs from the pillow upon which they reposed. He blessed them and reached for Tara's wrist. The time had come! The thing could go no further, for alive or dead, by all the laws of Barsoom she would be the wife of O-Tar of Manator the instant the two were locked together. Even should rescue come then or later she could never dissolve those bonds and Turan would be lost to her as surely as though death separated them.

Her hand stole toward the hidden blade, but instantly the hand of the groom shot out and seized her wrist. He had guessed her intention. Through the slits in the grotesque mask she could see his eyes upon her and she guessed the sardonic smile that the mask hid. For a tense moment the two stood thus. The people below them kept breathless silence for the play before the throne had not passed un-noticed.

Dramatic as was the moment it was suddenly rendered trebly so by the noisy opening of the doors leading to The Hall of Chiefs. All eyes turned in the direction of the interruption to see another figure framed in the massive opening – a half-clad figure buckling the half-adjusted harness hurriedly in place – the figure of O-Tar, Jeddak of Manator.

"Stop!" he screamed, springing forward along the aisle toward the throne. "Seize the impostor!"

All eyes shot to the figure of the groom before the throne. They saw him raise his hand and snatch off the golden mask, and Tara of Helium in wide-eyed incredulity looked up into the face of Turan the panthan.

"Turan the slave," they cried then. "Death to him! Death to him!"

"Wait!" shouted Turan, drawing his sword, as a dozen warriors leaped forward.

"Wait!" screamed another voice, old and cracked, as I-Gos, the ancient taxidermist, sprang from among the guests and reached the throne steps ahead of the foremost warriors.

At sight of the old man the warriors paused, for age is held in great veneration among the peoples of Barsoom, as is true, perhaps, of all peoples whose religion is based to any extent upon ancestor worship. But O-Tar gave no heed to him, leaping instead swiftly toward the throne. "Stop, coward!" cried I-Gos.

The people looked at the little old man in amazement. "Men of Manator," he cackled in his thin, shrill voice, "wouldst be ruled by a coward and a liar?"

"Down with him!" shouted O-Tar.

"Not until I have spoken," retorted I-Gos. "It is my right. If I fail my life is forfeit – that you all know and I know. I demand therefore to be heard. It is my right!"

"It is his right," echoed the voices of a score of warriors in various parts of the chamber.

"That O-Tar is a coward and a liar I can prove," continued I-Gos. "He said that he faced bravely the horrors of the chamber of O-Mai and saw nothing of the slave Turan. I was there, hiding behind the hangings, and I saw all that transpired. Turan had been hiding in the chamber and was even then lying upon the couch of O-Mai when O-Tar, trembling with fear, entered the room. Turan, disturbed, arose to a sitting position at the same time voicing a piercing shriek. O-Tar screamed and swooned."

"It is a lie!" cried O-Tar.

"It is not a lie and I can prove it," retorted I-Gos. "Didst notice the night that he returned from the chambers of O-Mai and was boasting of his exploit, that when he would summon slaves to bring wine he reached for his dagger to strike the gong with its pommel as is always his custom? Didst note that, any of you? And that he had no dagger? O-Tar, where is the dagger that you carried into the chamber of O-Mai? You do not know; but I know. While you lay in the swoon of terror I took it from your harness and hid it among the sleeping silks upon the couch of O-Mai. There it is even now, and if any doubt it let them go thither and there they will find it and know the cowardice of their jeddak."

"But what of this impostor?" demanded one. "Shall he stand with impunity upon the throne of Manator whilst we squabble about our ruler?"

"It is through his bravery that you have learned the cowardice of O-Tar," replied I-Gos, "and through him you will be given a greater jeddak."

"We will choose our own jeddak. Seize and slay the slave!" There were cries of approval from all parts of the room. Gahan was listening intently, as though for some hoped-for sound. He saw the warriors approaching the dais, where he now stood with drawn sword and with one arm about Tara of Helium. He wondered if his plans had miscarried after all. If they had it would mean death for him, and he knew that Tara would take her life if he fell. Had he, then, served her so futilely after all his efforts?

Several warriors were urging the necessity for sending at once to the chamber of O-Mai to search for the dagger that would prove, if found, the cowardice of O-Tar. At last three consented to go. "You need not fear," I-Gos assured them. "There is naught there to harm you. I have been there often of late and Turan the slave has slept there for these many nights. The screams and moans that frightened you and O-Tar were voiced by Turan to drive you away from his hiding place." Shame-facedly the three left the apartment to search for O-Tar's dagger.

And now the others turned their attention once more to Gahan. They approached the throne with bared swords, but they came slowly for they had seen this slave upon the Field of Jetan and they knew the prowess of his arm. They had reached the foot of the steps when from far above there sounded a deep boom, and another, and another, and Turan smiled and breathed a sigh of relief. Perhaps, after all, it had not come too late. The warriors stopped and listened as did the others in the chamber. Now there broke upon their ears a loud rattle of musketry and it all came from above as though men were fighting upon the roofs of the palace.

"What is it?" they demanded, one of the other.

"A great storm has broken over Manator," said one.

"Mind not the storm until you have slain the creature who dares stand upon the throne of your jeddak," demanded O-Tar. "Seize him!"

Even as he ceased speaking the arras behind the throne parted and a warrior stepped forth upon the dais. An exclamation of surprise and dismay broke from the lips of the warriors of O-Tar. "U-Thor!" they cried. "What treason is this?"

"It is no treason," said U-Thor in his deep voice. "I bring you a new jeddak for all of Manator. No lying poltroon, but a courageous man whom you all love."

He stepped aside then and another emerged from the corridor hidden by the arras. It was A-Kor, and at sight of him there rose exclamations of surprise, of pleasure, and of anger, as the various factions recognized the coup d'etat that had been arranged so cunningly. Behind A-Kor came other warriors until the dais was crowded with them – all men of Manator from the city of Manatos.

O-Tar was exhorting his warriors to attack, when a bloody and disheveled padwar burst into the chamber through a side entrance. "The city has fallen!" he cried aloud. "The hordes of Manatos pour through The Gate of Enemies. The slaves from Gathol have arisen and destroyed the palace guards. Great ships are landing warriors upon the palace roof and in the Fields of Jetan. The men of Helium and Gathol are marching through Manator. They cry aloud for the Princess of Helium and swear to leave Manator a blazing funeral pyre consuming the bodies of all our people. The skies are black with ships. They come in great processions from the east and from the south."

And then once more the doors from The Hall of Chiefs swung wide and the men of Manator turned to see another figure standing upon the threshold – a mighty figure of a man with white skin, and black hair, and gray eyes that glittered now like points of steel and behind him The Hall of Chiefs was filled with fighting men wearing the harness of far countries. Tara of Helium saw him and her heart leaped in exultation, for it was John Carter, Warlord of Barsoom, come at the head of a victorious host to the rescue of his daughter, and at his side was Djor Kantos to whom she had been betrothed.

The Warlord eyed the assemblage for a moment before he spoke. "Lay down your arms, men of Manator," he said. "I see my daughter and that she lives, and if no harm has befallen her no blood need be shed. Your city is filled with the fighting men of U-Thor, and those from Gathol and from Helium. The palace is in the hands of the slaves from Gathol, beside a thousand of my own warriors who fill the halls and chambers surrounding this room. The fate of your jeddak lies in your own hands. I have no wish to interfere. I come only for my daughter and to free the slaves from Gathol. I have spoken!" and without waiting for a reply and as though the room had been filled with his own people rather than a hostile band he strode up the broad main aisle toward Tara of Helium.

The chiefs of Manator were stunned. They looked to O-Tar; but he could only gaze helplessly about him as the enemy entered from The Hall of Chiefs and circled the throne room until they had surrounded the entire company. And then a dwar of the army of Helium entered.

"We have captured three chiefs," he reported to The Warlord, "who beg that they be permitted to enter the throne room and report to their fellows some matter which they say will decide the fate of Manator."

"Fetch them," ordered The Warlord.

They came, heavily guarded, to the foot of the steps leading to the throne and there they stopped and the leader turned toward the others of Manator and raising high his right hand displayed a jeweled dagger. "We found it," he said, "even where I-Gos said that we would find it," and he looked menacingly upon O-Tar.

"A-Kor, jeddak of Manator!" cried a voice, and the cry was taken up by a hundred hoarse-throated warriors.

"There can be but one jeddak in Manator," said the chief who held the dagger; his eyes still fixed upon the hapless O-Tar he crossed to where the latter stood and holding the dagger upon an outstretched palm proffered it to the discredited ruler. "There can be but one jeddak in Manator," he repeated meaningly.

O-Tar took the proffered blade and drawing himself to his full height plunged it to the guard into his breast, in that single act redeeming himself in the esteem of his people and winning an eternal place in The Hall of Chiefs.

As he fell all was silence in the great room, to be broken presently by the voice of U-Thor. "O-Tar is dead!" he cried. "Let A-Kor rule until the chiefs of all Manator may be summoned to choose a new jeddak. What is your answer?"

"Let A-Kor rule! A-Kor, Jeddak of Manator!" The cries filled the room and there was no dissenting voice.

A-Kor raised his sword for silence. "It is the will of A-Kor," he said, "and that of the Great Jed of Manatos, and the commander of the fleet from Gathol, and of the illustrious John Carter, Warlord of Barsoom, that peace lie upon the city of Manator and so I decree that the men of Manator go forth and welcome the fighting men of these our allies as guests and friends and show them the wonders of our ancient city and the hospitality of Manator. I have spoken." And U-Thor and John Carter dismissed their warriors and bade them accept the hospitality of Manator. As the room emptied Djor Kantos reached the side of Tara of Helium. The girl's happiness at rescue had been blighted by sight of this man whom her virtuous heart told her she had wronged. She dreaded the ordeal that lay before her and the dishonor that she must admit before she could hope to be freed from the understanding that had for long existed between them. And now Djor Kantos approached and kneeling raised her fingers to his lips.

"Beautiful daughter of Helium," he said, "how may I tell you the thing that I must tell you – of the dishonor that I have all unwittingly done you? I can but throw myself upon your generosity for forgiveness; but if you demand it I can receive the dagger as honorably as did O-Tar."

"What do you mean?" asked Tara of Helium. "What are you talking about – why speak thus in riddles to one whose heart is already breaking?"

Her heart already breaking! The outlook was anything but promising, and the young padwar wished that he had died before ever he had had to speak the words he now must speak.

"Tara of Helium," he continued, "we all thought you dead. For a long year have you been gone from Helium. I mourned you truly and then, less than a moon since, I wed with Olvia Marthis." He stopped and looked at her with eyes that might have said: "Now, strike me dead!"

"Oh, foolish man!" cried Tara. "Nothing you could have done could have pleased me more. Djor Kantos, I could kiss you!"

"I do not think that Olvia Marthis would mind," he said, his face now wreathed with smiles. As they spoke a body of men had entered the throne room and approached the dais. They were tall men trapped in plain harness, absolutely without ornamentation. Just as their leader reached the dais Tara had turned to Gahan, motioning him to join them.

"Djor Kantos," she said, "I bring you Turan the panthan, whose loyalty and bravery have won my love."

John Carter and the leader of the new come warriors, who were standing near, looked quickly at the little group. The former smiled an inscrutable smile, the latter addressed the Princess of Helium. "'Turan the panthan!'" he cried. "Know you not, fair daughter of Helium, that this man you call panthan is Gahan, Jed of Gathol?"

For just a moment Tara of Helium looked her surprise; and then she shrugged her beautiful shoulders as she turned her head to cast her eyes over one of them at Gahan of Gathol.

"Jed or panthan," she said; "what difference does it make what one's slave has been?" and she laughed roguishly into the smiling face of her lover.

His story finished, John Carter rose from the chair opposite me, stretching his giant frame like some great forest-bred lion.

"You must go?" I cried, for I hated to see him leave and it seemed that he had been with me but a moment.

"The sky is already red beyond those beautiful hills of yours," he replied, "and it will soon be day."

"Just one question before you go," I begged.

"Well?" he assented, good-naturedly.

"How was Gahan able to enter the throne room garbed in O-Tar's trappings?" I asked.

"It was simple – for Gahan of Gathol," replied The Warlord. "With the assistance of I-Gos he crept into The Hall of Chiefs before the ceremony, while the throne room and Hall of Chiefs were vacated to receive the bride. He came from the pits through the corridor that opened behind the arras at the rear of the throne, and passing into The Hall of Chiefs took his place upon the back of a riderless thoat, whose warrior was in I-Gos' repair room. When O-Tar entered and came near him Gahan fell upon him and struck him with the butt of a heavy spear. He thought that he had killed him and was surprised when O-Tar appeared to denounce him."

"And Ghek? What became of Ghek?" I insisted.

"After leading Val Dor and Floran to Tara's disabled flier which they repaired, he accompanied them to Gathol from where a message was sent to me in Helium. He then led a large party including A-Kor and U-Thor from the roof, where our ships landed them, down a spiral runway into the palace and guided them to the throne room. We took him back to Helium with us, where he still lives, with his single rykor which we found all but starved to death in the pits of Manator. But come! No more questions now."

I accompanied him to the east arcade where the red dawn was glowing beyond the arches.

"Good-bye!" he said.

"I can scarce believe that it is really you," I exclaimed. "Tomorrow I will be sure that I have dreamed all this."

He laughed and drawing his sword scratched a rude cross upon the concrete of one of the arches.

"If you are in doubt tomorrow," he said, "come and see if you dreamed this."

A moment later he was gone.

Jetan, or Martian Chess

FOR THOSE WHO CARE for such things, and would like to try the game, I give the rules of Jetan as they were given me by John Carter. By writing the names and moves of the various pieces on bits of paper and pasting them on ordinary checkermen the game may be played quite as well as with the ornate pieces used upon Mars.

The Board: Square board consisting of one hundred alternate black and orange squares.

The Pieces: In order, as they stand upon the board in the first row, from left to right of each player.

Warrior: 2 feathers; 2 spaces straight in any direction or combination.

Padwar: 2 feathers; 2 spaces diagonal in any direction or combination.

Dwar: 3 feathers; 3 spaces straight in any direction or combination.

Flier: 3 bladed propellor; 3 spaces diagonal in any direction or combination; and may jump intervening pieces.

Chief: Diadem with ten jewels; 3 spaces in any direction; straight or diagonal or combination.

Princess: Diadem with one jewel; same as Chief, except may jump intervening pieces.

Flier: See above.

Dwar: See above.

Padwar: See above.

Warrior: See above.

And in the second row from left to right:

Thoat: Mounted warrior 2 feathers; 2 spaces, one straight and one diagonal in any direction.

Panthans: (8 of them): 1 feather; 1 space, forward, side, or diagonal, but not backward.

Thoat: See above.

The game is played with twenty black pieces by one player and twenty orange by his opponent, and is presumed to have originally represented a battle between the Black race of the south and the Yellow race of the north. On Mars the board is usually arranged so that the Black pieces are played from the south and the Orange from the north.

The game is won when any piece is placed on same square with opponent's Princess, or a Chief takes a Chief.

The game is drawn when either Chief is taken by a piece other than the opposing Chief, or when both sides are reduced to three pieces, or less, of equal value and the game is not won in the ensuing ten moves, five apiece.

The Princess may not move onto a threatened square, nor may she take an opposing piece. She is entitled to one ten-space move at any time during the game. This move is called the escape.

Two pieces may not occupy the same square except in the final move of a game where the Princess is taken.

When a player, moving properly and in order, places one of his pieces upon a square occupied by an opponent piece, the opponent piece is considered to have been killed and is removed from the game.

The moves explained. Straight moves mean due north, south, east, or west; diagonal moves mean northeast, southeast, southwest, or northwest. A Dwar might move straight north three spaces, or north one space and east two spaces, or any similar combination of straight moves, so long as he did not cross the same square twice in a single move. This example explains combination moves.

The first move may be decided in any way that is agreeable to both players; after the first game the winner of the preceding game moves first if he chooses, or may instruct his opponent to make the first move.

Gambling: The Martians gamble at Jetan in several ways. Of course the outcome of the game indicates to whom the main stake belongs; but they also put a price upon the head of each piece, according to its value, and for each piece that a player loses he pays its value to his opponent.

THE MASTER MIND OF MARS

BOOK SIX

A LETTER

Helium, June 8th, 1925

My Dear Mr. Burroughs:

It was in the Fall of nineteen seventeen at an officers' training camp that I first became acquainted with John Carter, War Lord of Barsoom, through the pages of your novel "A Princess of Mars." The story made a profound impression upon me and while my better judgment assured me that it was but a highly imaginative piece of fiction, a suggestion of the verity of it pervaded my inner consciousness to such an extent that I found myself dreaming of Mars and John Carter, of Dejah Thoris, of Tars Tarkas and of Woola as if they had been entities of my own experience rather than the figments of your imagination.

It is true that in those days of strenuous preparation there was little time for dreaming, yet there were brief moments before sleep claimed me at night and these were my dreams. Such dreams! Always of Mars, and during my waking hours at night my eyes always sought out the Red Planet when he was above the horizon and clung there seeking a solution of the seemingly unfathomable riddle he has presented to the Earthman for ages.

Perhaps the thing became an obsession. I know it clung to me all during my training camp days, and at night, on the deck of the transport, I would lie on my back gazing up into the red eye of the god of battle – my god – and wishing that, like John Carter, I might be drawn across the great void to the haven of my desire.

And then came the hideous days and nights in the trenches – the rats, the vermin, the mud – with an occasional glorious break in the monotony when we were ordered over the top. I loved it then and I loved the bursting shells, the mad, wild chaos of the thundering guns, but the rats and the vermin and the mud – God! how I hated them. It sounds like boasting, I know, and I am sorry; but I wanted to write you just the truth about myself. I think you will understand.

And it may account for much that happened afterwards.

There came at last to me what had come to so many others upon those bloody fields. It came within the week that I had received my first promotion and my captaincy, of which I was greatly proud, though humbly so; realizing as I did my youth, the great responsibility that it placed upon me as well as the opportunities it offered, not only in service to my country but, in a personal way, to the men of my command. We had advanced a matter of two kilometers and with a small detachment I was holding a very advanced position when I received orders to fall back to the new line. That is the last that I remember until I regained consciousness after dark. A shell must have burst among us. What became of my men I never knew. It was cold and very dark when I awoke and at first, for an instant, I was quite comfortable – before I was fully conscious, I imagine – and then I commenced to feel pain. It grew until it seemed unbearable. It was in my legs. I reached down to feel them, but my hand recoiled from what it found, and when I tried to move my legs I discovered that I was dead from the waist down. Then the moon came out from behind a cloud and I saw that I lay within a shell hole and that I was not alone – the dead were all about me.

It was a long time before I found the moral courage and the physical strength to draw myself up upon one elbow that I might view the havoc that had been done me.

One look was enough, I sank back in an agony of mental and physical anguish – my legs had been blown away from midway between the hips and knees. For some reason I was not bleeding excessively, yet I know that I had lost a great deal of blood and that I was gradually losing enough to put me out of my misery in a short time if I were not soon found; and as I lay there on my back, tortured with pain, I prayed that they would not come in time, for I shrank more from the thought of going maimed through life than I shrank from the thought of death.

Then my eyes suddenly focussed upon the bright red eye of Mars and there surged through me a sudden wave of hope. I stretched out my arms towards Mars, I did not seem to question or to doubt for an instant as I prayed to the god of my vocation to reach forth and succour me. I knew that he would do it, my faith was complete, and yet so great was the mental effort that I made to throw off the hideous bonds of my mutilated flesh that I felt a momentary qualm of nausea and then a sharp click as of the snapping of a steel wire, and suddenly I stood naked upon two good legs looking down upon the bloody, distorted thing that had been I. Just for an instant did I stand thus before I turned my eyes aloft again to my star of destiny and with outstretched arms stand there in the cold of that French night – waiting.

Suddenly I felt myself drawn with the speed of thought through the trackless wastes of interplanetary space. There was an instant of extreme cold and utter darkness, then – But the rest is in the manuscript that, with the aid of one greater than either of us, I have found the means to transmit to you with this letter. You and a few others of the chosen will believe in it – for the rest it matters not as yet.

The time will come – but why tell you what you already know?

My salutations and my congratulations – the latter on your good fortune in having been chosen as the medium through which Earthmen shall become better acquainted with the manners and customs of Barsoom, against the time that they shall pass through space as easily as John Carter, and visit the scenes that he has described to them through you, as have I.

Your sincere friend, *Ulysses Paxton*, Late Captain, – th Inf., U.S. Army.

CHAPTER ONE

The House of the Dead

I MUST HAVE CLOSED my eyes involuntarily during the transition for when I opened them I was lying flat on my back gazing up into a brilliant, sun-lit sky, while standing a few feet from me and looking down upon me with the most mystified expression was as strange a looking individual as my eyes ever had rested upon.

He appeared to be quite an old man, for he was wrinkled and withered beyond description. His limbs were emaciated; his ribs showed distinctly beneath his shrunken hide; his cranium was large and well developed, which, in conjunction with his wasted limbs and torso, lent him the appearance of top heaviness, as though he had a head beyond all proportion to his body, which was, I am sure, really not the case.

As he stared down upon me through enormous, many-lensed spectacles I found the opportunity to examine him as minutely in return. He was, perhaps, five feet five in height, though doubtless he had been taller in youth, since he was somewhat bent; he was naked except for some rather plain and well-worn leather harness which supported his weapons and pocket pouches, and one great ornament a collar, jewel studded, that he wore around his scraggy neck – such a collar as a dowager empress of pork or real estate might barter her soul for, if she had one. His skin was red, his scant locks grey. As he looked at me his puzzled expression increased in intensity, he grasped his chin between the thumb and fingers of his left hand and slowly raising his right hand he scratched his head most deliberately. Then he spoke to me, but in a language I did not understand.

At his first words I sat up and shook my head. Then I looked about me. I was seated upon a crimson sward within a high-walled enclosure, at least two, and possibly three, sides of which were formed by the outer walls of a structure that in some respects resembled more closely a feudal castle of Europe than any familiar form of architecture that comes to my mind. The facade presented to my view was ornately carved and of most irregular design, the roof line being so broken as to almost suggest a ruin, and yet the whole seemed harmonious and not without beauty. Within the enclosure grew a number of trees and shrubs, all weirdly strange and all, or almost all, profusely flowering. About them wound walks of coloured pebbles among which scintillated what appeared to be rare and beautiful gems, so lovely were the strange, unearthly rays that leaped and played in the sunshine.

The old man spoke again, peremptorily this time, as though repeating a command that had been ignored, but again I shook my head. Then he laid a hand upon one of his two swords, but as he drew the weapon I leaped to my feet, with such remarkable results that I cannot even now say which of us was the more surprised. I must have sailed ten feet into the air and back about twenty feet from where I had been sitting; then I was sure that I was upon Mars (not that I had for one instant doubted it), for the effects of the lesser gravity, the colour of the sward and the skin-hue of the red Martians I had seen described in the manuscripts of John Carter, those marvellous and as yet unappreciated contributions to the scientific literature of a world. There could be no doubt of it, I stood upon the soil of the Red Planet, I had come to the world of my dreams – to Barsoom.

So startled was the old man by my agility that he jumped a bit himself, though doubtless involuntarily, but, however, with certain results. His spectacles tumbled from his nose to the sward, and then it was that I discovered that the pitiful old wretch was practically blind when deprived of these artificial aids to vision, for he got to his knees and commenced to grope frantically for the lost glasses, as though his very life depended upon finding them in the instant.

Possibly he thought that I might take advantage of his helplessness and slay him. Though the spectacles were enormous and lay within a couple of feet of him he could not find them, his hands, seemingly afflicted by that strange perversity that sometimes confounds our simplest acts, passing all about the lost object of their search, yet never once coming in contact with it.

As I stood watching his futile efforts and considering the advisability of restoring to him the means that would enable him more readily to find my heart with his sword point, I became aware that another had entered the enclosure.

Looking towards the building I saw a large red-man running rapidly towards the little old man of the spectacles. The newcomer was quite naked, he carried a club in one hand, and there was upon his face such an expression as unquestionably boded ill for the helpless husk of humanity grovelling, mole-like, for its lost spectacles.

My first impulse was to remain neutral in an affair that it seemed could not possibly concern me and of which I had no slightest knowledge upon which to base a predilection towards either of the parties involved; but a second glance at the face of the club-bearer aroused a question as to whether it might not concern me after all.

There was that in the expression upon the man's face that betokened either an inherent savageness of disposition or a maniacal cast of mind which might turn his evidently murderous attentions upon me after he had dispatched his elderly victim, while, in outward appearance at least, the latter was a sane and relatively harmless individual. It is true that his move to draw his sword against me was not indicative of a friendly disposition towards me, but at least, if there were any choice, he seemed the lesser of two evils.

He was still groping for his spectacles and the naked man was almost upon him as I reached the decision to cast my lot upon the side of the old man. I was twenty feet away, naked and unarmed, but to cover the distance with my Earthly muscles required but an instant, and a naked sword lay by the old man's side where he had discarded it the better to search for his spectacles. So it was that I faced the attacker at the instant that he came within striking distance of his victim, and the blow which had been intended for another was aimed at me. I side-stepped it and then I learned that the greater agility of my Earthly muscles had its disadvantages as well as its advantages, for, indeed, I had to learn to walk at the very instant that I had to learn to fight with a new weapon against a maniac armed with a bludgeon, or at least, so I assumed him to be and I think that it is not strange that I should have done so, what with his frightful show of rage and the terrible expression upon his face.

As I stumbled about endeavouring to accustom myself to the new conditions, I found that instead of offering any serious opposition to my antagonist I was hard put to it to escape death at his hands, so often did I stumble and fall sprawling upon the scarlet sward; so that the duel from its inception became but a series of efforts, upon his part to reach and crush me with his great club, and upon mine to dodge and elude him. It was mortifying but it is the truth.

However, this did not last indefinitely, for soon I learned, and quickly too under the exigencies of the situation, to command my muscles, and then I stood my ground and when he aimed a blow at me, and I had dodged it, I touched him with my point and brought blood along with a savage roar of pain. He went more cautiously then, and taking advantage of the change I pressed him so that he fell back. The effect upon me was magical, giving me new confidence, so that I set upon him in good earnest, thrusting and cutting until I had him bleeding in a half-dozen places, yet taking good care to avoid his mighty swings, any one of which would have felled an ox.

In my attempts to elude him in the beginning of the duel we had crossed the enclosure and were now fighting at a considerable distance from the point of our first meeting. It now happened that I stood facing towards that point at the moment that the old man regained his spectacles, which he quickly adjusted to his eyes. Immediately he looked about until he discovered us, whereupon he commenced to yell excitedly at us at the same time running in our direction and drawing his short-sword as he ran. The red-man was pressing me hard, but I had gained almost complete control of myself, and fearing that I was soon to have two antagonists instead of one I set upon him with redoubled intensity. He missed me by the fraction of an inch, the wind in the wake of his bludgeon fanning my scalp, but he left an opening into which I stepped, running my word fairly through his heart. At least I thought that I had pierced his heart but I had forgotten what I had once read in one of John Carter's manuscripts to the effect that all the Martian internal organs are not disposed identically with those of Earthmen. However, the immediate results were quite as satisfactory as though I had found his heart for the wound was sufficiently grievous to place him hors de combat, and at that instant the old gentleman arrived. He found me ready, but I had mistaken his intentions. He made no unfriendly gestures with his weapon, but seemed to be trying to convince me that he had no intention of harming me. He was very excited and apparently tremendously annoyed that I could not understand him, and perplexed, too. He hopped about screaming strange sentences at me that bore the tones of peremptory commands, rabid invective and impotent rage. But the fact that he had returned his sword to its scabbard had greater significance than all his jabbering, and when he ceased to yell at me and commenced to talk in a sort of pantomime I realized that he was making overtures of peace if not of friendship, so I lowered my point and bowed. It was all that I could think of to assure him that I had no immediate intention of spitting him.

He seemed satisfied and at once turned his attention to the fallen man. He examined his pulse and listened to his heart, then, nodding his head, he arose and taking a whistle from one of his pocket pouches sounded a single loud blast.

There emerged immediately from one of the surrounding buildings a score of naked red-men who came running towards us. None was armed. To these he issued a few curt orders, whereupon they gathered the fallen one in their arms and bore him off. Then the old man started towards the building, motioning me to accompany him. There seemed nothing else for me to do but obey. Wherever I might be upon Mars, the chances were a million to one that I would be among enemies; and so I was as well off here as elsewhere and must depend upon my own resourcefulness, skill and agility to make my way upon the Red Planet.

The old man led me into a small chamber from which opened numerous doors, through one of which they were just bearing my late antagonist. We followed into a large, brilliantly lighted chamber wherein there burst upon my astounded vision the most gruesome scene that I ever had beheld. Rows upon rows of tables arranged in parallel lines filled the room and with few exceptions each table bore a similar grisly burden, a partially dismembered or otherwise mutilated human corpse. Above each table was a shelf bearing containers of various sizes and shapes, while from the bottom of the shelf depended numerous surgical instruments, suggesting that my entrance upon Barsoom was to be through a gigantic medical college.

At a word from the old man, those who bore the Barsoomian I had wounded laid him upon an empty table and left the apartment. Whereupon my host if so I may call him, for certainly he was not as yet my captor, motioned me forward. While he conversed in ordinary tones, he made two incisions in the body of my late antagonist; one, I imagine, in a large vein and one in an artery, to which he deftly attached the ends of two tubes, one of which was connected with an empty glass receptacle and the other with a similar receptacle filled with a colourless, transparent liquid resembling clear water. The connections made, the old gentleman pressed a button controlling a small motor, whereupon the victim's blood was pumped into the empty jar while the contents of the other was forced into the emptying veins and arteries.

The tones and gestures of the old man as he addressed me during this operation convinced me that he was explaining in detail the method and purpose of what was transpiring, but as I understood no word of all he said I was as much in the dark when he had completed his discourse as I was before he started it, though what I had seen made it appear reasonable to believe that I was witnessing an ordinary Barsoomian embalming. Having removed the tubes the old man closed the openings he had made by covering them with bits of what appeared to be heavy adhesive tape and then motioned me to follow him. We went from room to room, in each of which were the same gruesome exhibits. At many of the bodies the old man paused to make a brief examination or to refer to what appeared to be a record of the case, that hung upon a hook at the head of each of the tables.

From the last of the chambers we visited upon the first floor my host led me up an inclined runway to the second floor where there were rooms similar to those below, but here the tables bore whole rather than mutilated bodies, all of which were patched in various places with adhesive tape. As we were passing among the bodies in one of these rooms a Barsoomian girl, whom I took to be a servant or slave, entered and addressed the old man, whereupon he signed me to follow him and together we descended another runway to the first floor of another building.

Here, in a large, gorgeously decorated and sumptuously furnished apartment an elderly red-woman awaited us. She appeared to be quite old and her face was terribly disfigured as by some injury. Her trappings were magnificent and she was attended by a score of women and armed warriors, suggesting that she was a person of some consequence, but the little old man treated her quite brusquely, as I could see, quite to the horror of her attendants.

Their conversation was lengthy and at the conclusion of it, at the direction of the woman, one of her male escort advanced and opening a pocket pouch at his side withdrew a handful of what appeared to me to be Martian coins. A quantity of these he counted out and handed to the little old man, who then beckoned the woman to follow him, a gesture which included me. Several of her women and guard started to accompany us, but these the old man waved back peremptorily; whereupon there ensued a heated discussion between the woman and one of her warriors on one side and the old man on the other, which terminated in his proffering the return of the woman's money with a disgusted air. This seemed to settle the argument, for she refused the coins, spoke briefly to her people and accompanied the old man and myself alone.

He led the way to the second floor and to a chamber which I had not previously visited. It closely resembled the others except that all the bodies therein were of young women, many of them of great beauty. Following closely at the heels of the old man the woman inspected the gruesome exhibit with painstaking care.

Thrice she passed slowly among the tables examining their ghastly burdens. Each time she paused longest before a certain one which bore the figure of the most beautiful creature I had ever looked upon; then she returned the fourth time to it and stood looking long and earnestly into the dead face. For awhile she stood there talking with the old man,

apparently asking innumerable questions, to which he returned quick, brusque replies, then she indicated the body with a gesture and nodded assent to the withered keeper of this ghastly exhibit.

Immediately the old fellow sounded a blast upon his whistle, summoning a number of servants to whom he issued brief instructions, after which he led us to another chamber, a smaller one in which were several empty tables similar to those upon which the corpses lay in adjoining rooms. Two female slaves or attendants were in this room and at a word from their master they removed the trappings from the old woman, unloosed her hair and helped her to one of the tables. Here she was thoroughly sprayed with what I presume was an antiseptic solution of some nature, carefully dried and removed to another table, at a distance of about twenty inches from which stood a second parallel table.

Now the door of the chamber swung open and two attendants appeared bearing the body of the beautiful girl we had seen in the adjoining room. This they deposited upon the table the old woman had just quitted and as she had been sprayed so was the corpse, after which it was transferred to the table beside that on which she lay. The little old man now made two incisions in the body of the old woman, just as he had in the body of the red-man who had fallen to my sword; her blood was drawn from her veins and the clear liquid pumped into them, life left her and she lay upon the polished ersite slab that formed the table top, as much a corpse as the poor, beautiful, dead creature at her side.

The little old man, who had removed the harness down to his waist and been thoroughly sprayed, now selected a sharp knife from among the instruments above the table and removed the old woman's scalp, following the hair line entirely around her head. In a similar manner he then removed the scalp from the corpse of the young woman, after which, by means of a tiny circular saw attached to the end of a flexible, revolving shaft he sawed through the skull of each, following the line exposed by the removal of the scalps. This and the balance of the marvellous operation was so skilfully performed as to baffle description.

Suffice it to say that at the end of four hours he had transferred the brain of each woman to the brain pan of the other, deftly connected the severed nerves and ganglia, replaced the skulls and scalps and bound both heads securely with his peculiar adhesive tape, which was not only antiseptic and healing but anaesthetic, locally, as well.

He now reheated the blood that he had withdrawn from the body of the old woman, adding a few drops of some clear chemical solution, withdrew the liquid from the veins of the beautiful corpse, replacing it with the blood of the old woman and simultaneously administering a hypodermic injection.

During the entire operation he had not spoken a word. Now he issued a few instructions in his curt manner to his assistants, motioned me to follow him, and left the room. He led me to a distant part of the building or series of buildings that composed the whole, ushered me into a luxurious apartment, opened the door to a Barsoomian bath and left me in the hands of trained servants.

Refreshed and rested I left the bath after an hour of relaxation to find harness and trappings awaiting me in the adjoining chamber. Though plain, they were of good material, but there were no weapons with them.

Naturally I had been thinking much upon the strange things I had witnessed since my advent upon Mars, but what puzzled me most lay in the seemingly inexplicable act of the old woman in paying my host what was evidently a considerable sum to murder her and transfer to the inside of her skull the brain of a corpse. Was it the outcome of some horrible religious fanaticism, or was there an explanation that my Earthly mind could not grasp?

I had reached no decision in the matter when I was summoned to follow a slave to another and near-by apartment where I found my host awaiting me before a table loaded with delicious foods, to which, it is needless to say, I did ample justice after my long fast and longer weeks of rough army fare.

During the meal my host attempted to converse with me, but, naturally, the effort was fruitless of results. He waxed quite excited at times and upon three distinct occasions laid his hand upon one of his swords when I failed to comprehend what he was saying to me, an action which resulted in a growing conviction upon my part that he was partially demented; but he evinced sufficient self-control in each instance to avert a catastrophe for one of us.

The meal over he sat for a long time in deep meditation, then a sudden resolution seemed to possess him. He turned suddenly upon me with a faint suggestion of a smile and dove headlong into what was to prove an intensive course of instruction in the Barsoomian language. It was long after dark before he permitted me to retire for the night, conducting me himself to a large apartment, the same in which I had found my new harness, where he pointed out a pile of rich sleeping silks and furs, bid me a Barsoomian good night and left me, locking the door after him upon the outside, and leaving me to guess whether I were more guest or prisoner.

CHAPTER TWO
Preferment

THREE WEEKS PASSED RAPIDLY. I had mastered enough of the Barsoomian tongue to enable me to converse with my host in a reasonably satisfactory manner, and I was also progressing slowly in the mastery of the written language of his nation, which is different, of course, from the written language of all other Barsoomian nations, though the spoken language of all is identical. In these three weeks I had learned much of the strange place in which I was half guest and half prisoner and of my remarkable host-jailer, Ras Thavas, the old surgeon of Toonol, whom I had accompanied almost constantly day after day until gradually there had unfolded before my astounded faculties an understanding of the purposes of the institution over which he ruled and in which he laboured practically alone; for the slaves and attendants that served him were but hewers of wood and carriers of water. It was his brain alone and his skill that directed the sometimes beneficent, the sometimes malevolent, but always marvellous activities of his life's work.

Ras Thavas himself was as remarkable as the things he accomplished. He was never intentionally cruel; he was not, I am sure, intentionally wicked. He was guilty of the most diabolical cruelties and the basest of crimes; yet in the next moment he might perform a deed that if duplicated upon Earth would have raised him to the highest pinnacle of man's esteem. Though I know that I am safe in saying that he was never prompted to a cruel or criminal act by base motives, neither was he ever urged to a humanitarian one by high motives. He had a purely scientific mind entirely devoid of the cloying influences of sentiment, of which he possessed none. His was a practical mind, as evidenced by the enormous fees he demanded for his professional services; yet I know that he would not operate for money alone and I have seen him devote days to the study of a scientific problem the solution of which could add nothing to his wealth, while the quarters that he furnished his waiting clients were overflowing with wealthy patrons waiting to pour money into his coffers.

His treatment of me was based entirely upon scientific requirements. I offered a problem. I was either, quite evidently, not a Barsoomian at all, or I was of a species of which he had no knowledge. It therefore best suited the purposes of science that I be preserved and studied. I knew much about my own planet. It pleased Ras Thavas' scientific mind to milk me of all I knew in the hope that he might derive some suggestion that would solve one of the Barsoomian scientific riddles that still baffle their savants; but he was compelled to admit that in this respect I was a total loss, not alone because I was densely ignorant upon practically all scientific subjects, but because the learned sciences on Earth have not advanced even to the swaddling-clothes stage as compared with the remarkable progress of corresponding activities on Mars. Yet he kept me by him, training me in many of the minor duties of his vast laboratory. I was entrusted with the formula of the "embalming fluid" and taught how to withdraw a subject's blood and replace it with this marvellous preservative that arrests decay without altering in the minutest detail the nerve or tissue structure of the body. I learned also the secret of the few drops of solution which, added to the rewarmed blood before it is returned to the veins of the subject revitalizes the latter and restores to normal and healthy activity each and every organ of the body.

He told me once why he had permitted me to learn these things that he had kept a secret from all others, and why he kept me with him at all times in preference to any of the numerous individuals of his own race that served him and me in lesser capacities both day and night.

"Vad Varo," he said, using the Barsoomian name that he had given me because he insisted that my own name was meaningless and impractical, "for many years I have needed an assistant, but heretofore I have never felt that I had discovered one who might work here for me wholeheartedly and disinterestedly without ever having reason to go elsewhere or to divulge my secrets to others. You, in all Barsoom, are unique – you have no other friend or acquaintance than myself. Were you to leave we you would find yourself in a world of enemies, for all are suspicious of a stranger. You would not survive a dozen dawns and you would be cold and hungry and miserable – a wretched outcast in a hostile world. Here you have every luxury that the mind of man can devise or the hand of man produce, and you are occupied with work of such engrossing interest that your every hour must be fruitful of unparalleled satisfaction. There is no selfish reason, therefore, why you should leave me and there is every reason why you should remain. I expect no loyalty other than that which may be prompted by egoism. You make an ideal assistant, not only for the reasons I have just given you, but because you are intelligent and quick-witted, and now I have decided, after observing you carefully for a sufficient time, that you can serve me in yet another capacity – that of personal bodyguard.

"You may have noticed that I alone of all those connected with my laboratory am armed. This is unusual upon Barsoom, where people of all classes, and all ages and both sexes habitually go unarmed. But many of these people I could not trust armed as they would slay me; and were I to give arms to those whom I might trust, who knows but that the others would obtain possession of them and slay me, or even those whom I had trusted turn against me, for there is not one who might not wish to go forth from this place back among his own people – only you, Vad Varo, for there is no other place for you to go. So I have decided to give you weapons.

"You saved my life once. A similar opportunity might again present itself. I know that being a reasoning and reasonable creature, you will not slay me, for you have nothing to gain and everything to lose by my death, which would leave you friendless and unprotected in a world of strangers where assassination is the order of society and natural death one of the rarest of phenomena. Here are your arms." He stepped to a cabinet which he unlocked, displaying an assortment of weapons, and selected for me a long-sword, a short-sword, a pistol and a dagger.

"You seem sure of my loyalty, Ras Thavas," I said.

He shrugged his shoulders. "I am only sure that I know perfectly where your interests lie – sentimentalists have words: love, loyalty, friendship, enmity, jealousy, hate, a thousand others; a waste of words – one word defines them all: self-interest. All men of intelligence realize this. They analyse an individual and by his predilections and his needs they classify him as friend or foe, leaving to the weak-minded idiots who like to be deceived the drooling drivel of sentiment."

I smiled as I buckled my weapons to my harness, but I held my peace. Nothing could be gained by arguing with the man and, too, I felt quite sure that in any purely academic controversy I should get the worst of it; but many of the matters of which he had spoken had aroused my curiosity and one had reawakened in my mind a matter to which I had given considerable thought. While partially explained by some of his remarks I still wondered why the red-man from whom I had rescued him had seemed so venomously bent upon slaying him the day of my advent upon Barsoom, and so, as we sat chatting after our evening meal, I asked him.

"A sentimentalist," he said. "A sentimentalist of the most pronounced type. Why that fellow hated me with a venom absolutely unbelievable by any of the reactions of a trained, analytical mind such as mine; but having witnessed his reactions I become cognizant of a state of mind that I cannot of myself even imagine. Consider the facts. He was the victim of assassination – a young warrior in the prime of life, possessing a handsome face and a splendid physique. One of my agents paid his relatives a satisfactory sum for the corpse and brought it to me. It is thus that I obtain practically all of my material. I treated it in the manner with which you are familiar. For a year the body lay in the laboratory, there being no occasion during that time that I had use for it; but eventually a rich client came, a not overly prepossessing man of considerable years. He had fallen desperately in love with a young woman who was attended by many handsome suitors. My client had more money than any of them, more brains, more experience, but he lacked the one thing that each of the others had that always weighs heavily with the undeveloped, unreasoning, sentiment-ridden minds of young females – good looks."

"Now 378-J-493811-P had what my client lacked and could afford to purchase. Quickly we reached an agreement as to price and I transferred the brain of my rich client to the head of 378-J-493811-P and my client went away and for all I know won the hand of the beautiful moron; and 378-J-493811-P might have rested on indefinitely upon his ersite slab until I needed him or a part of him in my work, had I not, merely by chance, selected him for resurgence because of an existing need for another male slave.

"Mind you now, the man had been murdered. He was dead. I bought and paid for the corpse and all there was in it. He might have lain dead forever upon one of my ersite slabs had I not breathed new life into his dead veins. Did he have the brains to view the transaction in a wise and dispassionate manner? He did not.

"His sentimental reactions caused him to reproach me because I had given him another body, though it seemed to me that, looking at the matter from a standpoint of sentiment, if one must, he should have considered me as a benefactor for having given him life again in a perfectly healthy, if somewhat used, body.

"He had spoken to me upon the subject several times, begging me to restore his body to him, a thing of which, of course, as I explained to him, was utterly out of the question unless chance happened to bring to my laboratory the corpse of the client who had purchased his carcass – a contingency quite beyond the pale of possibility for one as wealthy as my client. The fellow even suggested that I permit him to go forth and assassinate my client bringing the body back that I might reverse the operation and restore his body to his brain. When I refused to divulge the name of the present possessor of his body he grew sulky, but until the very hour of your arrival, when he attacked me, I did not suspect the depth of his hate complex.

"Sentiment is indeed a bar to all progress. We of Toonol are probably less subject to its vagaries than most other nations upon Barsoom, but yet most of my fellow countrymen are victims of it in varying degrees. It has its rewards and compensations, however. Without it we could preserve no stable form of government and the Phundahlians, or some other people, would overrun and conquer us; but enough of our lower classes have sentiment to a sufficient degree to give them loyalty to the Jeddak of Toonol and the upper classes are brainy enough to know that it is to their own best interests to keep him upon his throne.

"The Phundahlians, upon the other hand, are egregious sentimentalists, filled with crass stupidities and superstitions, slaves to every variety of brain-withering conceit. Why the very fact that they keep the old termagant, Xaxa, on the throne brands them with their stupid idiocy. She is an ignorant, arrogant, selfish, stupid, cruel virago, yet the Phundahlians would fight and die for her because her father was Jeddak of Phundahl. She taxes them until they can scarce stagger beneath their burden, she misrules them, exploits them, betrays them, and they fall down and worship at her feet. Why? Because her father was Jeddak of Phundahl and his father before him and so on back into antiquity; because they are ruled by sentiment rather than reason; because their wicked rulers play upon this sentiment.

"She had nothing to recommend her to a sane person – not even beauty. You know, you saw her."

"I saw her?" I demanded.

"You assisted me the day that we gave her old brain a new casket – the day you arrived from what you call your Earth."

"She! That old woman was Jeddara of Phundahl?"

"That was Xaxa," he assured me.

"Why, you did not accord her the treatment that one of the Earth would suppose would be accorded a ruler, and so I had no idea that she was more than a rich old woman."

"I am Ras Thavas," said the old man. "Why should I incline the head to any other? In my world nothing counts but brain and in that respect and without egotism, I may say that I acknowledge no superior."

"Then you are not without sentiment," I said, smiling. "You acknowledge pride in your intellect!"

"It is not pride," he said, patiently, for him, "it is merely a fact that I state. A fact that I should have no difficulty in proving. In all probability I have the most highly developed and perfectly functioning mind among all the learned men of my acquaintance, and reason indicates that this fact also suggests that I possess the most highly developed and perfectly functioning mind upon Barsoom. From what I know of Earth and from what I have seen of you, I am convinced that there is no mind upon your planet that may even faintly approximate in power that which I have developed during a thousand years of active study and research. Rasoom (Mercury) or Cosoom (Venus) may possibly support intelligences equal to or even greater than mine. While we have made some study of their thought waves, our instruments are not yet sufficiently developed to more than suggest that they are of extreme refinement, power and flexibility."

"And what of the girl whose body you gave to the Jeddara?" I asked, irrelevantly, for my mind could not efface the memory of that sweet body that must, indeed, have possessed an equally sweet and fine brain.

"Merely a subject! Merely a subject!" he replied with a wave of his hand.

"What will become of her?" I insisted.

"What difference does it make?" he demanded. "I bought her with a batch of prisoners of war. I do not even recall from what country my agent obtained them, or from whence they originated. Such matters are of no import."

"She was alive when you bought her?" I demanded.

"Yes. Why?"

"You-er-ah-killed her, then?"

"Killed her! No; I preserved her. That was some ten years ago. Why should I permit her to grow old and wrinkled? She would no longer have the same value then, would she? No, I preserved her. When Xaxa bought her she was just as fresh and young as the day she arrived. I kept her a long time. Many women looked at her and wanted her face and figure, but it took a Jeddara to afford her. She brought the highest price that I have ever been paid.

"Yes, I kept her a long time, but I knew that some day she would bring my price."

"She was indeed beautiful and so sentiment has its uses – were it not for sentiment there would be no fools to support this work that I am doing, thus permitting me to carry on investigations of far greater merit. You would be surprised, I know, were I to tell you that I feel that I am almost upon the point of being able to produce rational human beings through the action upon certain chemical combinations of a group of rays probably entirely undiscovered by your scientists, if I am to judge by the paucity of your knowledge concerning such things."

"I would not be surprised," I assured him. "I would not be surprised by anything that you might accomplish."

CHAPTER THREE

Valla Dia

I LAY AWAKE a long time that night thinking of 4296-E-2631-H, the beautiful girl whose perfect body had been stolen to furnish a gorgeous setting for the cruel brain of a tyrant. It seemed such a horrid crime that I could not rid my mind of it and I think that contemplation of it sowed the first seed of my hatred and loathing for Ras Thavas. I could not conjure a creature so utterly devoid of bowels of compassion as to even consider for a moment the frightful ravishing of that sweet and lovely body for even the holiest of purposes, much less one that could have been induced to do so for filthy pelf.

So much did I think upon the girl that night that her image was the first to impinge upon my returning consciousness at dawn, and after I had eaten, Ras Thavas not having appeared, I went directly to the storage room where the poor thing was. Here she lay, identified only by a small panel, bearing a number: 4296-E-2631-H. The body of an old woman with a disfigured face lay before me in the rigid immobility of death; yet that was not the figure that I saw, but instead, a vision of radiant loveliness whose imprisoned soul lay dormant beneath those greying locks.

The creature here with the face and form of Xaxa was not Xaxa at all, for all that made the other what she was had been transferred to this cold corpse. How frightful would be the awakening, should awakening ever come! I shuddered to think of the horror that must overwhelm the girl when first she realized the horrid crime that had been perpetrated upon her. Who was she? What story lay locked in that dead and silent brain? What loves must have been hers whose beauty was so great and upon whose fair face had lain the indelible imprint of graciousness! Would Ras Thavas ever arouse her from this happy semblance of death? – far happier than any quickening ever could be for her. I shrank from the thought of her awakening and yet I longed to hear her speak, to know that that brain lived again, to learn her name, to listen to the story of this gentle life that had been so rudely snatched from its proper environment and so cruelly handled by the hand of Fate. And suppose she were awakened! Suppose she were awakened and that I – A hand was laid upon my shoulder and I turned to look into the face of Ras Thavas.

You seem interested in this subject," he said.

"I was wondering," I replied, "what the reaction this girl's brain would be were she to awaken to the discovery that she had become an old, disfigured woman."

He stroked his chin and eyed me narrowly. "An interesting experiment," he mused.

"I am gratified to discover that you are taking a scientific interest in the labours that I am carrying on. The psychological phases of my work I have, I must confess, rather neglected during the past hundred years or so, though I formerly gave them a great deal of attention. It would be interesting to observe and study several of these cases. This one, especially, might prove of value to you as an initial study, it being simple and regular. Later we will let you examine into a case where a man's brain has been transferred to a woman's skull, and a woman's brain to a man's. There are also the interesting cases where a portion of diseased or injured brain has been replaced by a portion of the brain from another subject, and, for experimental purposes alone, those human brains that have been transplanted to the craniums of beasts, and vice versa, offer tremendous opportunities for observation. I have in mind one case in which I transferred half the brain of an ape to the skull of a man, after having removed half of his brain, which I grafted upon the remaining part of the brain in the ape's skull. That was a matter of several years ago and I have often thought that I should like to recall these two subjects and note the results. I shall have to have a look at them – as I recall it they are in vault L-42-X, beneath building 4-J-21. We shall have to have a look at them someday soon – it has been years since I have been below. There must be some very interesting specimens there that have escaped my mind. But come! let us recall 4296-E-2631-H.

"No!" I exclaimed, laying a hand upon his arm. "It would be horrible."

He turned a surprised look upon me and then a nasty, sneering smile curled his lips. "Maudlin, sentimental fool!" he cried. "Who dare say no to me?"

I laid a hand upon the hilt of my long-sword and looked him steadily in the eye.

"Ras Thavas," I said, "you are master in your own house; but while I am your guest treat me with courtesy."

He returned my look for a moment but his eyes wavered. "I was hasty," he said.

"Let it pass." That, I let answer for an apology – really it was more than I had expected – but the event was not unfortunate. I think he treated me with far greater respect thereafter; but now he turned immediately to the slab bearing the mortal remains of 4296-E-2631-H.

"Prepare the subject for revivification," he said, "and make what study you can of all its reactions." With that he left the room.

I was now fairly adept at this work which I set about with some misgivings but with the assurance that I was doing right in obeying Ras Thavas while I remained a member of his entourage. The blood that had once flowed through the veins of the beautiful body that Ras Thavas had sold to Xaxa reposed in an hermetically sealed vessel upon the shelf above the corpse. As I had before done in other cases beneath the watchful eyes of the old surgeon I now did for the first time alone. The blood heated, the incisions made, the tubes attached and the few drops of life-giving solution added to the blood, I was now ready to restore life to that delicate brain that had lain dead for ten years. As my finger rested upon the little button that actuated the motor that was to send the revivifying liquid into those dormant veins, I experienced such a sensation as I imagined no mortal man has ever felt.

I had become master of life and death, and yet at this moment that I stood there upon the point of resurrecting the dead I felt more like a murderer than a saviour. I tried to view the procedure dispassionately through the cold eye of science, but I failed miserably. I could only see a stricken girl grieving for her lost beauties. With a muffled oath I turned away. I could not do it! And then, as though an outside force had seized upon me, my finger moved unerringly to the button and pressed it. I cannot explain it, unless upon the theory of dual mentality, which may explain many things. Perhaps my subjective mind directed the act. I do not know. Only I know that I did it, the motor started, the level of the blood in the container commenced gradually to lower.

Spell-bound, I stood watching. Presently the vessel was empty. I shut off the motor, removed the tubes, sealed the openings with tape. The red glow of life tinged the body, replacing the sallow, purplish hue of death. The breasts rose and fell regularly, the head turned slightly and the eyelids moved. A faint sigh issued from between the parting lips. For a long time there was no other sign of life, then, suddenly, the eyes opened. They were dull at first, but presently they commenced to fill with questioning wonderment. They rested on me and then passed on about that portion of the room that was visible from the position of the body. Then they came back to me and remained steadily fixed upon my countenance after having once surveyed me up and down. There was still the questioning in them, but there was no fear.

"Where am I?" she asked. The voice was that of an old woman – high and harsh. A startled expression filled her eyes. "What is the matter with me? What is wrong with my voice? What has happened?"

I laid a hand upon her forehead. "Don't bother about it now," I said, soothingly. "Wait until sometime when you are stronger. Then I will tell you."

She sat up. "I am strong," she said, and then her eyes swept her lower body and limbs and a look of utter horror crossed her face. "What has happened to me? In the name of my first ancestor, what has happened to me?"

The shrill, harsh voice grated upon me. It was the voice of Xaxa and Xaxa now must possess the sweet musical tones that alone would have harmonized with the beautiful face she had stolen. I tried to forget those strident notes and think only of the pulchritude of the envelope that had once graced the soul within this old and withered carcass.

She extended a hand and laid it gently upon mine. The act was beautiful, the movements graceful. The brain of the girl directed the muscles, but the old, rough vocal cords of Xaxa could give forth no sweeter notes. "Tell me, please!" she begged. There were tears in the old eyes, I'll venture for the first time in many years. "Tell me! You do not seem unkind."

And so I told her. She listened intently and when I was through she sighed.

"After all," she said, "it is not so dreadful, now that I really know. It is better than being dead." That made me glad that I had pressed the button. She was glad to be alive, even draped in the hideous carcass of Xaxa. I told her as much.

"You were so beautiful," I told her.

"And now I am so ugly?" I made no answer.

"After all, what difference does it make?" she inquired presently. "This old body cannot change me, or make me different from what I have always been. The good in me remains and whatever of sweetness and kindness, and I can be happy to be alive and perhaps to do some good. I was terrified at first, because I did not know what had happened to me. I thought that maybe I had contracted some terrible disease that had so altered me – that horrified me; but now that I know – pouf! what of it?"

"You are wonderful," I said. "Most women would have gone mad with the horror and grief of it – to lose such wondrous beauty as was yours – and you do not care."

"Oh, yes, I care, my friend," she corrected me, "but I do not care enough to ruin my life in all other respects because of it, or to cast a shadow upon the lives of those around me. I have had my beauty and enjoyed it. It is not an unalloyed happiness I can assure you. Men killed one another because of it; two great nations went to war because of it; and perhaps my father lost his throne or his life – I do not know, for I was captured by the enemy while the war still raged. It may be raging yet and men dying because I was too beautiful. No one will fight for me now, though," she added, with a rueful smile.

"Do you know how long you have been here?" I asked.

"Yes," she replied. "It was the day before yesterday that they brought me hither."

"It was ten years ago," I told her.

"Ten years! Impossible."

I pointed to the corpses around us. "You have lain like this for ten years," I explained. "There are subjects here who have lain thus for fifty, Ras Thavas tells me."

"Ten years! Ten years! What may not have happened in ten years! It is better thus. I should fear to go back now. I should not want to know that my father, my mother too, perhaps, were gone. It is better thus. Perhaps you will let me sleep again? May I not?"

"That remains with Ras Thavas," I replied; "but for a while I am to observe you."

"Observe me?"

"Study you – your reactions."

"Ah! and what good will that do?"

"It may do some good in the world."

"It may give this horrid Ras Thavas some new ideas for his torture chamber – some new scheme for coining money from the suffering of his victims," she said, her harsh voice saddened.

"Some of his works are good," I told her. "The money he makes permits him to maintain this wonderful establishment where he constantly carries on countless experiments. Many of his operations are beneficent. Yesterday a warrior was brought in whose arm was crushed beyond repair. Ras Thavas gave him a new arm. A demented child was brought. Ras Thavas gave her a new brain. The arm and the brain were taken from two who had met violent deaths. Through Ras Thavas they were permitted, after death, to give life and happiness to others."

She thought for a moment. "I am content," she said. "I only hope that you will always be the observer."

Presently Ras Thavas came and examined her. "A good subject," he said. He looked at the chart where I had made a very brief record following the other entries relative to the history of Case No. 4296-E-2631-H. Of course this is, naturally, a rather free translation of this particular identification number. The Barsoomians have no alphabet such as ours and their numbering system is quite different. The thirteen characters above were represented by four Toonolian characters, yet the meaning was quite the same – they represented, in contracted form, the case number, the room, the table and the building.

"The subject will be quartered near you where you may regularly observe it," continued Ras Thavas. "There is a chamber adjoining yours. I will see that it is unlocked. Take the subject there. When not under your observation, lock it in."

It was only another case to him.

I took the girl, if I may so call her, to her quarters. On the way I asked her her name, for it seemed to me an unnecessary discourtesy always to address her and refer to her as 4296-E-2631-H, and this I explained to her.

"It is considerate of you to think of that," she said, "but really that is all that I am here – just another subject for vivisection."

"You are more than that to me," I told her. "You are friendless and helpless. I want to be of service to you – to make your lot easier if I can."

"Thank you again," she said. "My name is Valla Dia, and yours?"

"Ras Thavas calls me Vad Varo," I told her.

But that is not your name?"

"My name is Ulysses Paxton."

"It is a strange name, unlike any that I have ever heard, but you are unlike any man I have ever seen – you do not seem Barsoomian. Your colour is unlike that of any race."

"I am not of Barsoom, but from Earth, the planet you sometimes call Jasoom. That is why I differ in appearance from any you have known before."

"Jasoom! There is another Jasoomian here whose fame has reached to the remotest corners of Barsoom, but I never have seen him."

"John Carter?" I asked.

"Yes, The War Lord. He was of Helium and my people were not friendly with those of Helium. I never could understand how he came here. And now there is another from Jasoom – how can it be? How did you cross the great void?"

I shook my head. "I cannot even guess," I told her.

"Jasoom must be peopled with wonderful men," she said. It was a pretty compliment.

"As Barsoom is with beautiful women," I replied.

She glanced down ruefully at her old and wrinkled body.

"I have seen the real you," I said gently.

"I hate to think of my face," she said. "I know it is a frightful thing."

"It is not you, remember that when you see it and do not feel too bad."

"Is it as bad as that?" she asked.

I did not reply.

"Never mind," she said presently. "If I had not beauty of the soul, I was not beautiful, no matter how perfect my features may have been; but if I possessed beauty of soul then I have it now. So I can think beautiful thoughts and perform beautiful deeds and that, I think, is the real test of beauty, after all."

"And there is hope," I added, almost in a whisper.

"Hope? No, there is no hope, if what you mean to suggest is that I may some time regain my lost self. You have told me enough to convince me that that can never be."

"We will not speak of it," I said, "but we may think of it and sometimes thinking a great deal of a thing helps us to find a way to get it, if we want it badly enough."

"I do not want to hope," she said, "for it will but mean disappointment for me. I shall be happy as I am. Hoping, I should always be unhappy."

I had ordered food for her and after it was brought Ras Thavas sent for me and I left her, locking the door of her chamber as the old surgeon had instructed. I found Ras Thavas in his office, a small room which adjoined a very large one in which were a score of clerks arranging and classifying reports from various departments of the great laboratory. He arose as I entered.

"Come with me, Vad Varo," he directed. "We will have a look at the two cases in L-42-X, the two of which I spoke."

"The man with half a simian brain and the ape with a half human brain?" I asked.

He nodded and preceded me towards the runway that led to the vaults beneath the building. As we descended, the corridors and passageways indicated long disuse.

The floors were covered with an impalpable dust, long undisturbed; the tiny radium bulbs that faintly illuminated the sub-Barsoomian depths were likewise coated. As we proceeded, we passed many doorways on either side, each marked with its descriptive hieroglyphic. Several of the openings had been tightly sealed with masonry. What gruesome secrets were hid within? At last we came to L-42-X. Here the bodies were arranged on shelves, several rows of which almost completely filled the room from floor to ceiling, except for a rectangular space in the centre of the chamber, which accommodated an ersite-topped operating table with its array of surgical instruments, its motor and other laboratory equipment.

Ras Thavas searched out the subjects of his strange experiment and together we carried the human body to the table. While Ras Thavas attached the tubes I returned for the vessel of blood which reposed upon the same shelf with the corpse. The now familiar method of revivification was soon accomplished and presently we were watching the return of consciousness to the subject.

The man sat up and looked at us, then he cast a quick glance about the chamber; there was a savage light in his eyes as they returned to us. Slowly he backed from the table to the floor, keeping the former between us.

"We will not harm you," said Ras Thavas.

The man attempted to reply, but his words were unintelligible gibberish, then he shook his head and growled. Ras Thavas took a step towards him and the man dropped to all fours, his knuckles resting on the floor, and backed away, growling.

"Come!" cried Ras Thavas. "We will not harm you." Again he attempted to approach the subject, but the man only backed quickly away, growling more fiercely; and then suddenly he wheeled and climbed quickly to the top of the highest shelf, where he squatted upon a corpse and gibbered at us.

"We shall have to have help," said Ras Thavas and, going to the doorway, he blew a signal upon his whistle.

"What are you blowing that for?" demanded the man suddenly. "Who are you? What am I doing here? What has happened to me?"

"Come down," said Ras Thavas. "We are friends."

Slowly the man descended to the floor and came towards us, but he still moved with his knuckles to the pavement He looked about at the corpses and a new light entered his eyes.

"I am hungry!" he cried. "I will eat!" and with that he seized the nearest corpse and dragged it to the floor.

"Stop! Stop!" cried Ras Thavas, leaping forward. "You will ruin the subject," but the man only backed away, dragging the corpse along the floor after him. It was then that the attendants came and with their help we subdued and bound the poor creature. Then Ras Thavas had the attendants bring the body of the ape and he told them to remain, as we might need them.

The subject was a large specimen of the Barsoomian white ape, one of the most savage and fearsome denizens of the Red Planet, and because of the creature's great strength and ferocity Ras Thavas took the precaution to see that it was securely bound before resurgence.

It was a colossal creature about ten or fifteen feet tall, standing erect, and had an intermediary set of arms or legs midway between its upper and lower limbs. The eyes were close together and nonprotruding; the ears were high set, while its snout and teeth were strikingly like those of our African gorilla.

With returning consciousness the creature eyed us questioningly. Several times it seemed to essay to speak but only inarticulate sounds issued from its throat.

Then it lay still for a period.

Ras Thavas spoke to it. "If you understand my words, nod your head." The creature nodded.

"Would you like to be freed of your bonds?" asked the surgeon.

Again the creature nodded an affirmative.

"I fear that you will attempt to injure us, or escape," said Ras Thavas.

The ape was apparently trying very hard to articulate and at last there issued from its lips a sound that could not be misunderstood. It was the single word no.

"You will not harm us or try to escape?" Ras Thavas repeated his question.

"No," said the ape, and this time the word was clearly enunciated.

"We shall see," said Ras Thavas. "But remember that with our weapons we may dispatch you quickly if you attack us."

The ape nodded, and then, very laboriously: "I will not harm you."

At a sign from Ras Thavas the attendants removed the bonds and the creature sat up. It stretched its limbs and slid easily to the floor, where it stood erect upon two feet, which was not surprising, since the white ape goes more often upon two feet than six; a fact of which I was not cognizant at the time, but which Ras Thavas explained to we later in commenting upon the fact that the human subject had gone upon all fours, which, to Ras Thavas, indicated a reversion to type in the fractional ape-brain transplanted to the human skull.

Ras Thavas examined the subject at considerable length and then resumed his examination of the human subject which continued to evince more simian characteristics than human, though it spoke more easily than the ape, because, undoubtedly, of its more perfect vocal organs. It was only by exerting the closest attention that the diction of the ape became understandable at all.

"There is nothing remarkable about these subjects," said Ras Thavas, after devoting half a day to them. "They bear out what I had already determined years ago in the transplanting of entire brains; that the act of transplanting stimulates growth and activity of brain cells. You will note that in each subject the transplanted portions of the brains are more active – they, in a considerable measure, control. That is why we have the human subject displaying distinctly simian characteristics, while the ape behaves in a more human manner; though if longer and closer observation were desirable you would doubtless find that each reverted at times to his own nature – that is the ape would be more wholly an ape and the human more manlike – but it is not worth the time, of which I have already given too much to a rather unprofitable forenoon. I shall leave you now to restore the subjects to anaesthesia while I return to the laboratories above. The attendants will remain here to assist you, if required."

The ape, who had been an interested listener, now stepped forward. "Oh, please, I pray you," it mumbled, "do not again condemn me to these horrid shelves. I recall the day that I was brought here securely bound, and though I have no recollection of what has transpired since I can but guess from the appearance of my own skin and that of these dusty corpses that I have lain here long. I beg that you will permit me to live and either restore me to my fellows or allow me to serve in some capacity in this establishment, of which I saw something between the time of my capture and the day that I was carried into this laboratory, bound and helpless, to one of your cold, ersite slabs."

Ras Thavas made a gesture of impatience. "Nonsense!" he cried. "You are better off here, where you can be preserved in the interests of science."

"Accede to his request," I begged, "and I will myself take over all responsibility for him while I profit by the study that he will afford me."

"Do as you are directed," snapped Ras Thavas as he quit the room.

I shrugged my shoulders. "There is nothing for it, then," I said.

"I might dispatch you all and escape," mused the ape, aloud, "but you would have helped me. I could not kill one who would have befriended me – yet I shrink from the thought of another death. How long have I lain here?"

I referred to the history of his case that had been brought and suspended at the head of the table. "Twelve years," I told him.

"And yet, why not?" he demanded of himself. "This man would slay me – why should I not slay him first."

"It would do you no good," I assured him, "for you could never escape. Instead you would be really killed, dying a death from which Ras Thavas would probably think it not worth while ever to recall you, while I, who might find the opportunity at some later date and who have the inclination, would be dead at your hands and thus incapable of saving you."

I had been speaking in a low voice, close to his ear, that the attendants might not overhear me. The ape listened intently.

"You will do as you suggest?" he asked.

"At the first opportunity that presents itself," I assured him.

"Very well," he said, "I will submit, trusting to you."

A half hour later both subjects had been returned to their shelves.

CHAPTER FOUR

The Compact

Days ran into weeks, weeks into months, as day by day I labored at the side of Ras Thavas, and more and more the old surgeon took me into his confidence, more and more he imparted to me the secrets of his skill and his profession.

Gradually he permitted me to perform more and more important functions in the actual practice of his vast laboratory. I started transferring limbs from one subject to another, then internal organs of the digestive tract. Then he entrusted to me a complete operation upon a paying client I removed the kidneys from a rich old man, replacing them with healthy ones from a young subject The following day I gave a stunted child new thyroid glands. A week later I transferred two hearts and then, at last, came the great day for me – unassisted, with Ras Thavas standing silently beside me, I took the brain of an old man and transplanted it within the cranium of a youth.

When I had done Ras Thavas laid a hand upon my shoulder. "I could not have done better myself," he said. He seemed much elated and I could not but wonder at this unusual demonstration of emotion upon his part, he who so prided himself upon his lack of emotionalism. I had often pondered the purpose which influenced Ras Thavas to devote so much time to my training, but never had I hit upon any more satisfactory explanation than that he had need of assistance in his growing practice. Yet when I consulted the records, that were now open to me, I discovered that his practice was no greater than it had been for many years; and even had it been there was really no reason why he should have trained me in preference to one of his red-Martian assistants, his belief in my loyalty not being sufficient warrant, in my mind, for this preferment when he could, as well as not have kept me for a bodyguard and trained one of his own kind to aid him in his surgical work.

But I was presently to learn that he had an excellent reason for what he was doing – Ras Thavas always had an excellent reason for whatever he did. One night after we had finished our evening meal he sat looking at me intently as he so often did, as though he would read my mind, which, by the way, he was totally unable to do, much to his surprise and chagrin; for unless a Martian is constantly upon the alert any other Martian can read clearly his every thought; but Ras Thavas was unable to read mine. He said that it was due to the fact that I was not a Barsoomian. Yet I could often read the minds of his assistants, when they were off their guard, though never had I read aught of Ras Thavas' thoughts, nor, I am sure, had any other read them. He kept his brain sealed like one of his own blood jars, nor was he ever for a moment found with his barriers down.

He sat looking at me this evening for a long time, nor did it in the least embarrass me, so accustomed was I to his peculiarities. "Perhaps," he said presently, "one of the reasons that I trust you is due to the fact that I cannot ever, at any time, fathom your mind; so, if you harbor traitorous thoughts concerning me I do not know it, while the others, every one of them, reveal their inmost souls to my searching mind and in each one there is envy, jealousy or hatred of me. Them, I know, I cannot trust. Therefore I must accept the risk and place all my dependence upon you, and my reason tells me that my choice is a wise one – I have told you upon what grounds it based my selection of you as my bodyguard. The same holds true in my selection of you for the thing I have in mind. You cannot harm me without harming yourself and no man will intentionally do that; nor is there any reason why you should feel any deep antagonism towards me.

"You are, of course, a sentimentalist and doubtless you look with horror upon many of the acts of a sane, rational, scientific mind; but you are also highly intelligent and can, therefore, appreciate better than another, even though you may not approve them, the motives that prompt me to do many of those things of which your sentimentality disapproves. I may have offended you, but I have never wronged you, nor have I wronged any creature for which you might have felt some of your so-called friendship or love. Are my premises incorrect, or my reasoning faulty?"

I assured him to the contrary.

"Very well! Now let me explain why I have gone to such pains to train you as no other human being, aside from myself, has ever been trained. I am not ready to use you yet, or rather you are not ready;

but if you know my purpose you will realize the necessity for bending your energy to the consummation of my purpose, and to that end you will strive even more diligently than you have to perfect yourself in the high, scientific art I am imparting to you.

"I am a very old man," he continued after a brief pause, "even as age goes upon Barsoom. I have lived more than a thousand years. I have passed the allotted natural span of life, but I am not through with my life's work – I have but barely started it. I must not die. Barsoom must not be robbed of this wondrous brain and skill of mine. I have long had in mind a plan to thwart death, but it required another with skill equal to mine – two such might live for ever. I have selected you to be that other, for reasons that I already have explained – they are undefiled by sentimentalism. I did not choose you because I love you, or because I feel friendship for you, or because I think that you love me, or feel friendship towards me. I chose you because I knew that of all the inhabitants of a world you were the one least likely to fail me. For a time you will have my life in your hands. You will understand now why I have not been able to choose carelessly.

"This plan that I have chosen is simplicity itself provided that I can count upon just two essential factors – skill and self-interested loyalty in an assistant. My body is about worn out. I must have a new one. My laboratory is filled with wonderful bodies, young and complete with potential strength and health. I have but to select one of these and have my skilled assistant transfer my brain from this old carcass to the new one." He paused.

"I understand now, why you have trained me," I said. "It has puzzled me greatly."

"Thus and thus only may I continue my labors," he went on, "and thus may Barsoom be assured a continuance practically indefinitely, of the benefits that my brain may bestow upon her children. I may live for ever, provided I always have a skilled assistant, and I may assure myself of such by seeing to it that he never dies; when he wears out one organ, or his whole body, I can replace either from my great storehouse of perfect parts, and for me he can perform the same service. Thus may we continue to live indefinitely; for the brain, I believe, is almost deathless, unless injured or attacked by disease.

"You are not ready as yet to be entrusted with this important task. You must transfer many more brains and meet with and overcome the various irregularities and idiosyncrasies that constitute the never failing differences that render no two operations identical. When you gain sufficient proficiency I shall be the first to know it and then we shall lose no time in making Barsoom safe for posterity."

The old man was far from achieving hatred of himself. However, his plan was an excellent one, both for himself and for me. It assured us immortality – we might live for ever and always with strong, healthy, young bodies. The outlook was alluring – and what a wonderful position it placed me in. If the old man could be assured of my loyalty because of self-interest, similarly might I depend upon his loyalty; for he could not afford to antagonize the one creature in the world who could assure him immortality, or withhold it from him. For the first time since I had entered his establishment I felt safe.

As soon as I had left him I went directly to Valla Dia's apartment, for I wanted to tell her his wonderful news. In the weeks that had passed since her resurrection I had seen much of her and in our daily intercourse there had been revealed to me little by little the wondrous beauties of her soul, until at last I no longer saw the hideous, disfigured face of Xaxa when I looked upon her, but the eyes of my heart penetrated deeper to the loveliness that lay within that sweet mind. She had become my confidante, as I was hers, and this association constituted the one great pleasure of my existence upon Barsoom.

Her congratulations, when I told her of what had come to me, were very sincere and lovely. She said that she hoped I would use this great power of mine to do good in the world. I assured her that I would and that among the first things that I should demand of Ras Thavas was that he should give Valla Dia a beautiful body; but she shook her head.

"No, my friend," she said, "if I may not have my own body this old one of Xaxa's is quite as good for me as another. Without my own body I should not care to return to my native country; while were Ras Thavas to give me the beautiful body of another, I should always be in danger of the covetousness of his clients, any one of whom might see and desire to purchase it, leaving to me her old husk, conceivably one quite terribly diseased or maimed. No, my friend, I am satisfied with the body of Xaxa, unless I may again possess my own, for Xaxa at least bequeathed me a tough and healthy envelope, however ugly it may be; and for what do looks count here? You, alone, are my friend – that I have your friendship is enough. You admire me for what I am, not for what I look like, so let us leave well enough alone."

"If you could regain your own body and return to your native country, you would like that?" I demanded.

"Oh, do not say it!" she cried. "The simple thought of it drives me mad with longing. I must not harbour so hopeless a dream that at best may only tantalize me into greater abhorrence of my lot."

"Do not say that it is hopeless," I urged. "Death, only, renders hope futile."

"You mean to be kind," she said, "but you are only hurting me. There can be no hope."

"May I hope for you, then?" I asked. "For I surely see a way; however slight a possibility for success it may have, still, it is a way."

She shook her head. "There is no way," she said, with finality. "No more will Duhor know me."

"Duhor?" I repeated. "Your – someone you care for very much?"

"I care for Duhor very much," she answered with a smile, "but Duhor is not someone – Duhor is my home, the country of my ancestors."

"How came you to leave Duhor?" I asked. "You have never told me, Valla Dia."

"It was because of the ruthlessness of Jal Had, Prince of Amhor," she replied.

"Hereditary enemies were Duhor and Amhor; but Jal Had came disguised into the city of Duhor, having heard, they say, of the great beauty attributed to the only daughter of Kor San, Jeddak of Duhor, and when he had seen her he determined to possess her. Returning to Amhor he sent ambassadors to the court of Kor San to sue for the hand of the Princess of Duhor; but Kor San, who had no son, had determined to wed his daughter to one of his own Jeds, that the son of this union, with the blood of Kor San in his veins, might rule over the people of Duhor; and so the offer of Jal Had was declined.

"This so incensed the Amhorian that he equipped a great fleet and set forth to conquer Duhor and take by force that which he could not win by honorable methods. Duhor was, at that time, at war with Helium and all her forces were far afield in the south, with the exception of a small army that had been left behind to guard the city. Jal Had, therefore, could not have selected a more propitious time for an attack. Duhor fell, and while his troops were looting the fair city Jal Had, with a picked force, sacked the palace of the Jeddak and searched for the princess; but the princess had no mind to go back with him as Princess of Amhor. From the moment that the vanguard of the Amhorian fleet was seen in the sky she had known, with the others of the city, the purpose for which they came, and so she used her head to defeat that purpose.

"There was in her retinue a cosmetologist whose duty it was to preserve the lustrous beauty of the princess' hair and skin and prepare her for public audiences, for fetes and for the daily intercourse of the court. He was a master of his art; he could render the ugly pleasant to look upon, he could make the plain lovely, and he could make the lovely radiant. She called him quickly to her and commanded him to make the radiant ugly, and when he had done with her none might guess that she was the Princess of Duhor, so deftly had he wrought with his pigments and his tiny brushes.

"When Jal Had could not find the princess within the palace, and no amount of threat or torture could force a statement of her whereabouts from the loyal lips of her people, the Amhorian ordered that every woman within the palace be seized and taken to Amhor; there to be held as hostages until the Princess of Duhor should be delivered to him in marriage. We were, therefore, all seized and placed upon an Amhorian war ship which was sent back to Amhor ahead of the balance of the fleet, which remained to complete the sacking of Duhor.

"When the ship, with its small convoy, had covered some four thousand of the five thousand haads that separate Duhor from Amhor, it was sighted by a fleet from Phundahl which immediately attacked. The convoying ships were destroyed or driven off and that which carried us was captured. We were taken to Phundahl where we were put upon the auction block and I fell to the bid of one of Ras Thavas' agents. The rest you know."

"And what became of the princess?" I asked.

"Perhaps she died – her party was separated in Phundahl – but death could not more definitely prevent her return to Duhor. The Princess of Duhor will never again see her native country."

"But you may!" I cried, for I had suddenly hit upon a plan. "Where is Duhor?"

"You are going there?" she asked, laughingly.

"Yes!"

"You are mad, my friend," she said. "Duhor lies a full seven thousand, eight hundred haads from Toonol, upon the opposite side of the snow-clad Artolian Hills. You, a stranger and alone, could never reach it; for between lie the Toonolian Marshes, wild hordes, savage beasts and warlike cities. You would but die uselessly within the first dozen haads, even could you escape from the island upon which stands the laboratory of Ras Thavas; and what motive is there to prompt you to such a useless sacrifice?"

I could not tell her. I could not look upon that withered figure and into that hideous and disfigured face and say: "It is because I love you, Valla Dia." But that, alas, was my only reason. Gradually, as I had come to know her through the slow revealment of the wondrous beauty of her mind and soul, there had crept into my heart a knowledge of my love; and yet, explain it I cannot, I could not speak the words to that frightful old hag. I had seen the gorgeous mundane tabernacle that had housed the equally gorgeous spirit of the real Valla Dia – that I could love; her heart and soul and mind I could love; but I could not love the body of Xaxa. I was torn, too, by other emotions, induced by a great doubt – could Valla Dia return my love. Habilitated in the corpse of Xaxa, with no other suitor, nay, with no other friend she might, out of gratitude or through sheer loneliness, be attracted to me; but once again were she Valla Dia the beautiful and returned to the palace of her king, surrounded by the great nobles of Duhor, would she have either eyes or heart for a lone and friendless exile from another world? I doubted it – and yet that doubt did not deter me from my determination to carry out, as far as Fate would permit, the mad scheme that was revolving in my brain.

"You have not answered my question, Vad Varo," she interrupted my surging thoughts. "Why would you do this thing?"

"To right the wrong that has been done you, Valla Dia," I said.

She sighed. "Do not attempt it, please," she begged. "You would but rob me of my one friend, whose association is the only source of happiness remaining to me. I appreciate your generosity and your loyalty, even though I may not understand them; your unselfish desire to serve me at such suicidal risk touches me more deeply than I can reveal, adding still further to the debt I owe you; but you must not attempt it – you must not."

"If it troubles you, Valla Dia," I replied, "we will not speak of it again; but know always that it is never from my thoughts. Some day I shall find a way, even though the plan I now have fails me."

The days moved on and on, the gorgeous Martian nights, filled with her hurtling moons, followed one upon another. Ras Thavas spent more and more time in directing my work of brain transference. I had long since become an adept; and I realized that the time was rapidly approaching when Ras Thavas would feel that he could safely entrust to my hands and skill his life and future. He would be wholly within my power and he knew that I knew it. I could slay him; I could permit him to remain for ever in the preserving grip of his own anaesthetic; or I could play any trick upon him that I chose, even to giving him the body of a calot or a part of the brain of an ape; but he must take the chance and that I knew, for he was failing rapidly. Already almost stone blind, it was only the wonderful spectacles that he had himself invented that permitted him to see at all; long deaf, he used artificial means for hearing; and now his heart was showing symptoms of fatigue that he could not longer ignore.

One morning I was summoned to his sleeping apartment by a slave. I found the old surgeon lying, a shrunken, pitiful heap of withered skin and bones.

"We must hasten, Vad Varo," he said in a weak whisper. "My heart was like to have stopped a few tals ago. It was then that I sent for you." He pointed to a door leading from his chamber. "There," he said, "you will find the body I have chosen. There, in the private laboratory I long ago built for this very purpose, you will perform the greatest surgical operation that the universe has ever known, transferring its most perfect brain to the most beautiful and perfect body that ever has passed beneath these ancient eyes. You will find the head already prepared to receive my brain; the brain of the subject having been removed and destroyed – totally destroyed by fire. I could not possibly chance the existence of a brain desiring and scheming to regain its wondrous body. No, I destroyed it. Call slaves and have them bear my body to the ersite slab."

"That will not be necessary," I told him; and lifting his shrunken form in my arms as he had been an Earthly babe, I carried him into the adjoining room where I found a perfectly lighted and appointed laboratory containing two operating tables, one of which was occupied by the body of a red-man. Upon the surface of the other, which was vacant, I laid Ras Thavas, then I turned to look at the new envelope he had chosen. Never, I believe, had I beheld so perfect a form, so handsome a face – Ras Thavas had indeed chosen well for himself. Then I turned back to the old surgeon. Deftly, as he had taught me, I made the two incisions and attached the tubes. My finger rested upon the button that would start the motor pumping his blood from his veins and his marvellous preservative-anaesthetic into them. Then I spoke.

"Ras Thavas," I said, "you have long been training me to this end. I have labored assiduously to prepare myself that there might be no slightest cause for apprehension as to the outcome. You have, coincidentally, taught me that one's every act should be prompted by self-interest only. You are satisfied, therefore, that I am not doing this for you because I love you, or because I feel any friendship for you; but you think that you have offered me enough in placing before me a similar opportunity for immortality.

"Regardless of your teaching I am afraid that I am still somewhat of a sentimentalist I crave the redressing of wrongs. I crave friendship and love. The price you offer is not enough. Are you willing to pay more that this operation may be successfully concluded?"

He looked at me steadily for a long minute. "What do you want?" he asked. I could see that he was trembling with anger, but he did not raise his voice.

"Do you recall 4296-E-2631-H?" I inquired.

"The subject with the body of Xaxa? Yes, I recall the case. What of it?"

"I wish her body returned to her. That is the price you must pay for this operation."

He glared at me. "It is impossible. Xaxa has the body. Even if I cared to do so, I could never recover it. Proceed with the operation!"

"When you have promised me," I insisted.

"I cannot promise the impossible – I cannot obtain Xaxa. Ask me something else. I am not unwilling to grant any reasonable request."

"That is all I wish – just that; but I do not insist that you obtain the body. If I bring Xaxa here will you make the transfer?"

"It would mean war between Toonol and Phundahl," he fumed.

"That does not interest me," I said. "Quick! Reach a decision. In five tals I shall press this button. If you promise what I ask, you shall be restored with a new and beautiful body; if you refuse you shall lie here in the semblance of death for ever."

"I promise," he said slowly, "that when you bring the body of Xaxa to me I will transfer to that body any brain that you select from among my subjects."

"Good!" I exclaimed, and pressed the button.

CHAPTER FIVE
Danger

RAS THAVAS AWAKENED from the anaesthetic a new and gorgeous creature – a youth of such wondrous beauty that he seemed of heavenly
rather than worldly origin; but in that beautiful head was the hard,
cold, thousand-year-old brain of the master surgeon. As he opened his
eyes he looked upon me coldly.

"You have done well," he said.

"What I have done, I have done for friendship – perhaps for love," I
said, "so you can thank the sentimentalism you decry for the success of
the transfer."

He made no reply.

"And now," I continued, "I shall look to you for the fulfilment of the
promise you have made me."

"When you bring Xaxa's body I shall transfer to it the brain of any of
my subjects you may select," he said, "but were I you, I would not risk
my life in such an impossible venture – you cannot succeed. Select another body – there are many beautiful ones – and I will give it the brain
of 4296-E-2631-H.

"None other than the body now owned by the Jeddara Xaxa will fulfill your promise to me," I said.

He shrugged and there was a cold smile upon his handsome lips.
"Very well," he said, "fetch Xaxa. When do you start?"

"I am not yet ready. I will let you know when I am."

"Good and now begone – but wait! First go to the office and see what
cases await us and if there be any that do not require my personal attention,
and they fall within your skill and knowledge, attend to them yourself."

As I left him I noticed a crafty smile of satisfaction upon his lips. What
had aroused that? I did not like it and as I walked away I tried to con-

jure what could possibly have passed through that wondrous brain to call forth at that particular instant so unpleasant a smile. As I passed through the doorway and into the corridor beyond I heard him summon his personal slave and body servant, Yamdor, a huge fellow whose loyalty he kept through the bestowal of lavish gifts and countless favors. So great was the fellow's power that all feared him, as a word to the master from the lips of Yamdor might easily send any of the numerous slaves or attendants to an ersite slab for eternity. It was rumored that he was the result of an unnatural experiment which had combined the brain of a woman with the body of a man, and there was much in his actions and mannerisms to justify this general belief. His touch, when he worked about his master, was soft and light, his movements graceful, his ways gentle, but his mind was jealous, vindictive and unforgiving.

I believe that he did not like me, through jealousy of the authority I had attained in the establishment of Ras Thavas; for there was no questioning the fact that I was a lieutenant, while he was but a slave; yet he always accorded me the utmost respect. He was, however, merely a minor cog in the machinery of the great institution presided over by the sovereign mind of Ras Thavas, and as such I had given him little consideration; nor did I now as I bent my steps towards the office.

I had gone but a short distance when I recalled a matter of importance upon which it was necessary for me to obtain instructions from Ras Thavas immediately; and so I wheeled about and retraced my way towards his apartments, through the open doorway of which, as I approached, I heard the new voice of the master surgeon. Ras Thavas had always spoken in rather loud tones, whether as a vocal reflection of his naturally domineering and authoritative character, or because of his deafness, I do not know; and now, with the fresh young vocal cords of his new body, his words rang out clearly and distinctly in the corridor leading to his room.

"You will, therefore, Yamdor," he was saying, "go at once and, selecting two slaves in whose silence and discretion you may trust, take the subject from the apartments of Vad Varo and destroy it – let no vestige of body or brain remain. Immediately after, you will bring the two slaves to the laboratory F-30-L, permitting them to speak to no one, and I will consign them to silence and forgetfulness for eternity. Vad Varo will discover the absence of the subject and report the matter to me."

"During my investigation you will confess that you aided 4296-E-2631-H to escape, but that you have no idea where it intended going. I will sentence you to death as punishment, but at last explaining how urgently I need your services and upon your solemn promise never to transgress again, I will defer punishment for the term of your continued good behaviour. Do you thoroughly understand the entire plan?"

"Yes, master," replied Yamdor.

"Then depart at once and select the slaves who are to assist you."

Quickly and silently I sped along the corridor until the first intersection permitted me to place myself out of sight of anyone coming from Ras Thavas' apartment; then I went directly to the chamber occupied by Valla Dia. Unlocking the door I threw it open and beckoned her to come out. "Quick! Valla Dia!" I cried. "No time is to be lost. In attempting to save you I have but brought destruction upon you. First we must find a hiding place for you, and that at once – afterwards we can plan for the future."

The place that first occurred to me as affording adequate concealment was the half forgotten vaults in the pits beneath the laboratories, and towards these I hastened Valla Dia. As we proceeded I narrated all that had transpired, nor did she once reproach me; but, instead, expressed naught but gratitude for what she was pleased to designate as my unselfish friendship. That it had miscarried, she assured me, was no reflection upon me and she insisted that she would rather die in the knowledge that she possessed one such friend than to live on indefinitely, friendless.

We came at last to the chamber I sought – vault L-42-X, in building 4-J-21, where reposed the bodies of the ape and the man, each of which possessed half the brain of the other. Here I was forced to leave Valla Dia for the time, that I might hasten to the office and perform the duties imposed upon me by Ras Thavas, lest his suspicions be aroused when Yamdor reported that he had found her apartment vacant.

I reached the office without it being discovered by anyone who might report the fact to Ras Thavas that I had been a long time coming from his apartment. To my relief, I found there were no cases. Without appearing in any undue haste, I nevertheless soon found an excuse to depart and at once made my way towards my own quarters, moving in a leisurely and unconcerned manner and humming, as was my wont (a habit which greatly irritated Ras Thavas), snatches from some song that had been popular at the time that I quit Earth. In this instance it was "Oh, Frenchy."

I was thus engaged when I met Yamdor moving hurriedly along the corridor leading from my apartment, in company with two male slaves. I greeted him pleasantly, as was my custom, and he returned my greeting; but there was an expression of fear and suspicion in his eyes. I went at once to my quarters, opened the door leading to the chamber formerly occupied by Valla Dia and then hastened immediately to the apartment of Ras Thavas, where I found him conversing with Yamdor. I rushed in apparently breathless and simulating great excitement.

"Ras Thavas," I demanded, "what have you done with 4296-E-2631-H? She has disappeared; her apartment is empty; and as I was approaching it I met Yamdor and two other slaves coming from that direction." I turned then upon Yamdor and pointed an accusing finger at him. "Yamdor!" I cried. "What have you done with this woman?"

Both Ras Thavas and Yamdor seemed genuinely puzzled and I congratulated myself that I had thus readily thrown them off the track. The master surgeon declared that he would make an immediate investigation; and he at once ordered a thorough search of the ground and of the island outside the enclosure. Yamdor denied any knowledge of the woman and I, at least, was aware of the sincerity of his protestations, but not so Ras Thavas. I could see a hint of suspicion in his eyes as he questioned his body servant; but evidently he could conjure no motive for any such treasonable action on the part of Yamdor as would have been represented by the abduction of the woman and the consequent gross disobedience of orders.

Ras Thavas' investigation revealed nothing. I think as it progressed that he became gradually more and more imbued with a growing suspicion that I might know more about the disappearance of Valla Dia than my attitude indicated, for I presently became aware of a delicately concealed espionage. Up to this time I had been able to smuggle food to Valla Dia every night, after Ras Thavas had retired to his quarters. Then, on one occasion, I suddenly became subconsciously aware that I was being followed, and instead of going to the vaults I went to the office, where I added some observations to my report upon a case I had handled that day. Returning to my room I hummed a few bars from "Over There," that the suggestion of my unconcern might be accentuated. From the moment that I quit my quarters until I returned to them I was sure that eyes had been watching my every move. What was I to do? Valla Dia must have food, without it she would die; and were I to be followed to her hiding place while taking it to her, she would die; Ras Thavas would see to that.

Half the night I lay awake, racking my brains for some solution to the problem.

There seemed only one way – I must elude the spies. If I could do this but one single time I could carry out the balance of a plan that had occurred to me, and which was, I thought, the only one feasible that might eventually lead to the resurrection of Valla Dia in her own body. The way was long, the risks great; but I was young, in love and utterly reckless of consequences in so far as they concerned me; it was Valla Dia's happiness alone that I could not risk too greatly, other than under dire stress. Well, the stress existed and I must risk that even as I risked my life.

My plan was formulated and I lay awake upon my sleeping silks and furs in the darkness of my room, awaiting the time when I might put it into execution. My window, which was upon the third floor, overlooked the walled enclosure, upon the scarlet sward of which I had made my first bow to Barsoom. Across the open casement I had watched Cluros, the farther moon, take his slow deliberate way.

He had already set. Behind him, Thuria, his elusive mistress, fled through the heavens. In five xats (about 15 minutes) she would set; and then for about three and three quarters Earth hours the heavens would be dark, except for the stars.

In the corridor, perhaps, lurked those watchful eyes. I prayed God that they might not be elsewhere as Thuria sank at last beneath the horizon and I swung to my window ledge, in my hand a long rope fabricated from braided strips torn from my sleeping silks while I had awaited the setting of the moons. One end I had fastened to a heavy sorapus bench which I had drawn close to the window. I dropped the free end of the rope and started my descent. My Earthly muscles, un-tried in such endeavours, I had not trusted to the task of carrying me to my window ledge in a single leap, when I should be returning. I felt that they would, but I did not know; and too much depended upon the success of my venture to risk any unnecessary chance of failure. And so I had prepared the rope.

Whether I was being observed I did not know. I must go on as though none were spying upon me. In less then four hours Thuria would return (just before the sudden Barsoomian dawn) and in the interval I must reach Valla Dia, persuade her of the necessity of my plan and carry out its details, returning to my chamber before Thuria could disclose me to any accidental observer. I carried my weapons with me and in my heart was unbending determination to slay whoever might cross my path and recognize me during the course of my errand, however innocent of evil intent against me he might be.

The night was quiet except for the usual distant sounds that I had heard ever since I had been here – sounds that I had interpreted as the cries of savage beasts. Once I had asked Ras Thavas about them, but he had been in ill humor and had ignored my question. I reached the ground quickly and without hesitation moved directly to the near-est entrance of the building, having previously searched out and deter-mined upon the route I would follow to the vault. No one was visible and I was confident, when at last I reached the doorway, that I had come through undetected. Valla Dia was so happy to see me again that it almost brought the tears to my eyes.

"I thought that something had happened to you," she cried, "for I knew that you would not remain away so long of your own volition."

I told her of my conviction that I was being watched and that it would not be possible for me longer to bring food to her without incurring almost certain detection, which would spell immediate death for her.

"There is a single alternative," I said, "and that I dread even to suggest and would not were there any other way. You must be securely hidden for a long time, until Ras Thavas' suspicions have been allayed; for as long as he has me watched I cannot possibly carry out the plans I have formulated for your eventual release, the restoration of your own body and your return to Duhor."

"Your will shall be my law, Vad Varo."

I shook my head. "It will be harder for you than you imagine."

"What is the way?" she asked.

I pointed, to the ersite-topped table. "You must pass again though that ordeal that I may hide you away in this vault until the time is ripe for the carrying out of my plans. Can you endure it?"

She smiled. "Why not?" she asked. "It is only sleep – if it lasts for ever I shall be no wiser."

I was surprised that she did not shrink from the idea, but I was very glad since I knew that it was the only way that we had a chance for success. Without my help she disposed herself upon the ersite slab.

"I am ready, Vad Varo," she said, bravely; "but first promise me that you will take no risks in this mad venture. You cannot succeed. When I close my eyes I know that it will be for the last time if my resurrection depends upon the successful outcome of the maddest venture that ever man conceived; yet I am happy, because I know that it is inspired by the greatest friendship with which any mortal woman has ever been blessed."

As she talked I had been adjusting the tubes and now I stood beside her with my finger upon the starting button of the motor.

"Good-bye, Vad Varo," she whispered.

"Not good-bye, Valla Dia, but only a sweet sleep for what to you will be the briefest instant. You will seem but to close your eyes and open them again. As you see me now, I shall be standing here beside you as though I never had departed from you. As I am the last that you look upon to-night before you close your eyes, so shall I be the first that you shall look upon as you open them on that new and beautiful morning; but you shall not again look forth through the eyes of Xaxa, but from the limpid depths of your own beautiful orbs."

She smiled and shook her head. Two tears formed beneath her lids. I pressed her hand in mine and touched the button.

CHAPTER SIX

Suspicions

IN SO FAR as I could know I reached my apartment without detection. Hiding my rope where I was sure it would not be discovered, I sought my sleeping silks and furs and was soon asleep.

The following morning as I emerged from my quarters I caught a fleeting glimpse of a figure in a nearby corridor and from then on for a long time I had further evidence that Ras Thavas suspicioned me. I went at once to his quarters, as had been my habit. He seemed restless, but he gave me no hint that he held any assurance that I had been responsible for the disappearance of Valla Dia, and I think that he was far from positive of it. It was simply that his judgment pointed to the fact that I was the only person who might have any reason for interfering in any way with this particular subject, and he was having me watched to either prove or disprove the truth of his reasonable suspicions. His restlessness he explained to me himself.

"I have often studied the reaction of others who have undergone brain transference," he said, "and so I am not wholly surprised at my own. Not only has my brain energy been stimulated, resulting in an increased production of nervous energy, but I also feel the effects of the young tissue and youthful blood of my new body. They are affecting my consciousness in a way that my experiment had vaguely indicated, but which I now see must be actually experienced to be fully understood. My thoughts, my inclinations, even my ambitions have been changed, or at least coloured, by the transfer. It will take some time for me to find myself."

Though uninterested, I listened politely until he was through and then I changed the subject "Have you located the missing woman?" I asked.

He shook his head, negatively.

"You must appreciate, Ras Thavas," I said, "that I fully realize that you must have known that the removal or destruction of that woman would entirely frustrate my entire plan. You are master here. Nothing that passes is without your knowledge."

"You mean that I am responsible for the disappearance of the woman?" he demanded.

"Certainly. It is obvious. I demand that she be restored."

He lost his temper. "Who are you to demand?" he shouted. "You are naught but a slave. Cease your impudence or I shall erase you – erase you. It will be as though you never had existed."

I laughed in his face. "Anger is the most futile attribute of the sentimentalist," I reminded him. "You will not erase me, for I alone stand between you and mortality."

"I can train another," he parried.

"But you could not trust him," I pointed out.

"But you bargained with me for my life when you had me in your power," he cried.

"For nothing that it would have harmed you to have granted willingly. I did not ask anything for myself. Be that as it may, you will trust me again. You will trust, for no other reason than that you will be forced to trust me. So why not win my gratitude and my loyalty by returning the woman to me and carrying out in spirit as well as in fact the terms of our agreement?"

He turned and looked steadily at me. "Vad Varo," he said, "I give you the word of honor of a Barsoomian noble that I know absolutely nothing concerning the whereabouts of 4296-E-2631-H."

"Perhaps Yamdor does," I persisted.

"Nor Yamdor. Of my knowledge no person in any way connected with me knows what became of it. I have spoken the truth."

Well, the conversation was not as profitless as it might appear, for I was sure that it had almost convinced Ras Thavas that I was equally as ignorant of the fate of Valla Dia as was he. That it had not wholly convinced him was evidenced by the fact that the espionage continued for a long time, a fact which determined me to use Ras Thavas' own methods in my own defence. I had had allotted to me a number of slaves, and these I had won over by kindness and understanding until I knew that I had the full measure of their loyalty. They had no reason to love Ras Thavas and every reason to hate him; on the other hand they had no reason to hate me, and I saw to it that they had every reason to love me.

The result was that I had no difficulty in enlisting the services of a couple of them to spy upon Ras Thavas' spies, with the result that I was soon apprised that my suspicions were well founded – I was being constantly watched every minute that I was out of my apartments, but the spying did not come beyond my outer chamber walls. That was why I had been successful in reaching the vault in the manner that I had, the spies having assumed that I would leave my chamber only by its natural exit, had been content to guard that and permit my windows to go unwatched.

I think it was about two of our months that the spying continued and then my men reported that it seemed to have ceased entirely. All that time I was fretting at the delay, for I wanted to be about my plans which would have been absolutely impossible for me to carry out if I were being watched. I had spent the interval in studying the geography of the north-eastern Barsoomian hemisphere where my activities were to be carried on, and also in scanning a great number of case histories and inspecting the subjects to which they referred; but at last, with the removal of the spies, it began to look as though I might soon commence to put my plans in active operation.

Ras Thavas had for some time permitted me considerable freedom in independent investigation and experiment, and this I determined to take advantage of in every possible way that might forward my plans for the resurrection of Valla Dia. My study of the histories of many of the cases had been with the possibility in mind of discovering subjects that might be of assistance to me in my venture. Among those that had occupied my careful attention were, quite naturally, the cases with which I had been most familiar, namely: 378-J-493811-P, the red-man from whose vicious attack I had saved Ras Thavas upon the day of my advent upon Mars; and he whose brain had been divided with an ape.

The former, 378-J-493811-P, had been a native of Phundahl – a young warrior attached to the court of Xaxa, Jeddara of Phundahl – and a victim of assassination. His body had been purchased by a Phundahlian noble for the purpose, as Ras Thavas had narrated, of winning the favor of a young beauty. I felt that I might possibly enlist his services, but that would depend upon the extent of his loyalty towards Xaxa, which I could only determine by reviving and questioning him.

He whose brain had been divided with an ape had originated in Ptarth, which lay at a considerable distance to the west of Phundahl and a little south and about an equal distance from Duhor, which lay north and a little west of it. An inhabitant of Ptarth, I reasoned, would know much of the entire country included in the triangle formed by Phundahl, Ptarth and Duhor; the strength and ferocity of the great ape would prove of value in crossing beast-infested wastes; and I felt that I could hold forth sufficient promise to the human half of the great beast's brain, which really now dominated the creature, to win its support and loyalty. The third subject that I had tentatively selected had been a notorious Toonolian assassin, whose audacity, fearlessness and swordsmanship had won for him a reputation that had spread far beyond the boundaries of his country.

Ras Thavas, himself a Toonolian, had given me something of the history of this man whose grim calling is not without honor upon Barsoom, and which Gor Hajus had raised still higher in the esteem of his countrymen through the fact that he never struck down a woman or a good man and that he never struck from behind.

His killings were always the results of fair fights in which the victim had every opportunity to defend himself and slay his attacker; and he was famous for his loyalty to his friends. In fact this very loyalty had been a contributing factor in his downfall which had brought him to one of Ras Thavas' ersite slabs some years since, for he had earned the enmity of Vobis Kan, Jeddak of Toonol, through his refusal to assassinate a man who once had befriended Gor Hajus in some slight degree; following which Vobis Kan conceived the suspicion that Gor Hajus had him marked for slaying. The result was inevitable: Gor Hajus was arrested and condemned to death; immediately following the execution of the sentence, an agent of Ras Thavas had purchased the body.

These three, then, I had chosen to be my partners in my great adventure. It is true that I had not discussed the matter with any one of them, but my judgment assured me that I would have no difficulty in enlisting their services and loyalty in return for their total resurrection.

My first task lay in renewing the organs of 378-J-493811-P and of Gor Hajus, which had been injured by the wounds that had laid them low; the former requiring a new lung and the latter a new heart, his executioner having run him through with a short-sword. I hesitated to ask Ras Thavas' permission to experiment on these subjects for fear of the possibility of arousing his suspicions, in which event he would probably have them destroyed, and so I was forced to accomplish my designs by subterfuge and stealth. To this end I made it a practice for weeks to carry my regular laboratory work far into the night, often requiring the services of various assistants that all might become accustomed to the sight of me at work at unusual hours. In my selection of these assistants I made it a point to choose two of the very spies that Ras Thavas had set to watching me. While it was true that they were no longer employed in this particular service, I had hopes that they would carry word of my activities to their master; and I was careful to see that they received from me the proper suggestions that would mould their report in language far from harmful to me. By the merest suggestion I carried to them the idea that I worked thus late purely for the love of the work itself and the tremendous interest in it that Ras Thavas had awakened within my mind. Some nights I worked with assistants and as often I did not, but always I was careful to assure myself that the following morning those in the office were made aware that I had labored far into the preceding night.

This groundwork carefully prepared, I had comparatively little fear of the results of actual discovery when I set to work upon the warrior of Phundahl and the assassin of Toonol. I chose the former first. His lung was badly injured where my blade had passed through it, but from the laboratory where were kept fractional bodies I brought a perfect lung, with which I replaced the one that I had ruined. The work occupied but half the night. So anxious was I to complete my task that I immediately opened up the breast of Gor Hajus, for whom I had selected an unusually strong and powerful heart and by working rapidly I succeeded in completing the transference before dawn. Having known the nature of the wounds that had dispatched these two men, I had spent weeks in performing similar operations that I might perfect myself especially in this work; and having encountered no unusual pathological conditions in either subject, the work had progressed smoothly and with great rapidity. I had completed what I had feared would be the most difficult part of my task and now, having removed as far as possible all signs of the operation except the therapeutic tape which closed the incisions, I returned to my quarters for a few minutes of much-needed rest, praying that Ras Thavas would not by any chance examine either of the subjects upon which I had been working, although I had fortified myself against such a contingency by entering full details of the operation upon the history card of each subject that, in the event of discovery, any suspicion of ulterior motives upon my part might be allayed by my play of open frankness.

I arose at the usual time and went at once to Ras Thavas' apartment, where I was met with a bombshell that nearly wrecked my composure. He eyed me closely for a long minute before he spoke.

"You worked late last night, Vad Varo," he said.

"I often do," I replied, lightly; but my heart was heavy as a stone.

"And what might it have been that so occupied your interest?" he inquired.

I felt as a mouse with which the cat is playing. "I have been doing quite a little lung and heart transference of late," I replied, "and I became so engrossed with my work that I did not note the passage of time."

"I have known that you worked late at night. Do you think it wise?"

At that moment I felt that it had been very unwise, yet I assured him to the contrary.

"I was restless," he said. "I could not sleep and so I went to your quarters after midnight, but you were not there. I wanted someone with whom to talk, but your slaves knew only that you were not there – where you were they did not know – so I set out to search for you." My heart went into my sandals. "I guessed that you were in one of the laboratories, but though I visited several I did not find you." My heart arose with the lightness of a feather. "Since my own transference I have been cursed with restlessness and sleeplessness, so that I could almost wish for the return of my old corpse – the youth of my body harmonizes not with the antiquity of my brain. It is filled with latent urges and desires that comport illy with the serious subject matter of my mind."

"What your body needs," I said, "is exercise. It is young, strong, virile. Work it hard and it will let your brain rest at night."

"I know that you are right," he replied. "I have reached that same conclusion myself. In fact, not finding you, I walked in the gardens for an hour or more before returning to my quarters, and then I slept soundly. I shall walk every night when I cannot sleep, or I shall go into the laboratories and work as do you."

This news was most disquieting. Now I could never be sure but that Ras Thavas was wandering about at night and I had one more very important night's work to do, perhaps two. The only way that I could be sure of him was to be with him.

"Send for me when you are restless," I said, "and I will walk and work with you. You should not go about thus at night alone."

"Very well," he said, "I may do that occasionally."

I hoped that he would do it always, for then I would know that when he failed to send for me he was safe in his own quarters. Yet I saw that I must henceforth face the menace of detection; and knowing this I determined to hasten the completion of my plans and to risk everything on a single bold stroke.

That night I had no opportunity to put it into action as Ras Thavas sent for me early and informed me that we would walk in the gardens until he was tired. Now, as I needed a full night for what I had in mind and as Ras Thavas walked until midnight, I was compelled to forego everything for that evening, but the following morning I persuaded him to walk early on the pretext that I should like to go beyond the enclosure and see something of Barsoom besides the inside of his laboratories and his gardens. I had little confidence that he would grant my request, yet he did so. I am sure he never would have done it had he possessed his old body; but thus greatly had young blood changed Ras Thavas.

I had never been beyond the buildings, nor had I seen beyond, since there were no windows in the outside walls of any of the structures and upon the garden side the trees had grown to such a height that they obstructed all view beyond them. For a time we walked in another garden just inside the outer wall, and then I asked Ras Thavas if I might go even beyond this.

"No," he said. "It would not be safe."

"And why not?" I asked.

"I will show you and at the same time give you a much broader view of the outside world than you could obtain by merely passing through the gate. Come, follow me!" He led me immediately to a lofty tower that rose at the corner of the largest building of the group that comprised his vast establishment. Within was a circular runway which led not only upward, but down as well. This we ascended, passing openings at each floor, until we came at last out upon its lofty summit.

About me spread the first Barsoomian landscape of any extent upon which my eyes had yet rested during the long months that I had spent upon the Red Planet. For almost an Earthly year I had been immured within the grim walls of Ras Thavas' bloody laboratory, until, such creatures of habit are we, the weird life there had grown to seem quite natural and ordinary; but with this first glimpse of open country there surged up within me an urge for freedom, for space, for room to move about, such as I knew would not be long denied.

Directly beneath lay an irregular patch of rocky land elevated perhaps a dozen feet or more above the general level of the immediately surrounding country. Its extent was, at a rough guess, a hundred acres. Upon this stood the buildings and grounds, which were enclosed in a high wall. The tower upon which we stood was situated at about the centre of the total area enclosed. Beyond the outer wall was a strip of rocky ground on which grew a sparse forest of fair sized trees interspersed with patches of a jungle growth, and beyond all, what appeared to be an oozy marsh through which were narrow water courses connecting occasional open water – little lakes, the largest of which could have comprised scarce two acres. This landscape extended as far as the eye could reach, broken by occasional islands similar to that upon which we were and at a short distance by the skyline of a large city, whose towers and domes and minarets glistened and sparkled in the sun as though plated with shining metals and picked out with precious gems.

This, I knew, must be Toonol and all about us the Great Toonolian Marshes which extend nearly eighteen hundred Earth miles east and west and in some places have a width of three hundred miles. Little is known about them in other portions of Barsoom as they are frequented by fierce beasts, afford no landing places for fliers and are commanded by Phundahl at their western end and Toonol at the east, inhospitable kingdoms that invite no intercourse with the outside world and maintain their independence alone by their inaccessibility and savage aloofness.

As my eyes returned to the island at our feet I saw a huge form emerge from one of the nearby patches of jungle a short distance beyond the outer wall. It was followed by a second and a third. Ras Thavas saw that the creatures had attracted my notice.

"There," he said, pointing to them, "are three of a number of similar reasons why it would not have been safe for us to venture outside the enclosure."

They were great white apes of Barsoom, creatures so savage that even that fierce Barsoomian lion, the banth, hesitates to cross their path.

"They serve two purposes," explained Ras Thavas. "They discourage those who might otherwise creep upon me by night from the city of Toonol, where I am not without many good enemies, and they prevent desertion upon the part of my slaves and assistants."

"But how do your clients reach you?" I asked. "How are your supplies brought in?"

He tuned and pointed down toward the highest portion of the irregular roof of the building below us. Built upon it was a large, shed-like structure. "There," he said, "I keep three small ships. One of them goes every day to Toonol."

I was overcome with eagerness to know more about these ships, in which I thought I saw a much needed means of escape from the island; but I dared not question him for fear of arousing his suspicions.

As we turned to descend the tower runway I expressed interest in the structure which gave evidence of being far older than any of the surrounding buildings.

"This tower," said Ras Thavas, "was built some twenty-three thousand years ago by an ancestor of mine who was driven from Toonol by the reigning Jeddak of the time. Here, and upon other islands, he gathered a considerable following, dominated the surrounding marshes and defended himself successfully for hundreds of years. While my family has been permitted to return to Toonol since, this has been their home; to which, one by one, have been added the various buildings which you see about the tower, each floor of which connects with the adjacent building from the roof to the lowest pits beneath the ground."

This information also interested me greatly since I thought that I saw where it too might have considerable bearing upon my plan of escape, and so, as we descended the runway, I encouraged Ras Thavas to discourse upon the construction of the tower, its relation to the other buildings and especially its accessibility from the pits. We walked again in the outer garden and by the time we returned to Ras Thavas' quarters it was almost dark and the master surgeon was considerably fatigued.

"I feel that I shall sleep well to-night," he said as I left him.

"I hope so, Ras Thavas," I replied.

CHAPTER SEVEN
Escape

IT WAS USUALLY ABOUT three hours after the evening meal, which was served immediately after dark, that the establishment quieted down definitely for the night. While I should have preferred waiting longer before undertaking that which I had in mind, I could not safely do so, since there was much to be accomplished before dawn. So it was that with the first indications that the occupants of the building in which my work was to be performed had retired for the night, I left my quarters and went directly to the laboratory, where, fortunately for my plans, the bodies of Gor Hajus, the assassin of Toonol, and 378-J-493811-P both reposed. It was the work of a few minutes to carry them to adjoining tables, where I quickly strapped them securely against the possibility that one or both of them might not be willing to agree to the proposition I was about to make them, and thus force me to anaesthetize them again. At last the incisions were made, the tubes attached and the motors started. 378-J-493811-P, whom I shall hereafter call by his own name, Dar Tarus, was the first to open his eyes; but he had not regained full consciousness when Gor Hajus showed signs of life.

I waited until both appeared quite restored. Dar Tarus was eyeing me with growing recognition that brought a most venomous expression of hatred to his countenance. Gor Hajus was frankly puzzled. The last he remembered was the scene in the death chamber at the instant that his executioner had run a sword through his heart. It was I who broke the silence.

"In the first place" I said, "let me tell you where you are, if you do not already know."

"I know well enough where I am," growled Dar Tarus.

"Ah!" exclaimed Gor Hajus, whose eyes had been roaming about the chamber. "I can guess where I am. What Toonolian has not heard of Ras Thavas? So they sold my corpse to the old butcher did they? And what now? Did I just arrive?"

"You have been here six years," I told him, "and you may stay here for ever unless we three can reach an agreement within the next few minutes, and that goes for you too, Dar Tarus."

"Six years!" mused Gor Hajus. "Well, out with it, man. What do you want? If it is to slay Ras Thavas, no! He has saved me from utter destruction; but name me some other, preferably Vobis Kan, Jeddak of Toonol. Find me a blade and I will slay a hundred to regain life."

"I seek the life of none unless he stands in the way of the fulfilment of my desire in this matter that I have in hand. Listen! Ras Thavas had here a beautiful Duhorian girl. He sold her body to Xaxa, Jeddara of Phundahl, transplanting the girl's brain to the wrinkled and hideous body of the Jeddara. It is my intention to regain the body, restore it to its own brain and return the girl to Duhor."

Gor Hajus grinned. "You have a large contract on your hands," he said, "but I can see that you are a man after my own heart and I am with you. It will give freedom and fighting, and all that I ask is a chance for one thrust at Vobis Kan."

"I promise you life," I replied; "but with the understanding that you serve me faithfully and none other, undertaking no business of your own, until mine has been carried to a successful conclusion."

"That means that I shall have to serve you for life," he replied, "for the thing you have undertaken you can never accomplish; but that is better than lying here on a cold ersite slab waiting for old Ras Thavas to come along and carve out my gizzard. I am yours! Let me up, that I may feel a good pair of legs under me again."

"And you?" I asked, turning to Dar Tarus as I released the bonds that held Gor Hajus. For the first time I now noticed that the ugly expression that I had first noted upon the face of Dar Tarus had given place to one of eagerness.

"Strike off my bonds!" he cried. "I will follow you to the ends of Barsoom and the way leads thus far to the fulfilment of your design; but it will not. It will lead to Phundahl and to the chamber of the wicked Xaxa, where, by the generosity of my ancestors, I may be given the opportunity to avenge the hideous wrong the creature did me. You could not have chosen one better fitted for your mission than Dar Tarus, one time soldier of the Jeddara's Guard, whom she had slain that in my former body one of her rotten nobles might woo the girl I loved."

A moment later the two men stood at my side, and without more delay I led them towards the runway that descended to the path beneath the building. As we went, I described to them the creature I had chosen to be the fourth member of our strange party. Gor Hajus questioned the wisdom of my choice, saying that the ape would attract too much attention to us. Dar Tarus, however, believed that it might be helpful in many respects, since it was possible that we might be compelled to spend some time among the islands of the marshes which were often infested with these creatures; while, once in Phundahl, the ape might readily be used in the furtherance of our plans and would cause no considerable comment in a city where many of these beasts are held in captivity and often are seen performing for the edification of street crowds.

We went at once to the vault where the ape lay and where I had concealed the anaesthetized body of Valla Dia. Here I revived the great anthropoid and to my great relief found that the human half of its brain still was dominant. Briefly I explained my plan as I had to the other two and won the hearty promise of his support upon my engaging to restore his brain to its rightful place upon the completion of our venture.

First we must get off the island, and I outlined two plans I had in mind. One was to steal one of Ras Thavas' three fliers and set out directly for Phundahl, and the other, in the event that the first did not seem feasible, was to secrete ourselves aboard one of them on the chance that we might either overpower the crew and take over the ship after we had left the island, or escape undetected upon its arrival in Toonol. Dar Tarus liked the first plan; the ape, whom we now called by the name belonging to the human half of his brain, Hovan Du, preferred the first alternative of the second plan; and Gor Hajus the second alternative.

Dar Tarus explained that as our principal objective was Phundahl, the quicker we got there the better. Hovan Du argued that by seizing the ship after it had left the island we would have longer time in which to make our escape before the ship was missed and pursuit instituted, than by seizing it now in the full knowledge that its absence would be discovered within a few hours. Gor Hajus thought that it would be better if we could come into Toonol secretly and there, through one of his friends, secure arms and a flier of our own. It would never do, he insisted, to attempt to go far without arms for himself and Dar Tarus, nor could we hope to reach Phundahl without being overhauled by pursuers; for we must plan on the hypothesis that Ras Thavas would immediately discover my absence; that he would at once investigate; that he would find Dar Tarus and Gor

Hajus missing and thereupon lose no time in advising Vobis Kan, Jeddak of Toonol, that Gor Hajus the assassin was at large, whereupon the Jeddak's best ships would be sent in pursuit.

Gor Hajus' reasoning was sound and coupled with my recollection that Ras Thavas had told me that his three ships were slow, I could readily foresee that our liberty would be of short duration were we to steal one of the old surgeon's fliers.

As we discussed the matter we had made our way through the pits and I had found the exit to the tower. Silently we passed upward along the runway and out upon the roof. Both moons were winging low through the heavens and the scene was almost as light as day. If anyone was about, discovery was certain. We hastened towards the hangar and were soon within it where, for a moment at least, I breathed far more easily than I had beneath those two brilliant moons upon the exposed roof.

The fliers were peculiar-looking contrivances, low, squat, with rounded bows and stems and covered decks, their every line proclaiming them as cargo carriers built for anything but speed. One was much smaller than the other two and a second was evidently undergoing repairs. The third I entered and examined carefully. Gor Hajus was with me and pointed out several places where we might hide with little likelihood of discovery unless it were suspected that we might be aboard, and that of course constituted a very real danger; so much so that I had about decided to risk all aboard the small flier, which Gor Hajus assured me would be the fastest of the three, when Dar Tarus stuck his head into the ship and motioned me to come quickly.

"There is someone about," he said when I reached his side.

"Where?" I demanded.

"Come," he said, and led me to the rear of the hangar, which was flush with the wall of the building upon which it stood, and pointed through one of the windows into the inner garden where, to my consternation, I saw Ras Thavas walking slowly to and fro. For an instant I was sick with despair, for I knew that no ship could leave that roof unseen while anyone was abroad in the garden beneath, and Ras Thavas least of all people in the world; but suddenly a great light dawned upon me. I called the three close to me and explained my plan.

Instantly they grasped the possibilities in it and a moment later we had run the small flier out upon the roof and turned her nose toward the east, away from Toonol. Then Gor Hajus entered her, set the various controls as we had decided, opened the throttle, slipped back to the roof. The four of us hastened into the hangar and ran to the rear window where we saw the ship moving slowly and gracefully out over the garden and the head of Ras Thavas, whose ears must instantly have caught the faint purring of the motor, for he was looking up by the time we reached the window.

Instantly he hailed the ship and stepping back from the window that he might not see me I answered: "Good-bye, Ras Thavas! It is I, Vad Varo, going out into a strange world to see what it is like. I shall return. The spirits of your ancestors be with you until then."

That was a phrase I had picked up from reading in Ras Thavas' library and I was quite proud of it.

"Come back at once," he shouted up in reply, "or you will be with the spirits of your own ancestors before another day is done."

I made no reply. The ship was now at such a distance that I feared my voice might no longer seem to come from it and that we should be discovered. Without more delay we concealed ourselves aboard one of the remaining fliers, that upon which no work was being done, and there commenced as long and tiresome a period of waiting as I can recall ever having passed through.

I had at last given up any hope of the ship's being flown that day when I heard voices in the hangar, and presently the sound of footsteps aboard the flier. A moment later a few commands were given and almost immediately the ship moved slowly out into the open.

The four of us were crowded into a small compartment built into a tiny space between the forward and aft starboard buoyancy tanks. It was very dark and poorly ventilated, having evidently been designed as a storage closet to utilize otherwise waste space. We dared not converse for fear of attracting attention to our presence, and for the same reason we moved about as little as possible, since we had no means of knowing but that some member of the crew might be just beyond the thin door that separated us from the main cabin of the ship.

Altogether we were most uncomfortable; but the distance to Toonol is not so great but that we might hope that our situation would soon be changed – at least if Toonol was to be the destination of the ship. Of this we soon had cheering hope. We had been out but a short time when, faintly, we heard a hail and then the motors were immediately shut down and the ship stopped.

"What ship?" we heard a voice demand, and from aboard our own came the reply: "The Vosar, Tower of Thavas for Toonol." We heard a scraping as the other ship touched ours.

"We are coming aboard to search you in the name of Vobis Kan, Jeddak of Toonol. Make way!" shouted one from the other ship. Our cheer had been of short duration. We heard the shuffling of many feet and Gor Hajus whispered in my ear.

"What shall we do?" he asked.

I slipped my short-sword into his hand. "Fight!" I replied.

"Good, Vad Varo," he replied, and then I handed him my pistol and told him to pass it on to Dar Tarus. We heard the voices again, but nearer now.

"What ho!" cried one. "It is Bal Zak himself, my old friend Bal Zak!" "None other," replied a deep voice. "And whom did you expect to find in command of the Vosar other than Bal Zak?"

"Who could know but that it might have been this Vad Varo himself, or even Gor Hajus," said the other, "and our orders are to search all ships."

"I would that they were here," replied Bal Zak, "for the reward is high. But how could they, when Ras Thavas himself with his own eyes saw them fly off in the Pinsar before dawn this day and disappear in the east?"

"Right you are, Bal Zak," agreed the other, "and it were a waste of time to search your ship. Come men! to our own!" I could feel the muscles about my heart relax with the receding footfalls of Vobis Kan's warriors as they quitted the deck of the Vosar for their own ship, and my spirits rose with the renewed purring of our own motor as Ras Thavas' flier again got under way. Gor Hajus bent his lips close to my ear.

"The spirits of our ancestors smile upon us," he whispered. "It is night and the darkness will aid in covering our escape from the ship and the landing stage."

"What makes you think it is night?" I asked.

"Vobis Kan's ship was close by when it hailed and asked our name. By daylight it could have seen what ship we were."

He was right. We had been locked in that stuffy hole since before dawn, and while I had thought that it had been for a considerable time, I also had realized that the darkness and the inaction and the nervous strain would tend to make it seem much longer than it really had been; so that I would not have been greatly surprised had we made Toonol by daylight.

The distance from the Tower of Thavas to Toonol is inconsiderable, so that shortly after Vobis Kan's ship had spoken to us we came to rest upon the landing stage at our destination. For a long time we waited, listening to the sounds of movement aboard the ship and wondering, upon my part at least, as to what the intentions of the captain might be. It was quite possible that Bal Zak might return to Thavas this same night, especially if he had come to Toonol to fetch a rich or powerful patient to the laboratories; but if he had come only for supplies he might well lie here until the morrow. This much I had learned from Gor Hajus, my own knowledge of the movements of the fliers of Ras Thavas being considerably less than nothing; for, though I had been months a lieutenant of the master surgeon, I had learned only the day before of the existence of his small fleet, it being according to the policy of Ras Thavas to tell me nothing unless the telling of it coincided with and furthered his own plans.

Questions which I asked he always answered, if he reasoned that the effects would not be harmful to his own interests, but he volunteered nothing that he did not particularly wish me to know; and the fact that there were no windows in the outside walls of the building facing towards Toonol, that I had never before the previous day been upon the roof and that I never had seen a ship sail over the inner court towards the east all tended to explain my ignorance of the fleet and its customary operations.

We waited quietly until silence fell upon the ship, betokening either that the crew had retired for the night or that they had gone down into the city. Then, after a whispered consultation with Gor Hajus, we decided to make an attempt to leave the flier. It was our purpose to seek a hiding place within the tower of the landing stage from which we might investigate possible avenues of escape into the city, either at once or upon the morrow when we might more easily mix with the crowd that Gor Hajus said would certainly be in evidence from a few hours after sunrise.

Cautiously I opened the door of our closet and looked into the main cabin beyond. It lay in darkness. Silently we filed out. The silence of the tomb lay upon the flier, but from far below arose the subdued noises of the city. So far, so good! Then, without sound, without warning, a burst of brilliant fight illuminated the interior of the cabin. I felt my fingers tighten upon my sword-hilt as I glanced quickly about.

Directly opposite us, in the narrow doorway of a small cabin, stood a tall man whose handsome harness betokened the fact that he was no common warrior. In either hand he held a heavy Barsoomian pistol, into the muzzles of which we found ourselves staring.

CHAPTER EIGHT

Hands Up!

IN QUIET TONES he spoke the words of the Barsoomian equivalent of our Earthly hands up! The shadow of a grim smile touched his lips, and as he saw us hesitate to obey his commands he spoke again.

"Do as I tell you and you will be well off. Keep perfect silence. A raised voice may spell your doom; a pistol shot most assuredly."

Gor Hajus raised his hands above his head and we others followed his example.

"I am Bal Zak," announced the stranger. My heart slumped.

"Then you had better commence firing," said Gor Hajus, "for you will not take us alive and we are four to one."

"Not so fast, Gor Hajus," admonished the captain of the Vosar, until you learn what is in my mind."

"That, we already know for we heard you speak of the large reward that awaited the captor of Vad Varo and Gor Hajus," snapped the assassin of Toonol.

"Had I craved that reward so much I could have turned you over to the dwar of Vobis Kan's ship when he boarded us," said Bal Zak.

"You did not know we were aboard the Vosar," I reminded him.

"Ah, but I did."

Gor Hajus snorted his disbelief.

"How then," Bal Zak reminded us, "was I able to be ready upon this very spot when you emerged from your hiding place? Yes, I knew that you were aboard."

"But how?" demanded Dar Tarus.

"It is immaterial," replied Bal Zak, "but to satisfy your natural curiosity I will tell you that I have quarters in a small room in the Tower of

Thavas, my windows overlook the roof and the hangar. My long life spent aboard fliers has made me very sensitive to every sound of a ship-motors changing their speed will awaken me in the dead of night, as quickly as will their starting or their stopping. I was awakened by the starting of the motors of the Pinsar; I saw three of you upon the roof and the fourth drop from the deck of the flier as she started and my judgment told me that the ship was being sent out unmanned for some reason of which I had no knowledge. It was too late for me to prevent the act and so I waited in silence to learn what would follow. I saw you hasten into the hangar and I heard Ras Thavas' hail and your reply, and then I saw you board the Vosar. Immediately I descended to the roof and ran noiselessly to the hangar, apprehending that you intended making away with this ship; but there was no one about the controls; and from a tiny port in the control room, through which one has a view of the main cabin, I saw you enter the closet. I was at once convinced that your only purpose was to stow away for Toonol and consequently, aside from keeping an eye upon your hiding place, I went about my business as usual."

"And you did not advise Ras Thavas?" I asked.

"I advised no one," he replied. "Years ago I learned to mind my own business, to see all, to hear all and to tell nothing unless it profited me to do so."

"But you said that the reward is high for our apprehension," Gor Hajus reminded him. "Would it not be profitable to collect it?"

"There are in the breasts of honourable men," replied Bal Zak, "forces that rise superior to the lust for gold, and while Toonolians are supposedly a people free from the withering influences of sentiment yet I for one am not totally unconscious of the demand of gratitude. Six years ago, Gor Hajus, you refused to assassinate my father, holding that he was a good man, worthy to live and one that had once befriended you slightly. To-day, through his son, you reap your reward and in some measure are repaid for the punishment that was meted out to you by Vobis Kan because of your refusal to slay the sire of Bal Zak. I have sent my crew away that none aboard the Vosar but myself might have knowledge of your presence. Tell me your plans and command me in what way I may be of further service to you."

"We wish to reach the streets, unobserved," replied Gor Hajus. "Can you but help us in that we shall not put upon your shoulders further responsibility for our escape. You have our gratitude and in Toonol, I need not remind you, the gratitude of Gor Hajus is a possession that even the Jeddak has craved."

"Your problem is complicated," said Bal Zak, after a moment of thought, "by the personnel of your party. The ape would immediately attract attention and arouse suspicion. Knowing much of Ras Thavas' experiments I realized at once this morning, after watching him with you, that he had the brain of a man; but this very fact would attract to him and to you the closer attention of the masses."

"I do not need acquaint them with the fact," growled Hovan Du. "To them I need be but a captive ape. Are such unknown in Toonol?"

"Not entirely, though they are rare," replied Bal Zak. "But there is also the white skin of Vad Varo! Ras Thavas appears to have known nothing of the presence of the ape with you; but he full well knew of Vad Varo, and your description has been spread by every means at his command. You would be recognized immediately by the first Toonolian that lays eyes upon you, and then there is Gor Hajus. He has been as dead for six years, yet I venture there is scarce a Toonolian that broke the shell prior to ten years ago who does not know the face of Gor Hajus as well as he knows that of his own mother. The Jeddak himself was not better known to the people of Toonol than Gor Hajus. That leaves but one who might possibly escape suspicion and detection in the streets of Toonol."

"If we could but obtain weapons for these others," I suggested, "we might even yet reach the house of Gor Hajus' friend."

"Fight your way through the city of Toonol?" demanded Bal Zak.

"If there is no other way we should have to," I replied.

"I admire the will," commented the commander of the Vosar, "but fear that the flesh is without sufficient strength. Wait! there is a way – perhaps. On the stage just below this there is a public depot where equilibrimotors are kept and rented. Could we find the means to obtain four of these there would be a chance, at least, for you to elude the air patrols and reach the house of Gor Hajus' friend; and I think I see a way to the accomplishment of that. The landing tower is closed for the night but there are several watchmen distributed through it at different levels. There is one at the equilibrimotor depot and, as I happen to know, he is a devotee of jetan. He would rather play jetan than attend to his duties as watchman. I often remain aboard the Vosar at night and occasionally he and I indulge in a game. I will ask him up to-night and while he is thus engaged you may go to the depot, help yourselves to equilibrimotors and pray to your ancestors that no air patrol suspects you as you cross the city towards your destination. What think you of this plan, Gor Hajus?"

"It is splendid," replied the assassin. "And you, Vad Varo?"

"If I knew what an equilibrimotor is I might be in a better position to judge the merits of the plan," I replied. "However, I am satisfied to abide by the judgment of Gor Hajus. I can assure you, Bal Zak, of our great appreciation, and as Gor Hajus has put the stamp of his approval upon your plan I can only urge you to arrange that we may put it into effect with as little delay as possible."

"Good!" exclaimed Bal Zak. "Come with me and I will conceal you until I have lured the watchman to the jetan game within my cabin. After that your fate will be in your own hands."

We followed him from the ship on to the deck of the landing stage and close under the side of the Vosar opposite that from which the watchman must approach the ship and enter it. Then, bidding us good luck, Bal Zak departed.

From the summit of the landing tower I had my first view of a Martian city.

Several hundred feet below me lay spread the broad, well-lighted avenues of Toonol, many of which were crowded with people. Here and there, in this central district, a building was raised high upon its supporting, cylindrical metal shaft; while further out, where the residences predominated, the city took on the appearance of a colossal and grotesque forest. Among the larger palaces only an occasional suite of rooms was thus raised high above the level of the others, these being the sleeping apartments of the owners, their servants or their guests; but the smaller homes were raised in their entirety, a precaution necessitated by the constant activities of the followers of Gor Hajus' ancient profession that permitted no man to be free from the constant menace of assassination. Throughout the central district the sky was pierced by the lofty towers of several other landing stages; but, as I was later to learn, these were comparatively few in number. Toonol is in no sense a flying nation, supporting no such enormous fleets of merchant ships and vessels of war as, for example, the twin cities of Helium or the great capital of Ptarth.

A peculiar feature of the street lighting of Toonol, and in fact the same condition applies to the lighting of other Barsoomian cities I have visited, I noted for the first time that night as I waited upon the landing stage for the return of Bal Zak with the watchman. The luminosity below me seemed confined directly to the area to be lighted; there was no diffusion of light upward or beyond the limits the lamps were designed to light This was effected, I was told, by lamps designed upon principles resulting from ages of investigation of the properties of light waves and the laws governing them which permit Barsoomian scientists to confine and control light as we confine and control matter. The light waves leave the lamp, pass along a prescribed circuit and return to the lamp. There is no waste nor, strange this seemed to me, are there any dense shadows when lights are properly installed and adjusted, for the waves in passing around objects to return to the lamp, illuminate all sides of them.

The effect of this lighting from the great height of the tower was rather remarkable. The night was dark, there being no moons at that hour upon this night, and the effect was that obtained when sitting in a darkened auditorium and looking upon a brilliantly lighted stage. I was still intent upon watching the life and colour beneath when we heard Bal Zak returning. That he had been successful in his mission was apparent from the fact that he was conversing with another.

Five minutes later we crept quietly from our hiding place and descended to the stage below where lay the equilibrimotor depot. As theft is practically unknown upon Barsoom, except for purposes entirely disassociated from a desire to obtain pecuniary profit through the thing stolen, no precautions are taken against theft. We therefore found the doors of the depot open and Gor Hajus and Dar Tarus quickly selected four equilibrimotors and adjusted them upon us. They consist of a broad belt, not unlike the life belt used aboard trans-oceanic liners upon Earth; these belts are filled with the eighth Barsoomian ray, or ray of propulsion, to a sufficient degree to just about equalize the pull of gravity and thus to maintain a person in equilibrium between that force and the opposite force exerted by the eighth ray. Permanently attached to the back of the belt is a small radium motor, the controls for which are upon the front of the belt.

Rigidly attached to and projecting from each side of the upper rim of the belt is a strong, light wing with small hand levers for quickly altering its position.

Gor Hajus quickly explained the method of control, but I could apprehend that there might be embarrassment and trouble awaiting me before I mastered the art of flying in an equilibrimotor. He showed me how to tilt the wings downward in walking so that I would not leave the ground at every step, and thus he led me to the edge of the landing stage.

"We will rise here," he said, "and keeping in the darkness of the upper levels seek to reach the house of my friend without being detected. If we are pursued by air patrols we must separate; and later those who escape may gather just west of the city wall where you will find a small lake with a deserted tower upon its northern rim – this tower will be our rendezvous in event of trouble. Follow me!" He started his motor and rose gracefully into the air.

Hovan Du followed him and then it was my turn. I rose beautifully for about twenty feet, floating out over the city which lay hundreds of feet below, and then, quite suddenly, I turned upside down. I had done something wrong – I was quite positive of it. It was a most startling sensation, I can assure you, floating there with my head down, quite helpless; while below me lay the streets of a great city and no softer, I was sure, than the streets of Los Angeles or Paris. My motor was still going, and as I manipulated the controls which operated the wings I commenced to describe all sorts of strange loops and spirals and spins; and then Dar Tarus came to my rescue. First he told me to lie quietly and then directed the manipulation of each wing until I had gained an upright position. After that I did fairly well and was soon rising in the wake of Gor Hajus and Hovan Du.

I need not describe in detail the hour of flying, or rather floating, that ensued. Gor Hajus led us to a considerable altitude and there, through the darkness above the city, our slow motors drove us towards a district of magnificent homes surrounded by spacious grounds; and here, as we hovered over a large palace, we were suddenly startled by a sharp challenge coming from directly above us.

"Who flies by night?" a voice demanded.

"Friends of Mu Tel, Prince of the House of Kan," replied Gor Hajus: quickly.

"Let me see your night flying permit and your flier's licence," ordered the one above us, at the same time swooping suddenly to our level and giving me my first sight of a Martian policeman. He was equipped with a much swifter and handier equilibrimotor than ours. I think that was the first fact to impress us deeply, and it demonstrated the futility of flight; for he could have given us ten minutes' start and overhauled each of us within another ten minutes, even though we had elected to fly in different directions. The fellow was a warrior rather than a policeman, though detailed to duty such as our Earthly police officers perform; the city being patrolled both day and night by the warriors of Vobis Kan's army.

He dropped now close to the assassin of Toonol, again demanding permit and licence and at the same time flashing a light in the face of my comrade.

"By the sword of the Jeddak!" he cried. "Fortune heaps her favors upon me. Who would have thought an hour since that it would be I who would collect the reward for the capture of Gor Hajus?"

"Any other fool might have thought it," returned Gor Hajus, "but he would have been as wrong as you," and as he spoke he struck with the short-sword I had loaned him.

The blow was broken by the wing of the warrior's equilibrimotor, which it demolished, yet it inflicted a severe wound in the fellow's shoulder. He tried to back off, but the damaged wing caused him only to wheel around erratically; and then he seized upon his whistle and attempted to blow a mighty blast that was cut short by another blow from Gor Hajus' sword that split the man's head open to the bridge of his nose.

"Quick!" cried the assassin. "We must drop into the gardens of Mu Tel, for that signal will bring a swarm of air patrols about our heads."

The others I saw falling rapidly towards the ground, but again I had trouble.

Depress my wings as I would I moved only slightly downward and upon a path that, if continued, would have landed me at a considerable distance from the gardens of Mu Tel. I was approaching one of the elevated portions of the palace, what appeared to be a small suite that was raised upon its shining metal shaft far above the ground. From all directions I could hear the screaming whistles of the air patrols answering the last call of their comrade whose corpse floated just above me, a guide even in death to point the way for his fellows to search us out. They were sure to discover him and then I would be in plain view, of them and my fate sealed.

Perhaps I could find ingress to the apartment looming darkly near! There I might hide until the danger had passed, provided I could enter, undetected. I directed my course towards the structure; an open window took form through the darkness and then I collided with a fine wire netting – I had run into a protecting curtain that fends off assassins of the air from these high-flung sleeping apartments. I felt that I was lost. If I could but reach the ground I might find concealment among the trees and shrubbery that I had seen vaguely outlined beneath me in the gardens of this Barsoomian prince; but I could not drop at a sufficient angle to bring me to ground within the garden, and when I tried to spiral down I turned over and started up again. I thought of ripping open my belt and letting the eighth ray escape; but in my unfamiliarity with this strange force I feared that such an act might precipitate me to the ground with too great violence, though I was determined to have recourse to it as a last alternative if nothing less drastic presented itself.

In my last attempt to spiral downward I rose rapidly feet foremost to a sudden and surprising collision with some object above me. As I frantically righted myself, fully expecting to be immediately seized by a member of the air patrol, I found myself face to face with the corpse of the warrior Gor Hajus had slain.

The whistling of the air patrols sounded ever nearer – it could be only a question of seconds now before I was discovered – and with the stern necessity that confronted me, with death looking me in the face, there burst upon me a possible avenue of escape from my dilemma.

Seizing tightly with my left hand the harness of the dead Toonolian, I whipped out my dagger and slashed his buoyancy belt a dozen times. Instantly, as the rays escaped, his body started to drag me downward, Our descent was rapid, but not precipitate, and it was but a matter of seconds before we landed gently upon the scarlet sward of the gardens of Mu Tel, Prince of the House of Kan, close beside a clump of heavy shrubbery. Above me sounded the whistles of the circling patrols as I dragged the corpse of the warrior into the concealing depth of the foliage. Nor was I an instant too soon for safety, as almost immediately the brilliant rays of a searchlight shot downward from the deck of a small patrol ship, illuminating the open spaces of the garden all about me. A hurried glance through the branches and the leaves of my sanctuary revealed nothing of my companions and I breathed a sigh of relief in the thought that they, too, had found concealment.

The light played for a short time about the gardens and then passed on, as did the sound of the patrol's whistles, as the search proceeded elsewhere; thus giving me the assurance that no suspicion was directed upon our hiding place.

Left in darkness I appropriated such of the weapons of the dead warrior as I coveted, after having removed my equilibrimotor, which I was first minded to destroy, but which I finally decided to moor to one of the larger shrubs against the possibility that I might again have need for it; and now, secure in the conviction that the danger of discovery by the air patrol had passed, I left my concealment and started in search of my companions.

Keeping well in the shadows of the trees and shrubs I moved in the direction of the main building, which loomed darkly near at hand; for in this direction I believed Gor Hajus would lead the others as I knew that the palace of Mu Tel was to have been our destination. As I crept along, moving with utmost stealth, Thuria, the nearer moon, shot suddenly above the horizon, illuminating the night with her brilliant rays. I was close to the building's ornately carved wall at the moment; beside me was a narrow niche, its interior cast in deepest shadow by Thuria's brilliant rays; to my left was an open bit of lawn upon which, revealed in every detail of its terrifying presence, stood as fearsome a creature as my Earthly eyes ever had rested upon. It was a beast about the size of a Shetland pony, with ten short legs and a terrifying head that bore some slight resemblance to that of a frog, except that the jaws were equipped with three rows of long, sharp tusks.

The thing had its nose in the air and was sniffing about, while its great pop eyes moved swiftly here and there, assuring me, beyond the shadow of a doubt, that it was searching for someone. I am not inclined to be egotistical, yet I could not avoid the conviction that it was searching for me. It was my first experience of a Martian watch dog; and as I sought concealment within the dark shadows of the niche behind me, at the very instant that the creature's eyes alighted upon me, and heard his growl and saw him charge straight towards me, I had a premonition that it might prove my last experience with one.

I drew my long-sword as I backed into the niche, but with a sense of the utter inadequacy of the unaccustomed weapon in the face of this three or four hundred pounds of ferocity incarnate. Slowly I backed away into the shadows as the creature bore down upon me and then, as it entered the niche, my back collided with a solid obstacle that put an end to further retreat.

CHAPTER NINE
The Palace of Mu Tel

As the calot entered the niche I experienced, I believe, all of the reactions of the cornered rat, and I certainly know that I set myself to fight in that proverbial manner. The beast was almost upon me and I was metaphorically kicking myself for not having remained in the open where there were many tall trees when the support at my back suddenly gave way, a hand reached out of the darkness behind me and seized my harness and I was drawn swiftly into inky blackness. A door slammed and the silhouette of the calot against the moonlit entrance to the niche was blotted out.

A gruff voice spoke in my ear. "Come with me!" it said. A hand found mine and thus I was led along through the darkness of what I soon discovered was a narrow corridor from the constantly recurring collisions I had first with one side of it and then with the other.

Ascending gradually, the corridor turned abruptly at right angles and I saw beyond my guide a dim luminosity that gradually increased until another turn brought us to the threshold of a brilliantly lighted chamber – a magnificent apartment, the gorgeous furnishings and decorations of which beggar the meagre descriptive powers of my native tongue. Cold, ivory, precious stones, marvelous woods, resplendent fabrics, gorgeous furs and startling architecture combined to impress upon my earthly vision such a picture as I had never even dreamed of dreaming; and in the center of this room, surrounded by a little group of Martians, were my three companions.

My guide conducted me towards the party, the members of which had turned towards us as we entered the chamber, and stopped before a tall Barsoomian, resplendent in jewel-encrusted harness.

"Prince," he said, "I was scarce a tal too soon. In fact, as I opened the door to step out into the garden in search of him, as you directed, there he was upon the opposite side with one of the calots of the garden almost upon him."

"Good!" exclaimed he who had been addressed as prince, and then he turned to Gor Hajus. "This is he, my friend, of whom you told me?"

"This is Vad Varo, who claims to be from the planet Jasoom," replied Gor Hajus; "and this, Vad Varo, is Mu Tel, Prince of the House of Kan."

I bowed and the prince advanced and placed his right hand upon my left shoulder in true Barsoomian acknowledgment of an introduction; when I had done similarly, the ceremony was over. There was no silly pleased-to-meet-you, how-do-you-do? or it's-a-pleasure-I-assure-you.

At Mu Tel's request I narrated briefly what had befallen me between the time I had become separated from my companions and the moment that one of his officers had snatched me from impending disaster. Mu Tel gave instructions that all traces of the dead patrol be removed before dawn lest their discovery bring upon him the further suspicion of his uncle, Vobis Kan, Jeddak of Toonol, who it seemed had long been jealous of his nephew's growing popularity and fearful that he harbored aspirations for the throne.

It was later in the evening, during one of those elaborate meals for which the princes of Barsoom are justly famous, when mellowed slightly by the rare vintages with which he delighted his guests, that Mu Tel discoursed with less restraint upon his imperial uncle.

"The nobles have long been tired of Vobis Kan," he said, "and the people are tiring of him – he is a conscienceless tyrant – but he is our hereditary ruler, and so they hesitate to change. We are a practical people, little influenced by sentiment; yet there is enough to keep the masses loyal to their Jeddak even after he has ceased to deserve their loyalty, while the fear of the wrath of the masses keeps the nobles loyal. There is also the natural suspicion that I, the next in line for succession, would make them no less tyrannical a Jeddak than has Vobis Kan, while, having youth, I might be much more active in cruel and nefarious practices.

"For myself, I would not hesitate to destroy my uncle and seize his throne were I sure of the support of the army, for with the warriors of Vobis Kan at my back I might defy the balance of Toonol. It is because of this that I long since offered my friendship to Gor Hajus; not that he might slay my uncle, but that when I had slain him in fair fight Gor Hajus might win to me the loyalty of the Jeddak's warriors, for great is the popularity of Gor Hajus among the soldiers, who ever look up to such a great fighter with reverence and devotion. I have offered Gor

Hajus a high place in the affairs of Toonol should he cast his lot with me; but he tells me that he has first to fulfil his obligations to you, Vad Varo, and for the furtherance of your adventure he has asked me to give you what assistance I may. This I offer gladly, from purely practical motives, since your early success will hasten mine. Therefore I propose to place at your disposal a staunch flier that will carry you and your companions to Phundahl."

This offer I naturally accepted, after which we fell to discussing plans for our departure which we finally decided to attempt early the following night, at a time when neither of the moons would be in the heavens. After a brief discussion of equipment we were, at my request, permitted to retire since I had not slept for more than thirty-six hours and my companions for twenty-four.

Slaves conducted us to our sleeping apartments, which were luxuriously furnished, and arranged magnificent sleeping silks and furs for our comfort.

After they had left us Gor Hajus touched a button and the room rose swiftly upon its metal shaft to a height of forty or fifty feet; the wire netting automatically dropped about us, and we were safe for the night.

The following morning, after our apartment had been lowered to its daylight level and before I was permitted to leave it, a slave was sent to me by Mu Tel with instructions to stain my entire body the beautiful copper-red of my Barsoomian friends; furnishing me with a disguise which I well knew to be highly essential to the success of my venture, since my white skin would have drawn unpleasant notice upon me in any city of Barsoom. Another slave brought harness and weapons for Gor Hajus, Dar Tarus and myself, and a collar and chain for Hovan Du, the ape-man. Our harness, while of heavy material, and splendid workmanship, was quite plain, being free of all insignia either of rank or service – such harness as is customarily worn by the Barsoomian panthan, or soldier of fortune, at such times as he is not definitely in the service of any nation or individual. These panthans are virtually men without a country, being roving mercenaries ready to sell their swords to the highest bidder. Although they have no organization they are ruled by a severe code of ethics and while in the employ of a master are, almost without exception, loyal to him. They are generally supposed to be men who have flown from the wrath of their own Jeddaks or the justice of their own courts, but there is among them a sprinkling of adventurous souls who have adopted their calling because of the thrills and excitement it offers. While they are well paid, they are also great gamblers and notorious spenders, with the result that they are almost always without funds and often reduced to strange expedients for the gaining of their livelihood between engagements; a fact which gave great plausibility to our possession of a trained ape, which upon Mars would appear no more remarkable than would to us the possession of a monkey or parrot by an old salt just returned, from a long cruise, to one of our Earthly ports.

This day that I stayed in the palace of Mu Tel, I spent much in the company of the prince, who found pleasure in questioning me concerning the customs, the politics, the civilization and the geography of Earth, with much of which, I was surprised to note, he seemed quite familiar; a fact which he explained was due to the marvelous development of Barsoomian astronomical instruments, wireless photography and wireless telephony; the last of which has been brought to such a state of perfection that many Barsoomian savants have succeeded in learning several Earthly languages, notably Urdu, English and Russian, and, a few, Chinese also. These have doubtless been the first languages to attract their attention because of the fact that they are spoken by great numbers of people over large areas of the world.

Mu Tel took me to a small auditorium in his palace that reminded me somewhat of private projection rooms on Earth. It had, I should say, a capacity of some two hundred persons and was built like a large camera obscura; the audience sitting within the instrument, their backs towards the lens and in front of them, filling one entire end of the room, a large ground glass upon which is thrown the image to be observed.

Mu Tel seated himself at a table upon which was a chart of the heavens. Just above the chart was a movable arm carrying a pointer. This pointer Mu Tel moved until it rested upon the planet Earth, then he switched off the light in the room and immediately there appeared upon the ground glass plate a view such as one might obtain from an airplane riding at an elevation of a thousand feet.

There was something strangely familiar about the scene before me. It was of a desolate, wasted country. I saw shattered stumps whose orderly arrangement proclaimed that here once an orchard had blossomed and borne fruit. There were great, unsightly holes in the earth and over and across all a tangle of barbed wire. I asked Mu Tel how we might change the picture to another locality. He lighted a small radio bulb between us and I saw a globe there, a globe of Earth, and a small pointer fixed over it.

"The side of this globe now presented to you represents the face of the Earth turned towards us," explained Mu Tel. "You will note that the globe is slowly revolving. Place this pointer where you will upon the globe and that portion of Jasoom will be revealed for you."

I moved the pointer very slowly and the picture changed. A ruined village came into view. I saw some people moving among its ruins. They were not soldiers. A little further on I came upon trenches and dug-outs – there were no soldiers here, either. I moved the pointer rapidly north and south along a vast line of trenches. Here and there in villages there were soldiers, but they were all French soldiers and never were they in the trenches. There were no German soldiers and no fighting. The war was over, then! I moved the pointer to the Rhine and across. There were soldiers in Germany – French soldiers, English soldiers, American soldiers. We had won the war! I was glad, but it seemed very far away and quite unreal – as though no such world existed and no such peoples had ever fought – it was as though I were recalling through its illustrations a novel that I had read a long time since.

"You seem much interested in that war torn country," remarked Mu Tel.

"Yes," I explained, "I fought in that war. Perhaps I was killed. I do not know."

"And you won?" he asked.

"Yes, my people won," I replied. "We fought for a great principle and for the peace and happiness of a world. I hope that we did not fight in vain."

"If you mean that you hope that your principle will triumph because you fought and won, or that peace will come, your hopes are futile. War never brought peace – it but brings more and greater wars. War is Nature's natural state – it is folly to combat it. Peace should be considered only as a time for preparation for the principal business of man's existence. Were it not for constant warring of one form of life upon another, and even upon itself, the planets would be so overrun with life that it would smother itself out. We found upon Barsoom that long periods of peace brought plagues and terrible diseases that killed more than the wars killed and in a much more hideous and painful way. There is neither pleasure nor thrill nor reward of any sort to be gained by dying in bed of a loathsome disease. We must all die – let us therefore go out and die in a great and exciting game, and make room for the millions who are to follow us. We have tried it out upon Barsoom and we would not be without war."

Mu Tel told me much that day about the peculiar philosophy of Toonolians. They believe that no good deed was ever performed except for a selfish motive; they have no god and no religion; they believe, as do all educated Barsoomians, that man came originally from the Tree of Life, but unlike most of their fellows they do not believe that an omnipotent being created the Tree of Life. They hold that the only sin is failure – success, however achieved, is meritorious; and yet, paradoxical as it may seem, they never break their given word. Mu Tel explained that they overcame the baneful results of this degrading weakness – this sentimental bosh – by seldom, if ever, binding themselves to loyalty to another, and then only for a definitely prescribed period.

As I came to know them better, and especially Gor Hajus, I began to realize that much of their flaunted contempt of the finer sensibilities was specious. It is true that generations of inhibition had to some extent atrophied those characteristics of heart and soul which the noblest among us so highly esteem; that friendships ties were lax and that blood kinship awakened no high sense of responsibility or love even between parents and children; yet Gor Hajus was essentially a man of sentiment, though he would doubtless have run through the heart any who had dared accuse him of it, thus perfectly proving the truth of the other's accusation. His pride in his reputation for integrity and loyalty proved him a man of heart as truly as did his jealousy of his reputation for heartlessness prove him a man of sentiment; and in all this he was but typical of the people of Toonol. They denied deity, and in the same breath worshipped the fetish of science that they had permitted to obsess them quite as harmfully as do religious fanatics accept the unreasoning rule of their imaginary gods; and so, with all their vaunted knowledge, they were unintelligent because unbalanced.

As the day drew to a close I became the more anxious to be away. Far to the west across desolate leagues of marsh lay Phundahl, and in Phundahl the beauteous body of the girl I loved and that I was sworn to restore to its rightful owner.

The evening meal was over and Mu Tel himself had conducted us to a secret hangar in one of the towers of his palace. Here artisans had prepared a flier for us, having removed during the day all signs of its real ownership, even to slightly altering its lines; so that in the event of capture Mu Tel's name might in no way be connected with the expedition. Provisions were stored, including plenty of raw meat for Hovan Du, and, as the farther moon sank below the horizon and darkness fell, a panel of the tower wall, directly in front of the flier's nose, slid aside. Mu Tel wished us luck and the ship slipped silently out into the night. The flier, like many of her type, was without cockpit or cabin; a low, metal hand-rail surmounted her gunwale; heavy rings were set substantially in her deck and to these her crew was supposed to cling or attach themselves by means of their harness hooks provided for this and similar purposes; a low wind shield, with a rakish slant afforded some protection from the wind; the motor and controls were all exposed, as all the space below decks was taken up by the buoyancy tanks. In this type everything is sacrificed to speed; there is no comfort aboard. When moving at high speed each member of the crew lies extended at full length upon the deck, each in his allotted place to give the necessary trim, and hangs on for dear life. These Toonolian crafts, however, are not overly fast, so I was told, being far outstripped in speed by the fliers of such nations as Helium and Ptarth who have for ages devoted themselves to the perfection of their navies; but this one was quite fast enough for our purposes, to the consummation of which it would be pitted against fliers of no higher rating, and it was certainly fast enough for me. In comparison with the slow-moving Vosar, it seemed to shoot through the air like an arrow.

We wasted no time in strategy or stealth, but opened her wide as soon as we were in the clear, and directed her straight towards the west and Phundahl. Scarcely had we passed over the gardens of Mu Tel when we met with our first adventure.

We shot by a solitary figure floating in the air and almost simultaneously there shrilled forth the warning whistle of an air patrol. A shot whistled above us harmlessly and we were gone; but within a few seconds I saw the rays of a searchlight shining down from above and moving searchingly to and fro through the air.

"A patrol boat!" shouted Gor Hajus in my ear. Hovan Du growled savagely and shook the chain upon his collar. We raced on, trusting to the big gods and the little gods and all our ancestors that the relentless eye of light would not find us out; but it did. Within a few seconds it fell full upon our deck from above and in front of us and there it clung as the patrol boat dropped rapidly towards us while it maintained a high rate of speed upon a course otherwise identical with ours. Then, to our consternation, the ship opened fire on us with explosive bullets. These projectiles contain a high explosive that is detonated by light rays when the opaque covering of the projectile is broken by impact with the target. It is therefore not at all necessary to make a direct hit for a shot to be effective. If the projectile strikes the ground or the deck of a vessel or any solid substance near its target, it does considerably more damage when fired at a group of men than if it strikes but one of them, since it will then explode if its outer shell is broken and kill or wound several; while if it enters the body of an individual the light rays cannot reach it and it accomplishes no more than a non-explosive bullet. Moonlight is not powerful enough to detonate this explosive and so projectiles fired at night, unless touched by the powerful rays of searchlights, detonate at sunrise the following morning, making a battlefield a most unsafe place at that time even though the contending forces are no longer there. Similarly they make the removal of the unexploded projectiles from the bodies of the wounded a most ticklish operation which may well result in the instant death of both the patient and the surgeon.

Dar Tarus, at the controls, turned the nose of our flier upward directly towards the patrol boat and at the same time shouted to us to concentrate our fire upon her propellers. For myself, I could see little but the blinding eye of the searchlight, and at that I fired with the strange weapon to which I had received my first introduction but a few hours since when it was presented to me by Mu Tel. To me that all searching eye represented the greatest menace that confronted us, and could we blind it the patrol boat would have no great advantage over us. So I kept my rifle straight upon it my finger on the button that controlled the fire, and prayed for a hit.

Gor Hajus knelt at my side, his weapon spitting bullets at the patrol boat. Dar Tarus' hands were busy with the controls and Hovan Du squatted in the bow and growled.

Suddenly Dar Tarus voiced an exclamation of alarm. "The controls are hit!" he shouted. "We can't alter our course – the ship is useless." Almost the same instant the searchlight was extinguished – one of my bullets evidently having found it. We were quite close to the enemy now and heard their shout of anger.

Our own craft, out of control, was running swiftly towards the other. It seemed that if there was not a collision we would pass directly beneath the keel of the air patrol. I asked Dar Tarus if our ship was beyond repair.

"We could repair it if we had time," he replied, "but it would take hours and while we were thus delayed the whole air patrol force of Toonol would be upon us."

"Then we must have another ship," I said. Dar Tarus laughed. "You are right, Vad Varo," he replied, "but where shall we find it?"

I pointed to the patrol boat. "We shall not have to look far."

Dar Tarus shrugged his shoulders. "Why not!" he exclaimed. "It would be a glorious fight and a worthy death."

Gor Hajus slapped me on the shoulder. "To the death, my captain!" he cried.

Hovan Du shook his chain and roared.

The two ships were rapidly approaching one another. We had stopped firing now for fear that we might disable the craft we hoped to use for our escape; and for some reason the crew of the patrol ship had ceased firing at us – I never learned why. We were moving in a line that would

bring us directly beneath the other ship. I determined to board her at all costs. I could see her keel boarding tackle slung beneath her, ready to be lowered to the deck of a quarry when once her grappling hooks had seized the prey. Doubtless they were already manning the latter, and as soon as we were beneath her the steel tentacles would reach down and seize us as her crew swarmed down the board tackle to our deck.

I called Hovan Du and he crept back to my side where I whispered my instructions in his ear. When I was done he nodded his head with a low growl. I cast off the harness hook that held me to the deck, and the ape and I moved to our bow after I had issued brief, whispered instructions to Gor Hajus and Dar Tarus. We were now almost directly beneath the enemy craft; I could see the grappling hooks being prepared for lowering. Our bow ran beneath the stern of the other ship and the moment was at hand for which I had been waiting. Now those upon the deck of the patrol boat could not see Hovan Du or me. The boarding tackle of the other ship swung fifteen feet above our heads; I whispered a word of command to the ape and simultaneously we crouched and sprang for the tackle. It may sound like a mad chance – failure meant almost certain death – but I felt that if two of us could reach the deck of the patrol boat while her crew was busy with the grappling gear it would be well worth the risk.

Gor Hajus had assured me that there would not be more than six men aboard the patrol ship; that one would be at the controls and the others manning the grappling hooks. It would be a most propitious time to gain a footing on the enemy's deck.

Hovan Du and I made our leaps and Fortune smiled upon us, though the huge ape but barely reached the tackle with one outstretched hand, while my Earthly muscles carried me easily to my goal. Together we made our way rapidly towards the bow of the patrol craft and without hesitation, and as previously arranged, he clambered quickly up the starboard side and I the port. If I were the more agile jumper Hovan Du far outclassed me in climbing, with the result that he reached the rail and was clambering over while my eyes were still below the level of the deck, which was, perhaps, a fortunate thing for me since, by chance, I had elected to gain the deck directly at a point where, unknown to me, one of the crew of the ship was engaged with the grappling hooks. Had his eyes not been attracted elsewhere by the shout of one of his fellows who was first to see Hovan Du's savage face rise above the gunwale, he could have dispatched me with a single blow before ever I could have set foot upon the deck The ape had also come up directly in front of a Toonolian warrior and this fellow had let out a yell of surprise and sought to draw his sword, but the ape, for all his great bulk, was too quick for him; and as my eyes topped the rail I saw the mighty anthropoid seize the unfortunate man by the harness, drag him to the side and hurl him to destruction far below. Instantly we were both over the rail and squarely on deck while the remaining members of the craft's crew, abandoning their stations, ran forward to overpower us. I think that the sight of the great, savage beast must have had a demoralizing effect upon them, for they hesitated, each seeming to be willing to accord his fellow the honour of first engaging us; but they did come on, though slowly. This hesitation I was delighted to see, for it accorded perfectly with the plan that I had worked out, which depended largely upon the success which might attend the efforts of Gor Hajus and Dar Tarus to reach the deck of the patrol when our craft had risen sufficiently close beneath the other to permit them to reach the boarding tackle, which we were utilizing with reverse English, as one might say.

Gor Hajus had cautioned me to dispatch the man at the controls as quickly as possible, since his very first act would be to injure them the instant that there appeared any possibility that we might be successful in our attempt to take his ship, and so I ran quickly towards him and before he could draw I cut him down. There were now four against us and we waited for them to advance that we might gain time for our fellows to reach the deck.

The four moved slowly forward and were almost within striking distance when I saw Gor Hajus' head appear above the stern rail, quickly followed by that of Dar Tarus.

"Look!" I cried to the enemy, "and surrender," and I pointed astern.

One of them turned to look and what he saw brought an exclamation of surprise to his lips. "It is Gor Hajus," he cried, and then, to me: "What is your purpose with us if we surrender?"

"We have no quarrel with you," I replied. "We but wish to leave Toonol and go our way in peace – we shall not harm you."

He turned to his fellows while, at a sign from me, my three companions stopped their advance and waited. For a few minutes the four warriors conversed in low tones, then he who had first spoken addressed me.

"There are few Toonolians," he said, "who would not be glad to serve Gor Hajus, whom we had thought long dead, but to surrender our ship to you would mean certain death for us when we reported our defeat at our headquarters. On the other hand were we to continue our defence most of us here upon the deck of this flier would be killed. If you can assure us that your plans are not aimed at the safety of Toonol, I can make a suggestion that will afford an avenue of escape and safety for us all."

"We only wish to leave Toonol," I replied. "No harm can come to Toonol because of what I seek to accomplish."

"Good! and where do you wish to go?"

"That I may not tell you."

"You may trust us, if you accept my proposal," he assured me, "which is that we convey you to your destination, after which we can return to Toonol and report that we engaged you and that after a long running fight, in which two of our number were killed, you eluded us in the darkness and escaped."

"Can we trust these men?" I asked, addressing Gor Hajus, who assured me that we could, and thus the compact was entered into which saw us speeding rapidly towards Phundahl aboard one of Vobis Kan's own fliers.

CHAPTER TEN
Phundahl

THE FOLLOWING NIGHT the Toonolian crew set us down just inside the wall of the city of Phundahl, following the directions of Dar Tarus who was a native of the city, had been a warrior of the Jeddara's Guard and, prior to that seen service in Phundahl's tiny navy. That he was familiar with every detail of Phundahl's defences and her systems of patrols was evidenced by the fact that we landed without detection and that the Toonolian ship rose and departed apparently unnoticed.

Our landing place had been the roof of a low building built within and against the city wall. From this roof Dar Tarus led us down an inclined runway to the street, which, at this point, was quite deserted. The street was narrow and dark, being flanked upon one side by the low buildings built against the city wall and upon the other by higher buildings, some of which were windowless and none showing any light. Dar Tarus explained that he had chosen this point for our entrance because it was a district of storage houses, and while a hive of industry during the day, was always deserted at night, not even a watchman being required owing to the almost total absence of thievery upon Barsoom.

By devious and roundabout ways he led us finally to a section of second-rate shops, eating places and hotels such as are frequented by the common soldiers, artisans and slaves, where the only attention we attracted was due to the curiosity aroused by Hovan Du. As we had not eaten since leaving Mu Tel's palace, our first consideration was food. Mu Tel had furnished Gor Hajus with money, so that we had the means to gratify our wants. Our first stop was at a small shop where Gor Hajus purchased four or five pounds of thoat steak for Hovan Du, and then we repaired to an eating place of which Dar Tarus knew. At first the proprietor would not let us bring Hovan Du inside, but finally, after much argument, he permitted us to lock the great ape in an inner room where Hovan Du was forced to remain with his thoat meat while we sat at a table in the outer room.

I will say for Hovan Du that he played his role well, nor was there once when the proprietor of the place, or any of his patrons, or the considerable crowd that gathered to listen to the altercation, could have guessed that the body of the great savage beast was animated by a human brain. It was really only when feeding or fighting that the simian half of Hovan Du's brain appeared to exercise any considerable influence upon him; yet there seemed little doubt that it always coloured all his thoughts and actions to some extent, accounting for his habitual taciturnity and the quickness with which he was aroused to anger, as well as to the fact that he never smiled, nor appeared to appreciate in any degree the humor of a situation. He assured me, however, that the human half of his brain not only appreciated but greatly enjoyed the lighter episodes and occurrences of our adventure and the witty stories and anecdotes related by Gor Hajus, the Assassin, but that his simian anatomy had developed no muscles wherewith to evidence physical expression of his mental reactions.

We dined heartily, though upon rough and simple fare, but were glad to escape the prying curiosity of the garrulous and gossipy proprietor, who plied us with so many questions as to our past performances and future plans that Dar Tarus, who was our spokesman here, was hard put to it to quickly fabricate replies that would be always consistent. However, escape we did at last, and once again in the street, Dar Tarus set out to lead us to a public lodging house of which he knew. As we went we approached a great building of wondrous beauty in and out of which constant streams of people were pouring, and when we were before it Dar Tarus asked us to wait without as he must enter. When I asked him why, he told me that this was a temple of Tur, the god worshipped by the people of Phundahl.

"I have been away for a long time," he said, "and have had no opportunity to do honor to my god. I shall not keep you waiting long. Gor Hajus, will you loan me a few pieces of gold?"

In silence the Toonolian took a few pieces of money from one of his pocket pouches and handed them to Dar Tarus, but I could see that it was only with difficulty that he hid an expression of contempt, since the Toonolians are atheists.

I asked Dar Tarus if I might accompany him into the temple, which seemed to please him very much; and so we fell in with the stream approaching the broad entrance. Dar Tarus gave me two of the gold pieces that he had borrowed from Gor Hajus and told me to follow directly behind him and do whatever I saw him doing.

Directly inside the main entrance, and spread entirely across it at intervals that permitted space for the worshippers to pass between them, was a line of priests, their entire bodies, including their heads and faces, covered by a mantle of white cloth. In front of each was a substantial stand upon which rested a cash drawer. As we approached one of these we handed him a piece of gold which he immediately changed into many pieces of lesser value, one of which we dropped into a box at his side; whereupon he made several passes with his hands above our heads, dipped one of his fingers into a bowl of dirty water which he rubbed upon the ends of our noses, mumbled a few words which I could not understand and turned to the next in line as we passed on into the interior of the great temple. Never have I seen such a gorgeous display of wealth and lavish ornamentation as confronted my eyes in this, the first of the temples of Tur that it was my fortune to behold.

The enormous floor was unbroken by a single pillar and arranged upon it at regular intervals were carven images resting upon gorgeous pedestals. Some of these images were of men and some of women and many of them were beautiful; and there were others of beasts and of strange, grotesque creatures and many of these were hideous indeed. The first we approached was that of a beautiful female figure; and about the pedestal of this lay a number of men and women prone upon the floor against which they bumped their heads seven times and then arose and dropped a piece of money into a receptacle provided for that purpose, moving on then to another figure. The next that Dar Tarus and I visited was that of a man with a body of a silian, about the pedestal of which was arranged a series of horizontal wooden bars in concentric circles. The bars were about five feet from the floor and hanging from them by their knees were a number of men and women, repeating monotonously, over and over again, something that sounded to me like, bibble-babble-blup.

Dar Tarus and I swung to the bars like the others and mumbled the meaningless phrase for a minute or two, then we swung down, dropped a coin into the box, and moved on. I asked Dar Tarus what the words were that we had repeated and what they meant, but he said he did not know. I asked him if anyone knew, but he appeared shocked and said that such a question was sacrilegious and revealed a marked lack of faith. At the next figure we visited the people were all upon their hands and knees crawling madly in a circle about the pedestal. Seven times around they crawled and then they arose and put some money in a dish and went their ways. At another the people rolled about, saying, "Tur is Tur; Tur is Tur; Tur is Tur," and dropping money in a golden bowl when they were done.

"What god was that?" I whispered to Dar Tarus when we had quit this last figure, which had no head, but eyes, nose and mouth in the center of its belly.

"There is but one god," replied Dar Tarus solemnly, "and he is Tur!"

"Was that Tur?" I inquired.

"Silence, man," whispered Dar Tarus. "They would tear you to pieces were they to hear such heresy."

"Oh, I beg your pardon," I exclaimed. "I did not mean to offend. I see now that that is merely one of your idols."

Dar Tarus clapped a hand over my mouth. "S-s-s-t!" he cautioned to silence. "We do not worship idols – there is but one god and he is Tur!"

"Well, what are these?" I insisted, with a sweep of a hand that embraced the several score images about which were gathered the thousands of worshippers.

"We must not ask," he assured me. "It is enough that we have faith that all the works of Tur are just and righteous. Come! I shall soon be through and we may join our companions."

He led me next to the figure of a monstrosity with a mouth that ran entirely around its head. It had a long tail and the breasts of a woman. About this image were a great many people, each standing upon his head. They also were repeating, over and over, "Tur is Tur; Tur is Tur; Tur is Tur." When we had done this for a minute or two, during which I had a devil of a time maintaining my equilibrium, we arose, dropped a coin into the box by the pedestal and moved on.

"We may go now," said Dar Tarus. "I have done well in the sight of Tur."

"I notice," I remarked, "that the people repeated the same phrase before this figure that they did at the last – Tur is Tur."

"Oh, no," exclaimed Dar Tarus. "On the contrary they said just exactly the opposite from what they said at the other. At that they said, Tur is Tur; while at this they absolutely reversed it and said, Tur is Tur. Do you not see? They turned it right around backwards, which makes a very great difference."

"It sounded the same to me," I insisted.

"That is because you lack faith," he said sadly, and we passed out of the temple, after depositing the rest of our money in a huge chest, of which there were many standing about almost filled with coins.

We found Gor Hajus and Hovan Du awaiting us impatiently, the center of a large and curious throng among which were many warriors in the metal of Xaxa, the Jeddara of Phundahl. They wanted to see Hovan Du perform, but Dar Tarus told them that he was tired and in an ugly mood.

"To-morrow," he said, "when he is rested I shall bring him out upon the avenues to amuse you."

With difficulty we extricated ourselves, and passing into a quieter avenue, took a round-about way to the lodging place, where Hovan Du was confined in a small chamber while Gor Hajus, Dar Tarus and I were conducted by slaves to a large sleeping apartment where sleeping silks and furs were arranged for us upon a low platform that encircled the room and was broken only at the single entrance to the chamber. Here were already sleeping a considerable number of men, while two armed slaves patrolled the aisle to guard the guests from assassins.

It was still early and some of the other lodgers were conversing in low whispers so I sought to engage Dar Tarus in conversation relative to his religion, about which I was curious.

"The mysteries of religions always fascinate me, Dar Tarus," I told him.

"Ah, but that is the beauty of the religion of Tur," he exclaimed, "it has no mysteries. It is simple, natural, scientific and every word and work of it is susceptible of proof through the pages of Turgan, the great book written by Tur himself.

"Tur's home is upon the sun. There, one hundred thousand years ago, he made Barsoom and tossed it out into space. Then he amused himself by creating man in various forms and two sexes; and later he fashioned animals to be food for man and each other, and caused vegetation and water to appear that man and the animals might live. Do you not see how simple and scientific it all is?"

But it was Gor Hajus who told me most about the religion of Tur one day when Dar Tarus was not about. He said that the Phundahlians maintained that Tur still created every living thing with his own hands. They denied vigorously that man possessed the power to reproduce his kind and taught their young that all such belief was vile; and always they hid every evidence of natural procreation, insisting to the death that even those things which they witnessed with their own eyes and experienced with their own bodies in the bringing forth of their young never transpired.

Turgan taught them that Barsoom is flat and they shut their minds to every proof to the contrary. They would not leave Phundahl far for fear of falling off the edge of the world; they would not permit the development of aeronautics because should one of their ships circumnavigate Barsoom it would be a wicked sacrilege in the eyes of Tur, who made Barsoom flat.

They would not permit the use of telescopes, for Tur taught them that there was no other world than Barsoom and to look at another would be heresy; nor would they permit the teaching in their schools of any history of Barsoom that antedated the creation of Barsoom by Tur, though Barsoom has a well authenticated written history that reaches back more than one hundred thousand years; nor would they permit any geography of Barsoom except that which appears in Turgan, nor any scientific researches along biological lines. Turgan is their only text book – if it is not in Turgan it is a wicked lie.

Much of all this and a great deal more I gathered from one source or another during my brief stay in Phundahl, whose people are, I believe, the least advanced in civilization of any of the red nations upon Barsoom. Giving, as they do, all their best thought to religious matters, they have become ignorant, bigoted and narrow, going as far to one extreme as the Toonolians do to the other.

However, I had not come to Phundahl to investigate her culture but to steal her queen, and that thought was uppermost in my mind when I awoke to a new day – my first in Phundahl. Following the morning meal we set out in the direction of the palace to reconnoitre, Dar Tarus leading us to a point from which he might easily direct us the balance of the way, as he did not dare accompany us to the immediate vicinity of the royal grounds for fear of recognition, the body he now possessed having formerly belonged to a well-known noble.

It was arranged that Gor Hajus should act as spokesman and I as keeper of the ape. This arranged, we bade farewell to Dar Tarus and set forth, the three of us, along a broad and beautiful avenue that led directly to the palace gates. We had been planning and rehearsing the parts that we were to play and which we hoped would prove so successful that they would open the gates to us and win us to the presence of the Jeddara.

As we strolled with seeming unconcern along the avenue, I had ample opportunity to enjoy the novel and beautiful sights of this rich boulevard of palaces. The sun shone down upon vivid scarlet lawns, gorgeous flowered pimalia and a score of other rarely beautiful Barsoomian shrubs and trees, while the avenue itself was shaded by almost perfect specimens of the magnificent sorapus. The sleeping apartments of the buildings had all been lowered to their daytime level, and from a hundred balconies gorgeous silks and furs were airing in the sun. Slaves were briskly engaged with their duties about the grounds, while upon many a balcony women and children sat at their morning meal. Among the children we aroused considerable enthusiasm, or at least Hovan Du did, nor was he without interest to the adults. Some of them would have detained us for an exhibition, but we moved steadily on towards the palace, for nowhere else had we business or concern within the walls of Phundahl.

Around the palace gates was the usual crowd of loitering curiosity seekers; for after all human nature is much the same everywhere, whether skins be black or white, red or yellow or brown, upon Earth or upon Mars. The crowd before Xaxa's gates were largely made up of visitors from the islands of that part of the Great Toonolian Marshes which owes allegiance to Phundahl's queen, and like all provincials eager for a glimpse of royalty; though none the less to be interested by the antics of a simian, wherefore we had a ready made audience awaiting our arrival. Their natural fear of the great brute caused them to fall back a little at our approach so that we had a clear avenue to the very gates themselves, and there we halted while the crowds closed in behind, forming a half circle about us. Gor Hajus addressed them in a loud tone of voice that might be overheard by the warriors and their officers beyond the gates, for it was really them we had come to entertain, not the crowds in which we had not the slightest interest.

"Men and women of Phundahl," cried Gor Hajus, "behold two poor panthans, who, risking their lives, have captured and trained one of the most savage and ferocious and at the same time most intelligent specimens of the great white ape of Barsoom ever before seen in captivity and at great expense have brought it to Phundahl for your entertainment and edification. My friends, this wonderful ape is endowed with human intelligence; he understands every word that is spoken to him. With your kind attention, my friends, I will endeavor to demonstrate the remarkable intelligence of this ferocious, man-eating beast – an intelligence that has entertained the crowned heads of Barsoom and mystified the minds of her most learned savants."

I thought Gor Hajus did pretty well as a bally-hoo artist. I had to smile as I listened, here upon Mars, to the familiar lines that I had taught him out of my Earthly experience of county fairs and amusement parks, so highly ludicrous they sounded falling from the lips of the Assassin of Toonol; but they evidently interested his auditors and impressed them, too, for they craned their necks and stood in earnest eyed silence awaiting the performance of Hovan Du. Even better, several members of the Jeddara's Guard pricked up their ears and sauntered towards the gates; and among them was an officer.

Gor Hajus caused Hovan Du to lie down at word of command, to get up, to stand upon one foot, and to indicate the number of fingers that Gor Hajus held up by growling once for each finger, thus satisfying the audience that he could count; but these simple things were only by way of leading up to the more remarkable achievements which we hoped would win an audience before the Jeddara. Gor Hajus borrowed a set of harness and weapons from a man in the crowd and had Hovan Du don it and fence with him, and then indeed did we hear exclamations of amazement.

The warriors and the officer of Xaxa had drawn near the gates and were interested spectators, which was precisely what we wished, and now Gor Hajus was ready for the final, astounding revelation of Hovan Du's intelligence.

"These things that you have witnessed are as nothing," he cried. "Why this wonderful beast can even read and write. He was captured in a deserted city near Ptarth and can read and write the language of that country. Is there among you one who, by chance, comes from that distant country?"

A slave spoke up. "I am from Ptarth."

"Good!" said Gor Hajus. "Write some simple instructions and hand them to the ape. I will turn my back that you may know that I cannot assist him in any way."

The slave drew forth a tablet from a pocket pouch and wrote briefly. What he wrote he handed to Hovan Du. The ape read the message and without hesitation moved quickly to the gate and handed it to the officer standing upon the other side, the gate being constructed of wrought metal in fanciful designs that offered no obstruction to the view or to the passage of small articles. The officer took the message and examined it.

"What does it say?" he demanded of the slave that had penned it.

"It says," replied the latter: "Take this message to the officer who stands just within the gates."

There were exclamations of surprise from all parts of the crowd and Hovan Du was compelled to repeat his performance several times with different messages which directed him to do various things, the officer always taking a great interest in the proceedings.

"It is marvellous," said he at last "The Jeddara would be amused by the performance of this beast. Wait here, therefore, until I have sent word to her that she may, if she so desires, command your presence."

Nothing could have better suited us and so we waited with what patience we might for the messenger to return; and while we waited Hovan Du continued to mystify his audience with new proofs of his great intelligence.

CHAPTER ELEVEN

Xaxa

THE OFFICER RETURNED, the gates swung out and we were commanded to enter the courtyard of the palace of Xaxa, Jeddara of Phundahl. After that events transpired with great rapidity – surprising and totally unexpected events. We were led through an intricate maze of corridors and chambers until I became suspicious that we were purposely being confused, and convinced that whether such was the intention or not the fact remained that I could no more have retraced my steps to the outer courtyard than I could have flown without wings.

We had planned that, in the event of gaining admission to the palace, we would carefully note whatever might be essential to a speedy escape; but when, in a whisper, I asked Gor Hajus if he could find his way out again he assured me that he was as confused as I.

The palace was in no sense remarkable nor particularly interesting, the work of the Phundahlian artists being heavy and oppressing and without indication of high imaginative genius. The scenes depicted were mostly of a religious nature illustrating passages from Turgan, the Phundahlian bible, and, for the most part, were a series of monotonous repetitions. There was one, which appeared again and again, depicting Turgan creating a round, flat Mars and hurling it into Space, that always reminded me of a culinary artist turning a flap jack in a child's window.

There were also numerous paintings of what appeared to be court scenes delineating members of the Phundahlian royal line in various activities; it was noticeable that the more recent ones in which Xaxa appeared had had the principal figure repainted so that there confronted me from time to time portraits, none too well done, of the beautiful face and figure of Valla Dia in the royal trappings of a Jeddara. The effect of these upon me is not easy of description. They brought home to me the fact that I was approaching, and should presently be face to face with, the person of the woman to whom I had consecrated my love and my life, and yet in that same person I should be confronting one whom I loathed and would destroy.

We were halted at last before a great door and from the number of warriors and nobles congregated before it I was confident that we were soon to be ushered into the presence of the Jeddara. As we waited those assembled about us eyed us with, it seemed to me, more of hostility than curiosity and when the door swung open they accompanied us, with the exception of a few warriors, into the chamber beyond. The room was of medium size and at the farther side, behind a massive table, sat Xaxa. About her were grouped a number of heavily armed nobles. As I looked them over I wondered if among them was he for whom the body of Dar Tarus had been filched; for we had promised him that if conditions were favorable we would attempt to recover it.

Xaxa eyed us coldly as we were halted before her. "Let us see the beast perform," she commanded, and then suddenly: "What mean you by permitting strangers to enter my presence bearing arms?" she cried. "Sag Or, see that their weapons are removed!" and she turned to a handsome young warrior standing near her.

Sag Or! That was the name. Before me stood the noble for whom Dar Tarus had suffered the loss of his liberty, his body and his love. Gor Hajus had also recognized the name and Hovan Du, too; I could tell by the way they eyed the man as he advanced. Curtly he instructed us to hand our weapons to two warriors who advanced to receive them. Gor Hajus hesitated. I admit that I did not know what course to pursue.

Everyone seemed hostile and yet that might be, and doubtless was, but a reflection of their attitude towards all strangers. If we refused to disarm we were but three against a roomful, if they chose to resort to force; or if they turned us out of the palace because of it we would be robbed of this seemingly god given opportunity to win to the very heart of Xaxa's palace and to her very presence, where we must eventually win before we could strike. Would such an opportunity ever be freely offered us again? I doubted it and felt that we had better assume a vague risk now than, by refusing their demand, definitely arm their suspicions. So I quietly removed my weapons and handed them to the warrior waiting to receive them; and following my example, Gor Hajus did likewise, though I can imagine with what poor grace.

Once again Xaxa signified that she would see Hovan Du perform. As Gor Hajus put him through his antics she watched listlessly; nor did anything that the ape did arouse the slightest flicker of interest among the entire group assembled about the Jeddara. As the thing dragged on I became obsessed with apprehensions that all was not right. It seemed to me that an effort was being made to detain us for some purpose – to gain time. I could not understand, for instance, why Xaxa required that we repeat several times the least interesting of the ape's performances. And all the time Xaxa sat playing with a long, slim dagger, and I saw that she watched me quite as much as she watched Hovan Du, while I found it difficult to keep my eyes averted from that perfect face, even though I knew that it was but a stolen mask behind which lurked the cruel mind of a tyrant and a murderess.

At last came an interruption to the performance. The door opened and a noble entered, who went directly to the Jeddara whom he addressed briefly and in a low tone. I saw that she asked him several questions and that she seemed vexed by his replies. Then she dismissed him with a curt gesture and turned towards us.

"Enough of this!" she cried. Her eyes rested upon mine and she pointed her slim dagger at me. "Where is the other?" she demanded.

"What other?" I inquired.

"There were three of you, besides the ape. I know nothing about the ape, nor where, nor how you acquired it; but I do know all about you, Vad Varo, and Gor Hajus, the Assassin of Toonol, and Dar Tarus. Where is Dar Tarus?" her voice was low and musical and entirely beautiful – the voice of Valla Dia – but behind it I knew was the terrible personality of Xaxa, and I knew too that it would be hard to deceive her, for she must have received what information she had directly from Ras Thavas. It had been stupid of me not to foresee that Ras Thavas would immediately guess the purpose of my mission and warn Xaxa. I perceived instantly that it would be worse than useless to deny our identity, rather I must explain our presence – if I could.

"Where is Dar Tarus?" she repeated.

"How should I know?" I countered. "Dar Tarus has reasons to believe that he would not be safe in Phundahl and I imagine that he is not anxious that anyone should know his whereabouts – myself included. He helped me to escape from the Island of Thavas, for which his liberty was to be his reward. He has not chosen to accompany me further upon my adventures."

Xaxa seemed momentarily disarmed that I did not deny my identity – evidently she had supposed that I would do so.

"You admit then," she said, "that you are Vad Varo, the assistant of Ras Thavas?"

"Have I ever sought to deny it?"

"You have disguised yourself as a red-man of Barsoom."

"How could I travel in Barsoom otherwise, where every man's hand is against a stranger?"

"And why would you travel in Barsoom?" Her eyes narrowed as she waited for my reply.

"As Ras Thavas has doubtless sent you word, I am from another world and I would see more of this one," I told her. "Is that strange?"

"And you come to Phundahl and seek to gain entrance to my presence and bring with you the notorious Assassin of Toonol that you may see more of Barsoom?"

"Gor Hajus may not return to Toonol," I explained, "and so he must seek service for his sword at some other court than that of Vobis Kan – in Phundahl perhaps, or if not here he must move on. I hope that he will decide to accompany me as I am a stranger in Barsoom, unaccustomed to the manners and ways of her people. I would fare ill without a guide and mentor."

"You shall fare ill," she cried. "You have seen all of Barsoom that you are destined to see – you have reached the end of your adventure. You think to deceive me, eh? You do not know, perhaps, that I have heard of your infatuation for Valla Dia or that I am fully conversant with the purpose of your visit to Phundahl." Her eyes left me and swept her nobles and her warriors. "To the pits with them!" she cried. "Later we shall choose the manner of their passing."

Instantly we were surrounded by a score of naked blades. There was no escape for Gor Hajus or me, but I thought that I saw an opportunity for Hovan Du to get away. I had had the possibility of such a contingency in mind from the first and always I had been on the look-out for an avenue of escape for one of us, and so the open windows at the right of the Jeddara had not gone unnoticed, nor the great trees growing in the courtyard beneath. Hovan Du was close beside me as Xaxa spoke.

"Go!" I whispered. "The windows are open. Go, and tell Dar Tarus what has happened to us," and then I fell back away from him and dragged Gor Hajus with me as though we would attempt to resist arrest; and while I thus distracted their attention from him Hovan Du turned towards an open window. He had taken but a few steps when a warrior attempted to halt him; with that the ferocious brain of the anthropoid seemed to seize dominion over the great creature. With a hideous growl he leaped with the agility of a cat upon the unfortunate Phundahlian, swung him high in giant hands and using his body as a flail tumbled his fellows to right and left as he cut a swath towards the open window nearest him.

Instantly pandemonium reigned in the apartment. The attention of all seemed centered upon the great ape and even those who had been confronting us turned to attack Hovan Du. And in the midst of the confusion I saw Xaxa step to some heavy hangings directly behind her desk, part them and disappear.

"Come!" I whispered to Gor Hajus. Apparently intent only upon watching the conflict between the ape and the warriors I moved forward with the fighters but always to the left towards the desk that Xaxa had just quitted. Hovan Du was giving a good account of himself. He had discarded his first victim and one by one had seized others as they came within range of his long arms and powerful hands, sometimes four at a time as he stood well braced upon two of his hand-like feet and fought with the other four. His shock of bristling hair stood erect upon his skull and his fierce eyes blazed with rage as, towering high above his antagonists, he fought for his life – the most feared of all the savage creatures of Barsoom. Perhaps his greatest advantage lay in the inherent fear of him that was a part of every man in that room who faced him, and it forwarded my quickly conceived plan, too, for it kept every eye turned upon Hovan Du, so that Gor Hajus and I were able to work our way to the rear of the desk. I think Hovan Du must have sensed my intention then, for he did the one thing best suited to attract every eye from us to him and, too, he gave me notice that the human half of his brain was still alert and watchful of our welfare.

Heretofore the Phundahlians must have looked upon him as a remarkable specimen of great ape, marvelously trained, but now, of a sudden, he paralyzed them with awe, for his roars and growls took the form of words and he spoke with the tongue of a human. He was near the window now. Several of the nobles were pushing bravely forward. Among them was Sag Or. Hovan Du reached forth and seized him, wrenching his weapons from him. "I go," he cried, "but let harm befall my friends and I shall return and tear the heart from Xaxa. Tell her that, from the Great Ape of Ptarth."

For an instant the, warriors and the nobles stood transfixed with awe. Every eye was upon Hovan Du as he stood there with the struggling figure of Sag Or in his mighty grasp. Gor Hajus and I were forgotten. And then Hovan Du turned and leaped to the sill of the window and from there lightly to the branches of the nearest tree; and with him went Sag Or, the favorite of Xaxa, the Jeddara. At the same instant I drew Gor Hajus with me between the hangings in the rear of Xaxa's desk, and as they fell behind us we found ourselves in the narrow mouth of a dark corridor.

Without knowledge of where the passage led we could only follow it blindly, urged on by the necessity for discovering a hiding place or an avenue of escape from the palace before the pursuit which we knew would be immediately instituted, overtook us. As our eyes became accustomed to the gloom, which was partially dispelled by a faint luminosity, we moved more rapidly and presently came to a narrow spiral runway which descended into a dark hole below the level of the corridor and also arose into equal darkness above.

"Which way?" I asked Gor Hajus.

"They will expect us to descend," he replied, "for in that direction lies the nearest avenue of escape."

"Then we will go up."

"Good!" he exclaimed. "All we seek now is a place to hide until night has fallen, for we may not escape by day."

We had scarcely started to ascend before we heard the first sound of pursuit – the clank of accoutrements in the corridor beneath. Yet, even with this urge from behind, we were forced to move with great caution, for we knew not what lay before. At the next level there was a doorway, the door closed and locked, but there was no corridor, nor anywhere to hide, and so we continued on upward. The second level was identical with that just beneath, but at the third a single corridor ran straight off into darkness and at our right was a door, ajar. The sounds of pursuit were appreciably nearer now and the necessity for concealment seemed increasing as the square of their growing proportions until every other consideration was overwhelmed by it. Nor is this so strange when the purpose of my adventure is considered and that discovery now must as-suredly spell defeat and blast for ever the slender ray of hope that re-mained for the resurrection of Valla Dia in her own flesh.

There was scarce a moment for consideration. The corridor before us was shrouded in darkness – it might be naught but a blind alley. The door was close and ajar.

I pushed it gently inward. An odor of heavy incense greeted our nos-trils and through the small aperture we saw a portion of a large chamber garishly decorated. Directly before us, and almost wholly obstructing our view of the entire chamber, stood a colossal statue of a squatting man-like figure. Behind us we heard voices – our pursuers already were ascending the spiral – they would be upon us in a few seconds. I examined the door and discovered that it fastened with a spring lock. I looked again into the chamber and saw no one within the range of our vision, and then I motioned Gor Hajus to follow me and stepping into the room closed the door behind us. We had burned our bridges. As the door closed the lock engaged with a sharp, metallic click.

"What was that?" demanded a voice, originating, seemingly, at the far end of the chamber.

Gor Hajus looked at me and shrugged his shoulders in resignation (he must have been thinking what I was thinking – that with two av-enues we had chosen the wrong one) but he smiled and there was no reproach in his eyes.

"It sounded from the direction of the Great Tur," replied a second voice.

"Perhaps someone is at the door," suggested the first speaker.

Gor Hajus and I were flattened against the back of the statue that we might postpone as long as possible our inevitable discovery should the speakers decide to investigate the origin of the noise that had attracted their suspicions. I was facing against the polished stone of the figure's back, my hands outspread upon it. Beneath my fingers were the carven bits of its ornamental harness – jutting protuberances that were costly gems set in these trappings of stone, and there were gorgeous inlays of gold filagree; but these things I had no eyes for now. We could hear the two conversing as they came nearer. Perhaps I was nervous, I do not know. I am sure I never shrank from an encounter when either duty or expediency called; but in this instance both demanded that we avoid conflict and remain undiscovered. However that may be, my fingers must have been moving nervously over the jeweled harness of the figure when I became vaguely, perhaps subconsciously, aware that one of the gems was loose in its setting. I do not recall that this made any impression upon my conscious mind, but I do know that it seemed to catch the attention of my wandering fingers and they must have paused to play with the loosened stone.

The voices seemed quite close now – it could be but a matter of seconds before we should be confronted by their owners. My muscles seemed to tense for the anticipated encounter and unconsciously I pressed heavily upon the loosened setting – whereat a portion of the figure's back gave noiselessly inward revealing to us the dimly lighted interior of the statue. We needed no further invitation; simultaneously we stepped across the threshold and in almost the same movement I turned and closed the panel gently behind us. I think that there was absolutely no sound connected with the entire transaction; and following it we remained in utter silence, motionless – scarce breathing. Our eyes became quickly accustomed to the dim interior which we discovered was lighted through numerous small orifices in the shell of the statue, which was entirely hollow, and through these same orifices every outside sound came clearly to our ears.

We had scarcely closed the opening when we heard the voices directly outside it and simultaneously there came a hammering on the door by which we had entered the apartment from the corridor. "Who seeks entrance to Xaxa's Temple?" demanded one of the voices within the room.

"'Tis I, dwar of the Jeddara's Guard," boomed a voice from without. "We are seeking two who came to assassinate Xaxa."

"Came they this way?"

"Think you, priest, that I should be seeking them here had they not?"

"How long since?"

"Scarce twenty tals since," replied the dwar.

"Then they are not here," the priest assured him, "for we have been here for a full zode* and no other has entered the temple during that time. Look quickly to Xaxa's apartments above and to the roof and the hangars, for if you followed them up the spiral there is no other where they might flee."

*A tal is about one second, and a zode approximately two and one-half hours, Earth time.

"Watch then the temple carefully until I return," shouted the warrior and we heard him and his men moving on up the spiral.

Now we heard the priests conversing as they moved slowly past the statue.

"What could have caused the noise that first attracted our attention?" asked one.

"Perhaps the fugitives tried the door," suggested the other.

"It must have been that, but they did not enter or we should have seen them when they emerged from behind the Great Tur, for we were facing him at the time, nor have once turned our eyes from this end of the temple."

"Then at least they are not within the temple."

"And where else they may be is no concern of ours."

"No, nor if they reached Xaxa's apartment, if they did not pass through the temple."

"Perhaps they did reach it."

"And they were assassins!"

"Worse things might befall Phundahl."

"Hush! the gods have ears."

"Of stone."

"But the ears of Xaxa are not of stone and they hear many things that are not intended for them."

"The old she-banth!" "She is Jeddara and High Priestess."

"Yes, but – " the voices passed beyond the range of our ears at the far end of the temple, yet they had told me much – that Xaxa was feared and hated by the priesthood and that the priests themselves had none too much reverence for their deity as evidenced by the remark of one that the gods have ears of stone. And they had told us other things, important things, when they conversed with the dwar of the Jeddara's Guard.

Gor Hajus and I now felt that we had fallen by chance upon a most ideal place of concealment, for the very guardians of the temple would swear that we were not, could not be, where we were. Already had they thrown the pursuers off our track.

Now, for the first time, we had an opportunity to examine our hiding place. The interior of the statue was hollow and far above us, perhaps forty feet, we could see the outside light shining through the mouth, ears and nostrils, just below which a circular platform could be discerned running around the inside of the neck. A ladder with flat rungs led upward from the base to the platform. Thick dust covered the floor on which we stood, and the extremity of our position suggested a careful examination of this dust, with the result that I was at once impressed by the evidence that it revealed; which indicated that we were the first to enter the statue for a long time, possibly for years, as the fine coating of almost impalpable dust that covered the floor was undisturbed. As I searched for this evidence my eyes fell upon something lying huddled close to the base of the ladder and approaching nearer I saw that it was a human skeleton, while a closer examination revealed that the skull was crushed and one arm and several ribs broken. About it lay, dust covered, the most gorgeous trappings I had ever seen. Its position at the foot of the ladder, as well as the crushed skull and broken bones, appeared quite conclusive evidence of the manner in which death had come – the man had fallen head foremost from the circular platform forty feet above, carrying with him to eternity, doubtless, the secret of the entrance to the interior of the Great Tur.

I suggested this to Gor Hajus who was examining the dead man's trappings and he agreed with me that such must have been the manner of his death.

"He was a high priest of Tur," whispered Gor Hajus, "and probably a member of the royal house – possibly a Jeddak. He has been dead a long time."

"I am going up above," I said. "I will test the ladder. If it is safe, follow me up. I think we shall be able to see the interior of the temple through the mouth of Tur."

"Go carefully," Gor Hajus admonished. "The ladder is very old."

I went carefully, testing each rung before I trusted my weight to it, but I found the old sorapus wood of which it was constructed sound and as staunch as steel. How the high priest came to his death must always remain a mystery, for the ladder or the circular platform would have carried the weight of a hundred red-men.

From the platform I could see through the mouth of Tur. Below me was a large chamber along the sides of which were ranged other, though lesser, idols. They were even more grotesque than those I had seen in the temple in the city and their trappings were rich beyond the conception of man – Earthman – for the gems of Barsoom scintillate with rays unknown to us and of such gorgeous and blinding beauty as to transcend description. Directly in front of the Great Tur was an altar of palthon, a rare and beautiful stone, blood red, in which are traced in purest white Nature's most fanciful designs; the whole vastly enhanced by the wondrous polish which the stone takes beneath the hand of the craftsman.

Gor Hajus joined me and together we examined the interior of the temple. Tall windows lined two sides, letting in a flood of light. At the far end, opposite the Great Tur, were two enormous doors, closing the main entrance to the chamber, and here stood the two priests whom we had heard conversing. Otherwise the temple was deserted. Incense burned upon tiny altars before each of the minor idols, but whether any burned before the Great Tur we could not see.

Having satisfied our curiosity relative to the temple, we returned our attention to a further examination of the interior of Tur's huge head and were rewarded by the discovery of another ladder leading upward against the rear wall to a higher and smaller platform that evidently led to the eyes. It did not take me long to investigate and here I found a most comfortable chair set before a control that operated the eyes, so that they could be made to turn from side to side, or up or down, according to the whim of the operator; and here too was a speaking-tube leading to the mouth. This again I must needs investigate and so I returned to the lower platform and there I discovered a device beneath the tongue of the idol, and this device, which was in the nature of an amplifier, was connected with the speaking-tube from above. I could not repress a smile as I considered these silent witnesses to the perfidy of man and thought of the broken thing lying at the foot of the ladder. Tur, I could have sworn, had been silent for many years.

Together Gor Hajus and I returned to the higher platform and again I made a discovery – the eyes of Tur were veritable periscopes. By turning them we could see any portion of the temple and what we saw through the eyes was magnified.

Nothing could escape the eyes of Tur and presently, when the priests began to talk again, we discovered that nothing could escape Tur's ears, for every slightest sound in the temple came clearly to us. What a valuable adjunct to high priesthood this Great Tur must have been in the days when that broken skeleton lying below us was a thing of blood and life!

CHAPTER TWELVE

The Great Tur

THE DAY DRAGGED wearily for Gor Hajus and me. We watched the various priests who came in pairs at intervals to relieve those who had preceded them, and we listened to their prattle, mostly idle gossip of court scandals. At times they spoke of us and we learned that Hovan Du had escaped with Sag Or, nor had they been located as yet, nor had Dar Tarus. The whole court was mystified by our seemingly miraculous disappearance. Three thousand people, the inmates and attaches of the palace, were constantly upon the look-out for us. Every part of the palace and the palace grounds had been searched and searched again. The pits had been explored more thoroughly than they had been explored within the memory of the oldest retainer, and it seemed that queer things had been unearthed there – things of which not even Xaxa dreamed, and the priests whispered that at least one great and powerful house would fall because of what a dwar of the Jeddak's Guard had discovered in a remote precinct of the pits.

As the sun dropped below the horizon and darkness came, the interior of the temple was illuminated by a soft white light, brilliantly but without the glare of Earthly artificial illumination. More priests came and many young girls, priestesses. They performed before the idols, chanting meaningless gibberish.

Gradually the chamber filled with worshippers, nobles of the Jeddara's court with their women and their retainers, forming in two lines along either side of the temple before the lesser idols, leaving a wide aisle from the great entrance to the foot of the Great Tur and towards this aisle they all faced, waiting. For what were they waiting? Their eyes were turned expectantly towards the closed doors of the great entrance and Gor Hajus and I felt our eyes held there too, fascinated by the suggestion that they were about to open and reveal some stupendous spectacle.

And presently the doors did swing slowly open and all we saw was what appeared to be a great roll of carpet lying upon its side across the opening. Twenty slaves, naked but for their scant leather harness, stood behind the huge roll; and as the doors swung fully open they rolled the carpet inward to the very feet of the altar before the Great Tur, covering the wide aisle from the entranceway almost to the idol with a thick, soft rug of gold and white and blue. It was the most beautiful thing in the temple where all else was blatant, loud and garish or hideous, or grotesque. And then the doors closed and again we waited; but not for long. Bugles sounded from without, the sound increasing as they neared the entrance. Once more the doors swung in. Across the entrance stood a double rank of gorgeously trapped nobles. Slowly they entered the temple and behind them came a splendid chariot drawn by two banths, the fierce Barsoomian lion, held in leash by slaves on either side. Upon the chariot was a litter and in the litter, reclining at ease, lay Xaxa. As she entered the temple the people commenced to chant her praises in a monotonous sing-song. Chained to the chariot and following on foot was a red warrior and behind him a procession composed of fifty young men and an equal number of young girls.

Gor Hajus touched my arm. "The prisoner," he whispered, "do you recognize him?"

"Dar Tarus!" I exclaimed.

It was Dar Tarus – they had discovered his hiding place and arrested him, but what of Hovan Du? Had they taken him, also? If they had it must have been only after slaying him, for they never would have sought to capture the fierce beast, nor would he have brooked capture. I looked for Sag Or, but he was nowhere to be seen within the temple and this fact gave me hope that Hovan Du might be still at liberty.

The chariot was halted before the altar and Xaxa alighted; the lock that held Dar Tarus' chain to the vehicle was opened and the banths were led away by their attendants to one side of the temple behind the lesser idols. Then Dar Tarus was dragged roughly to the altar and thrown upon it and Xaxa, mounting the steps at its base, came close to his side and with hands outstretched above him looked up at the Great Tur towering above her. How beautiful she was! How richly trapped! Ah, Valla Dia! that your sweet form should be debased to the cruel purposes of the wicked mind that now animates you!

Xaxa's eyes now rested upon the face of the Great Tur. "O, Tur, Father of Barsoom," she cried, "behold the offering we place before you, All-seeing, All-knowing, All-powerful One, and frown no more upon us in silence. For a hundred years you have not deigned to speak aloud

to your faithful slaves; never since Hora San, the high priest, was taken away by you on that long-gone night of mystery have you unsealed your lips to your people. Speak, Great Tur! Give us some sign, ere we plunge this dagger into the heart of our offering, that our works are pleasing in thine eyes. Tell us whither went the two who came here to-day to assassinate your high priestess; reveal to us the fate of Sag Or. Speak Great Tur, ere I strike," and she raised her slim blade above the heart of Dar Tarus and looked straight upward into the eyes of Tur.

And then, as a bolt from the blue, I was struck by the great inspiration. My hand sought the lever controlling the eyes of Tur and I turned them until they completed a full circuit of the room and rested again upon Xaxa. The effect was magical. Never before had I seen a whole roomful of people so absolutely stunned and awestruck as were these. As the eyes returned to Xaxa she seemed turned to stone and her copper skin to have taken on an ashen purple hue. Her dagger remained stiffly poised above the heart of Dar Tarus. Not for a hundred years had they seen the eyes of the Great Tur move. Then I placed the speaking-tube to my lips and the voice of Tur rumbled through the chamber. As from one great throat a gasp arose from the crowded temple floor and the people fell upon their knees and buried their faces in their hands.

"Judgment is mine!" I cried. "Strike not lest ye be struck! To Tur is the sacrifice!" I was silent then, attempting to plan how best to utilize the advantage I had gained. Fearfully, one by one, the bowed heads were raised and frightened eyes sought the face of Tur. I gave them another thrill by letting the god's eyes wander slowly over the upturned faces, and while I was doing this I had another inspiration, which I imparted to Gor Hajus in a low whisper. I could hear him chuckle as he started down the ladder to carry my new plan into effect. Again I had recourse to the speaking-tube.

"The sacrifice is Tur's," I rumbled. "Tur will strike with his own hand. Extinguish the lights and let no one move under pain of instant death until Tur gives the word. Prostrate yourselves and bury your eyes in your palms, for whosoever sees shall be blinded when the spirit of Tur walks among his people."

Down they went again and one of the priests hurriedly extinguished the lights, leaving the temple in total darkness; and while Gor Hajus was engaged with his part of the performance I tried to cover any accidental noise he might make by keeping up a running fire of celestial revelation.

"Xaxa, the high priestess, asks what has become of the two whom she believed came to assassinate her. I, Tur took them to myself. Vengeance is Tur's! And Sag Or I took, also. In the guise of a great ape I came and took Sag Or and none knew me; though even a fool might have guessed, for who is there ever heard a great ape speak with tongue of man unless he was animated by the spirit of Tur?"

I guess that convinced them, it being just the sort of logic suited to their religion, or it would have convinced them if they had not already been convinced. I wondered what might be passing in the mind of the doubting priest who had remarked that the gods had ears of stone.

Presently I heard a noise upon the ladder beneath me and a moment later someone climbed upon the circular landing.

"All's well," whispered the voice of Gor Hajus. "Dar Tarus is with me."

"Light the temple!" I commanded through the speaking-tube. "Rise and look upon your altar."

The lights flashed on and the people rose, trembling, to their feet. Every eye was bent upon the altar and what they saw there seemed to crush them with terror. Some of the women screamed and fainted. It all impressed me with the belief that none of them had taken this god of theirs with any great amount of seriousness, and now when they were confronted with absolute proof of his miraculous powers they were swept completely off their feet. Where, a few moments before, they had seen a live sacrifice awaiting the knife of the high priestess they saw now only a dust-covered human skull. I grant you that without an explanation it might have seemed a miracle to almost anyone so quickly had Gor Hajus run from the base of the idol with the skull of the dead high priest and returned again leading Dar Tarus with him. I had been a bit concerned as to what the attitude of Dar Tarus might be, who was no more conversant with the hoax than were the Phundahlians, but Gor Hajus had whispered "For Valla Dia" in his ear and he had understood and come quickly.

"The Great Tur," I now announced, "is angry with his people. For a long time they had denied him in their hearts even while they made open worship of him. The Great Tur is angry with Xaxa. Only through Xaxa may the people of Phundahl be saved from destruction, for the Great Tur is angry. Go then from the temple and the palace leaving no human being here other than Xaxa, the high priestess of Tur. Leave her here in solitude beside the altar. Tur would speak with her alone."

I could see Xaxa fairly shrivel in fright.

"Is the Jeddara Xaxa, High Priestess of the Great God Tur, afraid to meet her master?" I demanded. The woman's jaw trembled so that she could not reply.

"Obey! or Xaxa and all her people shall be struck dead!" I fairly screamed at them.

Like cattle they turned and fled towards the entrance and Xaxa, her knees shaking so that she could scarce stand erect, staggered after them. A noble saw her and pushed her roughly back, but she shrieked and ran after him when he had left her. Then others dragged her to the foot of the altar and threw her roughly down and one menaced her with his sword, but at that I called aloud that no harm must befall the Jeddara if they did not wish the wrath of Tur to fall upon them all. They left her lying there and so weak from fright was she that she could not rise, and a moment later the temple was empty, but not until I had shouted after them to clear the whole palace within a quarter zode, for my plan required a free and unobstructed as well as unobserved field of action.

The last of them was scarce out of sight ere we three descended from the head of Tur and stepped out upon the temple floor behind the idol. Quickly I ran towards the altar, upon the other side of which Xaxa had dropped to the floor in a swoon. She still lay there and I gathered her into my arms and ran quickly back to the door in the wall behind the idol – the doorway through which Gor Hajus and I had entered the temple earlier in the day.

Preceded by Gor Hajus and followed by Dar Tarus, I ascended the runway towards the roof where the conversation of the priests had informed us were located the royal hangars. Had Hovan Du and Sag Or been with us my cup of happiness would have been full, for within half a day, what had seemed utter failure and defeat had been turned almost to assured success. At the landing where lay Xaxa's apartments we halted and looked within, for the long night voyage I contemplated would be cold and the body of Valla Dia must be kept warm with suitable robes even though it was inhabited by the spirit of Xaxa. Seeing no one we entered and soon found what we required. As I was adjusting a heavy robe of orluk about the Jeddara she regained consciousness. Instantly she recognized me and then Gor Hajus and finally Dar Tarus. Mechanically she felt for her dagger, but it was not there and when she saw my smile she paled with anger. At first she must have jumped to the conclusion that she had been the victim of a hoax, but presently a doubt seemed to enter her mind – she must have been recalling some of the things that had transpired within the temple of the Great Tur, and these, neither she nor any other mortal might explain.

"Who are you?" she demanded.

"I am Tur," I replied, brazenly.

"What is your purpose with me?"

"I am going to take you away from Phundahl," I replied.

"But I do not wish to go. You are not Tur. You are Vad Varo. I shall call for help and my guards will come and slay you."

"There is no one in the palace," I reminded her. "Did I, Tur, not send them away?' "I shall not go with you," she announced firmly. "Rather would I die."

"You shall go with me, Xaxa," I replied, and though she fought and struggled we carried her from her apartment and up the spiral runway to the roof where, I prayed, I should find the hangars and the royal fliers; and as we stepped out into the fresh night air of Mars we did see the hangars before us, but we saw something else – a group of Phundahlian warriors of the Jeddara's Guard whom they had evidently failed to notify of the commands of Tur. At sight of them Xaxa cried aloud in relief.

"To me! To the Jeddara!" she cried. "Strike down these assassins and save me!" There were three of them and there were three of us, but they were armed and between us we had but Xaxa's slender dagger. Gor Hajus carried that. Victory seemed turned to defeat as they rushed towards us; but it was Gor Hajus who gave them pause. He seized Xaxa and raised the blade, its point above her heart.

"Halt!" he cried, "or I strike."

The warriors hesitated; Xaxa was silent, stricken with fear. Thus we stood in stalemate when, just beyond the three Phundahlian warriors, I saw a movement at the roof's edge. What was it? In the dim light I saw something that seemed a human head, and yet unhuman, rise slowly above the edge of the roof, and then, silently, a great form followed, and then I recognized it – Hovan Du, the great white ape.

"Tell them," I cried to Xaxa in a loud voice that Hovan Du might hear, "that I am Tur, for see, I come again in the semblance of a white ape!" and I pointed to Hovan Du. "I would not destroy these poor warriors. Let them lay down their weapons and go in peace."

The men turned, and seeing the great ape standing there behind them, materialized, it might have been, out of thin air, were shaken.

"Who is he, Jeddara?" demanded one of the men.

"It is Tur," replied Xaxa in a weak voice; "but save me from him! Save me from him!"

"Throw down your weapons and your harness and fly!" I commanded, "or Tur will strike you dead. Heard you not the people rushing from the palace at Tur's command? How think you we brought Xaxa hither with a lesser power than Tur's when all her palace was filled with her fighting men? Go, while yet you may in safety."

One of them unbuckled his harness and threw it with his weapons upon the roof, and as he started at a run for the spiral his companions followed his example.

Then Hovan Du approached us.

"Well done, Vad Varo," he growled, "though I know not what it is all about."

"That you shall know later," I told him, "but now we must find a swift flier and be upon our way. Where is Sag Or? Does he still live?"

"I have him securely bound and safely hidden in one of the high towers of the palace," replied the ape. "It will be easy to get him when we have launched a flier."

Xaxa was eyeing us ragefully. "You are not Tur!" she cried. "The ape has exposed you."

"But too late to profit you in any way, Jeddara," I assured her. "Nor could you convince one of your people who stood in the temple this night that I am not Tur. Nor do you, yourself, know that I am not. The ways of Tur, the all-powerful, all-knowing, are beyond the conception of mortal man. To you then, Jeddara, I am Tur, and you will find me all-powerful enough for my purposes."

I think she was still perplexed as we found and dragged forth a flier, aboard which we placed her, and turned the craft's nose towards a lofty tower where Hovan Du told us lay Sag Or.

"I shall be glad to see myself again," said Dar Tarus, with a laugh.

"And you shall be yourself again, Dar Tarus," I told him, "as soon as ever we can come again to the pits of Ras Thavas."

"Would that I might be reunited with my sweet Kara Vasa," he sighed. Then, Vad Varo, the last full measure of my gratitude would be yours."

"Where may we find her?"

"Alas, I do not know. It was while I was searching for her that I was apprehended by the agents of Xaxa. I had been to her father's palace only to learn that he had been assassinated and his property confiscated. The whereabouts of Kara Vasa they either did not know or would not divulge; but they held me there upon one pretext or another until a detachment of the Jeddara's Guard could come and arrest me."

"We shall have to make inquiries of Sag Or," I said.

We were now coming to a stop alongside a window of the tower Hovan Du had indicated, and he and Dar Tarus leaped to the sill and disappeared within. We were all armed now, having taken the weapons discarded by the three warriors at the hangars, and with a good flier beneath our feet and all our little company reunited, with Xaxa and Sag Or, whom they were now conducting aboard, we were indeed in high spirits.

As we got under way again, setting our nose towards the east, I asked Sag Or if he knew what had become of Kara Vasa, but he assured me, in surly tones, that he did not.

"Think again, Sag Or," I admonished him, "and think hard, for perhaps upon your answer your life depends."

"What chance have I for life?" he sneered, casting an ugly look towards Dar Tarus.

"You have every chance," I replied. "Your life lies in the hollow of my hand; and you serve me well it shall be yours, though in your own body and not in that belonging to Dar Tarus."

"You do not intend destroying me?"

"Neither you nor Xaxa," I answered. "Xaxa shall live on in her own body and you in yours."

"I do not wish to live in my own body," snapped the Jeddara.

Dar Tarus stood looking at Sag Or – looking at his own body like some disembodied soul – as weird a situation as I have ever encountered.

"Tell me, Sag Or," he said, "what has become of Kara Vasa. When my body has been restored to me and yours to you I shall hold no enmity against you if you have not harmed Kara Vasa and will tell me where she be."

"I cannot tell you, for I do not know. She was not harmed, but the day after you were assassinated she disappeared from Phundahl. We were positive that she was spirited away by her father, but from him we could learn nothing. Then he was assassinated," the man glanced at Xaxa, "and since, we have learned nothing. A slave told us that Kara Vasa, with some of her father's warriors, had embarked upon a flier and set out for Helium, where she purposed placing herself under the protection of the great War Lord of Barsoom; but of the truth of that we know nothing. This is the truth. I, Sag Or, have spoken!" It was futile then to search Phundahl for Kara Vasa and so we held our course towards the east and the Tower of Thavas.

CHAPTER THIRTEEN

Back to Thavas

ALL THAT NIGHT we sped beneath the hurtling moons of Mars, as strange a company as was ever foregathered upon any planet, I will swear. Two men, each possessing the body of the other, an old and wicked empress whose fair body belonged to a youthful damsel beloved by another of this company, a great white ape dominated by half the brain of a human being, and I, a creature of a distant planet, with Gor Hajus, the Assassin of Toonol, completed the mad roster.

I could scarce keep my eyes from the fair form and face of Xaxa, and it is well that I was thus fascinated for I caught her in the act of attempting to hurl herself overboard, so repugnant to her was the prospect of living again in her own old and hideous corpse. After that I kept her securely bound and fastened to the deck though it hurt me to see the bonds upon those fair limbs.

Dar Tarus was almost equally fascinated by the contemplation of his own body, which he had not seen for many years.

"By my first ancestor," he ejaculated. "It must be that I was the least vain of fellows, for I give you my word I had no idea that I was so fair to look upon. I can say this now without seeming egotism, since I am speaking of Sag Or," and he laughed aloud at his little joke.

But the fact remained that the body and face of Dar Tarus were beautiful indeed, though there was a hint of steel in the eyes and the set of the jaw that betokened fighting blood. Little wonder, then, that his own, which Dar Tarus now possessed, was marked by dissipation and age; nor that Dar Tarus yearned to come again into his own.

Just before dawn we dropped to one of the numerous small islands that dot the Great Toonolian Marshes and nosing the ship between the boles of great trees we came to rest upon the surface of the ground, half buried in the lush and gorgeous jungle grasses, well hidden from the sight of possible pursuers. Here Hovan Du found fruits and nuts for us which the simian section of his brain pronounced safe for human consumption, and instinct led him to a nearby spring from which there bubbled delicious water. We four were half famished and much fatigued, so that the food and water were most welcome to us; nor did Xaxa and Sag Or refuse them. Having eaten, three of us lay down upon the ship's deck to sleep, after securely chaining our prisoners, while the fourth stood watch. In this way, taking turns, we slept away most of the day and when night fell, rested and refreshed, we were ready to resume our flight.

Making a wide detour to the south we avoided Toonol and about two hours before dawn we sighted the high Tower of Thavas. I think we were all keyed up to the highest pitch of excitement, for there was not one aboard that flier but whose whole life would be seriously affected by the success or failure of our venture.

As a first precaution we secured the hands of Xaxa and Sag Or behind their backs and placed gags in their mouths, lest they succeed in giving warning of our approach.

Cluros had long since set and Thuria was streaming towards the horizon as we stopped our motor and drifted without lights a mile or two south of the tower while we waited impatiently for Thuria to leave the heavens to darkness and the world to us. To the northwest the lights of Toonol shone plainly against the dark background of the windows of the great laboratory of Ras Thavas, but the tower itself was dark from plinth to pinnacle.

And now the nearer moon dropped plummetlike beneath the horizon and left the scene to darkness and to us. Dar Tarus started the motor, the wonderful, silent motor of Barsoom, and we moved slowly, close to the ground, towards Ras Thavas' island, with no sound other than the gentle whirring of our propeller; nor could that have been heard scarce a hundred feet so slowly was it turning. Close off the island we came to a stop behind a cluster of giant trees and Hovan Du, going into the bow, uttered a few low growls. Then we stood waiting in silence, listening. There was a rustling in the dense undergrowth upon the shore. Again Hovan Du voiced his low, grim call and this time there came an answer from the black shadows. Hovan Du spoke in the language of the great apes and the invisible creature replied.

For five minutes, during which time we were aware from the different voices that others had joined in the conversation from the shore, the apes conversed, and then Hovan Du turned to me.

"It is arranged," he said. "They will permit us to hide our ship beneath these trees and they will permit us to pass out again when we are ready and board her, nor will they harm us in any way. All they ask is that when we are through we shall leave the gate open that leads to the inner court."

"Do they understand that while an ape goes in with us none will return with us?"

I asked.

"Yes; but they will not harm us."

"Why do they wish the gate left open?"

"Do not inquire too closely, Vad Varo," replied Hovan Du. "It should be enough that the great apes make it possible for you to restore Valla Dia's body to her brain and escape with her from this terrible place."

"It is enough," I replied. "When may we land?"

"At once. They will help us drag the ship beneath the trees and make her fast."

"But first we must top the wall to the inner court," I reminded him.

"Yes, true – I had forgotten that we cannot open the gate from this side."

He spoke again, then, to the apes, whom we had not yet seen; and then he told us that all was arranged and that he and Dar Tarus would return with the ship after landing us inside the wall.

Again we got under way and rising slowly above the outer wall dropped silently to the courtyard beyond. The night was unusually dark, clouds having followed Thuria and blotted out the stars after the moon had set. No one could have seen the ship at a distance of fifty feet, and we moved almost without noise. Quietly we lowered our prisoners over the side and Gor Hajus and I remained with them while Dar Tarus and Hovan Du rose again and piloted the ship back to its hiding place.

I moved at once to the gate and, unlatching it, waited. I heard nothing. Never, I think, have I endured such utter silence. There came no sound from the great pile rising behind me, nor any from the dark jungle beyond the wall. Dimly I could see the huddled forms of Gor Hajus, Xaxa and Sag Or beside me – otherwise I might have been alone in the darkness and immensity of space.

It seemed an eternity that I waited there before I heard a soft scratching on the panels of the heavy gate. I pushed it open and Dar Tarus and Hovan Du stepped silently within as I closed and relatched it. No one spoke. All had been carefully planned so that there was no need of speech. Dar Tarus and I led the way, Gor Hajus and Hovan Du brought up the rear with the prisoners. We moved directly to the entrance to the tower, found the runway and descended to the pits. Every fortune seemed with us. We met no one, we had no difficulty in finding the vault we sought, and once within we secured the door so that we had no fear of interruption – that was our first concern – and then I hastened to the spot where I had hidden Valla Dia behind the body of a large warrior, tucked far back against the wall in a dark corner. My heart stood still as I dragged aside the body of the warrior, for always had I feared that Ras Thavas, knowing my interest in her and guessing the purpose of my venture, would cause every chamber and pit to be searched and every body to be examined until he found her for whom he sought; but my fears had been baseless, for there lay the body of Xaxa, the old and wrinkled casket of the lovely brain of my beloved, where I had hidden it against this very night. Gently I lifted it out and bore it to one of the two ersite-topped tables. Xaxa, standing there bound and gagged, looked on with eyes that shot hate and loathing at me and at that hideous body to which her brain was so soon to be restored.

As I lifted her to the adjoining slab she tried to wriggle from my grasp and hurl herself to the floor, but I held her and soon had strapped her securely in place. A moment later she was unconscious and the re-transference was well under way. Gor Hajus, Sag Or and Hovan Du were interested spectators, but to Dar Tarus, who stood ready to assist me, it was an old story, for he had worked in the laboratory and seen more than enough of similar operations. I will not bore you with a description of it – it was but a repetition of what I had done many times in preparation for this very event.

At last it was completed and my heart fairly stood still as I replaced the embalming fluid with Valla Dia's own life blood and saw the color mount to her cheeks and her rounded bosom rise and fall to her gentle breathing. Then she opened her eyes and looked up into mine.

"What has happened, Vad Varo?" she asked. "Has something gone amiss that you have recalled me so soon, or did I not respond to the fluid?"

Her eyes wandered past me to the faces of the others standing about. "What does it mean?" she asked. "Who are these?"

I raised her gently in my arms and pointed at the body of Xaxa lying deathlike on the ersite slab beside her. Valla Dia's eyes went wide. "It is done?" she cried, and clapped her hands to her face and felt of all her features and of the soft, delicate contours of her smooth neck; and yet she could scarce believe it and asked for a glass and I took one from Xaxa's pocket pouch and handed it to her. She looked long into it and the tears commenced to roll down her cheeks, and then she looked up at me through the mist of them and put her dear arms about my neck and drew my face down to hers. "My chieftain," she whispered – that was all. But it was enough. For those two words I had risked my life and faced unknown dangers, and gladly would I risk my life again for that same reward and always, for ever.

Another night had fallen before I had completed the restoration of Dar Tarus and Hovan Du. Xaxa, and Sag Or and the great ape I left sleeping the death-like sleep of Ras Thavas' marvelous anaesthetic. The great ape I had no intention of restoring, but the others I felt bound to return to Phundahl, though Dar Tarus, now resplendent in his own flesh and the gorgeous trappings of Sag Or, urged me not to inflict them again upon the long-suffering Phundahlians.

"But I have given my word," I told him.

"Then they must be returned," he said.

"Though what I may do afterward is another matter," I added, for there had suddenly occurred to me a bold scheme.

I did not tell Dar Tarus what it was nor would I have had time, for at the very instant we heard someone without trying the door and then we heard voices and presently the door was tried again, this time with force. We made no noise, but just waited. I hoped that whoever it was would go away. The door was very strong and when they tried to force it they must soon have realized the futility of it because they quickly desisted and we heard their voices for only a short time thereafter and then they seemed to have gone away.

"We must leave," I said, "before they return."

Strapping the hands of Xaxa and Sag Or behind them and placing gags in their mouths I quickly restored them to life, nor ever did I see two less grateful.

The looks they cast upon me might well have killed could looks do that, and with what disgust they viewed one another was writ plain in their eyes.

Cautiously unbolting the door I opened it very quietly, a naked sword in my right hand and Dar Tarus, Gor Hajus and Hovan Du ready with theirs at my shoulder, and as it swung back it revealed two standing in the corridor watching – two of Ras Thavas' slaves; and one of them was Yamdor, his body servant. At sight of us the fellow gave a loud cry of recognition and before I could leap through the doorway and prevent them, they had both turned and were flying up the corridor as fast as their feet would carry them.

Now there was no time to be lost – everything must be sacrificed to speed.

Without thought of caution or silence we hastened through the pits towards the runway in the tower; and when we stepped into the inner court it was night again, but the farther moon was in the heavens and there were no clouds. The result was that we were instantly discovered by a sentry, who gave the alarm as he ran forward to intercept us.

What was a sentry doing in the courtyard of Ras Thavas? I could not understand.

And what were these? A dozen armed warriors were hurrying across the court on the heels of the sentry.

"Toonolians!" shouted Gor Hajus. "The warriors of Vobis Kan, Jeddak of Toonol!" Breathlessly we raced for the gate. If we could but reach it first! But we were handicapped by our prisoners, who held back the moment they discovered how they might embarrass us, and so it was that we all met in front of the gate. Dar Tarus and Gor Hajus and Hovan Du and I put Valla Dia and our prisoners behind us and fought the twenty warriors of Toonol with the odds five to one against us; but we had more heart in the fight than they and perhaps that gave us an advantage, though I am sure that Gor Hajus was as ten men himself so terrible was the effect of his name alone upon the men of Toonol.

"Gor Hajus!" cried one, the first to recognize him.

"Yes, it is Gor Hajus," replied the assassin. "Prepare to meet your ancestors!" and he drove into them like a racing propeller, and I was upon his right and Hovan Du and Dar Tarus upon his left.

It was a pretty fight, but it must eventually have gone against us, so greatly were we outnumbered, had I not thought of the apes and the gate beside us.

Working my way to it I threw it open and there upon the outside, attracted by the noise of the conflict, stood a full dozen of the great beasts. I called to Gor Hajus and the others to fall back beside the gate, and as the apes rushed in I pointed to the Toonolian warriors.

I think the apes were at a loss to know which were friends and which were foes, but the Toonolians apprised them by attacking them, while we stood aside with our points upon the ground. Just a moment we stood thus waiting. Then as the apes rushed among the Toonolian warriors, we slipped into the darkness of the jungle beyond the outer wall and sought our flier. Behind us we could hear the growls and the roars of the beasts mingled with the shouts and the curses of the men; and the sound still rose from the courtyard as we clambered aboard the flier and pushed off into the night.

As soon as we felt that we were safely escaped from the Island of Thavas I removed the gags from the mouths of Xaxa and Sag Or and I can tell you that I immediately regretted it, for never in my life had I been subjected to such horrid abuse as poured from the wrinkled old lips of the Jeddara; and it was only when I started to gag her again that she promised to desist.

My plans were now well laid and they included a return to Phundahl since I could not start for Duhor with Valla Dia without provisions and fuel; nor could I obtain these elsewhere than in Phundahl, since I felt that I held the key that would unlock the resources of that city to me; whereas all Toonol was in arms against us owing to Vobis Kan's fear of Gor Hajus.

So we retraced our way towards Phundahl as secretly as we had come, for I had no mind to be apprehended before we had gained entrance to the palace of Xaxa.

Again we rested over daylight upon the same island that had given us sanctuary two days before, and at dark we set out upon the last leg of our journey to Phundahl. If there had been pursuit we had seen naught of it, and that might easily be explained by the great extent of the uninhabited marshes across which we flew and the far southerly course that we followed close above the ground.

As we neared Phundahl I caused Xaxa and Sag Or to be again gagged, and further, I had their heads bandaged so that none might recognize them; and then we sailed straight over the city towards the palace, hoping that we would not be discovered and yet ready in the event that we should be.

But we came to the hangars on the roof apparently unseen and constantly I coached each upon the part he was to play. As we were settling slowly to the roof Dar Tarus, Hovan Du and Valla Dia quickly bound Gor Hajus and me and wrapped our heads in bandages, for we had seen below the figures of the hangar guard. Had we found the roof unguarded the binding of Gor Hajus and me had been unnecessary.

As we dropped nearer one of the guard hailed us. "What ship?' he cried.

"The royal flier of the Jeddara of Phundahl," replied Dar Tarus, "returning with Xaxa and Sag Or."

The warriors whispered among themselves as we dropped nearer and I must confess that I felt a bit nervous as to the outcome of our ruse; but they permitted us to land without a word and when they saw Valla Dia they saluted her after the manner of Barsoom, as, with the regal carriage of an empress, she descended from the deck of the flier.

"Carry the prisoners to my apartments!" she commanded, addressing the guard, and with the help of Hovan Du and Dar Tarus the four bound and muffled figures were carried from the flier down the spiral runway to the apartments of Xaxa, Jeddara, of Phundahl. Here excited slaves hastened to do the bidding of the Jeddara. Word must have flown through the palace with the speed of light that Xaxa had returned, for almost immediately court functionaries began to arrive and be announced, but Valla Dia sent word that she would see no one for a while.

Then she dismissed her slaves, and at my suggestion Dar Tarus investigated the apartments with a view to finding a safe hiding place for Gor Hajus, me, and the prisoners. This he soon found in a small antechamber directly off the main apartment of the royal suite; the bonds were removed from the assassin and myself and together we carried Xaxa and Sag Or into the room.

The entrance here was furnished with a heavy door over which there were hangings that completely hid it. I bade Hovan Du, who, like the rest of us, wore Phundahlian harness, stand guard before the hangings and let no one enter but members of our own party. Gor Hajus and I took up our positions just within the hangings through which we cut small holes that permitted us to see all that went on within the main chamber, for I was greatly concerned for Valla Dia's safety while she posed as Xaxa, whom I knew to be both feared and hated by her people and therefore always liable to assassination.

Valla Dia summoned the slaves and bade them admit the officials of the court, and as the doors opened fully a score of nobles entered. They appeared ill at ease and I could guess that they were recalling the episode in the temple when they had deserted their Jeddara and even hurled her roughly at the feet of the Great Tur, but Valla Dia soon put them at their ease.

"I have summoned you," she said, "to hear the word of Tur. Tur would speak again to his people. Three days and three nights have I spent with Tur. His anger against Phundahl is great. He bids me summon all the higher nobles to the temple after the evening meal to-night, and all the priests, and the commanders and dwars of the Guard, and as many of the lesser nobles as be in the palace; and then shall the people of Phundahl hear the word and the law of Tur and all those who shall obey shall live and all those who shall not obey shall die; and woe be to him who, having been summoned, shall not be in the temple this night. I, Xaxa, Jeddara of Phundahl, have spoken! Go!" They went and they seemed glad to go. Then Valla Dia summoned the odwar of the Guard, who would be in our world a general, and she told him to clear the palace of every living being from the temple level to the roof an hour before the evening meal, nor to permit any one to enter the temple or the levels above it until the hour appointed for the assembling in the temple to hear the word of Tur, excepting however those who might be in her own apartments, which were not to be entered upon pain of death. She made it all very clear and plain and the odwar understood and I think he trembled a trifle, for all were in great fear of the Jeddara Xaxa; and then he went away and the slaves were dismissed and we were alone.

CHAPTER FOURTEEN

John Carter

HALF AN HOUR before the evening meal we carried Xaxa and Sag Or down the spiral runway and placed them in the base of the Great Tur and Gor Hajus and I took our places on the upper platform behind the eyes and voice of the idol. Valla Dia, Dar Tarus and Hovan Du remained in the royal apartments. Our plans were well formulated. There was no one between the door at the rear of the Great Tur and the flier that lay ready on the roof in the event that we were forced to flee through any miscarriage of our mad scheme.

The minutes dragged slowly by and darkness fell. The time was approaching. We heard the doors of the temple open and beyond we saw the great corridor brilliantly lighted. It was empty except for two priests who stood hesitating nervously in the doorway. Finally one of them mustered up sufficient courage to enter and switch on the lights. More bravely now they advanced and prostrated themselves before the altar of the Great Tur. When they arose and looked up into the face of the idol I could not resist the temptation to turn those huge eyes until they had rolled completely about the interior of the chamber and rested again upon the priests; but I did not speak and I think the effect of the awful silence in the presence of the living god was more impressive than would words have been. The two priests simply collapsed. They slid to the floor and lay there trembling, moaning and supplicating Tur to have mercy on them, nor did they rise before the first of the worshippers arrived.

Thereafter the temple filled rapidly and I could see the word of Tur had been well and thoroughly disseminated. They came as they had before; but there were more this time, and they ranged upon either side of the central aisle and there they waited, their eyes divided be-

tween the doorway and the god. About the time that I thought the next scene was about to be enacted I let Tur's eyes travel over the assemblage that they might be keyed to the proper pitch for what was to follow. They reacted precisely as had the priests, falling upon the floor and moaning and supplicating; and there they remained until the sounds of bugles announced the coming of the Jeddara. Then they rose unsteadily to their feet.

The great doors swung open and there was the carpet and the slaves behind it. As they rolled it down towards the altar the bugles sounded louder and the head of the royal procession came into view. I had ordered it thus to permit of greater pageantry than was possible when the doors opened immediately upon the head of the procession. My plan permitted the audience to see the royal retinue advancing down the long corridor and the effect was splendid. First came the double rank of nobles and behind these the chariot drawn by the two banths, bearing the litter upon which reclined Valla Dia. Behind her walked Dar Tarus, but all within that room thought they were looking upon the Jeddara Xaxa and her favorite, Sag Or. Hovan Du walked behind Sag Or and following came the fifty young men and the fifty maidens.

The chariot halted before the altar and Valla Dia descended and knelt and the voices that had been chanting the praises of Xaxa were stilled as the beautiful creature extended her hands towards the Great Tur and looked up into his face.

"We are ready, Master!" she cried. "Speak! We await the word of Tur!" A gasp arose from the kneeling assemblage, a gasp that ended in a sob. I felt that they were pretty well worked up and that everything ought to go off without a hitch. I placed the speaking-tube to my lips.

"I am Tur!" I thundered and the people trembled. "I come to pass judgment on the men of Phundahl. As you receive my word so shall you prosper or so shall you perish. The sins of the people may be atoned by two who have sinned most in my sight." I let the eyes of Tur rove about over the audience and then brought them to rest upon Valla Dia. "Xaxa, are you ready to atone for your sins and for the sins of your people?"

Valla Dia bowed her beautiful head. "Thy will is law, Master!" she replied.

"And Sag Or," I continued, "you have sinned. Are you prepared to pay?"

"As Tur shall require," said Dar Tarus.

"Then it is my will," I boomed, "that Xaxa and Sag Or shall give back to those from whom they stole them, the beautiful bodies they now wear; that he from whom Sag Or took this body shall become Jeddak of Phundahl and High Priest of Tur; and that she from whom Xaxa stole her body shall be returned in pomp to her native country. I have spoken. Let any who would revolt against my word speak now or for ever hold his peace."

There was no objection voiced. I had felt pretty certain that there would not be. I doubt if any god ever looked down upon a more subdued and chastened flock.

As I had talked, Gor Hajus had descended to the base of the idol and removed the bonds from the feet and legs of Xaxa and Sag Or.

"Extinguish the lights!" I commanded. A trembling priest did my bidding.

Valla Dia and Dar Tarus were standing side by side before the altar when the lights went out. In the next minute they and Gor Hajus must have worked fast, for when I heard a low whistle from the interior of the idol's base, the prearranged signal that Gor Hajus had finished his work, and ordered the lights on again, there stood Xaxa and Sag Or where Valla Dia and Dar Tarus: had been, and the latter were nowhere in sight. I think the dramatic effect of that transformation upon the people there was the most stupendous thing I have ever seen. There was no cord or gag upon either Xaxa or Sag Or, nothing to indicate that they had been brought hither by force – no one about who might have so brought them. The illusion was perfect – it was a gesture of omnipotence that simply staggered the intellect. But I wasn't through.

"You have heard Xaxa renounce her throne," I said, "and Sag Or submit to the judgment of Tur."

"I have not renounced my throne!" cried Xaxa. "It is all a – –"Silence!" I thundered. "Prepare to greet the new Jeddak, Dar Tarus of Phundahl!" I turned my eyes towards the great doors and the eyes of the assemblage followed mine. They swung open and there stood Dar Tarus, resplendent in the trappings of Hora San, the long dead Jeddak and high priest, whose bones we had robbed in the base of the idol an hour earlier. How Dar Tarus had managed to make the change so quickly is beyond me, but he had done it and the effect was colossal. He looked every inch a Jeddak as he moved with slow dignity up the wide aisle along the blue and gold and white carpet. Xaxa turned purple with rage. "Impostor!" she shrieked. "Seize him! Kill him!" and she ran forward to meet him as though she would slay him with her bare hands.

"Take her away," said Dar Tarus in a quiet voice, and at that Xaxa fell foaming to the floor. She shrieked and gasped and then lay still – a wicked old woman dead of apoplexy. And when Sag Or saw her lying there he must have been the first to realize that she was dead and that there was now no one to protect him from the hatreds that are leveled always at the person of a ruler's favorite. He looked wildly about for an instant and then threw himself at the feet of Dar Tarus.

"You promised to protect me!" he cried.

"None shall harm you," replied Dar Tarus. "Go your way and live in peace." Then he turned his eyes upward towards the face of the Great Tur. "What is thy will, Master?" he cried. "Dar Tarus, thy servant, awaits thy commands!" I permitted an impressive silence before I replied.

"Let the priests of Tur, the lesser nobles and a certain number of the Jeddara's Guard go forth into the city and spread the word of Tur among the people that they may know that Tur smiles again upon Phundahl and that they have a new Jeddak who stands high in the favor of Tur. Let the higher nobles attend presently in the chambers that were Xaxa's and do honor to Valla Dia in whose perfect body their Jeddara once ruled them, and effect the necessary arrangements for her proper return to Duhor, her native city. There also will they find two who have served Tur well and these shall be accorded the hospitality and friendship of every Phundahlian – Gor Hajus of Toonol and Vad Varo of Jasoom. Go! and when the last has gone let the temple be darkened. I, Tur, have spoken!" Valla Dia had gone directly to the apartments of the former Jeddara and the moment that the lights were extinguished Gor Hajus and I joined her. She could not wait to hear the outcome of our ruse, and when I assured her that there had been no hitch the tears came to her eyes for very joy.

"You have accomplished the impossible, my chieftain," she murmured, "and already can I see the hills of Duhor and the towers of my native city. Ah, Vad Varo, I had not dreamed that life might again hold for me such happy prospects. I owe you life and more than life."

We were interrupted by the coming of Dar Tarus, and with him were Hovan Du and a number of the higher nobles. The latter received us pleasantly, though I think they were mystified as to just how we were linked with the service of their god, nor, I am sure, did one of them ever learn. They were frankly delighted to be rid of Xaxa; and while they could not understand Tur's purpose in elevating a former warrior of the Guard to the throne, yet they were content if it served to relieve them from the wrath of their god, now a very real and terrible god, since the miracles that had been performed in the temple. That Dar Tarus had been of a noble family relieved them of embarrassment, and I noted that they treated him with great respect. I was positive that they would continue to treat him so, for he was also high priest and for the first time in a hundred years he would bring to the Great Tur in the royal temple the voice of god, for Hovan Du had agreed to take service with Dar Tarus, and Gor Hajus as well, so that there would never be lacking a tongue wherewith Tur might speak. I foresaw great possibilities for the reign of Dar Tarus, Jeddak of Phundahl.

At the meeting held in the apartments of Xaxa it was decided that Valla Dia should rest two days in Phundahl while a small fleet was preparing to transport her to Duhor. Dar Tarus assigned Xaxa's apartments for her use and gave her slaves from different cities to attend upon her, all of whom were to be freed and returned with Valla Dia to her native land.

It was almost dawn before we sought our sleeping silks and furs and the sun was high before we awoke. Gor Hajus and I breakfasted with Valla Dia, outside whose door we had spread our beds that we might not leave her unprotected for a moment that it was not necessary. We had scarce finished our meal when a messenger came from Dar Tarus summoning us to the audience chamber, where we found some of the higher officers of the court gathered about the throne upon which Dar Tarus sat, looking every inch an emperor. He greeted us kindly, rising and descending from his dais to receive Valla Dia and escort her to one of the benches be had placed beside the throne for her and for me.

"There is one," he said to me, "who has come to Phundahl over night and now begs audience of the Jeddak – one whom I thought you might like to meet again," and he signed to one of his attendants to admit the petitioner; and when the doors at the opposite end of the room opened I saw Ras Thavas standing there. He did not recognize me or Valla Dia or Gor Hajus until he was almost at the foot of the throne, and when he did he looked puzzled and glanced again quickly at Dar Tarus.

"Ras Thavas of the Tower of Thavas, Toonol," announced an officer.

"What would Ras Thavas of the Jeddak of Phundahl?" asked Dar Tarus.

"I came seeking audience of Xaxa," replied Ras Thavas, "not knowing of her death or your accession until this very morning; but I see Sag Or upon Xaxa's throne and beside him one whom I thought was Xaxa, though they tell me Xaxa is dead, and another who was my assistant at Thavas and one who is the Assassin of Toonol, and I am confused, Jeddak, and do not know whether I be among friends or foes."

"Speak as though Xaxa still sat upon the throne of Phundahl," Dar Tarus told him, "for though I am Dar Tarus, whom you wronged, and not Sag Or, yet need you have no fear in the court of Phundahl."

"Then let me tell you that Vobis Kan, Jeddak of Toonol, learning that Gor Hajus had escaped me, swore that I had set him free to assassinate him, and he sent warriors who took my island and would have imprisoned me had I not been warned in time to escape; and I came hither to Xaxa to beg her to send warriors to drive the men of Toonol from my island and restore it to me that I may carry on my scientific labors."

Dar Tarus turned to me. "Vad Varo, of all others you are most familiar with the work of Ras Thavas. Would you see him again restored to his island and his laboratory?"

"Only on condition that he devote his great skill to the amelioration of human suffering," I replied, "and no longer prostitute it to the foul purposes of greed and sin." This led to a discussion which lasted for hours, the results of which were of far-reaching significance. Ras Thavas agreed to all that I required and Dar Tarus commissioned Gor Hajus to head an army against Toonol.

But these matters, while of vast interest to those most directly concerned, have no direct bearing upon the story of my adventures upon Barsoom, as I had no part in them, since upon the second day I boarded a flier with Valla Dia and, escorted by a Phundahlian fleet, set out towards Duhor. Dar Tarus accompanied us for a short distance. When the fleet was stopped at the shore of the great marsh he bade us farewell, and was about to step to the deck of his own ship and return to Phundahl when a shout arose from the deck of one of the other ships and word was soon passed that a lookout had sighted what appeared to be a great fleet far to the south-west. Nor was it long before it became plainly visible to us all and equally plain that it was headed for Phundahl.

Dar Tarus told me then that as much as he regretted it, there seemed nothing to do but return at once to his capital with the entire fleet, since he could not spare a single ship or man if this proved an enemy fleet, nor could Valla Dia or I interpose any objection; and so we turned about and sped as rapidly as the slow ships of Phundahl permitted back towards the city.

The stranger fleet had sighted us at about the same time that we had sighted it, and we saw it change its course and bear down upon us; and as it came nearer it fell into single file and prepared to encircle us. I was standing at Dar Tarus' side when the colors of the approaching fleet became distinguishable and we first learned that it was from Helium.

"Signal and ask if they come in peace," directed Dar Tarus.

"We seek word with Xaxa, Jeddara of Phundahl." came the reply. "The question of peace or war will be hers to decide."

"Tell them that Xaxa is dead and that I, Dar Tarus, Jeddak of Phundahl, will receive the commander of Helium's fleet in peace upon the deck of this ship, or that I will receive him in war with all my guns. I, Dar Tarus, have spoken!" From the bow of a great ship of Helium there broke the flag of truce and when Dar Tarus' ship answered it in kind the other drew near and presently we could see the men of Helium upon her decks. Slowly the great flier came alongside our smaller ship and when the two had been made fast a party of officers boarded us.

They were fine-looking men, and at their head was one whom I recognized immediately though I never before had laid eyes upon him. I think he was the most impressive figure I have ever seen as he advanced slowly across the deck towards us – John Carter, Prince of Helium, Warlord of Barsoom.

"Dar Tarus," he said, "John Carter greets you and in peace, though it had been different, I think, had Xaxa still reigned."

"You came to war upon Xaxa?" asked Dar Tarus.

"We came to right a wrong," replied the Warlord. "But from what we know of Xaxa that could have been done only by force."

"What wrong has Phundahl done Helium?" demanded Dar Tarus.

"The wrong was against one of your own people – even against you in person."

"I do not understand," said Dar Tarus.

"There is one aboard my ship who may be able to explain to you, Dar Tarus," replied John Carter, with a smile. He turned and spoke to one of his aides in a whisper, and the man saluted and returned to the deck of his own ship. "You shall see with your own eyes, Dar Tarus." Suddenly his eyes narrowed. "This is indeed Dar Tarus who was a warrior of the Jeddara's Guard and supposedly assassinated by her command?"

"It is," replied Dar Tarus.

"I must be certain," said the Warlord.

"There is no question about it, John Carter," I spoke up in English.

His eyes went wide, and when they fell upon me and he noted my lighter skin, from which the dye was wearing away, he stepped forward and held out his hand.

"A countryman?" he asked.

"Yes, an American," I replied.

"I was almost surprised," he said. "Yet why should I be? I have crossed – there is no reason why others should not. And you have accomplished it! You must come to Helium with me and tell me all about it."

Further conversation was interrupted by the return of the aide, who brought a young woman with him. At sight of her Dar Tarus uttered a cry of joy and sprang forward, and I did not need to be told that this was Kara Vasa.

There is little more to tell that might not bore you in the telling – of how John Carter himself took Valla Dia and me to Duhor after attending the nuptials of Dar Tarus and Kara Vasa; and of the great surprise that awaited me in Duhor, where I learned for the first time that Kor San, Jeddak of Duhor, was the father of Valla Dia; and of the honors and the great riches that he heaped upon me when Valla Dia and I were wed.

John Carter was present at the wedding and we initiated upon Barsoom a good old American custom, for the Warlord acted as best man; and then he insisted that we follow that up with a honeymoon and bore us off to Helium, where I am writing this.

Even now it seems like a dream that I can look out of my window and see the scarlet and the yellow towers of the twin cities of Helium; that I have met, and see daily, Carthoris, Thuvia of Ptarth, Tara of Helium, Gahan of Gathol and that peerless creature, Dejah Thoris, Princess of Mars. Though to me, beautiful as she is, there is another even more beautiful – Valla Dia, Princess of Duhor – Mrs. Ulysses Paxton.

A FIGHTING MAN OF MARS

BOOK SEVEN

FOREWORD

To JASON GRIDLEY of Tarzana, discoverer of the Gridley Wave, belonged the credit of establishing radio communication between Pellucidar and the outer world.

It was my good fortune to be much in his laboratory while he was
carrying on his experiments and to be, also, the recipient of his confidences, so that I was fully aware that while he hoped to establish communication with Pellucidar he was also reaching out toward an even
more stupendous accomplishment – he was groping through space for
contact with another planet; nor did he attempt to deny that the present
goal of his ambition was radio communication with Mars.

Gridley had constructed a simple, automatic device for broadcast-
ing signals intermittently and for recording whatever might be received
during his absence.

For a period of five minutes the Gridley Wave carried a simple code
signal consisting of two letters, "J.G.," out into the ether, following
which there was a pause of ten minutes. Hour after hour, day after day,
week after week, these silent, invisible messengers sped out to the uttermost reaches of infinite space, and after Jason Gridley left Tarzana
to embark upon his expedition to Pellucidar, I found myself drawn to
his laboratory by the lure of the tantalizing possibilities of his dream, as
well as by the promise I had made him that I would look in occasionally to see that the device was functioning properly and to examine
the recording instruments for any indication that the signals had been
received and answered.

My considerable association with Gridley had given me a fair working knowledge of his devices and sufficient knowledge of the Morse
Code to enable me to receive with moderate accuracy and speed.

Months passed; dust accumulated thickly upon everything except
the working parts of Gridley's device, and the white ribbon of ticker

tape that was to receive an answering signal retained its virgin purity; then I went away for a short trip into Arizona.

I was absent for about ten days and upon my return one of the first things with which I concerned myself was an inspection of Gridley's laboratory and the instruments he had left in my care. As I entered the familiar room and switched on the lights it was with the expectation of meeting with the same blank unresponsiveness to which I was by now quite accustomed.

As a matter of fact, hope of success had never been raised to any considerable degree in my breast, nor had Gridley been over sanguine – his was merely an experiment. He considered it well worth while to make it, and I considered it equally worth while to lend him what small assistance I might.

It was, therefore, with feelings of astonishment that assumed the magnitude of a distinct shock that I saw upon the ticker tape the familiar tracings which stand for the dots and dashes of code.

Of course I realized that some other researcher might have duplicated Jason's discovery of the Gridley Wave and that the message might have originated upon earth, or, again, it might be a message from Jason himself in Pellucidar, but when I had deciphered it, all doubts were quickly put to rest. It was from Ulysses Paxton, one time captain, – the U.S. Infantry, who, miraculously transported from a battlefield in France to the bosom of the great Red Planet, had become the right hand man of Ras Thavas, the mastermind of Mars, and later the husband of Valla Dia, daughter of Kor San, Jeddak of Duhor.

In brief, the message explained that for months mysterious signals had been received at Helium, and while they were unable to interpret them, they felt that they came from Jasoom, the name by which the planet Earth is known upon Mars.

John Carter being absent from Helium, a fast flier had been dispatched to Duhor bearing an urgent request to Paxton to come at once to the twin cities and endeavor to determine if in truth the signals they were receiving actually originated upon the planet of his birth.

Upon his arrival at Helium, Paxton immediately recognized the Morse Code signals and no doubt was left in the minds of the Martian scientists that at last something tangible had been accomplished toward the solution of inter-communication between Jasoom and Barsoom.

Repeated attempts to transmit answering signals to Earth proved fruitless and then the best minds of Helium settled down to the task of analyzing and reproducing the Gridley Wave.

They felt that at last they had succeeded. Paxton had sent his message and they were eagerly awaiting an acknowledgment.

I have since been in almost constant communication with Mars, but out of loyalty to Jason Gridley, to whom all the credit and honor are due, I have made no official announcement, nor shall I give out any important information, leaving all that for his return to the outer world; but I believe that I am betraying no confidence if I narrate to you the interesting story of Hadron of Hastor, which Paxton told me one evening not long since.

I hope that you will enjoy it as much as I did.

But before I go on with the story a brief description of the principal races of Mars, their political and military organization and some of their customs may prove of interest to many of my readers. The dominant race in whose hands rest the progress and civilization – yes, the very life of Mars – differ but little in physical appearance from ourselves. The fact that their skins are a light reddish copper color and that they are oviparous constitute the two most marked divergences from Anglo-Saxon standards. No, there is another – their longevity. A thousand years is the natural span of life of a Martian, although, because of their war-like activities and the prevalence of assassination among them, few live their allotted span.

Their general political organization has changed little in countless ages, the unit still being the tribe, at the head of which is a chief or jed, corresponding in modern times to our king. The princes are known as lesser jeds, while the chief of chiefs, or the head of consolidated tribes, is the jeddak, or emperor, whose consort is a jeddara.

The majority of red Martians live in walled cities, though there are many who reside in isolated, though well walled and defended, farm homes along those rich irrigated ribbons of land that we of earth know as the Canals of Mars.

In the far south, that is in the south polar region, dwells a race of very handsome and highly intelligent black men. There, also, is the remnant of a white race; while the north polar regions are dominated by a race of yellow men.

In between the two poles and scattered over all the and waste lands of the dead sea bottoms, often inhabiting the ruined cities of another age, are the feared green hordes of Mars.

The terrible green warriors of Barsoom are the hereditary enemies of all the other races of this martial planet. They are of heroic size and in addition to being equipped with two legs and two arms apiece, they have an intermediary pair of limbs, which may be used at will either as arms or legs. Their eyes are set at the extreme sides of their heads, a trifle above the center, and protrude in such a manner that they may be directed either forward or back and also independently of each other, thus permitting these remarkable creatures to look in any direction, or in two directions at once without the necessity of turning their heads.

Their ears, which are slightly above the eyes and closer together are small cupped-shape antennae, protruding several inches from the head, while their noses are but longitudinal slits in the center of their faces, midway between their mouths and ears.

They have no hair on their bodies, which are of a very light yellow-ish-green color in infancy, deepening to an olive green toward maturity, the adult males being darker in color than the females.

The iris of the eyes is blood red, as an Albino's, while the pupil is dark. The eyeball itself is very white, as are the teeth and it is these latter which add a most ferocious appearance to an otherwise fearsome and terrible countenance, as the lower tusks curve upward to sharp points which end about where the eyes of earthly human beings are located. The whiteness of the teeth is not that of ivory, but of the snowiest and most gleaming of china. Against the dark background of their olive skins their tusks stand out in a most striking manner, causing these weapons to present a singularly formidable appearance.

They are a cruel and taciturn race, entirely devoid of love, sympathy or pity.

They are an equestrian race, never walking other than to move about their camps.

Their mounts, called thoats, are great savage beasts whose proportions harmonize with those of their giant masters. They have eight legs and broad flat tails larger at the tips than at the roots. They hold these tails straight out while running. Their mouths are enormous, splitting their heads from their snouts to their long, massive necks. Like their masters, they are entirely devoid of hair, their skins being a dark slate color and exceedingly smooth and glossy, with the exception of the belly, which is white, and the legs, which shade from the slate of the shoulders and hips to a vivid yellow at the feet. The feet are heavily padded and nailless.

Like the red men, the green hordes are ruled by jeds and jeddaks, but their military organization is not carried to the same detail of perfection as is that of the red men.

The military forces of the red men are highly organized, the principal arm of the service being the navy, an enormous air force of battleships, cruisers and an infinite variety of lesser craft down to one-man scout fliers. Next in size and importance is the infantry branch of the service, while the cavalry, mounted on a breed of small thoats, similar to those used by the green Martian giants, is utilized principally in patrolling the avenues of the cities and the rural districts that border the irrigating systems.

The principal basic unit, although not the smallest one of the military organization, is a utan, consisting of one hundred men, which is commanded by a dwar with several padwars or lieutenants junior to him. An odwar commands a umak of ten thousand men, while next above him is a jedwar, who is junior only to the jed or king.

Science, literature, art and architecture are in some of their departments further advanced upon Mars than upon Earth, a remarkable thing when one considers the constant battle for survival which is the most marked characteristic of life upon Barsoom.

Not only are they waging a continual battle against Nature, which is slowly diminishing their already scant atmosphere, but from birth to death they are constantly faced by the stern necessity of defending themselves against enemy nations of their own race and the great hordes of roving green warriors of the dead sea bottom; while within the walls of their own cities are countless professional assassins, whose calling is so well recognized that in some localities they are organized into guilds.

But notwithstanding all the grim realities with which they have to contend, the red Martians are a happy, social people. They have their games, their dances and their songs, and the social life of a great capital of Barsoom is as gay and magnificent as any that may be found in the rich capitals of Earth.

That they are a brave, noble and generous people is indicated by the fact that neither John Carter nor Ulysses Paxton would return to Earth if they might.

And now to return to the tale that I had from Paxton across forty-three million miles of space.

CHAPTER ONE

Sanoma Tora

THIS IS THE STORY of Hadron of Hastor, Fighting Man of Mars, as narrated by him to Ulysses Paxton:

I am Tan Hadron of Hastor, my father is Had Urtur, Odwar of the 1st Umak of the Troops of Hastor. He commands the largest ship of war that Hastor has ever contributed to the navy of Helium, accommodating as it does the entire ten thousand men of the 1st Umak, together with five hundred lesser fighting ships and all the paraphernalia of war. My mother is a princess of Gathol.

As a family we are not rich except in honor, and, valuing this above all mundane possessions, I chose the profession of my father rather than a more profitable career. The better to further my ambition I came to the capital of the empire of Helium and took service in the troops of Tardos Mors, Jeddak of Helium, that I might be nearer the great John Carter, Warlord of Mars.

My life in Helium and my career in the army were similar to those of hundreds of other young men. I passed through my training days without notable accomplishment, neither heading nor trailing my fellows, and in due course I was made a Padwar in the 91st Umak, being assigned to the 5th Utan of the 11th Dar.

What with being of noble lineage by my father and inheriting royal blood from my mother, the palaces of the twin cities of Helium were always open to me and I entered much into the gay life of the capital. It was thus that I met Sanoma Tora, daughter of Tor Hatan, Odwar of the 91st Umak.

Tor Hatan is only of the lower nobility, but he is fabulously rich from the loot of many cities well invested in farm land and mines, and because here in the capital of Helium riches count for more than they do in Hastor, Tor Hatan is a powerful man, whose influence reaches even to the throne of the Jeddak.

Never shall I forget the occasion upon which I first laid eyes upon Sanoma Tora. It was upon the occasion of a great feast at the marble palace of The Warlord. There were gathered under roof the most beautiful women of Barsoom, where, notwithstanding the gorgeous and radiant beauty of Dejah Thoris, Tara of Helium and Thuvid of Ptarth, the pulchritude of Sanoma Tora was such as to arrest attention. I shall not say that it was greater than that of those acknowledged queens of Barsoomian loveliness, for I know that my adoration of Sanoma Tora might easily influence my judgment, but there were others there who remarked her gorgeous beauty which differs from that of Dejah Thoris as the chaste beauty of a polar landscape differs from the beauty of the tropics, as the beauty of a white palace in the moonlight differs from the beauty of its garden at midday.

When at my solicitation I was presented to her, she glanced first at the insignia upon my armor, and noting therefrom that I was but a Padwar, she vouchsafed me but a condescending word and turned her attention again to the Dwar with whom she had been conversing.

I must admit that I was piqued and yet it was, indeed, the contumelious treatment she accorded me that fixed my determination to win her, for the goal most difficult of attainment has always seemed to me the most desirable.

And so it was that I fell in love with Sanoma Tora, the daughter of the commander of the Umak to which I was attached.

For a long time I found it difficult to further my suit in the slightest degree; in fact I did not even see Sanoma Tora for several months after our first meeting, since when she found that I was poor as well as low in rank I found it impossible to gain an invitation to her home and it chanced that I did not meet her elsewhere for a long time, but the more inaccessible she became the more I loved her until every waking moment of my time that was not actually occupied by the performance of my military duties was devoted to the devising of new and ever increasingly rash plans to possess her. I even had the madness to consider abducting her, and I believe that I should eventually have gone this far had there been no other way in which I could see her, but about this time a fellow officer of the 91st, in fact the Dwar of the Utan to which I was attached, took pity on me and obtained for me an invitation to a feast in the palace of Tor Hatan.

My host, who was also my commanding officer, had never noticed me before this evening and I was surprised to note the warmth and cordiality of his greetings.

"We must see more of you here, Hadron of Hastor," he had said. "I have been watching you and I prophesy that you will go far in the military service of the Jeddak."

Now I knew he was lying when he said that he had been watching me, for Tor Hatan was notoriously lax in his duties as a commanding officer, all of which were performed by the senior Teedwar of the Umak. While I could not fathom the cause of this sudden interest in me, it was nevertheless very pleasing since through it I might in some degree further my pursuit of the heart and hand of Sanoma Tora.

Sanoma Tora herself was slightly more cordial than upon the occasion of our first meeting, though she noticeably paid more attention to Sil Vagis than she did to me.

Now if there is any man in Helium whom I particularly detest more than another it is Sil Vagis, a nasty little snob who holds the title of Teedwar, though so far as I was ever able to ascertain he commands no troops, but is merely on the staff of Tor Hatan, principally, I presume, because of the great wealth of his father.

Such creatures we have to put up with in times of peace, but when war comes and the great Warlord takes command it is the fighting men who rank and riches do not count.

But be that as it may, while Sil Vagis spoiled this evening for me as he would spoil many others in the future, nevertheless I left the palace of Tor Hatan that night with a feeling bordering upon elation, for I had Sanoma Tora's permission to see her again in her father's home when my duties would permit me to pay my respects to her.

Returning to my quarters I was accompanied by my friend, the Dwar, and when I commented on the warmth of Tor Hatan's reception of me he laughed.

"You find it amusing," I said. "Why?"

"Tor Hatan, as you know," he said, "is very rich and powerful, and yet it is seldom, as you may have noticed, that he is invited to any one of the four places of Helium in which ambitious men most crave to be seen."

"You mean the palaces of the Warlord, the Jeddak, the Jed and Carthoris?" I asked.

"Of course," he replied. "What other four in Helium count for so much as these? Tor Hatan," he continued, "is supposed to come from the lower nobility, but there is a question in my mind as to whether there is a drop of noble blood in his veins, and one of the facts upon which I base my conjecture is his cringing and fawning reverence for anything pertaining to royalty – he would give his fat soul to be considered an intimate of any one of the four."

"But what has that to do with me?" I demanded.

"A great deal," he replied; "in fact, because of it you were invited to his palace tonight."

"I do not understand," I said.

"I chanced to be talking with Tor Hatan the morning of the day you received your invitation and in the course of our conversation I mentioned you. He had never heard of you, and as a Padwar in the 5th Utan you aroused his interest not a particle, but when I told him that your mother was a princess of Gathol, he pricked up his ears, and when he learned that you were received as a friend and equal in the palaces of the four demigods of Helium, he became almost enthusiastic about you. Now do you understand?" he concluded with a short laugh.

"Perfectly," I replied, "but none the less, I thank you. All that I wanted was the opportunity and inasmuch as I was prepared to achieve it criminally if necessary, I cannot quibble over any means that were employed to obtain it, however unflattering they may be to me."

For months I haunted the palace of Tor Hatan, and being naturally a good conversationalist and well schooled in the stately dances and joyous games of Barsoom, I was by no means an unwelcome visitor. Also I made it a point often to take Sanoma Tora to one or another of the four great palaces of Helium. I was always welcome because of the blood relationship which existed between my mother and Gahan of Gathol, who had married Tara of Helium.

Naturally I felt that I was progressing well with my suit, but my progress was not fast enough to keep pace with the racing desires of my passion. Never had I known love before and I felt that I should die if I did not soon possess Sanoma Tora, and so it was that upon a certain night I visited the palace of her father definitely determined to lay my heart and sword at her feet before I left, and, although the natural complexes of a lover convinced me that I was an unworthy worm, that she would be wholly justified in spurning, I was yet determined to declare myself so that I might openly be accounted a suitor, which, after all, gives one greater freedom even though he be not entirely a favored suitor.

It was one of those lovely nights that transform old Barsoom into a world of enchantment. Thuria and Cluros were racing through the heavens casting their soft light upon the garden of Tor Hatan, empurpling the vivid, scarlet sward and lending strange hues to the gorgeous blooms of pimalia and sorapus, while the winding walks, gravelled with semi-precious stones, shot back a thousand scintillant rays that, clothed in ever-changing colors, danced at the feet of the marble statuary that lent an added artistic charm to the ensemble.

In one of the spacious halls that overlooked the garden of the palace, a youth and a maiden sat upon a massive bench of rich sorapus wood, such a bench as might have graced the halls of the great Jeddak himself, so intricate its rich design, so perfect the carving of the master craftsman who produced it.

Upon the leathern harness of the youth were the insignia of his rank and service – a Padwar in the 91st Umak. The youth was I, Hadron of Hastor, and with me was Sanoma Tora, daughter of Tor Hatan. I had come filled with the determination boldly to plead my cause, but suddenly I had become aware of my unworthiness. What had I to offer this beautiful daughter of the rich Tor Hatan? I was only a Padwar, and a poor one at that. Of course, there was the royal blood of Gathol in my veins, and that, I knew, would have weight with Tor Hatan, but I am not given to boasting and I could not have reminded Sanoma Tora of the advantages to be derived because of it even had I known positively that it would influence her. I had, therefore, nothing to offer but my great love, which is, perhaps, after all, the greatest gift that man or woman can bring to another, and I had thought of late that Sanoma Tora might love me. Upon several occasions she had sent for me, and, although in each instance she had suggested going to the palace of Tara of Helium, I had been vain enough to hope that this was not her sole reason for wishing to be with me.

"You are uninteresting tonight, Hadron of Hastor," she said after a particularly long silence, during which I had been endeavoring to formulate my proposal in some convincing and graceful phrases.

"Perhaps," I replied, "it is because I am trying to find the words in which to clothe the most interesting thought I have ever entertained."

"And what is that?" she asked politely, though with no great show of interest.

"I love you, Sanoma Tora," I blurted awkwardly.

She laughed. It was like the tinkling of silver upon crystal – beautiful but cold. "That has been apparent for a long while," she said, "but why speak of it?"

"And why not?" I asked.

"Because even if I returned your love, I am not for you, Hadron of Hastor," she replied coldly.

"You cannot love me then, Sanoma Tora?" I asked.

"I did not say that," she replied.

"You could love me?"

"I could love you if I permitted myself the weakness," she said, "but what is love?"

"Love is everything," I told her.

Sanoma Tora laughed. "If you think that I would link myself for life to a threadbare Padwar even if I loved him, you are mistaken," she said haughtily. "I am the daughter of Tor Hatan, whose wealth and power are but little less than those of the royal families of Helium. I have suitors whose wealth is so great that they could buy you a thousand times over. Within the year an emissary of the Jeddak Tul Axtar of Jahar waited upon my father; he had seen me and he said that he would return, and, merely for love, you would ask me, who may some day be Jeddara of Jahar to become the wife of a poor Padwar."

I arose. "Perhaps you are right," I said. "You are so beautiful that it does not seem possible that you could be wrong, but deep in my heart I cannot but feel that happiness is the greatest treasure that one may possess, and love the greatest power. Without these, Sanoma Tora, even a Jeddara is poor indeed."

"I shall take my chance," she said.

"I hope that the Jeddak of Jahar is not as greasy as his emissary," I remarked rather peevishly, I am afraid.

"He may be an animated grease-pot for all I care if he will make me his Jeddara," said Sanoma Tora.

"Then there is no hope for me?" I asked.

"Not while you have so little to offer, Padwar," she replied.

It was then that a slave announced Sil Vagis, and I took my leave. I had never before plumbed such depths of despondency as that which engulfed me as I made my unhappy way back to my quarters, but even though hope seemed dead I had not relinquished my determination to win her. If wealth and power were her price, then I would achieve wealth and power. Just how I was going to accomplish it was not entirely clear, but I was young and to youth all things are possible.

I had tossed in wakefulness upon my sleeping silks and furs for some time when an officer of the guard burst suddenly into my quarters.

"Hadron!" he shouted, "are you here?"

"Yes," I replied.

"Praised be the ashes of my ancestors!" he exclaimed. "I feared that you were not."

"Why should I not be?" I demanded. "What is this all about?"

"Tor Hatan, the fat old treasure bag, is gone mad," he exclaimed.

"Tor Hatan gone mad? What do you mean? What has that got to do with me?"

"He swears that you have abducted his daughter."

In an instant I was upon my feet. "Abducted Sanoma Tora!" I cried. "Has something happened to her? Tell me, quickly."

"Yes, she is gone, all right," said my informant, "and there is something mighty mysterious about it."

But I did not wait to hear more. Seizing my harness, I adjusted it as I ran up the spiral runway toward the hangars on the roof of the barracks. I had no authority or permit to take out a flier, but what did that mean to me if Sanoma Tora was in danger?

The hangar guards sought to detain and question me. I do not recall what I told them; I know that I must have lied to them, for they let me run out a swift one-man flier and an instant later I was racing through the night toward the palace of Tor Hatan.

As it stands but little more than two haads from the barracks, I was there in but a few moments, and, as I landed in the garden, which was now brilliantly lighted, I saw a number of people congregated there, among whom were Tor Hatan and Sil Vagis.

As I leaped from the deck of the flier, the former came angrily toward me. "So it is you!" he cried. "What have you to say for yourself? Where is my daughter?"

"That is what I have come to ask, Tor Hatan," I replied.

"You are at the bottom of this," he cried. "You abducted her. She told Sil Vagis that this very night you had demanded her hand in marriage and that she had refused you."

"I did ask for her hand," I said, "and she refused me. That part is true; but if she has been abducted, in the name of your first ancestor, do not waste time trying to connect me with the diabolical plot. I had nothing to do with it. How did it happen? Who was with her?"

"Sil Vagis was with her. They were walking in the garden," replied Tor Hatan.

"You saw her abducted," I asked, turning to Sil Vagis, "and you are here unwounded and alive?"

He started to stammer. "There were many of them," he said. "They overpowered me."

"You saw them?" I asked.

"Yes."

"Was I among them?" I demanded.

"It was dark. I could not recognize any of them, perhaps they were disguised."

"They overpowered you?" I asked him.

"Yes," he said.

"You lie!" I exclaimed. "Had they laid hands upon you they would have killed you. You ran away and hid, never drawing a weapon to defend the girl."

"That is a lie," cried Sil Vagis. "I fought with them, but they overpowered me."

I turned to Tor Hatan. "We are wasting time," I said. "Is there no one who can give us a clue as to the identity of these men and the direction they took in their flight? How and whence came they? How and whence did they depart?"

"He is trying to throw you off the track, Tor Hatan," said Sil Vagis. "Who else could it have been but a disgruntled suitor? What would you say if I should tell you that the metal of the men who stole Sanoma Tora was the metal of the warriors of Hastor?"

"I would say that you are a liar," I replied. "If it was so dark that you could not recognize faces, how could you decipher the insignia upon their harness?"

At this juncture another officer of the 91st Umak joined us. "We have found one who may, perhaps, shed some light upon the subject," he said, "if he lives long enough to speak."

Men had been searching the grounds of Tor Hatan and that portion of the city adjacent to his palace, and now several approached bearing a man, whom they laid upon the sward at our feet. His broken and mangled body was entirely naked, and as he lay there gasping feebly for breath, he was a pitiful spectacle.

A slave dispatched into the palace returned with stimulants, and when some of these had been forced between his lips, the man revived slightly.

"Who are you?" asked Tor Hatan.

"I am a warrior of the city guard," replied the man feebly.

An officer approached Tor Hatan excitedly. "My men have just found six more bodies close to the point at which we discovered this man," he said. "They are all naked and similarly broken and mangled."

"Perhaps we shall get to the bottom of this yet," said Tor Hatan, and, turning again to the poor, broken thing upon the scarlet sward, he directed him to proceed.

"We were on night patrol over the city when we saw a craft running without lights. As we approached it and turned our searchlight upon it, I caught a single, brief glimpse of it. It bore no colors or insignia to denote its origin and its design was unlike that of any ship I have ever seen. It had a long, low, enclosed cabin upon either side of which were mounted two peculiar-looking guns. This was all I had time to note, except that I saw a man directing one of the guns in our direction. The Padwar in command of our ship immediately gave orders to fire upon the stranger, and at the same time he hailed him. At that instant our ship dissolved in mid-air; even my harness fell from me. I remember falling, that is all," and with these words he gasped once and died.

Tor Hatan called his people around him. "There must have been someone about the palace or the grounds who saw something of this occurrence," he said. "I command that no matter who may be involved, whoever has any knowledge whatsoever of this affair, shall speak."

A slave stepped forward, and as he approached Tor Hatan eyed him with haughty arrogance.

"Well," demanded the odwar, "what have you to say? Speak!"

"You have commanded it, Tor Hatan," said the slave; "otherwise I should not speak, for when I have told what I saw I shall have incurred the enmity of a powerful noble," and he glanced quickly toward Sil Vagis.

"And if you speak the truth, man, you will have won the friendship of a Padwar whose sword is not so mean but that it may protect you even from a powerful noble," I said quickly, and I, too, glanced at Sil Vagis, for it was in my mind that what the fellow had to tell might be none too flattering to the soft fop who masqueraded beneath the title of a warrior.

"Speak!" commanded Tor Hatan impatiently. "And see to it that thou dost not lie."

"For fourteen years I have served faithfully in your palace, Tor Hatan," replied the man, "ever since I was brought to Helium a prisoner of war after the fall and sack of Kobol, where I served in the body guard of the Jed of Kobol, and in all that time you have had no reason to question my truthfulness. Sanoma Tora trusted me, and had I had a sword this night she might still be with us."

"Come! Come!" cried Tor Hatan; "get to the point. What saw you?"

"The fellow saw nothing," snapped Sil Vagis. "Why waste time upon him? He seeks but to glory in a little brief notoriety.

"Let him speak," I exclaimed.

"I had just ascended the first ramp to the second level of the palace," explained the slave, "on my way to the sleeping quarters of Tor Hatan to arrange his sleeping silks and furs for the night as is my custom, and, pausing for a moment to look out into the garden, I saw Sanoma Tora and Sil Vagis walking in the moonlight. Conscious that I should not thus observe them, I was about to continue on my way about my duties when I saw a flier dropping silently out of the night toward the garden. Its motors were noiseless, it showed no light. It seemed a spectral ship and of such strange design that even if for no other reason it would have arrested my attention, but there were other reasons. Unlighted ships move through the night for no good purpose, and so I paused to watch it.

"It landed silently and quickly behind Sanoma Tora and Sil Vagis; nor did they seem aware of its presence until their attention was attracted by the slight clanking of the accoutrements of one of the several warriors who sprang from its low cabin as it grounded. Then Sil Vagis wheeled about. For just an instant he stood as though petrified and then as the strange warriors leaped toward him, he turned and fled into the concealing shrubbery of the garden."

"It is a lie," cried Sil Vagis.

"Silence, coward!" I commanded.

"Continue, slave!" directed Tor Hatan.

"Sanoma Tora was not aware of the presence of the strange warriors until she was seized roughly from behind. It all happened so quickly that I scarce had time to realize the purpose of the sinister visitation before they laid hands upon her. When I comprehended that my mistress was the object of this night attack, I rushed hurriedly down the ramp, but ere I reached the garden they had dragged her aboard the flier. Even then, however, had I had a sword I might at least have died in the service of Sanoma Tora, for I reached the ship of mystery as the last warrior was clambering aboard. I seized him by the harness and attempted to drag him to the ground, at the same time shouting loudly to attract the palace guard, but ere I did so one of his fellows on the deck above me drew his long sword and struck viciously at my head. The blade caught me but a glancing blow which, however, sufficed to stun me for a moment, so that I relaxed my hold upon the strange warrior and fell to the sward. When I regained consciousness the ship had gone and the tardy palace guard was pouring from the guard room. I have spoken – and spoken truthfully."

Tor Hatan's cold gaze sought out the lowered eyes of Sil Vagis. "What have you to say to this?" he demanded.

"The fellow is in the employ of Hadron of Hastor," shouted Sil Vagis. "He speaks nothing but lies. I attacked them when they came, but there were many and they overpowered me. This fellow was not present."

"Let me see thy head," I said to the slave, and when he had come and knelt before me I saw a great red welt the length of one side of his head above the ear, just such a welt as a glancing blow from the flat side of a long sword might have made. "Here," I said to Tor Hatan, pointing to the great welt, "is the proof of a slave's loyalty and courage. Let us see the wounds received by a noble of Helium who by his own testimony engaged in single-handed combat against great odds. Surely in such an encounter he must have received at least a single scratch."

"Unless he is as marvelous a swordsman as the great John Carter himself," said the dwar of the palace guard with a thinly veiled sneer.

"It is all a plot," cried Sil Vagis. "Do you take the word of a slave, Tor Hatan, against that of a noble of Helium?"

"I rely on the testimony of my eyes and my senses," replied the odwar, and he turned his back upon Sil Vagis and again addressed the slave. "Didst thou recognize any of those who abducted Sanoma Tora," he demanded, "or note their harness or their metal?"

"I got no good look at the face of any of them, but I did see the harness and the metal of him whom I tried to drag from the flier."

"Was it the metal of Hastor?" asked Tor Hatan.

"By my first ancestor, it was not," replied the slave emphatically; "nor was it the metal of any other city of the Empire of Helium. The design and the insignia were unknown to me, and yet there was a certain familiarity about them that tantalizes me. I feel that I have seen them before, but when and where I cannot recall. In the service of my jed I fought invaders from many lands and it may be that upon some of these I saw similar metal many years ago."

"Are you satisfied, Tor Hatan," I demanded, "that the aspersions cast upon me by Sil Vagis are without foundation?"

"Yes, Hadron of Hastor," replied the odwar.

"Then with your leave, I shall depart," I said.

"Where are you going?" he asked.

"To find Sanoma Tora," I replied.

"And if you find her," he said, "and return her safely to me, she is yours."

I made no other acknowledgment of his generous offer than to bow deeply, for I had it in my mind that Sanoma Tora might have something to say about that, and whether she had or not, I wished no mate who came not to me willingly.

Leaping to the deck of the flier that brought me I rose into the night and sped in the direction of the marble palace of the Warlord of Barsoom, for, even though the hour was late, I was determined to see him without an instant's unnecessary loss of time.

CHAPTER TWO

Brought Down

As I approached the Warlord's palace I saw signs of activity unusual for that hour of the night. Fliers were arriving and departing, and when I alighted upon that portion of the roof reserved for military ships, I saw the fliers of a number of high officers of the Warlord's staff.

Being a frequent visitor at the palace and being well known by all the officers of the Warlord's body guard, I had no difficulty in gaining admission to the palace, and presently I was waiting in the hall, just off the small compartment in which the Warlord is accustomed to give small, private audiences, while a slave announced me to his master.

I do not know how long I waited. It could not have been a long while, yet it seemed to me a veritable eternity, because my mind was harassed by the conviction that the woman I loved was in dire danger. I was possessed by a conviction, ridiculous perhaps, but none the less real, that I alone could save her and that every instant I was delayed reduced her chances for succor before it was too late.

But at last I was invited to enter, and when I stood in the presence of the great Warlord I found him surrounded by men high in the councils of Helium.

"I assume," said John Carter, coming directly to the point, "that what brings you here tonight, Hadron of Hastor, pertains to the matter of the abduction of the daughter of Tor Hatan. Have you any knowledge or any theory that might cast any light upon the subject?"

"No," I replied. "I have come merely to obtain your authority to depart at once in an attempt to pick up the trail of the abductors of Sanoma Tora."

"Where do you intend to search?" he demanded.

"I do not yet know, sir," I replied, "but I shall find her."

He smiled. "Such assurance is at least an asset," he said, "and know-ing as I do what prompts it, I shall grant you the permission you desire. While the abduction of a daughter of Helium is in itself of sufficient gravity to warrant the use of every resource to apprehend her abductors and return her to her home, there is also involved in this occurrence an element that may portend high danger to the empire. As you doubt-less know, the mysterious ship that bore her away mounted a gun from which emanated some force that entirely disintegrated all the metal parts of the patrol flier that sought to intercept and question it. Even the weapons and the metal portions of the harness of the crew were dis-sipated into nothing, a fact that was easily discernible from an exami-nation of the wreck of the patrol flier and the bodies of its crew. Wood, leather, flesh, everything of the animal and vegetable kingdom that was aboard the flier, has been found scattered about the ground where it fell, but no trace of any metallic substance remains.

"I am impressing this upon you because it suggests to my mind a pos-sible clue to the general location of the city of these new enemies of He-lium. I am convinced that this is but the first blow, since any navy armed with such guns could easily hold Helium at its mercy, and few indeed are the cities of Barsoom outside the empire that would not seize with avidity upon any instrument that would give them the sack of the Twin Cities.

"For some time now we have been deeply concerned by the increasing number of missing ships of the navy. In nearly all instances these were ships engaged in charting air currents and recording atmospheric pres-sures in different parts of Barsoom far from the empire, and recently it has become apparent that the vast majority of these ships which never re-turn were those cruising in the southern part of the western hemisphere, an unhospitable portion of our planet concerning which we have unfor-tunately but little knowledge owing to the fact that we have developed no trade with the unfriendly people inhabiting this vast domain.

"This, Hadron of Hastor, is only a suggestion; only the vaguest of clues, but I offer it to you for what it is worth. A thousand one-man scout fliers will be dispatched between now and noon tomorrow in search of the abductors of Sanoma Tora; nor will these be all. Cruisers and battleships will take the air as well, for Helium must know what city or what nation has developed a weapon of destruction such as that used above Helium this night.

"It is my belief that the weapon is of very recent invention and that whatever power possesses it, must be bending every effort to perfect it and produce it in such quantities as to make them masters of the world. I have spoken. Go, and may fortune be with you."

You may believe that I lost no time in setting out upon my mission now that I had authority from John Carter. Going to my quarters I hastened my preparation for departure, which consisted principally of making a careful selection of weapons and of exchanging a rather ornate harness I had been wearing for one of simpler design and of heavier and more durable leather. My fighting harness is always the best and plainest that I can procure and is made for me by a famous harnessmaker of Lesser Helium. My equipment of weapons was standard, consisting of a long sword, a short sword, a dagger and a pistol. I also provided myself with extra ammunition and a supply of the concentrated ration used by all Martian fighting men.

As I gathered together these simple necessities which, with a single sleeping fur, would constitute my equipment, my mind was given over to consideration of various explanations for the disappearance of Sanoma Tora. I searched my brain for any slightest memory that might suggest an explanation, or point toward the possible identity of her abductors. It was while thus engaged that I recalled her reference to the jeddak, Tul Axtar of Jahar nor was there within the scope of my recollection any other incident that might point a clue. I distinctly recalled the emissary of Tul Axtar who had visited the court of Helium not long since. I had heard him boast of the riches and power of his jeddak and the beauty of his women. Perhaps, then, it might be as well to search in the direction of Jahar as elsewhere, but before departing I determined once again to visit the palace of Tor Hatan and question the slave who had been the last to see Sanoma Tora.

As I was about to set out, another thought occurred to me. I knew that in the Temple of Knowledge might be found either illustrations or replicas of the metal and harness of every nation of Barsoom, concerning which aught was known in Helium. I therefore repaired immediately to the temple and with the assistance of a clerk I presently found a drawing of the harness and metal of a warrior of Jahar. By an ingenious photostatic process a copy of this illustration was made for me in a few seconds, and with this I hastened to the palace of Tor Hatan.

The odwar was absent, having gone to the palace of the Warlord, but his major-domo summoned the slave, Kal Tavan, who had witnessed the abduction of Sanoma Tora and grappled with one of her abductors.

As the man approached I noticed him more particularly than I had previously. He was well built, with clear cut features and that air which definitely bespeaks the fighting man.

"You said, I believe, that you were from Kobol?" I asked.

"I was born in Tjanath," he replied. "I had a wife and daughter there. My wife fell before the hand of an assassin and my daughter disappeared when she was very young. I never knew what became of her. The familiar scenes of Tjanath reminded me of happier days and so increased my grief that I could not remain. I turned panthan then and sought service in other cities; thus I served in Kobol."

"And there you became familiar with the harness and the metal of many cities and nations?" I asked.

"Yes," he replied.

"What harness and metal are these?" I demanded, handing him the copy of the illustration I had brought from the Temple of Knowledge.

He examined it briefly and then his eyes lighted with recognition. "It is the same," he said. "It is identical."

"Identical with what?" I asked.

"With the harness worn by the warrior with whom I grappled at the time that Sanoma Tora was stolen," he replied.

"The identity of the abductors of Sanoma Tora is established," I said, and then I turned to the major-domo. "Send a messenger at once to the Warlord informing him that the daughter of Tor Hatan was stolen by men from Jahar and that it is my belief that they are the emissaries of Tul Axtar, Jeddak of Jahar," and without more words I turned and left the palace, going directly to my flier.

As I arose above the towers and domes and lofty landing stages of Greater Helium, I turned the prow of my flier toward the west and opening wide the throttle sped swiftly through the thin air of dying Barsoom toward that great unknown expanse of her remote southwestern hemisphere, somewhere within the vast reaches of which lay Jahar toward which, I was now convinced, Sanoma Tora was being borne to become not the Jeddara of Tul Axtar, but his slave, for jeddaks take not their jeddaras by force upon Barsoom.

I believed that I understood the explanation of Sanoma Tora's abduction, an explanation that would have caused her intensive chagrin since it was far from flattery. I believed that Tul Axtar's emissary had reported to his master the charm and beauty of the daughter of Tor Hatan, but that she was not of sufficiently noble birth to become his jeddara, and so he had adopted the only expedient by which he might possess her. My blood boiled at the suggestion, but my judgment told me that it was doubtless right.

During the past few years – I should say the last ten or twenty – greater strides have been taken in the advancement of aeronautics than had been previously achieved in the preceding five hundred years.

The perfection of the destination control compass by Carthoris of Helium is considered by many authorities to have marked the beginning of a new era of invention. For centuries we seemed to have stagnated in a quiet pond of self-sufficiency, as though we had reached the acme of perfection beyond which it was useless to seek for improvement upon what we considered the highest possible achievements of science.

Carthoris of Helium, inheriting the restless, inquiring mind of his earth-born sire, awoke us. Our best minds took up the challenge and the result was rapid improvement in design and construction of air ships of all classes, leading to a revolution in motor building.

We had thought that our light, compact, powerful radium motors never could be improved upon and that man never would travel, either safely or economically, at a speed greater than that attained by our swift one-man scout fliers – about eleven hundred haads per zode (Note: Approximately one hundred and sixty-six earth miles per hour), when a virtually unknown padwar in the navy of Helium announced that he had perfected a motor that, with one-half the weight of our present motors, would develop twice the speed.

It was this type of motor with which my scout flier was equipped – a seemingly fuelless motor, since it derived its invisible and imponderable energy from the inexhaustible and illimitable magnetic field of the planet.

There are certain basic features of the new motor that only the inventor and the government of Helium are fully conversant with and these are most jealously guarded. The propeller shaft, which extends well within the hull of the flier, is constructed of numerous lateral segments insulated from one another. Around this shaft and supporting it is a series of armature-like bearings, through the center of which it passes.

These are connected in series with a device called an accumulator through which the planet's magnetic energy is directed to the peculiar armatures which encircle the propeller shaft.

Speed is controlled by increasing or diminishing the number of armature bearings in series with the accumulator – all of which is simply accomplished by a lever which the pilot moves from his position on deck where he ordinarily lies upon his stomach, his safety belt snapped to heavy rings in the deck.

The limit of speed, the inventor claims, is dependent solely upon the ratio of strength to weight in the construction of the hull. My one-man scout flier easily attains a speed of two thousand haads per zode (Note: Approximately three hundred miles per hour), nor could it have withstood the tremendous strain of a more powerful motor, though it would have been easy to have increased both the power of one and the speed of the other by the simple expedient of a longer propeller shaft carrying an additional number of armature bearings.

In experimenting with the new motor at Hastor last year, an attempt was made to drive a scout flier at the exceptional speed of thirty-three hundred haads per zode (Note: Approximately five hundred miles per hour; a haad being 1949.0592 earth feet and a zode 2462 earth hours), but before the ship had attained a speed of three thousand haads per zode it was torn to pieces by its own motor. Now we are trying to attain the greatest strength with the minimum of weight and as our engineers succeed we shall see speed increased until, I am sure, we shall easily attain to seven thousand haads per zode (Note: Over one thousand miles per hour), for there seems to be no limit to the power of these marvelous motors.

Little less marvelous is the destination control compass of Carthoris of Helium. Set your pointer upon any spot on either hemisphere; open your throttle and then lie down and go to sleep if you will. Your ship will carry you to your destination, drop within a hundred yards or so of the ground and stop, while an alarm awakens you. It is really a very simple device, but I believe that John Carter has fully described it in one of his numerous manuscripts.

In the adventure upon which I had embarked the destination control compass was of little value to me, since I did not know the exact location of Jahar. However, I set it roughly at a point about thirty degrees south latitude, thirty-five degrees east longitude, as I believed that Jahar lay somewhere to the southwest of that point.

Flying at high speed I had long since left behind the cultivated areas near Helium and was crossing above a desolate and deserted waste of ocher moss that clothed the dead sea bottoms where once rolled a mighty ocean bearing upon its bosom the shipping of a happy and prosperous people, now but a half-forgotten memory in the legends of Barsoom.

Upon the edges of plateaus that once had marked the shore line of a noble continent I passed above the lonely monuments of that ancient prosperity, the sad, deserted cities of old Barsoom. Even in their ruins there is a grandeur and magnificence that still has power to awe a modern man. Down toward the lowest sea bottoms other ruins mark the tragic trail that that ancient civilization had followed in pursuit of the receding waters of its ocean to where the last city finally succumbed, bereft of commerce, shorn of power, to fall at last an easy victim to the marauding hordes of fierce, green tribesmen, whose descendants now are the sole rulers of many of these deserted sea bottoms. Hating and hated, ignorant of love, laughter or happiness, they lead their long,

fierce lives quarreling among themselves and their neighbors and prey-
ing upon any chance adventurers who happen within the confines of
their bitter and desolate domain.

Fierce and terrible as are all green men, there are few whose cruel natures and bloody exploits have horrified the minds of red men to such
an extent as have the green hordes of Torquas.

The city of Torquas, from which they derive their name, was one of
the most magnificent and powerful of ancient Barsoom. Though it has
been deserted for ages by all but roaming tribes of green men, it is still
marked upon every map, and as it lay directly in the path of my search
for Jahar and as I had never seen it, I had purposely laid my course to
pass over it, and when, far ahead, I saw its lofty towers and battlements
I felt the thrill of excitement and the lure of adventure which these dead
cities of Barsoom proverbially exert upon us red men.

As I approached the city I reduced my speed and dropped lower that
I might obtain a better view of it. What a beautiful city it must have
been in its time! Even today, after all the ages that have passed since
its broad avenues surged with the life of happy, prosperous throngs, its
great palaces still stand in all their glorious splendor, that time and the
elements have softened and mellowed, but not yet destroyed.

As I circled low above the city I saw miles of avenues that have not
known the foot of man for countless ages. The stone flagging of their
pavement was overgrown with ocher moss, with here and there a stunted
tree or a grotesque shrub of one of those varieties that somehow find sustenance in the desert and wasteland. Silent, deserted courtyards looked
up at me, gorgeous gardens of another happier day. Here and there the
roof of a building had fallen in, but for the most part they remained intact, dreaming, doubtless, of the wealth and beauty that they had known
in days of yore, and in imagination I could see the gorgeous sleeping
silks and furs spread out in the sunlight, while the women idled beneath
gay canopies of silks, their jeweled harnesses scintillating with each move
of their bodies. I saw the pennons waving from countless thousands of
staffs and the great ships at anchor in the harbor rose and fell to the undulations of the restless sea. There were swaggering sailors upon the avenues, and burly, fighting men before the doors of every palace. Ah, what a
picture imagination conjured from the deathlike silence of that deserted
city, and then, as a long, swinging circle brought me above the courtyard
of a splendid palace that faced upon the city's great central square, my
eyes beheld that which shattered my beautiful dream of the past. Directly
below me I saw a score of great thoats penned in what once may have
been the royal garden of a jeddak.

The presence of these huge beasts meant but one thing, and that was that their green masters were to be found nearby.

As I passed above the courtyard one of the restless, vicious beasts looked up and saw me and instantly he commenced to squeal angrily. Immediately the other thoats, their short temper aroused by the squealing of their fellow and their attention directed by his upward gaze, discovered me and set up a perfect pandemonium of grunts and squeals, which brought the result that I had immediately foreseen. A green warrior leaped into the courtyard from the interior of the palace and looked up just in time to see me before I passed from his line of vision above the roof of the building.

Realizing immediately that this was no place for me to loiter, I opened my throttle and at the same time rose swiftly toward a greater altitude. As I passed over the building and out across the avenue in front of it, I saw some twenty green warriors pour out of the building, their upward gaze searching the skies. The warrior on guard had apprised them of my presence.

I cursed myself for a stupid fool in having taken this unnecessary chance merely to satisfy my idle curiosity. Instantly I took a zig-zag, upward course, rising as swiftly as I could, while from below a savage war cry rose plainly to my ears. I saw long, wicked-looking rifles aimed at me. I heard the hiss of projectiles hurtling by me, but, though the first volley passed close to us, not a bullet struck the ship. In a moment more I would be out of range and safe and I prayed to a thousand ancestors to protect me for the few brief minutes that would be necessary to place me entirely out of harm's way. I thought that I had made it and was just about to congratulate myself upon my good luck when I heard the thud of a bullet against the metal of my ship and almost simultaneously the explosion of the projectile, and then I was out of range.

Angry cries of disappointment came faintly to my ears as I sped swiftly toward the southwest, relieved that I had been so fortunate as to be able to get away without suffering any damage.

I had already flown about seventy karads (Note: A karad is equivalent to a degree of longitude) from Helium, but I was aware that Jahar might still be fifty to seventy-five karads distant and I made up my mind that I would take no more chances such as those from which I had just so fortunately escaped.

I was now moving at great speed again and I had scarcely finished congratulating myself upon my good fortune when it suddenly became apparent to me that I was having difficulty in maintaining my altitude. My flier was losing buoyancy and almost immediately I guessed, what investigation later revealed, that one of my buoyancy tanks had been punctured by the explosive bullet of the green warriors.

To reproach myself for my carelessness seemed a useless waste of mental energy, though I can assure you that I was keenly aware of my fault and of its possible bearing upon the fate of Sanoma Tora, from the active prosecution of whose rescue I might now be entirely eliminated. The results as they affected me did not appall me half so much as did the contemplation of the unquestioned danger in which Sanoma Tora must be, from which my determination to rescue her had so obsessed me that there had not entered into my thoughts any slightest consideration of failure.

The mishap was a severe blow to my hopes and yet it did not shatter them entirely, for I am so constituted that I know I shall never give up hope of success in any issue as long as life remains to me.

How much longer my ship would remain afloat it was difficult to say, and, having no means of making such repairs as would be necessary to conserve the remaining contents of the punctured buoyancy tank, the best that I could do was to increase my speed so that I might cover as much distance as possible before I was forced down. The construction of my ship was such that at high speed it tended to maintain itself in the air with a minimum of the eighth ray in its buoyancy tanks; yet I knew that the time was not far distant when I should have to make a landing in this dreary, desolate wasteland.

I had covered something in the neighborhood of two thousand haads since I had been fired upon above Torquas, crossing what had been a large gulf when the waters of the ocean rolled over the vast plains that now lay moss covered and arid beneath me. Far ahead I could see the outlines of low hills that must have marked the southwestern shore line of the gulf. Toward the northwest the dead sea bottom extended as far as the eye could reach, but this was not the direction I wished to take, and so I sped on toward the hills hoping that I might maintain sufficient altitude to cross them, but as they swiftly loomed closer this hope died in my breast and I realized that the end of my flight was now but a matter of moments. At the same time I discerned the ruins of a deserted city nestling at the foot of the hills; nor was this an unwelcome sight since water is almost always to be found in the wells of these ancient cities, which have been kept in repair by the green nomads of the wasteland.

By now I was skimming but a few ads above the surface of the ground. (Note: An ad is about 9.75 earth feet.) I had greatly diminished my speed to avoid a serious accident in landing and because of this the end was hastened so that presently I came gently to rest upon the ocher vegetation scarcely a haad from the water-front of the deserted city.

CHAPTER THREE
Cornered

My LANDING WAS most unfortunate in that it left me in plain sight of the city without any place of concealment in the event that the ruins happened to be occupied by one of the numerous tribes of green men who infest the dead sea bottoms of Barsoom, often making their headquarters in one or another of the deserted cities that line the ancient shore.

The fact that they usually choose to inhabit the largest and most magnificent of the ancient palaces and that these ordinarily stand back some little distance from the water-front rendered it quite possible that even in the event that there were green men in the city I might reach the concealing safety of one of the nearer buildings before I was discovered by them.

My flier being now useless, there was nothing to do but abandon it, and so, with only my weapons, ammunition and a little concentrated rations, I walked quickly in the direction of the age old water-front. Whether or not I reached the buildings unobserved, I was unable to determine, but at any rate I did reach them without seeing any sign of a living creature about.

Portions of many of these ancient, deserted cities are inhabited by the great white apes of Barsoom, which are in many respects more to be feared than the green warriors themselves, for not only are these man-like creatures endowed with enormous strength and characterized by intense ferocity, but they are also voracious man-eaters. So terrible are they that it is said that they are the only living creatures that can instill fear within the breasts of the green men of Barsoom.

Knowing the possible dangers that might lurk within the precincts of this ruin, it may be wondered that I approached it at all, but as a matter of fact there was no safe alternative. Out upon the dead monotony of the ocher moss of the sea bottom, I should have been discovered by the first white ape or green Martian that approached the city from that direction, or that chanced to come from the interior of the ruins to the water-front. It was, therefore, necessary for me to seek concealment until night had fallen, since only by night might I travel in safety across the sea bottom, and, as the city offered the only concealment nearby, I had no choice but to enter it. I can assure you that it was not without feelings of extreme concern that I clambered to the surface of the broad avenue that once skirted the shore of a busy harbor. Across its wide expanse rose the ruins of what once had been shops and warehouses, but whose eyeless windows now looked down upon a scene of and desolation. Gone were the great ships! Gone the busy, hurrying throngs! Gone the ocean!

Crossing the avenue I entered one of the taller buildings, which I noticed was surmounted by a high tower. The entire structure, including the tower, seemed to be in an excellent state of preservation and it occurred to me that if I could ascend into the latter, I should be able to obtain an excellent view of the city and of the country that lay beyond it to the southwest, which was the direction in which I intended to pursue my search for Jahar. I reached the building apparently unobserved, and, entering, found myself in a large chamber, the nature and purpose of which it was no longer possible to determine, since such decorations as may possibly have adorned its walls in the past were no longer discernible and whatever furniture it may have contained to give a clue to its identity had long since been removed. There was an enormous fireplace in the far end of the room and at one side of this fireplace a ramp led downward, and upon the other a similar ramp led upward.

Listening intently for a moment I heard no sound, either within or without the building, so that it was with considerable confidence that I started to ascend the ramp.

Upward I continued from floor to floor, each of which consisted of a single large chamber, a fact which finally convinced me that the building had been a warehouse for the storing of goods passing through this ancient port.

From the upper floor a wooden ladder extended upward through the center of the tower above. It was of solid skeel, which is practically indestructible, so that though I knew it might be anywhere from five hundred thousand to a million years old, I did not hesitate to trust myself to it.

The circular interior core of the tower, upward through which the ladder extended, was rather dark. At each landing there was an opening into the tower chamber at that point, but as many of these openings were closed only a subdued light penetrated to the central core.

I had ascended to the second level of the tower when I thought that I heard a strange noise beneath me.

Just the suggestion of a noise it was, but such utter silence had reigned over the deserted city that the faintest sound must have been appreciable to me.

Pausing in my ascent, I looked down, listening; but the sound which I had been unable to translate was not repeated, and I continued my way on upward.

Having it in my mind to climb as high up in the tower as possible, I did not stop to examine any of the levels that I passed.

Continuing upward for a considerable distance my progress was finally blocked by heavy planking that appeared to form the ceiling of the shaft. Some eight or ten feet below me was a small door that probably led to one of the upper levels of the tower and I could not but wonder why the ladder had been continued on upward above this doorway, since it could serve no practical purpose if it merely ended at the ceiling. Feeling above me with my fingers I traced the outlines of what appeared to be a trap door. Obtaining a firm footing upon the ladder as high up as I could climb, I placed a shoulder against the barrier. In this position I was able to exert considerable pressure upward with the result that presently I felt the planking rise above me and a moment later, to the accompaniment of subdued groans, the trap door swung upward upon ancient wooden hinges long unused. Clambering into the apartment above I found myself upon the top level of the tower, which rose to a height of some two hundred feet above the avenue below. Before me were the corroded remains of an ancient and long obsolete beacon-light, such as were used by the ancients long before the discovery of radium and its practical and scientific application to the lighting requirements of modern civilization upon Barsoom. These ancient lamps were operated by expensive machines which generated electricity, and this one was doubtless used as a beacon for the safe guidance of ancient mariners into the harbor, whose waters once rolled almost to the foot of the tower.

This upper level of the tower afforded an excellent view in all directions. To the north and northeast stretched a vast expanse. To the south was a range of low hills that curved gently in a northeasterly direction, forming in by-gone days the southern shore line of what is still known as the Gulf of Torquas. Toward the west I looked out over the ruins of a great city, which extended far back into low hills, the flanks of which it had mounted as it expanded from the sea shore. There in the distance I could still discern the ancient villas of the wealthy, while in the nearer foreground were enormous public buildings, the most pretentious of which were built upon the four sides of a large quadrangle that I could easily discern a short distance from the water-front. Here, doubtless, stood the official palace of the jeddak who once ruled the rich country of which this city was the capital and the principal port. There, now, only silence reigns. It was indeed a depressing sight and one fraught with poignant prophecy for us of present-day Barsoom.

Where they battled valiantly but futilely against the menace of a constantly diminishing water supply, we are faced with a problem that far transcends theirs in the importance of its bearing upon the maintenance of life upon our planet. During the past several thousand years only the courage, resourcefulness and wealth of the red men of Barsoom have made it possible for life to exist upon our dying planet, for were it not for the great atmosphere plants conceived and built and maintained by the red race of Barsoom, all forms of air-breathing creatures would have become extinct thousands of years ago.

As I gazed out over the city, my mind occupied with these dismal thoughts, I again became aware of a sound coming from the interior of the tower beneath me, and, stepping to the open trap, I looked down into the shaft and there, directly below me, I saw that which might well make the stoutest Barsoomian heart quail – the hideous, snarling face of a great white ape of Barsoom.

As our eyes met the creature voiced an angry growl and, abandoning its former stealthy approach, rushed swiftly up the ladder. Acting almost mechanically I did the one and only thing that might even temporarily stay its rush upon me – I slammed down the heavy trap door above its head, and as I did so I saw for the first time that the door was equipped with a heavy wooden bar, and you may well believe that I lost no time in securing this, thus effectually barring the creature's ascent by this route into the veritable cul de sac in which I had placed myself.

Now, indeed, was I in a pretty predicament – two hundred feet above the city with my only avenue of escape cut off by one of the most feared of all the savage beasts of Barsoom.

I had hunted these creatures in Thark as a guest of the great green jeddak, Tars Tarkas, and I knew something of their cunning and resourcefulness as well as of their ferocity. Extremely man-like in conformation, they also approach man more closely than any other of the lower orders in the size and development of their brain. Occasionally these creatures are captured when young and trained to perform, and so intelligent are they that they can be taught to do almost anything that man can do that lies within the range of their limited reasoning capacity. Man has, however, never been able to subdue their ferocious nature and they are always the most dangerous of animals to handle, which probably accounts more even than their intelligence for the interest displayed by the large audiences that they unfailingly attract.

In Hastor I have paid a good price to see one of these creatures and now I found myself in a position where I should very gladly pay a good deal more not to see one, but from the noise he was making in the shaft beneath me it appeared to me that he was determined that I should have a free show and he a free meal. He was hurling himself as best he could against the trap door, above which I stood with some misgivings which were presently allayed when I realized that not even the vast strength of a white ape could avail against the still staunch and sturdy skeel of the ancient door.

Finally convinced that he could not come at me by this avenue, I set about taking stock of my situation. Circling the tower I examined its outward architecture by the simple expedient of leaning far outward above each of the four sides. Three sides terminated at the roof of the building a hundred and fifty feet below me, while the fourth extended to the pavement of the courtyard two hundred feet below. Like much of the architecture of ancient Barsoom, the surface of the tower was elaborately carved from top to bottom and at each level there were window embrasures, some of which were equipped with small stone balconies. As a rule there was but a single window to a level, and as the window for the level directly beneath never opened upon the same side of the tower as the window for the level above, there was always a distance of from thirty to forty feet between windows upon the same side, and, as I was examining the outside of the tower with a view to its offering me an avenue of escape, this point was of great importance to me, since a series of window ledges, one below another, would have proved a most welcome sight to a man in my position.

By the time I had completed my survey of the exterior of the tower, the ape had evidently come to the conclusion that he could not demolish the barrier that kept him from me and I hoped that he would abandon the idea entirely and depart. But when I lay down on the floor and placed an ear close to the door I could plainly hear him just below as he occasionally changed from one uncomfortable position to another upon the small ladder beneath me. I did not know to what extent these creatures might have developed pertinacity of purpose, but I hoped that he might soon tire of his vigil and his thoughts be diverted into some other channel. However, as the day wore to a close this possibility seemed to grow more and more remote until at last I became almost convinced that the creature had determined to lay siege until hunger or desperation forced me from my retreat.

How longingly I gazed at the beckoning hills beyond the city where lay my route toward the southwest – toward fabled Jahar.

The sun was low in the west. Soon would come the sudden transition from daylight to darkness, and then what? Perhaps the creature would abandon its vigil; hunger or thirst might attract it elsewhere, but how was I to know? How easily it might descend to the bottom of the tower and await me there, confident that sooner or later I must come down.

One unfamiliar with the traits of these savage creatures might wonder why, armed as I was with sword and pistol, I did not raise the trap door and give battle to my jailer. Had I known positively that he was the only white ape in the vicinity I should not have hesitated to do so, but experience assured me that there was doubtless an entire herd of them quartered in the ruined city. So scarce is the flesh they crave that it is their ordinary custom to hunt alone, so that in the event that they make a kill they may be more certain of retaining the prize for themselves, but if I should attack him he would most certainly raise such a row as to attract his fellows, in which event my chance for escape would have been reduced to the ultimate zero.

A single shot from my pistol might have dispatched him, but it was equally possible that it would not, for these great white apes of Barsoom are tremendous creatures, endowed with almost unbelievable vitality. Many of them stand fully fifteen feet in height and are endowed by nature with tremendous strength. Their very appearance is demoralizing to an enemy; their white, hairless bodies are in themselves repulsive to the eye of a red man; the great shock of white hair bristling erect upon their pates accentuates the brutality of their countenances, while their intermediary set of limbs, which they use either as arms or legs as necessity or whim suggests, render them most formidable antagonists. Quite generally they carry a club, in the use of which they are terribly proficient. One of them, therefore, seemed sufficiently a menace in itself, so that I had no desire to attract others of its kind, though I was fully aware that eventually I might be forced to carry the battle to him.

Just as the sun was setting my attention was attracted toward the waterfront where the long shadows of the city were stretching far out across the dead sea bottom. Riding up the gentle acclivity toward the city was a party of green warriors, mounted upon their great savage thoats. There were perhaps twenty of them, moving silently over the soft moss that carpeted the bottom of the ancient harbor, the padded feet of their mounts giving forth no sound. Like specters, they moved in the shadows of the dying day, giving me further proof that Fate had led me to a most unfriendly shore, and then, as though to complete the trilogy of fearsome Barsoomian menaces, the roar of a banth rolled down out of the hills behind the city.

Safe from observation in the high tower above them, I watched the party as it emerged from the hollow of the harbor and rode out upon the avenue below me, and then for the first time I noted a small figure seated in front of one of the warriors. Darkness was coming swiftly now, but before the little cavalcade passed out of sight momentarily behind the corner of the building, as it entered another avenue leading toward the heart of the city, I thought that I recognized the little figure as that of a woman of my own race. That she was a captive was a foregone conclusion and I could not but shudder as I contemplated the fate that lay in store for her. Perhaps my own Sanoma Tora was in equal jeopardy. Perhaps – but no, that could not be possible – how could Sanoma Tora have fallen into the clutches of warriors of the fierce horde of Torquas?

It could not be she. No, that was impossible. But the fact remained that the captive was a red woman, and whether she were Sanoma Tora or another, whether she were from Helium or Jahar, my heart went out in sympathy to her and I forgot my own predicament as something within me urged me to pursue her captors and seek to snatch her from them; but, alas, how futile seemed my fancy. How might I, who might not even save himself, aspire to the rescue of another?

The thought galled me, it hurt my pride, and forthwith I determined that if I would not chance dying to save myself, I might at least chance it for a woman of my own race, and always in the back of my head was the thought that perhaps the object of my solicitude might, indeed, be the woman I loved.

Darkness had fallen as I pressed my ear again to the trap door. All was silent below so that presently I became assured that the creature had departed. Perhaps he was lying in wait for me further down, but what of that? I must face him eventually if he elected to remain. I loosened my pistol in its holster and was upon the point of slipping the bar that secured the door when I distinctly heard the beast directly beneath me.

For an instant I paused. What was the use? It meant certain death to raise that door, and in what way might I be profiting either myself or the poor captive if I gave my life thus uselessly? But there was an alternative – one that I had been planning to adopt in case of necessity from the moment that I had first examined the exterior construction of the tower. It offered a slender chance of escape from my predicament and even a very slender chance was better than what would confront me should I raise the trap door.

I stepped to one of the windows of the tower and looked down upon the city. Neither moon was in the sky; I could see nothing. Toward the interior of the city I heard the squealing of thoats. There would the camp of the green men be located. Thus by the squealing of their vicious mounts would I be guided to it. Again a hunting banth roared in the hills. I sat upon the sill and swung both legs across and then turning on my belly slipped silently over the edge until I hung only by my hands. Groping with my sandaled toes, I felt for a foothold upon the deep-cut carvings of the tower's face. Above me was a blue-black void shot with stars; below me a blank and empty void. It might have been a thousand sofads to the roof below me, or it might have been one; but though I could see nothing I knew that it was one hundred and fifty and that at the bottom lay death if a foot or a hand slipped.

In daylight the sculpturing had seemed large and deep and bold, but by night how different! My toes seemed to find but hollow scratches in a smooth surface of polished stone. My arms and fingers were tiring. I must find a foothold or fall, and then, when hope seemed gone, the toe of my right sandal slipped into a horizontal groove and an instant later my left found a hold.

Flattened against the sheer wall of the tower I lay there resting my tired fingers and arms for a moment and when I felt that they would bear my weight again I sought for hand holds. Thus painfully, perilously, monotonously, I descended inch by inch. I avoided the windows, which naturally greatly increased the difficulty and danger of my descent; yet I did not care to pass directly in front of them for fear that by chance the ape might have descended from the summit of the ladder and would see me.

I cannot recall that ever in my life I felt more alone than I did that night as I was descending the ancient beacon-tower of that deserted city for not even hope was with me. So precarious were my holds upon the rough stone that my fingers were soon numb and exhausted. How they clung at all to those shallow cuts, I do not know. The only redeeming feature of the descent was the darkness, and a hundred times I blessed my first ancestors that I could not see the dizzy depths below me; but on the other hand it was so dark that I could not tell how far I had descended; nor did I dare to look up where the summit of the tower must have been silhouetted against the starlit sky for fear that in doing so I should lose my balance and be precipitated to the courtyard or the roof below. The air of Barsoom is thin; it does not greatly diffuse the starlight, and so, while the heavens above were shot with brilliant points of light, the ground beneath was obliterated in darkness.

Yet I must have been nearer the roof than I thought when that happened which I had been assiduously endeavoring to prevent the scabbard of my long sword pattered noisily against the face of the tower. In the darkness and the silence it seemed a veritable din, but, however exaggerated it might appear to me, I knew that it was sufficient to reach the ears of the great ape in the tower. Whether a suggestion of its import would occur to him, I could not guess – I could only hope that he would be too dull to connect it with me or my escape.

But I was not to be left long in doubt, for almost immediately afterward a sound came from the interior of the tower that sounded to my over-wrought nerves like a heavy body rapidly descending a ladder. I realize now that imagination might easily have construed utter silence into such a sound, since I had been listening so intensely for that very thing that I might easily have worked myself into such a state of nervous apprehension that almost any sort of an hallucination was possible.

With redoubled speed and with a measure of recklessness that was almost suicidal, I hastened my descent and an instant later I felt the solid roof beneath my feet.

I breathed a sigh of relief, but it was destined to be but a short sigh and but brief relief, for almost instantly I was made aware that the sound from the interior of the tower had been no hallucination as the huge bulk of a great white ape loomed suddenly from a doorway not a dozen paces from me.

As he charged me he gave forth no sound. Evidently he had not held his solitary vigil this long with any intention of sharing his feast with another. He would dispatch me in silence, and, with similar intent I drew my long sword, rather than my pistol, to meet his savage charge.

What a puny, futile thing I must have appeared confronting that towering mountain of bestial ferocity.

Thanks be to a thousand fighting ancestors that I wielded a long sword with swiftness and with strength; otherwise I must have been gathered into that savage embrace in the brute's first charge. Four powerful hands were reached out to seize me, but I swung my long sword in a terrific cut that severed one of them cleanly at the wrist and at the same instant I leaped quickly to one side, and as the beast rushed past me, carried onward by its momentum, I ran my blade deep into its body. With a savage scream of rage and pain it sought to turn upon me, but its foot slipped upon its own dismembered hand and it stumbled awkwardly on trying to regain its equilibrium, but that it never accomplished, and still stumbling grotesquely it lunged over the edge of the roof to the courtyard below.

Fearing that the beast's scream might attract others of its kind to the roof, I ran swiftly to the north edge of the building where I had noted from the tower earlier in the afternoon a series of lower buildings adjoining, over the roofs of which I might possibly accomplish my descent to the street level.

Cold Cluros was rising above the distant horizon, shedding his pale light upon the city so that I could plainly see the roofs below me as I came to the north edge of the building. It was a long drop, but there was no safe alternative, since it was quite probable that should I attempt to descend through the building, I would meet other members of the ape's herd who had been attracted by the scream of their fellow.

Slipping over the edge of the roof I hung an instant by my hands and then dropped. The distance was about two ads, but I alighted safely and without injury. Upon your own planet, with its larger bulk and greater gravity, I presume that a fall of that distance might be serious, but not so, necessarily, upon Barsoom.

From this roof I had a short drop to the next, and from that I leaped to a low wall and thence to the ground below.

Had it not been for the fleeting glimpse of the girl captive that I had caught just at sunset, I should have set out directly for the hills west of the town, banth or no banth, but now I felt strongly upon me a certain moral obligation to make the best efforts that I could for succoring the poor unfortunate that had fallen into the clutches of these cruelest of creatures.

Keeping well within the shadows of the buildings I moved stealthily toward the central plaza of the city, from which direction I had heard the squealing of the thoats.

The plaza was a full haad from the water-front and I was compelled to cross several intersecting avenues as I cautiously made my way toward it, guided by an occasional squeal from the thoats quartered in some deserted palace courtyard.

I reached the plaza in safety, confident that I had not been observed.

Upon the opposite side I saw light within one of the great buildings that faced it, but I dared not cross the open space in the moonlight and so still clinging to the shadows I moved to the far end of the quadrangle where Cluros cast his densest shadows, and thus at last I won to the building in which the green men were quartered. Directly before me was a low window that must have opened into a room adjoining the one in which the warriors were congregated. Listening intently I heard nothing within the chamber and slipping a leg over the sill I entered the dark interior with the utmost stealth.

Tiptoeing across the room to find a door through which I might look into the adjoining chamber, I was suddenly arrested as my foot touched a soft body and I froze into rigidity, my hand upon my long sword, as the body moved.

CHAPTER FOUR

Tavia

THERE ARE OCCASIONS in the life of every man when he becomes impressed by the evidence of the existence of an extraneous power which guides his acts, which is sometimes described as the hand of providence, or is again explained on the hypothesis of a sixth sense which transports to the part of our brain that controls our actions, perceptions of which we are not objectively aware; but, account for it as one may, the fact remains that as I stood there that night in the dark chamber of the ancient palace of the deserted city I hesitated to thrust my sword into the soft body moving at my feet. This might after all have been the most reasonable and logical course for me to pursue. Instead I pressed my sword point firmly against yielding flesh and whispered a single word: "Silence!"

A thousand times since then have I given thanks to my first ancestors that I did not follow my natural impulse, for, in response to my admonition a voice whispered: "Do not thrust, red man; I am of your own race and a prisoner," and the voice was that of a girl.

Instantly I withdrew my blade and kneeled beside her. "If you have come to help me, cut my bonds," she said, "and be quick for they will soon return for me."

Feeling rapidly over her body I found that her wrists and ankles were secured with leather thongs and drawing my dagger I quickly severed these. "Are you alone?" I asked as I helped her to her feet.

"Yes," she replied. "In the next room they are playing for me to decide to which one I shall belong." At that moment there came the clank of side arms from the adjoining room. "They are coming," she said. "They must not find us here."

Taking her by the hand I moved to the window through which I had entered the apartment, but fortunately I reconnoitered before stepping out into the avenue and it was well for us that I did so, for as I looked to the right along the face of the building, I saw a green Martian warrior emerging from the main entrance. Evidently it had been the rattling of his side arms that we had heard as he moved across the adjoining apartment to the doorway.

"Is there another exit from this room?" I asked in a low whisper.

"Yes," she replied. "Opposite this window there is a doorway leading into a corridor. It was open when they brought me in, but they closed it."

"We shall be better off inside the building than out for a while at least," I said. "Come!" And together we crossed the apartment, groping along the wall for the door which I soon located. With the utmost care I drew it ajar, fearing that its ancient hinges might betray us by their complaining. Beyond the doorway lay a corridor dark as the depths of Omean and into this I drew the girl, closing the door silently behind us. Groping our way to the right away from the apartment occupied by the green warriors, we moved slowly through a black void until presently we saw just ahead a faint light, which investigation revealed as coming through the open doorway of an apartment that faced upon the central courtyard of the edifice. I was about to pass this doorway and seek a hiding place further within the remote interior of the building when my attention was attracted by the squealing of a thoat in the courtyard beyond the apartment we were passing.

From earliest boyhood I have had a great deal of experience with the small breed of thoats used as saddle animals by the men of my race and while I was visiting Tars Tarkas of Thark I became quite familiar with the methods employed by the green men in controlling their own huge vicious beasts.

For travel over the surface of the ground the thoat compares to other methods of land transportation as the one-man scout flier does to all other ships of the air in aerial navigation. He is at once the swiftest and the most dangerous, so that, faced as I was with a problem of land transportation, it was only natural that the squeal of the thoats, should suggest a plan to my mind.

"Why do you hesitate?" asked the girl. "We cannot escape in that direction since we cannot cross the courtyard."

"On the contrary," I replied, "I believe that in this direction may lie our surest avenue of escape."

"But their thoats are penned in the courtyard," she remonstrated, "and green warriors are never far from their thoats."

"It is because the thoats are there that I wish to investigate the court-yard," I replied.

"The moment they catch our scent," she said, "they will raise a disturbance that will attract the attention of their masters and we shall immediately be discovered and captured."

"Perhaps," I said; "but if my plan succeeds it will be well worth the risk, but if you are very much afraid I will abandon it."

"No," she said, "it is not for me to choose or direct. You have been generous enough to help me and I may only follow where you lead, but if I knew your plan perhaps I might follow more intelligently."

"Certainly," I said; "it is very simple. There are thoats. We shall take one of them and ride away. It will be much easier than walking and our chances for escape will be considerably greater, at the same time we shall leave the courtyard gates open, hoping that the other thoats will follow us out, leaving their masters unable to pursue us."

"It is a mad plan," said the girl, "but is a brave one. If we are discovered, there will be fighting and I am unarmed. Give me your short sword, warrior, that we may at least make the best account of ourselves that is possible."

I unsnapped the scabbard of my short sword from my harness and attached it to hers at her left hip, and, as I touched her body in doing so, I could not but note that there was no sign of trembling such as there would have been had she been affected by fright or excitement. She seemed perfectly cool and collected and her tone of voice was almost reassuring to me. That she was not Sanoma Tora I had known when she had first spoken in the darkness of the room in which I had stumbled upon her, and while I had been keenly disappointed I was still determined to do the best that I could to assist in the escape of the stranger, although I was confident that her presence might greatly delay and embarrass me while it subjected me to far greater danger than would have fallen to the lot of a warrior traveling alone. It was, therefore reassuring to find that my unwelcome companion would not prove entirely helpless.

"I trust you will not have to use it," I said as I finished hooking my short sword to her harness.

"You will find," she said, "that if necessity arises I can use it."

"Good," I said. "Now follow me and keep close to me."

A careful survey of the courtyard from the window of the chamber overlooking it revealed about twenty huge thoats, but no green warriors, evidence that they felt perfectly secure against enemies.

The thoats were congregated in the far end of the courtyard; a few of them had lain down for the night, but the balance were moving restlessly about as is their habit. Across the courtyard from us and at the same end stood a pair of massive gates. As far as I could determine they barred the only opening into the courtyard large enough to admit a thoat and I assumed that beyond them lay an alley leading to one of the avenues nearby.

To reach the gates unobserved by the thoats, was the first step in my plan and the better to do this I decided to seek an apartment near the gate, on either side of which I saw windows similar to that from which we were looking. Therefore, motioning my companion to follow me, I returned to the corridor and again groping through the darkness we made our way along it. In the third apartment which I explored I found a window letting into the courtyard close beside the gate. And in the wall which ran at right angles to that in which the window was set I found a doorway that opened into a large vaulted corridor upon the opposite side of the gate. This discovery greatly encouraged me since it harmonized perfectly with the plan I had in mind, at the same time reducing the risk which my companion must run in the attempted adventure of escape.

"Remain here," I said to her, placing her just behind the gate. "If my plan is successful I shall ride into this corridor upon one of the thoats and as I do so you must be ready to seize my hand and mount behind me. If I am discovered and fail I shall cry out 'For Helium!' and that must be your signal to escape as best you may."

She laid her hand upon my arm. "Let me go into the courtyard with you," she begged. "Two swords are better than one."

"No," I said. "Alone I have a better chance of handling the thoats than if their attention is distracted by another."

"Very well," she said, and with that I left her, and re-entering the chamber, went directly to the window. For a moment I reconnoitered the interior of the courtyard and finding conditions unchanged, I slipped stealthily through the window and edged slowly toward the gate. Cautiously I examined the latch and discovering it easy to manipulate, I was soon silently pushing one of the gates back upon its hinges. When it was opened sufficiently wide to permit the passage of a thoat, I turned my attention to the beasts within the enclosure. Practically untamed, these savage creatures are as wild as their uncaptured fellows of the remote sea bottoms, and, being controlled solely by telepathic means, they are amenable only to the suggestion of the more powerful minds of their masters and even so it requires considerable skill to dominate them.

I had learned the method from Tar Tarkas himself and had come to feel considerable proficiency so that I approached this crucial test of my power with the confidence that was absolutely requisite to success.

Placing myself close beside the gate, I concentrated every faculty of my mind to the direction of my will, telepathically, upon the brain of the thoat I had selected for my purpose, the selection being determined solely by the fact that he stood nearest to me. The effect of my effort was immediately apparent. The creature, which had been searching for the occasional tufts of moss that grew between the stone flags of the courtyard, raised his head and looked about him. At once he became restless, but he gave forth no sound since I was willing him to silence. Presently his eyes moved in my direction and halted upon me. Then, slowly, I drew him toward me. It was slow work, for he evidently sensed that I was not his master, but on he came. Once, when he was quite near me, he stopped and snorted angrily. He must have caught my scent then and realized that I was not even of the same race as that to which he was accustomed. Then it was that I exerted to their fullest extent every power of my mind. He stood there shaking his ugly head to and fro, his snarling lips baring his great fangs. Beyond him I could see that the other thoats, had been attracted by his actions. They were looking toward us and moving about restlessly, always drawing closer. Should they discover me and start to squeal, which is the first and always ready sign of their easily aroused anger, I knew that I should have their riders upon me in no time, since because of his nervous and irritable nature the thoat is the watchdog as well as the beast of burden of the green Barsoomians.

For a moment the beast I had selected hesitated before me as though undecided whether to retreat or to charge, but he did neither; instead he came slowly up to me and as I backed through the gate into the vaulted corridor beyond, he followed me. This was better than I had expected for it permitted me to compel him to lie down, so that the girl and I were able to mount with ease.

Before us lay a long vaulted corridor at the far end of which I could discern a moonlit archway, through which we presently passed onto a broad avenue.

To the left lay the hills, and, turning this way, I urged the fleet animal along the ancient deserted thoroughfare between rows of stately ruins toward the west and – what?

Where the avenue turned to wind upward into the hills, I glanced back; nor could I refrain a feeling of exultation as I saw strung out behind us in the moonlight a file of great thoats, which I was confident would well know what to do with their new found liberty.

"Your captors will not pursue us far," I said to the girl, indicating the thoats with a nod of my head.

"Our ancestors are with us tonight," she said. "Let us pray that they may never desert us."

Now, for the first time, I had a fairly good look at my companion, for both Cluros and Thuria were in the heavens and it was quite light. If I revealed my surprise it is not to be wondered at for, in the darkness, having only my companion's voice for a guide, I had been perfectly confident that I had given aid to a female, but now as I looked at that short hair and boyish face I did not know what to think; nor did the harness that my companion wore aid me in justifying my first conclusion, since it was quite evidently the harness of a man.

"I thought you were a girl," I blurted out.

A fine mouth spread into a smile that revealed strong, white teeth. "I am," she said.

"But your hair – your harness – even your figure belies your claim."

She laughed gayly. That, I was to find later, was one of her chiefest charms – that she could laugh so easily, yet never to wound.

"My voice betrayed me," she said. "It is too bad."

"Why is it too bad?" I asked.

"Because you would have felt better with a fighting man as a companion, whereas now you feel that you have only a burden."

"A light one," I replied, recalling how easily I had lifted her to the thoat's back. "But tell me who you are and why you are masquerading as a boy."

"I am a slave girl," she said; "just a slave girl who has run away from her master. Perhaps that will make a difference," she added a little sadly. "Perhaps you will be sorry that you have defended just a slave girl."

"No," I said, "that makes no difference. I myself, am only a poor padwar, not rich enough to afford a slave. Perhaps you are the one to be sorry that you were not rescued by a rich man."

She laughed. "I ran away from the richest man in the world," she said. "At least I guess he must have been the richest man in the world, for who could be richer than Tul Axtar, Jeddak of Jahar?"

"You belong to Tul Axtar, Jeddak of Jahar?" I exclaimed.

"Yes," she said. "I was stolen when I was very young from a city called Tjanath and ever since I have lived in the palace of Tul Axtar. He has many women – thousands of them. Sometimes they live all their lives in his palace and never see him. I have seen him," she shuddered; "he is terrible. I was not unhappy there for I had never known my mother; she died when I was young, and my father was only a memory. You see I was very, very young, indeed, when the emissaries of Tul Axtar stole me from my home in Tjanath. I made friends with everyone about the palace of

Tul Axtar. They all liked me, the slaves and the warriors and the chiefs, and because I was always boyish it amused them to train me in the use of arms and even to navigate the smaller fliers; but then came a day when my happiness was ended forever – Tul Axtar saw me. He saw me and he sent for me. I pretended that I was ill and did not go, and when night came I went to the quarters of a soldier whom I knew to be on guard and stole harness and I cut off my long hair and painted my face that I might look more like a man, and then I went to the hangars on the palace roof and by a ruse deceived the guards there and stole a one-man flier.

"I thought," she continued, "that if they searched for me at all they would search in the direction of Tjanath and so I flew in the opposite direction, toward the northeast, intending to make a great circle to the north, turning back toward Tjanath. After I passed over Xanator I discovered a large grove of mantalia growing out upon the dead sea bottom and I immediately descended to obtain some of the milk from these plants, as I had left the palace so hurriedly that I had no opportunity to supply myself with provisions. The mantalia grove was an unusually large one and as the plants grew to a height of from eight to twelve sofads, the grove offered excellent protection from observation. I had no difficulty in finding a landing place well within its confines. In order to prevent detection from above, I ran my plane in among the concealing foliage of two over-arching mantalias and then set about obtaining a supply of milk.

"As near objects never appear as attractive as those more distant, I wandered some little distance from my flier before I found the plants that seemed to offer a sufficiently copious supply of rich milk.

"A band of green warriors had also entered the grove to procure milk, and, as I was tapping the tree I had selected, one of them discovered me and a moment later I was captured. From their questions I became assured that they had not seen me enter the grove and that they knew nothing of the presence of my flier. They must have been in a portion of the grove very thickly overhung by foliage while I was approaching from above by making my landing; but be that as it may, they were ignorant of the presence of my flier and I determined to keep them in ignorance of it.

"When they had obtained as much milk as they required they returned to Xanator, bringing me with them. The rest you know."

"This is Xanator?" I asked.

"Yes," she replied.

"And what is your name?" I asked.

"Tavia," she replied. "And what is yours?"

"Tan Hadron of Hastor," I replied.

"It is a nice name," she said. There was a certain boyish frankness about the way she said it that convinced me that she would have been just as quick to tell me had she not liked my name. There was no suggestion of brainless flattery in her tone and I was to learn, as I became better acquainted with her, that honesty and candor were two of her marked characteristics, but at the moment I was giving such matters little thought since my mind was occupied with a portion of her narrative that had suggested to me an easy and swift method of escape from our predicament.

"Do you believe," I asked, "that you can find the mantalia grove where you hid your flier?"

"I am positive of it," she replied.

"Will the craft carry two?" I asked.

"It is a one-man flier," she replied, "but it will carry both of us, though both its speed and altitude will be reduced."

She told me that the grove lay to the southeast of Xanator and accordingly I turned the thoat's head toward the east. After we had passed well beyond the limits of the city we moved in a southerly direction down out of the hills onto the dead sea bottom.

Thuria was winging her swift flight through the heavens, casting strange and ever moving shadows upon the ocher moss that covered the ground, while far above cold Cluros took his slow and stately way. The light of the two moons clearly illuminated the landscape and I was sure that keen eyes could easily have detected us from the ruins of Xanator, although the swiftly moving shadows cast by Thuria were helpful to us since the shadows of every shrub and stunted tree produced a riot of movement upon the surface of the sea bottom in which our own moving shadow was less conspicuous, but the hope that I entertained most fondly was that all of the thoats, had followed our beast from the courtyard and that the green Martian warriors were left dismounted, in which event no pursuit could overtake us.

The great beast that was carrying us moved swiftly and silently so that it was not long before we saw in the distance the shadowy foliage of the mantalia grove and shortly afterward we entered its gloomy confines. It was not without considerable difficulty, however, that we located Tavia's flier, and mighty glad was I, too, when we found it in good condition for we had seen more than a single shadowy form slinking through the forest and I knew that the fierce animals of the barren hills and the great white apes of the ruined cities were equally fond of the milk of the mantalia and that we should be fortunate, indeed, if we escaped an encounter.

I rode as close to the flier as possible, and, leaving Tavia on the thoat, slipped quickly to the ground and dragged the small craft out into the open. An examination of the controls showed that they had not been tampered with, which was a great relief to me as I had feared that the flier might have been damaged by the great apes, which are inclined to be both inquisitive and destructive.

Assured that all was well I assisted Tavia to the ground, and a moment later we were upon the deck of the flier. The craft responded satisfactorily, though a little sluggishly, to the controls, and immediately we were floating gently upward into the temporary safety of a Barsoomian night.

The flier, which was of a design now almost obsolete in Helium, was not equipped with a destination control compass, which rendered it necessary for the pilot to be constantly at the controls. Our quarters on the narrow deck were exceedingly cramped and I foresaw a most uncomfortable journey ahead of us. Our safety belts were snapped to the same deck ring as we lay almost touching one another upon the hard skeel. The cowl which protected our faces from the rush of the wind that was generated even by our relatively slow speed was not sufficiently high to permit us to change our positions to any considerable degree, though occasionally we found it a relief to sit up with our backs toward the bow and thus relieve the tedium of remaining constantly prone in one position. When I thus rested my cramped muscles, Tavia guided the flier, but the cold wind of the Barsoomian night always brought me down behind the cowl in a very few moments.

By mutual consent, we were heading in a south-westerly direction while we discussed our eventual destination.

I had told Tavia that I wished to go to Jahar and why. She appeared much interested in the story of the abduction of Sanoma Tora, and, from her knowledge of Tul Axtar and the customs of Jahar, she thought it most probable that the missing girl might be found there, but as to the possibility of rescuing her, that was another matter over which she shook her head dubiously.

It was obvious to me that Tavia did not desire to return to Jahar, yet she put no obstacles in the path of my search for this my great objective; in fact, she gave me Jahar's position and herself set the nose of the flier upon the right course.

"Will there be any great danger to you in returning to Jahar?" I asked her.

"The danger will be very great," she said, "but where the master goes, the slave must follow."

"I am not your master," I said, "and you are not my slave. Let us consider ourselves rather as comrades in arms."

"That will be nice," she said simply, and then after a pause, "and if we are to be comrades then let me warn you against going directly to Jahar. This flier would be recognized immediately. Your harness would mark you as an alien and you would accomplish nothing more toward rescuing your Sanoma Tora than to achieve the pits of Tul Axtar and sooner or later the games in the great arena, where eventually you must be slain."

"What would you suggest then?" I asked.

"Beyond Jahar, to the southwest, lies Tjanath, the city of my birth. Of all the cities upon Barsoom that is the only one where I may hope to be received in a friendly manner and as they receive me, so will they receive you. There you may better prepare to enter Jahar, which you may only accomplish by disguising yourself as a Jaharian, for Tul Axtar permits no alien within the confines of his empire other than those who are brought as prisoners of war and as slaves. In Tjanath you can obtain the harness and metal of Jahar and there I can coach you in the customs and manners of the empire of Tul Axtar so that in a short time you may enter it with some reasonably slight assurance that you may deceive them as to your identity. To enter without proper preparation would be fatal."

I saw the wisdom of her counsel and accordingly we altered our course so as to pass south of Jahar, as we headed straight toward Tjanath, six thousand haads away.

All the balance of the night we traveled steadily at the rate of about six hundred haads per zode – a slow speed when compared with that of the good one-man flier that I had brought out of Helium.

As the sun rose the first thing that attracted my particular attention was the ghastly blue of the flier.

"What a color for a flier!" I exclaimed.

Tavia looked up at me. "There is an excellent reason for it, though," she said; "a reason that you must fully understand before you enter Jahar."

CHAPTER FIVE

To the Pits

BELOW US, in the ever changing light of the two moons, stretched the weird landscape of Barsoomian night as our little craft sorely overloaded, winged slowly away from Xanator above the low hills that mark the southwestern boundary of the fierce, green hordes of Torquas. With the coming of the new day we discussed the advisability of making a landing and waiting until night before proceeding upon our journey, since we realized that should we be sighted by an enemy craft we could not possibly hope to escape.

"Few fliers pass this way," said Tavia, "and if we keep a sharp lookout I believe that we shall be as safe in the air as on the ground for although we have passed beyond the limits of Torquas, there would still be danger from their raiding parties, which often go far afield."

And so we proceeded slowly in the direction of Tjanath, our eyes constantly scanning the heavens in all directions.

The monotony of the landscape, combined with our slow rate of progress, would ordinarily have rendered such a journey unendurable to me, but to my surprise the time passed quickly, a fact which I attributed solely to the wit and intelligence of my companion for there was no gainsaying the fact that Tavia was excellent company. I think that we must have talked about everything upon Barsoom and naturally a great deal of the conversation revolved about our own experiences and personalities, so that long before we reached Tjanath I felt that I knew Tavia better than I had ever known any other woman and I was quite sure that I had never confided so completely in any other person.

Tavia had a way with her that seemed to compel confidences so that, to my own surprise, I found myself discussing the most intimate details of my past life, my hopes, ambitions and aspirations, as well as the fears and doubts which, I presume, assail the minds of all young men.

When I realized how fully I had unbosomed myself to this little slave girl, I experienced a distinct shock of embarrassment, but the sincerity of Tavia's interest dispelled this feeling as did the realization that she had been almost as equally free with her confidences as had I.

We were two nights and a day covering the distance between Xanator and Tjanath and as the towers and landing stages of our destination appeared upon the distant horizon toward the end of the first zode of the second day, I realized that the hours that stretched away behind us to Xanator were, for some unaccountable reason, as happy a period as I had ever experienced.

Now it was over. Tjanath lay before us, and, with the realization, I experienced a distinct regret that Tjanath did not lie upon the opposite side of Barsoom.

With the exception of Sanoma Tora, I had never been particularly keen to be much in the company of women. I do not mean to convey the impression that I did not like them, for that would not be true. Their occasional company offered a diversion, which I enjoyed and of which I took advantage, but that I could be for so many hours in the exclusive company of a woman I did not love and thoroughly enjoy every minute of it would have seemed to me quite impossible; yet such had been the fact and I found myself wondering if Tavia had shared my enjoyment of the adventure.

"That must be Tjanath," I said nodding in the direction of the distant city.

"Yes," she replied.

"You must be glad that the journey is over," I ventured.

She looked up at me quickly, her brows contracting suddenly in conjecture. "Perhaps I should be," she replied enigmatically.

"It is your home," I reminded her.

"I have no home," she replied.

"But your friends are here," I insisted.

"I have no friends," she said.

"You forget Hadron of Hastor," I reminded her.

"No," she said, "I do not forget that you have been kind to me, but I remember that I am only an incident in your search for Sanoma Tora. Tomorrow, perhaps, you will be gone and we shall never see each other again."

I had not thought of that and I found that I did not like to think about it, and yet I knew that it was true. "You will soon make friends here," I said.

"I hope so," she replied; "but I have been gone a very long time and I was so young when I was taken away that I have but the faintest of memories of my life in Tjanath. Tjanath really means nothing to me. I could be as happy anywhere else in Barsoom with – with a friend."

We were now close above the outer wall of the city and our conversation was interrupted by the appearance of a flier, evidently a patrol, bearing down upon us. She was sounding an alarm – the shrill screaming of her horn shattering the silence of the early morning. Almost immediately the warning was taken up by gongs and shrieking sirens throughout the city. The patrol boat changed her course and rose swiftly above us, while from landing stages all about rose scores of fighting planes until we were entirely surrounded.

I tried to hail the nearer of them, but the infernal din of the warning signals drowned my voice. Hundreds of guns covered us, their crews standing ready to hurl destruction upon us.

"Does Tjanath always receive visitors in this hostile manner?" I inquired of Tavia.

She shook her head. "I do not know," she replied. "Had we approached in a strange ship of war, I might understand it; but why this little scout flier should attract half the navy of Tjanath is – Wait!" she exclaimed suddenly. "The design and color of our flier mark its origin as Jahar. The people of Tjanath have seen this color before and they fear it; yet if that is true, why is it that they have not fired upon us?"

"I do not know why they did not fire upon us at first," I replied, "but it is obvious why they do not now. Their ships are so thick about us that they could not fire without endangering their own craft and men."

"Can't you make them understand that we are friends?" she asked.

Immediately I made the signs of friendship and of surrender, but the ships seemed afraid to approach. The alarms had ceased and the ships were circling silently about us.

Again I hailed a nearby ship. "Do not fire," I shouted; "we are friends."

"Friends do not come to Tjanath in the blue death ships of Jahar," replied an officer upon the deck of the ship I had hailed.

"Let us come alongside," I insisted, "and at least I can prove to you that we are harmless."

"You will not come alongside my ship," he replied. "If you are friends you can prove it by doing as I instruct you."

"What are your wishes?" I asked.

"Come about and take your flier beyond the city walls. Ground her at least a haad beyond the east gate and then, with your companion, walk toward the city."

"Can you promise that we will be well received?" I asked.

"You will be questioned," he replied, "and if you are all right, you have nothing to fear."

"Very well," I replied, "we will do as you say. Signal your other ships to make way for us," and then, through the lane that they opened, we passed slowly back above the walls of Tjanath and came to the ground about a haad beyond the east gate.

As we approached the city the gates swung open and a detachment of warriors marched out to meet us. It was evident that they were very suspicious and fearful of us. The padwar in charge of them ordered us to halt while there were yet fully a hundred sofads between us.

"Throw down your weapons," he commanded, "and then come forward."

"But we are not enemies," I replied. "Do not the people of Tjanath know how to receive friends?"

"Do as you are told or we will destroy you both," was his only reply.

I could not refrain a shrug of disgust as I divested myself of my weapons, while Tavia threw down the short sword that I had loaned her. Unarmed we advanced toward the warriors, but even then the padwar was not entirely satisfied, for he searched our harness carefully before he finally conducted us into the city, keeping us well surrounded by warriors.

As the east gate of Tjanath closed behind us I realized that we were prisoners rather than the guests that we had hoped to be, but Tavia tried to reassure me by insisting that when they had heard our story we would be set at liberty and accorded the hospitality that she insisted was our due.

Our guards conducted us to a building that stood upon the opposite side of the avenue, facing the east gate, and presently we found ourselves upon a broad landing stage upon the roof of the building. Here a patrol flier awaited us and our padwar turned us over to the officer in charge, whose attitude toward us was marked by ill-concealed hatred and distrust.

As soon as we had been received on board, the patrol flier rose and proceeded toward the center of the city.

Below us lay Tjanath, giving the impression of a city that had not kept abreast of modern improvements. It was marked by signs of antiquity; the buildings reflected the architecture of the ancients and many of them were in a state of disrepair, though much of the city's ugliness was hidden or softened by the foliage of great trees and climbing vines, so that on the whole the aspect was more pleasing than otherwise. Toward the center of the city was a large plaza, entirely surrounded by imposing public buildings, including the palace of the Jed. It was upon the roof of one of these buildings that the flier landed.

Under a strong guard we were conducted into the interior of the building and after a brief wait were ushered into the presence of some high official. Evidently he had already been advised of the circumstances surrounding our arrival at Tjanath, for he seemed to be expecting us and was familiar with all that had transpired up to the present moment.

"What do you at Tjanath, Jaharian?" he demanded.

"I am not from Jahar," I replied. "Look at my metal."

"A warrior may change his metal," he replied, gruffly.

"This man has not changed his metal," said Tavia. "He is not from Jahar; he is from Hastor, one of the cities of Helium. I am from Jahar."

The official looked at her in surprise. "So you admit it!" he cried.

"But first I was from Tjanath," said the girl.

"What do you mean?" he demanded.

"As a little child I was stolen from Tjanath," replied Tavia. "All my life since I have been a slave in the palace of Tul Axtar, Jeddak of Jahar. Only recently I escaped in the same flier upon which we arrived at Tjanath. Near the dead city of Xanator I landed and was captured by the green men of Torquas. This warrior, who is Hadron of Hastor, rescued me from them. Together we came to Tjanath, expecting a friendly reception."

"Who are your people in Tjanath?" demanded the official.

"I do not know," replied Tavia; "I was very young. I remember practically nothing about my life in Tjanath."

"What is your name?"

"Tavia."

The man's interest in her story, which had seemed wholly perfunctory, seemed suddenly altered and galvanized.

"You know nothing about your parents or your family?" he demanded.

"Nothing," replied Tavia.

He turned to the padwar who was in charge of our escort. "Hold them here until I return," he said, and, rising from his desk, he left the apartment.

"He seemed to recognize your name," I said to Tavia.

"How could he?" she asked.

"Possibly he knew your family," I suggested; "at least his manner suggested that we are going to be given some consideration."

"I hope so," she said.

"I feel that our troubles are about over, Tavia," I assured her; "and for your sake I shall be very happy."

"And you, I suppose," she said, "will endeavor to enlist aid in continuing your search for Sanoma Tora?"

"Naturally," I replied. "Could anything less be expected of me?"

"No," she admitted in a very low voice.

Notwithstanding the fact that something in the demeanor of the official who had interrogated us had raised my hope for our future, I was still conscious of a feeling of depression as our conversation emphasized the near approach of our separation. It seemed as though I had always known Tavia, for the few days that we had been thrown together had brought us very close indeed. I knew that I should miss her sparkling wit, her ready sympathy and the quiet companionship of her silences, and then the beautiful features of Sanoma Tora were projected upon memory's screen and, knowing where my duty lay, I cast vain regrets aside, for love, I knew, was greater than friendship and I loved Sanoma Tora.

After a considerable lapse of time the official re-entered the apartment. I searched his face to read the first tidings of good news there, but his expression was inscrutable; however, his first words, addressed to the padwar, were entirely understandable.

"Confine the woman in the East Tower," he said, "and send the man to the pits."

That was all. It was like a blow in the face. I looked at Tavia and saw her wide eyes upon the official. "You mean that we are to be held as prisoners?" she demanded; "I, a daughter of Tjanath, and this warrior who came here from a friendly nation seeking your aid and protection?"

"You will each have a hearing later before the Jed," snapped the official. "I have spoken. Take them away."

Several of the warriors seized me rather roughly by the arms. Tavia had turned away from the official and was looking at me. "Good-bye, Hadron of Hastor!" she said. "It is my fault that you are here. May my ancestors forgive me!"

"Do not reproach yourself, Tavia," I begged her, "for who might have foreseen such a stupid reception?"

We were taken from the apartment by different doorways and there we turned, each for a last look at the other, and in Tavia's eyes there were tears, and in my heart.

The pits of Tjanath, to which I was immediately conducted, are gloomy, but they are not enveloped in impenetrable darkness as are the pits beneath most Barsoomian cities. Into the dungeon dim light filtered through the iron grating from the corridors, where ancient radium bulbs glowed faintly. Yet it was light and I gave thanks for that, for I have always believed that I should go mad imprisoned in utter darkness.

I was heavily fettered and unnecessarily so, it seemed to me, as they chained me to a massive iron ring set deep in the masonry wall of my dungeon, and then, leaving me, locked also the ponderous iron grating before the doorway.

As the footfalls of the warriors diminished to nothingness in the distance I heard the faint sound of something moving nearby me in my dungeon. What could it be? I strained my eyes into the gloomy darkness.

Presently, as my eyes became more accustomed to the dim light in my cell, I saw the figure of what appeared to be a man crouching against the wall near me. Again I heard a sound as he moved and this time it was accompanied by the rattle of a chain, and then I saw a face turn toward me, but I could not distinguish the features.

"Another guest to share the hospitality of Tjanath," said a voice that came from the blurred figure beside me. It was a clear voice – the voice of a man – and there was a quality to its timbre that I liked.

"Do our hosts entertain many such as we?" I asked.

"In this cell there was but one," he replied; "now there are two. Are you from Tjanath or elsewhere?"

"I am from Hastor, city of the Empire of Tardos Mors, Jeddak of Helium."

"You are a long way from home," he said.

"Yes," I replied; "and you?"

"I am from Jahar," he answered. "My name is Nur An."

"And mine is Hadron," I said. "Why are you here?"

"I am a prisoner because I am from Jahar," he replied. "What is your crime?"

"It is that they think I am from Jahar," I told him.

"What made them think that? Do you wear the metal of Jahar?"

"No, I wear the metal of Helium, but I chanced to come to Tjanath in a Jaharian flier."

He whistled. "That would be hard to explain," he said.

"I found it so," I admitted. "They would not believe a word of my story, nor of that of my companion."

"You had a companion, then?" he asked. "Where is he?"

"It was a woman. She was born in Tjanath, but for long years had been a slave in Jahar. Perhaps later they will believe her story, but for the present we are in prison. I heard them order her to the East Tower, while they sent me here to the prison."

"And here you will stay until you rot, unless you are lucky enough to be called for the games, or unlucky enough to be sentenced to The Death."

"What is The Death?" I asked, my curiosity piqued by his emphasis of the words.

"I do not know," he replied. "The warriors who come here often speak of it as though it was something quite horrible. Perhaps they do it to frighten me, but if that is true, then they have had very little satisfaction, for, whether or not I have been frightened, I have not let them see it."

"Let us hope for the games, then," I said.

"They are dull and stupid people here in Tjanath," said my companion. "The warriors have told me that sometimes many years elapse between games in the arena, but we may hope at least, for surely it would be better to die there with a good long sword in one's hand rather than to rot here in the darkness, or die The Death, whatever it may be."

"You are right," I said. "Let us beseech our ancestors that the Jed of Tjanath decrees games in the near future."

"So you are from Hastor," he said, musingly, after a moment's silence. "That is a long way from Tjanath. Pressing must have been the service that brought you so far afield!"

"I was searching for Jahar," I replied.

"Perhaps you are as well off that you found Tjanath first," he said, "for, though I am a Jaharian, I cannot boast the hospitality of Jahar."

"You think I would not have been accorded a cordial welcome there, then?" I asked.

"By my first ancestor, no," he exclaimed most emphatically. "Tul Axtar would have had you in the pits before he asked your name, and the pits of Jahar are not as light nor as pleasant as these."

"I did not intend that Tul Axtar should know that I was visiting him," I said.

"You are a spy?" he asked.

"No," I replied. "The daughter of the commander of the umak to which I was attached was abducted by Jaharians, and, I have reason to believe, by the orders of Tul Axtar himself. To effect her rescue was the object of my journey."

"You tell this to a Jaharian?" he asked lightly.

"With perfect impunity," I replied. "In the first place, I have read in your words and your tone that you are no friend to Tul Axtar, Jeddak of Jahar, and, secondly, there is evidently little chance that you ever will return to Jahar."

"You are right in both conjectures," he said. "I most assuredly have no love for Tul Axtar. He is a beast, hated by all decent men. The cause of my hatred for him so closely parallels your own reason to hate Tul Axtar that we are indeed bound by a common tie."

"How is that?" I demanded.

"All my life I have never felt aught but contempt for Tul Axtar, Jeddak of Jahar, but this contempt was not transmuted into hatred until he stole a woman, and it was the stealing of a woman, also, that directed your venom against him."

"A woman of your family?" I asked.

"My sweetheart, the woman I was to marry," replied Nur An. "I am a noble. My family is of ancient lineage and great wealth. For these reasons Tul Axtar knew that he had good cause to fear me, and urged on by this fear, he confiscated my property and sentenced me to death, but I have many friends in Jahar and one of these, a common warrior of the guard, connived at my escape after I had been imprisoned in the pits.

"I made my way to Tjanath and told my story to Haj Osis, the Jed, and, laying my sword at his feet, I offered him my services, but Haj Osis is a suspicious old fool and saw in me only a spy from Jahar. He ordered me to the pits and here I have lain for a long time."

"Jahar must be, indeed, an unhappy country," I said, "ruled over, as she is, by such a man as Tul Axtar. Recently I have heard much of him, but as yet I have not heard him credited with a single virtue."

"He has none," said Nur An. "He is a cruel tyrant, rotten with corruption and vice. If any of the great powers of Barsoom could have guessed what was in his mind, Jahar would have been reduced long ago and Tul Axtar destroyed."

"What do you mean?" I asked.

"For at least two hundred years Tul Axtar has fostered a magnificent dream, the conquest of all Barsoom. During all this time he has made manpower his fetish; no eggs might be destroyed, each woman being compelled to preserve all that she laid. (Note: Martians are oviparous.) An army of officials and inspectors took a record of the production of each female. Those that had the greatest number of males were rewarded; the unproductive were destroyed. When it was discovered that marriage tended to reduce the productivity of the females of Jahar, marriage among any classes beneath the nobility was proscribed by imperial edict.

"The result has been an appalling increase in population until many of the provinces of Jahar cannot support the incalculable numbers that swarm like ants in a hill. The richest agricultural land upon Barsoom could not support such numbers; every natural resource has been exhausted; millions are starving, and in large districts cannibalism is prevalent.

"During all this time Tul Axtar's officers have been training the males for war. From earliest consciousness the thought of war has been implanted within their minds. To war and to war alone do they look for relief from the hideous conditions which oppress them until today countless millions are clamoring for war, realizing that victory means loot, and that loot means food and riches. Already Tul Axtar commands an army of such vast proportions that the fate of Barsoom might readily lie in the palm of his hand were it not for but a single obstacle."

"And what is that?" I asked.

"Tul Axtar is a coward," replied Nur An. "Having fulfilled his dream of manpower, he is afraid to use it lest by some accident of fate his military plans should fail and his troops meet defeat. Therefore, he has waited while he urged on the scientists of Jahar to produce some weapon that would be so far superior in its destructive power to anything possessed by any other nation of Barsoom that his armies would be invincible.

"For years the best minds of Jahar labored with the problem until at last one of our most eminent scientists, an old man named Phor Tak, developed a rifle of amazing properties.

"The success of Phor Tak aroused the jealousies of other scientists, and though the old man had given Tul Axtar what he sought, yet the tyrant showed no gratitude, and Phor Tak was subjected to such indignities and oppressions that eventually he fled from Jahar.

"That, however, is of no import; all that Phor Tak could do for Tul Axtar he had done, and with the new rifle in his possession, the Jeddak was glad to be rid of the old scientist."

Naturally I was much interested in the rifle which Nur An had mentioned and I hoped that he would go into a further and more detailed description of it, but I dared not suggest that for fear that the natural loyalty which every man feels for the country of his birth might restrain him from divulging her military secrets to a stranger. I was to learn, however, that those lofty sentiments of patriotism, which are a part of every man of Helium, were induced as much by the love and respect in which we held our great jeddaks as by our natural attachment to the land of our birth; while, upon the other hand, the Jaharians looked only with contempt and loathing upon the head of their state and feeling no loyalty for him, who was in effect the state, they looked upon patriotism as nothing more than an empty catchword, which an unworthy master had used to his own end until it had become meaningless, and so, while at the moment I was surprised, I later came to understand why it was that Nur An voluntarily explained in detail to me all that he knew about the strange new weapon of Jahar and the means of defense against it.

"This new rifle," he continued after a moment's silence, "would render all the other armies and navies of Barsoom impotent before us. It projects an invisible ray, the vibrations of which effect such a change in the constitution of metals as to cause them to disintegrate. I am not a scientist; I do not fully understand the exact explanation of the phenomenon, but from what I was able to gather while the new weapon was being discussed in Jahar I am under the impression that these rays change the polarity of the protons in metallic substances, releasing the whole mass as free electrons. I have also heard the theory expounded that Phor Tak, in his investigation, discovered that the fundamental principle underlying time, matter and space are identical, and that what the rays projected from his rifle really accomplish is to translate any mass of metal upon which it is directed into the most elementary constituents of space.

"But be that as it may, Tul Axtar had the manpower and the weapon, yet still he hesitated. He was afraid and he sought for some excuse further to delay the war of conquest and loot which his millions of subjects now demanded, and to this end he hit upon the plan of insisting upon some medium of defense against this new rifle, basing his demands upon the possibility that some other power might also have discovered a similar weapon or would eventually, by the use of spies or informers, learn the secret from Jahar. Probably greatly to his surprise and unquestionably to his embarrassment, a man who had been an assistant in Phor Tak's laboratory presently developed a substance which dissipated the rays of the new weapon, rendering them harmless. With this substance, which is of a bluish color, the metal portions of the ships, weapons and harness of Jahar are now painted.

"But yet again Tul Axtar postponed his war, insisting upon the production of an enormous quantity of the new rifles and a mighty fleet of warships upon which to mount them. Then, he says, he will sail forth and conquer all Barsoom."

The destruction of the patrol boat above Helium the night of the abduction of Sanoma Tora was now quite clear to me, and when Nur An told me later that Tul Axtar had sent experimental fliers to attack Tjanath, I understood why it was that the blue flier in which Tavia and I had arrived had caused such consternation, but the thought that upset my mind almost to the exclusion of the plight of Sanoma Tora was that somewhere in the thin air of dying Barsoom a great Heliumetic fleet was moving to attack Jahar, or at least that was what I supposed since I had no reason to doubt that the message that I had given to the major-domo of Tor Hatan's palace had not been delivered to the Warlord. To lie here enchained in the pits of Tjanath, while the great fleet of Helium sped to its destruction, filled me with horror. With my own eyes had I seen the effects of this terrible new weapon and I knew that it was no idle dream upon the part of Nur An when he had stated that with it Tul Axtar could conquer a world; but there was a defense against it. If I could but regain my freedom, I might not only warn the ships of Helium and save them from inevitable doom, but also in connection with my quest for Sanoma Tora in the city of Jahar, I might discover the secret of the defense against the weapon which the Jaharians had evolved.

Freedom! Before it had only seemed the most desirable thing in the world; now it had become imperative.

CHAPTER SIX
Sentenced to Die

I WAS NOT LONG in the pits of Tjanath before warriors came, and, re-moving my fetters, led me from my dungeon. There were only two of them and I could not but note their carelessness and the laxness of their discipline as they escorted me to an upper level of the palace, but at the time I thought it meant only that the attitude of the officials had altered and that I was to be free.

There was nothing remarkable about the palace of the Jed of Tjanath. It was a poor place by comparison with the palaces of some of the great nobles of Helium, yet never before, I imagined, had I challenged with greater interest every detail of architecture, every corridor and door-way, or the manners, harness and decorations of the people that passed us, for, though in my heart was the hope that I was about to be free, yet I considered this place my prison and these people my jailers, and, as my one object in life was to escape, I was determined to let no detail elude my eye that might possibly in any way aid me if the time should come when I must make a break for liberty.

It was such thoughts that were uppermost in my mind as I was ush-ered through wide portals into the presence of a bejeweled warrior. As my eyes first alighted upon him I knew at once that I was in the pres-ence of Haj Osis, Jed of Tjanath.

As my guard halted me before him, the Jed scrutinized me intently with that air of suspicion which is his most marked characteristic.

"Your name and country?" he demanded.

"I am Hadron of Hastor, padwar in the navy of Helium," I replied.

"You are from Jahar," he accused. "You came here from Jahar with a woman of Jahar in a flier of Jahar. Can you deny it?"

I told Haj Osis in detail everything that had led up to my arrival at Tjanath. I told him Tavia's story as well, and I must at least credit him with listening to me in patience, though I was constantly impressed by a feeling that my appeal was being directed at a mind already so prejudiced against me that nothing that I might say could alter its convictions.

The chiefs and courtiers that surrounded the Jed evidenced open skepticism in their manner until I became convinced that fear of Tul Axtar so obsessed them that they were unable to consider intelligently any matter connected with the activities of the Jeddak of Jahar. Terror made them suspicious and suspicion sees everything through distorted lenses.

When I had finished my story, Haj Osis ordered me removed from the room and I was held in a small ante-chamber for some time while, I imagined, he discussed my case with his advisors.

When I was again ushered into his presence I felt that the whole atmosphere of the chamber was charged with antagonism, as for the second time I was halted before the dais upon which the Jed sat in his carved throne-chair.

"The laws of Tjanath are just," proclaimed Haj Osis, glaring at me, "and the Jed of Tjanath is merciful. The enemies of Tjanath shall receive justice, but they may not expect mercy. You, who call yourself Hadron of Hastor, have been adjudged a spy of our most malignant enemy, Tul Axtar of Jahar, and as such I, Haj Osis, Jed of Tjanath, sentence you to die The Death. I have spoken." With an imperious gesture he signalled the guards to remove me.

There was no appeal. My doom was sealed, and in silence I turned and left the chamber, escorted by a guard of warriors, but for the honor of Helium I may say that my step was firm and my chin high.

On my return to the pits I questioned the padwar in charge of my escort relative to Tavia, but if the fellow knew aught of her, he refused to divulge it to me and presently I found myself again fettered in the gloomy dungeon by the side of Nur An of Jahar.

"Well?" he asked.

"The Death," I replied.

He extended a manacled hand through the darkness and placed it upon one of mine. "I am sorry, my friend," he said.

"Man has but one life," I replied; "if he is permitted to give it in a good cause, he should not complain."

"You die for a woman," he said.

"I die for a woman of Helium," I corrected.

"Perhaps we shall die together," he said. "What do you mean?"

"While you were gone a messenger came from the major-domo of the palace advising me to make peace with my ancestors as I should die The Death in a short time."

"I wonder what The Death is like," I said.

"I do not know," replied Nur An, "but from the awe-hushed tones in which they mention it, I imagine that it must be very terrible."

"Torture, do you imagine?" I asked.

"Perhaps," he replied.

"They will find that the men of Helium who know so well how to live, know also how to die," I said.

"I shall hope to render a good account of myself also," said Nur An. "I shall not give them the satisfaction of knowing that I suffer. Still, I wish I might know beforehand what it is like that I might better be prepared to meet it."

"Let us not depress our thoughts by dwelling upon it," I suggested. "Let us rather take the part of men and consider only plans for thwarting our enemies and effecting our escape."

"I am afraid that is hopeless," he said.

"I may answer that," I said, "in the famous words of John Carter: 'I still live!'"

"The blind philosophy of absolute courage," he said admiringly, "but yet futile."

"It served him well many a time," I insisted, "for it gave him the will to attempt the impossible and to succeed. We still live, Nur An; do not forget that – we still live!"

"Make the best of it while you can," said a gruff voice from the corridor, "for it will not long be true."

The speaker entered our dungeon – a warrior of the guard, and with him was a single companion. I wondered how much of our conversation they had overheard, but I was soon reassured, for the very next words of the warrior that had first spoken revealed the fact that they had heard nothing but my assertion that we still lived.

"What did you mean by that," he asked, "'remember, Nur An, we still live?'"

I pretended not to hear his question and he did not repeat it, but came directly to me and unlocked my fetters. As he turned to unlock those which held Nur An, he turned his back to me and I could not but note his inexcusable carelessness. His companion lolled at the doorway while the first warrior bent over the padlock that held the fetters of Nur An.

My ancestors were kind to me; little had I expected such an opportunity as this, yet I waited – like a great banth ready to spring I waited until he should have released Nur An, and then, as the fetters fell away from my companion, I flung myself upon the back of the warrior. He sprawled forward upon his face on the stone flagging, falling heavily beneath my weight, and as he did so I snatched his dagger from its sheath and plunged it between his shoulder blades. With a single cry he died, but I had no fear that the echo of that cry would carry upward out of the gloomy pits of Tjanath to warn his fellows upon the level above.

But the fellow's companion had seen and heard and with a bound he was across the dungeon, his long sword ready in his hand, and now I was to see the mettle of which Nur An was made.

The affair had occurred so quickly, like a bolt of lightning out of a clear sky, that any man might have been excused had he been momentarily stunned into inactivity by the momentousness of my act, but Nur An was guilty of no fatal delay. As though we had planned the thing together it seemed that he leaped forward the instant that I sprang for the warrior and ran to meet his companion. Barehanded, he faced the long sword of his antagonist.

The gloom of the dungeon reduced the advantage of the armed man. He saw a figure leaping to meet his attack and in the excitement of the moment and in the dark of the cell, he did not know that Nur An was unarmed. He hesitated, paused and stepped back to receive the impetuous attack coming out of the darkness, and in that instant I had whipped the long sword of the fallen warrior from its scabbard and was charging the fellow at a slightly different angle from Nur An.

An instant later we were engaged and I found the fellow no mean swordsman; yet from the instant that our blades crossed I knew that I was his master and he must soon have realized it, too, for he fell back, fully on the defensive, evidently bent upon escaping to the corridor. This, however, I was determined not to permit and so I pressed him so closely that he dared not turn to run; nor did he call for help, and this, I guess, was because he realized the futility of so doing.

With the desperation of caged animals, Nur An and I were fighting for our lives. There could be no question here of the scrupulous observance of the niceties of combat. It was his life or ours. Realizing this, Nur An snatched the short sword from the corpse of the fallen warrior and an instant later the second man was lying in a pool of his own blood.

"And now what?" asked Nur An.

"Are you familiar with the palace?" I asked.

"No," he replied.

"Then we must depend upon what little I was able to glean from my observation of it," I said. "Let us get into the harnesses of these two men at once. Perhaps they will offer a sufficient disguise to permit us to reach one of the upper levels at least, for without an intimate knowledge of the pits it is useless for us to try to seek escape below ground."

"You are right," he said, and a few moments later we emerged into the corridors, to all intents and purposes, two warriors of the guard of Haj Osis, Jed of Tjanath. Believing that up to a certain point boldness of demeanor would be our best safeguard against detection, I led the way toward the ground level of the palace without attempting in any way to resort to stealth or secrecy.

"There are many warriors at the main entrance of the palace," I told Nur An, "and without knowing something of the regulations governing the coming and going of the inmates of the building, it would be suicidal to attempt to reach the avenue beyond the palace by that route."

"What do you suggest then?" he asked.

"The ground level of the palace is a busy place, people are coming and going constantly through the corridors. Doubtless some of the upper levels are less frequented. Let us therefore seek a hiding place higher up and from the vantage point of some balcony we may be able to work out a feasible plan of escape."

"Good!" he said. "Lead on!"

Ascending the winding ramp from the lower pits, we passed two levels before we reached the ground level of the palace, without meeting a single person, but the instant that we emerged upon the ground level we saw people everywhere. Officers, courtiers, warriors, slaves and merchants moved to and fro upon their various duties or in pursuit of the business that had brought them to the palace, but their very numbers proved a safeguard for us.

Upon the side of the corridor opposite from the point at which we entered it lay an arched entrance to another ramp running upward. Without an instant's hesitation I crossed through the throng of people, and, with Nur An at my side, passed beneath the arch and entered the ascending ramp.

Scarcely had we started upward when we met a young officer descending. He accorded us scarcely a glance as we passed and I breathed more easily as I realized that our disguises did, in fact, disguise us.

There were fewer people on the second level of the palace, but yet far too many to suit me and so we continued on upward to the third level, the corridors of which we found almost deserted.

Near the mouth of the ramp lay the intersection of two main corridors. Here we hesitated for an instant to reconnoiter. There were people approaching from both directions along the corridor into which we had emerged, but in one direction the transverse corridor seemed deserted and we quickly entered it. It was a very long corridor, apparently extending the full length of the palace. It was flanked at intervals upon both sides by doorways, the doors to some of which were open, while others were closed or ajar. Through some of the open doorways we saw people, while the apartments revealed through others appeared vacant. The location of these we noted carefully as we moved slowly along, carefully observing every detail that might later prove of value to us.

We had traversed about two-thirds of this long corridor when a man stepped into it from a doorway a couple of hundred feet ahead of us. He was an officer, apparently a padwar of the guard. He halted in the middle of the corridor as a file of warriors emerged from the same doorway, and, forming in a column of twos, marched in our direction, the officer bringing up the rear.

Here was a test for our disguises that I did not care to risk. There was an open doorway at our left; beyond it I could see no one. "Come!" I said to Nur An, and without accelerating our speed we walked nonchalantly into the chamber, and as Nur An crossed the threshold, I closed the door behind him and as I did so I saw a young woman standing at the opposite side of the apartment looking squarely at us.

"What do you here, warriors?" she demanded.

Here, indeed, was an embarrassing situation. In the corridor without I could hear the clank of the accoutrements of the approaching warriors and I knew that the girl must hear it, too. If I did aught to arouse her suspicion, she had but to call for help, and how might I allay her suspicion when I had not the faintest conception of what might pass for a valid excuse for the presence of two warriors in this particular apartment, which for all I knew, might be the apartment of a princess of the royal house, to enter which without permission might easily mean death to a common warrior. I thought quickly, or perhaps I did not think at all; often we act rightly upon impulse and then credit the result to super-intelligence.

"We have come for the girl," I stated brusquely. "Where is she?"

"What girl?" demanded the young woman in surprise.

"The prisoner, of course," I replied.

"The prisoner?" she looked more puzzled than before.

"Of course," said Nur An, "the prisoner. Where is she?" and I almost smiled for I knew that Nur An had not the faintest idea of what was in my mind.

"There is no prisoner here," said the young woman. "These are the apartments of the infant son of Haj Osis."

"The fool misdirected us," I said. "We are sorry that we intruded. We were sent to fetch the girl, Tavia, who is a prisoner in the palace."

It was only a guess. I did not know that Tavia was a prisoner, but after the treatment that had been accorded me I surmised as much.

"She is not here," said the young woman, "and as for you, you had better leave these apartments at once for if you are discovered here it will go ill with you."

Nur An, who was standing beside me, had been looking at the young woman intently. He stepped forward now, closer to her.

"By my first ancestor," he exclaimed in a low voice, "it is Phao!"

The girl stepped back, her eyes wide with surprise and then slowly recognition dawned within them. "Nur An!" she exclaimed.

Nur An came close to the girl and took her hand in his. "All these years, Phao, I have thought that you were dead," he said. "When the ship returned the captain reported that you and a number of others were killed."

"He lied," said the girl. "He sold us into slavery here in Tjanath; but you, Nur An, what are you doing here in the harness of Tjanath?"

"I am a prisoner," replied my companion, "as is this warrior also. We have been confined in the pits beneath the palace and today we were to have died The Death, but we killed the two warriors who were sent to fetch us and now we are trying to find our way out of the palace."

"Then you are not looking for the girl, Tavia?" she asked.

"Yes," I said, "we are looking for her, too. She was made a prisoner at the same time that I was."

"Perhaps I can help you," said Phao; "perhaps," she added wistfully, "we may all escape together."

"I shall not escape without you, Phao," said Nur An.

"My ancestors have been good to me at last," said the girl.

"Where is Tavia?" I asked.

"She is in the East Tower," replied Phao.

"Can you lead us there, or tell us how we may reach it?" I asked.

"It would do no good to lead you to it," she replied, "as the door is locked and guards stand before it. But there is another way."

"And that?" I asked.

"I know where the keys are," she said, "and I know other things that will prove helpful."

"May our ancestors protect and reward you, Phao," I said. "And now tell me where I may find the keys."

"I shall have to lead you to the place myself," she replied, "but we shall stand a better chance to succeed if there are not too many of us. I, therefore, suggest that Nur An remain here. I shall place him in hiding where he will not be found. I will then lead you to the prisoner, and, if possible, we will make our way back to this apartment. I am in charge here. Only at regular hours, twice a day, night and morning, does any other visit the apartment of the little prince. Here I can hide you and feed you for a long time and perhaps eventually we shall be able to evolve some feasible plan for escape."

"We are in your hands, Phao," said Nur An. "If there is to be fighting, though, I should like to accompany Hadron."

"If we succeed there will be no fighting," replied the girl. She stepped quickly across the room to a door, which she opened, revealing a large closet. "Here, Nur An," she said, "is where you must remain until we return. There is no reason why anyone should open this door, and in so far as I know, it never has been opened since I have occupied these quarters, except by me."

"I do not like the idea of hiding," said Nur An with a grimace, "but – I have had to do many things recently that I did not like," and without more words he crossed the apartment and entered the closet. Their eyes met for an instant before Phao closed the door, and I read in the depth of both that which made me wonder, remembering as I did the story that Nur An had told me of the other woman whom Tul Axtar had stolen from him. But such matters were no concern of mine, nor had they any bearing upon the business at hand.

"Here is my plan, warrior," said Phao as she returned to my side. "When you entered this apartment you came saying that you were looking for the prisoner, Tavia. Although she was not here, I believed you. We will go, therefore, to Yo Seno, the keeper of the keys, and you will tell him the same story that you have been sent to fetch the prisoner, Tavia. If Yo Seno believes you, all will be well, for he will go himself and release the prisoner, turning her over to you."

"And if he does not believe me?" I asked.

"He is a beast," she said, "who is better dead than alive. Therefore you will know what to do."

"I understand," I said. "Lead the way."

The office of Yo Seno, the keeper of the keys, was upon the fourth level of the palace, almost directly above the quarters of the infant prince. At the doorway Phao halted, and drawing my ear down to her lips, whispered her final instructions. "I shall enter first," she said, "upon some trivial errand. A moment later you may enter, but pay no attention to me. It must not appear that we have come together."

"I understand," I said, and walked a few paces along the corridor so that I should not be in sight when the door opened. She told me afterward that she asked Yo Seno to have a new key made for one of the numerous doors in the apartment of the little prince.

I waited but a moment, and then I, too, entered the apartment. It was a gloomy room without windows. Upon its walls hung keys of every imaginable size and shape. Behind a large desk sat a coarse-looking man, who looked up quickly and scowled at the interruption as I entered.

"Well?" he demanded.

"I have come for the woman, Tavia," I said, "the prisoner from Jahar."

"Who sent you? What do you want of her?" he demanded.

"I have orders to bring her to Haj Osis," I replied.

He looked at me suspiciously. "You bring a written order?" he asked.

"Of course not," I replied, "it is not necessary. She is not to be taken out of the palace; merely from one apartment to another."

"I must have a written order," he snapped.

"Haj Osis will not be pleased," I said, "when he learns that you have refused to obey his command."

"I am not refusing," said Yo Seno. "Do not dare to say that I refuse. I cannot turn a prisoner over without a written order. Show me your authority and I will give you the keys."

I saw that the plan had failed; other measures must be taken. I whipped out my long sword. "Here is my authority!" I exclaimed, leaping toward him.

With an oath he drew his own sword, but instead of facing me with it he stepped quickly back, the desk still between us and, turning, struck a copper gong heavily with the flat of his blade.

As I rushed toward him I heard the sound of hurrying feet and the clank of metal from an adjoining room. Yo Seno, still backing away, sneered sardonically, and then the lights went out and the windowless room was plunged into darkness. Soft fingers grasped my left hand and a low voice whispered in my ear, "Come with me."

Quickly I was drawn to one side and through a narrow aperture just as a door upon the opposite side of the chamber was flung open, revealing the forms of half a dozen warriors silhouetted against the light from the room behind them. Then the door closed directly in front of my face and I was again in utter darkness, but Phao's fingers still grasped my hand.

"Silence!" a soft voice whispered.

From beyond the panels I heard angry and excited voices. Above the others one voice rose in tones of authority. "What is wrong here?"

There were muttered exclamations and curses as men bumped against pieces of furniture and ran into one another.

"Give us a light," cried a voice, and a moment later, "That is better."

"Where is Yo Seno? Oh, there you are, you fat rascal. What is amiss?"

"By Issus! he is gone." The voice was that of Yo Seno.

"Who is gone?" demanded the other voice. "Why did you summon us?"

"I was attacked by a warrior," explained Yo Seno, "who came demanding the key to the apartment where Haj Osis keeps the daughter of – -" I could not hear the rest of the sentence.

"Well, where is the man?" demanded the other.

"He is gone – and the key, too. The key is gone," Yo Seno's voice rose almost to a wail.

"Quick, then, to the apartment where the girl is kept," cried first speaker, doubtless the officer of the guard, and almost at once I heard them hasten from the apartment.

The girl at my side moved a little and I heard a low laugh. "They will not find the key," she said.

"Why?" I asked.

"Because I have it," she replied.

"Little good it will do us," I said ruefully. "They will keep the door well guarded now and we cannot use the key."

Phao laughed again. "We do not need the key," she said. "I took it to throw them off the track. They will watch the door while we enter elsewhere."

"I do not understand," I said.

"This corridor leads between the partitions to the room where the prisoner is kept. I know that because, when I was a prisoner in that room, Yo Seno came thus to visit me. He is a beast. I hope he has not visited this girl – I hope it for your sake, if you love her."

"I do not love her," I said. "She is only a friend." But I scarcely knew what I was saying, the words seemed to come mechanically for I was in the grip of such an emotion as I never before had experienced or endured. It had seized me the instant that Phao had suggested that Yo Seno might have visited Tavia through this secret corridor. I experienced a sensation that was almost akin to a convulsion – a sensation that left me a changed man. Before, I could have killed Yo Seno with my sword and been glad; now I wanted to tear him to pieces; I wanted to mutilate him and make him suffer. Never before in my life had I experienced such a bestial desire. It was hideous, and yet I gloated in its possession.

"What is the matter?" exclaimed Phao. "I thought I felt you tremble then."

"I trembled," I said.

"For what?" she asked.

"For Yo Seno," I replied, "but let us hasten. If this corridor leads to the apartment where Tavia is in prison, I cannot reach her too soon, for when Haj Osis learns that the key has been stolen he will have her removed to another prison."

"He will not learn it if Yo Seno and the padwar of the guard can prevent," said Phao, "for if this reached the ears of Haj Osis it might easily cost them both their lives. They will wait for you to come that they may kill you and get the key, but they will wait outside the prison door and you will not come that way."

As she spoke she started to walk along the narrow, dark corridor, leading me by the hand behind her. It was slow work for Phao had to grope her way slowly because the corridor turned sharply at right angles as it followed the partitions of the apartments between which it passed, and there were numerous stairways that led up over doorways and finally a ladder to the level above.

Presently she halted. "We are there," she whispered, "but we must listen first to make sure that no one has entered the apartment with the prisoner."

I could see absolutely nothing in the darkness, and how Phao knew that she had reached her destination, I could not guess.

"It is all right," she said presently, and simultaneously she pushed a wooden panel ajar and in the opening I saw a portion of the interior of a circular apartment with narrow windows heavily barred. Opposite the opening, upon a pile of sleeping silks and furs, I saw a woman reclining. Only a bare shoulder, a tiny ear and a head of tousled hair were visible. At the first glance I knew that they were Tavia's.

As we stepped into the apartment Phao closed the panel behind us. Attracted by the sound of our entrance, quietly executed though it was, Tavia sat up and looked at us and then, as she recognized me, sprang to her feet. Her eyes were wide with surprise and there was an exclamation upon her lips, which I silenced by a warning forefinger placed against my own. I crossed the apartment toward her, and she came to meet me, almost running. As I looked into her eyes I saw an expression there that I have never seen in the eyes of any other woman – at least not for me – and if I had ever doubted Tavia's friendship, such a doubt would have vanished in that instant, but I had not doubted it and I was only surprised now to realize the depth of it. Had Sanoma Tora ever looked at me like that I should have read love in the expression, but I had never spoken of love to Tavia and so I knew that it was only friendship that she felt. I had always been too much engrossed in my profession to make any close friendships so that I had never realized until that moment what a wonderful thing friendship might be.

As we met in the center of the room her eyes, moist with tears were upturned to mine. "Hadron," she whispered, her voice husky with emotion, and then I put my arm about her slender shoulders and drew her to me and something that was quite beyond my volition impelled me to kiss her upon the forehead. Instantly she disengaged herself and I feared that she had misunderstood that impulsive kiss of friendship, but her next words reassured me.

"I thought never to see you again, Hadron of Hastor," she said. "I feared that they had killed you. How comes it that you are here and in the metal of a warrior of Tjanath?"

I told her briefly of what had occurred to me since we had been separated and of how I had temporarily, at least, escaped The Death. She asked me what The Death was, but I could not tell her.

"It is very horrible," said Phao.

"What is it?" I asked.

"I do not know," replied the girl, "only that it is horrible. There is a deep pit, some say a bottomless pit, beneath the lower pits of the palace; horrible noises – groans and moans arise perpetually from it and into this pit those that are to die The Death are cast, but in such a way that the fall will not kill them. They must reach the bottom alive to endure all the horrors of The Death that await them there. That the torture is almost interminable is evidenced by the fact that the moans and groans of the victims never cease, no matter how long a period may have elapsed between executions."

"And you have escaped it," exclaimed Tavia. "My prayers have been answered. For days and nights have I been praying to my ancestors that you might be spared. Now if you can but escape this hateful place. Have you a plan?"

"We have a plan that with the help of Phao here may prove successful. Nur An, of whom I told you, is hiding in a closet in one of the apartments of the little prince. We shall return to that apartment at the first opportunity and here Phao will hide all three of us until some opportunity for escape presents itself."

"And we should lose no more time in returning," said Phao. "Come, let us go at once."

As we turned toward the panel through which we had entered I saw that it was ajar, though I was confident that Phao had closed it after us when we entered and simultaneously I could have sworn that I saw an eye glued to the narrow crack, as though someone watched us from the dark interior of the secret corridor.

In a single bound I was across the room and had drawn the panel aside. My sword was ready in my hand, but there was no one in the corridor beyond.

CHAPTER SEVEN
The Death

WITH PHAO IN THE LEAD and Tavia between us, we traversed the dark corridor back toward the apartment of Yo Seno. When we reached the panel marking the end of our journey, Phao halted and together we listened intently for any sound that might evidence the presence of an occupant in the room beyond. All was silent as the tomb.

"I believe," said Phao, "that it will be safer if you and Tavia remain here until night. I shall return to my apartment and go about my duties in the usual manner and after the palace has quieted down, these levels will be almost deserted; then I can come and get you with far less danger of detection than were I to take you to the apartment now."

We agreed that her plan was a good one, and bidding us a temporary farewell, she opened the panel sufficiently to permit her to survey the apartment beyond. It was quite empty. She stepped from the corridor, closing the panel behind her, and once again Tavia and I were plunged into darkness.

The long hours of our wait in the darkness of the corridor should have seemed interminable, but they did not. We made ourselves as comfortable as possible upon the floor, our backs against one of the walls, and, leaning close together so that we might converse in low whispers, we found more entertainment than I should have guessed possible, both in our conversation and in the long silences that broke it, so that it really did not seem a long time at all before the panel was swung open and we saw Phao in the subdued light of the apartment beyond. She motioned us to follow her, and, in silence, we obeyed. The corridor beyond the chamber of Yo Seno was deserted, as also was the ramp leading to the level below and the corridor upon which it opened. Fortune seemed to favor us at every step and there was a prayer of thanksgiving upon my lips as Phao pushed open the door leading into the apartment of the prince and motioned us to enter.

But at the same instant my heart sank within me, for, as I entered the apartment with Tavia, I saw warriors standing upon either side of the room awaiting us. With an exclamation of warning I drew Tavia behind me and backed quickly toward the door, but as I did so I heard a rush of feet and the clank of accoutrements in the corridor behind me, and, casting a quick glance over my shoulder, I saw other warriors running from the doorway of an apartment upon the opposite side of the corridor.

We were surrounded. We were lost, and my first thought was that Phao had betrayed us, leading us into this trap from which there could be no escape. They hustled us back into the room and surrounded us, and for the first time I saw Yo Seno. He stood there, a sneering grin upon his face, and but for the fact that Tavia had assured me that he had not harmed her I should have leaped upon him there, though a dozen swords had been at my vitals the next instant.

"So!" sneered Yo Seno. "You thought to fool me, did you? Well, I am not so easily fooled. I guessed the truth and I followed you through the corridor and overheard all your plans as you discussed them with the woman, Tavia. We have you all now," and turning to one of the warriors, he motioned to the closet upon the opposite side of the chamber. "Fetch the other," he commanded.

The fellow crossed to the door and, opening it, revealed Nur An lying bound and gagged upon the floor.

"Cut his bonds and remove the gag," ordered Yo Seno. "It is too late now for him to thwart my plans by giving the others a warning."

Nur An came toward us, with a firm step, his head high and a glance of haughty contempt for our captors.

The four of us stood facing Yo Seno, the sneer upon whose face had been replaced by a glare of hatred.

"You have been sentenced to die The Death," he said. "It is the death for spies. No more terrible punishment can be inflicted. Could there be, it would be meted to you two," as he looked first at me and then at Nur An, "that you might suffer more for the murder of our two comrades."

So they had found the warriors we had dispatched. Well, what of it? Evidently it had not rendered our position any worse than it had been before. We were to die The Death and that was the worst that they could accord us.

"Have you anything to say?" demanded Yo Seno.

"We still live," I exclaimed, and laughed in his face.

"Before long you will be beseeching your first ancestors for death," hissed the keeper of the keys, "but you will not have death too soon, and remember that no one knows how long it takes to die The Death. We cannot add to your physical suffering, but for the torment of your mind let me remind you that we are sending you to The Death without letting you know what the fate of your accomplices will be," and he nodded toward Tavia and Phao.

That was a nice point, well chosen. He could not have hit upon any means more certain to inflict acute torture upon me than this, but I would not give him the satisfaction of witnessing my true emotion, and so, once again, I laughed in his face. His patience had about reached the limit of its endurance, for he turned abruptly to a padwar of the guard and ordered him to remove us at once.

As we were hustled from the room, Nur An called a brave good-bye to Phao.

"Good-bye, Tavia!" I cried, "and remember that we still live."

"We still live, Hadron of Hastor!" she called back. "We still live!" and then she was swept from my view as we were pushed along down the corridor.

Down ramp after ramp we were conducted to the uttermost depths of the palace pits and then into a great chamber where I saw Haj Osis sitting upon a throne, surrounded again by his chiefs and his courtiers as he had been upon the occasion that he had interviewed me. Opposite the Jed, and in the middle of the chamber, hung a great iron cage, suspended from a heavy block set in the ceiling. Into this cage we were roughly pushed; the door was closed and secured with a large lock. I wondered what it was all about and what this had to do with The Death, and while I wondered a dozen men pushed a huge trap door from beneath the cage. A rush of cold, clammy air enveloped us and I experienced a chill that seemed to enter my marrow, as though I lay in the cold arms of death. Hollow moans and groans came faintly to my ears and I knew that we were above the pits where The Death lay.

No word was spoken within the chamber, but at a signal from Haj Osis strong men lowered the cage slowly into the aperture beneath us. Here the cold and the damp were more obvious and penetrating than before, while the ghastly sounds appeared to redouble in volume.

Down, down we slid into an abyss of darkness. The horror of the silence in the chamber above was forgotten in the horror of the pandemonium of uncanny sounds that rose from beneath.

How far we were lowered thus I may not even guess, but to Nur An it seemed at least a thousand feet and then we commenced to detect a slight luminosity about us. The moaning and the groaning had become a constant roar. As we approached, it seemed less like moans and groans and more like the sound of wind and rushing waters.

Suddenly, without the slightest warning, the bottom of the cage, which evidently must have been hinged upon one side, and held by a catch that could be sprung from above, swung downward. It happened so quickly that we hardly had time for conjecture before we were plunged into rushing water.

As I rose to the surface I discovered that I could see. Wherever we were, it was not shrouded in impenetrable darkness, but was lighted dimly.

Almost immediately Nur An's head bobbed up at arm's length from me. A strong current was bearing us onward and I realized at once that we were in the grip of a great underground river, one of those to which the remaining waters of dying Barsoom have receded. In the distance I descried a shoreline dimly visible in the subdued light, and, shouting to Nur An to follow me, I struck out toward it. The water was cold, but not sufficiently so to alarm me and I had no doubt but that we would reach the shore.

By the time that we had attained our goal and crawled out upon the rocky shore, our eyes had become accustomed to the dim light of the interior, and now, with astonishment, we gazed about us. What a vast cavern! Far, far above us its ceiling was discernible in the light of the minute radium particles with which the rock that formed its walls and ceiling was impregnated, but the opposite bank of the rushing torrent was beyond the range of our vision.

"So this is The Death!" exclaimed Nur An.

"I doubt if they know what it is themselves," I replied. "From the roaring of the river and the moaning of the wind, they have conjured something horrible in their own imaginations."

"Perhaps the greatest suffering that the victim must endure lies in his anticipation of what awaits him in these seemingly horrid depths," suggested Nur An, "whereas the worst that realization might bring would be death by drowning."

"Or by starvation," I suggested.

Nur An nodded. "Nevertheless," he said, "I wish I might return just long enough to mock them and witness their disappointment when they find that The Death is not so horrible after all."

"What a mighty river," he added after a moment's silence. "Could it be a tributary of Iss?"

"Perhaps it is Iss herself," I said.

"Then we are bound upon the last long pilgrimage down to the lost sea of Korus in the valley Dor," said Nur An gloomily. "It may be a lovely place, but I do not wish to go there yet."

"It is a place of horror," I replied.

"Hush," he cautioned; "that is sacrilege."

"It is sacrilege no longer since John Carter and Tars Tarkas snatched the veil of secrecy from the valley Dor and disposed of the myth of Issus, Goddess of Life Eternal." Even after I had told him the whole tragic story of the false gods of Mars, Nur An remained skeptical, so closely are the superstitions of religion woven into every fiber of our being.

We were both a trifle fatigued after our battle with the strong current of the river, and perhaps, too, we were suffering from reaction from the nervous shock of the ordeal through which we had passed. So we remained there, resting upon the rocky shore of the river of mystery. Eventually our conversation turned to what was uppermost in the minds of both and yet which each hesitated to mention – the fate of Tavia and Phao.

"I wish that they, too, had been sentenced to The Death," I said, "for then at least we might be with them and protect them."

"I am afraid that we shall never see them again," said Nur An gloomingly. "What a cruel fate that I should have found Phao only to lose her again irretrievably so quickly."

"It is indeed a strange trick of fate that after Tul Axtar stole her from you, he should have lost her too, and then that you should find her in Tjanath."

He looked at me with a slightly puzzled expression for a Moment and then his face cleared. "Phao is not the woman of whom I told you in the dungeon at Tjanath," he said. "Phao I loved long before; she was my first love. After I lost her I thought that I never could care for a woman again, but this other one came into my life and, knowing that Phao was gone forever, I found some consolation in my new love, but I realize now that was not the same, that no love could ever displace that which I felt for Phao."

"You lost her irretrievably once before," I reminded him, "but you found her again; perhaps you will find her once more."

"I wish that I might share your optimism," he said.

"We have little else to buoy us up," I reminded him.

"You are right," he said, and then with a laugh, added, "we still live!"

Presently, feeling rested, we set out along the shore in the direction that the river ran, for we had decided that that would be our course if for no other reason than that it would be easier going down hill than up. Where it would lead, we had not the slightest idea; perhaps to Korus; perhaps to Omean, the buried sea where lay the ships of the First Born.

Over tumbled rock masses we clambered and along level stretches of smooth gravel we pursued our rather aimless course, knowing not whither we were going, having no goal toward which to strive. There was some vegetation, weird and grotesque, but almost colorless for want of sunlight. There were tree-like plants with strange, angular branches that snapped off at the lightest touch, and as the trees did not look like trees, there were blossoms that did not look like flowers. It was a world as unlike the outer world as the figments of imagination are unlike realities.

But whatever musing upon the flora of this strange land I may have been indulging in was brought to a sudden termination as we rounded the shoulder of a jutting promontory and came face to face with as hideous a creature as ever I had laid my eyes upon. It was a great white lizard with gaping jaws large enough to engulf a man at a single swallow. At sight of us it emitted an angry hiss and advanced menacingly toward us.

Being unarmed and absolutely at the mercy of any creature that attacked us, we pursued the only plan that our intelligence could dictate – we retreated – and I am not ashamed to admit that we retreated rapidly.

Running quickly around the end of the promontory, we turned sharply up the bank away from the river. The bottom of the cavern rose sharply and as I clambered upward I glanced behind me occasionally to note the actions of our pursuer. He was now in plain sight, having followed us around the end of the promontory and there he stood looking about as though in search of us. Though we were not far from him, he did not seem to see us, and I soon became convinced that his eyesight was faulty; but not wishing to depend upon this I kept on climbing until presently we came to the top of the promontory, and, looking down upon the other side, I saw a considerable stretch of smooth gravel, stretching out into the dim distance along the river shore. If we could clamber down the opposite side of the barrier and reach this level stretch of gravel, I felt that we might escape the attentions of the huge monster. A final glance at him showed him still standing, peering first in one direction and then in another as though in search of us.

Nur An had followed close behind me and now together we slipped over the edge of the escarpment, and, though the rough rocks scratched us severely, we finally reached the gravel below, whereupon, having eluded our menacer, we set out upon a brisk run down the river. We had covered scarcely more than fifty paces when Nur An stumbled over an obstacle and as I stooped to give him a hand up, I saw that the thing that had tripped him was the rotting harness of a warrior and a moment later I saw the hilt of a sword protruding from the gravel. Seizing it, I wrenched it from the ground. It was a good long sword and I may tell you that the feel of it in my hand did more to restore my self-confidence than aught else that might have transpired. Being made of noncorrosive metal, as are all Barsoomian weapons, it remained as sound today as the moment that it had been abandoned by its owner.

"Look," said Nur An, pointing, and there at a little distance we saw another harness and another sword. This time there were two, a long sword and a short sword, and these Nur An took. No longer did we run. I have always felt that there is little upon Barsoom that two well-armed warriors need run from.

As we continued along our way across the level stretch of gravel we sought to solve the mystery of these abandoned weapons, a mystery that was still further heightened by our discovery of many more. In some cases the harness had rotted away entirely, leaving nothing but the metal parts, while in others it was comparatively sound and new. Presently we discerned a white mound ahead of us, but in the dim light of the cavern we could not at first determine of what it consisted. When we did, we were filled with horror, for the white mound was of the bones and skulls of human beings. Then, at last, I thought I had an explanation of the abandoned harness and weapons. This was the lair of the great lizard. Here he took his toll of the unhappy creatures that passed down the river, but how was it that armed men had come here. We had been cast into the cavern unarmed, as I was positive all of the condemned prisoners of Tjanath must have been. From whence came the others? I do not know, doubtless I shall never know. It was a mystery from the first. It will remain a mystery to the last.

As we passed on we found harness and weapons scattered all about, but there was infinitely more harness than weapons.

I had added a good short sword to my equipment, as well as a dagger, as had also Nur An, and I was stooping to examine another weapon which we had found – a short sword with a beautifully ornamented hilt and guard – when Nur An suddenly voiced an exclamation of warning.

"On guard," he cried, "Hadron! It comes!"

Leaping to my feet, I wheeled about, the short sword still in my hand, and there, bearing down upon us at considerable speed and with wide distended jaws, came the great white lizard hissing ominously. He was a hideous sight, a sight such as to make even a brave man turn and run, which I am now convinced is what practically all of his victims did; but here were two who did not run. Perhaps he was so close that we realized the futility of flight without giving the matter conscious thought, but be that as it may, we stood here – Nur An with his long sword in his hand, I with the ornately carved short sword that I had been examining, though instantly I realized that it was not the weapon with which to defend myself against this great hulking brute.

Yet I could not bear to waste a weapon already in my hand, especially in view of an accomplishment of mine in which I took considerable pride.

In Helium, both officers and men often wager large amounts upon the accuracy with which they can hurl daggers and short swords and I have seen considerable sums change hands within an hour, but so proficient was I that I had added considerably to my pay through my winning until my fame had spread to such an extent that I could find no one willing to pit his skill against mine.

Never had I hurled a weapon with a more fervent prayer for the accuracy of my throw than now as I launched the short sword swiftly at the mouth of the oncoming lizard. It was not a good throw. It would have lost me money in Helium, but in this instance, I think, it saved my life. The sword, instead of speeding in a straight line, point first, as it should have, turned slowly upward until it was travelling at an angle of about forty-five degrees, with the point forward and downward. In this position the point struck just inside of the lower jaw of the creature, while the heavy hilt, carried forward by its own momentum, lodged in the roof of the monster's mouth.

Instantly it was helpless; the point of the sword had passed through its tongue into the bony substance of its lower jaw, while the hilt was lodged in its upper jaw behind its mighty fangs. It could not dislodge the sword, either forward or backward, and for an instant it halted in hissing dismay, and simultaneously Nur An and I leaped to opposite sides of its ghastly white body. It tried to defend itself with its tail and talons, but we were too quick for it and presently it was lying in a pool of its own purple blood in the final spasmodic muscular reaction of dissolution.

There was something peculiarly disgusting and loathsome about the purple blood of the creature, not only in its appearance, but in its odor, which was almost nauseating, and Nur An and I lost no time in quitting the scene of our victory. At the river we washed our blades and then continued on upon our fruitless quest.

As we had washed our blades we had noticed fish in the river and after we had put sufficient distance between the lair of the lizard and ourselves, we determined to bend our energies for awhile toward filling our larder and our stomachs.

Neither one of us had ever caught a fish or eaten one, but we knew from history that they could be caught and that they were edible. Being swordsmen, we naturally looked to our swords as the best means for procuring our flesh and so we waded into the river with drawn long swords prepared to slaughter fish to our heart's content, but wherever we went there was no fish. We could see them elsewhere, but not within reach of our swords.

"Perhaps," said Nur An, "fish are not such fools as they appear. They may see us approaching and question our motive."

"I can readily believe that you are right," I replied. "Suppose we try strategy."

"How?" he asked.

"Come with me," I said, "and return to the bank." After a little search down stream I found a rocky ledge overhanging the river. "We will lie here at intervals," I said, "with only our eyes and the points of our swords over the edge of the bank. We must not talk or move, lest we frighten the fish. Perhaps in this way we shall procure one," for I had long since given up the idea of a general slaughter.

To my gratification my plan worked and it was not long before we each had a large fish.

Naturally, like other men, we prefer our flesh cooked, but being warriors we were accustomed to it either way, and so we broke our long fast upon raw fish from the river of mystery.

Both Nur An and I felt greatly refreshed and strengthened by our meal, however unpalatable it might have been. It had been some time since we had slept and though we had no idea whether it was still night upon the outer surface of Barsoom, or whether dawn had already broken, we decided that it would be best for us to sleep and so Nur An stretched out where we were while I watched. After he awoke, I took my turn. I think that neither one of us slept more than a single zode, but the rest did us quite as much good as the food that we had eaten and I am sure that I have never felt more fit than I did when we set out again upon our goalless journey.

I do not know how long we had been travelling after our sleep, for by now the journey was most monotonous, there being little change in the dimly seen landscape surrounding us and only the ceaseless roar of the river and the howling of the wind to keep us company.

Nur An was the first to discern the change; he seized my arm and pointed ahead. I must have been walking with my eyes upon the ground in front of me, else I must have seen what he saw simultaneously.

"It is daylight," I exclaimed. "It is the sun."

"It can be nothing else," he said.

There, far ahead of us, lay a great archway of light. That was all that we could see from the point at which we discovered it, but now we hastened on almost at a run, so anxious were we for a solution, so hopeful that it was indeed the sunlight and that in some inexplicable and mysterious way the river had found its way to the surface of Barsoom. I knew that this could not be true and Nur An knew it, and yet each knew how great his disappointment would be when the true explanation of the phenomenon was revealed.

When we approached the great patch of light it became more and more evident that the river had broken from its dark cavern out into the light of day, and when we reached the edge of that mighty portal we looked out upon a scene that filled our hearts with warmth and gladness, for there, stretching before us, lay a valley – a small valley it is true – a valley hemmed in, as far as we could see, by mighty cliffs, but yet a valley of life and fertility and beauty bathed in the hot light of the sun.

"It is not quite the surface of Barsoom," said Nur An, "but it is the next best thing."

"And there must be a way out," I said. "There must be. If there is not, we will make one."

"Right you are, Hadron of Hastor," he cried. "We will make a way. Come!"

Before us the banks of the roaring river were lined with lush vegetation; great trees raised their leafy branches far above the waters; the brilliant, scarlet sward was lapped by the little wavelets and everywhere bloomed gorgeous flowers and shrubs of many hues and shapes. Here was a vegetation such as I had never seen before upon the surface of Barsoom. Here were forms similar to those with which I was familiar and others totally unknown to me, yet all were lovely, though some were bizarre.

Emerging, as we had, from the dark and gloomy bowels of the earth, the scene before us presented a view of wondrous beauty, and, while doubtless enhanced by contrast, it was nevertheless such an aspect as is seldom given to the eyes of a Barsoomian of today to view. To me it seemed a little garden spot upon a dying world preserved from an ancient era when Barsoom was young and meteorological conditions were such as to favor the growth of vegetation that has since become extinct over practically the entire area of the planet. In this deep valley, surrounded by lofty cliffs, the atmosphere doubtless was considerably denser than upon the surface of the planet above. The sun's days were reflected by the lofty escarpment, which must also hold the heat during the colder periods of night, and, in addition to this, there was ample water for irrigation which nature might easily have achieved through percolation of the waters of the river through and beneath the top soil of the valley.

For several minutes Nur An and I stood spellbound by the bewitching view, and then, espying luscious fruit hanging in great clusters from some of the trees, and bushes loaded with berries we subordinated the esthetic to the corporeal and set forth to supplement our meal of raw fish with the exquisite offerings which hung so temptingly before us.

As we started to move through the vegetation we became aware of thin threads of a gossamerlike substance festooned from tree to tree and bush to bush. So fine as to be almost invisible, yet they were so strong as to impede our progress. It was surprisingly difficult to break them, and when there were a dozen or more at a time barring our way, we found it necessary to use our daggers to cut a way through them.

We had taken only a few steps into the deeper vegetation, cutting our way through the gossamer strands, when we were confronted by a new and surprising obstacle to our advance – a large, venomous-looking spider that scurried toward us in an inverted position, clinging with a dozen legs to one of the gossamer strands, which served both as its support and its pathway, and if its appearance was any index to its venomousness it must, indeed, have been a deadly insect.

As it came toward me, apparently with the most sinister intentions, I hastily returned my dagger to its scabbard and drew my short sword, with which I struck at the fearsome-looking creature. As the blow descended, it drew back so that my point only slightly scratched it, whereupon it opened its hideous mouth and emitted a terrific scream so out of proportion to its size and to the nature of such insects with which I was familiar that it had a most appalling effect upon my nerves. Instantly the scream was answered by an unearthly chorus of similar cries all about us and immediately a swarm of these horrid insects came racing toward us upon their gossamer threads. Evidently this was the only position which they assumed in moving about and their webs the only means to that end, for their twelve legs grew upward from their backs, giving them a most uncanny appearance.

Fearing that the creatures might be poisonous, Nur An and I retreated hastily to the mouth of the cavern, and as the spiders could not go beyond the ends of their threads, we were soon quite safe from them and now the luscious fruit looked more tempting than ever, since it seemed to be denied to us.

"The road down the river is well guarded," said Nur An with a rueful smile, "which might indicate a most desirable goal."

"At present that fruit is the most desirable thing in the world to me," I replied, "and I am going to try to discover some means of obtaining it."

Moving to the right, away from the river, I sought for an entrance into the forest that would be free from the threads of the spiders and presently I came to a point where there was a well-defined trail about four or five feet wide, apparently cut by man from the vegetation. Across the mouth of it, however, were strung thousands of gossamer strands. To touch them, we knew, would be the signal for myriads of the angry spiders to swarm upon us. While our greatest fear was, of course, that the insects might be poisonous, their cruelly fanged mouths also suggested that, poisonous or not, they might in their great numbers constitute a real menace.

"Do you notice," I said to Nur An, "that these threads seem stretched across the entrance to the pathway only. Beyond them I cannot detect any, though of course they are so tenuous that they might defy one's vision even at a short distance."

"I do not see any spiders here," said Nur An. "Perhaps we can cut our way through with impunity at this point."

"We shall experiment," I said, drawing my long sword.

Advancing, I cut a few strands, when immediately there swarmed out of the trees and bushes upon either side great companies of the insects, each racing along its own individual strand. Where the strands were intact the creatures crossed and recrossed the trail, staring at us with their venomous, beady eyes, their powerful, gleaming fangs bared threateningly toward us.

The cut strands floated in the air until borne down by the weight of the approaching spiders who followed to the severed ends but no further. Here they either hung glaring at us or else clambered up and down excitedly, but not one of them ever ventured from his strand.

As I watched them, their antics suggested a plan. "They are helpless when their web is severed," I said to Nur An. "Therefore if we cut all their webs they cannot reach us." Whereupon, advancing, I swung my long sword above my head and cut downward through the remaining strands. Instantly the creatures set up their infernal screaming. Several of them, torn from their webs by the blow of my sword, lay upon the ground upon their bellies, their feet sticking straight up into the air. They seemed utterly helpless, and though they screamed loudly and frantically waved their legs, they were clearly unable to move; nor could those hanging, at either side of the trail reach us. With my sword I destroyed those that lay in the path and then, followed by Nur An, I entered the forest. Ahead of us I could see no webs; the way seemed clear, but before we advanced further into the forest I turned about to have a last look at the discomfited insects to see what they might be about. They had stopped screaming now and were slowly returning into the foliage, evidently to their lairs, and as they seemed to offer no further menace we continued upon our way. The trees and bushes along the pathway were innocent of fruit or berries, though just beyond reach we saw them growing in profusion, behind a barrier of those gossamer webs that we had so quickly learned to avoid.

"This trail appears to have been made by man," said Nur An.

"Whoever made it, or when," I said, "there is no doubt but that some creature still uses it. The absence of fruit along it would alone be ample proof of that."

We moved cautiously along the winding trail, not knowing at what moment we might be confronted by some new menace in the form of man or beast. Presently we saw ahead of us what appeared to be an opening in the forest and a moment later we emerged into a clearing. Looming in front of us at a distance of perhaps less than a haad was a towering pile of masonry. It was a gloomy pile, apparently built of black volcanic rock. For some thirty feet above the ground there was a blank wall, pierced by but a single opening – a small doorway almost directly in front of us. This part of the structure appeared to be a well, beyond it rose buildings of weird and grotesque outlines and dominating all was a lofty tower, from the summit of which a wisp of smoke curled upward into the quiet air.

From this new vantage point we had a better view of the valley than had at first been accorded us, and now, more marked than ever, were the indications that it was the crater of some gigantic and long extinct volcano. Between us and the buildings, which suggested a small walled city, the clearing contained a few scattered trees, but most of the ground was given over to cultivation, being traversed by irrigation ditches of an archaic type which has been abandoned upon the surface for many ages, having been superseded by a system of subirrigation when the diminishing water supply necessitated the adoption of conservation measures.

Satisfied that no further information could be gained by remaining where we were, I started boldly into the clearing toward the city. "Where are you going?" asked Nur An.

"I am going to find out who dwells in that gloomy place," I replied. "Here are fields and gardens, so they must have food and that, after all, is the only favor that I shall ask of them."

Nur An shook his head. "The very sight of the place depresses me," he said. But he came with me as I knew he would, for Nur An is a splendid companion upon whose loyalty one may always depend.

We had traversed about two-thirds of the distance across the clearing toward the city before we saw any signs of life and then a few figures appeared at the top of the wall above the entrance. They carried long, thin scarfs, which they seemed to be waving in greeting to us and when we had come yet closer I saw that they were young women. They leaned over the parapet and smiled and beckoned to us.

As we came within speaking distance below the wall, I halted. "What city is this," I asked, "and who is jed here?"

"Enter, warriors," cried one of the girls, "and we will lead you to the jed." She was very pretty and she was smiling sweetly, as were her companions.

"This is not such a depressing place as you thought," I said in a low voice to Nur An.

"I was mistaken," said Nur An. "They seem to be a kindly, hospitable people. Shall we enter?"

"Come," called another of the girls; "behind these gloomy walls lie food and wine and love."

Food! I would have entered a far more forbidding place than this for food.

As Nur An and I strode toward the small door, it slowly withdrew to one side. Beyond, across a black paved avenue, rose buildings of black volcanic rock. The avenue seemed deserted as we stepped within. We heard the faint click of a lock as the door slid into place behind us and I had a sudden foreboding of ill that made my right hand seek the hilt of my long sword.

CHAPTER EIGHT
The Spider of Ghasta

FOR A MOMENT we stood undecided in the middle of the empty avenue, looking about us, and then our attention was attracted to a narrow stairway running up the inside of the wall, upon the summit of which the girls had appeared and welcomed us.

Down the stairway the girls were coming. There were six of them. Their beautiful faces were radiant with happy smiles of welcome that instantly dispelled the gloom of the dark surroundings as the rising sun dissipates night's darkness and replaces her shadows with light and warmth and happiness.

Beautifully wrought harness, enriched by many a sparkling jewel, accentuated the loveliness of faultless figures. As they approached a vision of Tavia sprang to my mind. Beautiful as these girls unquestionably were, how much more beautiful was Tavia!

I recall distinctly, even now, that in that very instant with all that was transpiring to distract my attention, I was suddenly struck by wonder that it should have been Tavia's face and figure that I saw rather than those of Sanoma Tora. You may believe that I brought myself up with a round turn and thereafter it was a vision of Sanoma Tora that I saw, and that, too, without any disloyalty to my friendship for Tavia – that blessed friendship which I looked upon as one of my proudest and most valuable possessions.

As the girls reached the pavement they came eagerly toward us. "Welcome, warriors," cried one, "to happy Ghasta. After your long journey you must be hungry. Come with us and you shall be fed, but first the great jed will wish to greet you and welcome you to our city, for visitors to Ghasta are few."

As they led us along the avenue I could not but note the deserted appearance of the city. There was no sign of life about any of the buildings that we passed nor did we see another human being until we had come to an open plaza, in the center of which rose a mighty building surmounted by the lofty tower that we had seen when we first emerged from the forest. Here we saw a number of people, both men and women – sad, dejected-looking people, who moved with bent shoulders and downcast eyes. There was no animation in their step and their whole demeanor seemed that of utter hopelessness. What a contrast they presented to the gay and happy girls who so joyously conducted us toward the main entrance of what I assumed to be the palace of the jed. Here, burly warriors were on guard – fat, oily-looking fellows, whose appearance was not at all to my liking. As we approached them an officer emerged from the interior of the building. If possible, he was even fatter and more greasy-looking than his men, but he smiled and bowed as he welcomed us.

"Greetings!" he exclaimed. "May the peace of Ghasta be upon the strangers who enter her gates."

"Send word to Ghron, the great jed," said one of the girls to him, "that we are bringing two strange warriors who wish to do honor to him before partaking of the hospitality of Ghasta."

As the officer dispatched a warrior to notify the jed of our coming, we were escorted into the interior of the palace. The furnishings were striking, but extremely fantastic in design and execution. The native wood of the forests had been used to fine advantage in the construction of numerous pieces of beautifully carved furniture, the grain of the woods showing lustrously in their various natural colors, the beauties of which were sometimes accentuated by delicate stain and by high polishes, but perhaps the most striking feature of the interior decorations was the gorgeously painted fabric that covered the walls and ceilings. It was a fabric of unbelievable lightness, which gave the impression of spun silver. So closely woven was it that, as I was to learn later, it would hold water and of such great strength that it was almost impossible to tear it.

Upon it were painted in brilliant colors the most fantastic scenes that imagination might conceive. There were spiders with the heads of beautiful women, and women with the heads of spiders. There were flowers and trees that danced beneath a great red sun, and great lizards, such as we had passed within the gloomy cavern on our journey down from Tjanath. In all the figures that were depicted there was nothing represented as nature had created it. It was as though some mad mind had conceived the whole.

As we waited in the great entrance hall of the palace of the jed, four of the girls danced for our entertainment – a strange dance such as I had never before seen upon Barsoom. Its steps and movements were as weird and fantastic as the mural decorations of the room in which it was executed, and yet with all there was a certain rhythm and suggestiveness in the undulations of those lithe bodies that imparted to us a feeling of well-being and content.

The fat and greasy padwar of the guard moistened his thick lips as he watched them and though he had doubtless seen them dance upon many occasions, he seemed to be much more affected than we, but perhaps he had no Phao or Sanoma Tora to occupy his thoughts.

Sanoma Tora! The chiseled beauty of her noble face stood out clearly upon the screen of memory for a brief instant and then slowly it began to fade. I tried to recall it, to see again the short, haughty lip and the cold, level gaze, but it receded into a blur from which there presently emerged a pair of wondrous eyes, moist with tears, a perfect face and a head of tousled hair.

It was then that the warrior returned to say that Ghron, the Jed, would receive us at once. Only the girls accompanied us, the fat padwar remaining behind, though I could have sworn that it was not through choice.

The room in which the jed received us was upon the second level of the palace. It was a large room, even more grotesquely decorated than those through which we had passed. The furniture was of weird shapes and sizes, nothing harmonized with anything else and yet the result was a harmony of discord that was not at all unpleasing.

The jed sat upon a perfectly enormous throne of volcanic glass. It was, perhaps, the most ornate and remarkable piece of furniture that I have ever seen and was the outstanding specimen of craftsmanship in the entire city of Ghasta, but if it caught my eye at the time it was only for an instant as nothing could for long distract one's attention from the jed himself. In the first glance he looked more like a hairy ape than a man. He was massively built with great, heavy, stooping shoulders and long arms covered with shaggy, black hair, the more remarkable, perhaps, because there is no race of hairy men upon Barsoom. His face was broad and flat and his eyes were so far apart that they seemed literally to be set in the corners of his face. As we were halted before him, he twisted his mouth into what I imagined at the time was intended for a smile, but which only succeeded in making him look more horrible than before.

As is customary, we laid our swords at his feet and announced our names and our cities.

"Hadron of Hastor, Nur An of Jahar," he repeated. "Ghron, the Jed, welcomes you to Ghasta. Few are the visitors who find their way to our beautiful city. It is an event, therefore, when two such illustrious warriors honor us with a visit. Seldom do we receive word from the outer world. Tell us, then of your journey and of what is transpiring upon the surface of Barsoom above us."

His words and his manner were those of a most solicitous host bent upon extending a proper and cordial welcome to strangers, but I could not rid myself of the belying suggestion of his repulsive countenance, though I could do no less than play the part of a grateful and appreciative guest.

We told our stories and gave him much news of those portions of Barsoom with which each of us was familiar and as Nur An spoke, I looked about me at the assemblage of the great chamber. They were mostly women and many of them were young and beautiful. The men, for the most part, were gross-looking, fat and oily, and there were certain lines of cruelty about their eyes and their mouths that did not escape me, though I tried to attribute it to the first depressing impression that the black and somber buildings and the deserted avenues had conveyed to my mind.

When we had finished our recitals, Ghron announced that a banquet had been prepared in our honor and in person he led the procession from the throne-room down a long corridor to a mighty banquet hall, in the center of which stood a great table, down the entire length of which was a magnificent decoration consisting entirely of the fruits and flowers of the forest through which we had passed. At one end of the table was the jed's throne and at the other were smaller thrones, one for Nur An and one for me. Seated on either side of us were the girls who had welcomed us to the city and whose business, it seemed, now was to entertain us.

The design of the dishes with which the table was set was quite in keeping with all the other mad designs of the palace of Ghron. No two plates or goblets or platters were of the same shape or size or design and nothing seemed suited to the purpose for which it was intended. My wine was served in a shallow, triangular-shaped saucer, while my meat was crammed into a tall, slender-stemmed goblet. However, I was too hungry to be particular, and, I hoped, too well conversant with the amenities of polite society to reveal the astonishment that I felt.

Here, as in other parts of the palace, the wall coverings were of the gossamer-like silver fabric that had attracted my attention and admiration the moment that I had entered the building and so fascinated was I by it that I could not refrain from mentioning it to the girl who sat at my right.

"There is no such fabric anywhere else in Barsoom," she said.

"It is made here and only here."

"It is very beautiful," I said. "Other nations would pay well for it."

"If we could get it to them," she said, "but we have no intercourse with the world above us."

"Of what is it woven?" I asked.

"When you entered the valley Hohr," she said, "you saw a beautiful forest, running down to the banks of the river Syl. Doubtless you saw fruit in the forest and, being hungry, you sought to gather it, but you were set upon by huge spiders that sped along silver threads, finer than a woman's hair."

"Yes," I said, "that is just what happened."

"It is from this web, spun by those hideous spiders, that we weave our fabric. It is as strong as leather and as enduring as the rocks of which Ghasta is built."

"Do women of Ghasta spin this wonderful fabric?" I asked.

"The slaves," she said, "both men and women."

"And from whence come your slaves?" I asked, "if you have no intercourse with the upper world?"

"Many of them come down the river from Tjanath, where they have died The Death, and there are others who come from further up the river, but why they come or from whence we never know. They are silent people, who will not tell us, and sometimes they come from down the river, but these are few and usually are so crazed by the horrors of their journey that we can glean no knowledge from them."

"And do any ever go on down the river from Ghasta?" I asked; for it was in that direction that Nur An and I hoped to make our way in search of liberty, as deep within me was the hope that we might reach the valley Dor and the lost sea of Korus, from which I was convinced I could escape, as did John Carter and Tars Tarkas.

"A few, perhaps," she said, "but we never know what becomes of these, for none returns."

"You are happy here?" I asked.

She forced a smile to her beautiful lips, but I thought that a shudder ran through her frame.

The banquet was elaborate and the food delicious. There was a great deal of laughter at the far end of the table where the jed sat, for those about him watched him closely, and when he laughed, which he always did at his own jokes, the others all laughed uproariously.

Toward the end of the meal a troupe of dancers entered the apartment. My first view of them almost took my breath away, for, with but a single exception, they were all horribly deformed. That one exception was the most beautiful girl I have ever seen – the most beautiful girl I have ever seen, with the saddest face that I have ever seen. She danced divinely and about her hopped and crawled the poor, unhappy creatures whose sad afflictions should have made them the objects of sympathy rather than ridicule and yet it was obvious that they had been selected for their part for the sole purpose of giving the audience an opportunity to vent its ridicule upon them. The sight of them seemed to incite Ghron to a pitch of frenzied mirth, and, to add to his own pleasure and to the discomforts of the poor, pathetic performers, he hurled food and plates at them as they danced about the banquet table.

I tried not to look at them, but there was a fascination in their deformities which attracted my gaze and presently it became apparent to me that the majority of them were artificially deformed, that they had been thus broken and bent at the behest of some malign mind and as I looked down the long board at the horrid face of Ghron, distorted by maniacal laughter, I could not but guess the author of their disfigurement.

When at last they were gone, three large goblets of wine were borne into the banquet hall by a slave; two of them were red goblets and one was black. The black goblet was set before Ghron and the red ones before Nur An and me. Then Ghron rose and the whole company followed his example.

"Ghron, the Jed, drinks to the happiness of his honored guests," announced the ruler, and, raising the goblet to his lips, he drained it to the bottom.

It seemed obvious that this little ceremony would conclude the banquet and that it was intended Nur An and I should drink the health of our host. I, therefore, raised my goblet. It was the first time that anything had been served to me in the proper receptacle and I was glad that at last I might drink without incurring the danger of spilling most of the contents of the receptacle into my lap.

"To the health and power of the great jed, Ghron," I said, and following my host's example, drained the contents of the goblet.

As Nur An followed my example with some appropriate words, I felt a sudden lethargy stealing over me and in the instant before I lost consciousness I realized that I had been given drugged wine.

When I regained consciousness I found myself lying upon the bare floor of a room of a peculiar shape that suggested it was the portion of the arc of a circle lying between the peripheries of two concentric circles. The narrow end of the room curved inward, the wider end outward. In the latter was a single, grated window; no door or other openings appeared in any of the walls, which were covered with the same silver fabric that I had noticed upon the walls and ceilings of the palace of the jed. Near me lay Nur An, evidently still under the influence of the opiate that had been administered to us in the wine.

Again I looked about the room. I arose and went to the window. Far below me I saw the roofs of the city. Evidently we were imprisoned in the lofty tower that rose from the center of the palace of the jed, but how had we been brought into the room? Certainly not through the window, which must have been fully two hundred feet above the city. While I was pondering this seemingly unanswerable problem, Nur An regained consciousness. At first he did not speak; he just lay there looking at me with a rueful smile upon his lips.

"Well?" I asked.

Nur An shook his head. "We still live," he said dismally, "but that is about the best that one may say."

"We are in the palace of a maniac, Nur An," I said. "There is no doubt in my mind as to that. Every one here lives in constant terror of Ghron and from what I have seen today they are warranted in feeling terror."

"Yet I believe we saw little or nothing at that," said Nur An.

"I saw enough," I replied.

"Those girls were so beautiful," he said after a moment's silence. "I could not believe that such beauty and such duplicity could exist together."

"Perhaps they were the unwilling tools of a cruel master," I suggested.

"I shall always like to think so," he said.

The day waned and night fell; no one came near us, but in the meantime I discovered something. Accidentally leaning against the wall at the narrow end of our room I found that it was very warm, in fact quite hot, and from this I inferred that the flue of the chimney from which we had seen the smoke issuing rose through the center of the tower and the wall of the chimney formed the rear wall of our apartment. It was a discovery, but at the moment it meant nothing to us.

There were no lights in our apartment, and, as only Cluros was in the heavens and upon the opposite side of the tower, our prison was in almost total darkness. We were sitting in gloomy contemplation of our predicament, each wrapped in his own unhappy thoughts, when I heard footsteps apparently approaching from below. They came nearer and nearer until finally they ceased in an adjoining apartment, seemingly the one next to ours. A moment later there was a scraping sound and a line of light appeared at the bottom of one of the side walls. It kept growing in width until I finally realized that the entire partition wall was rising. In the opening we saw at first the sandaled feet of warriors, and finally, little by little, their entire bodies were revealed – two stalwart, brawny men, heavily armed.

They carried manacles and with them they fastened our wrists behind our backs. They did not speak, but with a gesture one of them directed us to follow him, and, as we filed out of the room, the second warrior fell in behind us. In silence we entered a steep, spiral ramp, which we descended to the main body of the palace, but yet our escorts conducted us still lower until I knew that we must be in the pits beneath the palace.

The pits! Inwardly I shuddered. I much preferred the tower for I have always possessed an inherent horror of the pits. Perhaps these would be utterly dark and doubtless overrun by rats and lizards.

The ramp ended in a gorgeously decorated apartment in which was assembled about the same company of men and women that had partaken of the banquet with us earlier in the day. Here, too, was Ghron upon a throne. This time he did not smile as we entered the room. He did not seem to realize our presence. He was sitting, leaning forward, his eyes fixed upon something at the far end of the room over which hung a deadly silence that was suddenly shattered by a piercing scream of anguish. The scream was but a prelude to a series of similar cries of agony.

I looked quickly in the direction from which the screams came, the direction in which Ghron's gaze was fastened. I saw a naked woman chained to a grill before a hot fire. Evidently they had just placed her there as I had entered the room and it was her first shrill scream of agony that had attracted my attention.

The grill was mounted upon wheels so that it could be removed to any distance from the fire that the torturer chose, or completely turned about presenting the other side of the victim to the blaze.

As my eyes wandered back to the audience I saw that most of the girls sat there glaring straight ahead, their eyes fixed with horror upon the horrid scene. I do not believe that they enjoyed it; I know that they did not. They were equally the unwilling victims of the cruel vagaries of Ghron's diseased mind, but like the poor creature upon the grill they were helpless.

Next to the torture itself, the most diabolical conceit of the mind that had directed it was the utter silence enjoined upon all spectators against the background of which the shrieks and moans of the tortured victim evidently achieved their highest effectiveness upon the crazed mind of the jed.

The spectacle was sickening. I turned my eyes away. Presently one of the warriors who had fetched us touched me on the arm and motioned me to follow him.

He led us from this apartment to another and there we witnessed a scene infinitely more terrible than the grilling of the human victim. I cannot describe it; it tortures my memory even to think of it. Long before we reached that hideous apartment we heard the screams and curses of its inmates. In utter silence, our guard ushered us within. It was the chamber of horrors in which the Jed of Ghasta was creating abnormal deformities for his cruel dance of the cripples.

Still in silence, we were led from this horrid place and now our guide conducted us upward to a luxuriously furnished apartment. Upon divans lay two of the beautiful girls who had welcomed us to Ghasta.

For the first time since we had left our room in the tower one of our escort broke the silence. "They will explain," he said, pointing to the girls. "Do not try to escape. There is only one exit from this room. We will be waiting outside." He then removed our manacles and with his companion left the apartment, closing the door after them.

One of the occupants of the room was the same girl who had sat at my right during the banquet. I had found her most gracious and intelligent and to her I now turned.

"What is the meaning of this?" I demanded. "Why are we made prisoners? Why have we been brought here?"

She beckoned me to come to the divan on which she reclined and as I approached she motioned to me to sit down beside her.

"What you have seen tonight," she said, "represents the three fates that lie in store for you. Ghron has taken a fancy to you and he is giving you your choice."

"I do not yet quite understand," I said.

"You saw the victim before the grill?" she asked.

"Yes," I replied.

"Would you care to suffer that fate?"

"Scarcely."

"You saw the unhappy ones being bent and broken for the dance of the cripples," she pursued.

"I did," I answered.

"And now you see this luxurious room – and me. Which would you choose?"

"I cannot believe," I replied, "that the final alternative is without conditions, which might make it appear less attractive than it now seems, for otherwise there could be no possible question as to which I would chose."

"You are right," she said. "There are conditions."

"What are they?" I asked.

"You will become an officer in the palace of the jed and as such you will conduct tortures similar to those you have witnessed in the pits of the palace. You will be guided by whatever whim may possess your master."

I drew myself to my full height. "I choose the fire," I said.

"I knew that you would," she said sadly, "and yet I hoped that you might not."

"It is not because of you," I said quickly. "It is the other conditions which no man of honor could accept."

"I know," she said, "and had you accepted them I must eventually have despised you as I despise the others."

"You are unhappy here?" I asked.

"Of course," she said. "Who but a maniac could be happy in this horrid place? There are, perhaps, six hundred people in the city and there is not one who knows happiness. A hundred of us form the court of the jed; the others are slaves. As a matter of fact, we are all slaves, subject to every mad whim or caprice of the maniac who is our master."

"And there is no escape?" I asked.

"None."

"I shall escape," I said.

"How?"

"The fire," I replied.

She shuddered. "I do not know why I should care so much," she said, "unless it is that I liked you from the first. Even while I was helping to lure you into the city for the human spider of Ghasta, I wished that I might warn you not to enter, but I was afraid, just as I am afraid to die. I wish that I had your courage to escape through the fire."

I turned to Nur An, who had been listening to our conversation. "You have reached your decision?" I asked.

"Certainly," he said. "There could be but one decision for a man of honor."

"Good!" I exclaimed, and then I turned to the girl. "You will notify, Ghron of our decision?" I asked.

"Wait," she said; "ask for time in which to consider it. I know that it will make no difference in the end, but yet – Oh, even yet there is a germ of hope within me that even utter hopelessness cannot destroy."

"You are right," I said. "There is always hope. Let him think that you have half persuaded us to accept the life of luxury and ease that he has offered as an alternative to death or torture, and that if you are given a little more time you may succeed. In the meantime we may be able to work out some plan of escape."

"Never," she said.

CHAPTER NINE

Phor Tak of Jhama

BACK IN OUR QUARTERS in the chimney tower, Nur An and I discussed every mad plan of escape that entered our brains. For some reason our fetters had not been replaced, which gave us at least as much freedom of action as our apartment afforded and you may rest assured that we took full advantage of it, examining minutely every square inch of the floor and the walls as far up as we could reach, but our combined efforts failed to reveal any means for raising the partition which closed the only avenue of escape from our prison, with the exception of the window which, while heavily barred and some two hundred feet above the ground, was by no means, therefore, eliminated from our plans.

The heavy vertical bars which protected the window withstood our combined efforts when we sought to bend them, though Nur An is a powerful man, while I have always been lauded for my unusual muscular development. The bars were set a little too close together to permit our bodies to pass through, but the removal of one of them would leave an opening of ample size; yet to what purpose? Perhaps the same answer was in Nur An's mind that was in mine – that when hope was gone and the sole alternative remaining was the fire within the grill, we might at least cheat Ghron could we but hurl ourselves from this high window to the ground far below.

But whatever end each of us may have had in view, he kept it to himself and when I started digging at the mortar at the bottom of one of the bars with the prong of a buckle from my harness, Nur An asked no questions but set to work similarly upon the mortar at the top of the same bar. We worked in silence and with little fear of discovery, as no one had entered our prison since we had been incarcerated there. Once a day the partition was raised a few inches and food slipped in to us beneath it, but we did not see the person who brought it, nor did anyone communicate with us from the time that the guards had taken us to the palace that first night up to the moment that we had finally succeeded in loosening the bar so that it could by easily removed from its seat.

I shall never forget with what impatience we awaited the coming of night, that we might remove the bar and investigate the surrounding surface of the tower, for it had occurred to me that it might offer a means of descent to the ground below, or rather to the roof of the building which it surmounted, from where we might hope to make our way to the summit of the city wall undetected. Already, in view of this possibility, I had planned to tear strips from the fabric covering our walls wherewith to make a rope down which we might lower ourselves to the ground beyond the city wall.

As night approached I commenced to realize how high I had built my hopes upon this idea. It already seemed as good as accomplished, especially when I had utilized the possibilities of the rope to its fullest extent, which included making one of sufficient length to reach from our window to the bottom of the tower. Thus every obstacle was overcome. It was then, just at dusk, that I explained my plan to Nur An.

"Fine," he exclaimed. "Let us start at once making our rope. We know how strong this fabric is and that a slender strand of it will support our weight. There is enough upon one wall to make all the rope we need."

Success seemed almost assured as we started to remove the fabric from one of the larger walls, but here we met with our first obstacle. The fabric was fastened at the top and at the bottom with large-headed nails, set close together, which withstood our every effort to tear it loose. Thin and light in weight, this remarkable fabric appeared absolutely indestructible and we were almost exhausted by our efforts when we were finally forced to admit defeat.

The quick Barsoomian night had fallen and we might now, with comparative safety, remove the bar from the window and reconnoiter for the first time beyond the restricted limits of our cell, but hope was now low within our breasts and it was with little anticipation of encouragement that I drew myself to the sill and projected my head and shoulders through the aperture.

Below me lay the somber, gloomy city, its blackness relieved by but a few dim lights, most of which shone faintly from the palace windows. I passed my palm over the surface of the tower that lay within arm's reach, and again my heart sank within me. Smooth, almost glass-like volcanic rock, beautifully cut and laid, offered not the slightest handhold – indeed an insect might have found it difficult to have clung to its polished surface.

"It is quite hopeless," I said as I drew my head back into the room. "The tower is as smooth as a woman's breast."

"What is above?" asked Nur An.

Again I leaned out, this time looking upward. Just above me were the eaves of the tower – our cell was at the highest level of the structure. Something impelled me to investigate in that direction – an insane urge, perhaps, born of despair.

"Hold my ankles, Nu An," I said, "and in the name of your first ancestor, hold tightly!"

Clinging to two of the remaining bars I raised myself to a standing position upon the window ledge, while Nur An clung to my ankles. I could just reach the top of the eaves with my extended fingers. Lowering myself again to the sill, I whispered to Nur An. "I am going to attempt to reach the roof of the tower," I exclaimed.

"Why?" he asked.

I laughed. "I do not know," I admitted, "but something within my inner consciousness seems insistently to urge me on."

"If you fall," he said, "you will have escaped the fire – and I will follow you. Good luck, my friend from Hastor!"

Once again I raised myself to a standing position upon the sill and reached upward until my fingers bent above the edge of the lofty roof. Slowly I drew myself upward; below me, two hundred feet, lay the palace roof and death. I am very strong – only a very strong man could have hoped to succeed, for I had at best but a precarious hold upon the flat roof above me, but, at last, I succeeded in getting an elbow over and then I drew my body slowly over the edge until, at last, I lay panting upon the basalt flagging that topped the slender tower.

Resting a few moments, I arose to my feet. Mad, passionate Thuria raced across the cloudless sky; Cluros, her cold spouse, swung his aloof circle in splendid isolation; below me lay the valley of Hohr like some enchanted fairyland of ancient lore; above me frowned the beetling cliff that hemmed in this madman's world.

A puff of hot air struck me suddenly in the face, recalling to my mind that far below in the pits of Ghasta an orgy of torture was occurring. Faintly a scream arose from the black mouth of the flue behind me. I shuddered, but my attention was centered upon the yawning opening now and I approached it. Almost unbearable waves of heat were billowing upward from the mouth of the chimney. There was little smoke, so perfect was the combustion, but what there was shot into the air at terrific velocity. It almost seemed that were I to cast myself upon it I should be carried far aloft.

It was then that a thought was born – a mad, impossible idea, it seemed, and yet it clung to me as I lowered myself gingerly over the outer edge of the tower and finally regained the greater security of my cell.

I was about to explain my insane plan to Nur An when I was interrupted by sounds from the adjoining chamber and an instant later the partition started to rise. I thought they were bringing us food again, but the partition rose further than was necessary for the passing of food receptacles beneath it and a moment later we saw the ankles and legs of a woman beneath the base of the rising wall. Then a girl stooped and entered our cell. In the light from the adjoining room I recognized her – she who had been selected by Ghron to lure me to his will. Her name was Sharu.

Nur An had quickly replaced the bar on the window and when the girl entered there was nothing to indicate that aught was amiss, or that one of us had so recently been outside our cell, The partition remained half raised, permitting light to enter the apartment, and the girl, looking at me, must have noticed my gaze wandering to the adjoining room.

"Do not let your hopes rise," she said with a rueful smile. "There are guards waiting at the level next below."

"Why are you here, Sharu?" I asked.

"Ghron sent me," she replied. "He is impatient for your decision."

I thought quickly. Our only hope lay in the sympathy of this girl, whose attitude in the past had at least demonstrated her friendliness. "Had we a dagger and a needle," I said in a low whisper, "we could give Ghron his answer upon the morning of the day after tomorrow."

"What reason can I give him for this further delay?" she asked after a moment's thought.

"Tell him," said Nur An, "that we are communing with our ancestors and that upon their advice shall depend our decision."

Sharu smiled. She drew a dagger from its sheath at her side and laid it upon the floor and from a pocket pouch attached to her harness she produced a needle, which she laid beside the dagger. "I shall convince Ghron that it is best to wait," she said. "My heart had hoped, Hadron of Hastor, that you would decide to remain with me, but I am glad that I have not been mistaken in my estimate of your character. You will die, my warrior, but at least you will die as a brave man should and undefiled. Good-bye! I look upon you in life for the last time, but until I am gathered to my ancestors your image shall remain enshrined within my heart."

She was gone; the partition dropped, and again we were left in the semi-darkness of a moonlit night, but now we had the two things that I most desired – a dagger and a needle.

"Of what good are those?" asked Nur An as I gathered the two articles from the floor.

"You will see," I replied, and immediately I set to work cutting the fabric from the walls of our cell and then, standing upon Nur An's shoulders, I removed also that which covered the ceiling. I worked quickly for I knew that we had little time in which to accomplish that which I had set out to do. A mad scheme it was, and yet withal within the realms of practicability.

Working in the dark, more by sense of feel than by sight, I must have been inspired by some higher power to have accomplished with any degree of perfection the task that I had set myself.

The balance of that night and all of the following day Nur An and I labored without rest until we had fashioned an enormous bag from the fabric that had covered the walls and ceiling of our cell and from the scraps that remained we fashioned long ropes and when night fell again our task was completed.

"May luck be with us," I said.

"The scheme is worthy of the mad brain of Ghron himself," said Nur An; "yet it has within it the potentialities of success."

"Night has fallen," I said; "we need not delay longer. Of one thing, however, we may be sure, whether we succeed or fail we shall have escaped the fire and in either event may our ancestors look with love and compassion upon Sharu, whose friendship has made possible our attempt."

"Whose love," corrected Nur An.

Once again I made the perilous ascent to the roof, taking one of our new-made ropes with me. Then, from the summit, I lowered it to Nur An, who fastened the great bag to it; after which I drew the fruits of our labors carefully to the roof beside me. It was as light as a feather, yet stronger than the well-tanned hide of a zitidar. Next, I lowered the rope and assisted Nur An to my side, but not until he had replaced the bar that we had removed from the window.

Attached to the bottom of our bag, which was open, were a number of long cords, terminating in loops. Through these loops we passed the longest rope that we had made – a rope so long that it entirely encircled the circumference of the tower – when we lowered it below the projecting eaves. We made it fast there, but with a slip knot that could be instantly released with a single jerk.

Next, we slid the loops at the end of the ropes attached to the bottom of the bag along the cord that encircled the tower below the eaves until we had maneuvered the opening of the bag directly over the mouth of the flue leading down into the furnace of death in the pits of Ghasta.

Standing upon either side of the flue Nur An and I lifted the bag until it commenced to fill with the hot air rushing from the chimney. Presently it was sufficiently inflated to remain in an erect position, whereupon, leaving Nur An to steady it, I moved the loops until they were at equal distances from one another, thus anchoring the bag directly over the center of the flue. Then I passed another rope loosely through the loops and secured its end together, and to opposite sides of this rope Nur An and I snapped the boarding hooks that are a part of the harness of every Barsoomian warrior, the primary purpose of which is to lower boarding parties from the deck of one ship to that of another directly below, but which in practice are used in countless ways and numerous emergencies.

Then we waited; Nur An ready to slip the knot that held the rope around the tower beneath the eaves and I, upon the opposite side, with Sharu's sharp dagger prepared to cut the rope upon my side.

I saw the great bag that we had made filling with hot air. At first, loosely inflated, it rocked and swayed, but presently, its sides distended, it strained upward. Its fabric stretched tightly until I thought that it should burst. It tugged and pulled at its restraining cords, and yet I waited.

Down in the valley of Hohr there was little or no wind, which greatly facilitated the carrying out of our rash venture.

The great bag, almost as large as the room in which we had been confined, bellied above us. It strained upon its guy ropes in its impatience to be aloft until I wondered that they held, and then I gave the word.

Simultaneously Nur An slipped his knot and I severed the rope upon the opposite side. Freed, the great bag leaped aloft, snapping us in its wake. It shot upward with a velocity that was astounding until the valley of Hohr was but a little hollow in the surface of the great world that lay below us.

Presently a wind caught us and you may be assured that we gave thanks to our ancestors as we realized that we were at last drifting from above the cruel city of Ghasta. The wind increased until it was blowing rapidly in a northeasterly direction, but little did we care where it wafted us as long as it took us away from the river Syl and the valley of Hohr.

After we had passed beyond the crater of the ancient volcano, which formed the bed of the valley in which lay somber Ghasta, we saw below us, in the moonlight, a rough volcanic country that presented a weird and impressive appearance of unreality; deep chasms and tumbled piles of basalt seemed to present an unsurmountable barrier to man, which may explain why in this remote and desolate corner of Barsoom the valley of Hohr had lain for countless ages undiscovered.

The wind increased. Floating at a great altitude we were being carried at considerable speed, yet I could see that we were very slowly falling as the hot air within our bag cooled. How much longer it would keep us up I could not guess, but I hoped it would bear us at least beyond the uninviting terrain beneath us.

With the coming of dawn we were floating but a few hundred feet above the ground; the volcanic country was far behind us and as far as we could see stretched lovely, rolling hills, sparsely timbered with the drought-resisting skeel upon which it has been said the civilization of Barsoom has been erected.

As we topped a low hill, passing over it by a scant fifty sofads we saw below us a building of gleaming white. Like all the cities and isolated buildings of Barsoom, it was surrounded by a lofty wall, but in other respects it differed materially from the usual Barsoomian type of architecture. The edifice, which was made up of a number of buildings, was not surmounted by the usual towers, domes and minarets that mark all Barsoomian cities and which only in recent ages have been giving way slowly to the flat landing stages of an aerial world. The structure below us was composed of a number of flat-roofed buildings of various heights, none of which, however, appeared to rise over four levels. Between the buildings and the outer walls and in several open courts between the buildings, there was a profusion of trees and shrubbery with scarlet sward and well kept paths. It was, in fact, a striking and beautiful sight, yet having so recently been lured to near destruction by the beauties of Hohr and the engaging allurements of her beautiful women, we had no mind to be deceived again by external appearances. We would float over the palace of enchantment and take our chances in the open country beyond.

But Fate willed otherwise. The wind had abated; we were dropping rapidly; beneath us we saw people in the garden of the building and simultaneously, as they discovered us, it was evident that they were filled with consternation. They hastened quickly to the nearest entrances and there was not a human being in sight when we finally came to rest upon the roof of one of the taller sections of the structure.

As we extricated ourselves from the loops in which we had been sitting, the great bag, relieved of our weight, rose quickly into the air for a short distance, turned completely over and dropped to the ground just beyond the outer wall. It had served us well and now it seemed like a living thing that had given up its life for our salvation.

We were to have little time, however, for sentimental regrets, for almost immediately a head appeared through a small opening in the roof upon which we stood. The head was followed by the body of a man, whose harness was so scant as to leave him almost nude. He was an old man with a finely shaped head, covered with scant, gray locks.

Apparent physical old age is so rare upon Barsoom as always to attract immediate attention. In the natural span of life we live often to a thousand years, but during that long period our appearance seldom changes but little. It is true that most of us meet violent death long before we reach old age, but there are some who pass the allotted span of life and others who do not care for themselves so well and these few constitute the physically old among us; evidently of such was the little old man who confronted us.

At sight of him Nur An voiced an exclamation of pleased surprise. "Phor Tak!" he cried.

"Heigh-oo!" cackled the old man in a high falsetto. "Who cometh from the high heavens who knows old Phor Tak?"

"It is I – Nur An!" exclaimed my friend.

"Heigh-oo!" cried Phor Tak. "Nur An – one of Tul Axtar's pets."

"As you once were, Phor Tak."

"But not now – not now," almost screamed the old man. "The tyrant squeezed me like some juicy fruit and then cast the empty rind aside. Heigh-oo! He thought it was empty, but I pray daily to all my ancestors that he may live to know that he was wrong. I can say this with safety to you. Nur An, for I have you in my power and I promise you that you shall never live to carry word of my whereabouts to Tul Axtar."

"Do not fear, Phor Tak," said Nur An. "I, too, have suffered from the villainy of the Jeddak of Jahar. You were permitted to leave the capital in peace, but all my property was confiscated and I was sentenced to death."

"Heigh-oo! Then you hate him, too," exclaimed the old man.

"Hate is a weak word to describe my feeling for Tul Axtar," replied my friend.

"It is well," said Phor Tak. "When I saw you descending from the skies I thought that my ancestors had sent you to help me, and I know that it was indeed true. Be this another warrior from Jahar?" he added, nodding his old head toward me.

"No, Phor Tak," replied Nur An. "This is Hadron of Hastor, a noble of Helium, but he, too, has been wronged by Jahar."

"Good!" exclaimed the old man. "Now there are three of us. Heretofore I have had only slaves and women to assist me, but now with two trained warriors, young and strong, the goal of my triumph appears almost in sight."

As the two men conversed I had recalled that part of the story that Nur An had told me in the pits of Tjanath which related to Phor Tak and his invention of the rifle that projected the disintegrating rays which had proved so deadly against the patrol boat above Helium the night of Sanoma Tora's abduction. Strange, indeed, was fate that it should have brought me into the palace of the man who held the secret that might mean so much to Helium and to all Barsoom. Strange, too, and devious had been the path along which Fate had led me, yet I knew that my ancestors were guiding me and that all must have been arranged to some good end.

When Phor Tak had heard only a portion of our story he insisted that we must be both fatigued and hungry and, like the good host that he proved to be, he conducted us down to the interior of his palace and, summoning slaves, ordered that we be bathed and fed and then permitted to retire until we were rested. We thanked him for his kindness and consideration, of which we were glad to avail ourselves.

The days that followed were both interesting and profitable. Phor Tak, surrounded only by a few faithful slaves who had followed him into his exile, was delighted with our company and with the assistance which we could give him in his experiment, which, once assured of our loyalty, he explained to us in detail.

He told us the story of his wanderings after he had left Jahar and of how he had stumbled upon this long deserted castle, whose builder and occupants had left no record other than their bones. He told us that when he discovered it skeletons had strewn the courtyard and in the main entrance were piled the bones of a score of warriors, attesting the fierce defense that the occupants had waged against some unknown enemy, while in many of the upper rooms he had found other skeletons – the skeletons of women and children.

"I believe," he said, "that the place was beset by members of some savage horde of green warriors that left not a single survivor. The courts and gardens were overgrown with weeds and the interior of the building was filled with dust, but otherwise little damage had been done. I call it Jhama, and here I am carrying on my life's work."

"And that?" I asked.

"Revenge upon Tul Axtar," said the old man. "I gave him the disintegrating ray; I gave him the insulating paint that protects his own ships and weapons from it, and now some day I shall give him something else – something that will be as revolutionary in the art of war as the disintegrating ray itself; something that will cast the fleet of Jahar broken wrecks upon the ground; something that will search out the palace of Tul Axtar and bury the tyrant beneath its ruins."

We had not been long at Jhama before both Nur An and I became convinced that Phor Tak's mind was at least slightly deranged from long brooding over the wrongs inflicted upon him by Tul Axtar; though naturally possessed of a kindly disposition he was obsessed by a maniacal desire to wreak vengeance upon the tyrant with utter disregard of the consequences to himself and to others. Upon this single subject he was beyond the influence of reason and having established to his own satisfaction that Nur An and I were potential factors in the successful accomplishment of his design, he would fly into a perfect frenzy of rage whenever I broached the subject of our departure.

Fretting as I was beneath the urge to push on to Jahar and the rescue of Sanoma Tora, I could but illy brook this enforced delay, but Phor Tak was adamant – he would not permit me to depart – and the absolute loyalty of his slaves made it possible for him to enforce his will. In our hearing he explained to them that we were guests, honored guests as long as we made no effort to depart without his permission, but should they discover us in an attempt to leave Jhama surreptitiously they were to destroy us.

Nur An and I discussed the matter at length. We had discovered that four thousand haads of difficult and unfriendly country lay between us and Jahar. Being without a ship and without thoats there was little likelihood that we should be able to reach Jahar in time to be of service to Sanoma Tora, if we ever reached it at all, and so we agreed to bide our time, impressing Phor Tak with our willingness to aid him in the hope that eventually we should be able to enlist his aid and support, and so successful were we that within a short time we had so won the confidence of the old scientist that we began to entertain hope that he would take us into his innermost confidence and reveal the nature of the instrument of destruction which he was preparing for Tul Axtar.

I must admit that I was principally interested in his invention because I was confident that in order to utilize it against Tul Axtar he must find some means of transporting it to Jahar and in this I saw an opportunity for reaching the capital of the tyrant myself.

We had been in Jhama about ten days during which time Phor Tak exhibited signs of extreme nervousness and irritability. He kept us with him practically all of the time that he was not closeted in the innermost recesses of his secret laboratory.

During the evening meal upon the tenth day Phor Tak seemed more distraught than ever. Talking, as usual, interminably about his hatred of Tul Axtar, his countenance assumed an expression of maniacal fury.

"But I am helpless," he almost screamed at last. "I am helpless because there is no one to whom I may entrust my secret, who also has the courage and intelligence to carry out my plan. I am too old, too weak to undergo the hardships that would mean nothing to young men like you, but which must be undergone if I am to fulfill my destiny as the savior of Jahar. If I could but trust you! If I could but trust you!"

"Perhaps you can, Phor Tak," I suggested.

The words or my tone seemed to soothe him. "Heigh-oo!" he exclaimed. "Sometimes I almost think that I can."

"We have a common aim," I said; "or at least different aims which converge at the same point – Jahar. Let us work together then. We wish to reach Jahar. If you can help us, we will help you."

He sat in silent thought for a long moment. "I'll do it," he said. "Heigh-oo! I'll do it. Come," and rising from his chair he led us toward the locked doorway that barred the entrance to his secret laboratory.

CHAPTER TEN
The Flying Death

Phor Tak's laboratory occupied an entire wing of the building and consisted of a single, immense room fully fifty feet in height. His benches, tables, instruments and cabinets, located in one corner, were lost in the great interior. Near the ceiling and encircling the room was a single track from which was suspended a miniature cruiser, painted the ghastly blue of Jahar. Upon one of the benches was a cylindrical object about as long as one's hand. These were the only noticeable features of the laboratory other than its immense emptiness.

As Phor Tak ushered us within, he closed the door behind him and I heard the ominous click of the ponderous lock. There was something depressing in the suggestiveness of the situation induced, perhaps, by our knowledge that Phor Tak was mad and accentuated by the eerie mystery of the vasty chamber.

Leading us to the bench upon which lay the cylindrical object which had attracted my attention, he lifted it carefully, almost caressingly, from its resting place. "This," he said, "is a model of the device that will destroy Jahar. In it you behold the concentrated essence of scientific achievement. In appearance it is but a small metal cylinder, but within it is a mechanism as delicate and as sensitive as the human brain and you will perceive that it functions almost as though animated by a mind within itself, but it is purely mechanical and may be produced in quantities quickly and at low cost. Before I explain it further I shall demonstrate one phase of its possibilities. Watch!"

Still holding the cylinder in his hand, Phor Tak stepped to a shallow cabinet against the wall and opening it revealed an elaborate equipment of switches, levers and push buttons. "Now watch the miniature flier suspended from the track near the ceiling," he directed, at the same time closing a switch. Immediately the flier commenced to travel along the track at considerable speed. Now Phor Tak pressed a button upon the top of the cylinder, which immediately sped from his extended palm, turned quickly in the air and rushed straight for the speeding flier. Slowly the distance between the two closed; the cylinder, curving gradually into the line of flight of the flier, was now trailing directly behind it, its pointed nose but a few feet from the stern of the miniature ship. Then Phor Tak pulled a tiny lever upon his switchboard and the flier leaped forward at accelerated speed. Instantly the speed of the cylinder increased and I could see that it was gaining in velocity much more rapidly than the flier. Half way around the room again its nose struck the stem of the fleeing craft with sufficient severity to cause the ship to tremble from stem to stern; then the cylinder fell away and floated gently toward the floor. Phor Tak opened a switch that stopped the flier in its flight and then, running forward, caught the descending cylinder in his hand.

"This model," he explained, as he returned to where we stood, "is so constructed that when it makes contact with the flier it will float gently downward to the floor, but as you have doubtless fully realized ere this, the finished product in practical use will explode upon contact with the ship. Note these tiny buttons with which it is covered. When any one of these comes in contact with an object, the model stops and descends, whereas the full-sized device, properly equipped, will explode, absolutely demolishing whatever it may have come in contact with. As you are aware every substance in the universe has its own fixed vibratory rate. This mechanism can be so attuned as to be attracted by the vibratory rate of any substance. The model, for example, is attracted by the blue protective paint with which the flier is covered. Imagine a fleet of Jaharian warship moving majestically through the air in battle formation. From an enemy ship or from the ground and at a distance so far as to be unobservable by the ships of Jahar, I release as many of these devices as there are ships in the fleet, allowing a few moments to elapse between launchings. The first torpedo rushes toward the fleet and destroys the nearest ship. All the torpedoes in the rear, strung out in line, are attracted by the combined masses of all the blue protecting coverings of the entire fleet. The first ship is falling to the ground and though all of its paint may not have been destroyed, it has not the power to deflect any of the succeeding torpedoes, which one by one destroy the nearest of the remaining ships until the fleet has been absolutely erased. I have destroyed a great fleet without risking the life of a single man of my own following."

"But they will see the torpedoes coming," suggested Nur An, "and they will devise some defense. Even gunfire might stop many of them."

"Heigh-oo! But I have thought of that," cackled Phor Tak. He laid the torpedo upon a bench and opened another cabinet.

In this cabinet were a number of receptacles, some tightly sealed and others opened, revealing their contents which appeared to be different colored paints. From a number of these receptacles protruded the handles of paint brushes. One such handle, however, appeared to hang in midair, a few inches above one of the shelves, while just beneath it was a section of the rim of a receptacle that also appeared to be resting upon nothing. Phor Tak placed his open hand directly beneath this floating rim and when he removed his hand from the cabinet, the rim of the receptacle and the portion of the handle of the paint brush, floating just above it, followed, hovering just over his extended fingers, which were cupped in the position that they might assume were they holding a glass jar, such as would ordinarily have belonged to a rim like that which I could see floating about an inch above his fingers.

Going to the bench where he had laid the cylinder, Phor Tak went through the motions of setting a jar upon it, and, though there was no jar visible other than the floating rim, I distinctly heard a noise that was identical with the sound which the bottom of a glass jar would have made in coming in contact with the bench.

I can assure you that I was greatly mystified, but still more so by the events immediately following. Phor Tak seized the handle of the paint brush and made a pass a few inches above the metal torpedo. Instantly a portion of the torpedo, about an inch wide and three or four inches long, disappeared. Pass after pass he made until finally the whole surface of the torpedo had disappeared. Where it had rested the bench was empty. Phor Tak returned the handle of the paint brush to its floating position just above the floating jar rim and then he turned to us with an expression of child-like pride upon his face, as much to say, "Well, what do you think of that? Am I not wonderful?" And I was certainly forced to concede that it was wonderful and that I was entirely baffled and mystified by what I had seen.

"There, Nur An," exclaimed Phor Tak, "is the answer to your criticism of The Flying Death."

"I do not understand," said Nur An with a puzzled expression upon his face.

"Heigh-oo!" cried Phor Tak. "Have you not seen me render the device invisible?"

"But it is gone," said Nur An.

Phor Tak laughed his high cackling laugh. "It is still there," he said, "but you cannot see it. Here," and he took Nur An's hand and guided it toward the spot where the device had been.

I could see Nur An's fingers apparently feeling over the surface of something several inches above the top of the table. "By my first ancestor, it is still there!" he exclaimed.

"It is wonderful," I exclaimed. "You did not even touch it; you merely made passes above it with the handle of a paint brush and it disappeared."

"But I did touch it," insisted Phor Tak. "The brush was there, but you did not see it because it was covered by the substance which renders The Flying Death invisible. Notice this transparent glass receptacle in which I keep the compound of invisibility and all that you can see of it is that part of the rim which, by chance, has not been coated with the compound."

"Marvelous!" I exclaimed. "Even now, although I have witnessed it with my own eyes I can scarce conceive of the possibility of such a miracle."

"It is no miracle," said Phor Tak. "It is merely the application of scientific principles well known to me for hundreds of years. Nothing moves in straight lines; light, vision, electromagnetic forces follow lines that curve. The compound of invisibility merely bows outward the reflected light, which, entering our eyes and impinging upon our optic nerves, results in the phenomenon which we call vision, so that they pass around any object which is coated with the compound. When I first started to apply the compound to The Flying Death, your line of vision was deflected around the small portions so coated, but when I coated the entire surface of the torpedo, the curve of your vision passed completely around it on both sides so that you could plainly see the bench upon which it was resting precisely as though the device had not been there."

I was astounded at the apparent simplicity of the explanation, and, naturally, being a soldier, I saw the tremendous advantage that the possession of these two scientific secrets would impart to the nation which controlled them. For the safety; yes, for the very existence of Helium, I must possess them and if that were impossible, then Phor Tak must be destroyed before the secret of this infernal power could be passed on to any other nation. Perhaps I could so ingratiate myself with old Phor Tak as to be able to persuade him to turn these secrets over to Helium in return for Helium's assistance in the work of wreaking his vengeance upon Tul Axtar.

"Phor Tak," I said, "you hold here within your grasp two secrets which in the hands of a kindly and beneficent power would bring eternal peace to Barsoom."

"Heigh-oo!" he cried. "I do not want peace. I want war. War! War!"

"Very well," I agreed, realizing that my suggestion had not been in line with the mad processes of his crazed brain. "Let us have war then, and what country upon Barsoom is better equipped to wage war than Helium? If you want war, form an alliance with Helium."

"I do not need Helium," he cried. "I do not need to form alliances. I shall make war – I shall make war alone. With the invisible Flying Death I can destroy whole navies, whole cities, entire nations. I shall start with Jahar. Tul Axtar shall be the first to feel the weight of my devastating powers. When the fleet of Jahar has tumbled upon the roofs of Jahar and the walls of Jahar have fallen about the ears of Tul Axtar, then shall I destroy Tjanath. Helium shall know me next. Proud and mighty Helium shall tremble and bow at the feet of Phor Tak. I shall be Jeddak of Jeddaks, ruler of a world." As he spoke his voice rose to a piercing shriek and he trembled in the grip of the frenzy that held him.

He must be destroyed, not alone for the sake of Helium, but for the sake of all Barsoom; this mad mind must be removed if I found that it was impossible to direct or cajole it to my own ends. I determined, however, to omit no sacrifice that might tend to bring about a satisfactory conclusion to this strange adventure. I knew that mad minds were sometimes fickle minds and I hoped that in a moment of insane caprice Phor Tak might reveal to me the secret of The Flying Death and the compound of invisibility. This hope was his temporary reprieve from death; its fulfillment would be his pardon, but I knew that I must work warily – that at the slightest suggestion of duplicity, Phor Tak's suspicions would be aroused and that I should then be the one to be destroyed.

I tossed long upon my sleeping silks and furs that night in troubled thought and planning. I felt that I must possess these secrets; yet how? That they existed within his brain alone, I knew, for he had told me that there were no written formulas, or plans or specifications for either of them. Somehow I must wheedle them out of him and the best way to start was to ingratiate myself with him. To this end I must further his plans insofar as I possibly could.

Just before I fell asleep my thoughts reverted to Sanoma Tora and to the urgent mission that had led me to enter upon what had developed into the strangest adventure of my career. I felt a twinge of self-reproach as I suddenly realized that Sanoma Tora had not been uppermost in my mind while I had lain there making plans for the future, but now with recollection of her a plan was suggested whereby I might not only succor her but also advance myself in the good graces of Phor Tak at the same time, and, thus relieved, I fell asleep.

It was late the following morning before I had an opportunity to speak with the old inventor when I immediately broached the subject that was uppermost in my mind. "Phor Tak," I said, "you are handicapped by lack of knowledge of conditions existing in Jahar and the size and location of the fleet. Nur An and I will go to Jahar for you and obtain the information that you must have if your plans are to be successful. In this way, Nur An and I will also be striking a blow at Tul Axtar while we will be in a position to attend to those matters which require our presence in Jahar."

"But how will you get to Jahar?" demanded Phor Tak.

"Could not you let us take a flier?" I asked.

"I have none," replied Phor Tak. "I know nothing about them. I am not interested in them. I could not even build one."

To say that I was both surprised and shocked would be putting it mildly, but if I had previously entertained any doubts that Phor Tak's brain was abnormally developed, it would have vanished with his admission that he knew nothing about fliers, for it seemed to me that there was scarcely a man, woman or child in any of the flying nations of Barsoom but could have constructed some sort of a flier.

"But how without fliers did you expect to transport The Flying Death to the vicinity of the Jaharian fleet? How did you expect to demolish the palace of Tul Axtar, or reduce the city of Jahar to ruins?"

"Now that you and Nur An are here to help me, I can set my slaves to work under you and easily turn out a dozen torpedoes a day. As these are completed they will immediately be launched and eventually they will find their way to Jahar and the fleet. Of that there is no doubt, even if it takes a year they will eventually find their prey."

"If nothing chances to get in their way," I suggested; "but even so what pleasure will you derive from your revenge if you are unable to witness any part of it?"

"Heigh-oo! I have thought of that," replied Phor Tak, "but one may not have everything."

"You may have that," I told him.

"And how?" he demanded.

"By taking your torpedoes aboard a ship and flying to Jahar," I replied.

"No," he exclaimed stubbornly, "I shall do it my own way. What right have you to interfere with my plans?"

"I merely want to help you," I said, attempting to mollify him by a conciliatory tone and attitude.

"And there is another thought," said Nur An, "that suggests that it might be expedient to follow Hadron's plans."

"You are both against me," said Phor Tak.

"By no means," Nur An assured him. "It is our keen desire to aid you that prompts the suggestion."

"Well, what is yours then?" asked the old man.

"Your plan contemplates the destruction of the navies of Tjanath and Helium following the fall of Jahar," exclaimed Nur An. "This, at least in respect to the navy of Helium, you cannot possibly hope to accomplish at so great a distance and without any knowledge of the number of ships to be destroyed, nor will your torpedoes be similarly attracted to them as they are to the ships of Jahar because the ships of these other nations are not protected by the blue paint of Jahar. It will, therefore, be necessary for you to proceed to the vicinity of Tjanath and later to Helium and for your own protection you will use the blue paint of Jahar upon your ship, for you may never be certain unless you are on the ground at the time that you have destroyed all of the navy of Jahar, or all of their disintegrating ray rifles."

"That is true," said Phor Tak thoughtfully.

"And furthermore," continued Nur An, "if you dispatch more than the necessary number of torpedoes, those that remain at large will certainly be attracted by the blue paint of your own ship and you will be destroyed by your own devices."

"You ruin all my plans," screamed Phor Tak. "Why did you think of this?"

"If I had not thought of it you would have been destroyed," Nur An reminded him.

"Well, what am I to do about it? I have no ship. I cannot build a ship."

"We can get you one," I said.

"How?"

The conversation between Nur An and Phor Tak had suggested a plan to me and this I now explained roughly to them. Nur An was enthusiastic over the idea, but Phor Tak was not particularly keen for it. I could not understand the grounds for his objection, nor, as a matter of fact, did they interest me greatly since he finally admitted that he would be compelled to act in accordance with my suggestion.

Immediately adjacent to Phor Tak's laboratory was a well equipped machine shop and here Nur An and I labored for weeks utilizing the services of a dozen slaves until we had succeeded in constructing what I am sure was the most remarkable-looking airship that it had ever fallen to my lot to behold. Briefly, it was a cylinder pointed at each end and closely resembled the model of The Flying Death. Within the outer shell was another smaller cylinder; between the walls of these two we placed the buoyancy tanks. The tanks and the sides of the two envelopes were pierced by observation ports along each side of the ship and at the bow and stern. These ports could be completely covered by shutters hinged upon the outside, but operated from within. There were two hatchways in the keel and two above which led to a narrow walkway along the top of the cylinder. In turrets, forward, and aft were mounted two disintegrating ray rifles. Above the controls was a periscope that transmitted an image of all that came within its range to a ground glass plate in front of the pilot. The entire outside of the ship was first painted the ghastly blue that would protect it from the disintegrating ray rifles of Jahar, while over this was spread a coating of the compound of invisibility. The shutters that covered the ports being similarly coated, the ship could attain practically total invisibility by closing them, the only point remaining visible being the tiny eye of the periscope.

Not possessing sufficient technical knowledge to enable me to build one of the new type motors, I had to content myself with one of the old types of much less efficiency.

At last the work was done. We had a ship that would accommodate four with ease and it was uncanny to realize this fact and yet, at the same time, be unable to see anything but the tiny eyes of the periscope when the covers were lowered over the ports, and even the eye of the periscope was invisible unless it was turned in the direction of the observer.

As the work neared completion I had noticed that Phor Tak's manner became more marked by nervousness and irritability. He found fault with everything and on several occasions he almost stopped the work upon the ship.

Now, at last, we were ready to sail. The ship was stocked with ammunition, water and provisions, and at the last minute I installed a destination control compass for which I was afterward to be devoutly thankful.

When I suggested immediate departure, however, Phor Tak demurred, but would give me no reason for his objection.

Presently, however, I lost patience and told the old man that we were going anyway whether he liked it or not.

He did not fly into a rage as I had expected, but laughed instead, and there was something in the laugh that seemed more terrible than anger.

"You think I am a fool," he said, "and that I will let you go and carry my secrets to Tul Axtar, but you are mistaken."

"So are you," I snapped. "You are mistaken in thinking that we would betray you and you are also mistaken in thinking that you can prevent our departure."

"Heigh-oo!" he cackled. "I do not need to prevent your departure, but I can prevent your arrival at Jahar or elsewhere. I have not been idle while you worked upon this ship. I have constructed a full-size Flying Death. It is attuned to search out this ship. If you depart against my wishes, it will follow and destroy you. Heigh-oo! What do you think of that?"

"I think that you are an old fool," I cried in exasperation. "You have the opportunity to enlist the loyal aid of two honorable warriors and yet you choose to turn them into enemies."

"Enemies who cannot harm me," he reminded me. "I hold your lives in the hollow of my hand. Well have you concealed your thoughts from me, but not quite well enough. I have read enough of them to know that you think me mad and I have also received the impression that you would stop at nothing to prevent me from using my power against Helium. I have no doubt but that you will help me against Jahar, and against Tjanath, too, perhaps, but Helium, the mightiest and proudest empire of Barsoom, is my real goal. Helium shall proclaim me Jeddak of Jeddaks if I have to wreck a world to accomplish my design."

"Then all our work has been for nothing?" I demanded. "We are not going to use the ship we have constructed?"

"We may use it," he said, "but under my terms."

"And what are they?" I asked.

"You may go alone to Jahar, but I shall keep Nur An here as hostage. If you betray me, he dies."

There was no moving him; no amount of argument could alter his determination. I tried to convince him that one man could accomplish little, that, in fact, he might not be able to accomplish anything, but he was adamant – I should go alone or not at all.

CHAPTER ELEVEN

"Let the Fire be Hot!"

As I AROSE THAT NIGHT into the starlit splendor of a Barsoomian night, the white castle of Phor Tak lay a lovely gem below me bathed in the soft light of Thuria. I was alone; Nur An remained behind the hostage of the mad scientist. Because of him I must return to Jhama. Nur An had exacted no promise from me, but he knew that I would return.

Twenty-five hundred haads to the east lay Jahar and Sanoma Tora. Fifteen hundred haads to the southwest were Tjanath and Tavia. I turned the nose of my flier toward the goal of duty, toward the woman I loved, and, with throttle wide, my invisible craft sped toward distant Jahar.

But my thoughts I could not control. Despite my every effort to keep them concentrated upon the purpose of my adventure, they persisted in wandering to a prison tower, to a tousled head of refractory hair, to a rounded shoulder that had once pressed mine. I shook myself to be rid of the vision as I sped through the night, but it constantly returned and in its wake came harrowing thoughts of the fate that might have overtaken Tavia during my absence.

I set my destination control compass upon Jahar, the exact position of which I had obtained from Phor Tak, and thus relieved of the necessity of constantly remaining at the controls, I busied myself about the interior of the ship. I looked to the ammunition of the disintegrating ray rifles and rearranged it to suit my own ideas.

Phor Tak had equipped me with three types of rays; one would disintegrate metal, another would disintegrate wood and the third would disintegrate human flesh. I had also brought along something which Phor Tak had refused me when I had asked him for it. I pressed the pocket pouch in which I had placed it to make sure that I still had the vial, the contents of which I imagined might prove of inestimable value to me.

I raised all the port shutters and adjusted the ventilators, for at best the interior of this strange ship seemed close and stuffy to one who was accustomed to the open deck of the fast scout fliers of Helium. Then I spread my sleeping silks and furs and settled myself down to rest, knowing that when I arrived at Jahar my destination control compass would stop the ship and an alarm would awaken me if I still slept, but sleep would not come. I thought of Sanoma Tora. I visualized her cold and stately beauty, but always her haughty eyes dissolved into the eyes of Tavia, sparkling with the joy of life, soft with the light of friendship.

I was far from Jhama when at last I sprang determinedly from my sleeping silks and furs, and going to the controls, I cut off the destination control compass and with a single, swift turn swung the nose of the flier toward Tjanath.

The die was cast. I felt that I should experience remorse and self loathing, but I experienced neither. I joyed in the thought that I was rushing to the service of a friend and I knew in the most innermost recesses of my heart that of the two, Tavia had more claim upon my friendship than had Sanoma Tora, from, whom I had received at best only scant courtesy.

I did not again try to sleep. I did not feel like sleeping; instead I remained at the controls and watched the desolate landscape as it rushed forward to pass beneath me. With the coming of dawn I saw Tjanath directly ahead of me and as I approached the city it was difficult for me to realize that I could do so with utter impunity and that my ship with its closed ports was entirely invisible. Moving slowly now, I circled above the palace of Haj Osis. Those portions of the palace that were topped by flat roofs revealed sleepy guardsmen. At the main hangar a single guardsman watched.

I floated above the east tower; beneath me, cuddled in her sleeping silks and furs, I could picture Tavia. How surprised she would he could she know that I hovered thus close above her.

Dropping lower I circled the tower, coming to a stop finally opposite the windows of the room in which Tavia had been confined. I maneuvered the ship to bring one of the ports opposite the window and close enough to give me a view of the interior of the room. But though I remained there for some time, I could see no one and at last I became convinced that Tavia had been removed to other quarters. I was disappointed for this must necessarily greatly complicate my plans for rescue. I had foreseen but little difficulty in transferring Tavia by night through the tower window to the flier; now I must make my plans all anew. Everything hinged, of course, upon my ability to locate Tavia. To do that it was evident that I must enter the palace. The moment that I quitted the invisibility of my flier, I should be menaced by the greatest danger at every turn, and, clothed as I was in home-made harness fashioned by the hands of the slaves of Phor Tak, I should arouse the active suspicion of the first person who laid eyes upon me.

I must enter the palace and to do it in any degree of safety I must have a disguise.

All my ports were now closed, the periscope being my only eye. I turned it slowly about as I tried to plan some method of procedure that might have within it some tiny seed of success.

As the panorama slowly unfolded itself upon the ground glass before me there appeared the main palace hangar and the single warrior upon watch. Here my periscope came to rest, for here was an entrance to the palace and here a disguise.

Slowly maneuvering my ship in the direction of the hangar, I brought it down upon the roof of that structure. I should have been glad to moor it, but here there were no means at hand. I must depend upon its own weight and hope that no high wind would rise.

Realizing that the instant that I emerged from the interior of the flier I should be entirely visible, I waited, watching through my periscope until the warrior upon the roof just below me turned his back; then I emerged quickly from the ship through one of the upper hatches and dropped to the roof upon the side closest to the warrior. I was about four feet from the edge of the roof and he was standing almost below me, his back toward me. Should he turn he would discover me instantly and would give an alarm before I could be upon him. My only hope of success, therefore, was to silence him before he realized that he was menaced.

I have learned from the experiences of John Carter that first thoughts are often inspirations, while sober afterthought may lead to failure, or so delay action as to nullify all its effect.

Therefore, in this instance, I acted upon inspiration. I did not hesitate. I stepped quickly to the edge of the roof and hurled myself straight at the broad shoulders of the sentry. In my hand was a slim dagger.

The end came quickly. I think the poor fellow never knew what happened to him. Dragging his body to the interior of the hangar I stripped the harness from it, at the same time, though almost mechanically, I noted the ships within the hangar. With the exception of one, a patrol boat, they all bore the personal insignia of the Jed of Tjanath. They were the king's ships – an ornate cruiser heavily armed, two smaller pleasure crafts, a two-man scout flier and a one-man scout flier. They were not much, of course, by comparison with the ships of Helium, but I was quite sure that they were absolutely the best that Tjanath could afford. However, having my own ship, I was not particularly concerned with these other than that I am always interested in ships of all descriptions.

Not far from where I stood was the entrance to a ramp leading down into the palace. Realizing that only through boldness might I succeed, I walked directly to the ramp and entered it. As I rounded the first turn I was appalled to see that the ramp passed directly through a guard room. Upon the floor fully a score of warriors were stretched upon their sleeping silks and furs.

I did not dare to pause; I must keep on. Perhaps I could pass them without arousing their curiosity. I had had but a brief glimpse of the room before I entered it and in that glimpse I had seen only men apparently wrapped in sleep and an instant later, as I emerged into the room itself, I saw that it contained only those whom I had first seen. No one within it was awake, but I heard voices in an adjoining room. Hurrying quickly across the apartment I entered the ramp upon the opposite side.

I think my heart had stood still as I strode silently across that room among those sleeping men, for had a single one of them awakened he would have inevitably known that I was no fellow member of the guard.

Further down within the palace itself I should be in less danger, for so great is the number of retainers in the palace of a jed that no one may know them all by sight, so that strange and unfamiliar faces are almost as customary as they are upon the avenues of a city.

My plan was to try to reach the tower room in which Tavia had been confined, for I was positive that, from my position in the flier, I could not see the entire interior and it was just possible that Tavia was there.

Owing to the construction of my ship I had been unable to attract her attention without raising a hatch and taking the chance of revealing my presence, which would have, I felt, jeopardized Tavia's chances for escape far too greatly to warrant my doing so.

Perhaps I should have waited until night; perhaps I was overanxious and in my zeal I might be running far greater risks than were necessary. I thought of these things now and perhaps I upbraided myself, but I had gone too far now to retreat. I was properly in for it, whatever might follow.

As I followed the ramp down to different levels I tried to discover some familiar landmark that might lead me to the east tower, and as I emerged into a corridor at one of the levels I saw almost directly in front of me a door which I instantly recognized – it was the door to the office of Yo Seno, the keeper of the keys.

"Good!" I thought. "Fate certainly has led me here."

Crossing to the door I opened it and stepped quickly within the room, closing the door behind me. Yo Seno was sitting at his desk. He was alone. He did not look up. He was one of those arrogant men – a small man with a little authority – who liked to impress his importance upon all inferiors. Therefore, doubtless, it was his way to ignore his visitors for a moment or two. This time he made a mistake. After quietly locking the door behind me I crossed to the door at the opposite end of the room and bolted it, too.

It was then that, doubtless compelled by curiosity, Yo Seno looked up. At first he did not recognize me. "What do you want?" he demanded gruffly.

"You, Yo Seno," I said.

He looked at me steadily for a moment with growing astonishment, then with his eyes wide he leaped to his feet. "You?" he screamed. "By Issus, no! You are dead!"

"I have returned from the grave, Yo Seno. I have come back to haunt you," I said.

"What do you want?" he demanded. "Stand aside! You are under arrest."

"Where is Tavia?" I asked.

"How do I know?" he demanded.

"You are the keeper of the keys, Yo Seno. Who should know better than you where the prisoners are?"

"Well, what if I do know? I shall not tell," he said.

"You shall tell, Yo Seno, or you shall die." I warned him.

He had walked from behind his desk and was standing not far from me when, without warning and with far greater celerity than I gave him credit for possessing, he snatched his long sword from its scabbard and was upon me.

I was forced to jump backward quickly to avoid his first cut, but when he swung the second time my own sword was out and I was on my guard. Yo Seno proved himself no mean antagonist. He was clever with the sword and he knew that he was fighting for his life. I wondered at first why he did not call for help and then I came to the conclusion that it was because there were no warriors in the adjoining room, as there had been upon my previous visit to Yo Seno's quarters. We fought in silence, only the din of metal upon metal reflecting the deadliness of the combat.

I was in a hurry to be done with him and I was pressing him closely when he resorted to a trick which came near to proving my undoing. I had backed him up against his desk and thought that I had him where he could not escape. I could not see his left hand behind him; nor the heavy vase for which it was groping, but an instant later I saw the thing flying straight at my head and I also saw the opening which Yo Seno made in the instant that he cast the missile, for so occupied was he with his aim that he let his point drop. Stooping beneath the vase I sprang into close quarters, driving my sword through the heart of Yo Seno.

As I wiped the blood from my blade upon the hair of my victim I could not repress a feeling of elation that it had been my hand that had cut down the seducer of Phao and in some measure avenged the honor of my friend, Nur An.

Now, however, was no time for meditation. I heard footsteps approaching in the corridor without and hastily seizing the harness of the corpse, I dragged it toward the panel which hid the entrance to the secret corridor that led to the room in the east tower – that familiar corridor where I had passed happy moments alone with Tavia.

With more haste than reverence, I dumped the corpse of Yo Seno into the dark interior and then, closing the panel after me, I groped my way through the darkness toward the tower room, my heart high with the hope that I might find Tavia still there.

As I approached the panel at the tower end of the corridor I could feel my heart beating rapidly – a sensation to which I was unaccustomed and which I could not explain. I was positive that I was in excellent physical condition, and, while it is not at all unusual that surprise or imminent danger causes the heart of some men to palpitate, even though they may be endowed with exceptional courage, yet, for my part, I had never experienced such a sensation and I must admit that I was deeply mystified.

The anticipation of seeing Tavia again soon caused me to forget the unpleasant sensation and as I stopped behind the panel my whole mind was occupied with pleasurable consideration of what I hoped awaited me beyond – the longed for reunion with this best of friends.

I was upon the point of springing the catch and opening the panel when my attention was attracted by voices from the room beyond. I heard a man's voice and that of a woman, but I could understand no words. Cautiously, I opened the panel sufficiently to permit me to view the interior of the apartment.

The scene that met my gaze sent the hot fighting blood surging through my frame. In the center of the room a young warrior in rich trappings had Tavia in his grasp and was dragging her across the room toward the doorway. Tavia struggled, striking at him.

"Don't be a fool," snarled the man. "Haj Osis has given you to me. You will lead a better life as my slave than most free women live."

"I prefer prison or death," replied Tavia.

Phao was standing helplessly at one side, her eyes filled with compassion for Tavia. It was obvious that she could do nothing to defend her friend, for the trappings of the warrior proclaimed him of high rank, but just what that rank was I did not discern at the time for I was not interested. In a bound I was in the center of the room and seizing the warrior roughly by the shoulder, I hurled him backward so heavily that he fell sprawling to the floor. I heard gasps of astonishment from both Phao and Tavia and my name breathed in the soft accents of the latter.

As I drew my sword the warrior scrambled to his feet, but did not draw. "Fool! Idiot! Knave!" he shrieked. "Do you not realize what you have done? Do you not know who I am?"

"In a moment it will be 'who you were,'" I told him in a low voice. "On guard!"

"No," he cried, backing away. "You wear the harness and the metal of a warrior of the guard. You cannot dare draw your sword against the son of Haj Osis. Back, fellow, I am Prince Haj Alt."

"I could pray to Issus that you might be Haj Osis himself," I replied, "but at least there will be some recompense in the knowledge that I have destroyed his spawn. On guard, you fool, unless you wish to die like a sorak."

He was still backing away and now he looked about him with every evidence of terror written upon his weak countenance. He espied the panel door that I had inadvertently left open and before I could prevent he had darted through and closed it behind him. I leaped in pursuit, but the lock had clicked and I did not know where to find the mechanism to release it.

"Quick, Phao!" I cried. "You know the secret of the panel. Open it for me. We must not permit this fellow to escape or he will sound the alarm and we shall all be lost."

Phao ran quickly to my side and placed her thumb upon a button cleverly hidden in the ornate carving of the wood paneling that covered the wall. I waited in breathless expectancy, but the panel did not open. Phao pushed frantically again and again, and then she turned to me with a gesture of helplessness and defeat.

"He has tampered with the lock upon the other side," she said. "He is a clever rogue and he would have thought of that."

"We must follow," I said, and raising my long sword I struck the panel a heavy blow that would have shattered much thicker planking, but I only made a scratch upon it, tearing away a little piece scarce thicker than a fingernail, but the scar that I had made revealed the harrowing truth – the panel was constructed of forandus, the hardest and the lightest metal known to Barsoomians. I turned away. "It is useless," I said "to attempt to pierce forandus with cold steel."

Tavia had crossed to us and was standing in silence, looking up into my face. Her eyes were bathed with unshed tears and I saw her lips tremble. "Hadron!" she breathed. "You have come back from the dead. Oh, why did you come, for this time they will make no mistake."

"You know why I came, Tavia," I told her.

"Tell me," she said, very soft and low.

"For friendship, Tavia," I replied; "for the best friend that a man ever had."

At first she seemed surprised and then an odd little smile curved her lips. "I would rather have the friendship of Hadron of Hastor," she said, "than any other gift the world might give me."

It was a nice thing for her to say and I certainly appreciated it, but I did not understand that little smile. However, I had no time then in which to solve riddles; the problem of our safety was the all important question, and then it was that I thought of the vial in my pocket pouch. I looked quickly about the room. In one corner I espied a pile of sleeping silks and furs; something there might answer my purpose; the contents of the vial might yet give us all freedom if I had but time enough. I ran quickly across the room and searched rapidly until I had found three pieces of fabric that were at least best suited to my purpose than any of the others. I opened my pocket pouch to withdraw the vial and at the same instant I heard the pounding of running feet and the clank and clatter of arms.

Too late! They were already at the door. I closed my pocket pouch and waited. At first it was in my mind to take them on in combat as they entered, but I put that idea aside as worse than useless, since it could result in nothing but my death, whereas time might conjure an opportunity to use the contents of the vial.

The door swung open, fully fifty warriors were revealed in the corridor without. A padwar of the guard entered followed by his men. "Surrender!" he commanded.

"I have not drawn," I replied. "Come and take it."

"You admit that you are the warrior who attacked the prince, Haj Alt?" he demanded.

"I do," I replied.

"What have these women to do with it?"

"Nothing. I do not know them. I followed Haj Alt here because I thought that it would give me the opportunity that I have long sought to kill him."

"Why did you want to kill him?" demanded the padwar. "What grievance have you against the prince?"

"None," I replied. "I am a professional assassin and I was hired by others."

"Who are they?" he demanded.

I laughed at him, for I knew that he knew better than to ask a professional assassin of Barsoom such a question as that. The members of this ancient fraternity are guided by a code of ethics which they scrupulously observe and seldom, if ever, can anything persuade or force one of their number to divulge the name of his principal.

I saw Tavia's eyes upon me and it seemed to me that there was a little questioning expression in them, but I knew that she must know that I was lying thus to protect her and Phao.

I was hustled from the chamber and as I was being conducted along the corridors and down the ramps of the palace, the padwar questioned me in an endeavor to learn my true identity. I was greatly relieved to discover that they did not recognize me and I hoped that I might continue to escape recognition, not that it would make any difference in my fate for I realized that the direst would be inflicted upon one who had attempted to assassinate the prince of the house of Haj Osis, but I was afraid that were I to be recognized they might accuse Tavia of complicity in the attack upon Haj Alt and that she would be made to suffer accordingly.

Presently I found myself in the pits again and by chance in the very cell that Nur An and I had occupied. I experienced almost the sensations of a homecoming, but with variations. Once again I was alone, fettered to a stone wall. My only hope, the vial which they had overlooked and which still reposed at the bottom of my pocket pouch. But this was no time or place to use its contents, nor had I the requisite materials at hand even had I been unfettered.

I was not long in the pits this time before warriors came and, unlocking my fetters, conducted me to the great throne room of the palace, where Haj Osis sat upon his dais surrounded by the high officers and functionaries of his army and his court.

Haj Alt, the prince, was there and when he saw me being led toward the throne he trembled with rage. As I was halted in front of the jed, he turned to his son. "Is this the warrior who attacked you, Haj Alt?" he asked.

"This is the scoundrel," replied the younger man. "He took me by surprise and would have stabbed me in the back had I not managed to outwit him."

"He drew his sword against you," demanded Haj Osis – "against the person of a prince?"

"He did and he would have killed me with it, too, as he did kill Yo Seno, whose corpse I found in the corridor that leads from Yo Seno's office to the tower."

So, they had found the body of Yo Seno. Well, they would not kill me any deader for that crime than for menacing the life of the prince.

At this juncture an officer entered the throne room rather hurriedly. He was breathing rapidly as he stopped at the foot of the throne. He was standing right beside me and I saw him turn and look quickly at me, his eyes running rapidly up and down me between head and feet. Then he addressed the man upon the throne.

"Haj Osis, Jed of Tjanath," he said, "I came quickly to tell you that the body of a warrior of the hangar guard was just found within the Jed's hangar. His harness had been stripped from him and his weapons, while strange harness and strange weapons were left beside his corpse and as I approached your throne, Haj Osis, I recognized the harness of my dead warrior upon the body of this man here," and he pointed an accusing finger at me.

Haj Osis was scrutinizing me very carefully now. There was a strange look in his eyes that I did not like. It betokened half recognition and then of a sudden I saw the dawning of full recognition there, and the Jed of Tjanath swore a loud oath that resounded through the great throne room.

"Breath of Issus!" he shouted. "Look at him! Do you not know him? He is the spy from Jahar who called himself Hadron of Hastor. He died The Death. With my own eyes I saw him, and yet he is back here in my palace murdering my people and threatening my son, but this time he shall die." Haj Osis had arisen from his throne and with upraised hands that seemed to claw the air above me he appeared like some hideous corphal pronouncing a curse upon its victim. "But first we shall know who sent him here. He did not come of his own volition to kill me and my son; behind him is some malignant mind that yearns to destroy the Jed of Tjanath and his family. Burn him slowly, but do not let him die until he has divulged the name. Away with him! Let the fire be hot, but slow."

CHAPTER TWELVE
The Cloak of Invisibility

As Haj Osis, Jed of Tjanath, pronounced sentence of death upon me I knew whatever I might do to save myself must be done at once, for the instant that the guards laid hold upon me again my final hope would have vanished for it was evident that the torture and the death would take place immediately.

The warriors forming the guard that had escorted me from the pits were lined up several paces behind me. The dais upon which Haj Osis stood was raised but a little over three feet above the floor of the throne room. Between me and the Jed of Tjanath there was no one, for as he had sentenced me he had advanced from his throne to the very edge of the platform.

The action that I took was not delayed as long as it has taken me to tell it. Had it been, it could never have been taken for the guards would have been upon me. Instantly the last word fell from his mouth my plan was formulated and in that instant I leaped cat-like to the dais, full upon Haj Osis, Jed of Tjanath. So sudden, so unexpected was my attack that there was no defense. I seized him by the throat with one hand and with the other I snatched his dagger from its sheath and raising it above him I shouted my warning in a voice that all might hear.

"Stand back, or Haj Osis dies!" I cried.

They had started to rush me, but as the full import of my threat came home to them, they halted.

"It is my life, or yours, Haj Osis," I said, "unless you do what I tell you to do."

"What?" he asked, his face black with terror.

"Is there an anteroom behind the throne?" I asked.

"Yes," he replied. "What of it?"

"Take me there alone," I said. "Command your people to stand aside."

"And let you kill me when you get me there?" he demanded, trembling.

"I shall kill you now if you do not," I replied. "Listen, Haj Osis, I did not come here to kill you or your son. What I told the padwar of the guard was a lie. I came for another purpose, far transcending in importance to me the life of Haj Osis or that of his son. Do as I tell you and I promise that I shall not kill you. Tell your people that we are going into the anteroom and that I promise not to harm you if we are left alone there for five xats (about fifteen minutes)."

He hesitated. "Make haste," I said, "I have no time to waste," and I let the point of his own dagger touch his throat.

"Don't!" he screamed, shrinking back. "I will do whatever you say. Stand back all of you!" he shouted to his people. "I am going to the anteroom with this warrior and I command you upon pain of death not to enter there for five xats. At the end of that time, come; but not before."

I took a firm hold upon Haj Osis' harness between his shoulders and I kept the point of his dagger pressed against the flesh beneath his left shoulder blade as I followed him toward the anteroom, while those who had crowded the dais behind the throne fell back to make an aisle for us. At the doorway I halted and turned toward them.

"Remember," I said, "five full xats and not a tal before."

Entering the anteroom I closed and bolted the door, and then, still forcing Haj Osis ahead of me, I crossed the room and closed and bolted the only other door to the chamber. Then I pushed the Jed to one side of the room.

"Lie down here upon your face," I said.

"You promised not to kill me," he wailed.

"I shall not kill you unless they come before the five xats are up and you do otherwise than as I bid you so as not to delay me. I am going to bind you, but it will not hurt you."

With poor grace he lay down upon his belly and with his own harness I strapped his arms together behind his back. Then I blindfolded him and left him lying there.

As I had entered the room I had taken in its contents with a single, quick glance and I had seen there precisely the things that I most needed, and now that I had disposed of Haj Osis I crossed quickly to one of the windows and tore down a part of the silk hangings that covered it. It was a full length of fine, light silk and very wide, since it had been intended to hang in graceful folds as an under-drape with heavier hangings. At the ornate desk where the Jed of Tjanath signed his decrees, I went to work. First I took the vial from my pocket pouch and unstoppered it; then I wadded the silk into a ball and because of its wonderful fineness I could compress it within my two hands. Fastening the ball of silk into a loosely compressed mass with strips torn from another hanging, I slowly poured the contents of the vial over it, turning the ball with the point of Haj Osis' dagger. Remembering Phor Tak's warning, I was careful not to let any of the contents of the vial come in contact with my flesh and I could readily see why one had to be careful as I watched the ball of silk disappear before my eyes.

Knowing that the compound of invisibility would dry almost as rapidly as it impregnated the silk, I waited only a brief instant after emptying about half the contents of the vial upon the ball. Then, groping with my fingers, I found the strings that held it into its roughly spherical shape and cut them, after which I shook the silk out as best I could. For the most part it was invisible, but there were one or two spots that the compound had not reached. These I quickly daubed with some of the liquid remaining in my pocket pouch.

So much depended upon the success of my experiment that I almost feared to put it to the test, but it must be tested and there could be only a few xats remaining before the warriors of Haj Osis would burst into the antechamber.

By feel alone I draped the silk over my head so that it fell all about me. Through its thin and delicate meshes I could see objects at close range quite well enough to make my way about. I crossed to Haj Osis and took the blind from his eyes, at the same time stepping quickly back. He looked hurriedly and affrightedly about him.

"Who did that?" he demanded, and then half to himself, "He is gone." For a moment he was silent, rolling his eyes about in all directions, searching every nook and corner of the apartment. Then an expression that was part hope and part relief came to his eyes.

"Quick!" he shouted in a loud voice. "The guard! He has escaped!"

I breathed a sigh of relief – if Haj Osis could not see me, no one could – my plan had succeeded.

I dared not return to the throne-room and make my escape that way along corridors with which I was familiar for I could already hear the rush of feet toward the anteroom door and I was well aware that, although they could not see me, they could feel me and that unquestionably in the rush my mantle of invisibility, or at least a portion of it, would be torn from me, which would indubitably spell my doom.

I ran quickly to the other doorway and unbolted it and as I opened it I looked back at Haj Osis. His eyes were upon the doorway and they were wide with incredulity and horror. For an instant I did not realize the cause and looked quickly behind me to see if I could see what had caused Haj Osis fright and then it dawned upon me and I smiled. He had seen and heard the bolt shot and the door open as though by ghostly hands.

He must have sensed a vague suspicion of the truth, for he turned quickly toward the other door and screamed a warning in a high falsetto voice. "Do not enter," he cried, "until the five xats are up. It is I who commands – Haj Osis, the Jed."

Closing the door after me and still smiling, I hastened along the corridor, searching for a ramp that would carry me to the upper levels of the palace from which I could easily locate the guard room and the hangar where I had left my ship.

The corridor I had entered led directly into the royal apartments.

At first it was difficult to accustom myself to my invisibility and as I suddenly entered an apartment in which there were several people, my first impulse was to turn and flee, but though I had stepped directly into the view of one of the occupants of the room and at a distance of little more than five or six feet without attracting his attention, although his eyes were apparently directly upon me, my confidence was quickly restored. I continued on across the room as nonchalantly as though I had been in my own quarters in Helium.

The royal apartment seemed interminable and though I was constantly seeking a way out of them into one of the main corridors of the palace, I was instead constantly stumbling into places where I did not care to be and where I had no business, sometimes with considerable embarrassment, as when I entered a cozy, private apartment in the women's quarters at a moment when I was convinced they were not expecting strange gentlemen.

I would not turn back, however, for I had no time to lose, and crossing the room I followed another short corridor only to leap from the frying pan into the fire – I had entered the forbidden apartment of the Jeddara herself. It is a good thing for the royal lady that it was I and not Haj Osis who came thus unexpectedly upon her, for her position was most compromising, and from his harness I judged that her good-looking companion was a slave. In disgust I retreated, for there was no other exit from the apartment, and presently I stumbled, entirely by accident, upon one of the main corridors of the palace – a busy corridor filled with slaves, warriors and courtiers, with men, women and children passing to and fro upon whatever business called them, or perhaps seated upon the carved benches that lined the walls.

I was not yet accustomed to my new and surprising state of invisibility. I could see the people about me and it seemed inevitable that I must be seen. For a moment I had hesitated in the doorway that had led me to the corridor. A slave girl, approaching along the corridor, turned suddenly toward the doorway where I stood. She was looking directly at me, yet her gaze appeared to pass entirely through me. For an instant I was filled with consternation, and then, realizing that she was about to collide with me, I stepped quickly to one side. She passed by me, but it was evident that she sensed my presence for she paused and looked quickly about, an expression of surprise in her eyes. Then, to my immense relief, she passed through the doorway. She had not seen me, though doubtless she had heard me as I stepped aside. With a feeling of renewed confidence I now joined the throng in the corridor, threading my way in and out among the people to avoid contact with them and searching diligently all the while for the entrance to a ramp leading upward. This I presently discovered, and it was not long thereafter that I reached the upper level of the palace, where a short search brought me to the guard room at the foot of the ramp leading to the royal hangars.

Idling in the guard room, the warriors then off duty were engaged in various pursuits. Some where cleaning their harness and polishing their metal; two were playing at jetan, while others were rolling tiny numbered spheres at a group of numbered holes – a fascinating game of chance, called yano, which is, I presume, almost as old as Barsoomian civilization. The room was filled with the laughter and oaths of fighting men. How alike are warriors the world over! But for their harness and their metal they might have been a detachment of the palace guard at Helium.

Passing among them I ascended the ramp to the roof where the hangars stood. Two warriors on duty at the top of the ramp almost blocked my further progress. It would be a narrow squeeze to pass between them and I feared detection. As I paused I could not but over-hear their conversation.

"I tell you that he was struck from behind," said one. "He never knew what killed him," and I knew that they were talking about the guards-man I had killed.

"But from whence came his assassin?" demanded the other.

"The padwar believes it may have been a fellow member of the guard. There will be an investigation and we shall all be questioned."

"It was not I," said the other. "He was my best friend."

"Nor was it I."

"He had a way with women. Perhaps–"

My attention was distracted and their conversation terminated by the footsteps of a warrior running rapidly up the ramp. My position was now most precarious. The ramp was narrow and the man coming from behind might easily bump into me. I must, therefore, pass the sentries immediately and make my way to the roof. There was just sufficient room between the warrior at my left and the sidewall of the ramp for me to pass through, if he did not step back, and with all the stealth that I could summon I edged myself slowly behind him and you may rest assured that I breathed a sigh of relief when I had passed him.

The warrior ascending the ramp had now reached the two men. "The assassin of the hangar sentry has been discovered," he said.

"He is none other than the spy from Jahar who called himself Hadron of Hastor and who, with the other spy, Nur An, was sentenced to die The Death. Through some miracle he escaped and has returned to the palace of Haj Osis. Besides the hangar sentry, he has slain Yo Seno, but he was captured after attacking the prince, Haj Alt. Again he has escaped and he is now at large in the palace. The padwar of the guard has sent me to direct you to redouble your watchfulness. Great will be the reward of him who captures Hadron of Hastor, dead or alive."

"By my metal, I'd like to see him try to escape this way," said one of the sentries.

"He'll never come here by daylight."

I smiled as I walked quickly toward the hangar. To reach the roof without disarranging my robe of invisibility was difficult, but I finally accomplished it. Before me lay the empty roof; no ship was in sight, but I smiled again to myself, knowing well that it was there. I looked about for the eye of the periscope that would reveal the craft's presence to me, but it was not visible. However, that did not concern me greatly since I realized that it might be turned in the opposite direction. It was only necessary for me to walk where I had left the ship, and this I did, feeling ahead of me with extended hands.

I crossed the roof from one side to the other, but found no ship. That I was perplexed goes without saying. I most certainly knew where I had left the ship, but it no longer was there. Perhaps a wind had moved it slightly, and with this thought in mind I searched another section of the roof, but with equal disappointment. By now I was truly apprehensive, and thereupon I set about a systematic search of the roof until I had covered every square foot of it and was convinced beyond doubt that the worst of disasters had befallen me – my ship was gone; but where? Indeed the compound of invisibility had its drawbacks. My ship might be and probably was at no great distance from me, yet I could not see it. A gentle wind was blowing from the southwest. If my ship had risen from the roof, it would drift in a northeasterly direction, but though I strained my eyes toward that point of the compass I could discern nothing of the tiny eye of the periscope.

I must admit that for a moment I was well-nigh discouraged. It seemed that always when success was about within my grasp some malign fate snatched it from me, but presently I shook this weak despondency from me and with squared shoulders faced the future and whatever it might bring.

For a few moments I considered my position in all its aspects and sought to discover the best solution of my problem. I must rescue Tavia, but I felt that it would be useless to attempt to do so without a ship, therefore I must have a ship, and I knew that ships were just beneath me in the royal hangars. At night these hangars would be closed and locked and watched over by sentries in the bargain. If I would have a ship I must take it now and depend upon the swiftness and boldness of my act for its success.

Royal fliers are usually fast fliers and if the ships of Haj Osis were no exception to this general Barsoomian rule, I might hope to outdistance pursuit could I but pass the hangar sentry.

Of one thing I was certain, I could not accomplish that by remaining upon the roof of the hangar and so I cautiously descended, choosing a moment when the attention of the sentries was directed elsewhere, for there was always danger that my robe might blow aside, revealing my limbs.

Once on the roof again I slipped quickly into the hangar and inspecting the ships I selected one that I was sure would carry four with ease, and which, from its lines, gave token of considerable speed.

Clambering to the deck I took my place at the controls; very gradually I elevated the ship about a foot from the floor; then I opened the throttle wide.

Directly ahead of me, through the open doorways of the hangar, the sentries were standing upon the opposite side of the room. As the ship leaped into the sunlight they voiced simultaneously a cry of surprise and alarm. Like brave warriors they sprang forward with drawn long swords and I could see that they were going to try to board me before I could gain altitude, but presently one of them halted wide-eyed and stood aside.

"Blood of our first ancestors!" he cried. "There is no one at the controls."

The second man had evidently discovered this simultaneously, for he, too, shrank aside, and with whirling propeller I shot upward from the royal hangar of the Jed of Tjanath.

But only for an instant were the two sentries overwhelmed by astonishment. Immediately I heard the shriek of sirens and the clang of great gongs and then, glancing behind, I saw that already they had launched a flier in pursuit. It was a two-man flier and almost immediately I realized that it was far swifter than the one I had chosen, and then to make matters even worse for me I saw patrol boats arising from hangars located elsewhere upon the palace roof. That they all saw my ship and were converging upon it was evident; escape seemed impossible; each way I turned a patrol boat was approaching; already I had been driven into an ascending spiral, my eyes constantly alert for any avenue of escape that might open to me.

How hopeless it looked! My ship was too slow; my pursuers too many.

It would not be long now, I thought, and at that very instant I saw something off my port bow at a little greater altitude that gave me one of the greatest thrills I had ever experienced in my life. It was only a little round eye of glass, but to me it meant life and more than life, for it might mean also life and happiness for Tavia – and of course for Sanoma Tora.

A patrol boat coming diagonally from below was almost upon me as I drew my flier beneath that floating eye, judging the distance so nicely that I just had clearance for my head beneath the keel of my own ship. Locating one of the hatches, which were so constructed that they opened either from the inside or the out, I scrambled quickly into the interior of the Jhama, as Phor Tak had christened it.

Closing the hatch and springing to the controls, I rose quickly out of immediate danger. Then, standing to one side, I watched my former pursuers.

I could read the consternation in their faces as they came alongside the royal flier that I had stolen, and realized that it was unmanned. Not having seen either me or my ship, they must have been hard put to it to find any sort of an explanation for the phenomenon.

As I watched them I found it constantly necessary to change my position, owing to the number of patrol boats and other craft that congregating. I did not wish to leave the vicinity of the palace entirely for it was my intention to remain here until after dark when I should make an attempt to take Tavia and Phao aboard the Jhama. I also had it in my mind to reconnoiter the East Tower during the day and try to get into communication with Tavia if possible. It was already the fifth zode. In fifty xats (three hours) the sun would set.

I wished to initiate my plan of rescue as soon after dark as possible, as experience had taught me that plans do not always develop as smoothly in execution as they do in contemplation.

A warrior from one of the patrol ships had boarded the royal craft that I had purloined and was returning it to the hangar. Some of the ships were following and others were returning to their stations. A single patrol boat remained cruising about and as I watched it I suddenly became aware that a young officer standing upon its deck had espied the eye of my periscope. I saw him pointing toward it and immediately thereafter the craft altered its course and came directly toward me. This was not so good and I lost no time in moving to one side, turning the eye of my periscope away from them so that they could not see it or follow me.

I moved a short distance out of their course and then swung my periscope toward them again. To my astonishment I discovered that they, too, had altered their course and were following me.

Now I rose swiftly and took a new direction, but when I looked again the craft was bearing down upon me and not only that, but she was training a gun on me.

What had happened? It was evident that something had gone wrong and that I was no longer clothed in total invisibility, but whatever it was, it was too late now to rectify it even if I could. I had but a single recourse and I prayed to my first ancestor that it might not now be too late to put it into execution. Should they fire upon me, I was lost.

I brought the Jhama to a full stop and sprang quickly aft to where the rear rifle was mounted on a platform just within the after turret.

In that instant I had occasion to rejoice in the foresight that had prompted me to rearrange the projectiles properly against the necessity for instant use in such an emergency as this. Selecting one, I jammed it into the chamber and closed the breech block. The turret, crudely and hastily constructed though it had been, responded to my touch and an instant later my sight covered the approaching patrol vessel, and through the tiny opening provided for the sight I witnessed the effect of my first shot with Phor Taks disintegrating ray rifle.

I had used a metal disintegrating projectile and the result was appalling.

I loved a ship and it tore my heart to see that staunch craft fall apart in midair as its metal parts disappeared before the disintegrating ray.

But that was not all, as wood and leather and fabric sank with increasing swiftness toward the ground, brave warriors hurtled to their doom. It was horrifying.

I am a true son of Barsoom; I joy in battle; armed conflict is my birthright, and war the goal of my ambition, but this was not war; it was murder.

I took no joy in my victory as I had when I laid Yo Seno low in mortal combat, and now, more than ever, was I determined that this frightful instrument of destruction must in some way be forever banned upon Barsoom. War with such a weapon completely hidden by the compound of invisibility would be too horrible to contemplate. Navies, cities, whole nations could be wiped out by a single battle thus equipped. The mad dream of Phor Tak might easily come true and a maniac yet rule all Barsoom.

But meditation and philosophizing were not for me at this time. I had work to do and though it necessitated wiping out all Tjanath, I purposed doing it.

Again the sirens and the gongs raised their wild alarm; again patrol boats gathered. I felt that I must depart until after nightfall, for I had no stomach to again be forced to turn that deadly rifle upon my fellow men while any alternative existed.

As I started to turn back the controls my eyes chanced to fall upon one of the stern ports and, to my surprise, I saw that the shutter was raised. How this occurred I do not know; it has always remained a mystery, but at least it explained how it had been possible for the patrol boat to follow me. That round port hole moving through the air must have filled them with wonder, but at the same time it was a clue to follow and though they did not understand it, they, like the brave warriors that they were, followed it in the line of their duty.

I quickly closed it, and, after examining the others and finding them all closed, I was now confident that, with the exception of the small eye of my periscope, I was entirely surrounded by invisibility and hence under no immediate necessity for leaving the vicinity of the palace, as I could easily maneuver the ship to keep out of the way of the patrol boats that were now again congregating near the royal hangar.

I think they were pretty much upset by what had happened and evidently there was no unanimity of opinion as to what should be done. The patrol ships hovered about, evidently waiting orders, and it was not until almost dark that they set out in a systematic search of the air above the city; nor had they been long at this before I understood their orders as well as though I had read them myself. The lower ships moved at an altitude of not over fifty feet above the higher buildings; two hundred feet above these moved the second line. The ships at each level cruised in a series of concentric circles and in opposite directions, thereby combing the air above the city so closely that no enemy ship could possibly approach. The air below was watched by a thousand eyes; at every point of vantage sentries were on watch and upon the roof of every public building guns appeared as if by magic.

I began to be quite apprehensive that even the small eye of my periscope might not go undetected and so I dropped my ship into a little opening among some lofty trees that grew within the palace garden, and here I waited some twenty feet above the ground, my periscope completely screened from view, unseen and, in consequence, myself unseeing, until the swift night of Barsoom descended upon Tjanath; then I rose slowly from my leafy retreat.

Above the trees I paused to have a look about me through the periscope. Far above me were the twinkling lights of the circling patrol boats and from a thousand windows of the palace shone other lights. Before me rose the dark outlines of the East Tower silhouetted against the starry sky.

Rising slowly I circled the tower until I had brought the Jhama opposite Tavia's window.

My ship carried no lights, of course, and I had not switched on any of the lights within her cabin, so that I felt that I might with impunity raise one of the upper hatches, and this I did. The Jhama lay with her upper deck a foot or two beneath the sill of Tavia's window. Before venturing from below I replaced my cloak of invisibility about me.

There was no light in Tavia's room. I placed my ear close against the iron bars and listened. I could hear no sound. My heart sank within me. Could it be that they had removed her to some other part of the palace? Could it be that Haj Alt had come and taken her away? I shuddered at the mere suggestion and cursed the luck that had permitted him to escape my blade.

With all those eyes and ears straining through the darkness I feared to make the slightest sound, though I felt that there was little likelihood that the open hatch would be noticed in the surrounding darkness; yet I must ascertain whether or not Tavia was within that room. I leaned close against the bars and whispered her name. There was no response.

"Tavia!" I whispered, this time much louder, and it seemed to me that my voice went booming to high heaven in tones that the dead might hear.

This time I heard a response from the interior of the room. It sounded like a gasp and then I heard someone moving – approaching the window. It was so dark in the interior that I could see nothing, but presently I heard a voice close to me.

"Hadron! Where are you?"

She had recognized my voice. For some reason I thrilled to the thought of it. "Here at the window, Tavia," I said.

She came very close. "Where?" she asked. "I cannot see you."

I had forgotten my robe of invisibility. "Never mind," I said. "You cannot see me, but I will explain that later. Is Phao with you?"

"Yes."

"And no one else?"

"No."

"I am going to take you with me, Tavia – you and Phao. Stand aside well out of line of the window so that you will not be hurt while I remove the bars. Then be ready to board my ship immediately."

"Your ship!" she said. "Where is it?"

"Never mind now. There is a ship here. Do just as I tell you. Do you trust me?"

"With my life, Hadron, forever," she whispered.

Something within me sang. It was more than a mere thrill; I cannot explain it; nor did I understand it, but now there were other things to think of.

"Stand aside quickly, Tavia, and keep Phao away from the window until I call you again." Dimly I could see her figure for a moment and than I saw it withdraw from the window. Returning to the controls I brought the forward turret of the ship opposite the window, upon the bars of which I trained the rifle. I loaded it and pressed the button. Through the tiny sight aperture and because of the darkness I could see nothing of the result, but I knew perfectly well what had happened, and when I lowered the ship again and went on deck I found that the bars had vanished in thin air.

"Quick, Tavia," I said. "Come!"

With one foot upon the deck of the flier and the other upon the sill of the window, I held the ship close to the wall of the tower and as best I could I held the cloak of invisibility like a canopy to shield the girls from sight as they boarded the Jhama.

It was difficult and risky business. I wished I might have had grappling hooks, but I had none and so I must do the best I could, holding the cloak with one hand and assisting Tavia to the sill with the other.

"There is no ship," she said in slightly frightened tone.

"There is a ship, Tavia," I said. "Think only of your confidence in me and do as I bid." I grasped her firmly by the harness where the straps crossed upon her back. "Have no fear," I said and then I swung her out over the hatch and lowered her gently into the interior of the Jhama.

Phao was behind her and I must give her credit for being as courageous as Tavia. It must have been a terrifying experience to those two girls to feel that they were being lowered into thin air a hundred feet above the ground, for they could see no ship – only a darker hole within the darkness of the night.

As soon as they were both aboard, I followed them, closing the hatch after me.

They were huddled in the darkness on the floor of the cabin, weak and exhausted from the brief ordeal through which they had just passed, but I could not take the time then to answer the questions with which I knew their heads must be filled.

If we passed the watchers on the roofs and the patrol boats above, there would be plenty of time for questions and answers. If we did not, there would be no need for either.

CHAPTER THIRTEEN

Tul Axtar's Women

WITH PROPELLERS MOVING only enough to give us headway, we moved slowly and silently from the tower. I did not dare to rise to the altitude of the circling fliers for fear of almost inevitable collision, owing to the limited range of visibility permitted by the periscope, and so I held to a course that carried me only above the roof of the lower part of the palace until I reached a broad avenue that led in an easterly direction to the outer wall of the city. I kept well down below the roofs of the buildings, where there was little likelihood of encountering other craft. Our only danger of detection now, and that was slight indeed, was that our propeller might be overheard by some of the watchers on the roofs, but the hum and drone of the propellers of the ships above the city must have drowned out whatever slight sound our slowly revolving blades gave forth, and at last we came to the gate at the end of the avenue, and rising to top its battlements, we passed out of Tjanath into the night beyond. The lights of the city and of the circling patrol boats above grew fainter and fainter as we left them far behind.

We had maintained absolute silence during our escape from the city, but as soon as our escape appeared assured, Tavia unlocked the flood gates of her curiosity. Phao's first question was relative to Nur An. Her sigh of relief held as great assurance of her love for him as could words have done. The two listened in breathless attention to the story of our miraculous escape from The Death. Then they wanted to know all about the Jhama, the compound of invisibility and the disintegrating ray with which I had dissolved the bars from their prison window. Nor was it until their curiosity had been appeased that we were able to discuss our plans for the future.

"I feel that I should go at once to Jahar," I said.

"Yes," said Tavia in a low voice. "It is your duty. You must go there first and rescue Sanoma Tora."

"If there was only some place where I might leave you and Phao in safety, I should feel that I could carry on this mission with far greater peace of mind, but I know of no other place than Jhama and I hesitate to return there and let Phor Tak know that I failed to go immediately to Jahar as I had intended. The man is quite insane. There is no telling what he might do if he learns the truth; nor am I certain that you two would be safe there in his power. He trusts only his slaves and he might easily become obsessed with an hallucination that you are spies."

"You need not think of me at all," said Tavia, "for no matter where you might find a place to leave us, I should not remain. The place of the slave is with her master."

"Do not say that, Tavia. You are not my slave."

"I am a slave girl," she replied. "I must be someone's slave. I prefer to be yours."

I was touched by her loyalty, but I did not like to think of Tavia as a slave; yet however much I might loathe the idea the fact remained that she was one. "I give you your freedom, Tavia," I said.

She smiled. "I do not want it and now that it is decided that I am to remain with you" (she had done all the deciding), "I wish to learn all that I can about navigating the Jhama, for it may be that in that way I may help you."

Tavia's knowledge of aerial navigation made the task of instructing her simple indeed; in fact she had no trouble whatsoever in handling the craft.

Phao also manifested an interest and it was not long before she, too, took her turn at the controls, while Tavia insisted upon being inducted into all the mysteries of the disintegrating ray rifle.

Long before we saw the towers of Tul Axtar's capital, we sighted a one-man flier painted the ghastly blue of Jahar, and then far to the right and to the left we saw others. They were circling slowly at a great altitude. I judged that they were scouts watching for the coming of an expected enemy fleet. We passed below them and a little later encountered the second line of enemy ships. These were all scout cruisers, carrying from ten to fifteen men. Approaching one of them quite closely I saw that it carried four disintegrating ray rifles, two mounted forward and two aft. As far as I could see in either direction these ships were visible, and if, as I presumed, they formed a circle entirely about Jahar, they must have been numerous indeed.

Passing on beyond them we presently encountered the third line of Jaharian ships. Here were stationed huge battleships, carrying crews of a thousand men and more and fairly bristling with big guns.

While none of these ships was as large as the major ships of Helium, they constituted a most formidable force and it was obvious that they had been built in great numbers.

What I had already seen impressed me with the fact that Tul Axtar was entertaining no idle dream in his contemplated subjection of all Barsoom. With but a fraction of the ships I had already seen I would guarantee to lay waste all of Barsoom, provided my ships were armed with disintegrating ray rifles, and I felt sure that I had seen but a pitiful fraction of Tul Axtar's vast armament.

The sight of all these ships filled me with the direct forebodings of calamity. If the fleet of Helium had not already arrived and been destroyed, it certainly must be destroyed when it did arrive. No power on earth could save it. The best that I could hope, had the fleet already arrived, was that an encounter with the disintegrating ray rifles of the first line might have proved sufficient warning to turn the balance of the fleet back.

Far behind the line of battleships I could see the towers of Jahar rising in the distance, and as we reached the vicinity of the city I descried a fleet of the largest ships I have ever seen, resting upon the ground just outside the city wall. These ships, which completely encircled the city wall that was visible to us, must have been capable of accommodating at least ten thousand men each, and from their construction and their light armaments, I assumed them to be transports. These, doubtless, were to carry the hordes of hungry Jaharian warriors upon the campaign of loot and pillage that it was planned should destroy a world.

Contemplation of this vast armada prompted me to abandon all other plans and hasten at once to Helium, that the alarm might be spread and plans be made to thwart the mad ambition of Tul Axtar. My mind was a seething caldron of conflicting demands upon me. Countless times had I risked my life to reach Jahar for but a single purpose and now that I had arrived I was called upon to turn back for the fulfillment of another purpose – a larger, a more important one, perhaps, but I am only human and so I turned first to the rescue of the woman that I loved, determined immediately thereafter to throw myself wholeheartedly into the prosecution of the other enterprise that duty and inclination demanded of me. I argued that the slight delay that would result would in no way jeopardize the greater cause, while should I abandon Sanoma Tora now there was little likelihood that I would ever be able to return to Jahar to her succor.

With the great ghastly blue fleet of Jahar behind us, we topped the city's walls and moved in the direction of the palace of the jeddak.

My plans were well formulated. I had discussed them again and again with Tavia, who had grown up in the palace of Tul Axtar.

At her suggestion we were to maneuver the Jhama to a point directly over the summit of a slender tower, upon which there was not room to land the flier, but through which I could gain ingress to the palace at a point close to the quarters of the women.

As we had passed through the three lines of Jaharian ships, protected by our coating of the compound of invisibility, so we passed the sentries on the city wall and the warriors upon watch in the towers and upon the ramparts of the palace of the towers and upon the ramparts of the palace of the jeddak, and without incident worthy of note I stopped the Jhama just above the summit of the tower that Tavia indicated.

"In about ten xats (approximately thirty minutes) it will be dark," I said to Tavia. "If you find it impractical to remain here constantly, try and return when dark has fallen, for whether I am successful in finding Sanoma Tora I shall not attempt to return to the Jhama until night has fallen."

She had told me that there was a possibility that the women's quarters might be locked at sunset and for this reason I was entering the palace by daylight, though I should have much preferred not to risk it until after nightfall. Tavia had also assured me that if I once entered the women's quarters I would have no difficulty in leaving even after they were locked, as the doors could be opened from the inside, the precaution of locking being taken not for fear that the inmates would leave the quarters, but to protect them against the dangers of assassins and others with evil intent.

Adjusting the robe of invisibility about me, I raised the forward keel hatch, which was directly over the summit of the tower that had once been used as a lookout in some distant age before newer and loftier portions of the palace had rendered it useless for this purpose.

"Good-bye and good luck," whispered Tavia. "When you return I hope that you will bring your Sanoma Tora with you. While you are gone I shall pray to my ancestors for your success."

Thanking her, I lowered myself through the hatch to the summit of the tower, in which was set a small trap door.

As I raised this door I saw below me the top of the ancient ladder that long dead warriors had used and which evidently was seldom, if ever, used now as was attested by the dust upon its rungs. The ladder led me down to a large room in the upper level of this portion of the palace – a room that had doubtless originally been a guard room, but which was now the receptacle for odds and ends of discarded furniture, hangings and ornaments. Filled as it was with specimens of the craftsmanship of ancient Jahar, together with articles of more modern fabrication, it would have been a most interesting room to explore; yet I passed through it with nothing more than a single searching glance for live enemies. Closely following Tavia's instructions I descended two spiral ramps, where I found myself in a most ornately decorated corridor, opening upon which were the apartments of the women of Tul Axtar. The corridor was long, stretching away fully a thousand sofads to a great, arched window at the far end, through which I could see the waving foliage of trees.

Many of the countless doors that lined the corridor on either side were open or ajar, for the corridor itself was forbidden to all but the women and their slaves, with the exception of Tul Axtar. The foot of the single ramp leading to it from the level watched over by a guard of picked men, composed exclusively of eunuchs, and Tavia assured me that short shrift was made of any adventurous spirit who sought to investigate the precincts above; yet here was I, a man and an enemy, safely within the forbidden territory.

As I looked about me in attempt to determine where to commence my investigation, several women emerged from one of the apartments and approached me along the corridor. They were beautiful women, young and richly trapped, and from their light conversation and their laughter I judged that they were not unhappy. My conscience pricked me as I realized the mean advantage that I was taking of them, but it could not be avoided and so I waited and listened, hoping that I might overhear some snatch of conversation that would aid me in my quest for Sanoma Tora; but I learned nothing from them other than that they referred to Tul Axtar contemptuously as the old zitidar. Some of their references to him were extremely personal and none was complimentary.

They passed me and entered a large room at the end of the corridor. Almost immediately thereafter other women emerged from other apartments and followed the first party into the same apartment.

It soon became evident to me that they were congregating there and I thought that perhaps this might be the best way in which to start my search for Sanoma Tora – perhaps she, too, might be among the company.

Accordingly I fell in behind one of the groups and followed it through the large doorway and a short corridor, which opened into a great hall that was so gorgeously appointed and decorated as to suggest the throne room of a jeddak, and in fact such appeared to have been a part of its purpose, for at one end rose an enormous, highly-carved throne.

The floor was highly polished wood, in the center of which was a large pool of water. Along the sides of the room were commodious benches, piled with pillows and soft silks and furs. Here it was that Tul Axtar occasionally held unique court, surrounded solely by his women. Here they danced for him; here they disported themselves in the limpid waters of the pool for his diversion; here banquets were spread and to the strains of music high revelry persisted long into the night.

As I looked about me at those who had already assembled I saw that Sanoma Tora was not among them and so I took my place close to the entrance where I might scrutinize the face of each who entered. They were coming in droves now. I believe that I have never seen so many women alone together before. As I watched for Sanoma Tora I tried to count them, but I soon gave, it up as hopeless, though I estimated that fully fifteen hundred women were congregated in the great hall when at last they ceased to enter.

They seated themselves upon the benches about the room, which was filled with a babel of feminine voices. There were women of all ages and of every type, but there was none that was not beautiful. The secret agents of Tul Axtar must have combed the world for such an aggregation of loveliness as this.

A door at one side of the throne opened and a file of warriors entered. At first I was surprised because Tavia had told me that no men other than Tul Axtar ever were permitted upon this level, but presently I saw that the warriors were women dressed in the harness of men, their hair cut and their faces painted, after the fashion of the fighting men of Barsoom. After they had taken their places on either side of the throne, a courtier entered by the same door – another woman masquerading as a man.

"Give thanks!" she cried. "Give thanks! The Jeddak comes!"

Instantly the women arose and a moment later Tul Axtar, Jeddak of Jahar, entered the hall, followed by a group of women disguised as courtiers.

As Tul Axtar lowered his great bulk into the throne, he signalled for the women in the room to be seated. Then he spoke in a low voice to a woman courtier at his side.

The woman stepped to the edge of the dais. "The great Jeddak designs to honor you individually with his royal observation," she announced in stilted tones. "From my left you will pass before him, one by one. In the name of the Jeddak, I have spoken."

Immediately the first woman at the left arose and walked slowly past the throne, pausing in front of Tul Axtar long enough to turn completely about, and then walked slowly on around the apartment and out through the doorway beside which I stood. One by one in rapid succession the others followed her. The whole procedure seemed meaningless to me. I could not understand it – then.

Perhaps a hundred women had passed before the Jeddak and come down the long hall toward me when something in the carriage of one of them attracted my attention as she neared me, and an instant later I recognized Sanoma Tora. She was changed, but not greatly and I could not understand why it was that I had not discovered her in the room previously. I had found her! After all these long months I had found her – the woman I loved. Why did my heart not thrill?

As she passed through the doorway leading from the great hall, I followed her and along the corridor to an apartment near the far end, and when she entered, I entered behind her. I had to move quickly, too, for she turned immediately and closed the door after her.

We were alone in a small room, Sanoma Tora and I. In one corner were her sleeping silks and furs; between two windows was a carved bench upon which stood those toilet articles that are essential to a woman of Barsoom.

It was not the apartment of a Jeddara; it was a little better than the cell of a slave.

As Sanoma Tora crossed the room listlessly toward a stool which stood before the toilet bench, her back was toward me and I dropped the robe of invisibility from about me.

"Sanoma Tora!" I said in a low voice.

Startled, she turned toward me. "Hadron of Hastor!" she exclaimed; "or am I dreaming?"

"You are not dreaming, Sanoma Tora. It is Hadron of Hastor."

"Why are you here? How did you get here? It is impossible. No men but Tul Axtar are permitted upon this level."

"Here I am, Sanoma Tora, and I have come to take you back to Helium – if you wish to return."

"Oh name of my first ancestor, if I could but hope," she cried.

"You may hope, Sanoma Tora," I assured her. "I am here and I can take you back."

"I cannot believe it," she said. "I cannot imagine how you gained entrance here. It is madness to think that two of us could leave without being detected."

I threw the cloak about me. "Where are you, Tan Hadron? What has become of you? What has happened?" cried Sanoma Tora.

"This is how I gained entrance," I explained. "This is how we shall escape." I removed the cloak from about me.

"What forbidden magic is this?" she demanded, and, as best I might in few words, I explained to her the compound of invisibility and how I had come by it.

"How have you fared here, Sanoma Tora?" I asked her. "How have they treated you?"

"I have not been ill treated," she replied; "no one has paid any attention to me." I could scent the wounded vanity in her tone. "Until tonight I had not seen Tul Axtar. I have just come from the hall where he holds court among his women."

"Yes," I said, "I know. I was there. It was from there that I followed you here."

"When can you take me away?" she asked.

"Very quickly now," I replied.

"I am afraid that it will have to be quickly," she said.

"Why?" I asked.

"When I passed Tul Axtar he stopped me for a moment and I heard him speak to one of the courtiers at his side. He told her to ascertain my name and where I was quartered. The women have told me what happens after Tul Axtar has noticed one of us, and I am afraid; but what difference does it make, I am only a slave."

What a change had come over the haughty Sanoma Tora! Was this the same arrogant beauty who had refused my hand? Was this the Sanoma Tora who had aspired to be a jeddara? She was humbled now – I read it in the droop of her shoulders, in the trembling of her lips, in the fear-haunted light that shone from her eyes.

My heart was filled with compassion for her, but I was astonished and dismayed to discover that no other emotion overwhelmed me. The last time that I had seen Sanoma Tora I would have given my soul to have been able to take her into my arms. Had the hardships that I had undergone so changed me? Was Sanoma Tora, a slave, less desirable to me than Sanoma Tora, daughter of the rich Tor Hatan? No; I knew that that could not be true. I had changed, but doubtless it was only a temporary metamorphosis induced by the nervous strain which I was undergoing consequent upon the responsibility imposed upon me by the necessity for carrying word to Helium in time to save her from destruction at the hands of Tul Axtar – to save not only Helium, but a world. It was a grave responsibility. How might one thus burdened have time for thoughts of love? No, I was not myself; yet I knew that I still loved Sanoma Tora.

Realizing the necessity for haste, I made a speedy examination of the room and discovered that I could easily effect Sanoma Tora's rescue by taking her through the window, just as I had taken Tavia and Phao from the east tower at Tjanath.

Briefly, but carefully, I explained my plan to her and bid her prepare herself while I was gone that there might be no delay when I was ready to take her aboard the Jhama.

"And now, Sanoma Tora," I said, "for a few moments, good-bye! The next that you will hear will be a voice at your window, but you will see no one nor any ship. Extinguish the light in your room and step to the sill. I will take your hand. Put your trust in me then and do as I bid."

"Good-bye, Hadron!" she said. "I cannot express now in adequate words the gratitude that I feel, but when we are returned to Helium there is nothing you can demand of me that I shall not grant you, not only willingly, but gladly."

I raised her fingers to my lips and had turned toward the door when Sanoma Tora laid a detaining hand upon my arm. "Wait!" she said. "Someone is coming."

Hastily I resumed my cloak of invisibility and stepped to one side of the room as the door, leading into the corridor, was thrown open, revealing one of the female courtiers of Tul Axtar in gorgeous harness. The woman entered the room and stepped to one side of the doorway which remained opened.

"The Jeddak! Tul Axtar, Jeddak of Jahar!" she announced.

A moment later Tul Axtar entered the room, followed by half a dozen of his female courtiers. He was a gross man with repulsive features, which reflected a combination of strength and weakness, of haughty arrogance, of pride and of doubt – an innate questioning of his own ability.

As he faced Sanoma Tora his courtiers formed behind him.

They were masculine-looking women, who had evidently been selected because of this very characteristic. They were good-looking in a masculine way and their physiques suggested that they might prove a very effective body guard for the Jeddak.

For several minutes Tul Axtar examined Sanoma Tora with appraising eyes. He came closer to her and there was that in his attitude which I did not like, and when he laid a hand upon her shoulder, I could scarce retrain myself.

"I was not wrong," he said. "You are gorgeous. How long have you been here?"

She shuddered, but did not reply.

"You are from Helium?"

No answer.

"The ships of Helium are on their way to Jahar." He laughed. "My scouts bring word that they will soon be here. They will meet with a warm welcome from the great fleet of Tul Axtar." He turned to his courtiers. "Go!" he said, "and let none return until I summon her."

They bowed and retired, closing the door after them, and then Tul Axtar laid his hand again upon the bare flesh of Sanoma Tora's shoulder.

"Come!" he said. "I shall not war with all of Helium – with you I shall love – by my first ancestor, but you are worthy the love of a jeddak."

He drew her toward him. My blood boiled – so hot was my anger that it boiled over and without thought of the consequences I let the cloak fall from me.

CHAPTER FOURTEEN

The Cannibals of U-Gor

As I DROPPED THE CLOAK of invisibility aside I drew my long sword and as it slithered from its sheath, Tul Axtar heard and faced me. His craven blood rushed to his heart and left his face pale at the sight of me. A scream was in his throat when my point touched him in warning.

"Silence!" I hissed.

"Who are you?" he demanded.

"Silence!"

Even in the instant my plans were formed. I made him turn with his back toward me and then I disarmed him, after which I bound him securely and gagged him.

"Where can I hide him, Sanoma Tora?" I asked.

"There is a little closet here," she said, pointing toward a small door in one side of the room, and then she crossed to it and opened it, while I dragged Tul Axtar behind her and cast him into the closet – none too gently I can assure you.

As I closed the closet door I turned to find Sanoma Tora white and trembling. "I am afraid," she said. "If they come back and find him thus, they will kill me."

"His courtiers will not return until he summons them," I reminded her. "You heard him tell them that such were his wishes – his command." She nodded.

"Here is his dagger," I told her. "If worse comes to worst you can hold them off by threatening to kill Tul Axtar," but the girl seemed terrified, she trembled in every limb and I feared that she might fail if put to the test. How I wished that Tavia were here. I knew that she would not fail, and, in the name of my first ancestor, how much depended upon success!

"I shall return soon," I said, as I groped about the floor for the robe of invisibility. "Leave that large window open and when I return, be ready."

As I replaced the cloak about me I saw that she was trembling so that she could not reply; in fact, she was even having difficulty in holding the dagger, which I expected momentarily to see drop from her nerveless fingers, but there was naught that I could do but hasten to the Jhama and try to return before it was too late.

I gained the summit of the tower without incident. Above me twinkled the brilliant stars of a Barsoomian night, while just above the palace roof hung the gorgeous planet, Jasoom (Earth).

The Jhama, of course, was invisible, but so great was my confidence in Tavia that when I stretched a hand upward I knew that I should feel the keel of the craft and sure enough I did. Three times I rapped gently upon the forward hatch, which was the signal that we had determined upon before I had entered the palace. Instantly the hatch was raised and a moment later I had clambered aboard.

"Where is Sanoma Tora?" asked Tavia.

"No questions now," I replied. "We must work quickly. Be ready to take over the controls the moment that I leave them."

In silence she took her place at my side, her soft shoulder touching my arm, and in silence I dropped the Jhama to the level of the windows in the women's quarters. In a general way I knew the location of Sanoma Tora's apartment, and as I moved slowly along I kept the periscope pointed toward the windows and presently I saw the figure of Sanoma Tora upon the ground glass before me. I brought the Jhama close to the sill, her upper deck just below it.

"Hold her here, Tavia," I said. Then I raised the upper hatch a few inches and called to the girl within the room.

At the sound of my voice she trembled so that she almost dropped the dagger, although she must have known that I was coming and had been awaiting me.

"Darken your room," I whispered to her. I saw her stagger across to a button that was set in the wall and an instant later the room was enveloped in darkness. Then I raised the hatch and stepped to the sill. I did not wish to be bothered with the enveloping folds of the mantle of invisibility and so I had folded it up and tucked it into my harness, where I could have it instantly ready for use in the event of an emergency. I found Sanoma Tora in the darkness and so weak with terror was she that I had to lift her in my arms and carry her to the window, where with Phao's help I managed to draw her through the open hatch into the interior. Then I returned to the closet where Tul Axtar lay bound and gagged. I stopped and cut the bonds which held his ankles.

"Do precisely as I tell you, Tul Axtar," I said, "or my steel will have its way yet and find your heart. It thirsts for your blood, Tul Axtar, and I have difficulty in restraining it, but if you do not fail me perhaps I shall be able to save you yet. I can use you, Tul Axtar, and upon your usefulness to me depends your life, for dead you are no value to me."

I made him rise and walk to the window and there I assisted him to the sill. He was terror-stricken when I tried to make him step out into space, as he thought, but when I stepped to the deck of the Jhama ahead of him and he saw me apparently floating there in the air, he took a little heart and I finally succeeded in getting him aboard.

Following him I closed the hatch and lighted a single dim light within the hull. Tavia turned and looked at me for orders.

"Hold her where she is, Tavia," I said.

There was a tiny desk in the cabin of the Jhama where the officer of the ship was supposed to keep his log and attend to any other records or reports that it might be necessary to make. Here were writing materials, and as I got them out of the drawer in which they were kept, I called Phao to my side.

"You are of Jahar." I said. "You can write in the language of your country?"

"Of course," she said.

"Then write what I dictate," I instructed her.

She prepared to do my bidding.

"If a single ship of Helium is destroyed," I dictated, "Tul Axtar dies. Now sign it Hadron of Hastor, Padwar of Helium."

Tavia and Phao looked at me and then at the prisoner, their eyes wide in astonishment, for in the dim light of the ship's interior they had not recognized the prisoner.

"Tul Axtar of Jahar." breathed Tavia incredulously. "Tan Hadron of Hastor, you have saved Helium and Barsoom tonight."

I could not but note how quickly her mind functioned, with what celerity she had seen the possibilities that lay in the possession of the person of Tul Axtar, Jeddak of Jahar.

I took the note that Phao had written, and, returning quickly to Sanoma Tora's room, I laid it upon her dressing table. A moment later I was again in the cabin of the Jhama and we were rising swiftly above the roofs of Jahar.

Morning found us beyond the uttermost line of Jaharian ships, beneath which we had passed, guided by their lights – evidence to me that the fleet was poorly officered, for no trained man, expecting an enemy in force, would show lights aboard his ships at night.

We were speeding now in the direction of far Helium, following the course that I hoped would permit us to intercept the fleet of the Warlord in the event that it was already bound for Jahar as Tul Axtar had announced.

Sanoma Tora had slightly recovered her poise and control of her nerves. Tavia's sweet solicitude for her welfare touched me deeply. She had soothed and quieted her as she might have soothed and quieted a younger sister, though she herself was younger than Sanoma Tora, but with the return of confidence Sanoma Tora's old haughtiness was return-ing and it seemed to me that she showed too little gratitude to Tavia for her kindliness, but I realized that that was Sanoma Tora's way, that it was born in her and that doubtless deep in her heart she was fully appreciative and grateful. However that may be, I cannot but admit that I wished at the time that she would show it by some slight word or deed. We were flying smoothly, slightly above the normal altitude of battleships. The destina-tion control compass was holding the Jhama to her course, and after all that I had passed through, I felt the need of sleep. Phao, at my suggestion, had rested earlier in the night, and as all that was needed was a lookout to keep a careful watch for ships, I entrusted this duty to Phao, and Tavia and I rolled up in our sleeping silks and furs and were soon asleep.

Tavia and I were about mid-ship, Phao was forward at the controls, constantly swinging the periscope to and fro searching the sky for ships. When I retired Sanoma Tora was standing at one of the starboard ports looking out into the night, while Tul Axtar lay down in the stern of the ship. I had long since removed the gag from his mouth, but he seemed too utterly cowed even to address us and lay there in morose silence, or perhaps he was asleep, I do not know.

I was thoroughly fatigued and must have slept like a log from the moment that I laid down until I was suddenly awakened by the impact of a body upon me. As I struggled to free myself, I discovered to my chagrin that my hands had been deftly bound while I slept, a feat that had been rendered simple by the fact that it is my habit to sleep with my hands together in front of my face.

A man's knee was upon my chest, pressing me heavily against the deck and one of his hands clutched me by the throat. In the dim light of the cabin I saw that it was Tul Axtar and that his other hand held a dagger. "Silence!" he whispered. "If you would live, make no sound," and then to make assurance doubly sure he gagged me and bound my an-kles. Then he crossed quickly to Tavia. and bound her, and as he did so my eyes moved quickly about the interior of the cabin in search of aid. On the floor, near the controls, I saw Phao lying bound and gagged as was I. Sanoma Tora crouched against the wall, apparently overcome by terror. She was neither bound nor gagged. Why had she not warned me? Why had she not come to my help? If it had been Tavia who remained unbound instead of Sanoma Tora, how different would have been the outcome of Tul Axtar's bid for liberty and revenge.

How had it all happened? I was sure that I had bound Tul Axtar so securely that he could not possibly have freed himself, and yet I must have been mistaken and I cursed myself for the carelessness that had upset all my plans and that might easily eventually spell the doom of Helium.

Having disposed of Phao, Tavia and me, Tul Axtar moved quickly to the controls, ignoring Sanoma Tora as he passed by her. In view of the marked terror that she displayed, I could readily understand why he did not consider her any menace to his plans – she was as harmless to him free as bound.

Putting the ship about he turned back toward Jahar and though he did not understand the mechanism of the destination control compass and could not cut it out, this made no difference as long as he remained at the controls, the only effect that the compass might have being to return the ship to its former course should the controls be again abandoned while the ship was in motion.

Presently he turned toward me. "I should destroy you, Hadron of Hastor," he said, "had I not given the word of a jeddak that I would not."

Vaguely I had wondered to whom he had given his word that he would not kill me, but other and more important thoughts were racing through my mind, crowding all else into the background. Uppermost among them, of course, were plans for regaining control of the Jhama and, secondarily, apprehension as to the fate of Tavia, Sanoma Tora and Phao.

"Give thanks for the magnanimity of Tul Axtar," he continued, "who exacts no penalty for the affront you have put upon him. Instead you are to be set free. I shall land you." He laughed. "Free! I shall land you in the province of U-Gor!"

There was something nasty in the tone of his voice which made his promise sound more like a threat. I had never heard of U-Gor, but I assumed that it was some remote province from which it would be difficult or impossible for me to make my way either to Jahar or Helium. Of one thing I was confident – that Tul Axtar would not set me free any place that I might become a menace to him.

For hours the Jhama moved on in silence. Tul Axtar had not had the decency or the humanity to remove our gags. He was engrossed with the business of the controls, and Sanoma Tora, crouching against the side of the cabin, never spoke; nor once in all that time did her eyes turn toward me. What thoughts were passing in that beautiful head? Was she trying to find some plan by which she might turn the tables upon Tul Axtar, or was she merely crushed by the hopeless outlook – the prospect of being returned to the slavery of Jahar? I did not know; I could not guess; she was an enigma to me.

How far we traveled or in what direction, I did not know. The night had long since passed and the sun was high when I became aware that Tul Axtar was bringing the ship down. Presently the purring of the motor ceased and the ship came to a stop. Leaving the controls he walked back to where I lay.

"We have arrived in U-Gor," he said. "Here I shall set you at liberty, but first give me the strange thing that rendered you invisible in my palace."

The cloak of invisibility! How had he learned of that? Who could have told him? There seemed but one explanation, but every fiber of my being shrank even from considering it. I had rolled it up into a small ball and tucked it into the bottom of my pocket pouch, its sheer silk permitting it to be compressed into a very small space. He took the gag from my mouth.

"When you return to your palace at Jahar," I said, "look upon the floor beneath the window in the apartment that was occupied by Sanoma Tora. If you find it there you are welcome to it. As far as I am concerned it has served its purpose well."

"Why did you leave it there?" he demanded.

"I was in a great hurry when I quit the palace and accidents will happen." I will admit that my lie may not have been very clever, but neither was Tul Axtar and he was deceived by it.

Grumbling, he opened one of the keel hatches and very unceremoniously dropped me through it. Fortunately the ship lay close to the ground and I was not injured. Next he lowered Tavia to my side, and then he, himself, descended to the ground. Stooping, he cut the bonds that secured Tavia's wrists.

"I shall keep the other," he said. "She pleases," and somehow I knew that he meant Phao. "This one looks like a man and I swear that she would be as easy to subdue as a she-banth. I know the type. I shall leave her with you." It was evident that he had not recognized Tavia as one of the former occupants of the women's quarters in his palace and I was glad that he had not.

He re-entered the Jhama, but before he closed the hatch he spoke to us again. "I shall drop your weapons when we are where you cannot use them against me and you may thank the future Jeddara of Jahar for the clemency I have shown you!"

Slowly the Jhama rose. Tavia was removing the cords from her ankles and when she was free she came and fell to work upon the bonds that secured me, but I was too dazed, too crushed by the blow that had been struck me to realize any other fact than that Sanoma Tora, the woman I loved, had betrayed me, for I fully realized now what any one but a fool would have guessed before – that Tul Axtar had bribed her to set him free by the promise that he would make her Jeddara of Jahar.

Well, her ambition would be fulfilled, but at what a hideous cost. Never, if she lived for a thousand years could she look upon herself or her act with aught but contempt and loathing, unless she was far more degraded than I could possible believe. No; she would suffer, of that I was sure; but that thought gave me no pleasure. I loved her and I could not even now wish her unhappiness.

As I sat there on the ground, my head bowed in misery. I felt a soft arm steal about my shoulders and a tender voice spoke close to my ear. "My poor Hadron!"

That was all; but those few words embodied such a wealth of sympathy and understanding that, like some miraculous balm, they soothed the agony of my tortured heart.

No one but Tavia could have spoken them. I turned and taking one of her little hands in mine, I pressed it to my lips. "Loved friend," I said. "Thanks be to all my ancestors that it was not you."

I do not know what made me say that. The words seemed to speak themselves without my volition, and yet when they were spoken there came to me a sudden realization of the horror that I would have felt had it been Tavia who had betrayed me. I could not even contemplate it without an agony of pain. Impulsively I took her in my arms.

"Tavia," I cried, "promise me that you will never desert me. I could not live without you."

She put her strong, young arms about my neck and clung to me. "Never this side of death," she whispered, and then she tore herself from me and I saw that she was weeping.

What a friend! I knew that I could never again love a woman, but what cared I for that if I could have Tavia's friendship for life.

"We shall never part again, Tavia," I said. "If our ancestors are kind and we are permitted to return to Helium, you shall find a home in the house of my father and a mother in my mother."

She dried her eyes and looked at me with a strange wistful expression that I could not fathom, and then, through her tears, she smiled – that odd, quizzical little smile that I had seen before and that I did not understand any more than I understood a dozen of her moods and expressions, which made her so different from other girls and which, I think, helped to attract me toward her. Her characteristics lay not all upon the surface – there were depths and undercurrents which one might not easily fathom. Sometimes when I expected her to cry, she laughed; and when I thought she should be happy, she wept, but she never wept as I have seen other women weep – never hysterically, for Tavia never lost control of herself, but quietly as though from a full heart rather than from over-wrought nerves, and through her tears there might burst a smile at the end.

I think that Tavia was quite the most wonderful girl that I have ever known and as I had come to know her better and see more of her, I had grown to realize that despite her attempt at mannish disguise to which she still clung, she was quite the most beautiful girl that I had ever seen. Her beauty was not like that of Sanoma Tora, but as she looked up into my face now the realization came to me quite suddenly, and for what reason I do not know, that the beauty of Tavia far transcended that of Sanoma Tora because of the beauty of the soul that, shining through her eyes, transfigured her whole countenance.

Tul Axtar, true to his promise, dropped our weapons through a lower hatch of the Jhama and as we buckled them on we listened to the rapidly diminishing sound of the propellers of the departing craft. We were alone and on foot in a strange and, doubtless, an unhospitable country,

"U-Gor!" I said. "I have never heard of it. Have you, Tavia?"

"Yes," she said. "This is one of the outlaying provinces of Jahar. Once it was a rich and thriving agricultural country, but as it fell beneath the curse of Tul Axtar's mad ambition for man power, the population grew to such enormous proportions that U-Gor could not support its people. Then cannibalism started. It began justly with the eating of the officials that Tul Axtar had sent to enforce his cruel decrees. An army was dispatched to subdue the province, but the people were so numerous that they conquered the army and ate the warriors. By this time their farms were ruined. They had no seed and they had developed a taste for human flesh. Those who wished to till the ground were set upon by bands of roving men and devoured. For a hundred years they have been feeding upon one another until now it is no longer a populous province, but a wasteland inhabited by roving bands, searching for one another that they may eat."

I shuddered at her recital. It was obvious that we must escape this accursed place as rapidly as possible. I asked Tavia if she knew the location of U-Gor and she told me that it lay southeast of Jahar, about a thousands haads and about two thousand haads southwest of Xanator.

I saw that it would be useless to attempt to reach Helium from here. Such a journey on foot, if it could be accomplished at all, would require years. The nearest friendly city toward which we could turn was Gathol, which I estimated lay some seven thousand haads almost due north. The possibility of reaching Gathol seemed remote in the extreme, but it was our only hope and so we turned our faces toward the north and set out upon our long and seemingly hopeless journey toward the city of my mother's birth.

The country about us was rolling, with here and there a range of low hills, while far to the north I could see the outlines of higher hills against the horizon. The land was entirely denuded of all but noxious weeds, attesting the grim battle for survival waged by its unhappy people. There were no reptiles; no insects; no birds – all had been devoured during the century of misery that had lain upon the land.

As we plodded onward through this desolate and depressing waste, we tried to keep up one another's spirit as best we could and a hundred times I had reason to give thanks that it was Tavia who was my companion and no other.

What could I have done under like circumstances burdened with Sanoma Tora? I doubt that she could have walked a dozen haads, while Tavia swung along at my side with the lithe grace of perfect health and strength. It takes a good man to keep up with me on a march, but Tavia never lagged; nor did she show signs of fatigue more quickly than I.

"We are well matched, Tavia," I said.

"I had thought of that – a long time ago," she said quietly.

We continued on until almost dusk without seeing a sign of any living thing and were congratulating ourselves upon our good fortune when Tavia glanced back, as one of us often did.

She touched my arm and nodded toward the rear. "They come!" she said simply.

I looked back and saw three figures upon our trail. They were too far away for me to be able to do more than identify them as human beings. It was evident that they had seen us and they were closing the distance between us at a steady trot.

"What shall we do?" asked Tavia. "Stand and fight, or try to elude them until night falls?"

"We shall do neither," I said. "We shall elude them now without exerting ourselves in the least."

"How?" she asked.

"Through the inventive genius of Phor Tak, and the compound of invisibility that I filched from him."

"Splendid!" exclaimed Tavia. "I had forgotten your cloak. With it we should have no difficulty in eluding all dangers between here and Gathol."

I opened my pocket pouch and reached in to withdraw the cloak. It was gone! As was the vial containing the remainder of the compound. I looked at Tavia and she must have read the truth in my expression.

"You have lost it?" she asked.

"No, it has been stolen from me," I replied.

She came again and laid her hand upon my arm in sympathy and I knew that she was thinking what I was thinking, that it could have been none other than Sanoma Tora who had stolen it. I hung my head. "And to think that I jeopardized your safety, Tavia, to save such as she."

"Do not judge her hastily," she said. "We cannot know how sorely she may have been tempted, or what threats were used to turn her from the path of honor. Perhaps she is not as strong as we."

"Let us not speak of her," I said. "It is a hideous sensation, Tavia, to feel love turned to hatred."

She pressed my arm. "Time heals all hurts," she said, "and some day you will find a woman worthy of you, if such a one exists."

I looked down at her. "If such a one exists," I mused, but she interrupted my meditation with a question.

"Shall we fight or run, Hadron of Hastor?" she demanded.

"I should prefer to fight and die," I replied, "but I must think of you, Tavia."

"Then we shall remain and fight," she said; "but Hadron, you must not die."

There was a note of reproach in her tone that did not escape me and I was ashamed of myself for having seemed to forget the great debt that I owed her for her friendship.

"I am sorry," I said. "Tavia, I could not wish to die while you live."

"That is better," she said. "How shall we fight? Shall I stand upon your right or upon your left?"

"You shall stand behind me, Tavia," I told her. "While my hand can hold a sword, you will need no other defense."

"A long time ago, after we first met," she said, "you told me that we should be comrades in arms. That means that we fight together, shoulder to shoulder, or back to back. I hold you to your word, Tan Hadron of Hastor."

I smiled, and, though I felt that I could fight better alone than with a woman at my side, I admired her courage. "Very well," I said; "fight at my right, for thus you will be between two swords."

The three upon our trail had approached us so closely by this time that I could discern what manner of creatures they were and I saw before me naked savages with tangled, unkempt hair, filthy bodies and degraded faces. The wild light in their eyes, their snarling lips exposing yellow fangs, their stealthy, slinking carriage gave them more the appearance of wild beasts than men.

They were armed with swords which they carried in their hands, having neither harness nor scabbard. They halted at a short distance from us, eyeing us hungrily, and doubtless they were hungry for their flabby bellies suggested that they went often empty and were then gorged when meat fell to their lot in sufficient quantities. Tonight these three had hoped to gorge themselves; I could see it in their eyes. They whispered together in low tones for a few minutes and then they separated to rush us from different points simultaneously.

"We'll carry the battle to them, Tavia," I whispered. "When they have taken their positions around us, I shall give the word and then I shall rush the one in front of me and try to dispatch him before the others can set upon us. Keep close beside me so that they cannot cut you off."

"Shoulder to shoulder until the end," she said.

CHAPTER FIFTEEN

The Battle of Jahar

GLANCING ACROSS MY SHOULDER I saw that the two circling to our rear were already further away from us than he who stood facing us and realizing that the unexpectedness of our act would greatly enhance the chances of success, I gave the word.

"Now, Tavia," I whispered, and together we leaped forward at a run straight for the naked savage facing us.

It was evident that he had not expected this and it was also evident that he was a slow-witted beast, for as he saw us coming his lower jaw dropped and he just stood there, waiting to receive us; whereas if he had had any intelligence he would have fallen back to give his fellows time to attack us from the rear.

As our swords crossed I heard a savage growl from behind, such a growl as might issue from the throat of a wild beast. From the corner of my eye I saw Tavia glance back and then before I could realize what she intended, she sprang forward and ran her sword through the body of the man in front of me as he lunged at me with his own weapon, and now, wheeling together, we faced the other two who were running rapidly toward us and I can assure you that it was with a feeling of infinite relief that I realized that the odds were no longer so greatly against us.

As the two engaged us, I was handicapped at first by the necessity of constantly keeping an eye upon Tavia, but not for long.

In an instant I realized that a master hand was wielding that blade. Its point wove in and out past the clumsy guard of the savage and I knew, and I guessed he must have sensed, that his life lay in the hollow of the little hand that gripped the hilt. Then I turned my attention to my own antagonist.

These were not the best swordsmen that I have ever met, but they were far from being poor swordsmen. Their defense, however, far excelled their offense and this, I think, was due to two things, natural cowardice and the fact that they usually hunted in packs, which far outnumbered the quarry. Thus a good defense only was required, since the death blow might always be struck from behind by a companion of the one who engaged the quarry from in front.

Never before had I seen a woman fight and I should have thought that I should have been chagrined to have one fighting at my side, but instead I felt a strange thrill that was partly pride and partly something else that I could not analyze.

At first, I think, the fellow facing Tavia did not realize that she was a woman, but he must have soon as the scant harness of Barsoom hides little and certainly did not hide the rounded contours of Tavia's girlish body. Perhaps, therefore, it was surprise that was his undoing, or possibly when he discovered her sex he became overconfident, but at any rate Tavia slipped her point into his heart just an instant before I finished my man.

I cannot say that we were greatly elated over our victory. Each of us felt compassion for the poor creatures who had been reduced to their horrid state by the tyranny of cruel Tul Axtar, but it had been their lives or ours and we were glad it had not been ours.

As a matter of precaution I took a quick look about us as the last of our antagonists fell and I was glad that I had, for I immediately discerned three creatures crouching at the top of a low hill not far distant.

"We are not done yet, Tavia," I said. "Look!" and pointed in the direction of the three.

"Perhaps they do not care to share the fate of their fellows," she said. "They are not approaching."

"They can have peace if they want it as far as I am concerned," I said. "Come, let us go on. If they follow us, then will be time enough to consider them."

As we walked on toward the north we glanced back occasionally and presently we saw the three rise and come down the hill toward the bodies of their slain fellows, and as they did so we saw that they were women and that they were unarmed.

When they realized that we were departing and had no intention of attacking them, they broke into a run and, uttering loud, uncanny shrieks, raced madly toward the corpses.

"How pathetic," said Tavia sadly. "Even these poor degraded creatures possess human emotions. They, too, can feel sorrow at the loss of loved ones."

"Yes," I said. "Poor things, I am sorry for them."

Fearing that in the frenzy of their grief they might attempt to avenge their fallen mates, we kept a close eye upon them or we might not have witnessed the horrid sequel of the fray. I wish that we had not.

When the three women reached the corpses they fell upon them, but not with weeping and lamentation – they fell upon them to devour them.

Sickened, we turned away and walked rapidly toward the north until long after darkness had descended.

We felt that there was little danger of attack at night since there were no savage beasts in a country where there was nothing to support them and also that it was reasonable to assume that the hunting men would be abroad by day rather than by night, since at night they would be far less able to find quarry or follow it.

I suggested to Tavia that we rest for a short time and then push on for the balance of the night, find a place of concealment early in the day and remain there until night had fallen again, as I was sure that if we followed this plan we would make better time and suffer less exhaustion by traveling through the cool hours of darkness and at the same time would greatly minimize the danger of discovery and attack by whatever hostile people lay between us and Gathol.

Tavia agreed with me and so we rested for a short time, taking turns at sleeping and watching.

Later we pushed on and I am sure that we covered a great distance before dawn, though the high hills to the north of us still looked as far away as they had upon the previous day.

We now set about searching for some comfortable place of concealment where we might spend the daylight hours. Neither of us was suffering to any extent from either hunger or thirst, as the ancients would have done under like circumstances, for with the gradual diminution of water and vegetable matter upon Mars during countless ages all her creatures have by a slow process of evolution been enabled to go for long periods without either food or drink and we have also learned so to control our minds that we do not think of food or drink until we are able to procure it, which doubtless greatly assists us in controlling the cravings of our appetite.

After considerable search we found a deep and narrow ravine which seemed a most favorable place in which to hide, but, scarcely had we entered it, when I chanced to see two eyes looking down upon us from the summit of one of the ridges that flanked it. As I looked, the head in which the eyes were set was withdrawn below the summit.

"That puts an end to this place," I said to Tavia, telling her what I had seen. "We must move on and look for a new sanctuary."

As we emerged from the ravine at its upper end I glanced back, and again I saw the creature looking at us and once again he tried to hide himself from us. As we moved on I kept glancing back and occasionally I would see him – one of the hunting men of U-Gor. He was stalking us as the wild beast stalks its prey. The very thought of it filled me with disgust. Had he been a fighting man stalking us merely to kill, I should not have felt as I did, but the thought that he was stealthily trailing us because he desired to devour us was repellent – it was horrifying.

Hour after hour the thing kept upon our trail; doubtless he feared to attack because we outnumbered him, or perhaps he thought we might become separated, or lie down to sleep or do one of the number of things that travelers might do that would give him the opportunity he sought, but after awhile he must have given up hope. He no longer sought to conceal himself from us and once, as he mounted a low hill, he stood there silhouetted against the sky and throwing his head back, he gave voice to a shrill, uncanny cry that made the short hairs upon my neck stand erect. It was the hunting cry of the wild beast calling the pack to the kill.

I could feel Tavia shudder and press more closely to me and I put my arm about her in a gesture of protection, and thus we walked on in silence for a long time.

Twice again the creature voiced his uncanny cry until at last it was answered ahead of us and to the right.

Again we were forced to fight, but this time only two, and when we pushed on again it was with a feeling of depression that I could not shake off – depression for the utter hopelessness of our situation.

At the summit of a higher hill than we had before crossed, I halted. Some tall weeds grew there. "Let us lie down here, Tavia," I said. "From here we can watch; let us be the watchers for a while. Sleep, and when night comes we shall move on."

She looked tired and that worried me, but I think she was suffering more from the nervous strain of the eternal stalking than from physical fatigue. I know that it affected me and how much more might it affect a young girl than a trained fighting man. She lay very close to me, as though she felt safer thus and was soon asleep, while I watched.

From this high vantage point I could see a considerable area of country about us and it was not long before I detected figures of men prowling about like hunting banths and often it was apparent that one was stalking another. There were at least a half dozen such visible to me at one time. I saw one overtake his prey and leap upon it from behind.

They were at too great a distance from me for me to discern accurately the details of the encounter, but I judged that the stalker ran his sword through the back of his quarry and then, like a hunting banth, he fell upon his kill and devoured it. I do not know that he finished it, but he was still eating when darkness fell.

Tavia had had a long sleep and when she awoke she reproached me for having permitted her to sleep so long and insisted that I must sleep.

From necessity I have learned to do with little sleep when conditions are such that I cannot spare the time, though I always make up for it later, and I have also learned to limit my sleep to any length of time that I choose, so that now I awoke promptly when my allotted time had elapsed and again we set out toward far Gathol.

Again this night, as upon the preceding one, we moved unmolested through the horrid land of U-Gor and when morning dawned we saw the high hills rising close before us.

"Perhaps these hills mark the northern limits of U-Gor," I suggested.

"I think they do," replied Tavia.

"They are only a short distance away now," I said; "let us keep on until we have passed them. I cannot leave this accursed land behind me too soon."

"Nor I," said Tavia. "I sicken at the thought of what I have seen."

We had crossed a narrow valley and were entering the hills when we heard the hateful hunting cry behind us. Turning, I saw a single man moving across the valley toward us. He knew that I had seen him, but he kept steadily on, occasionally stopping to voice his weird scream. He heard an answer come from the east and then another and another from different directions. We hastened onward, climbing the low foot-hills that led upward toward the summit far above, and as we looked back we saw the hunting men converging upon us from all sides. We had never seen so many of them at one time before.

"Perhaps if we get well up into the mountains we can elude them," I said.

Tavia shook her head. "At least we have made a good fight, Hadron," she said.

I saw that she was discouraged; nor could I wonder; yet a moment later she looked up at me and smiled brightly. "We still live, Hadron of Hastor!" she exclaimed.

"We still live and we have our swords," I reminded her.

As we climbed they pressed upward behind us and presently I saw others coming through the hills from the right and from the left. We were turned from the low saddle over which I had hoped to cross the summit of the range, for hunting men had entered it from above and were coming down toward us. Directly ahead of us now loomed a high peak, the highest in the range as far as I could see, and only there, up its steep side, were there no hunting men to bar our way.

As we climbed, the sides of the mountain grew steeper until the ascent was not only most arduous, but sometimes difficult and dangerous; yet there was no alternative and we pressed onward toward the summit, while behind us came the hunting men of U-Gor. They were not rushing us and from that I felt confident that they knew that they had us cornered. I was looking for a place in which we might make a stand, but I found none and at last we reached the summit, a circular, level space perhaps a hundred feet in diameter.

As our pursuers were yet some little distance below us, I walked quickly around the outside of the table-like top of the peak. The entire northern face dropped sheer from the summit for a couple of hundred feet, definitely blocking our retreat. At every other point the hunting men were ascending. Our situation appeared hopeless; it was hopeless, and yet I refused to admit defeat.

The summit of the mountain was strewn with loose rock. I hurled a rock down at the nearest cannibal. It struck him upon the head and sent him hurtling down the mountain side, carrying a couple of his fellows with him. Then Tavia followed my example and together we bombarded them, but more often we scored misses than hits and there were so many of them and they were so fierce and so hungry that we did not even stem their advance. So numerous were they now that they reminded me of insects, crawling up there from below – huge, grotesque insects that would soon fall upon us and devour us.

As they came nearer they gave voice to a new cry that I had not heard before. It was a cry that differed from the hunting call, but was equally as terrible.

"Their war-cry," said Tavia.

On and on with relentless persistency the throng swarmed upward toward us. We drew our swords; it was our last stand. Tavia pressed closer to me and for the first time I thought I felt her tremble.

"Do not let them take me," she said. "It is not death that I fear."

I knew what she meant and I took her in my arms. "I cannot do it, Tavia," I said. "I cannot."

"You must," she replied in a firm voice. "If you care for me even as a friend, you cannot let these beasts take me alive."

I know that I choked then so that I could not reply, but I knew that she was right and I drew my dagger.

"Good-bye, Hadron – my Hadron!"

Her breast was bared to receive my dagger, her face was upturned toward mine. It was still a brave face with no fear upon it, and oh how beautiful it was.

Impulsively, guided by a power I could not control, I bent and crushed my lips to hers. With half closed eyes she pressed her own lips upward more tightly against mine.

"Oh, Issus!" she breathed as she took them away, and then, "They come! Strike now, Hadron, and strike deep!"

The creatures were almost at the summit. I swung my hand upward that I might bury the slim dagger deeply in that perfect breast. To my surprise my knuckles struck something hard above me. I glanced upward. There was nothing there; yet something impelled me to feel again, to solve that uncanny mystery even in that instant of high tragedy.

Again I felt above me. By Issus, there was something there! My fingers passed over a smooth surface – a familiar surface.

It could not be, and yet I knew that it must be – the Jhama.

I asked no questions of myself nor of fate at that instant. The hunting men of U-Gor were almost upon us as my groping fingers found one of the mooring rings in the bow of the Jhama. Quickly I swung Tavia above my head.

"It is the Jhama. Climb to her deck," I cried.

The dear girl, as quick to seize upon the fortuitous opportunities as any trained fighting man, did not pause to question, but swung herself upward to the deck with the agility of an athlete, and as I seized the mooring ring and drew myself upward she lay flat upon her belly and reaching down assisted me; nor was the strength in that slender frame unequal to the task.

The leaders of the horde had reached the summit. They paused in momentary confusion when they saw us climb into thin air and stand there apparently just above their heads, but hunger urged them on and they leaped for us, clambering upon one another's back and shoulders to seize us and drag us down.

Two almost gained the deck as I fought them all back single-handed while Tavia had raised a hatch and leaped to the controls.

Another foul-faced thing reached the deck upon the opposite side and only chance revealed him to me before he had run his sword through my back. The Jhama was already rising as I turned to engage him. There was little room there in which to fight, but I had the advantage in that I knew the extent of the deck beneath my feet, while he could see nothing but thin air. I think it frightened him, too, and when I rushed him he stepped backward out into space and, with a scream of terror, hurtled downward toward the ground.

We were saved, but how in the name of all our ancestors had the Jhama chanced to be at this spot?

Perhaps Tul Axtar was aboard! The thought filled me with alarm for Tavia's safety and with my sword ready I leaped through the hatchway into the cabin, but only Tavia was there.

We tried to arrive at some explanation of the miracle that had saved us, but no amount of conjecture brought forth any thing that was at all satisfactory.

"She was there when we needed her most," said Tavia; "that fact should satisfy us."

"I guess it will have to for the time being at least," I said, "and now once more we can turn a ship's nose toward Helium."

We had passed but a short distance beyond the mountains when I sighted a ship in the distance and shortly thereafter another and another until I was aware that we were approaching a great fleet moving toward the east. As we came closer I descried the hulls painted with the ghastly blue of Jahar and I knew that this was Tul Axtar's formidable armada.

And then we saw ships approaching from the east and I knew that it was the fleet of Helium. It could be no other; yet I must make certain, and so I sped in the direction of the nearest ship of this other fleet until I saw the banners and pennons of Helium floating from her upper works and the battle insignia of the Warlord painted upon her prow. Behind her came the other ships – a noble fleet moving to inevitable doom.

A Jaharian cruiser was moving toward the first great battleship as I raced to intercept them and bring one of my rifles into action.

I was forced to come close to my target as was the Jaharian cruiser, since the effective range of the disintegrating ray rifle is extremely limited.

Everything aboard the battleship of Helium was ready for action, but I knew why they had not fired a gun. It has ever been the boast of John Carter, Warlord of Barsoom, that he would not start a war. The enemy must fire the first shot. If I could have reached them in time he would have realized the fatal consequences of this magnanimous and chivalrous code and the ships of Helium, with their long-range guns, might have annihilated Jahar's entire fleet before it could have brought its deadly rifles within range, but fate had ordained otherwise and now the best that I could hope was that I might reach the Jaharian ship before it was too late.

Tavia was at the controls. We were racing toward the blue cruiser of Jahar. I was standing at the forward rifle. In another moment we should be within range and then I saw the great battleship of Helium crumble in mid-air. Its wooden parts dropped slowly toward the ground and a thousand warriors plunged to a cruel death upon the barren land beneath.

Almost immediately the other ships of Helium were brought to a stop. They had witnessed the catastrophe that had engulfed the first ship of the line and the commander of the fleet had realized that they were menaced by a new force of which they had no knowledge.

The ships of Tul Axtar, encouraged by this first success, were now moving swiftly to the attack. The cruiser that had destroyed the great battleship was in the lead, but now I was within range of it.

Realizing that the blue protective paint of Jahar would safeguard the ship itself against the disintegrating ray, I had rammed home a cartridge of another type in the chamber and swinging the muzzle of the rifle so that it would rake the entire length of the ship, I pressed the button.

Instantly the men upon deck dissolved into thin air – only their harness and their metal and their weapons were left.

Directing Tavia to run the Jhama alongside, I raised the upper hatch and leaped to the deck of the cruiser and a moment later I had raised the signal of surrender above her. One can imagine the consternation aboard the nearer ships of Jahar as they saw that signal flying from her forward mast, for there was none sufficiently close to have witnessed what actually transpired aboard her.

Returning to the cabin of the Jhama I lowered the hatch and went at once to the periscope. Far in the rear of the first line of Jaharian ships I could just discern the royal insignia upon a great battleship, which told me that Tul Axtar was there, but in a safe position. I should have liked to reach his ship next, but the fleet was moving forward toward the ships of Helium and I dared not spare the time.

By now the ships of Helium had opened fire and shells were exploding about the leading ships of the Jaharian fleet – shells so nicely timed that they can be set to explode at any point up to the extreme range of the gun that discharges them. It takes nice gunnery to synchronize the timing with the target.

As ship after ship of the Jaharian fleet was hit, the others brought their big guns into action. Temporarily, at least, the disintegrating ray rifles had failed, but that they would succeed I knew if a single ship could get through the Heliumetic line, where among the great battleships she could destroy a dozen in the space of a few minutes.

The gunnery of the Jaharians was poor; their shells usually exploded high in air before they reached their target, but as the battle continued it improved; yet I knew that Jahar never could hope to defeat Helium with Helium's own weapons.

A great battleship of Tul Axtar's fleet was hit three times in succession almost alongside of me. I saw her drop by the stern and I knew that she was done for, and then I saw her commander rush to the bow and take the last long dive and I knew that there were brave men in Tul Axtar's fleet as well as in the fleet of Helium, but Tul Axtar was not one of them, for in the distance I could see his flagship racing toward Jahar.

Despite the cowardice of the jeddak, the great fleet pushed on to the attack. If they had the courage they could still win, for their ships outnumbered the ships of Helium ten to one and as far as the eye could reach I could see them speeding from the north, from the south and from the west toward the scene of battle.

Closer and closer the ships of Helium were pressing toward the ships of Jahar. In his ignorance the Warlord was playing directly into the hands of the enemy. With their superior marksmanship and twenty battleships protected by the blue paint of Jahar, Helium could wipe out Tul Axtar's great armada; of that I was confident, and with that thought came an inspiration. It might be done and only Tan Hadron of Hastor could do it.

Shells were falling all about us. The force of the explosions rocked the Jhama until she tossed and pitched like an ancient ship upon an ancient sea. Again and again were we perilously close to the line of fire of the Jaharian disintegrating ray rifles. I felt that I might no longer risk Tavia thus, yet I must carry out the plan that I had conceived.

It is strange how men change and for what seemingly trivial reasons. I had thought all my life that I would make any sacrifice for Helium, but now I knew that I would not sacrifice a single hair of that tousled head for all Barsoom. This, I soliloquized, is friendship.

Taking the controls I turned the bow of the Jhama toward one of the ships of Helium, that was standing temporarily out of the line of fire, and as we approached her side I turned the controls back over to Tavia, and, raising the forward hatch, sprang to the deck of the Jhama, raising both hands above my head in signal of surrender in the event that they might take me for a Jaharian.

What must they have thought when they saw me apparently floating upright upon thin air? That they were astonished was evident by the expressions on the faces of those nearest to me as the Jhama touched the side of the battleship.

They kept me covered as I came aboard, leaving Tavia to maneuver the Jhama.

Before I could announce myself I was recognized by a young officer of my own umak. With a cry of surprise he leaped forward and threw his arms about me. "Hadron of Hastor!" he cried. "Have I witnessed your resurrection from death; but no, you are too real, too much alive to be any wraith of the other world."

"I am alive now," I cried, "but none of us will be unless I can get word to your commander. Where is he?"

"Here," said a voice behind me and I turned to see an old odwar who had been a great friend of my father's. He recognized me immediately, but there was no time even for greetings.

"Warn the fleet that the ships of Jahar are armed with disintegrating ray rifles that can dissolve every ship as you saw the first one dissolve. They are only effective at short range.

"Keep at least a haad distance from them and you are relatively safe. And now if you will give me three men and direct the fire of your fleet away from the Jaharian ships on the south of their line, I will agree to have twenty ships for you in an hour – ships protected by the blue of Jahar in which you may face their disintegrating ray rifles with impunity."

The odwar knew me well and upon his own responsibility he agreed to do what I asked.

Three padwars of my own class guaranteed to accompany me. I fetched Tavia aboard the battleship and turned her over to the protection of the old odwar, though she objected strenuously to being parted from me.

"We have gone through so much together, Hadron of Hastor," she said, "let us go on to the end together."

She had come quite close to me and spoken in a low voice that none might overhear. Her eyes, filled with pleading, were upturned to mine.

"I cannot risk you further, Tavia," I said.

"There is so much danger then, you think?" she asked.

"We shall be in danger, of course," I said; "this is war and one can never tell. Do not worry though. I shall come back safely."

"Then it is that you fear that I shall be in the way," she said, "and another can do the work better than I."

"Of course not," I replied. "I am thinking only of your safety."

"If you are lost, I shall not live. I swear it," she said, "so if you can trust me to do the work of a man, let me go with you instead of one of those."

I hesitated. "Oh, Hadron of Hastor, please do not leave me here without you," she said.

I could not resist her. "Very well, then," I said, "come with me. I would rather have you than any other," and so it was that Tavia replaced one of the padwars on the Jhama, much to the officer's chagrin.

Before entering the Jhama I turned again to the old odwar. "If we are successful," I said, "a number of Tul Axtar's battleships will move slowly toward the Helium line beneath signals of surrender. Their crews will have been destroyed. Have boarding parties ready to take them over."

Naturally every one aboard the battleship was intensely interested in the Jhama though all that they could see of her was the open hatch and the eye of the periscope. Officers and men lined the rail as we went aboard our invisible craft and as I closed the hatch, a loud cheer rang out above me.

My first act thoroughly evidenced my need of Tavia, for I put her at the after turret in charge of the rifle there, while one of the padwars took the controls and turned the prow of the Jhama toward the Jaharian fleet.

I was standing in a position where I could watch the changing scene upon the ground glass beneath the periscope and when a great battleship swung slowly into the miniature picture before me, I directed the padwar to lay a straight course for her, but a moment later I saw another battleship moving abreast of her, This was better and we changed our course to pass between the two.

They were moving gallantly toward the fleet of Helium, firing their big guns now and reserving their disintegrating ray rifles for closer range. What a magnificent sight they were, and yet how helpless. The tiny, invisible Jhama, with her little rifles, constituted a greater menace to them than did the entire fleet of Helium. On they drove, unconscious of the inevitable fate bearing down upon them.

"Sweep the starboard ship from stem to stern," I called to Tavia. "I will take this fellow on our port," and then to the padwar at the controls, "Half speed!"

Slowly we passed their bows. I touched the button upon my rifle and through the tiny sighting aperture I saw the crew dissolve in the path of those awful rays, as the two ships passed. We were very close – so close that I could see the expressions of consternation and horror on the faces of some of the warriors as they saw their fellows disappear before their eyes, and then their turn would come and they would be snuffed out in the twinkling of an eye, their weapons and their metal clattering to the deck.

As we dropped astern of them, our work completed, I had the padwar bring the Jhama about and alongside one of the ships, which I quickly boarded, running up the signal of surrender. With the death of the officer at her controls she had fallen off with the wind, but I quickly brought her up again and, setting her at half speed, her bow toward the ships of Helium, I locked the controls and left her.

Returning to the Jhama we crossed quickly to the other ship and a few moments later it, too, was moving slowly toward the fleet of the Warlord, the signal of surrender fluttering above it.

So quickly had the blow been struck that even the nearer ships of Jahar were some time in realizing that anything was amiss. Perhaps they were unable to believe their own eyes when they saw two of their great battleships surrender before having been struck by a single shot, but presently the commander of a light cruiser seemed to awaken to the seriousness of the situation, even though he could not fully have understood it. We were already moving toward another battleship when I saw the cruiser speeding directly toward one of our prizes and I knew that it would never reach the fleet of Helium if he boarded it, a thing which I must prevent at all costs. His course would bring him across our bow and as he passed I raked him with the forward rifle.

I saw that it would be impossible for the Jhama to overtake this swift cruiser, which was moving at full speed and so we had to let her go her way. At first I was afraid she would ram the nearer prize and had she hit her squarely at the rate that she was traveling, the cruiser would have plowed half way through the hull of the battleship. Fortunately, she missed the great ship by a hair and went speeding on into the midst of the fleet of Helium.

Instantly she was the target for a hundred guns, a barrage of shells was bursting about her and then there must have been a dozen hits simultaneously, for the cruiser simply disappeared – a mass of flying debris.

As I turned back to our work I saw the havoc being wrought by the big guns of Helium upon the enemy ships to the north of me. In the instant that I glanced I saw three great battleships take the final dive, while at least four others were drifting helplessly with the wind, but other ships of that mighty armada were swinging into action. As far as I could see they were coming from the north, from the south and from the west. There seemed no end to them and now, at last, I realized that only a miracle could give victory to Helium.

In accordance with my suggestion our own fleet was holding off, concentrating the fire of its big guns upon the nearer ships of Jahar – constantly seeking to keep those deadly rifles out of range.

Again we fell to work – to the grim work that the god of battle had allotted to us. One by one, twenty great battleships surrendered their deserted decks to us and as we worked I counted fully as many more destroyed by the guns of the Warlord.

In the prosecution of our work we had been compelled to destroy at least half a dozen small craft, such as scout fliers and light cruisers, and now these were racing erratically among the remaining ships of the Jaharian fleet, carrying consternation and doubtless terror to the hearts of Tul Axtar's warriors, for all the nearer ships must have realized long since that some strange, new force had been loosed upon them by the ships of Helium.

By this time we had worked so far behind the Jaharian first line that we could no longer see the ships of Helium, though bursting shells attested the fact that they were still there.

From past experience I realized that it would be necessary to protect the captured Jaharian ships from being re-taken and so I turned back, taking a position where I could watch as many of them as possible and it was well that I did so, for we found it necessary to destroy the crews of three more ships before we reached the battle line of Helium.

Here they had already manned a dozen of the captured battleships of Jahar, and, with the banners and pennons of Helium above them, they had turned about and were moving into action against their sister ships.

It was then that the spirit of Jahar was broken. This, I think, was too much for them as doubtless the majority of them believed that these ships had gone over to the enemy voluntarily with all their officers and crews, for few, if any, could have known that the latter had been destroyed.

Their Jeddak had long since deserted them. Twenty of their largest ships had gone over to the enemy and now protected by the blue of Jahar and manned by the best gunners of Barsoom, were plowing through them, spreading death and destruction upon every hand.

A dozen of Tul Axtar's ships surrendered voluntarily and then the others turned and scattered; very few of them headed toward Jahar and I knew by that that they believed that the city must inevitably fall.

The Warlord made no effort to pursue the fleeing craft; instead he stationed the ships that we had captured from the enemy, more than thirty all told now, entirely around the fleet of Helium to protect it from the disintegrating ray rifles of the enemy in the event of a renewed attack, and then slowly we moved on Jahar.

CHAPTER SIXTEEN

Despair

IMMEDIATELY AFTER THE CLOSE of the battle the Warlord sent for me and a few moments later Tavia and I stepped aboard the flagship.

The Warlord himself came forward to meet us. "I knew," he said, "that the son of Had Urtur would give a good account of himself. Helium can scarcely pay the debt of gratitude that you have placed upon her today. You have been to Jahar; your work today convinces me of that. May we with safety approach and take the city?"

"No," I replied, and then briefly I explained the mighty force that Tul Axtar had gathered and the armament with which he expected to subdue the world. "But there is a way," I said.

"And what is that?" he asked.

"Send one of the captured Jaharian ships with a flag of truce and I believe that Tul Axtar will surrender. He is a coward. He fled in terror when the battle was still young."

"Will he honor a flag of truce?"

"If it is carried aboard one of his own ships, protected by the blue paint of Jahar, I believe that he will," I said; "but at the same time I shall accompany the ship in the invisible Jhama.

"I know how I may gain entrance to the palace. I have abducted Tul Axtar once and perchance I may be able to do it again. If you have him in your hands, you can dictate terms to the nobles, all of whom fear the terrific power of the hungry multitude that is held in check now only by the instinctive terror they feel for their Jeddak."

As we waited for the former Jaharian cruiser that was to carry the flag of truce to come alongside, John Carter told me what had delayed the expedition against Jahar for so many months.

The major-domo of Tor Hatan's palace, to whom I had entrusted the message to John Carter and which would have led immediately to the descent upon Jahar, had been assassinated while on his way to the palace of the Warlord. Suspicion, therefore, did not fall upon Tul Axtar and the ships of Helium scoured Barsoom for many months in vain search for Sanoma Tora.

It was only by accident that Kal Tavan, the slave who had overheard my conversation with the major-domo, learned that the ships of Helium had not been dispatched to Jahar, for a slave ordinarily is not taken into the confidences of his master and the arrogant Tor Hatan was, of all men, least likely to do so; but Kal Tavan did hear eventually and he went himself to the Warlord and told his story.

"For his services," said John Carter, "I gave him his freedom and as it was apparent from his demeanor that he had been born to the nobility in his native country, though he did not tell me this, I gave him service aboard the fleet. He has turned out to be an excellent man and recently I have made him a dwar. Having been born in Tjanath and served in Kobol, he was more familiar with this part of Barsoom than any other man in Helium. I, therefore, assigned him to duty with the navigating officer of the fleet and he is now aboard the flagship."

"I had occasion to notice the man immediately after Sanoma Tora's abduction," I said, "and I was much impressed by him. I am glad that he has found his freedom and the favor of the Warlord."

The cruiser that was to bear the flag of truce was now alongside. The officer in command reported to the Warlord and as he received his instructions, Tavia and I returned to the Jhama. We had decided to carry on our part of the plan alone, for if it became necessary to abduct Tul Axtar again I had hoped, also, that I might find Phao and Sanoma Tora, and if so the small cabin of the Jhama would be sufficiently crowded without the addition of the two padwars. They were reluctant to leave her for I think they had had the most glorious experience of their lives during the short time that they had been aboard her, but I gained permission from the Warlord for them to accompany the cruiser to Jahar.

Once again Tavia and I were alone. "Perhaps this will be our last cruise aboard the Jhama," I said.

"I think I shall be glad to rest," she replied.

"You are tired?" I asked.

"More tired than I realized until I felt the safety and security of that great fleet of Helium about me. I think that I am just tired of being always in danger."

"I should not have brought you now," I said. "There is yet time to return you to the flagship."

She smiled. "You know better than that, Hadron," she said.

I did know better. I knew that she would not leave me. We were silent for a while as the Jhama slid through the air slightly astern of the cruiser. As I looked at Tavia's face, it seemed to reflect a great weariness and there were little lines of sadness there that I had not seen before. Presently she spoke again in a dull tone that was most unlike her own.

"I think that Sanoma Tora will be glad to come away with you this time," she said.

"I do not know," I said. "It makes no difference to me whether she wishes to come or not. It is my duty to fetch her."

She nodded. "Perhaps it is best," she said; "her father is a noble and very rich."

I did not understand what that had to do with it and not being particularly interested further in either Sanoma Tora or her father, I did not pursue the conversation. I knew that it was my duty to return Sanoma Tora to Helium if possible, and that was the only interest that I had in the affair.

We were well within sight of Jahar before we encountered any warships and then a cruiser came to meet ours which bore the flag of truce. The commanders of the two boats exchanged a few words and then the Jaharian craft turned and led the way toward the palace of Tul Axtar. It moved slowly and I forged on ahead, my plans already made, and the Jhama, being clothed with invisibility, needed no escort. I steered directly to that wing of the palace which contained the women's quarters and slowly circled it, my periscope on a line with the windows.

We had rounded the end of the wing, in which the great hall lay where Tul Axtar held court with his women, when the periscope came opposite the windows of a gorgeous apartment. I brought the ship to a stop before it, as I had before some of the others which I wished to examine, and while the slowly moving periscope brought different parts of the large room to the ground glass plate before me I saw the figures of two women and instantly I recognized them. One was Sanoma Tora and the other Phao, and upon the figure of the former hung the gorgeous trappings of a Jeddara. The woman I had loved had achieved her goal, but it caused me no pang of jealousy. I searched the balance of the apartment and finding no other occupant, I brought the deck of the Jhama close below the sill of the window. Then I raised a hatch and leaped into the room.

At sight of me Sanoma Tora arose from the divan upon which she had been sitting and shrank back in terror. I thought that she was about to scream for help, but I warned her to silence, and at the same instant Phao sprang forward and, seizing Sanoma Tora's arm, clapped a palm over her mouth. A moment later I had gained her side.

"The fleet of Jahar has gone down to defeat before the ships of Helium," I told Sanoma Tora, "and I have come to take you back to your own country."

She was trembling so that she could not reply. I had never seen such a picture of abject terror, induced no doubt by her own guilty conscience.

"I am glad you have come, Hadron of Hastor," said Phao, "for I know that you will take me, too."

"Of course," I said. "The Jhama lies just outside that window. Come! We shall soon be safe aboard the flagship of the Warlord."

While I had been talking I had become aware of a strange noise that seemed to come from a distance and which rose and fell in volume and now it appeared to be growing nearer and nearer. I could not explain it; perhaps I did not attempt to, for at best I could be only mildly interested. I had found two of those whom I sought. I would get them aboard the Jhama and then I would try to locate Tul Axtar.

At that instant the door burst open and a man rushed into the room. It was Tul Axtar. He was very pale and he was breathing hard. At sight of me he halted and shrank back and I thought that he was going to turn and run, but he only looked fearfully back through the open door and then he turned to me, trembling.

"They are coming!" he cried in a voice of terror. "They will tear me to pieces."

"Who is coming?" I demanded.

"The people," he said. "They have forced the gates and they are coming, Do you not hear them?"

So that was the noise that had attracted my attention – the hungry hordes of Jahar searching out the author of their misery.

"The Jhama is outside that window," I said. "If you will come aboard her as a prisoner of war, I will take you to the Warlord of Barsoom."

"He will kill me, too," wailed Tul Axtar.

"He should," I assured him.

He stood looking at me for a moment and I could see in his eyes and the expression of his face the reflection of a dawning idea. His countenance lightened. He looked almost hopeful. "I will come," he said; "but first let me get one thing to take with me. It is in yonder cabinet."

"Hasten," I said.

He went quickly to the cabinet, which was a tall affair reaching from the floor almost to the ceiling, and when he opened the door it hid him from our view.

As I waited I could hear the crash of weapons upon levels below and the screams and shrieks and curses of men and I judged that the palace guard was holding the mob, temporarily at least. Finally I became impatient. "Hasten, Tul Axtar," I called, but there was no reply. Again I called him, with the same result, and then I crossed the room to the cabinet, but Tul Axtar was not behind the door.

The cabinet contained many drawers of different sizes, but there was not one large enough to conceal a man, nor any through which he could have passed to another apartment. Hastily I searched the room, but Tul Axtar was nowhere to be found and then I chanced to glance at Sanoma Tora. She was evidently trying to attract my attention, but she was so terrified that she could not speak. With trembling fingers she was pointing toward the window. I looked in that direction, but I could see nothing.

"What is it? What are you trying to say, Sanoma Tora?" I demanded as I rushed to her side.

"Gone!" she managed to say. "Gone!"

"Who is gone?" I demanded.

"Tul Axtar."

"Where? What do you mean?" I insisted.

"The hatch of the Jhama – I saw it open and close."

"But it cannot be possible. We have been standing here looking-" and then a thought struck me that left me almost dazed. I turned to Sanoma Tora. "The cloak of invisibility?" I whispered.

She nodded.

Almost in a single bound I crossed the room to the window and was feeling for the deck of the Jhama. It was not there. The ship had gone. Tul Axtar had taken it and Tavia was with him.

I turned back and crossed the room to Sanoma Tora. "Accursed woman!" I cried. "Your selfishness, your vanity, your treachery has jeopardized the safety of one whose footprints you are not fit to touch." I wanted to close my fingers upon that perfect throat, I yearned to see the agony of death upon that beautiful face; but only turned away, my hands dropping at my sides, for I am a man – a noble of Helium – and the women of Helium are sacred, even such as Sanoma Tora.

From below came the sounds of renewed fighting. If the mob broke through I knew that we should all be lost, There was but one hope for even temporary safety and that was the slender tower above the women's quarters.

"Follow me," I said curtly. As we entered the main corridor I caught a glimpse of the interior of the great hall where Tul Axtar had held court. It was filled with terrified women. Well they knew what the fate of the women of a Jeddak would be at the hands of an infuriated mob. My heart went out to them, but I could not save them. Lucky, indeed, should I be if I were able to save these two.

Crossing the corridor we ascended the spiral ramp to the storeroom, where, after entering, I took the precaution to bolt the door, then I ascended the ladder toward the trap door at the summit of the tower, the two women following me. As I raised the trap and looked about me I could have cried aloud with joy, for circling low above the roof of the palace was the cruiser flying the flag of truce. I apprehended no danger of discovery by Jaharian warriors since I knew that they were all well occupied below – those who were not fleeing for their lives – and so I sprang to the summit of the tower and hailed the cruiser in a voice that they might well hear above the howling of the mob. An answering hail came from the deck of the craft and a moment later she dropped to the level of the tower roof. With the help of the crew I assisted Phao and Sanoma Tora aboard.

The officer in command of the cruiser stepped to my side. "Our mission here is fruitless," he said. "Word has just been brought me that the palace has fallen before the onslaught of a mob of infuriated citizens. The nobles have commandeered every craft upon which they could lay hands and have fled. There is no one with whom we can negotiate a peace. No one knows what has become of Tul Axtar."

"I know," I told him, and then I narrated what had happened in the apartment of the Jeddara.

"We must pursue him," he said. "We must overtake him and carry him back to the Warlord."

"Where shall we look?" I asked. "The Jhama may lie within a dozen sofads of us and even so we could not see her. I shall search for him; never fear, and some day I shall find him, but it is useless now to try to find the Jhama. Let us return to the flagship of the Warlord."

I do not know that John Carter fully realized the loss that I had sustained, but I suspect that he did for he offered me all the resources of Helium in my search for Tavia.

I thanked him, but asked only for a fast ship; one in which I might devote the remainder of my life in what I truly believed would prove a futile search for Tavia, for how could I know where in all wide Barsoom Tul Axtar would elect to hide. Doubtless there were known to him many remote spots in his own empire where he could live in safety for the balance of his allotted time on Barsoom. To such a place he would go and because of the Jhama no man would see him pass; there would be no clue by which to follow him and he would take Tavia with him and she would be his slave. I shuddered and my nails sank into my palms at the thought.

The Warlord ordered one of the newest and swiftest fliers of Helium to be brought alongside the flagship. It was a trim craft of the semi-cabin type that would easily accommodate four or five in comfort. From his own stores he had provisions and water transferred to it and he added wine from Ptarth and jars of the famous honey of Dusar.

Sanoma Tora and Phao had been sent at once to a cabin by the Warlord, for the deck of a man-of-war on duty is no place for women. I was about to depart when a messenger came saying that Sanoma Tora wished to see me.

"I do not wish to see her," I replied.

"Her companion also begged that you would come," replied the messenger.

That was different. I had almost forgotten Phao, but if she wished to see me I would go, and so I went at once to the cabin where the two girls were. As I entered Sanoma Tora came forward and threw herself upon her knees before me.

"Have pity on me, Hadron of Hastor," she cried. "I have been wicked, but it was my vanity and not my heart that sinned. Do not go away. Come back to Helium and I will devote my life to your happiness. Tor Hatan, my father, is rich. The mate of his only child may live forever in luxury."

I am afraid that my lips curled to the sneer that was in my heart. What a petty soul was hers! Even in her humiliation and her penitence she could see no beauty and no happiness greater than wealth and power. She thought that she was changed, but I knew that Sanoma Tora never could change.

"Forgive me, Tan Hadron," she cried. "Come back to me, for I love you. Now I know that I love you."

"Your love has come too late, Sanoma Tora," I said.

"You love another?" she asked.

"Yes," I replied.

"The Jeddara of some of the strange countries you have been through?" she asked.

"A slave girl," I replied.

Her eyes went wide in incredulity. She could not conceive that one might choose a slave girl to the daughter of Tor Hatan. "Impossible," she said.

"It is true, though," I assured her; "a little slave girl is more desirable to Tan Hadron of Hastor than is Sanoma Tora, the daughter of Tor Hatan," and with that I turned my back upon her and faced Phao. "Good-bye, dear friend," I said. "Doubtless we shall never meet again, but I shall see to it that you have a good home in Hastor. I shall speak to the Warlord before I leave and have him send you directly to my mother."

She laid her hand upon my shoulder. "Let me go with you, Tan Hadron," she said, "for perhaps while you are searching for Tavia you will pass near Jhama."

I understood instantly what she meant, and I reproached myself for having even temporarily forgotten Nur An. "You shall come with me,

Phao," I said, "and my first duty shall be to return to Jhama. and rescue Nur An from poor old Phor Tak."

Without another glance at Sanoma Tora I led Phao from the cabin, and after a few parting words with the Warlord we boarded my new ship and with friendly farewells in our ears, headed west toward Jhama.

Being no longer protected by the invisibility compound of Phor Tak, or the disintegrating ray resisting paint of Jahar, we were forced to keep a sharp lookout for enemy ships, of which I had but little fear if we sighted them in time for I knew that I could outdistance any of them.

I set the destination control compass upon Jhama and opened the throttle wide; the swift Barsoomian night had fallen; the only sound was the rush of thin air along our sides which drowned out the quiet purring of our motor.

For the first time since I had found her again on the quarters of the Jeddara at Jahar, I had an opportunity to talk with Phao and the first thing I asked her was for an explanation of the abandonment of the Jhama after Tul Axtar had grounded Tavia and me in U-Gor.

"It was an accident," she said, "that threw Tul Axtar into a great fit of rage. We were headed for Jahar when he sighted one of his own ships, which took us aboard as soon as they discovered the identity of the jeddak. It was night and in the confusion of boarding the Jaharian warship Tul Axtar momentarily forgot the Jhama which must have drifted away from the larger craft the moment that we left her. They cruised about searching for her for awhile, but at last they had to give it up and the ship proceeded toward Jahar."

The miracle of the presence of the Jhama at the top of the peak, where we had so providentially found it in time to escape from the hunting men of U-Gor, was now no longer a miracle. The prevailing winds in this part of Barsoom are from the northwest at this time of year. The Jhama had merely drifted with the wind and chanced to lodge upon the highest peak of the range.

Phao also told me why Tul Axtar had originally abducted Sanoma Tora from Helium. He had had his secret agents at Helium for some time previous and they had reported to him that the best way to lure the fleet of Helium to Jahar was to abduct a woman of some noble family. He had instructed them to select a beautiful one, and so they had decided upon the daughter of Tor Hatan.

"But how did they expect to lure the fleet of Helium to Jahar if they left no clue as to the identity of the abductors of Sanoma Tora?" I asked.

"They left no clue at the time because Tul Axtar was not ready to receive the attack of Helium," explained Phao; "but he had already sent his agents word to drop a hint as to the whereabouts of Sanoma Tora when John Carter learned through other sources the identity of her abductors."

"So it all worked out the way Tul Axtar had planned," I said, "except the finish."

We passed the hours with brief snatches of conversation and long silences, each occupied with his own thoughts – Phao's doubtless a mixture of hope and fear, but there was little room for hope in mine. The only pleasant prospects that lay before me lay in rescuing Nur An and reuniting him and Phao. After that I would take them to any country to which they wished to go and then return to the vicinity of Jahar and prosecute my hopeless search.

"I heard what you said to Sanoma Tora in the cabin of the flagship," said Phao after a long silence, "and I was glad."

"I said a number of things," I reminded her; "to which do you refer?"

"You said that you loved Tavia," she replied.

"I said nothing of the kind," I rejoined rather shortly, for I almost loathed that word.

"But you did," she insisted. "You said that you loved a little slave girl and I know that you love Tavia. I have seen it in your eyes."

"You have seen nothing of the kind. Because you are in love, you think that everyone must be."

She laughed. "You love her and she loves you."

"We are only friends – very good friends," I insisted, "and furthermore I know that Tavia does not love me."

"How do you know?"

"Let us not speak of it any more," I said, but though I did not speak of it, I thought about it. I recalled that I had told Sanoma Tora that I loved a little slave girl and I knew that I had had Tavia in my mind at the time, but I thought that I had said it more to wound Sanoma Tora than for any other purpose. I tried to analyze my own feelings, but at last I gave it up as a foolish thing to do. Of course, I did not love Tavia; I loved no one; love was not for me – Sanoma Tora had killed it within my breast, and I was equally sure that Tavia did not love me; if she had, she would have shown it and I was quite sure that she had never demonstrated any other feeling for me than the finest of comradeship. We were just what she had said we were – comrades in arms and nothing else.

It was still dark when I saw the gleaming white palace of Phor Tak shining softly in the moonlight far below us. Late as it was, there were lights in some of the rooms. I had hoped that all would be asleep, for my plans depended upon my ability to enter the palace secretly. I knew that Phor Tak never kept any watch at night, feeling that none was needed in such an isolated spot.

Silently I dropped the flier until it rested upon the roof of the building where Nur An and I had first landed, for I knew that there I would find a passage to the palace below.

"Wait here at the controls, Phao," I whispered. "Nur An and I may have to come away in a hurry and you must be ready."

She nodded her head understandingly, and a moment later I had slipped quietly to the roof and was approaching the opening that led down into the interior.

As I paused at the top of the spiral ramp I felt quickly of my weapons to see that each was in its place. John Carter had fitted me out anew. Once more I stood in the leather and metal of Helium, with a full complement of weapons such as belong to a fighting man of Barsoom. My long sword was of the best steel, for it was one of John Carter's own. Besides this, I carried a short sword and a dagger, and once again a heavy radium pistol hung at my hip. I loosened the latter in its holster as I started down the spiral ramp.

As I approached the bottom I heard a voice. It was coming from the direction of Phor Tak's laboratory, the door of which opened upon the corridor at the bottom of the ramp. I crept slowly downward. The door leading to the laboratory was closed. Two men were conversing. I could recognize the thin, high voice of Phor Tak; the other voice was not that of Nur An; yet it was strangely familiar.

" – riches beyond your dream," I heard the second man say.

"I do not need riches," cackled Phor Tak. "Heigh-oo! Presently I shall own all the riches in the world."

"You will need help," I could hear the other man say in a pleading tone. "I can give you help; you shall have every ship of my great fleet."

That remark brought me upstanding – "every ship of my great fleet!" It could not be possible and yet –

Gently I tried the door. To my surprise it swung open revealing the interior of the room. Beneath a bright light stood Tul Axtar. Fifty feet from him Phor Tak was standing behind a bench upon which was mounted a disintegrating ray rifle, aimed full at Tul Axtar.

Where was Tavia? Where was Nur An? Perhaps this man alone knew where Tavia was and Phor Tak was about to destroy him. With a cry of warning I leaped into the room. Tul Axtar and Phor Tak looked at me quickly, surprise large upon their countenances.

"Heigh-oo!" screamed the old inventor. "So you have come back! Knave! Ingrate! Traitor! But you have come back only to die."

"Wait," I cried, raising my hand. "Let me speak."

"Silence!" screamed Phor Tak. "You shall see Tul Axtar die. I hated to kill him without someone to see – someone to witness his death agony. I shall have my revenge on him first and then on you."

"Stop!" I cried. His finger was already hovering over the button that would snatch Tul Axtar into oblivion, perhaps with the secret of the whereabouts of Tavia.

I drew my pistol. Phor Tak made a sudden motion with his hands and disappeared. He vanished as though turned to thin air by his own disintegrating rays, but I knew what had happened. I knew that he had thrown a mantle of invisibility around himself and I fired at the spot where he had last been visible.

At the same instant the floor opened beneath me and I shot into utter darkness.

I felt myself hurtling along a smooth surface which gradually became horizontal and an instant later I shot into a dimly lighted apartment, which I knew must be located in the pits beneath the palace.

I had clung to my pistol as I fell and now, as I arose to my feet, I thrust it back into its holster; at least I was not unarmed.

The dim light in the apartment, which was little better than no light at all, I discovered, came from a ventilator in the ceiling and that aside from the shaft that had conducted me to the cell, there was no other opening in the wall or ceiling or floor. The ventilator was about two feet in diameter and led straight up from the center of the ceiling to the roof of the building, several levels above. The lower end of the shaft was about two feet above my finger tips when I extended them high above my head. This avenue of escape, then, was useless, but, alas, how tantalizing. It was maddening to see daylight and an open avenue to the outer world just above me and be unable to reach it. I was glad that the sun had risen, throwing its quick light over the scene, for had I fallen here in utter darkness my plight would have seemed infinitely worse than now, and my first ancestor knew that it was bad enough. I turned my attention now to the chute through which I had descended and I found that I could ascend it quite a little distance, but presently it turned steeply upward and its smoothly polished walls were unscalable.

I returned to the pits. I must escape, but now, as my eyes became accustomed to the dim light, I saw strewn about the floor, that which snatched away my last hope and filled me with horror. Everywhere upon the stone flagging were heaps and mounds of human bones picked clean by gnawing rats. I shuddered as I contemplated the coming of night. How long before my bones, too, would be numbered among the rest?

The thought made me frantic, not for myself but for Tavia. I could not die. I must not die. I must live until I had found her.

Hastily I circled the room, searching for some clue to hope, but I found only rough-hewn stone set in soft mortar.

Soft mortar! With the realization, hope dawned anew. If I could remove a few of these blocks and pile them one on top of the other, I might easily reach the shaft that terminated in the ceiling above my head. Drawing my dagger I fell to work, scraping and scratching at the mortar about one of the stones in the nearest wall. It seemed slow work, but in reality I had loosened the stone in an incredibly short time. The mortar was poor stuff and crumbled away easily. As I drew the block out my first plan faded in the light of what I saw in front of me. Beyond the opening I saw a corridor at the foot of a spiral ramp leading upward, and from somewhere above, daylight was filtering down.

I knew that if I could remove three more of those stones before I was detected I could worm my body through the opening into the corridor beyond, and you may well believe that I worked rapidly.

One by one the blocks were loosened and removed and it was with a feeling of exultation that I slipped through into the corridor. Above me rose a spiral ramp. Where it led, I did not know, but at least it led out of the pits. Cautiously, and yet without any hesitation, I ascended. I must try to reach the laboratory before Phor Tak had slain Tul Axtar. This time I would make sure of the old inventor before I entered the room and I prayed to all my ancestors that I should be in time.

Doors, leading from the ramp to various levels of the palace, were all locked and I was forced to ascend to the roof. As it chanced the wing upon which I found myself was more or less detached, so that at first glance I could see no way whereby I could make my way from it to any of the adjoining roofs.

As I walked around the edge of the building hurriedly, looking for some means of descent to the roof below, I saw something one level below me that instantly charged my attention. It was a man's leg protruding from a window, as though he had thrown one limb across the sill. A moment later I saw an arm emerge, and the top of a man's head and his shoulders were visible as he leaned out. He reached down and up and I saw something appear directly beneath him that had not been there before, and at the same instant I caught a glimpse of a girl, lying a few feet further down, and then I saw the man slide over the sill quickly and drop down and disappear, and all that lay below me was the flagging of a courtyard.

But in that brief instant I knew precisely what I had seen. I had seen Tul Axtar raise the hatch of the Jhama. I had seen Tavia lying bound upon the floor of the ship beneath the hatch. I had seen Tul Axtar enter the interior of the craft and close the hatch above his head.

It takes a long while to tell it when compared with the time in which it actually transpired; nor was I so long in acting as I have been in telling.

As the hatch closed, I leaped.

CHAPTER SEVENTEEN

I Find a Princess

IT WOULD BE AS UNREASONABLE to aver that I fully visualized the outcome of my act as I leaped out into space with nothing visible between
me and the flagstones of the courtyard forty feet below as it would be to
assume that I acted solely upon unreasoning impulse. There are emergencies in which the mind functions with inconceivable celerity. Perceptions are received, judgments arrived at and reason operates to a definite
conclusion all so swiftly that the three acts appear simultaneous. Thus
must have been the process in this instance.

I knew where the narrow walkway upon the upper deck of the
Jhama must lie in the seemingly empty space below me, for I had
jumped almost the instant that the hatch had closed. Of course I know
now, and I knew then, that it would have been a dangerous feat and
difficult of achievement even had I been able to see the Jhama below
me; yet as I look back upon it now there was nothing else that I could
have done. It was my one, my last chance to save Tavia from a fate
worse than death – it was perhaps my last opportunity ever to see her
again. As I jumped then I should jump again under like conditions
even though I knew that I should miss the Jhama, for now as then I
know that I should rather die than lose Tavia; although then I did not
know why, while now I do.

But I did not miss. I landed squarely upon my feet upon the narrow walkway. The impact of my weight upon the upper deck of the
craft must have been noticeable to Tul Axtar, for I could feel the Jhama
drop a little beneath me. Doubtless he wondered what had happened,
but I do not think that he guessed the truth. However, he did not raise
the hatch as I hoped he would, but instead he must have leaped to the
controls at once for almost immediately the Jhama rose swiftly at an

acute angle, which made it difficult for me to cling to her since her upper deck was not equipped with harness rings. By grasping the forward edge of the turret, however, I managed to hold on.

As Tul Axtar gained sufficient altitude and straightened out upon his course he opened the throttle wide so that the wind rushing at me at terrific velocity seemed momentarily upon the point of carrying me from my precarious hold and hurtling me to the ground far below. Fortunately I am a strong man – none other could have survived that ordeal – yet how utterly helpless I was.

Had Tul Axtar guessed the truth he could have raised the after hatch and had me at his mercy, for though my pistol hung at my side I could not have released either hand to use it, but doubtless Tul Axtar did not know, or if he did he hoped that the high speed of the ship would dislodge whoever or whatever it might have been that he felt drop upon it.

I had hung there but a short time before I realized that eventually my hold must weaken and be torn loose. Something must be done to rectify my position. Tavia must be saved and because I alone could save her, I must not die.

Straining every thew I dragged myself further forward until I lay with my chest upon the turret. Slowly, inch by inch, I wormed myself forward. The tubular sheeting of the periscope was just in front of me. If I could but reach that with one hand I might hope to attain greater safety. The wind was buffeting me, seeking to tear me away. I sought a better hold with my left forearm about the turret and then I reached quickly forward with my right hand and my fingers closed about the sheathing.

After that it was not difficult to stretch a part of my harness about the front of the turret. Now I found that I could have one hand free, but until the ship stopped I could not hope to accomplish anything more.

What was transpiring beneath me? Could Tavia be safe even for a brief time in the power of Tul Axtar? The thought drove me frantic. The Jhama must be stopped, and then an inspiration came to me.

With my free hand I unsnapped my pocket pouch from my harness and drawing myself still further forward, I managed to place the opened pouch over the eye of the periscope.

Immediately Tul Axtar was blind; he could see nothing, nor was it long before the reaction that I had expected and hoped for came – the Jhama slowed down and finally came to a stop.

I had been lying partially upon the forward hatch and now I drew myself away from and in front of it. I hoped that it would be the forward hatch that he would open. It was the closer to him. I waited, and then glancing forward I saw that he was opening the ports. In this way he could see to navigate the ship and my plan was blocked.

I was disappointed, but I would not give up hope. Very quietly I tried the forward hatch, but it was locked upon the inside. Then I made my way swiftly and silently to the after hatch. If he should start the Jhama again at full speed now, doubtless I should be lost, but I felt that I was forced to risk the chance. Already the Jhama was in motion again as I laid my hand upon the hatch cover. This time I was neither silent nor gentle. I heaved vigorously and the hatch opened. Not an instant did I hesitate and as the Jhama leaped forward again at full speed, I dropped through the hatchway to the interior of the craft.

As I struck the deck Tul Axtar heard me and wheeling from the controls to face me, he recognized me. I think I never before beheld such an expression of mingled astonishment, hatred and fear as convulsed his features. At his feet lay Tavia, so quietly still that I thought her dead, and then Tul Axtar reached for his pistol and I for mine, but I had led a cleaner life than Tul Axtar had. My mind and muscles coordinate with greater celerity than can those of one who has wasted his fiber in dissipation.

Point blank I fired at his putrid heart and Tul Axtar, Jeddak and tyrant of Jahar, lunged forward upon the lower deck of the Jhama dead.

Instantly I sprang to Tavia's side and turned her over. She had been bound and gagged and, for some unaccountable reason, blindfolded as well, but she was not dead. I almost sobbed for joy when I realized that. How my fingers seemed to fumble in their haste to free her; yet it was only a matter of seconds ere it was done and I was crushing her in my arms.

I know that my tears fell upon her upturned face as our lips were pressed together, but I am not ashamed of that, and Tavia wept too and clung to me and I could feel her dear body tremble. How terrified she must have been, and yet I know she had never shown it to Tul Axtar. It was the reaction – the mingling of relief and joy at the moment that the despair had been blackest.

In that instant, as our hearts beat together and she drew me closer to her, a great truth dawned upon me. What a stupid fool I had been! How could I ever have thought that the sentiment that I entertained for Sanoma Tora was love? How could I ever believe that my love for Tavia had been such a weak thing as friendship? I drew her closer, if such were possible.

"My princess," I whispered.

Upon Barsoom those two words, spoken by man to maid, have a peculiar and unalterable significance, for no man speaks thus to any woman that he does not wish for wife.

"No, no," sobbed Tavia, "Take me, I am yours; but I am only a slave girl. Tan Hadron of Hastor cannot mate with such."

Even then she thought only of me and my happiness, and not of herself at all. How different she was from such as Sanoma Tora? I had risked my life to win a clod of dirt and I had found a priceless jewel.

I looked her in the eyes, those beautiful, fathomless wells of love and understanding. "I love you, Tavia," I said. "Tell me that I may have the right to call you my princess."

"Even though I be a slave?" she asked.

"Even though you were a thousand times less than a slave," I told her.

She sighed and snuggled closer to me. "My chieftain," she whispered in a low, low voice.

That, as far as I, Tan Hadron of Hastor, is concerned, is the end of the story. That instant marked the highest pinnacle to which I may ever hope to achieve, but there is more that may interest those who have come thus far with me upon adventures that have carried me half way around the southern hemisphere of Barsoom.

When Tavia and I could tear ourselves apart, which was not soon, I opened the lower hatch and let the corpse of Tul Axtar find its last resting place upon the barren ground below. Then we turned back toward Jhama, where we discovered that earlier in the morning Nur An had come to one of the roofs of the palace and been discovered by Phao.

When Nur An had learned that I had entered the palace just before dawn, he had become apprehensive and instituted a search for me. He had not known of the coming of Tul Axtar and believed that the Jeddak must have arrived after he had retired for the night; nor had he known how close Tavia had been, lying bound in the Jhama close beside the palace wall.

His search of the palace, however, had revealed the fact that Phor Tak was missing. He had summoned the slaves and a careful search had been made, but no sign of Phor Tak was visible.

It occurred to me then that I might solve the question as to the whereabouts of the old scientist. "Come with me," I said to Nur An; "Perhaps I can find Phor Tak for you."

I led him to the laboratory. "There is no use searching there," he said, "we have looked in a hundred times today. A glance will reveal the fact that the laboratory is deserted."

"Wait," I said. "Let us not be in too much of a hurry. Come with me; perhaps yet I may disclose the whereabouts of Phor Tak."

With a shrug he followed me as I entered the vast laboratory and walked toward the bench upon which a disintegrating rifle was mounted. Just back of the bench my foot struck something that I could not see, but that I had rather expected to find there, and stooping I felt a huddled form beneath a covering of soft cloth.

My fingers closed upon the invisible fabric and I drew it aside. There, before us on the floor, lay the dead body of Phor Tak, a bullet hole in the center of his breast.

"Name of Issus!" cried Nur An. "Who did this?"

"I," I replied, and then I told him what had happened in the laboratory as the last night waned.

He looked around hurriedly. "Cover it up quickly," he said. "The slaves must not know. They would destroy us. Let us get out of here quickly."

I drew the cloak of invisibility over the body of Phor Tak again. "I have work here before I leave," I said.

"What?" he demanded.

"Help me gather all of the disintegrating rays shells and rifles into one end of the room."

"What are you going to do?" he demanded.

"I am going to save a world, Nur An," I said.

Then he fell to and helped me and when they were all collected in a pile at the far end of the laboratory, I selected a single shell and returning to the rifle mounted upon the bench I inserted it in the chamber, closed the block and turned the muzzle of the weapon upon that frightful aggregation of death and disaster.

As I pressed the button all that remained in Jhama of Phor Tak's dangerous invention disappeared in thin air, with the exception of the single rifle, for which there remained no ammunition. With it had gone his model of The Flying Death and with him the secret had been lost.

Nur An told me that the slaves were becoming suspicious of us and as there was no necessity of risking ourselves further, we embarked upon the flier that John Carter had given me, and, taking the Jhama in tow, set our course toward Helium.

We overtook the fleet shortly before it reached the Twin Cities of Greater Helium and Lesser Helium and upon the deck of John Carter's flagship we received a welcome and a great ovation, and shortly thereafter there occurred one of the most remarkable and dramatic incidents that I have ever beheld. We were holding something of an informal reception upon the forward deck of the great battleship. Officers and nobles were pressing forward to be presented and numerous were the appreciative eyes that admired Tavia.

It was the turn of the Dwar, Kal Tavan, who had been a slave in the palace of Tor Hatan. As he came face to face with Tavia, I saw a look of surprise in his eyes.

"Your name is Tavia?" he repeated.

"Yes," she said, "and yours is Tavan. They are similar."

"I do not need to ask from what country you are," he said. "You are Tavia of Tjanath."

"How do you know?" she asked.

"Because you are my daughter," he replied. "Tavia is the name your mother gave you. You look like her. By that alone I should have known my daughter anywhere."

Very gently he took her in his arms and I saw tears in his eyes, and hers too, as he pressed his lips against her forehead, and then he turned to me.

"They told me that the brave Tan Hadron of Hastor had chosen to mate with a slave girl," he said; "but that is true. Your princess is in truth a princess – the granddaughter of a jed. She might have been the daughter of a jed had I remained in Tjanath."

How devious are the paths of fate! How strange and unexpected the destinations to which they lead. I had set out upon one of these paths with the intention of marrying Sanoma Tora at the end. Sanoma Tora had set out upon another in the hopes of marrying a Jeddak. At the end of her path, she had found only ignominy and disgrace. At the end of mine I had found a princess.

A Glossary of Names and Terms Used in the Martian Books

Aaanthor. A dead city of ancient Mars.

Aisle of Hope. An aisle leading to the court-room in Helium.

Apt. An Arctic monster. A huge, white-furred creature with six limbs, four of which, short and heavy, carry it over the snow and ice; the other two, which grow forward from its shoulders on either side of its long, powerful neck, terminate in white, hairless hands with which it seizes and holds its prey. Its head and mouth are similar in appearance to those of a hippopotamus, except that from the sides of the lower jawbone two mighty horns curve slightly downward toward the front. Its two huge eyes extend in two vast oval patches from the centre of the top of the cranium down either side of the head to below the roots of the horns, so that these weapons really grow out from the lower part of the eyes, which are composed of several thousand ocelli each. Each ocellus is furnished with its own lid, and the apt can, at will, close as many of the facets of his huge eyes as he chooses. (See *The Warlord of Mars*.)

Astok. Prince of Dusar.

Avenue of Ancestors. A street in Helium.

Banth. Barsoomian lion. A fierce beast of prey that roams the low hills surrounding the dead seas of ancient Mars. It is almost hairless, having only a great, bristly mane about its thick neck. Its long, lithe body is supported by ten powerful legs, its enormous jaws are equipped with several rows of long needle-like fangs, and its mouth reaches to a point far back of its tiny ears. It has enormous protruding eyes of green. (See *The Gods of Mars*.)

Bar Comas. Jeddak of Warhoon. (See *A Princess of Mars*.)

Barsoom. *Mars*

Black pirates of Barsoom. Men six feet and over in height. Have clear-cut and handsome features; their eyes are well set and large, though a slight narrowness lends them a crafty appearance. The iris is extremely black while the eyeball itself is quite white and clear. Their skin has the appearance of polished ebony. (See *The Gods of Mars*.)

Calot. A dog. About the size of a Shetland pony and has ten short legs. The head bears a slight resemblance to that of a frog, except that the jaws are equipped with three rows of long, sharp tusks. (See *A Princess of Mars*.)

Carter, John. Warlord of Mars.

Carthoris of Helium. Son of John Carter and Dejah Thoris.

Dak Kova. Jed among the Warhoons (later jeddak).

Darseen. Chameleon-like reptile.

Dator. Chief or prince among the First Born.

Dejah Thoris. Princess of Helium.

Djor Kantos. Son of Kantos Kan; padwar of the Fifth Utan.

Dor. Valley of Heaven.

Dotar Sojat. John Carter's Martian name, from the surnames of the first two warrior chieftains he killed.

Dusar. A Martian kingdom.

Dwar. Captain.

Ersite. A kind of stone.

Father of Therns. High Priest of religious cult.

First Born. Black race; black pirates.

Kar Komak. Odwar of Lotharian bowmen.

Gate of Jeddaks. A gate in Helium.

Gozava. Tars Tarkas' dead wife.

Gur Tus. Dwar of the Tenth Utan.

Haad. Martian mile.

Hal Vas. Son of Vas Kor the Dusarian noble.

Hastor. A city of Helium.

Hekkador. Title of Father of Therns.

Helium. The empire of the grandfather of Dejah Thoris.

Holy Therns. A Martian religious cult.

Hortan Gur. Jeddak of Torquas.

Hor Vastus. Padwar in the navy of Helium.

Horz. Deserted city; Barsoomian Greenwich.

Illall. A city of Okar.

Iss. River of Death. (See *A Princess of Mars*.)

Issus. Goddess of Death, whose abode is upon the banks of the Lost Sea of Korus. (See *The Gods of Mars*.)

Jav. A Lotharian.

Jed. King.

Jeddak. Emperor.

Kab Kadja. Jeddak of the Warhoons of the south.

Kadabra. Capital of Okar.

Kadar. Guard.

Kalksus. Cruiser; transport under Vas Kor.

Kantos Kan. Padwar in the Helium navy.

Kaol. A Martian kingdom in the eastern hemisphere.

Kaor. Greeting.

Karad. Martian degree.

Komal. The Lotharian god; a huge banth.

Korad. A dead city of ancient Mars. (See *A Princess of Mars.*)

Korus. The Lost Sea of Dor.

Kulan Tith. Jeddak of Kaol. (See *The Warlord of Mars.*)

Lakor. A thern.

Larok. A Dusarian warrior; artificer.

Lorquas Ptomel. Jed among the Tharks. (See *A Princess of Mars.*)

Lothar. The forgotten city.

Marentina. A principality of Okar.

Matai Shang. Father of Therns. (See *The Gods of Mars.*)

Mors Kajak. A jed of lesser Helium.

Notan. Royal Psychologist of Zodanga.

Nutus. Jeddak of Dusar.

Od. Martian foot.

Odwar. A commander, or general.

Okar. Land of the yellow men.

Old Ben (or Uncle Ben). The writer's body-servant (coloured).

Omad. Man with one name.

Omean. The buried sea.

Orluk. A black and yellow striped Arctic monster.

Otz Mountains. Surrounding the Valley Dor and the Lost Sea of Korus.

Padwar. Lieutenant.

Panthan. A soldier of fortune.

Parthak. The Zodangan who brought food to John Carter in the pits of Zat Arras. (See *The Gods of Mars.*)

Pedestal of Truth. Within the courtroom of Helium.

Phaidor. Daughter of Matai Shang. (See *The Gods of Mars.*)

Pimalia. Gorgeous flowering plant.

Plant men of Barsoom. A race inhabiting the Valley Dor. They are ten or twelve feet in height when standing erect; their arms are very short and fashioned after the manner of an elephant's trunk, being sinuous; the body is hairless and ghoulish blue except for a broad band of white which encircles the protruding, single eye, the pupil, iris and ball of which are dead white. The nose is a ragged, inflamed, circular hole in the centre of the blank face, resembling a fresh bullet wound which has not yet commenced to bleed. There is no mouth in the head. With the exception of the face, the head is covered by a tangled mass of jet-black hair some eight or ten inches in length. Each hair is about the thickness of a large angleworm. The body, legs and feet are of human shape but of monstrous proportions, the feet being fully three feet long and very flat and broad. The method of feeding consists in running their odd hands over the surface of the turf, cropping off the tender vegetation with razor-like talons and sucking it up from two mouths, which lie one in the palm of each hand. They are equipped with a massive tail about six feet long, quite round where it joins the body, but tapering to a flat, thin blade toward the end, which trails at right angles to the ground. (See *The Gods of Mars.*)

Prince Soran. Overlord of the navy of Ptarth.

Ptarth. A Martian kingdom.

Ptor. Family name of three Zodangan brothers.

Sab Than. Prince of Zodanga. (See *A Princess of Mars.*)

Safad. A Martian inch.

Sak. Jump.

Salensus Oll. Jeddak of Okar. (See *The Warlord of Mars.*)

Saran Tal. Carthoris' major-domo.

Sarkoja. A green Martian woman. (See *A Princess of Mars.*)

Sator Throg. A Holy Thern of the Tenth Cycle.

Shador. Island in Omean used as a prison.

Silian. Slimy reptiles inhabiting the Sea of Korus.

Sith. Hornet-like monster. Bald-faced and about the size of a Hereford bull. Has frightful jaws in front and mighty poisoned sting behind. The eyes, of myriad facets, cover three-fourths of the head, permitting the creature to see in all directions at one and the same time. (See *The Warlord of Mars.*)

Skeel. A Martian hardwood.

Sola. A young green Martian woman.

Solan. An official of the palace.

Sompus. A kind of tree.

Sorak. A little pet animal among the red Martian women, about the size of a cat.

Sorapus. A Martian hardwood.

Sorav. An officer of Salensus Oll.

Tal. A Martian second.

Tal Hajus. Jeddak of Thark.

Talu. Rebel Prince of Marentina.

Tan Gama. Warhoon warrior.

Tardos Mors. Grandfather of Dejah Thoris and Jeddak of Helium.

Tario. Jeddak of Lothar.

Tars Tarkas. A green man, chieftain of the Tharks.

Temple of Reward. In Helium.

Tenth Cycle. A sphere, or plane of eminence, among the Holy Therns.

Thabis. Issus' chief.

Than Kosis. Jeddak of Zodanga. (See *A Princess of Mars.*)

Thark. City and name of a green Martian horde.

Thoat. A green Martian horse. Ten feet high at the shoulder, with four legs on either side; a broad, flat tail, larger at the tip than at the root which it holds straight out behind while running; a mouth splitting its head from snout to the long, massive neck. It is entirely devoid of hair and is of a dark slate colour and exceedingly smooth and glossy. It has a white belly and the legs are shaded from slate at the shoulders and hips to a vivid yellow at the feet. The feet are heavily padded and nailless. (See *A Princess of Mars.*)

Thor Ban. Jed among the green men of Torquas.

Thorian. Chief of the lesser Therns.

Throne of Righteousness. In the court-room of Helium.

Throxus. Mightiest of the five oceans.

Thurds. A green horde inimical to Torquas.

Thuria. The nearer moon.

Thurid. A black dator.

Thuvan Dihn. Jeddak of Ptarth.

Thuvia. Princess of Ptarth.

Torith. Officer of the guards at submarine pool.

Torkar Bar. Kaolian noble; dwar of the Kaolian Road.

Torquas. A green horde.

Turjun. Carthoris' alias.

Utan. A company of one hundred men (military).

Vas Kor. A Dusarian noble.

Warhoon. A community of green men; enemy of Thark.

Woola. A Barsoomian calot.

Xat. A Martian minute.

Xavarian. A Helium warship.

Xodar. Dator among the First Born.

Yersted. Commander of the submarine.

Zad. Tharkian warrior.

Zat Arras. Jed of Zodanga.

Zithad. Dator of the guards of Issus. (See *The Gods of Mars.*)

Zitidars. Mastodonian draught animals.

Zodanga. Martian city of red men at war with Helium.

Zode. A Martian hour.

eBook *bundled* with purchase

bitlit.com

Claim your eBook edition for any Engage Books title:
1. Download the BitLip app for Android or iOS
2. Write your name in UPPERCASE on the copyright page
3. Use the BitLit app to submit two photos
4. Download your eBook to any device

SNAP A PICTURE   WRITE YOUR NAME   CHECK YOUR EMAIL

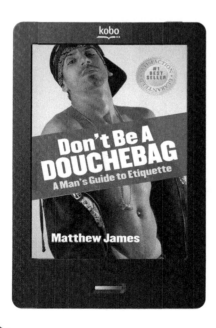
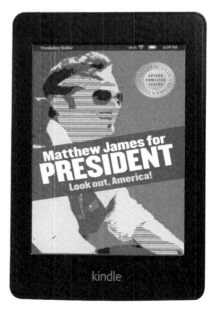

Printed by BoD™in Norderstedt, Germany